# the GRAPHIC CANON OF CHILDREN'S LITERATURE

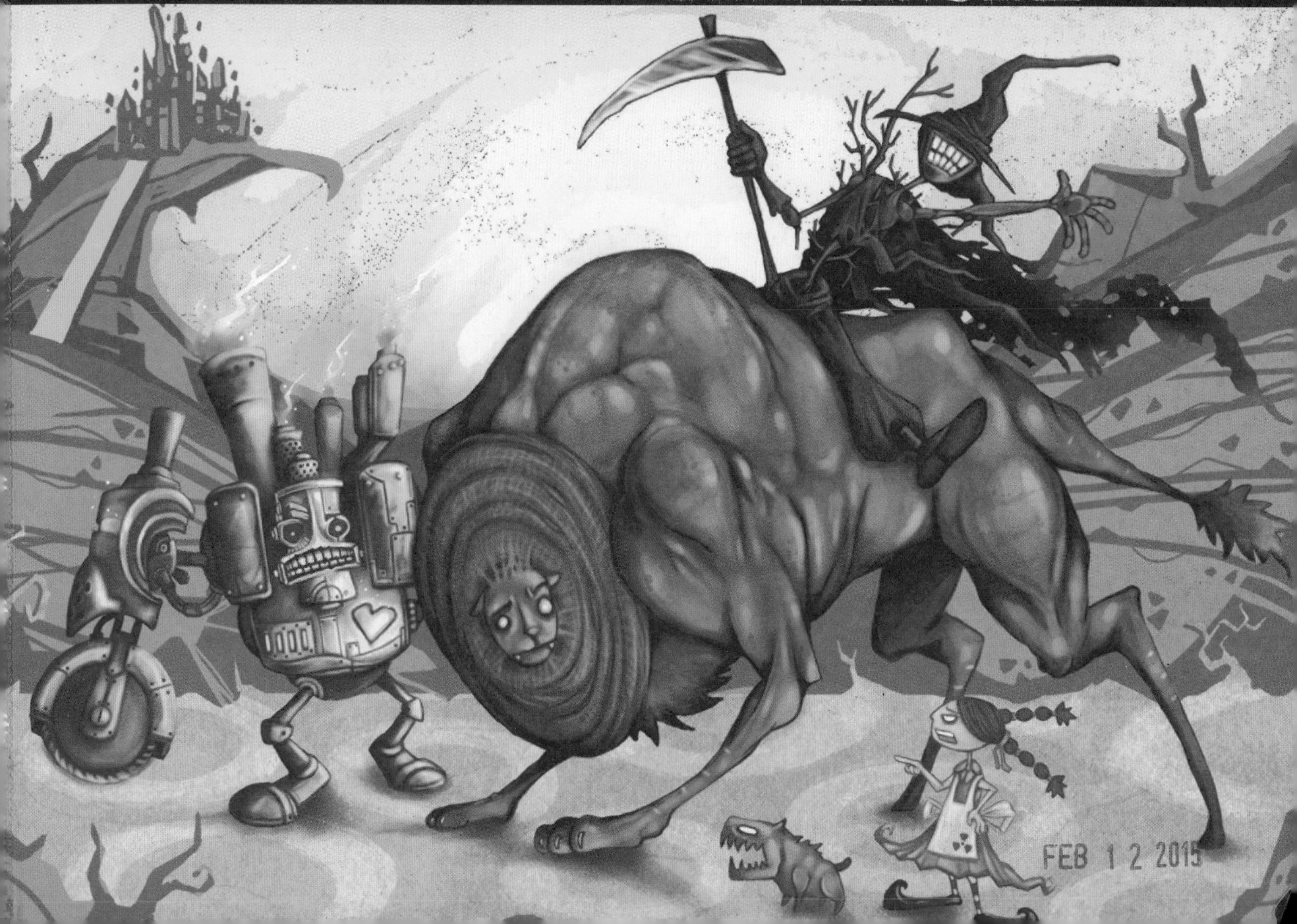

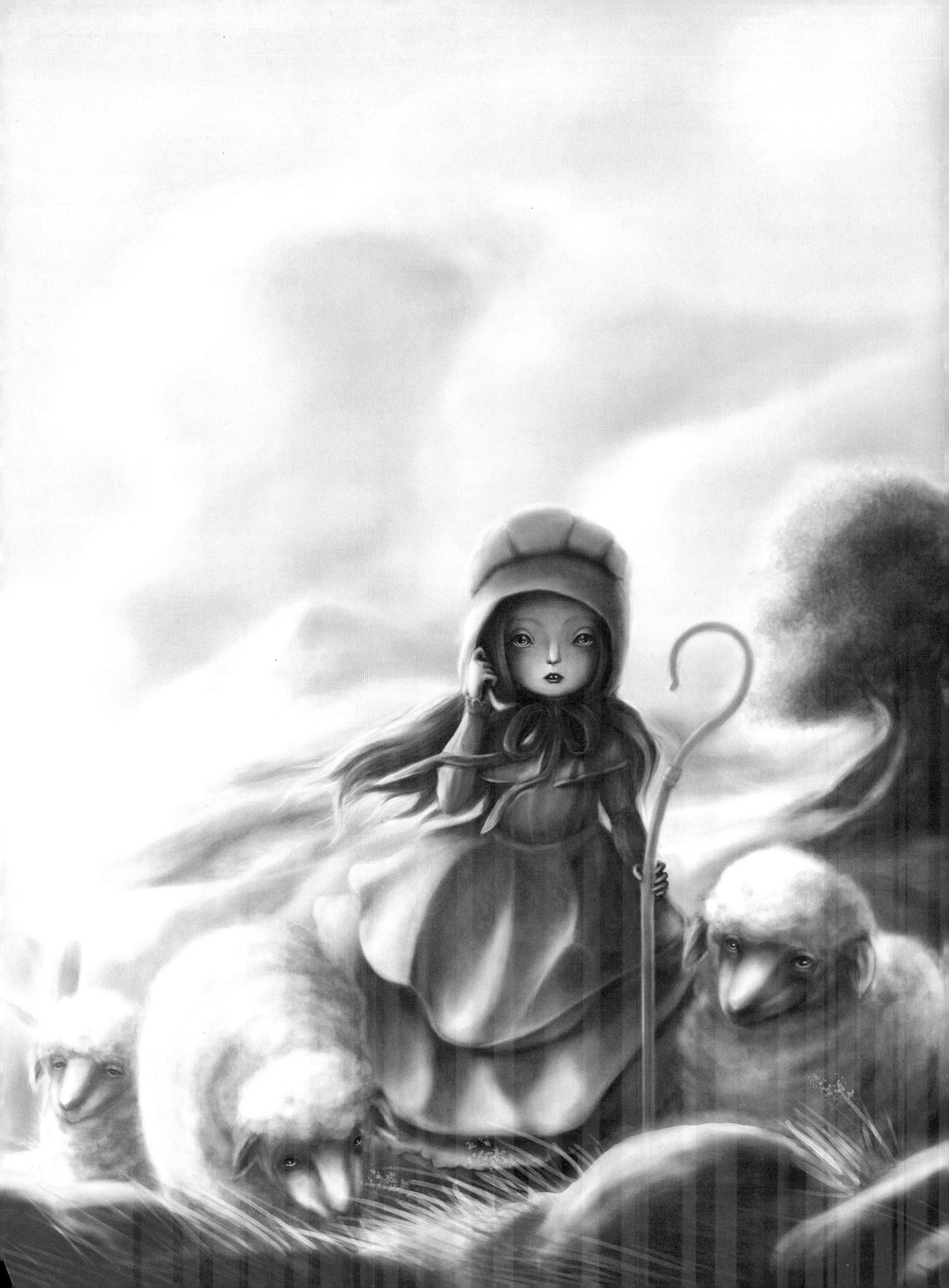

THE WORLD'S GREAT KIDS' LIT
AS COMICS AND VISUALS

# the GRAPHIC CANON
## OF CHILDREN'S LITERATURE

Edited by
# RUSS KICK

SEVEN STORIES PRESS
New York • Oakland

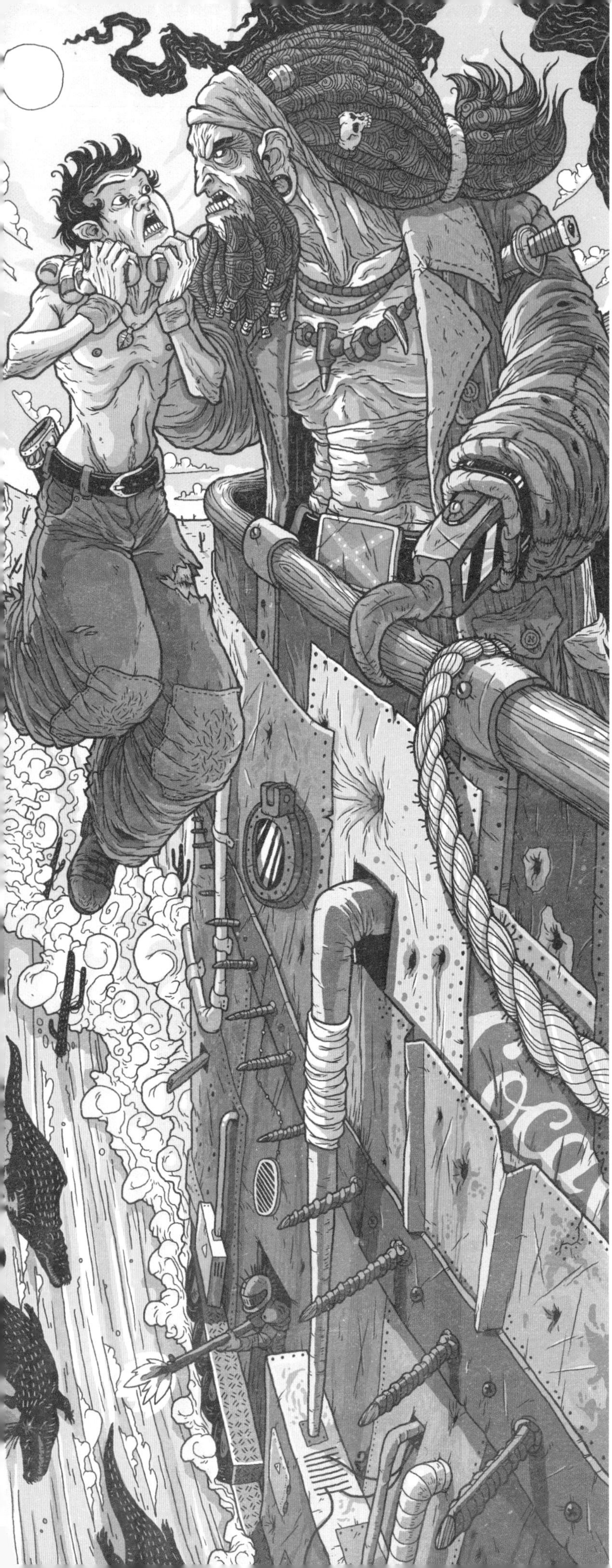


For permissions information see page 468.

A SEVEN STORIES PRESS FIRST EDITION



**SEVEN STORIES PRESS**
140 Watts Street
New York, NY 10013
www.sevenstories.com

College professors and high school and middle school teachers may order free examination copies of Seven Stories Press titles. To order, email academic@sevenstories.com or send a fax on school letterhead to (212) 226-1411.

Book design by Stewart Cauley, New York

**Library of Congress Cataloging-in-Publication Data**
The graphic canon of children's literature : the world's great kids' lit as comics and visuals / edited by Russ Kick. —A Seven Stories Press First Edition.
pages cm
ISBN 978-1-60980-530-2 (paperback)
1. Comic books, strips, etc.
2. Children's literature.
3. Literature—Adaptations.
4. Graphic novels in education.
I. Kick, Russ.
PN6714.G734 2014
741.5—dc23
2014010178

Printed in Hong Kong

9 8 7 6 5 4 3 2 1

ART CREDITS

Front cover: from "The Firebird" adapted by Lesley Barnes
Half title page: *The Wonderful Wizard of Oz* adapted by Polawat Darapong
Frontispiece: "Little Bo Peep" adapted by Karyl Gil
Copyright page: *Peter Pan* adapted by Artem Bizyaev
Page v: from "The Weardale Fairies" adapted by Rachael Ball
Pages vi-vii: "The Wizard of Oz Supporting Actor Audition Queue" by Mattias Adolfsson
Pages viii & ix: "Harry Potter Series" adapted by Katie Cook
Page 1: from "The Tinderbox" adapted by Isabel Greenberg
Page 464: *A Wrinkle in Time* adapted by Jeremy Sorese
Page 467: "Hansel and Gretel" adapted by Rada Azolina
Page 468: *Where the Wild Things Are* adapted by Lars Henkel
Inside back cover: "Beauty and the Beast" adapted by Manuel Šumberac
Back cover: "Little Red Riding Hood" adapted by Anna Lensch

# CONTENTS



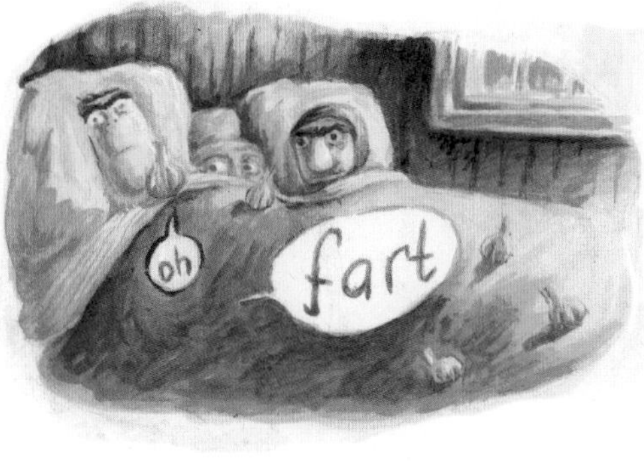
oh
fart

the Wizard of OZ

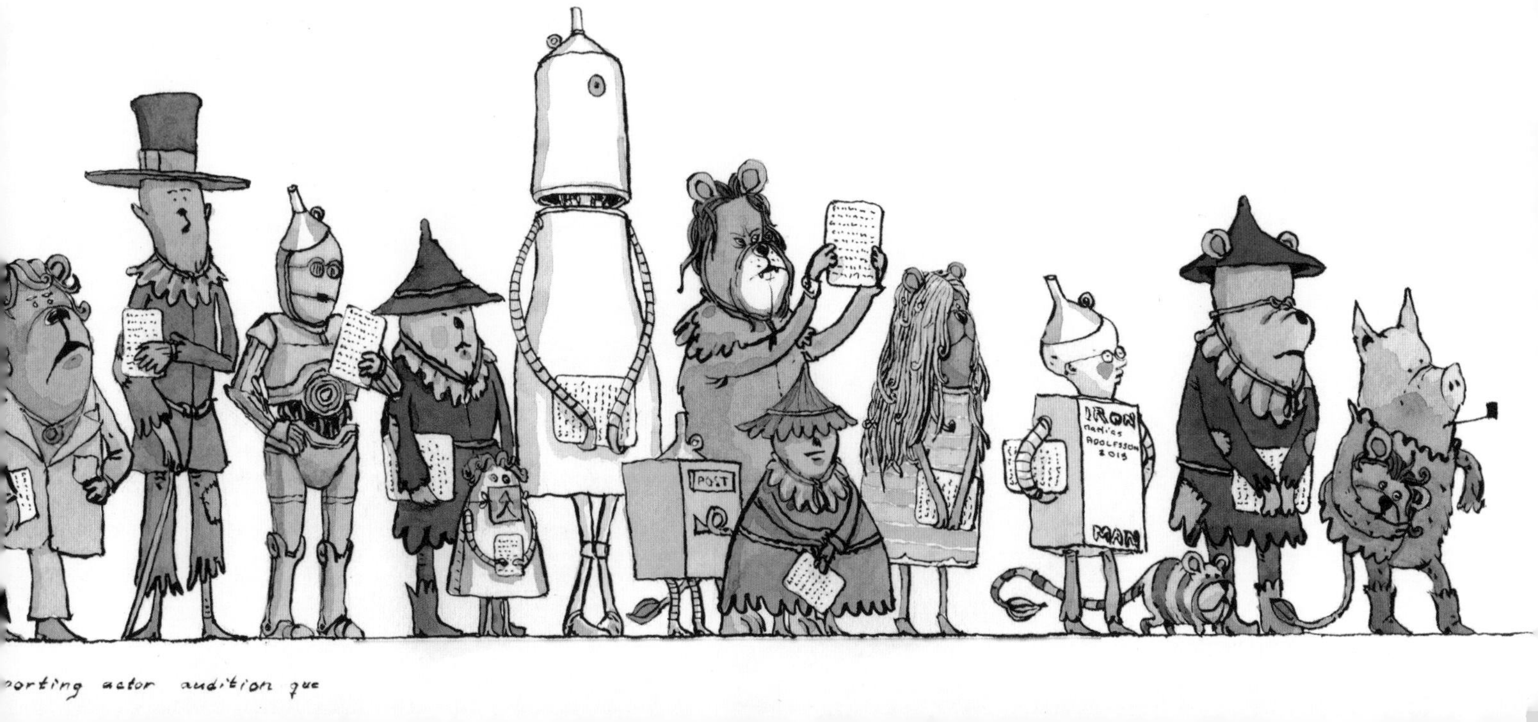
POST
IRON
MAN
porting actor audition que

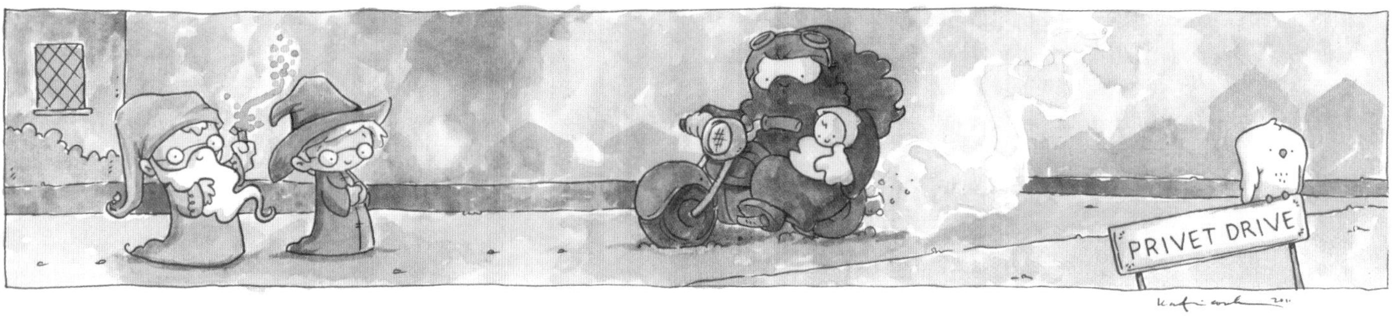

PRIVET DRIVE

# EDITOR'S INTRODUCTION

*There are some themes, some subjects, too large for adult fiction; they can only be dealt with adequately in a children's book.*
—Philip Pullman

*When I'm grappling with ideas which are radical enough to upset grown-ups, then I am likely to put these ideas into a story which will be marketed for children, because children understand what their parents have rejected and forgotten.*
—Madeleine L'Engle

*Boys and girls may have to shield their parents from this book. Parents are very easily scared.*
—*Cleveland Press* review of *Where the Wild Things Are* by Maurice Sendak

**IN THE INITIAL THREE-VOLUME SET** *THE GRAPHIC Canon*, over 120 illustrators, comics artists, and other types of artists visually adapted great works of world literature, from ancient Sumeria to the late twentieth-century United States. Seven Stories Press and I always knew we wanted to continue the project, so the question became, Where do we go now? Children's literature was an immediate strong candidate, and in the end we couldn't resist the lure of creating a twenty-first-century treasury of visual adaptations.

Part of the appeal is my belief that "children's literature" can be great literature, period. Works meant primarily for children or teens are usually ghettoized, considered unworthy of serious treatment and study. But the best of it achieves a greatness through heightened use of language, through examination of universal themes and human dilemmas, and through nuance and layers of meaning. One sign of a great work of literature or art is that it can be interpreted multiple ways, that it remains ambiguous, refusing to provide clear-cut answers.

In fact, the original *Graphic Canon* trilogy sported several works of children's lit. Mixed in with Dostoevsky, Dickinson, and Milton were Hans Christian Andersen, Lewis Carroll, and L. Frank Baum. It felt logical to move these works and others like them to the front and center. The volume you're now holding contains newly created adaptations of "The Little Mermaid,"

*Alice's Adventures in Wonderland*, the fourteen original Oz novels, and dozens of other works for young'uns.

As you'll be forcefully reminded—and this is another reason we wanted to do this volume—children's literature is *wild*. It's often bizarre, grotesque, dark, and violent. It seems odd that many of these works are considered children's literature. The fairy tales of the Brothers Grimm are the most well-known example, filled as they are with murder, mayhem, and mutilation. Hans Christian Andersen's "The Little Mermaid" ends with the mermaid committing suicide after considering stabbing the prince in the heart because he married another woman. *The Adventures of Pinocchio* is completely twisted, with the wooden boy being subject to repeated brutality, including a lynching. Aesop's fables often end with the death of at least one animal. Kidnapping/abduction is central to a number of works, including "The Weardale Fairies," "The Shepherdess and the Condor," "The Water-Sprite," *Peter Pan*, *The Jungle Book*, and *20,000 Leagues Under the Sea*. Danger everywhere! Wolves, dogs, tigers, condors, thieves, wicked stepmothers, witches, giants, pirates, disease, Nazis. . . . Aye-yi-yi!

This hasn't gone unnoticed. Any number of now-classic children's works have been decried as inappropriate through the decades. *Pippi Longstocking* triggered an ugly nationwide brawl over its rowdy, undisciplined, unparented protagonist. *Are You There God? It's Me, Margaret.* by Judy Blume is still—more than forty years after its publication—one of the most banned/challenged books in schools and public libraries throughout the United States. For several years, no British publisher would touch Roald Dahl's first two children's books—*Charlie and the Chocolate Factory* and *James and the Giant Peach*—because they were "too adult." Fifty years later it's easy to still marvel at the cruelty and darkness in them. One of the most enduring picture books of all time caused a furor, as its author related on *NOW*:

Bill Moyers: With *Where the Wild Things Are*, it created a big sensation. I mean, librarians would not put it in the shelves; in fact, there's one librarian who said, "This is not a book you leave in the presence of sensitive children to find in the twilight."
Maurice Sendak: Yes. There was a torrent of "Keep this book away from children."

There's something about seeing a children's work fully illustrated sequentially to make the terror and weirdness that much more visceral, that undeniable. While there are lots of picture books, such as *Wild Things*, many children's books are text-based, sometimes with accompanying spot illustrations. We don't often see "Little Red Riding Hood" faithfully related in pictures. It's a shock to see Pinocchio hanging from a tree, Ratty brandishing a pistol in *The Wind in the Willows*, the wasp ruthlessly torturing the snake in Aesop's fable, Humpty Dumpty cracked wide open and dead, and the three blind mice getting tailectomies, to say nothing of the nightmarish seven-headed Mouse King from *The Nutcracker*.

The fact that children's books are often illustrated was another enticement to do this book. So many of these books contain images that have become synonymous with the work: Sir John Tenniel's line illustrations for *Alice's Adventures in Wonderland* and *Through the Looking-Glass* have taken on a life of their own. William Wallace Denslow's plentiful illustrations for *The Wonderful Wizard of Oz* rivaled or bested the text in the opinion of many reviewers. You can't look at Quentin Blake's whimsical drawings without thinking of Roald Dahl. Antoine de Saint-Exupéry's watercolor line drawings for *The Little Prince* mesh seamlessly with his words. Likewise, Beatrix Potter tenderly illustrated her own works, and Edward Lear whimsically illustrated his.

Then there are the picture books, with full-page images and minimal text, the visuals forming the main part of the equation. Dr. Seuss was the master. And Maurice Sendak. Richard Scarry. *The Giving Tree*, *The Very Hungry Caterpillar*, *The Berenstain Bears*, *Babar*, *Curious George*, *Chitty-Chitty-Bang-Bang*, *The Little Engine That Could*.... Those canonical images are probably whipping through your head right now.

Beyond this, there are the artists who illustrated later editions of classic children's lit. Arthur Rackham specialized in this, bringing the skills of an old master to the Grimms, Aesop, Mother Goose, Kenneth Grahame, and lots more. Maxfield Parrish, who had a supernatural command of color, provided dazzling paintings for several children's books in the first part of the twentieth century. The number of illustrated editions of the Grimms, Andersen, and Alice is beyond reckoning. Artists from Salvador Dalí to Ralph Steadman to S. Clay Wilson have put their visual stamps on these tales.

Illustrations aren't the only images of these works that have imprinted themselves on us. Movies made from fairy tales and children's books in many cases monopolize how we picture certain characters. Disney has given us the defining looks of Pinocchio, Bambi, Mary Poppins, the Little Mermaid, Winnie-the-Pooh, Cinderella, Beauty and the Beast, Peter Pan and Tinkerbell, and others. If you don't picture Alice in Wonderland as Tenniel drew her, you're probably visualizing her as a yellow-haired girl in a blue dress and white smock, courtesy of Disney. And it goes beyond the Empire of the Mouse. Movies from other studios have tattooed our psyches with Dorothy and the Oz crew, Harry Potter and Hermione, Willy Wonka and his factory, the rabbits of *Watership Down*, and Bilbo, Gandalf, and Gollum, among others.

Yet each of these represents just a single conception of how these characters could look. I'm interested in seeing new conceptions. I want to see how twenty-first-century illustrators, cartoonists, comics artists, and painters view these age-old characters, these figures that have embedded themselves in the childhoods of generation after generation for decades, sometimes for centuries. Could we see Alice as a chubby, literally snot-nosed brat? Thank you, Vicki Nerino. Could someone demolish everything we think we know about Oz and rebuild it from the ground up, with a drawing style from the cutting edge and a color scheme from the golden age of Sunday comics? Thank you, Shawn Cheng. How about a Pinocchio that actually looks like he was carved from a tree, a Captain Nemo via Ziggy Stardust, a Tom Sawyer via *The Family Circus*, a hypercute Peter Pan, an avant-garde *Secret Garden*, a highly stylized Nutcracker, a Chinese Goldilocks, a male Snow White, a brown Winnie-the-Pooh...?

We ended up with over forty adaptations and over sixty stand-alone illustrations that treat children's literature with the respect, daring, and verve it deserves. In a strange twist, we created a book that many people may think isn't suitable for children, especially those under the age of, say, ten or twelve. They might be right. The book has obvious appeal for teens and adults, and maybe they're the only audiences for a work that shows so many bizarre, upsetting, and nightmarish images. Or perhaps we should keep in mind something Sendak said in one of his final interviews: "I refuse to lie to children. I refuse to cater to the bullshit of innocence."

—RUSS KICK

# "The Miller, His Son, and the Donkey" and "The Eagle, the Cat, and the Sow"

**Aesop**

ART/ADAPTATION BY **Roberta Gregory**

**WE'RE NOT POSITIVE THAT THE ANCIENT GREEK** known as Aesop existed, but most scholars now think that he was a real person, albeit one buried under more than two millennia of legends and mythmaking. The Penguin Classics edition *The Complete Fables* gives us the most unvarnished biography: "Aesop was probably a prisoner of war, sold into slavery in the early sixth century BC, who represented his masters in court and negotiations, and relied on animal stories to put across his key points."

None of Aesop's writings survive, but the hundreds of tales written by him or attributed to him (questionably

or wrongly) exist in ancient Greek and Latin sources. The fables have been immensely popular since their creation, but, like so much so-called children's literature from long ago, they've been watered down, bowdlerized, mistranslated, and rewritten through the ages.

Roberta Gregory gives us two of Aesop's lesser-known fables, darkly humorous tales about the perils of listening to other people (or, um, felines). Roberta is part of the early generation of underground comics artists, the ones who created the genre, with her feminist comics that started appearing in the mid-1970s. Her sweet, colorful style belies the cruel, harsh nature of this pair of fables.

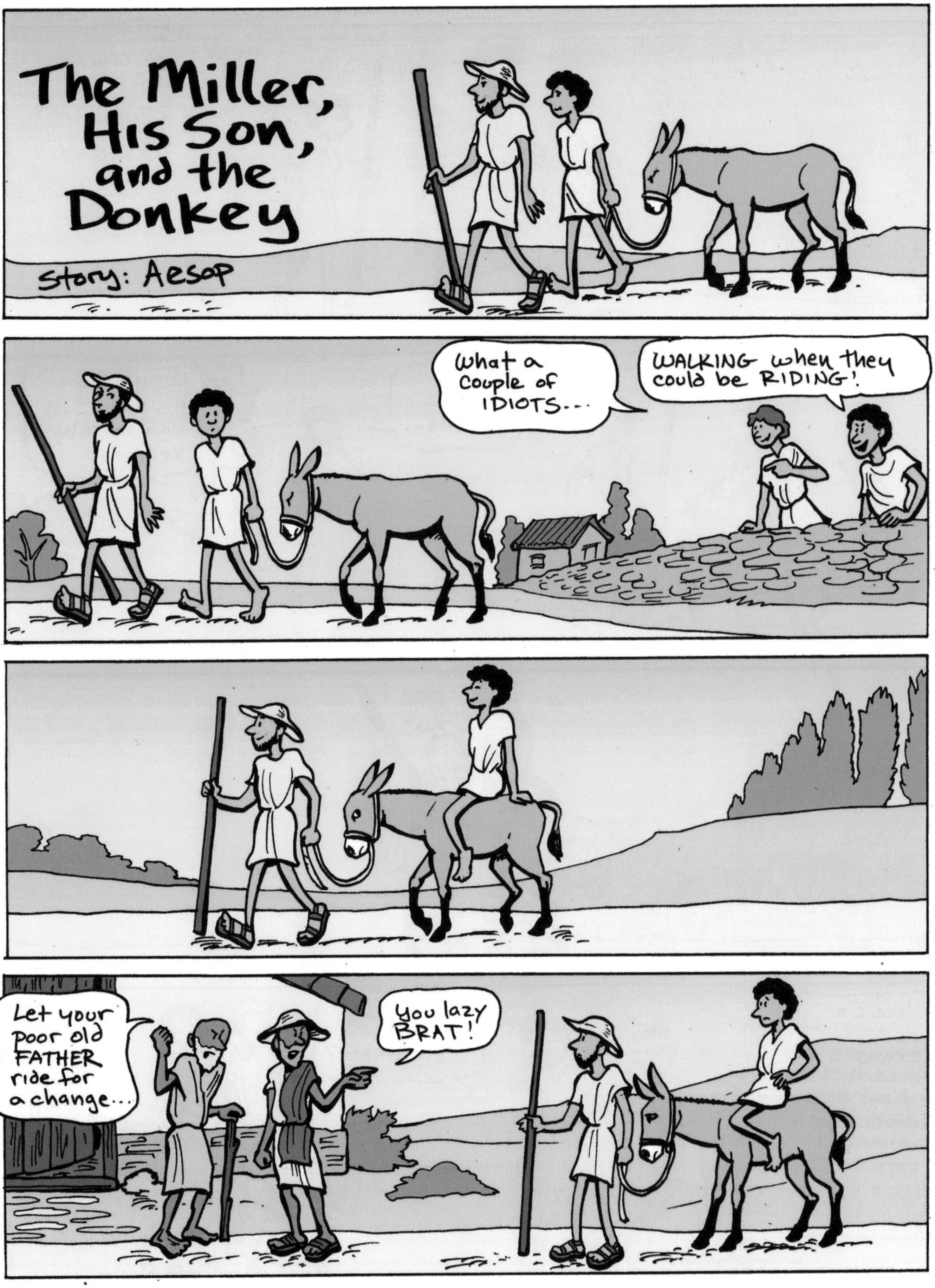
The Miller, His Son, and the Donkey
Story: Aesop
What a couple of IDIOTS...
WALKING when they could be RIDING!
Let your poor old FATHER ride for a change...
You lazy BRAT!

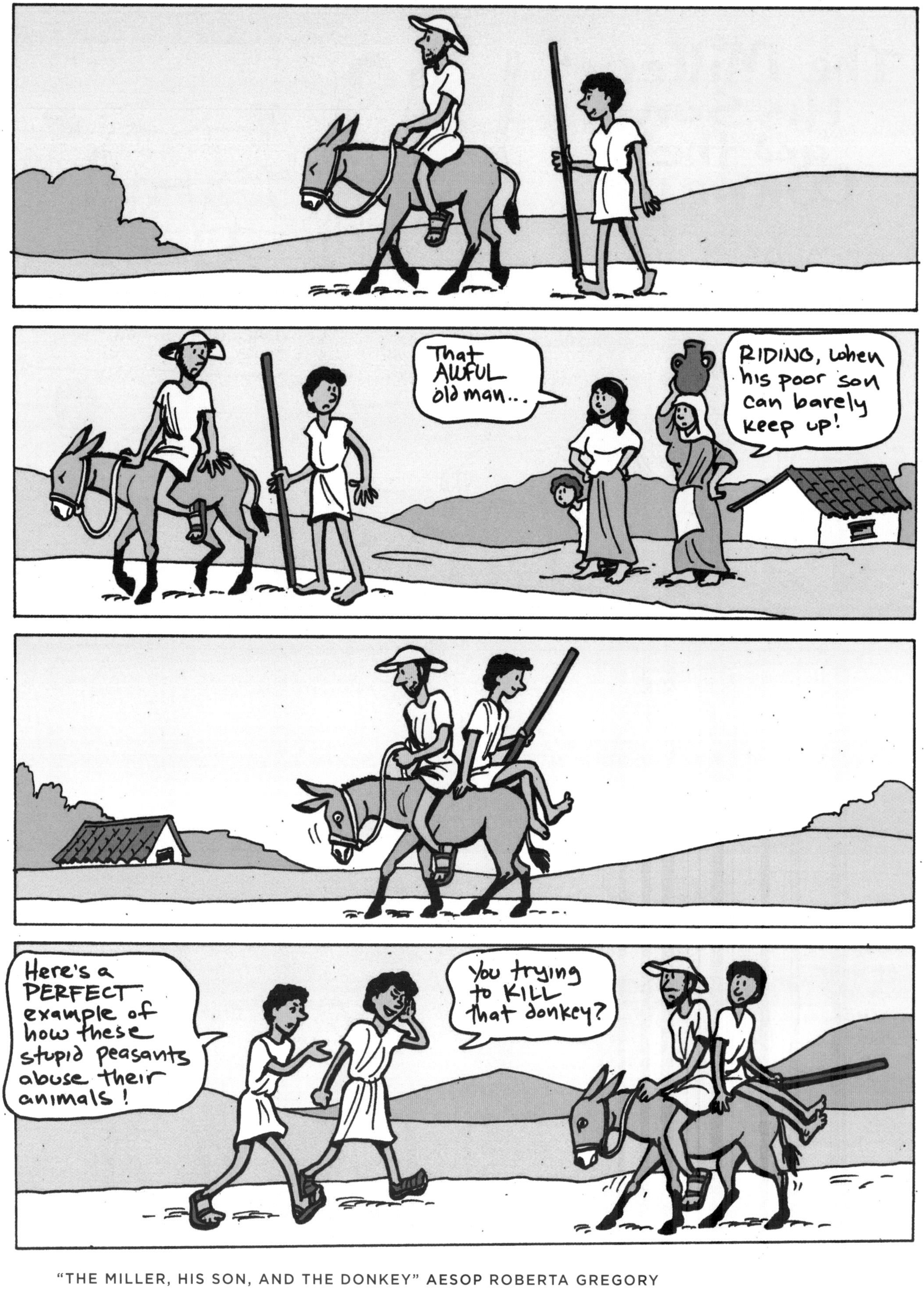
That AWFUL old man...
RIDING, when his poor son can barely keep up!
Here's a PERFECT example of how these stupid peasants abuse their animals!
You trying to KILL that donkey?

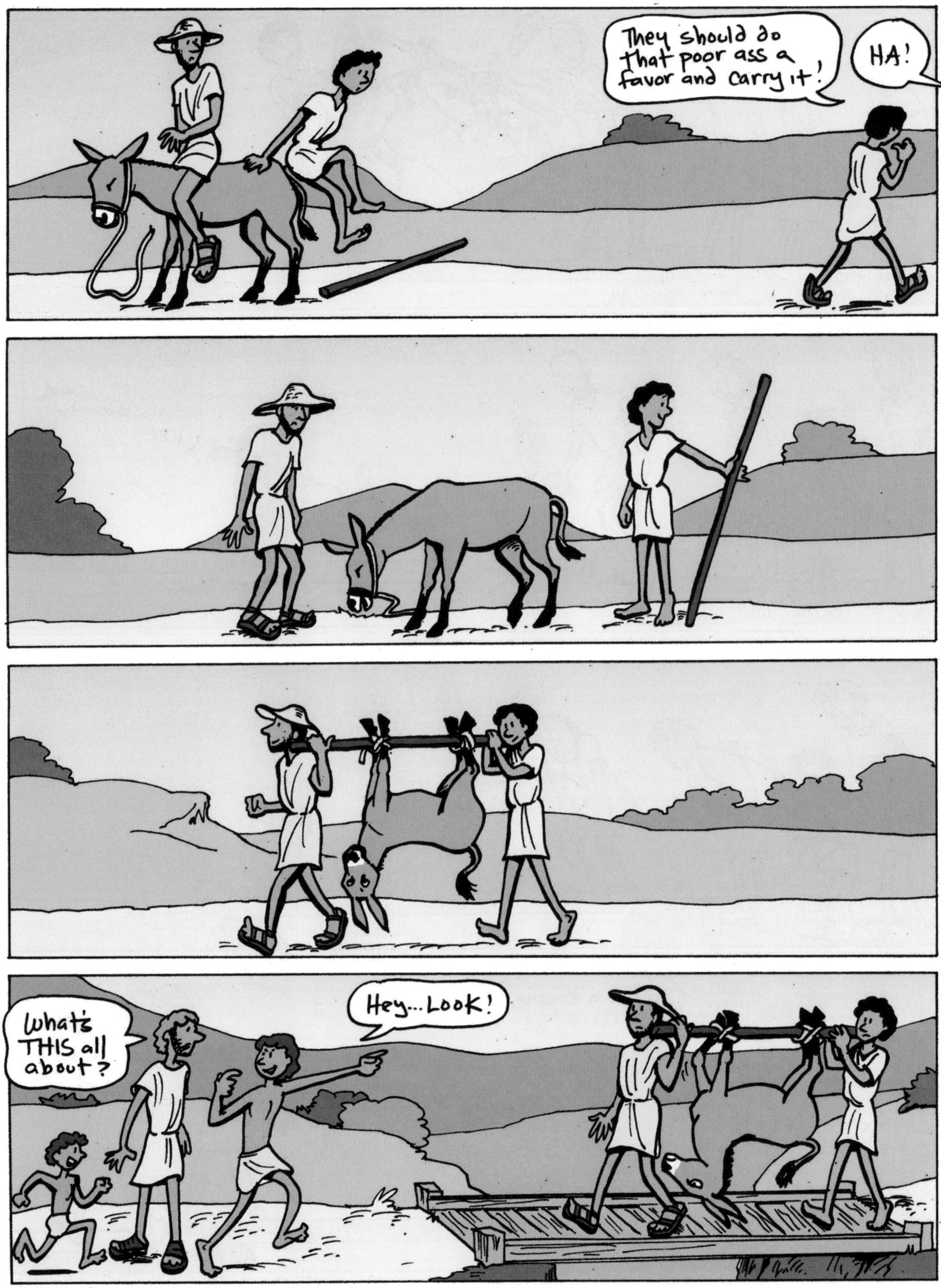
They should do that poor ass a favor and carry it!
HA!
What's THIS all about?
Hey...LOOK!

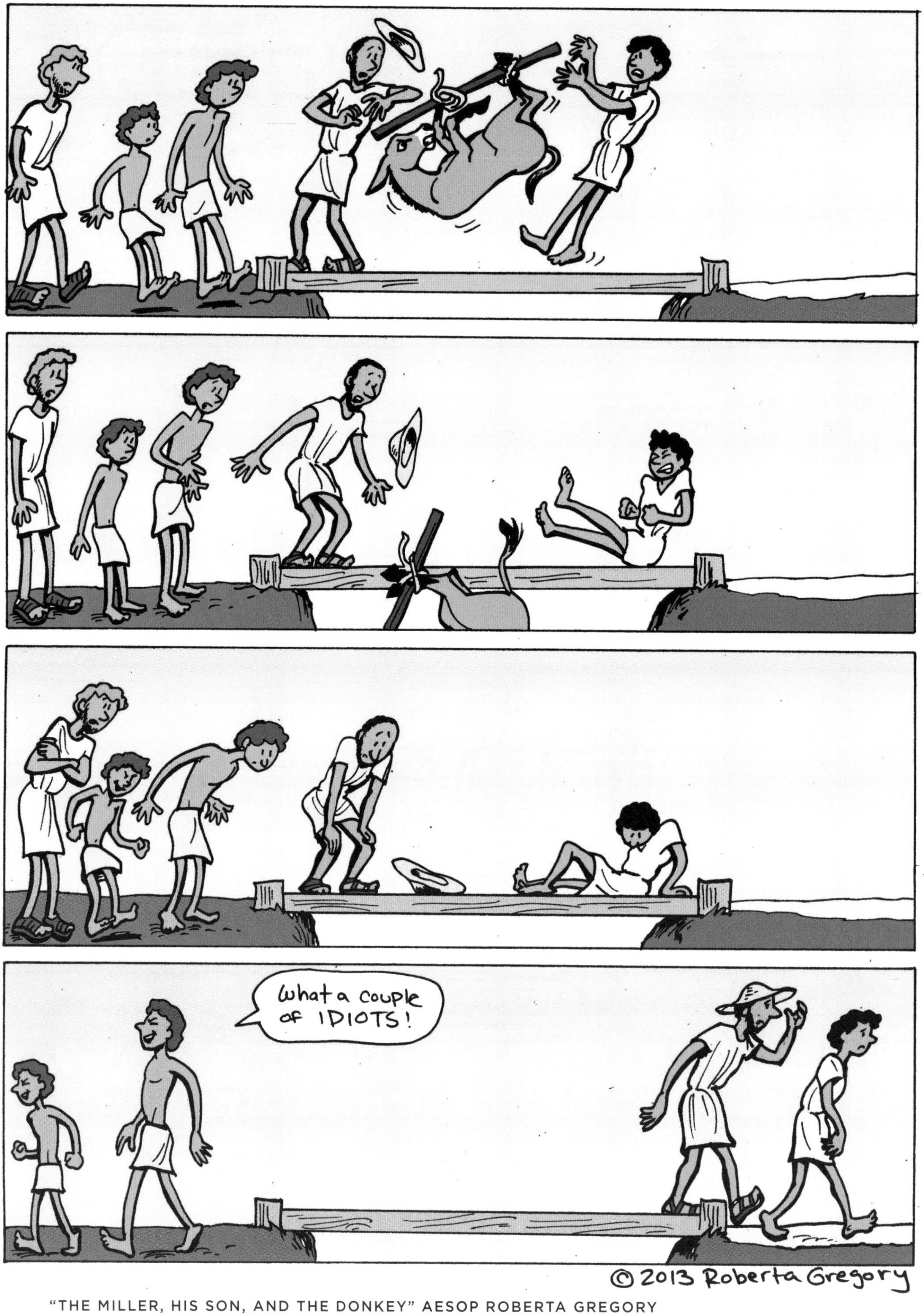
What a couple of IDIOTS!
© 2013 Roberta Gregory

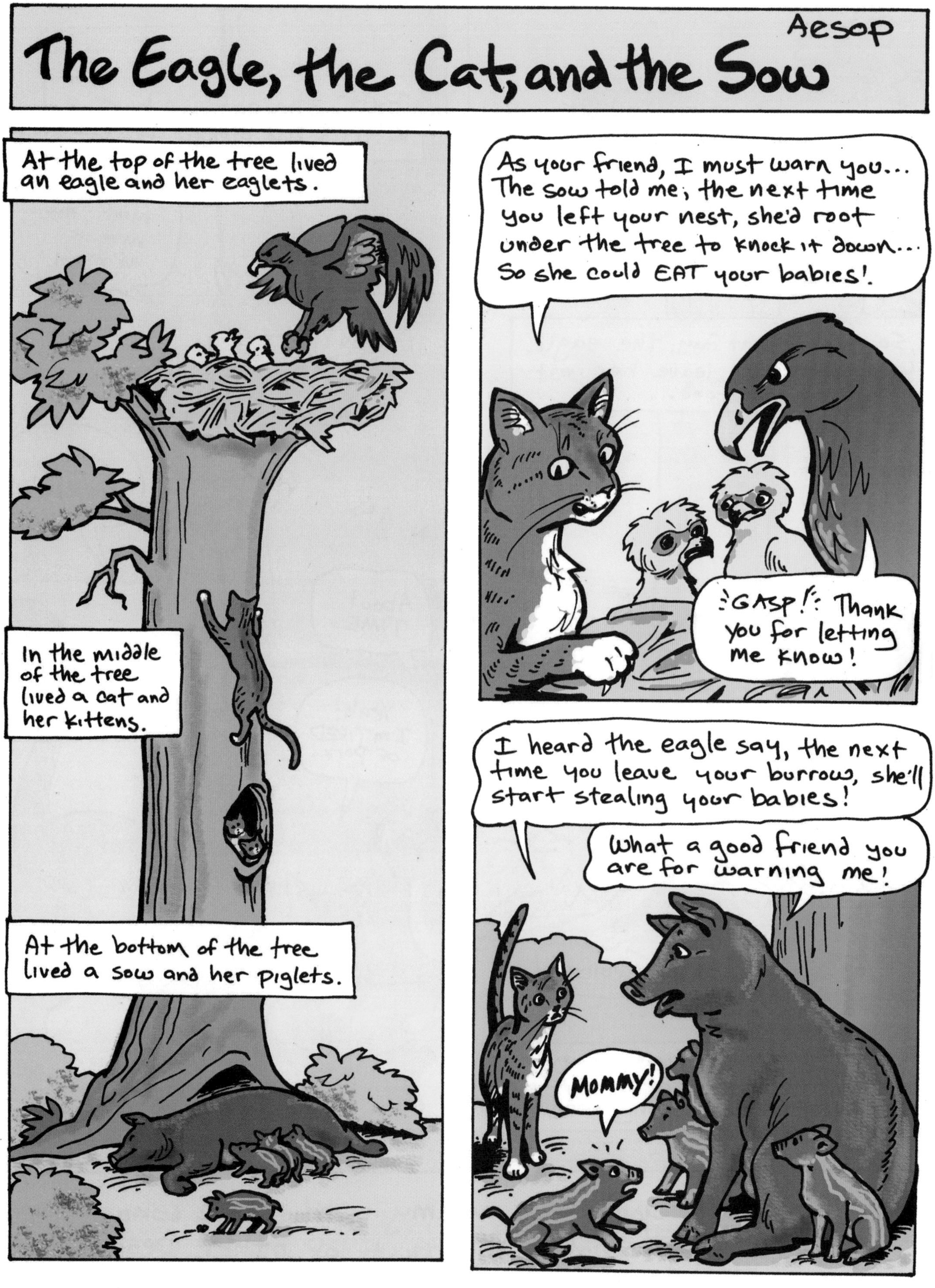
Aesop
The Eagle, the Cat, and the Sow
At the top of the tree lived an eagle and her eaglets.
In the middle of the tree lived a cat and her kittens.
At the bottom of the tree lived a sow and her piglets.
As your friend, I must warn you... The sow told me, the next time you left your nest, she'd root under the tree to knock it down... So she could EAT your babies!
GASP! Thank you for letting me know!
I heard the eagle say, the next time you leave your burrow, she'll start stealing your babies!
What a good friend you are for warning me!
MOMMY!

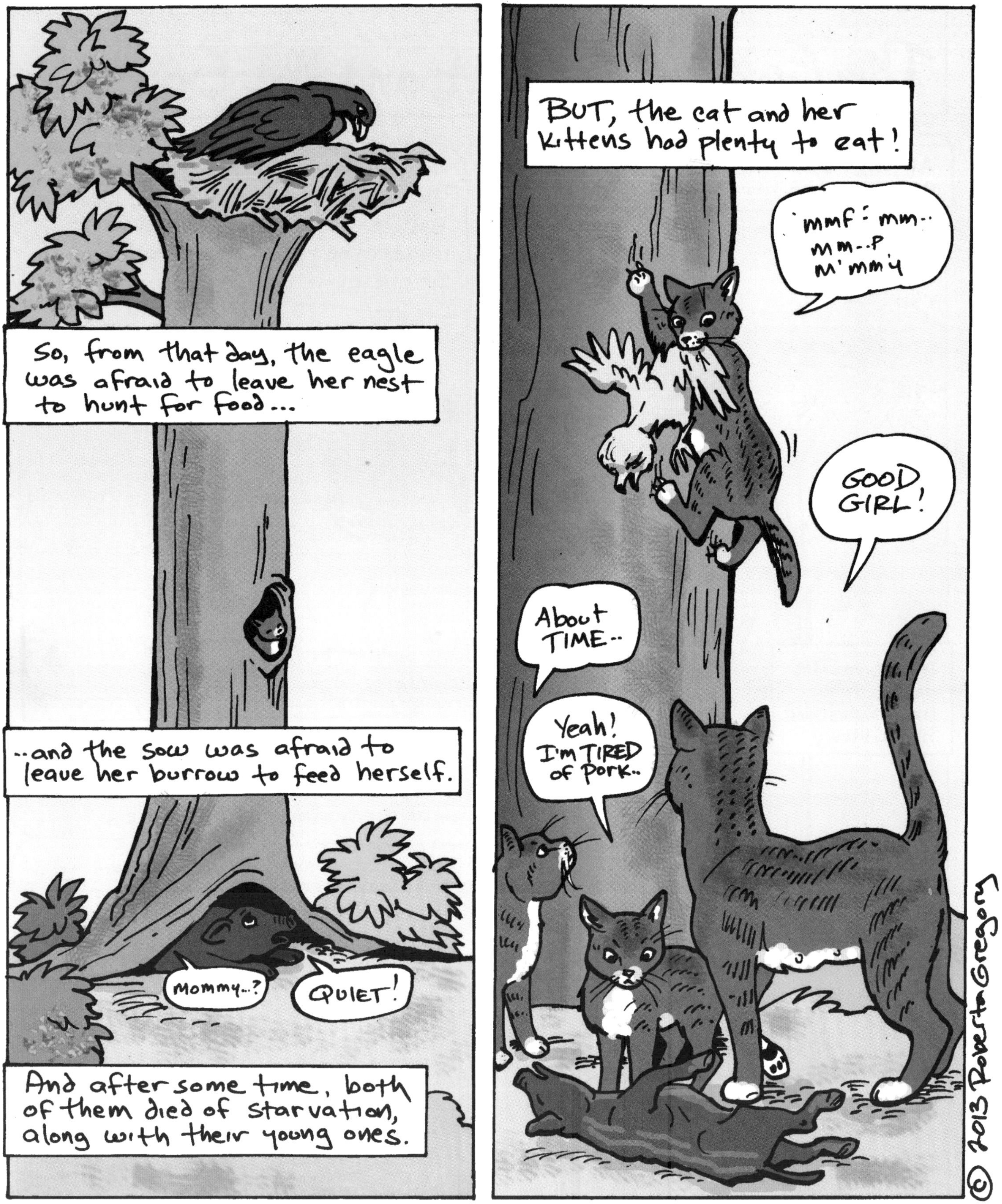
So, from that day, the eagle was afraid to leave her nest to hunt for food...
..and the sow was afraid to leave her burrow to feed herself.
Mommy...?
QUIET!
And after some time, both of them died of starvation, along with their young ones.
BUT, the cat and her kittens had plenty to eat!
mmf: mm.. mm..p M'mm'y
GOOD GIRL!
About TIME..
Yeah! I'm TIRED of Pork..
© 2013 Roberta Gregory

**The Moral:** Your true enemy is the one who promotes mistrust of other people.

# "The Ape and the Fisherman" and "The Wasp and the Snake"

## Aesop

ART/ADAPTATION BY **Peter Kuper**

**MORE AESOP, MORE DARKNESS. THIS TIME, THE HUMAN** foibles of greed, laziness, and cruelty lead to violent death among the animals. Artist Peter Kuper is known for his sociopolitical work (including cofounding *World War 3 Illustrated*), his long-running "Spy vs. Spy" feature for *Mad* magazine, and his adaptations of classic literature, including *The Jungle* (Upton Sinclair) and *The Metamorphosis* (Franz Kafka). The bright colors and lively action of his style provide a counterpoint to the savage nature of the tales.

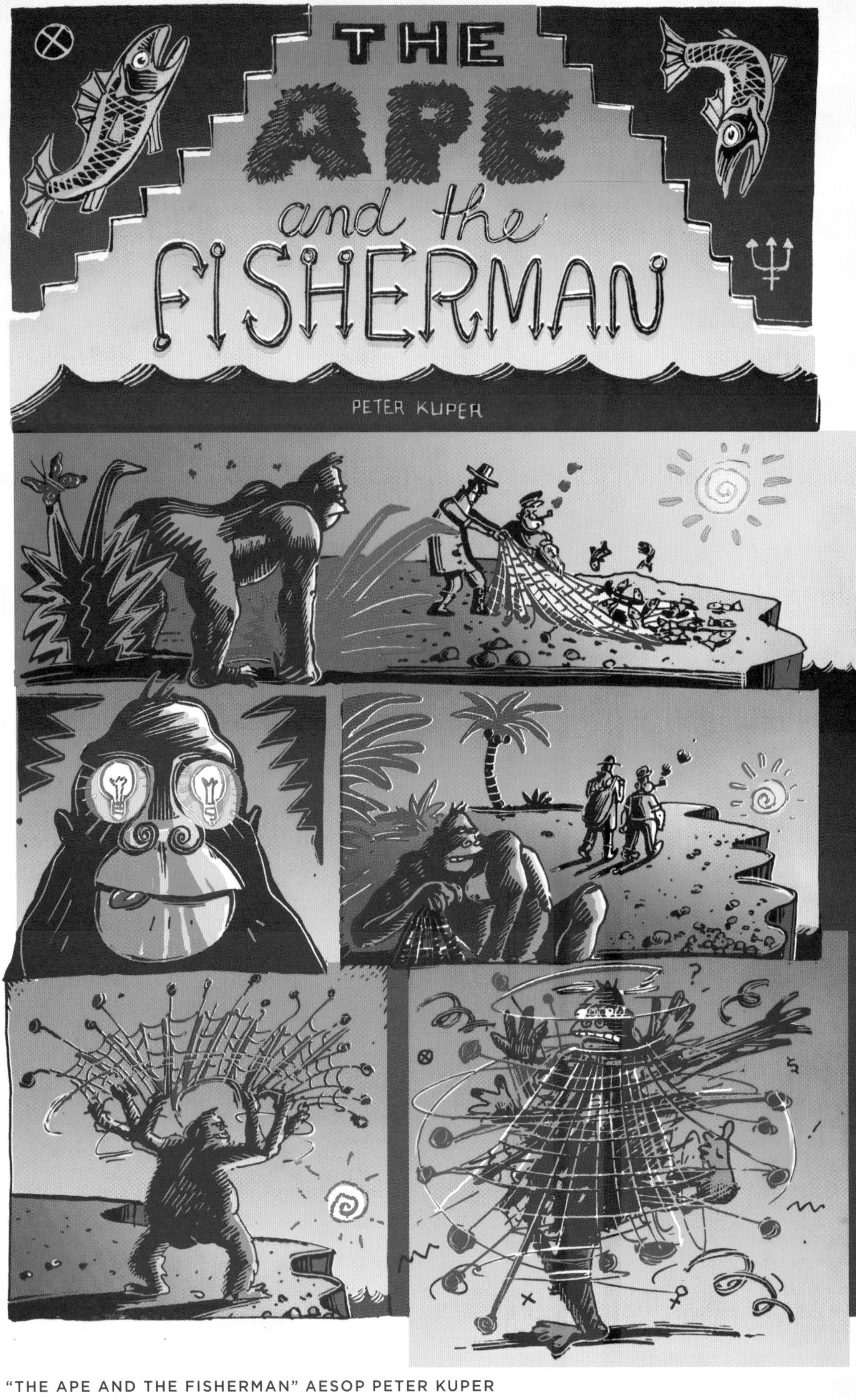
THE APE and the FISHERMAN
PETER KUPER

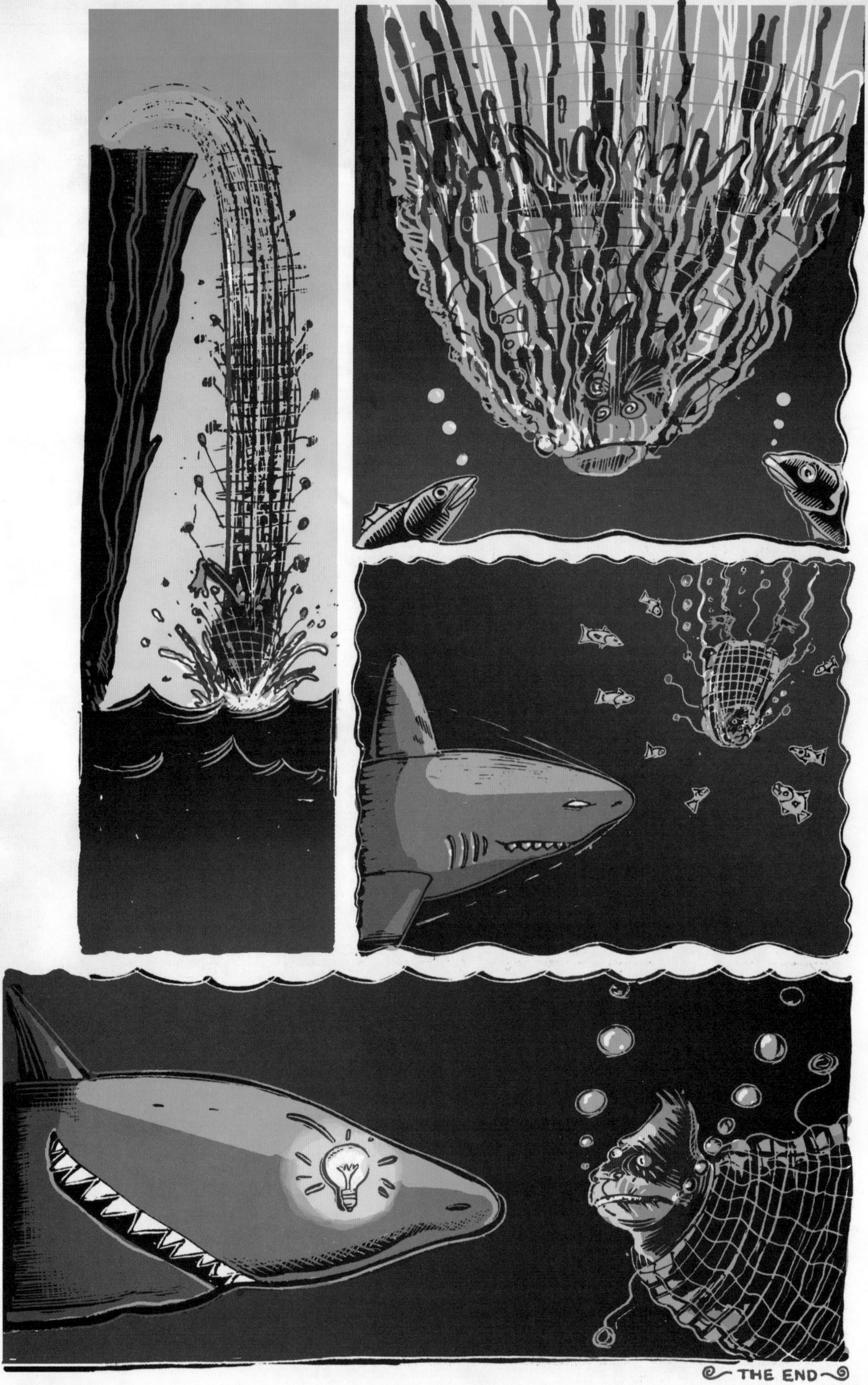
THE END

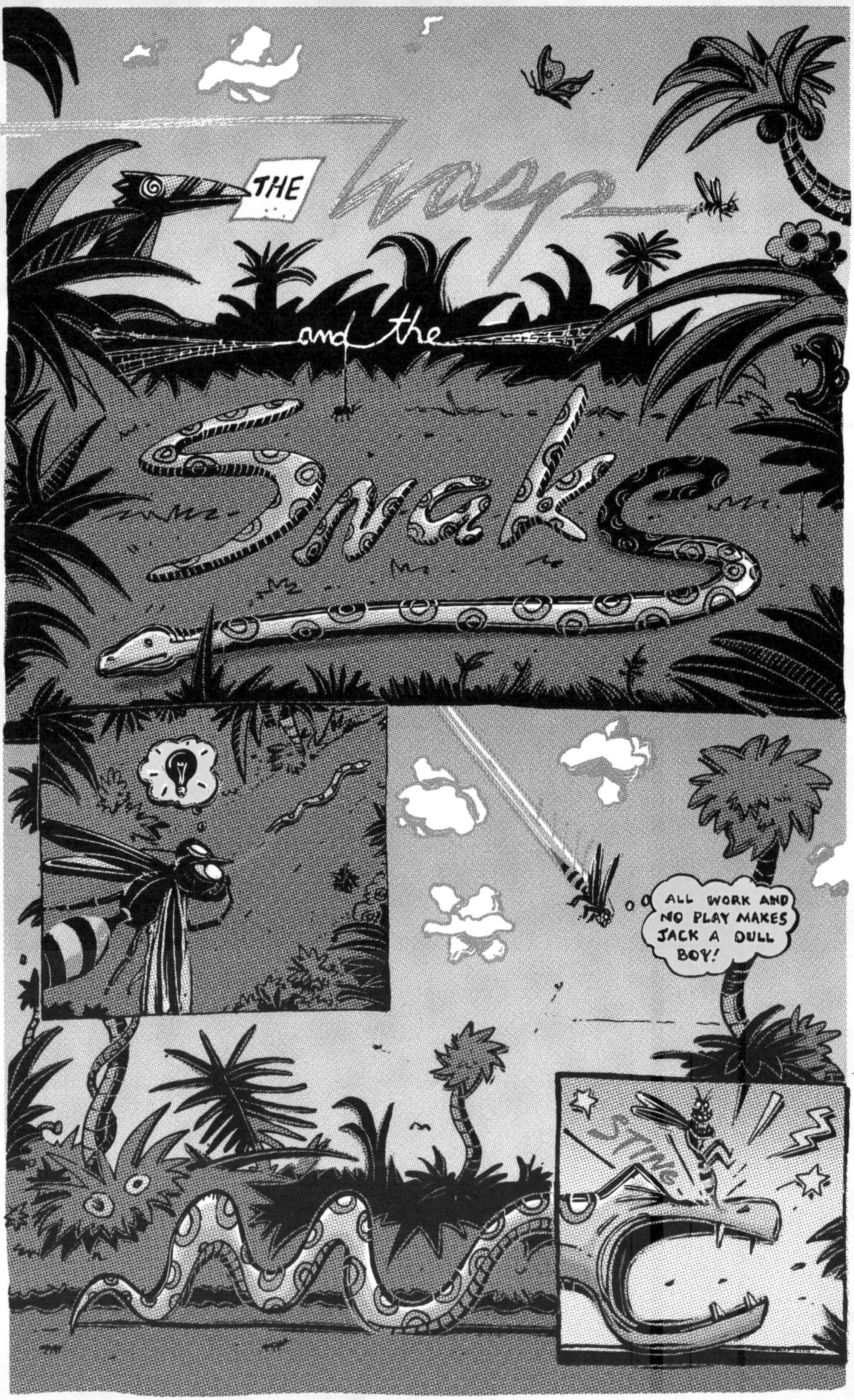
THE Wasp
and the
Snake
ALL WORK AND NO PLAY MAKES JACK A DULL BOY!
STING

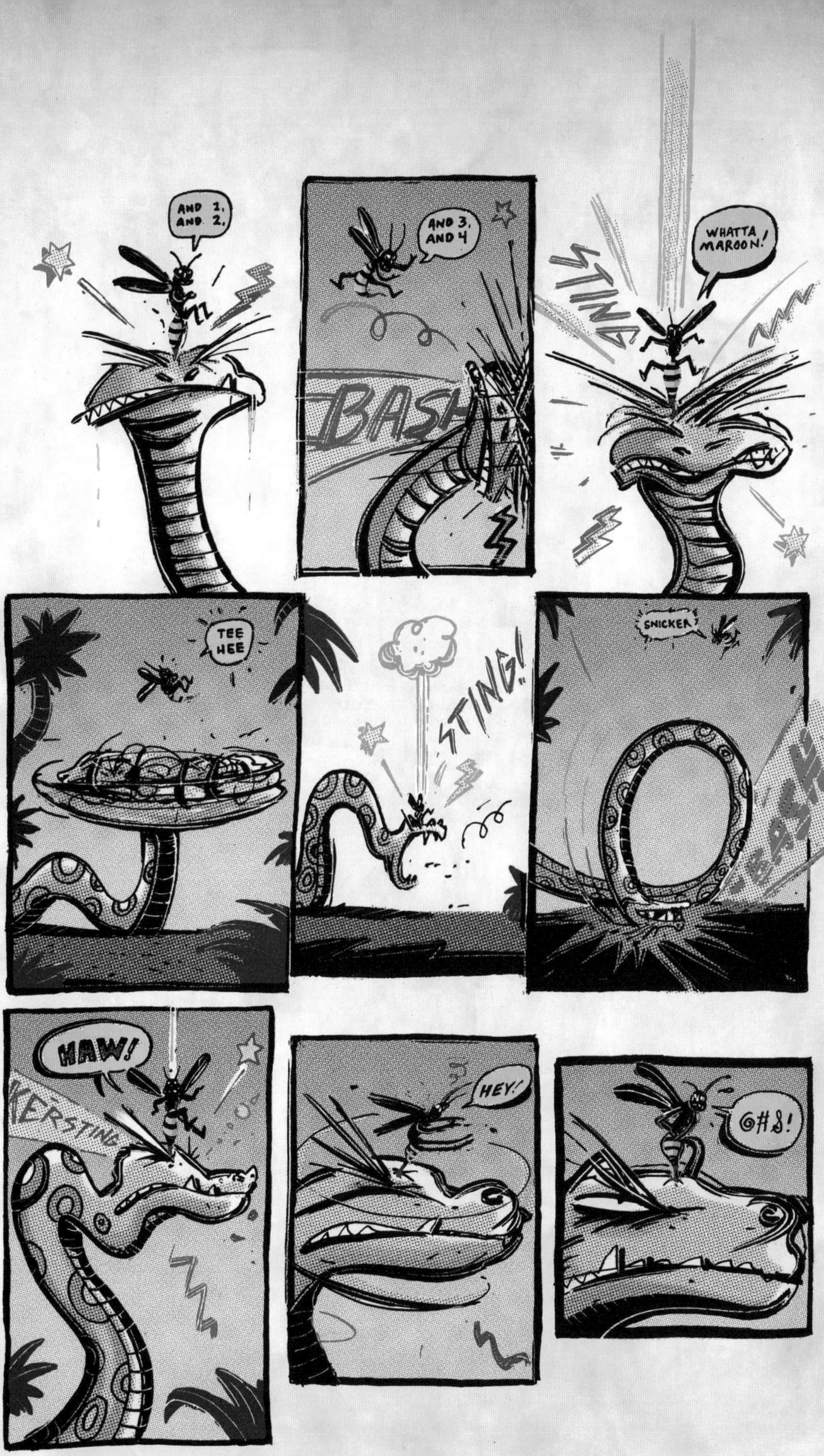
AND 1, AND 2,
AND 3, AND 4
BASH
WHATTA MAROON!
STING
TEE HEE
STING!
SNICKER
BASH
HAW!
KERSTING
HEY!
@#$!

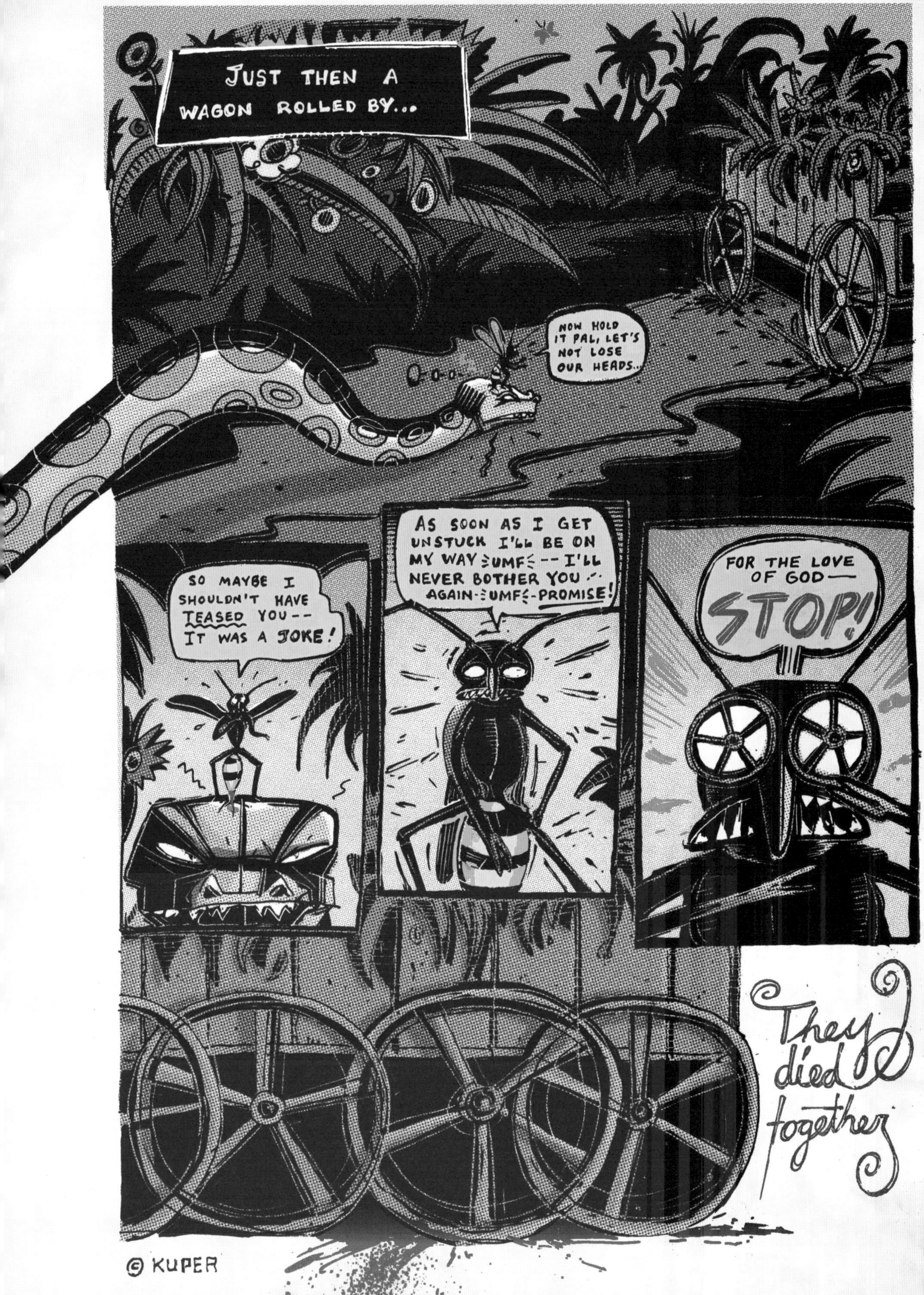
JUST THEN A WAGON ROLLED BY...
NOW HOLD IT PAL, LET'S NOT LOSE OUR HEADS...
SO MAYBE I SHOULDN'T HAVE TEASED YOU-- IT WAS A JOKE!
AS SOON AS I GET UNSTUCK I'LL BE ON MY WAY -UMF- -- I'LL NEVER BOTHER YOU AGAIN -UMF- PROMISE!
FOR THE LOVE OF GOD— STOP!
They died together
© KUPER

# "The Lion in Love," "The Fox and the Grapes," and "The City Mouse and the Country Mouse"

## Aesop

ART/ADAPTATION BY **Lance Tooks**

**ONE OF THE BEAUTIFUL ASPECTS OF FABLES AND** fairy tales is how easily they can be transplanted to other times and cultures, while the plot and message can remain essentially the same. In this trio of fables from Aesop, animals in ancient Greece become people in big cities of the twenty-first century. "The Lion in Love" takes place in the hood; "The Fox and the Grapes" is set among nightclubs; and the city mouse introduces the country mouse to life among Russian gangsters and drug lords.

A former assistant editor at Marvel Comics, Lance Tooks has worked extensively in animation (including Nickelodeon's cult-classic series *Doug*) and has created several highly praised graphic novels. His work integrates illustration, photos, text, and design in a marvelously unique way.

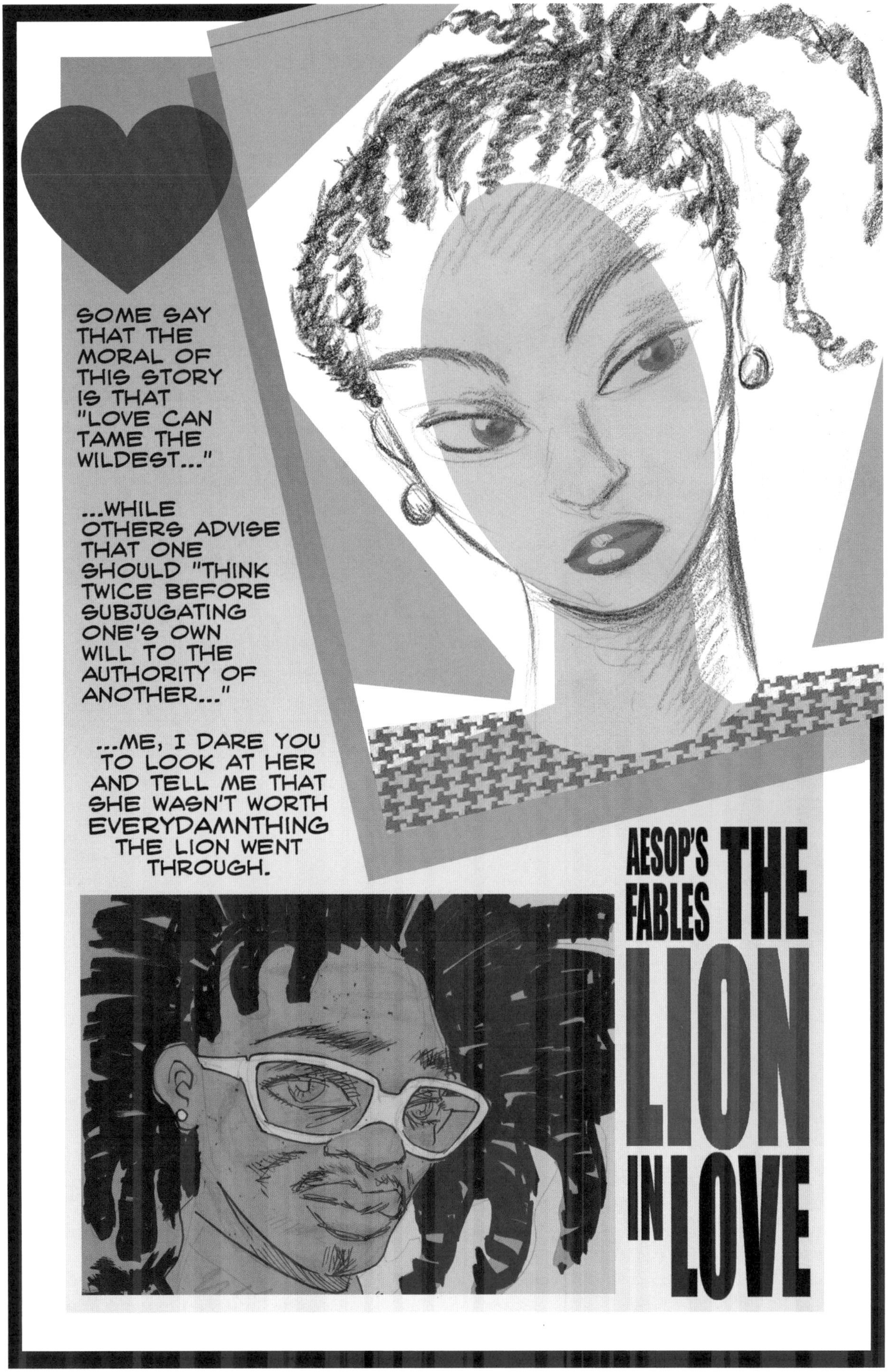
SOME SAY THAT THE MORAL OF THIS STORY IS THAT "LOVE CAN TAME THE WILDEST..."
...WHILE OTHERS ADVISE THAT ONE SHOULD "THINK TWICE BEFORE SUBJUGATING ONE'S OWN WILL TO THE AUTHORITY OF ANOTHER..."
...ME, I DARE YOU TO LOOK AT HER AND TELL ME THAT SHE WASN'T WORTH EVERYDAMNTHING THE LION WENT THROUGH.
AESOP'S FABLES
THE LION IN LOVE

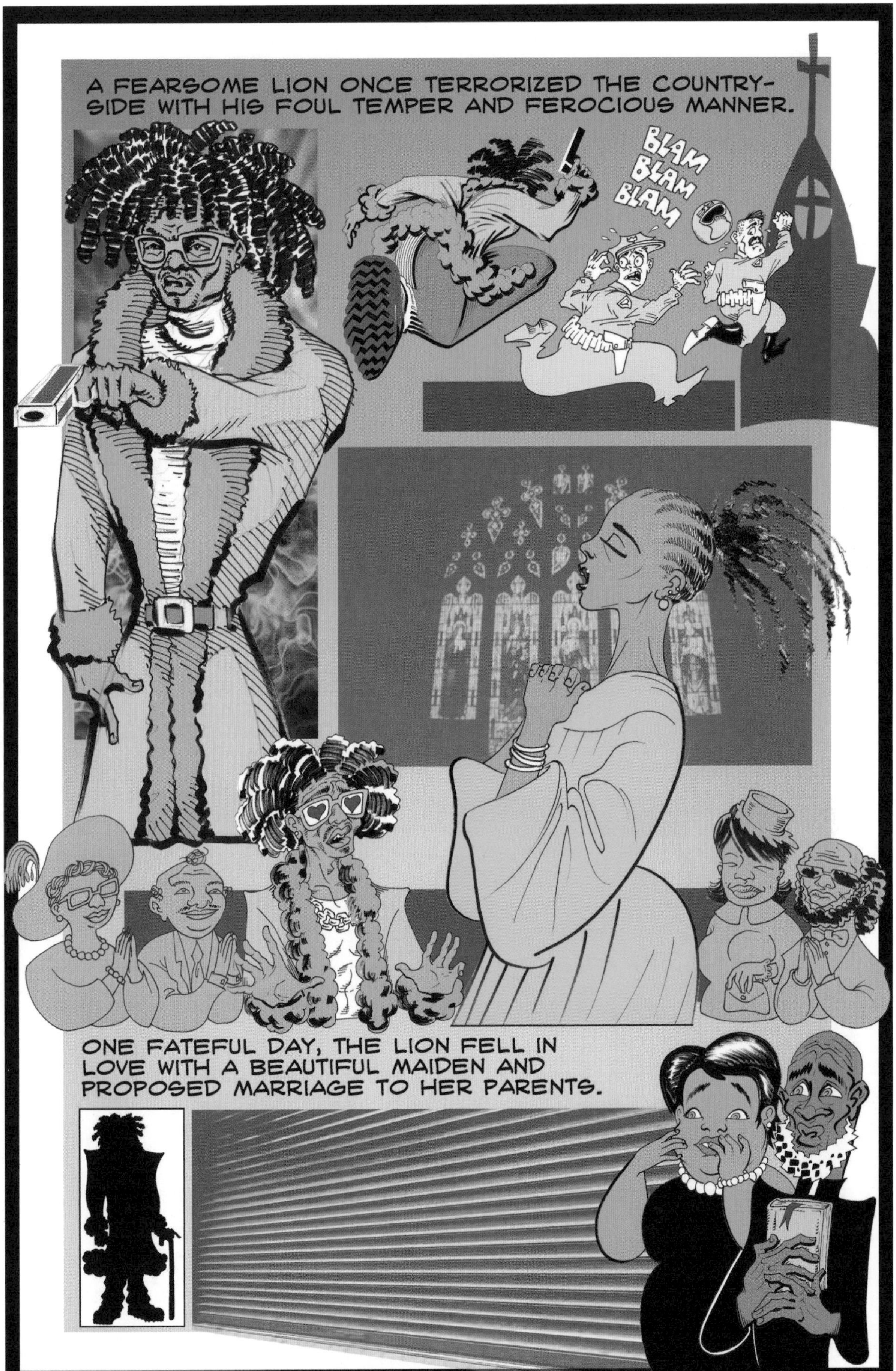
A FEARSOME LION ONCE TERRORIZED THE COUNTRY-SIDE WITH HIS FOUL TEMPER AND FEROCIOUS MANNER.
BLAM BLAM BLAM
ONE FATEFUL DAY, THE LION FELL IN LOVE WITH A BEAUTIFUL MAIDEN AND PROPOSED MARRIAGE TO HER PARENTS.

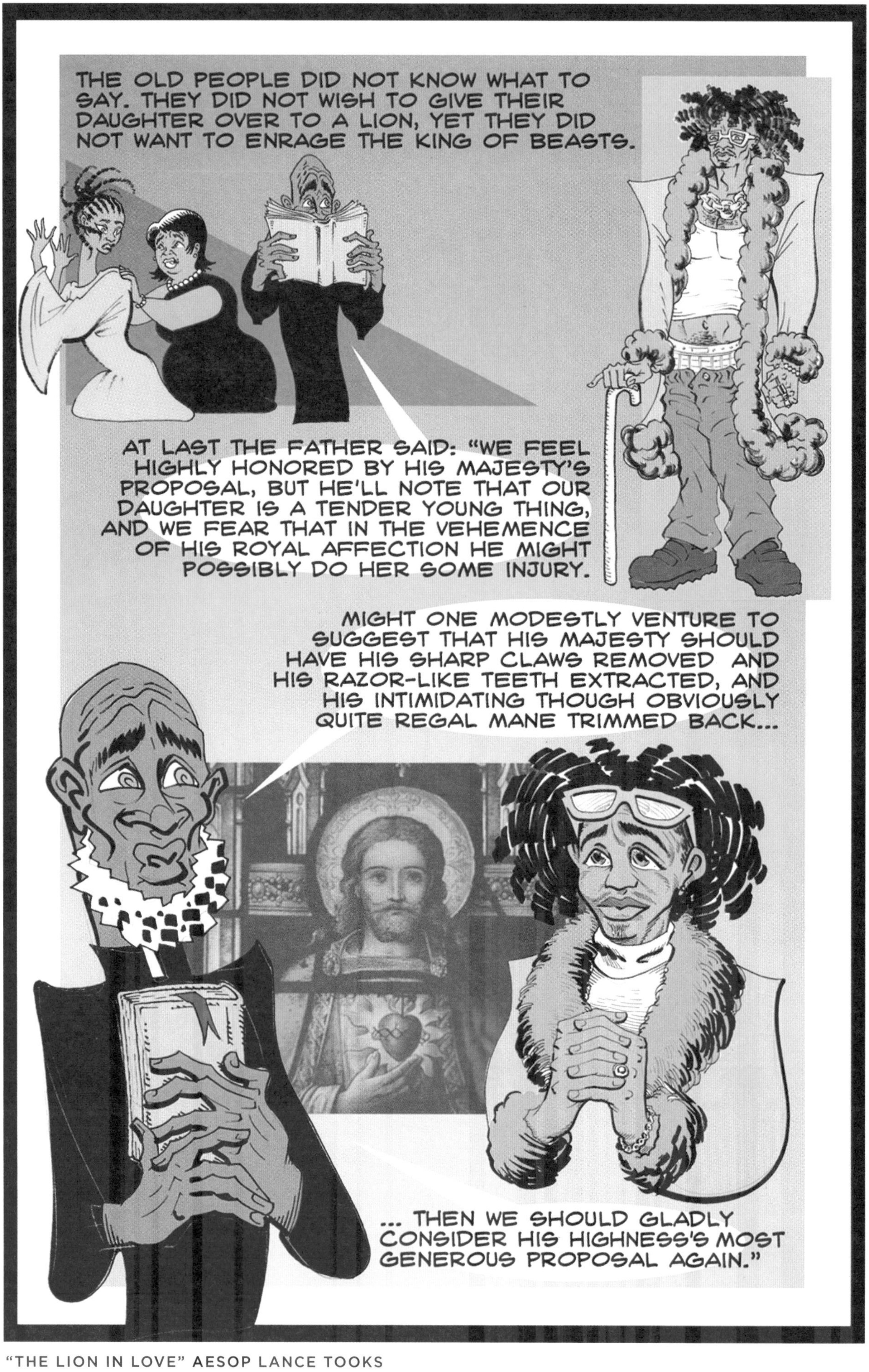
THE OLD PEOPLE DID NOT KNOW WHAT TO SAY. THEY DID NOT WISH TO GIVE THEIR DAUGHTER OVER TO A LION, YET THEY DID NOT WANT TO ENRAGE THE KING OF BEASTS.
AT LAST THE FATHER SAID: "WE FEEL HIGHLY HONORED BY HIS MAJESTY'S PROPOSAL, BUT HE'LL NOTE THAT OUR DAUGHTER IS A TENDER YOUNG THING, AND WE FEAR THAT IN THE VEHEMENCE OF HIS ROYAL AFFECTION HE MIGHT POSSIBLY DO HER SOME INJURY.
MIGHT ONE MODESTLY VENTURE TO SUGGEST THAT HIS MAJESTY SHOULD HAVE HIS SHARP CLAWS REMOVED AND HIS RAZOR-LIKE TEETH EXTRACTED, AND HIS INTIMIDATING THOUGH OBVIOUSLY QUITE REGAL MANE TRIMMED BACK...
... THEN WE SHOULD GLADLY CONSIDER HIS HIGHNESS'S MOST GENEROUS PROPOSAL AGAIN."

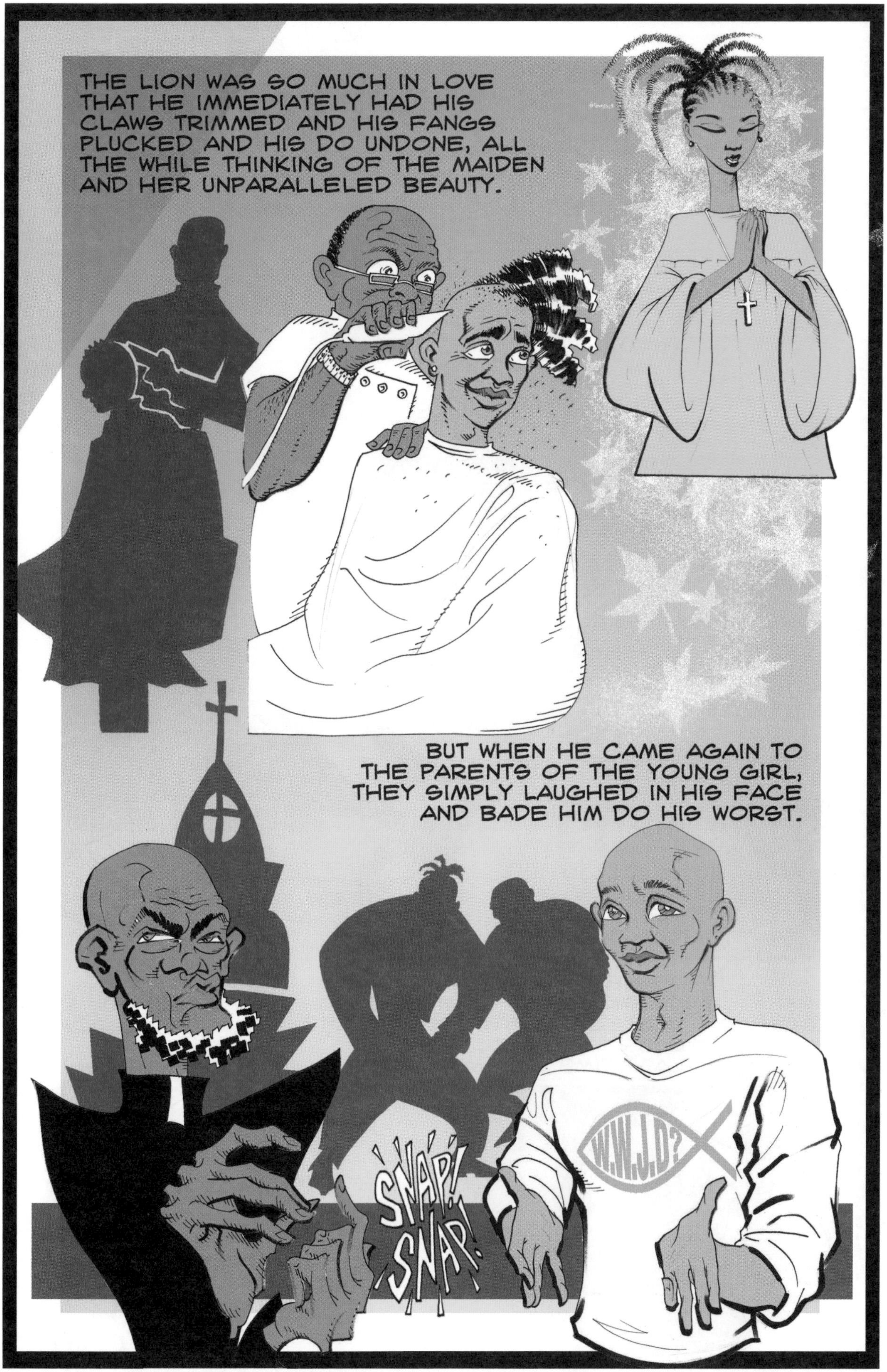
THE LION WAS SO MUCH IN LOVE THAT HE IMMEDIATELY HAD HIS CLAWS TRIMMED AND HIS FANGS PLUCKED AND HIS DO UNDONE, ALL THE WHILE THINKING OF THE MAIDEN AND HER UNPARALLELED BEAUTY.
BUT WHEN HE CAME AGAIN TO THE PARENTS OF THE YOUNG GIRL, THEY SIMPLY LAUGHED IN HIS FACE AND BADE HIM DO HIS WORST.
W.W.J.D?
SNAP!
SNAP!

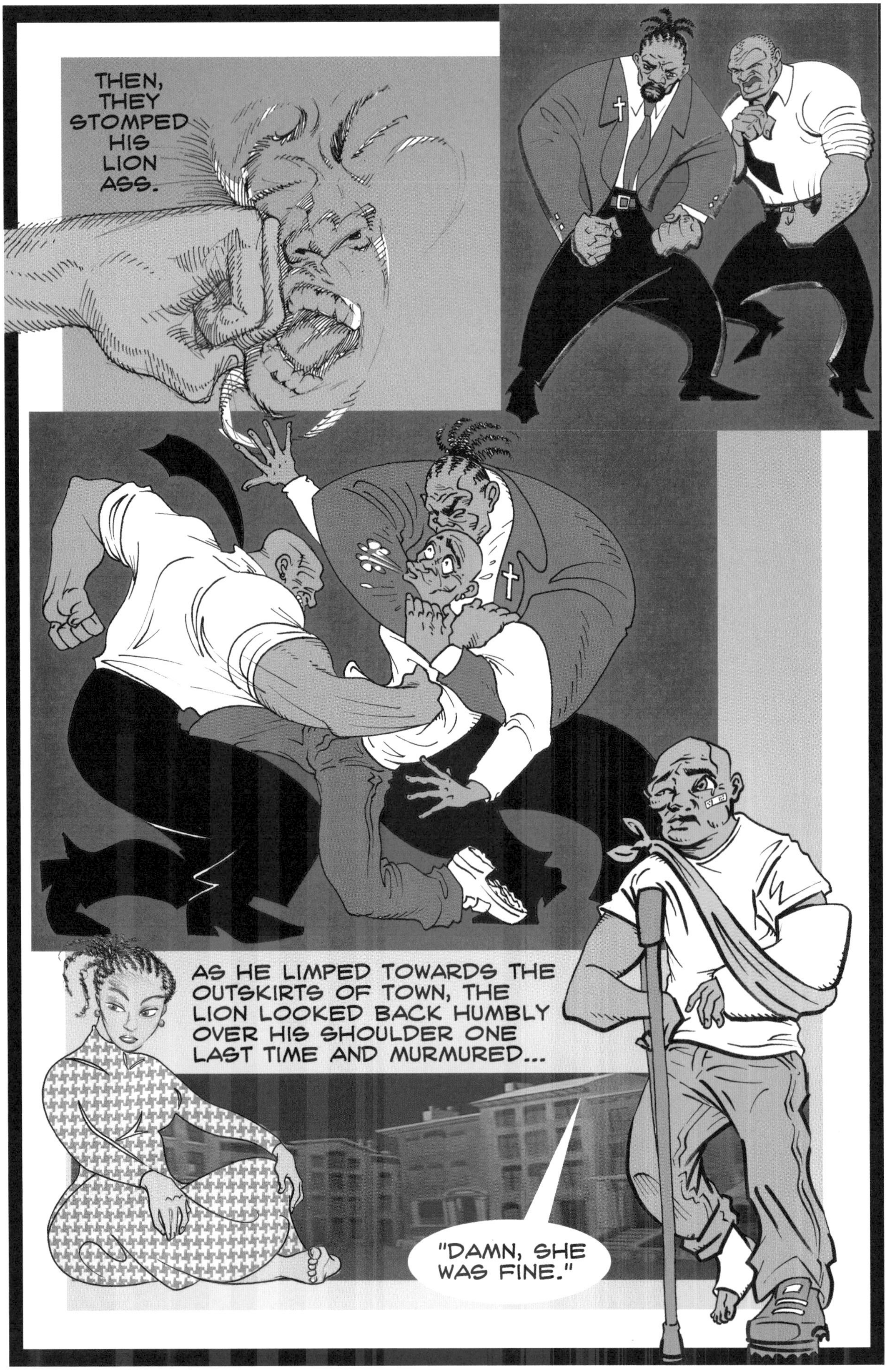
THEN, THEY STOMPED HIS LION ASS.
AS HE LIMPED TOWARDS THE OUTSKIRTS OF TOWN, THE LION LOOKED BACK HUMBLY OVER HIS SHOULDER ONE LAST TIME AND MURMURED...
"DAMN, SHE WAS FINE."

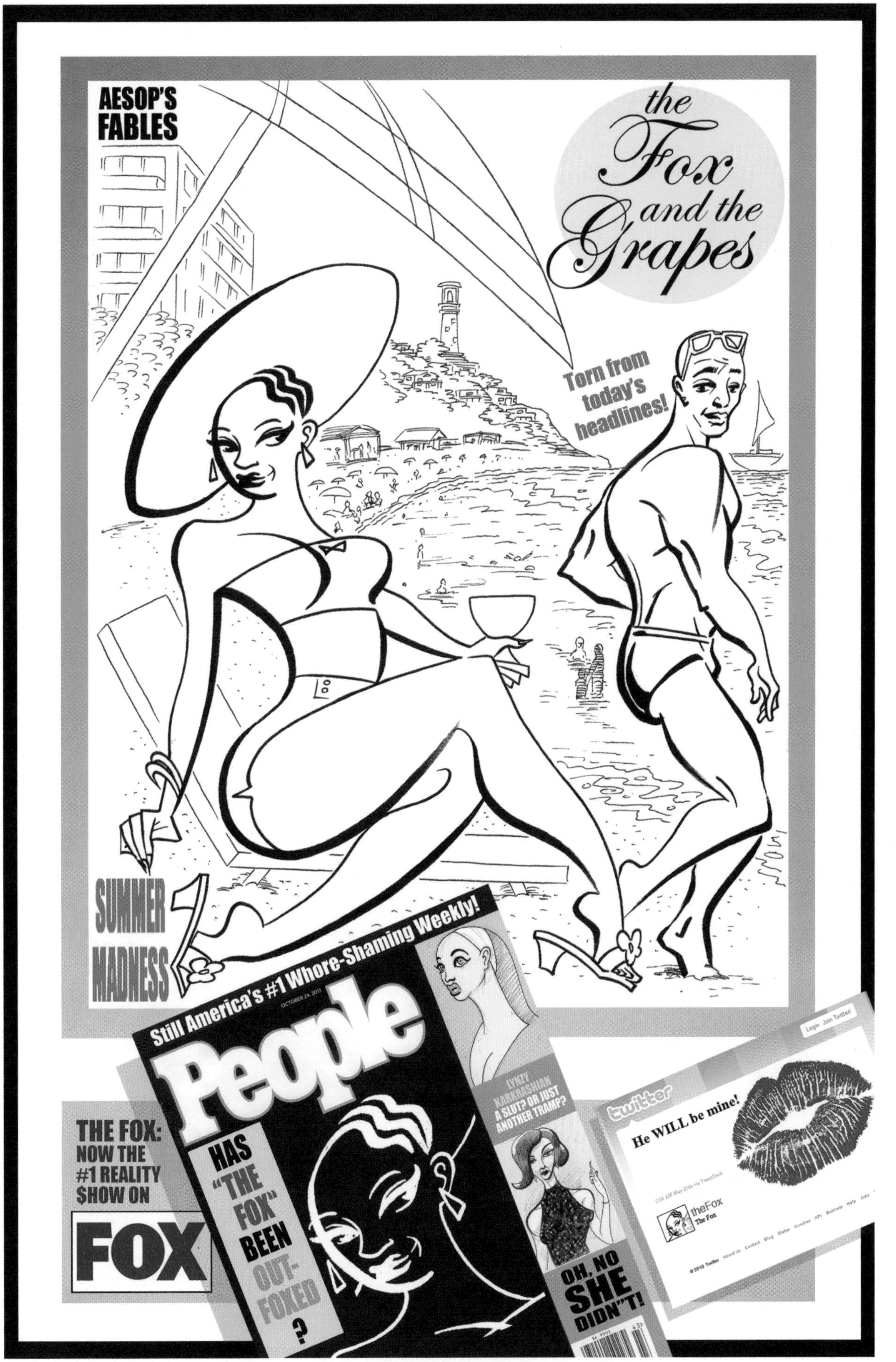
AESOP'S FABLES
the Fox and the Grapes
Torn from today's headlines!
SUMMER MADNESS
Still America's #1 Whore-Shaming Weekly!
People
LYNZY KARKRASHIAN A SLUT? OR JUST ANOTHER TRAMP?
HAS "THE FOX" BEEN OUT-FOXED?
OH, NO SHE DIDN'T!
THE FOX: NOW THE #1 REALITY $HOW ON
FOX
twitter
He WILL be mine!
theFox
The Fox

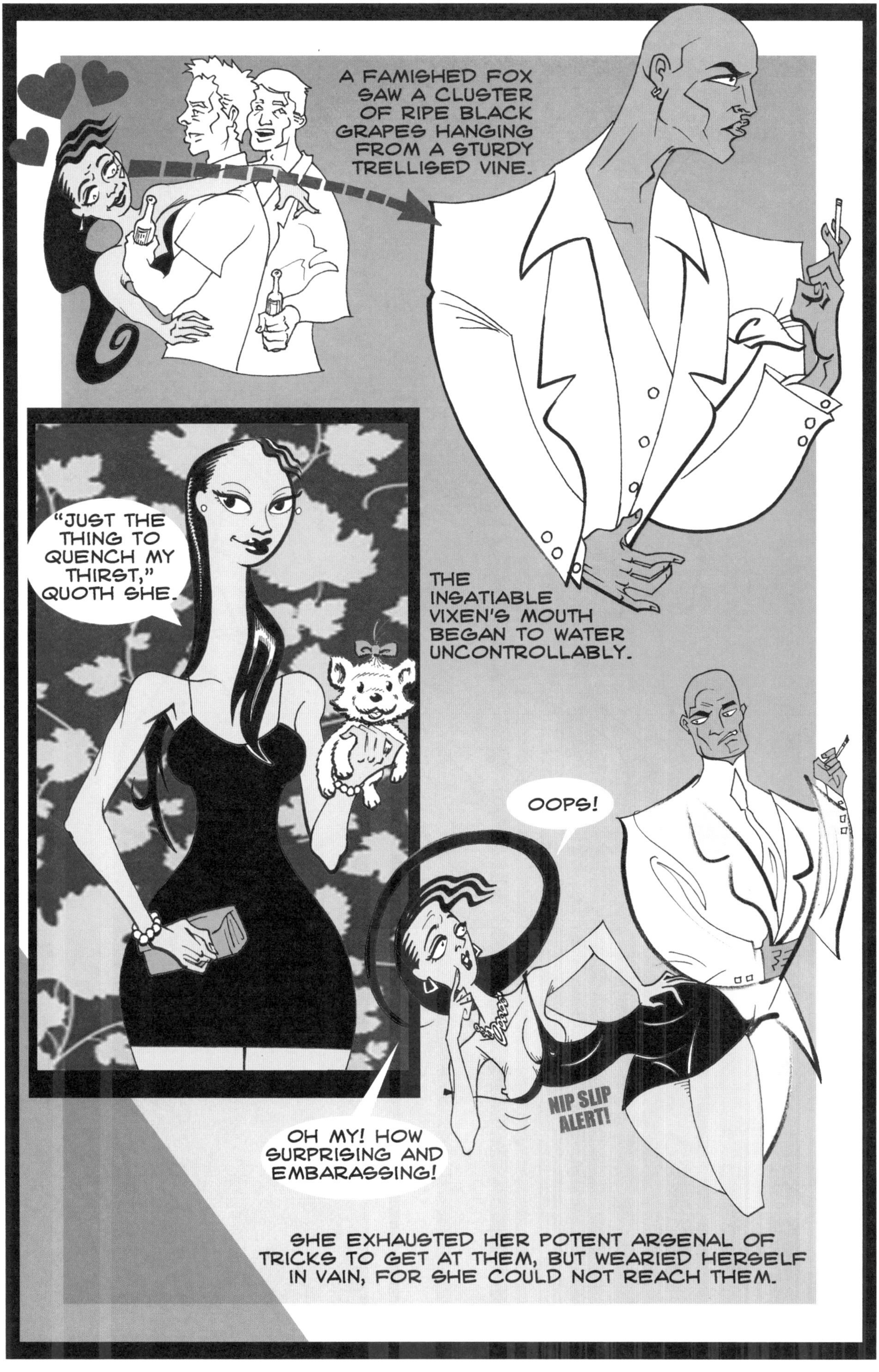
A FAMISHED FOX SAW A CLUSTER OF RIPE BLACK GRAPES HANGING FROM A STURDY TRELLISED VINE.
"JUST THE THING TO QUENCH MY THIRST," QUOTH SHE.
THE INSATIABLE VIXEN'S MOUTH BEGAN TO WATER UNCONTROLLABLY.
OOPS!
OH MY! HOW SURPRISING AND EMBARASSING!
NIP SLIP ALERT!
SHE EXHAUSTED HER POTENT ARSENAL OF TRICKS TO GET AT THEM, BUT WEARIED HERSELF IN VAIN, FOR SHE COULD NOT REACH THEM.

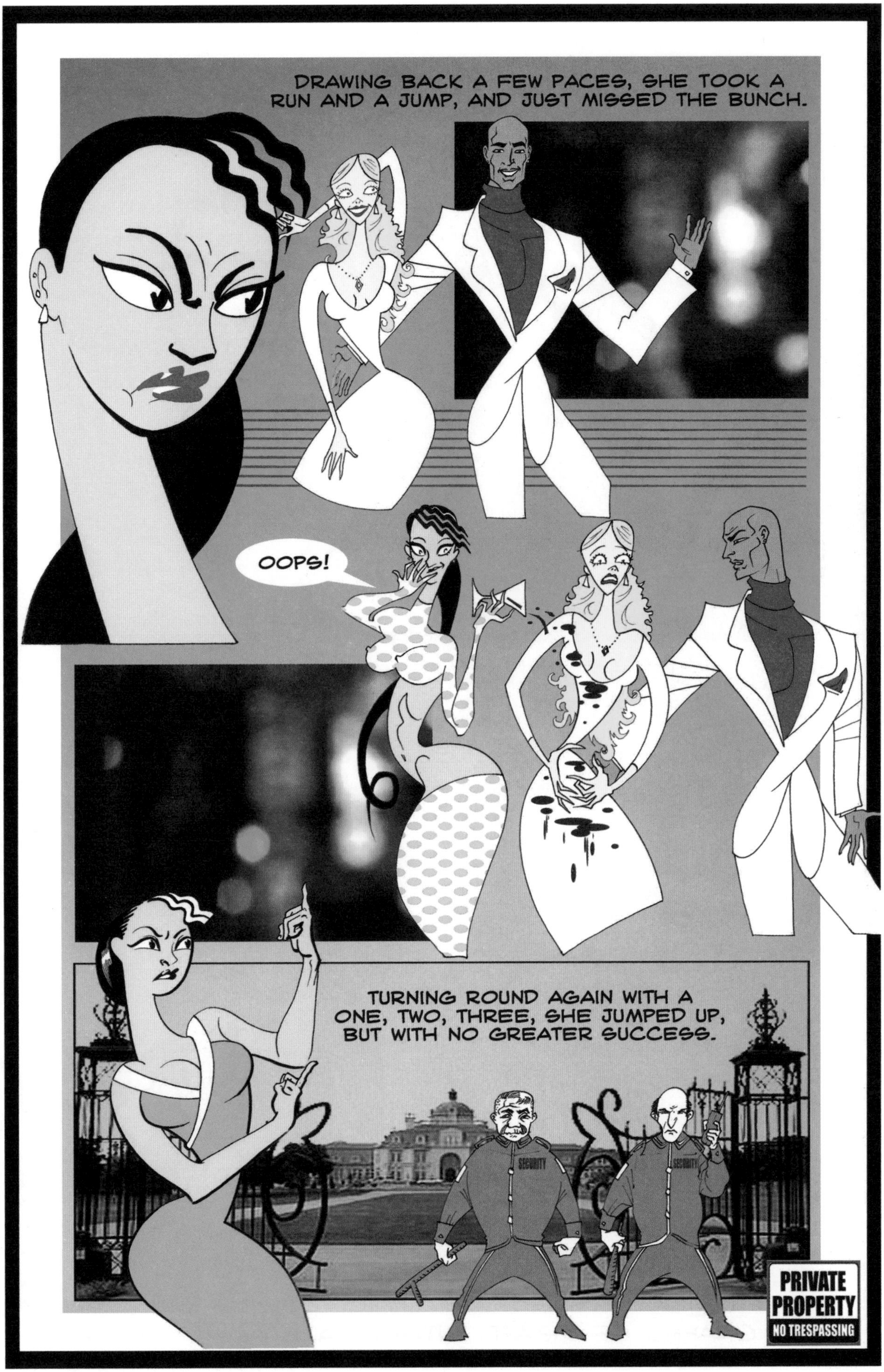
DRAWING BACK A FEW PACES, SHE TOOK A RUN AND A JUMP, AND JUST MISSED THE BUNCH.
OOPS!
TURNING ROUND AGAIN WITH A ONE, TWO, THREE, SHE JUMPED UP, BUT WITH NO GREATER SUCCESS.
SECURITY
SECURITY
PRIVATE PROPERTY
NO TRESPASSING

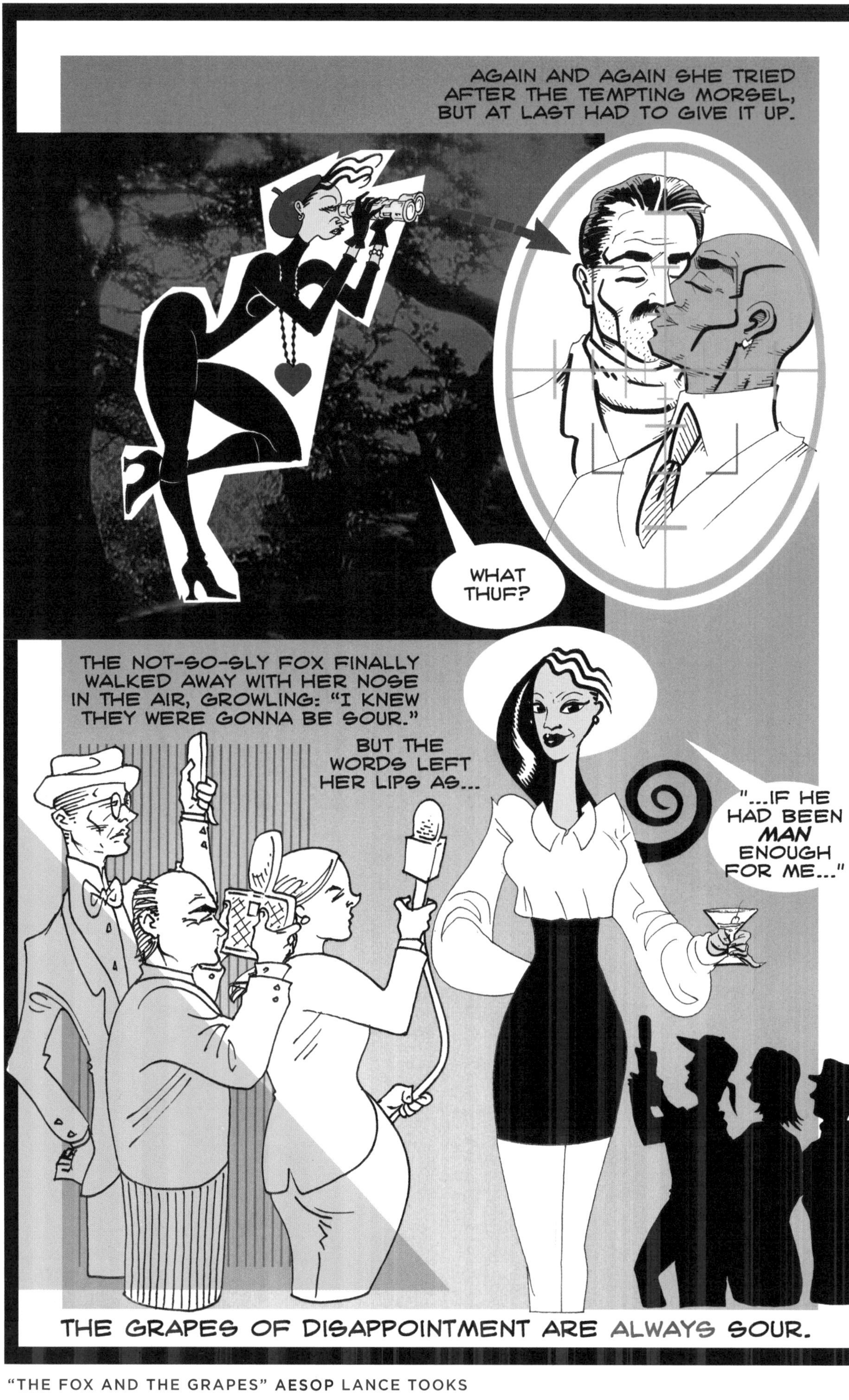
AGAIN AND AGAIN SHE TRIED AFTER THE TEMPTING MORSEL, BUT AT LAST HAD TO GIVE IT UP.
WHAT THUF?
THE NOT-SO-SLY FOX FINALLY WALKED AWAY WITH HER NOSE IN THE AIR, GROWLING: "I KNEW THEY WERE GONNA BE SOUR."
BUT THE WORDS LEFT HER LIPS AS...
"...IF HE HAD BEEN *MAN* ENOUGH FOR ME..."
THE GRAPES OF DISAPPOINTMENT ARE ALWAYS SOUR.

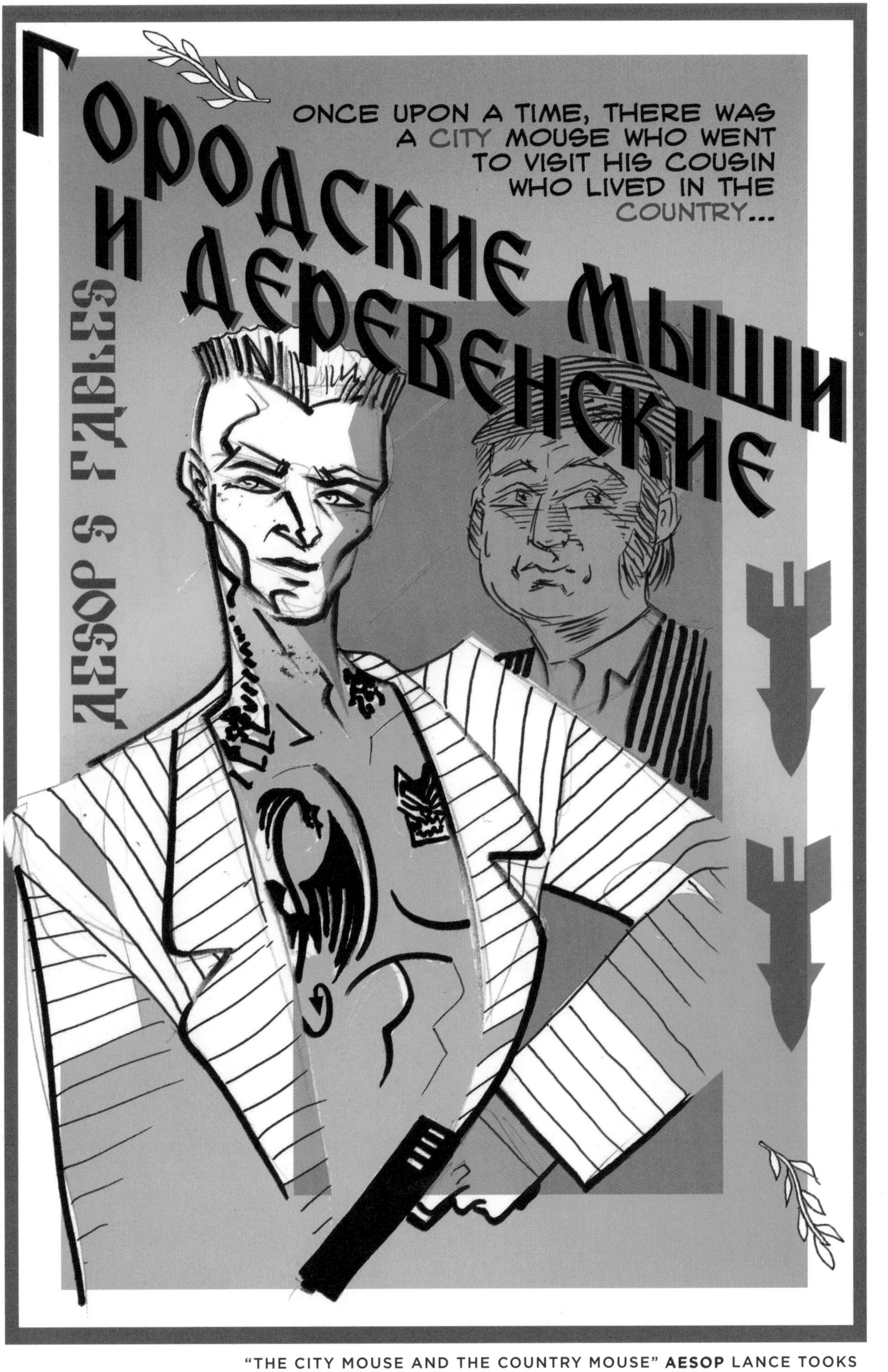
ГОРОДСКИЕ И ДЕРЕВЕНСКИЕ МЫШИ
AESOP'S FABLES
ONCE UPON A TIME, THERE WAS A CITY MOUSE WHO WENT TO VISIT HIS COUSIN WHO LIVED IN THE COUNTRY...

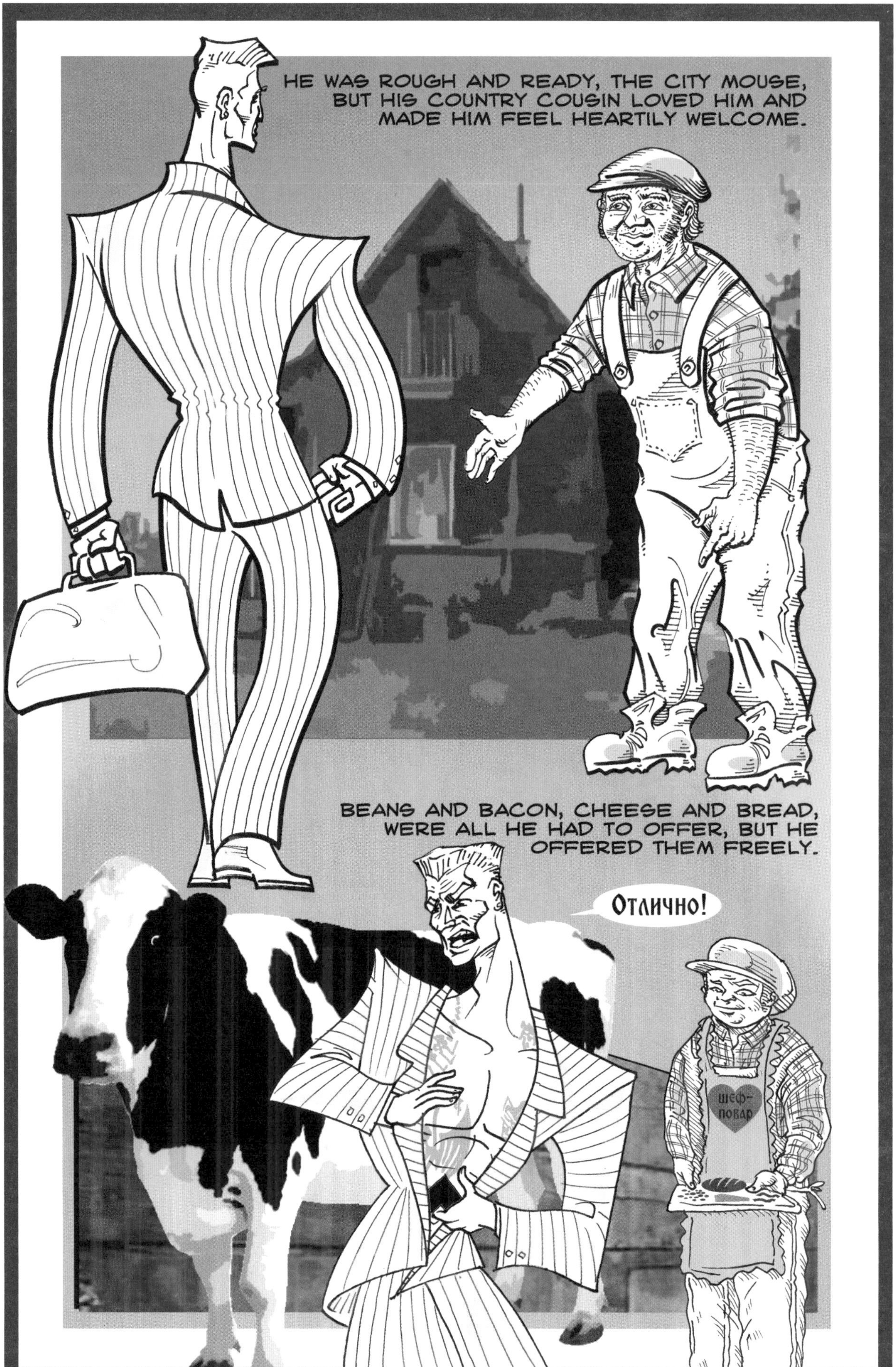
HE WAS ROUGH AND READY, THE CITY MOUSE, BUT HIS COUNTRY COUSIN LOVED HIM AND MADE HIM FEEL HEARTILY WELCOME.
BEANS AND BACON, CHEESE AND BREAD, WERE ALL HE HAD TO OFFER, BUT HE OFFERED THEM FREELY.
Отлично!
шеф-повар

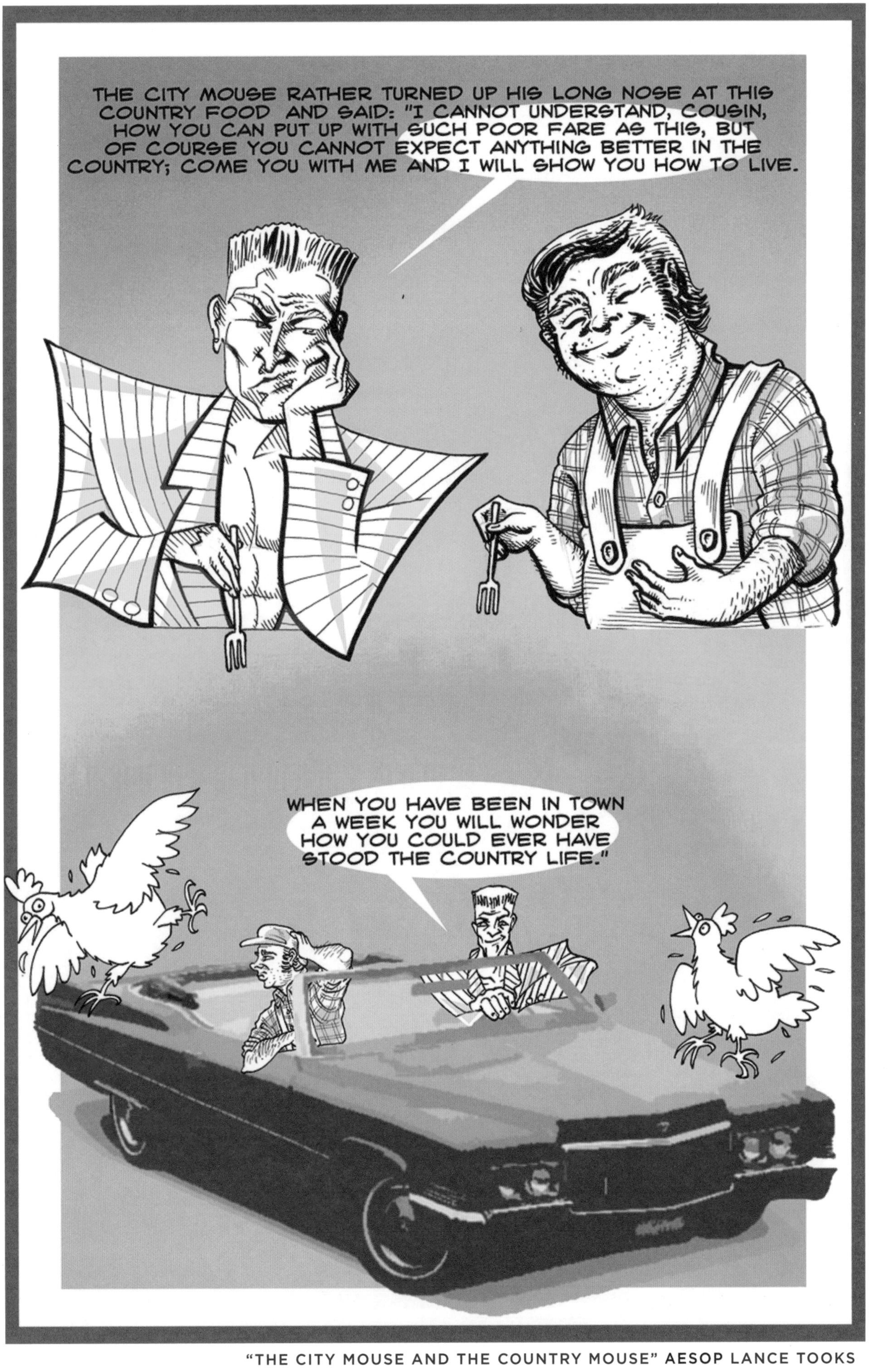
THE CITY MOUSE RATHER TURNED UP HIS LONG NOSE AT THIS COUNTRY FOOD AND SAID: "I CANNOT UNDERSTAND, COUSIN, HOW YOU CAN PUT UP WITH SUCH POOR FARE AS THIS, BUT OF COURSE YOU CANNOT EXPECT ANYTHING BETTER IN THE COUNTRY; COME YOU WITH ME AND I WILL SHOW YOU HOW TO LIVE.
WHEN YOU HAVE BEEN IN TOWN A WEEK YOU WILL WONDER HOW YOU COULD EVER HAVE STOOD THE COUNTRY LIFE."

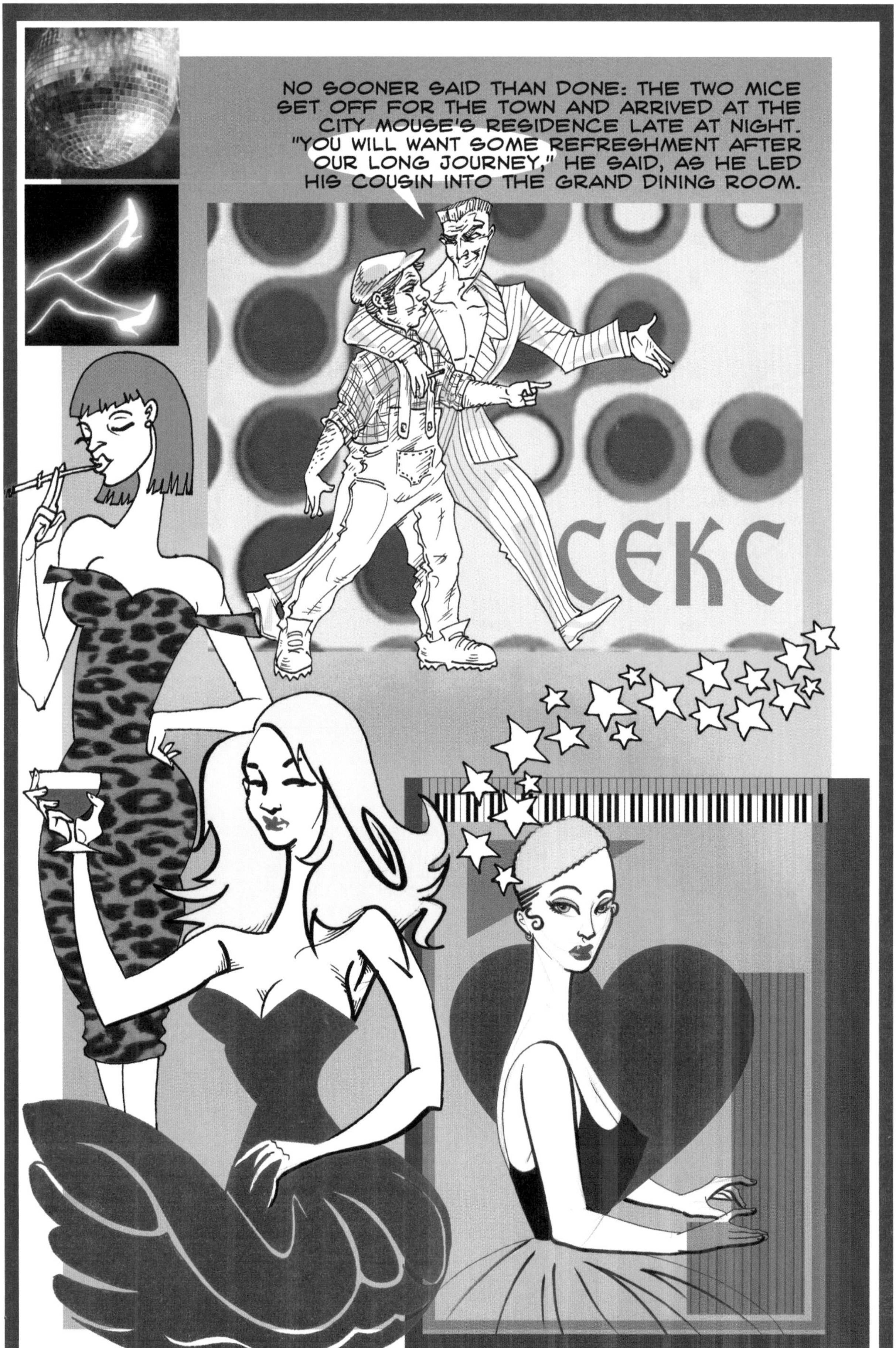
NO SOONER SAID THAN DONE: THE TWO MICE SET OFF FOR THE TOWN AND ARRIVED AT THE CITY MOUSE'S RESIDENCE LATE AT NIGHT. "YOU WILL WANT SOME REFRESHMENT AFTER OUR LONG JOURNEY," HE SAID, AS HE LED HIS COUSIN INTO THE GRAND DINING ROOM.
CEKC

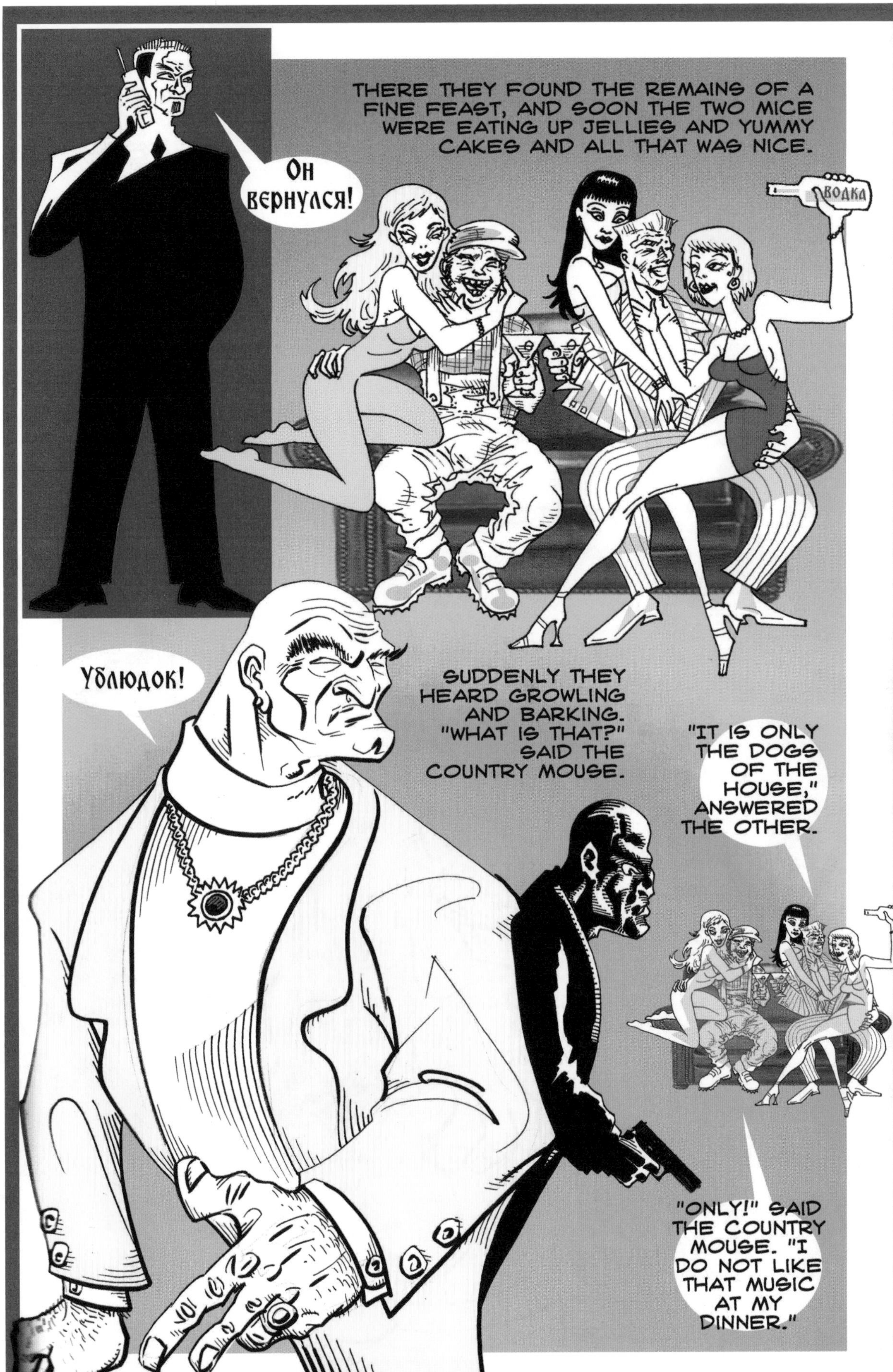
Он вернулся!
THERE THEY FOUND THE REMAINS OF A FINE FEAST, AND SOON THE TWO MICE WERE EATING UP JELLIES AND YUMMY CAKES AND ALL THAT WAS NICE.
ВОДКА
Ублюдок!
SUDDENLY THEY HEARD GROWLING AND BARKING. "WHAT IS THAT?" SAID THE COUNTRY MOUSE.
"IT IS ONLY THE DOGS OF THE HOUSE," ANSWERED THE OTHER.
"ONLY!" SAID THE COUNTRY MOUSE. "I DO NOT LIKE THAT MUSIC AT MY DINNER."

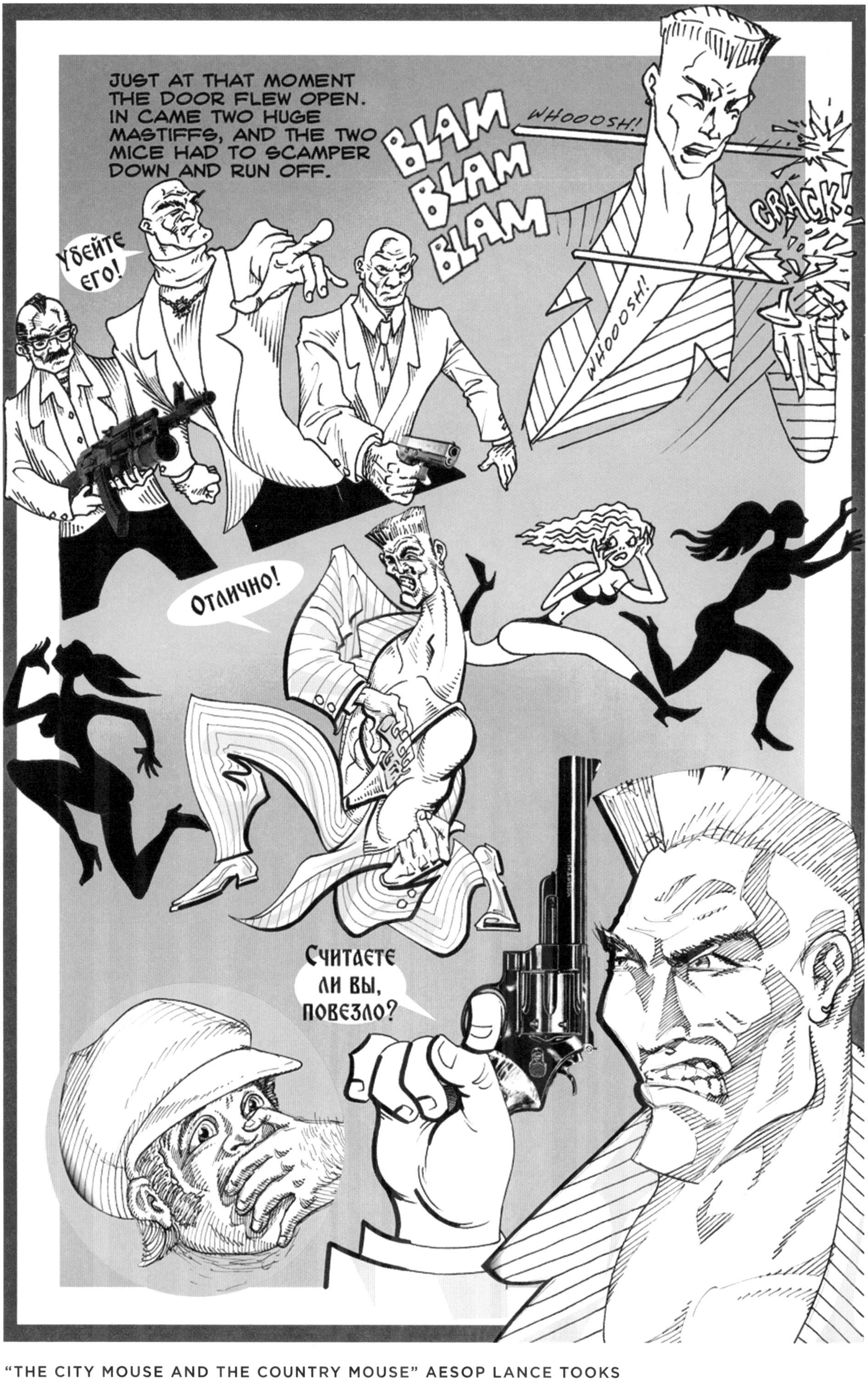
JUST AT THAT MOMENT THE DOOR FLEW OPEN. IN CAME TWO HUGE MASTIFFS, AND THE TWO MICE HAD TO SCAMPER DOWN AND RUN OFF.
BLAM BLAM BLAM
WHOOOSH!
CRACK!
WHOOOSH!
WHOOOSH!
Убейте его!
Отлично!
Считаете ли вы, повезло?

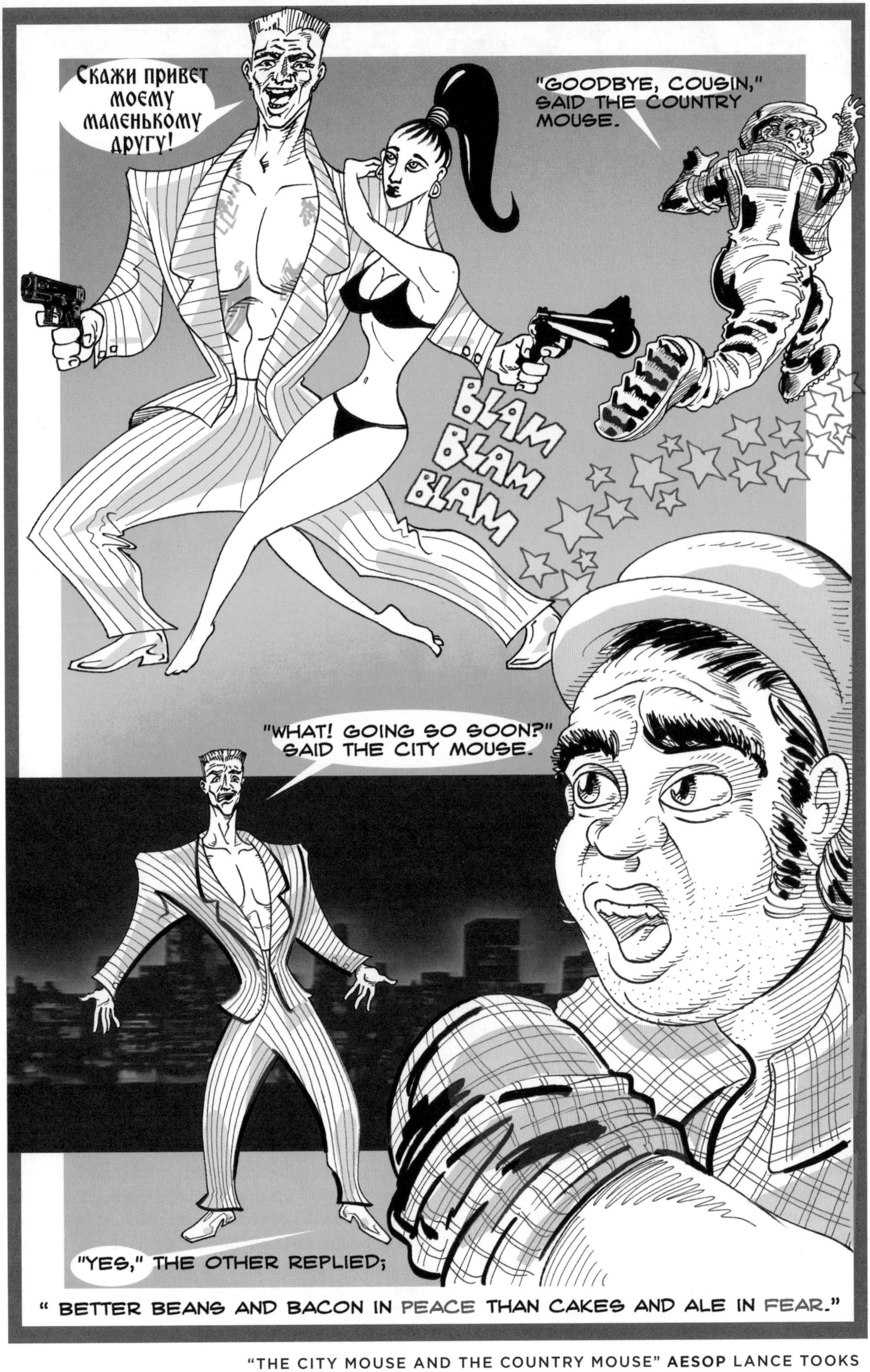
Скажи привет моему маленькому другу!
"GOODBYE, COUSIN," SAID THE COUNTRY MOUSE.
BLAM BLAM BLAM
"WHAT! GOING SO SOON?" SAID THE CITY MOUSE.
"YES," THE OTHER REPLIED;
" BETTER BEANS AND BACON IN PEACE THAN CAKES AND ALE IN FEAR."

# European fairy tale

ART/ADAPTATION BY **David W. Tripp**

**A YOUNG GIRL MENACED BY A BEAST WHO WILL** soon kill her and her grandmother . . . the tale of Little Red Riding Hood is harsh stuff. And the further back you go, to the first published versions and to the original folktales being told in southern France and northern Italy in the 1600s, the more grotesque and violent it gets. A werewolf or an ogre tricks the girl into eating her grandmother's heart and drinking her blood; it then has the girl strip naked and climb into bed, where she is devoured. No hunter bursts through the door to liberate the pair from the fiend's stomach. The implications of, or parallels to, rape and lust-murder are impossible to miss.

Jack Zipes, one of the leading scholars of fairy tales and children's lit, wrote: "It is because rape and violence are at the core of the history of *Little Red Riding Hood* that it is the most widespread and notorious fairy tale in the Western world, if not the entire world." No fairy tale has been analyzed and theorized about more than this one. It's the sole subject of at least five books, including one in which Zipes gathers almost forty published versions of the tale, from 1697 to 1990, and another in which scholars dissect the story from various theoretical viewpoints.

There are any number of variations on the tale. Sometimes Red Riding Hood escapes the wolf/werewolf/ogre through her cleverness. Sometimes she's an older girl, perhaps a teenager or even a young woman. She was never mentioned as wearing red clothing until Charles Perrault added that detail when he first put the folktale in writing.

Pennsylvania illustrator and woodblock artist David W. Tripp chose a version told in Italy and Austria, first collected in a German book from 1867. David has been illustrating the Alice novels paragraph by paragraph for a while, and now he brings his elongated, willowy figures to another piece of (alleged) children's literature.

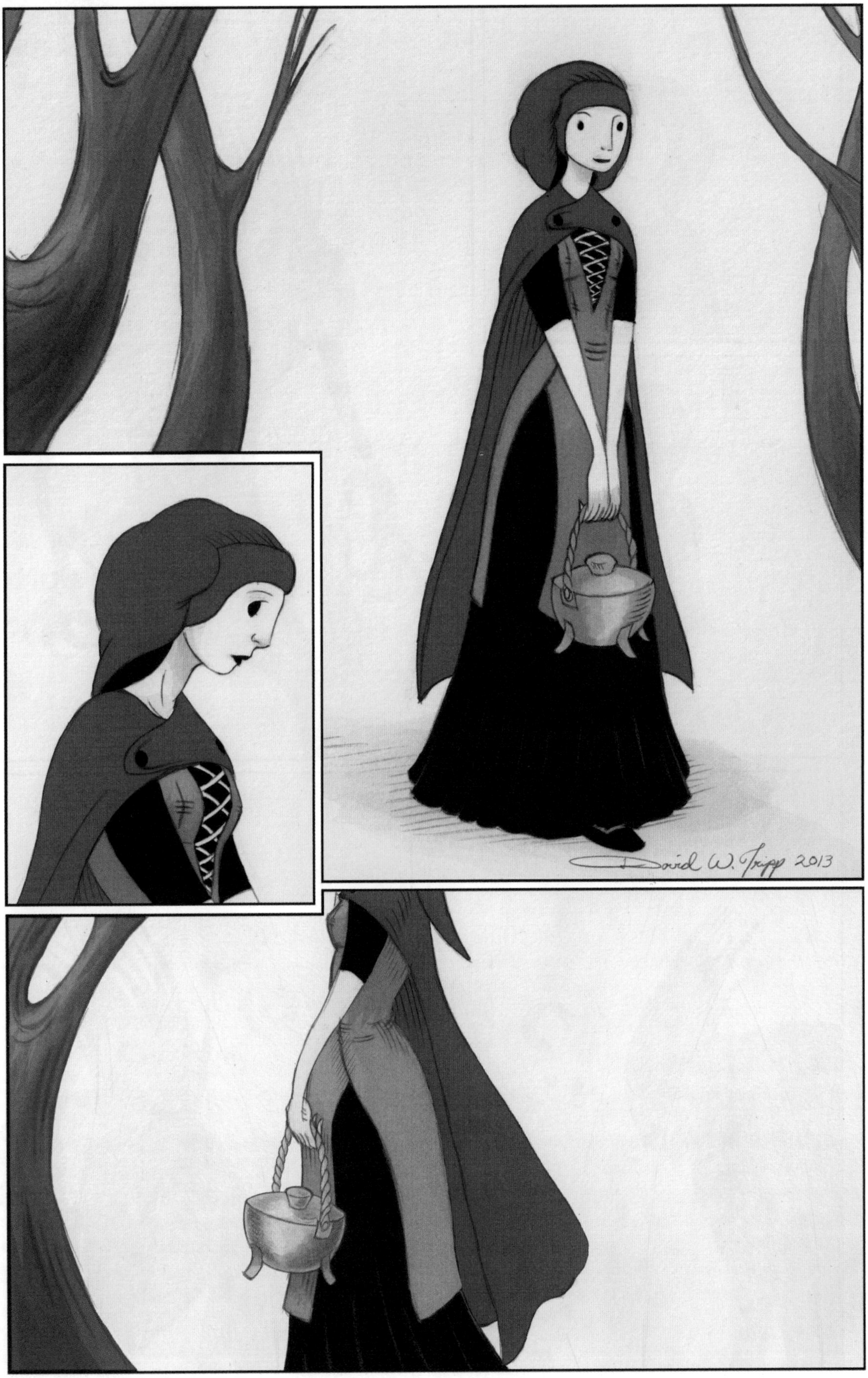
David W. Tripp 2013

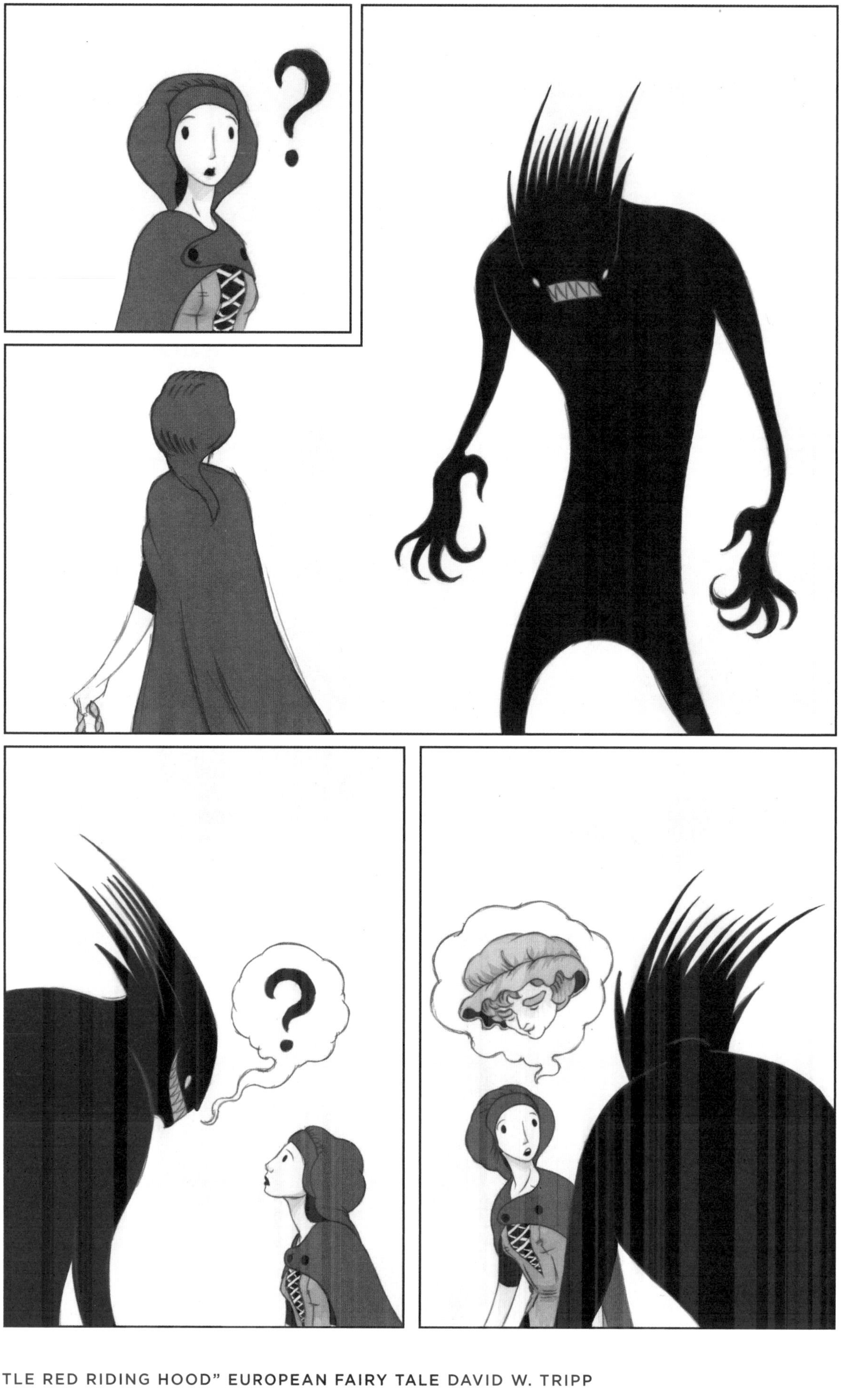
?
?

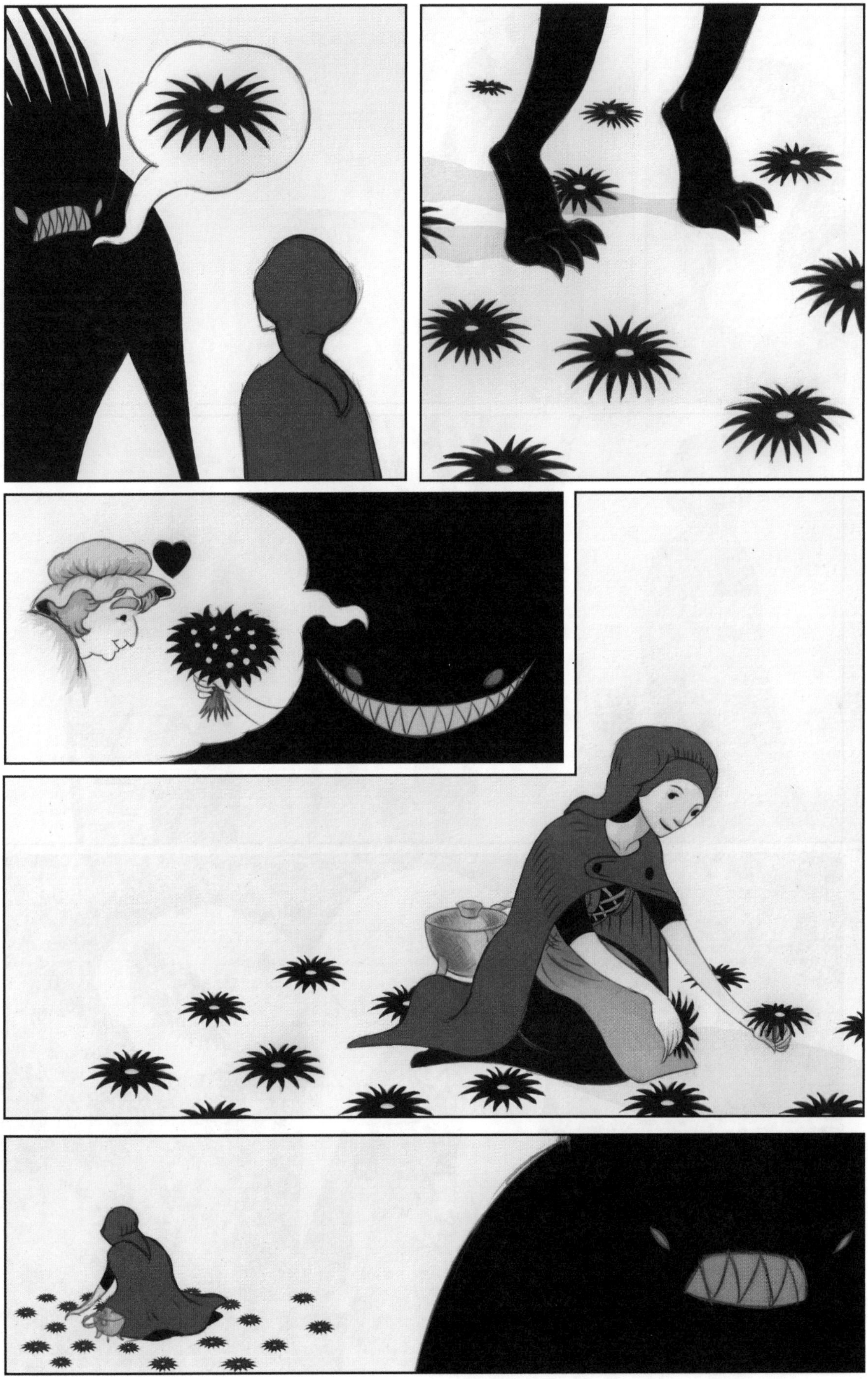

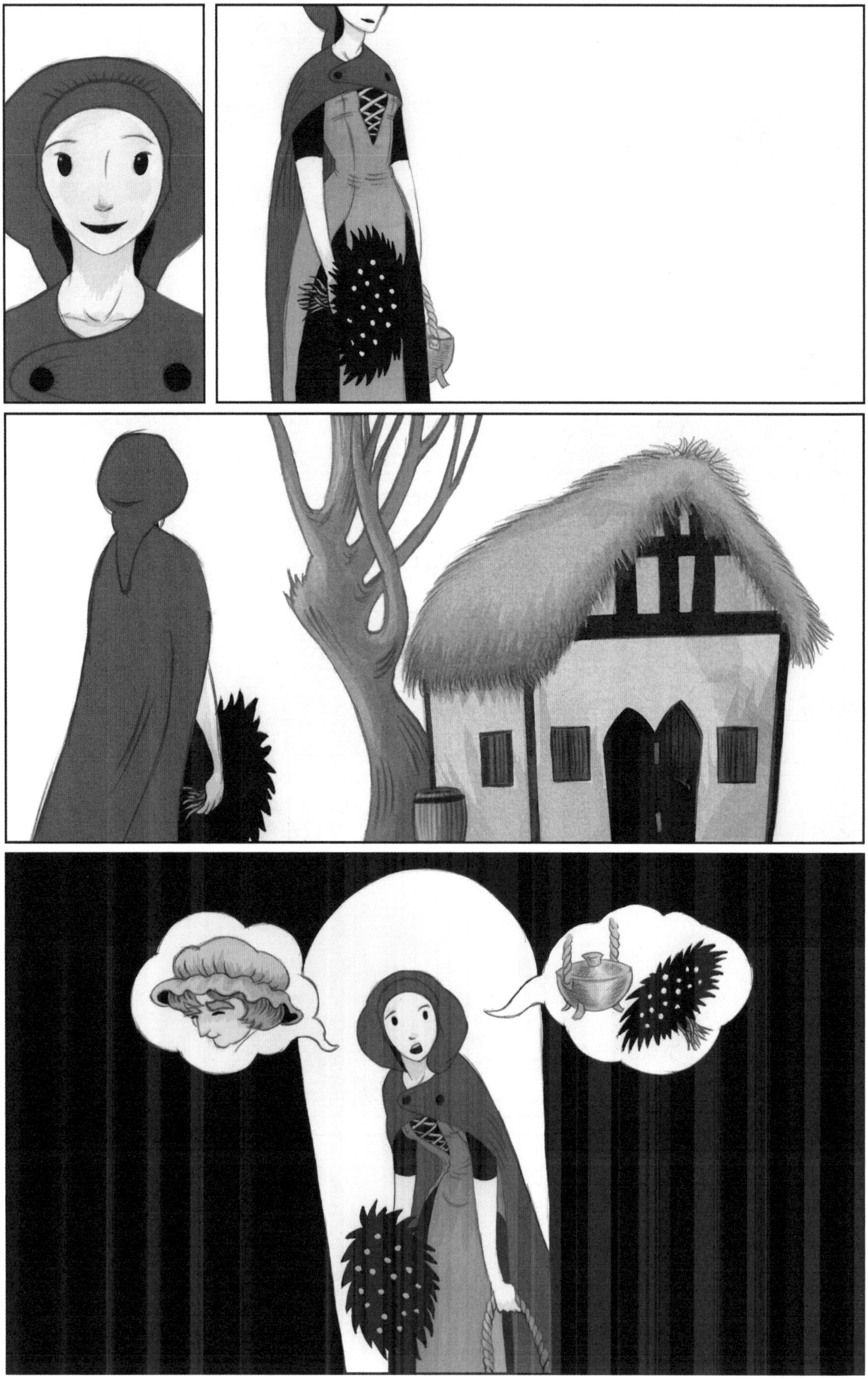

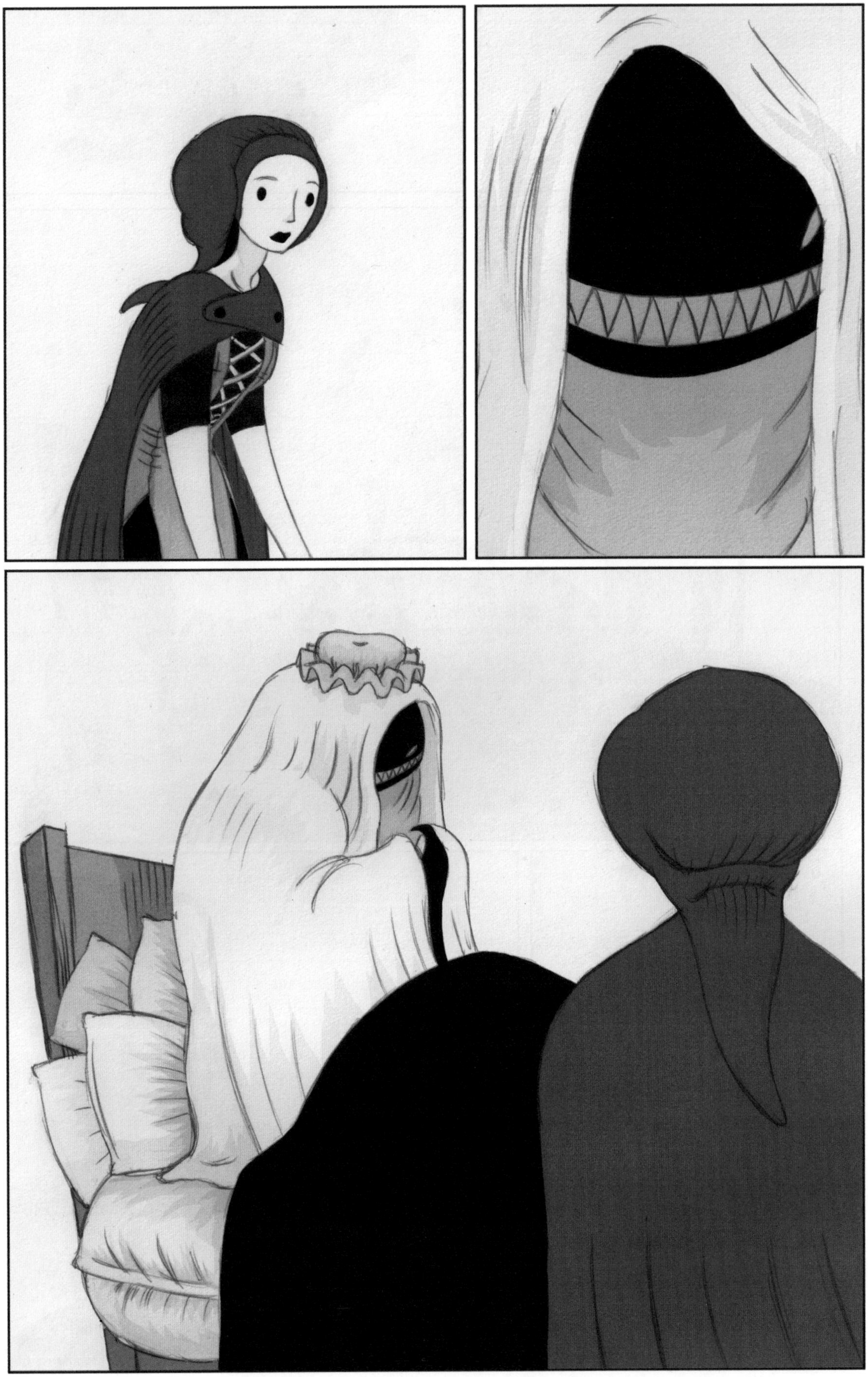

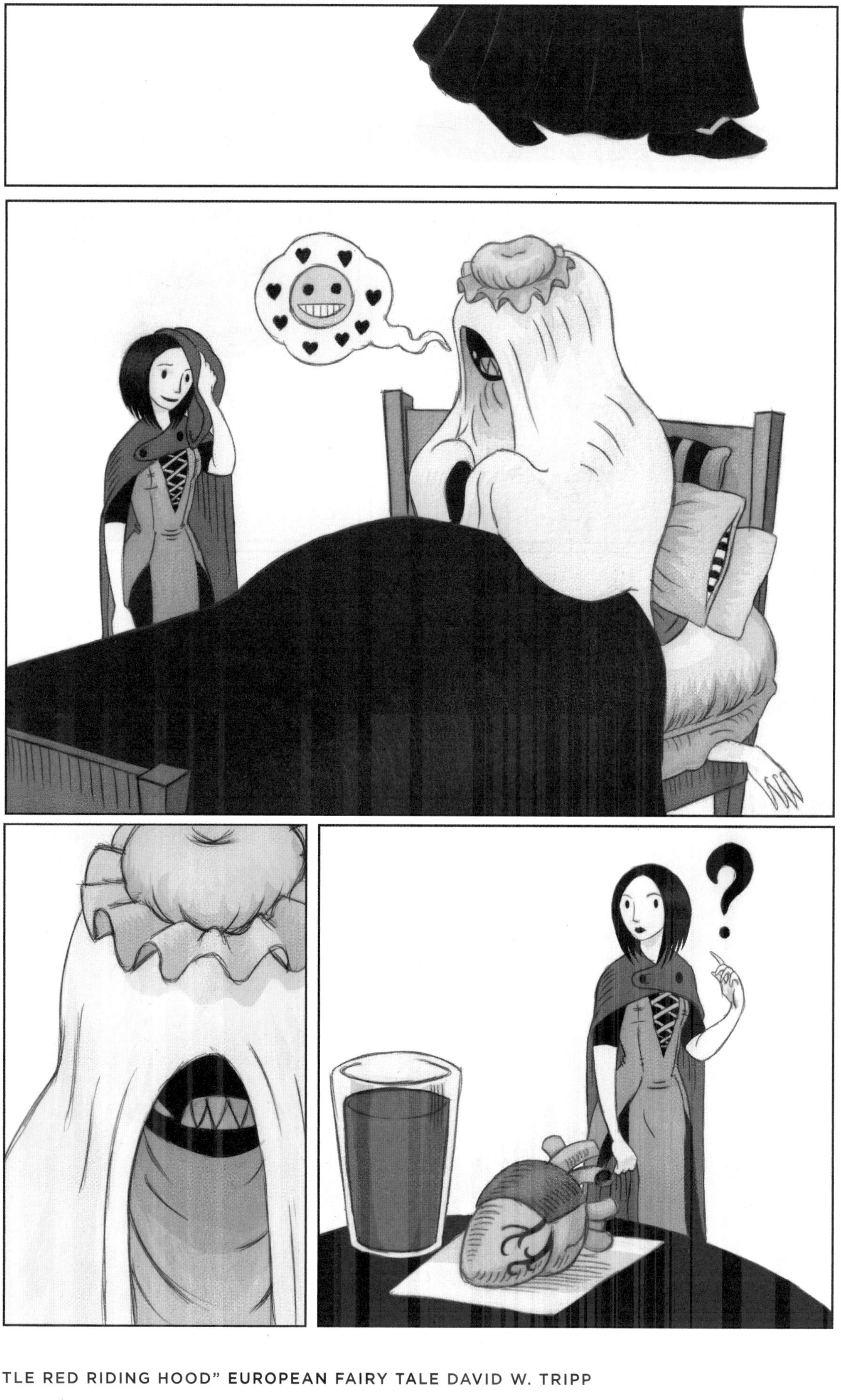
?

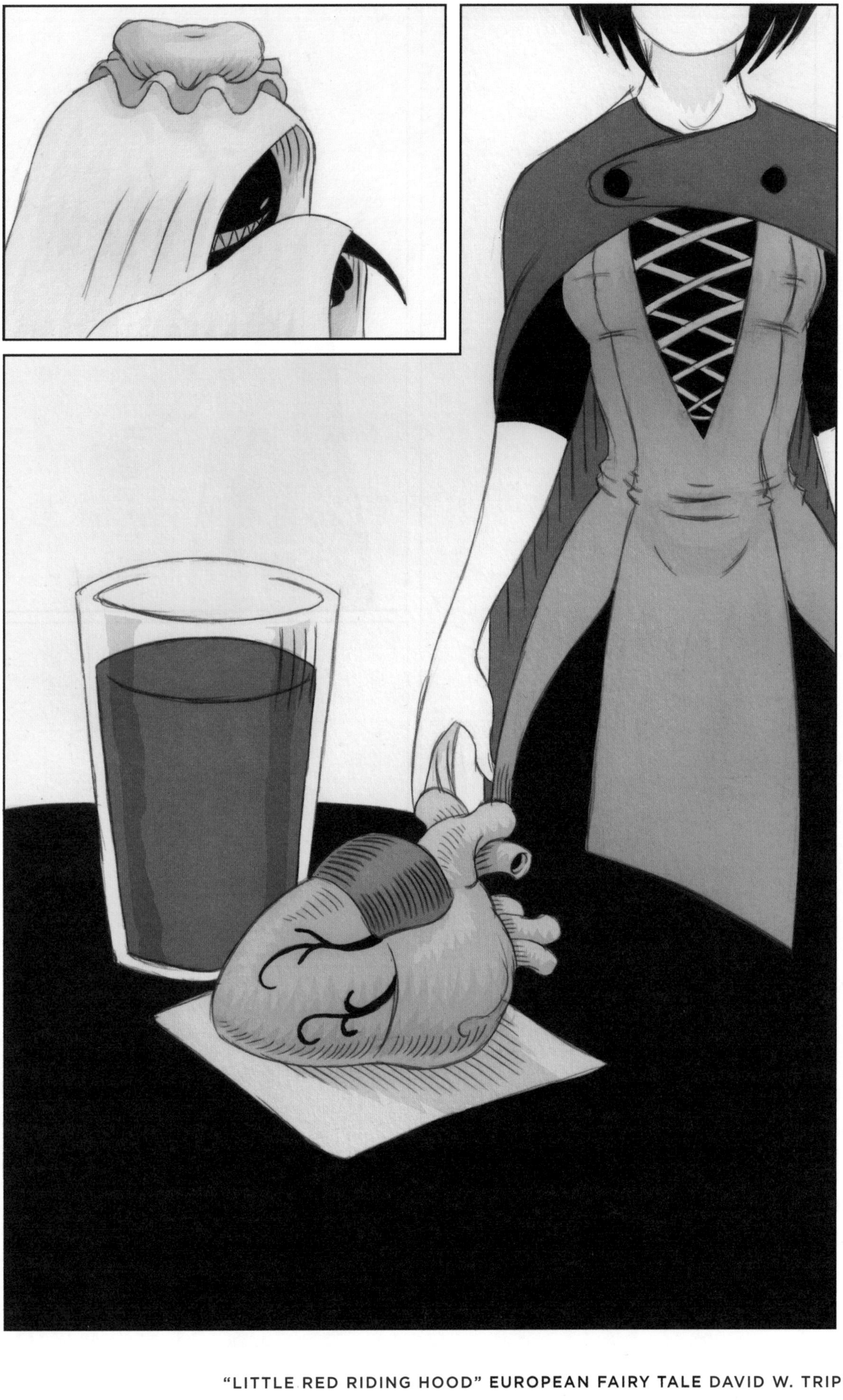

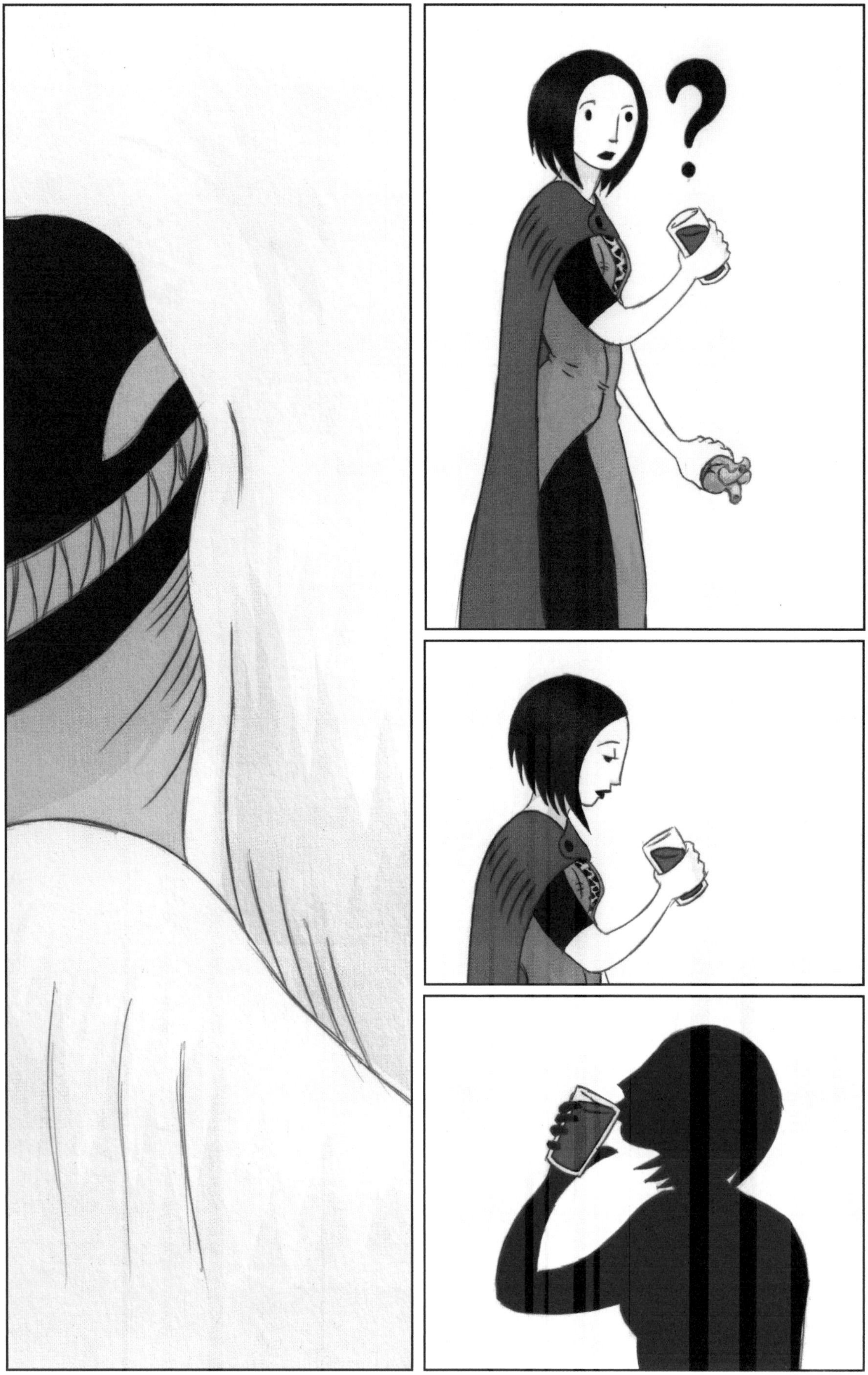
?

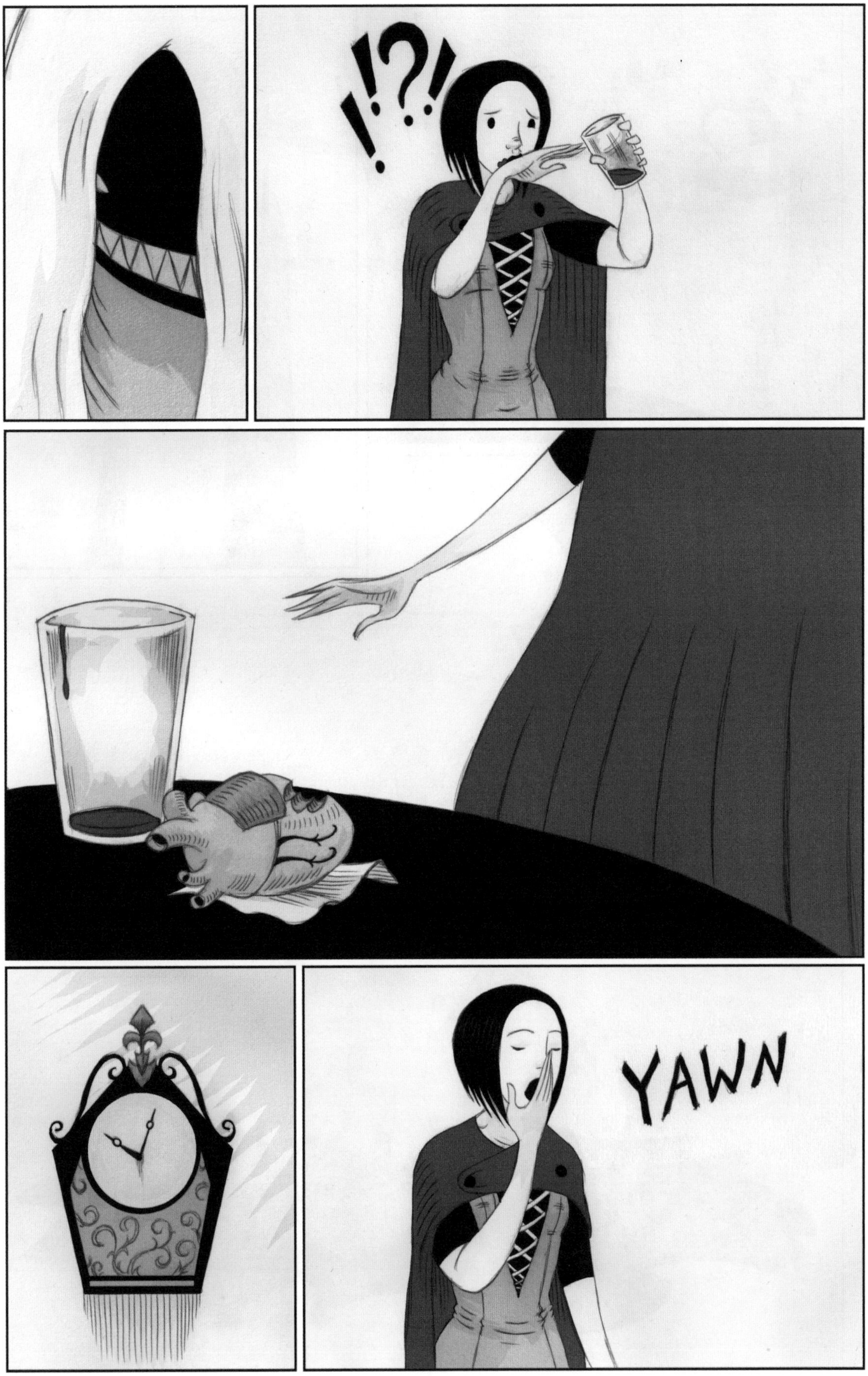
!?!
YAWN

"LITTLE RED RIDING HOOD" EUROPEAN FAIRY TALE DAVID W. TRIPP

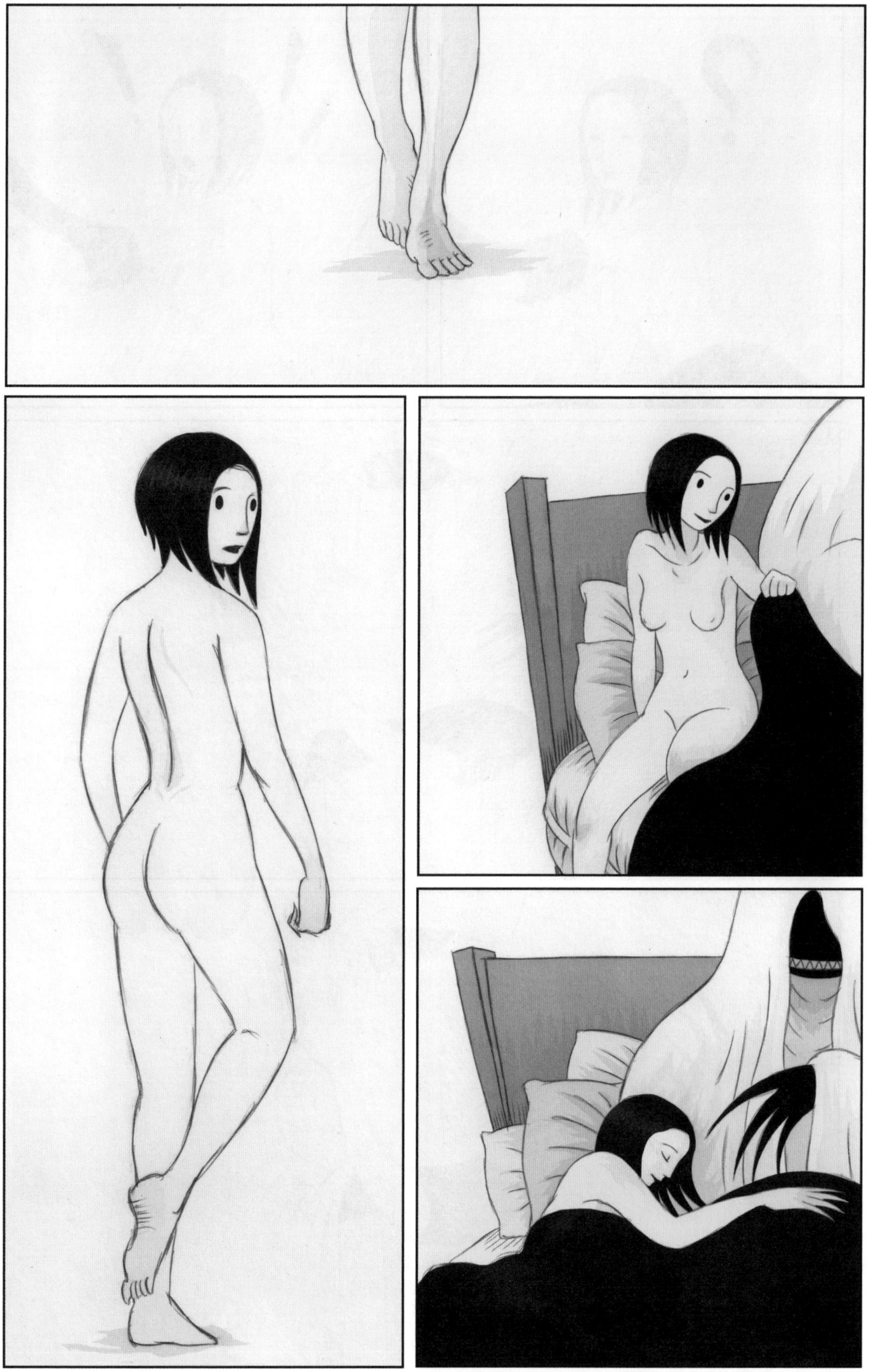

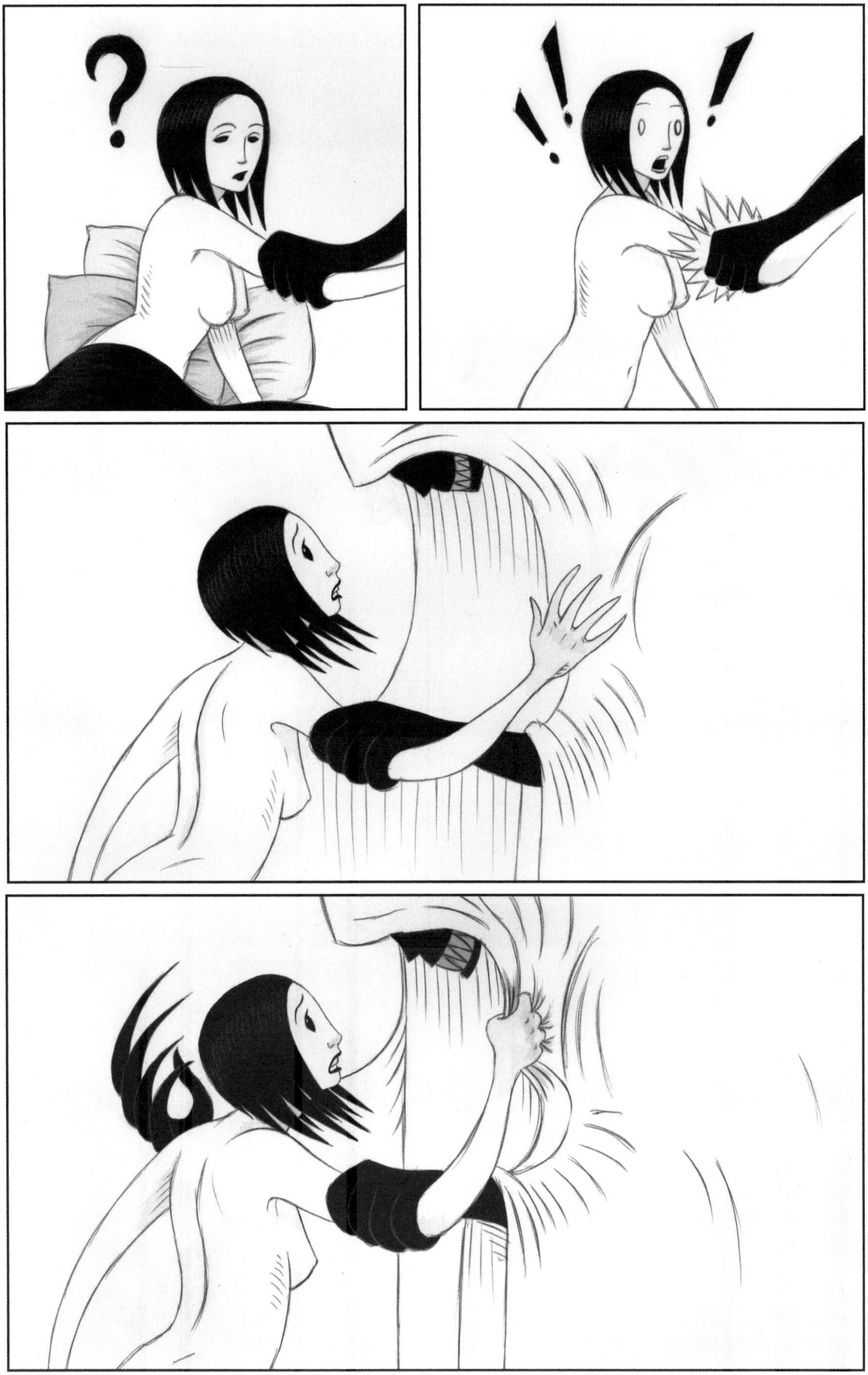
?
!!!

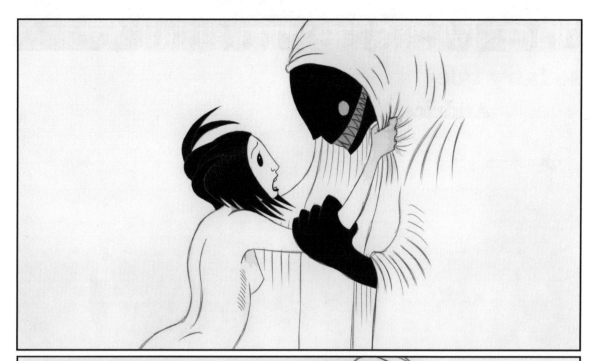

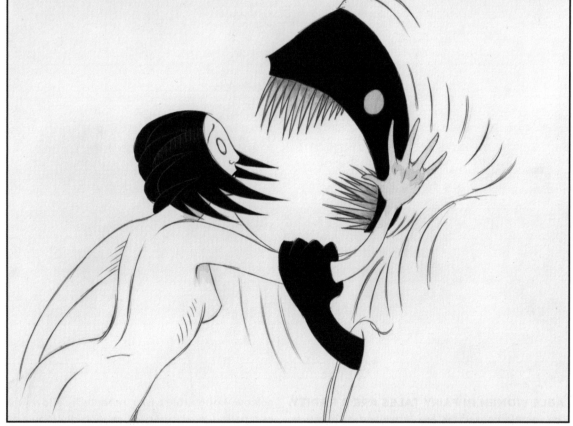

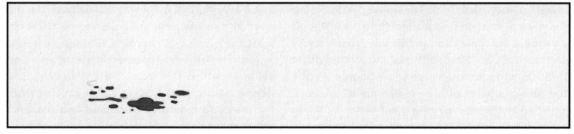

# Norse fairy tale

ART/ADAPTATION BY **Andrice Arp**

**BRAVE, ABLE WOMEN IN FAIRY TALES ARE A RARITY.** Usually, the female characters are terrorized by baddies (Little Red Riding Hood, Goldilocks) or are waiting for someone—preferably a prince—to rescue them from peril (Rapunzel, Snow White, Cinderella). But in this tale from Norway, the woman is the rescuer. First collected and written down in the mid-1800s, and translated here by Sir George Webbe Dasent, the title character of "The Mastermaid" is apparently a magician in the employ of a giant. After falling in love with a prince (sigh), she repeatedly tells him how to achieve impossible tasks, repeatedly allows the couple to escape the giant's pursuit, repeatedly repels other suitors, and finally figures out a way to win back her man. Yes, she does all this because she loves some royal clown, but at least she's a kick-ass heroine with girl power to spare.

Andrice Arp, who appeared in the original *Graphic Canon* volumes, with a tale from *The Arabian Nights* and a story from a leading postmodern writer, creates work that often features odd creatures from land and sea, and this quasi-feminist fairy tale is no exception.

# The Mastermaid

A Norwegian fairy tale adapted by Andrice Arp from a translation by George Webbe Dasent

**ONCE** upon a time, there was a King who had several sons. The youngest had no rest at home, and after a long time the King was forced to give him leave to go.

**NOW** after he had traveled some days, he came one night to a Giant's house

And there he got a place in the Giant's service. In the morning, the Giant went off to herd his goats.

Clean out the stable, and as soon as you have done that you needn't do anything else today...

for you must know it is an easy master you have come to.

But what is set to you to do, you must do well, and you mustn't think of going into any of the rooms but yours, for if you do I'll TAKE YOUR LIFE!

Sure enough it is an easy master...

but still it would be good fun...

to peep into his other rooms.

Oh in Heaven's name! What do you want here?

I got a place here yesterday!

A place indeed! Heaven help you out of it!

Well after all I've got an easy master, after I have cleaned out the stable my day's work is over.

Yes but how will you do it? For if you set to work to clean it, ten pitchforks full will come in for every one you toss out!

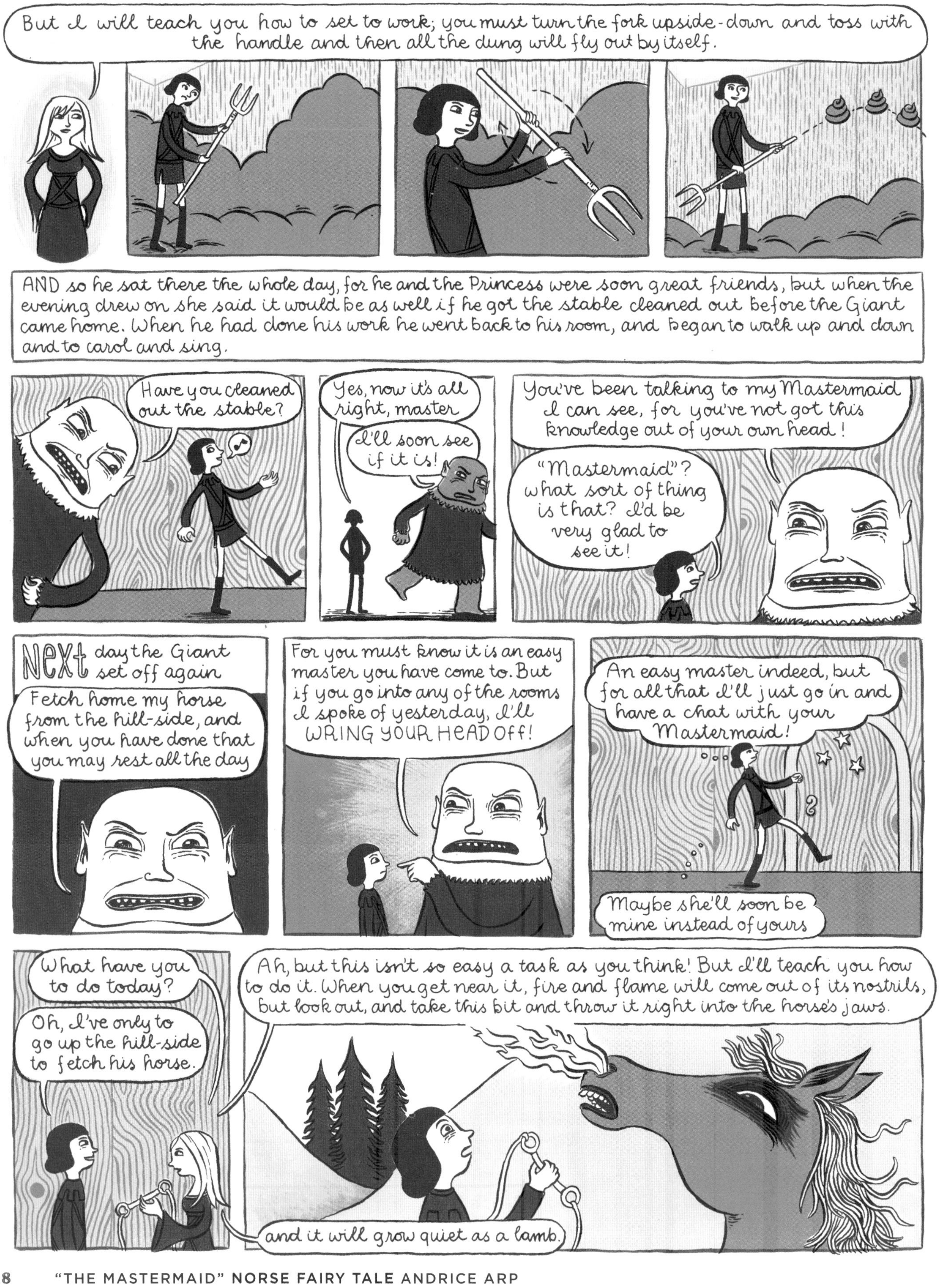
But I will teach you how to set to work; you must turn the fork upside-down and toss with the handle and then all the dung will fly out by itself.
AND so he sat there the whole day, for he and the Princess were soon great friends, but when the evening drew on she said it would be as well if he got the stable cleaned out before the Giant came home. When he had done his work he went back to his room, and began to walk up and down and to carol and sing.
Have you cleaned out the stable?
Yes, now it's all right, master
I'll soon see if it is!
You've been talking to my Mastermaid I can see, for you've not got this knowledge out of your own head!
"Mastermaid"? what sort of thing is that? I'd be very glad to see it!
Next day the Giant set off again
Fetch home my horse from the hill-side, and when you have done that you may rest all the day
For you must know it is an easy master you have come to. But if you go into any of the rooms I spoke of yesterday, I'll WRING YOUR HEAD OFF!
An easy master indeed, but for all that I'll just go in and have a chat with your Mastermaid!
Maybe she'll soon be mine instead of yours
What have you to do today?
Oh, I've only to go up the hill-side to fetch his horse.
Ah, but this isn't so easy a task as you think! But I'll teach you how to do it. When you get near it, fire and flame will come out of its nostrils, but look out, and take this bit and throw it right into the horse's jaws.
and it will grow quiet as a lamb.

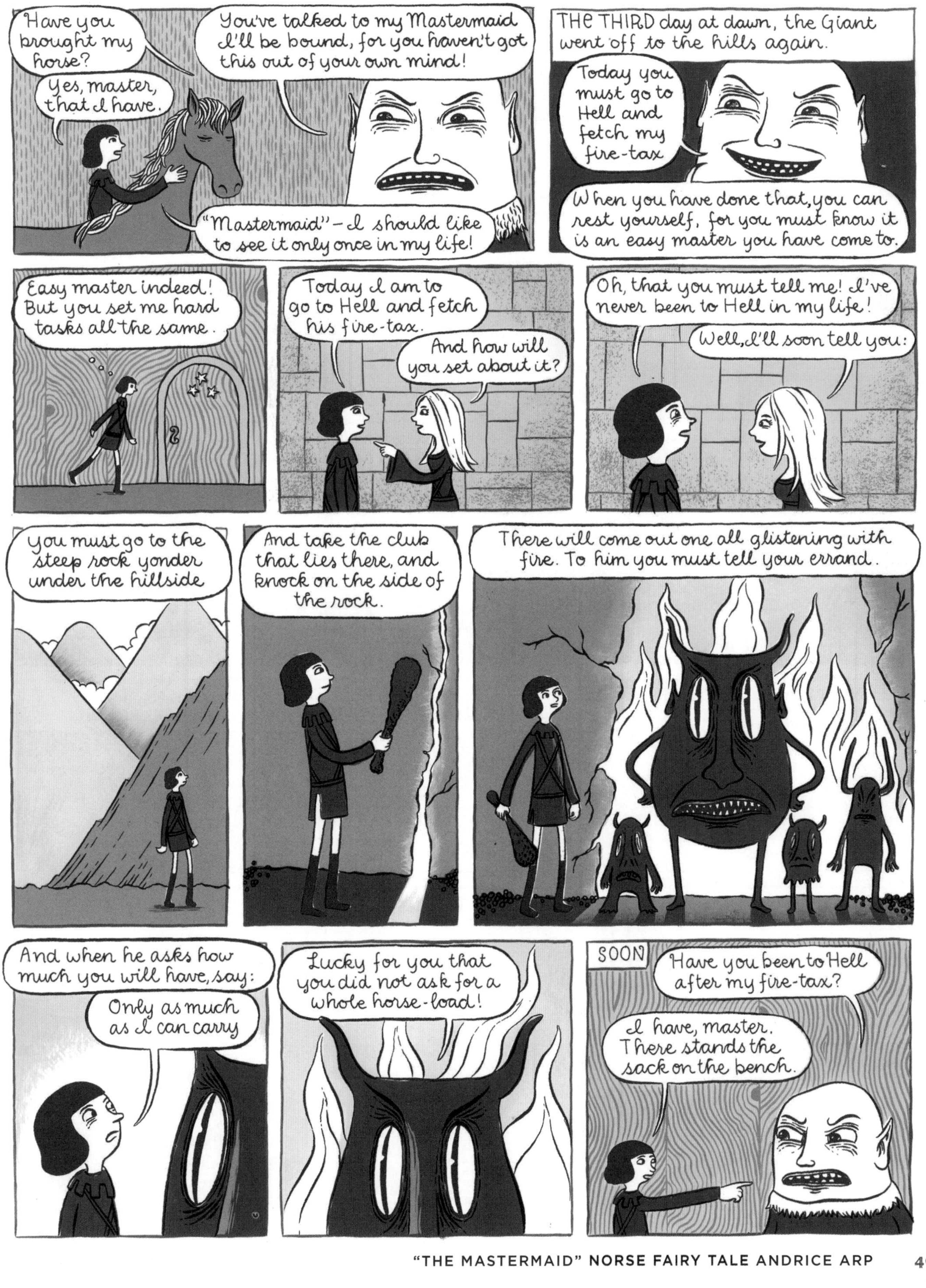
Have you brought my horse?
Yes, master, that I have.
You've talked to my Mastermaid I'll be bound, for you haven't got this out of your own mind!
"Mastermaid"—I should like to see it only once in my life!
THE THIRD day at dawn, the Giant went off to the hills again.
Today you must go to Hell and fetch my fire-tax
When you have done that, you can rest yourself, for you must know it is an easy master you have come to.
Easy master indeed! But you set me hard tasks all the same.
Today I am to go to Hell and fetch his fire-tax.
And how will you set about it?
Oh, that you must tell me! I've never been to Hell in my life!
Well, I'll soon tell you:
You must go to the steep rock yonder under the hillside
And take the club that lies there, and knock on the side of the rock.
There will come out one all glistening with fire. To him you must tell your errand.
And when he asks how much you will have, say:
Only as much as I can carry
Lucky for you that you did not ask for a whole horse-load!
SOON
Have you been to Hell after my fire-tax?
I have, master. There stands the sack on the bench.

You've been talking to my Mastermaid, that I can see. But if you have, I'll WRING YOUR HEAD OFF!

"Mastermaid"! I only wish I could see what sort of thing she is!

Well, well, wait until tomorrow, then I will take you to her myself.

Thank you kindly, master, but it is only a joke, I'll be bound.

NEXT DAY

Cut his throat, and boil him in the great big pot, and when the broth is ready, just give me a call.

After that he lay down on the bench to sleep, and began to snore so that it sounded like thunder over the hills.

So the Mastermaid took a knife and cut the Prince in his little finger, and let three drops of blood fall on a three-legged stool.

And after that she took old rags and soles of shoes and all the rubbish she could lay hands on, and put them into the pot.

Then she filled a chest full of ground gold...

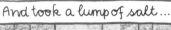
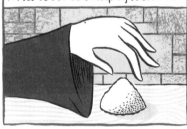

And took a lump of salt...

...a flask of water that hung behind the door...

And she took, besides, a golden apple and two golden chickens.

And off they set from the Giant's house as fast as they could.

When they had gone a little way, they came to the sea

And after that they sailed on a ship over the sea.

50    "THE MASTERMAID" NORSE FAIRY TALE ANDRICE ARP

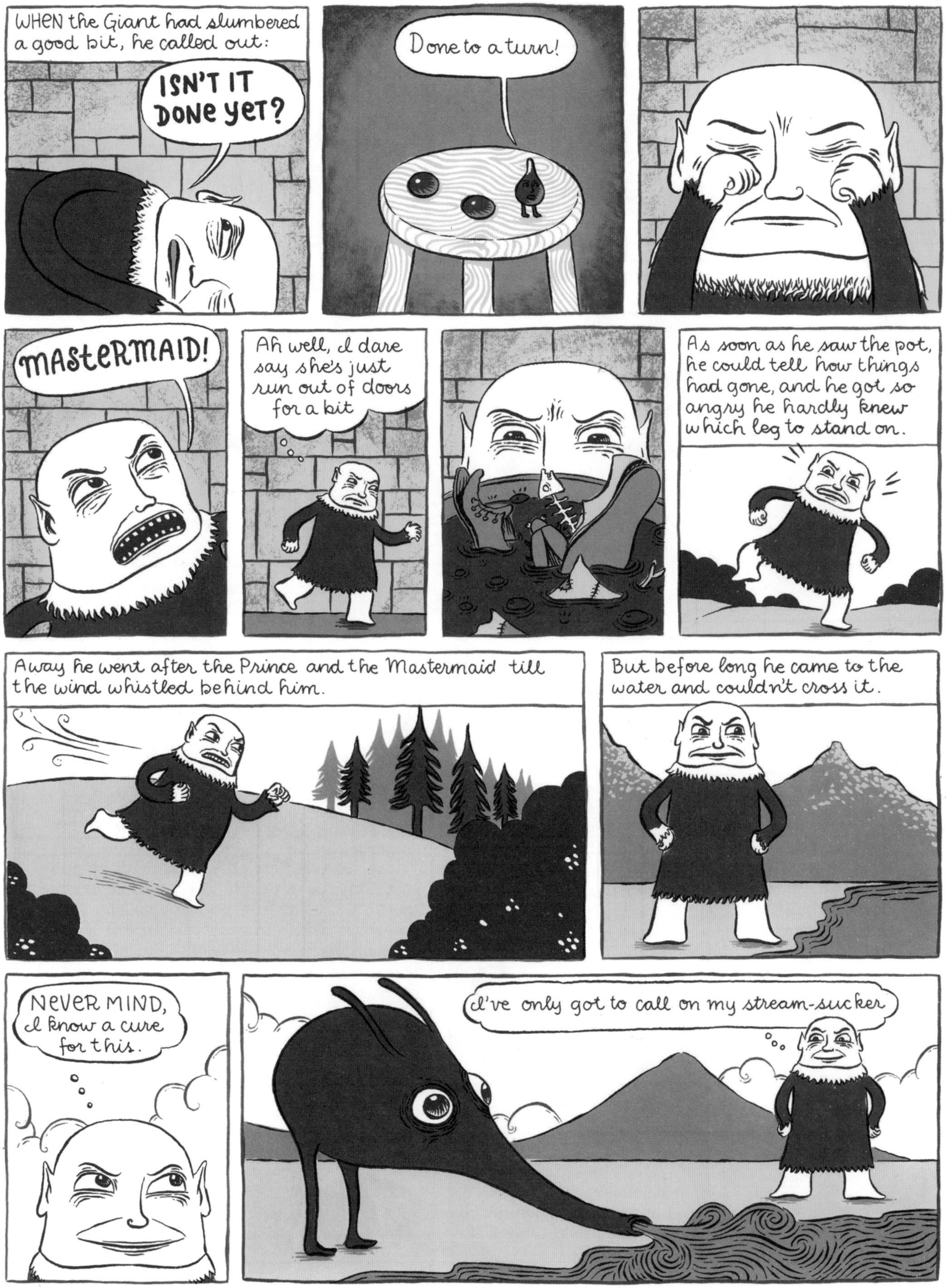
WHEN the Giant had slumbered a good bit, he called out:
ISN'T IT DONE YET?
Done to a turn!
MASTERMAID!
Ah well, I dare say she's just run out of doors for a bit
As soon as he saw the pot, he could tell how things had gone, and he got so angry he hardly knew which leg to stand on.
Away he went after the Prince and the Mastermaid till the wind whistled behind him.
But before long he came to the water and couldn't cross it.
NEVER MIND, I know a cure for this.
I've only got to call on my stream-sucker

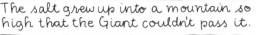

Now you must cast out the lump of salt.

The salt grew up into a mountain so high that the Giant couldn't pass it.

NEVER MIND! THERE'S A CURE FOR THIS TOO!

So he called on his hill-borer so that the stream-sucker might creep through and take another swill.

Throw overboard a drop out of the flask.

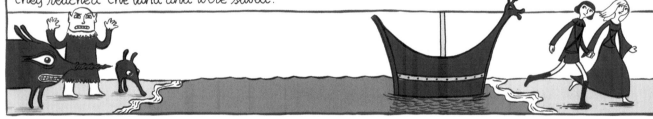
Then the sea was just as full as ever, and before the stream-sucker could take another gulp, they reached the land and were saved.

THEY made up their minds to go home to the Prince's father.

Just wait here ten minutes while I go home after a coach, for I will not hear of my sweetheart walking to my father's palace!

Ah! Don't leave me, for if you once get to the palace you will forget me, I know you will!

Oh! How can I forget you with whom I have gone through so much, and who I love so dearly!?

There was no help for it; he went home to fetch the coach and seven horses, and she was to wait for him by the seaside.

Now, when you go home, don't so much as say good-day to anyone. Go straight to the stable and drive back as quick as you can. They will all come about you, but act as if you did not see them.

Above all things, do not taste a morsel of food, for if you do, we will both come to grief.

NOW, just as he came to the palace, one of his brothers was thinking of holding his bridal feast, and the Bride and all her kith and kin had just arrived.

So they all thronged 'round him, and asked him about this thing and that, but he made as though he did not see them, and went straight to the stall and got out the horses.

And when they could not get him to come in, they came out to him with meat and drink, but the Prince would not taste so much as a crumb.

At last the Bride's sister rolled an apple to him.

Well, if you won't eat anything else, you may as well take a bite of this

For you must be both hungry and thirsty after so long a journey!

But he had scarce taken a bite before he forgot the Mastermaid.

Well, I think I must be mad! What am I to do with this coach and horses?

So he put the horses up again and went along with the others into the palace.

And it was soon settled that he should have as his wife the Bride's sister.

There sat the Mastermaid by the seaside and waited and waited, but no Prince came.

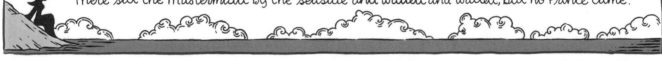

So at last she went up from the shore, and after she had gone a bit she came to a little hut which lay by itself in a copse close to the King's palace.

Now, the hut was as dark and dirty as a pigsty. She threw into the fire a handful of gold from her chest, and it bubbled and boiled all over the hut till it was gilded both outside and in.

NEXT day the Constable passed that way

To make a long story short, he fell in love at the sight of the Mastermaid and begged her to become his wife.

Well, but have you much money?

I am not so badly off

Then I will have you.

But they were scarce in bed before:

I have forgotten to make up the fire!

Don't stir out of bed, I'll see to it!

As soon as you have got hold of the shovel, tell me.

Well, I am holding it now

May you hold the shovel, and the shovel you, and may you heap hot coals over yourself till morning breaks

As soon as day broke, he did not stay long, but set off as if the Evil One or the Bailiff were at his heels.

He told no one where he had been, for shame's sake.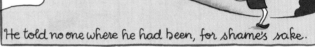

Next day the Attorney passed by the place

And when he saw the lovely maiden, he fell more in love than the Constable and began to woo her in hot haste.

Have you a good lot of money?

I am not so badly off

And they went to bed.

I have forgotten to shut the door of the porch!

Lie still while I go do it!

Tell me when you have got hold of the door-latch.

I've got hold of it now

May you hold the door, and the door you, and may you go from wall to wall until the day dawns

As soon as it let go its hold, off set the Attorney, leaving behind him his money and forgetting his courtship all together...

for he was afraid lest the house door come dancing after him.

The third day the Sheriff passed that way

And he had scarce set his eyes on the Mastermaid before he began to woo her.

If you have lots of money, I will have you; if not you may go about your business.

I am not so badly off

But they had scarce gone to bed before:

I have forgotten to bring home the calf from the meadow! I must get up!

By all the powers, that shall never be!

Well only tell me when you've got hold of the calf's tail.

Now I have hold of it

May you hold the calf's tail, and the tail you, and may you take a tour of the world until dawn

At dawn, the poor Sherriff was so glad to let go of the calf's tail that he forgot his sack of money and everything else.

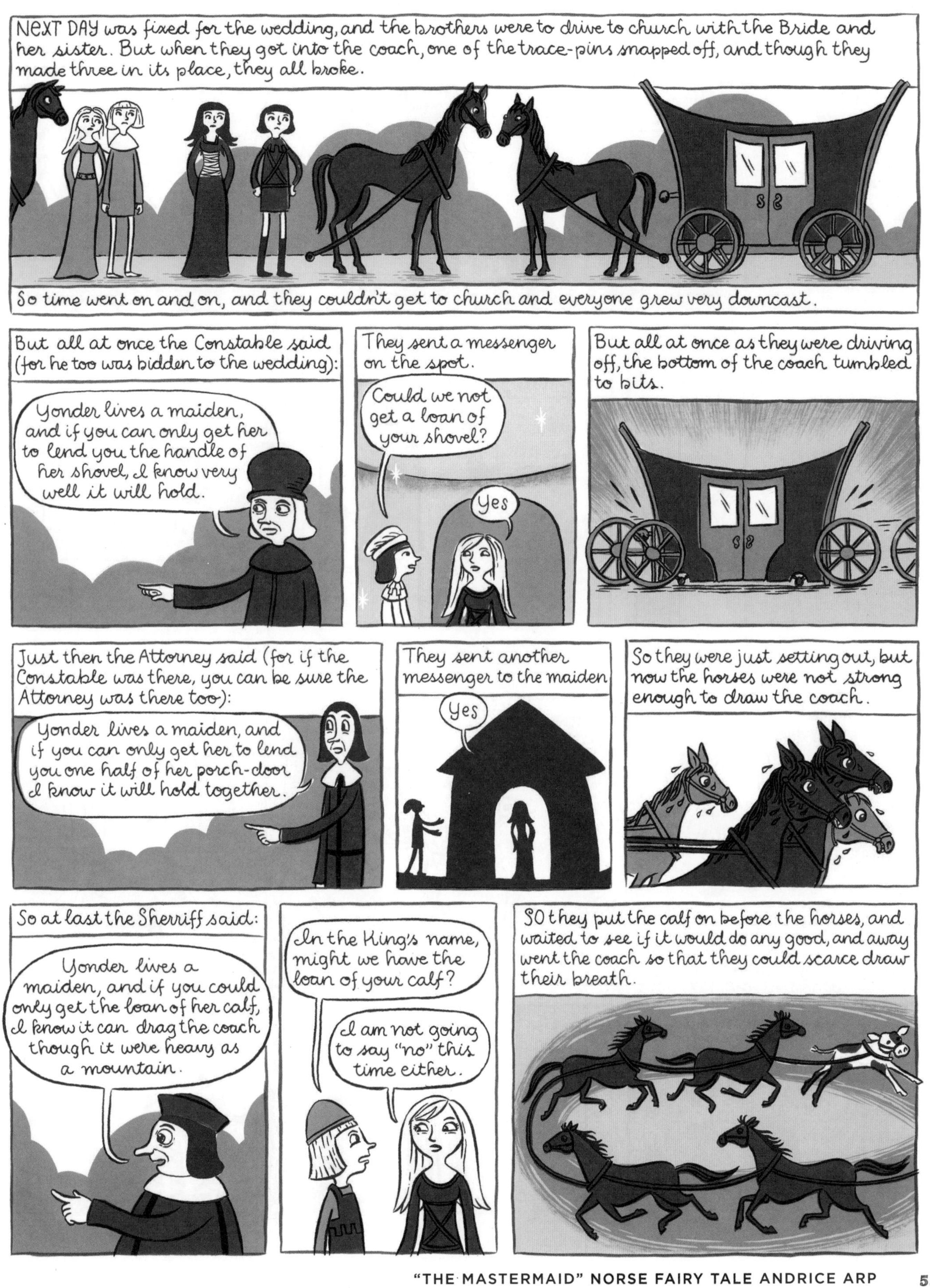

NEXT DAY was fixed for the wedding, and the brothers were to drive to church with the Bride and her sister. But when they got into the coach, one of the trace-pins snapped off, and though they made three in its place, they all broke.
So time went on and on, and they couldn't get to church and everyone grew very downcast.
But all at once the Constable said (for he too was bidden to the wedding):
Yonder lives a maiden, and if you can only get her to lend you the handle of her shovel, I know very well it will hold.
They sent a messenger on the spot.
Could we not get a loan of your shovel?
Yes
But all at once as they were driving off, the bottom of the coach tumbled to bits.
Just then the Attorney said (for if the Constable was there, you can be sure the Attorney was there too):
Yonder lives a maiden, and if you can only get her to lend you one half of her porch-door I know it will hold together.
They sent another messenger to the maiden
Yes
So they were just setting out, but now the horses were not strong enough to draw the coach.
So at last the Sherriff said:
Yonder lives a maiden, and if you could only get the loan of her calf, I know it can drag the coach though it were heavy as a mountain.
In the King's name, might we have the loan of your calf?
I am not going to say "no" this time either.
SO they put the calf on before the horses, and waited to see if it would do any good, and away went the coach so that they could scarce draw their breath.

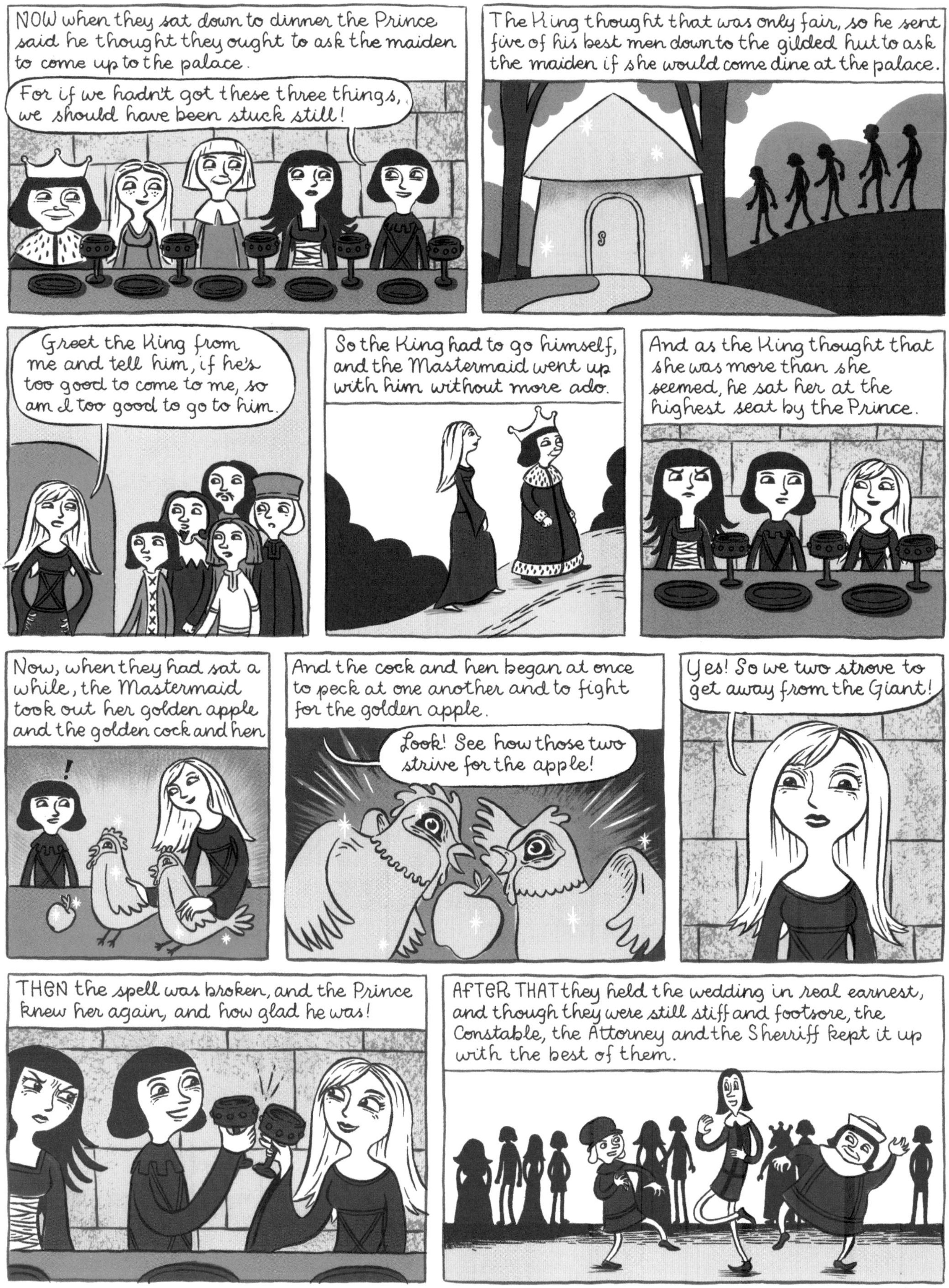
NOW when they sat down to dinner the Prince said he thought they ought to ask the maiden to come up to the palace.
For if we hadn't got these three things, we should have been stuck still!
The King thought that was only fair, so he sent five of his best men down to the gilded hut to ask the maiden if she would come dine at the palace.
Greet the King from me and tell him, if he's too good to come to me, so am I too good to go to him.
So the King had to go himself, and the Mastermaid went up with him without more ado.
And as the King thought that she was more than she seemed, he sat her at the highest seat by the Prince.
Now, when they had sat a while, the Mastermaid took out her golden apple and the golden cock and hen
!
And the cock and hen began at once to peck at one another and to fight for the golden apple.
Look! See how those two strive for the apple!
Yes! So we two strove to get away from the Giant!
THEN the spell was broken, and the Prince knew her again, and how glad he was!
AFTER THAT they held the wedding in real earnest, and though they were still stiff and footsore, the Constable, the Attorney and the Sherriff kept it up with the best of them.

# "The Firebird"

## Russian fairy tale

ART/ADAPTATION BY **Lesley Barnes**

**THE FIGURE OF A BIRD OF FIRE OCCURS IN A NUMBER** of mythologies and folktales throughout the world. Perhaps its most famous appearance is in the Russian fairy tale "Ivan Tsarevich, the Firebird, and the Gray Wolf." Lesley Barnes of London—whose work has appeared on or in book covers for Penguin, greeting cards, Post-It Notes, gift wrap, the *Economist*, museum shows, and elsewhere—illustrated the tale in a series of stunning images that she self-published as a long, unfolding concertina. She has adapted it for publication here, and she explained the modified version of the tale that she created:

The Tsar had an extraordinary tree on which there grew many Golden Apples. But during the night these rare fruits began to disappear, so the Tsar asked his son, Prince Ivan, to guard the tree. One night as the Prince was dozing under the tree, a bird made of fire swooped down and plucked a Golden Apple. The flames woke the Prince, and he unsuccessfully grabbed at the Firebird but could only capture a single fiery feather.

Prince Ivan put the feather in his hat and jumped on his horse to chase after the Firebird. As he was galloping out of his father's kingdom, a wolf jumped out at them. The Prince fell from his horse, who fled, and stared up at the wolf in terror. But the wolf was friendly, and he told the Prince that if he jumped on his back he would take him to the Firebird's garden.

When they reached the garden, the Prince finally managed to capture the Firebird. But the bird belonged to Tsar Dolmat, and as soon as his guards spotted the Prince they captured him and took him to the Tsar. Tsar Dolmat was angry but said to the Prince: "If you steal the Horse with the Golden Mane for me I will give you my Firebird."

The wolf offered to take the Prince to the kingdom of Tsar Afron, who owned the Horse with the Golden Mane. Prince Ivan saw the horse shining in the distance and managed to capture it and jump on its back. But just as the Prince was about to gallop away, Tsar Afron's guards surrounded him. The guards took the Prince to Tsar Afron, who said to him: "If you steal Princess Helen for me you can have my horse!"

So Prince Ivan stole Princess Helen . . . but they fell in love, so Prince Ivan took her back to his kingdom, where they married, surrounded by Golden Apples.

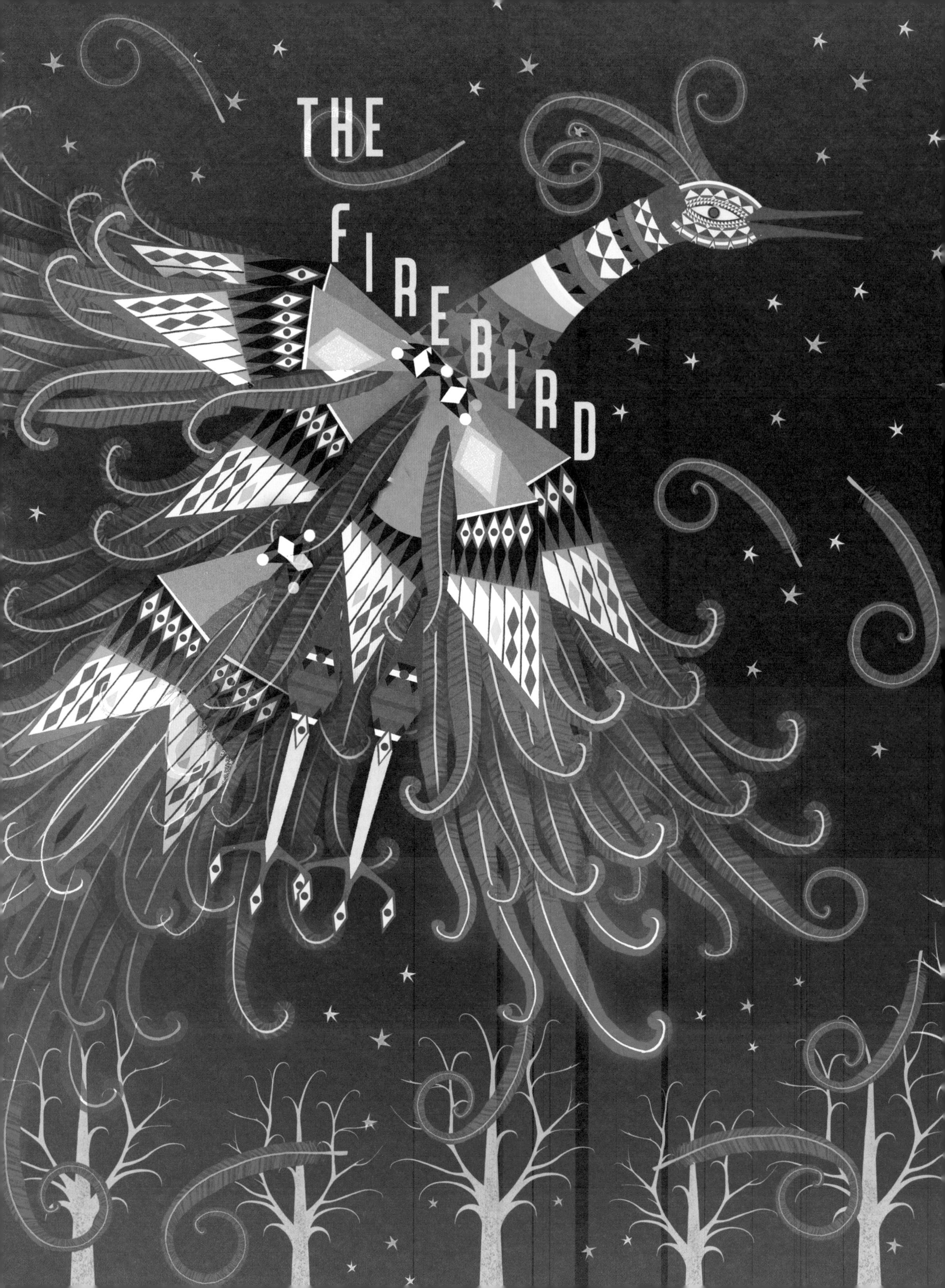
THE FIREBIRD

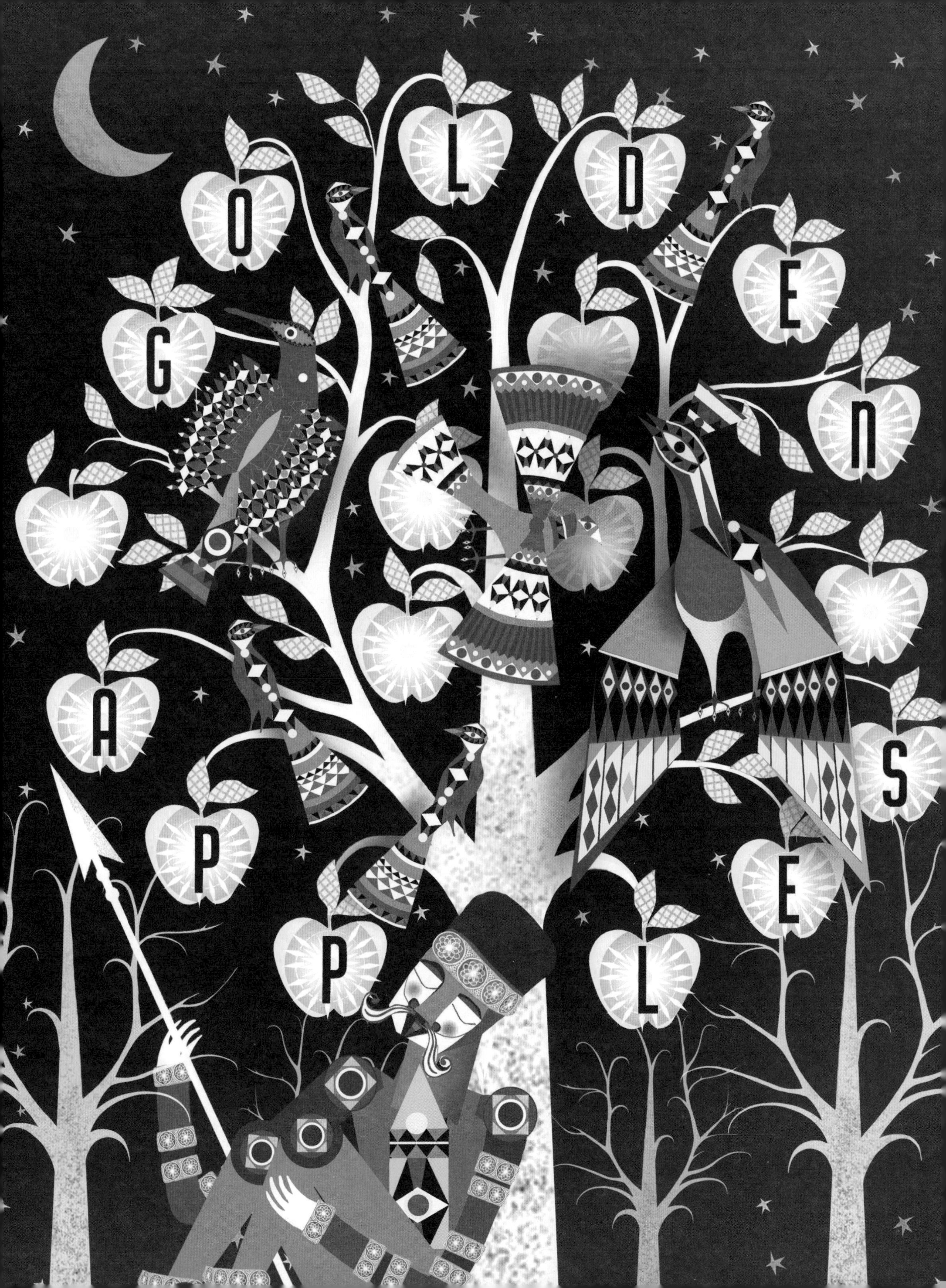
GOLDEN
APPLES

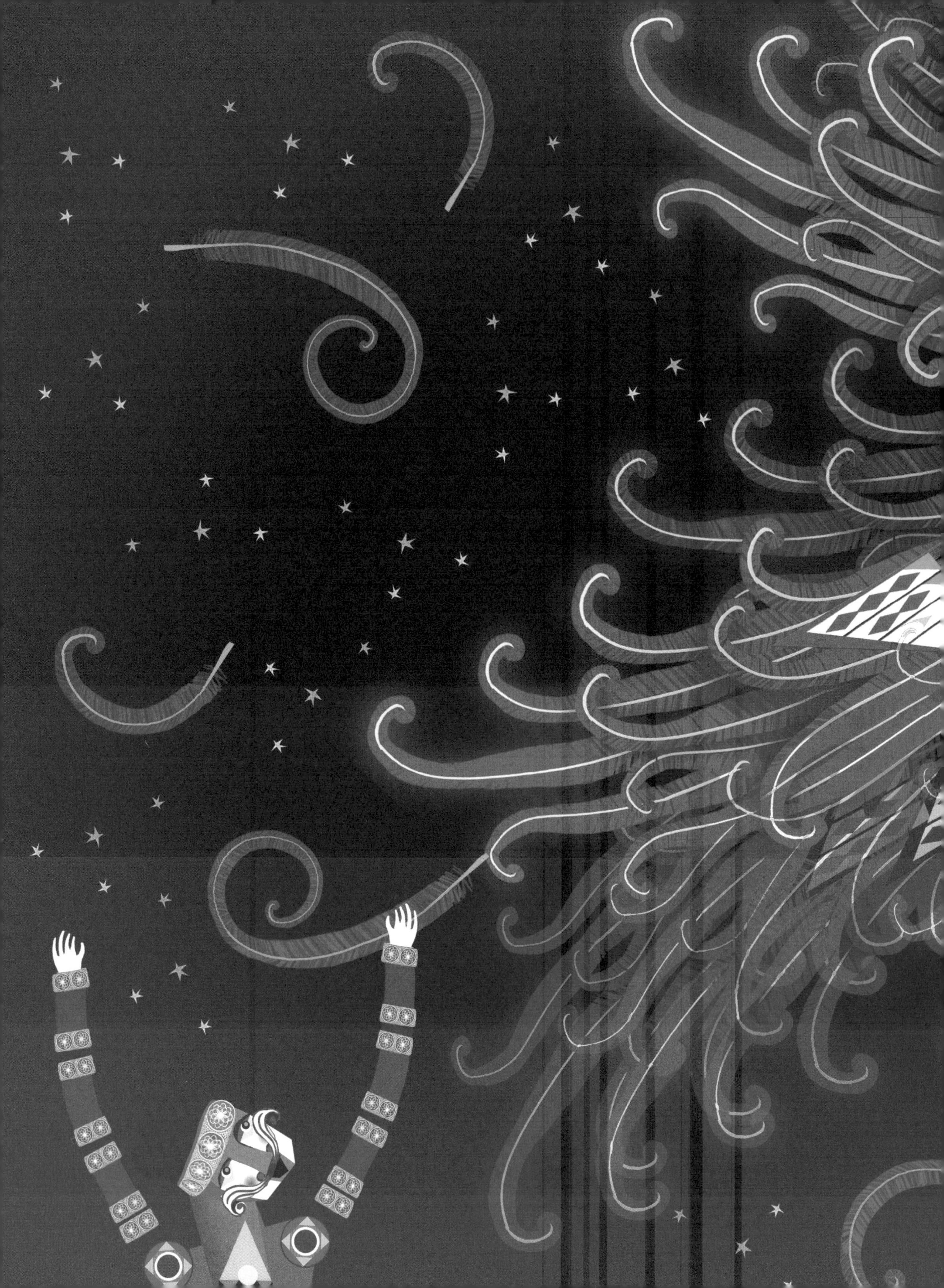

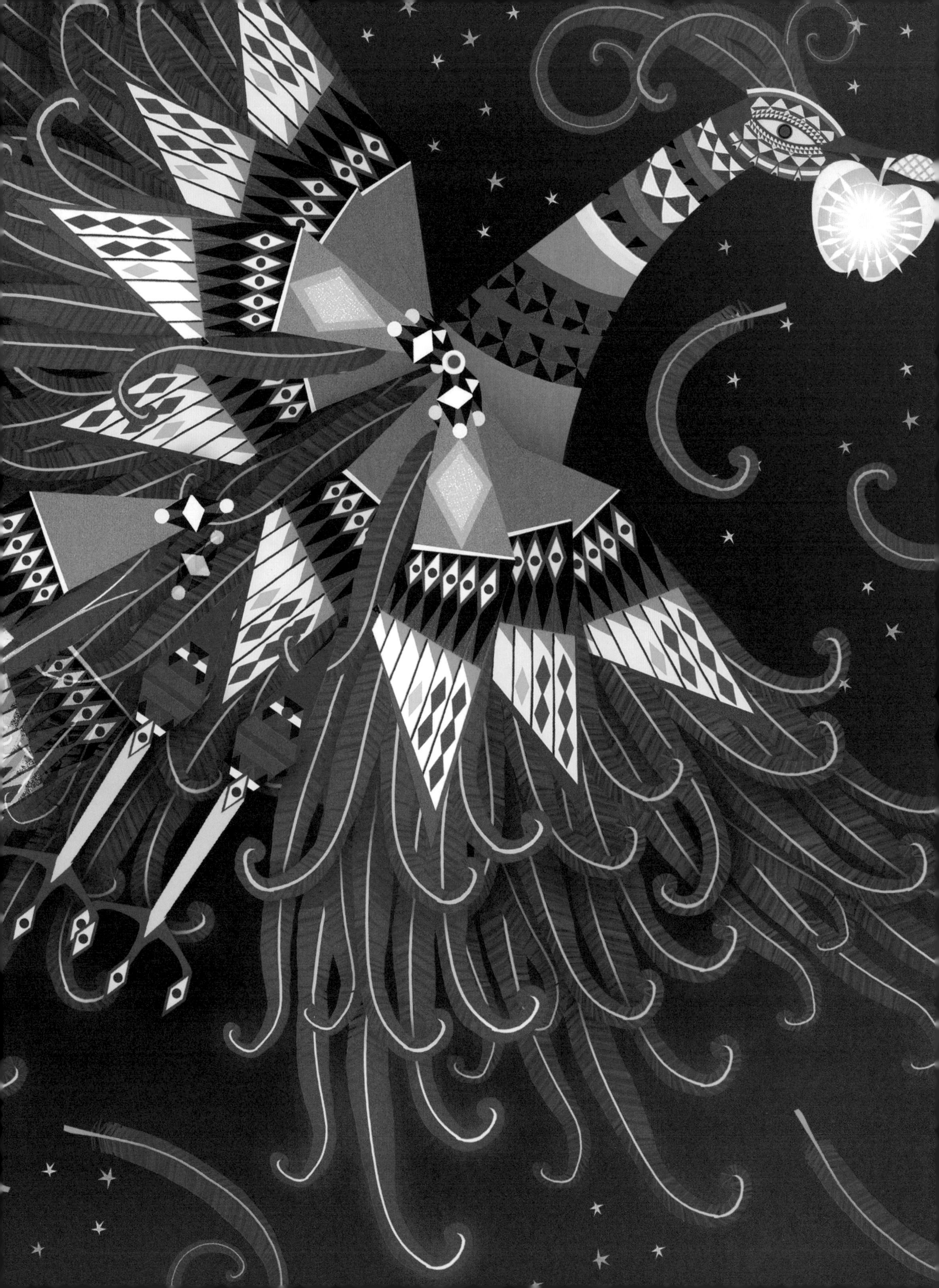

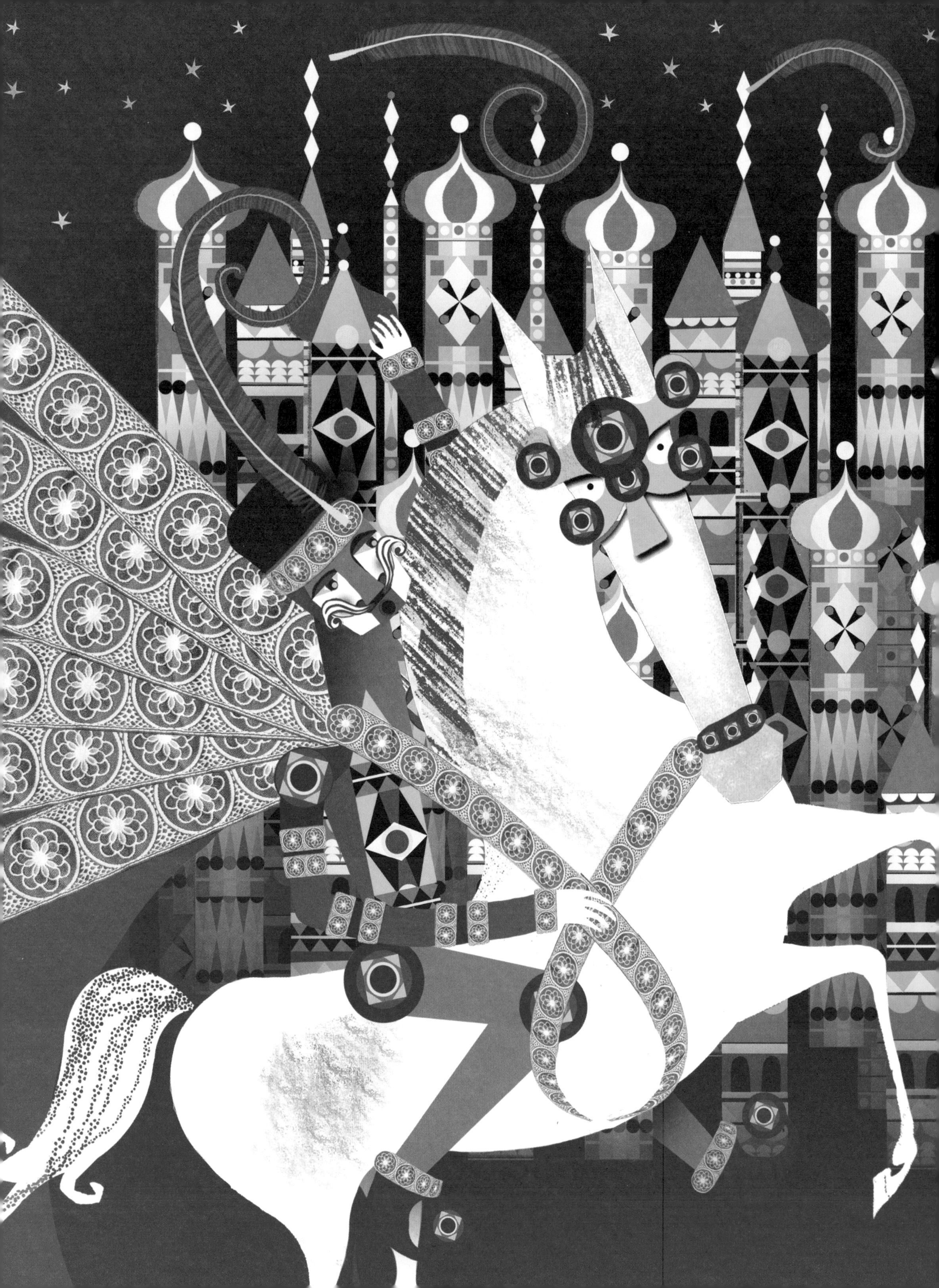

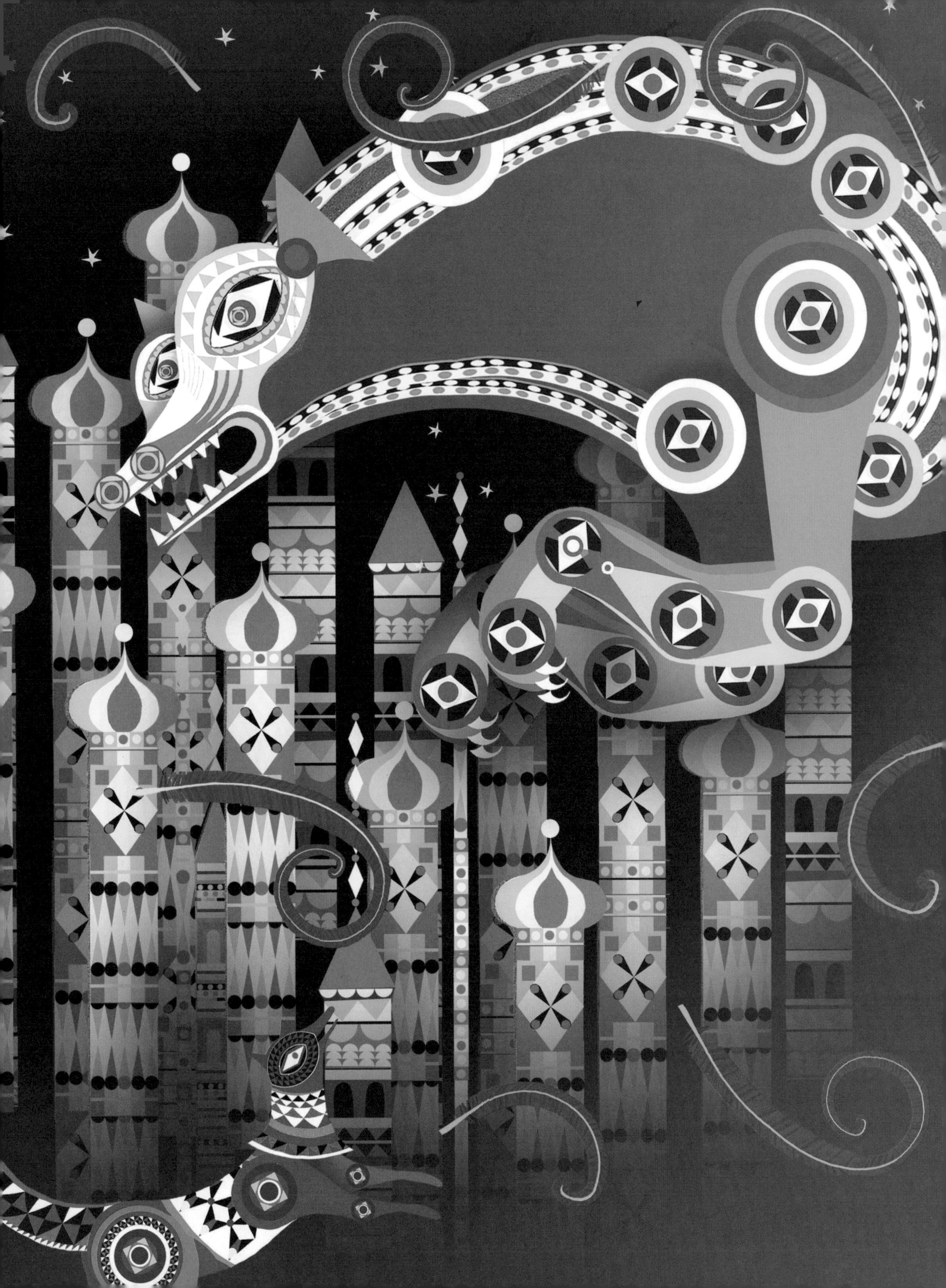

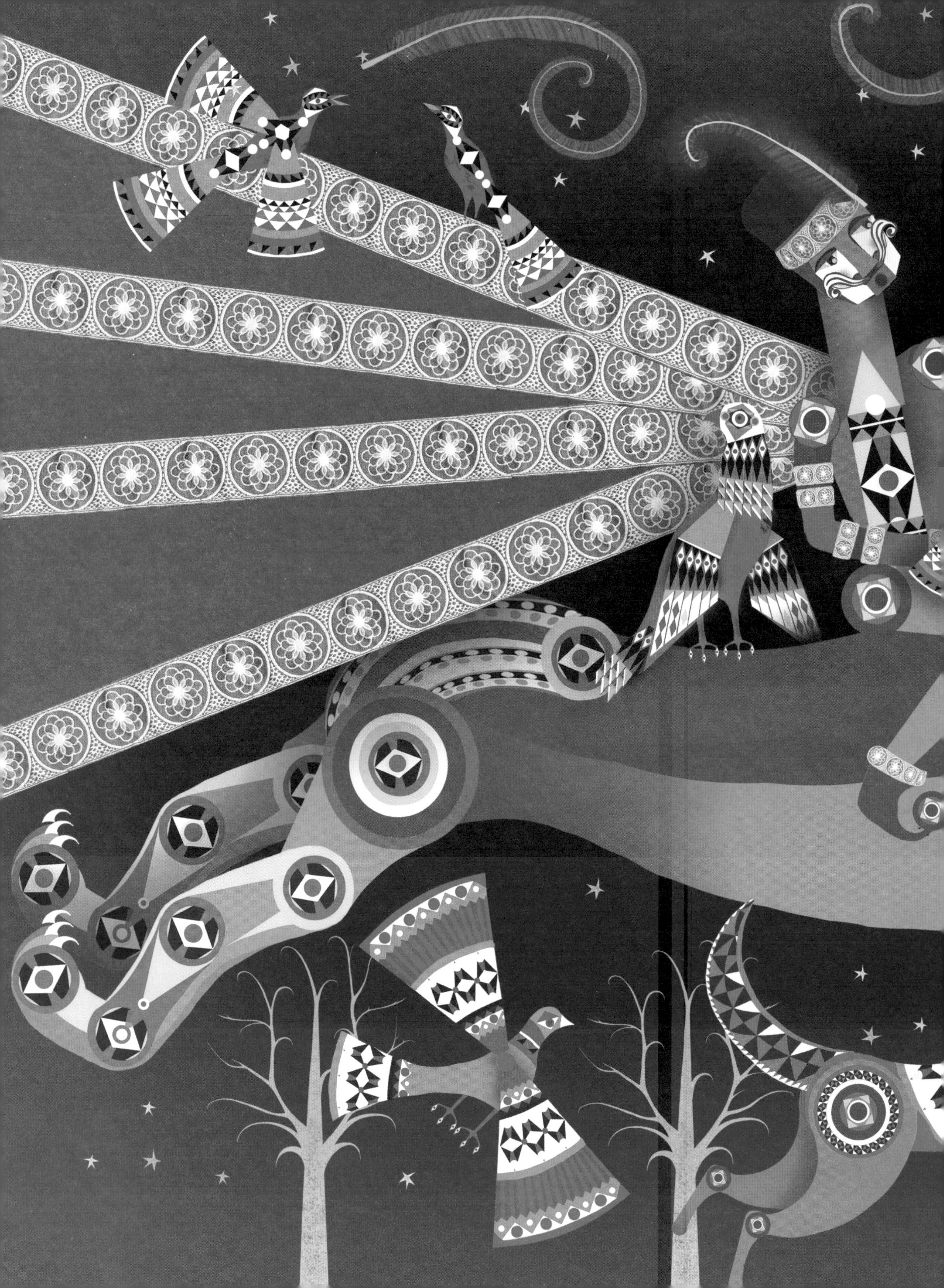

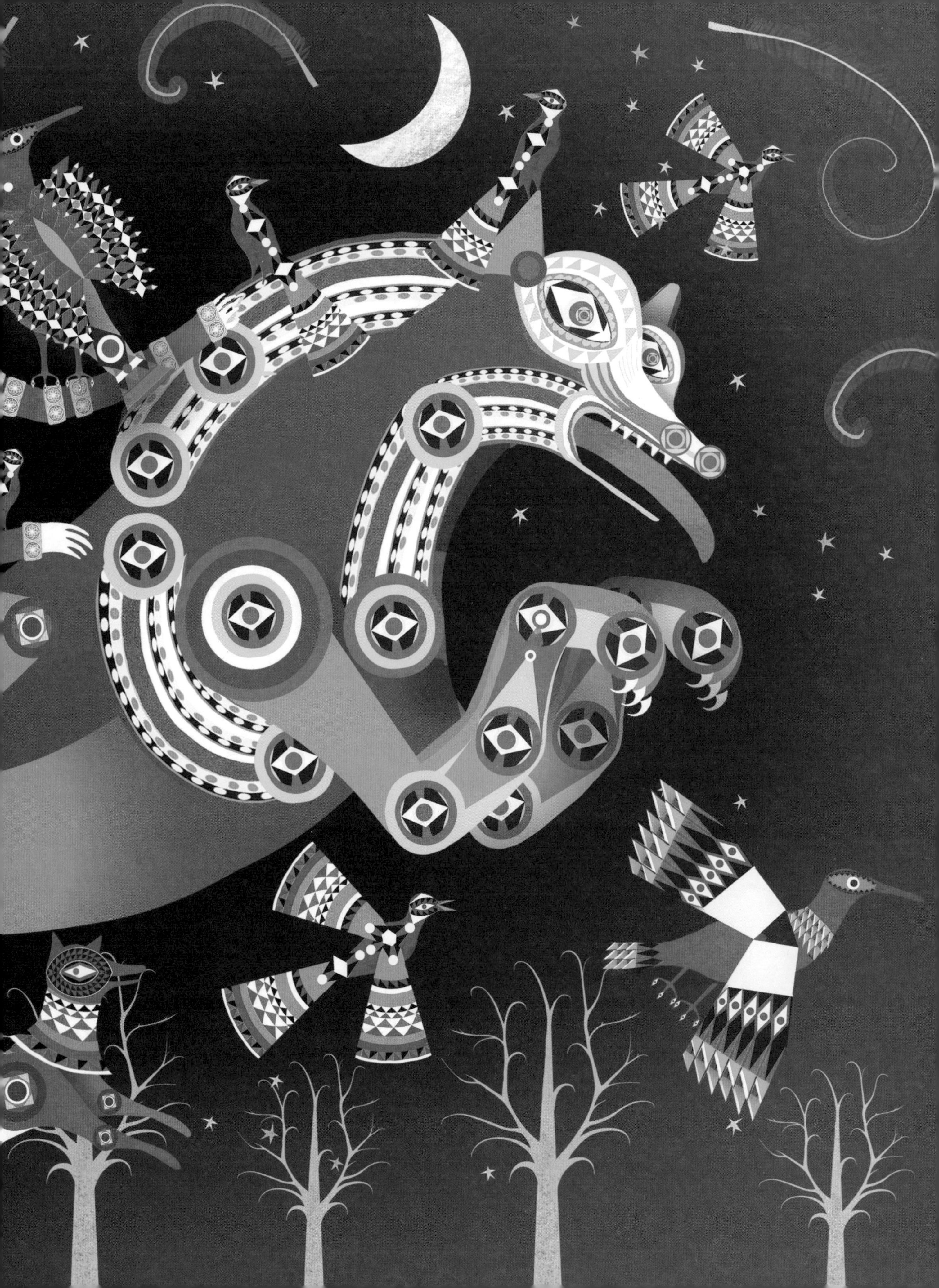

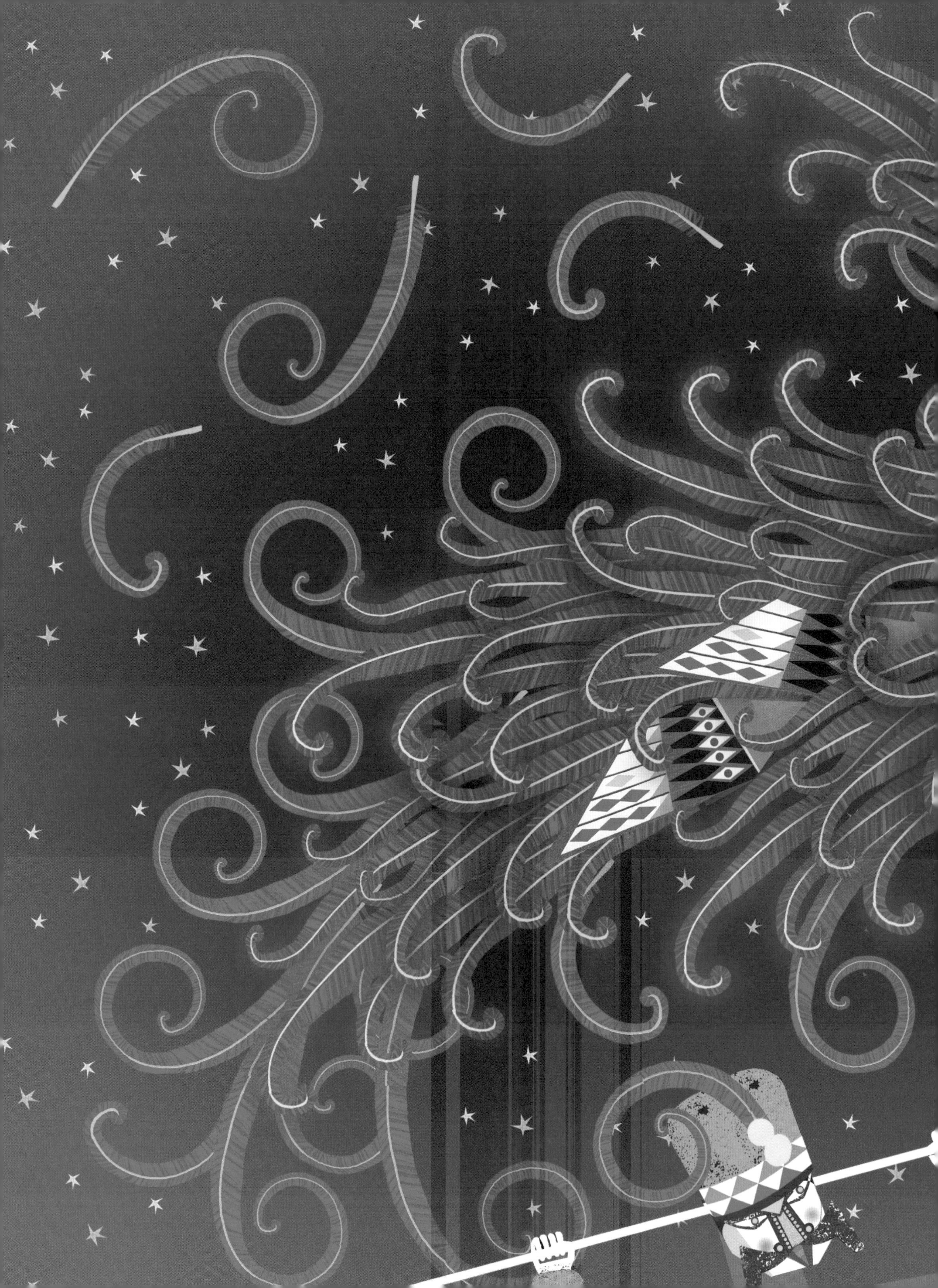

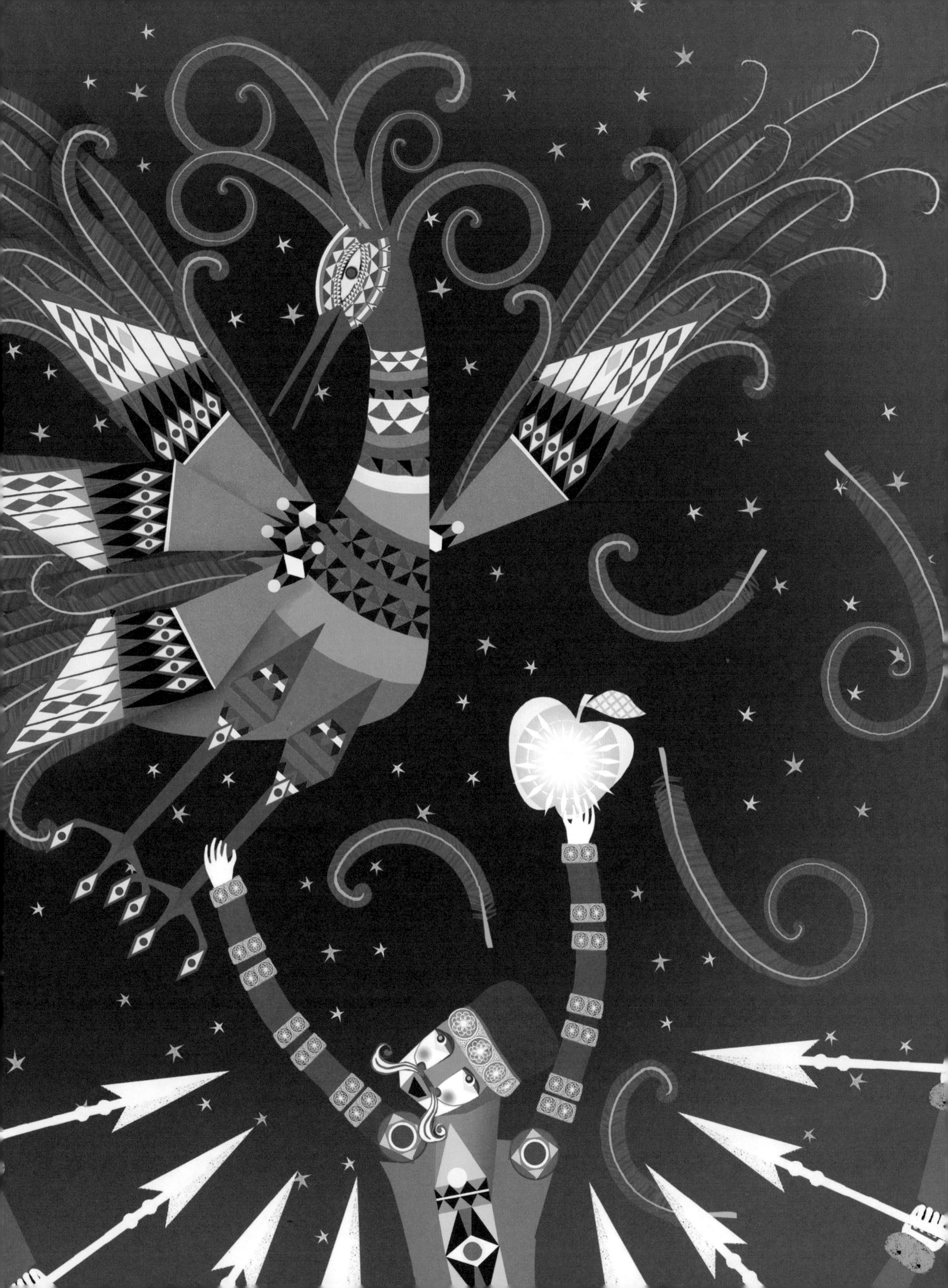

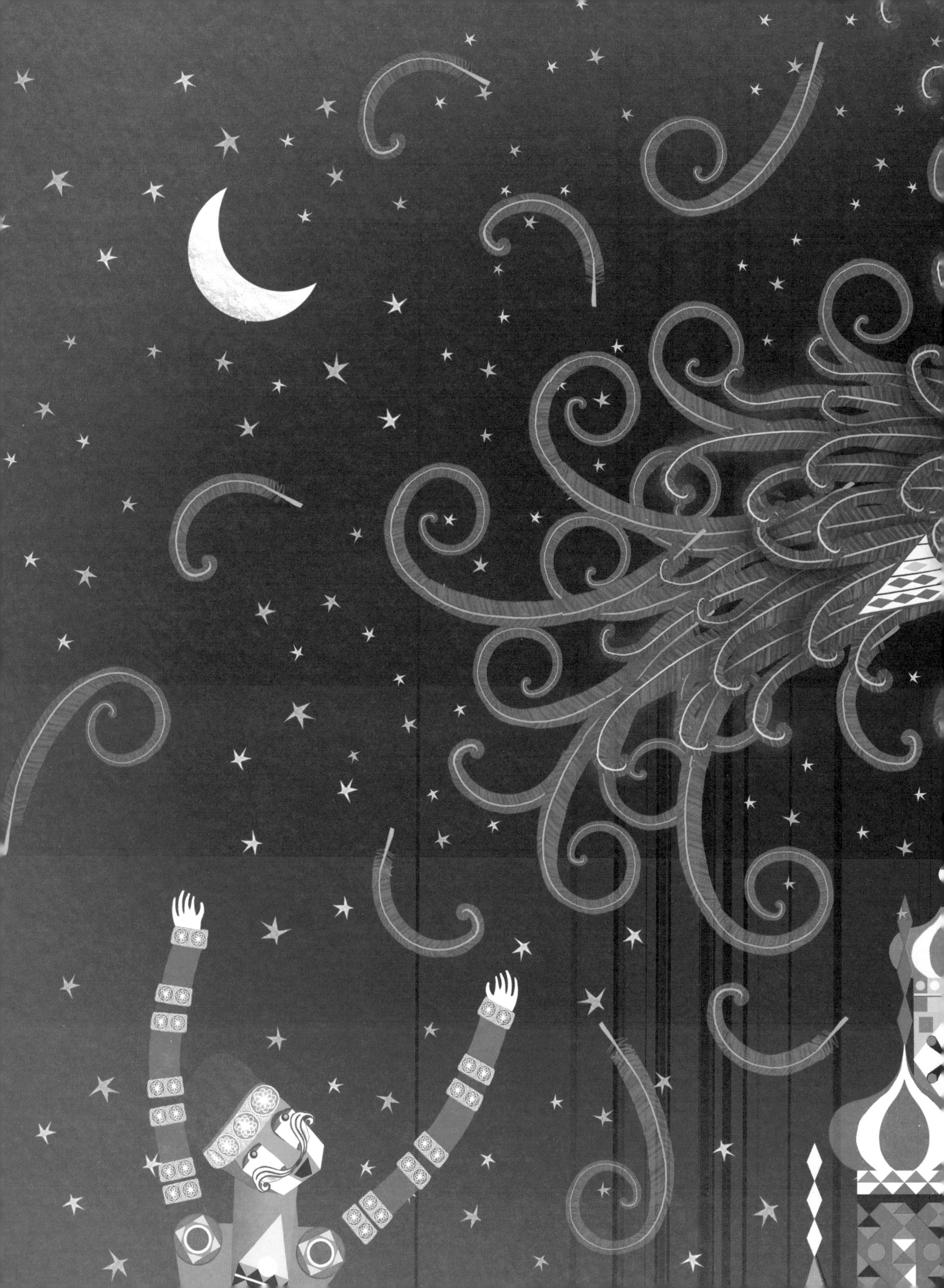

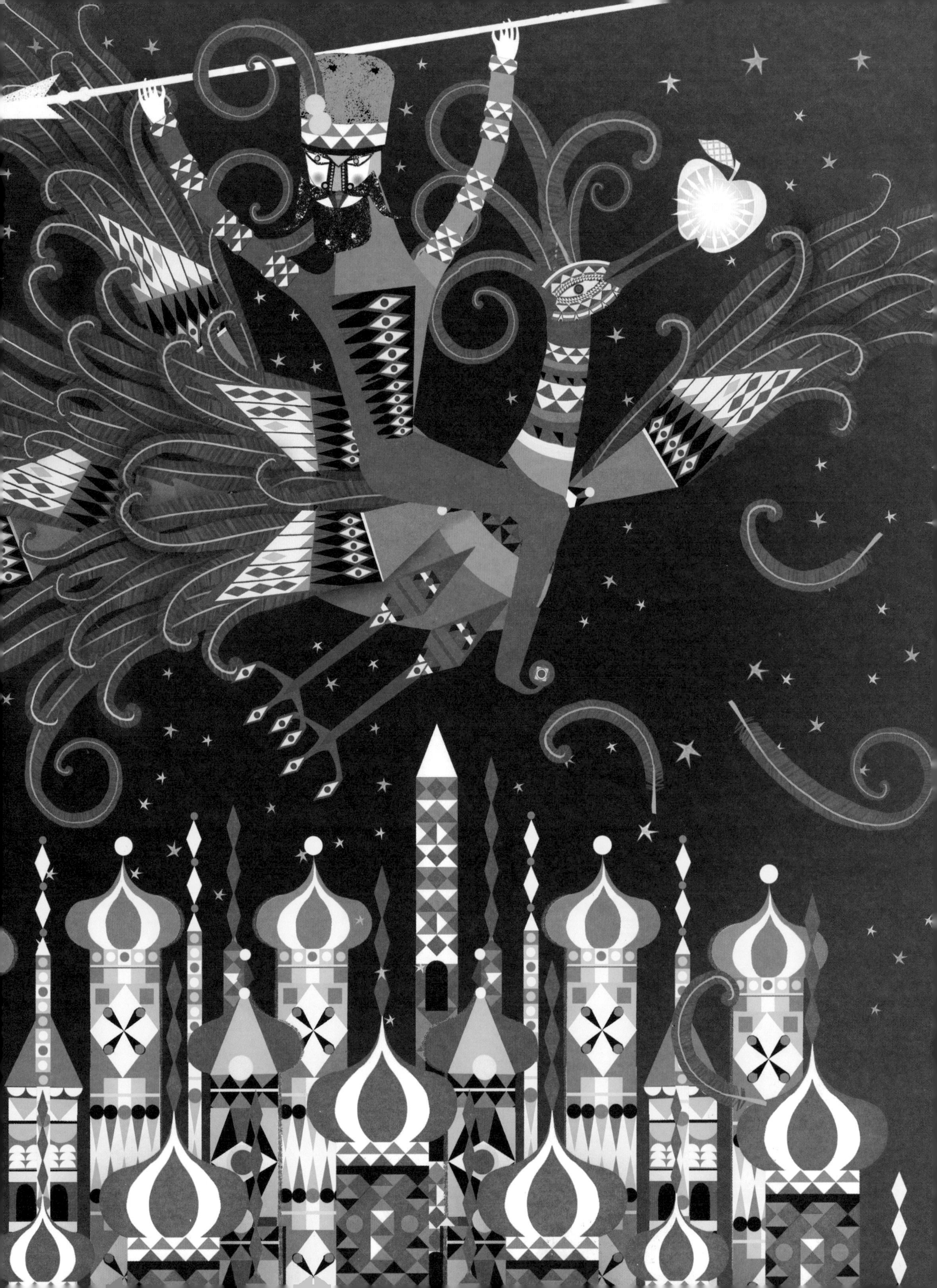

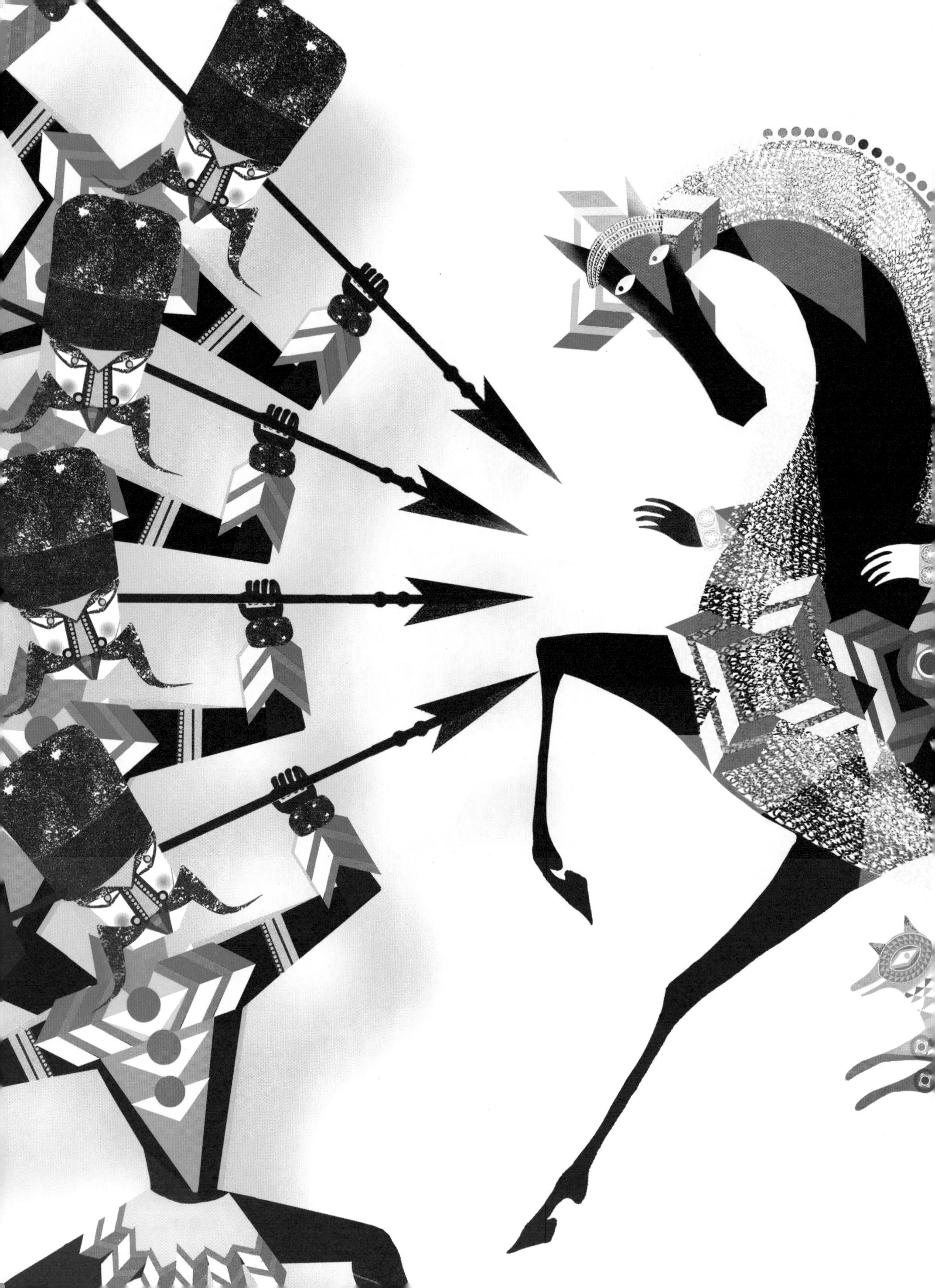

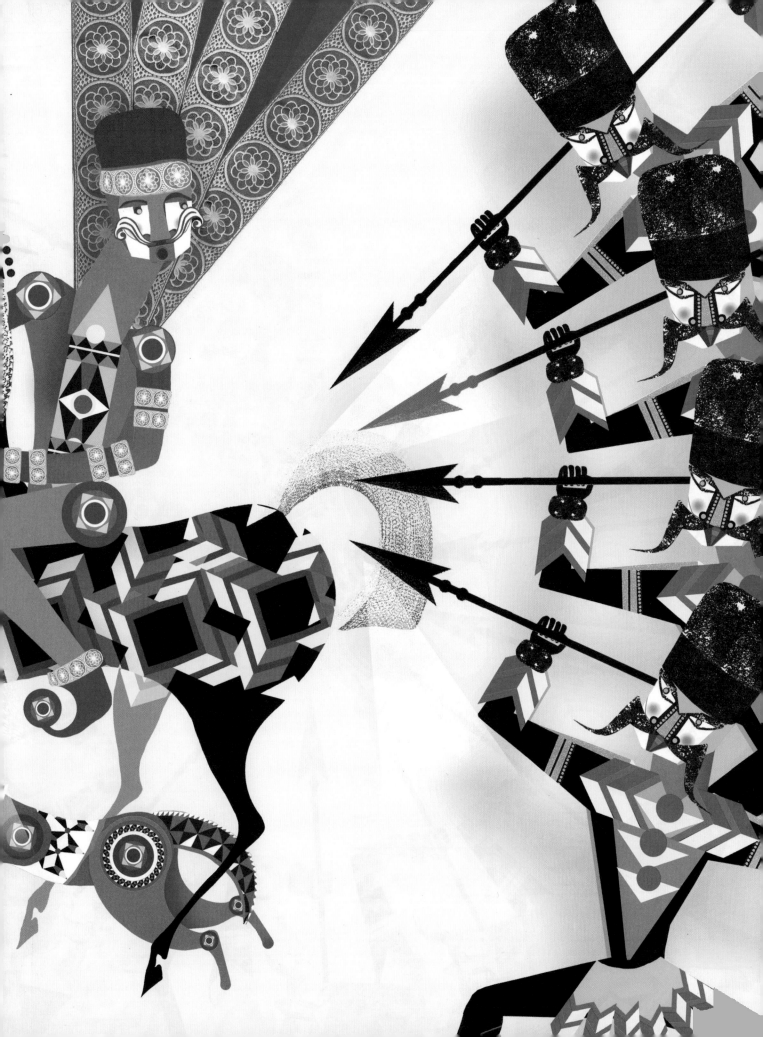

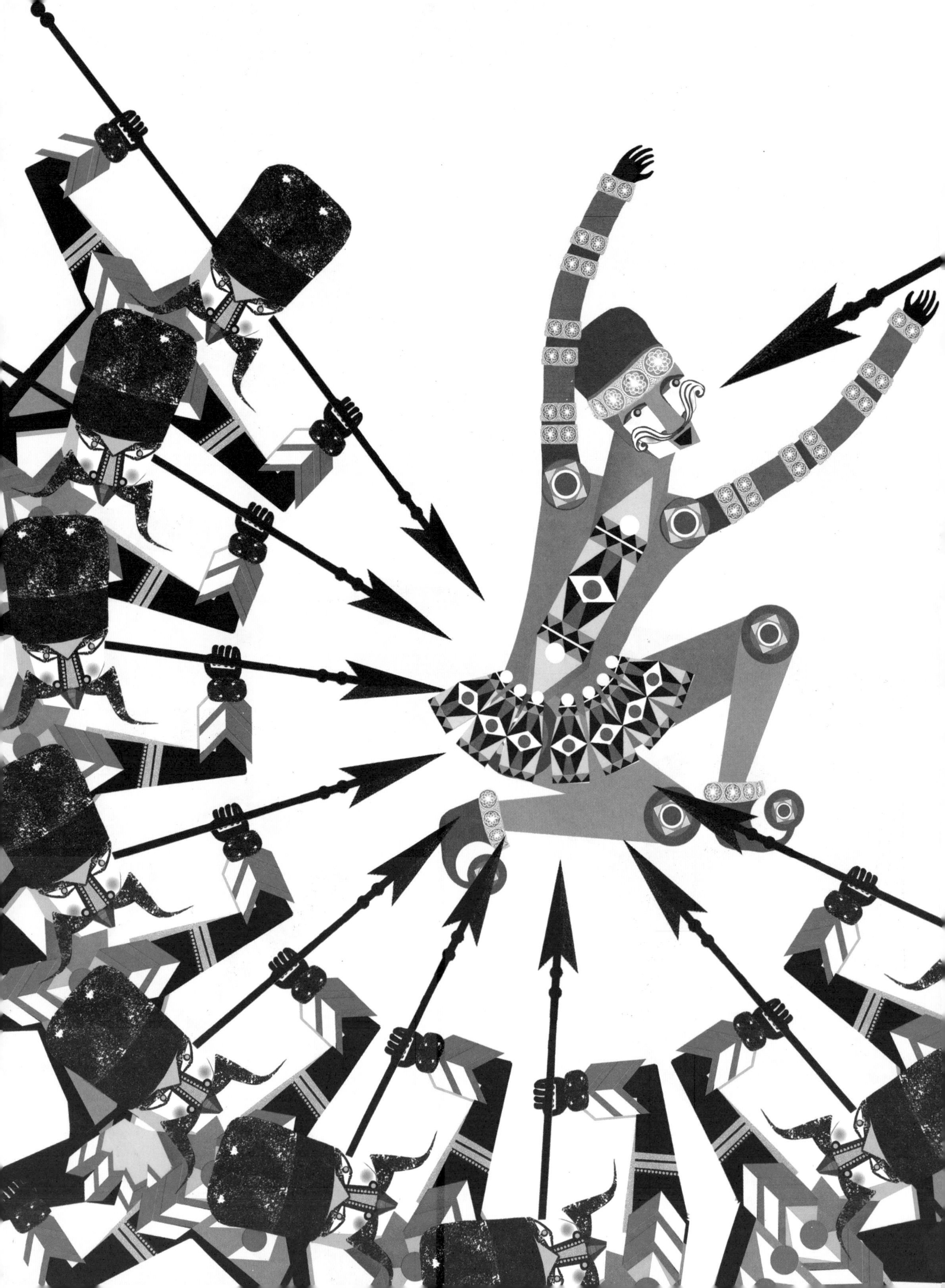

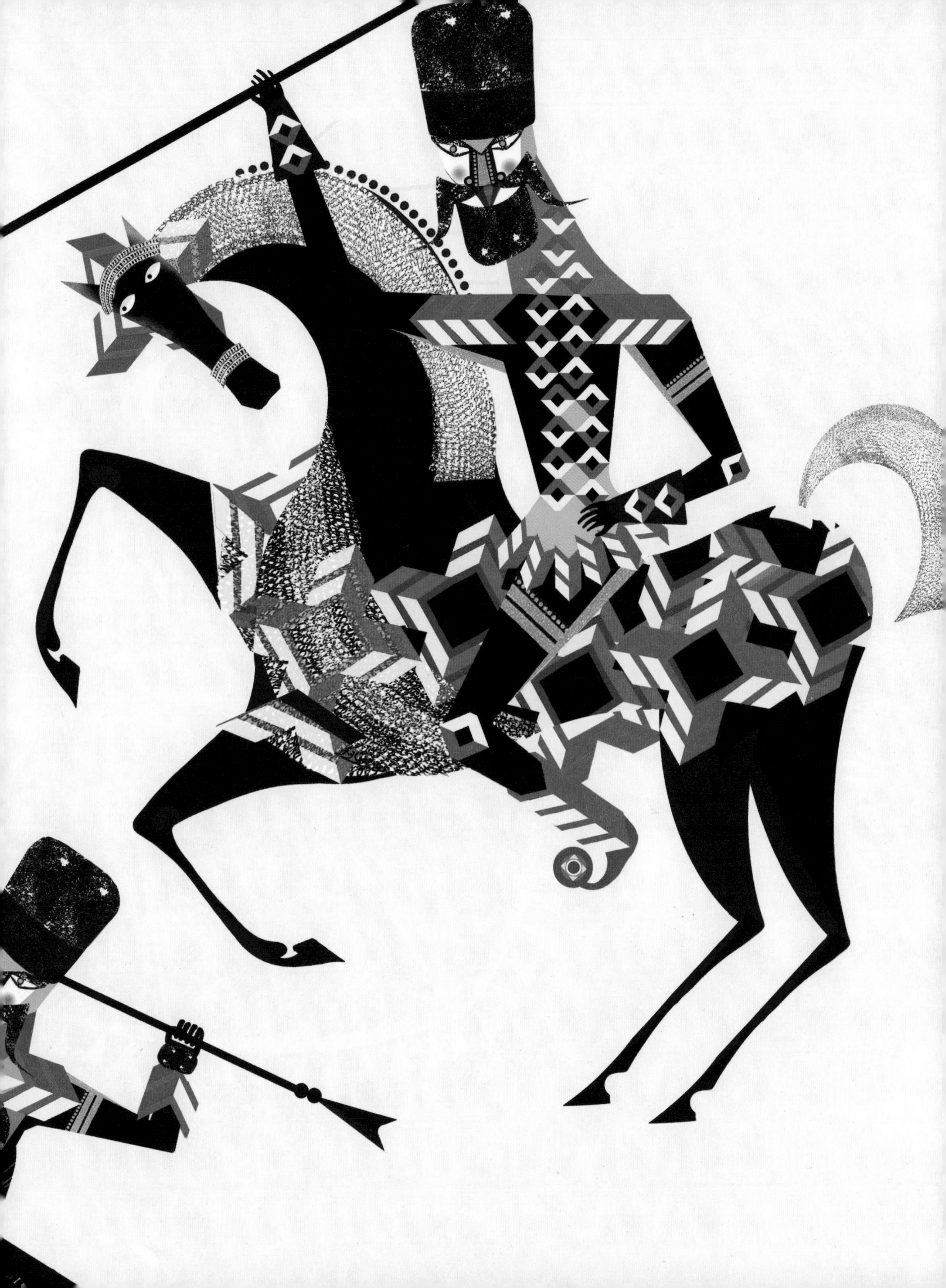

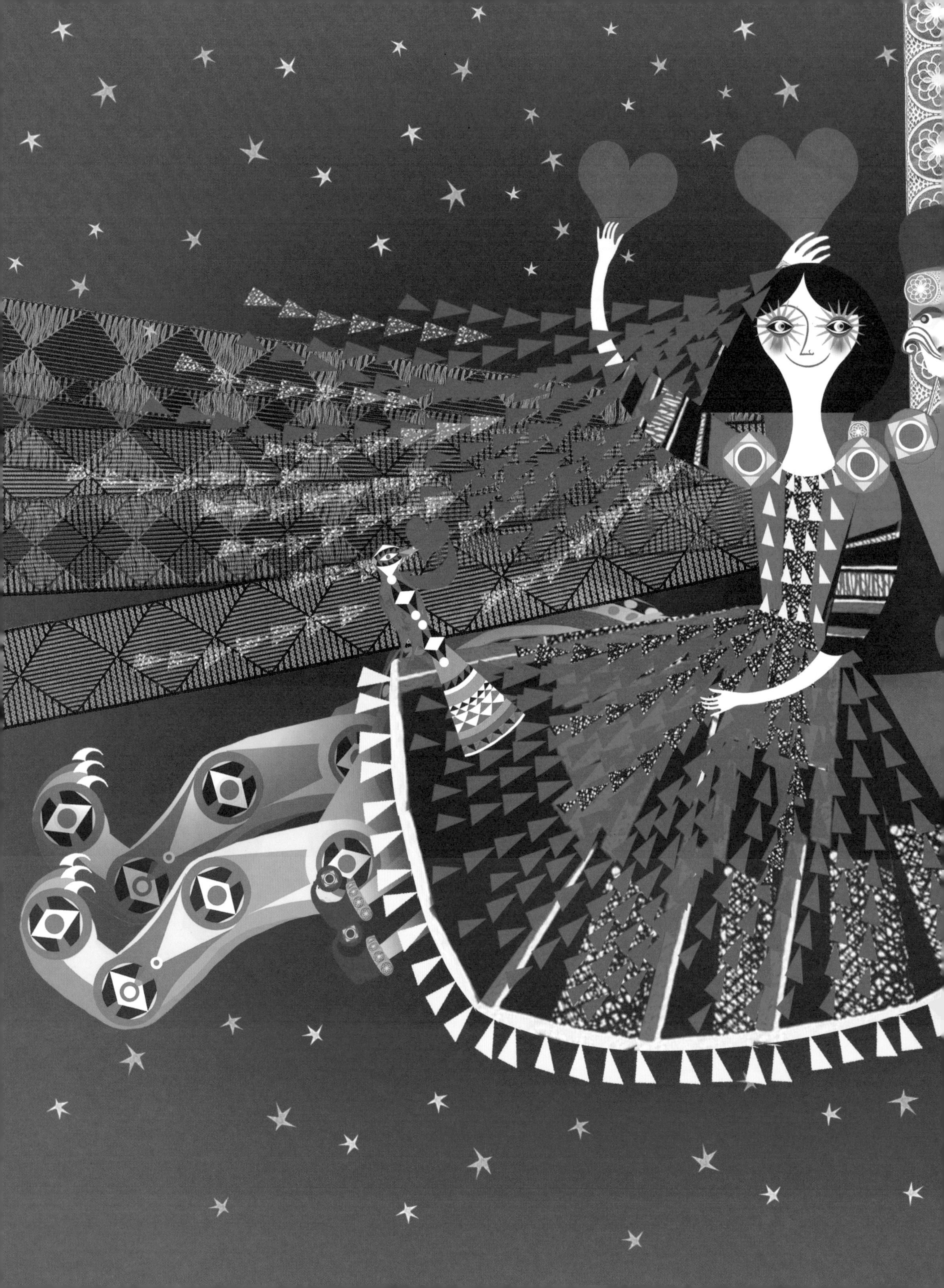

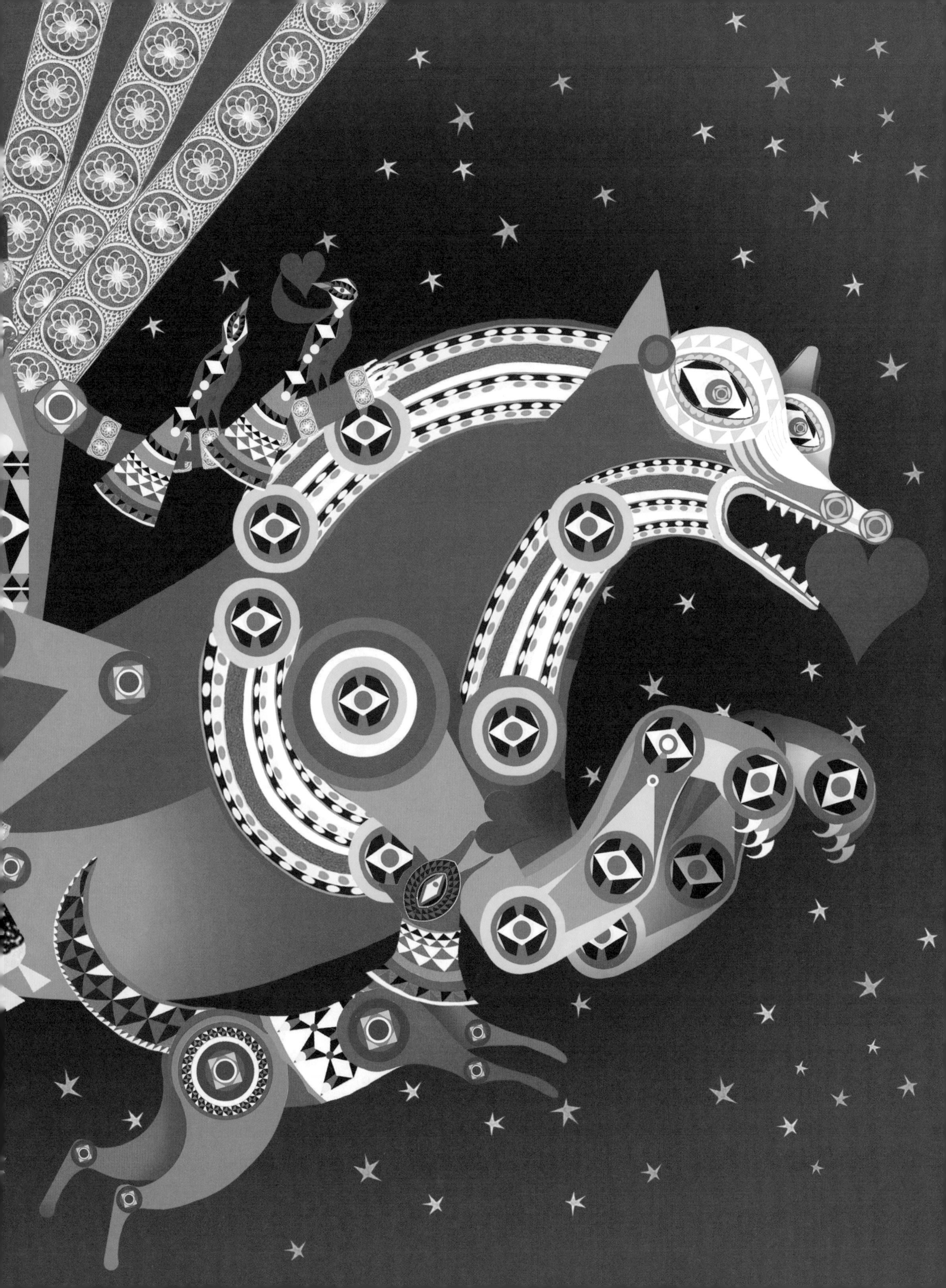

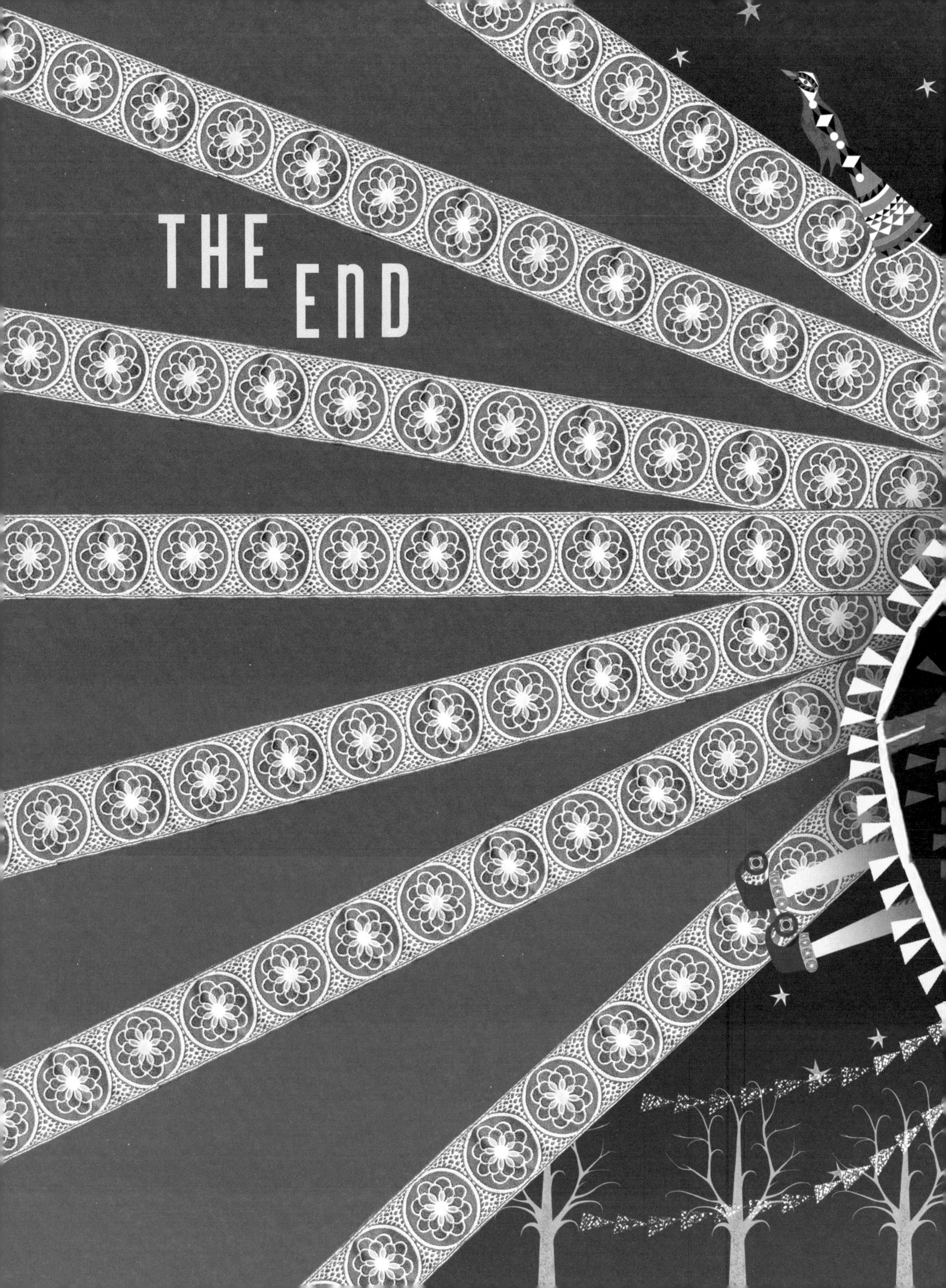
THE END

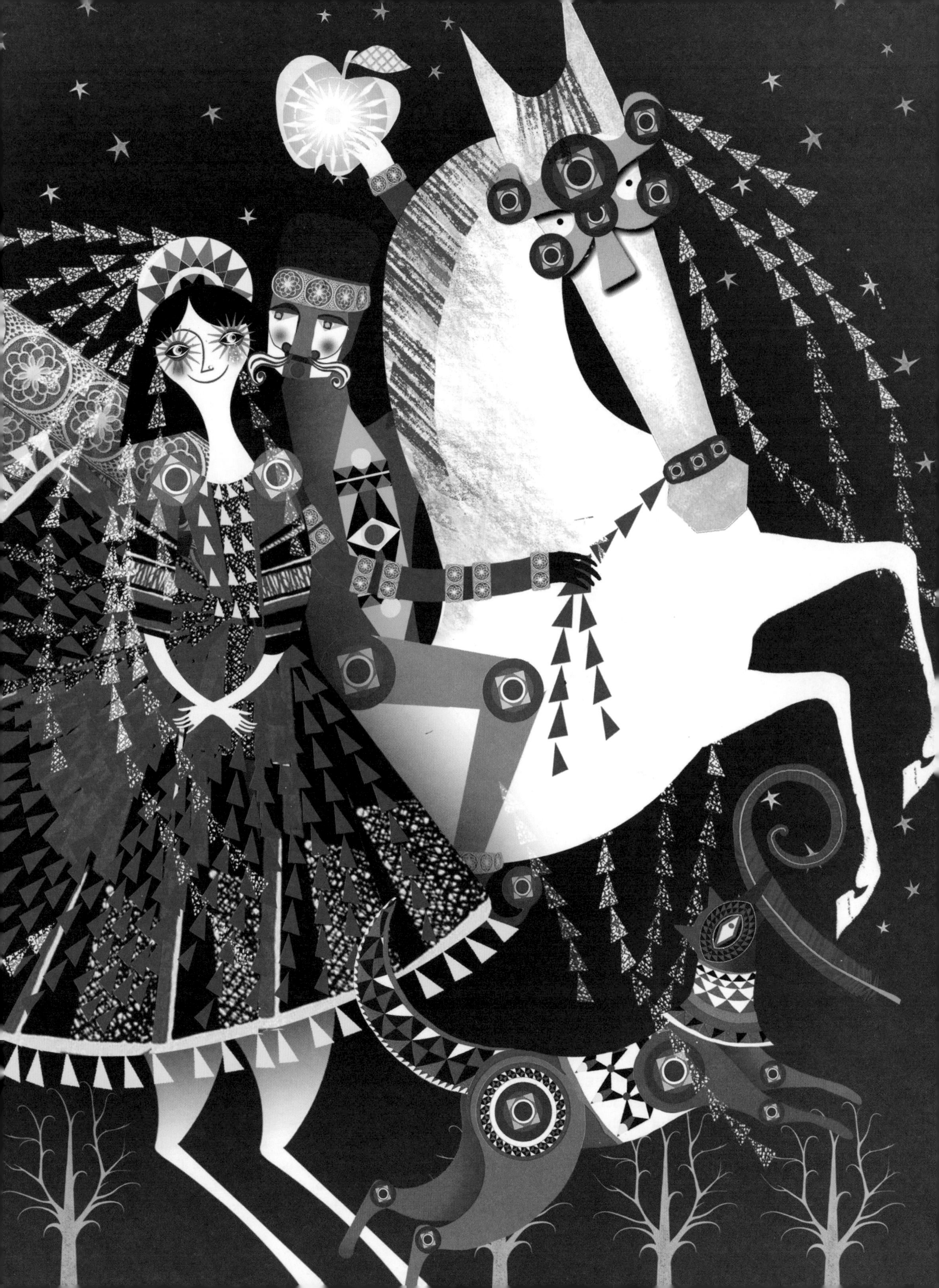

# "The Shepherdess and the Condor"

## Peruvian fairy tale

ILLUSTRATIONS BY **Miguel Molina**

**"LA PASTORA Y EL CÓNDOR" ("THE SHEPHERDESS** and the Condor") is a folktale aimed at children, told among indigenous peoples throughout South America. In the tradition of disturbing fairy tales from around the world, it's an abduction story apparently meant to frighten girls away from strange men. In some versions, the hummingbird who rescues the girl is rewarded with the green necklace she was wearing, thus explaining the brilliant green sheen of many hummingbirds.

Miguel Molina chose to illustrate the version he heard as a child in Peru. Besides being a wonder on the Native American flute, Miguel is a painter and illustrator whose illustrations for a CD of Peruvian jazz earned a Latin Grammy nomination for best album cover/packaging.

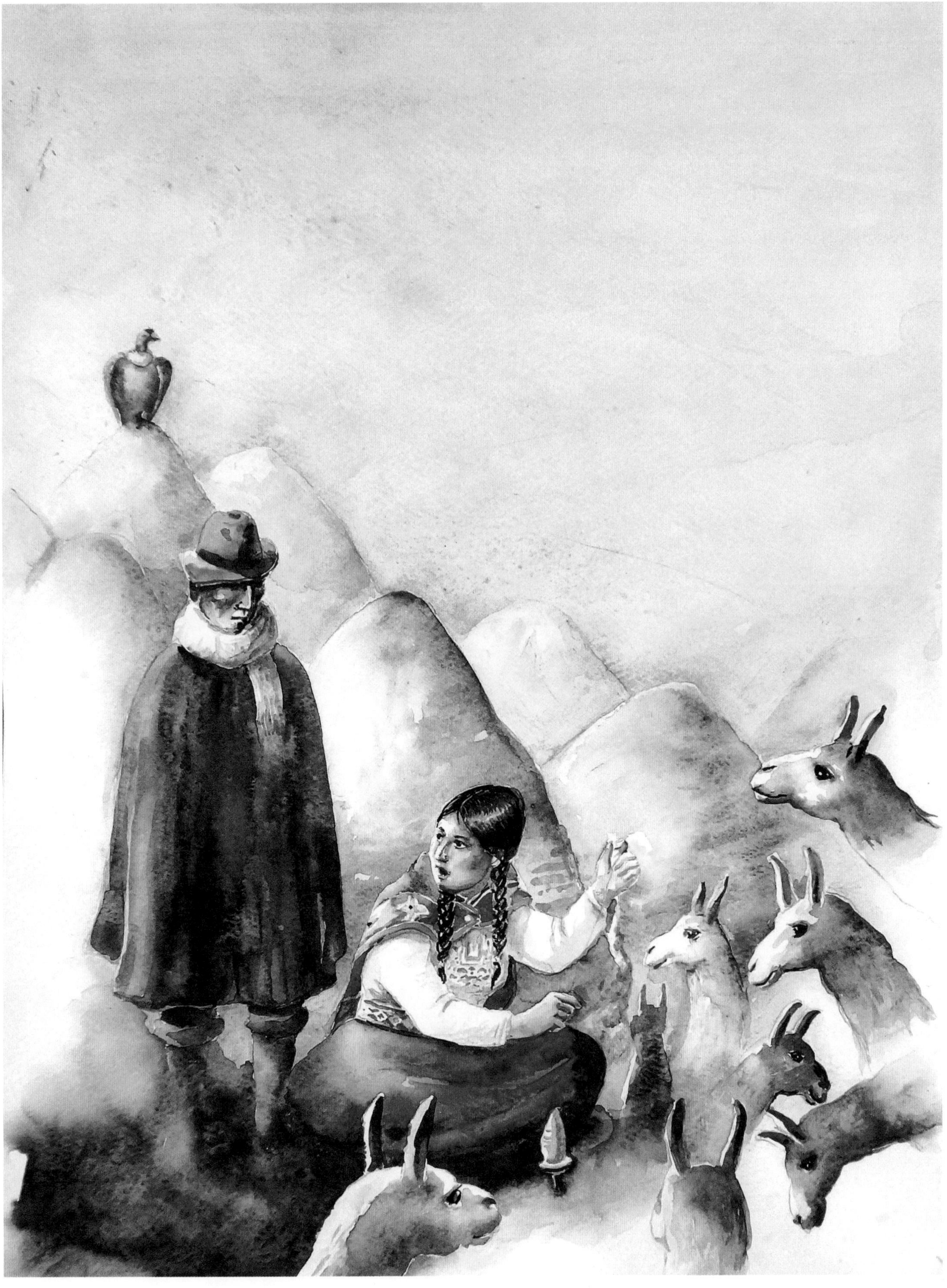

"THE SHEPHERDESS AND THE CONDOR" PERUVIAN FAIRY TALE MIGUEL MOLINA

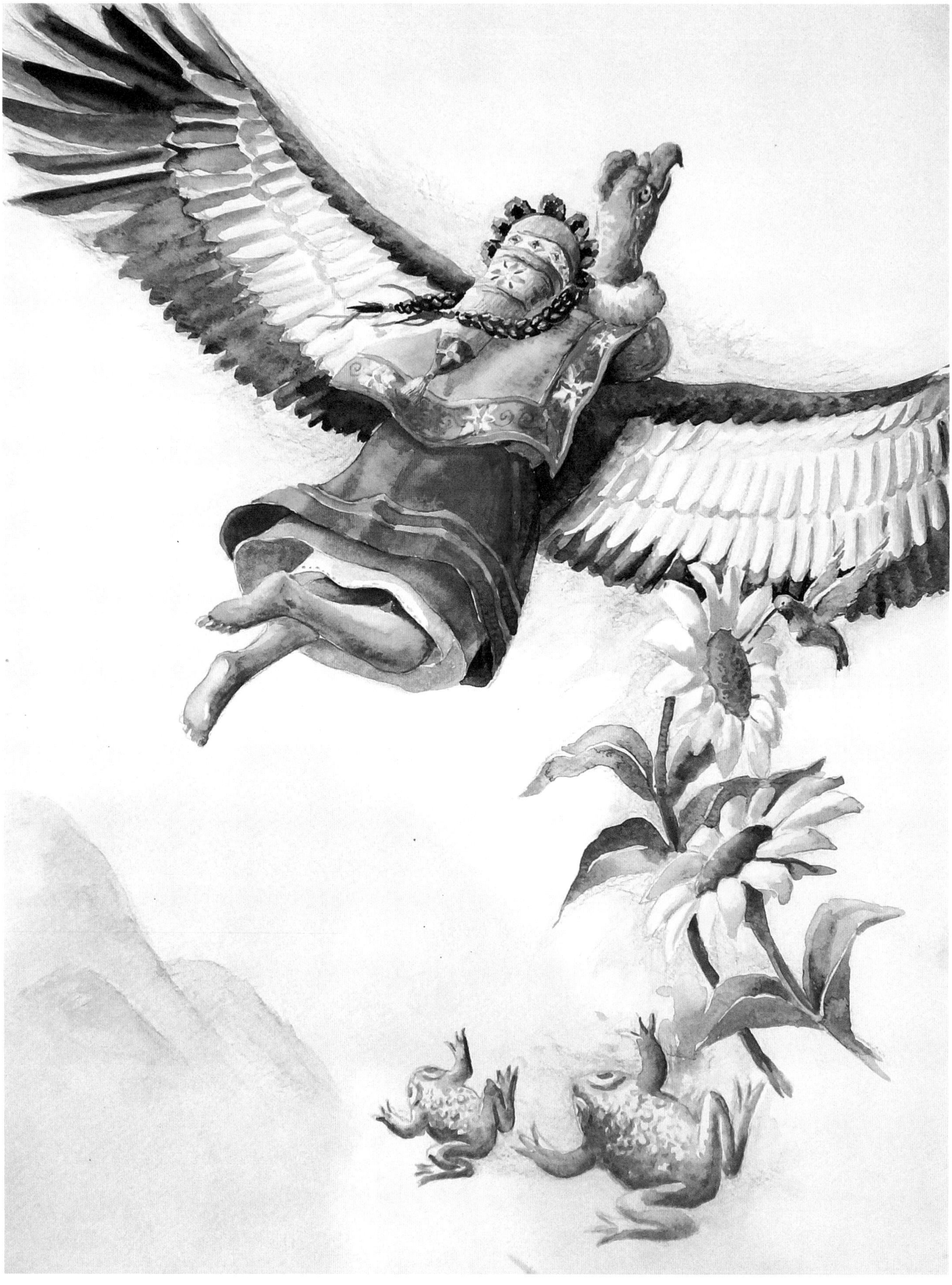

# British fairy tale

ART/ADAPTATION BY **Rachael Ball**

**THE FAIRIES WHO APPEAR IN FAIRY TALES SEEM LIKE** charming figments of the imagination to our jaded twenty-first-century sensibilities, but back when these stories were still primarily oral culture, the lines were much blurrier. In *English Fairy Tales and Legends*, Rosalind Kerven wrote that, although we think of fairies as being for children, "until comparatively recently, adults in country areas also believed in them. [Thomas] Keightley, writing in the late nineteenth century, cites people in Cumbria, Devon, Durham, Hampshire, Norfolk, Northumberland, Suffolk and Yorkshire who claimed they had actually seen fairies."

Although "The Weardale Fairies" has its roots in County Durham, it relates the widespread belief that fairies sometimes steal human children (this shows up in Shakespeare's *A Midsummer Night's Dream*). It also contains the universal trope of having to solve a riddle in order to win a favor from supernatural beings (stretching back at least to ancient Egypt).

While working on a fairy tale graphic novel and teaching art in London, Rachael Ball created this atmospheric take on the story of fae kidnappers and maternal love, which manages to be brooding and whimsical at once.

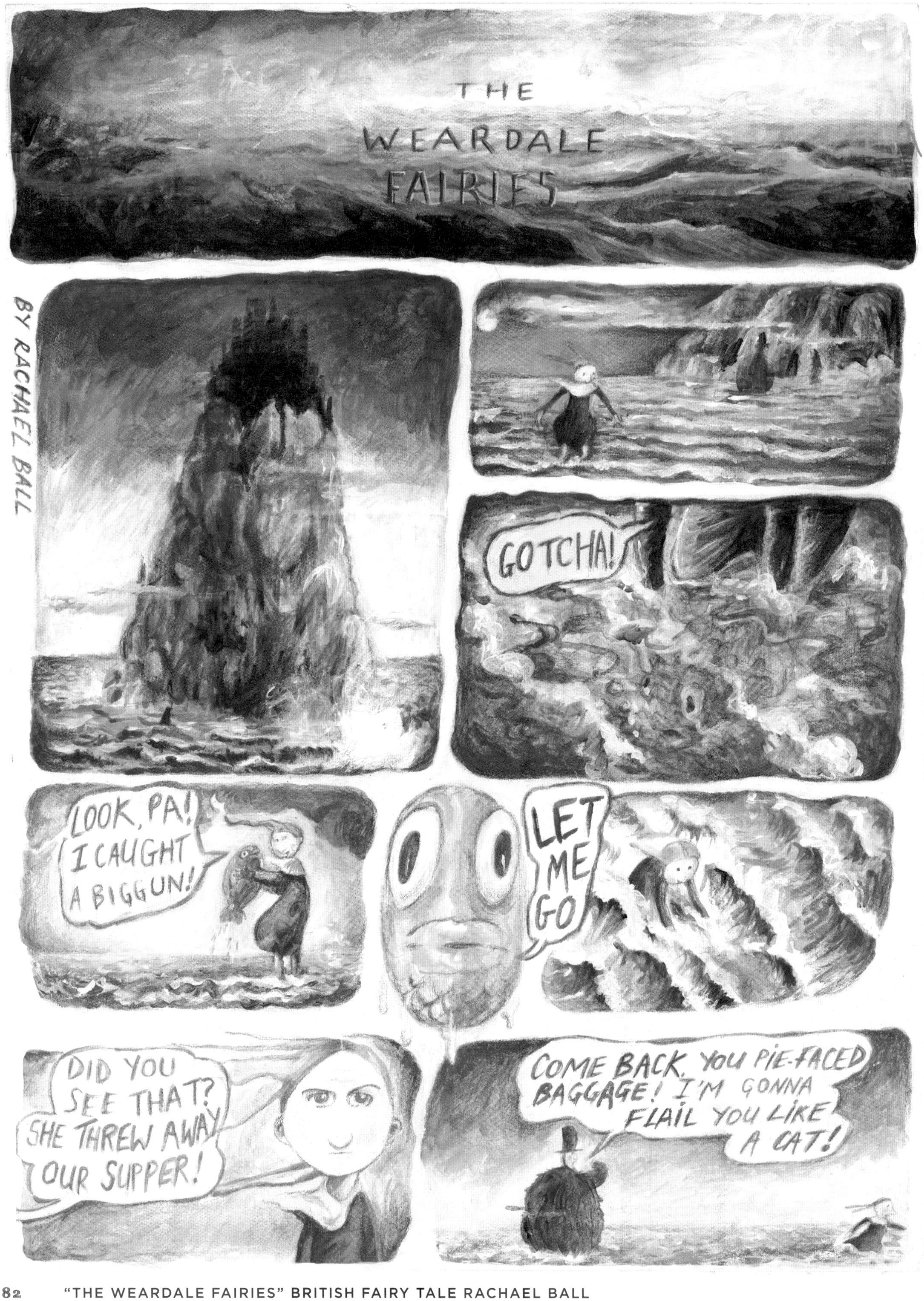
THE WEARDALE FAIRIES
BY RACHAEL BALL
GOTCHA!
LOOK, PA! I CAUGHT A BIGGUN!
LET ME GO
DID YOU SEE THAT? SHE THREW AWAY OUR SUPPER!
COME BACK, YOU PIE-FACED BAGGAGE! I'M GONNA FLAIL YOU LIKE A CAT!

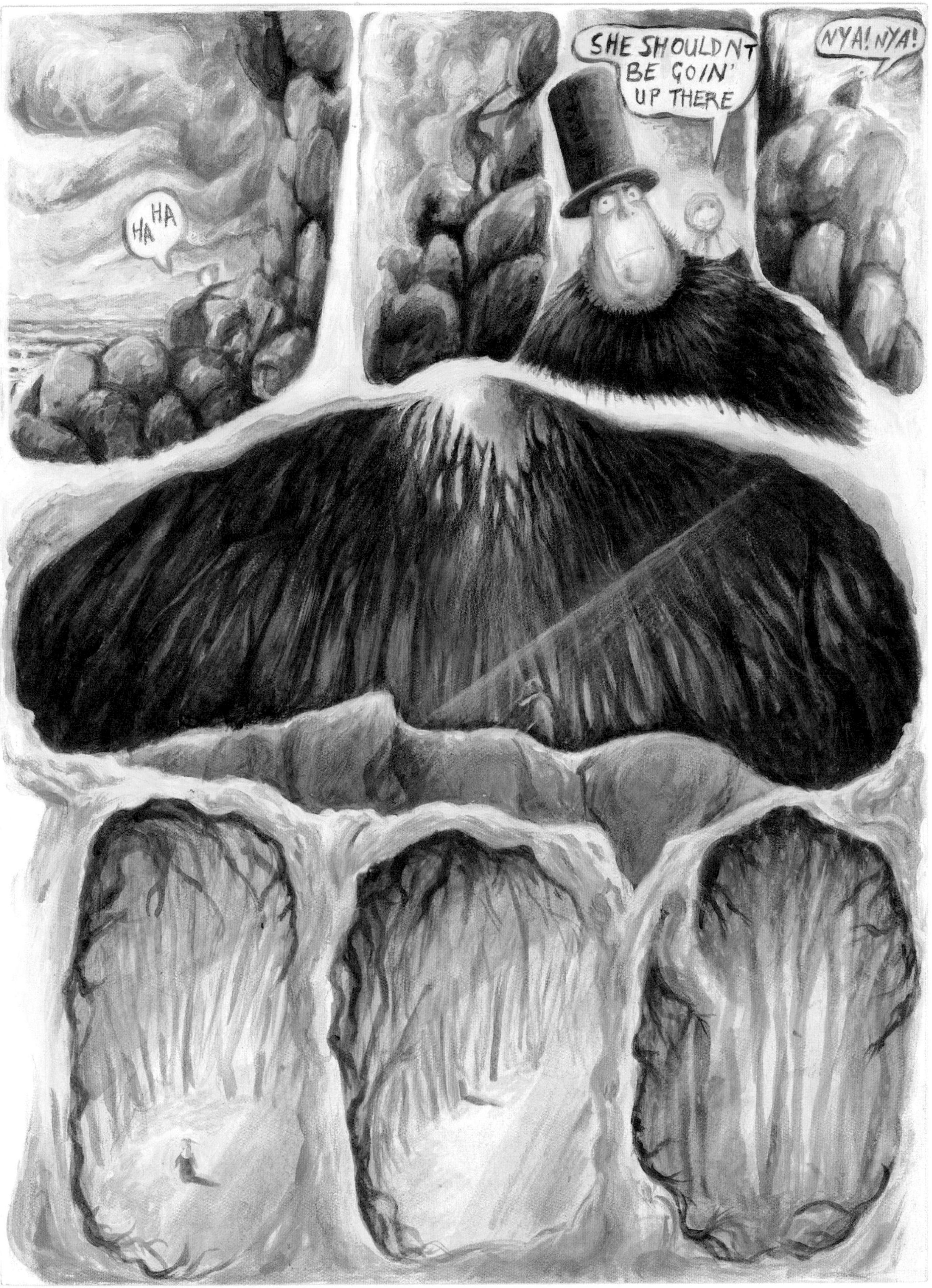
HA HA
SHE SHOULDN'T BE GOIN' UP THERE
NYA! NYA!

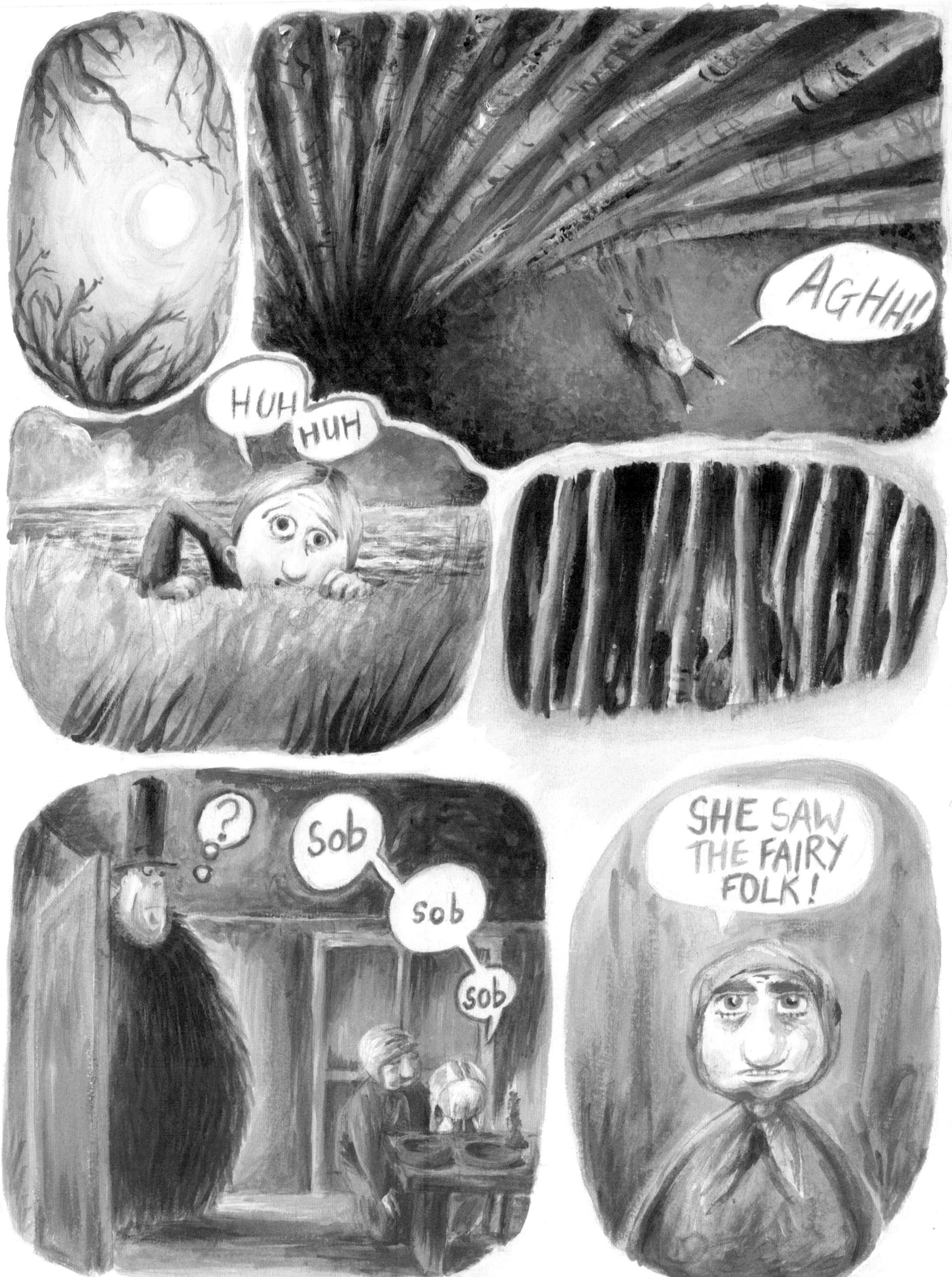
AGHH!
HUH
HUH
?
Sob
sob
sob
SHE SAW THE FAIRY FOLK!

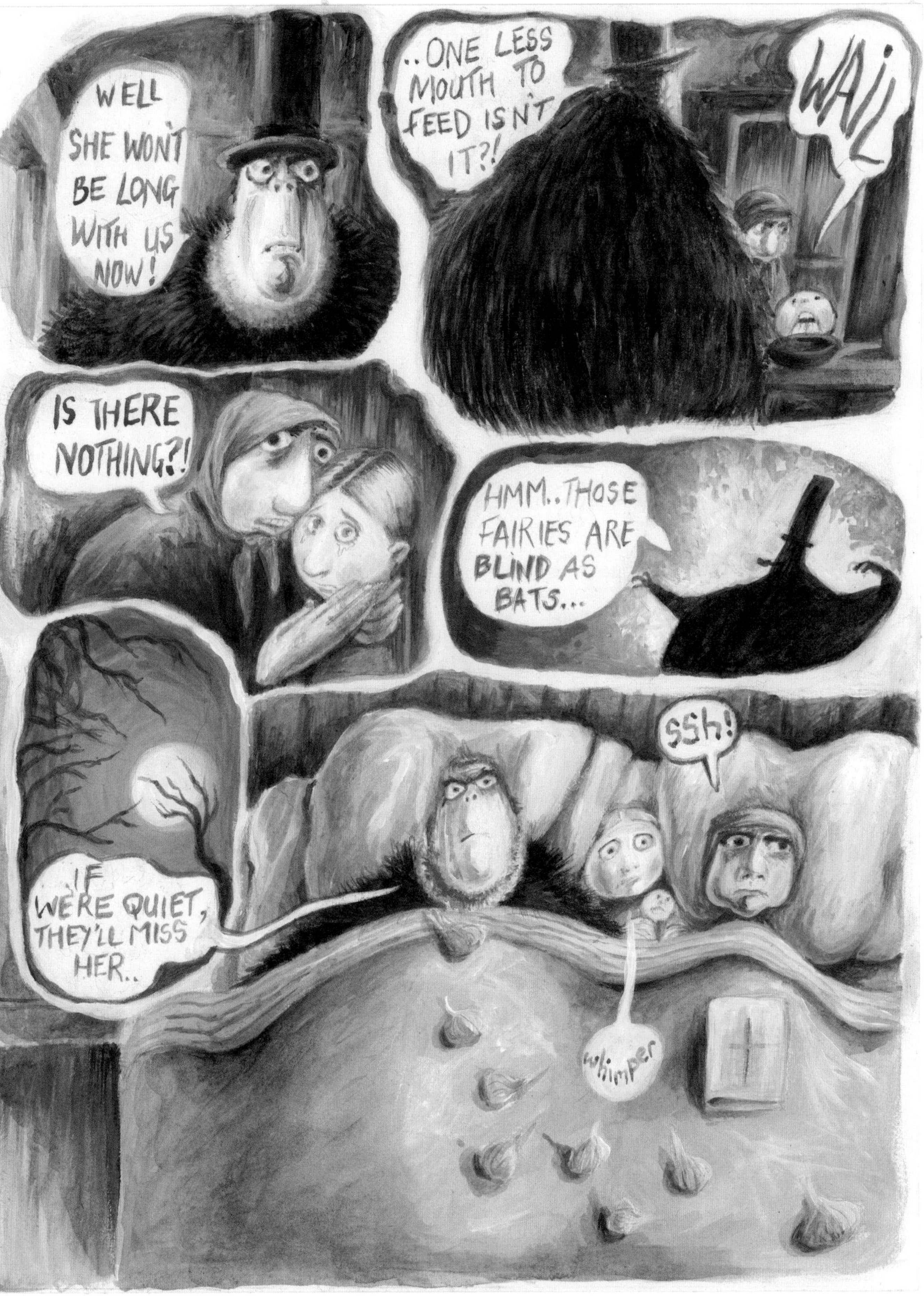
WELL SHE WON'T BE LONG WITH US NOW!
..ONE LESS MOUTH TO FEED ISN'T IT?!
WAIL
IS THERE NOTHING?!
HMM..THOSE FAIRIES ARE BLIND AS BATS...
IF WE'RE QUIET, THEY'LL MISS HER..
SSh!
whimper

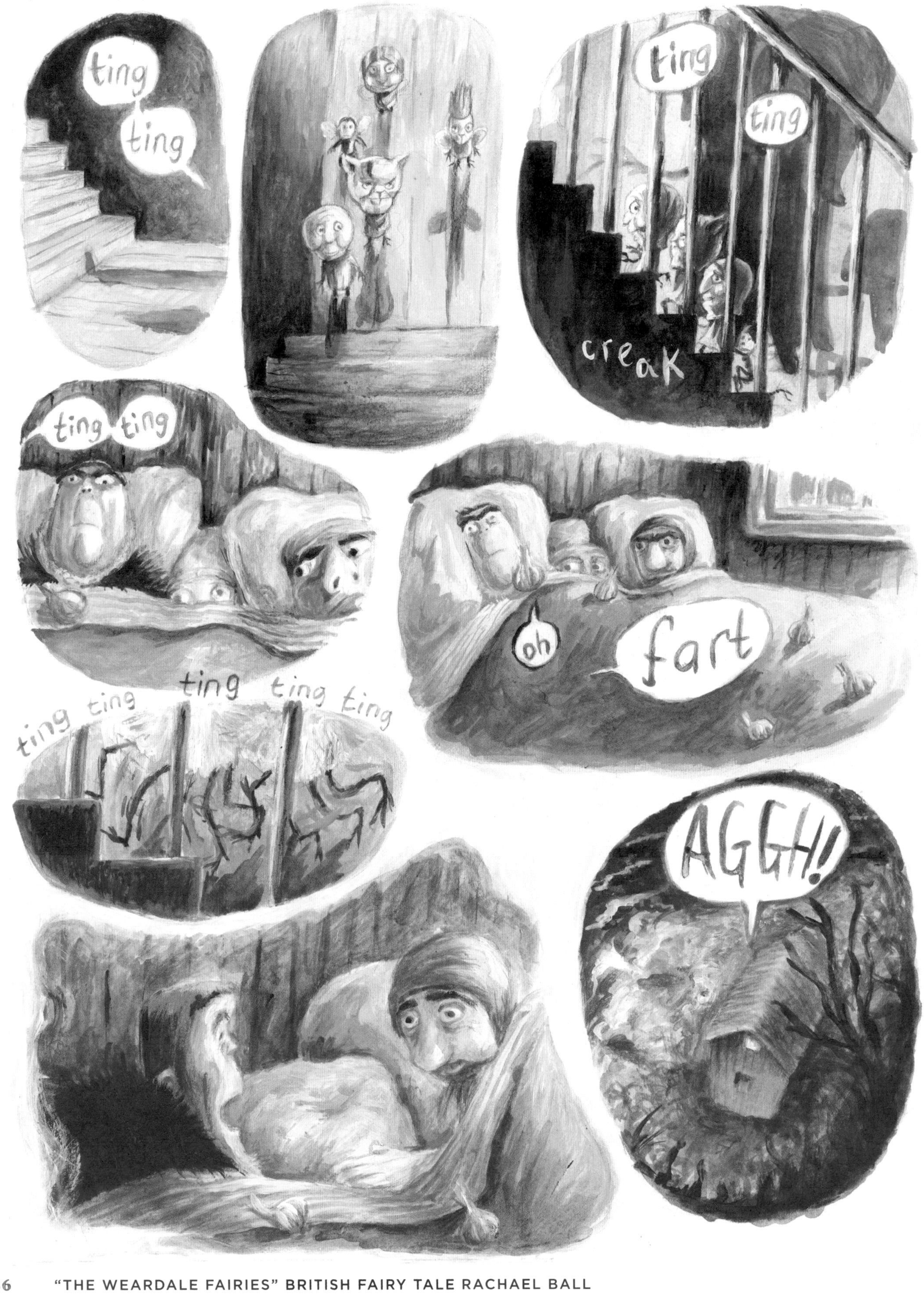
ting
ting
ting
ting
creak
ting ting
oh
fart
ting ting
ting
ting ting
AGGH!!

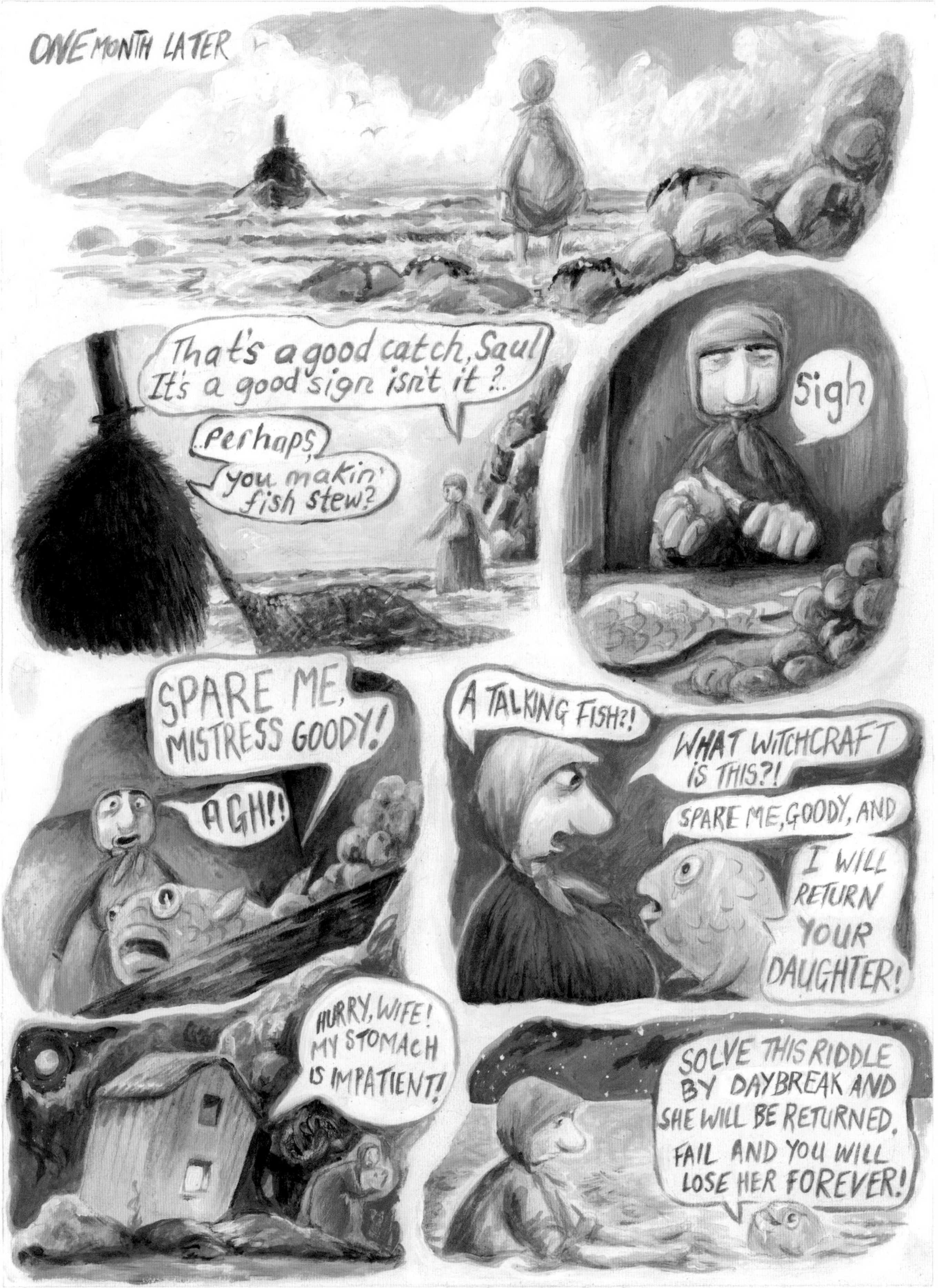
ONE MONTH LATER
That's a good catch, Saul
It's a good sign isn't it?..
..perhaps,
you makin' fish stew?
sigh
SPARE ME, MISTRESS GOODY!
AGH!!
A TALKING FISH?!
WHAT WITCHCRAFT IS THIS?!
SPARE ME, GOODY, AND
I WILL RETURN YOUR DAUGHTER!
HURRY, WIFE! MY STOMACH IS IMPATIENT!
SOLVE THIS RIDDLE BY DAYBREAK AND SHE WILL BE RETURNED.
FAIL AND YOU WILL LOSE HER FOREVER!

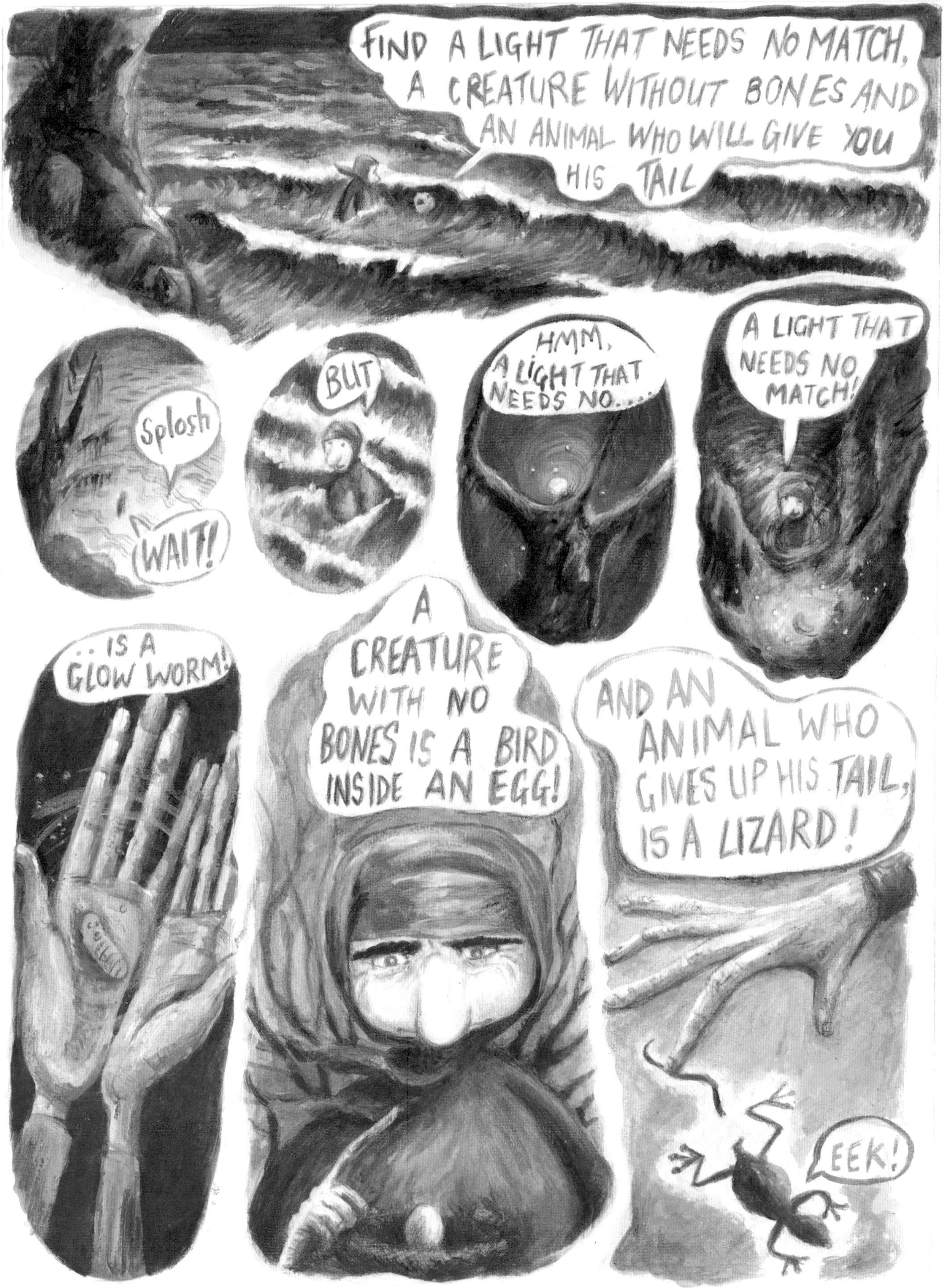
FIND A LIGHT THAT NEEDS NO MATCH, A CREATURE WITHOUT BONES AND AN ANIMAL WHO WILL GIVE YOU HIS TAIL
Splosh
WAIT!
BUT
HMM, A LIGHT THAT NEEDS NO....
A LIGHT THAT NEEDS NO MATCH!
..IS A GLOW WORM!
A CREATURE WITH NO BONES IS A BIRD INSIDE AN EGG!
AND AN ANIMAL WHO GIVES UP HIS TAIL, IS A LIZARD!
EEK!

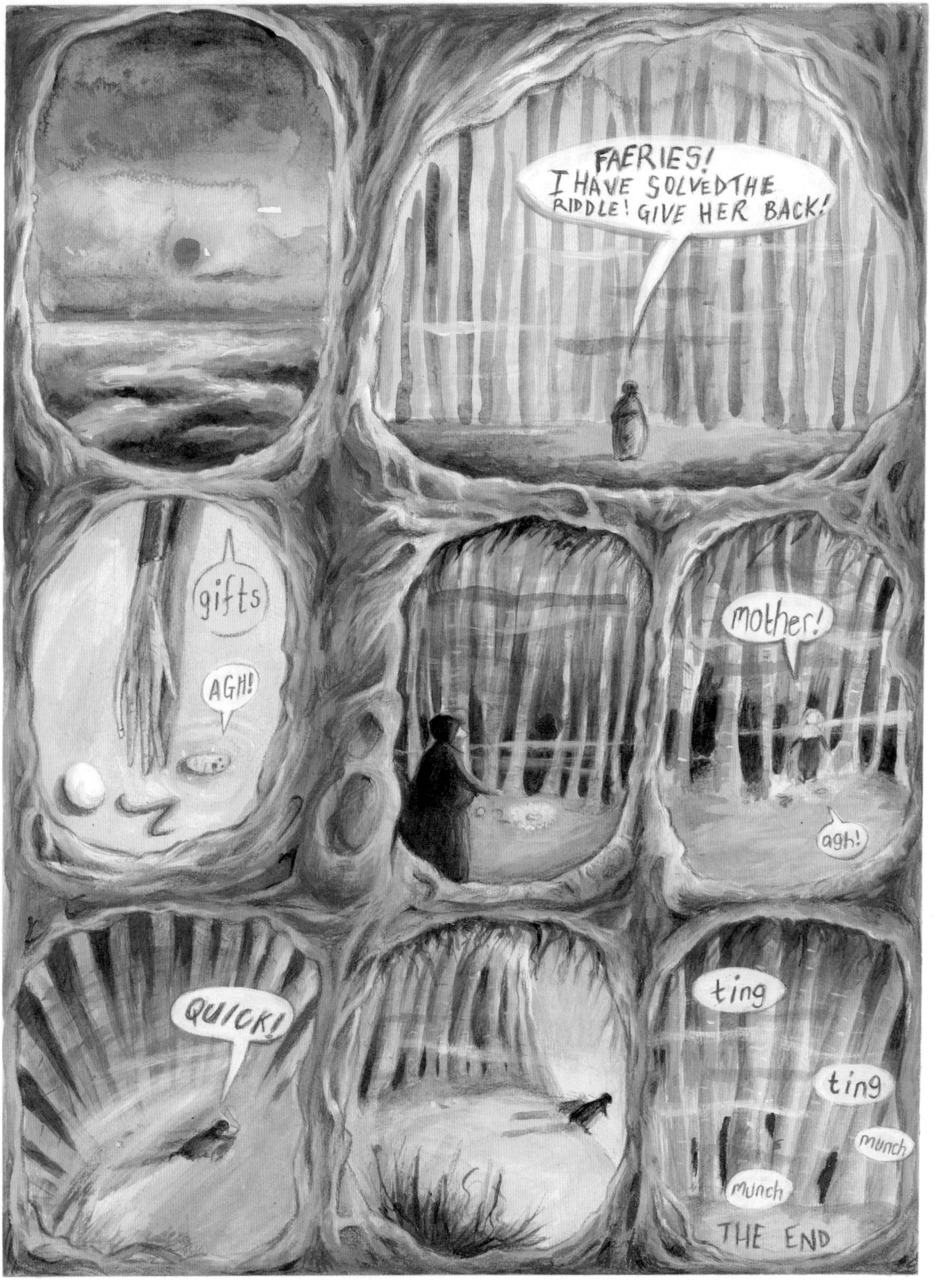
FAERIES! I HAVE SOLVED THE RIDDLE! GIVE HER BACK!
gifts
AGH!
mother!
agh!
QUICK!
ting
ting
munch
munch
THE END

# Jean de La Fontaine

ART/ADAPTATION BY **Maëlle Doliveux**

**THE FRENCH POET JEAN DE LA FONTAINE WROTE** around 237 fables in verse during the last third of the 1600s. Not since Aesop, who lived well over two millennia earlier, have fables primarily about animals secured such a prominent spot in literature and culture. The *Encyclopedia Britannica* declared that they "rank among the greatest masterpieces of French literature." La Fontaine, in fact, took many of Aesop's tales—as well as those of other ancient Greeks and Romans, earlier French and Italian writers, and some folktales from India—added lots of humor and panache, then wrote them in rhyming couplets.

Maëlle Doliveux, a New Yorker of French-Swiss extraction, has gotten lots of recognition for her illustrations (usually silkscreens or etchings), but she—as will become obvious momentarily—is also a master of cut-paper, an overlooked artform that happens to be one of my favorites. In fact, as this book was going to press, Maëlle's *Four Fables* won a silver medal from the venerable Society of Illustrators. The images on the following pages are actually photographs of tabloid-sized works, three-dimensional assemblages of cut paper, arranged to seamlessly relate four of La Fontaine's fables.

In "The Fox, the Ape, and the Animals," a new king of the beasts must be named when the lion dies. For some reason, the monkey's silly tricks earn him the vote of the other animals. But the fox is upset, and shows the monkey to be a fool by trapping him with tales of nonexistent treasure. In "The Fox and the Stork," a fox laughingly serves soup to a stork, who is unable to eat it with her long beak. She invites the fox over for dinner, serving him a delicious meal at the bottom of a tall, slender vessel, which he can't access. "The Heron" and "The Damsel"—two tales often presented together—tell of the dangers of passing up good meals and good suitors, respectively. At some point, you'll take what you can get. Finally, in "The Lion in Love," a lion falls for a shepherdess, proposing to her. Her father suggests that, in order to be passionate without maiming her, the lion should let his claws and teeth be removed. The lovesick beast consents to being made defenseless, with disastrous results.

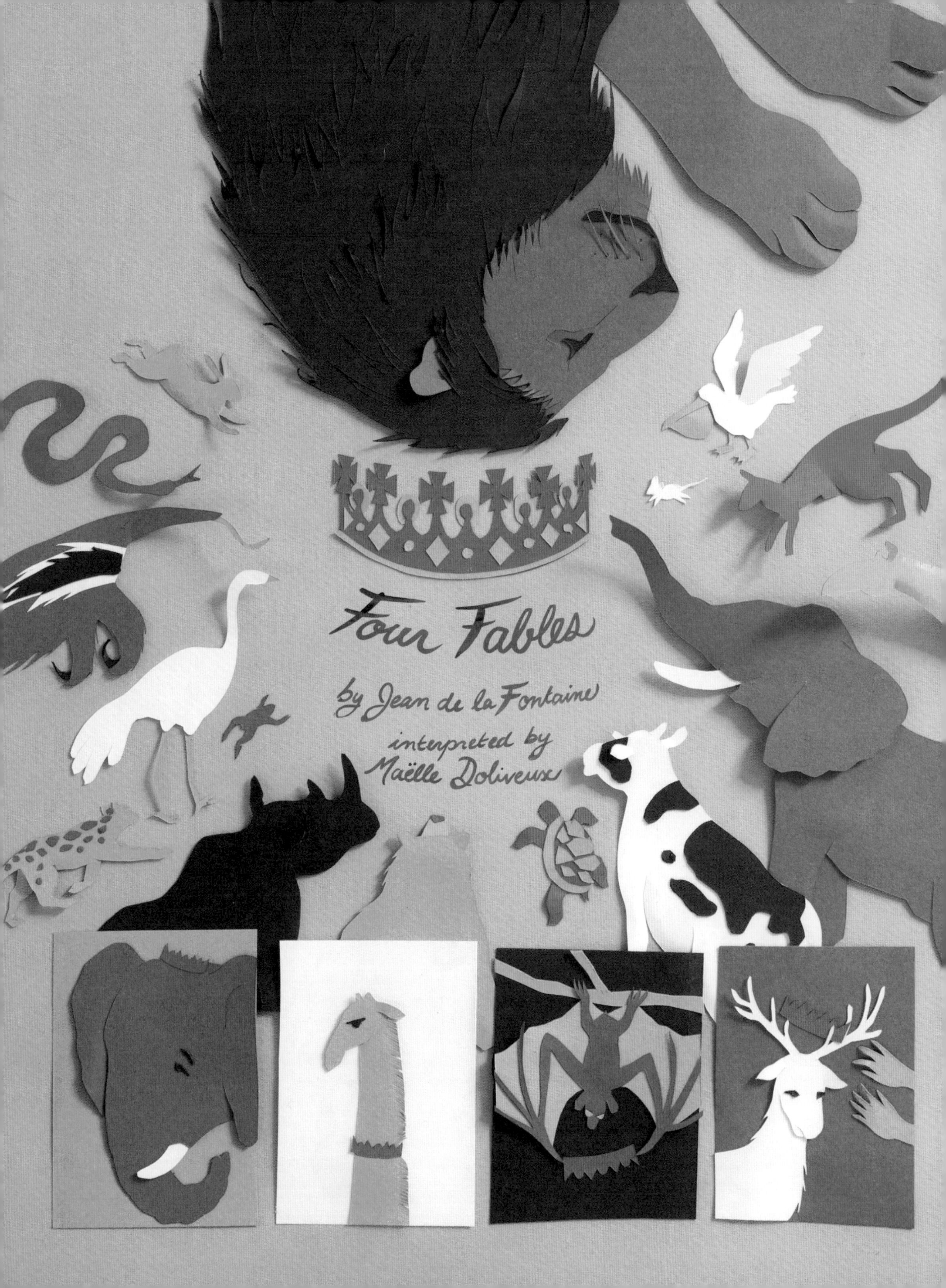
Four Fables
by Jean de la Fontaine
interpreted by
Maëlle Doliveux

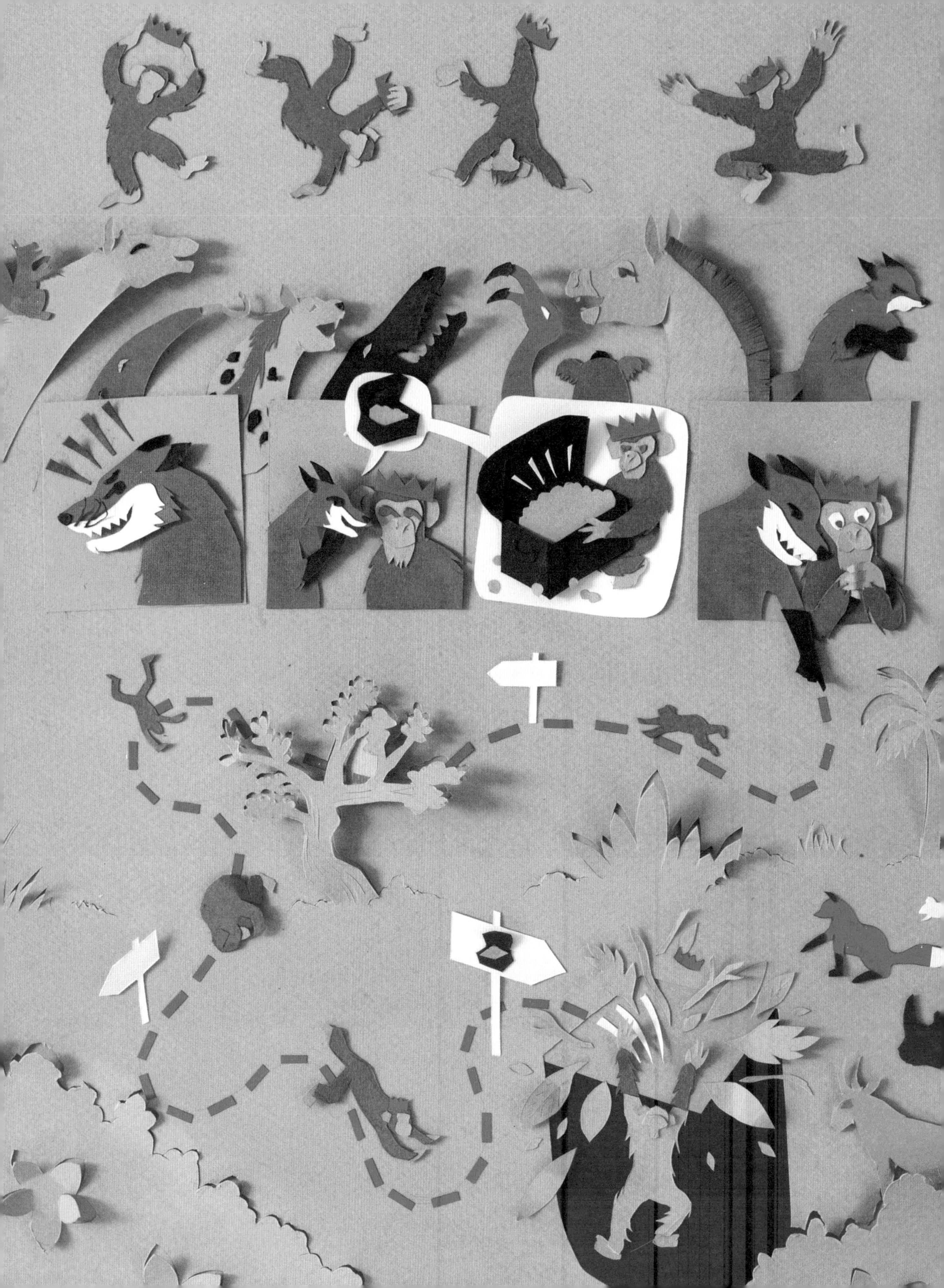

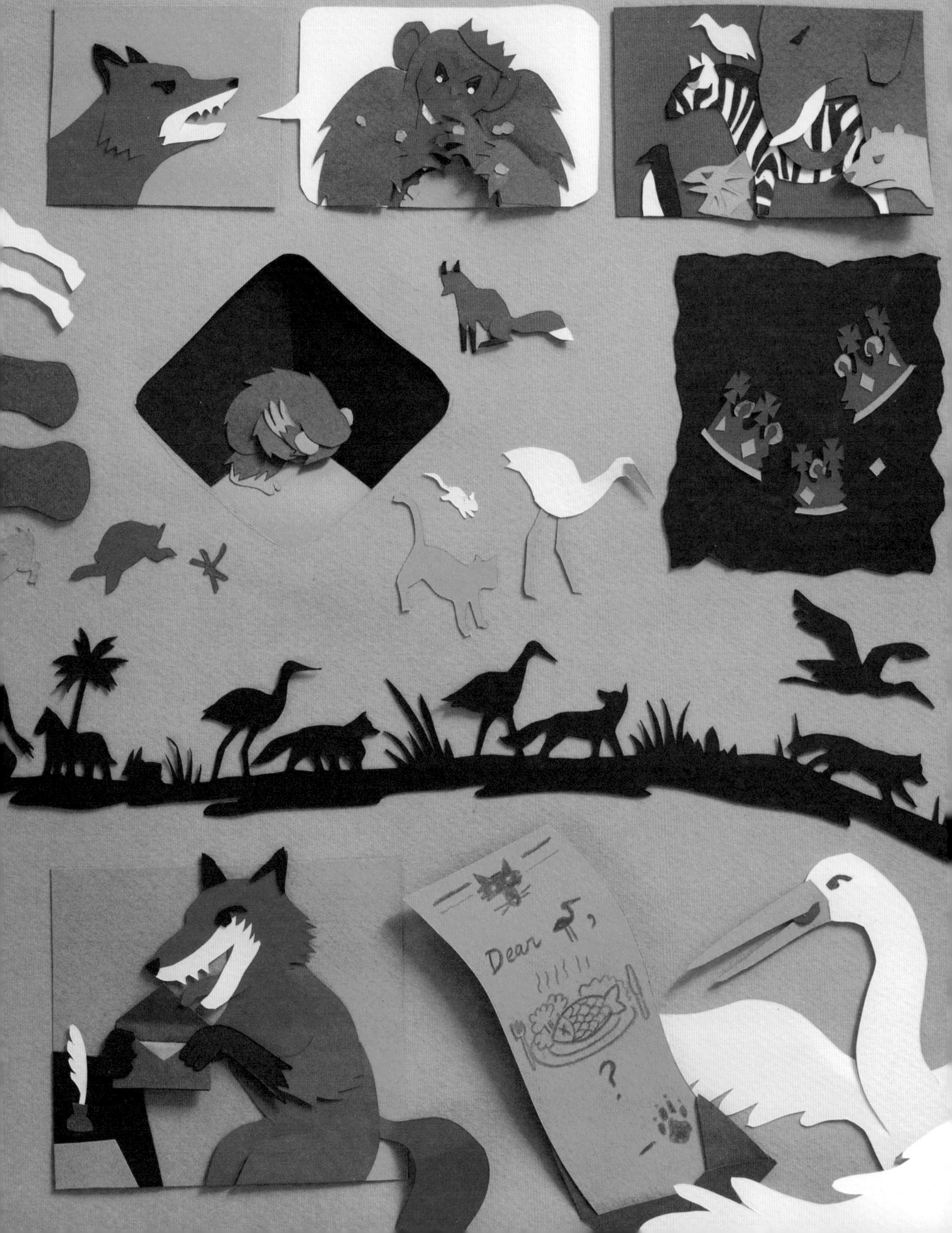
Dear

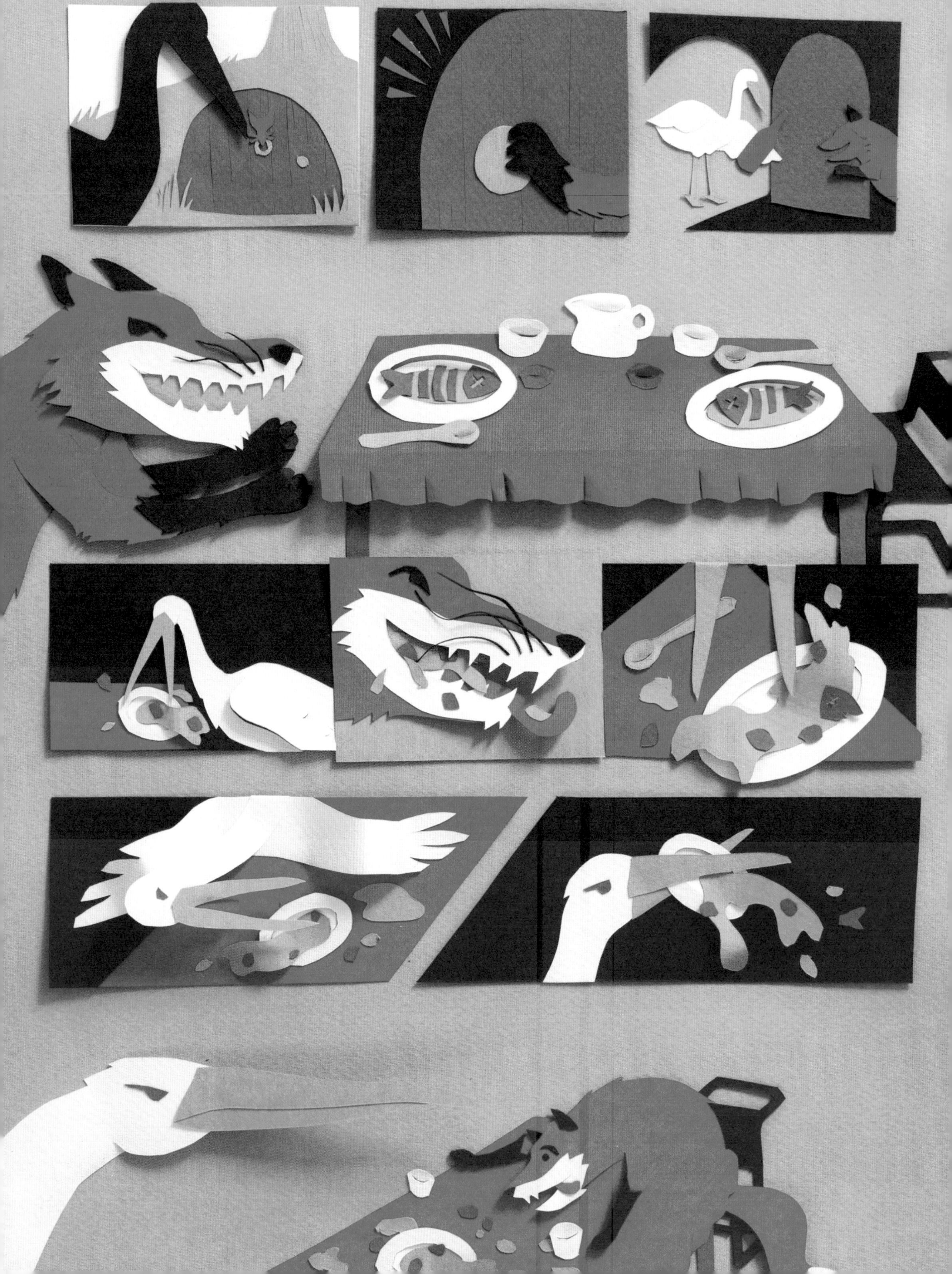

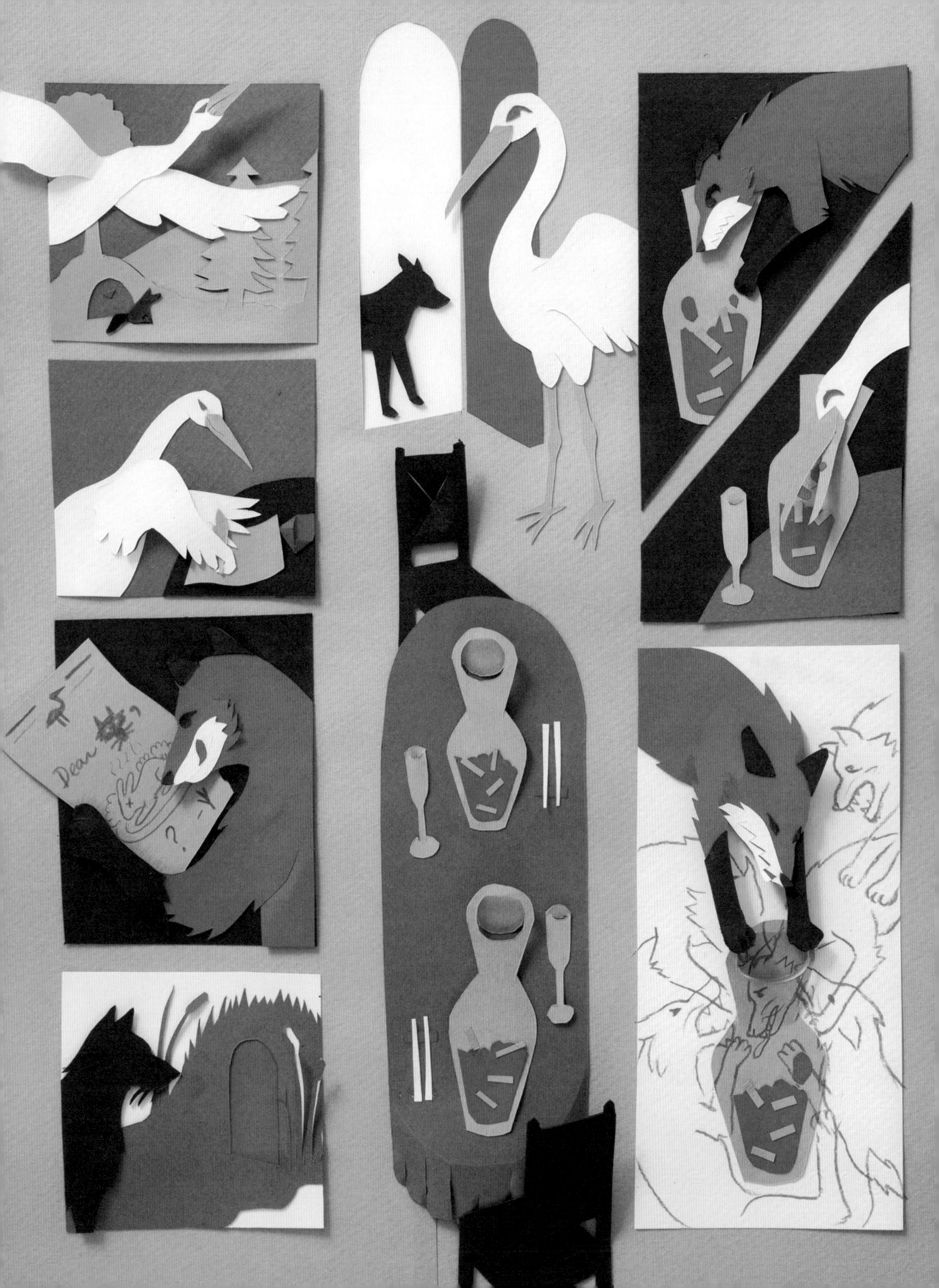
Dear

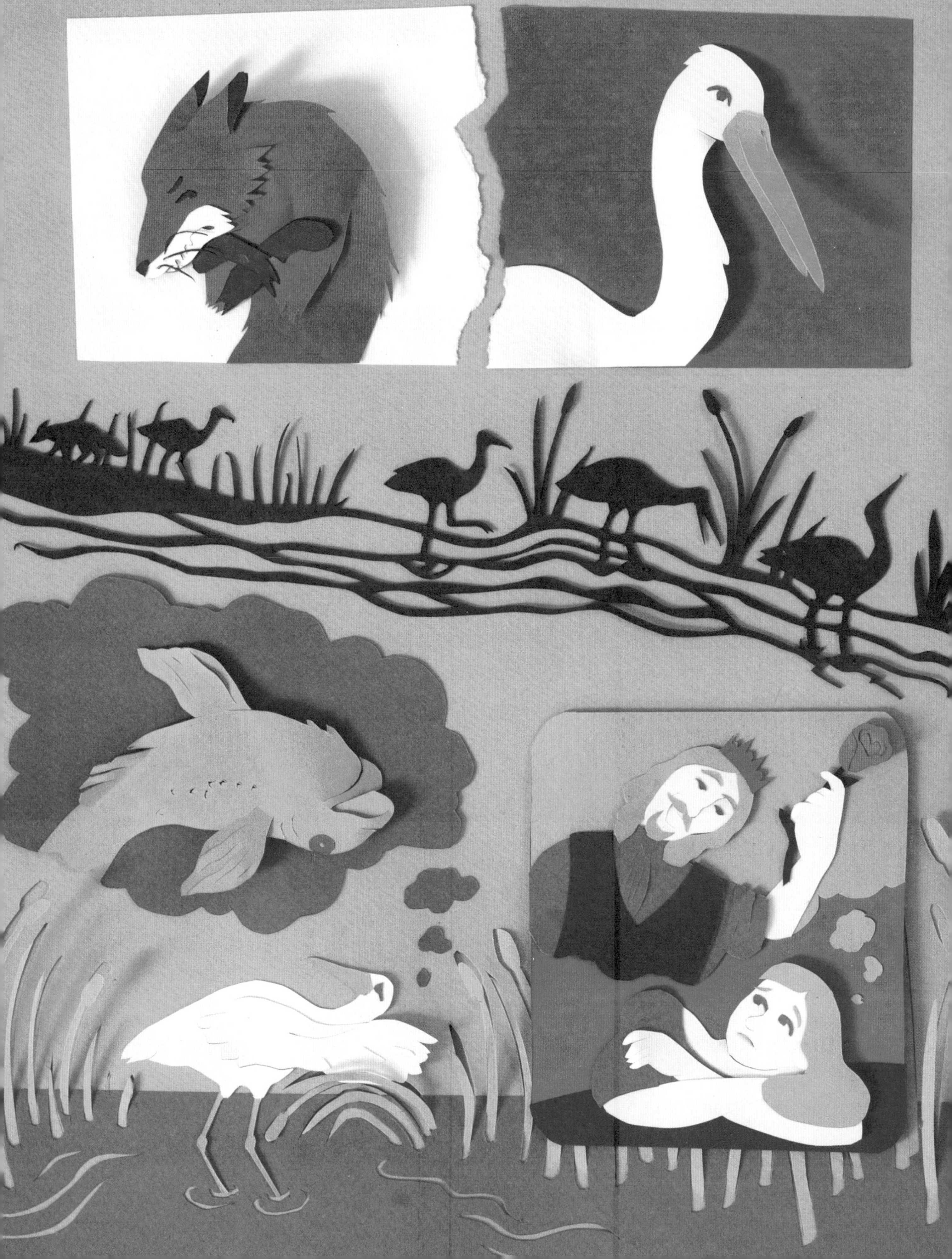

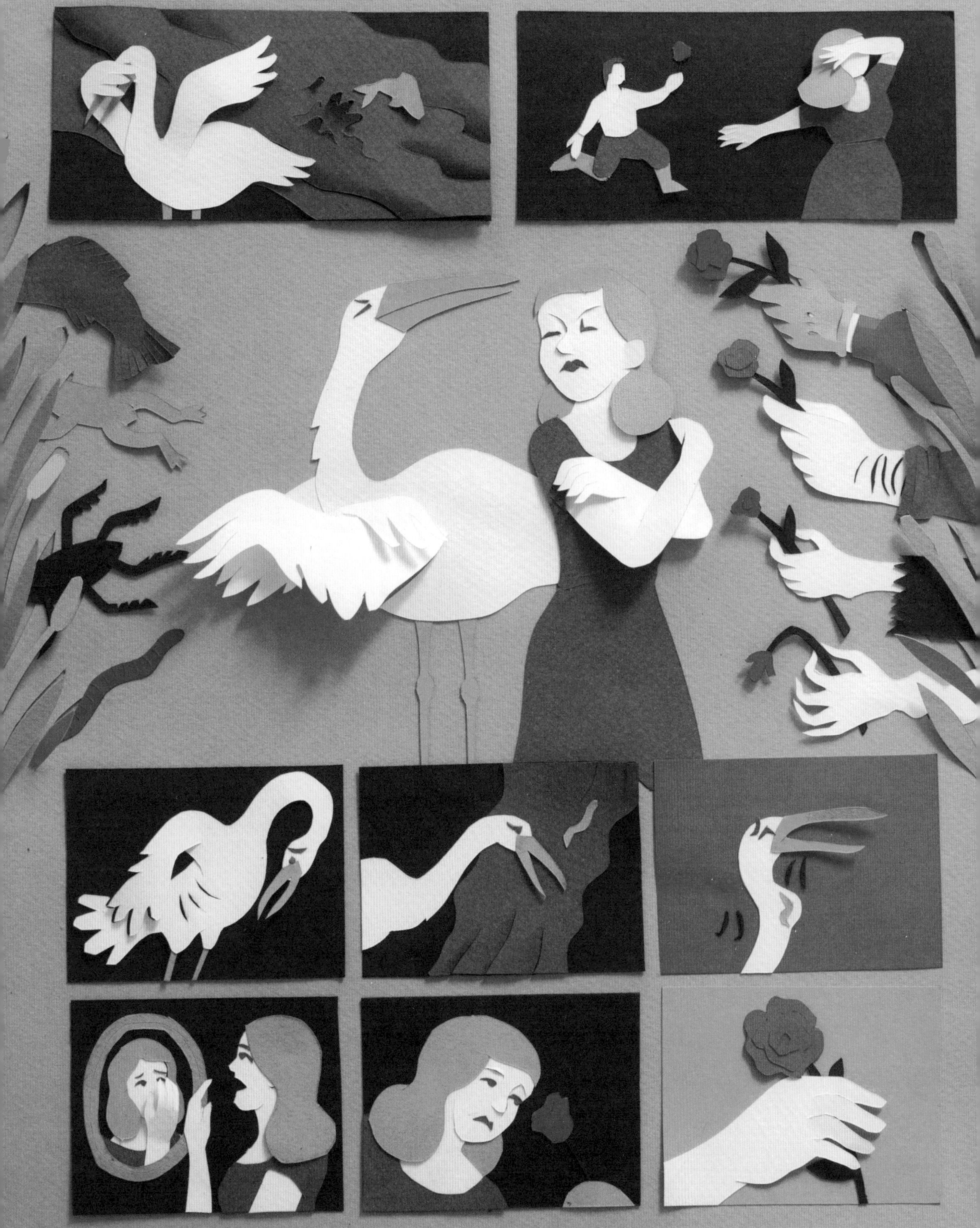

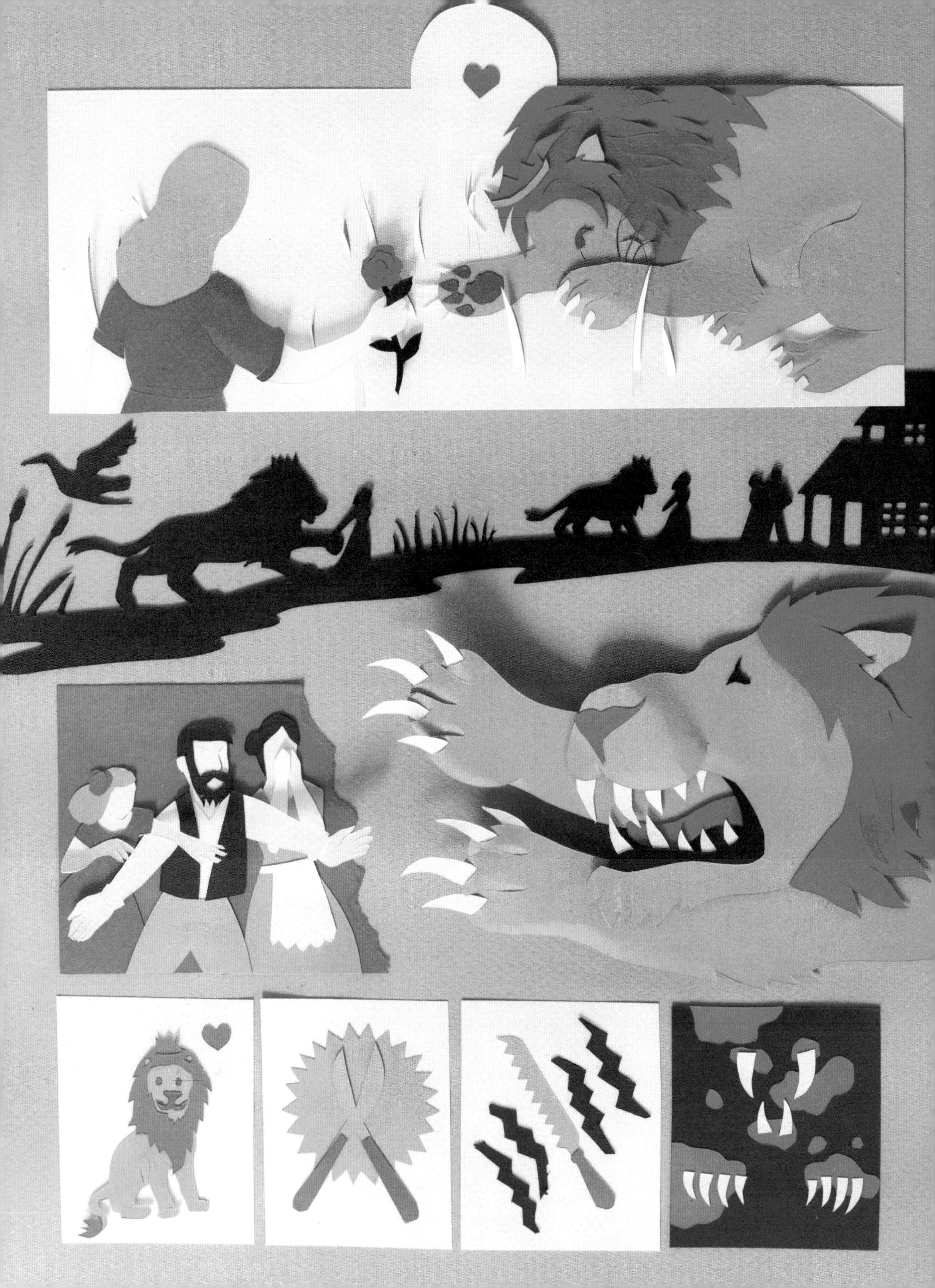

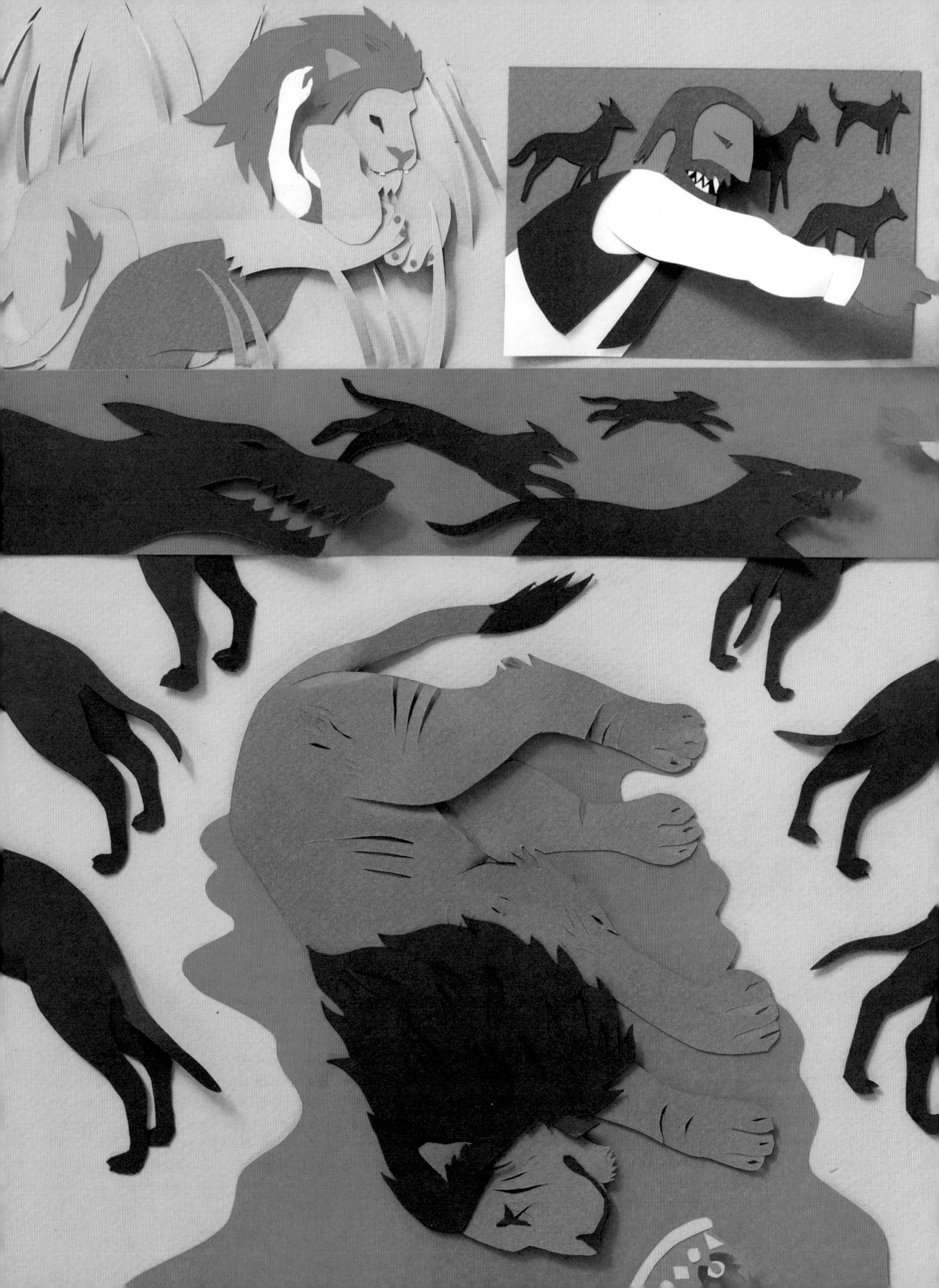

# "Town Musicians of Bremen"

## Brothers Grimm

ART/ADAPTATION BY **Kevin H. Dixon**

**BROTHERS JACOB AND WILHELM GRIMM WERE** scholarly types—librarians, linguists, lexicographers, university lecturers. As one of their many, often Herculean, projects, they set in writing folktales told across Germany, often in rural areas, the aim simply to preserve these traditional stories, many of which they later realized had their roots in France, Italy, Russia, Japan, and elsewhere.

They realized something else after the first edition of their massive book, *Kinder-und Hausmärchen* (*Children's and Household Tales*), was published in two parts in 1812 and 1815: their scholarly work—filled with footnotes and so on—was a huge hit among parents, who read it to their children. Over subsequent editions, they toned down the violence and grotesquery while chopping out the academic bits.

Kevin H. Dixon has created numerous comics, including *Mickey Death: Winds of Impotence*, with his masterpiece being a completely accurate, unabridged adaptation of *The Epic of Gilgamesh*, the world's oldest surviving work of narrative literature. Here Kevin employs his sense of humor, visual allusions, and trademark sound effects to bring us the Grimm-recorded tale of four old domestic animals who get a new lease on life.

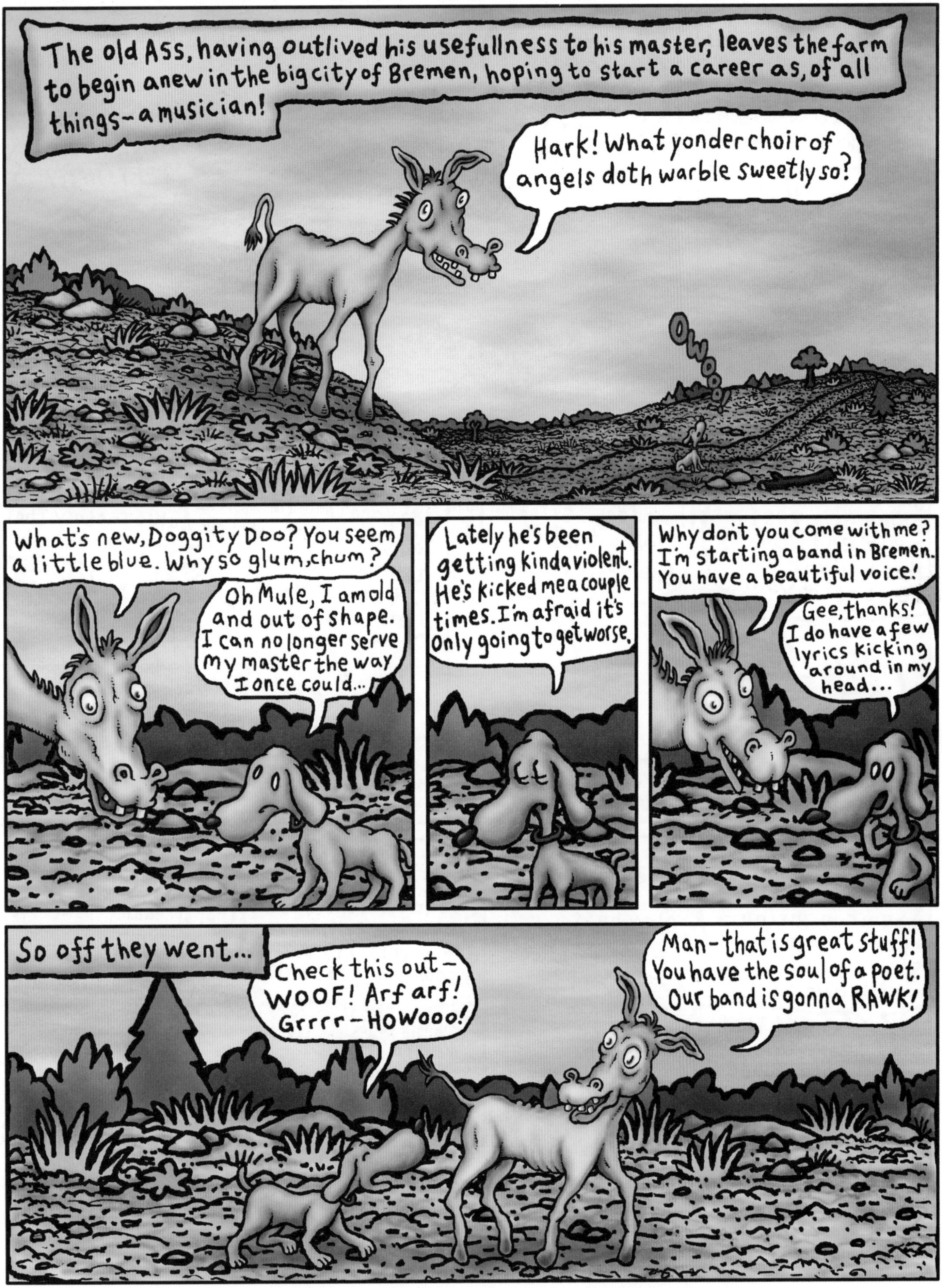
The old Ass, having outlived his usefullness to his master, leaves the farm to begin anew in the big city of Bremen, hoping to start a career as, of all things—a musician!
Hark! What yonder choir of angels doth warble sweetly so?
OWOOO!
What's new, Doggity Doo? You seem a little blue. Why so glum, chum?
Oh Mule, I am old and out of shape. I can no longer serve my master the way I once could...
Lately he's been getting kinda violent. He's kicked me a couple times. I'm afraid it's only going to get worse.
Why don't you come with me? I'm starting a band in Bremen. You have a beautiful voice!
Gee, thanks! I do have a few lyrics kicking around in my head...
So off they went...
Check this out—WOOF! Arf arf! Grrrr—HOWooo!
Man—that is great stuff! You have the soul of a poet. Our band is gonna RAWK!

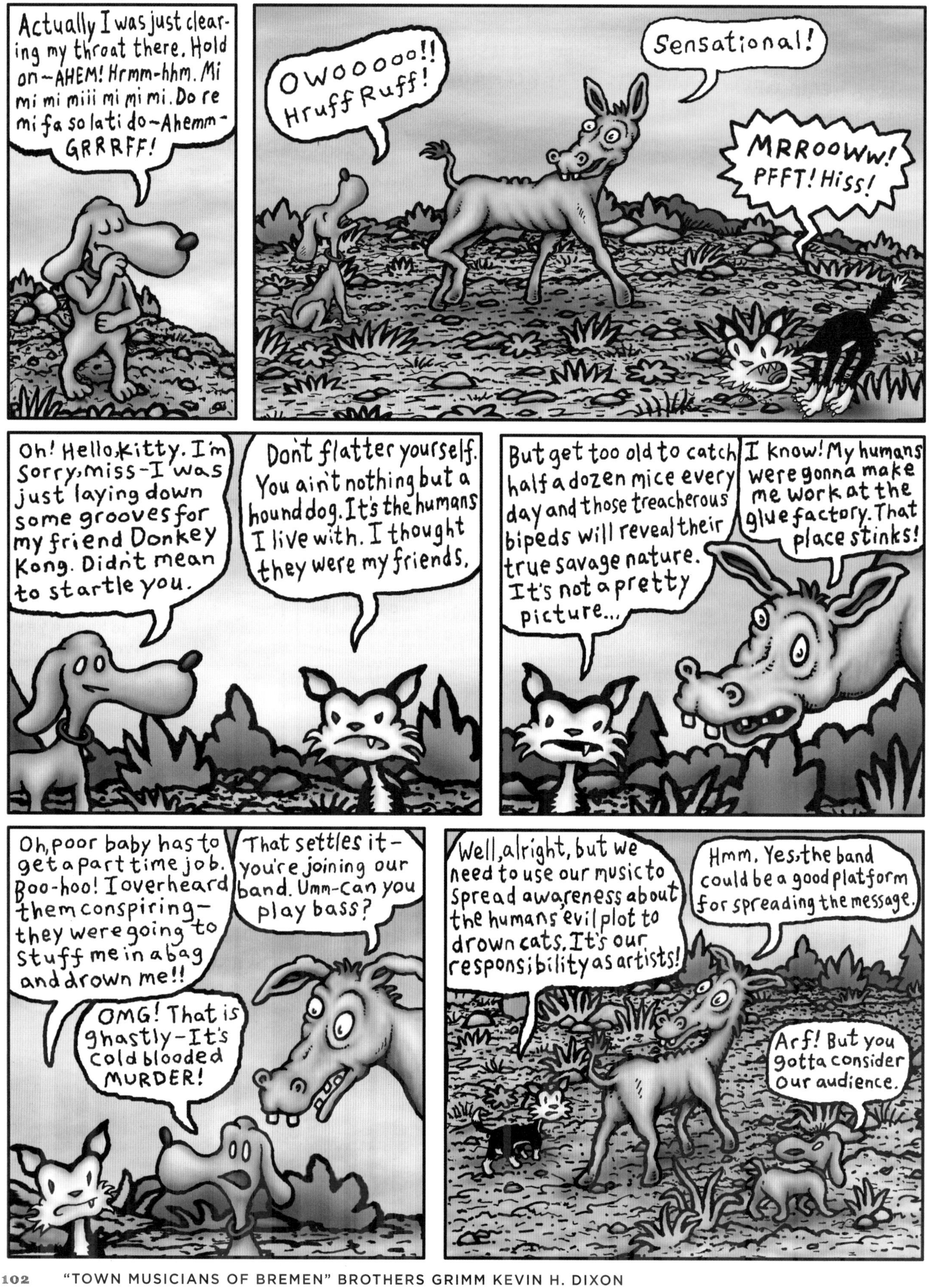

Actually I was just clearing my throat there. Hold on—AHEM! Hrmm-hhm. Mi mi mi miii mi mi mi. Do re mi fa so la ti do—Ahemm- GRRRFF!
OWOOOOO!! Hruff Ruff!
Sensational!
MRROOWW! PFFT! Hiss!
Oh! Hello, kitty. I'm sorry, miss-I was just laying down some grooves for my friend Donkey Kong. Didn't mean to startle you.
Don't flatter yourself. You ain't nothing but a hound dog. It's the humans I live with. I thought they were my friends.
But get too old to catch half a dozen mice every day and those treacherous bipeds will reveal their true savage nature. It's not a pretty picture...
I know! My humans were gonna make me work at the glue factory. That place stinks!
Oh, poor baby has to get a part time job. Boo-hoo! I overheard them conspiring—they were going to stuff me in a bag and drown me!!
That settles it—you're joining our band. Umm-can you play bass?
OMG! That is ghastly-It's cold blooded MURDER!
Well, alright, but we need to use our music to spread awareness about the humans' evil plot to drown cats. It's our responsibility as artists!
Hmm. Yes, the band could be a good platform for spreading the message.
Arf! But you gotta consider our audience.

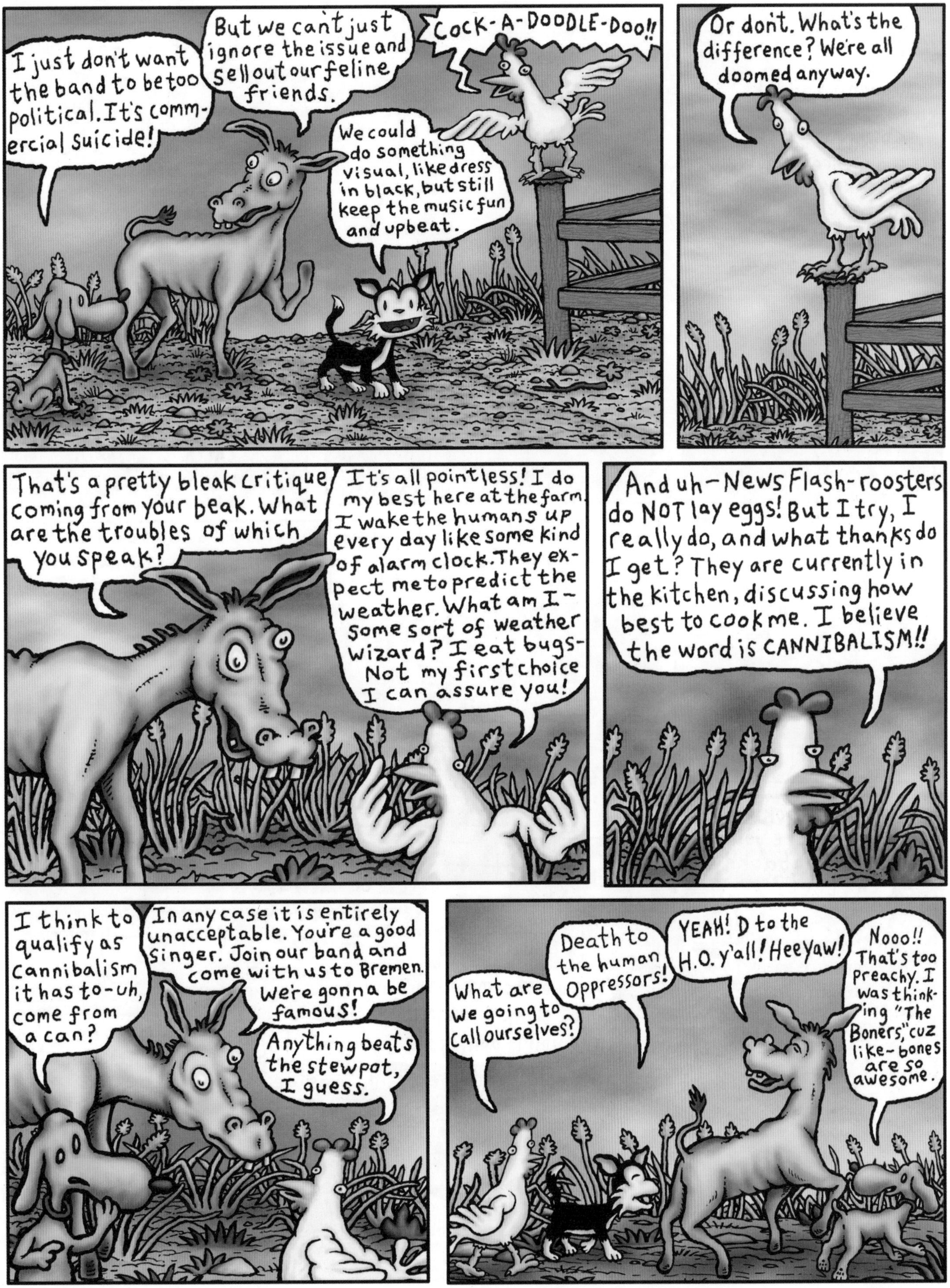

I just don't want the band to be too political. It's commercial suicide!
But we can't just ignore the issue and sell out our feline friends.
COCK-A-DOODLE-DOO!!
We could do something visual, like dress in black, but still keep the music fun and upbeat.
Or don't. What's the difference? We're all doomed anyway.
That's a pretty bleak critique coming from your beak. What are the troubles of which you speak?
It's all pointless! I do my best here at the farm. I wake the humans up every day like some kind of alarm clock. They expect me to predict the weather. What am I— some sort of weather wizard? I eat bugs- Not my first choice I can assure you!
And uh—News Flash—roosters do NOT lay eggs! But I try, I really do, and what thanks do I get? They are currently in the kitchen, discussing how best to cook me. I believe the word is CANNIBALISM!!
I think to qualify as cannibalism it has to—uh, come from a can?
In any case it is entirely unacceptable. You're a good singer. Join our band and come with us to Bremen. We're gonna be famous!
Anything beats the stewpot, I guess.
What are we going to call ourselves?
Death to the human Oppressors!
YEAH! D to the H.O. y'all! Heeyaw!
Nooo!! That's too preachy. I was thinking "The Boners," cuz like—bones are so awesome.

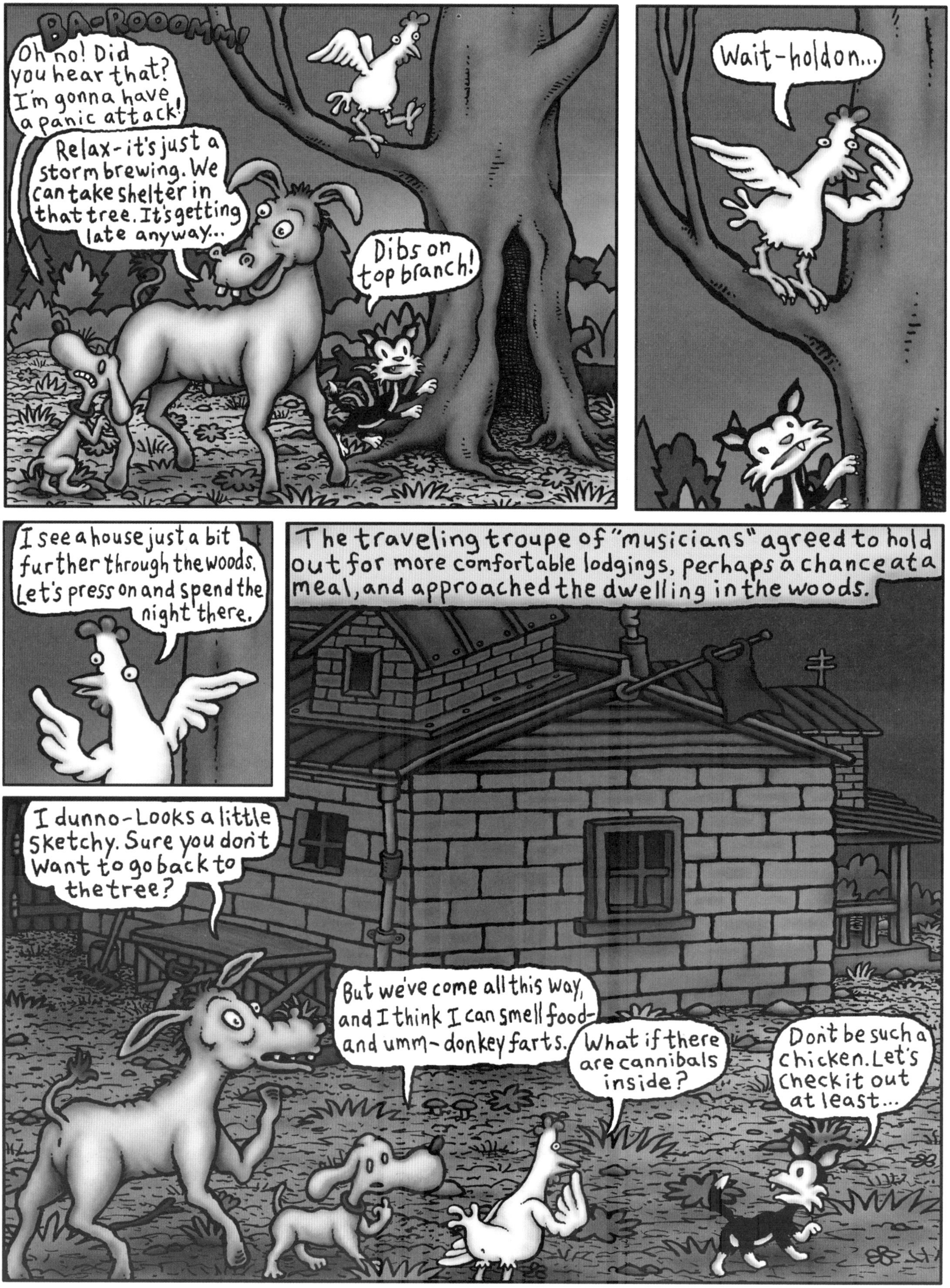
BA-ROOOMM!
Oh no! Did you hear that? I'm gonna have a panic attack!
Relax - it's just a storm brewing. We can take shelter in that tree. It's getting late anyway...
Dibs on top branch!
Wait - hold on...
I see a house just a bit further through the woods. Let's press on and spend the night there.
The traveling troupe of "musicians" agreed to hold out for more comfortable lodgings, perhaps a chance at a meal, and approached the dwelling in the woods.
I dunno - Looks a little sketchy. Sure you don't want to go back to the tree?
But we've come all this way, and I think I can smell food - and umm - donkey farts.
What if there are cannibals inside?
Don't be such a chicken. Let's check it out at least...

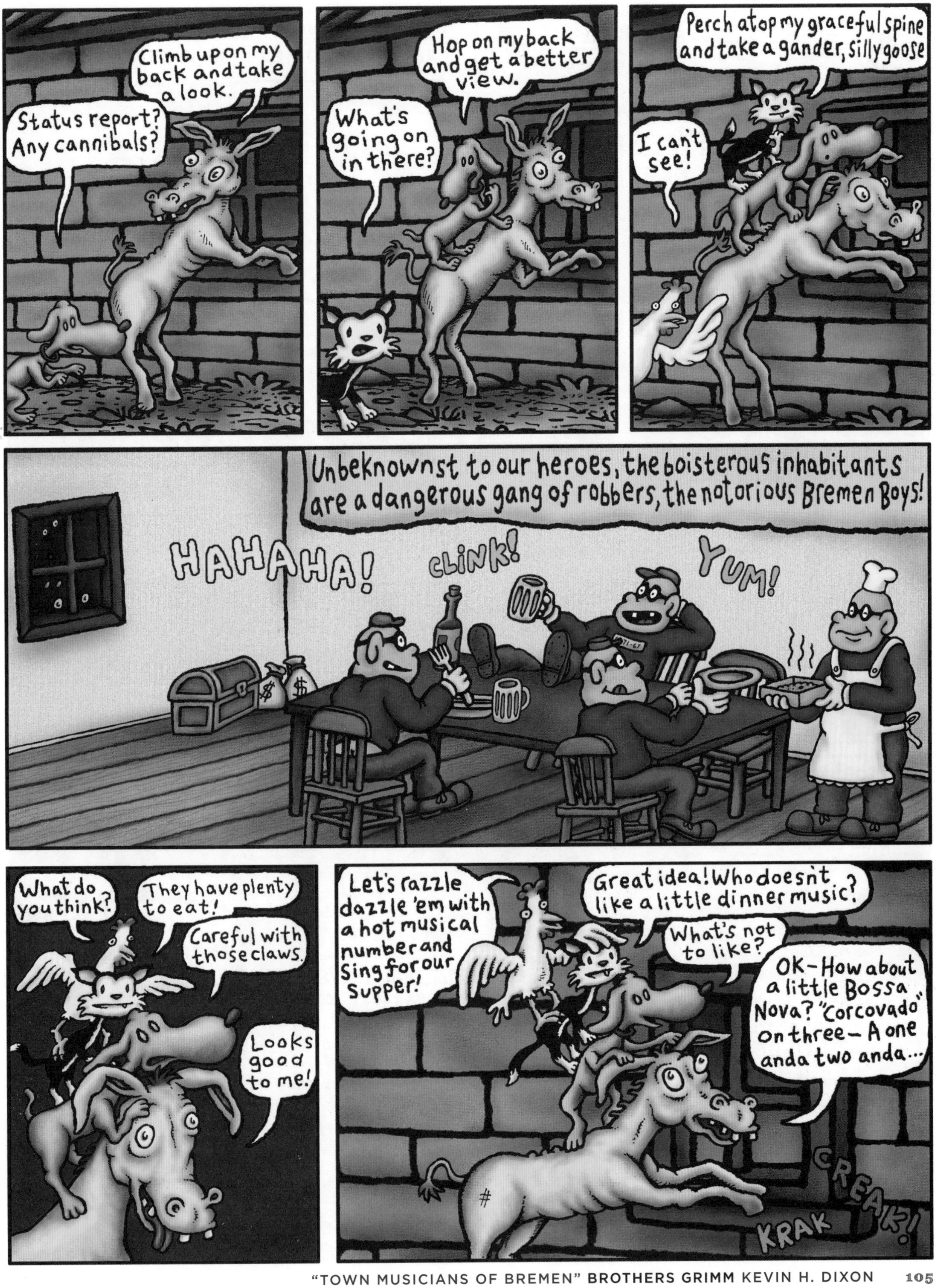
Climb upon my back and take a look.
Status report? Any cannibals?
Hop on my back and get a better view.
What's going on in there?
Perch atop my graceful spine and take a gander, silly goose
I can't see!
Unbeknownst to our heroes, the boisterous inhabitants are a dangerous gang of robbers, the notorious Bremen Boys!
HAHAHA!
CLINK!
YUM!
What do you think?
They have plenty to eat!
Careful with those claws.
Looks good to me!
Let's razzle dazzle 'em with a hot musical number and sing for our supper!
Great idea! Who doesn't like a little dinner music?
What's not to like?
OK-How about a little Bossa Nova? "Corcovado" on three- A one anda two anda...
CREAK!
KRAK

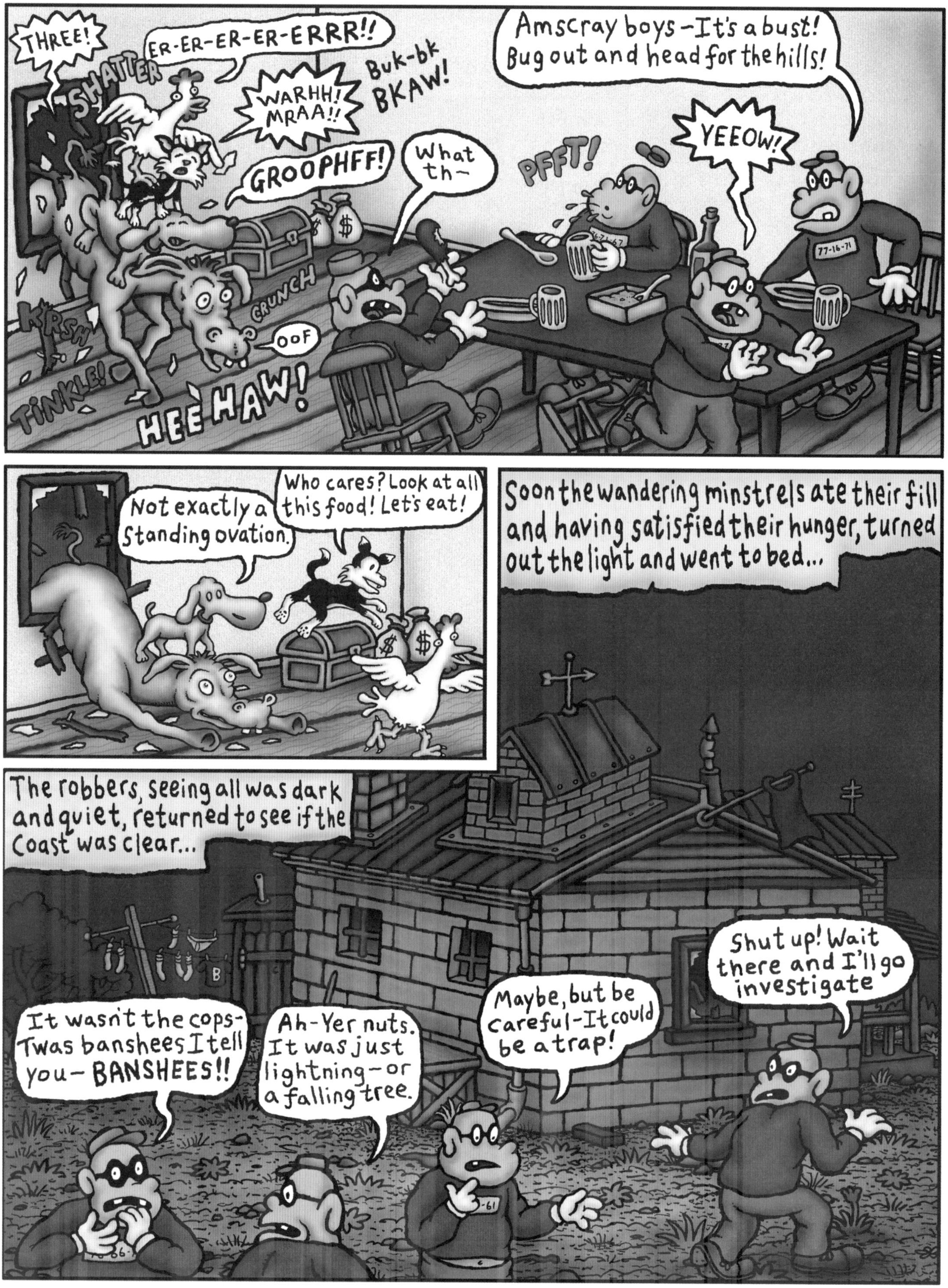
THREE!
SHATTER
ER-ER-ER-ER-ERRR!!
WARHH! MRAA!!
Buk-bk BKAW!
GROOPHFF!
What th~
Amscray boys–It's a bust! Bug out and head for the hills!
YEEOW!
PFFT!
CRUNCH
K'RSH
OOF
TINKLE!
HEE HAW!
Not exactly a standing ovation.
Who cares? Look at all this food! Let's eat!
Soon the wandering minstrels ate their fill and having satisfied their hunger, turned out the light and went to bed...
The robbers, seeing all was dark and quiet, returned to see if the Coast was clear...
It wasn't the cops–Twas banshees I tell you– BANSHEES!!
Ah-Yer nuts. It was just lightning–or a falling tree.
Maybe, but be careful–It could be a trap!
Shut up! Wait there and I'll go investigate

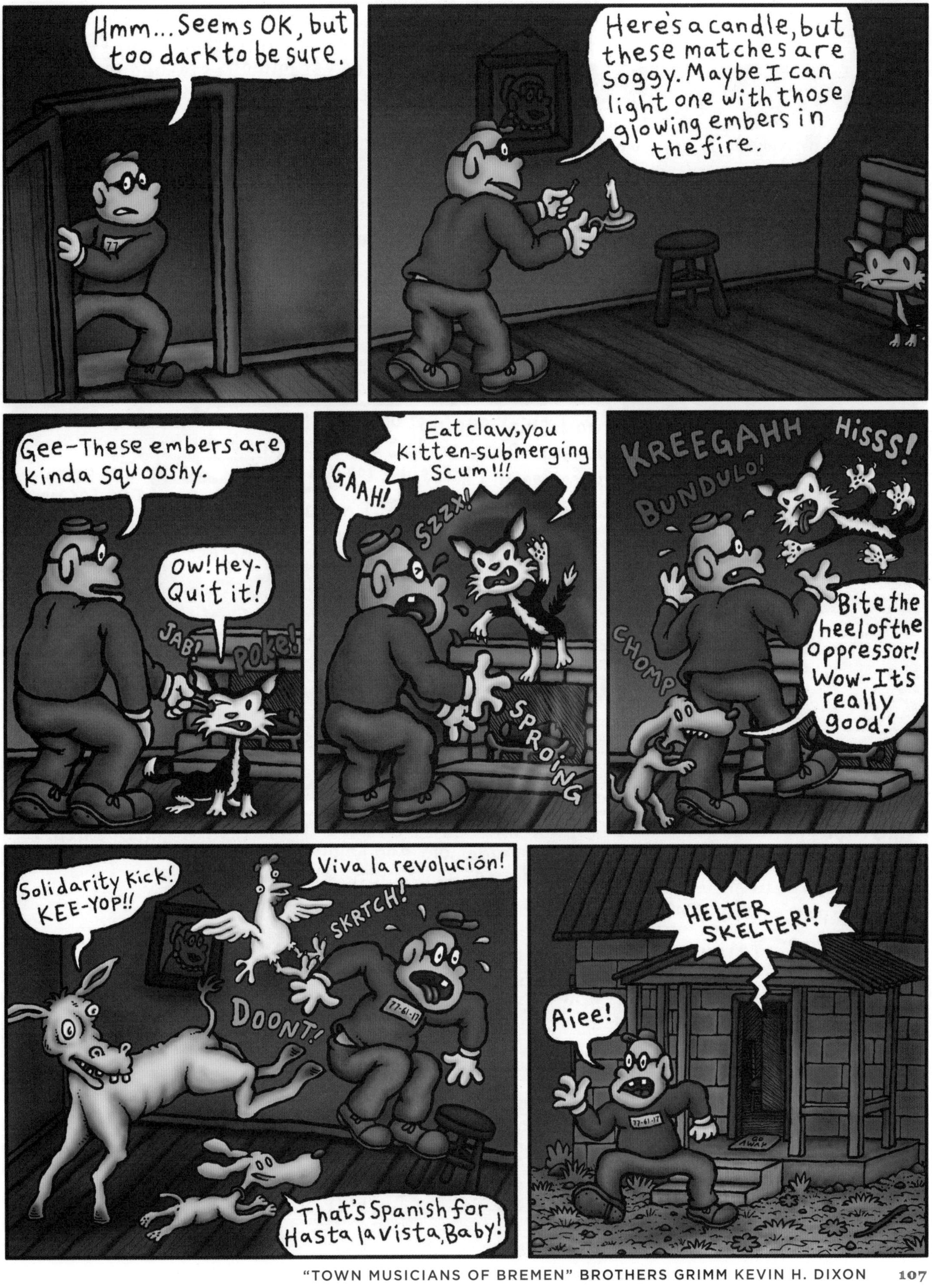

Hmm... Seems OK, but too dark to be sure.
Here's a candle, but these matches are soggy. Maybe I can light one with those glowing embers in the fire.
Gee–These embers are kinda squooshy.
JAB!
POKE!
Ow! Hey-Quit it!
GAAH!
Eat claw, you kitten-submerging scum!!!
SZZX!
SPROING
KREEGAHH
HISSS!
BUNDULO!
CHOMP
Bite the heel of the oppressor! Wow-It's really good!
Solidarity kick! KEE-YOP!!
Viva la revolución!
SKRTCH!
DOONT!
77-61-17
That's Spanish for Hasta la vista, Baby!
HELTER SKELTER!!
Aiee!
77-61-17
GO AWAY

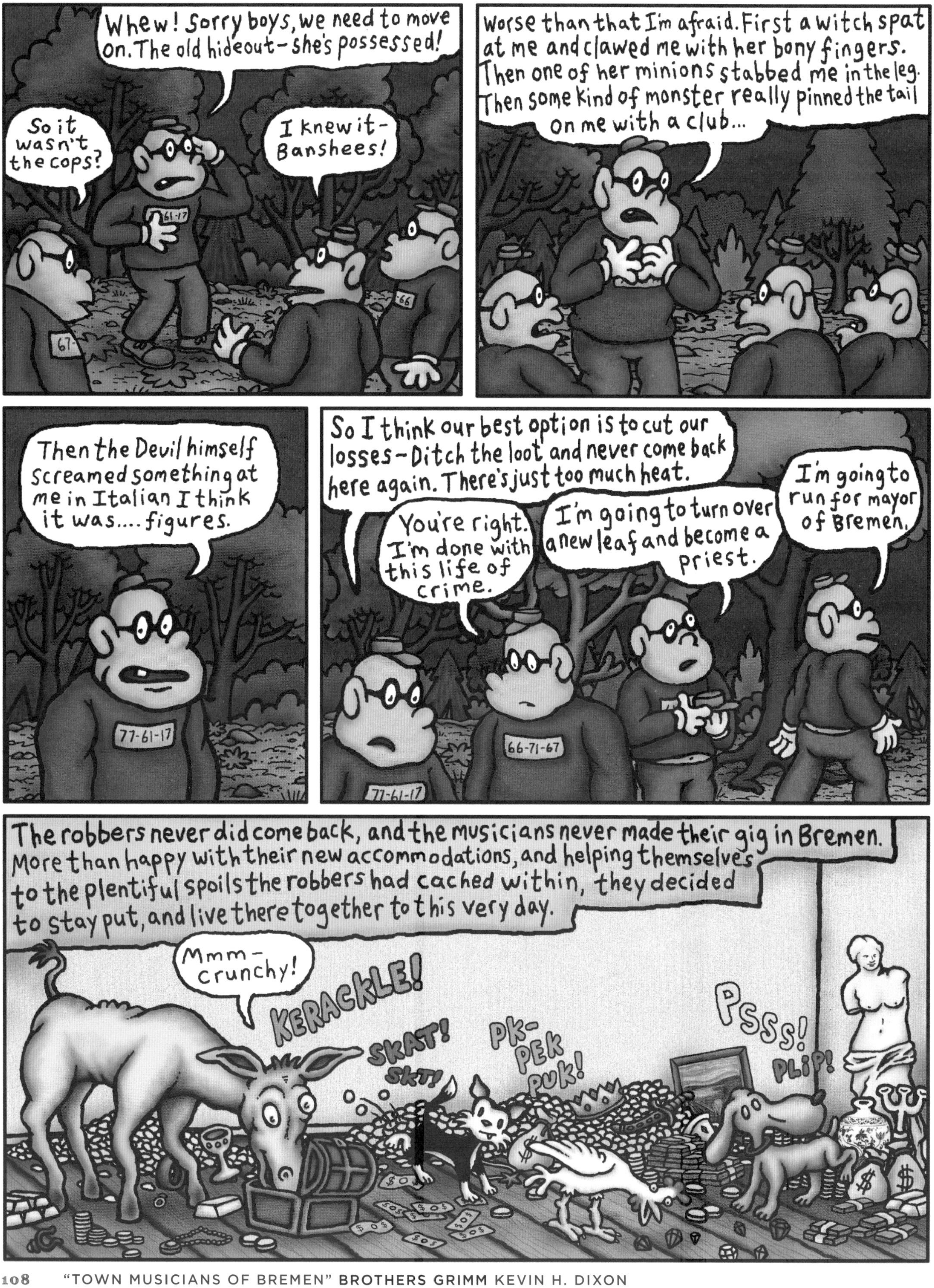
Whew! Sorry boys, we need to move on. The old hideout–she's possessed!
So it wasn't the cops?
I knew it–Banshees!
61-17
67-
-66
Worse than that I'm afraid. First a witch spat at me and clawed me with her bony fingers. Then one of her minions stabbed me in the leg. Then some kind of monster really pinned the tail on me with a club...
Then the Devil himself screamed something at me in Italian I think it was.... figures.
77-61-17
So I think our best option is to cut our losses–Ditch the loot and never come back here again. There's just too much heat.
You're right. I'm done with this life of crime.
I'm going to turn over a new leaf and become a priest.
I'm going to run for mayor of Bremen.
66-71-67
77-61-17
The robbers never did come back, and the musicians never made their gig in Bremen. More than happy with their new accommodations, and helping themselves to the plentiful spoils the robbers had cached within, they decided to stay put, and live there together to this very day.
Mmm–crunchy!
KERACKLE!
SKAT!
SKT!
PK-PEK PUK!
PSSS!
PLIP!

# "A Tale of One Who Traveled to Learn What Shivering Meant"

**Brothers Grimm**

ART/ADAPTATION BY **Chandra Free**

TECHNICAL ASSISTS BY **BLAM! Ventures**

**AMONG THE GRIMMS' CREEPIEST YET FUNNIEST YARNS** is the story of a young man who never quivers or trembles. Being stupid, it would seem, can have advantages.

Chandra Free, a.k.a. Spooky Chan, creator of *The God Machine* graphic novel, brings her instantly recognizable style to this story. *The Graphic Canon* volumes have always been open to approaches that differ from the standard comic format, so Chandra chose to meld images and text in a different way—full-page illustrations integrated with the entire text of the tale.

# A Tale of One Who Traveled to Learn What Shivering Meant

A father had two sons, the elder of whom was forward and clever enough to do almost anything; but the younger was so stupid that he could learn nothing, and when the people saw him they said, 'Will thy father still keep thee as a burden to him?' So, if anything was to be done, the elder had at all times to do it; but sometimes the father would call him to fetch something in the dead of night, and perhaps the way led through the churchyard or by a dismal place, and then he used to answer, 'No, father, I cannot go there, I am afraid,' for he was a coward. Or sometimes in the evening, tales were told by the fireside which made one shudder, and the listeners exclaimed, 'Oh, it makes us shiver!' In a corner, meanwhile, sat the younger son, listening, but he could not comprehend what was said, and he thought, 'They say continually, 'Oh, it makes us shiver, it makes us shiver!' but perhaps shivering is an art which I cannot understand.'

One day, however, his father said to him, 'Do you hear, you there in the corner? You are growing stout and big; you must learn some trade to get your living by. Do you see how your brother works? But as for you, you are not worth malt and hops.'
'Ah, father,' answered he, 'I would willingly learn something. When shall I begin? I want to know what shivering means, for of that I can understand nothing.'
The elder brother laughed when he heard this speech, and thought to himself, 'Ah! my brother is such a simpleton that he cannot earn his own living. He who would make a good hedge must learn betimes to bend.' But the father sighed and said, 'What shivering means you may learn soon enough, but you will never get your bread by that.'

Soon after the parish sexton came in for a gossip, so the father told him his troubles, and how that his younger son was such a simpleton that he knew nothing and could learn nothing. 'Just fancy, when I asked him how he intended to earn his bread, he desired to learn what shivering meant!' 'Oh, if that be all,' answered the sexton, 'he can learn that soon enough with me; just send him to my place, and I will soon teach him.' The father was very glad, because he thought that it would do the boy good; so the sexton took him home to ring the bells. About two days afterward he called him up at midnight to go into the church-tower to toll the bell. 'You shall soon learn what shivering means,' thought the sexton, and getting up he went out too.

As soon as the boy reached the belfry, and turned himself round to seize the rope, he saw upon the stairs, near the sounding-hole, a white figure. "Who's there?" he called out; but the figure gave no answer, and neither stirred nor spoke. "Answer," said the boy, "or make haste off; you have no business here to-night." But the sexton did not stir, so that the boy might think it was a ghost.

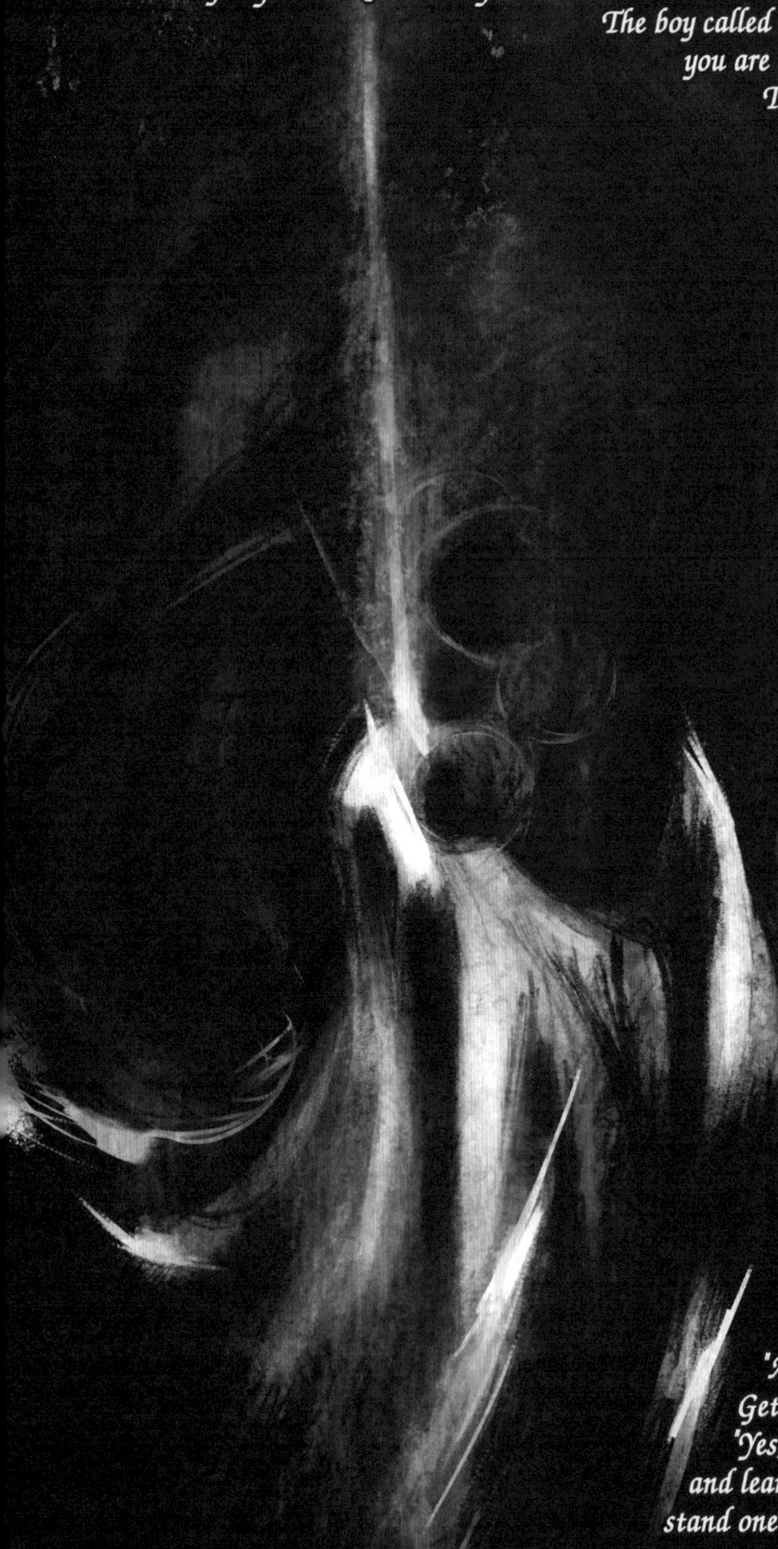

The boy called out a second time, "What are you doing here? Speak, if you are an honest fellow, or else I will throw you downstairs."

The sexton said to himself, "That is not a bad thought"; but he remained quiet as if he were a stone. Then the boy called out for the third time, but it produced no effect; so, making a spring, he threw the ghost down the stairs so that it rolled ten steps and then lay motionless in a corner. Thereupon he rang the bell, and then going home, he went to bed without saying a word, and fell fast asleep.

The sexton's wife waited some time for her husband, but he did not come; so at last she became anxious, woke the boy, and asked him if he knew where her husband was, who had gone before him to the belfry.

"No," answered the boy; "but there was someone standing on the steps who would not give any answer, nor go away, so I took him for a thief and threw him downstairs. Go now and see where he is; perhaps it may be he, but I should be sorry for it." The wife ran off and found her husband lying in a corner, groaning, with one of his ribs broken.

She took him up and ran with loud outcries to the boy's father, and said to him, "Your son has brought a great misfortune on us; he has thrown my husband down and broken his bones. Take the good-for-nothing fellow from our house."

The terrified father came in haste and scolded the boy. "What do these wicked tricks mean? They will only bring misfortune upon you."

"Father," answered the lad, "hear me! I am quite innocent. He stood there at midnight like one who had done some evil; I did not know who it was, and cried three times, 'Speak, or be off!'"

"Ah!" said the father, "everything goes badly with you. Get out of my sight; I do not wish to see you again!"

"Yes, father, willingly; wait but one day, then I will go out and learn what shivering means, that I may at least understand one business which will support me."

"Learn what you will," replied the father, "all is the same to me. Here are fifty dollars; go forth with them into the world, and tell no man whence you came, or who your father is, for I am ashamed of you."

"Yes, father, as you wish; but if you desire nothing else, I shall esteem that very lightly."

"Oh, if I could but shiver!"

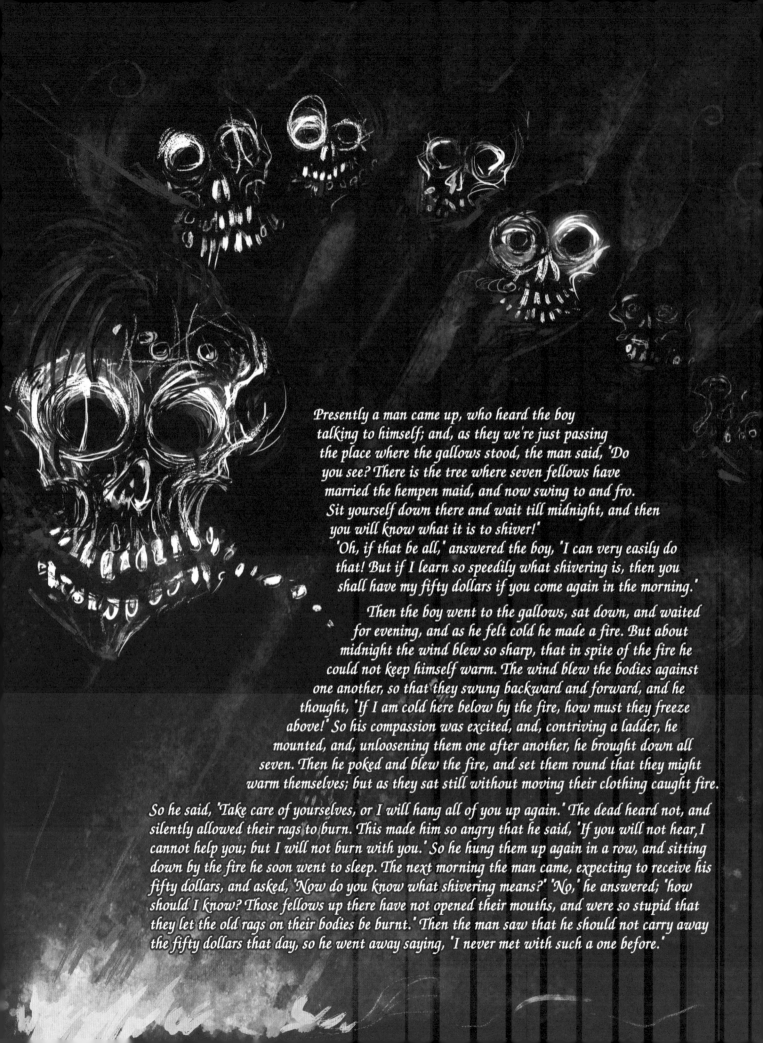

Presently a man came up, who heard the boy
talking to himself; and, as they we're just passing
the place where the gallows stood, the man said, 'Do
you see? There is the tree where seven fellows have
married the hempen maid, and now swing to and fro.
Sit yourself down there and wait till midnight, and then
you will know what it is to shiver!'
'Oh, if that be all,' answered the boy, 'I can very easily do
that! But if I learn so speedily what shivering is, then you
shall have my fifty dollars if you come again in the morning.'

Then the boy went to the gallows, sat down, and waited
for evening, and as he felt cold he made a fire. But about
midnight the wind blew so sharp, that in spite of the fire he
could not keep himself warm. The wind blew the bodies against
one another, so that they swung backward and forward, and he
thought, "If I am cold here below by the fire, how must they freeze
above!" So his compassion was excited, and, contriving a ladder, he
mounted, and, unloosening them one after another, he brought down all
seven. Then he poked and blew the fire, and set them round that they might
warm themselves; but as they sat still without moving their clothing caught fire.

So he said, 'Take care of yourselves, or I will hang all of you up again.' The dead heard not, and
silently allowed their rags to burn. This made him so angry that he said, "If you will not hear, I
cannot help you; but I will not burn with you." So he hung them up again in a row, and sitting
down by the fire he soon went to sleep. The next morning the man came, expecting to receive his
fifty dollars, and asked, 'Now do you know what shivering means?' 'No,' he answered; 'how
should I know? Those fellows up there have not opened their mouths, and were so stupid that
they let the old rags on their bodies be burnt.' Then the man saw that he should not carry away
the fifty dollars that day, so he went away saying, 'I never met with such a one before.'

The boy also went on his way and began again to say, 'Ah, if only I could but shiver—if I could but shiver!' A wagoner walking behind overheard him, and asked, 'What is it you are continually grumbling about?'

'Oh,' replied the youth, 'I wish to learn what shivering is, but nobody can teach me.'

'Cease your silly talk,' said the wagoner. 'Come with me, and I will see what I can do for you.' So the boy went with the wagoner, and about evening time they arrived at an inn where they put up for the night, and while they were going into the parlor he said, quite aloud, 'Oh, if I could but shiver—if I could but shiver!' The host overheard him and said, laughingly, 'Oh, if that is all you wish, you shall soon have the opportunity.' 'Hold your tongue,' said his wife; 'so many imprudent people have already lost their lives, it were a shame and sin to such beautiful eyes that they should not see the light again.' But the youth said, 'If it were ever so difficult I would at once learn it; for that reason I left home'; and he never let the host have any peace till he told him that not far off stood an enchanted castle, where any one might soon learn to shiver if he would watch there three nights. The King had promised his daughter in marriage to whoever would venture, and she was the most beautiful young lady that the sun ever shone upon. And he further told him that inside the castle there was an immense amount of treasure guarded by evil spirits; enough to make any one free, and turn a poor man into a very rich one. Many, he added, had already ventured into this castle, but no one had ever come out again. The next morning this youth went to the King, and said, 'If you will allow me, I wish to watch three nights in the enchanted castle.' The King looked at him, and because his appearance pleased him, he said, 'You may make three requests, but they must be inanimate things you ask for, and such as you can take with you into the castle.' So the youth asked for a fire, a lathe, and a cutting board. The King let him take these things by day into the castle, and when it was evening the youth went in and made himself a bright fire in one of the rooms, and, placing his cutting board and knife near it, he sat down upon his lathe. 'Ah, if I could but shiver!' said he. 'But even here I shall never learn.' At midnight, he got up to stir the fire, and, as he poked it, there shrieked suddenly in one corner, 'Miau, miau! how cold I am!' 'You simpleton!' he exclaimed, 'what are you shrieking for? If you are so cold, come and sit down by the fire and warm yourself!' As he was speaking, two great black cats sprang up to him with an immense jump and sat down one on each side, looking at him quite wildly with their fiery eyes. When they had warmed themselves for a little while they said, 'Comrade, shall we have a game of cards?' 'Certainly,' he said. So they stretched out their claws, and he said, 'Ah, what long nails you have got; wait a bit, I must cut them off first'; and so saying he caught them up by the necks, and put them on his board and screwed their feet down. 'Since I have seen what you are about, I have lost my relish for a game at cards,' said he; and, instantly killing them, threw them away into the water. But no sooner had he quieted these two and thought of sitting down again by his fire, than there came out of every hole and corner black cats and black dogs with glowing chains, continually more and more so that he could not hide himself. They howled fearfully and jumped upon his fire, and scattered it about as if they would extinguish it. He looked on quietly for some time, but at last, getting angry, he took up his knife and called out, 'Away with you, you vagabonds!' and chased them about until a part ran off, and the rest he killed and threw into the pond.

As soon as he returned, he blew up the sparks of his fire again and warmed himself, and while he sat, his eyes began to feel very heavy and he wished to go to sleep. So looking around, he saw a great bed in one corner, in which he lay down; but no sooner had he closed his eyes, than the bed began to move of itself and travelled all round the castle. "Just so," said he, "only better still"; whereupon the bed galloped away as if six horses pulled it up and down steps and stairs, until at last, all at once, it overset, bottom upward, and lay upon him like a mountain; but up he got, threw pillows and mattresses into the air, and saying, "Now he who wishes may travel," laid himself down by the fire and slept till day broke. In the morning the King came, and, seeing the youth lying on the ground, he thought that the spectres had killed him, and that he was dead; so he said, "It is a great misfortune that the finest men are thus killed"; but the youth, hearing this, sprang up, saying, "It is not come to that with me yet!" The King was much astonished, but very glad, and asked him how he had fared. "Very well," replied he; "as one night has passed, so also may the other two." Soon after, he met his landlord, who opened his eyes when he saw him. "I never thought to see you alive again," said he; "have you learnt now what shivering means?" "No," said he; "it is all of no use. Oh, if any one would but tell me!"

The second night, he went up again into the castle, and sitting down by the fire, began his old song, "If I could but shiver!" When midnight came, a ringing and a rattling noise was heard, gentle at first and louder and louder by degrees; then there was a pause, and presently with a loud outcry half a man's body came down the chimney and fell at his feet. "Holloa," he exclaimed; "only half a man answered that ringing; that is too little." Then the ringing began afresh, and a roaring and howling was heard, and the other half fell down. "Wait a bit," said he; "I will poke up the fire first." When he had done so and looked round again, the two pieces had joined themselves together, and an ugly man was sitting in his place. "I did not bargain for that," said the youth; "the bench is mine." The man tried to push him away, but the youth would not let him, and giving him a violent push sat himself down in his old place. Presently more men fell down the chimney, one after the other, who brought nine thigh-bones and two skulls, which they set up, and then they began to play at ninepins. At this, the youth wished also to play, so he asked whether he might join them. "Yes, if you have money!" "Money enough," he replied, "but your balls are not quite round"; so saying he took up the skulls, and, placing them on his lathe, turned them round. "Ah, now you will roll well," said he. "Holloa! Now we will go at it merrily." So he played with them and lost some of his money, but as it struck twelve everything disappeared. Then he lay down and went to sleep quietly. On the morrow the King came for news, and asked him how he had fared this time. "I have been playing ninepins," he replied, "and lost a couple of dollars." "Have you not shivered?" "No! I have enjoyed myself very much; but I wish some one would teach me that!"

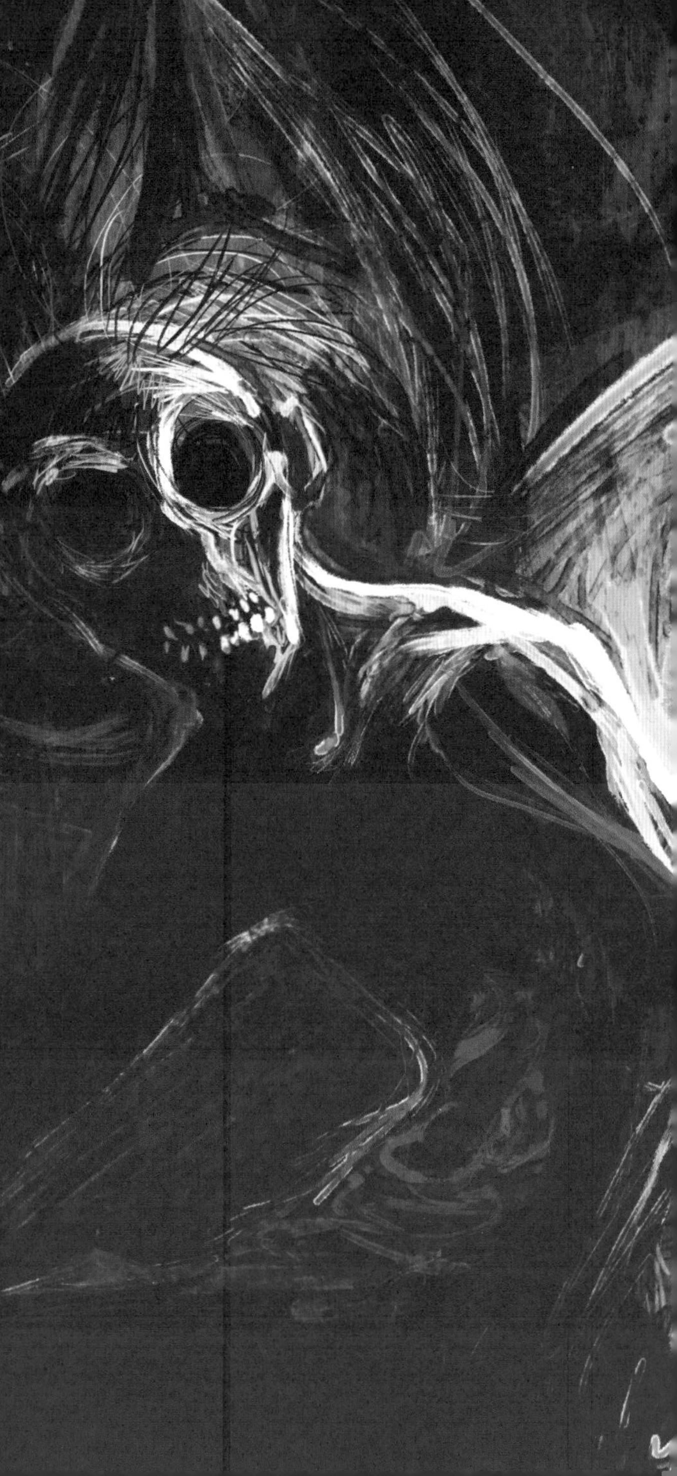

On the third night, he sat down again on his bench, saying in great vexation, 'Oh, if I could only shiver!' When it grew late, six tall men came in bearing a coffin between them. 'Ah, ah,' said he, 'that is surely my little cousin, who died two days ago'; and beckoning with his finger he called, 'Come, little cousin, come!' The men set down the coffin upon the ground, and he went up and took off the lid, and there lay a dead man within, and as he felt the face it was as cold as ice. 'Stop a moment,' he cried; 'I will warm it in a trice'; and stepping up to the fire he warmed his hands, and then laid them upon the face, but it remained cold. So he took up the body, and sitting down by the fire, he laid it on his lap and rubbed the arms so that the blood might circulate again. But all this was of no avail, and he thought to himself if two lie in a bed together, they warm each other; so he put the body in the bed, and covering it up laid himself down by its side.

After a little while, the body became warm and began to move about. 'See, my cousin,' he exclaimed, 'have I not warmed you?' But the body got up and exclaimed, 'Now I will strangle you.' 'Is that your gratitude?' cried the youth. 'Then you shall get into your coffin again'; and taking it up, he threw the body in, and made the lid fast. Then the six men came in again and bore it away. 'Oh, deary me,' said he, 'I shall never be able to shiver if I stop here all my lifetime!' At these words in came a man who was taller than all the others, and looked more horrible; but he was very old and had a long white beard. 'Oh, you wretch,' he exclaimed, 'now thou shalt learn what shivering means, for thou shalt die!'

"Not so quick," answered the youth; "if I die, I must be brought to it first."

"I will quickly seize you," replied the ugly one.

"Softly, softly; be not too sure. I am as strong as you, and perhaps stronger."

"That we will see," said the ugly man. "If you are stronger than I, I will let you go; come, let us try"; and he led him away through a dark passage to a smith's forge. Then taking up an axe he cut through the anvil at one blow down to the ground. "I can do that still better," said the youth, and went to another anvil, while the old man followed him and watched him, with his long beard hanging down. Then the youth took up an axe, and, splitting the anvil at one blow, wedged the old man's beard in it. "Now I have you; now death comes upon you!" and taking up an iron bar he beat the old man until he groaned, and begged him to stop, and he would give him great riches. So the youth drew out the axe, and let him loose. Then the old man, leading him back into the castle, showed him three chests full of gold in a cellar. "One share of this," said he, "belongs to the poor, another to the King, and a third to yourself." And just then it struck twelve and the old man vanished, leaving the youth in the dark. "I must help myself out here," said he, and groping round he found his way back to his room and went to sleep by the fire.

The next morning, the King came and inquired, 'Now have you learnt to shiver?' 'No,' replied the youth; 'What is it? My dead cousin came here, and a bearded man, who showed me a lot of gold down below; but what shivering means, no one has showed me!' Then the King said, 'You have won the castle, and shall marry my daughter.' 'That is all very fine,' replied the youth, 'but still I don't know what shivering means.' So the gold was fetched, and the wedding was celebrated, but the young Prince (for the youth was a Prince now), notwithstanding his love for his bride, and his great contentment, was still continually crying, 'If I could but shiver! If I could but shiver!' At last it fell out in this wise: one of the chambermaids said to the Princess, 'Let me bring in my aid to teach him what shivering is.' So she went to the brook which flowed through the garden, and drew up a pail of water full of little fish; and, at night, when the young Prince was asleep, his bride drew away the covering and poured the pail of cold water and the little fishes over him, so that they slipped all about him. Then the Prince woke up directly, calling out, 'Oh! that makes me shiver! Dear wife, that makes me shiver!"

"Yes, now I know what shivering means!'

*The End*

# "Star Dollars" and "The Water-Sprite"

## Brothers Grimm

ART/ADAPTATION BY **Noah Van Sciver**

**NOAH VAN SCIVER GIVES US TWO OF THE LESS-KNOWN** tales collected by the Grimm brothers. "Star Dollars" is charmingly didactic (sacrifice for others, and God will reward you many times over), while "The Water-Sprite" is a capture-and-escape tale with some truly odd twists thrown in.

Besides regularly contributing to *Mad* magazine, Noah wrote and drew one of the most highly regarded works of graphic biography, *The Hypo: The Melancholic Young Lincoln*, which examines the epic fails and crippling depression of the future president. His dark, heavily hatched and cross-hatched style amplifies the broodiness of these stories.

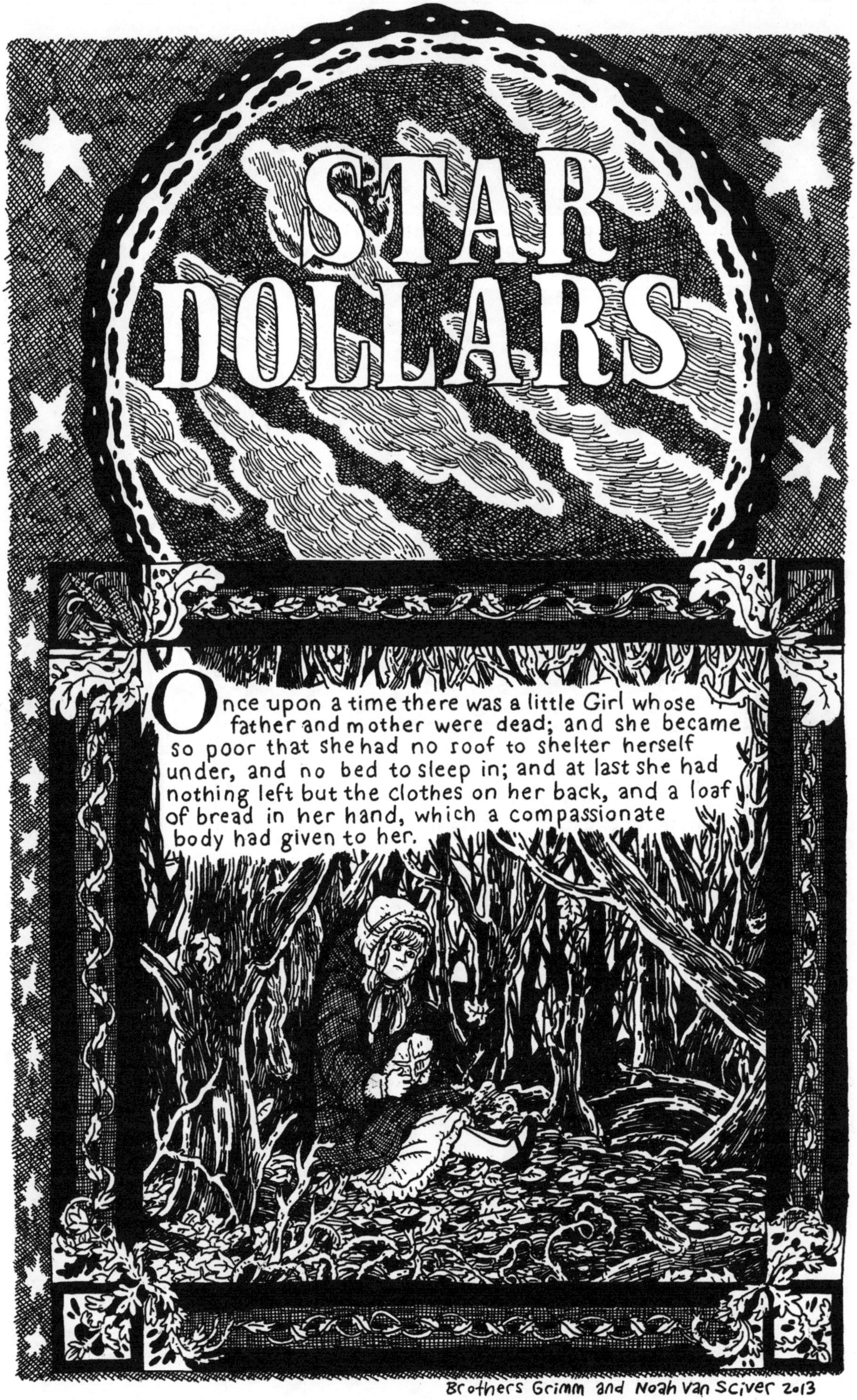
STAR DOLLARS
Once upon a time there was a little Girl whose father and mother were dead; and she became so poor that she had no roof to shelter herself under, and no bed to sleep in; and at last she had nothing left but the clothes on her back, and a loaf of bread in her hand, which a compassionate body had given to her.
Brothers Grimm and Noah Van Sciver 2013

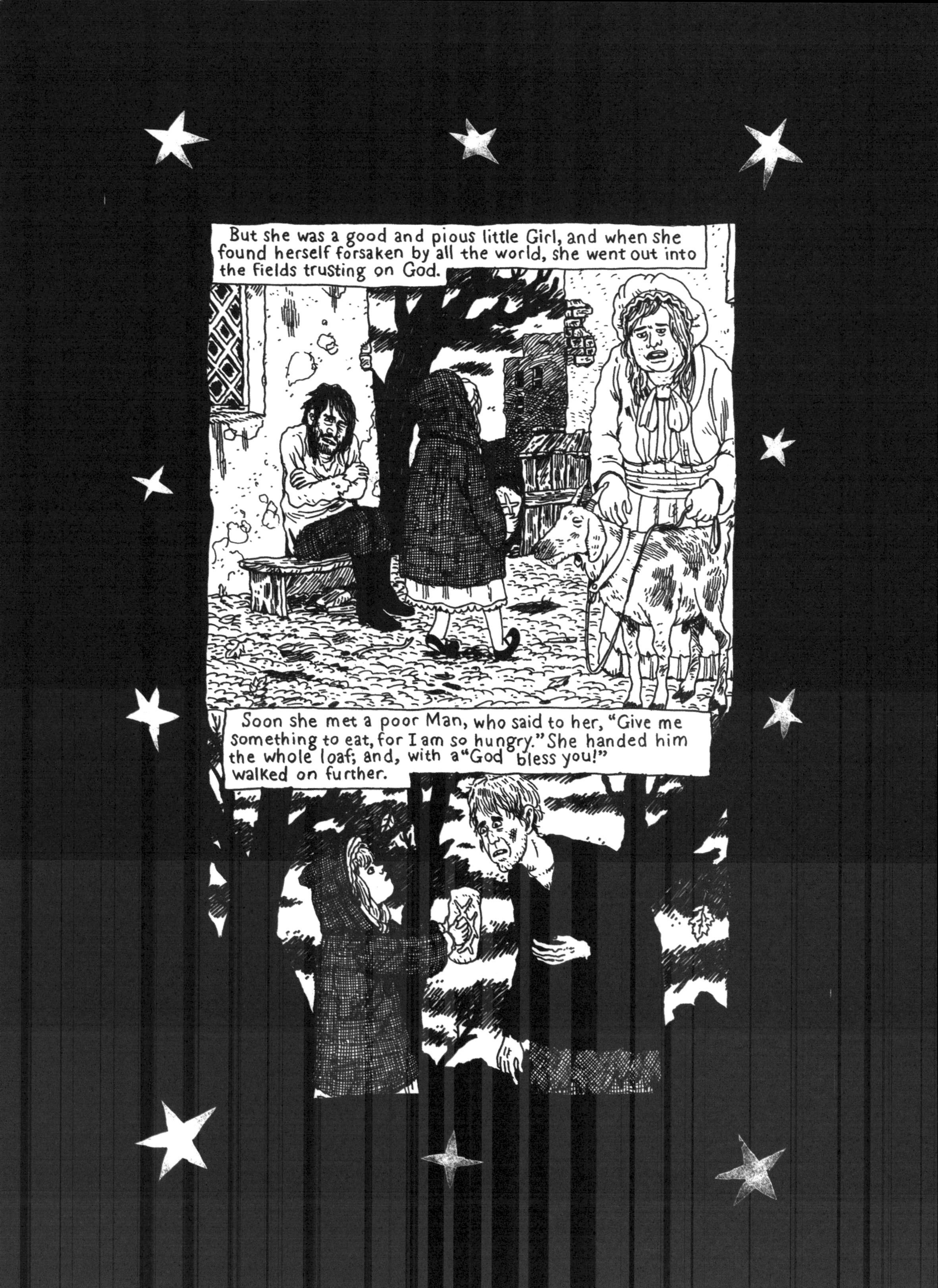
But she was a good and pious little Girl, and when she found herself forsaken by all the world, she went out into the fields trusting on God.
Soon she met a poor Man, who said to her, "Give me something to eat, for I am so hungry." She handed him the whole loaf; and, with a "God bless you!" walked on further.

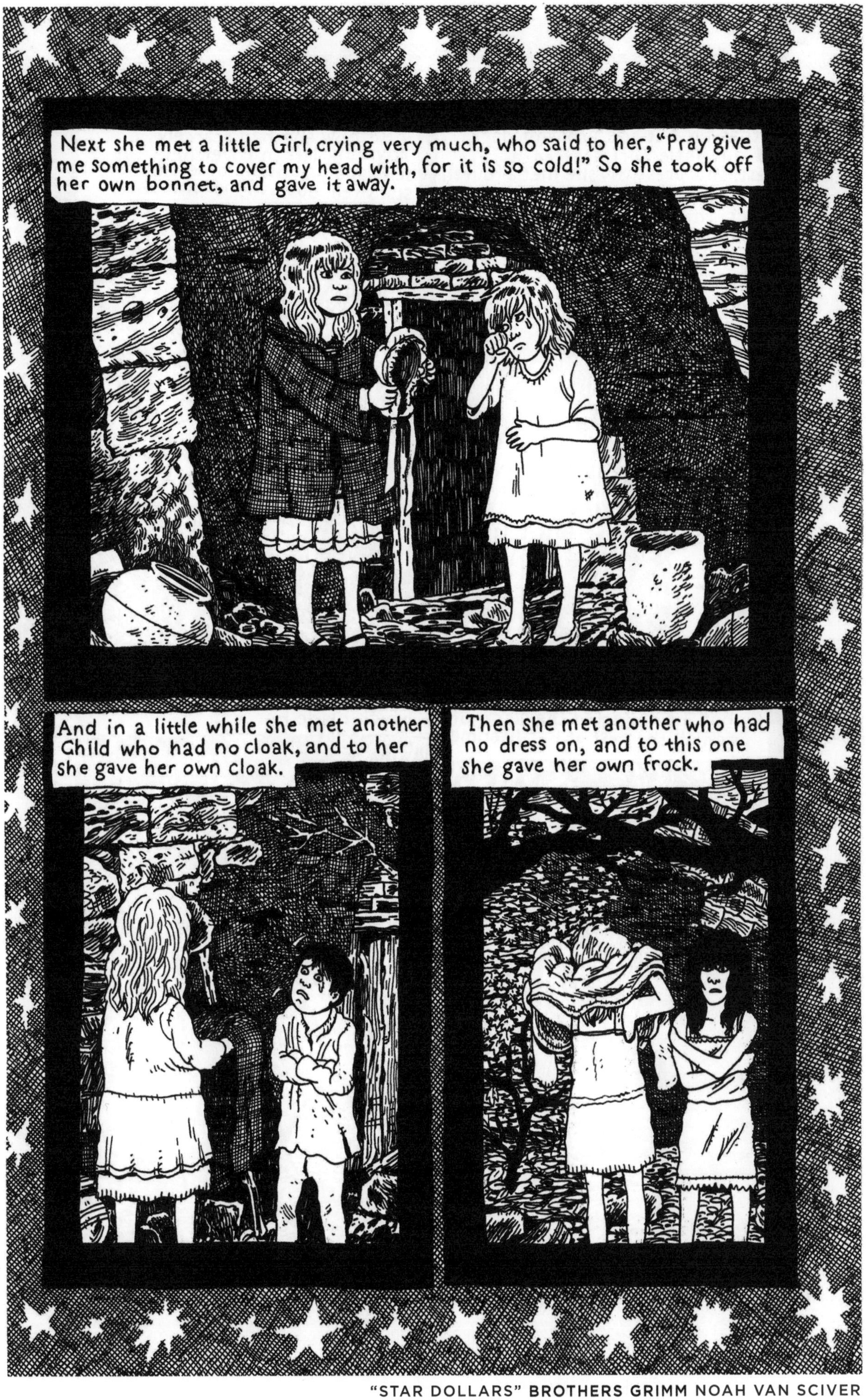
Next she met a little Girl, crying very much, who said to her, "Pray give me something to cover my head with, for it is so cold!" So she took off her own bonnet, and gave it away.
And in a little while she met another Child who had no cloak, and to her she gave her own cloak.
Then she met another who had no dress on, and to this one she gave her own frock.

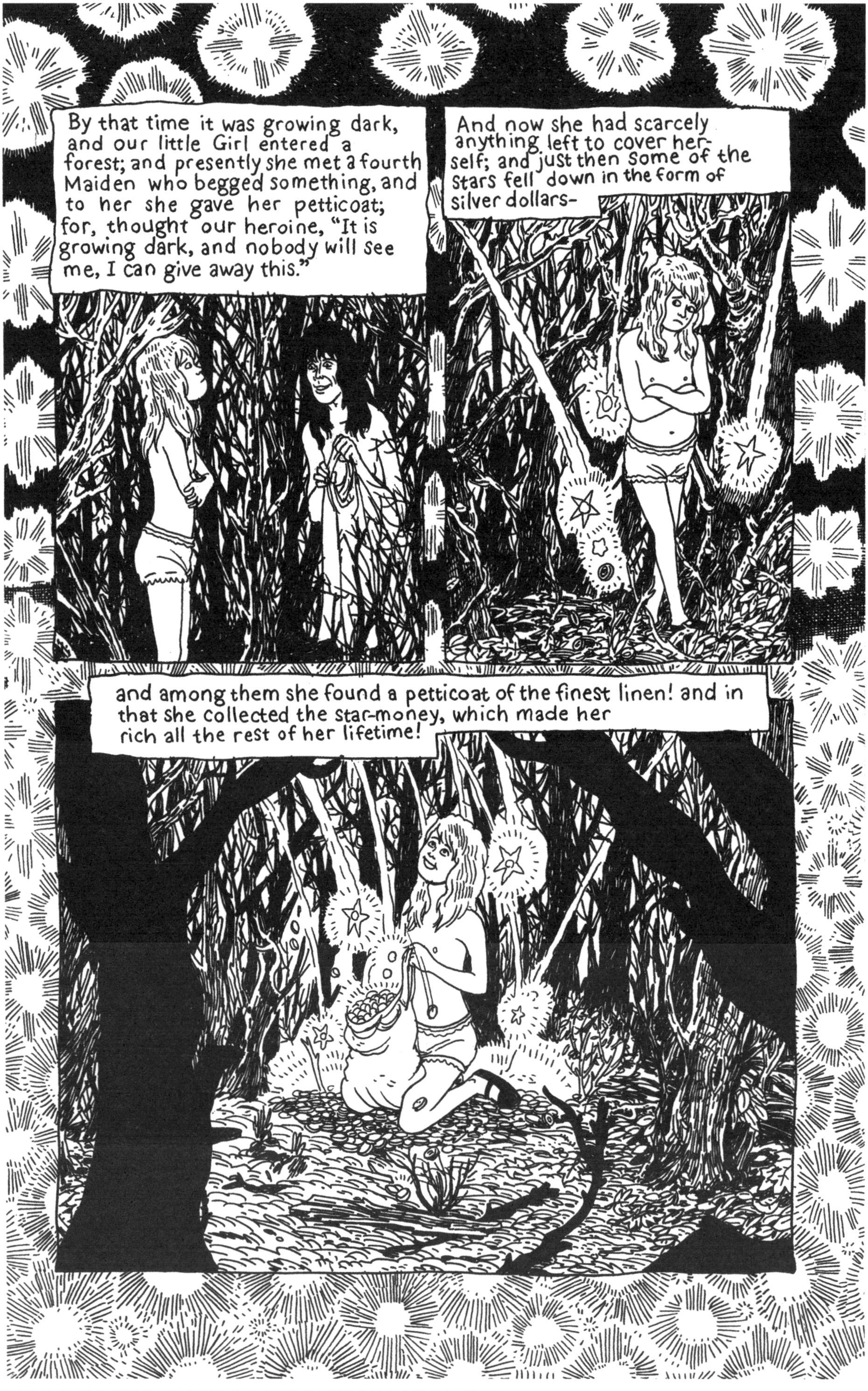
By that time it was growing dark, and our little Girl entered a forest; and presently she met a fourth Maiden who begged something, and to her she gave her petticoat; for, thought our heroine, "It is growing dark, and nobody will see me, I can give away this."
And now she had scarcely anything left to cover herself; and just then some of the stars fell down in the form of silver dollars-
and among them she found a petticoat of the finest linen! and in that she collected the star-money, which made her rich all the rest of her lifetime!

# THE WATER-SPRITE

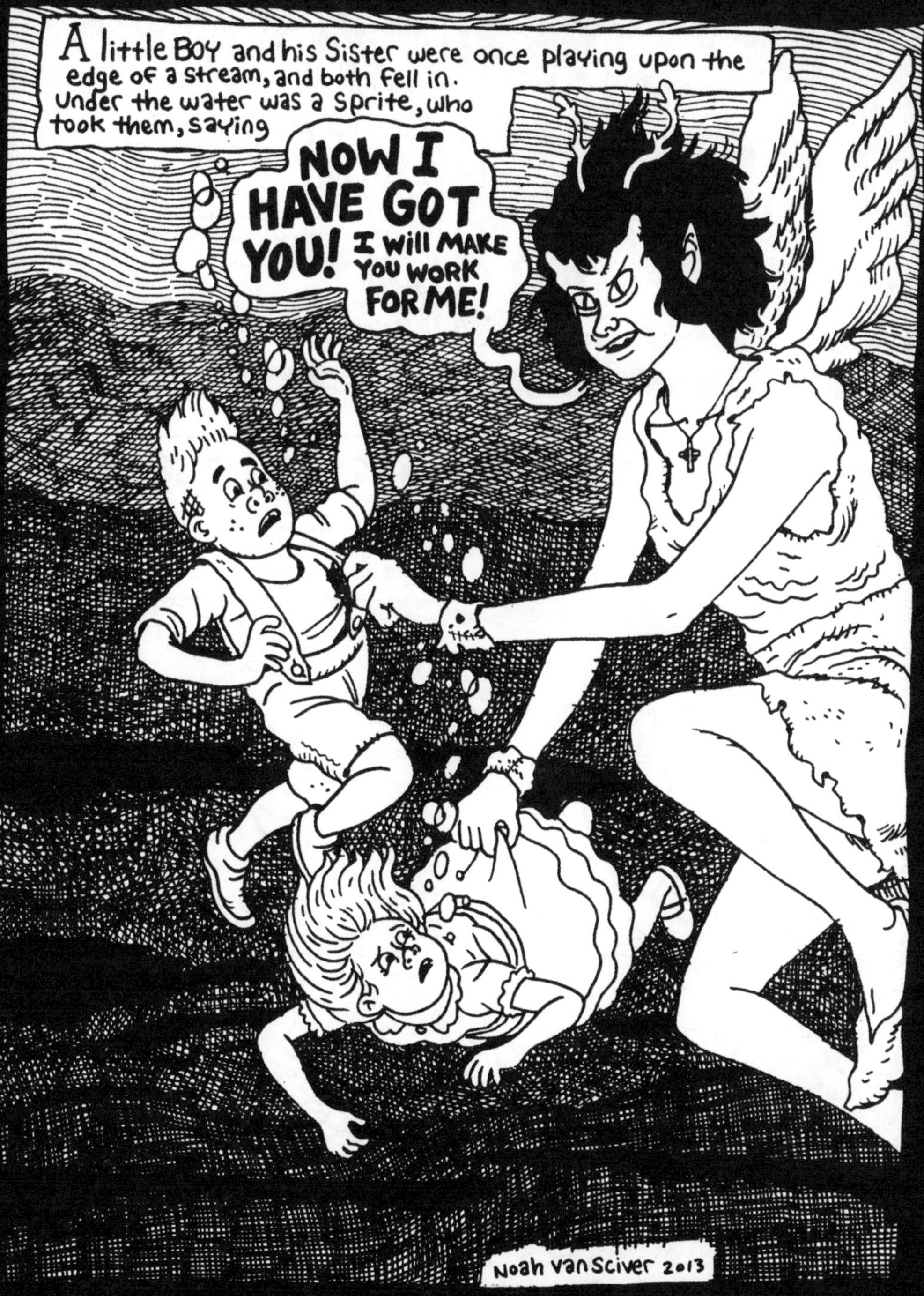
A little Boy and his Sister were once playing upon the edge of a stream, and both fell in. Under the water was a Sprite, who took them, saying
NOW I HAVE GOT YOU! I WILL MAKE YOU WORK FOR ME!
Noah Van Sciver 2013

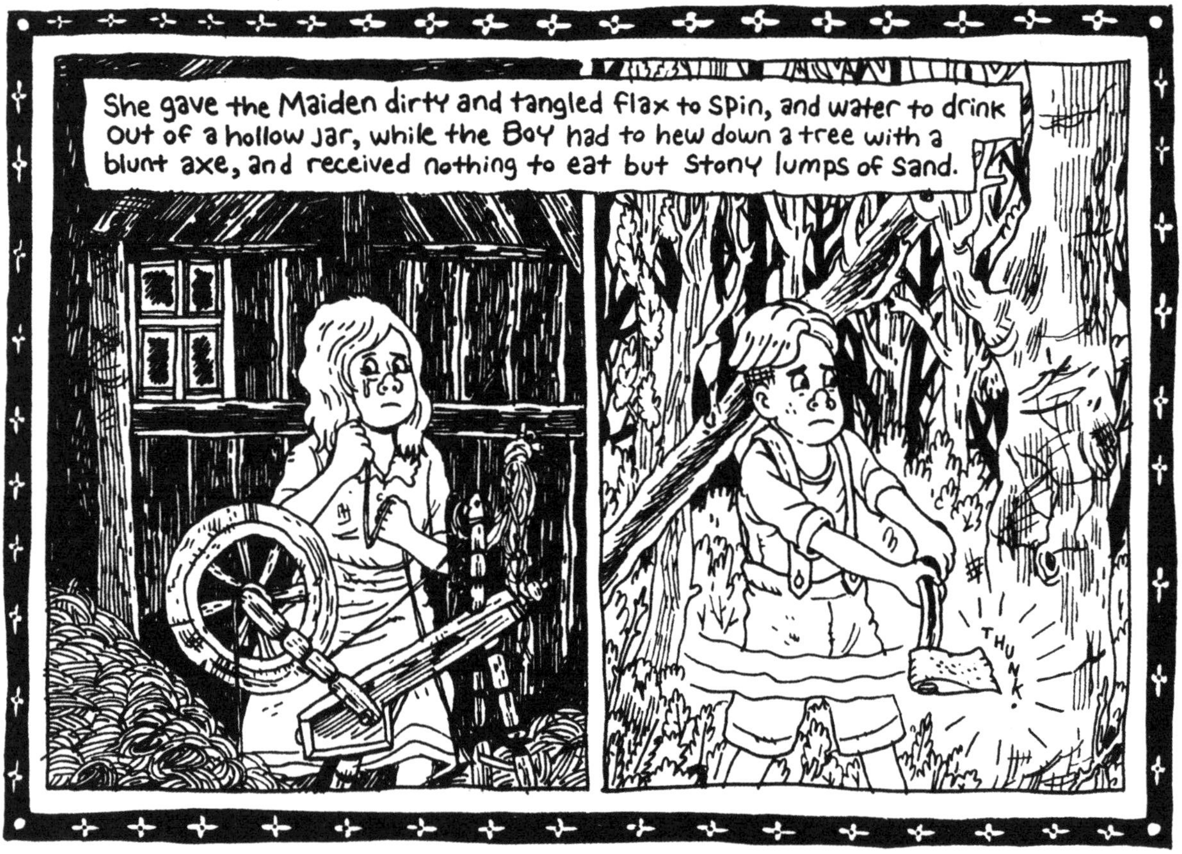
She gave the Maiden dirty and tangled flax to spin, and water to drink out of a hollow jar, while the Boy had to hew down a tree with a blunt axe, and received nothing to eat but stony lumps of sand.
THUNK

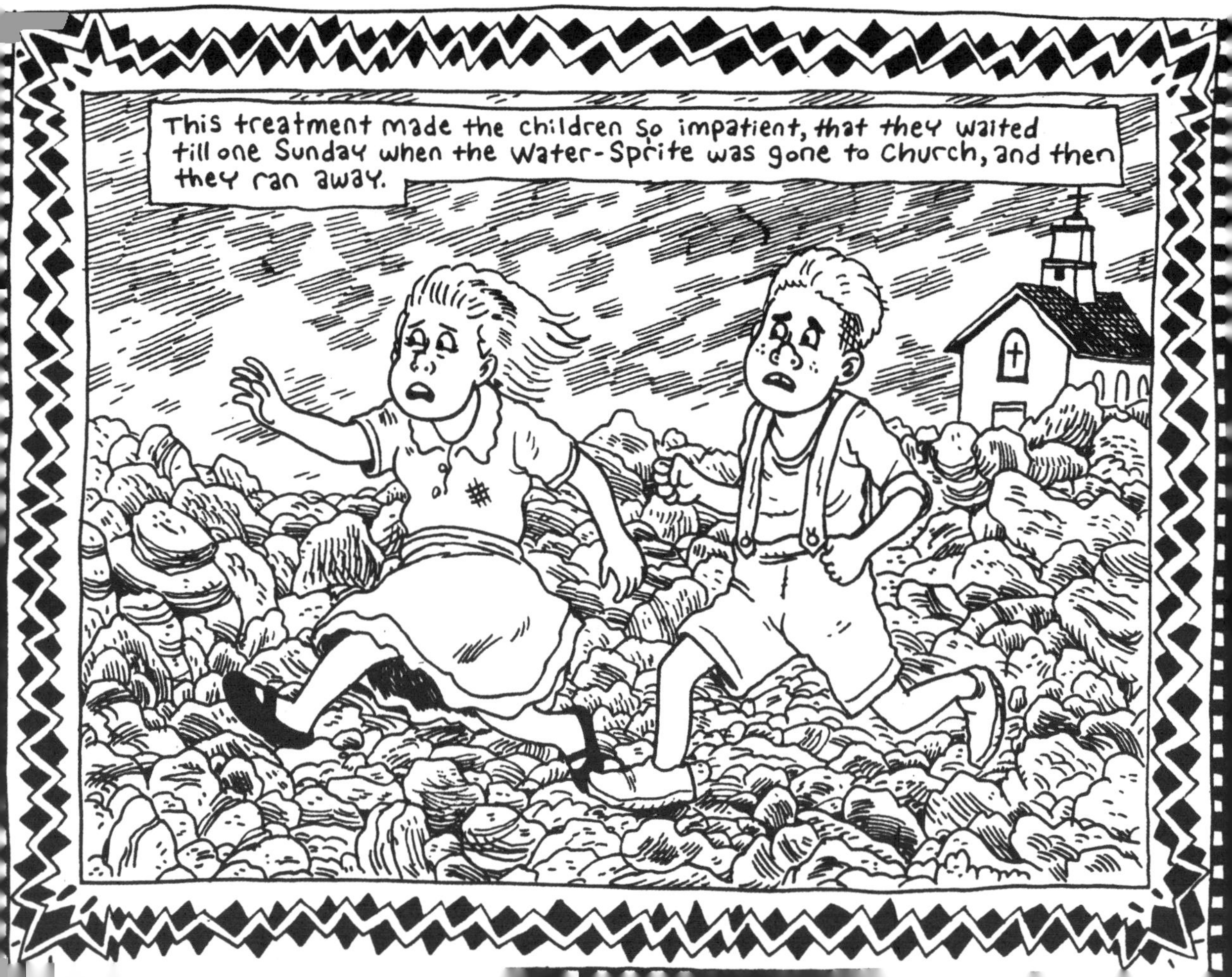
This treatment made the children so impatient, that they waited till one Sunday when the Water-Sprite was gone to church, and then they ran away.

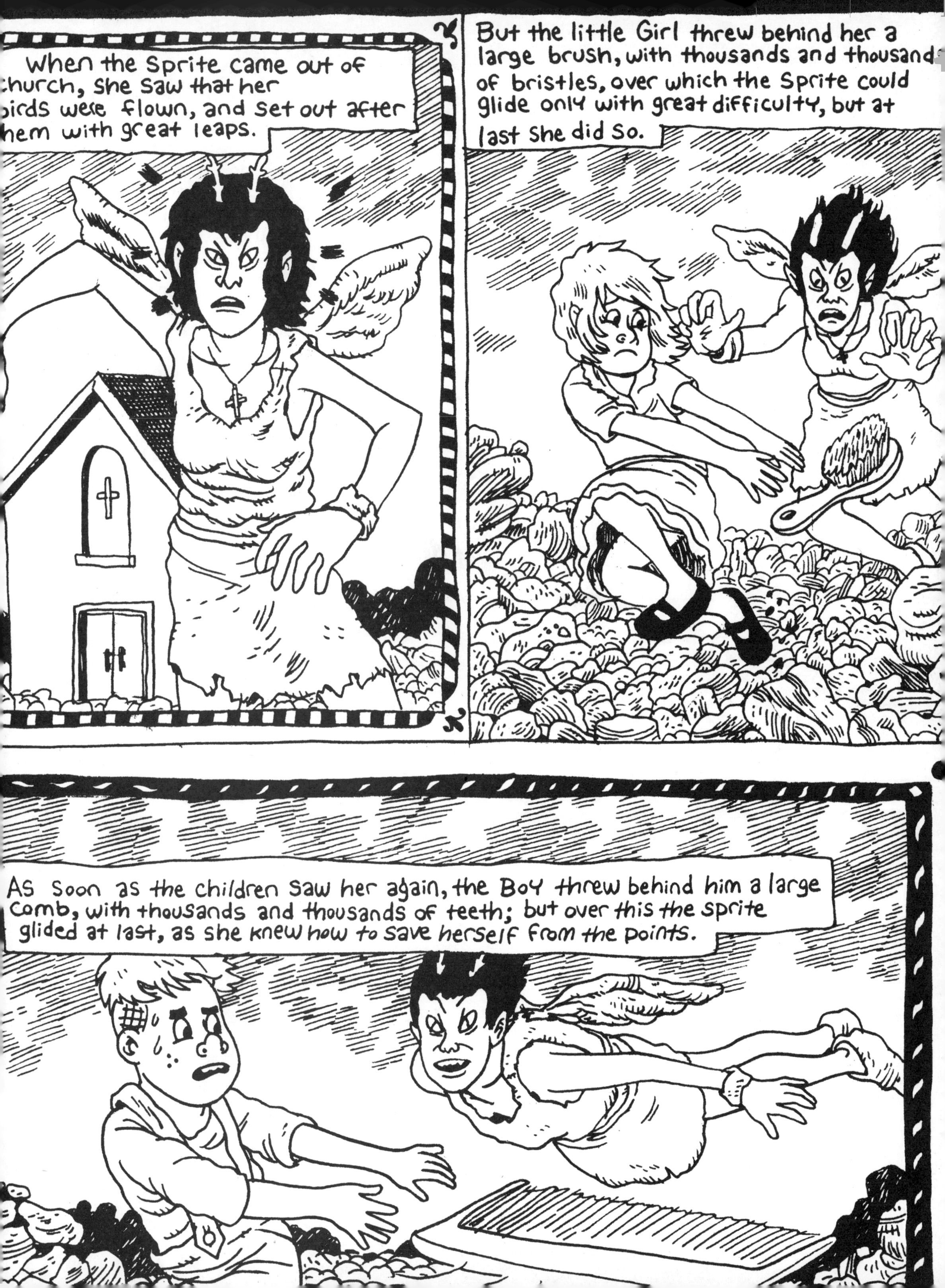
When the Sprite came out of church, she saw that her birds were flown, and set out after them with great leaps.
But the little Girl threw behind her a large brush, with thousands and thousands of bristles, over which the Sprite could glide only with great difficulty, but at last she did so.
As soon as the children saw her again, the Boy threw behind him a large comb, with thousands and thousands of teeth; but over this the sprite glided at last, as she knew how to save herself from the points.

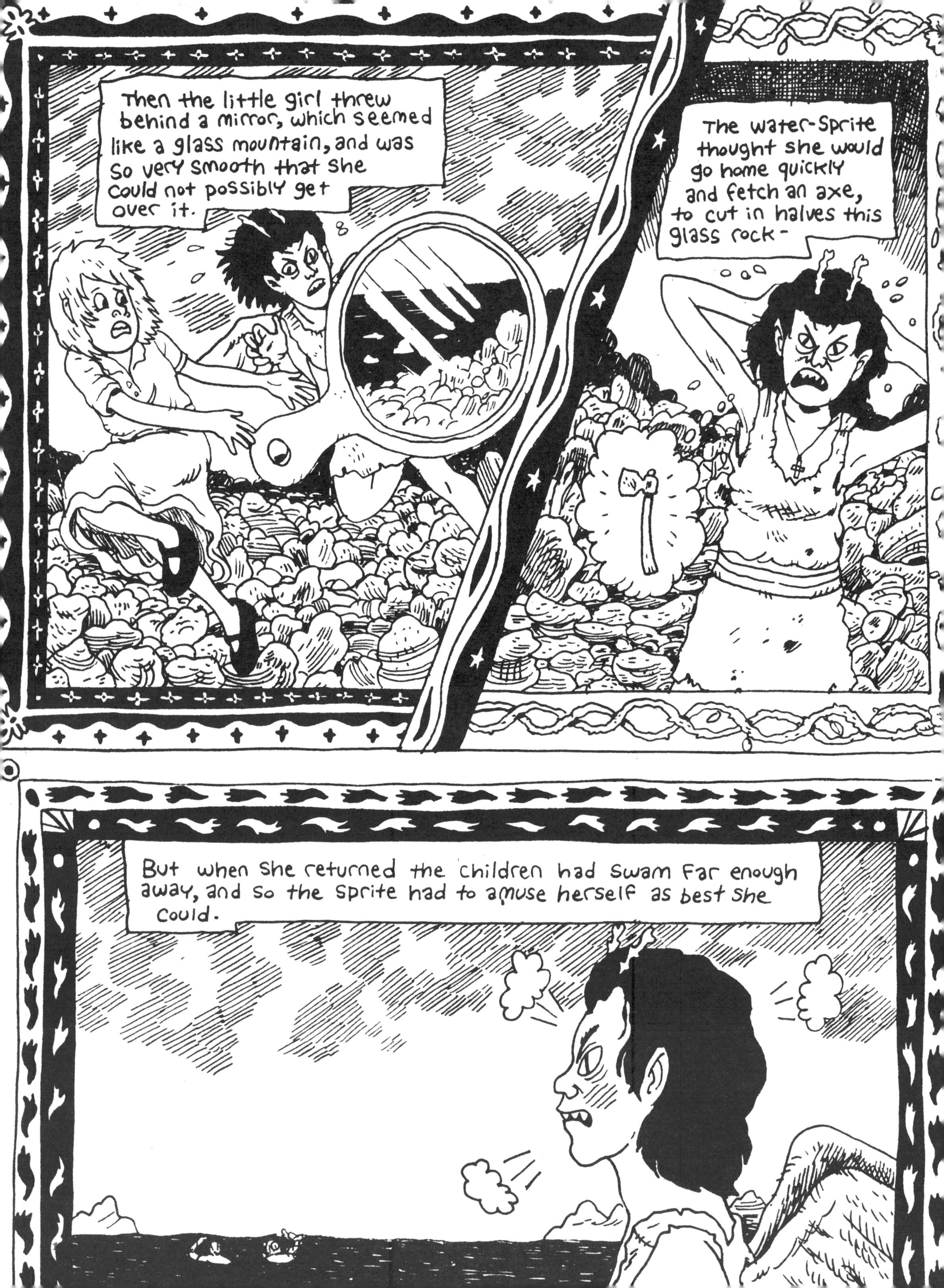

Then the little girl threw behind a mirror, which seemed like a glass mountain, and was so very smooth that she could not possibly get over it.
The water-sprite thought she would go home quickly and fetch an axe, to cut in halves this glass rock -
But when she returned the children had swam far enough away, and so the sprite had to amuse herself as best she could.

# The Nutcracker and the Mouse King

## E. T. A. Hoffmann

ILLUSTRATIONS BY **Sanya Glisic**

**PRETTY MUCH ANY NORTH AMERICAN CITY WITH A** ballet troupe is home to a performance of *The Nutcracker* in November/December every year. It's often the financial lifeblood of dance companies and is widely considered to be the most-performed ballet in the world. It's a yearly ritual for attendees and dancers alike, and is often the only dance performance many people will ever attend. The score for the 1892 ballet was written by Tchaikovsky, with the action based on Alexander Dumas's 1844 short story, which was actually—stay with me here—a simplified reworking of an 1816 novella by E. T. A. Hoffmann, a German Romantic writer and composer.

Sanya Glisic, an artist and printmaker from Chicago, works with silkscreening, woodblock printing, and tradi-tional illustration. Her stunning and terrifying images for *The Tibetan Book of the Dead* and the classic piece of scare-lit for children *Der Struwwelpeter* can be seen in the first two volumes of *The Graphic Canon*. For the current volume, Sanya says she chose to illustrate the original Hoffmann story because it's "much darker and weirder than the later, more well-known version by Dumas."

In these India-ink drawings, which were colored digitally, we see the dastardly Mouse King, which, like something out of the Book of Revelation, has seven heads; the Nutcracker himself, who comes to life to save little Marie and her fam-ily; the epic battle between the dolls and the mice; and the beautiful, whimsical Doll Kingdom (with the capital on the last page), where Marie is taken for a visit by the Nutcracker.

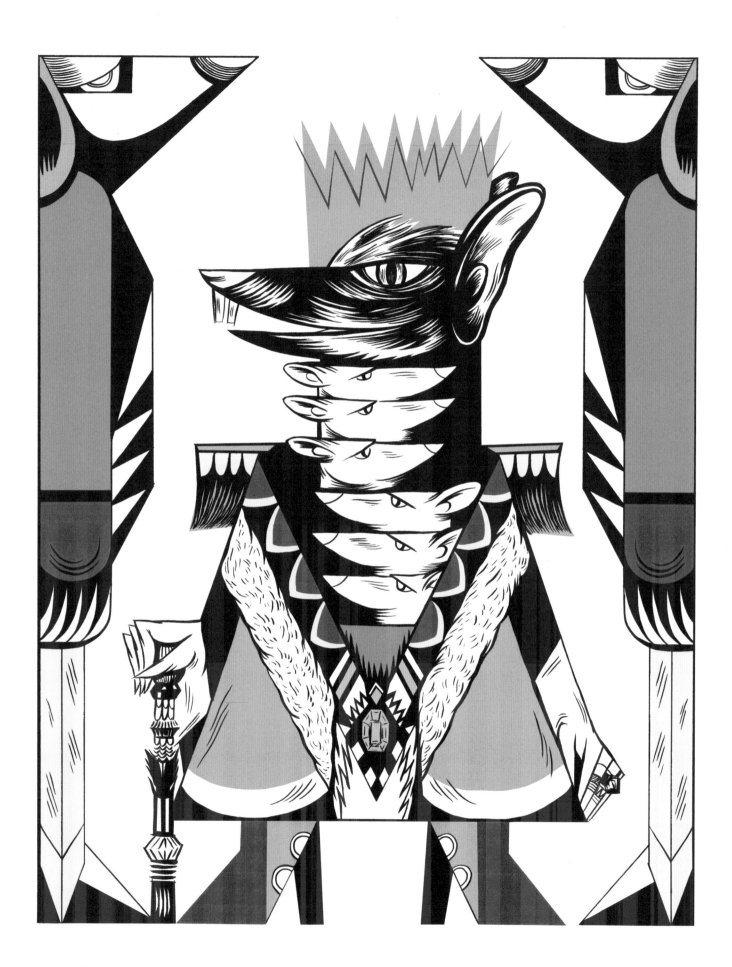

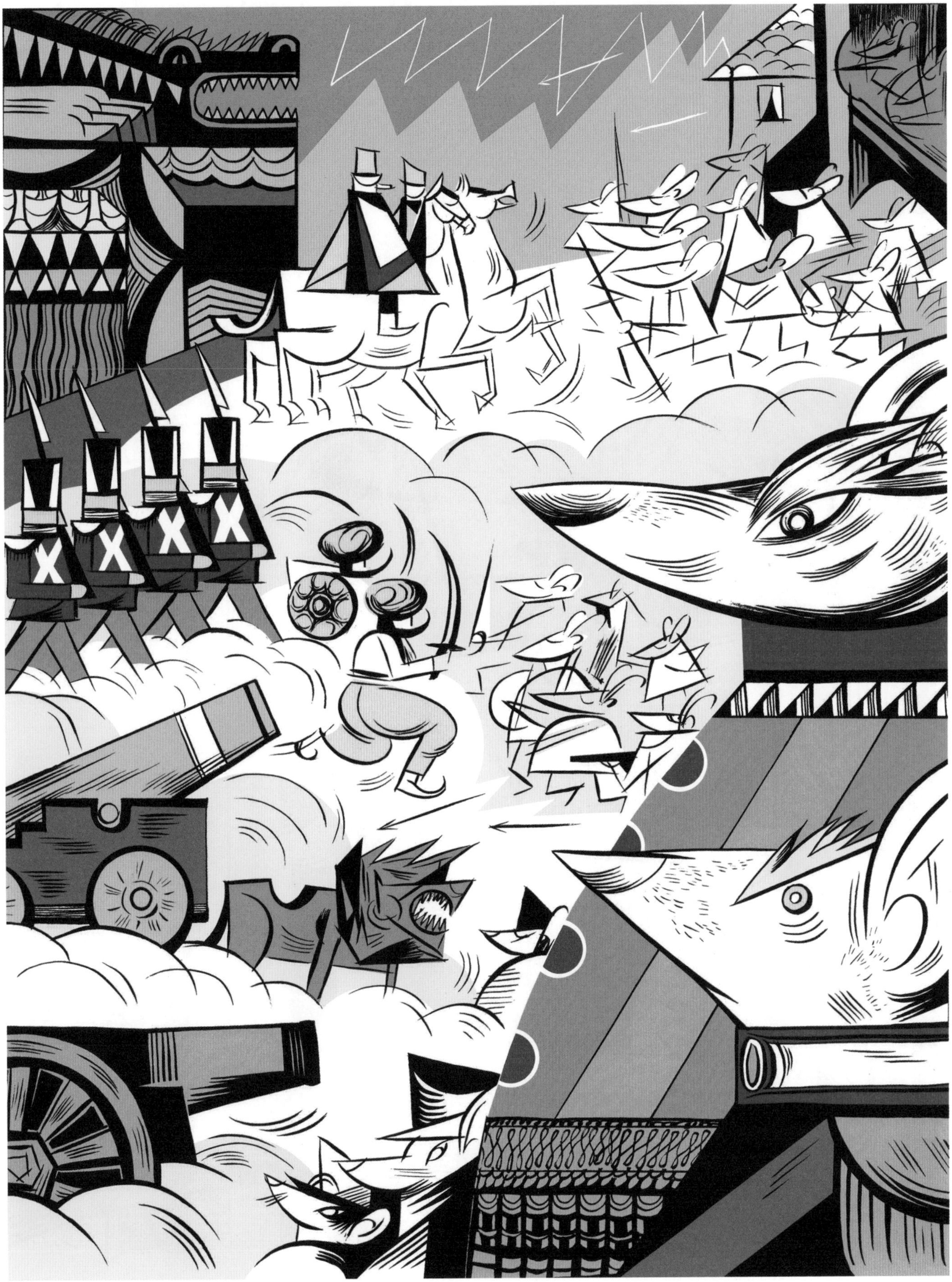

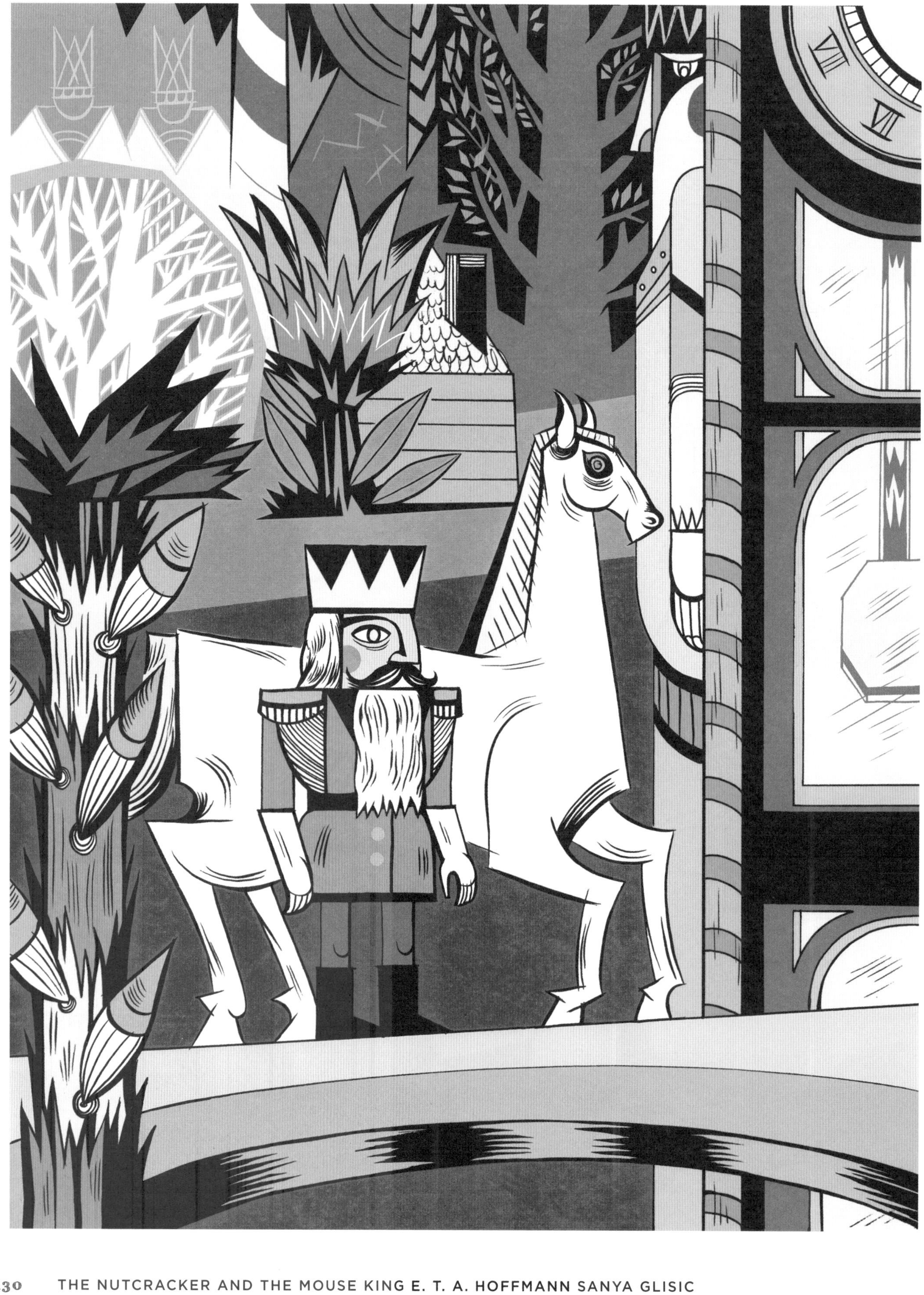

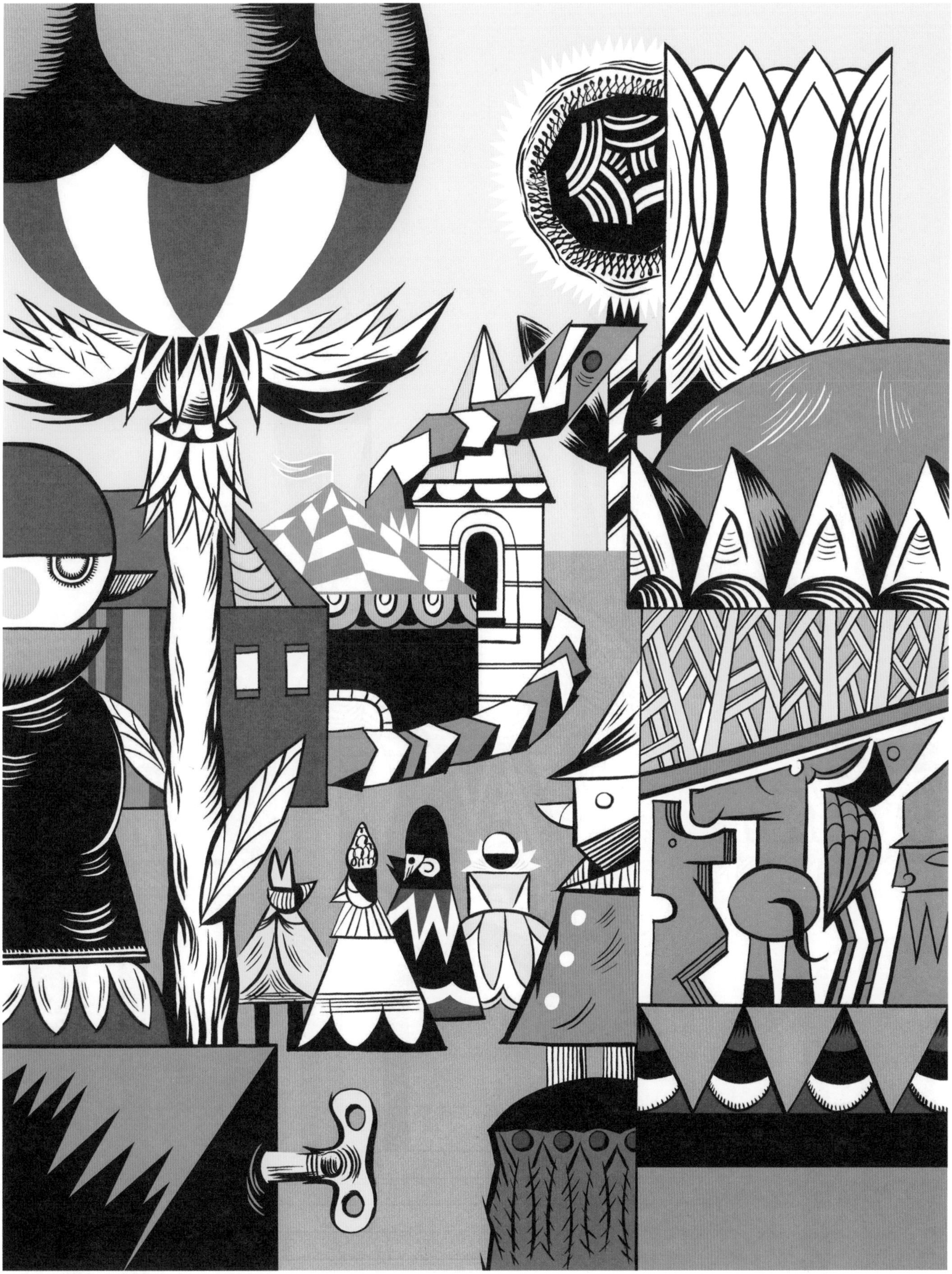

THE NUTCRACKER AND THE MOUSE KING E. T. A. HOFFMANN SANYA GLISIC

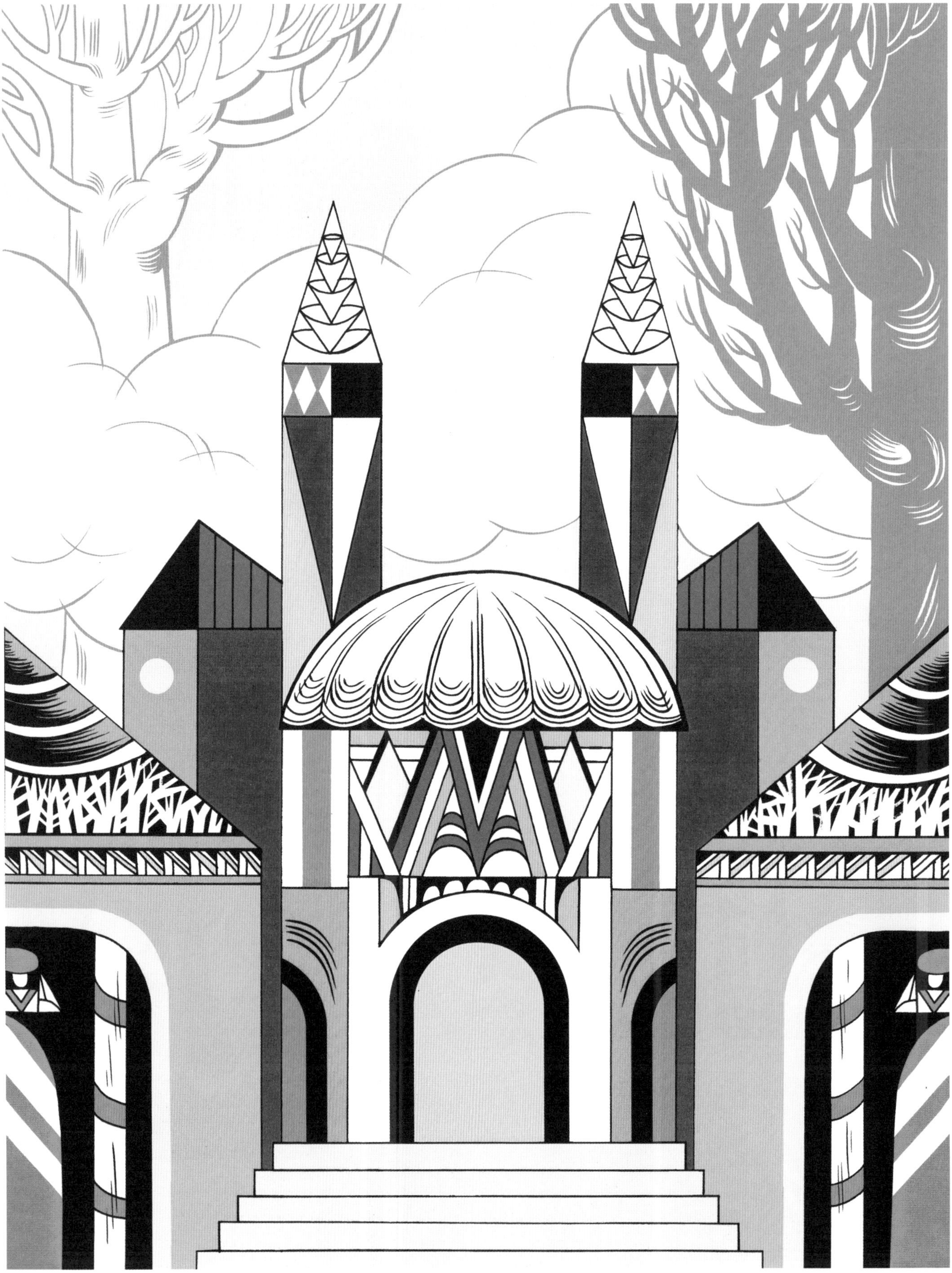

# Hans Christian Andersen

ART/ADAPTATION BY **Dame Darcy**

**FROM 1835 TO 1872, HANS CHRISTIAN ANDERSEN** wrote around 170 "fantastic" or "wonderful" stories for children. He also wrote plays, novels, and poems, but it is these "fairy tales"—including "The Emperor's New Clothes," "The Little Match Girl," and "Thumbelina"—that earned him international fame and literary immortality. We pretty much think of him as a kid-lit author, but in his native Denmark he's considered a Great Writer, and indeed the reigning literature critic Harold Bloom has compared the quality of Andersen's writing to Tolstoy's.

One of Andersen's earliest children's stories, "The Little Mermaid" was made into a hugely successful animated film in 1989 by Disney, forever giving the wrong impression about the tale. It's actually a dark, violent story, and it most assuredly does not have a "happily ever after" ending. Various live-action versions—which would allegedly stay true to the disturbing tale—have been planned by Hollywood for years. We'll see if one ever comes to fruition.

In the meantime, we have Dame Darcy, who was delighted to give us a true adaptation of the little mermaid's torturous, fruitless, fatal quest for romantic love. Mermaids have made frequent appearances in the legendary Dame's work for more than two decades. We agreed that it was high time that she put her unmistakable stamp on the most famous mermaid tale of them all. Darcy's dark sensibilities couldn't be more perfectly matched to Andersen's macabre tale.

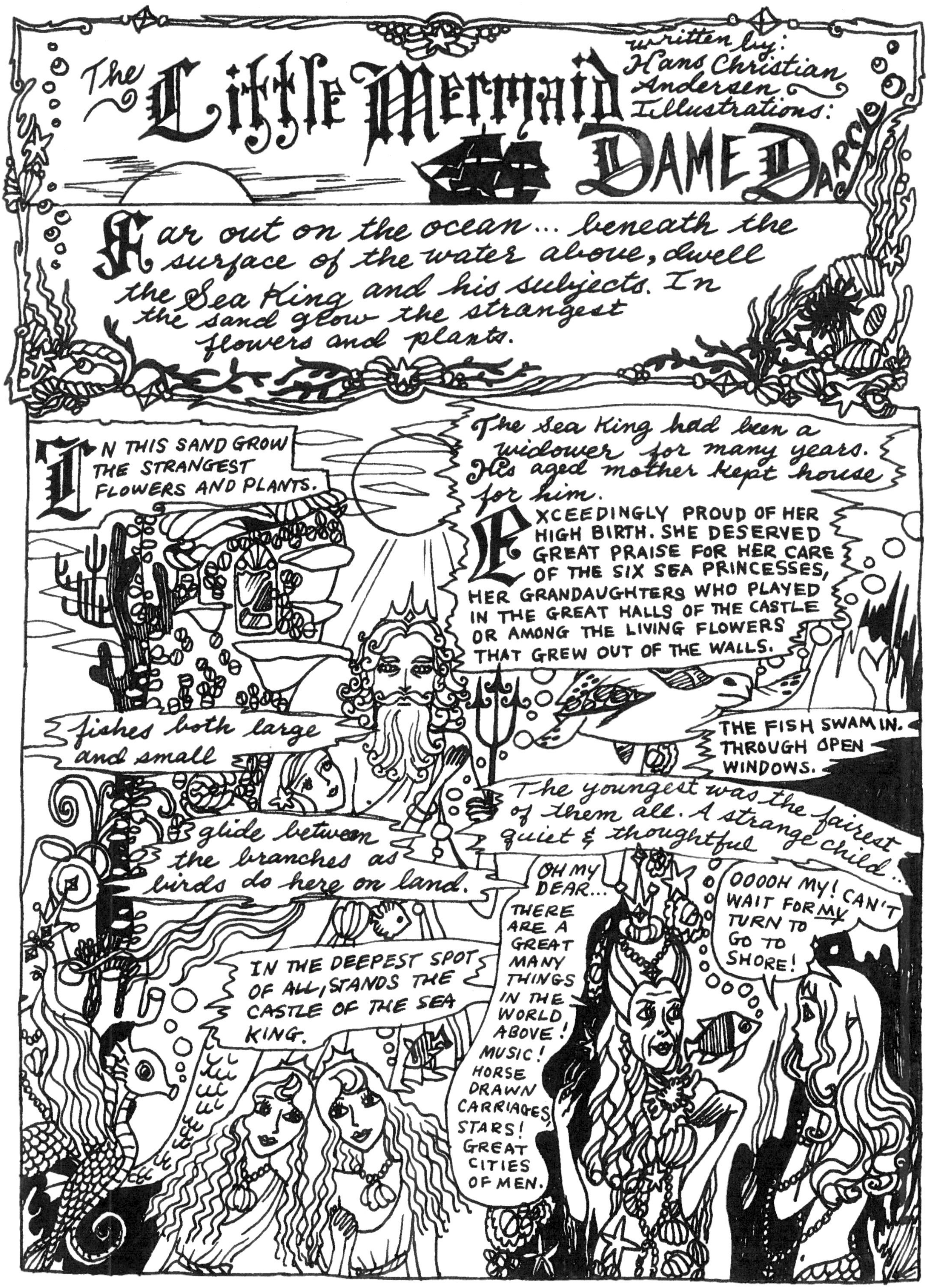
The Little Mermaid
written by: Hans Christian Andersen
Illustrations: Dame Darcy
Far out on the ocean... beneath the surface of the water above, dwell the Sea King and his subjects. In the sand glow the strangest flowers and plants.
IN THIS SAND GROW THE STRANGEST FLOWERS AND PLANTS.
The Sea King had been a widower for many years. His aged mother kept house for him.
EXCEEDINGLY PROUD OF HER HIGH BIRTH. SHE DESERVED GREAT PRAISE FOR HER CARE OF THE SIX SEA PRINCESSES, HER GRANDAUGHTERS WHO PLAYED IN THE GREAT HALLS OF THE CASTLE OR AMONG THE LIVING FLOWERS THAT GREW OUT OF THE WALLS.
fishes both large and small
THE FISH SWAM IN. THROUGH OPEN WINDOWS.
glide between the branches as birds do here on land.
The youngest was the fairest of them all. A strange child quiet & thoughtful...
IN THE DEEPEST SPOT OF ALL, STANDS THE CASTLE OF THE SEA KING.
OH MY DEAR... THERE ARE A GREAT MANY THINGS IN THE WORLD ABOVE! MUSIC! HORSE DRAWN CARRIAGES, STARS! GREAT CITIES OF MEN.
OOOOH MY! CAN'T WAIT FOR MY TURN TO GO TO SHORE!

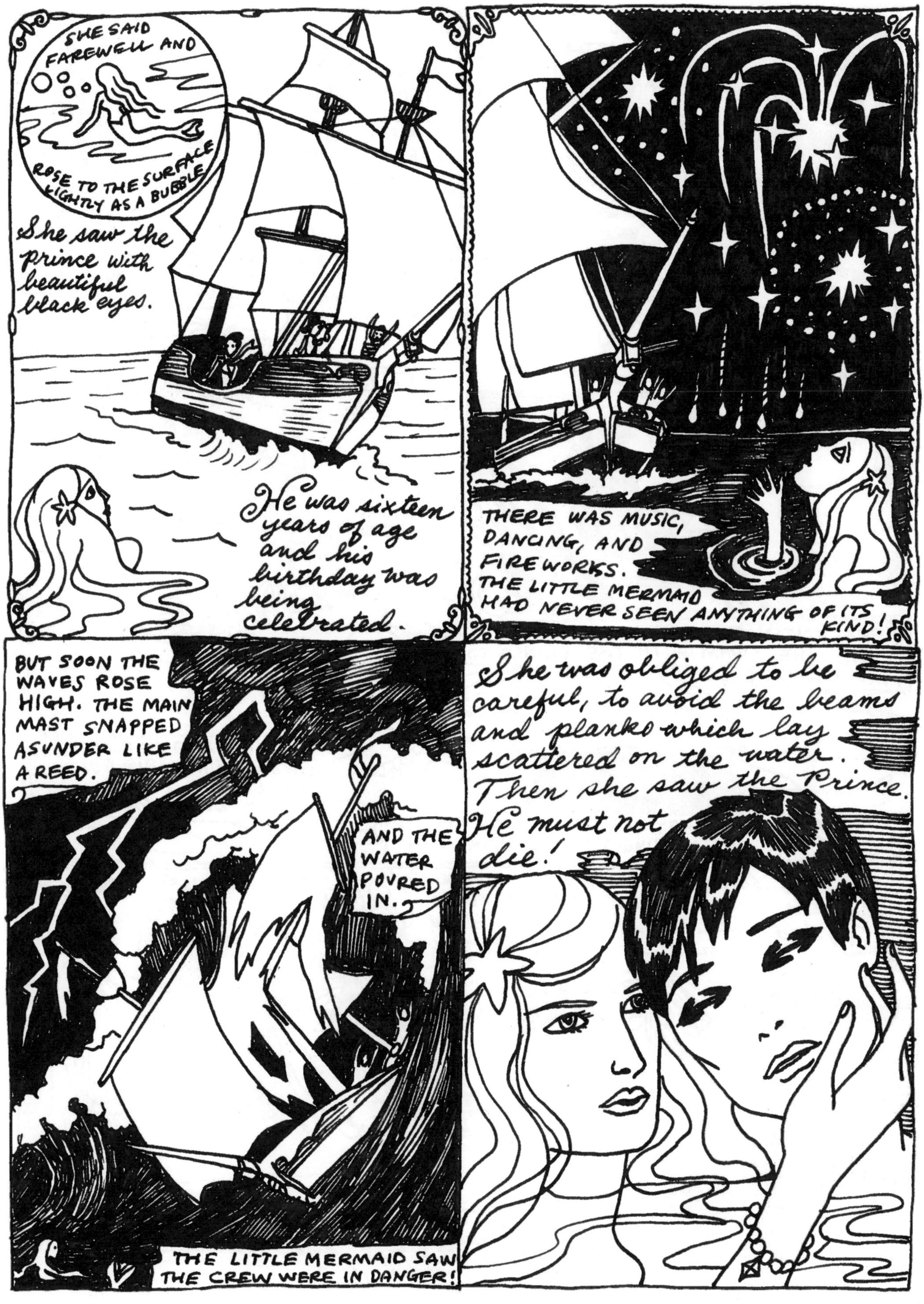
SHE SAID FAREWELL AND
ROSE TO THE SURFACE LIGHTLY AS A BUBBLE
She saw the prince with beautiful black eyes.
He was sixteen years of age and his birthday was being celebrated.
THERE WAS MUSIC, DANCING, AND FIREWORKS. THE LITTLE MERMAID HAD NEVER SEEN ANYTHING OF ITS KIND!
BUT SOON THE WAVES ROSE HIGH. THE MAIN MAST SNAPPED ASUNDER LIKE A REED.
AND THE WATER POURED IN.
THE LITTLE MERMAID SAW THE CREW WERE IN DANGER!
She was obliged to be careful, to avoid the beams and planks which lay scattered on the water. Then she saw the Prince. He must not die!

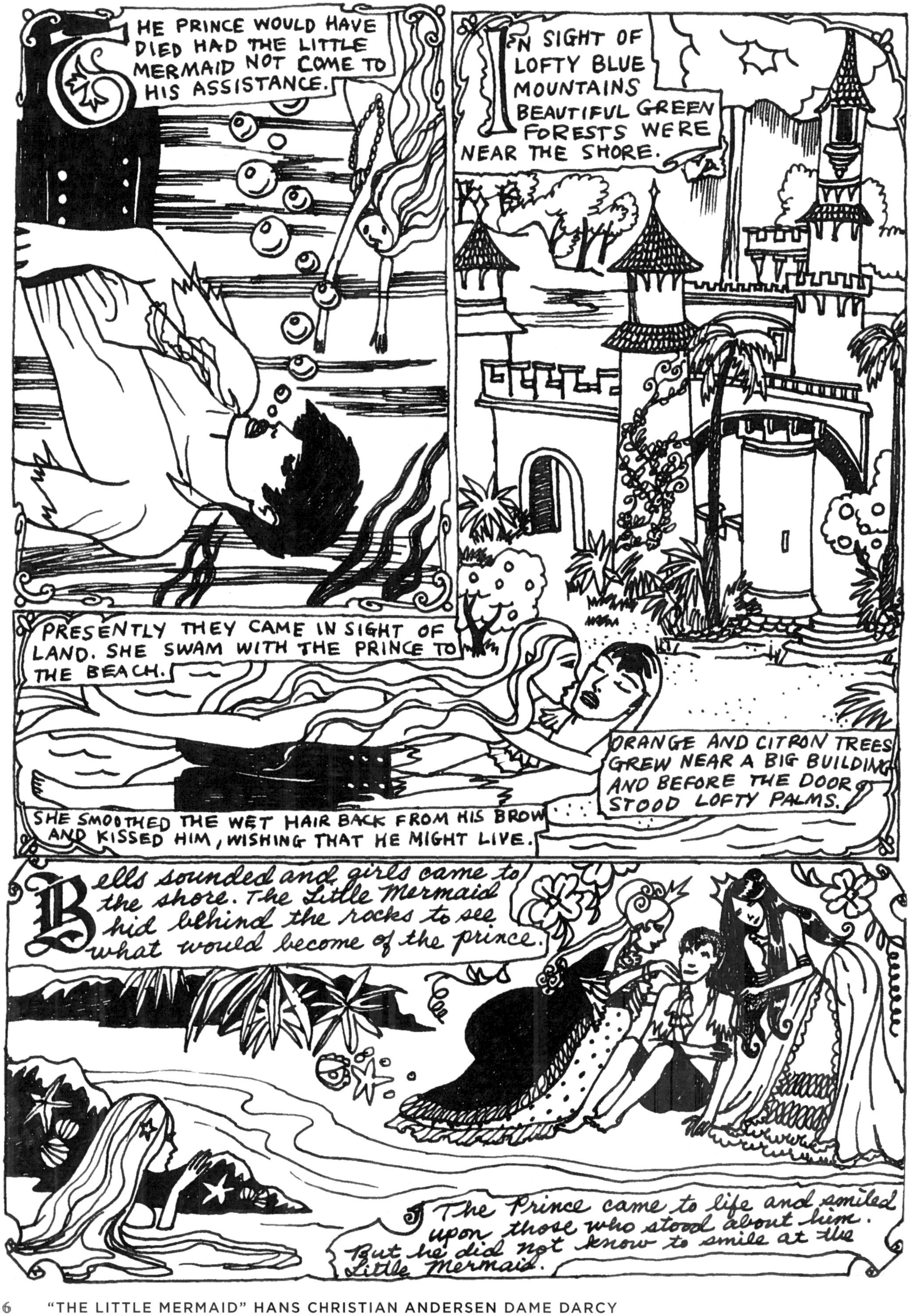
THE PRINCE WOULD HAVE DIED HAD THE LITTLE MERMAID NOT COME TO HIS ASSISTANCE.
IN SIGHT OF LOFTY BLUE MOUNTAINS BEAUTIFUL GREEN FORESTS WERE NEAR THE SHORE.
PRESENTLY THEY CAME IN SIGHT OF LAND. SHE SWAM WITH THE PRINCE TO THE BEACH.
ORANGE AND CITRON TREES GREW NEAR A BIG BUILDING AND BEFORE THE DOOR STOOD LOFTY PALMS.
SHE SMOOTHED THE WET HAIR BACK FROM HIS BROW AND KISSED HIM, WISHING THAT HE MIGHT LIVE.
Bells sounded and girls came to the shore. The Little Mermaid hid behind the rocks to see what would become of the prince.
The Prince came to life and smiled upon those who stood about him. But he did not know to smile at the Little Mermaid.

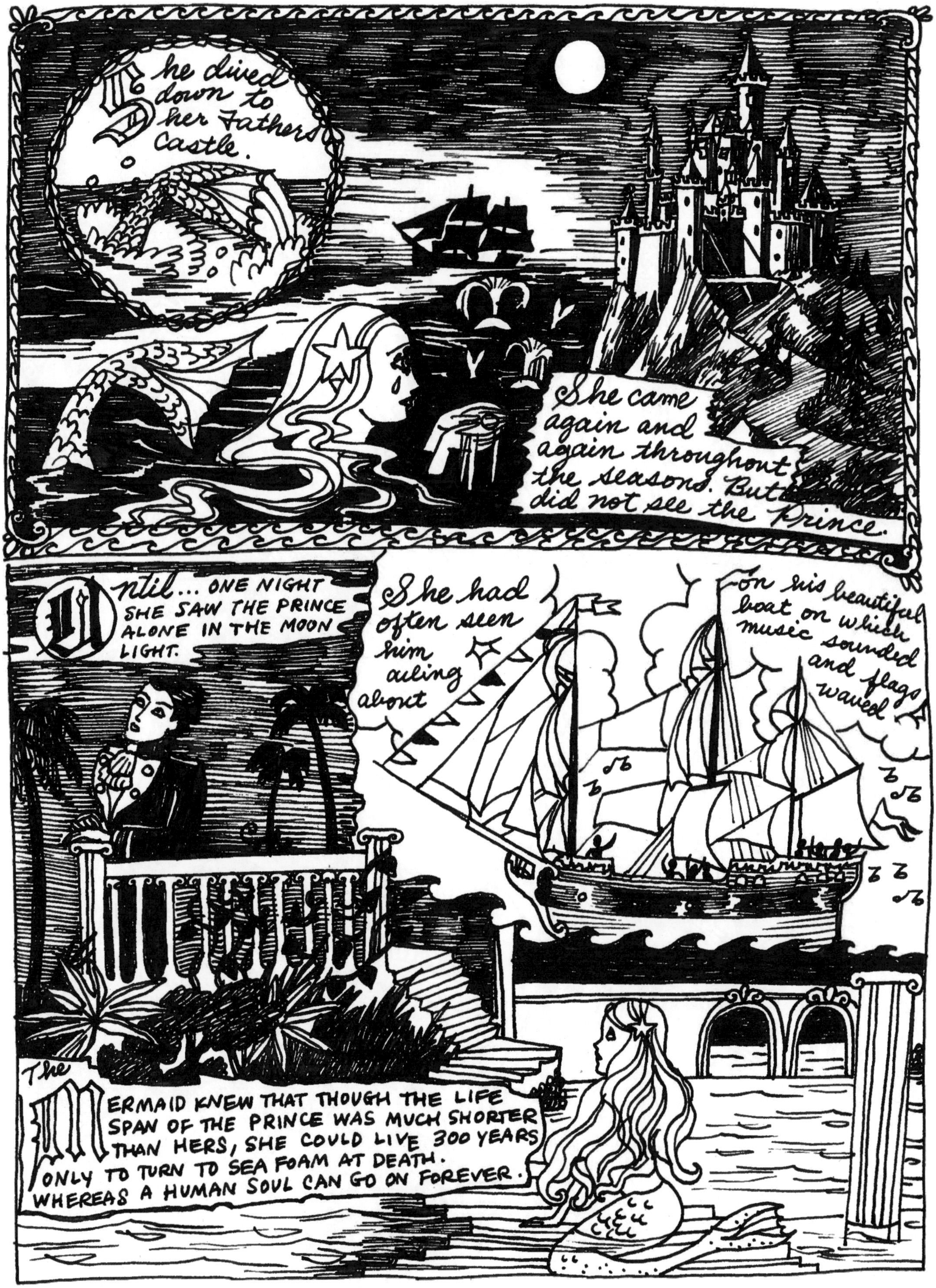
She dived down to her Fathers Castle.
She came again and again throughout the seasons. But did not see the Prince.
Until... ONE NIGHT SHE SAW THE PRINCE ALONE IN THE MOON LIGHT.
She had often seen him sailing about
on his beautiful boat on which music sounded and flags waved
The Mermaid KNEW THAT THOUGH THE LIFE SPAN OF THE PRINCE WAS MUCH SHORTER THAN HERS, SHE COULD LIVE 300 YEARS ONLY TO TURN TO SEA FOAM AT DEATH. WHEREAS A HUMAN SOUL CAN GO ON FOREVER.

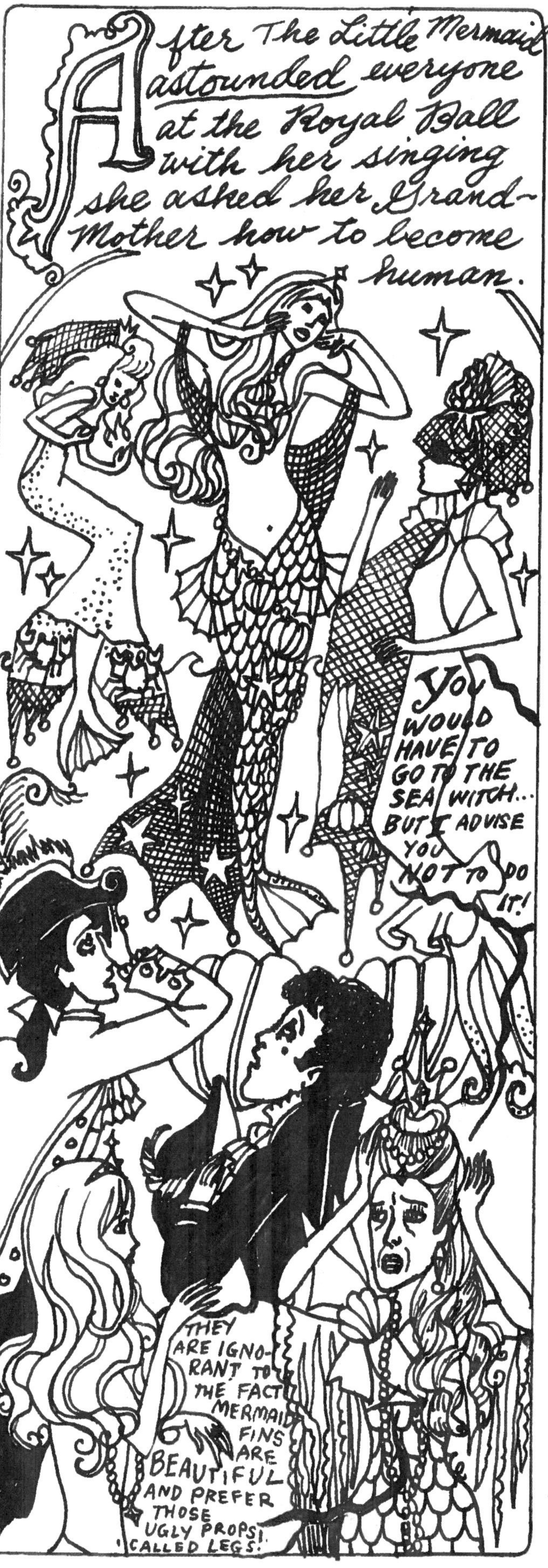
After The Little Mermaid astounded everyone at the Royal Ball with her singing she asked her Grand-Mother how to become human.
YOU WOULD HAVE TO GO TO THE SEA WITCH... BUT I ADVISE YOU NOT TO DO IT!
THEY ARE IGNO-RANT TO THE FACT MERMAID FINS ARE BEAUTIFUL AND PREFER THOSE UGLY PROPS! CALLED LEGS!

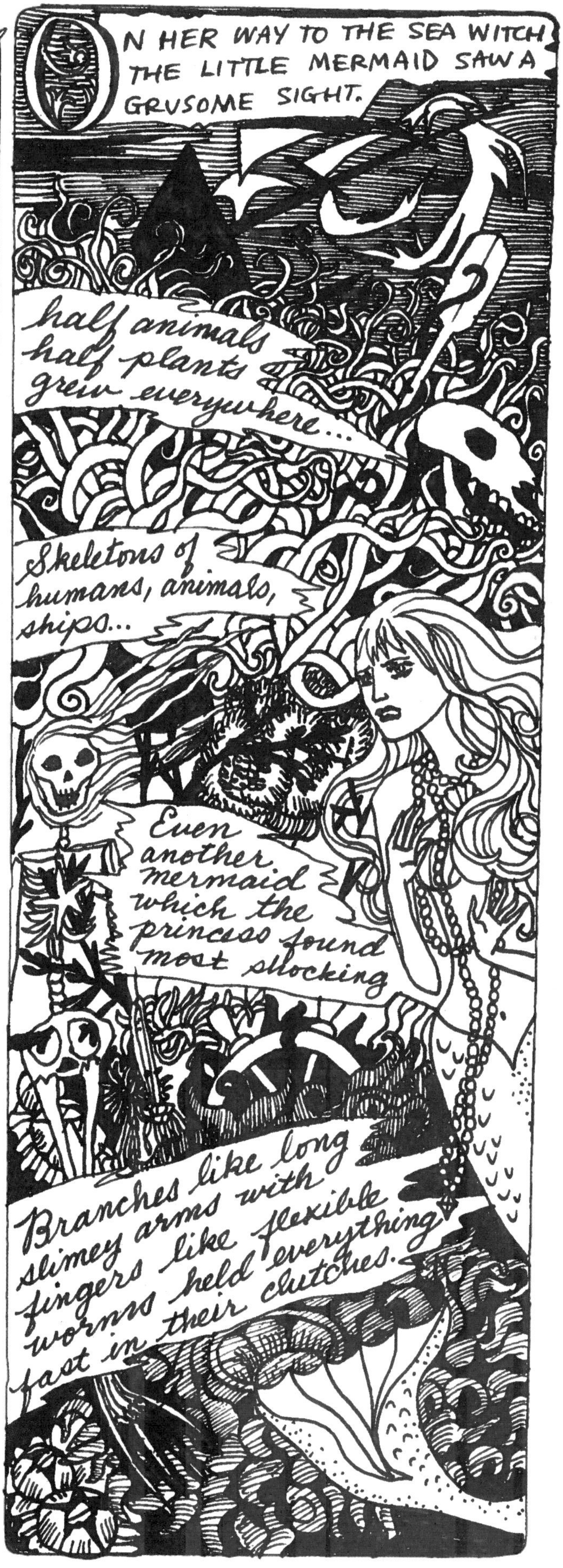
ON HER WAY TO THE SEA WITCH THE LITTLE MERMAID SAW A GRUSOME SIGHT.
half animals half plants grew everywhere...
Skeletons of humans, animals, ships...
Even another mermaid which the princess found most shocking
Branches like long slimey arms with fingers like flexible worms held everything fast in their clutches.

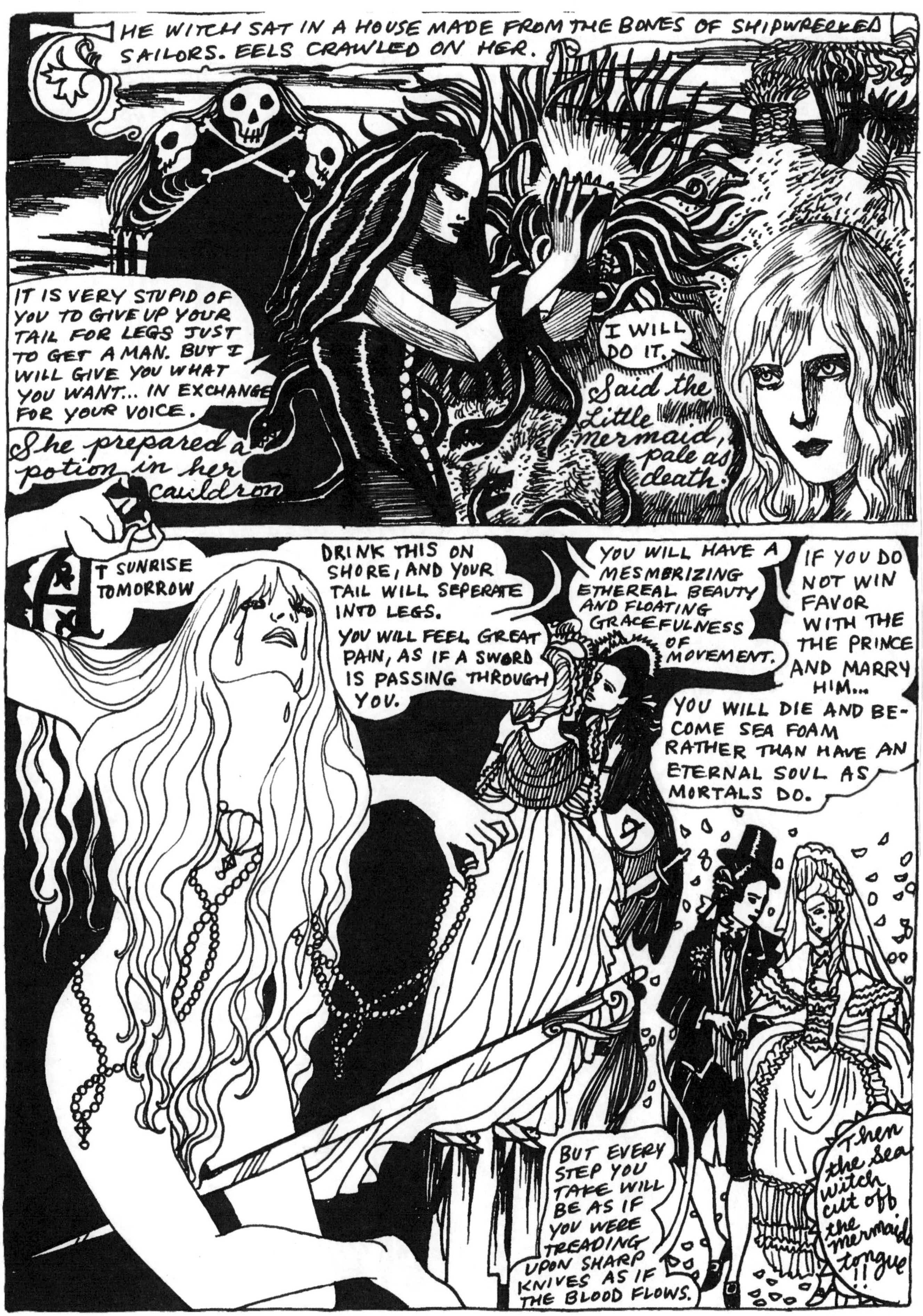
THE WITCH SAT IN A HOUSE MADE FROM THE BONES OF SHIPWRECKED SAILORS. EELS CRAWLED ON HER.
IT IS VERY STUPID OF YOU TO GIVE UP YOUR TAIL FOR LEGS JUST TO GET A MAN. BUT I WILL GIVE YOU WHAT YOU WANT... IN EXCHANGE FOR YOUR VOICE.
She prepared a potion in her cauldron
I WILL DO IT.
Said the Little mermaid, pale as death.
AT SUNRISE TOMORROW
DRINK THIS ON SHORE, AND YOUR TAIL WILL SEPERATE INTO LEGS.
YOU WILL FEEL GREAT PAIN, AS IF A SWORD IS PASSING THROUGH YOU.
YOU WILL HAVE A MESMERIZING ETHEREAL BEAUTY AND FLOATING GRACEFULNESS OF MOVEMENT.
IF YOU DO NOT WIN FAVOR WITH THE THE PRINCE AND MARRY HIM...
YOU WILL DIE AND BECOME SEA FOAM RATHER THAN HAVE AN ETERNAL SOUL AS MORTALS DO.
BUT EVERY STEP YOU TAKE WILL BE AS IF YOU WERE TREADING UPON SHARP KNIVES AS IF THE BLOOD FLOWS.
Then the Sea witch cut off the mermaid tongue!!

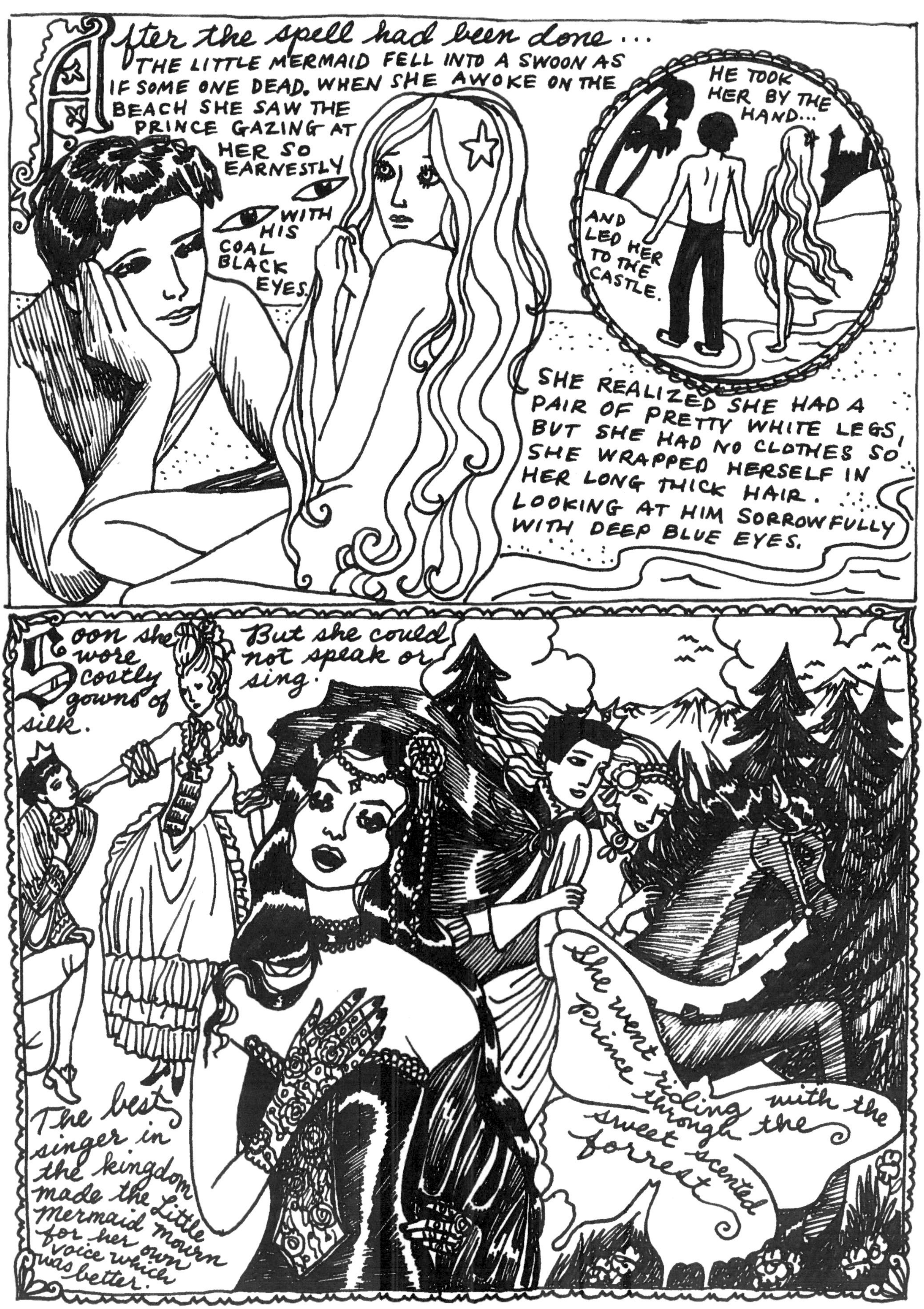
After the spell had been done...
THE LITTLE MERMAID FELL INTO A SWOON AS IF SOME ONE DEAD. WHEN SHE AWOKE ON THE BEACH SHE SAW THE PRINCE GAZING AT HER SO EARNESTLY
WITH HIS COAL BLACK EYES.
HE TOOK HER BY THE HAND...
AND LED HER TO THE CASTLE.
SHE REALIZED SHE HAD A PAIR OF PRETTY WHITE LEGS, BUT SHE HAD NO CLOTHES SO SHE WRAPPED HERSELF IN HER LONG THICK HAIR. LOOKING AT HIM SORROWFULLY WITH DEEP BLUE EYES.
Soon she wore costly gowns of silk.
But she could not speak or sing.
The best singer in the kingdom made the Little Mermaid mourn for her own voice which was better.
She went riding with the Prince through the sweet-scented forrest

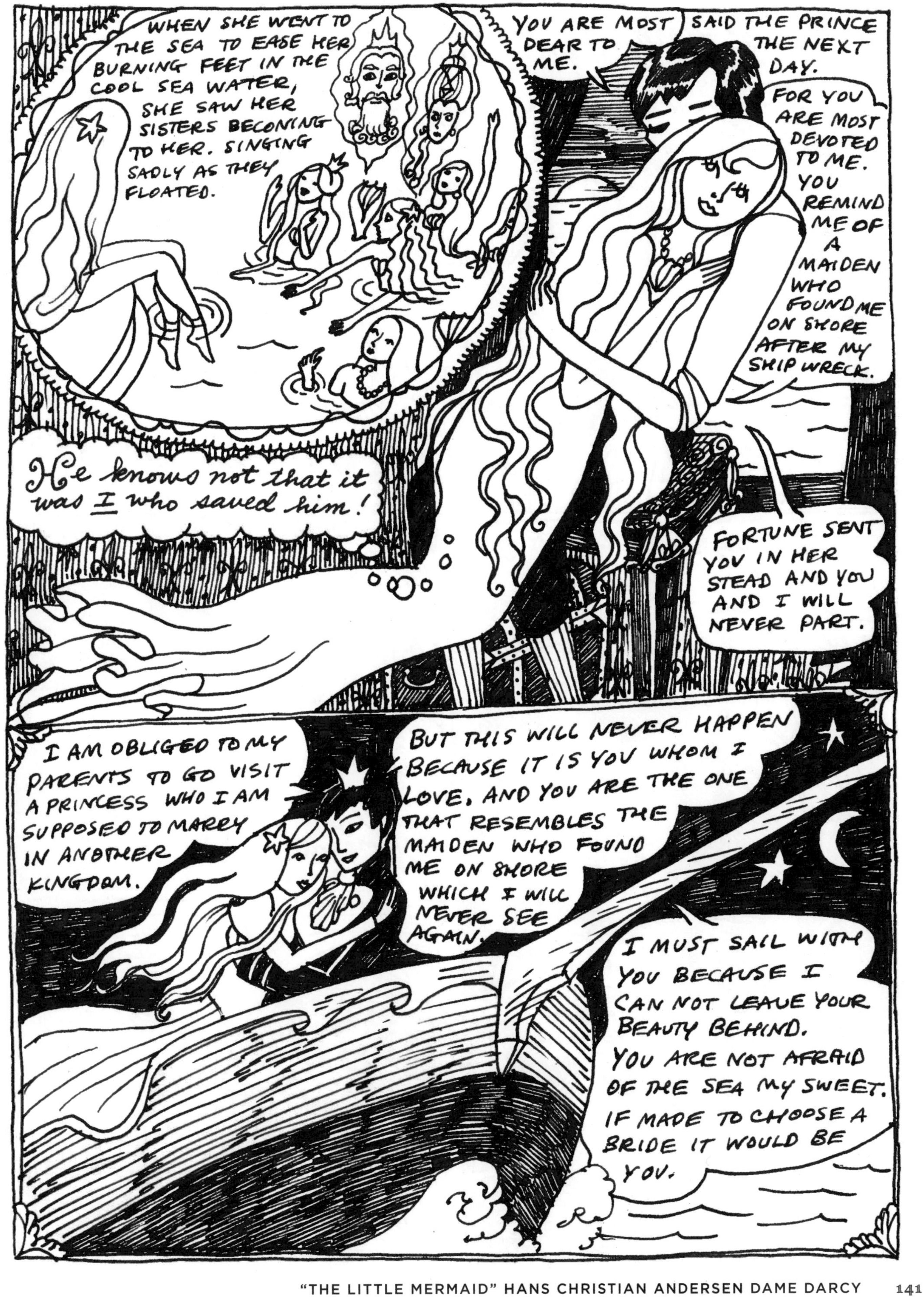
WHEN SHE WENT TO THE SEA TO EASE HER BURNING FEET IN THE COOL SEA WATER, SHE SAW HER SISTERS BECONING TO HER. SINGING SADLY AS THEY FLOATED.
YOU ARE MOST DEAR TO ME.
SAID THE PRINCE THE NEXT DAY.
FOR YOU ARE MOST DEVOTED TO ME. YOU REMIND ME OF A MAIDEN WHO FOUND ME ON SHORE AFTER MY SHIP WRECK.
He knows not that it was I who saved him!
FORTUNE SENT YOU IN HER STEAD AND YOU AND I WILL NEVER PART.
I AM OBLIGED TO MY PARENTS TO GO VISIT A PRINCESS WHO I AM SUPPOSED TO MARRY IN ANOTHER KINGDOM.
BUT THIS WILL NEVER HAPPEN BECAUSE IT IS YOU WHOM I LOVE, AND YOU ARE THE ONE THAT RESEMBLES THE MAIDEN WHO FOUND ME ON SHORE WHICH I WILL NEVER SEE AGAIN.
I MUST SAIL WITH YOU BECAUSE I CAN NOT LEAVE YOUR BEAUTY BEHIND. YOU ARE NOT AFRAID OF THE SEA MY SWEET. IF MADE TO CHOOSE A BRIDE IT WOULD BE YOU.

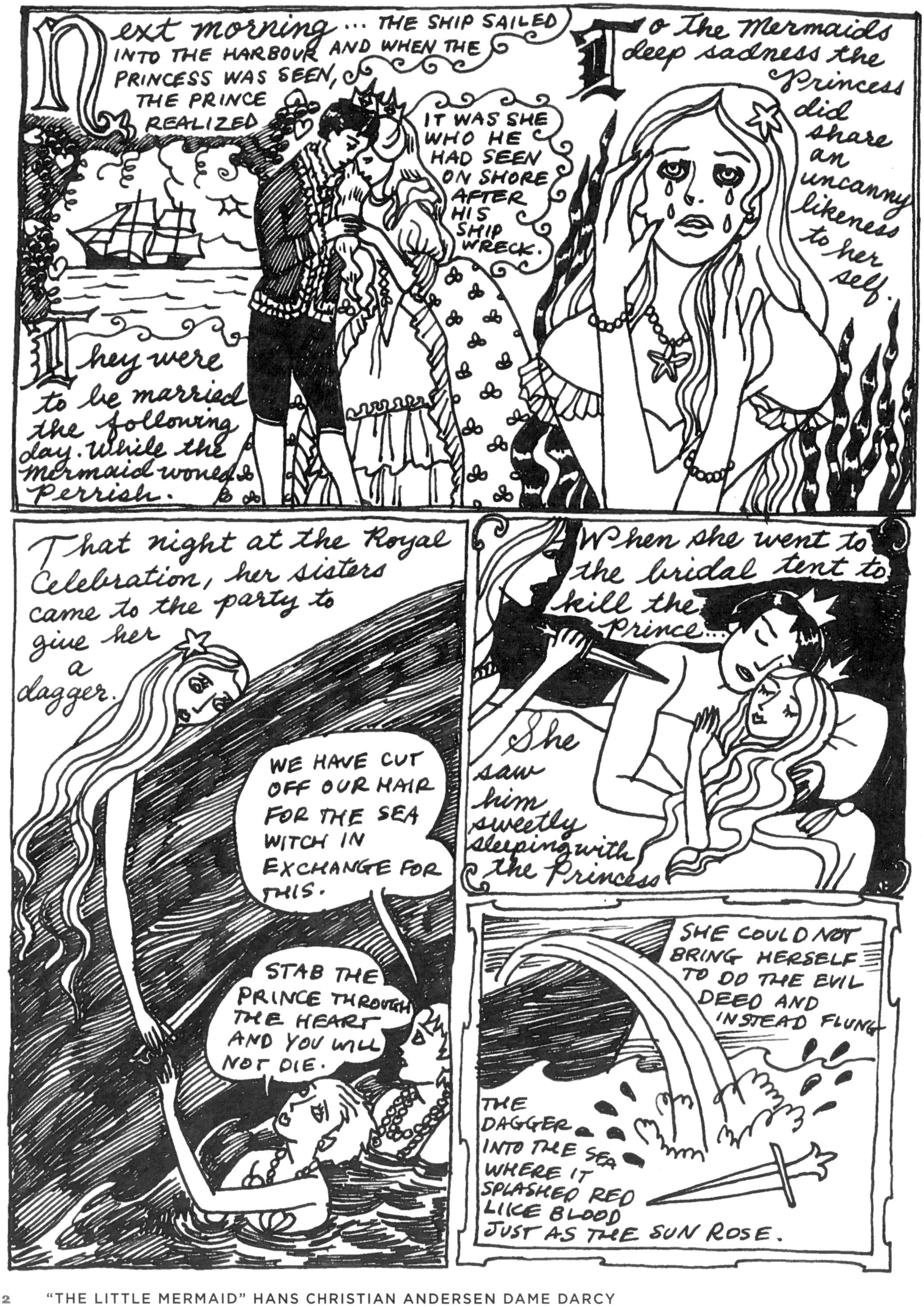
Next morning... THE SHIP SAILED INTO THE HARBOUR AND WHEN THE PRINCESS WAS SEEN, THE PRINCE REALIZED
IT WAS SHE WHO HE HAD SEEN ON SHORE AFTER HIS SHIP WRECK.
They were to be married the following day. While the mermaid woned Perrish.
To the Mermaids deep sadness the Princess did share an uncanny likeness to her self.
That night at the Royal Celebration, her sisters came to the party to give her a dagger.
WE HAVE CUT OFF OUR HAIR FOR THE SEA WITCH IN EXCHANGE FOR THIS.
STAB THE PRINCE THROUGH THE HEART AND YOU WILL NOT DIE.
When she went to the bridal tent to kill the Prince...
She saw him sweetly sleeping with the Princess
SHE COULD NOT BRING HERSELF TO DO THE EVIL DEED AND INSTEAD FLUNG
THE DAGGER INTO THE SEA WHERE IT SPLASHED RED LIKE BLOOD JUST AS THE SUN ROSE.

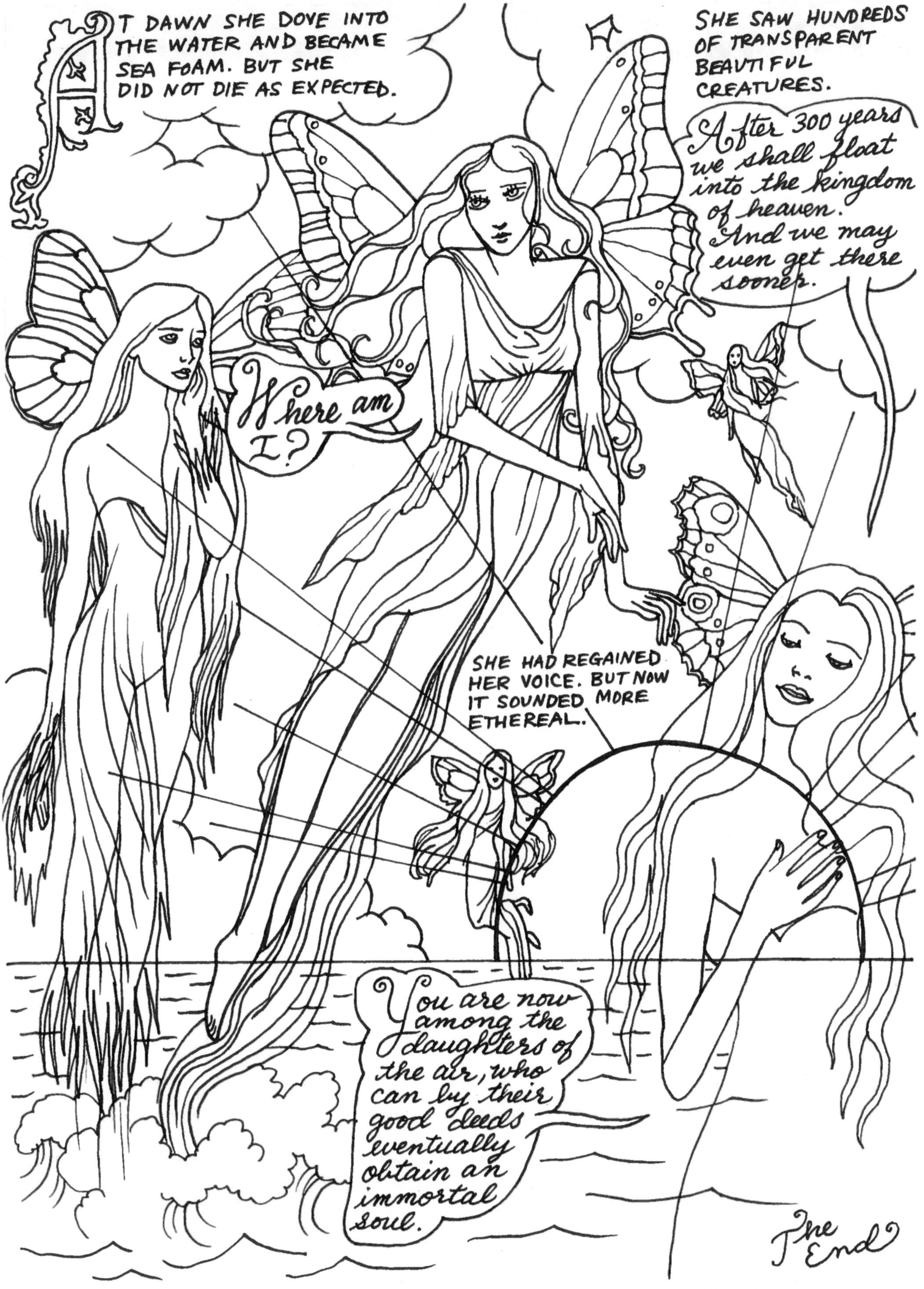
AT DAWN SHE DOVE INTO THE WATER AND BECAME SEA FOAM. BUT SHE DID NOT DIE AS EXPECTED.
SHE SAW HUNDREDS OF TRANSPARENT BEAUTIFUL CREATURES.
After 300 years we shall float into the kingdom of heaven. And we may even get there sooner.
Where am I?
SHE HAD REGAINED HER VOICE. BUT NOW IT SOUNDED MORE ETHEREAL.
You are now among the daughters of the air, who can by their good deeds eventually obtain an immortal soul.
The End

# Hans Christian Andersen

ART/ADAPTATION BY **Isabel Greenberg**

**INCLUDED IN HANS CHRISTIAN ANDERSEN'S FIRST** booklet of stories for children—along with "The Princess and the Pea"—"The Tinderbox" carries on the tradition of violence and abduction in fairy tales. Add a trio of the creepiest dogs this side of hellhounds, and you have one wild and disturbing adventure.

London artist and writer Isabel Greenberg made a splash early; she was twenty-three when she won the annual Graphic Short Story Contest put on by the London *Observer* and the storied publisher Jonathan Cape Ltd. Two years later, Cape published her debut graphic novel, *The Encyclopedia of Early Earth*, to rave reviews. Isabel's visual style, reminiscent of woodblock carving, suits the feel of much of her work, which is based on myths, legends, and folktales from around the world.

# THE TINDERBOX

## BY HANS CHRISTIAN ANDERSON, ADAPTED BY ISABEL GREENBERG

A Soldier came marching down the road. He had a pack on his back and a sword at his side. He had been in the war and was on his way home. Along the road he met a witch.

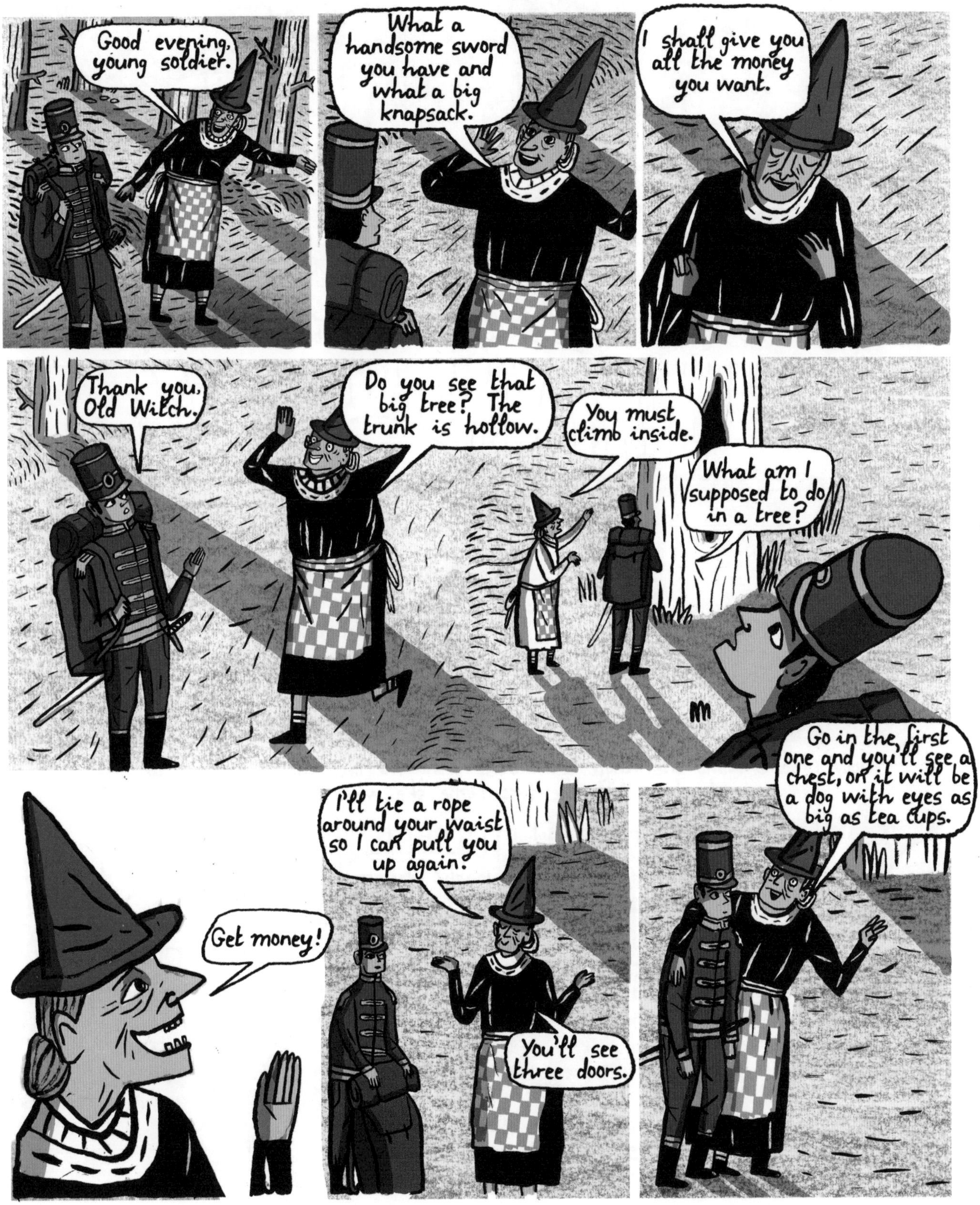
Good evening, young soldier.
What a handsome sword you have and what a big knapsack.
I shall give you all the money you want.
Thank you, Old Witch.
Do you see that big tree? The trunk is hollow.
You must climb inside.
What am I supposed to do in a tree?
Get money!
I'll tie a rope around your waist so I can pull you up again.
You'll see three doors.
Go in the first one and you'll see a chest, on it will be a dog with eyes as big as tea cups.

"Don't let that worry you. You will have my blue checked apron, just put the dog down on top of it, and it won't do you any harm. In the chest you will find copper."

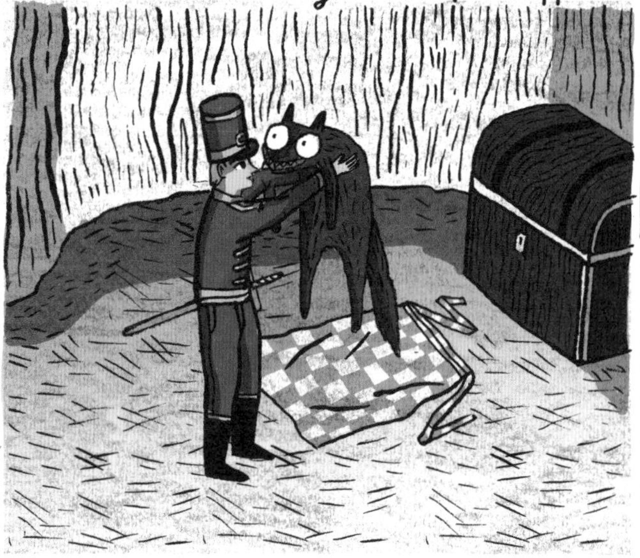

If it's silver you're after, then go into the next room. There you'll find a dog with eyes as big as millstones."

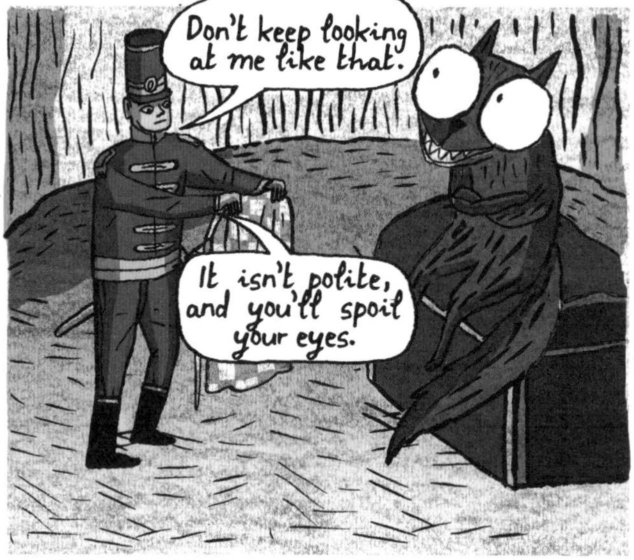
Don't keep looking at me like that.
It isn't polite, and you'll spoil your eyes.

"But if you'd rather have gold you can have that too, its in the third room. Wait til you see that dog, he's got eyes as big as the round tower in Copenhagen."

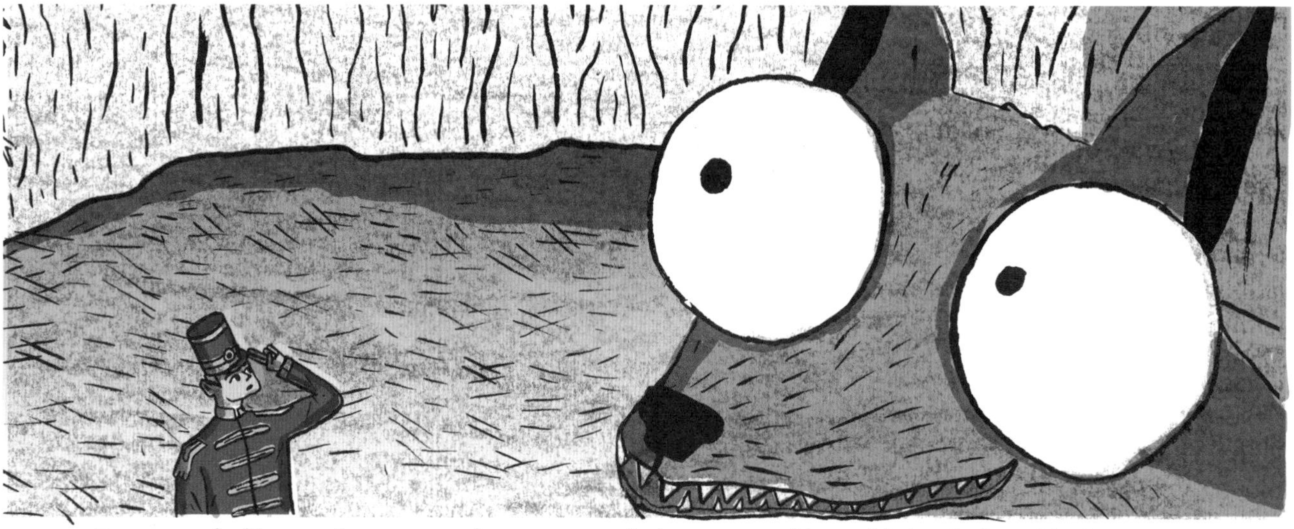

"Now I don't want one single coin. Just bring me the old tinderbox that my grandmother left the last time she was down there."

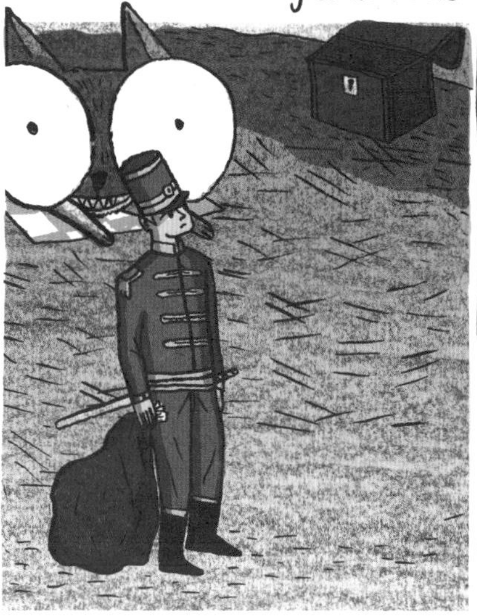

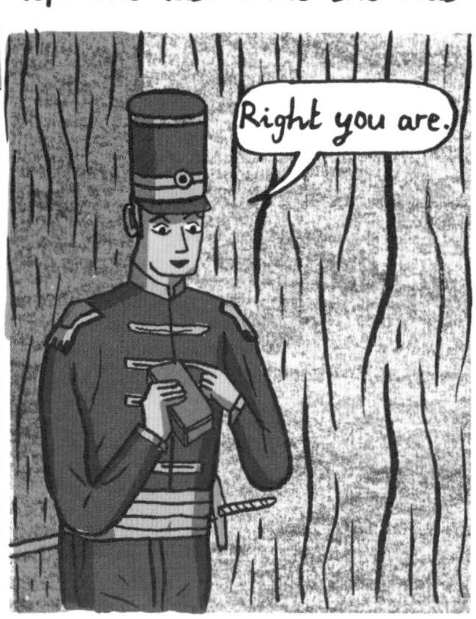
Right you are.

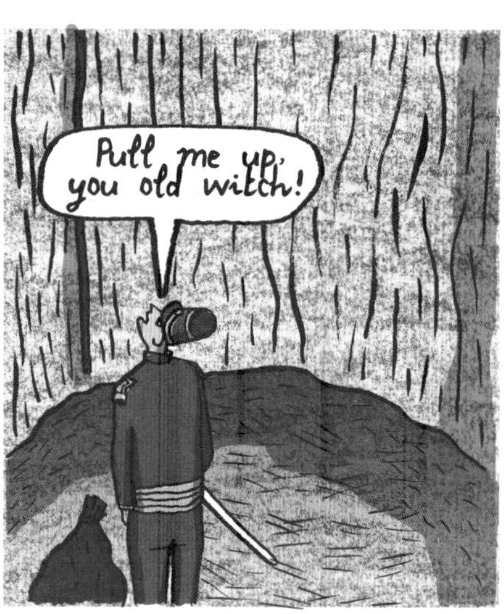
Pull me up, you old witch!

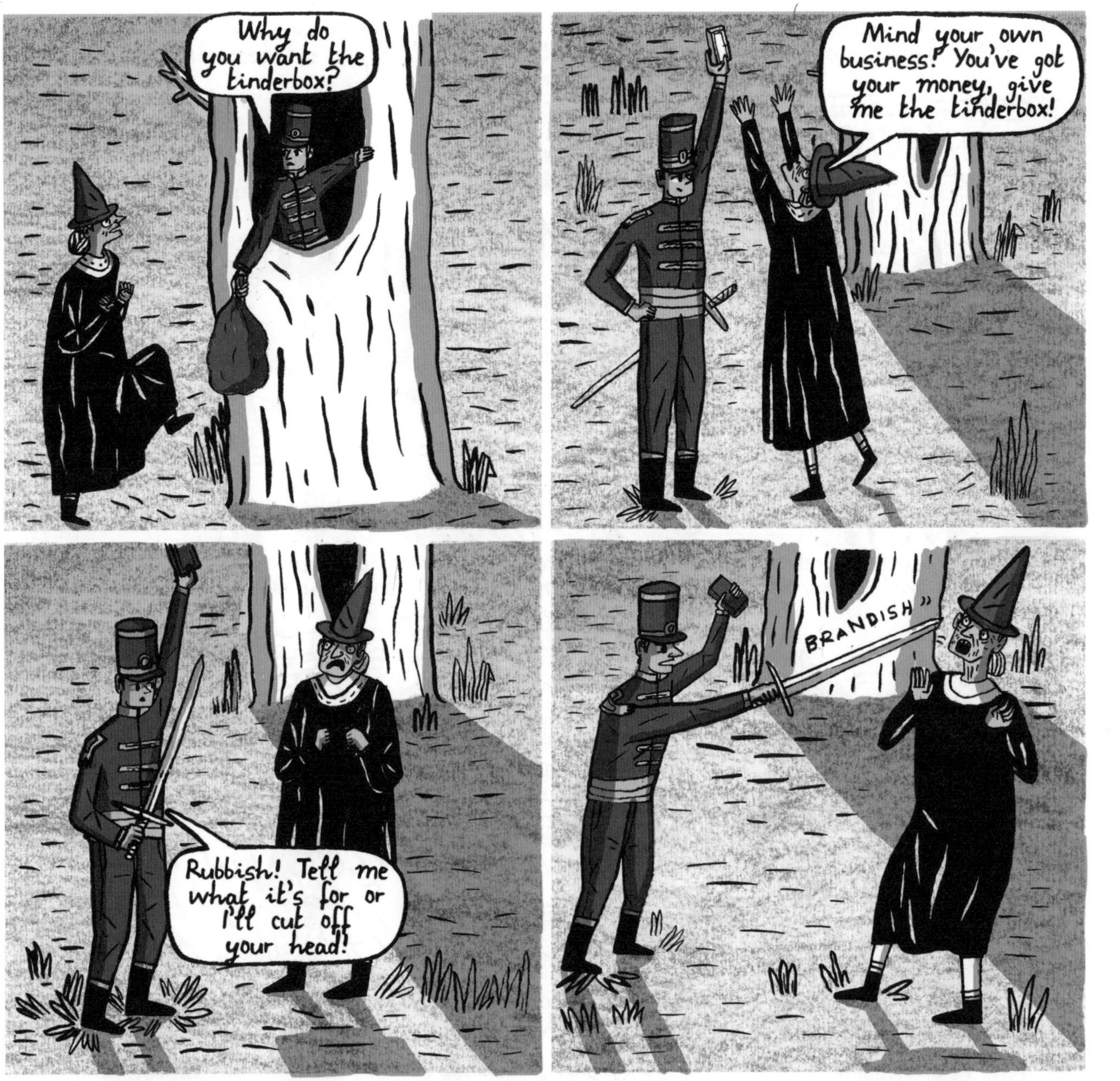
Why do you want the tinderbox?
Mind your own business! You've got your money, give me the tinderbox!
Rubbish! Tell me what it's for or I'll cut off your head!
BRANDISH

So he chopped off her head, dropped the tinderbox into his pocket and off to town he went.

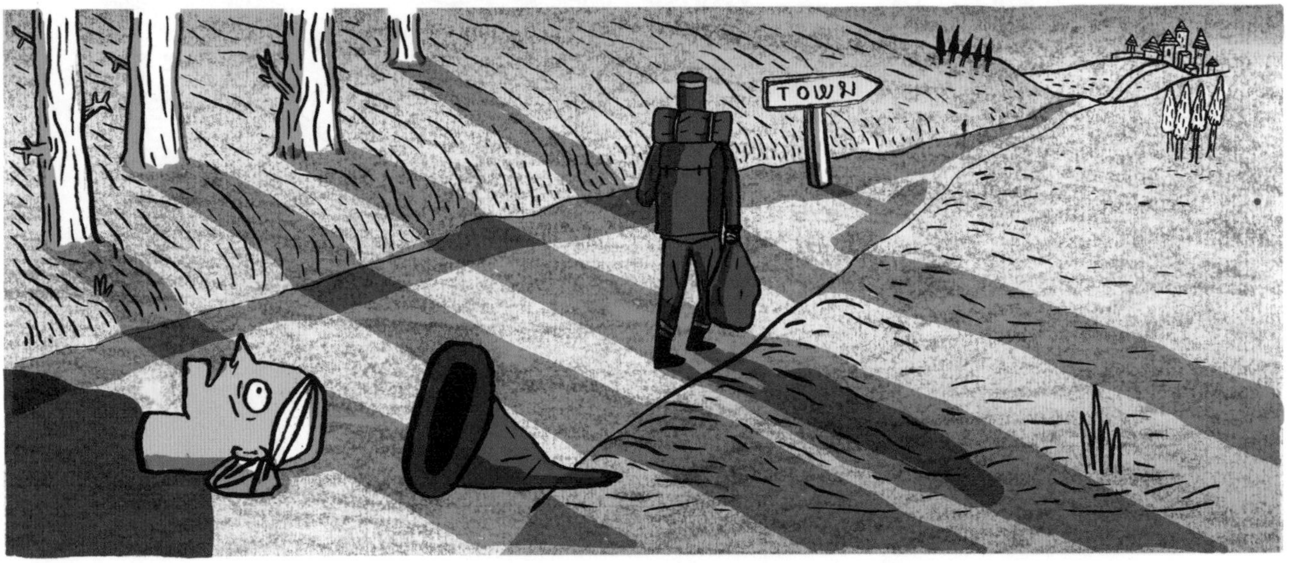
TOWN

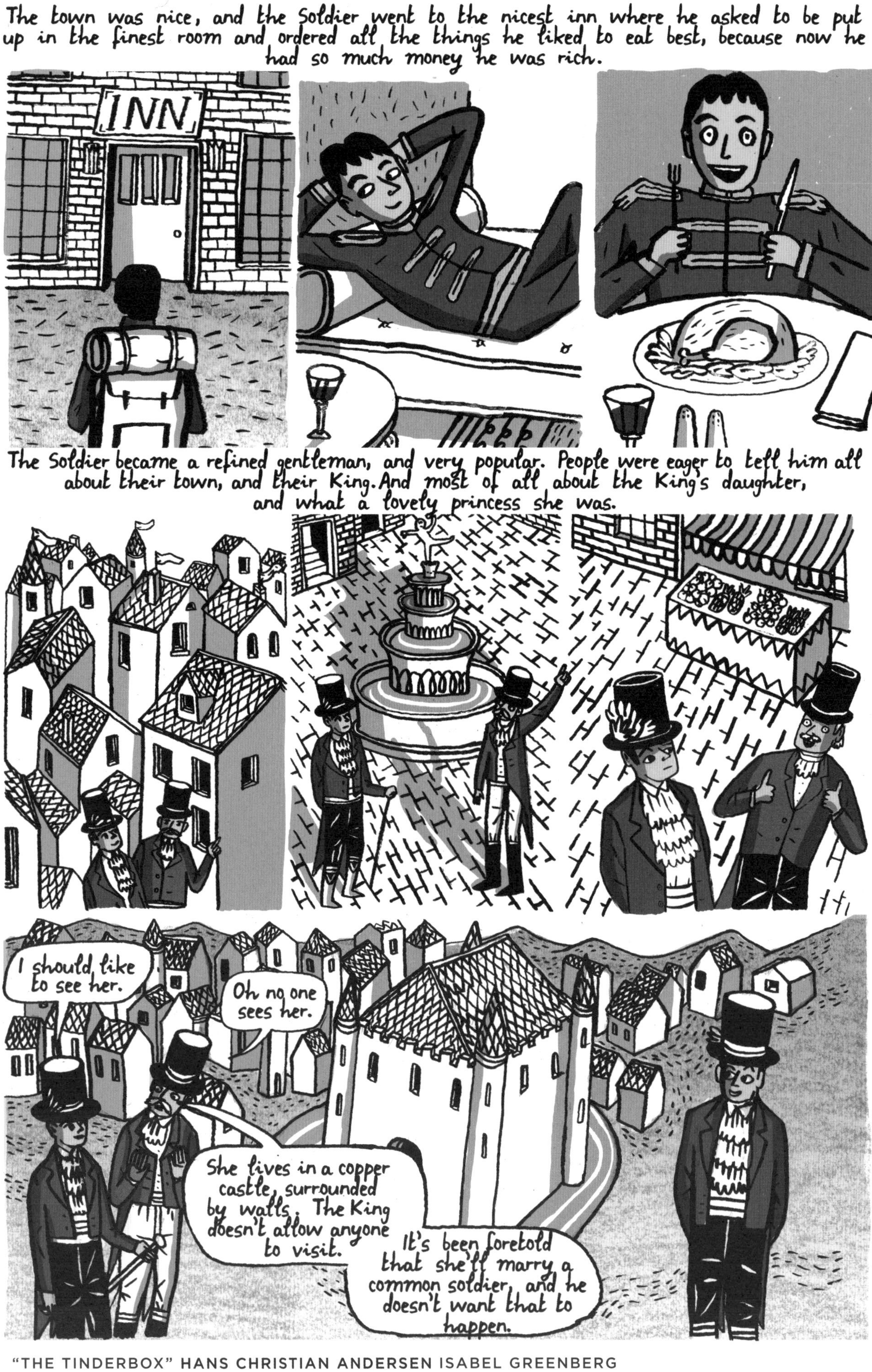
The town was nice, and the Soldier went to the nicest inn where he asked to be put up in the finest room and ordered all the things he liked to eat best, because now he had so much money he was rich.
INN
The Soldier became a refined gentleman, and very popular. People were eager to tell him all about their town, and their King. And most of all about the King's daughter, and what a lovely princess she was.
I should like to see her.
Oh no one sees her.
She lives in a copper castle, surrounded by walls. The King doesn't allow anyone to visit.
It's been foretold that she'll marry a common soldier, and he doesn't want that to happen.

Well, because the Soldier used his money every day and never recieved any, he soon had only two copper coins left. He had to move to a tiny garret and mend his own shoes. Soon he could not even afford to buy a candle.

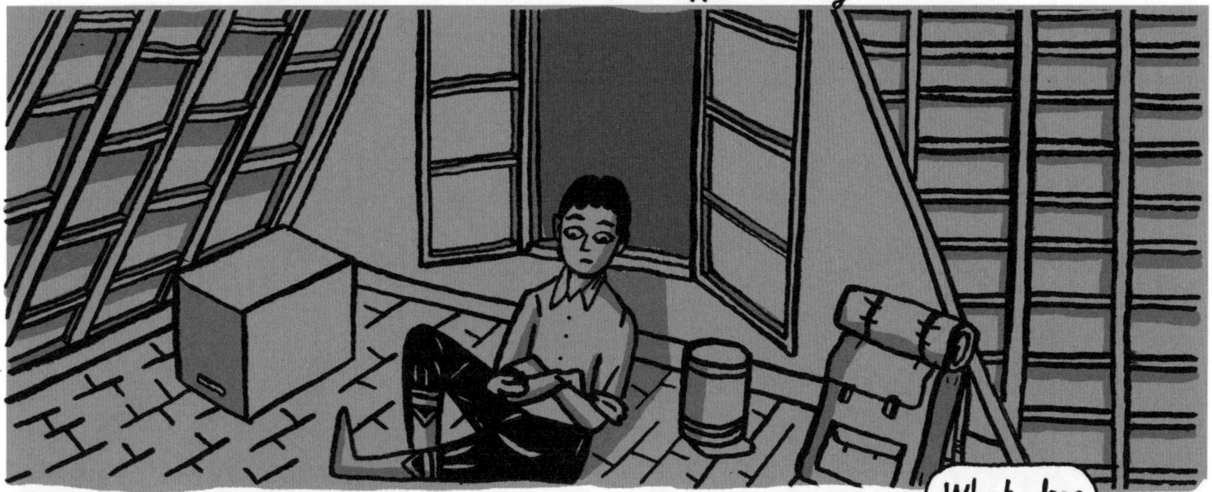

Suddenly he remembered that he had seen the stub of a candle in the tinderbox. He took out the candle, and struck the flint...

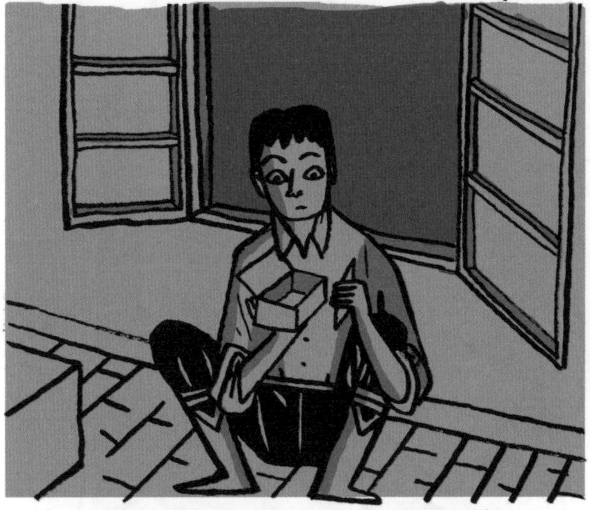

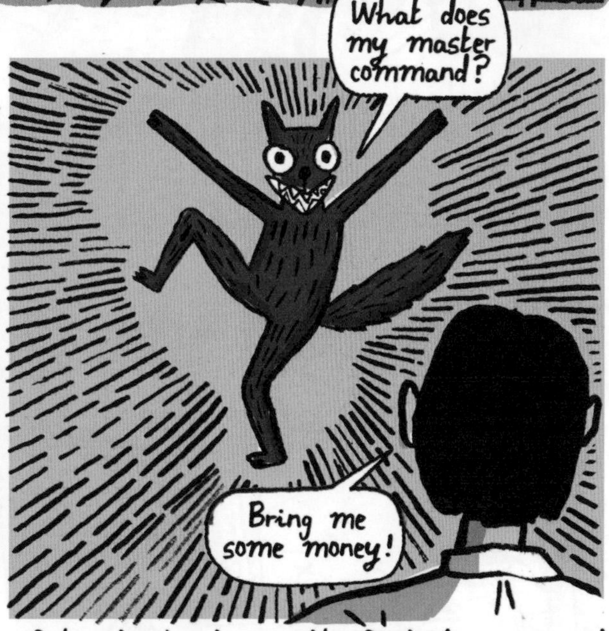
What does my master command?
Bring me some money!

In less time than it took to say thank you, the dog came back with a big sack of copper coins. Now the Soldier understood why the Tinderbox was so valuable.

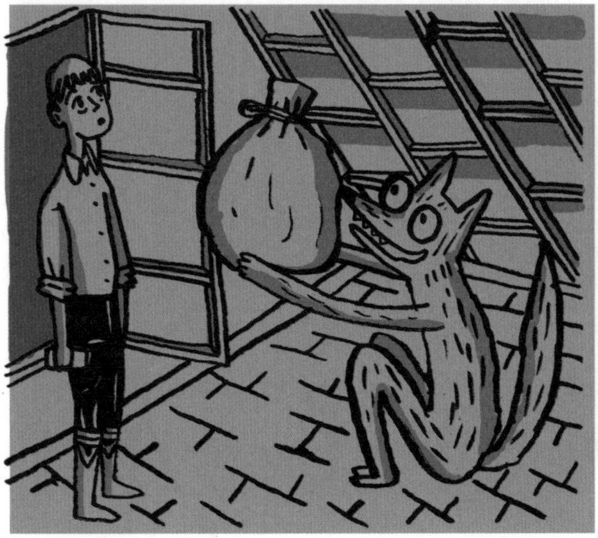

If he struck it once the first dog appeared, twice the second and three times the third dog.

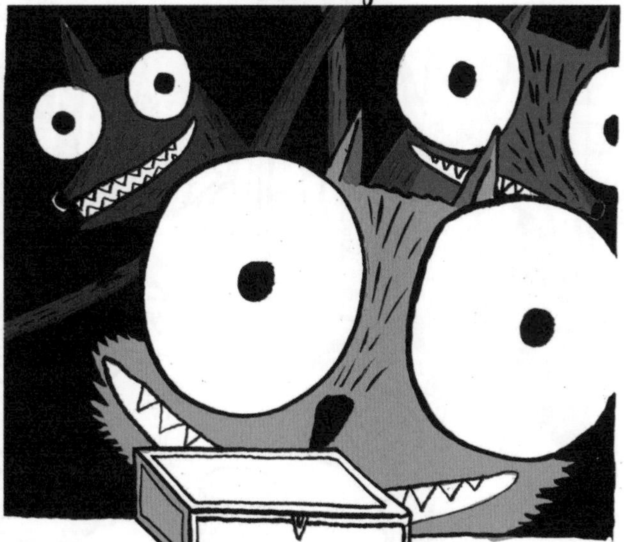

So the Soldier had fine clothes and fine friends once more. But one night, after his friends had gone, he struck his tinderbox.

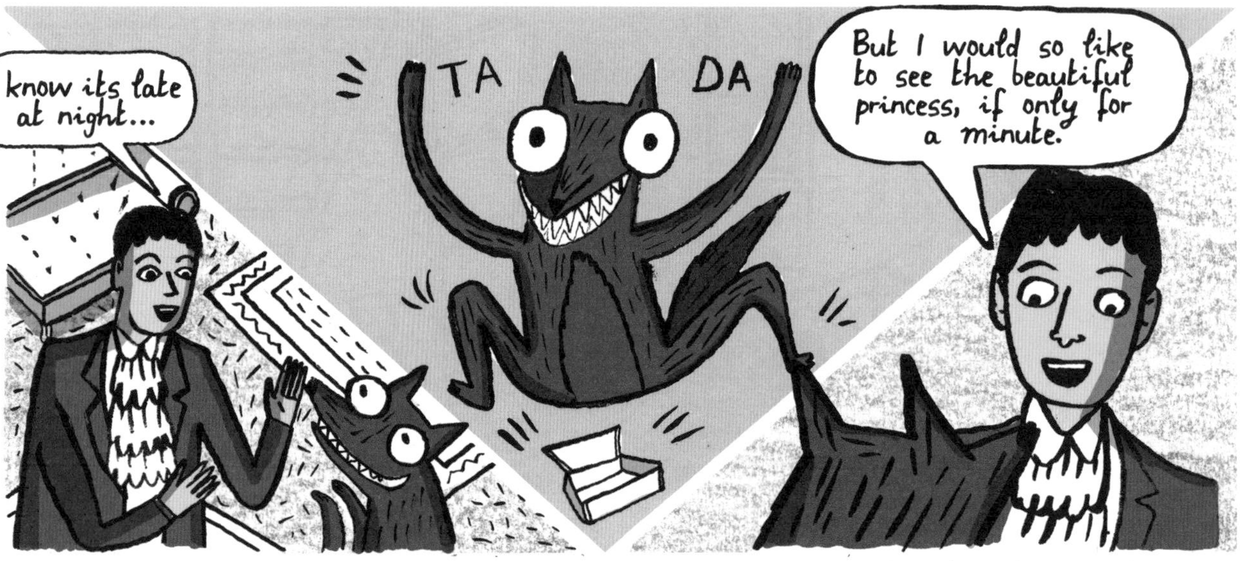
I know its late at night...
TA
DA
But I would so like to see the beautiful princess, if only for a minute.

Away went the dog and faster than thought returned with the sleeping princess.

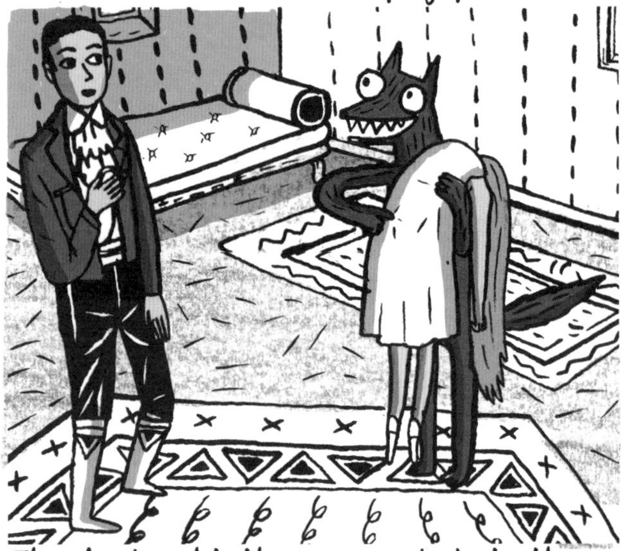

She was so lovely. The soldier could not help kissing her, for he was a true soldier.

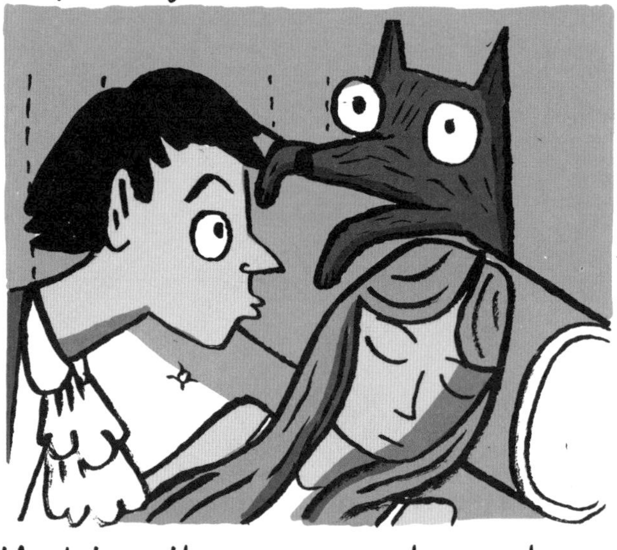

The dog brought the princess back to the castle, but in the morning as she was haing tea with her father and mother, she told them she had had a very strange dream.

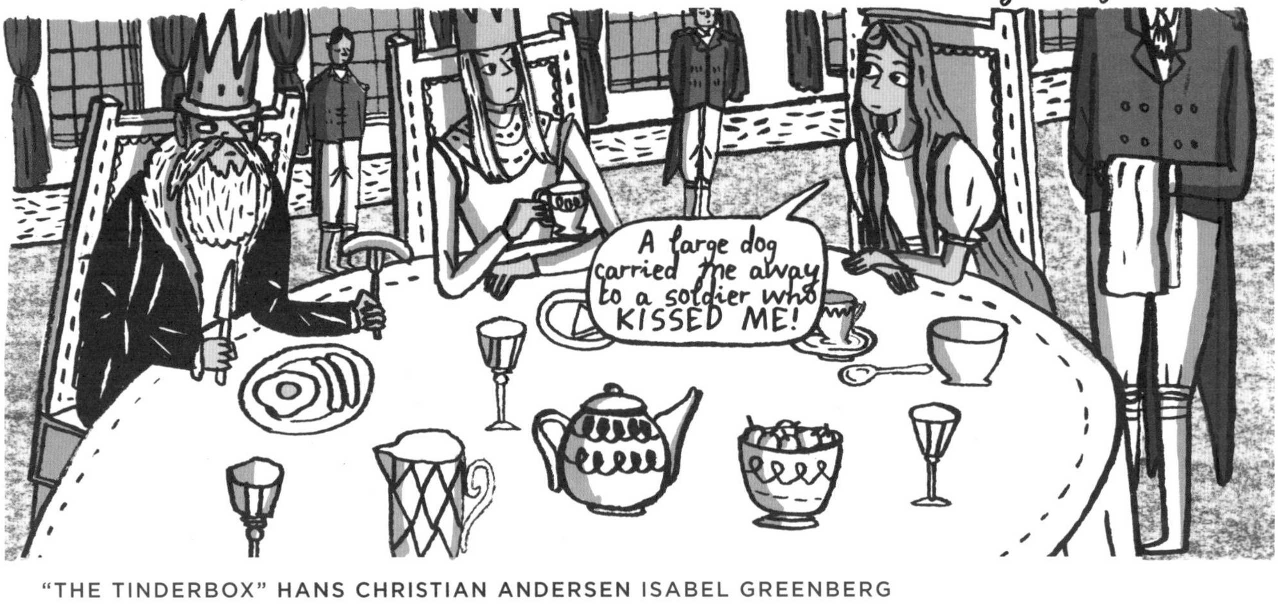
A large dog carried me away to a soldier who KISSED ME!

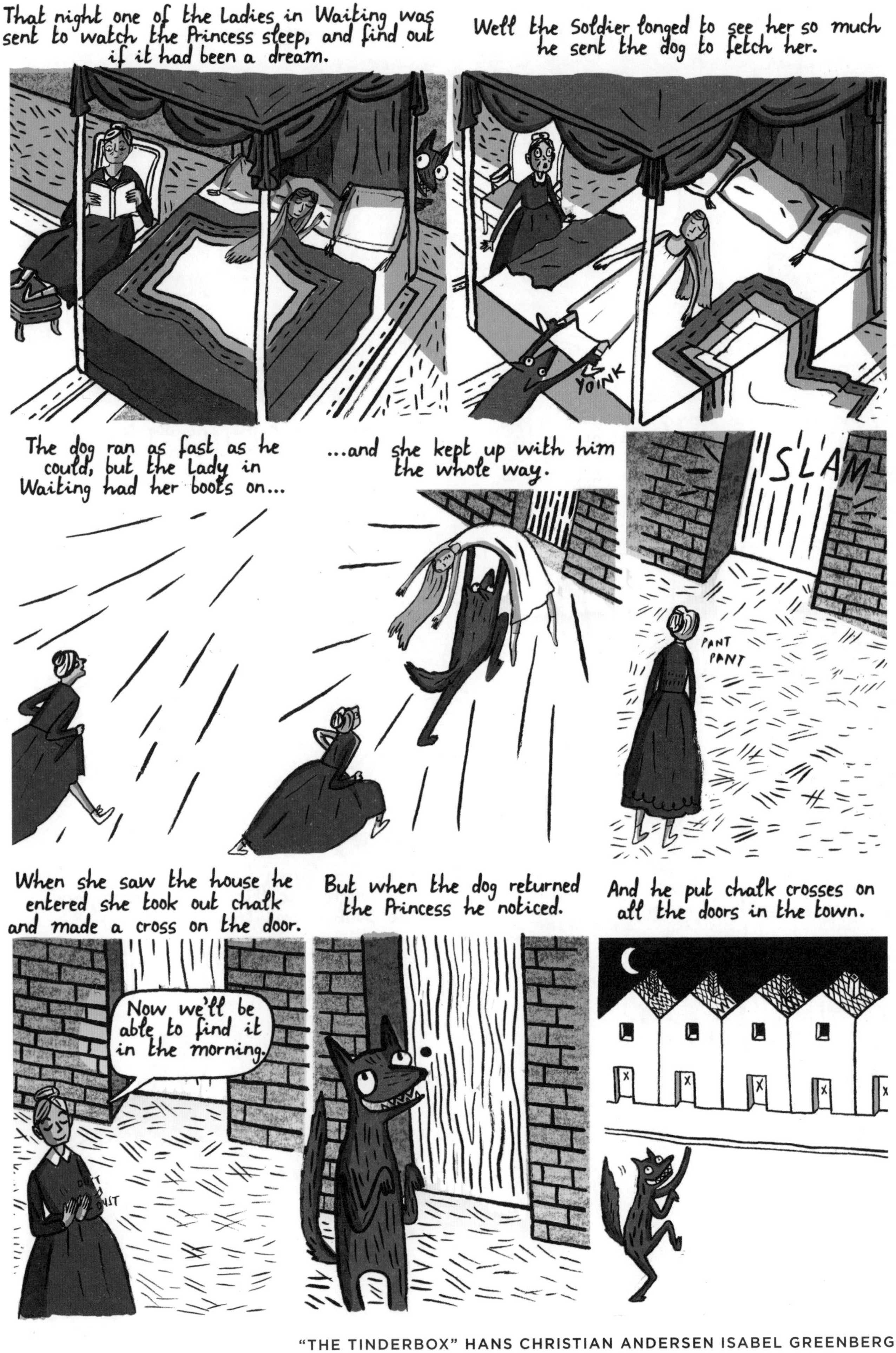
That night one of the Ladies in Waiting was sent to watch the Princess sleep, and find out if it had been a dream.
Well the Soldier longed to see her so much he sent the dog to fetch her.
YOINK
The dog ran as fast as he could, but the Lady in Waiting had her boots on...
...and she kept up with him the whole way.
SLAM
PANT PANT
When she saw the house he entered she took out chalk and made a cross on the door.
Now we'll be able to find it in the morning.
But when the dog returned the Princess he noticed.
And he put chalk crosses on all the doors in the town.

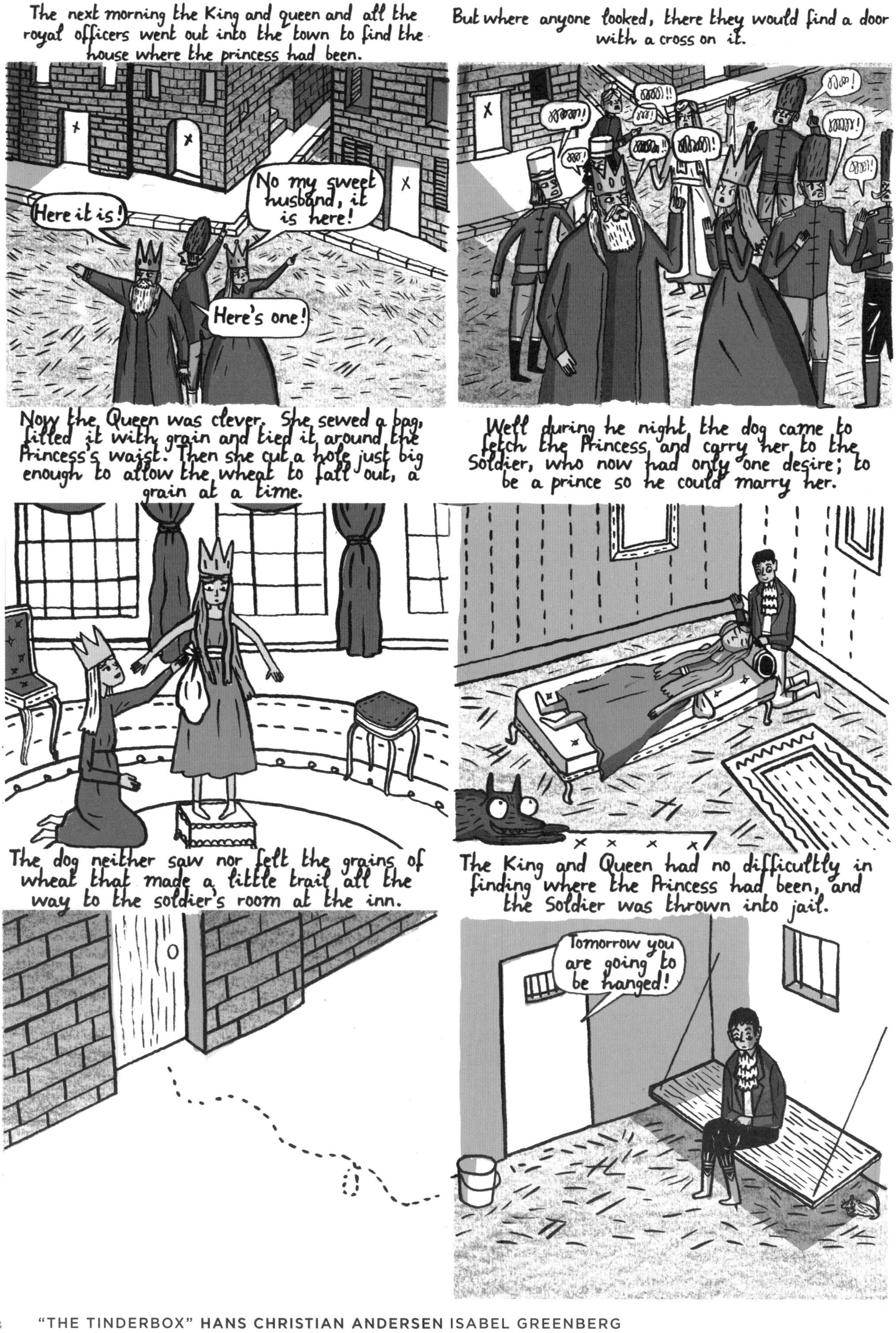
The next morning the King and queen and all the royal officers went out into the town to find the house where the princess had been.
Here it is!
No my sweet husband, it is here!
Here's one!
But where anyone looked, there they would find a door with a cross on it.
Now the Queen was clever. She sewed a bag, filled it with grain and tied it around the Princess's waist. Then she cut a hole just big enough to allow the wheat to fall out, a grain at a time.
Well during he night the dog came to fetch the Princess, and carry her to the Soldier, who now had only one desire; to be a prince so he could marry her.
The dog neither saw nor felt the grains of wheat that made a little trail all the way to the soldier's room at the inn.
The King and Queen had no difficultly in finding where the Princess had been, and the Soldier was thrown into jail.
Tomorrow you are going to be hanged!

Well that was not an amusing thing to hear. If only he had the tinderbox...

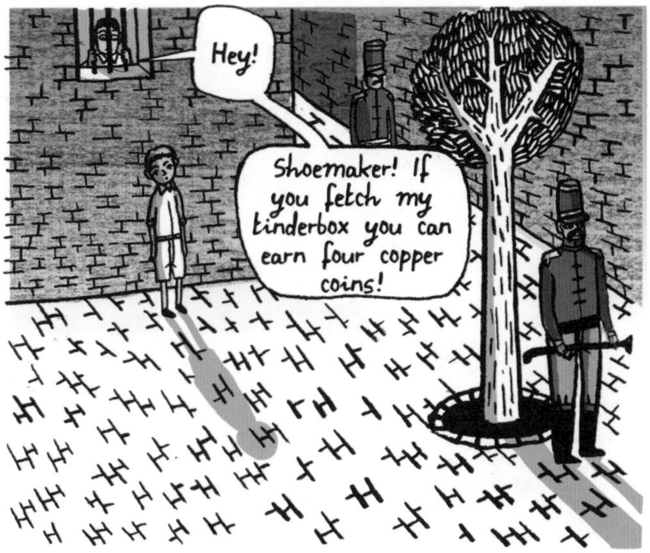
Hey!
Shoemaker! If you fetch my tinderbox you can earn four copper coins!

The Shoemaker's Apprentice, who didn't have one copper coin was eager to earn four. And now you shall hear what happened after that!

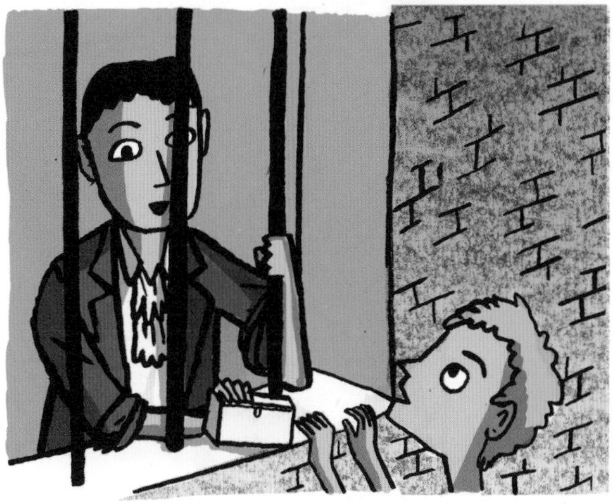

A gallows had been built and around it stood the royal soldiers and the King and Queen on their thrones.

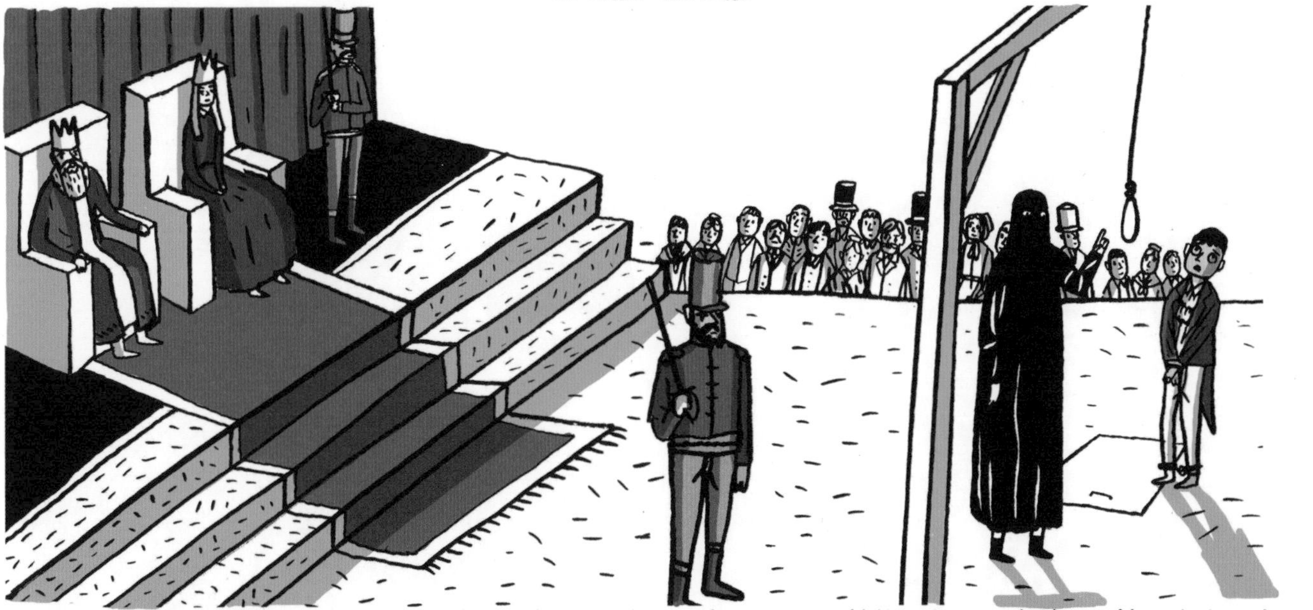

But the soldier declared that he had one last wish. He wanted to smoke a pipe.

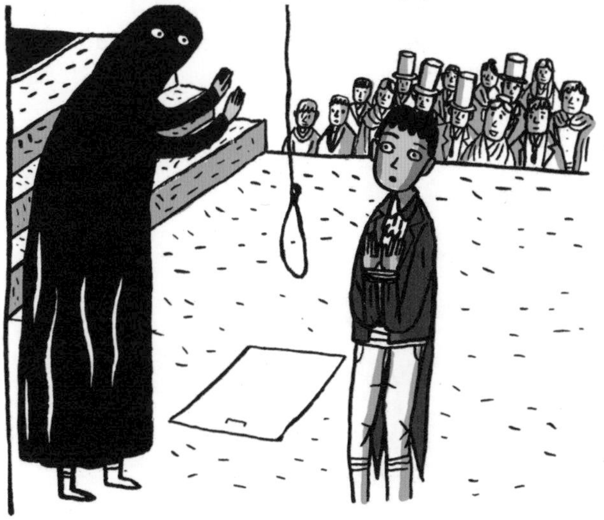

The King couldn't refuse and the Soldier took out his tinderbox and struck it once, twice, three times!

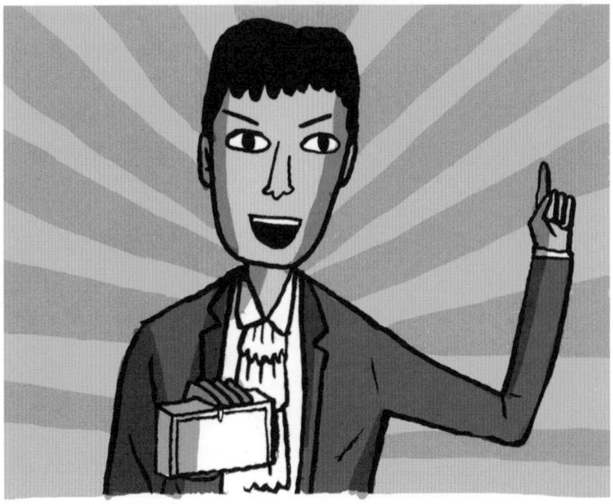

Standing before him were the three dogs.

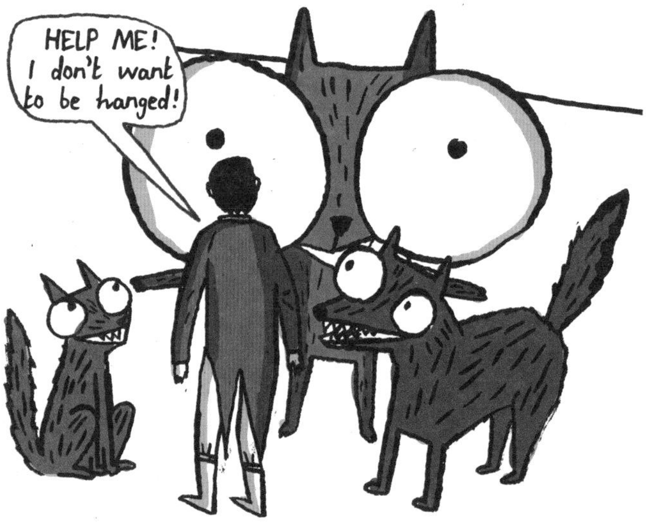
HELP ME! I don't want to be hanged!

The dogs ran towards the King and Queen and the Royal council.

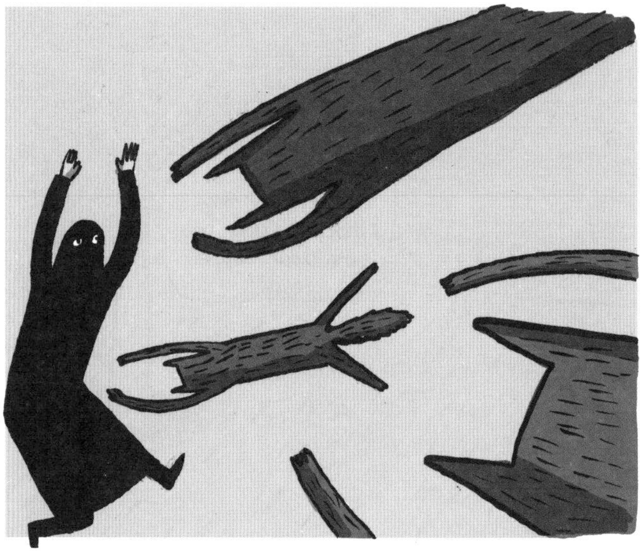

They threw them up in the air, so high that when they hit the earth they broke into little pieces.

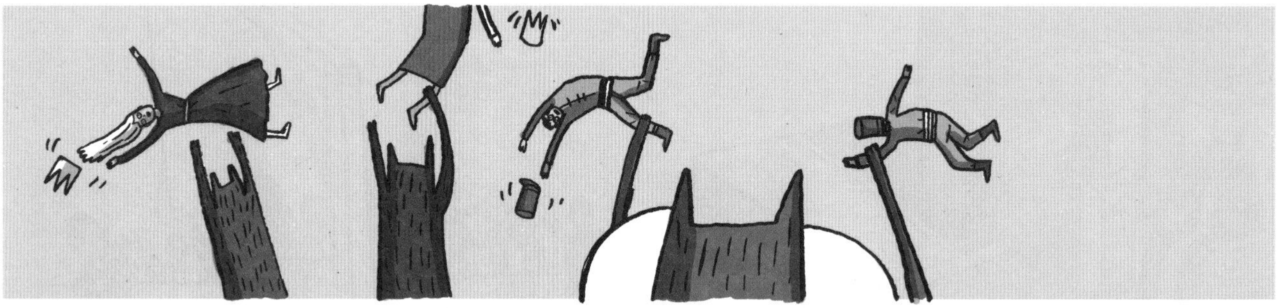

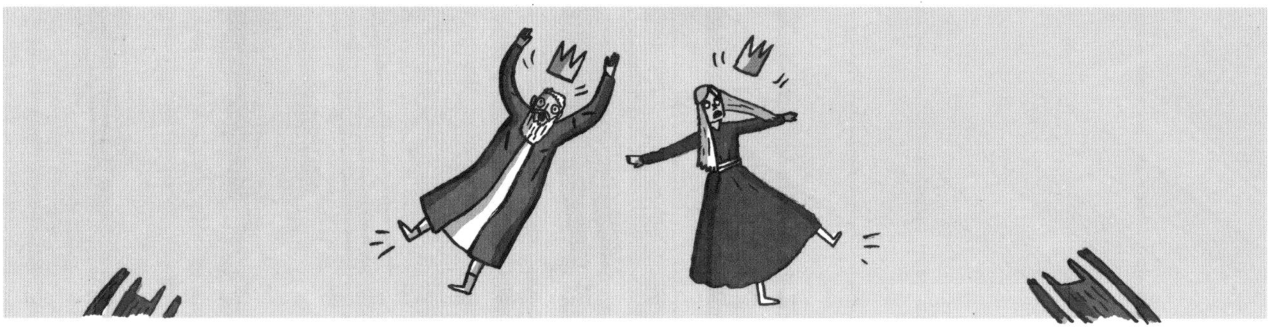

The people all cheered and the Princess came out of her copper castle and became queen and married the Soldier, which she liked very much. The wedding feast lasted a week and the three dogs sat at the table and made eyes at everyone.

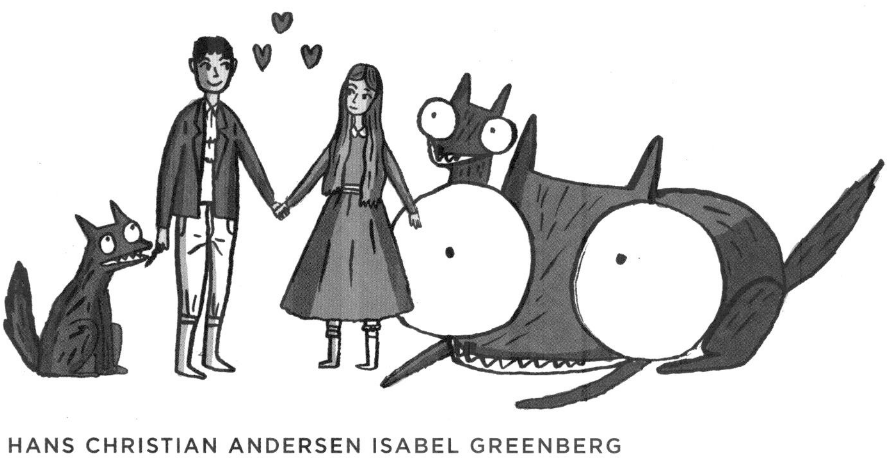

# "Goldilocks and the Three Bears"

## British fairy tale

ART/ADAPTATION BY **Billy Nunez**

**THE STORY OF GOLDILOCKS APPEARS TO BE FROM THE** British oral tradition, originally featuring a fox or an old woman as the intruder. (In some versions of the tale, the old lady is brutally killed by the bears.) The story was popularized in 1837 when poet laureate Robert Southey included a version in one of his books. Southey's "The Story of the Three Bears" was modified in many subsequent books of fairy tales and "nursery stories"; twelve years later the trespasser first became a little girl. It wasn't until 1904 that she was given the sobriquet Goldilocks.

Given her name, and the provenance of the tale, Goldilocks has been resolutely pictured as a Caucasian breaking into the domicile of brown bears. Billy Nunez—an illustrator, animator, and beatmaster from New York—decided to transplant the story to sixteenth-century China, with all the changes that implies.

"GOLDILOCKS AND THE THREE BEARS" BRITISH FAIRY TALE BILLY NUNEZ

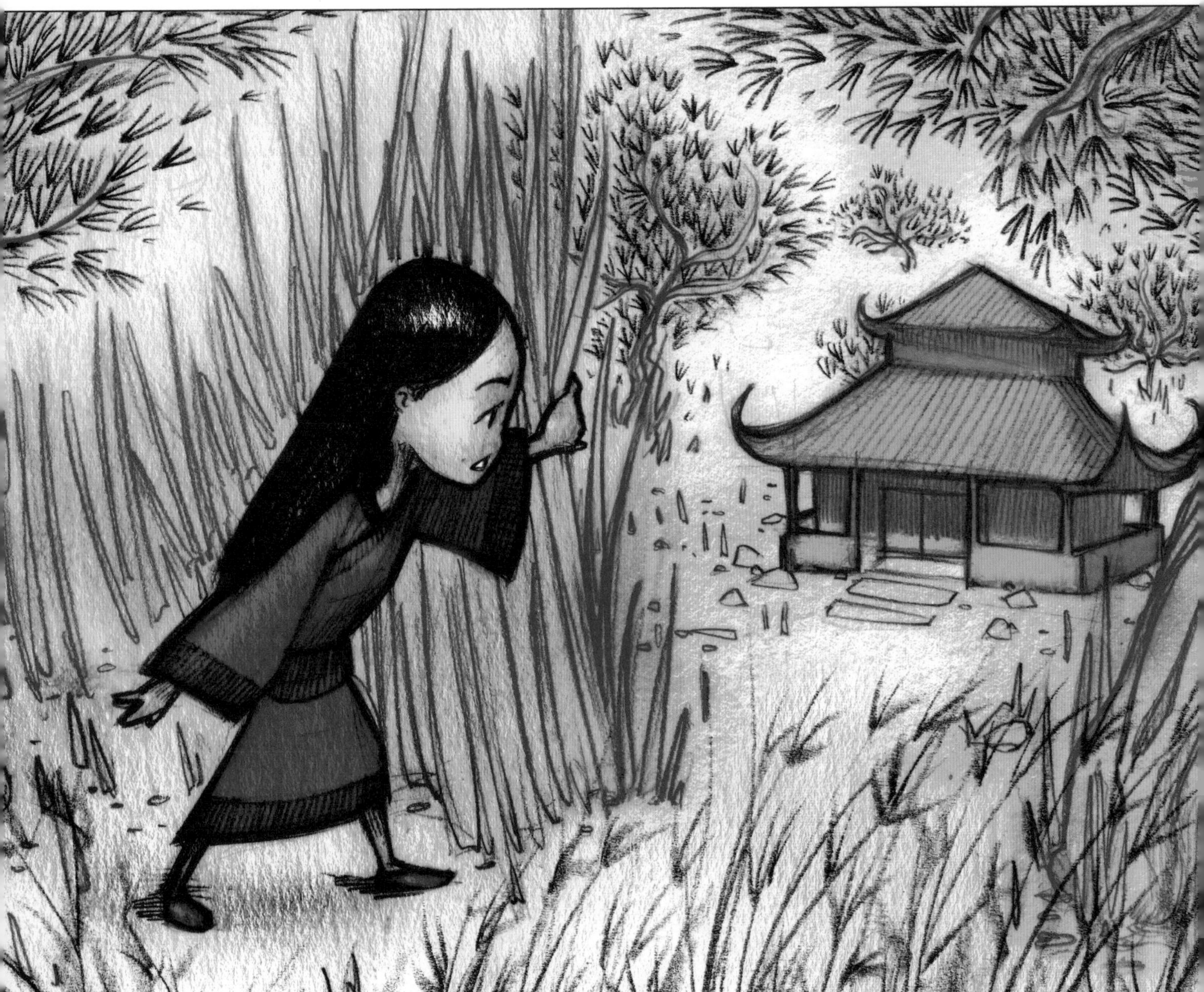

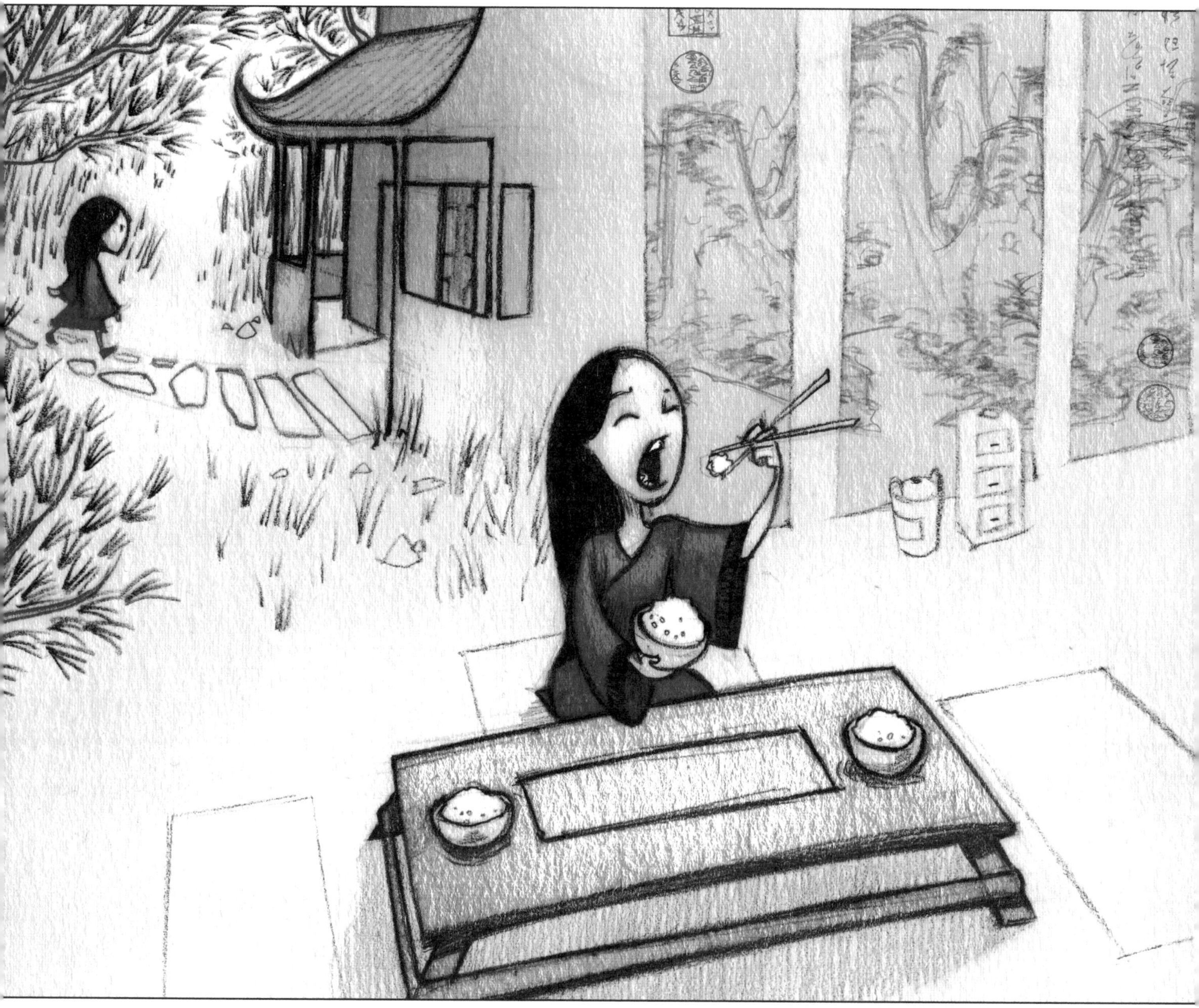

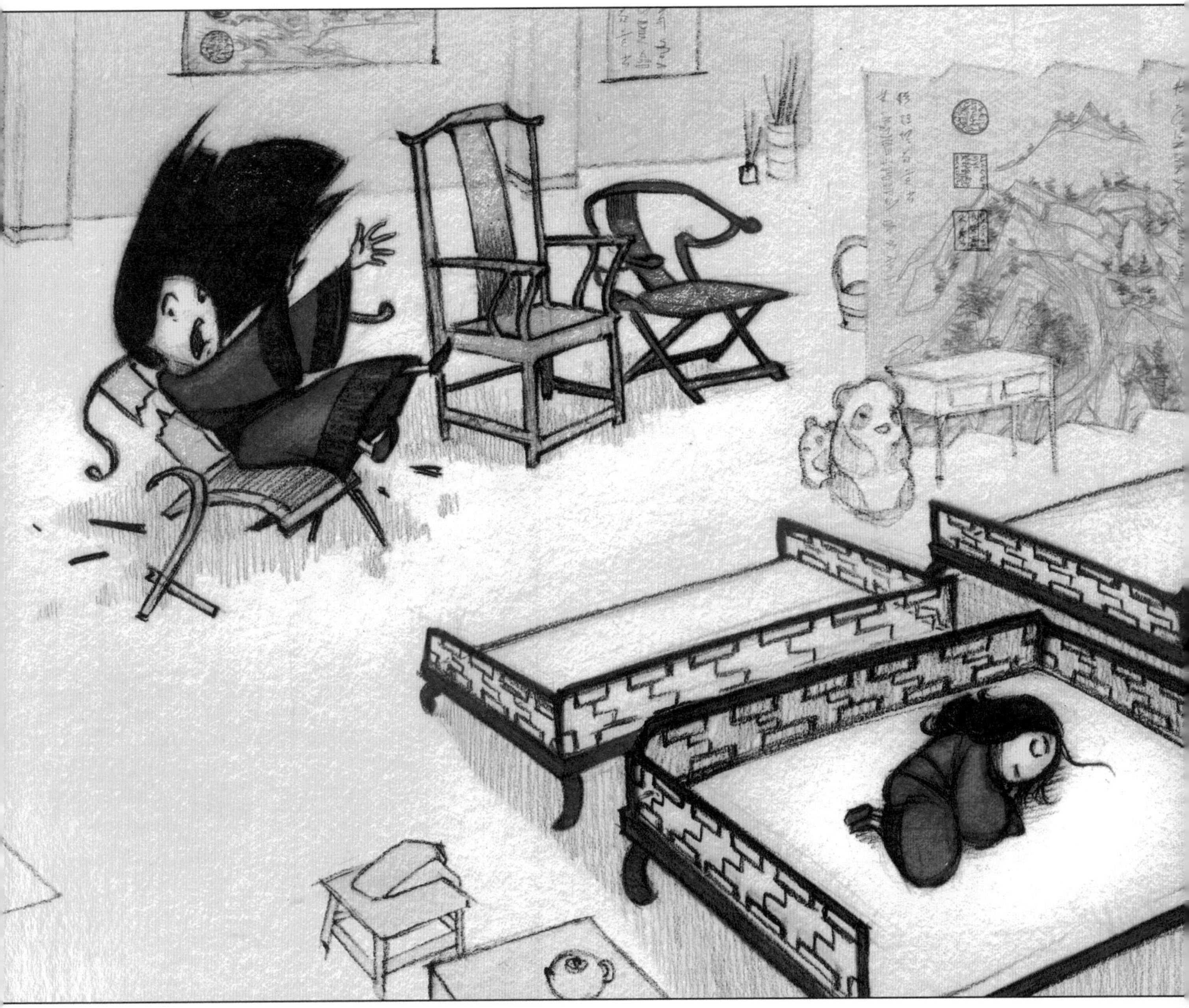

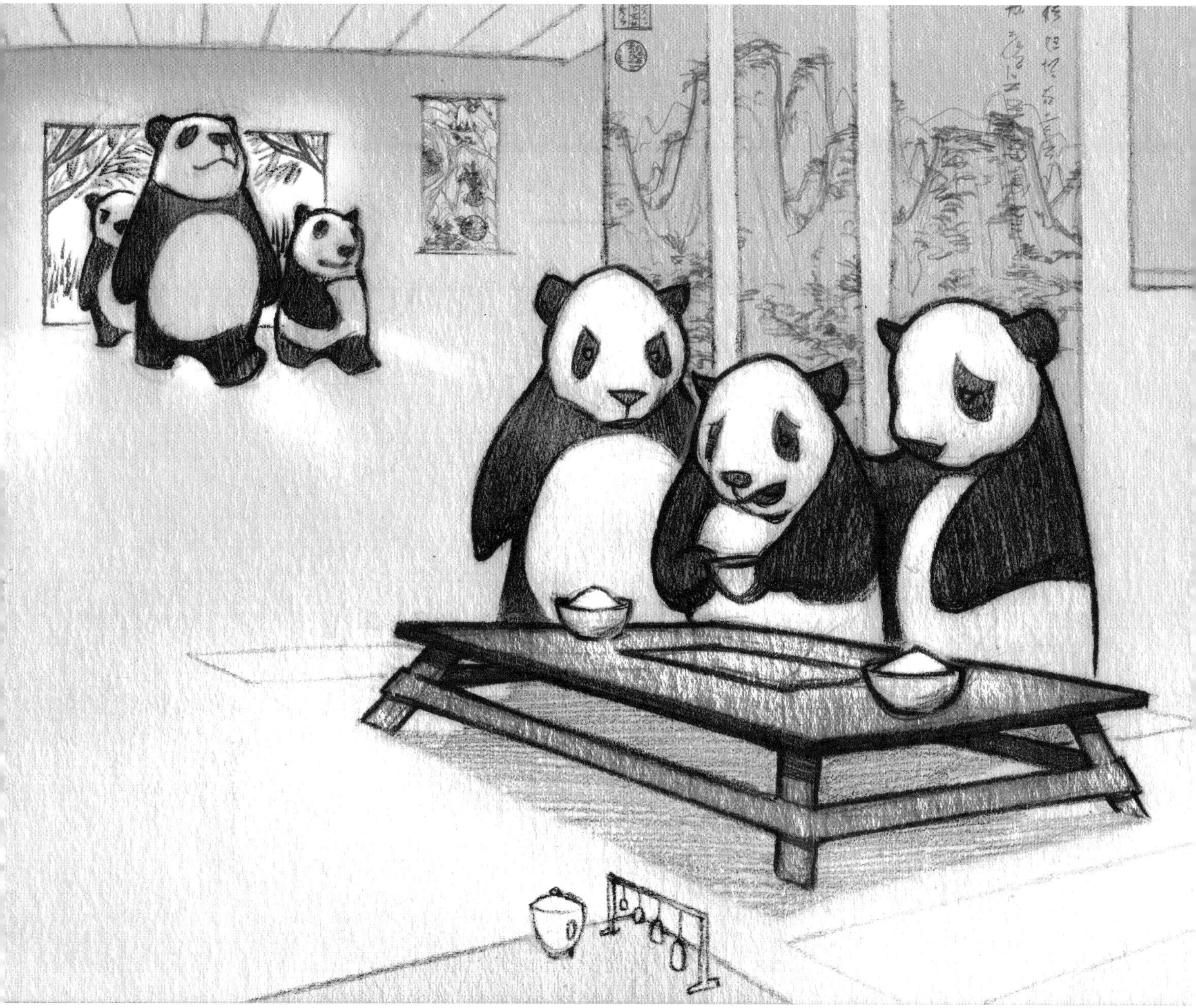

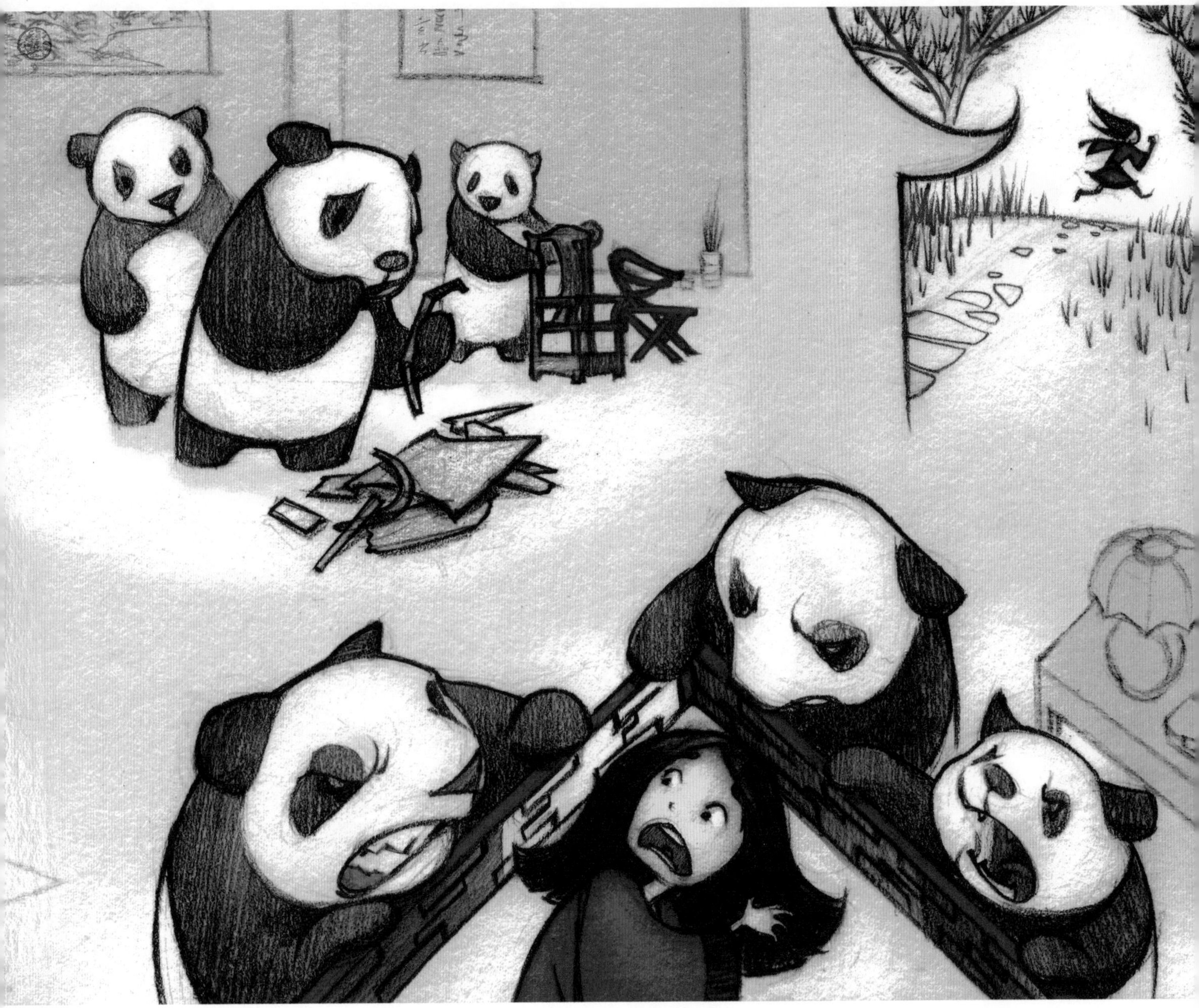

# "Advice to Little Girls"

**Mark Twain**

ART/ADAPTATION BY **Frank M. Hansen**

**SOME OF LITERATURE'S GREATEST WRITERS HAVE** been unable to resist the lure of writing for a younger audience. Mary Shelley, Gertrude Stein, William Faulkner, Sylvia Plath, Ted Hughes, James Joyce, T. S. Eliot, Virginia Woolf, and Aldous Huxley are among those who have penned works for kids. (Children's books by Leo Tolstoy and Carl Sandburg are adapted later in this volume.)

Mark Twain (a.k.a. Samuel Clemens) felt the lure, too. While his novel *The Adventures of Tom Sawyer* occupies some gray area between children's lit and works meant for adults, his essay "Advice to Little Girls" was directed squarely at the young'uns. Sort of. We think. This is Twain at his tongue-in-cheek best, telling tween girls how to deal with parents, teachers, selfish friends, and bratty siblings. It's tempting to say that this is truly meant for adults to chuckle at, but here's the rub—it was first published in a magazine for children: *California Youth's Companion* (in the issue of June 24, 1865). It is hysterical to think of girls taking Twain's advice (although I sicken at the thought that some of them might've actually dumped boiling water on their little brothers).

Frank M. Hansen brings his most whimsical touch to this complete subversion of the earnest etiquette manuals for children that were so popular at the time.

# ADVICE TO LITTLE GIRLS

BY MARK TWAIN

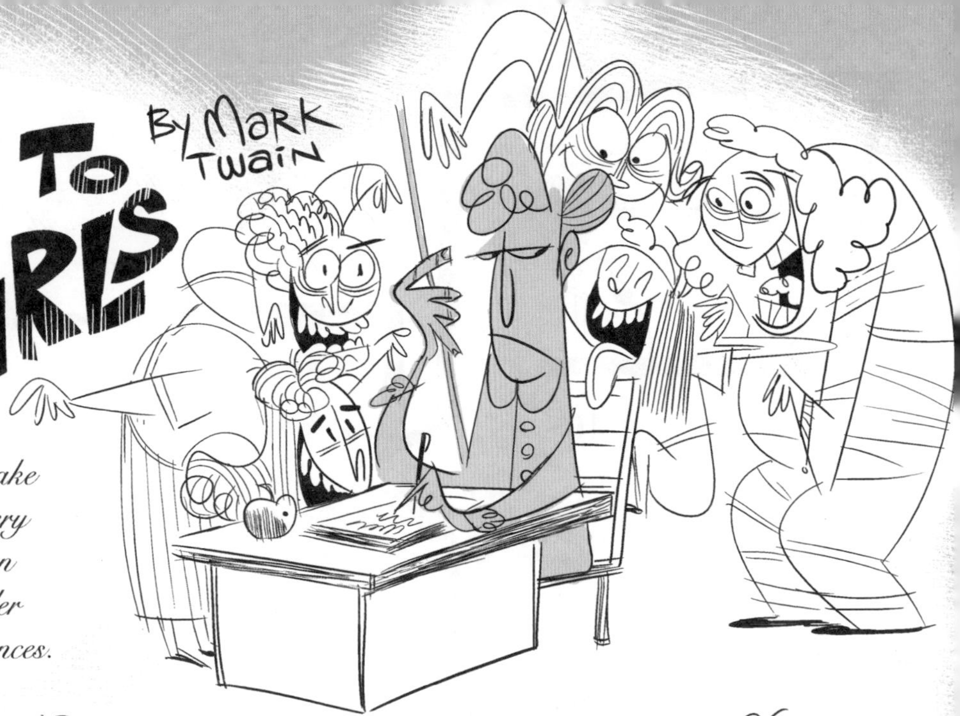

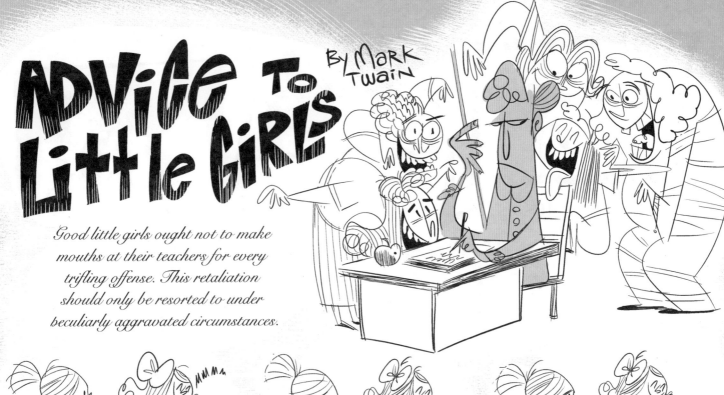

*Good little girls ought not to make mouths at their teachers for every trifling offense. This retaliation should only be resorted to under beculiarly aggravated circumstances.*

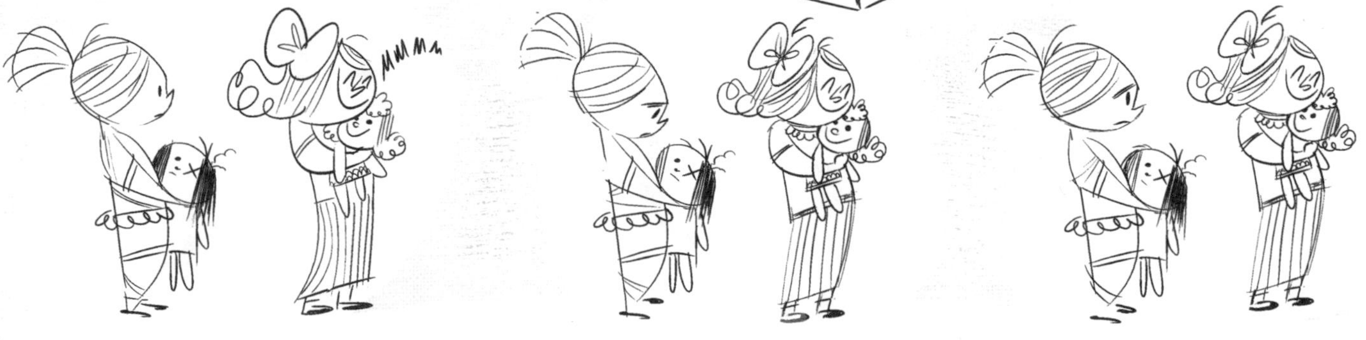
MMMM

*And you ought not to attempt to make a forcible swap with her unless your conscience would justify you in it, and you know you are able to do it.*

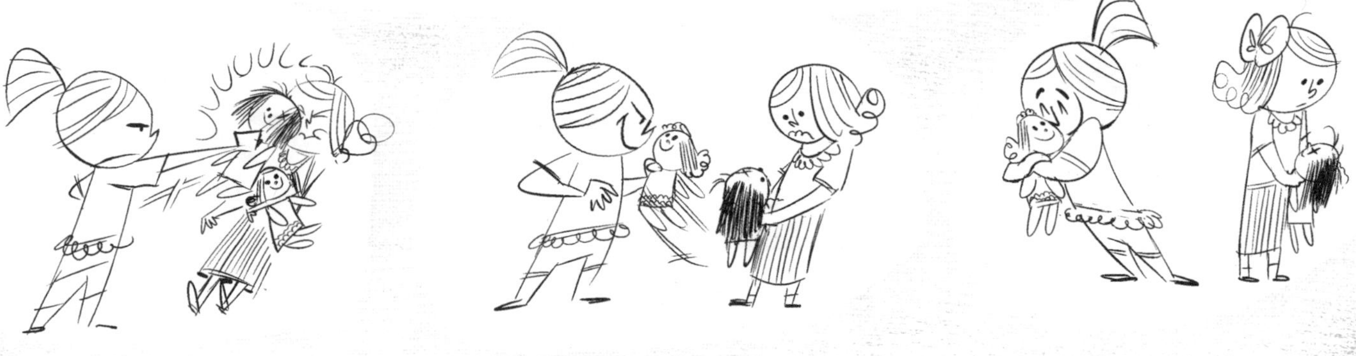
UUUULC

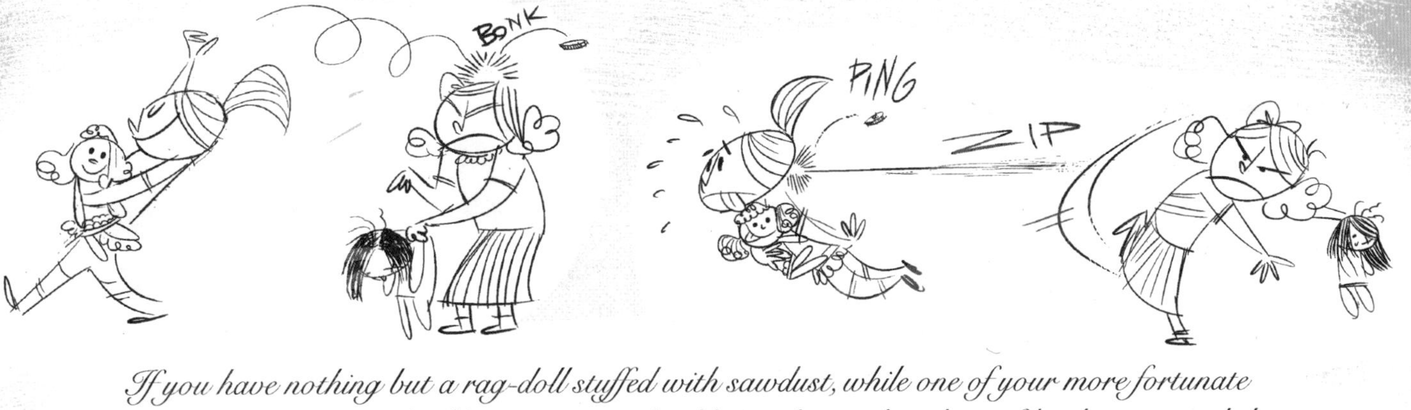
BONK
PING
ZIP

*If you have nothing but a rag-doll stuffed with sawdust, while one of your more fortunate little playmates has a costly China one, you should treat her with a show of kindness nevertheless.*

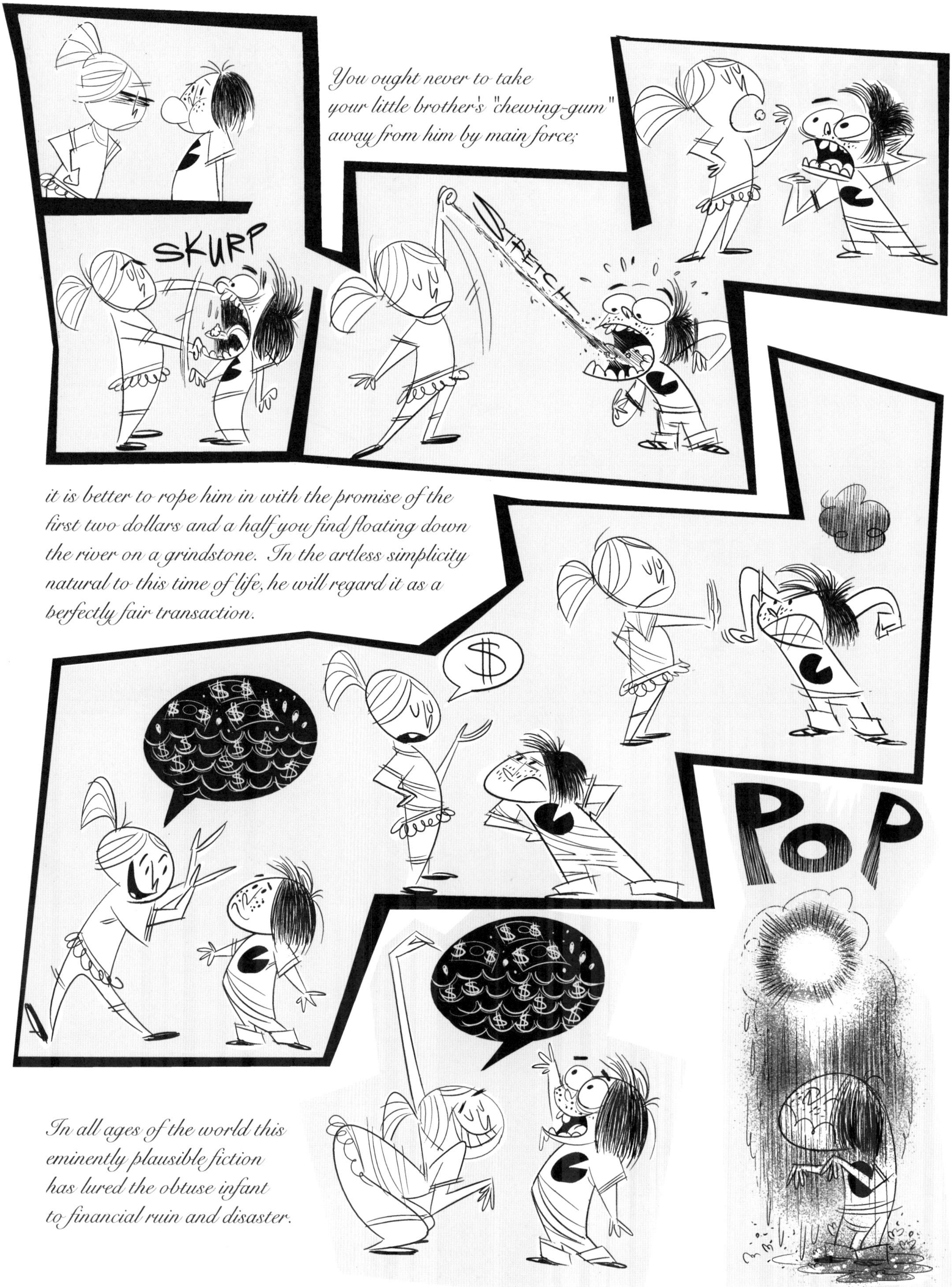
You ought never to take
your little brother's "chewing-gum"
away from him by main force;
SKURP
STRETCH
it is better to rope him in with the promise of the
first two dollars and a half you find floating down
the river on a grindstone. In the artless simplicity
natural to this time of life, he will regard it as a
perfectly fair transaction.
$
POP
In all ages of the world this
eminently plausible fiction
has lured the obtuse infant
to financial ruin and disaster.

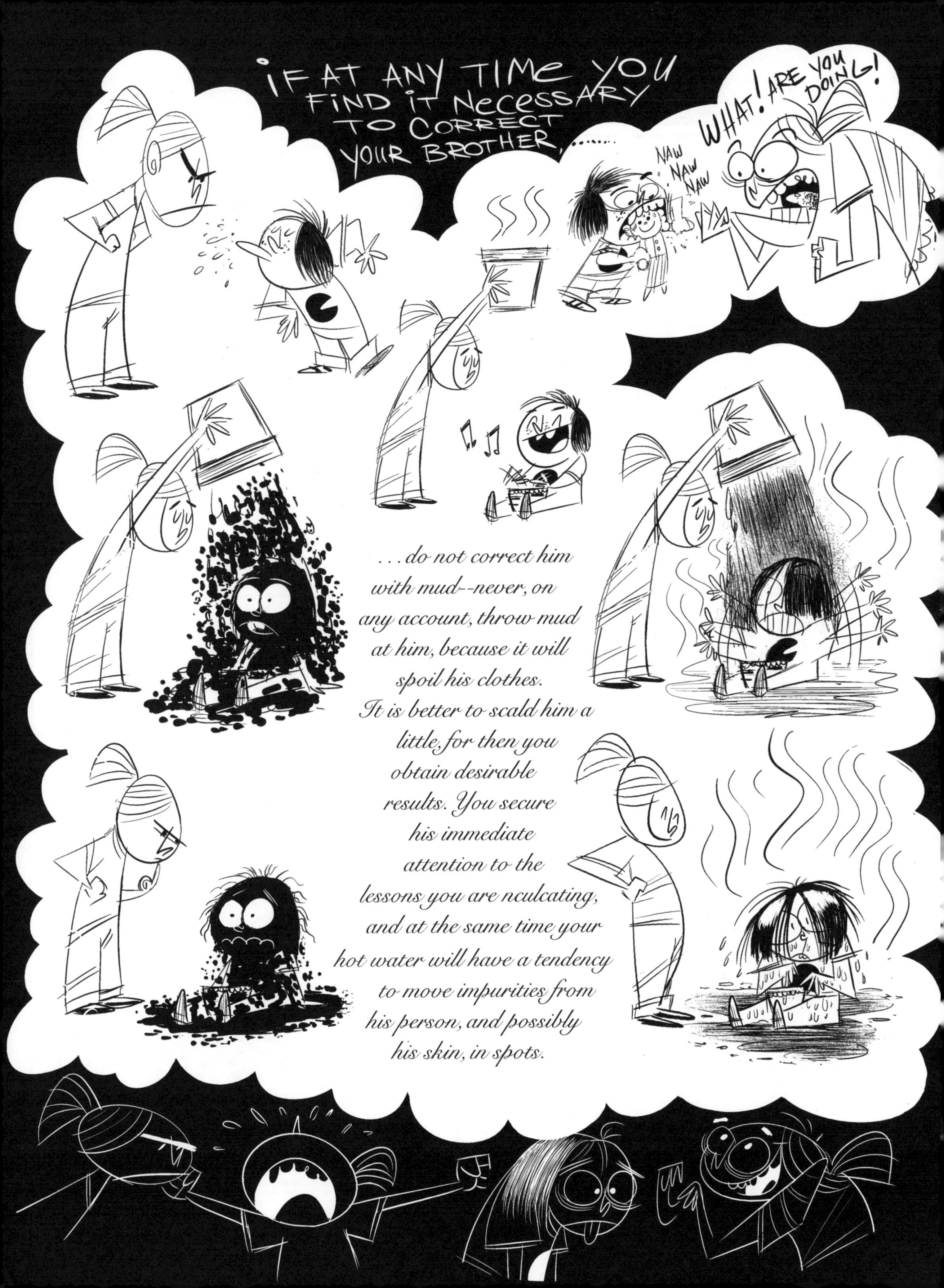
IF AT ANY TIME YOU FIND IT NECESSARY TO CORRECT YOUR BROTHER, ......
NAW NAW NAW
WHAT! ARE YOU DOING!
. . . do not correct him with mud--never, on any account, throw mud at him, because it will spoil his clothes. It is better to scald him a little, for then you obtain desirable results. You secure his immediate attention to the lessons you are nculcating, and at the same time your hot water will have a tendency to move impurities from his person, and possibly his skin, in spots.

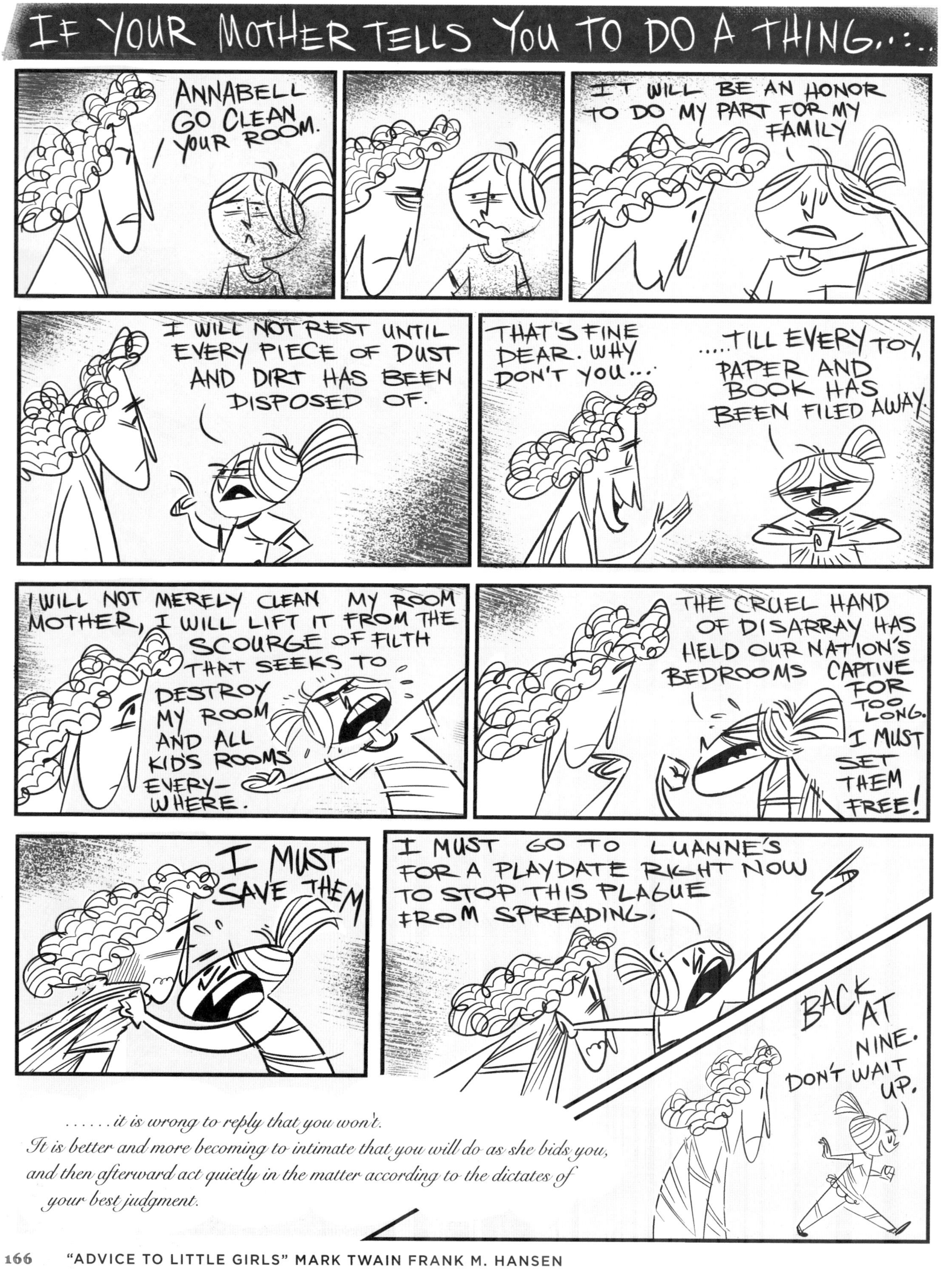
IF YOUR MOTHER TELLS YOU TO DO A THING. . : . .
ANNABELL GO CLEAN YOUR ROOM.
IT WILL BE AN HONOR TO DO MY PART FOR MY FAMILY
I WILL NOT REST UNTIL EVERY PIECE OF DUST AND DIRT HAS BEEN DISPOSED OF.
THAT'S FINE DEAR. WHY DON'T YOU....
.....TILL EVERY TOY, PAPER AND BOOK HAS BEEN FILED AWAY.
I WILL NOT MERELY CLEAN MY ROOM MOTHER, I WILL LIFT IT FROM THE SCOURGE OF FILTH THAT SEEKS TO DESTROY MY ROOM AND ALL KID'S ROOMS EVERY-WHERE.
THE CRUEL HAND OF DISARRAY HAS HELD OUR NATION'S BEDROOMS CAPTIVE FOR TOO LONG. I MUST SET THEM FREE!
I MUST SAVE THEM
I MUST GO TO LUANNE'S FOR A PLAYDATE RIGHT NOW TO STOP THIS PLAGUE FROM SPREADING.
BACK AT NINE. DON'T WAIT UP.

*. . . . . . it is wrong to reply that you won't.*
*It is better and more becoming to intimate that you will do as she bids you, and then afterward act quietly in the matter according to the dictates of your best judgment.*

*You should ever bear in mind that it is to your kind parents that you are ndebted for your food, and for the privilege of staying home from school when you let on that you are sick. Therefore you ought to respect their little prejudices, and humor their little whims, and put up with their little foibles until they get to crowding you too much.*

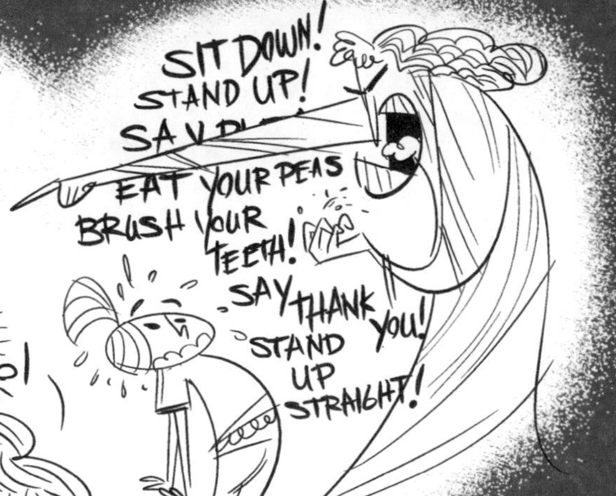
SIT DOWN!
STAND UP!
SAY PL...
EAT YOUR PEAS
BRUSH YOUR TEETH!
SAY THANK YOU!
STAND UP STRAIGHT!

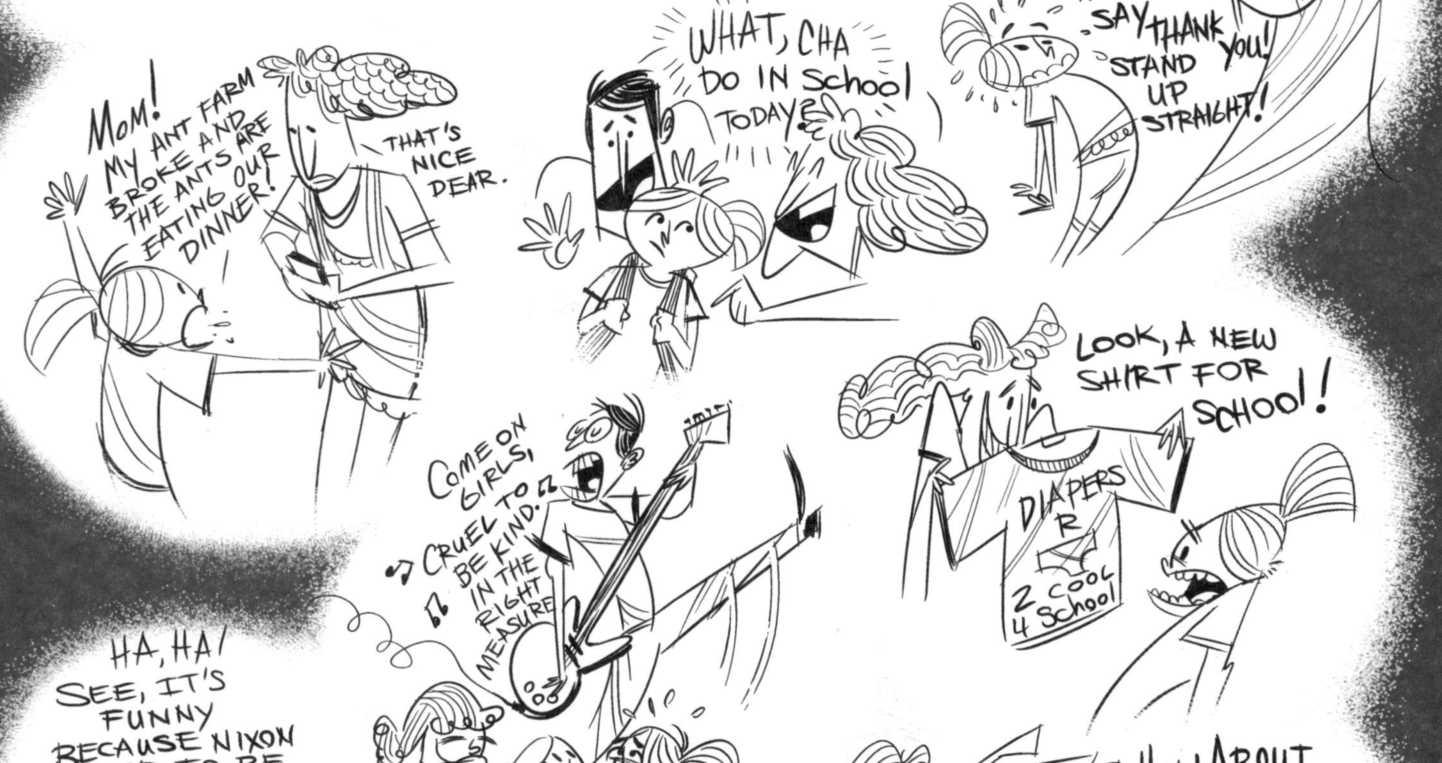
MOM! MY ANT FARM BROKE AND THE ANTS ARE EATING OUR DINNER!
THAT'S NICE DEAR.
WHAT, CHA DO IN School TODAY?
LOOK, A NEW SHIRT FOR SCHOOL!
DIAPERS R 2 COOL 4 School
Come on girls,
CRUEL TO BE KIND IN THE RIGHT MEASURE

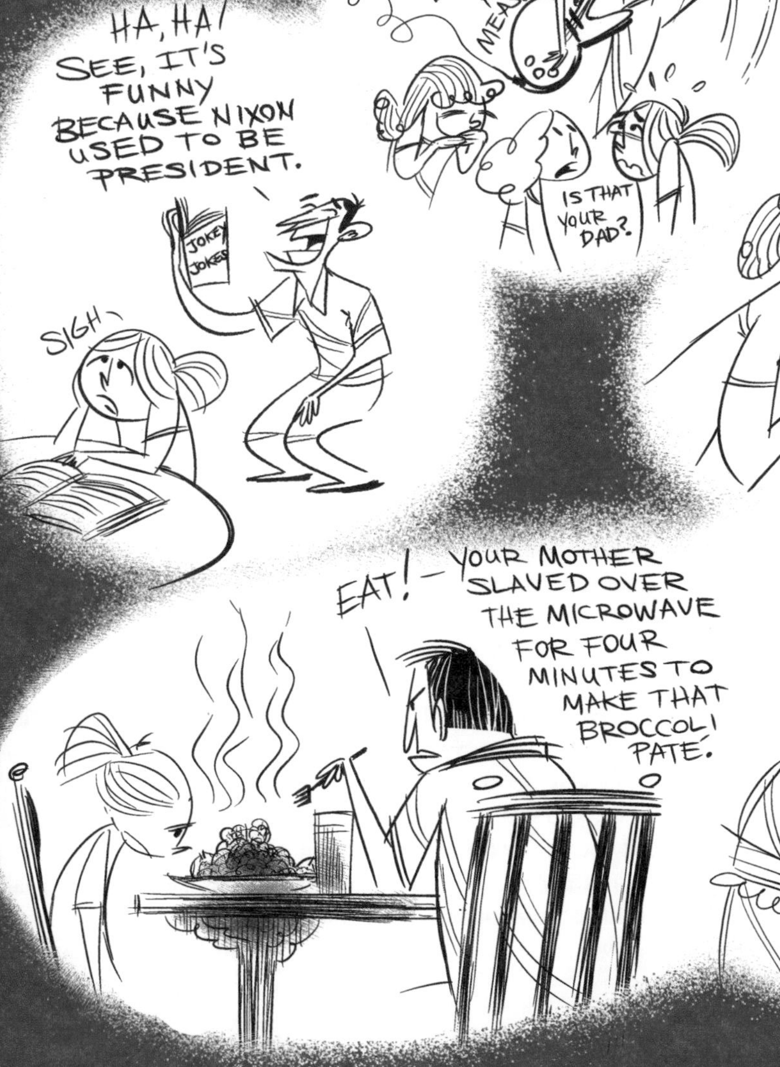
HA, HA! SEE, IT'S FUNNY BECAUSE NIXON USED TO BE PRESIDENT.
JOKEY JOKES
SIGH
IS THAT YOUR DAD?
EAT! — YOUR MOTHER SLAVED OVER THE MICROWAVE FOR FOUR MINUTES TO MAKE THAT BROCCOLI PATE.

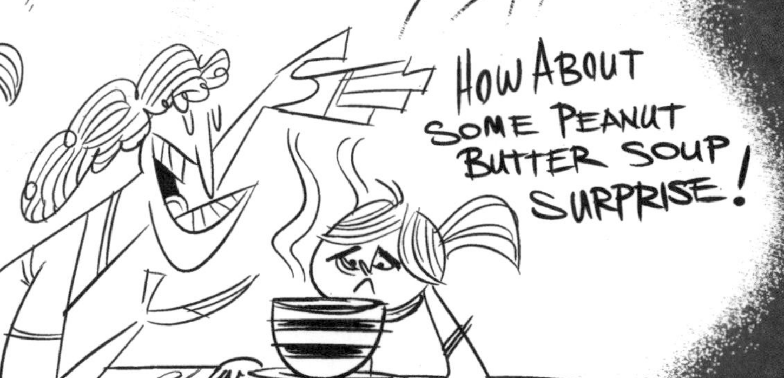
HOW ABOUT SOME PEANUT BUTTER SOUP SURPRISE!

*Good little girls always show marked deference f or the aged. You ought never to "sass" old people unless they "sass" you first.*

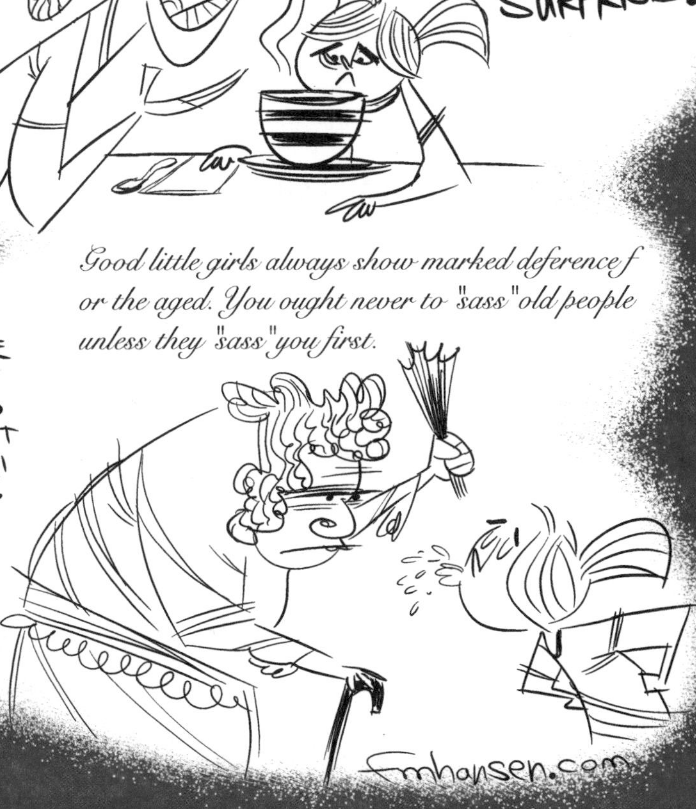
fmhansen.com

# Alice's Adventures in Wonderland

## Lewis Carroll

ART/ADAPTATION BY **Vicki Nerino**

**THE ALICE NOVELS SEEM LIKE THEY NEED NO** introduction. *Alice's Adventures in Wonderland* (1865) and its sequel, *Through the Looking-Glass, and What Alice Found There* (1871), comprise arguably the greatest work of children's literature ever published. The fertile mind of Charles Dodgson (a.k.a. Lewis Carroll)—Oxford professor, mathematician, deacon—created a huge number of characters and scenes that embedded themselves in our cultural imagination and are at least as popular as ever. It's impossible to tally the movies, TV shows, music videos, videogames, plays, paintings, graphic adaptations, and other works based on those books.

Which led to a predicament. With the number of illustrated editions—not to mention other visualizations—beyond counting, how could we bring something new to the table? So many artists have taken a crack at Alice, the White Rabbit, the Caterpillar, the Mad Hatter . . . is there a new way to approach what must be the most visually adapted work of fiction in history?

Then it occurred to me: Vicki Nerino. Vicki's style is grotesque, purposely ugly. Distorted and disturbing. Nobody had ever done the Alice books like that, I realized. She was all for the idea. While rereading the books, she noticed something that gets mentioned in in-depth analyses of the novels but isn't much-noticed otherwise. Like most great works of literature, there are many ways to read the Alice books. Among other viewpoints, you can see Alice as a bewildered child facing the weirdness of the adult world (i.e., Wonderland). But you can also make the case that Alice is a brat—judgmental, narrow-minded, selfish, dismissive. As Vicki said, "a real entitled little butthead." So that's the way Vicki approached it, giving us what may be the first non-cute Alice ever seen. . . .

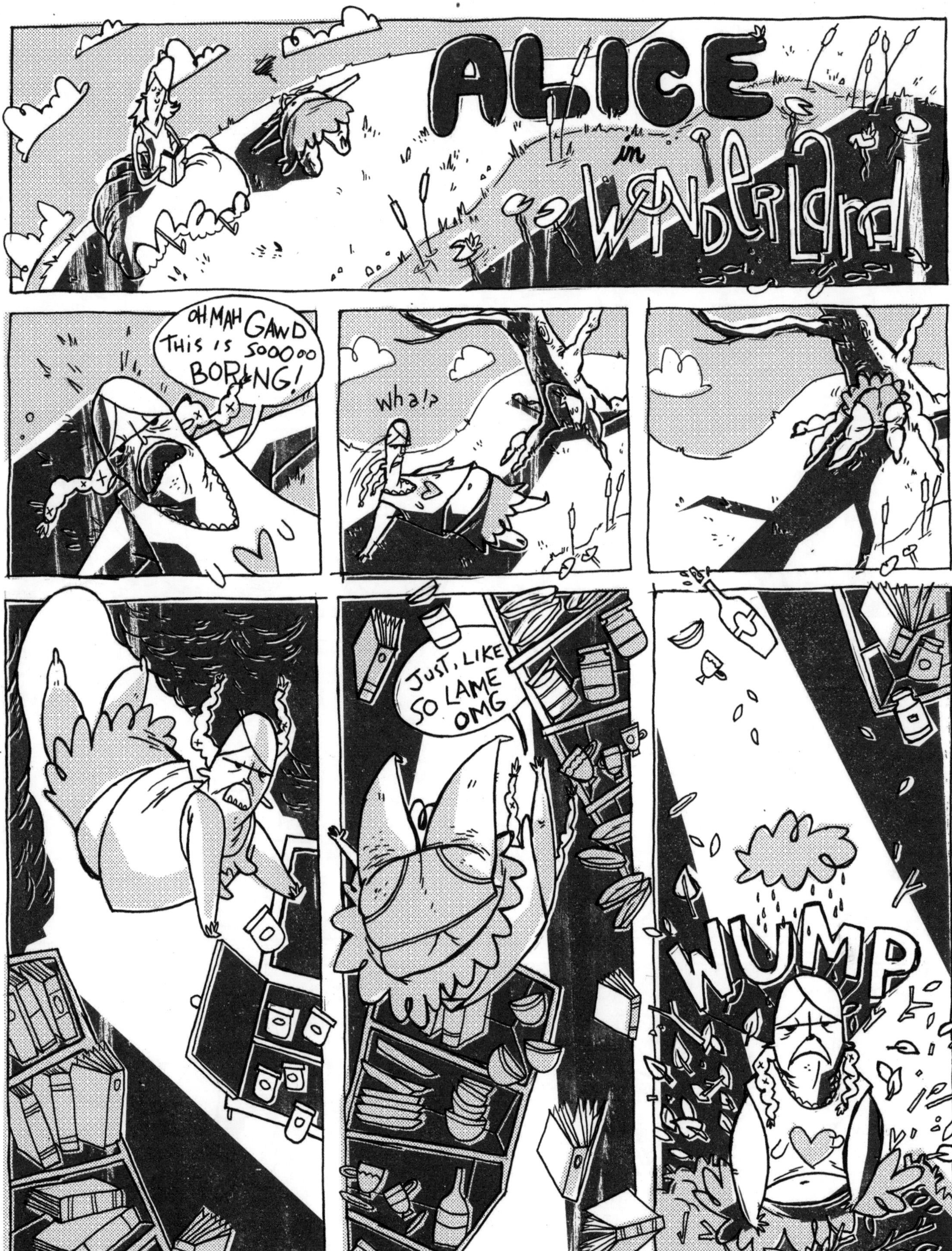
ALICE in WONDERLAND
OH MAH GAWD THIS IS SOOOOOO BORING!
wha!?
JUST, LIKE SO LAME OMG
WUMP

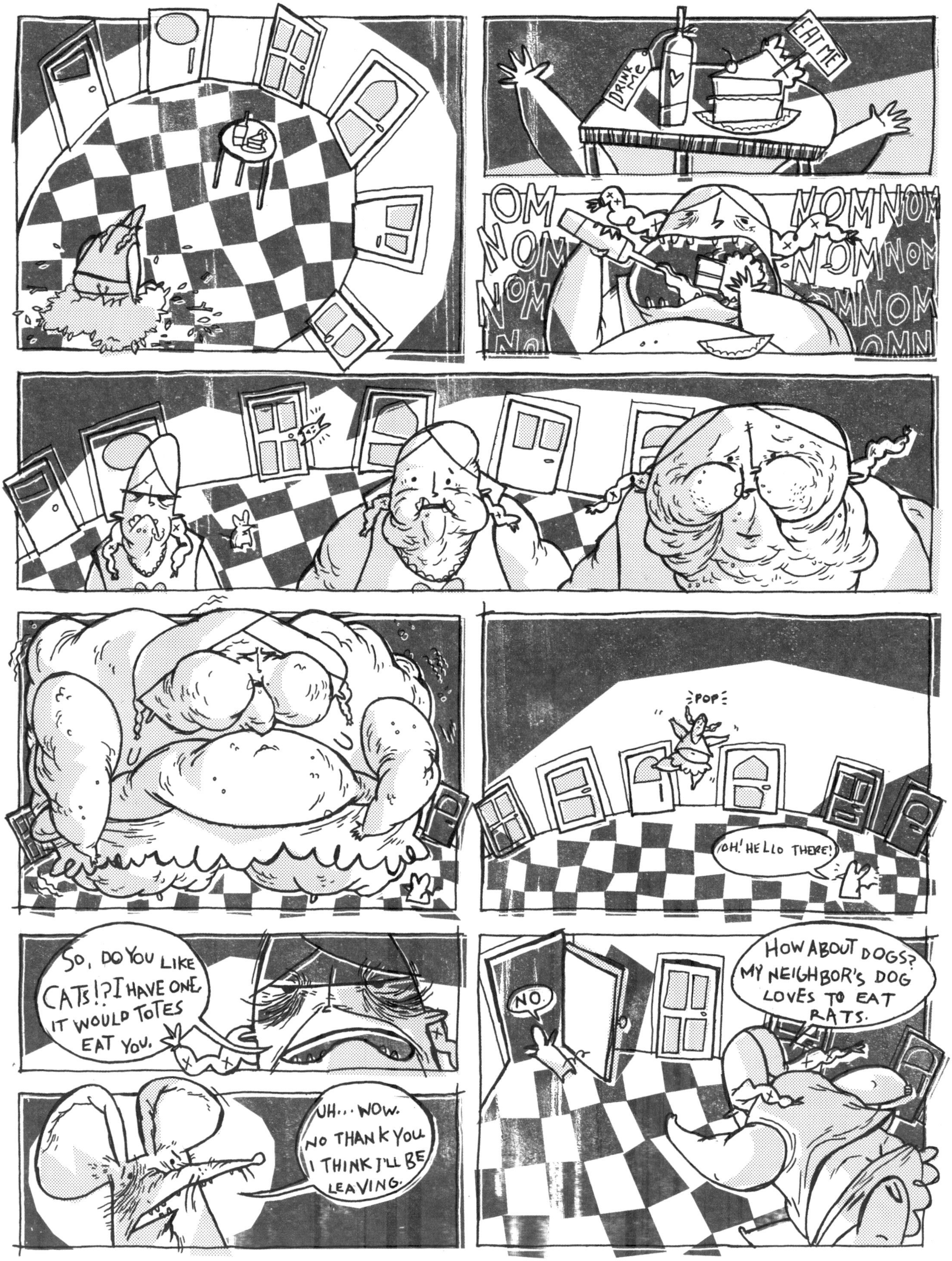
DRINK ME
EAT ME
OM NOM NOM NOM
NOMNOM NOMNOM NOMNOM
POP
OH! HELLO THERE!
SO, DO YOU LIKE CATS!? I HAVE ONE, IT WOULD TOTES EAT YOU.
UH... WOW. NO THANK YOU. I THINK I'LL BE LEAVING.
HOW ABOUT DOGS? MY NEIGHBOR'S DOG LOVES TO EAT RATS.
NO.

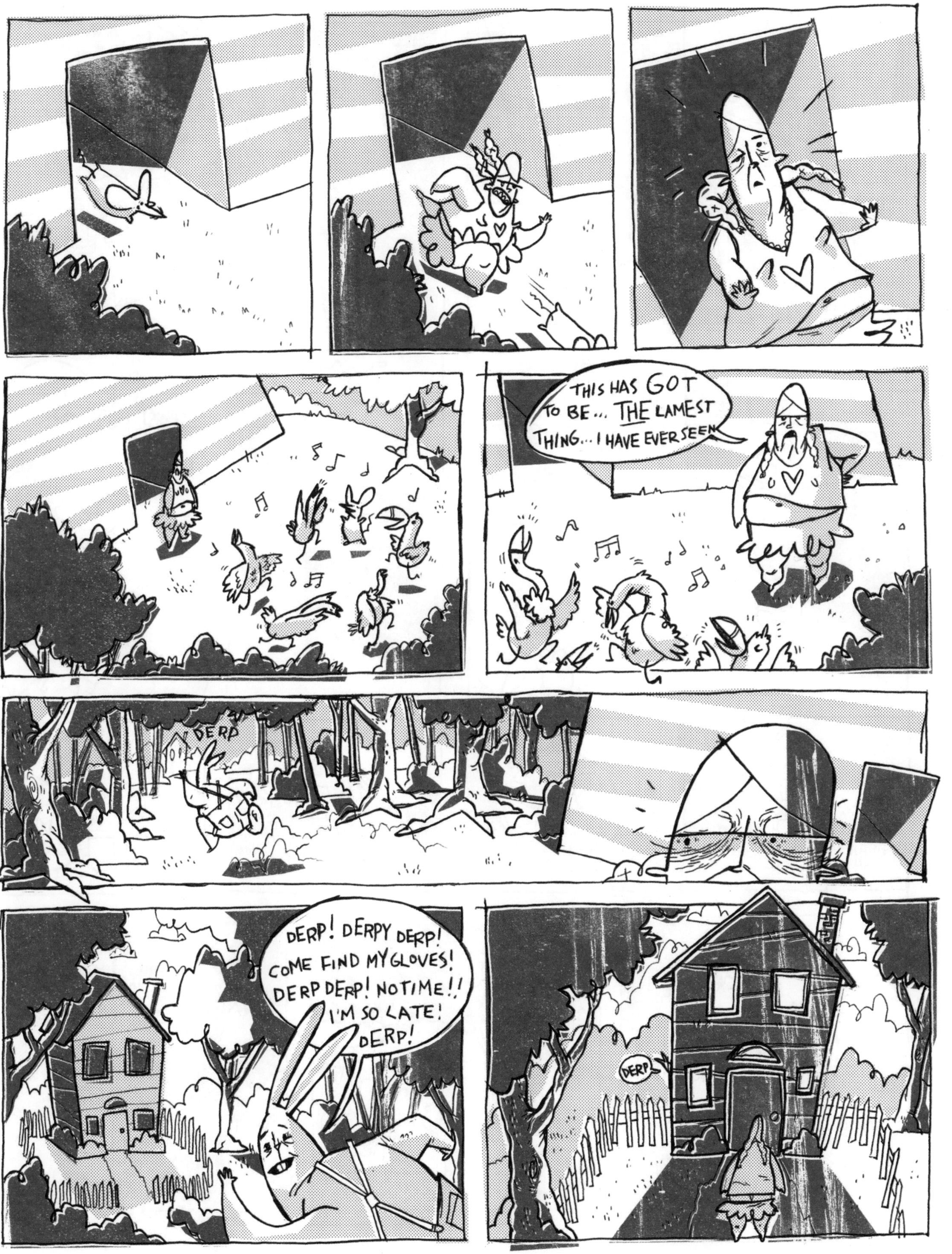
THIS HAS GOT TO BE... THE LAMEST THING... I HAVE EVER SEEN
DERP
DERP! DERPY DERP! COME FIND MY GLOVES! DERP DERP! NO TIME!! I'M SO LATE! DERP!
DERP

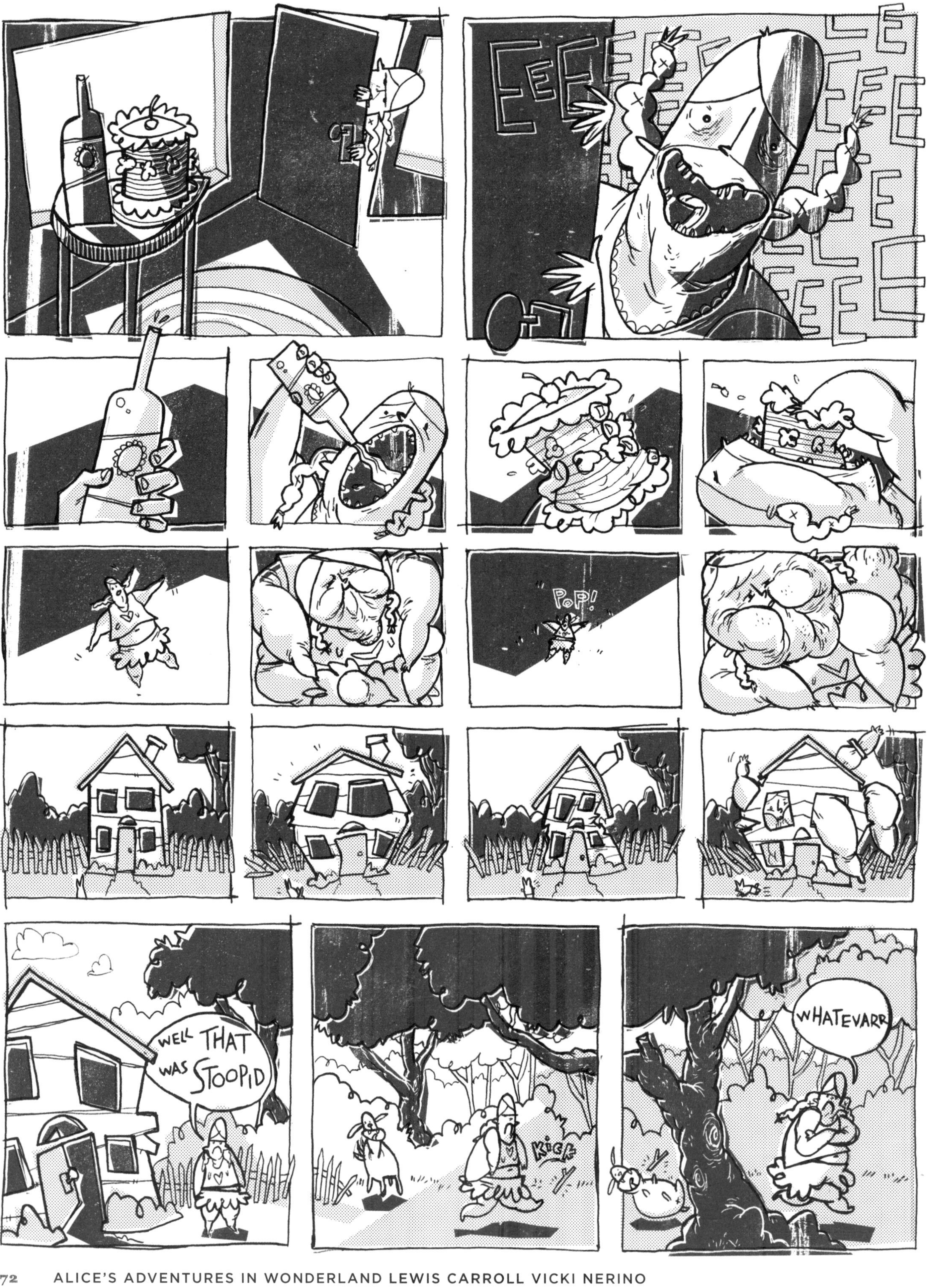
EEEEEEEEEEEEEEEEEEE
POP!
WELL THAT WAS STOOPID
KICK
WHATEVARR

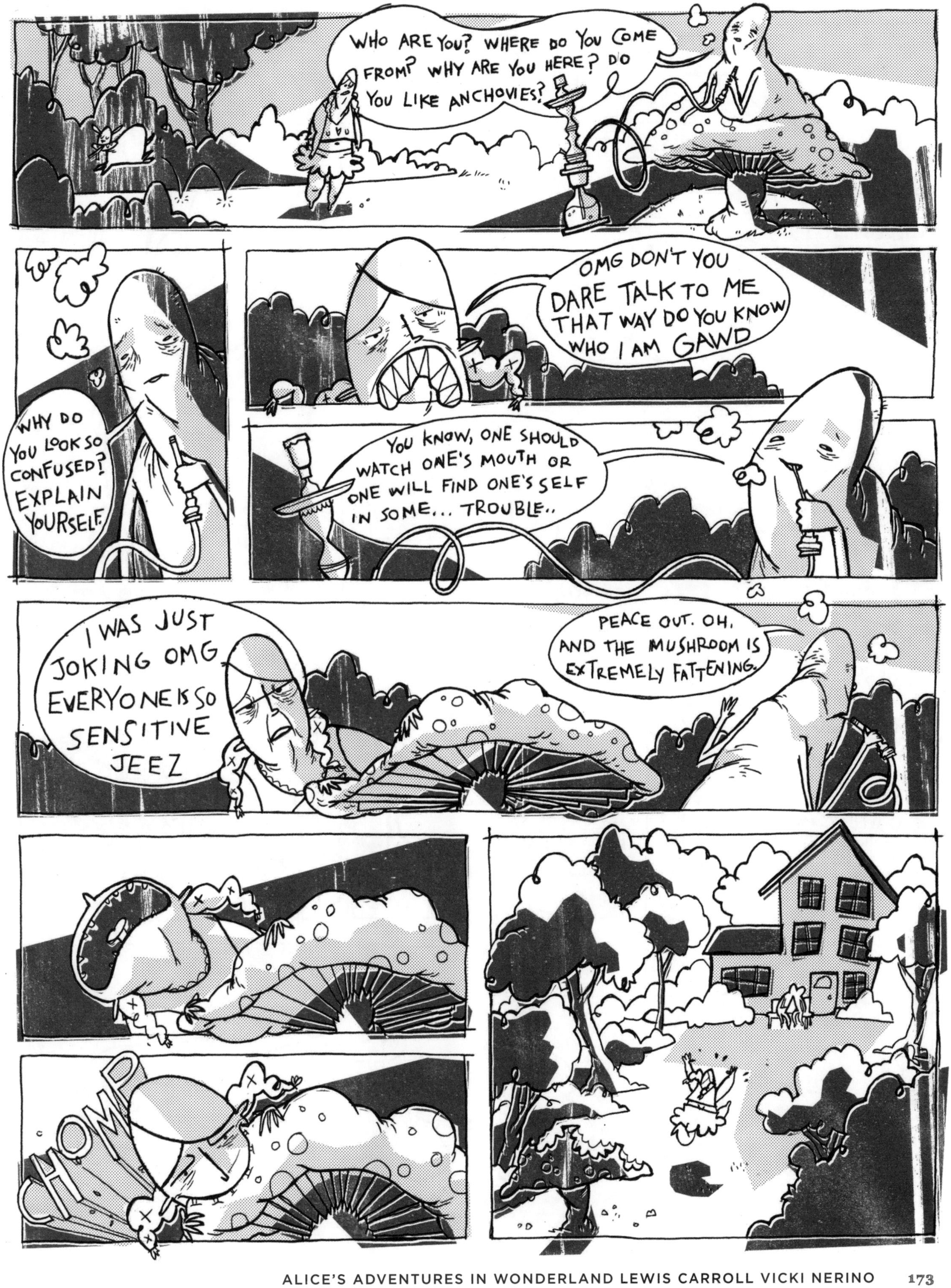

WHO ARE YOU? WHERE DO YOU COME FROM? WHY ARE YOU HERE? DO YOU LIKE ANCHOVIES?
WHY DO YOU LOOK SO CONFUSED? EXPLAIN YOURSELF.
OMG DON'T YOU DARE TALK TO ME THAT WAY DO YOU KNOW WHO I AM GAWD
YOU KNOW, ONE SHOULD WATCH ONE'S MOUTH OR ONE WILL FIND ONE'S SELF IN SOME... TROUBLE..
I WAS JUST JOKING OMG EVERYONE IS SO SENSITIVE JEEZ
PEACE OUT. OH, AND THE MUSHROOM IS EXTREMELY FATTENING.
CHOMP

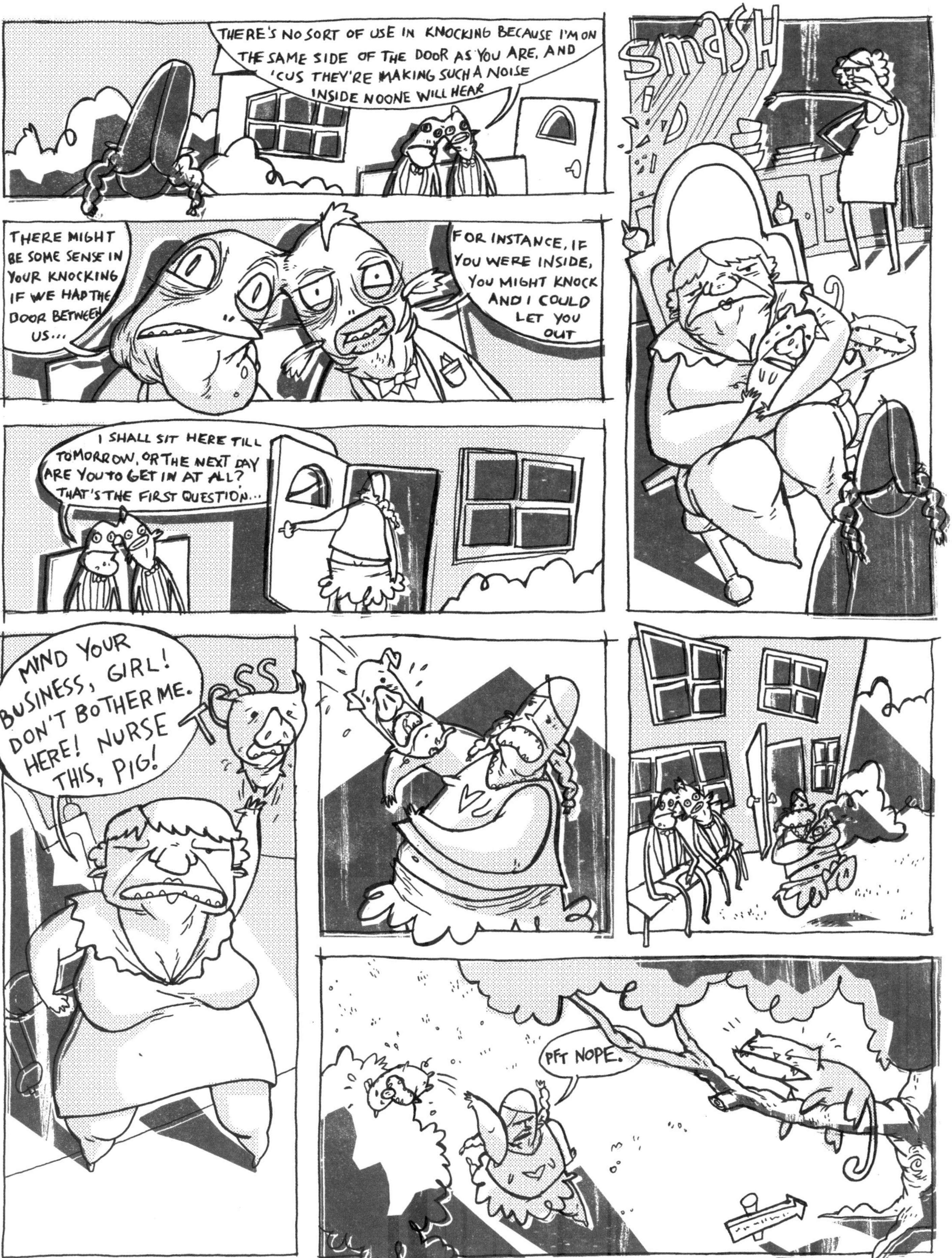
THERE'S NO SORT OF USE IN KNOCKING BECAUSE I'M ON THE SAME SIDE OF THE DOOR AS YOU ARE, AND 'CUS THEY'RE MAKING SUCH A NOISE INSIDE NOONE WILL HEAR
SMASH
THERE MIGHT BE SOME SENSE IN YOUR KNOCKING IF WE HAD THE DOOR BETWEEN US...
FOR INSTANCE, IF YOU WERE INSIDE, YOU MIGHT KNOCK AND I COULD LET YOU OUT
I SHALL SIT HERE TILL TOMORROW, OR THE NEXT DAY
ARE YOU TO GET IN AT ALL? THAT'S THE FIRST QUESTION...
MIND YOUR BUSINESS, GIRL! DON'T BOTHER ME. HERE! NURSE THIS, PIG!
TOSS
PFT NOPE.

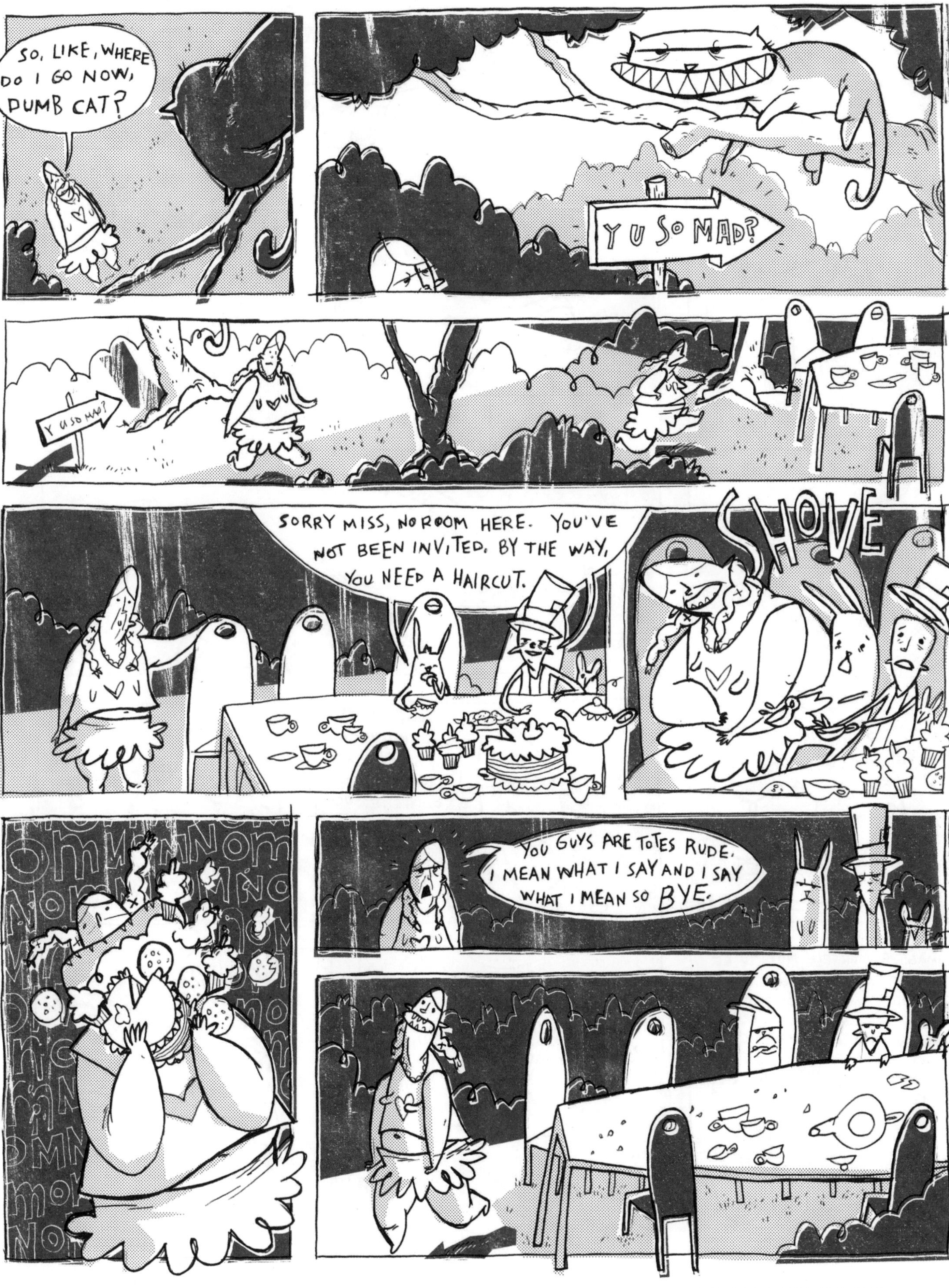
SO, LIKE, WHERE DO I GO NOW, DUMB CAT?
Y U SO MAD?
Y U SO MAD?
SORRY MISS, NO ROOM HERE. YOU'VE NOT BEEN INVITED. BY THE WAY, YOU NEED A HAIRCUT.
SHOVE
YOU GUYS ARE TOTES RUDE. I MEAN WHAT I SAY AND I SAY WHAT I MEAN SO BYE.

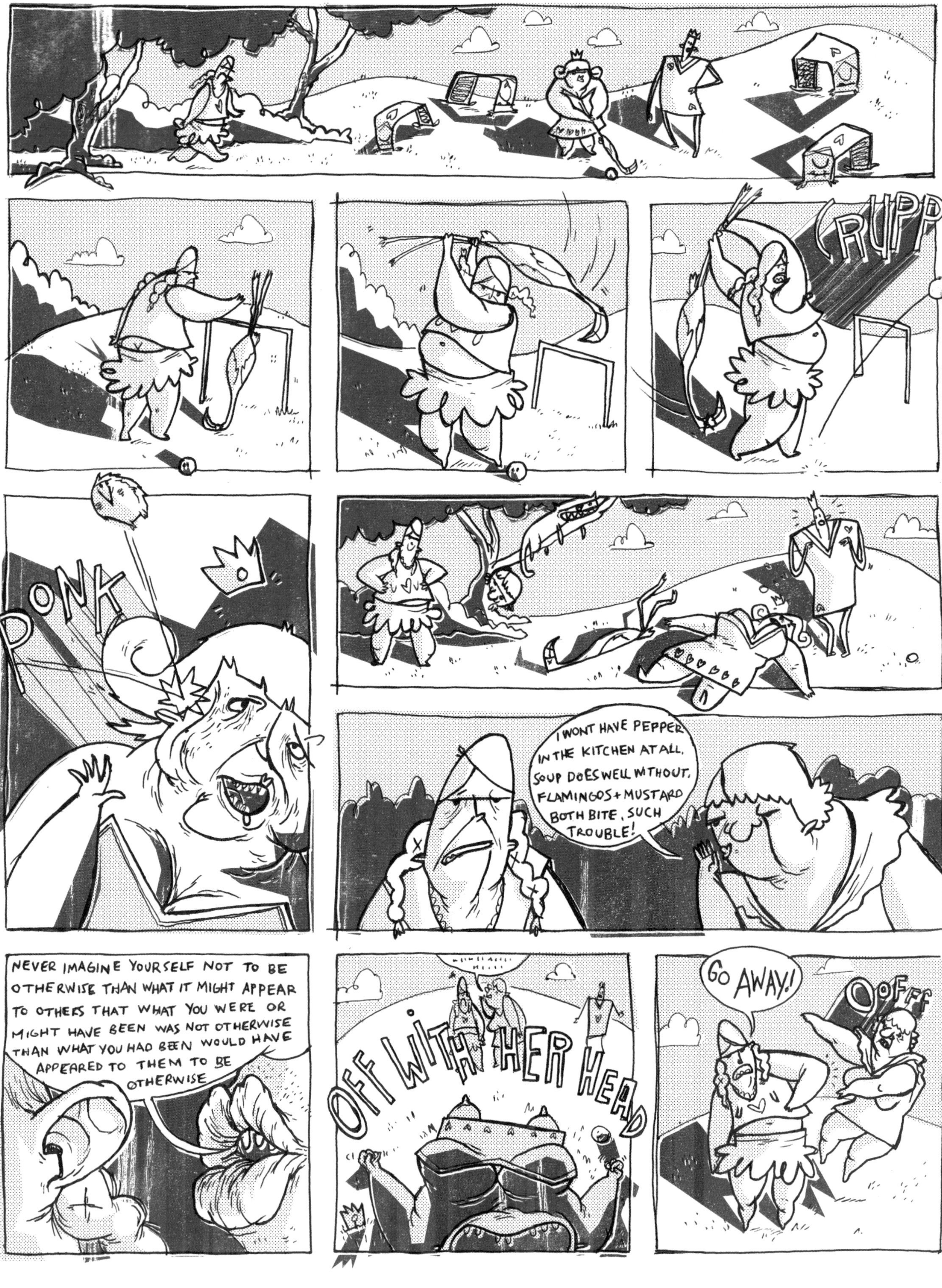
CRUPP
PONK
I WONT HAVE PEPPER IN THE KITCHEN AT ALL. SOUP DOES WELL WITHOUT. FLAMINGOS + MUSTARD BOTH BITE. SUCH TROUBLE!
NEVER IMAGINE YOURSELF NOT TO BE OTHERWISE THAN WHAT IT MIGHT APPEAR TO OTHERS THAT WHAT YOU WERE OR MIGHT HAVE BEEN WAS NOT OTHERWISE THAN WHAT YOU HAD BEEN WOULD HAVE APPEARED TO THEM TO BE OTHERWISE
OFF WITH HER HEAD
GO AWAY!
OOFFF

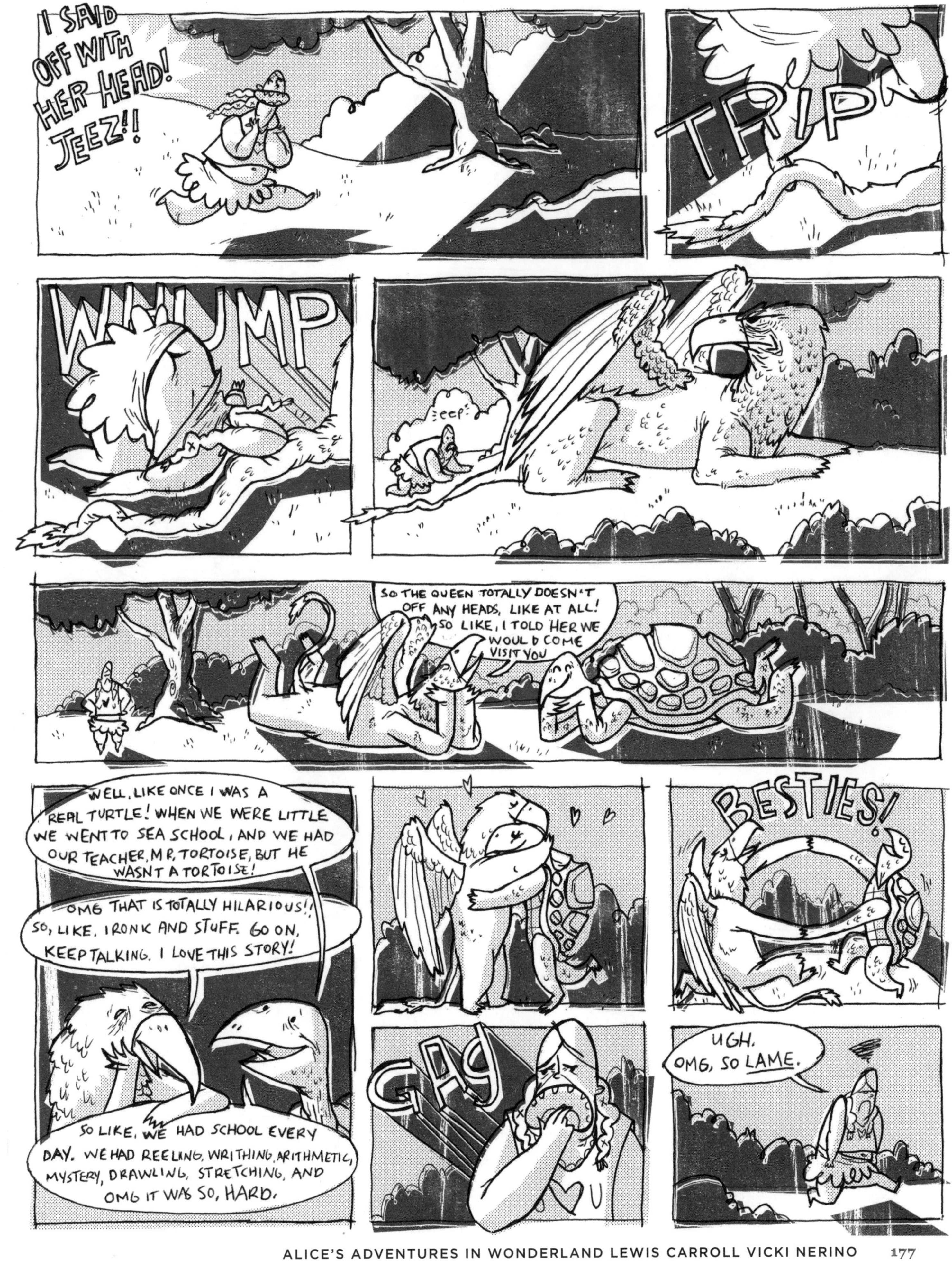

I SAID OFF WITH HER HEAD! JEEZ!!
TRIP
WHUMP
EEP
SO THE QUEEN TOTALLY DOESN'T OFF ANY HEADS, LIKE AT ALL! SO LIKE, I TOLD HER WE WOULD COME VISIT YOU
WELL, LIKE ONCE I WAS A REAL TURTLE! WHEN WE WERE LITTLE WE WENT TO SEA SCHOOL, AND WE HAD OUR TEACHER, MR. TORTOISE, BUT HE WASN'T A TORTOISE!
OMG THAT IS TOTALLY HILARIOUS!! SO, LIKE, IRONIC AND STUFF. GO ON, KEEP TALKING. I LOVE THIS STORY!
SO LIKE, WE HAD SCHOOL EVERY DAY. WE HAD REELING, WRITHING, ARITHMETIC, MYSTERY, DRAWLING, STRETCHING, AND OMG IT WAS SO, HARD.
BESTIES!
GAG
UGH. OMG, SO LAME.

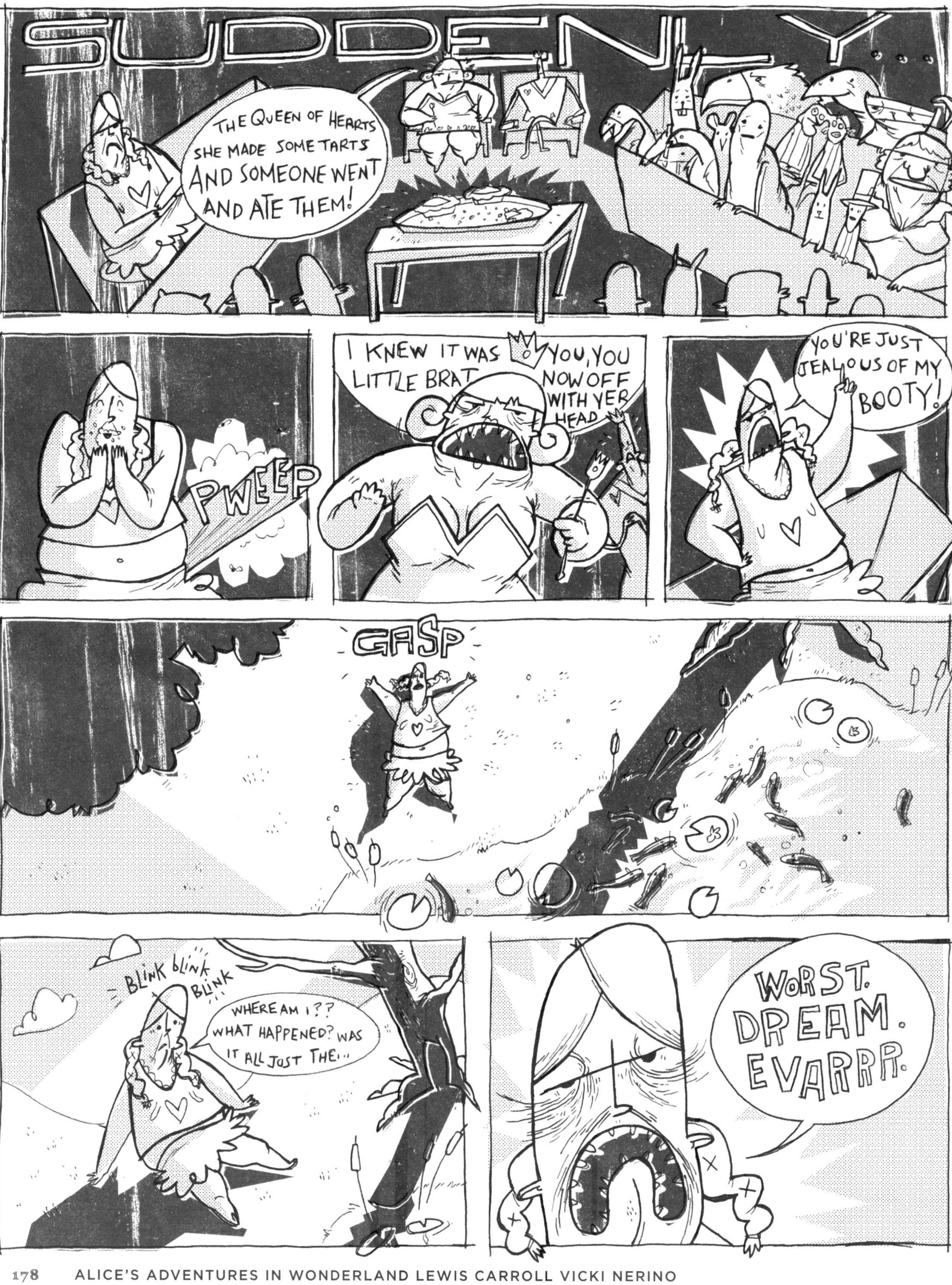
SUDDENLY...
THE QUEEN OF HEARTS SHE MADE SOME TARTS AND SOMEONE WENT AND ATE THEM!
PWEEP
I KNEW IT WAS YOU, YOU LITTLE BRAT NOW OFF WITH YER HEAD
YOU'RE JUST JEALOUS OF MY BOOTY!
GASP
BLINK BLINK BLINK
WHERE AM I?? WHAT HAPPENED? WAS IT ALL JUST THE...
WORST. DREAM. EVARRR.

# Leo Tolstoy

ART/ADAPTATION BY **Keren Katz**

**WHEN YOU HEAR THE NAME LEO TOLSTOY, YOU** probably don't think "children's writing." Yet, like a number of other literary greats, he sometimes wrote for the young'uns, too. I admit this gives rise to jokes among friends and colleagues. We imagine Anna Karenina throwing herself under the Little Engine That Could. Or *War and Peace* as a Little Golden Book.

But seriously, Tolstoy wrote over twenty stories for children—including "Where Love Is, God Is There Also" and "A Prisoner in the Caucasus"—as well as the novella *The Decembrists* and the fairy tale "Ivan the Fool." From 1869 to 1872, he adapted a slew of Aesop's fables and Hindu fables. It's five of the latter tales that Keren Katz chose to adapt in her unique style involving colored pencils and hand-lettering done in pencil (both highly unusual choices for comics artists and illustrators in general).

# The Birds in The Net

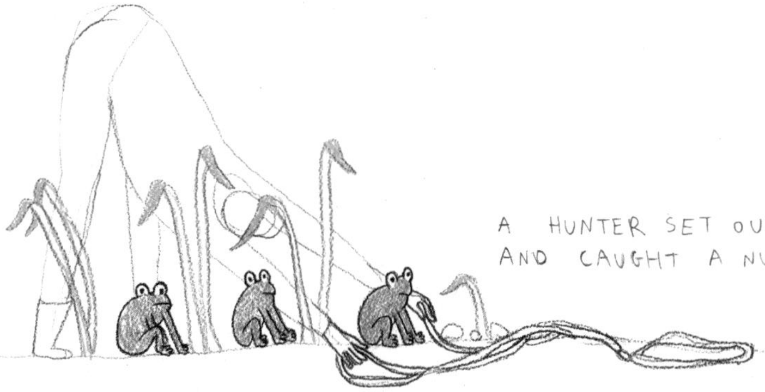

A HUNTER SET OUT A NET NEAR A LAKE AND CAUGHT A NUMBER OF BIRDS.

THE BIRDS WERE LARGE, AND THEY RAISED THE NET AND FLEW AWAY WITH IT.

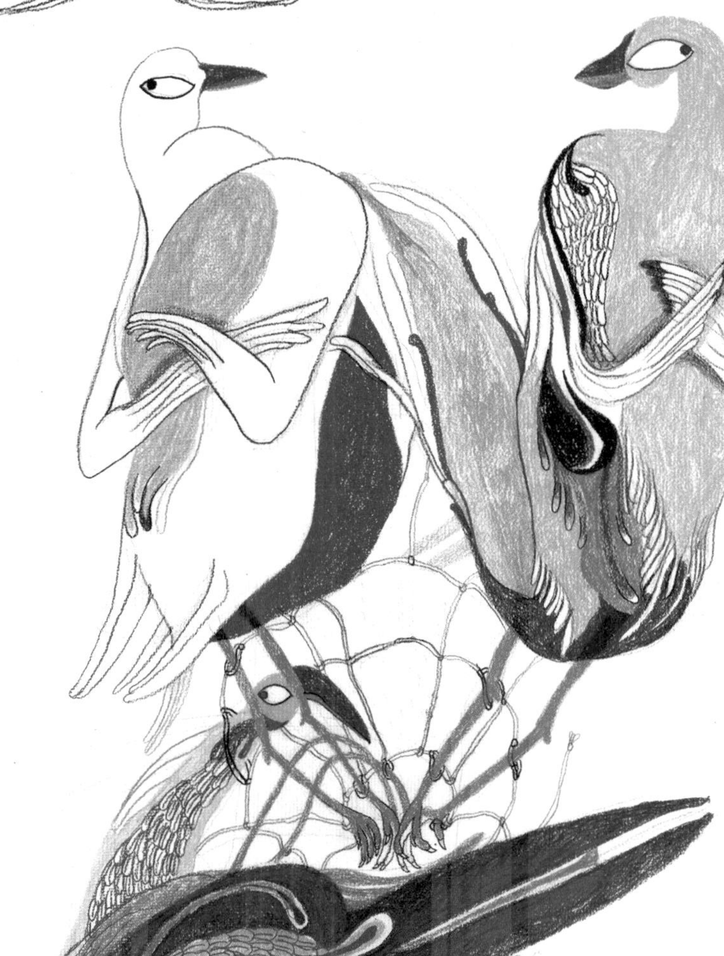

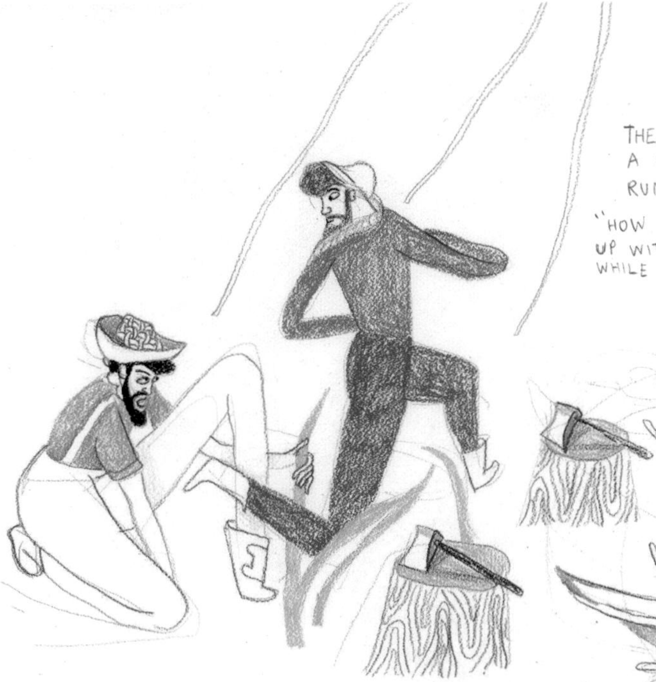

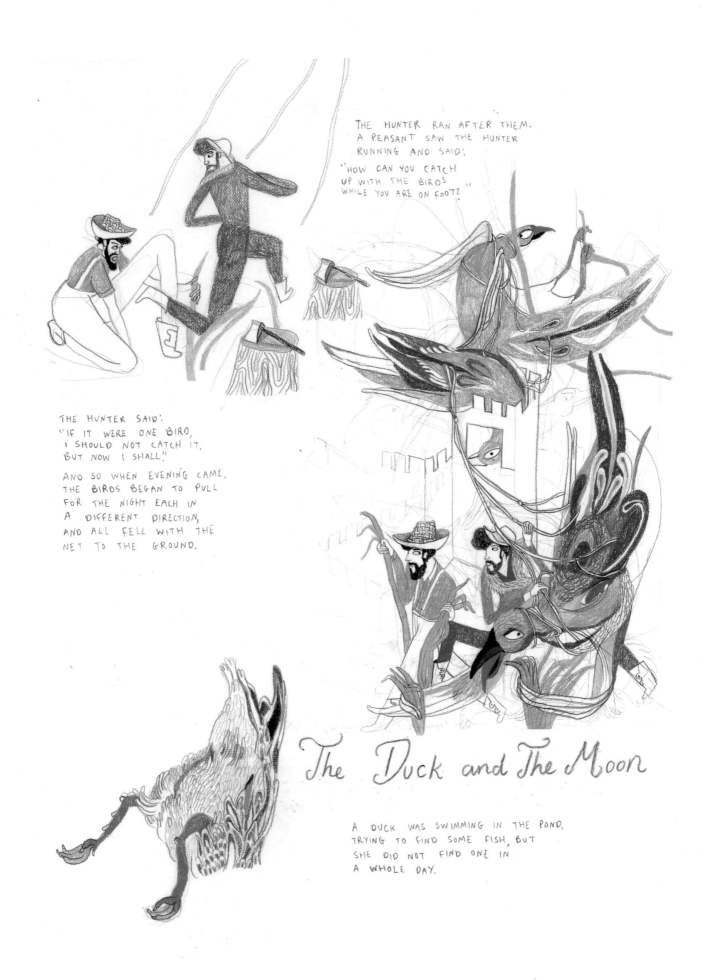

THE HUNTER RAN AFTER THEM. A PEASANT SAW THE HUNTER RUNNING AND SAID: "HOW CAN YOU CATCH UP WITH THE BIRDS WHILE YOU ARE ON FOOT?"

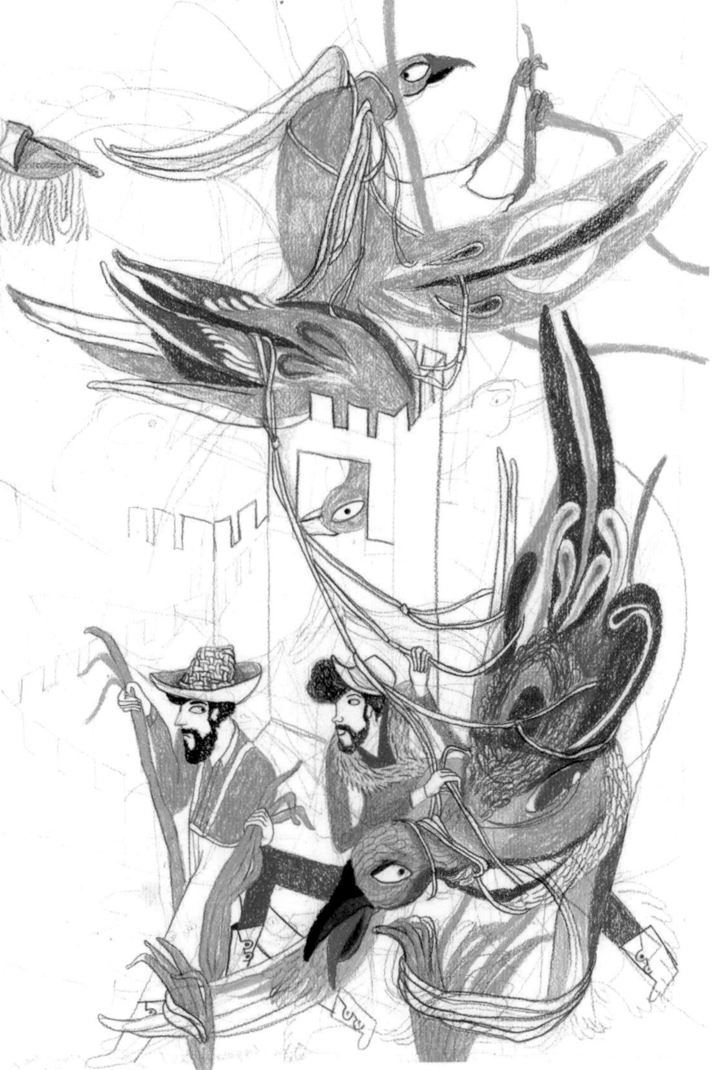

THE HUNTER SAID: "IF IT WERE ONE BIRD, I SHOULD NOT CATCH IT, BUT NOW I SHALL."

AND SO WHEN EVENING CAME, THE BIRDS BEGAN TO PULL FOR THE NIGHT EACH IN A DIFFERENT DIRECTION, AND ALL FELL WITH THE NET TO THE GROUND.

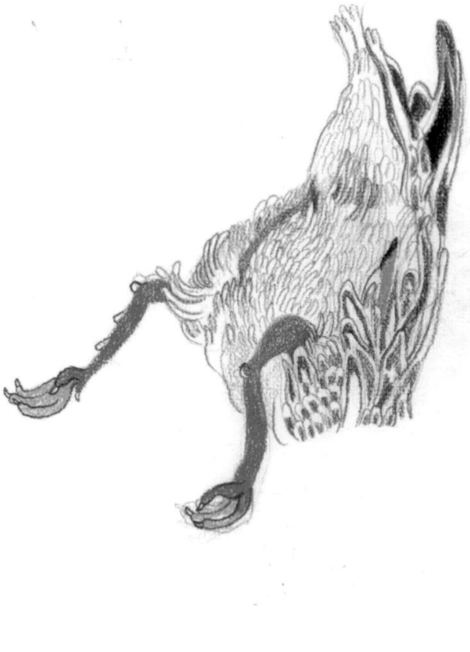

# The Duck and The Moon

A DUCK WAS SWIMMING IN THE POND, TRYING TO FIND SOME FISH, BUT SHE DID NOT FIND ONE IN A WHOLE DAY.

WHEN NIGHT CAME, SHE SAW THE MOON IN THE WATER; SHE THOUGHT THAT IT WAS A FISH, AND PLUNGED TO CATCH THE MOON.

THE OTHER DUCKS SAW HER DO THIS AND LAUGHED AT HER.

THAT MADE THE DUCK FEEL SO ASHAMED AND BASHFUL THAT WHEN SHE SAW A FISH, SHE DID NOT TRY TO CATCH IT.

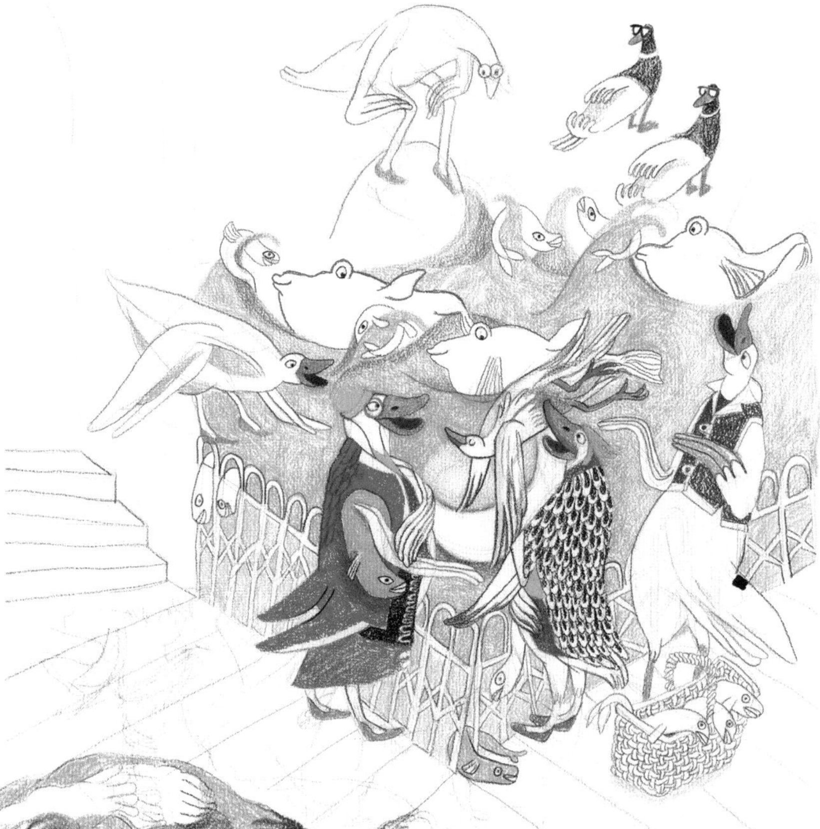

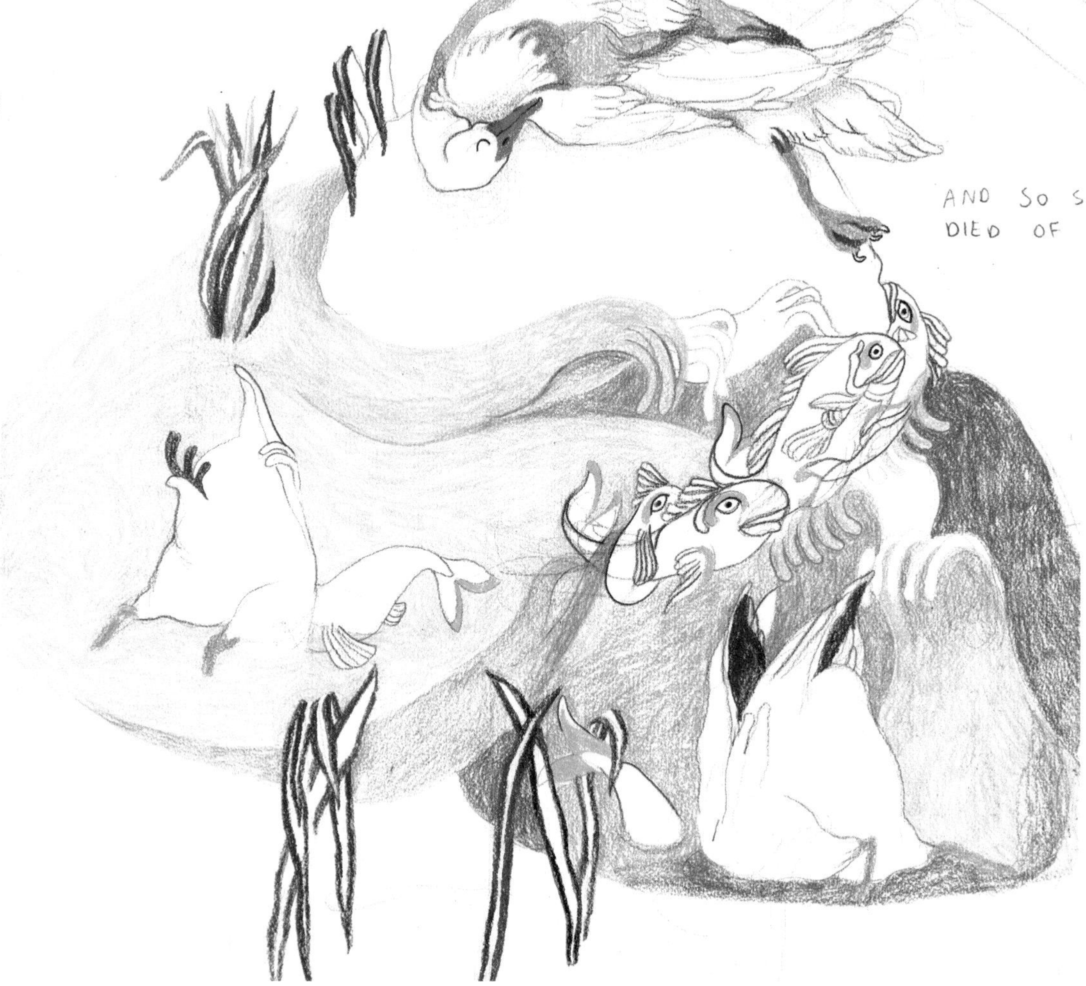

AND SO SHE DIED OF HUNGER.

# The Water Sprite and The Pearl

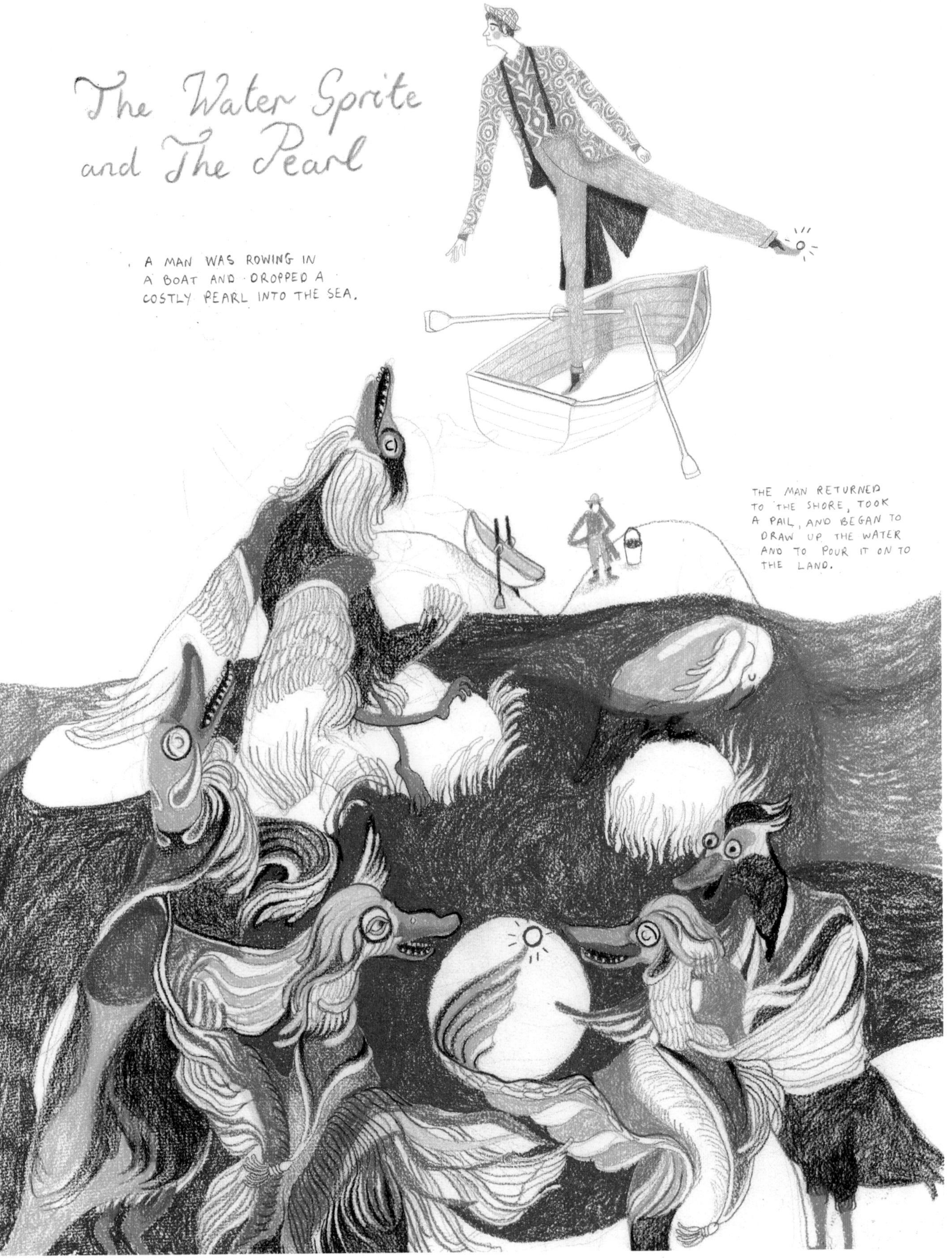
A MAN WAS ROWING IN A BOAT AND DROPPED A COSTLY PEARL INTO THE SEA.
THE MAN RETURNED TO THE SHORE, TOOK A PAIL, AND BEGAN TO DRAW UP THE WATER AND TO POUR IT ON TO THE LAND.

HE DREW THE WATER AND POURED
IT OUT FOR THREE DAYS WITHOUT STOPPING.

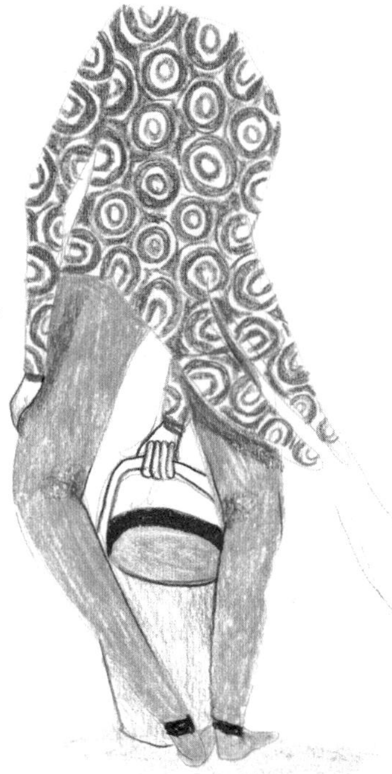

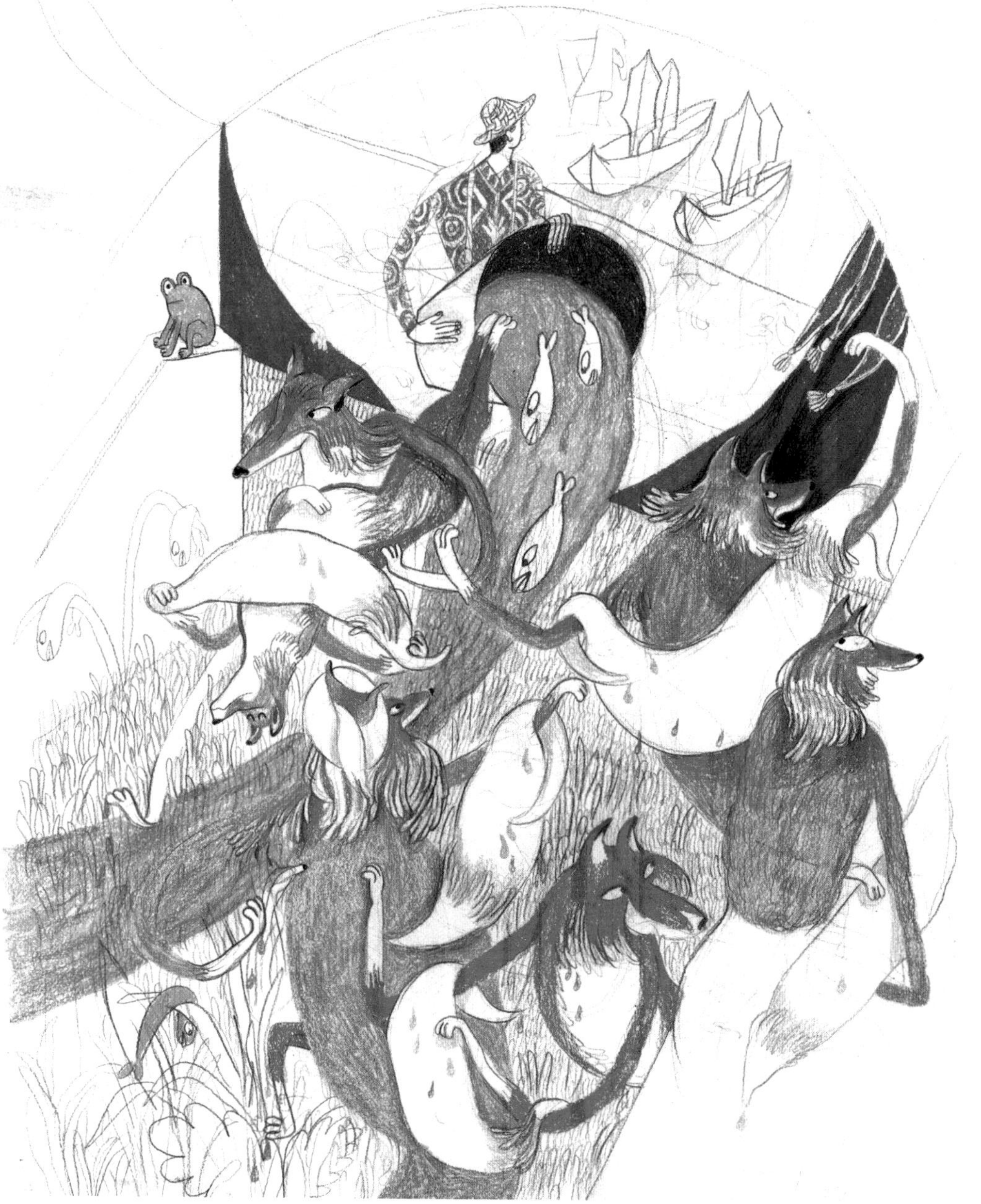

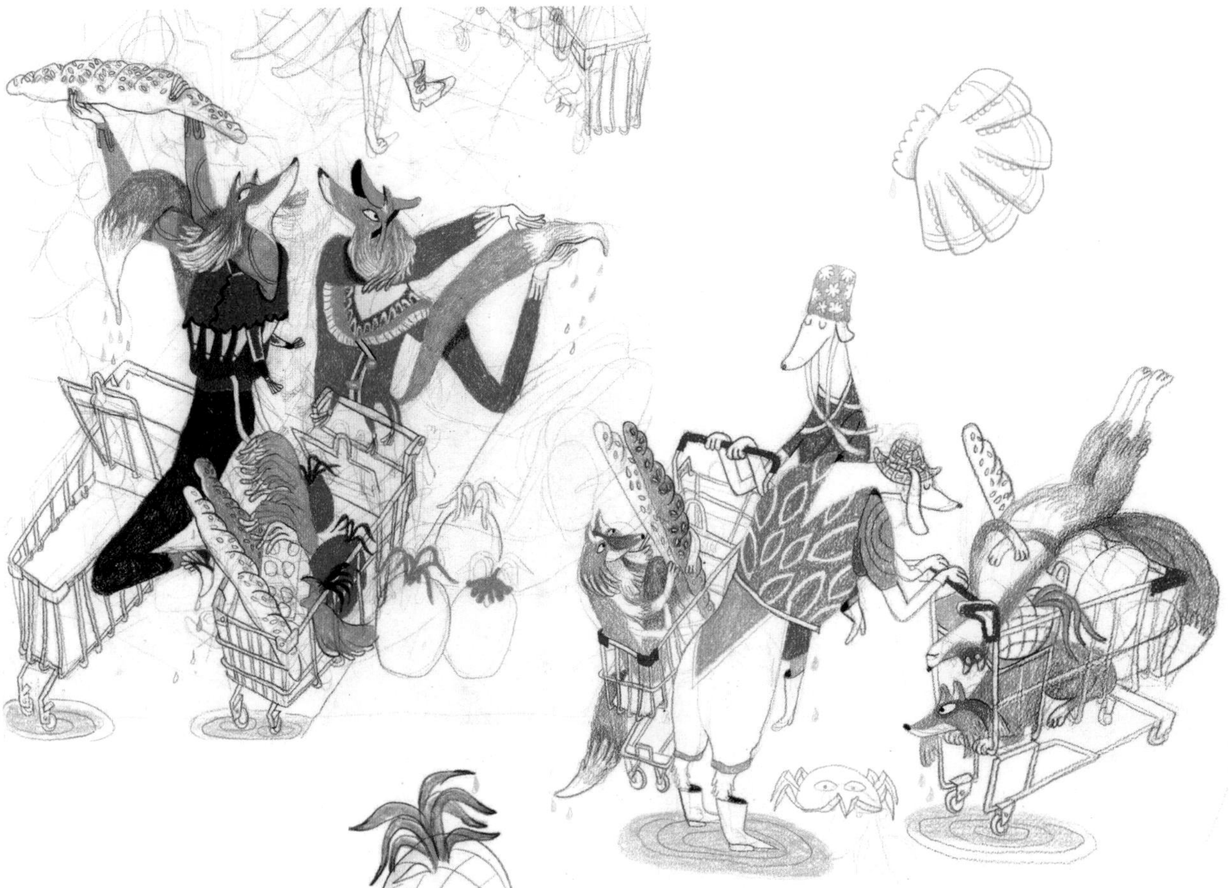

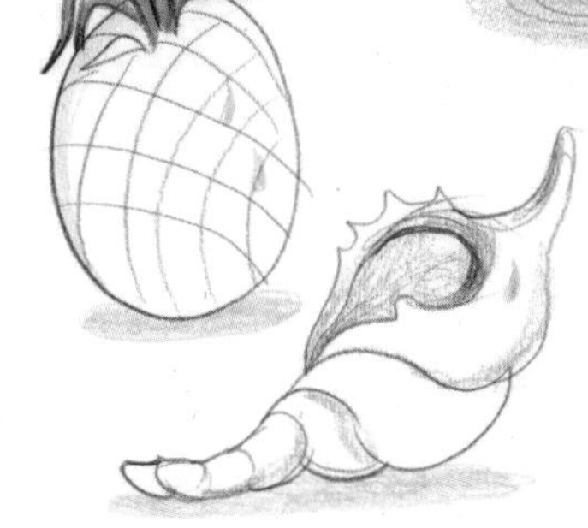

ON THE FOURTH DAY, THE WATER SPRITE CAME OUT OF THE WATER AND ASKED:

"WHY ARE YOU DRAWING THE WATER?"

THE MAN SAID:

"I'M DRAWING IT BECAUSE I'VE DROPPED A PEARL INTO IT.

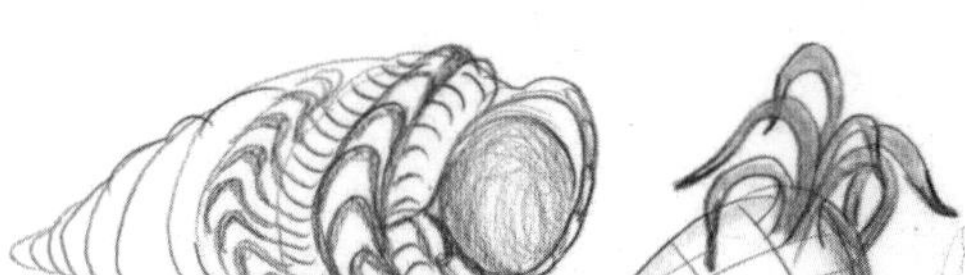

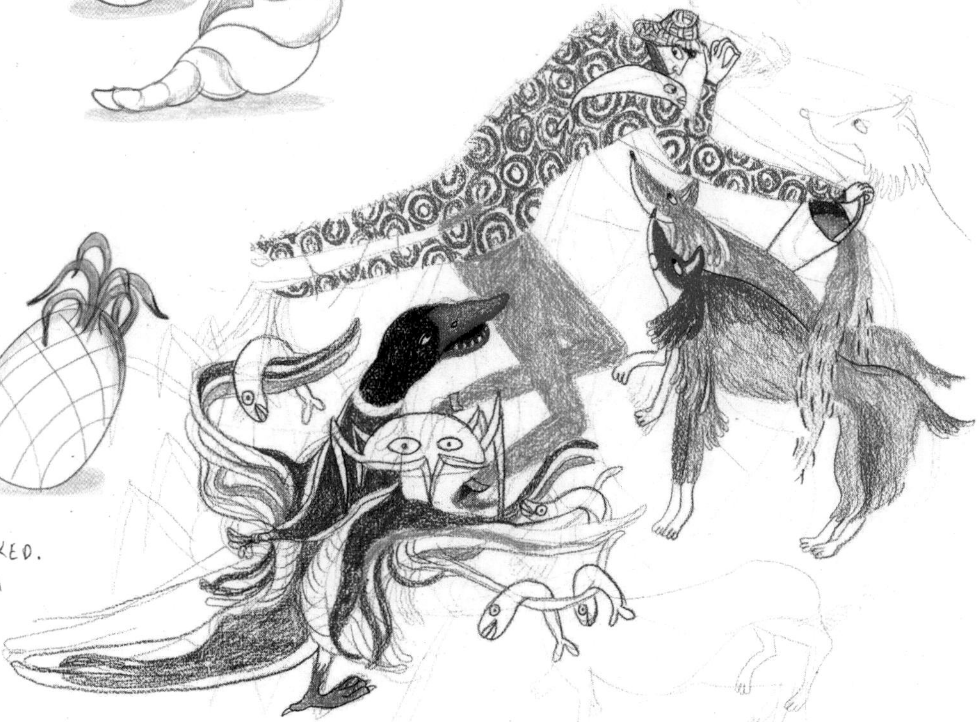

"WILL YOU STOP SOON?"

THE WATER SPRITE ASKED.

"I WILL STOP WHEN I DRY UP THE SEA",

SAID THE MAN.

THEN THE WATER SPRITE RETURNED TO THE SEA, BROUGHT BACK THAT PEARL, AND GAVE IT TO THE MAN.

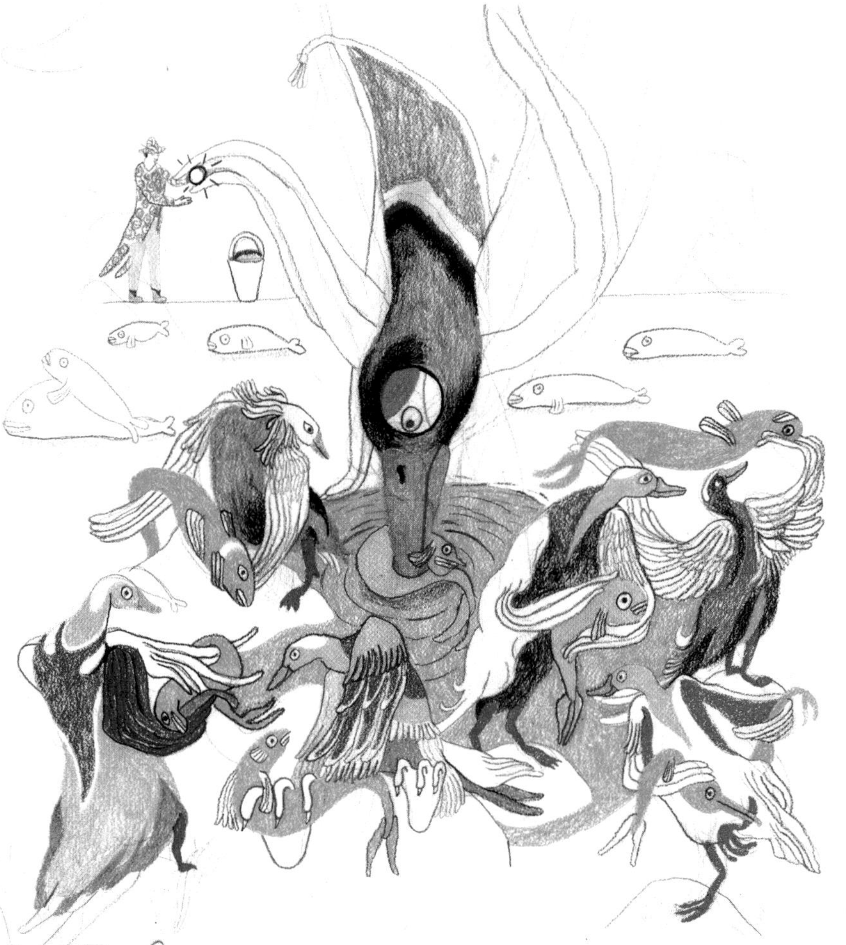

## The Mouse Under The Granary

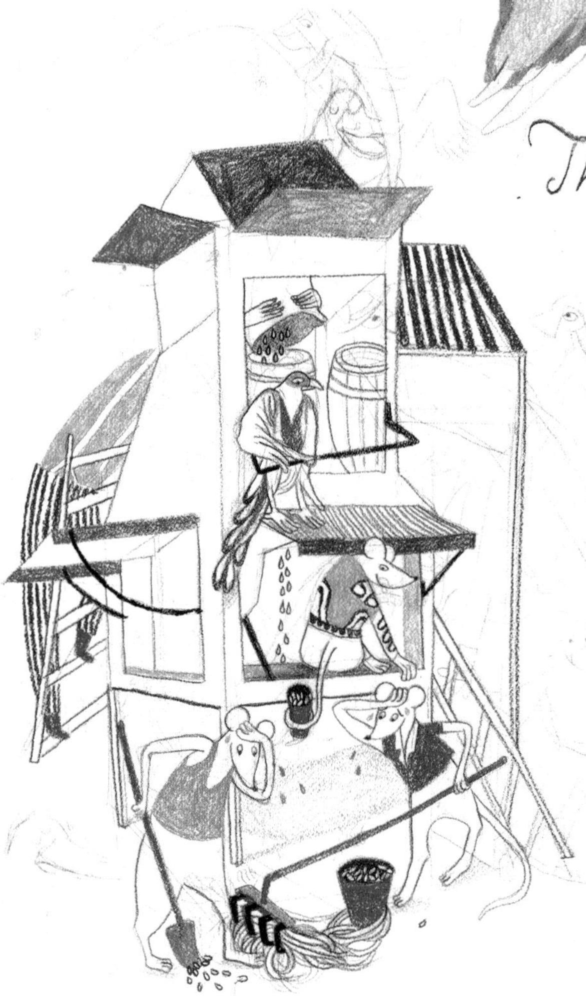

IN THE FLOOR OF THE GRANARY THERE WAS A LITTLE HOLE, AND THE GRAIN FELL DOWN THROUGH IT.

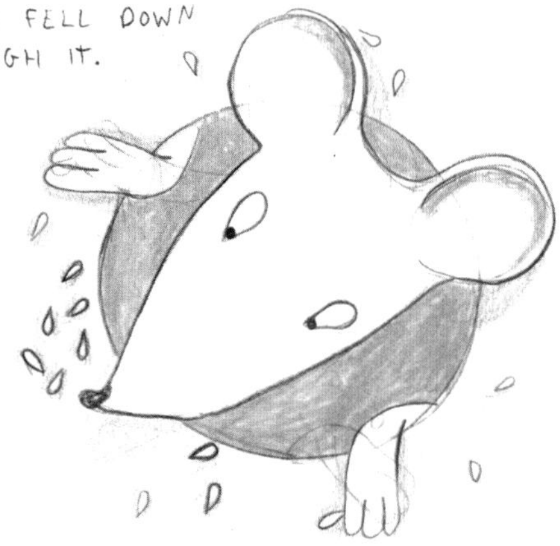

THE MOUSE HAD AN EASY LIFE OF IT BUT SHE WANTED TO BRAG OF HER EASE. SHE GNAWED A LARGER HOLE IN THE FLOOR AND INVITED OTHER MICE TO FEAST.

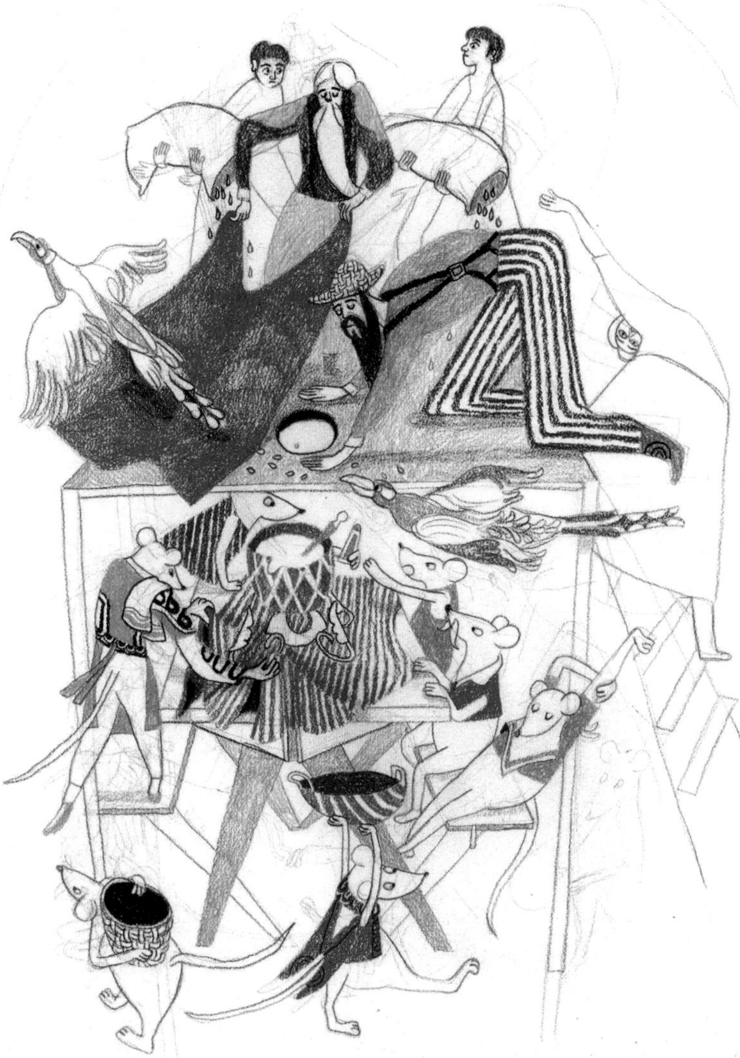

WHEN SHE BROUGHT THE MICE, SHE SAW THERE WAS NO HOLE. THE PEASANT HAD NOTICED THE BIG HOLE IN THE FLOOR, AND HAD STOPPED IT.

# The Falcon and The Cock

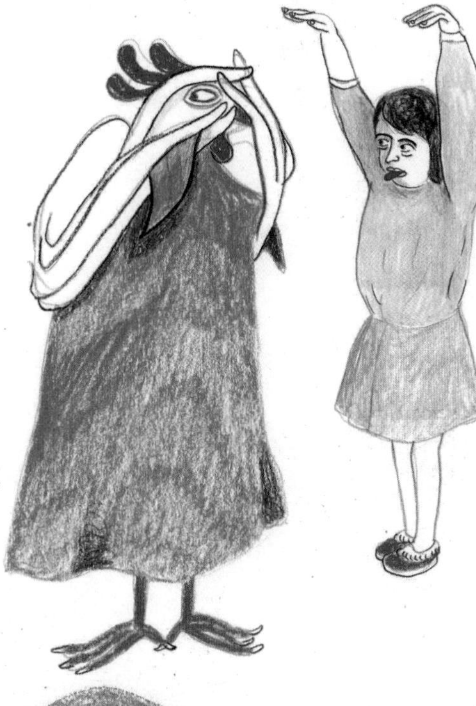

FALCON SAID TO THE COCK: "IN YOU COCKS THERE IS NO GRATITUDE. ONE CAN SEE THAT YOU'RE OF A COMMON BREED. YOU GO TO YOUR MASTERS WHEN YOU ARE HUNGRY.

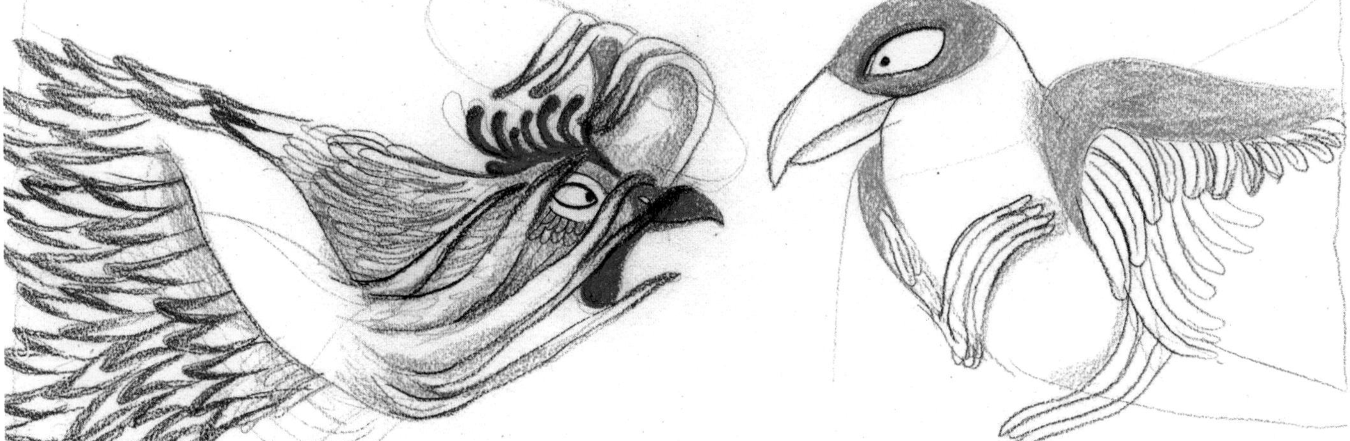

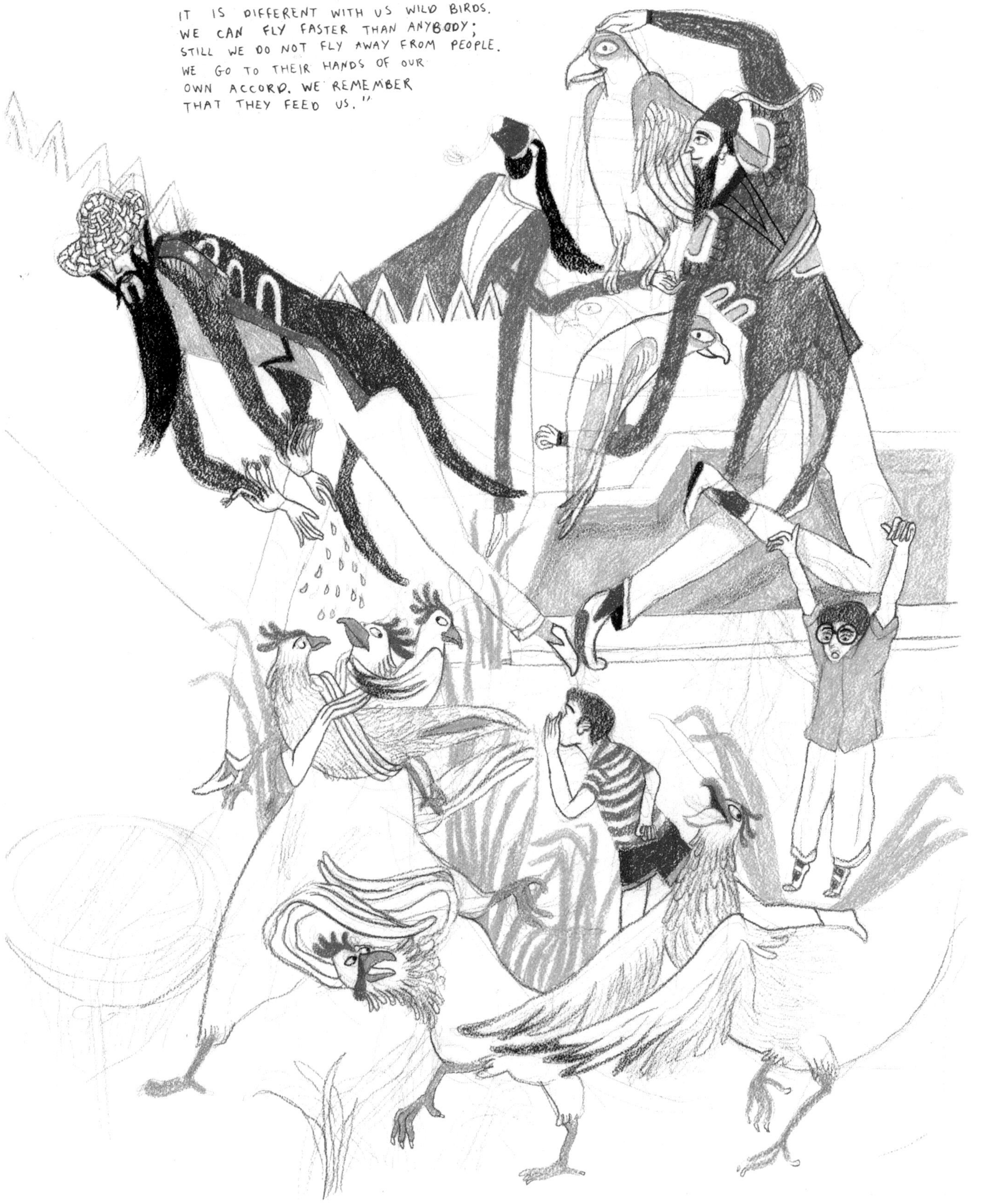
IT IS DIFFERENT WITH US WILD BIRDS.
WE CAN FLY FASTER THAN ANYBODY;
STILL WE DO NOT FLY AWAY FROM PEOPLE.
WE GO TO THEIR HANDS OF OUR
OWN ACCORD. WE REMEMBER
THAT THEY FEED US."

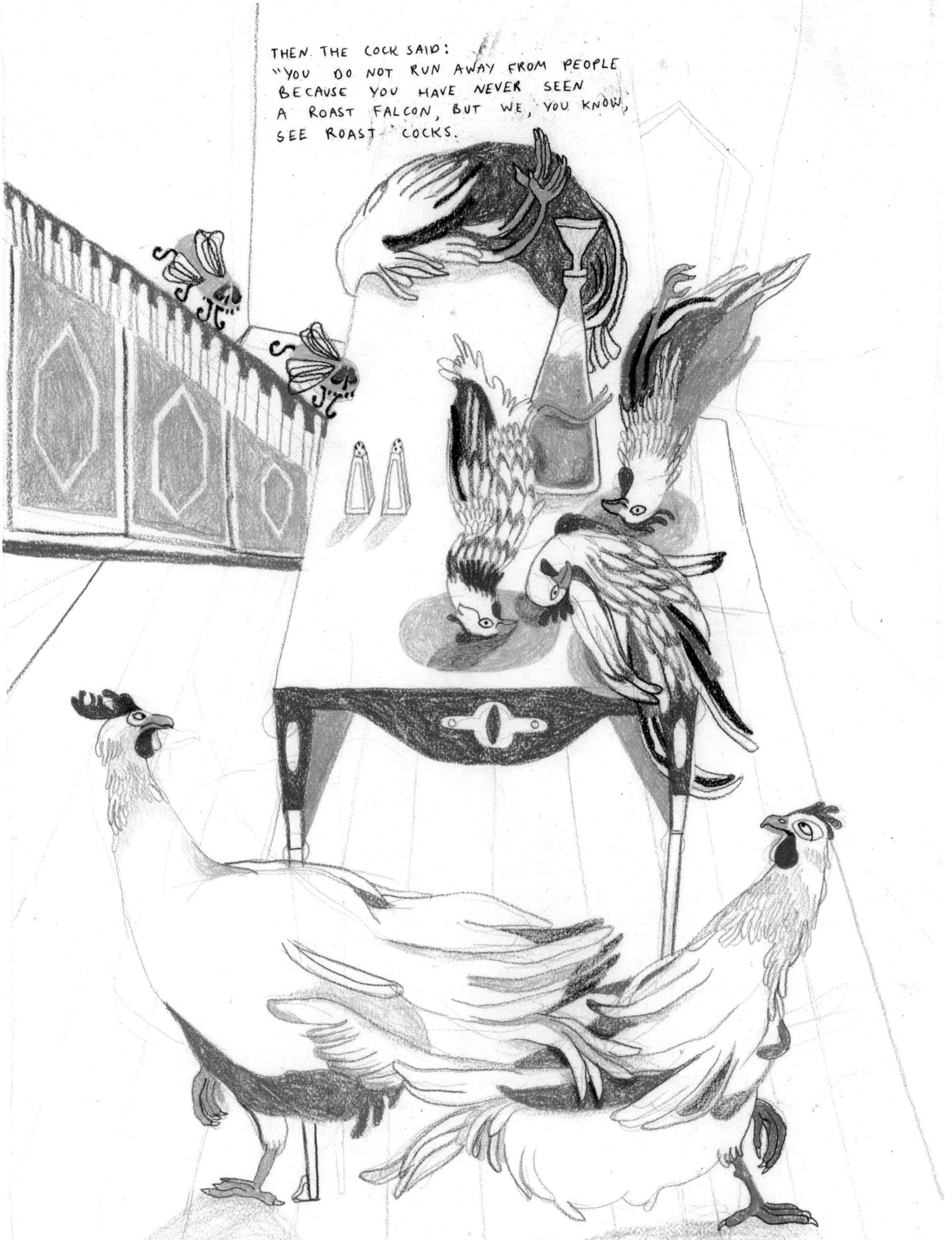
THEN THE COCK SAID:
"YOU DO NOT RUN AWAY FROM PEOPLE
BECAUSE YOU HAVE NEVER SEEN
A ROAST FALCON, BUT WE, YOU KNOW,
SEE ROAST COCKS.

# 20,000 Leagues Under the Sea

## Jules Verne

ART/ADAPTATION BY **Sandy Jimenez**

**ANY NUMBER OF FAMOUS WORKS OF CHILDREN'S** lit sprang from stories the authors were making up to entertain children they knew (either their own or family friends)— *Alice's Adventures in Wonderland*, Edward Lear's nonsense poems, *The Wonderful Wizard of Oz*, *The Wind in the Willows*, *Peter Pan*, *Watership Down*, and so on. An even more intriguing category of classic kid lit contains those works that were never intended for children at all. The Grimms' two-volume collection was originally meant to be a scholarly work of folklore that would preserve German culture. The gloomy, sociopolitically charged *The Time Machine* by H. G. Wells was not meant to entertain kiddies. And *20,000 Leagues Under the Sea*—in the English-speaking world, considered a wonderful adventure yarn for youngsters—is actually a complex work of literature, and Captain Nemo is one of the most beguiling antiheroes ever created. Jules Verne was never a children's writer.

Part of the misunderstanding comes from the large number of horrible translations of the 1870 French novel, including the earliest and most widespread ones. One-fifth to one-quarter of the book was routinely chopped out; Verne's style was dumbed down; and numerous words and phrases were either badly translated or flat-out botched. Plus, you have numerous adaptations of the novel created expressly for a young audience, keeping the adventure and the exotic locales while deleting the nuances.

Bearing markers and watercolors, Sandy Jimenez adapts the novel—highly condensed, of course—and remains faithful to the text and plot, while providing a dazzlingly unexpected visual twist. Nemo is David Bowie in his Ziggy Stardust incarnation. Ned Land, the great harpooner, is the late Freddie Mercury from Queen. Other musical references abound. Sandy explains: "I did it as a Glam-Rock/New Romantics/'80s punk/synth pop–themed meditation on the effects of the AIDS crisis on pop culture and many of my boyhood heroes in music." Nemo's grief at the deaths of crew members takes on new meaning, even as Verne's original remains untouched. . . .

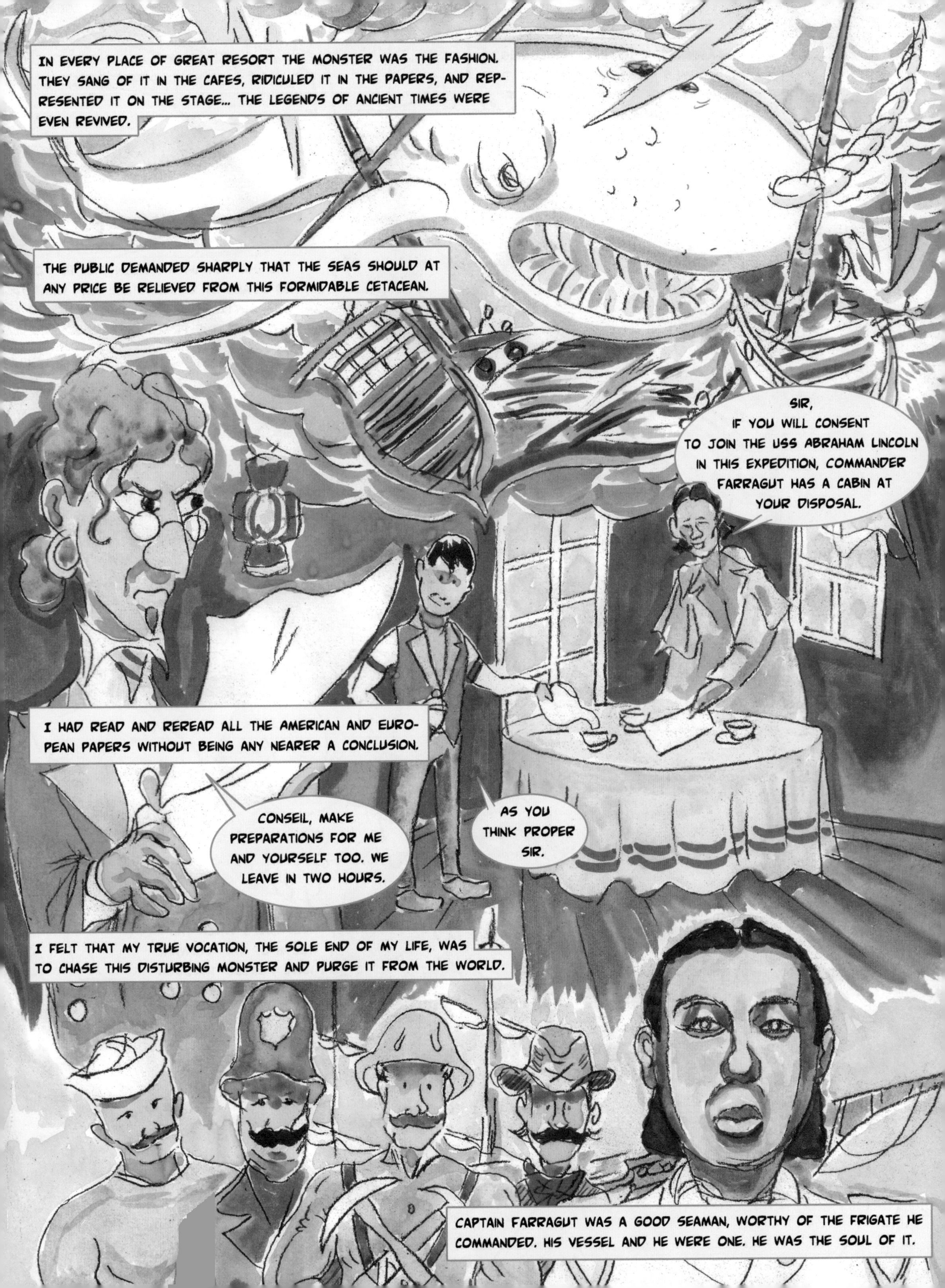

IN EVERY PLACE OF GREAT RESORT THE MONSTER WAS THE FASHION. THEY SANG OF IT IN THE CAFES, RIDICULED IT IN THE PAPERS, AND REPRESENTED IT ON THE STAGE... THE LEGENDS OF ANCIENT TIMES WERE EVEN REVIVED.
THE PUBLIC DEMANDED SHARPLY THAT THE SEAS SHOULD AT ANY PRICE BE RELIEVED FROM THIS FORMIDABLE CETACEAN.
SIR, IF YOU WILL CONSENT TO JOIN THE USS ABRAHAM LINCOLN IN THIS EXPEDITION, COMMANDER FARRAGUT HAS A CABIN AT YOUR DISPOSAL.
I HAD READ AND REREAD ALL THE AMERICAN AND EUROPEAN PAPERS WITHOUT BEING ANY NEARER A CONCLUSION.
CONSEIL, MAKE PREPARATIONS FOR ME AND YOURSELF TOO. WE LEAVE IN TWO HOURS.
AS YOU THINK PROPER SIR.
I FELT THAT MY TRUE VOCATION, THE SOLE END OF MY LIFE, WAS TO CHASE THIS DISTURBING MONSTER AND PURGE IT FROM THE WORLD.
CAPTAIN FARRAGUT WAS A GOOD SEAMAN, WORTHY OF THE FRIGATE HE COMMANDED. HIS VESSEL AND HE WERE ONE. HE WAS THE SOUL OF IT.

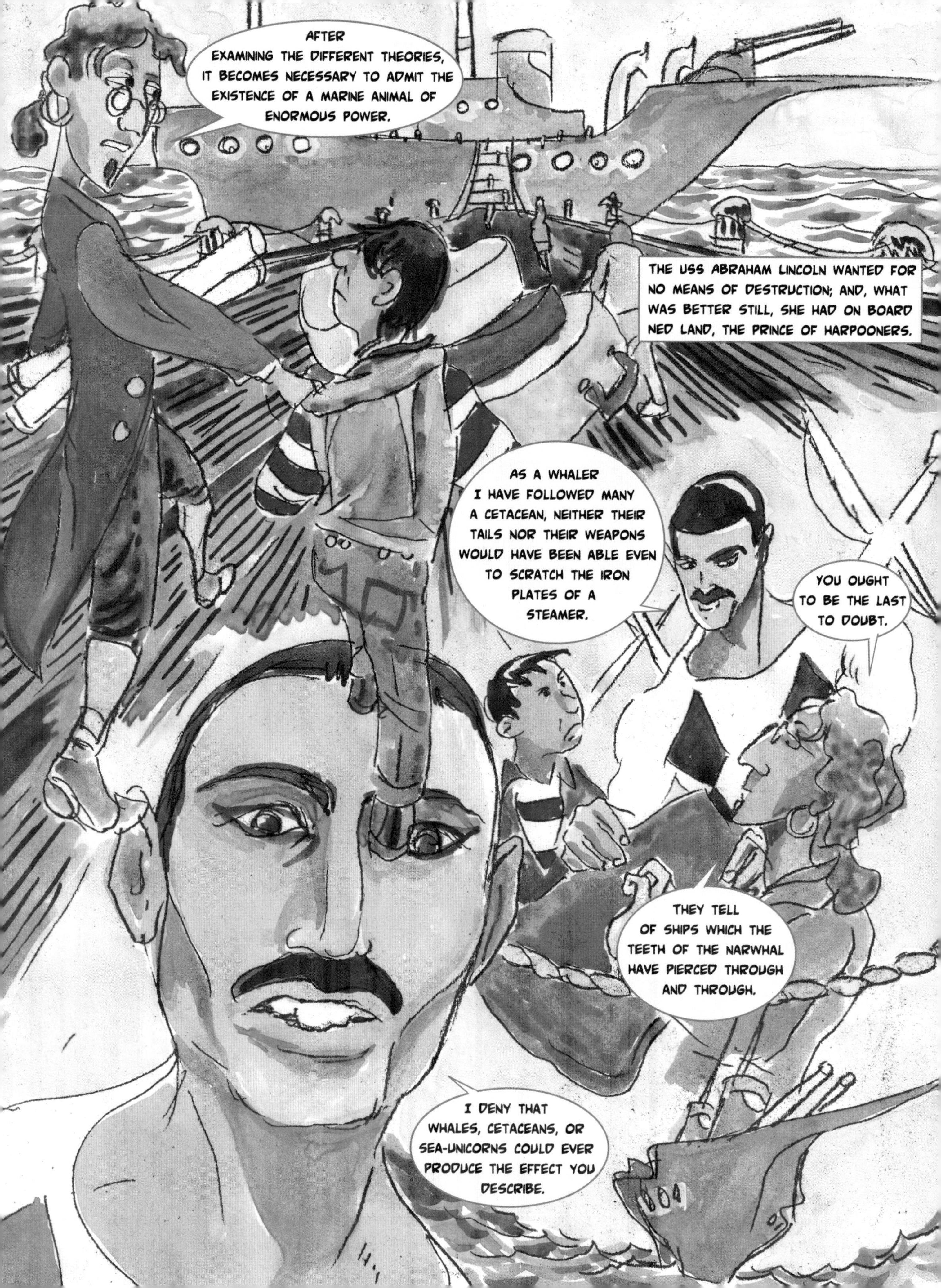
AFTER EXAMINING THE DIFFERENT THEORIES, IT BECOMES NECESSARY TO ADMIT THE EXISTENCE OF A MARINE ANIMAL OF ENORMOUS POWER.
THE USS ABRAHAM LINCOLN WANTED FOR NO MEANS OF DESTRUCTION; AND, WHAT WAS BETTER STILL, SHE HAD ON BOARD NED LAND, THE PRINCE OF HARPOONERS.
AS A WHALER I HAVE FOLLOWED MANY A CETACEAN, NEITHER THEIR TAILS NOR THEIR WEAPONS WOULD HAVE BEEN ABLE EVEN TO SCRATCH THE IRON PLATES OF A STEAMER.
YOU OUGHT TO BE THE LAST TO DOUBT.
THEY TELL OF SHIPS WHICH THE TEETH OF THE NARWHAL HAVE PIERCED THROUGH AND THROUGH.
I DENY THAT WHALES, CETACEANS, OR SEA-UNICORNS COULD EVER PRODUCE THE EFFECT YOU DESCRIBE.

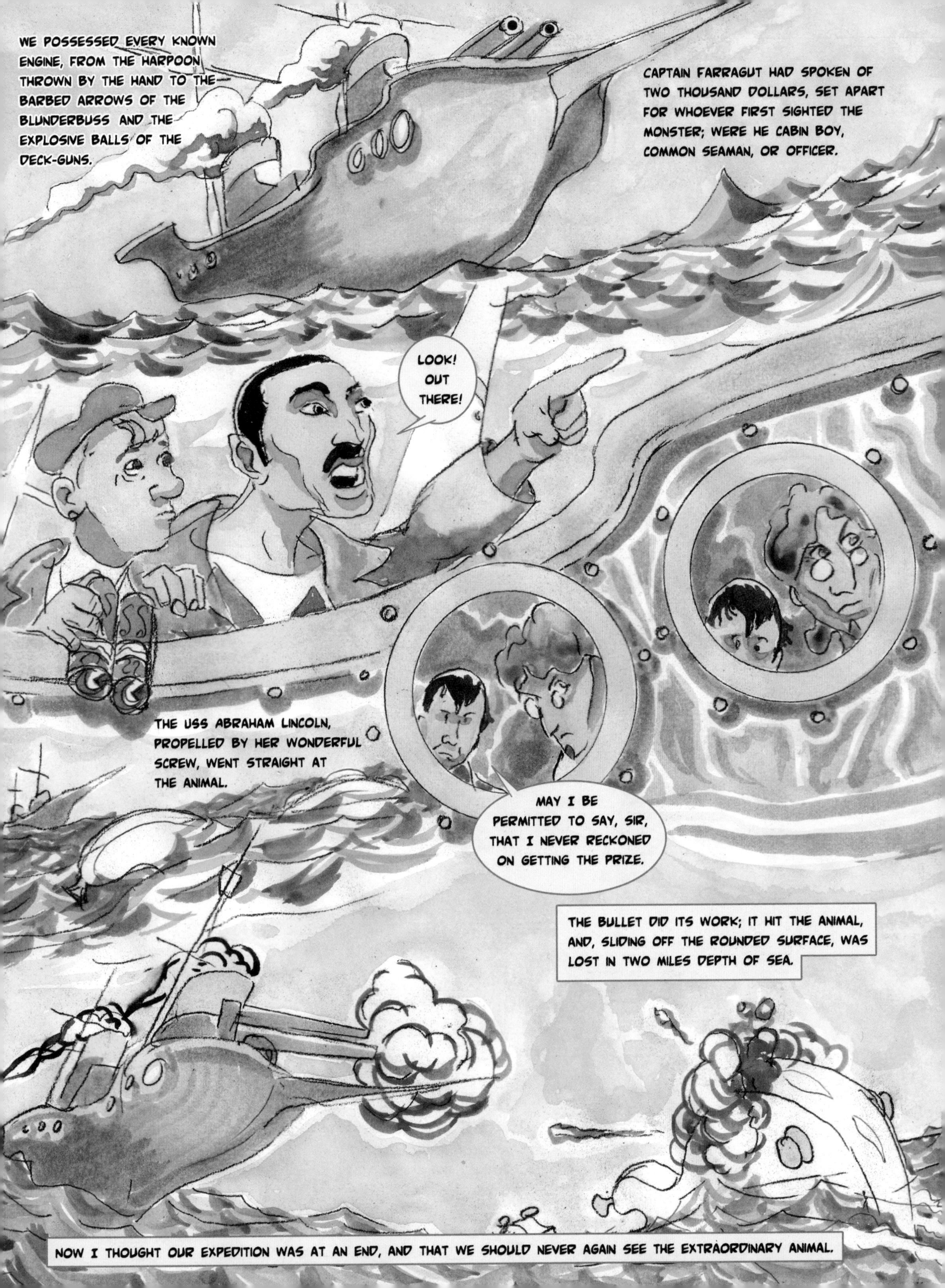
WE POSSESSED EVERY KNOWN ENGINE, FROM THE HARPOON THROWN BY THE HAND TO THE BARBED ARROWS OF THE BLUNDERBUSS AND THE EXPLOSIVE BALLS OF THE DECK-GUNS.
CAPTAIN FARRAGUT HAD SPOKEN OF TWO THOUSAND DOLLARS, SET APART FOR WHOEVER FIRST SIGHTED THE MONSTER; WERE HE CABIN BOY, COMMON SEAMAN, OR OFFICER.
LOOK! OUT THERE!
THE USS ABRAHAM LINCOLN, PROPELLED BY HER WONDERFUL SCREW, WENT STRAIGHT AT THE ANIMAL.
MAY I BE PERMITTED TO SAY, SIR, THAT I NEVER RECKONED ON GETTING THE PRIZE.
THE BULLET DID ITS WORK; IT HIT THE ANIMAL, AND, SLIDING OFF THE ROUNDED SURFACE, WAS LOST IN TWO MILES DEPTH OF SEA.
NOW I THOUGHT OUR EXPEDITION WAS AT AN END, AND THAT WE SHOULD NEVER AGAIN SEE THE EXTRAORDINARY ANIMAL.

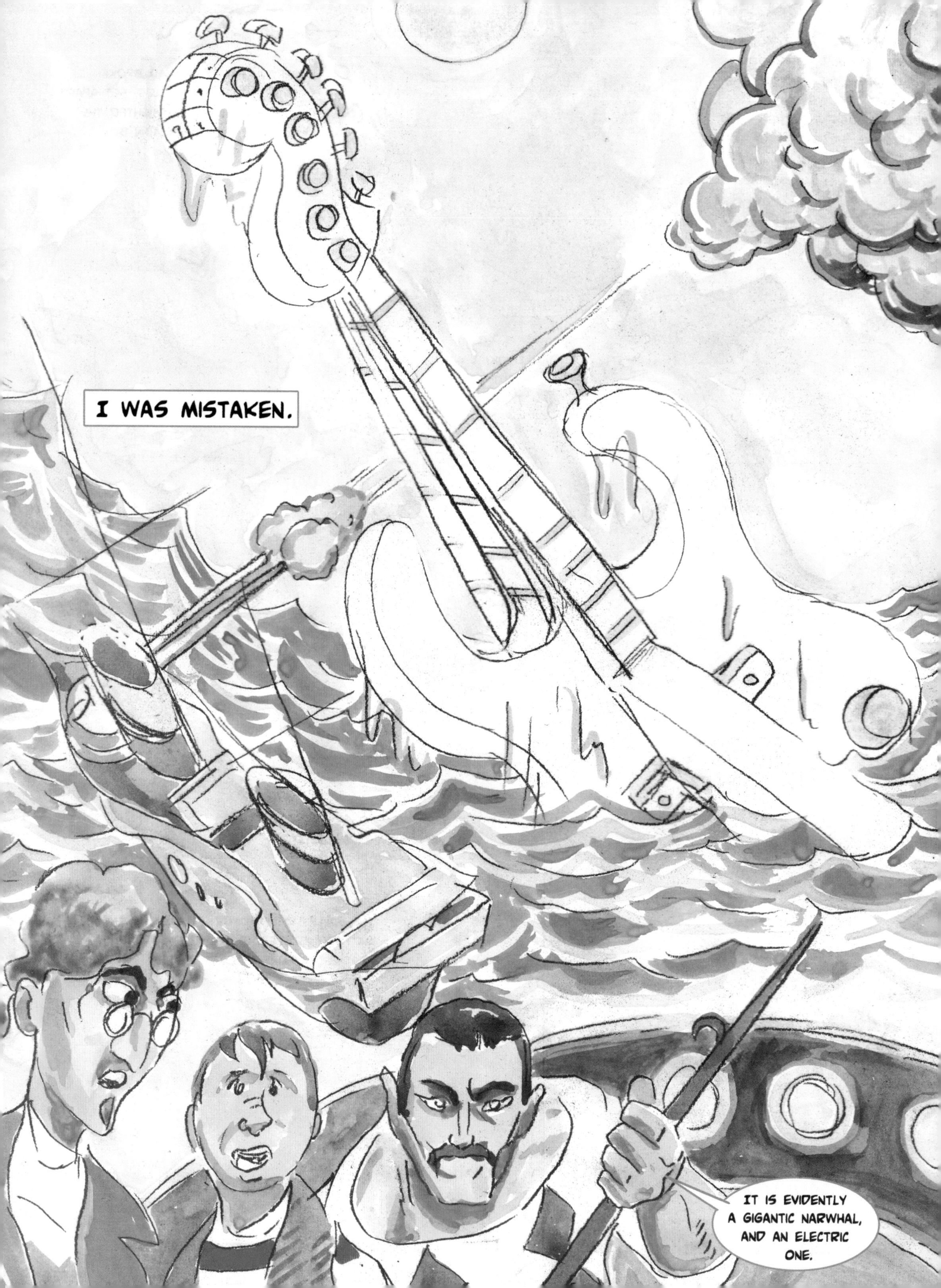
I WAS MISTAKEN.
IT IS EVIDENTLY A GIGANTIC NARWHAL, AND AN ELECTRIC ONE.

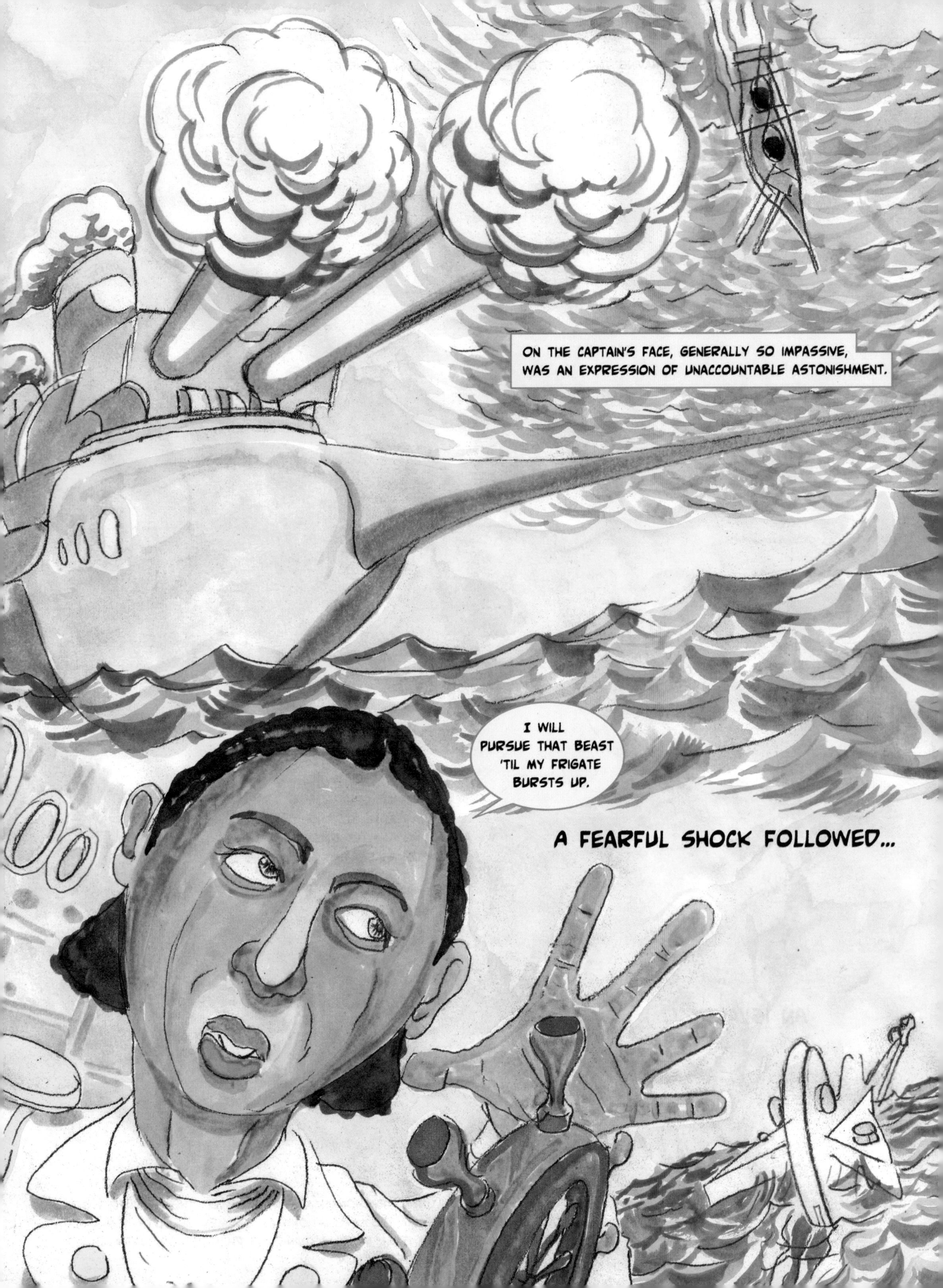
ON THE CAPTAIN'S FACE, GENERALLY SO IMPASSIVE, WAS AN EXPRESSION OF UNACCOUNTABLE ASTONISHMENT.
I WILL PURSUE THAT BEAST 'TIL MY FRIGATE BURSTS UP.
A FEARFUL SHOCK FOLLOWED...

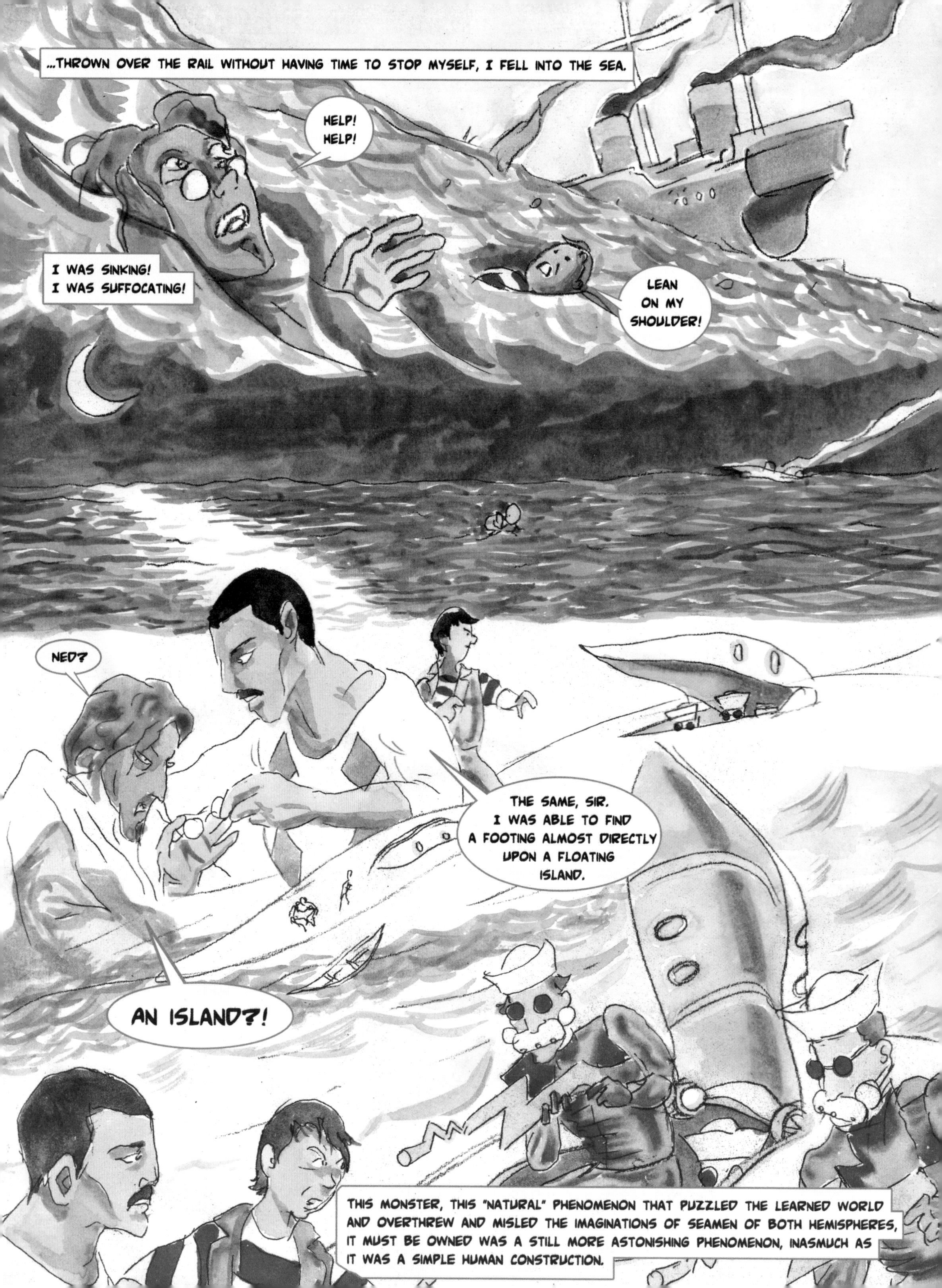
...THROWN OVER THE RAIL WITHOUT HAVING TIME TO STOP MYSELF, I FELL INTO THE SEA.
HELP! HELP!
I WAS SINKING! I WAS SUFFOCATING!
LEAN ON MY SHOULDER!
NED?
THE SAME, SIR. I WAS ABLE TO FIND A FOOTING ALMOST DIRECTLY UPON A FLOATING ISLAND.
AN ISLAND?!
THIS MONSTER, THIS "NATURAL" PHENOMENON THAT PUZZLED THE LEARNED WORLD AND OVERTHREW AND MISLED THE IMAGINATIONS OF SEAMEN OF BOTH HEMISPHERES, IT MUST BE OWNED WAS A STILL MORE ASTONISHING PHENOMENON, INASMUCH AS IT WAS A SIMPLE HUMAN CONSTRUCTION.

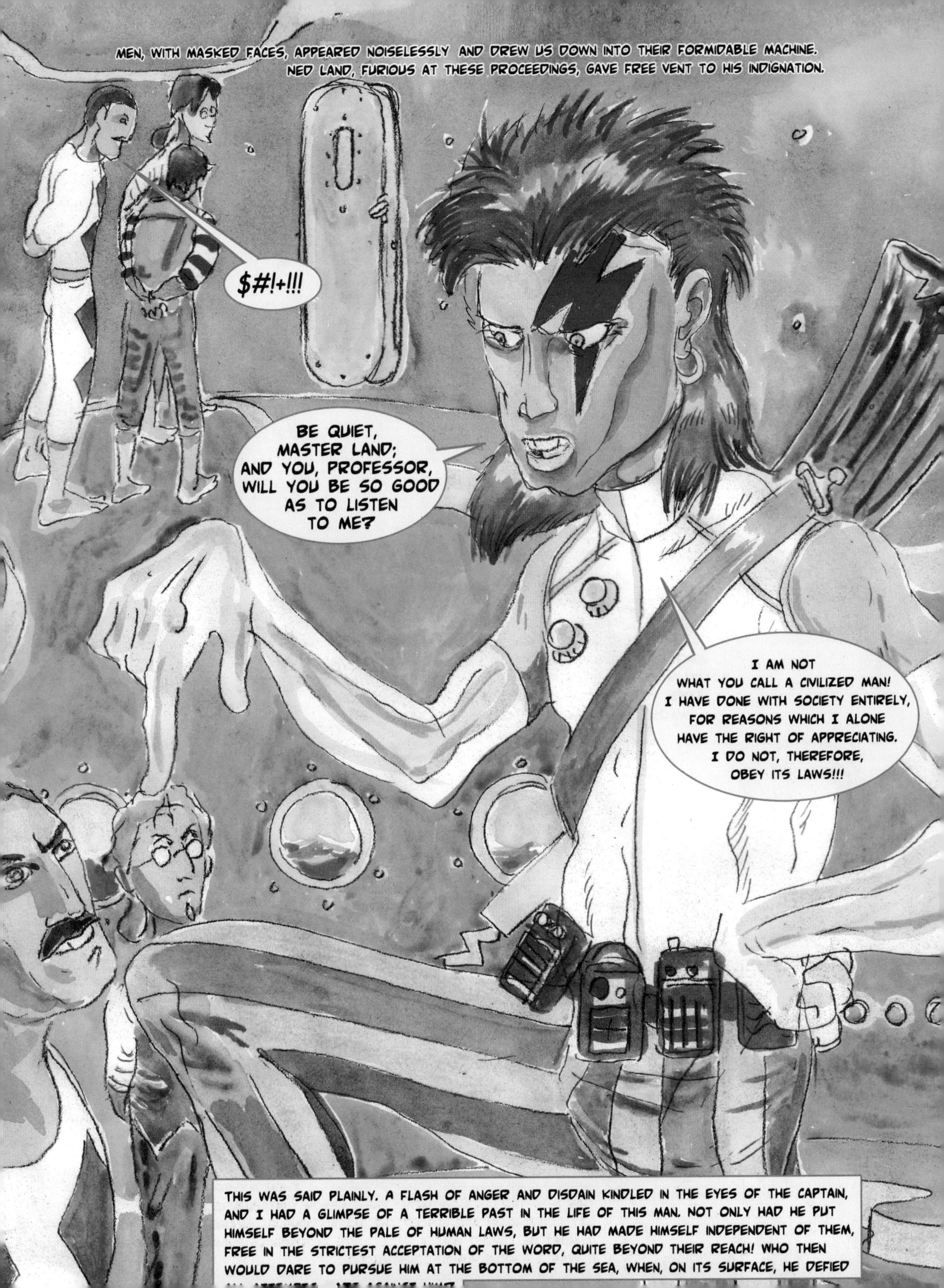
MEN, WITH MASKED FACES, APPEARED NOISELESSLY AND DREW US DOWN INTO THEIR FORMIDABLE MACHINE. NED LAND, FURIOUS AT THESE PROCEEDINGS, GAVE FREE VENT TO HIS INDIGNATION.
$#!+!!!
BE QUIET, MASTER LAND; AND YOU, PROFESSOR, WILL YOU BE SO GOOD AS TO LISTEN TO ME?
I AM NOT WHAT YOU CALL A CIVILIZED MAN! I HAVE DONE WITH SOCIETY ENTIRELY, FOR REASONS WHICH I ALONE HAVE THE RIGHT OF APPRECIATING. I DO NOT, THEREFORE, OBEY ITS LAWS!!!
THIS WAS SAID PLAINLY. A FLASH OF ANGER AND DISDAIN KINDLED IN THE EYES OF THE CAPTAIN, AND I HAD A GLIMPSE OF A TERRIBLE PAST IN THE LIFE OF THIS MAN. NOT ONLY HAD HE PUT HIMSELF BEYOND THE PALE OF HUMAN LAWS, BUT HE HAD MADE HIMSELF INDEPENDENT OF THEM, FREE IN THE STRICTEST ACCEPTATION OF THE WORD, QUITE BEYOND THEIR REACH! WHO THEN WOULD DARE TO PURSUE HIM AT THE BOTTOM OF THE SEA, WHEN, ON ITS SURFACE, HE DEFIED

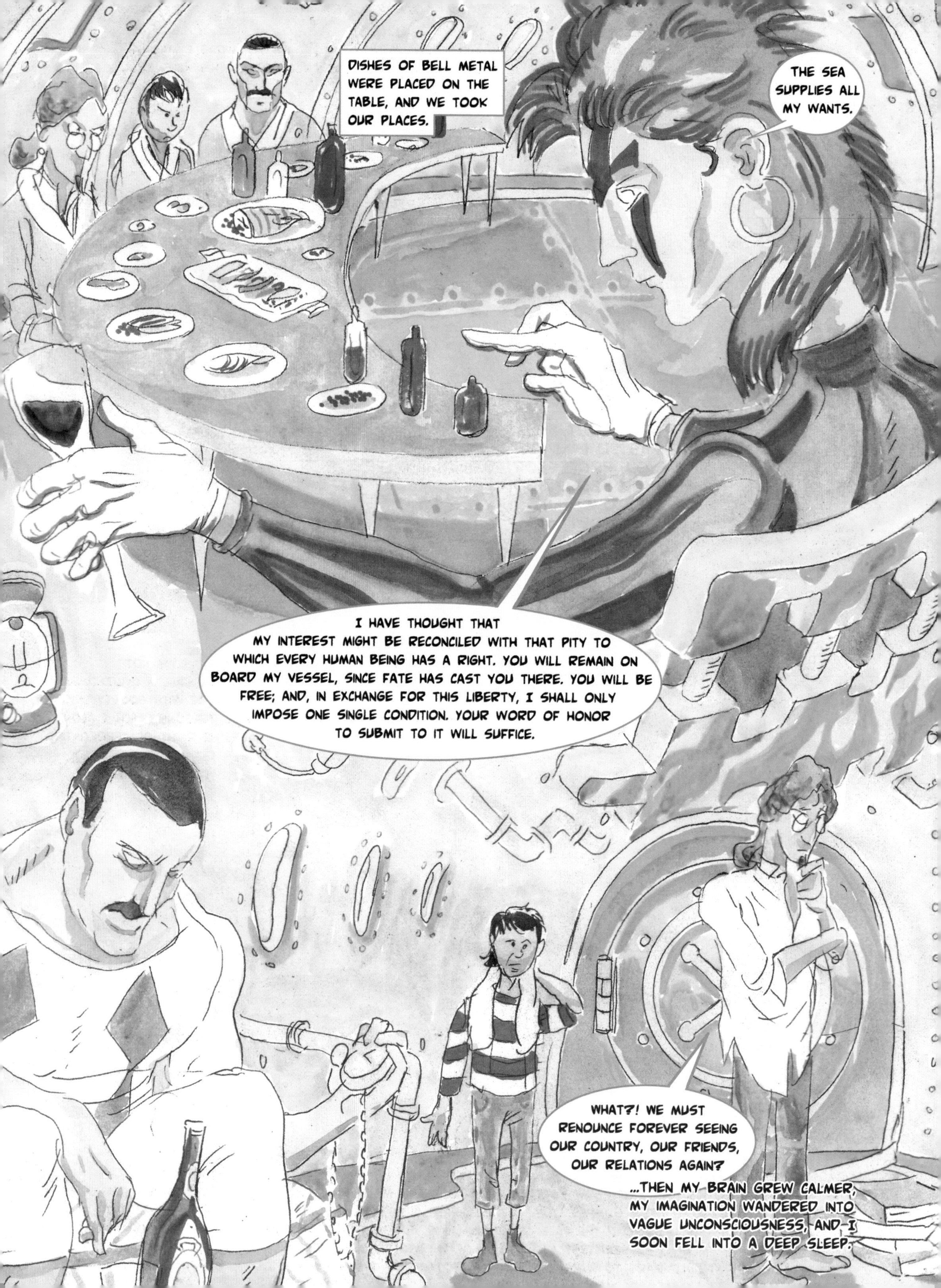
DISHES OF BELL METAL WERE PLACED ON THE TABLE, AND WE TOOK OUR PLACES.
THE SEA SUPPLIES ALL MY WANTS.
I HAVE THOUGHT THAT MY INTEREST MIGHT BE RECONCILED WITH THAT PITY TO WHICH EVERY HUMAN BEING HAS A RIGHT. YOU WILL REMAIN ON BOARD MY VESSEL, SINCE FATE HAS CAST YOU THERE. YOU WILL BE FREE; AND, IN EXCHANGE FOR THIS LIBERTY, I SHALL ONLY IMPOSE ONE SINGLE CONDITION. YOUR WORD OF HONOR TO SUBMIT TO IT WILL SUFFICE.
WHAT?! WE MUST RENOUNCE FOREVER SEEING OUR COUNTRY, OUR FRIENDS, OUR RELATIONS AGAIN?
...THEN MY BRAIN GREW CALMER, MY IMAGINATION WANDERED INTO VAGUE UNCONSCIOUSNESS, AND I SOON FELL INTO A DEEP SLEEP.

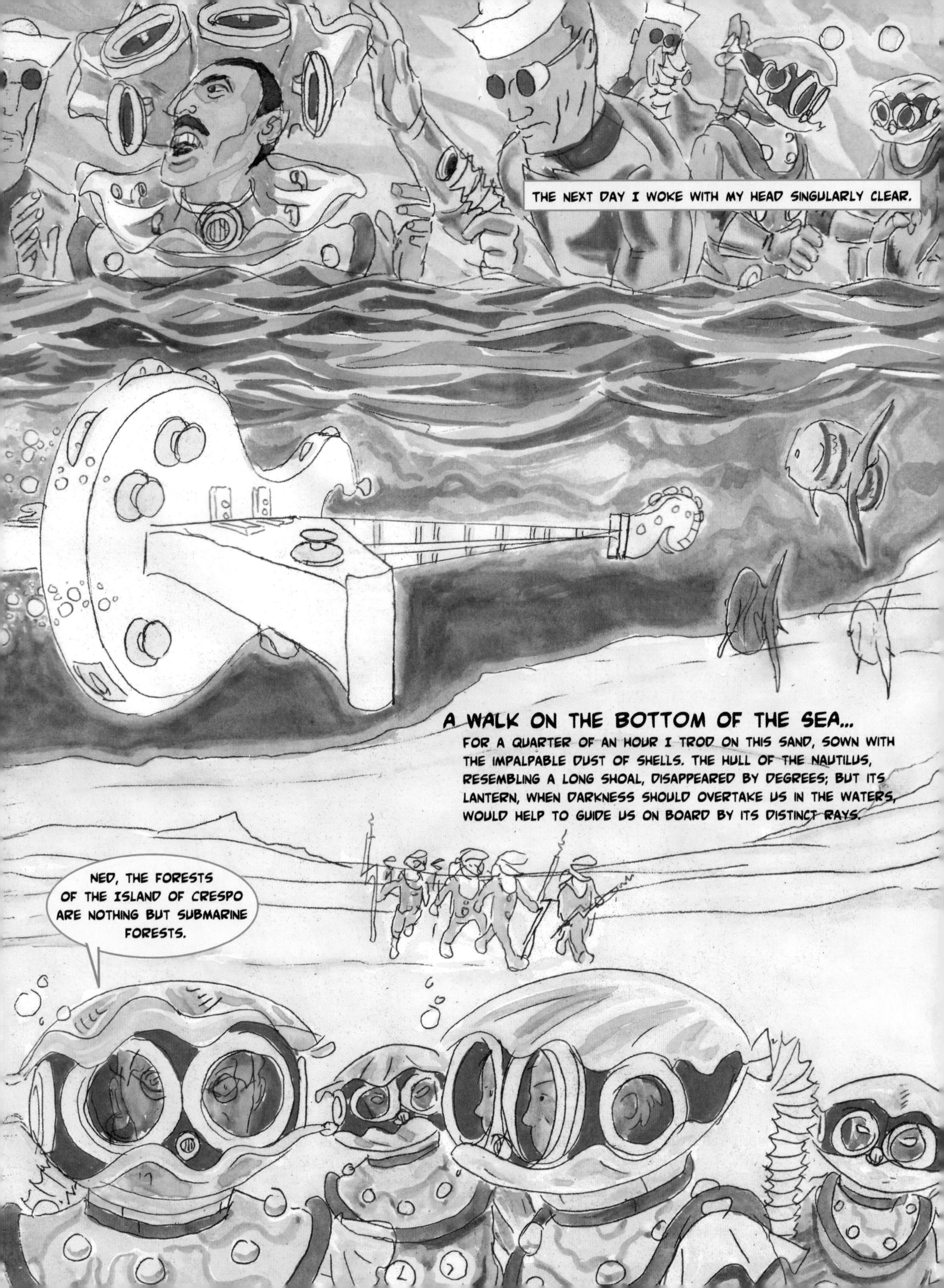
THE NEXT DAY I WOKE WITH MY HEAD SINGULARLY CLEAR.
A WALK ON THE BOTTOM OF THE SEA...
FOR A QUARTER OF AN HOUR I TROD ON THIS SAND, SOWN WITH THE IMPALPABLE DUST OF SHELLS. THE HULL OF THE NAUTILUS, RESEMBLING A LONG SHOAL, DISAPPEARED BY DEGREES; BUT ITS LANTERN, WHEN DARKNESS SHOULD OVERTAKE US IN THE WATERS, WOULD HELP TO GUIDE US ON BOARD BY ITS DISTINCT RAYS.
NED, THE FORESTS OF THE ISLAND OF CRESPO ARE NOTHING BUT SUBMARINE FORESTS.

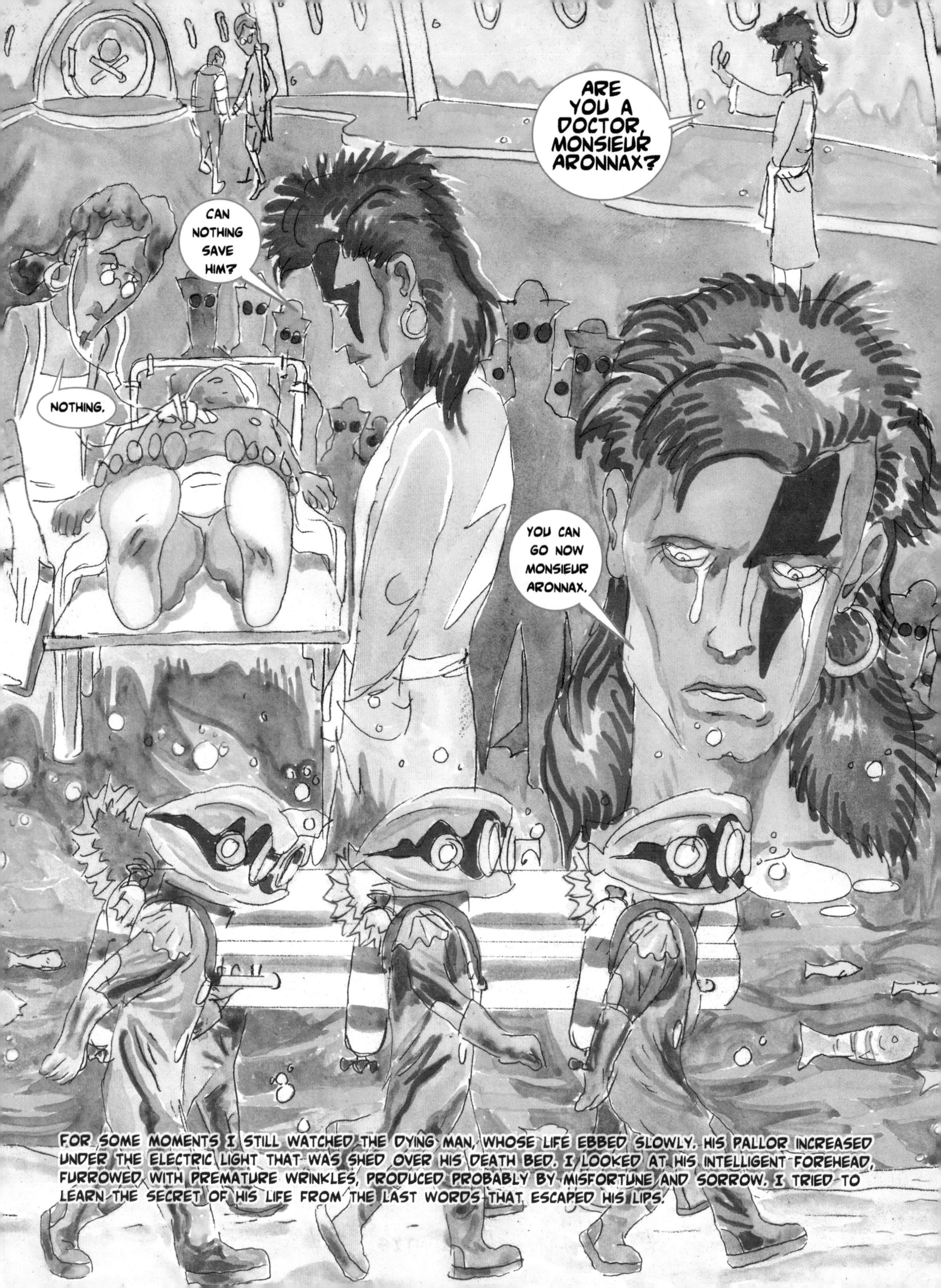

ARE YOU A DOCTOR, MONSIEUR ARONNAX?
CAN NOTHING SAVE HIM?
NOTHING.
YOU CAN GO NOW MONSIEUR ARONNAX.
FOR SOME MOMENTS I STILL WATCHED THE DYING MAN, WHOSE LIFE EBBED SLOWLY. HIS PALLOR INCREASED UNDER THE ELECTRIC LIGHT THAT WAS SHED OVER HIS DEATH BED. I LOOKED AT HIS INTELLIGENT FOREHEAD, FURROWED WITH PREMATURE WRINKLES, PRODUCED PROBABLY BY MISFORTUNE AND SORROW. I TRIED TO LEARN THE SECRET OF HIS LIFE FROM THE LAST WORDS THAT ESCAPED HIS LIPS.

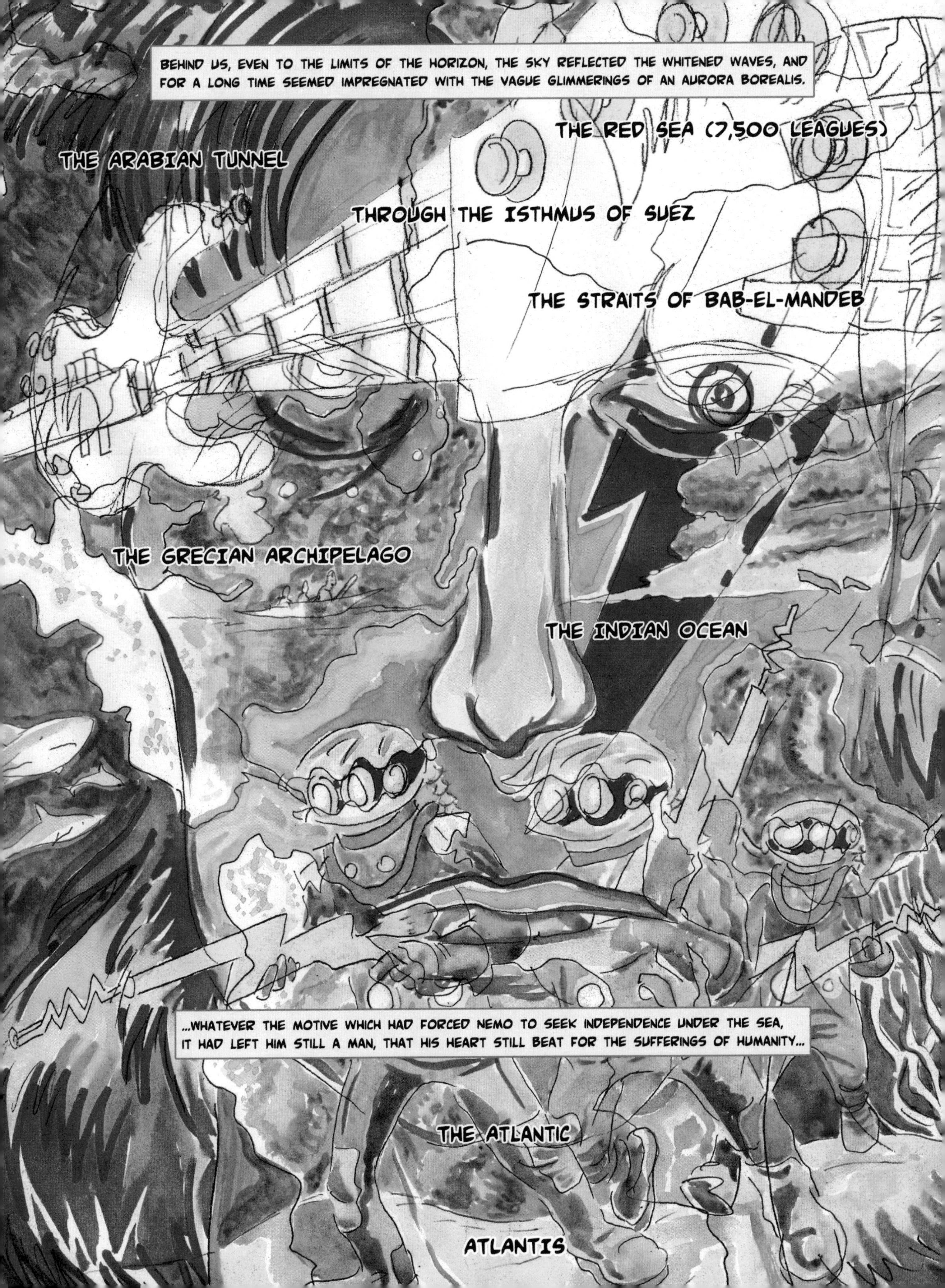
BEHIND US, EVEN TO THE LIMITS OF THE HORIZON, THE SKY REFLECTED THE WHITENED WAVES, AND FOR A LONG TIME SEEMED IMPREGNATED WITH THE VAGUE GLIMMERINGS OF AN AURORA BOREALIS.
THE RED SEA (7,500 LEAGUES)
THE ARABIAN TUNNEL
THROUGH THE ISTHMUS OF SUEZ
THE STRAITS OF BAB-EL-MANDEB
THE GRECIAN ARCHIPELAGO
THE INDIAN OCEAN
...WHATEVER THE MOTIVE WHICH HAD FORCED NEMO TO SEEK INDEPENDENCE UNDER THE SEA, IT HAD LEFT HIM STILL A MAN, THAT HIS HEART STILL BEAT FOR THE SUFFERINGS OF HUMANITY...
THE ATLANTIC
ATLANTIS

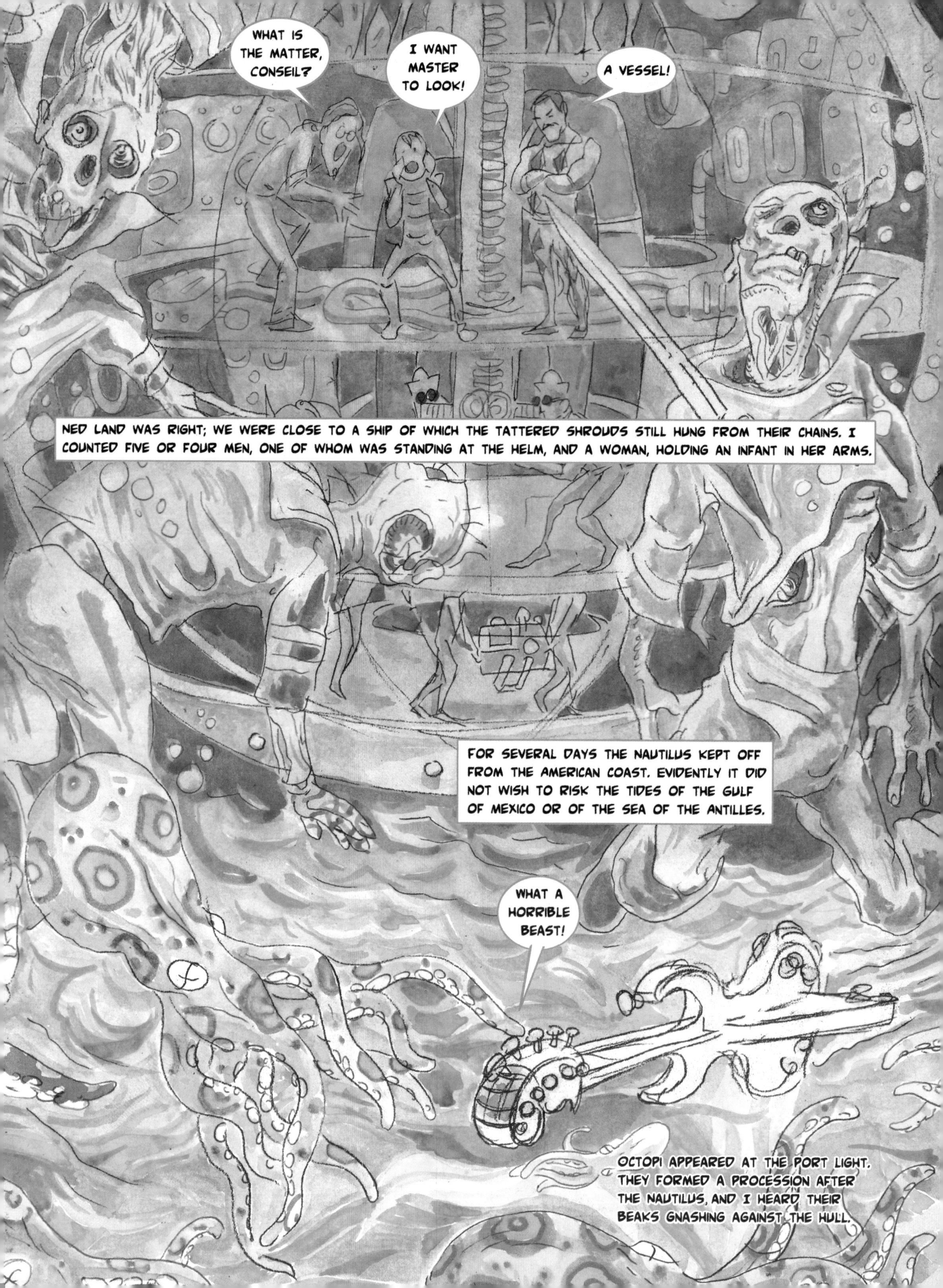
WHAT IS THE MATTER, CONSEIL?
I WANT MASTER TO LOOK!
A VESSEL!
NED LAND WAS RIGHT; WE WERE CLOSE TO A SHIP OF WHICH THE TATTERED SHROUDS STILL HUNG FROM THEIR CHAINS. I COUNTED FIVE OR FOUR MEN, ONE OF WHOM WAS STANDING AT THE HELM, AND A WOMAN, HOLDING AN INFANT IN HER ARMS.
FOR SEVERAL DAYS THE NAUTILUS KEPT OFF FROM THE AMERICAN COAST. EVIDENTLY IT DID NOT WISH TO RISK THE TIDES OF THE GULF OF MEXICO OR OF THE SEA OF THE ANTILLES.
WHAT A HORRIBLE BEAST!
OCTOPI APPEARED AT THE PORT LIGHT. THEY FORMED A PROCESSION AFTER THE NAUTILUS, AND I HEARD THEIR BEAKS GNASHING AGAINST THE HULL.

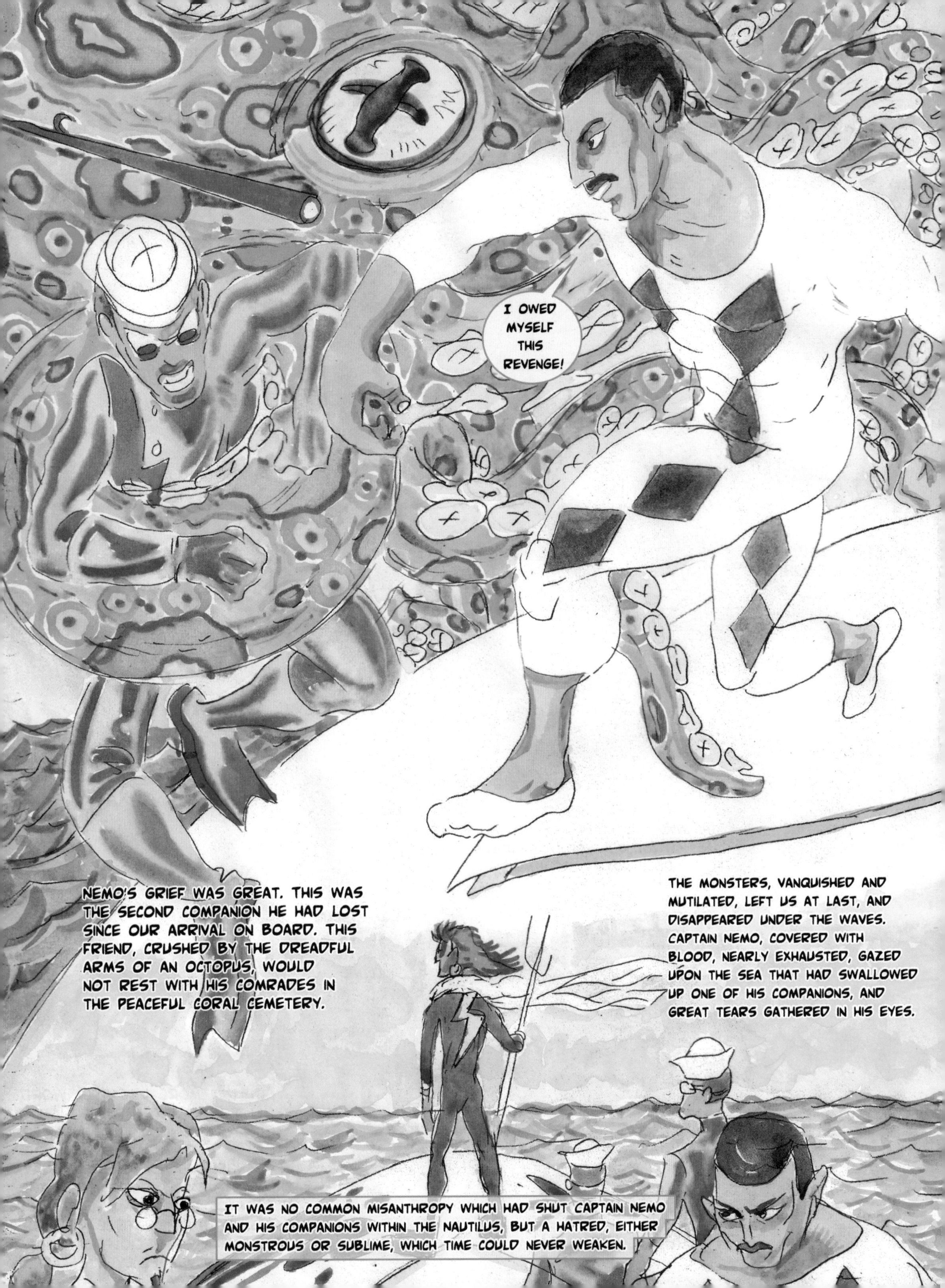
I OWED MYSELF THIS REVENGE!
NEMO'S GRIEF WAS GREAT. THIS WAS THE SECOND COMPANION HE HAD LOST SINCE OUR ARRIVAL ON BOARD. THIS FRIEND, CRUSHED BY THE DREADFUL ARMS OF AN OCTOPUS, WOULD NOT REST WITH HIS COMRADES IN THE PEACEFUL CORAL CEMETERY.
THE MONSTERS, VANQUISHED AND MUTILATED, LEFT US AT LAST, AND DISAPPEARED UNDER THE WAVES. CAPTAIN NEMO, COVERED WITH BLOOD, NEARLY EXHAUSTED, GAZED UPON THE SEA THAT HAD SWALLOWED UP ONE OF HIS COMPANIONS, AND GREAT TEARS GATHERED IN HIS EYES.
IT WAS NO COMMON MISANTHROPY WHICH HAD SHUT CAPTAIN NEMO AND HIS COMPANIONS WITHIN THE NAUTILUS, BUT A HATRED, EITHER MONSTROUS OR SUBLIME, WHICH TIME COULD NEVER WEAKEN.

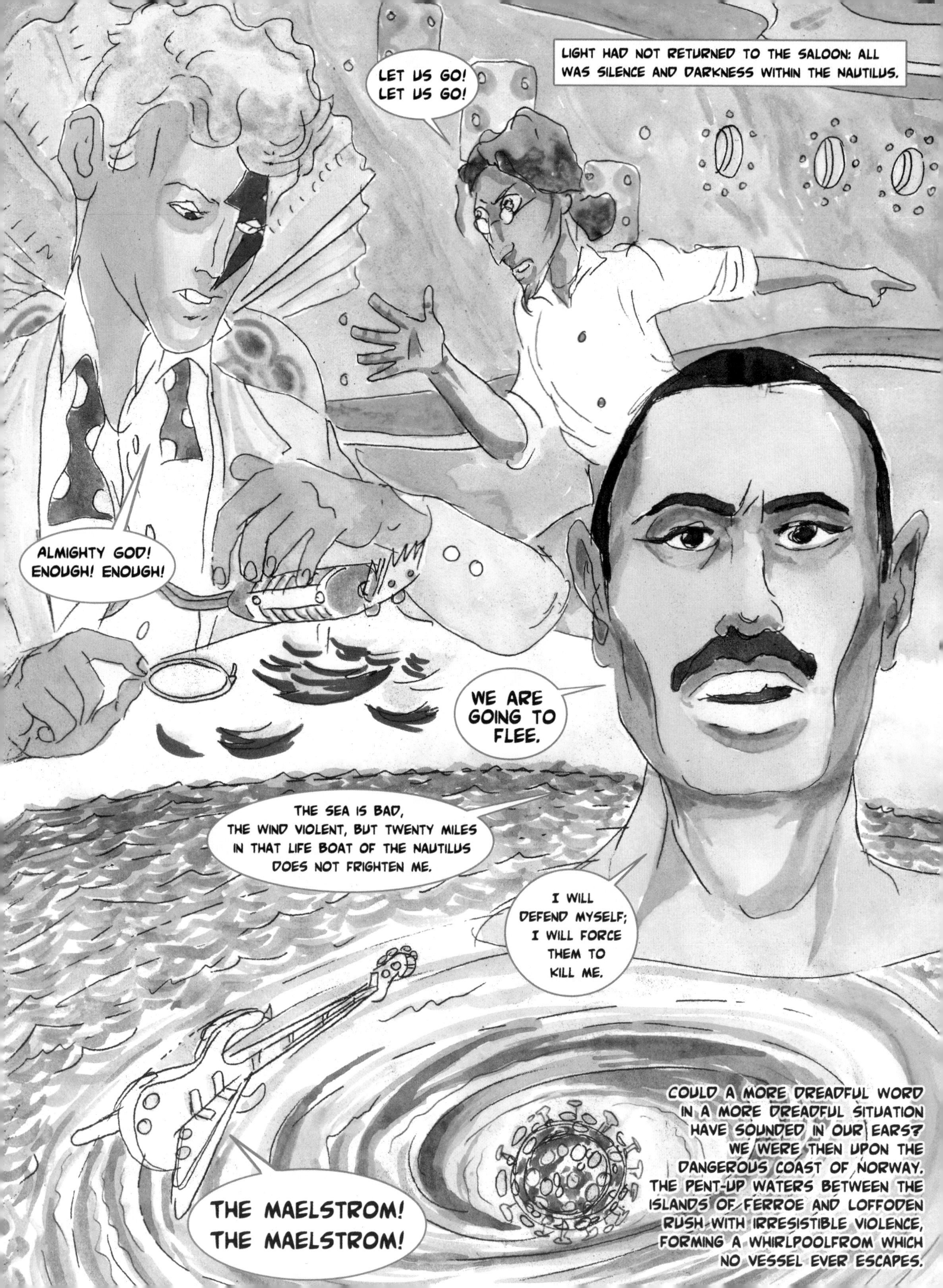
LIGHT HAD NOT RETURNED TO THE SALOON: ALL WAS SILENCE AND DARKNESS WITHIN THE NAUTILUS.
LET US GO! LET US GO!
ALMIGHTY GOD! ENOUGH! ENOUGH!
WE ARE GOING TO FLEE.
THE SEA IS BAD, THE WIND VIOLENT, BUT TWENTY MILES IN THAT LIFE BOAT OF THE NAUTILUS DOES NOT FRIGHTEN ME.
I WILL DEFEND MYSELF; I WILL FORCE THEM TO KILL ME.
THE MAELSTROM! THE MAELSTROM!
COULD A MORE DREADFUL WORD IN A MORE DREADFUL SITUATION HAVE SOUNDED IN OUR EARS? WE WERE THEN UPON THE DANGEROUS COAST OF NORWAY. THE PENT-UP WATERS BETWEEN THE ISLANDS OF FERROE AND LOFFODEN RUSH WITH IRRESISTIBLE VIOLENCE, FORMING A WHIRLPOOLFROM WHICH NO VESSEL EVER ESCAPES.

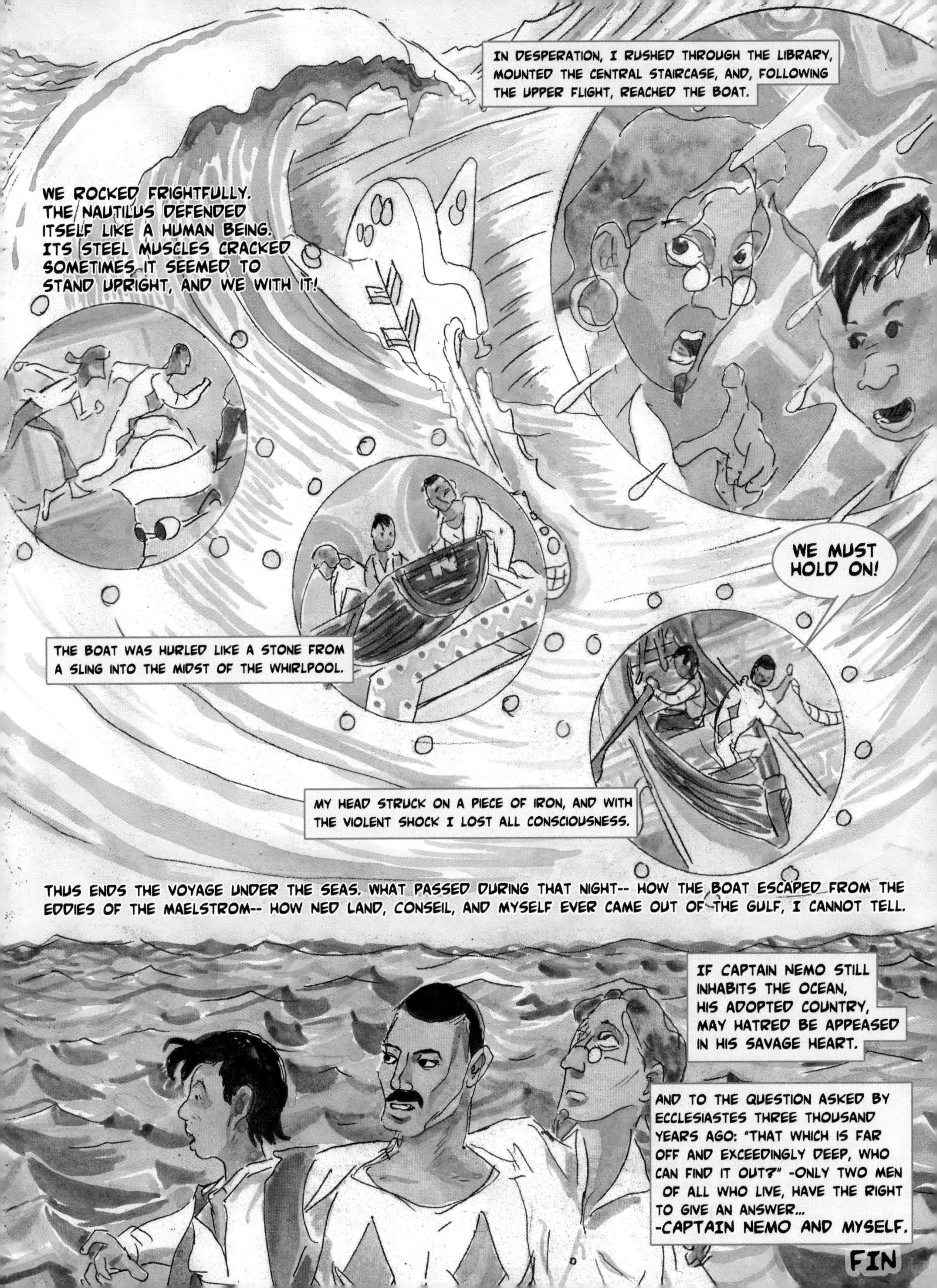
IN DESPERATION, I RUSHED THROUGH THE LIBRARY, MOUNTED THE CENTRAL STAIRCASE, AND, FOLLOWING THE UPPER FLIGHT, REACHED THE BOAT.
WE ROCKED FRIGHTFULLY. THE NAUTILUS DEFENDED ITSELF LIKE A HUMAN BEING. ITS STEEL MUSCLES CRACKED SOMETIMES IT SEEMED TO STAND UPRIGHT, AND WE WITH IT!
WE MUST HOLD ON!
THE BOAT WAS HURLED LIKE A STONE FROM A SLING INTO THE MIDST OF THE WHIRLPOOL.
MY HEAD STRUCK ON A PIECE OF IRON, AND WITH THE VIOLENT SHOCK I LOST ALL CONSCIOUSNESS.
THUS ENDS THE VOYAGE UNDER THE SEAS. WHAT PASSED DURING THAT NIGHT-- HOW THE BOAT ESCAPED FROM THE EDDIES OF THE MAELSTROM-- HOW NED LAND, CONSEIL, AND MYSELF EVER CAME OUT OF THE GULF, I CANNOT TELL.
IF CAPTAIN NEMO STILL INHABITS THE OCEAN, HIS ADOPTED COUNTRY, MAY HATRED BE APPEASED IN HIS SAVAGE HEART.
AND TO THE QUESTION ASKED BY ECCLESIASTES THREE THOUSAND YEARS AGO: "THAT WHICH IS FAR OFF AND EXCEEDINGLY DEEP, WHO CAN FIND IT OUT?" -ONLY TWO MEN OF ALL WHO LIVE, HAVE THE RIGHT TO GIVE AN ANSWER... -CAPTAIN NEMO AND MYSELF.
FIN

# "The Owl and the Pussycat"

## Edward Lear

ART/ADAPTATION BY **Rick Geary**

**ENGLISHMAN EDWARD LEAR WAS AN ACCOMPLISHED** landscape artist and a painter of birds who garnered comparisons to John James Audubon. He hoped to be remembered for his painting, but his most lasting, ceaselessly popular gift to the world is his nonsense poetry. Happily, "nonsense" is a recognized form of literature, and Lear was one of its pioneers. Non sequiturs, impossibilities, garbled syntax, made-up words, and general silliness and whimsy are the hallmarks of nonsense, along with (perhaps surprisingly) macabre and melancholy tones. (A number of the foremost nonsense writers—including Lear, Lewis Carroll, Shel Silverstein, and even John Lennon—displayed this dark tendency.)

During his lifetime, Lear put out four books of nonsense verse (which included limericks, a form he introduced to the masses but, contrary to popular belief, did not invent). "The Owl and the Pussycat"—perhaps his single most enduring poem—was written for the young daughter of his friend, poet John Addington Symonds, and came out in 1870. Here we see it jovially and crisply adapted by Rick Geary, a longtime contributor to *National Lampoon* and *Heavy Metal*, creator of graphic biographies of Trostsky and Hoover, writer-illustrator of a series of graphic nonfiction on famous murders in the nineteenth and twentieth centuries, and adapter of several works of classic lit, including *Great Expectations* and *Wuthering Heights*.

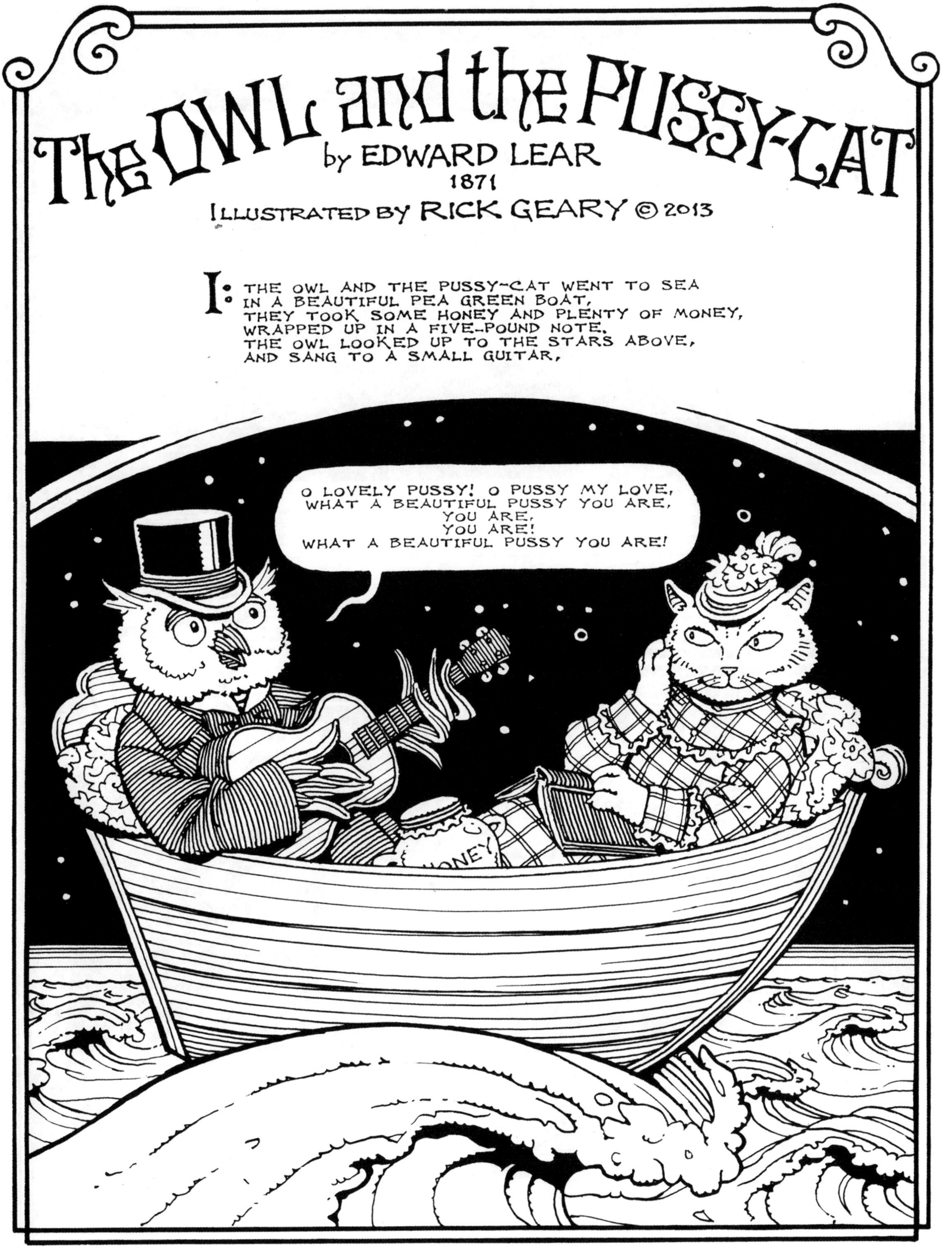
The OWL and the PUSSY-CAT
by EDWARD LEAR
1871
ILLUSTRATED BY RICK GEARY © 2013
I: THE OWL AND THE PUSSY-CAT WENT TO SEA
IN A BEAUTIFUL PEA GREEN BOAT,
THEY TOOK SOME HONEY AND PLENTY OF MONEY,
WRAPPED UP IN A FIVE-POUND NOTE.
THE OWL LOOKED UP TO THE STARS ABOVE,
AND SANG TO A SMALL GUITAR,
O LOVELY PUSSY! O PUSSY MY LOVE,
WHAT A BEAUTIFUL PUSSY YOU ARE,
YOU ARE,
YOU ARE!
WHAT A BEAUTIFUL PUSSY YOU ARE!
HONEY

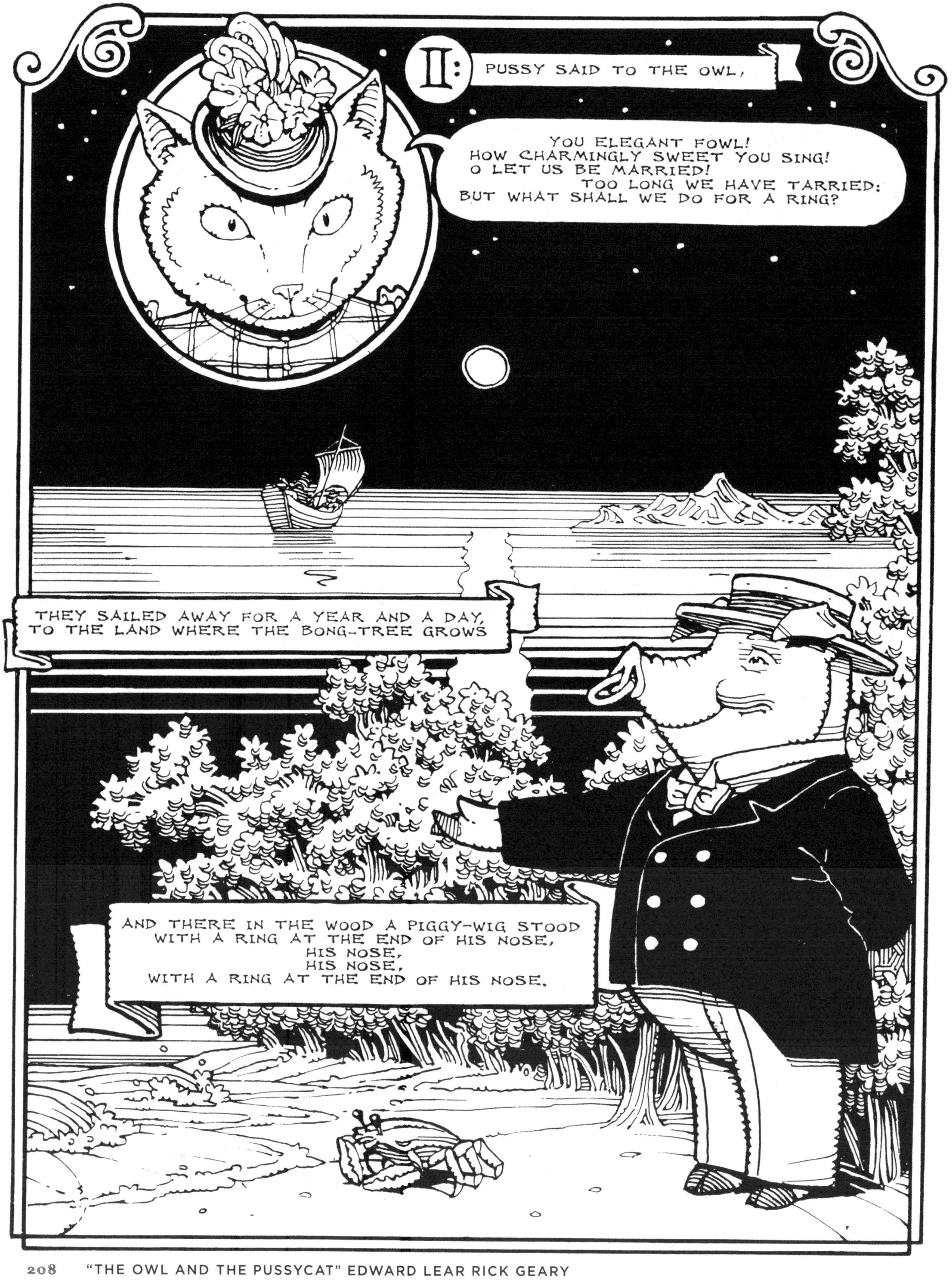
II:
PUSSY SAID TO THE OWL,
YOU ELEGANT FOWL! HOW CHARMINGLY SWEET YOU SING! O LET US BE MARRIED! TOO LONG WE HAVE TARRIED: BUT WHAT SHALL WE DO FOR A RING?
THEY SAILED AWAY FOR A YEAR AND A DAY, TO THE LAND WHERE THE BONG-TREE GROWS
AND THERE IN THE WOOD A PIGGY-WIG STOOD WITH A RING AT THE END OF HIS NOSE, HIS NOSE, HIS NOSE, WITH A RING AT THE END OF HIS NOSE.

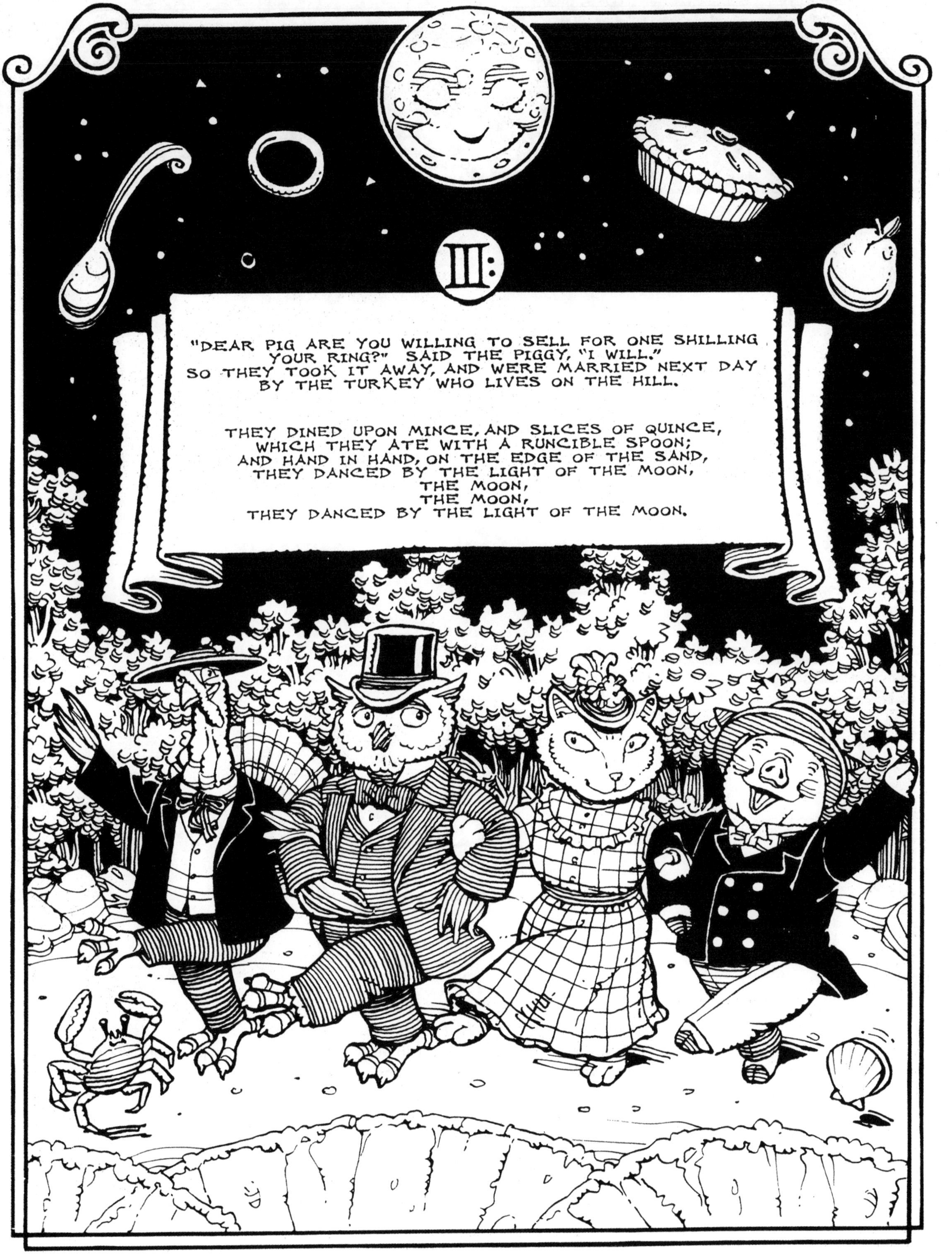
III:
"DEAR PIG ARE YOU WILLING TO SELL FOR ONE SHILLING
YOUR RING?" SAID THE PIGGY, "I WILL."
SO THEY TOOK IT AWAY, AND WERE MARRIED NEXT DAY
BY THE TURKEY WHO LIVES ON THE HILL.
THEY DINED UPON MINCE, AND SLICES OF QUINCE,
WHICH THEY ATE WITH A RUNCIBLE SPOON;
AND HAND IN HAND, ON THE EDGE OF THE SAND,
THEY DANCED BY THE LIGHT OF THE MOON,
THE MOON,
THE MOON,
THEY DANCED BY THE LIGHT OF THE MOON.

# "Calico Pie" and "The New Vestments"

## Edward Lear

ART/ADAPTATION BY **Joy Kolitsky**

**ALONG WITH THE AFORESEEN "THE OWL AND THE** Pussycat," "Calico Pie" appeared in Edward Lear's 1871 book *Nonsense Songs, Stories, Botany, and Alphabets*. Typical of the morose painter-poet, the adorable charm of each stanza gives way to a quatrain repeatedly grieving loss.

"The New Vestments"—appearing in the last nonsense book published in Lear's lifetime, *Laughable Lyrics* (1877)—is a more complex poem describing the most over-the-top outfit in all of literature and the problems it causes its ostentatious owner.

Joy Kolitsky dazzled us with adaptations of two works from a much different poet—Edna St. Vincent Millay—in *The Graphic Canon, Volume 3*. She's done animation work for Sony and MTV, among others, and her illustrations have graced the *New York Times* and the *Wall Street Journal*, as well as her own line of greeting cards.

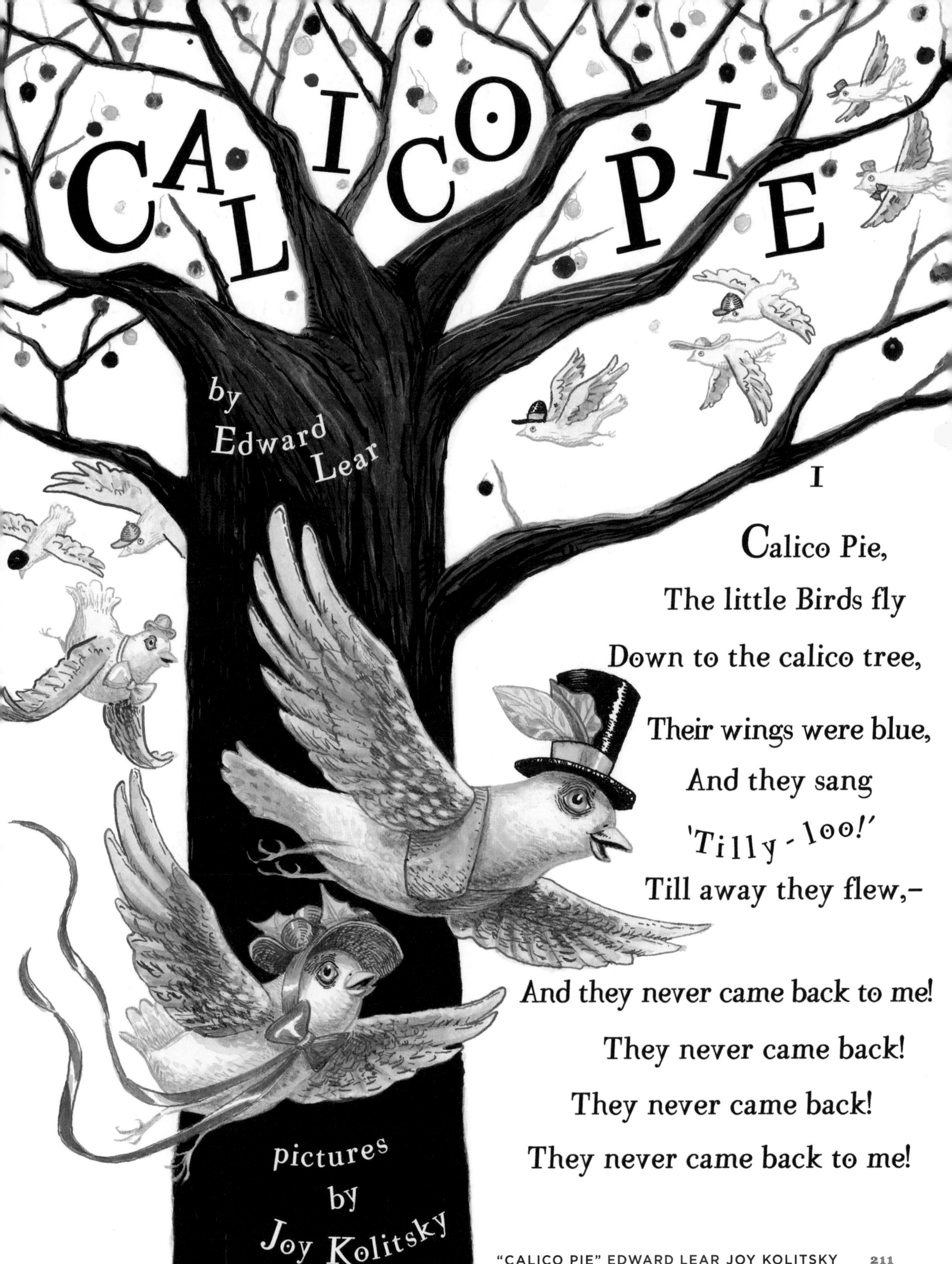

# CALICO PIE

by Edward Lear

pictures by Joy Kolitsky

I

Calico Pie,
The little Birds fly
Down to the calico tree,
Their wings were blue,
And they sang
'Tilly-loo!'
Till away they flew,–
And they never came back to me!
They never came back!
They never came back!
They never came back to me!

# II

Calico Jam, the little Fish swam, over the syllabub sea,

He took off his hat, to the Sole and the Sprat,

And the Willeby-Wat,–

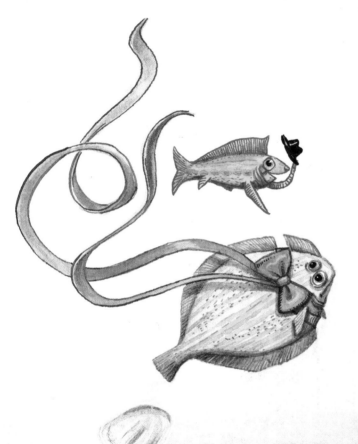

But he never came back to me!

He never came back!

He never came back!

He never came back to me!

## III

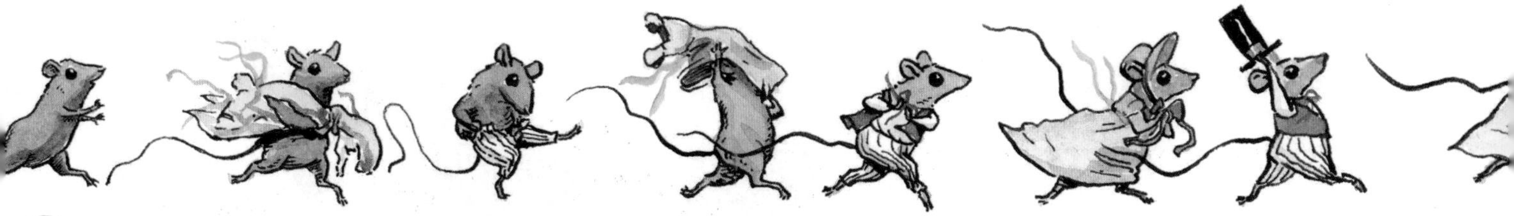

Calico Ban, the little Mice ran, to be ready in time for tea,

Flippity flup,
They drank it all up,
And danced in the cup,–

But they never came back to me!
They never came back!
They never came back!
They never came back to me!

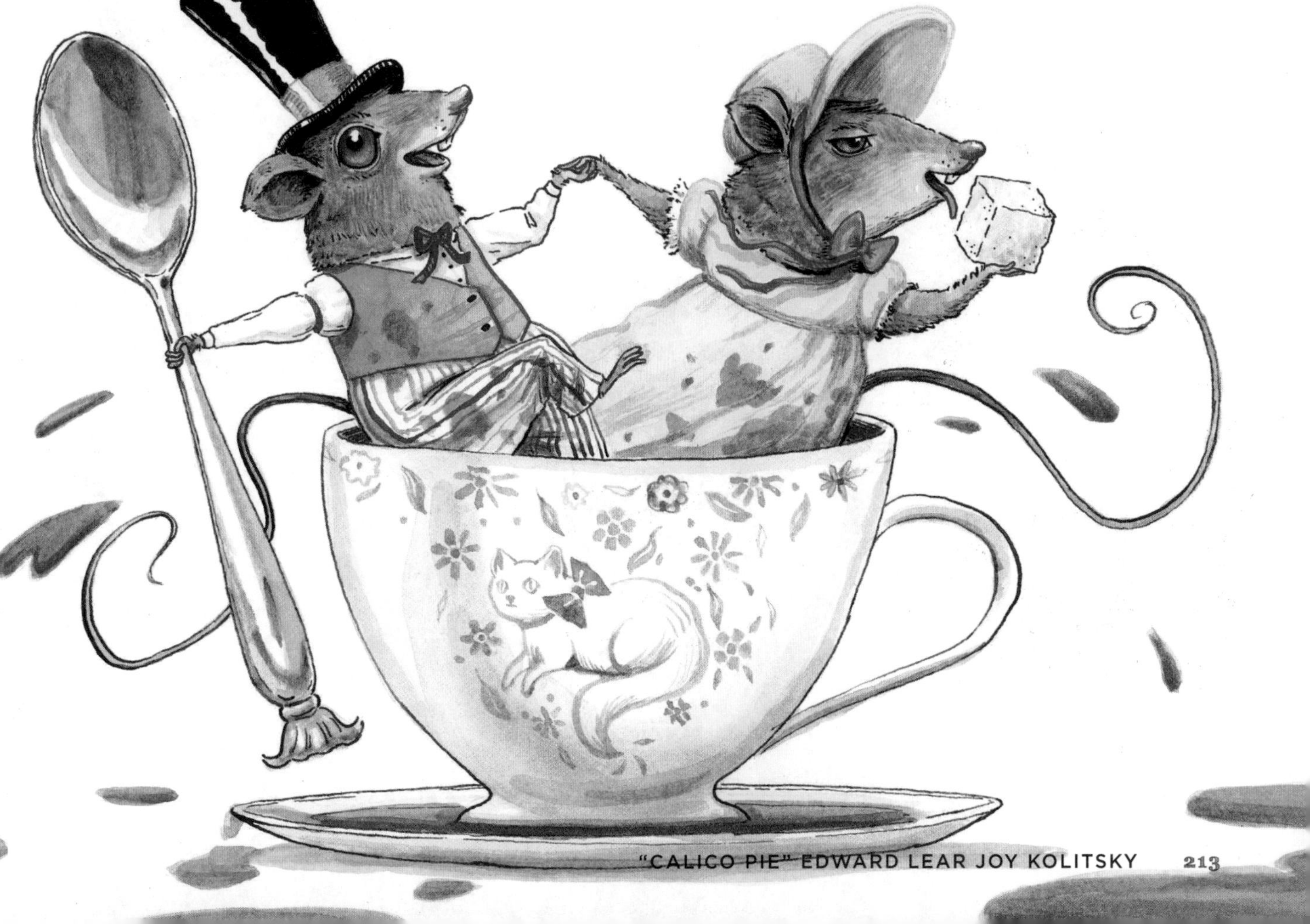

IV

Calico Drum,
The Grasshoppers come,
The Butterfly, Beetle, and Bee,

Over the ground,
Around and around,
With a hop and a bound,

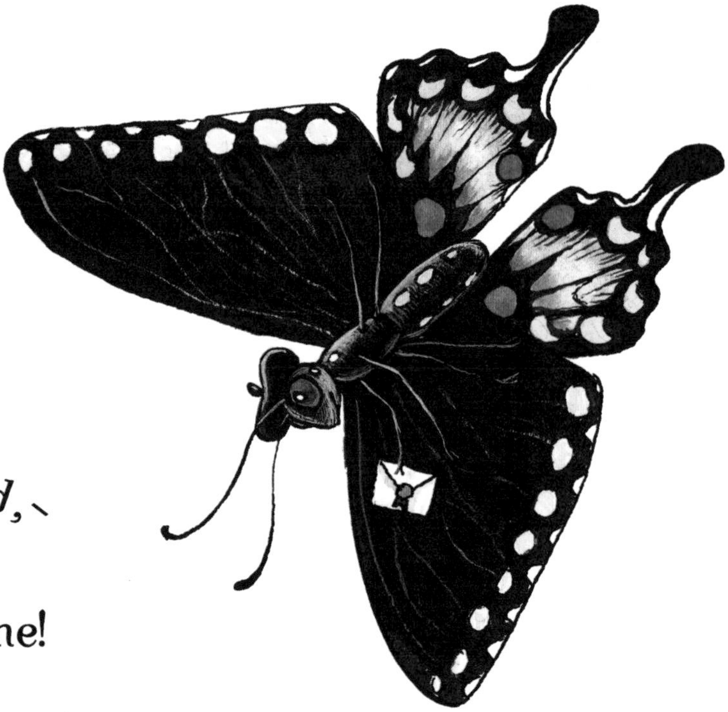

But they never came back to me!
They never came back!
They never came back!
They never came back to me!

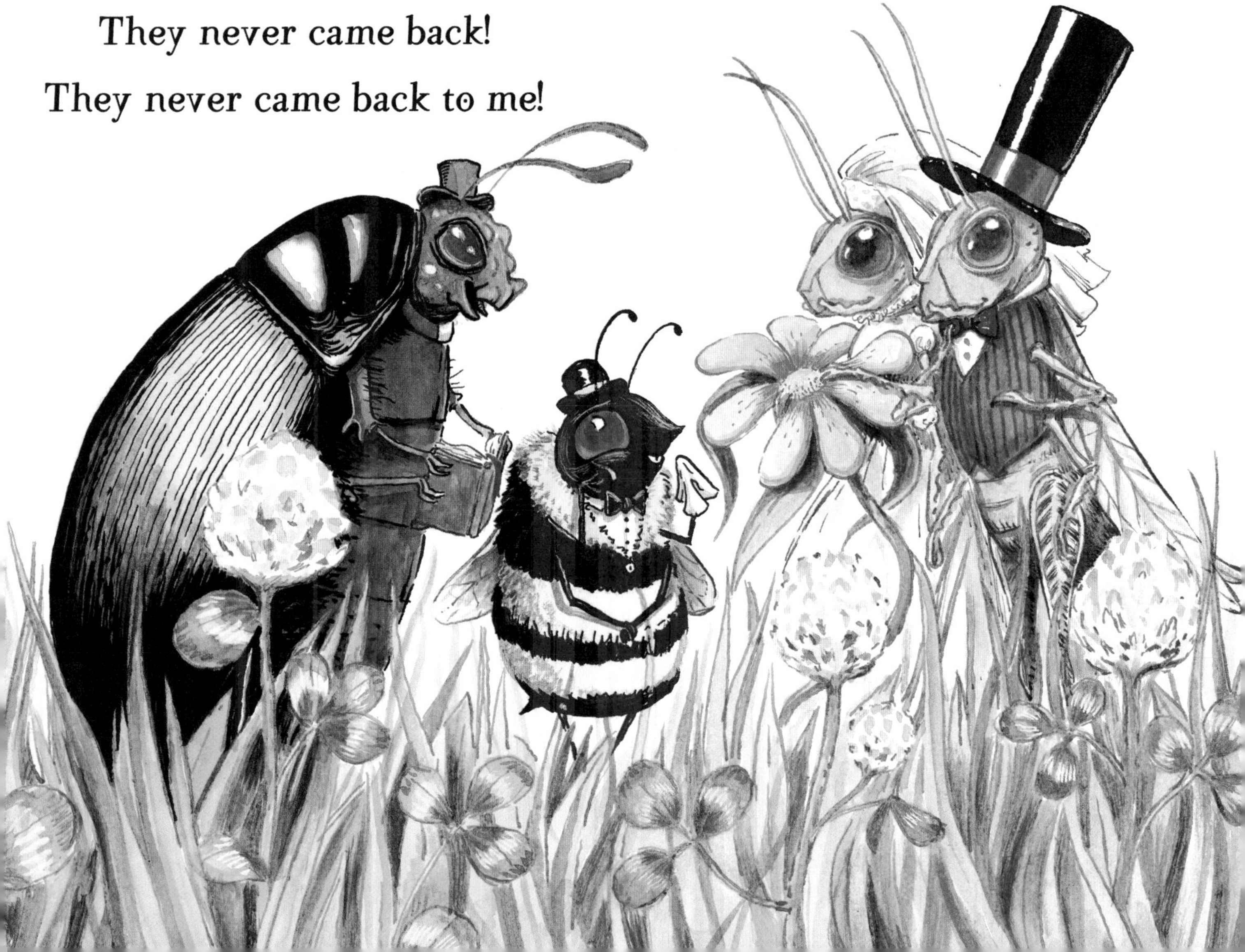

# The New Vestments

## by Edward Lear with pictures by Joy Kolitsky

There lived an old man in the kingdom of Tess, who invented a purely original dress;
And when it was perfectly made and complete, he opened the door, and walked into the street.

By way of a hat,
he'd a loaf of Brown Bread,
In the middle of which
he inserted his head;—

His Shirt was made up of
no end of dead Mice,
The warmth of whose skins
was quite fluffy and nice;—

His Drawers were of Rabit-skins,—
but it is not known whose;—

His Waistcoat and Trousers
were made of Pork Chops;—
His Buttons were Jujubes,
and Chocolate Drops;—

His Coat was all Pancakes
with Jam for a border,
And a girdle of Biscuits
to keep it in order;

And he wore over all,
as a screen from bad weather,
A Cloak of green Cabbage-leaves
stitched all together.

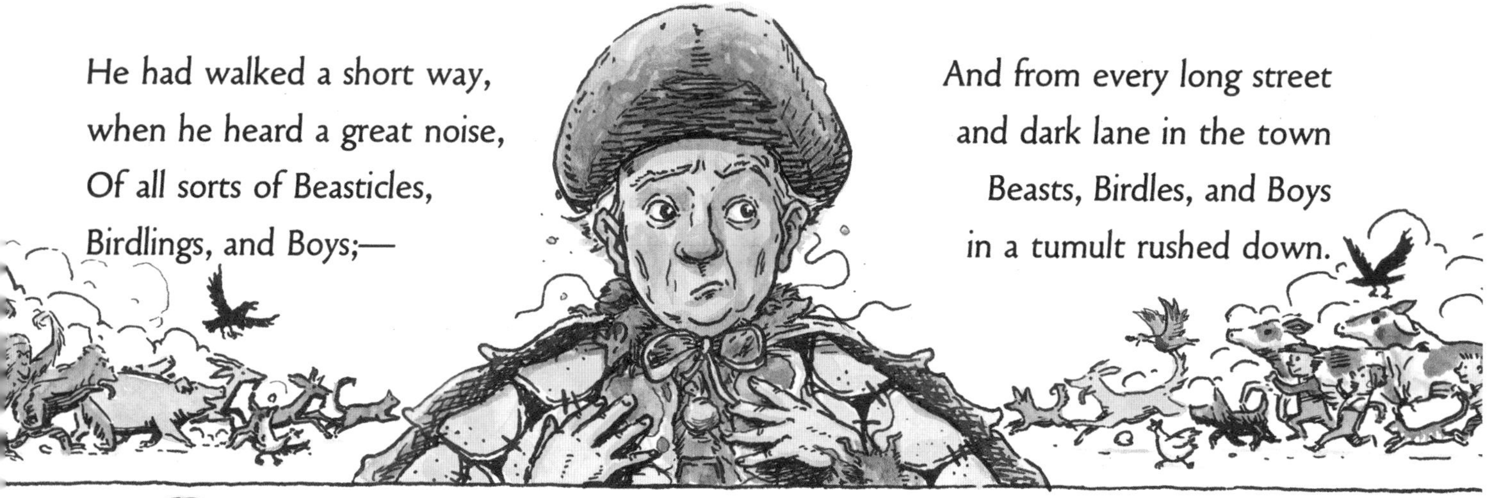

He had walked a short way,
when he heard a great noise,
Of all sorts of Beasticles,
Birdlings, and Boys;—

And from every long street
and dark lane in the town
Beasts, Birdles, and Boys
in a tumult rushed down.

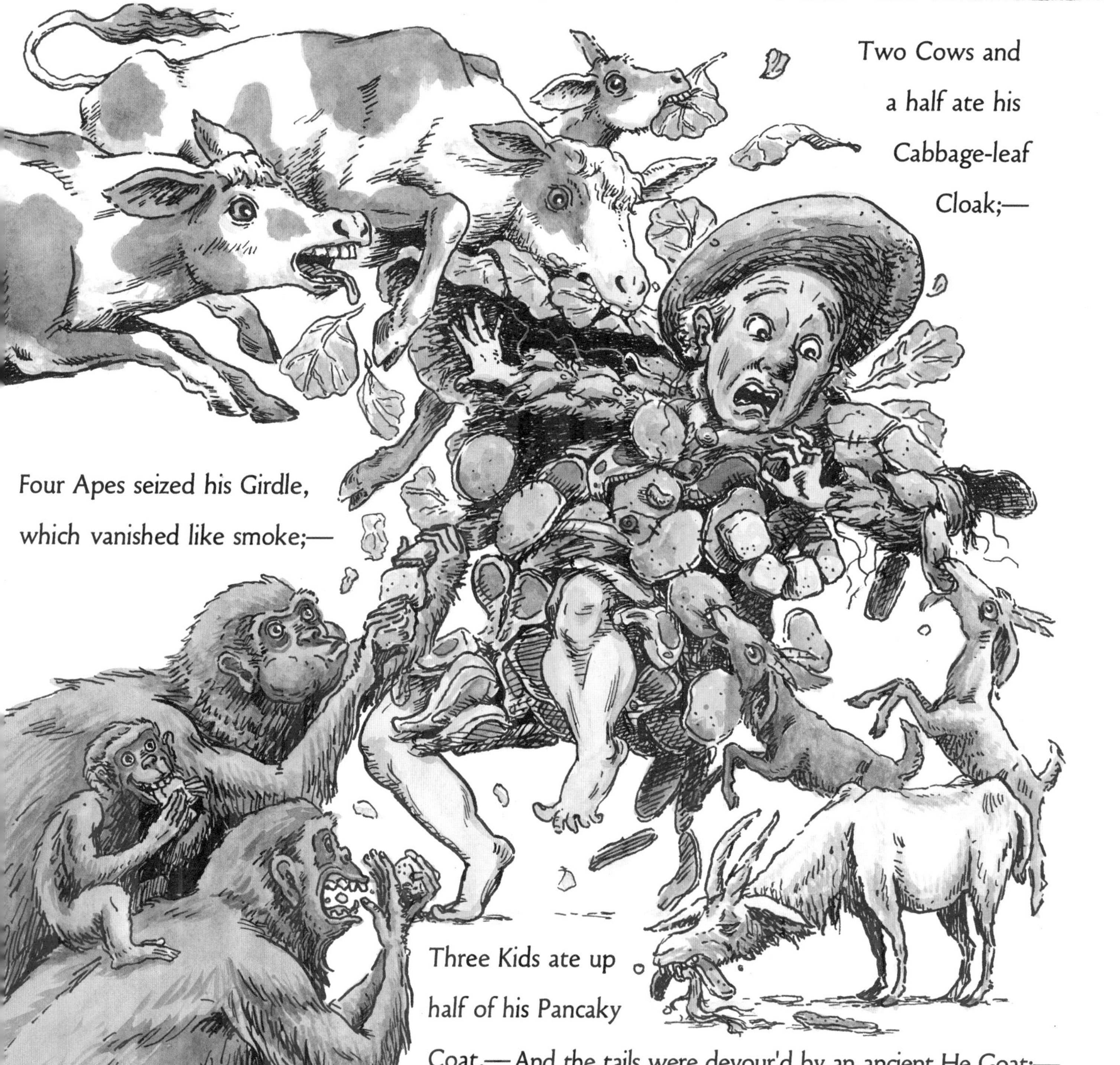

Two Cows and
a half ate his
Cabbage-leaf
Cloak;—

Four Apes seized his Girdle,
which vanished like smoke;—

Three Kids ate up
half of his Pancaky
Coat,—And the tails were devour'd by an ancient He Goat;—

An army of Dogs in a twinkling tore up his
Pork Waistcoat and Trousers to give to their Puppies;—
And while they were growling, and mumbling the Chops,

Ten boys
prigged the
Jujubes and
Chocolate
Drops.—

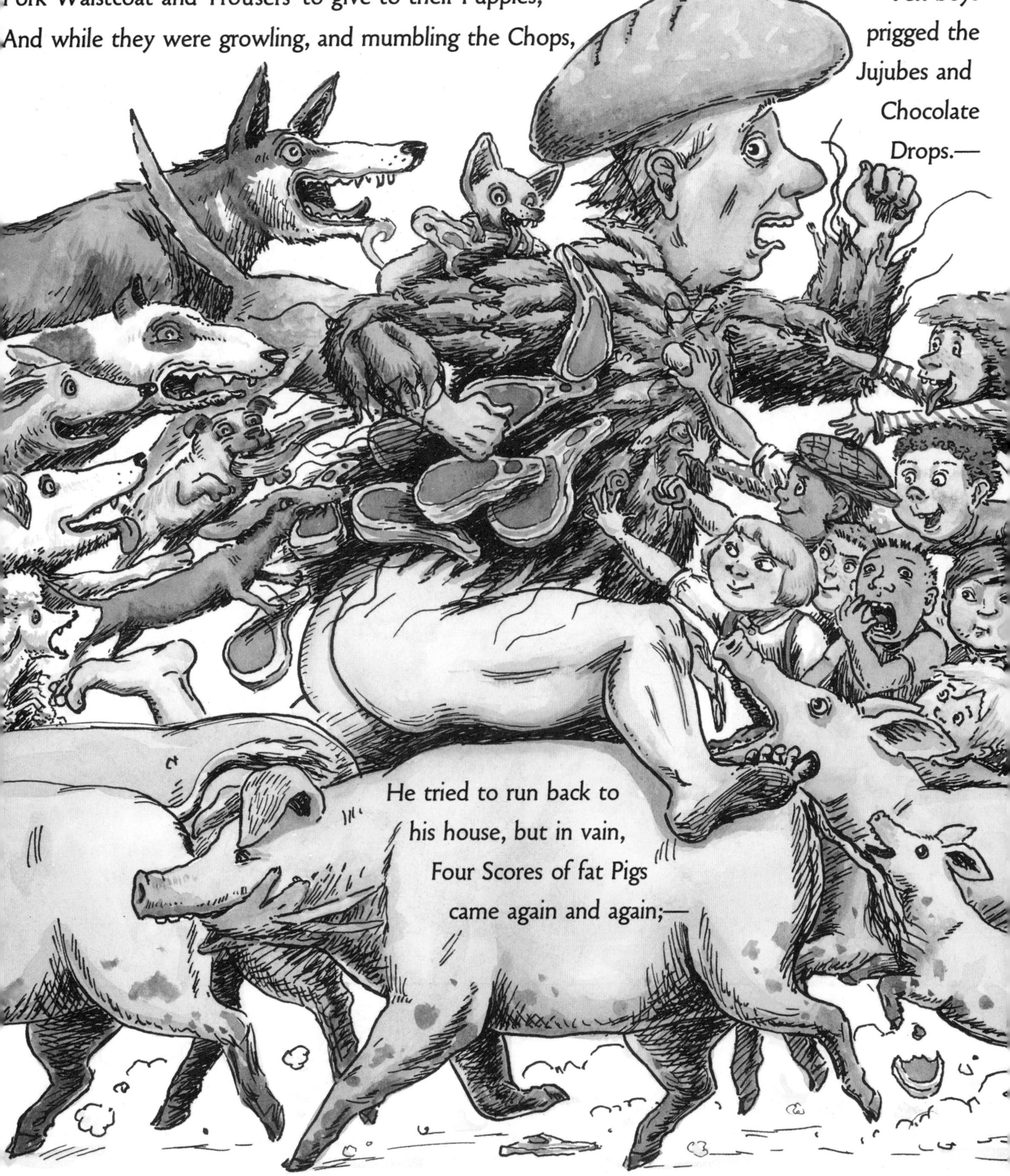

He tried to run back to
his house, but in vain,
Four Scores of fat Pigs
came again and again;—

They rushed out of stables and hovels and doors,— They tore off his stockings, his shoes, and his drawers;—

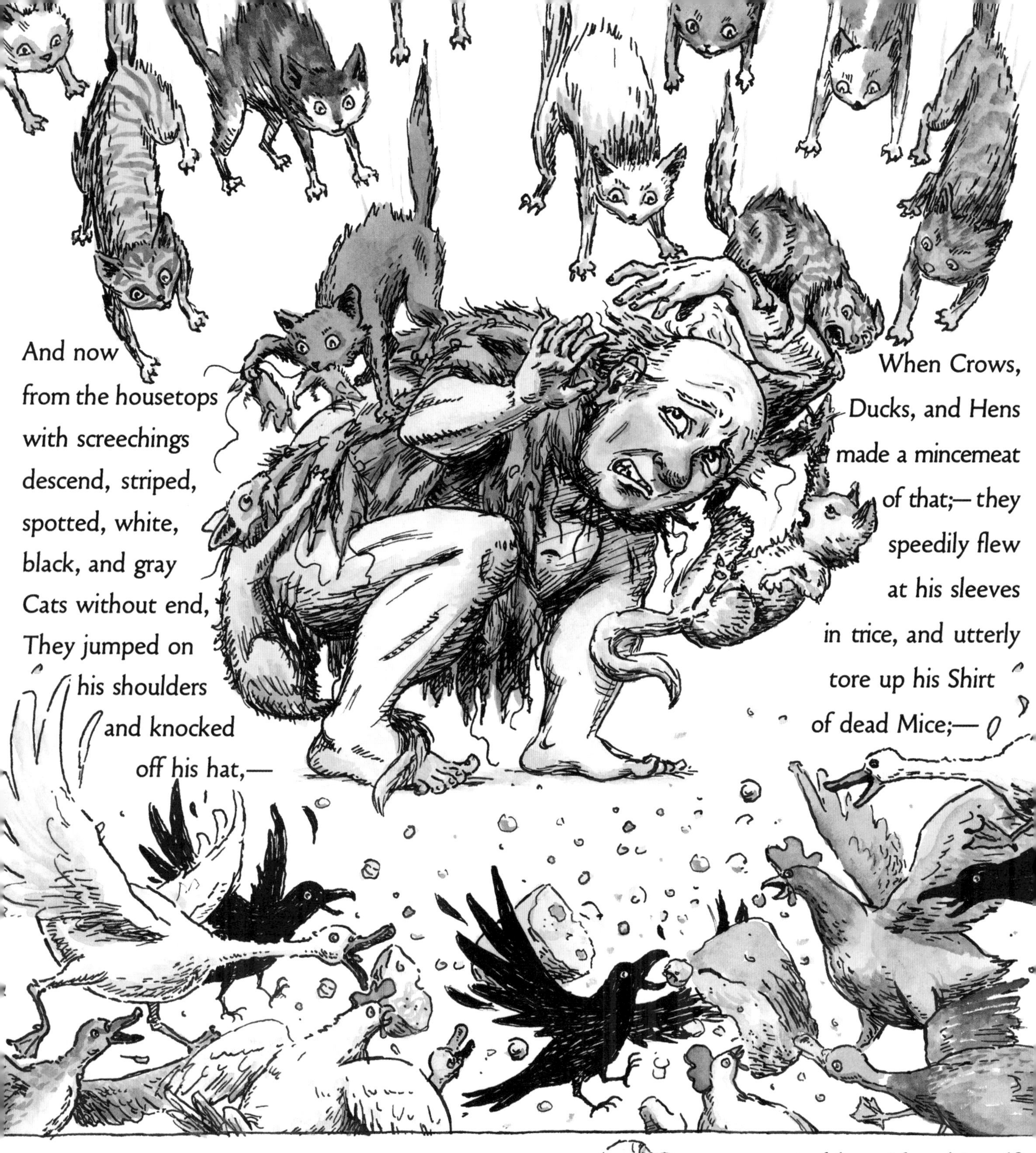

And now
from the housetops
with screechings
descend, striped,
spotted, white,
black, and gray
Cats without end,
They jumped on
his shoulders
and knocked
off his hat,—

When Crows,
Ducks, and Hens
made a mincemeat
of that;— they
speedily flew
at his sleeves
in trice, and utterly
tore up his Shirt
of dead Mice;—

They swallowed the last of his Shirt with a squall,—

Whereon he ran home with no clothes on at all.

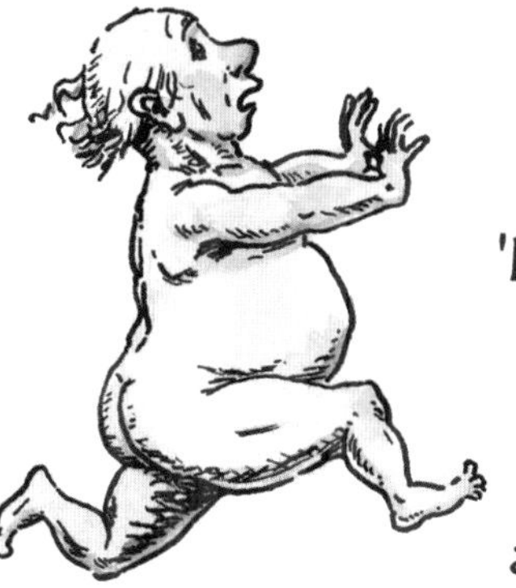

And he said to himself
as he bolted the door,
'I will not wear a similar
dress any more,
'any more, any more,
any more, never more!'

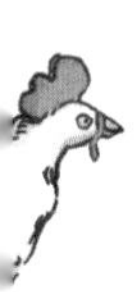

# The Adventures of Tom Sawyer

## Mark Twain

ART/ADAPTATION BY **R. Sikoryak**

**WITH *THE ADVENTURES OF TOM SAWYER*, MARK** Twain wrote the greatest boys' adventure novel. (With its sequel, *Adventures of Huckleberry Finn*, he wrote the Great American Novel.) Twain—born Samuel Clemens—based Tom's fictional town of St. Petersburg, Missouri, on his own Missouri hometown, and most of the characters had real-life counterparts. Tom himself blended three boys that Twain had grown up with.

Telling you the plot of this 1876 masterpiece would be redundant, since R. Sikoryak has amazingly covered the entire book in four panels. But these aren't just any panels. Fans of Sunday newspaper comics will instantly recognize the maps, festooned with meandering dotted lines, of Bil Keane's *The Family Circus*. Every so often, Keane would offer an annotated overview of little Billy's (or Dolly's, or Jeffy's, or P. J.'s) manic activities in the neighborhood, schoolyard, campgrounds, and so on.

Bob specializes in melding classic literature with classic cartoons and comics (mashing up, for example, *Dennis the Menace* with *Hamlet*, or *Peanuts* with Kafka's *The Metamorphosis*). This time he has applied the iconic *Family Circus* map to the activities of America's ultimate rambunctious boy, and, as always in Bob's works, the overlooked parallels become obvious and delightful.

# TOM SAWYER CIRCUS

By R. Sikoryak

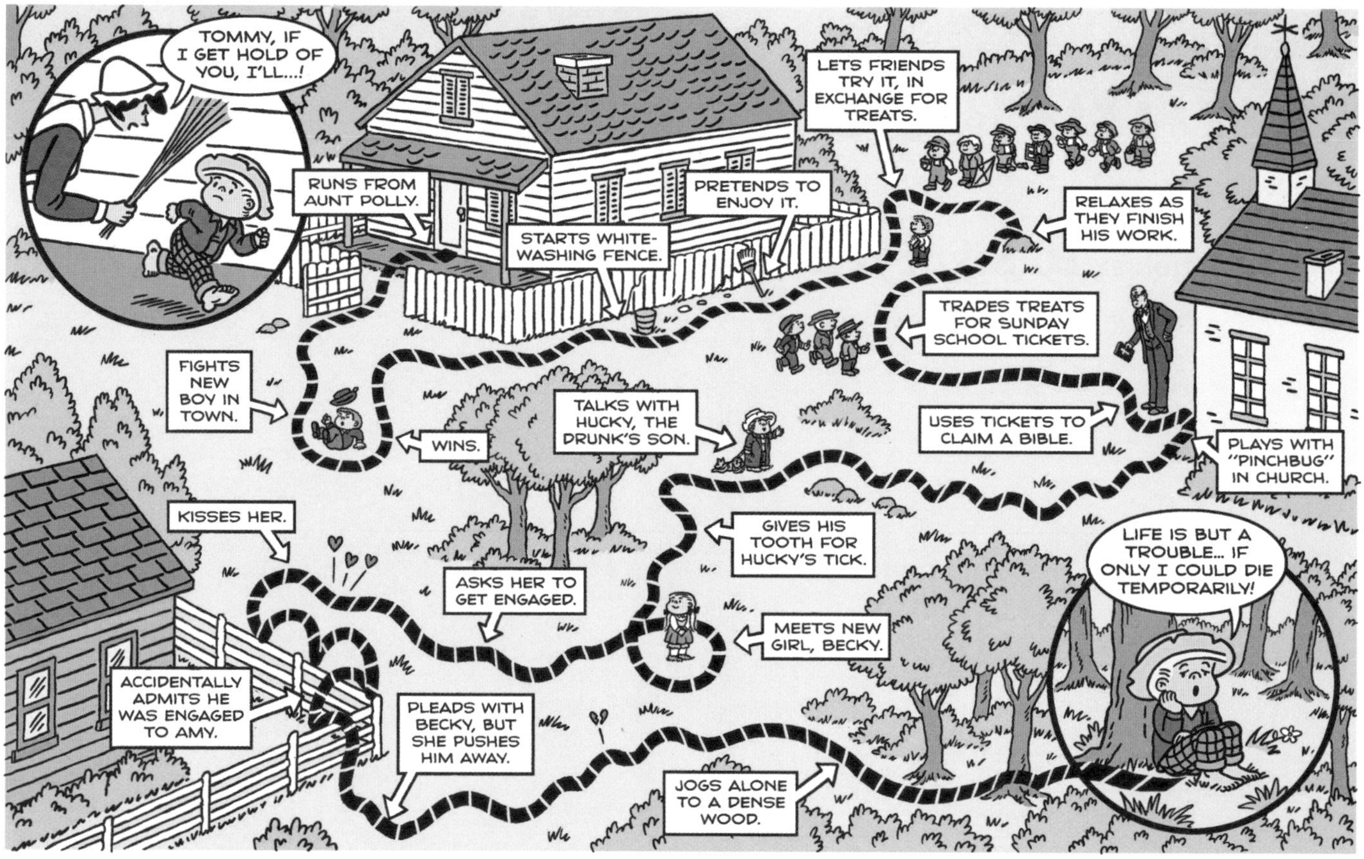
TOMMY, IF I GET HOLD OF YOU, I'LL...!
RUNS FROM AUNT POLLY.
STARTS WHITE-WASHING FENCE.
PRETENDS TO ENJOY IT.
LETS FRIENDS TRY IT, IN EXCHANGE FOR TREATS.
RELAXES AS THEY FINISH HIS WORK.
TRADES TREATS FOR SUNDAY SCHOOL TICKETS.
FIGHTS NEW BOY IN TOWN.
WINS.
TALKS WITH HUCKY, THE DRUNK'S SON.
USES TICKETS TO CLAIM A BIBLE.
PLAYS WITH "PINCHBUG" IN CHURCH.
GIVES HIS TOOTH FOR HUCKY'S TICK.
KISSES HER.
ASKS HER TO GET ENGAGED.
MEETS NEW GIRL, BECKY.
ACCIDENTALLY ADMITS HE WAS ENGAGED TO AMY.
PLEADS WITH BECKY, BUT SHE PUSHES HIM AWAY.
JOGS ALONE TO A DENSE WOOD.
LIFE IS BUT A TROUBLE... IF ONLY I COULD DIE TEMPORARILY!

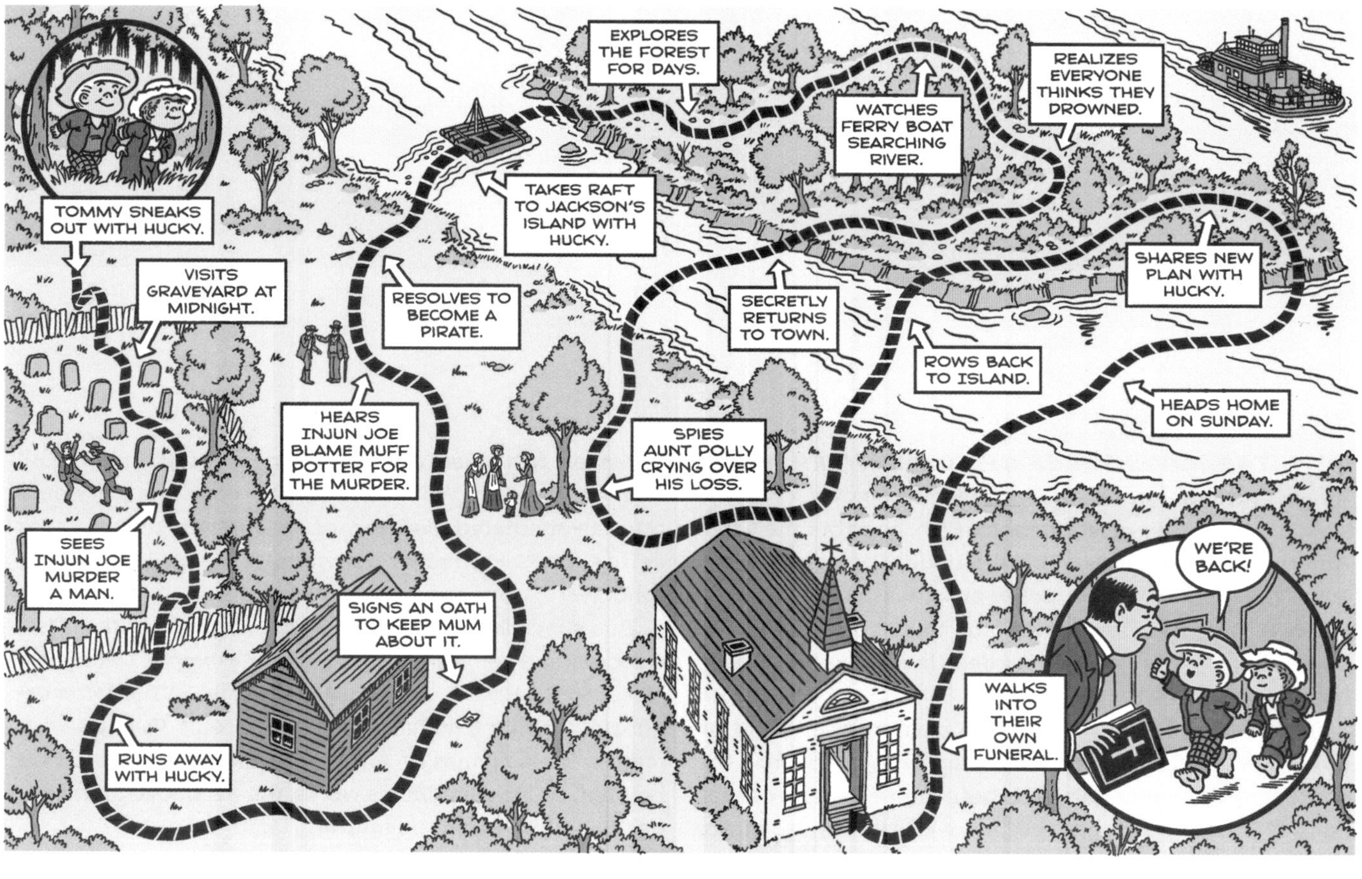
TOMMY SNEAKS OUT WITH HUCKY.
VISITS GRAVEYARD AT MIDNIGHT.
SEES INJUN JOE MURDER A MAN.
HEARS INJUN JOE BLAME MUFF POTTER FOR THE MURDER.
SIGNS AN OATH TO KEEP MUM ABOUT IT.
RUNS AWAY WITH HUCKY.
RESOLVES TO BECOME A PIRATE.
TAKES RAFT TO JACKSON'S ISLAND WITH HUCKY.
EXPLORES THE FOREST FOR DAYS.
WATCHES FERRY BOAT SEARCHING RIVER.
REALIZES EVERYONE THINKS THEY DROWNED.
SECRETLY RETURNS TO TOWN.
SPIES AUNT POLLY CRYING OVER HIS LOSS.
ROWS BACK TO ISLAND.
SHARES NEW PLAN WITH HUCKY.
HEADS HOME ON SUNDAY.
WALKS INTO THEIR OWN FUNERAL.
WE'RE BACK!

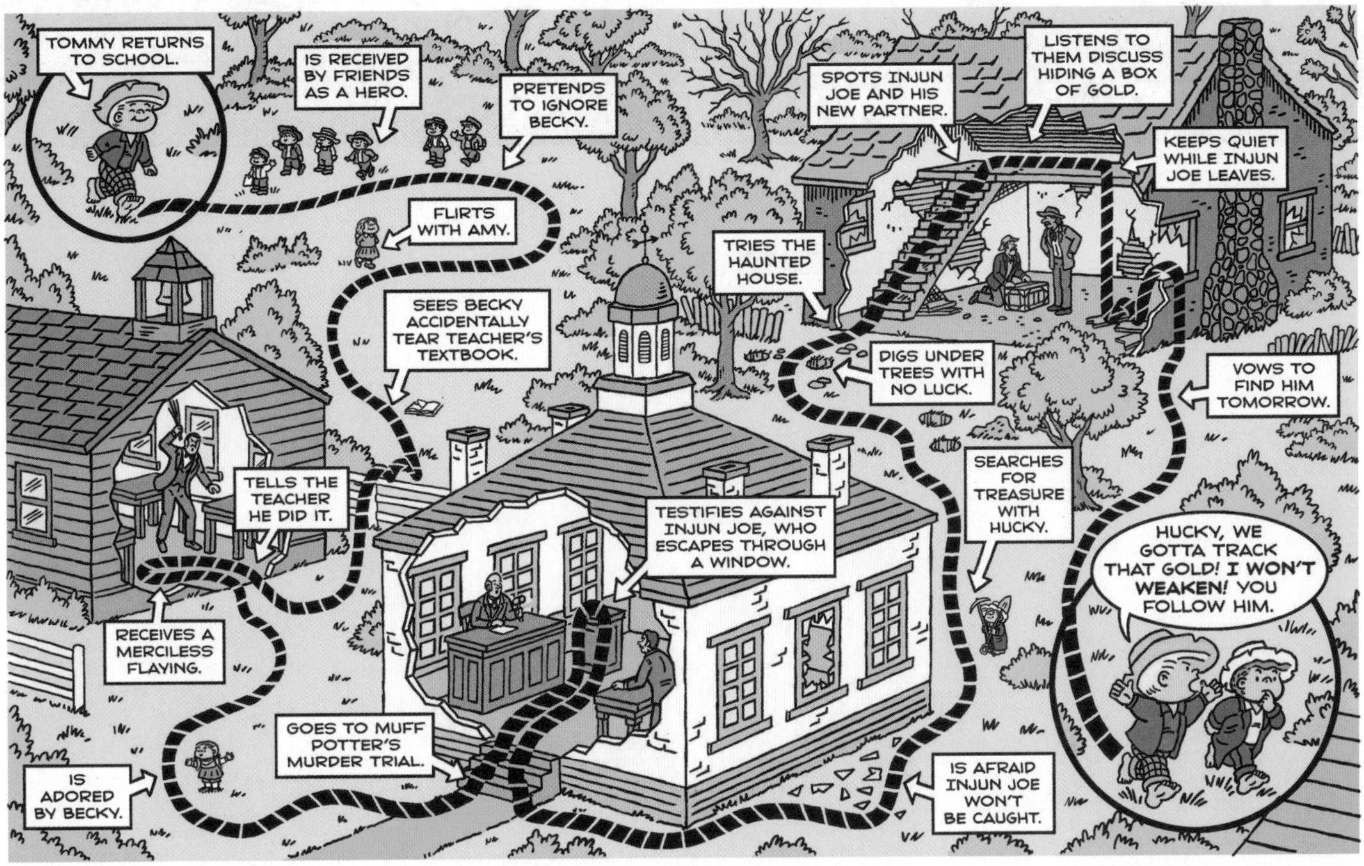
TOMMY RETURNS TO SCHOOL.
IS RECEIVED BY FRIENDS AS A HERO.
PRETENDS TO IGNORE BECKY.
FLIRTS WITH AMY.
SEES BECKY ACCIDENTALLY TEAR TEACHER'S TEXTBOOK.
TELLS THE TEACHER HE DID IT.
RECEIVES A MERCILESS FLAYING.
IS ADORED BY BECKY.
GOES TO MUFF POTTER'S MURDER TRIAL.
TESTIFIES AGAINST INJUN JOE, WHO ESCAPES THROUGH A WINDOW.
IS AFRAID INJUN JOE WON'T BE CAUGHT.
SEARCHES FOR TREASURE WITH HUCKY.
DIGS UNDER TREES WITH NO LUCK.
TRIES THE HAUNTED HOUSE.
SPOTS INJUN JOE AND HIS NEW PARTNER.
LISTENS TO THEM DISCUSS HIDING A BOX OF GOLD.
KEEPS QUIET WHILE INJUN JOE LEAVES.
VOWS TO FIND HIM TOMORROW.
HUCKY, WE GOTTA TRACK THAT GOLD! I WON'T WEAKEN! YOU FOLLOW HIM.

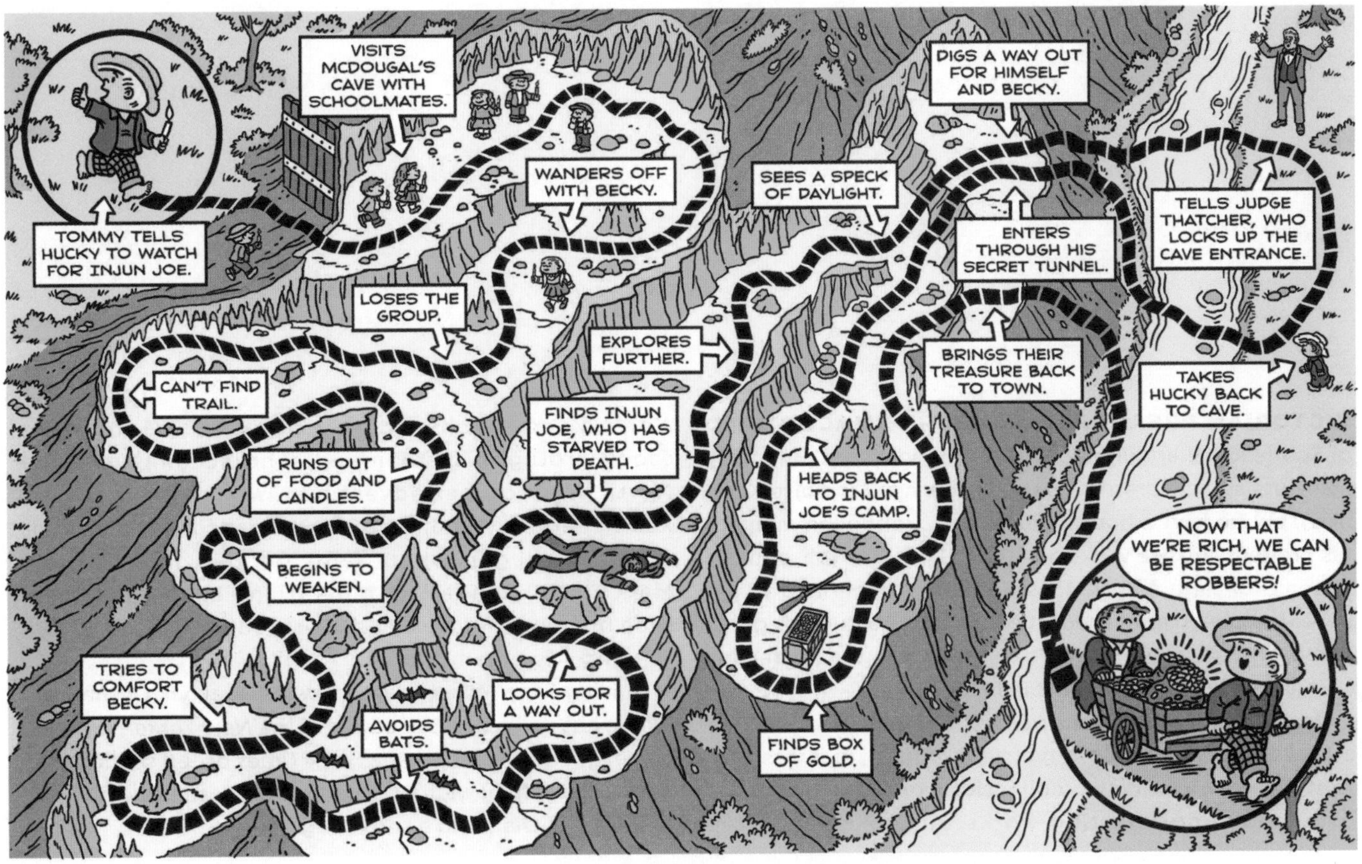
TOMMY TELLS HUCKY TO WATCH FOR INJUN JOE.
VISITS MCDOUGAL'S CAVE WITH SCHOOLMATES.
WANDERS OFF WITH BECKY.
LOSES THE GROUP.
CAN'T FIND TRAIL.
RUNS OUT OF FOOD AND CANDLES.
BEGINS TO WEAKEN.
TRIES TO COMFORT BECKY.
AVOIDS BATS.
LOOKS FOR A WAY OUT.
FINDS INJUN JOE, WHO HAS STARVED TO DEATH.
EXPLORES FURTHER.
SEES A SPECK OF DAYLIGHT.
DIGS A WAY OUT FOR HIMSELF AND BECKY.
TELLS JUDGE THATCHER, WHO LOCKS UP THE CAVE ENTRANCE.
TAKES HUCKY BACK TO CAVE.
ENTERS THROUGH HIS SECRET TUNNEL.
HEADS BACK TO INJUN JOE'S CAMP.
FINDS BOX OF GOLD.
BRINGS THEIR TREASURE BACK TO TOWN.
NOW THAT WE'RE RICH, WE CAN BE RESPECTABLE ROBBERS!

# At the Back of the North Wind

## George MacDonald

ART/ADAPTATION BY **Dasha Tolstikova**

**VICTORIAN PREACHERMAN GEORGE MACDONALD** of Scotland never quite got his due. Serious fans of fantasy literature and children's literature know him (and often love him), but he isn't a household name . . . although many of his progeny are. He was a mentor to Lewis Carroll, and if it weren't for him, *Alice's Adventures in Wonderland* might never have been published. The twentieth century's biggest names in fantasy—J. R. R. Tolkien, C. S. Lewis, Madeleine L'Engle—cite him as a direct influence.

MacDonald published poetry, sermons, and highly successful "realistic" novels for adults, but his five fantasy novels and two collections of fairy tales have proven his most lasting works. *At the Back of the North Wind*, published as a book in 1871, features a boy protagonist, Diamond, who accompanies the North Wind on her adventures, which include, well, killing people. A millimeter below its surface action is Christian allegory about faith, good, evil, and death. Mark Twain, in a letter to his friend MacDonald, said that his own children had worn out their copy from reading it so many times.

Hailing from Moscow and now in Brooklyn, Dasha Tolstikova has enlivened the pages of the *New Yorker*, the *Wall Street Journal*, and the *New York Times* op-ed section. She uses a beautifully wide gray palette to present the opening chapters of Diamond's surprising journey.

# AT THE BACK OF THE NORTH WIND

## Adapted from George MacDonald by D. Tolstikova

I AM GOING TO TELL YOU NOW HOW IT FARED WITH A BOY WHO WENT
TO THE BACK OF THE NORTH WIND.
HIS FATHER, WHO WAS A COACHMAN, NAMED HIM AFTER A FAVOURITE ·DIAMOND·
HORSE, AND HIS MOTHER HAD HAD NO OBJECTION.
SOMETIMES, WHEN HIS MOTHER HAD UNDRESSED HIM IN HER
ROOM, AND TOLD HIM TO TROT AWAY TO BED BY HIMSELF,
HE WOULD CREEP INTO THE HEART OF THE HAY & LIE THERE
THINKING HOW COLD IT WAS OUTSIDE IN THE WIND & HOW
WARM IT WAS INSIDE IN HIS BED.

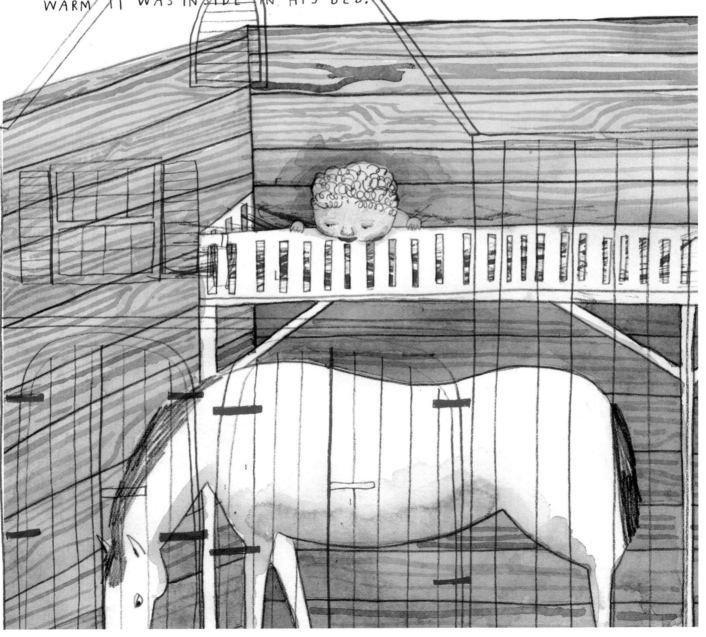

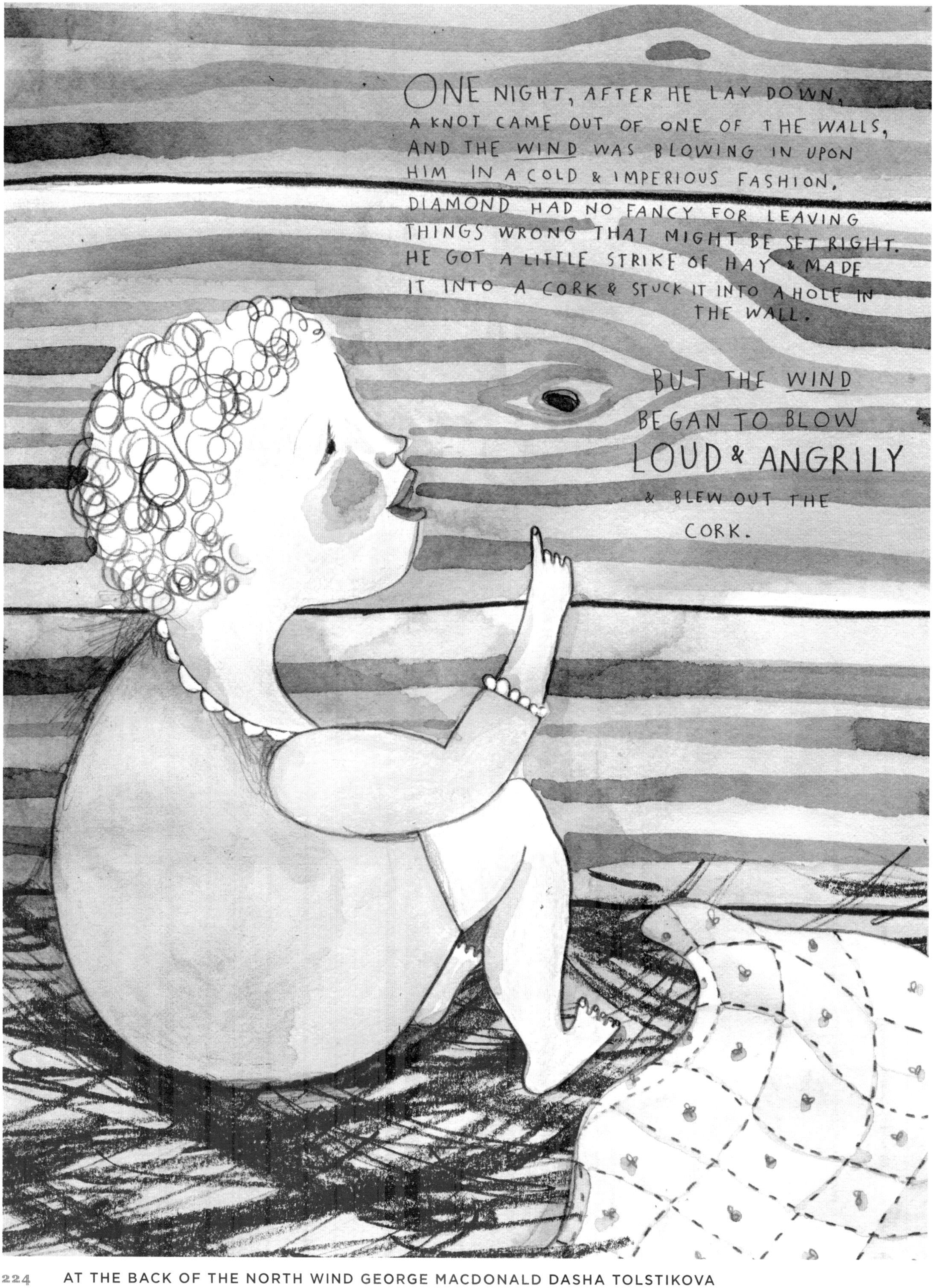
ONE NIGHT, AFTER HE LAY DOWN, A KNOT CAME OUT OF ONE OF THE WALLS, AND THE WIND WAS BLOWING IN UPON HIM IN A COLD & IMPERIOUS FASHION.
DIAMOND HAD NO FANCY FOR LEAVING THINGS WRONG THAT MIGHT BE SET RIGHT. HE GOT A LITTLE STRIKE OF HAY & MADE IT INTO A CORK & STUCK IT INTO A HOLE IN THE WALL.
BUT THE WIND BEGAN TO BLOW LOUD & ANGRILY & BLEW OUT THE CORK.

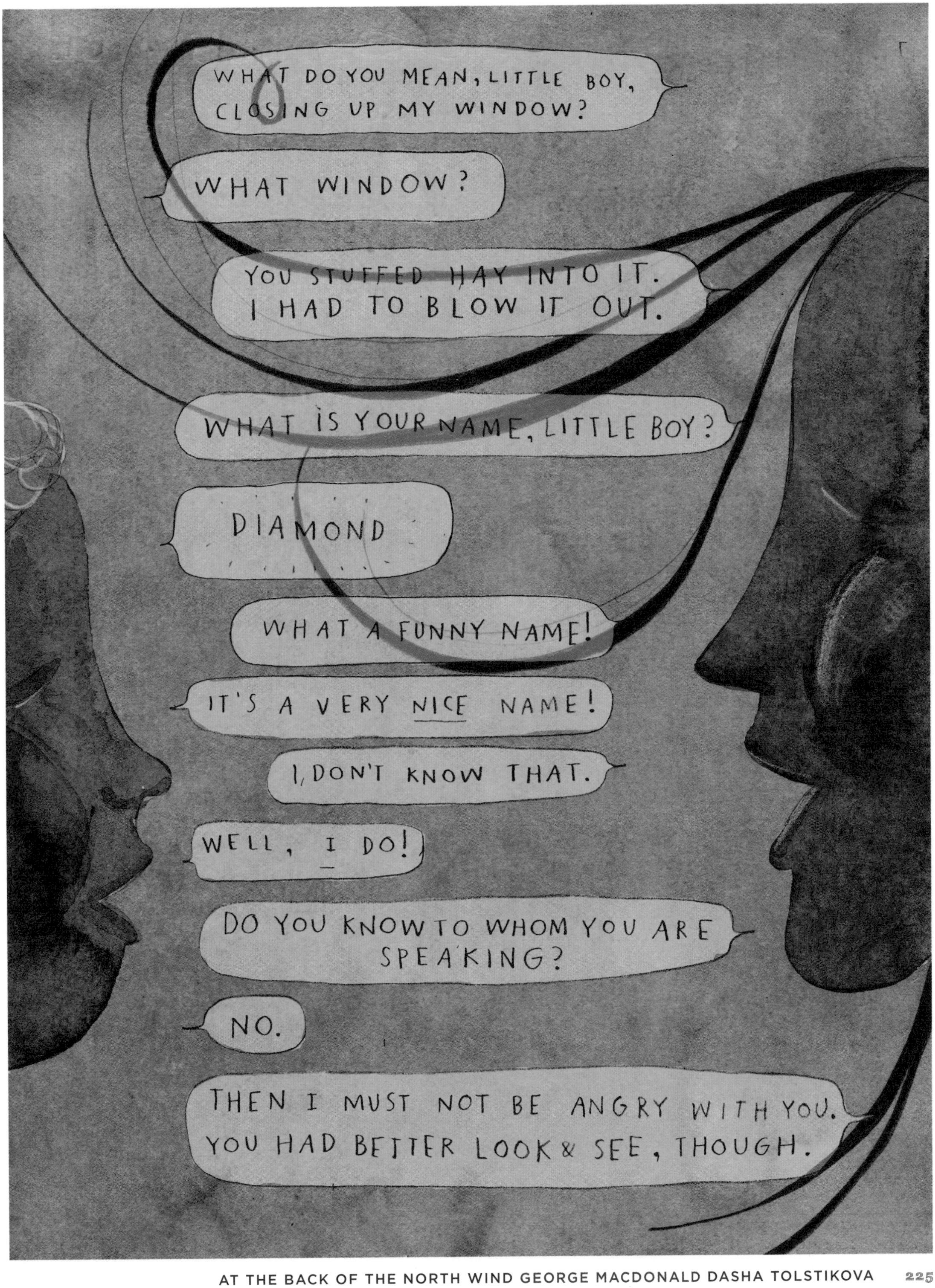
WHAT DO YOU MEAN, LITTLE BOY, CLOSING UP MY WINDOW?
WHAT WINDOW?
YOU STUFFED HAY INTO IT. I HAD TO BLOW IT OUT.
WHAT IS YOUR NAME, LITTLE BOY?
DIAMOND
WHAT A FUNNY NAME!
IT'S A VERY NICE NAME!
I DON'T KNOW THAT.
WELL, I DO!
DO YOU KNOW TO WHOM YOU ARE SPEAKING?
NO.
THEN I MUST NOT BE ANGRY WITH YOU. YOU HAD BETTER LOOK & SEE, THOUGH.

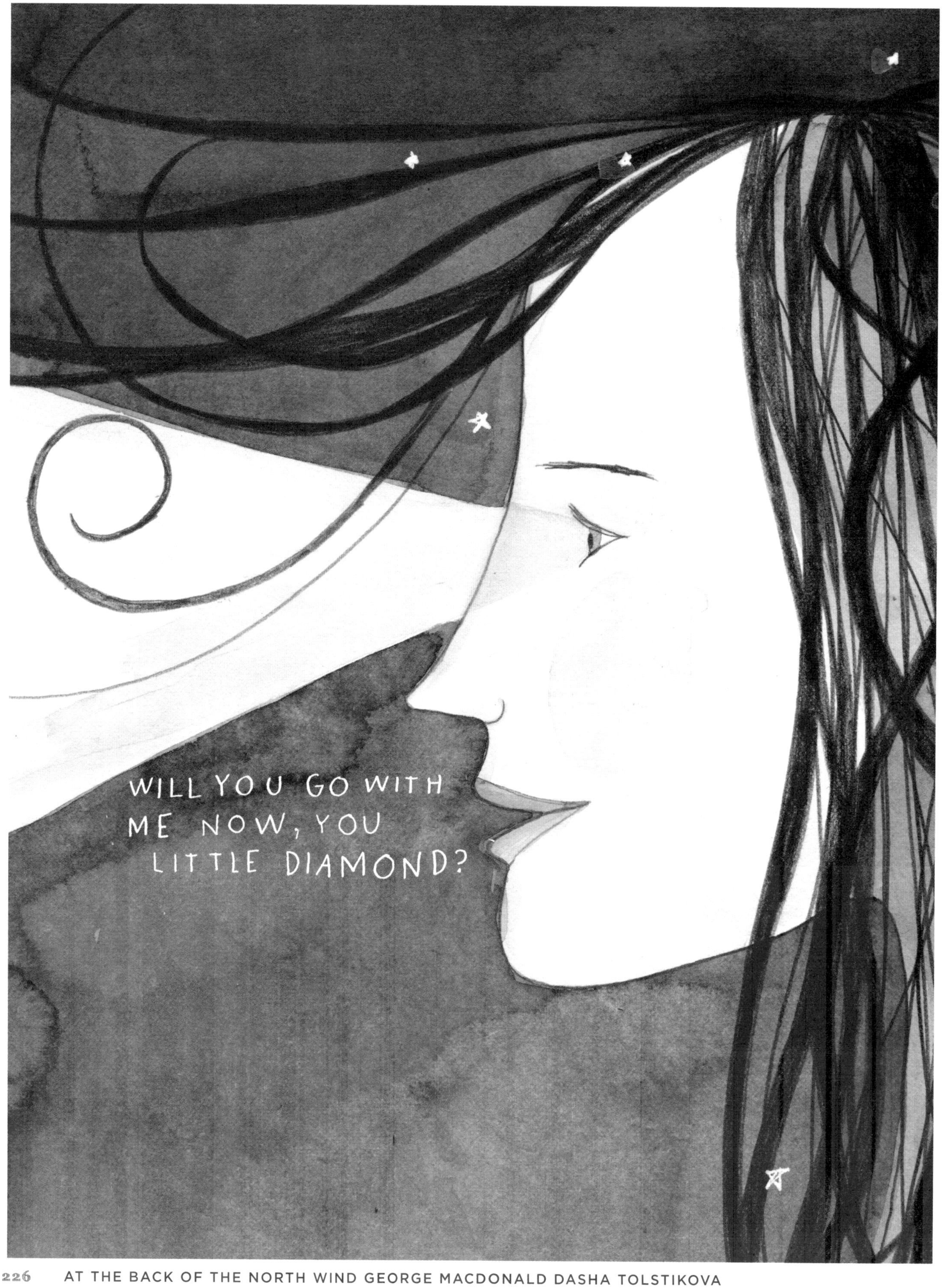
WILL YOU GO WITH
ME NOW, YOU
LITTLE DIAMOND?

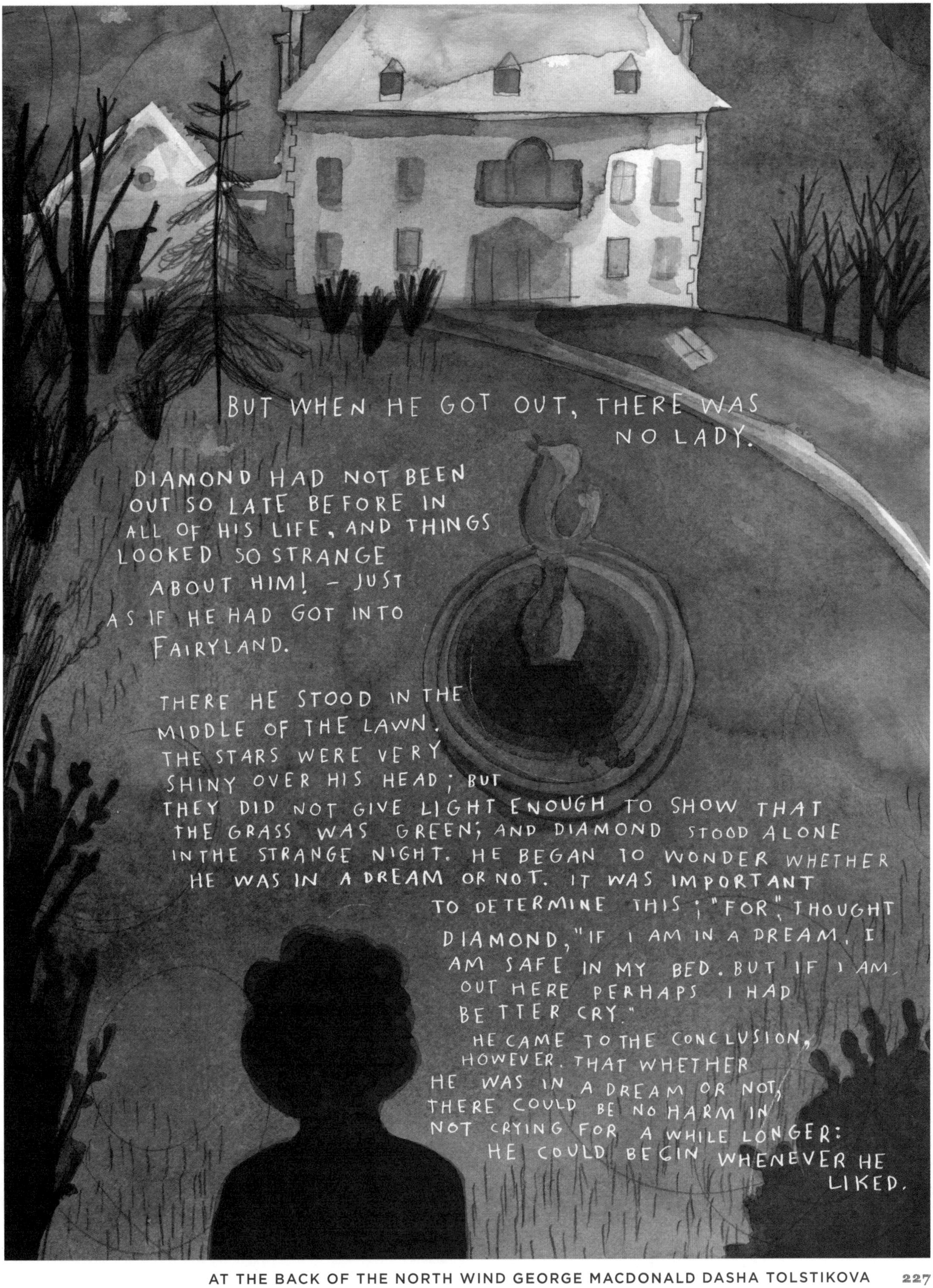
BUT WHEN HE GOT OUT, THERE WAS NO LADY.
DIAMOND HAD NOT BEEN OUT SO LATE BEFORE IN ALL OF HIS LIFE, AND THINGS LOOKED SO STRANGE ABOUT HIM! – JUST AS IF HE HAD GOT INTO FAIRYLAND.
THERE HE STOOD IN THE MIDDLE OF THE LAWN. THE STARS WERE VERY SHINY OVER HIS HEAD; BUT THEY DID NOT GIVE LIGHT ENOUGH TO SHOW THAT THE GRASS WAS GREEN; AND DIAMOND STOOD ALONE IN THE STRANGE NIGHT. HE BEGAN TO WONDER WHETHER HE WAS IN A DREAM OR NOT. IT WAS IMPORTANT TO DETERMINE THIS; "FOR," THOUGHT DIAMOND, "IF I AM IN A DREAM, I AM SAFE IN MY BED. BUT IF I AM OUT HERE PERHAPS I HAD BETTER CRY."
HE CAME TO THE CONCLUSION, HOWEVER, THAT WHETHER HE WAS IN A DREAM OR NOT, THERE COULD BE NO HARM IN NOT CRYING FOR A WHILE LONGER: HE COULD BEGIN WHENEVER HE LIKED.

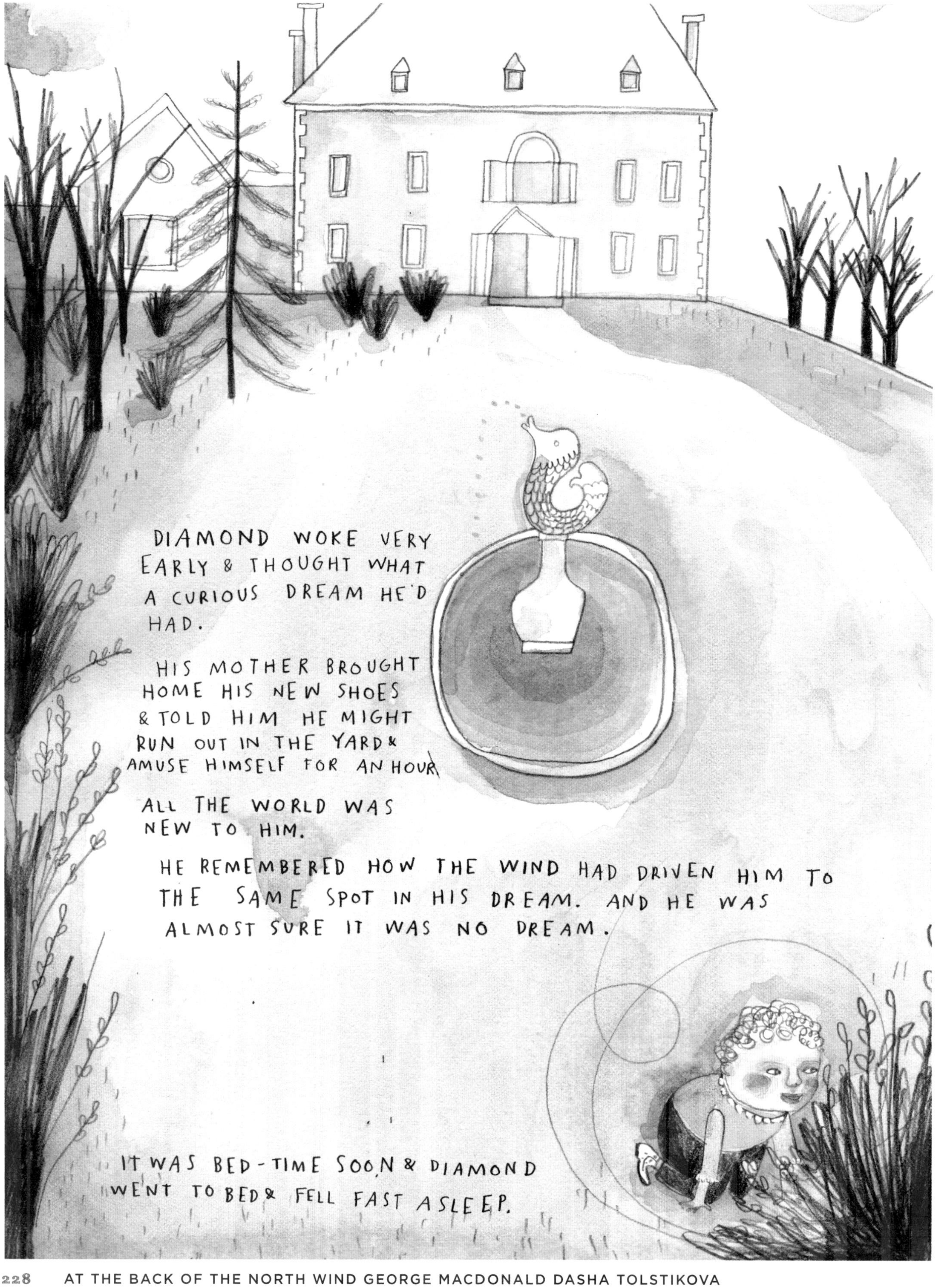
DIAMOND WOKE VERY EARLY & THOUGHT WHAT A CURIOUS DREAM HE'D HAD.
HIS MOTHER BROUGHT HOME HIS NEW SHOES & TOLD HIM HE MIGHT RUN OUT IN THE YARD & AMUSE HIMSELF FOR AN HOUR.
ALL THE WORLD WAS NEW TO HIM.
HE REMEMBERED HOW THE WIND HAD DRIVEN HIM TO THE SAME SPOT IN HIS DREAM. AND HE WAS ALMOST SURE IT WAS NO DREAM.
IT WAS BED-TIME SOON & DIAMOND WENT TO BED & FELL FAST ASLEEP.

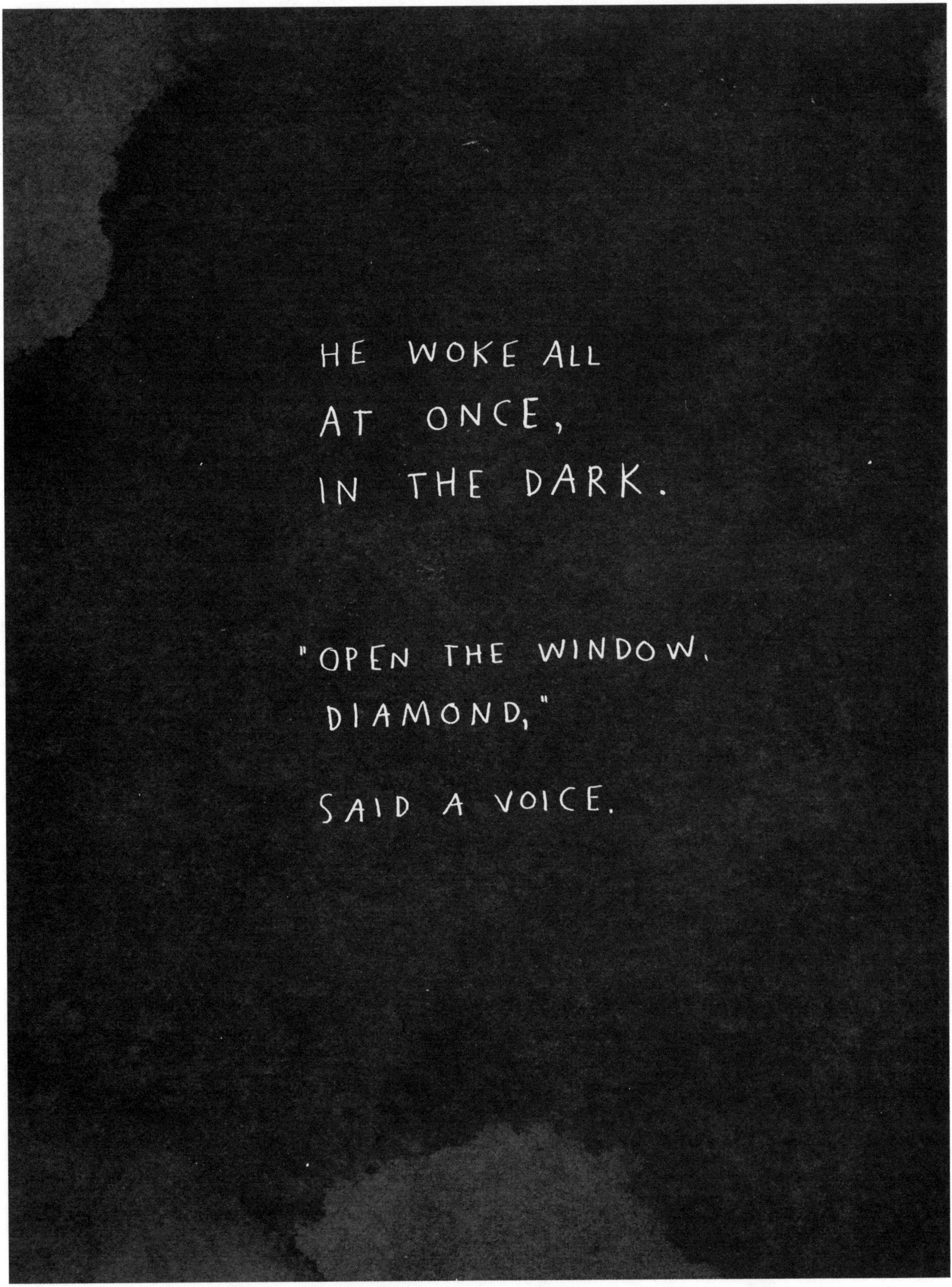
HE WOKE ALL
AT ONCE,
IN THE DARK.
"OPEN THE WINDOW,
DIAMOND,"
SAID A VOICE.

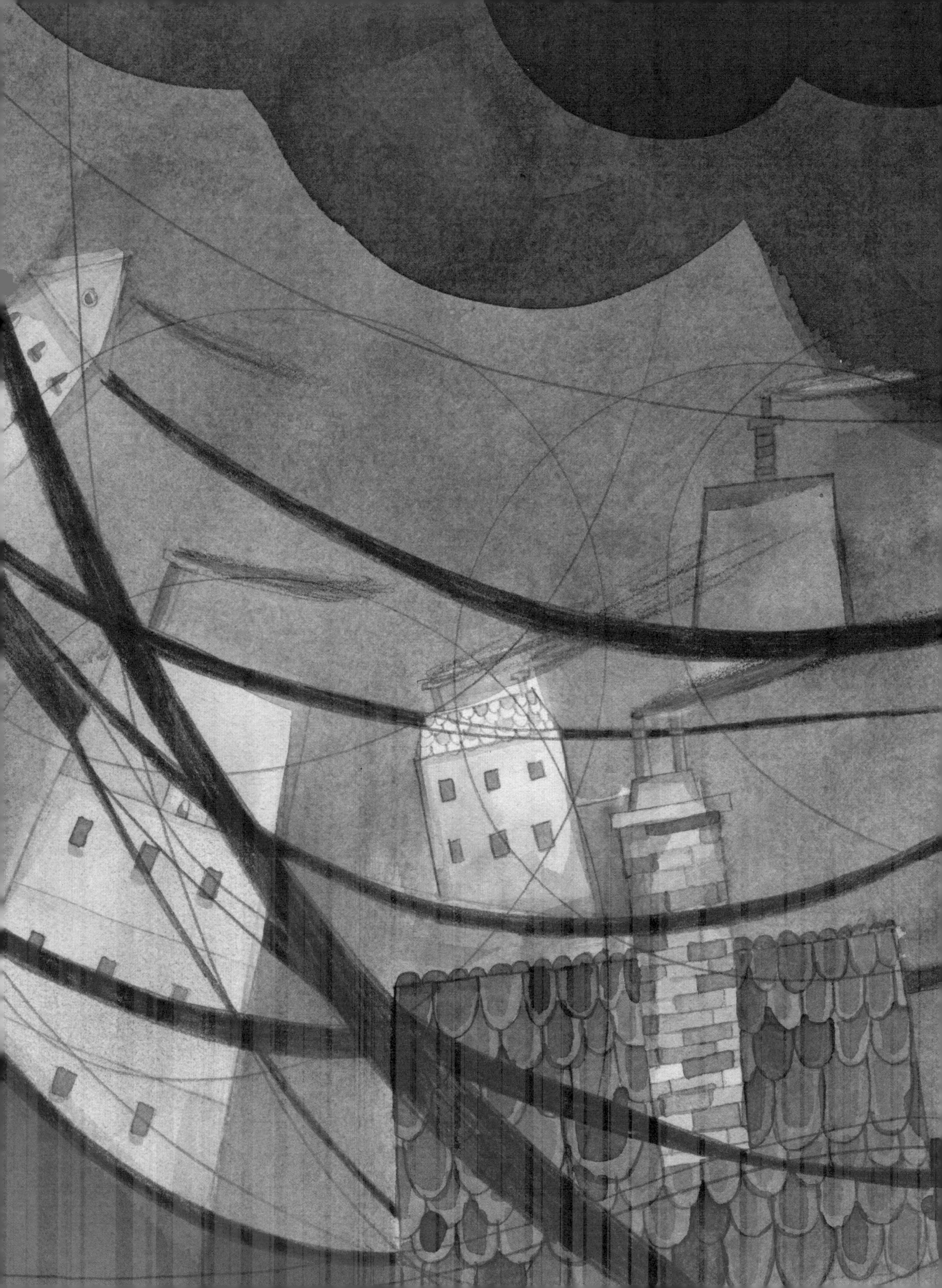

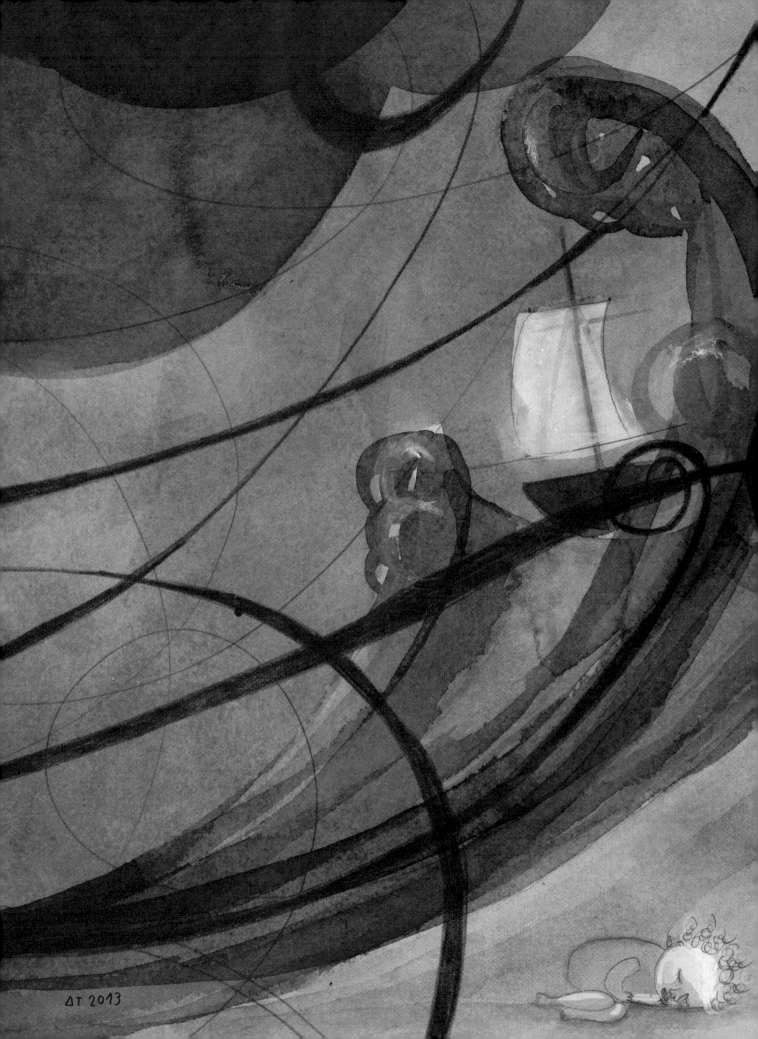

ΔT 2013

# Johanna Spyri

ART/ADAPTATION BY **Molly Brooks**

**THE REST OF THE WORLD HAS AN INDELIBLE IMPRESSION** of the Alps—sprawling green and blue as far as the eye can see, pure mountain air, crystal lakes, pristine, idyllic, rejuvenating. This apparently accurate picture comes mainly from a book and a movie: *Heidi* (1880) and *The Sound of Music* (1965). Written in a month by Johanna Spyri in Zurich, *Heidi* follows the childhood of a five-year-old orphan left in the care of her reclusive, embittered grandfather in the Swiss mountains. Later, she must leave in order to be a companion to a rich, disabled girl in Frankfurt. City life and formal education quickly start to destroy the naïve, carefree child of nature, although she quickly takes to Christianity. Heidi returns to the Alps, where, reborn, she reintroduces her grandfather to the power of prayer. Her friend comes to visit her and is soon able to walk, thanks to the invigorating mountains.

The healing power of nature (and of the child-savior Heidi) is a huge theme here. The overtly Christian aspect of the work—Spyri was quite pious—is often downplayed or eliminated in movie adaptations and abridged versions of the book. Not so with Molly Brooks's adaptation of the opening chapter. We see the introduction of Heidi to the high Alps and to her grandfather, and already the roles of nature, God, and freedom (in this case, from smothering clothing put on by her grouchy aunt) are coming into focus. Molly's crisp, pleasing colors give me a Swiss Alps boost by proxy.

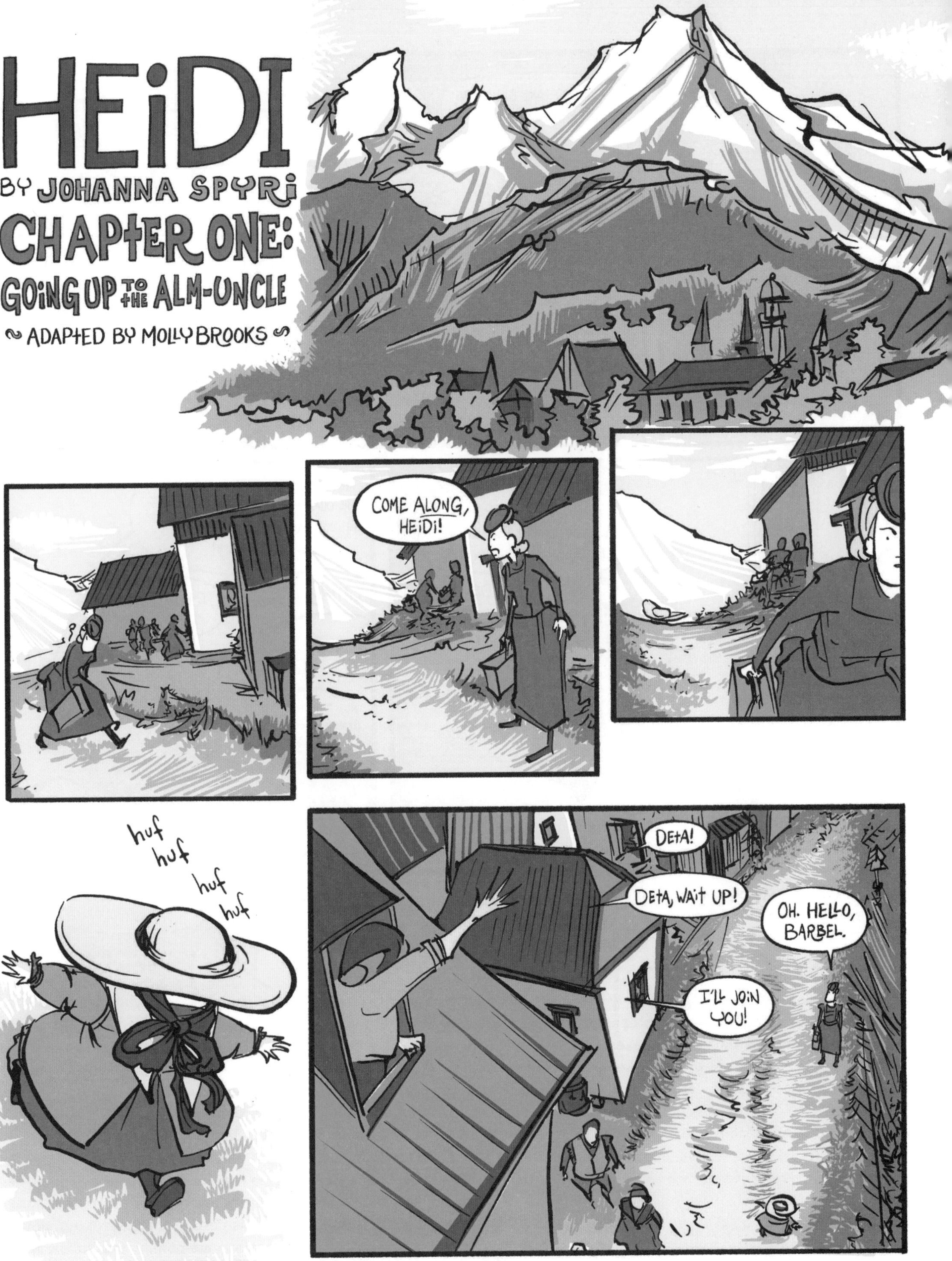
HEiDI
BY JOHANNA SPYRi
CHAPtER ONE:
GOiNG UP TO THE ALM-UNCLE
ADAPtED BY MOLLY BROOKS
COME ALONG, HEiDi!
huf
huf
huf
huf
DEtA!
DEtA, WAit UP!
OH. HELLO, BARBEL.
I'LL JOIN YOU!

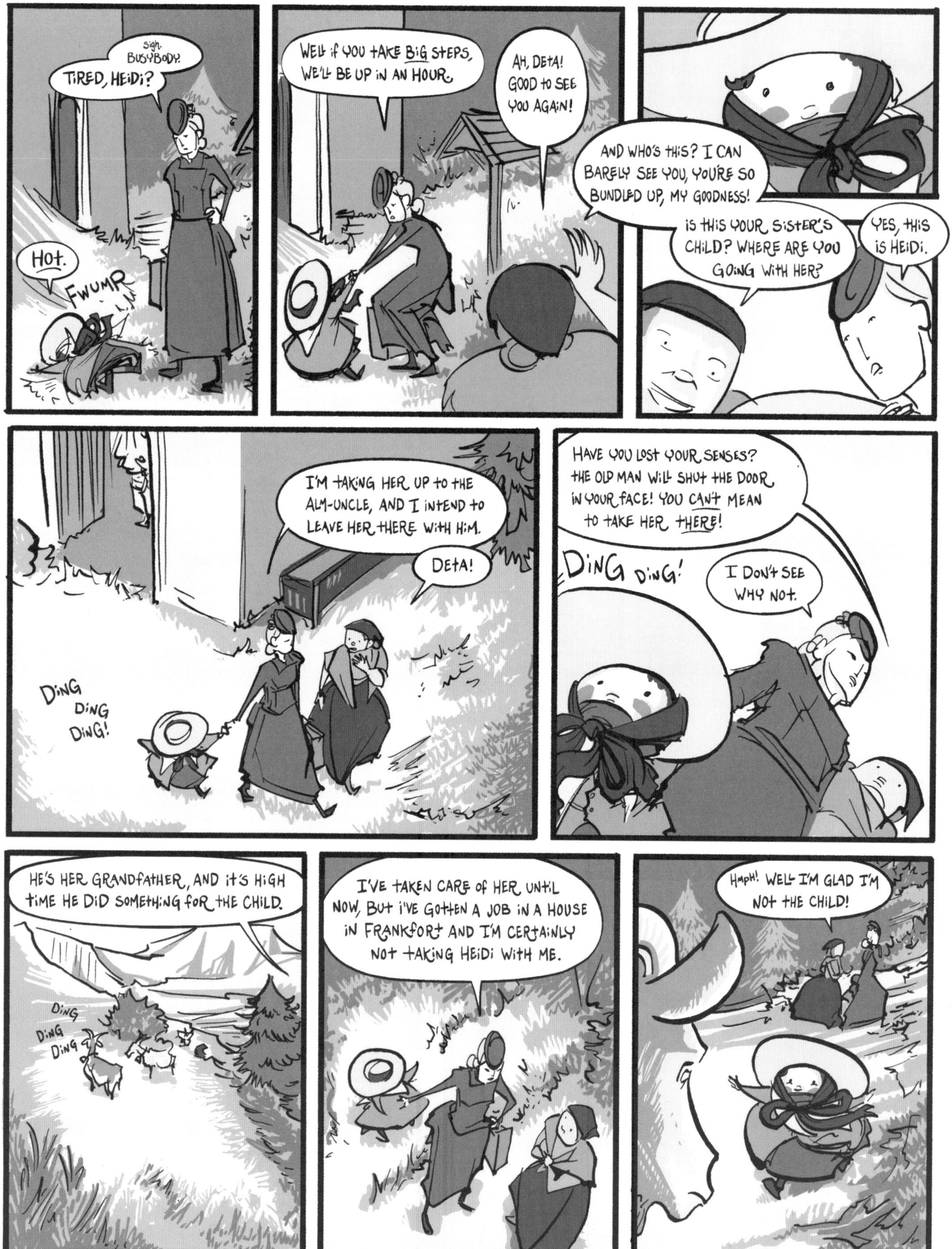
Sigh. BUSYBODY.
TIRED, HEIDI?
Hot.
FWUMR
WELL if YOU TAKE BIG STEPS, WE'LL BE UP IN AN HOUR.
AH, DETA! GOOD to SEE YOU AGAIN!
AND WHO'S THIS? I CAN BARELY SEE YOU, YOU'RE SO BUNDLED UP, MY GOODNESS!
IS THIS YOUR SISTER'S CHILD? WHERE ARE YOU GOING WITH HER?
YES, THIS IS HEIDI.
I'M TAKING HER UP TO THE ALM-UNCLE, AND I INTEND TO LEAVE HER THERE WITH HIM.
DETA!
DING DING DING!
HAVE YOU LOST YOUR SENSES? THE OLD MAN WILL SHUT THE DOOR IN YOUR FACE! YOU CAN'T MEAN TO TAKE HER THERE!
DING DING!
I DON'T SEE WHY NOT.
HE'S HER GRANDFATHER, AND IT'S HIGH TIME HE DID SOMETHING FOR THE CHILD.
DING DING DING
I'VE TAKEN CARE OF HER UNTIL NOW, BUT I'VE GOTTEN A JOB IN A HOUSE IN FRANKFORT AND I'M CERTAINLY NOT TAKING HEIDI WITH ME.
HMPH! WELL I'M GLAD I'M NOT THE CHILD!

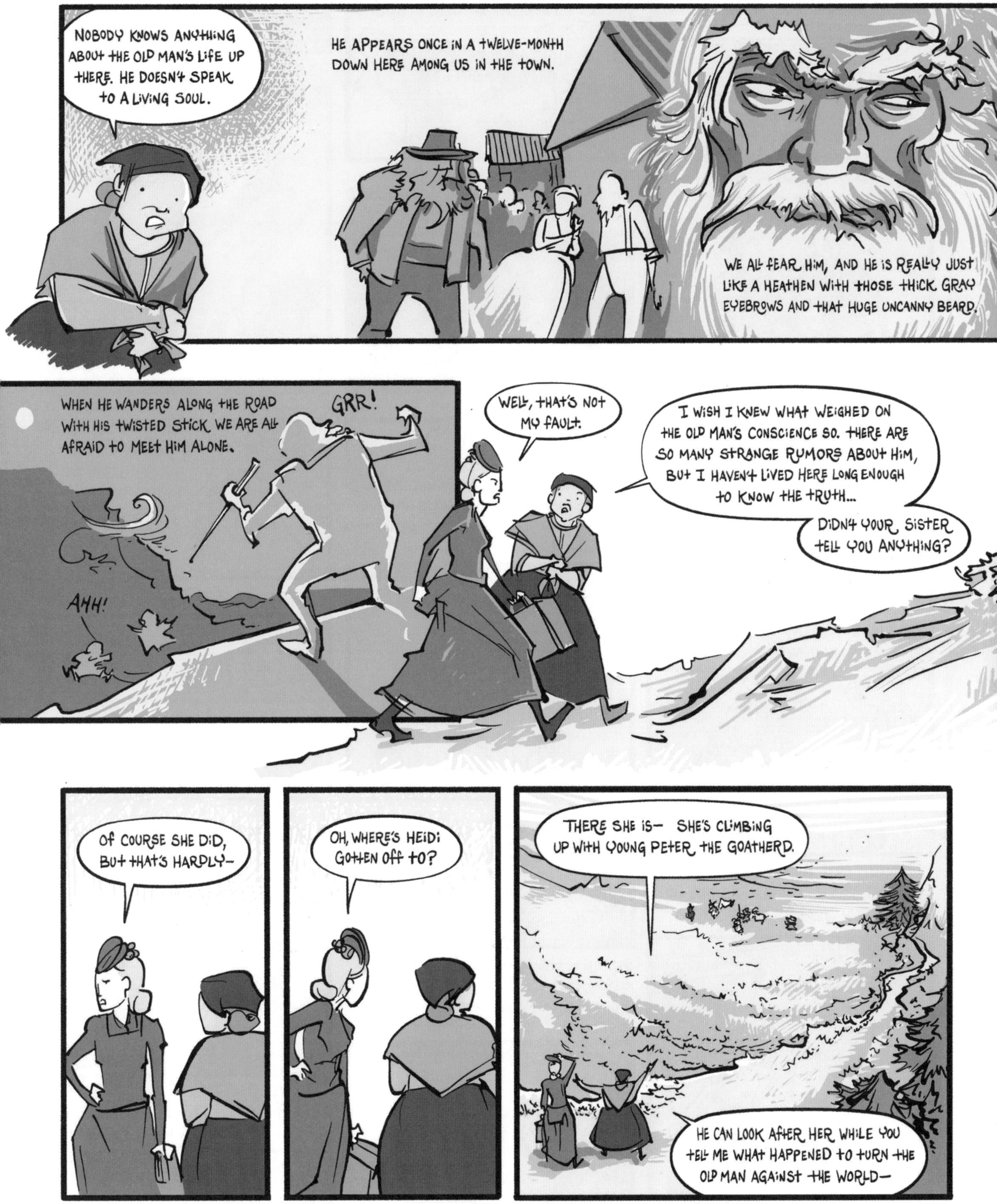

NOBODY KNOWS ANYTHING ABOUT THE OLD MAN'S LIFE UP THERE. HE DOESN'T SPEAK TO A LIVING SOUL.
HE APPEARS ONCE IN A TWELVE-MONTH DOWN HERE AMONG US IN THE TOWN.
WE ALL FEAR HIM, AND HE IS REALLY JUST LIKE A HEATHEN WITH THOSE THICK GRAY EYEBROWS AND THAT HUGE UNCANNY BEARD.
WHEN HE WANDERS ALONG THE ROAD WITH HIS TWISTED STICK WE ARE ALL AFRAID TO MEET HIM ALONE.
GRR!
AHH!
WELL, THAT'S NOT MY FAULT.
I WISH I KNEW WHAT WEIGHED ON THE OLD MAN'S CONSCIENCE SO. THERE ARE SO MANY STRANGE RUMORS ABOUT HIM, BUT I HAVEN'T LIVED HERE LONG ENOUGH TO KNOW THE TRUTH...
DIDN'T YOUR SISTER TELL YOU ANYTHING?
OF COURSE SHE DID, BUT THAT'S HARDLY—
OH, WHERE'S HEIDI GOTTEN OFF TO?
THERE SHE IS— SHE'S CLIMBING UP WITH YOUNG PETER THE GOATHERD.
HE CAN LOOK AFTER HER WHILE YOU TELL ME WHAT HAPPENED TO TURN THE OLD MAN AGAINST THE WORLD—

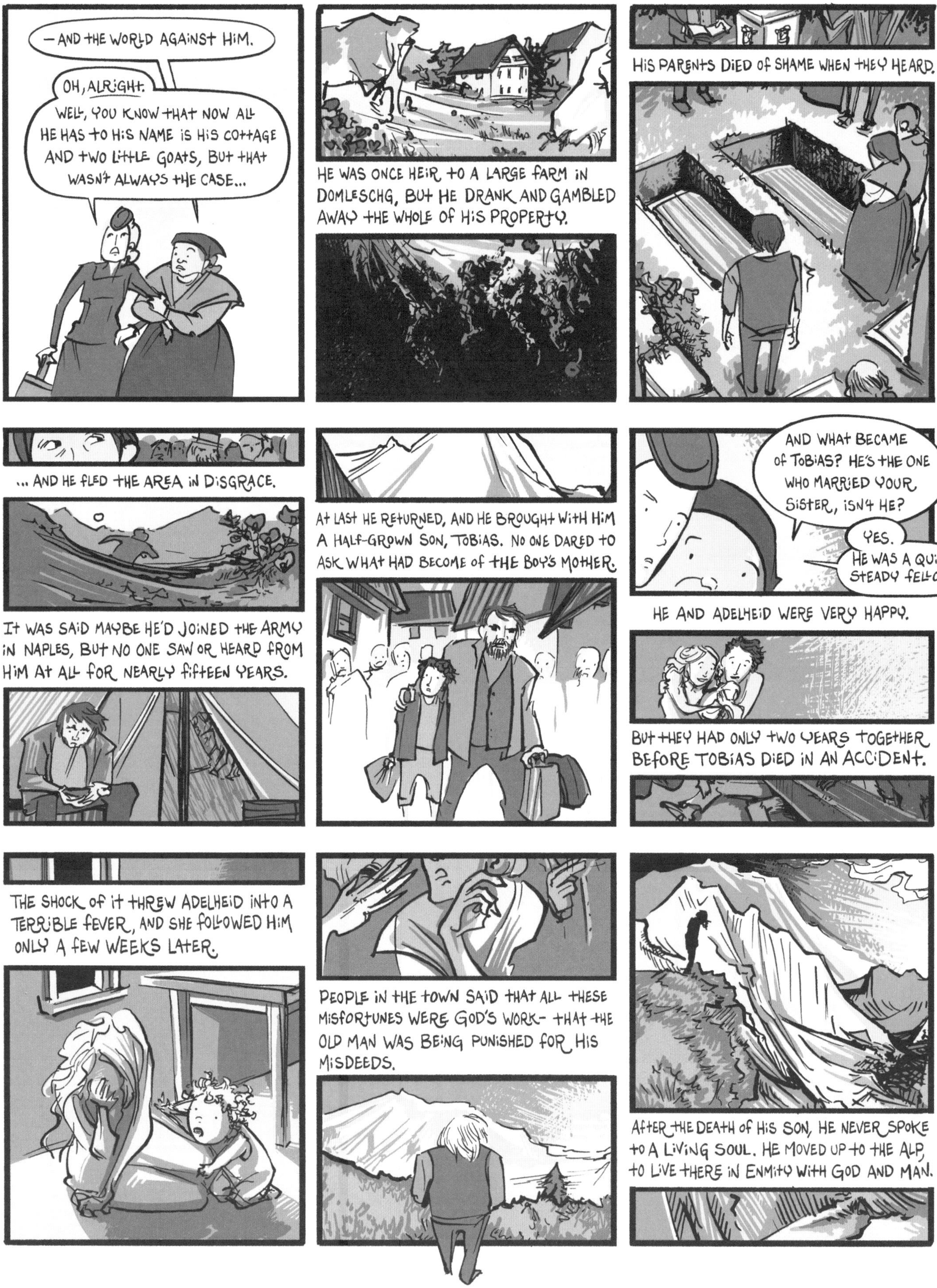
—AND THE WORLD AGAINST HIM.
OH, ALRIGHT.
WELL, YOU KNOW THAT NOW ALL HE HAS TO HIS NAME IS HIS COTTAGE AND TWO LITTLE GOATS, BUT THAT WASN'T ALWAYS THE CASE...
HE WAS ONCE HEIR TO A LARGE FARM IN DOMLESCHG, BUT HE DRANK AND GAMBLED AWAY THE WHOLE OF HIS PROPERTY.
HIS PARENTS DIED OF SHAME WHEN THEY HEARD.
...AND HE FLED THE AREA IN DISGRACE.
IT WAS SAID MAYBE HE'D JOINED THE ARMY IN NAPLES, BUT NO ONE SAW OR HEARD FROM HIM AT ALL FOR NEARLY FIFTEEN YEARS.
AT LAST HE RETURNED, AND HE BROUGHT WITH HIM A HALF-GROWN SON, TOBIAS. NO ONE DARED TO ASK WHAT HAD BECOME OF THE BOY'S MOTHER.
AND WHAT BECAME OF TOBIAS? HE'S THE ONE WHO MARRIED YOUR SISTER, ISN'T HE?
YES. HE WAS A QUIET, STEADY FELLOW.
HE AND ADELHEID WERE VERY HAPPY.
BUT THEY HAD ONLY TWO YEARS TOGETHER BEFORE TOBIAS DIED IN AN ACCIDENT.
THE SHOCK OF IT THREW ADELHEID INTO A TERRIBLE FEVER, AND SHE FOLLOWED HIM ONLY A FEW WEEKS LATER.
PEOPLE IN THE TOWN SAID THAT ALL THESE MISFORTUNES WERE GOD'S WORK— THAT THE OLD MAN WAS BEING PUNISHED FOR HIS MISDEEDS.
AFTER THE DEATH OF HIS SON, HE NEVER SPOKE TO A LIVING SOUL. HE MOVED UP TO THE ALP, TO LIVE THERE IN ENMITY WITH GOD AND MAN.

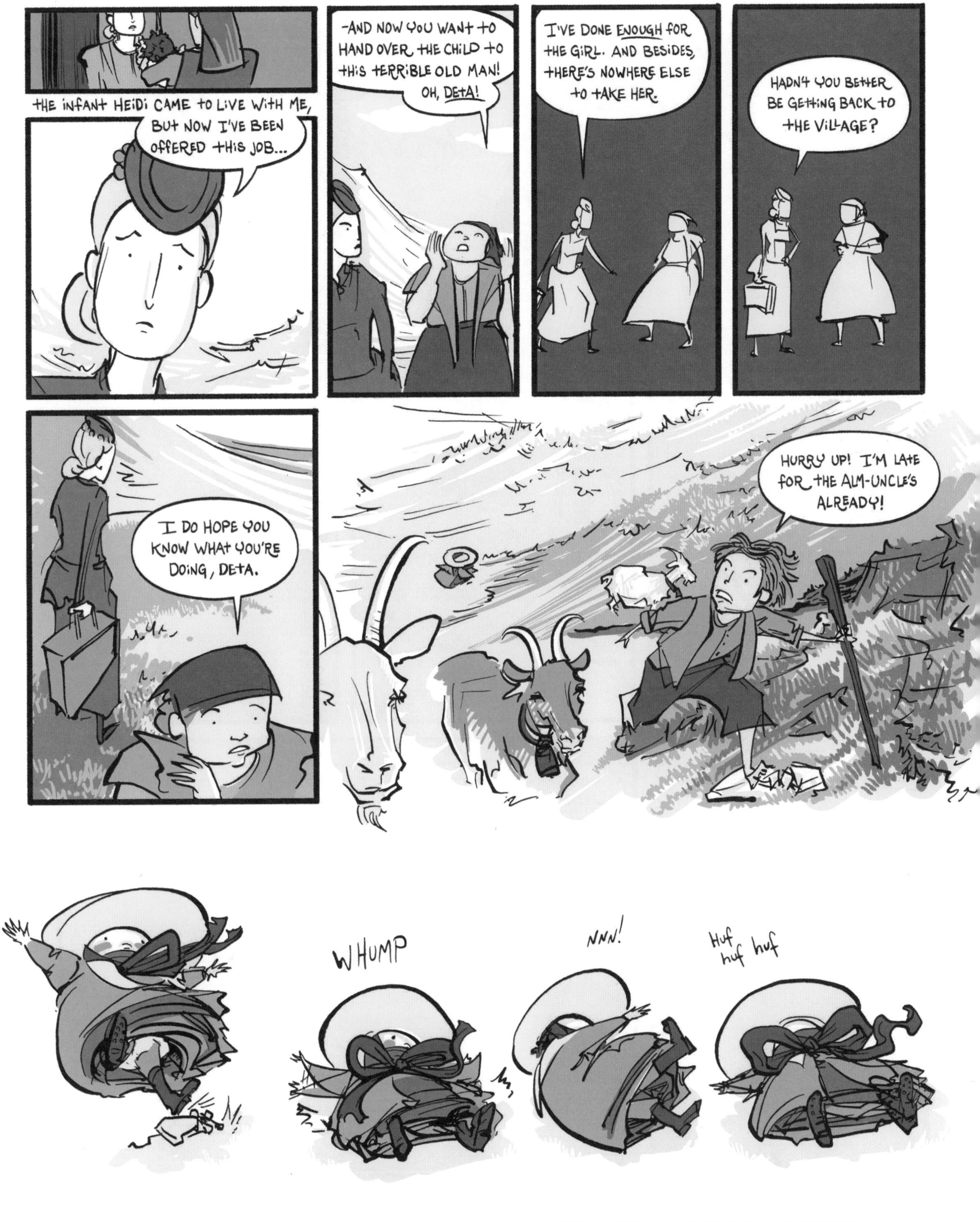

THE INFANT HEIDI CAME TO LIVE WITH ME,
BUT NOW I'VE BEEN OFFERED THIS JOB...
-AND NOW YOU WANT TO HAND OVER THE CHILD TO THIS TERRIBLE OLD MAN! OH, DETA!
I'VE DONE ENOUGH FOR THE GIRL. AND BESIDES, THERE'S NOWHERE ELSE TO TAKE HER.
HADN'T YOU BETTER BE GETTING BACK TO THE VILLAGE?
I DO HOPE YOU KNOW WHAT YOU'RE DOING, DETA.
HURRY UP! I'M LATE FOR THE ALM-UNCLE'S ALREADY!
WHUMP
NNN!
Huf huf huf

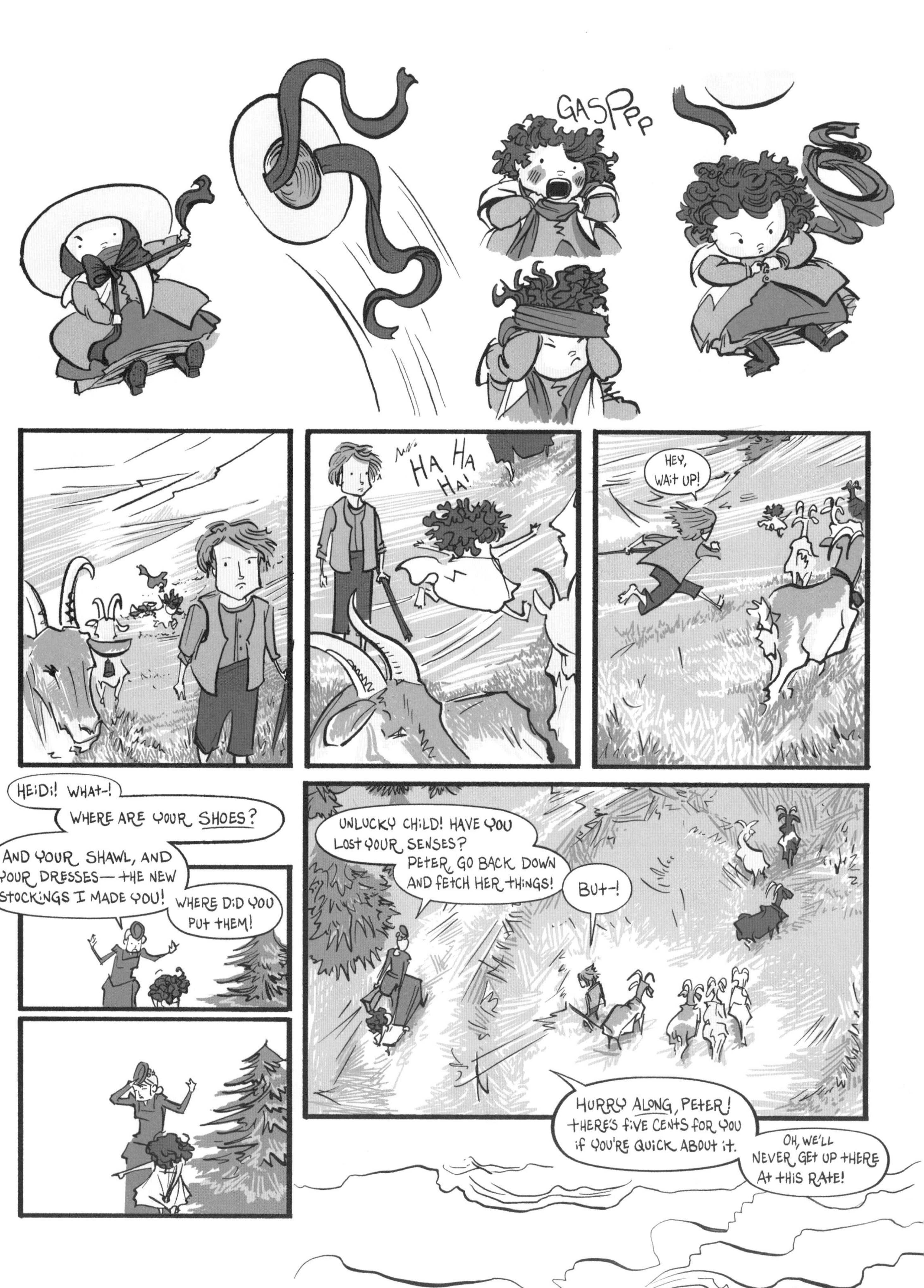
GASPPP
HA HA HA!
HEY, WAIT UP!
HEIDI! WHAT-!
WHERE ARE YOUR SHOES?
AND YOUR SHAWL, AND YOUR DRESSES— THE NEW STOCKINGS I MADE YOU!
WHERE DID YOU PUT THEM!
UNLUCKY CHILD! HAVE YOU LOST YOUR SENSES?
PETER, GO BACK DOWN AND FETCH HER THINGS!
BUT-!
HURRY ALONG, PETER! THERE'S FIVE CENTS FOR YOU IF YOU'RE QUICK ABOUT IT.
OH, WE'LL NEVER GET UP THERE AT THIS RATE!

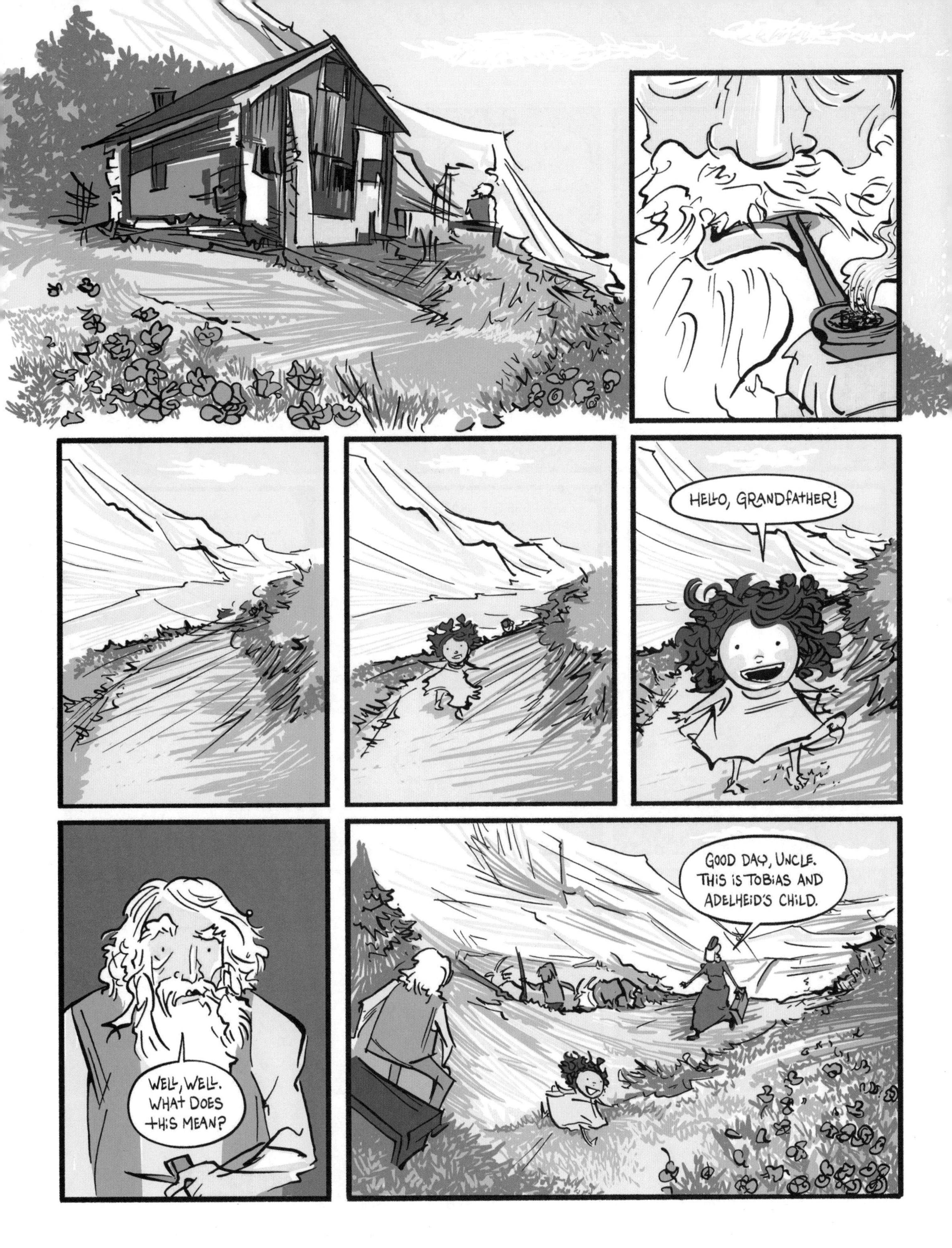
HELLO, GRANDFATHER!
WELL, WELL. WHAT DOES THIS MEAN?
GOOD DAY, UNCLE. THIS IS TOBIAS AND ADELHEID'S CHILD.

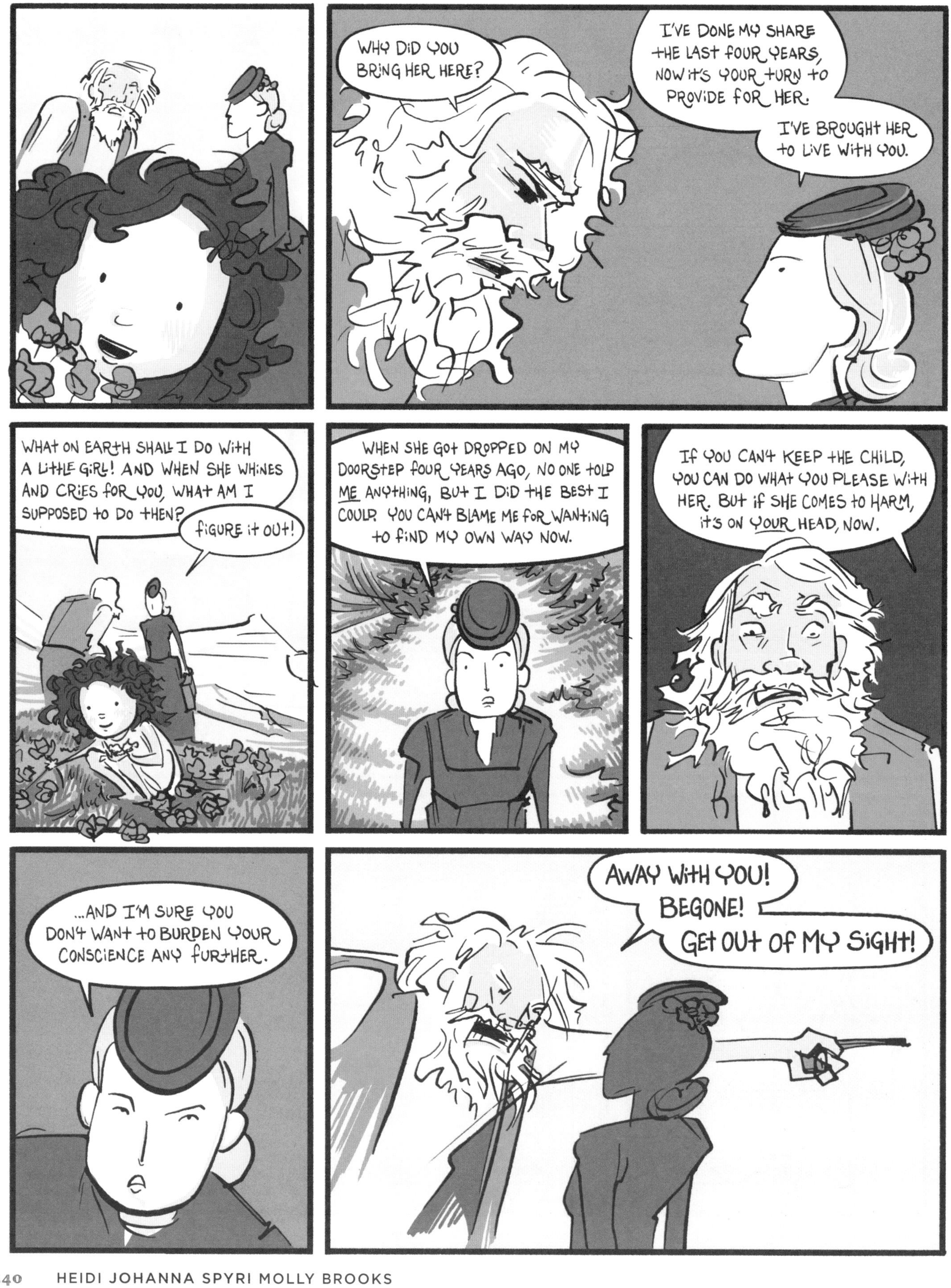
WHY DID YOU BRING HER HERE?
I'VE DONE MY SHARE THE LAST FOUR YEARS, NOW IT'S YOUR TURN TO PROVIDE FOR HER.
I'VE BROUGHT HER TO LIVE WITH YOU.
WHAT ON EARTH SHALL I DO WITH A LITTLE GIRL! AND WHEN SHE WHINES AND CRIES FOR YOU, WHAT AM I SUPPOSED TO DO THEN?
FIGURE IT OUT!
WHEN SHE GOT DROPPED ON MY DOORSTEP FOUR YEARS AGO, NO ONE TOLD ME ANYTHING, BUT I DID THE BEST I COULD. YOU CAN'T BLAME ME FOR WANTING TO FIND MY OWN WAY NOW.
IF YOU CAN'T KEEP THE CHILD, YOU CAN DO WHAT YOU PLEASE WITH HER. BUT IF SHE COMES TO HARM, IT'S ON YOUR HEAD, NOW.
...AND I'M SURE YOU DON'T WANT TO BURDEN YOUR CONSCIENCE ANY FURTHER.
AWAY WITH YOU! BEGONE! GET OUT OF MY SIGHT!

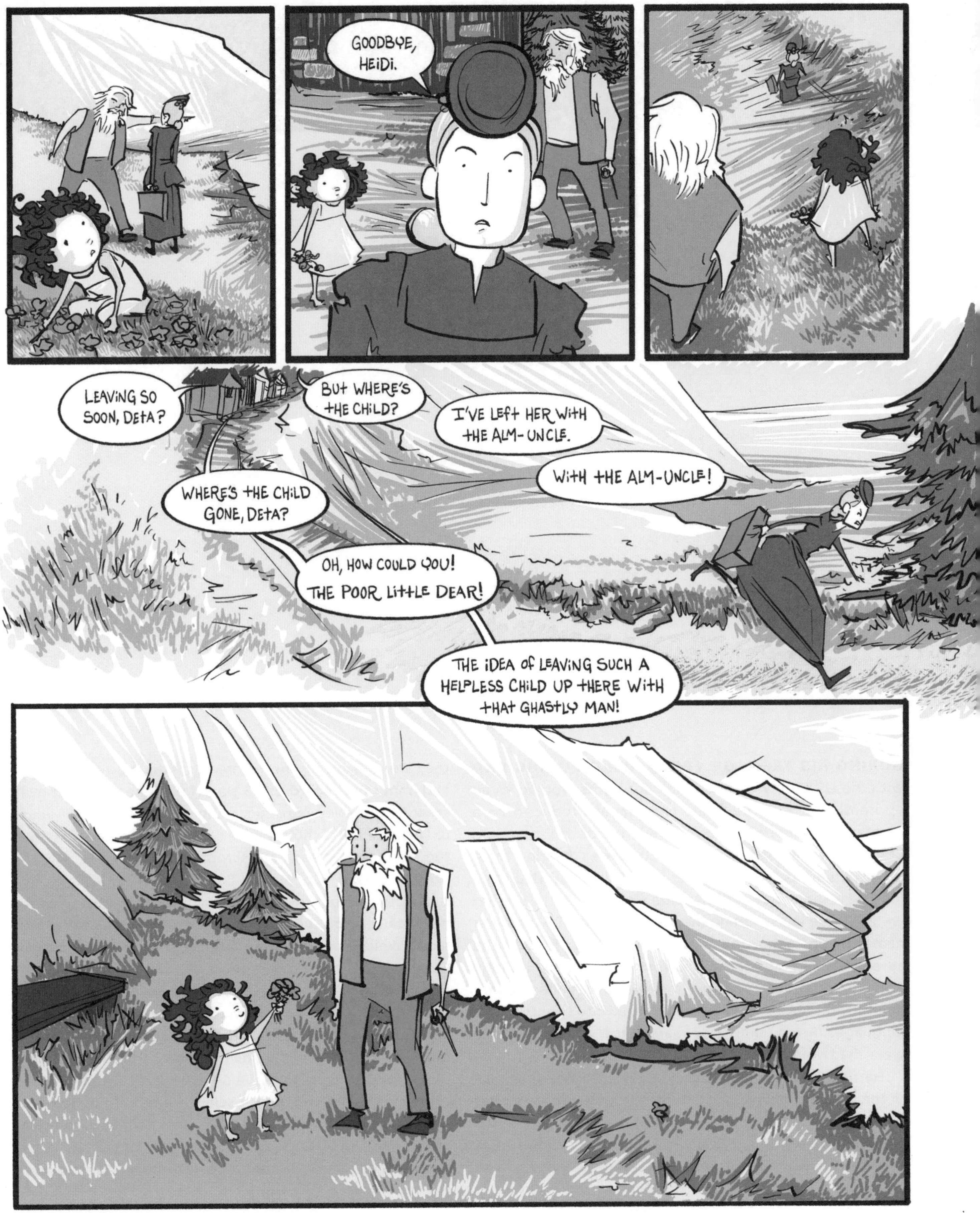
GOODBYE, HEIDI.
LEAVING SO SOON, DETA?
BUT WHERE'S THE CHILD?
I'VE LEFT HER WITH THE ALM-UNCLE.
WITH THE ALM-UNCLE!
WHERE'S THE CHILD GONE, DETA?
OH, HOW COULD YOU! THE POOR LITTLE DEAR!
THE IDEA OF LEAVING SUCH A HELPLESS CHILD UP THERE WITH THAT GHASTLY MAN!

# "The Tar Baby"

## (from *Tales of Uncle Remus*)

### Joel Chandler Harris

ART/ADAPTATION BY **Eric Knisley**

**DURING HIS TEENAGE YEARS, WHICH COINCIDED** with the US Civil War, Joel Chandler Harris worked as an apprentice at a Confederate newspaper produced on a plantation in Georgia, living on the grounds. He spent lots of his free time hanging out with the slaves, hearing them relate numerous folktales. Later, in 1879, while working as a journalist and editor at the Atlanta *Constitution*, he started writing these tales, putting them in the mouth of a character named Uncle Remus, an ex-slave spinning yarns for Billy, the seven-year-old grandson of his former master. Immensely popular and widely reprinted, the tales were collected into at least seven books and were translated into twenty-seven languages. For a number of years, Harris and Mark Twain were the two most popular authors in the US.

Harris wrote Uncle Remus's dialog—which forms the bulk of the tales—in slave dialect. He thought the slaves' stories not only had entertainment value but also needed to be preserved as a part of Southern culture. He didn't think they had any lasting historical or literary value, and he was wrong on both these counts. The *Tales of Uncle Remus*, as they are collectively known, are by far the most voluminous and important record of US slave folklore and dialect ever created, and they introduced the African American voice to US literature. Scholars have confirmed that the tales and the manner of speech are scrupulously authentic and are not the creations of Harris. Despite all this, the tales are radioactively controversial. Although completely accurate historical records, they are widely considered insensitive and racist. While other depictions of slave speech—most notably *Gone With the Wind* and *Adventures of Huckleberry Finn*— are held in high regard, *Tales of Uncle Remus* is an outcast. Still, in addition to their historical and literary import, they're among the most popular children's books ever published in the US, and no survey of kid lit is complete without them.

Eric Knisley hails from the South—North Carolina, to be exact—where he works at a science museum, in addition to creating hundreds of pages of comic strips and graphic novels. He bravely chose to adapt the most famous Uncle Remus tale, "The Tar Baby." All text is taken directly from the story as Harris wrote it.

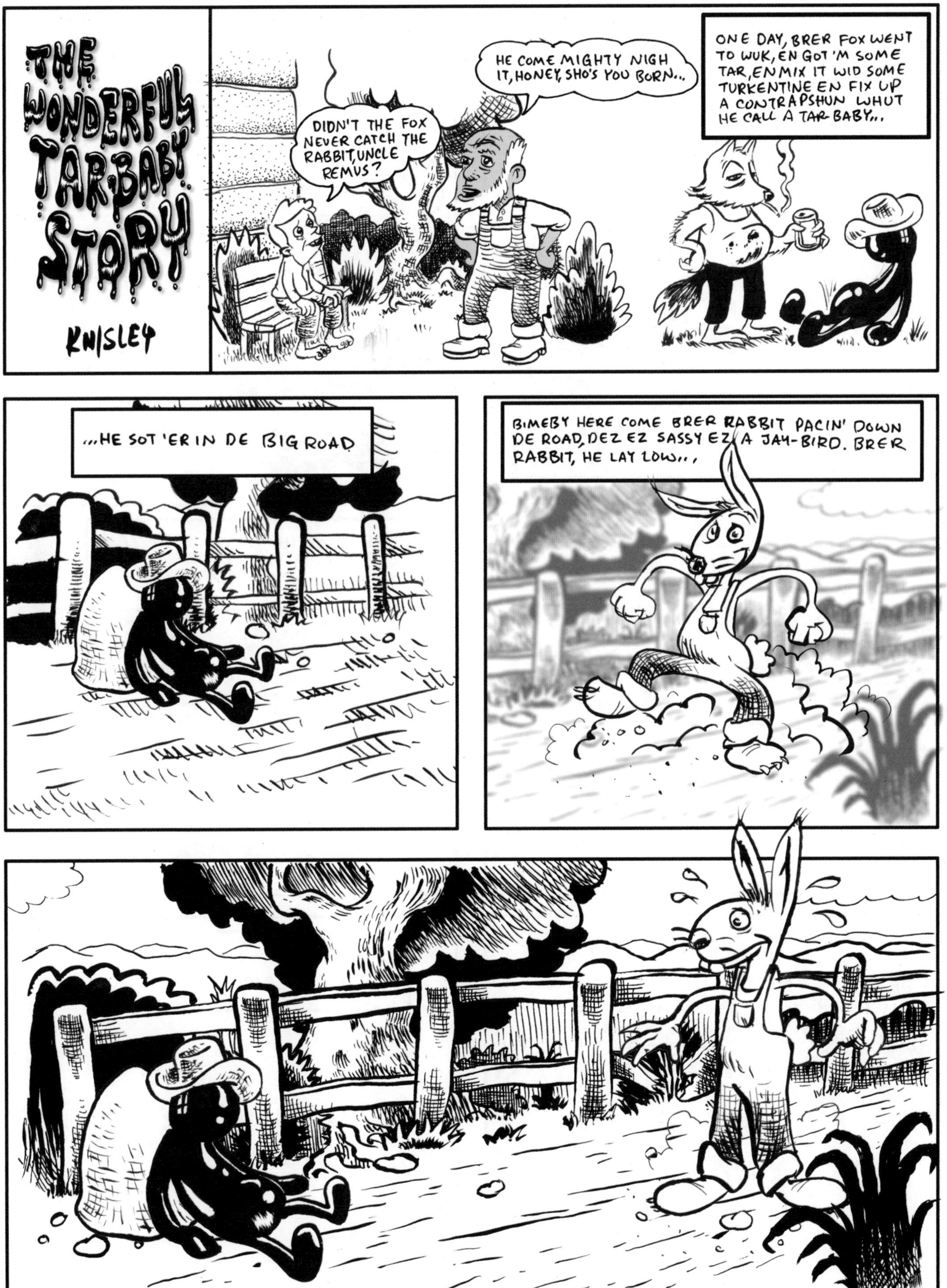
THE WONDERFUL TAR-BABY STORY
KNISLEY
DIDN'T THE FOX NEVER CATCH THE RABBIT, UNCLE REMUS?
HE COME MIGHTY NIGH IT, HONEY, SHO'S YOU BORN...
ONE DAY, BRER FOX WENT TO WUK, EN GOT 'M SOME TAR, EN MIX IT WID SOME TURKENTINE EN FIX UP A CONTRAPSHUN WHUT HE CALL A TAR-BABY...
...HE SOT 'ER IN DE BIG ROAD
BIMEBY HERE COME BRER RABBIT PACIN' DOWN DE ROAD, DEZ EZ SASSY EZ A JAY-BIRD. BRER RABBIT, HE LAY LOW...

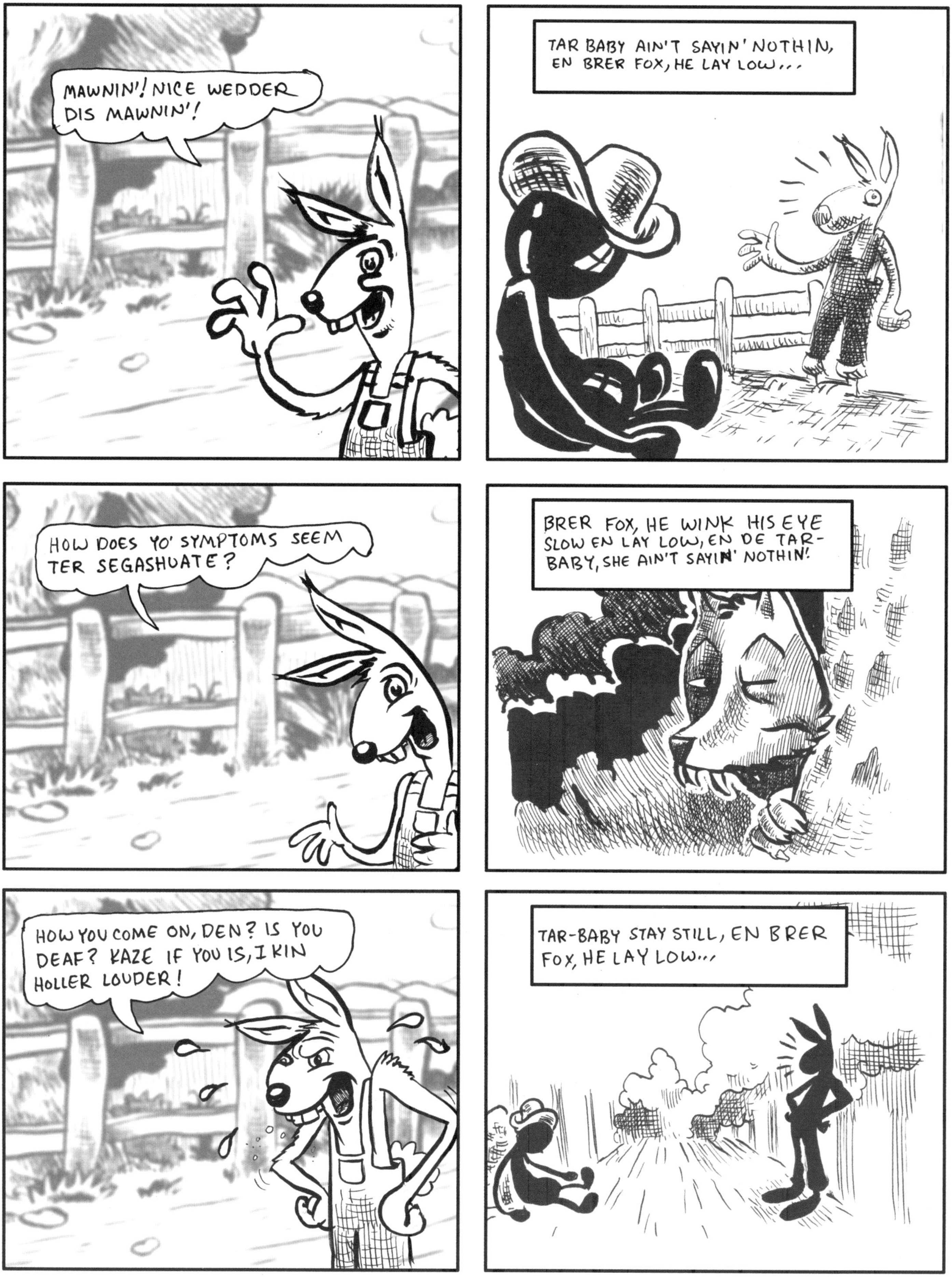

MAWNIN'! NICE WEDDER DIS MAWNIN'!
TAR BABY AIN'T SAYIN' NOTHIN, EN BRER FOX, HE LAY LOW...
HOW DOES YO' SYMPTOMS SEEM TER SEGASHUATE?
BRER FOX, HE WINK HIS EYE SLOW EN LAY LOW, EN DE TAR-BABY, SHE AIN'T SAYIN' NOTHIN'.
HOW YOU COME ON, DEN? IS YOU DEAF? KAZE IF YOU IS, I KIN HOLLER LOUDER!
TAR-BABY STAY STILL, EN BRER FOX, HE LAY LOW...

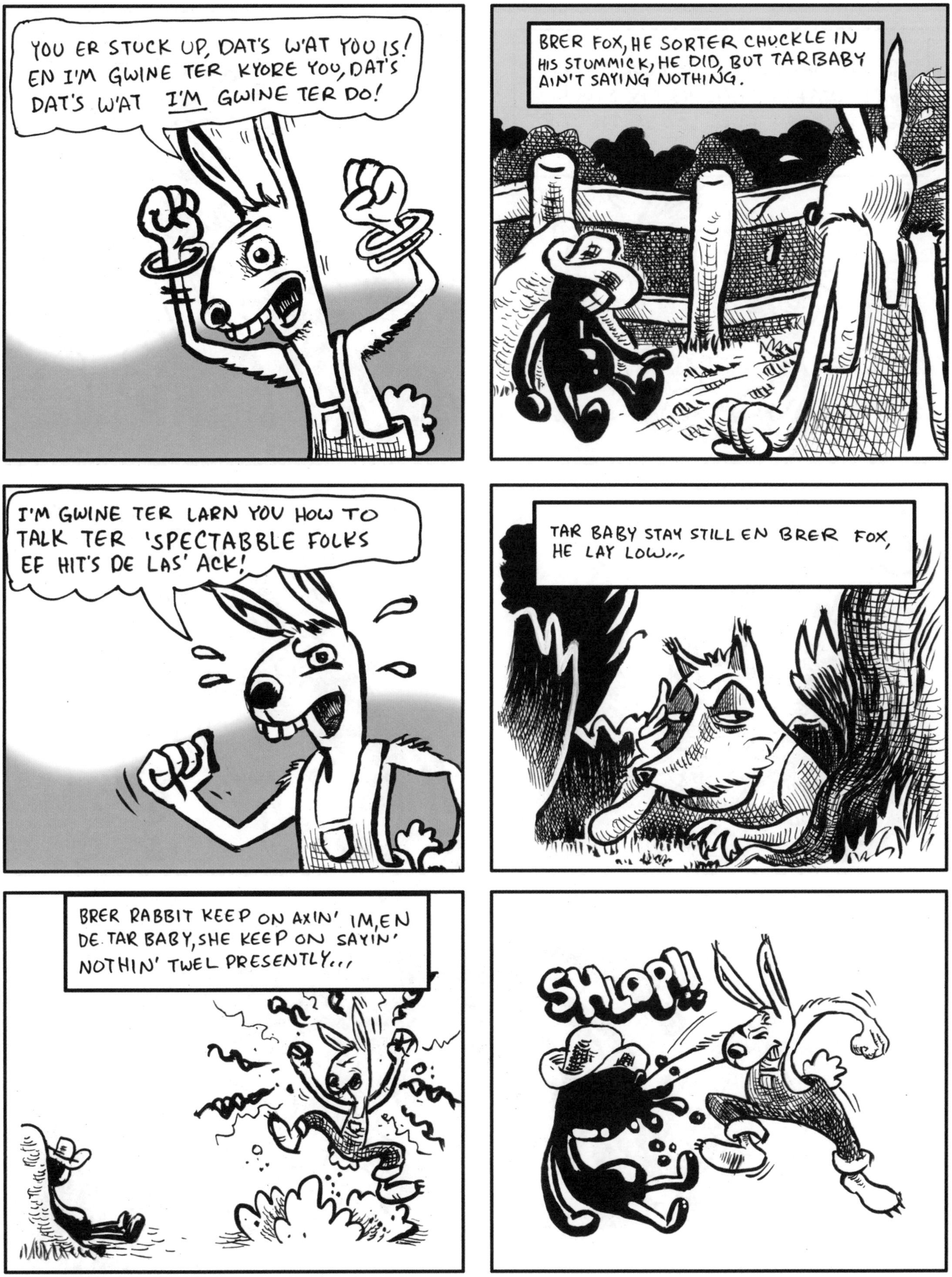
YOU ER STUCK UP, DAT'S W'AT YOU IS! EN I'M GWINE TER KYORE YOU, DAT'S DAT'S W'AT I'M GWINE TER DO!
BRER FOX, HE SORTER CHUCKLE IN HIS STUMMICK, HE DID, BUT TARBABY AIN'T SAYING NOTHING.
I'M GWINE TER LARN YOU HOW TO TALK TER 'SPECTABBLE FOLKS EF HIT'S DE LAS' ACK!
TAR BABY STAY STILL EN BRER FOX, HE LAY LOW...
BRER RABBIT KEEP ON AXIN' IM, EN DE TAR BABY, SHE KEEP ON SAYIN' NOTHIN' TWEL PRESENTLY...
SHLOP!!

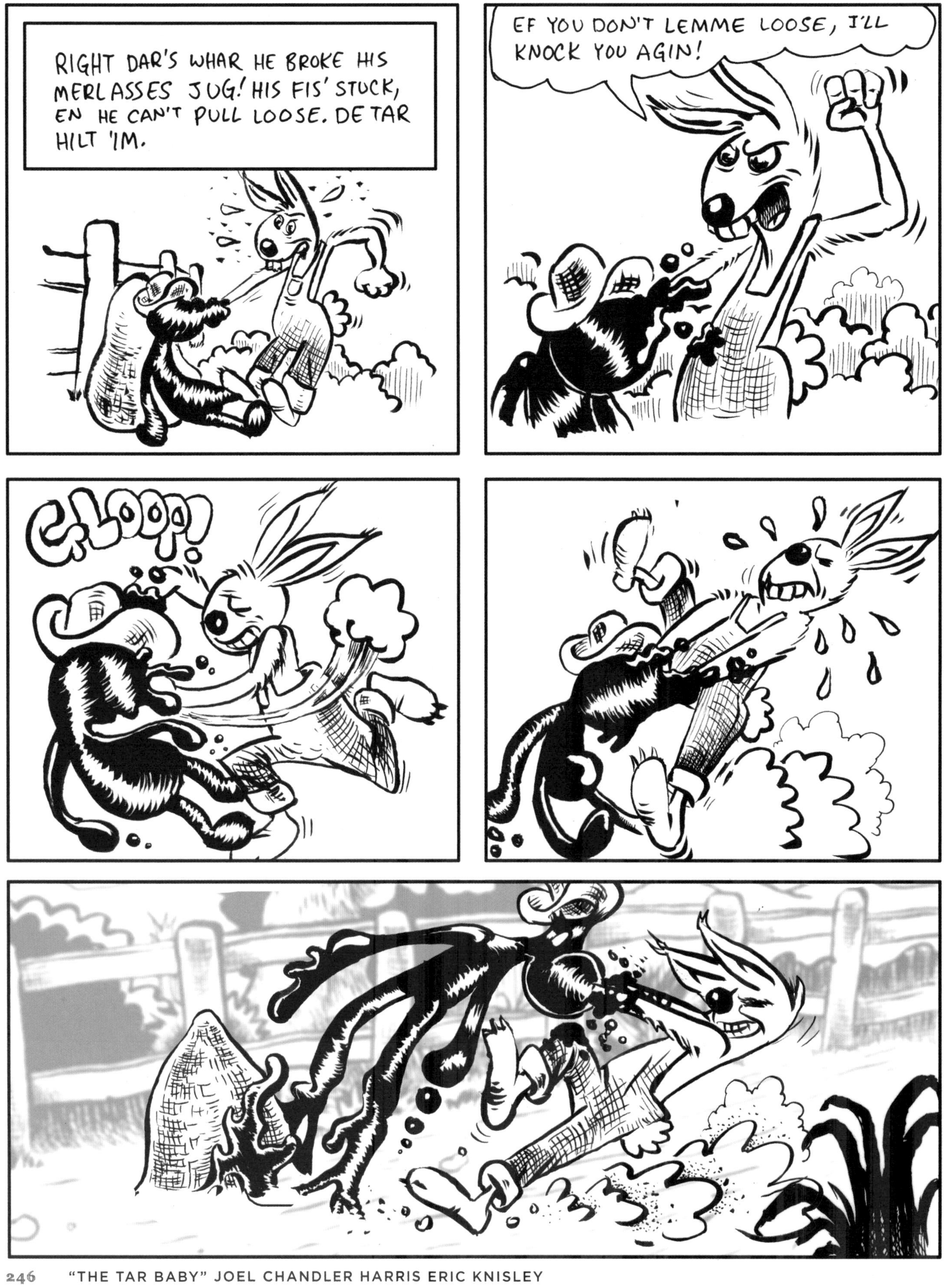
RIGHT DAR'S WHAR HE BROKE HIS MERLASSES JUG! HIS FIS' STUCK, EN HE CAN'T PULL LOOSE. DE TAR HILT 'IM.
EF YOU DON'T LEMME LOOSE, I'LL KNOCK YOU AGIN!
GLOOP!

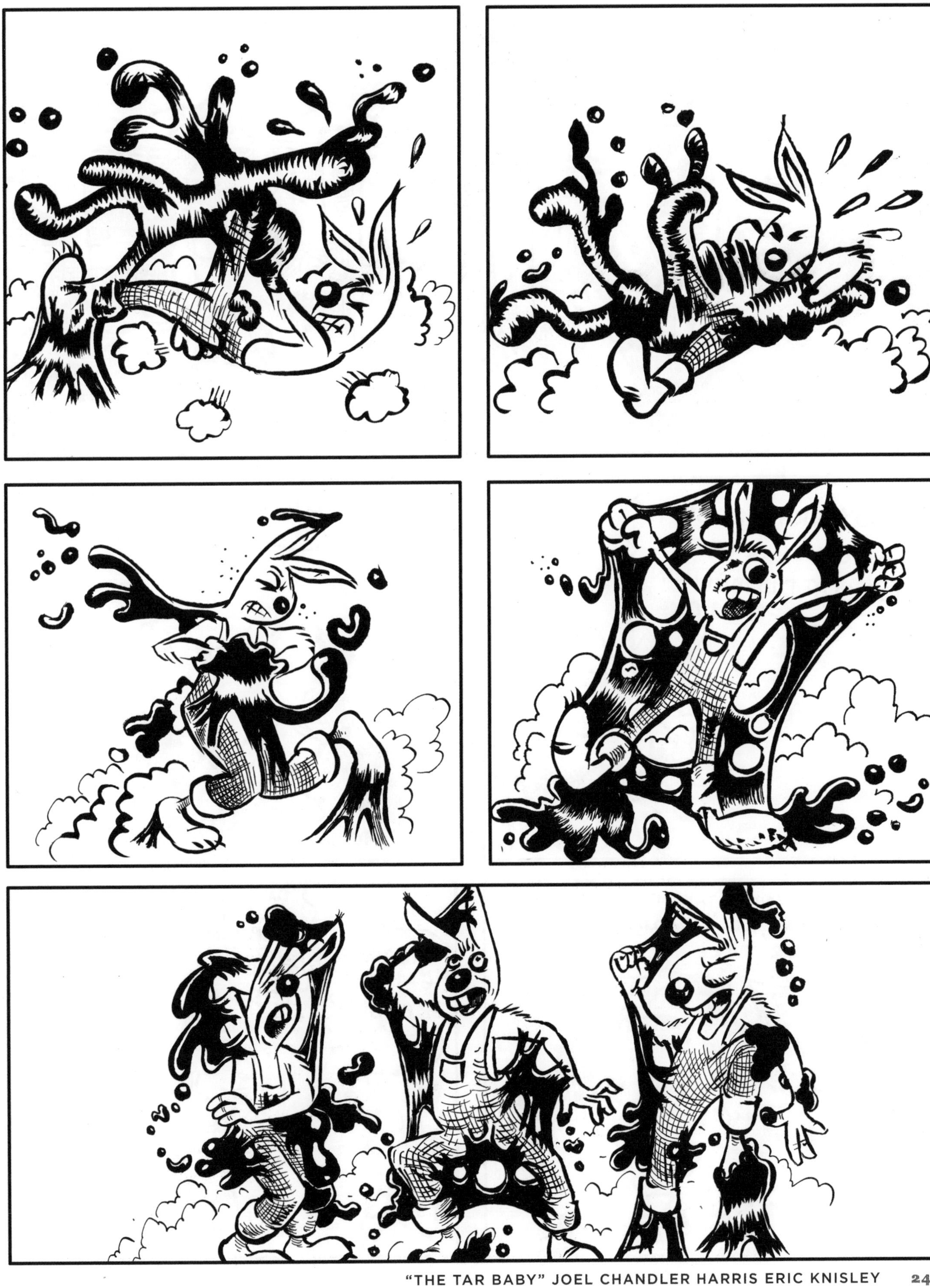

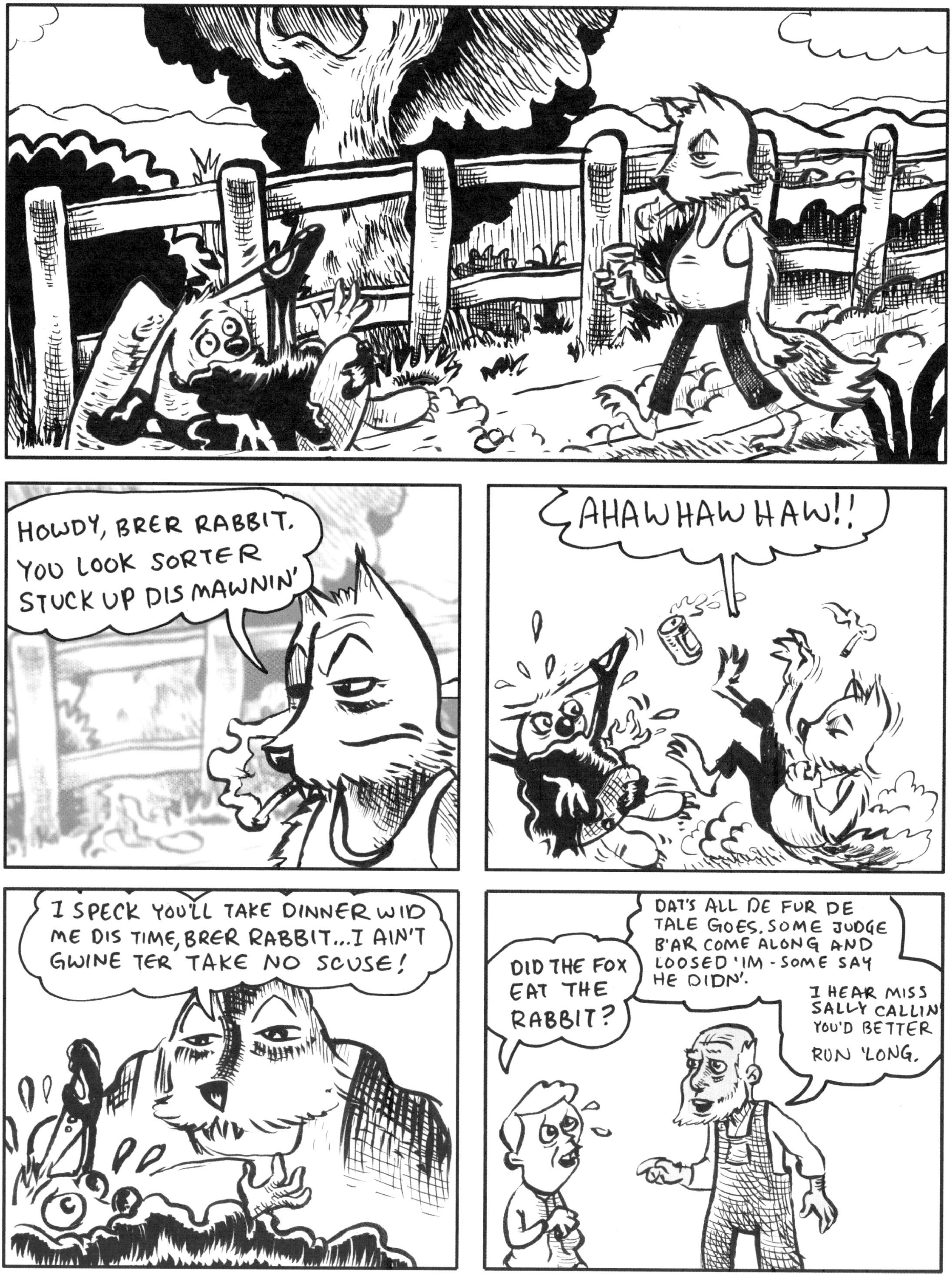
HOWDY, BRER RABBIT. YOU LOOK SORTER STUCK UP DIS MAWNIN'
AHAWHAWHAW!!
I SPECK YOU'LL TAKE DINNER WID ME DIS TIME, BRER RABBIT... I AIN'T GWINE TER TAKE NO SCUSE!
DID THE FOX EAT THE RABBIT?
DAT'S ALL DE FUR DE TALE GOES. SOME JUDGE B'AR COME ALONG AND LOOSED 'IM - SOME SAY HE DIDN'.
I HEAR MISS SALLY CALLIN' YOU'D BETTER RUN 'LONG.

# The Adventures of Pinocchio

## Carlo Collodi

ART/ADAPTATION BY **Molly Colleen O'Connell**

**PINOCCHIO GETS LYNCHED. THIS, IN FACT, IS THE** original ending of the story. *The Adventures of Pinocchio: The Story of a Puppet/Marionette* is a prime example of a dark, violent children's book that has entered our cultural brain in a completely false way. The novelist, satirical newspaperman, fighter for Italian independence, and translator of fairy tales Carlo Collodi hated children and intended *Pinocchio* as a warning, especially to boys, to behave properly. His wooden boy is a rapscallion, a selfish troublemaker who constantly gets his comeuppance in the form of severe beatings, mutilation, being transformed into a donkey that almost gets skinned, and getting hanged in a tree by the fox and cat who are robbing him. When a certain talking cricket lectures him about obeying one's parents and going to school, Pinocchio kills him with a hammer.

Collodi's tale originally appeared as a serial in an Italian children's magazine starting in 1881. He wrote children's literature reluctantly, referring to *Pinocchio* as "childish twaddle" in a letter to the publisher. He ended it with Pinocchio's apparent death by hanging, but public demand spurred him to continue this heavy-handed, pitch-black morality play (albeit one with complex mythological and psychological aspects). Pinocchio is rescued by a fairy with turquoise hair and continues getting the crap kicked out of him until he finally acts selflessly toward his father/creator Geppetto and the blue-haired fairy, and is granted his wish of becoming a real boy. See, lads, if you are respectful to your elders and stop being such crazed little bastards, you will be rewarded.

The number of Italian, English, and other editions of *The Adventures of Pinocchio* is in the hundreds, and most of them are illustrated. The boy made of wood has inspired legions of illustrators for over 130 years, yet, once again, Disney has provided the likeness that has a monopoly on our brains. It's virtually impossible to hear the name Pinocchio and not picture the oval-eyed, phallic-nosed, hat-wearing character from the highly sanitized 1940 animated film.

Baltimore-based artist Molly Colleen O'Connell gives us back the darkness and weirdness of the tale. Pinocchio looks like he truly was carved from a tree. We get the shocking lynching scene—the original end of the tale, but now the conclusion of part one of the novel—plus the beginning of part two, with the dramatic rescue by the fairy and her helpers.

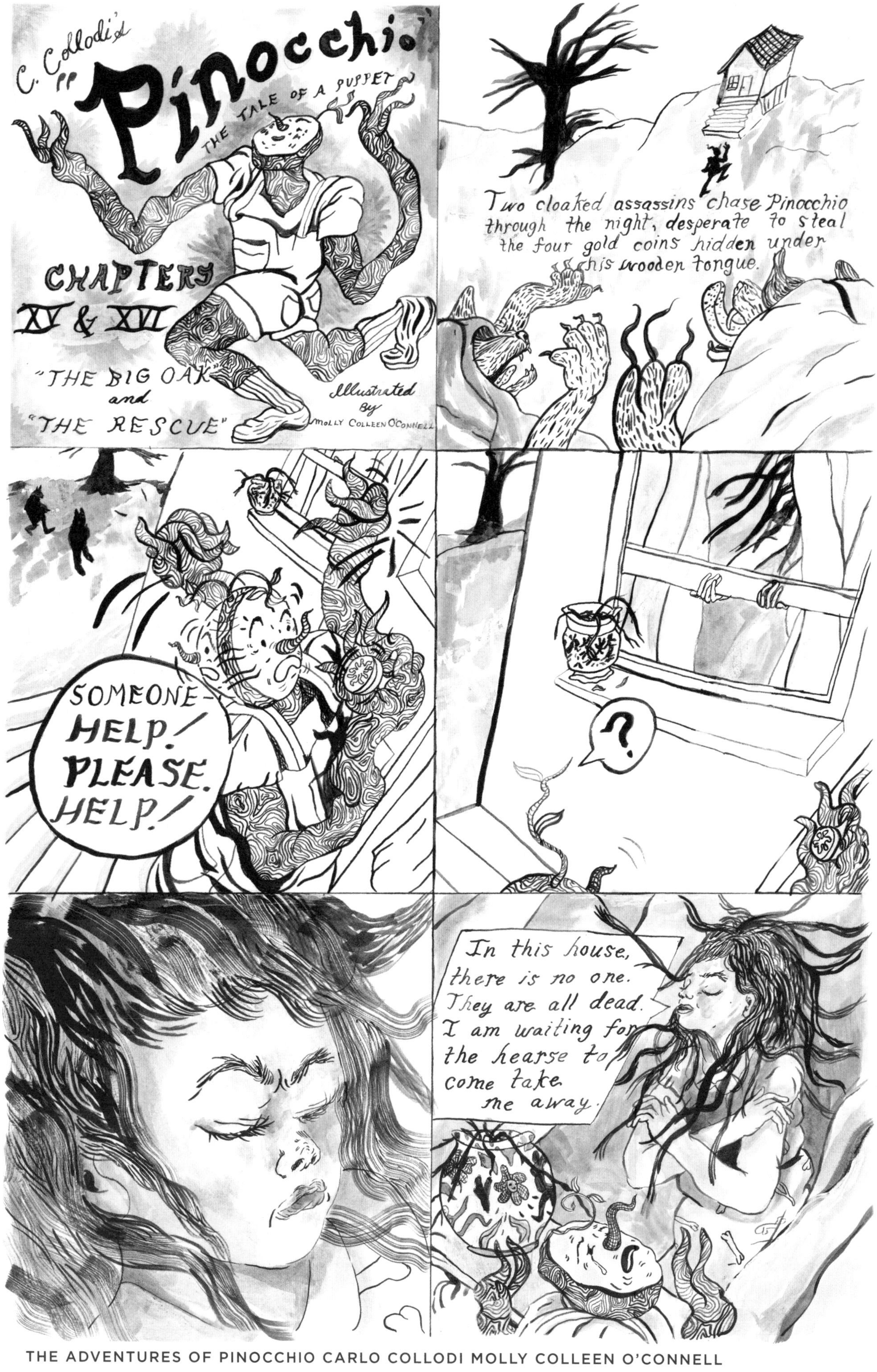
C. Collodi's
"Pinocchio"
THE TALE OF A PUPPET
CHAPTERS XV & XVI
"THE BIG OAK
and
"THE RESCUE"
Illustrated By MOLLY COLLEEN O'CONNELL
Two cloaked assassins chase Pinocchio through the night, desperate to steal the four gold coins hidden under his wooden tongue.
SOMEONE-
HELP!
PLEASE.
HELP!
?
In this house, there is no one. They are all dead. I am waiting for the hearse to come take me away.

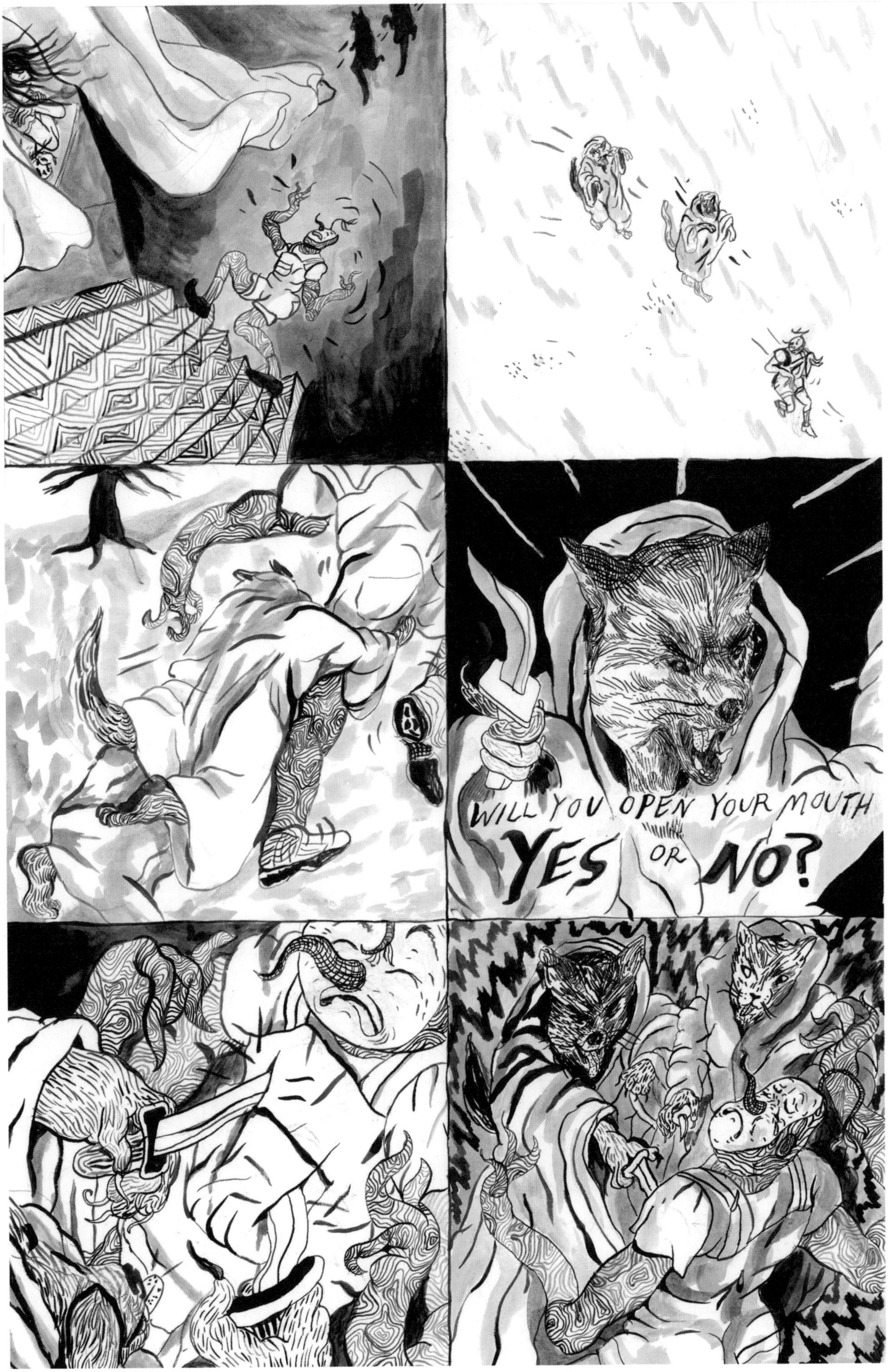
WILL YOU OPEN YOUR MOUTH
YES OR NO?

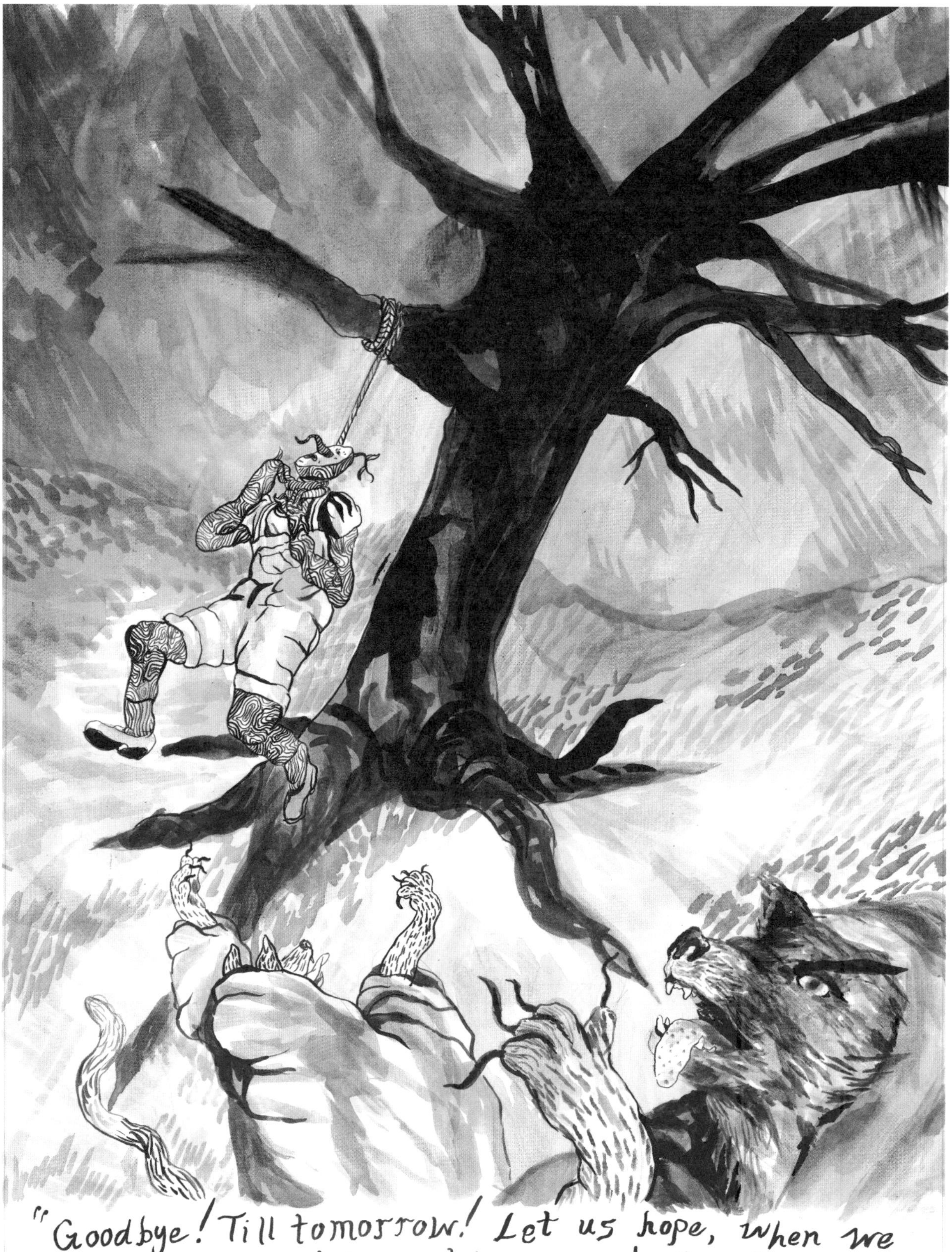
"Goodbye! Till tomorrow! Let us hope, when we return, you will be polite enough to allow yourself to be found quite dead...
& with your mouth wide open."

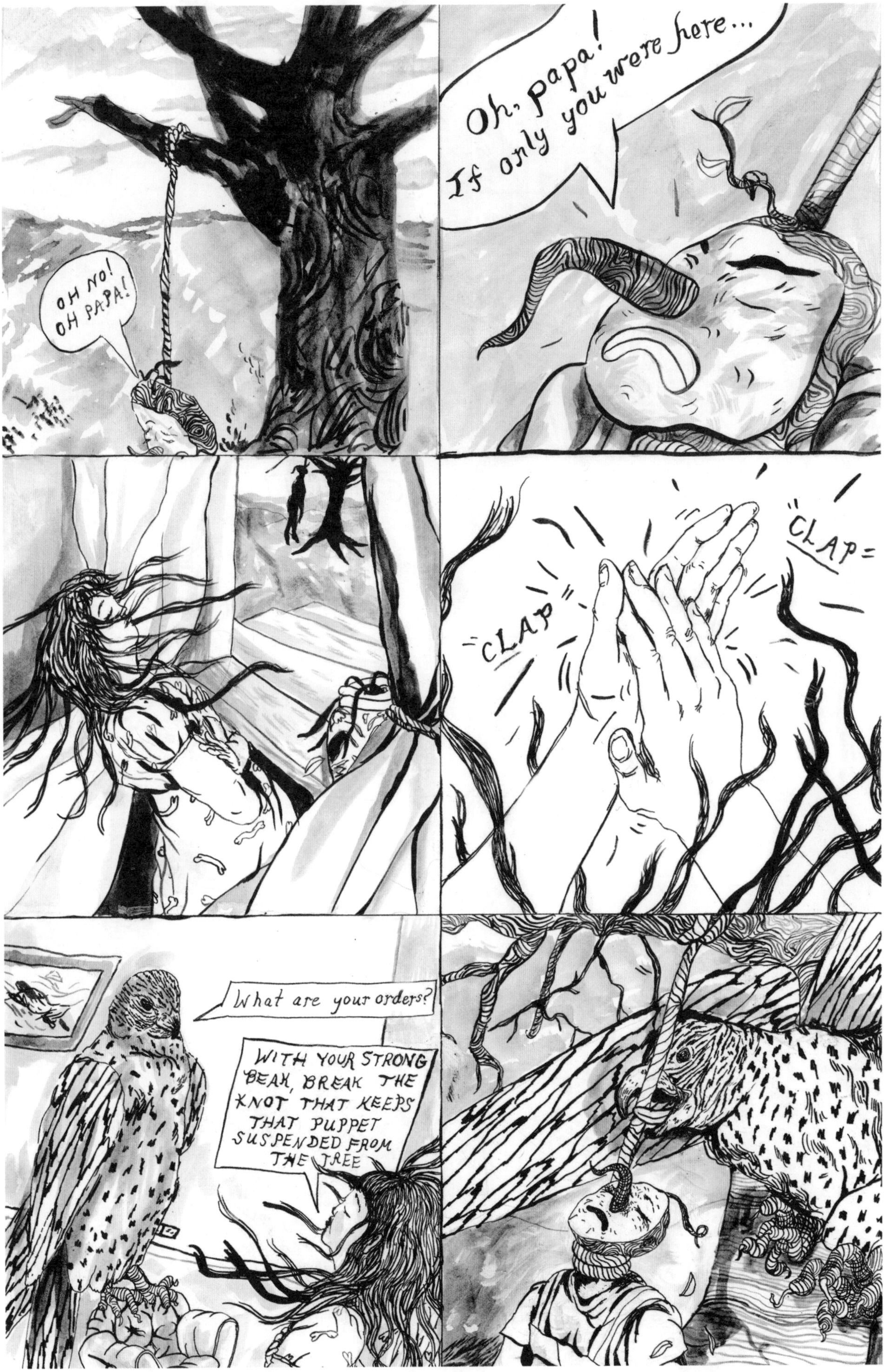
OH NO! OH PAPA!
Oh, papa! If only you were here...
CLAP
CLAP
What are your orders?
WITH YOUR STRONG BEAK, BREAK THE KNOT THAT KEEPS THAT PUPPET SUSPENDED FROM THE TREE

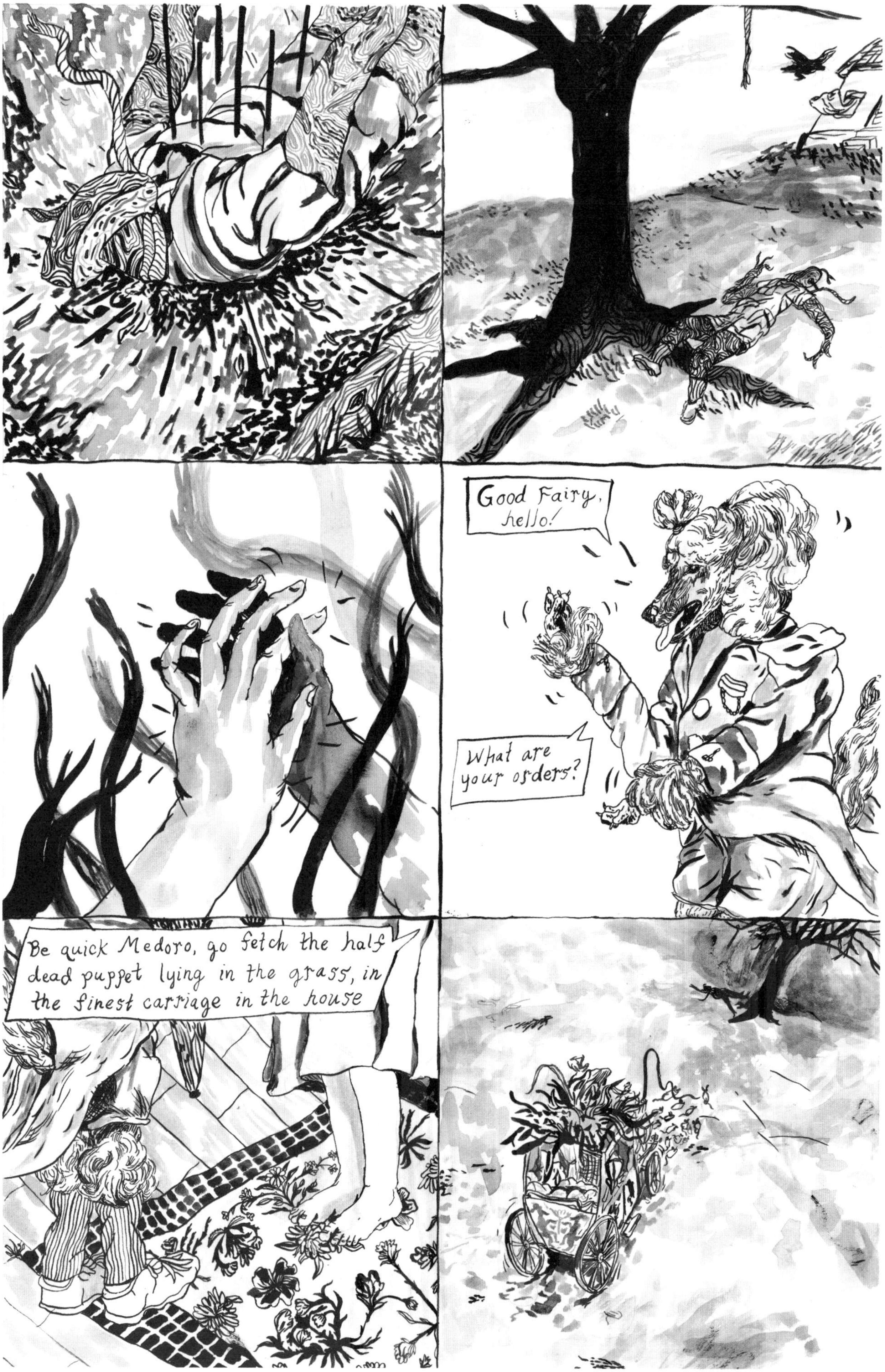
Good Fairy, hello!
What are your orders?
Be quick Medoro, go fetch the half dead puppet lying in the grass, in the finest carriage in the house

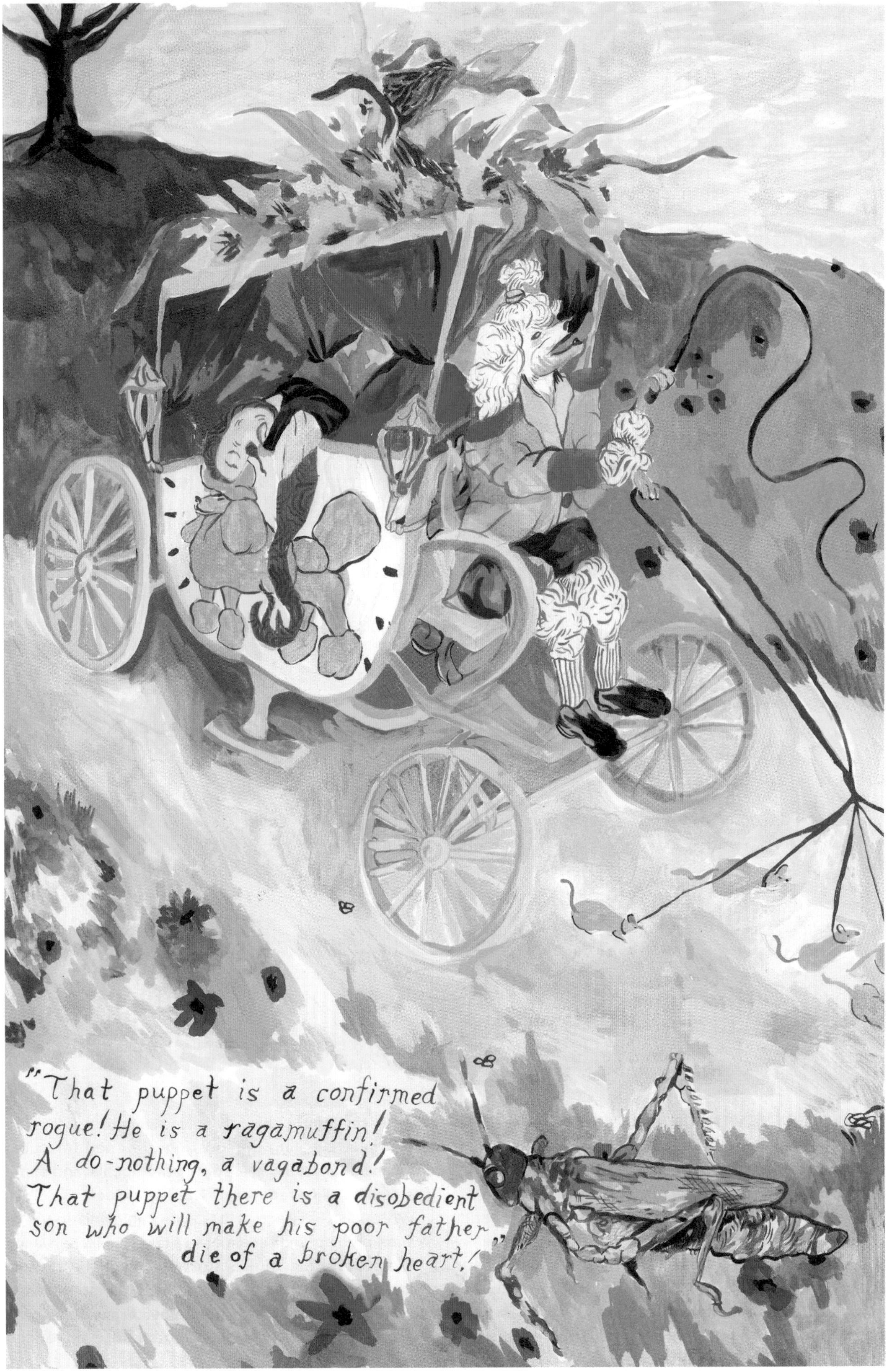
"That puppet is a confirmed rogue! He is a ragamuffin! A do-nothing, a vagabond! That puppet there is a disobedient son who will make his poor father die of a broken heart!"

# Robert Louis Stevenson

ADAPTATION BY **Lisa Fary**

ART BY **Kate Eagle** AND **John Dallaire**

**ROBERT LOUIS STEVENSON KNEW HOW TO WRITE** an adventure with flair and page-turning intensity. Even his "penny dreadful" (a lurid, cheaply printed horror tale meant to shock and titillate the masses)—*Strange Case of Dr. Jekyll and Mr. Hyde*—had enough style, nuance, and hidden meanings to enter the canon of world literature.

Inspired to spin a tale based on the map his twelve-year-old stepson had drawn, Stevenson wrote the "boys' novel" *Treasure Island* at the beginning of the 1880s. This hero's quest and coming-of-age story tells of an English lad who, recently having lost his father, comes into possession of a pirate map revealing the location of buried treasure on a tiny Caribbean island. He, some other locals, and some real pirates set sail to recover it. Trouble ensues.

Writer Lisa Fary and artists Kate Eagle and John Dallaire have teamed up to offer a meta-take on *Treasure Island*, with illustrations for the original story running in the background while in the foreground we watch as a young girl runs into weird reactions when she finds herself drawn to an old book supposedly meant for boys . . . but her dad understands.

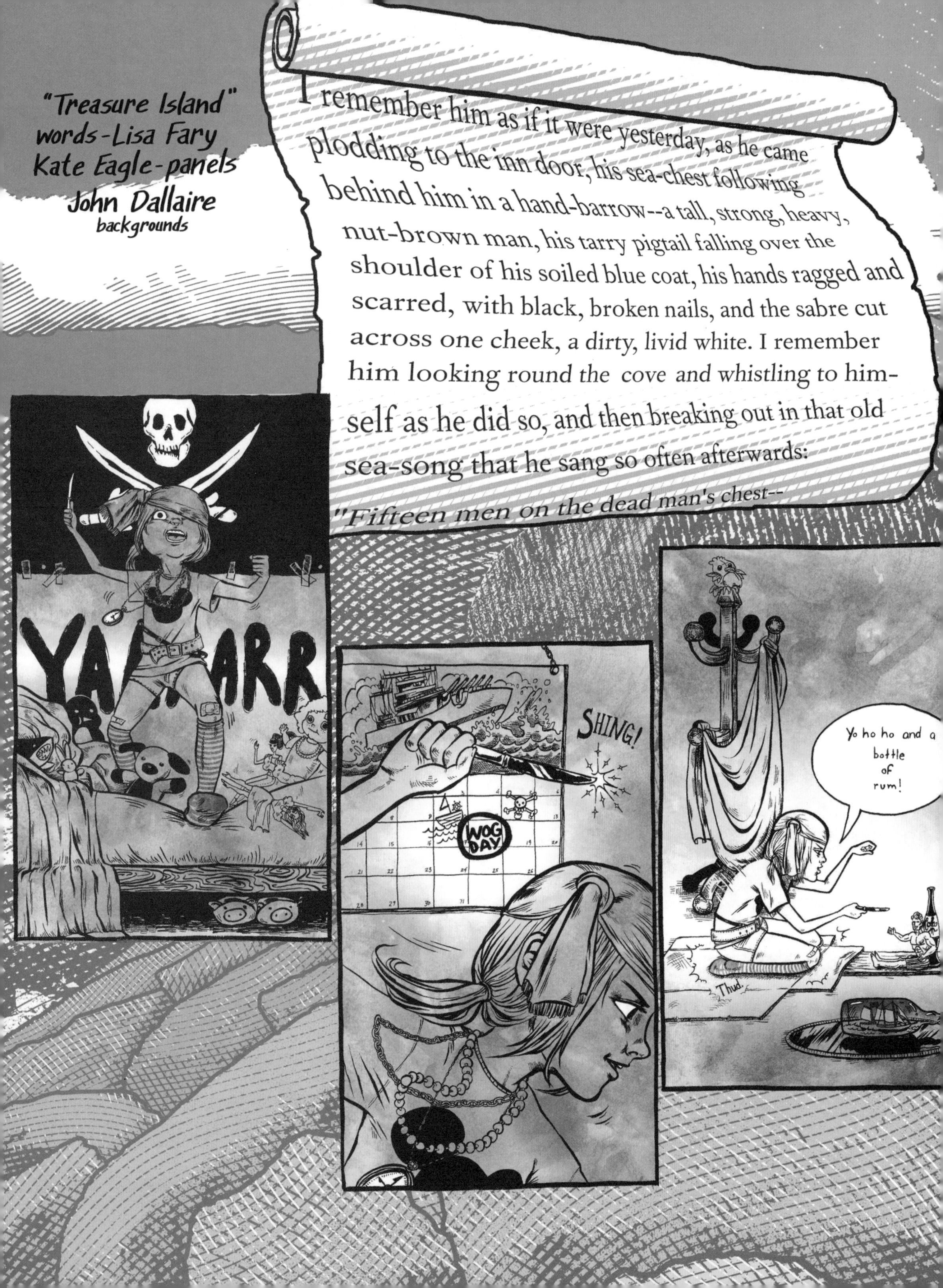
"Treasure Island"
words-Lisa Fary
Kate Eagle-panels
John Dallaire
backgrounds
I remember him as if it were yesterday, as he came plodding to the inn door, his sea-chest following behind him in a hand-barrow--a tall, strong, heavy, nut-brown man, his tarry pigtail falling over the shoulder of his soiled blue coat, his hands ragged and scarred, with black, broken nails, and the sabre cut across one cheek, a dirty, livid white. I remember him looking round the cove and whistling to him-self as he did so, and then breaking out in that old sea-song that he sang so often afterwards:
"Fifteen men on the dead man's chest--
SHING!
WOG DAY
Yo ho ho and a bottle of rum!
Thud.

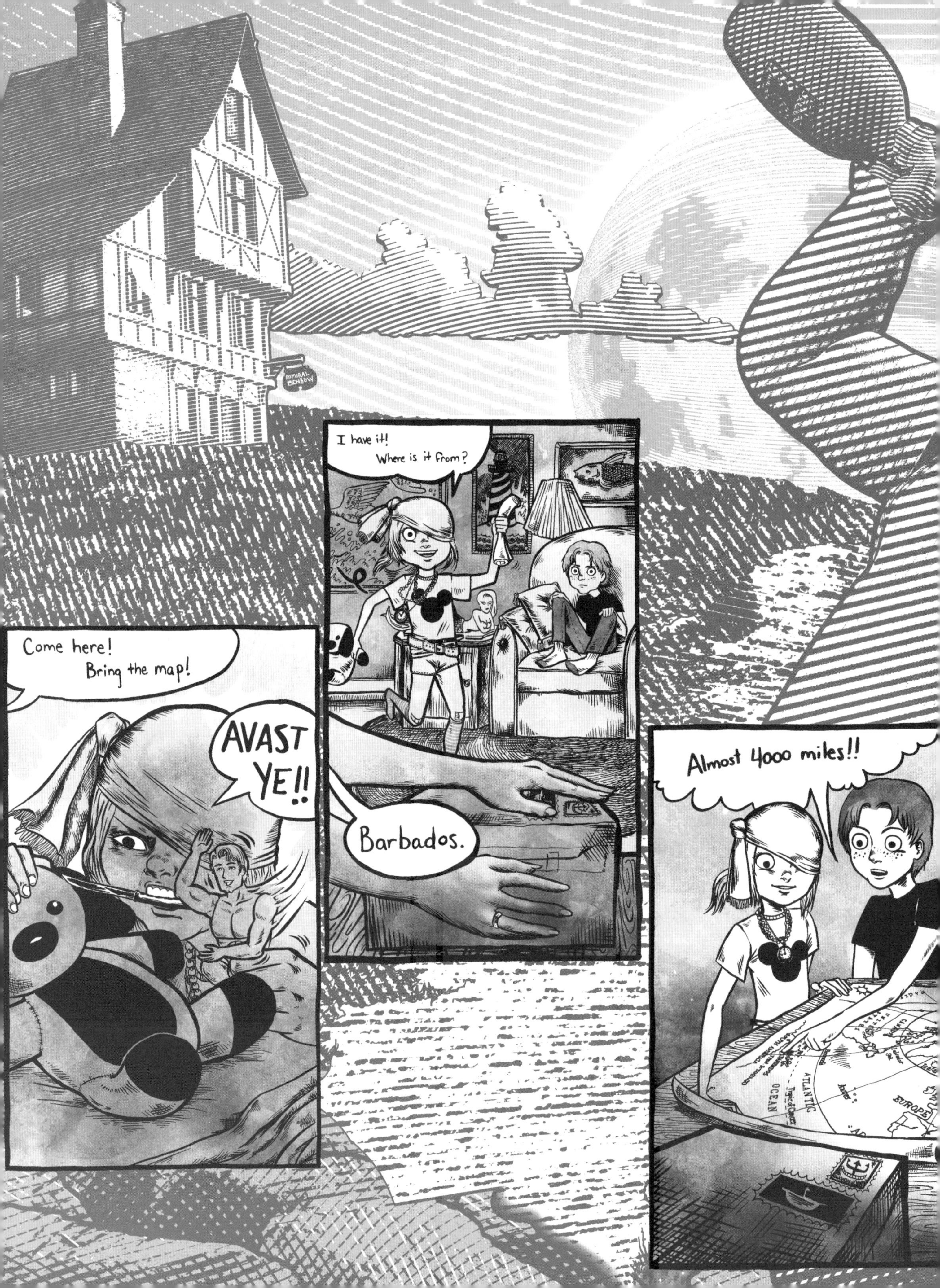
ADMIRAL BENBOW
I have it!
Where is it from?
Come here!
Bring the map!
AVAST YE!!
Barbados.
Almost 4000 miles!!
ATLANTIC
OCEAN
EUROPE

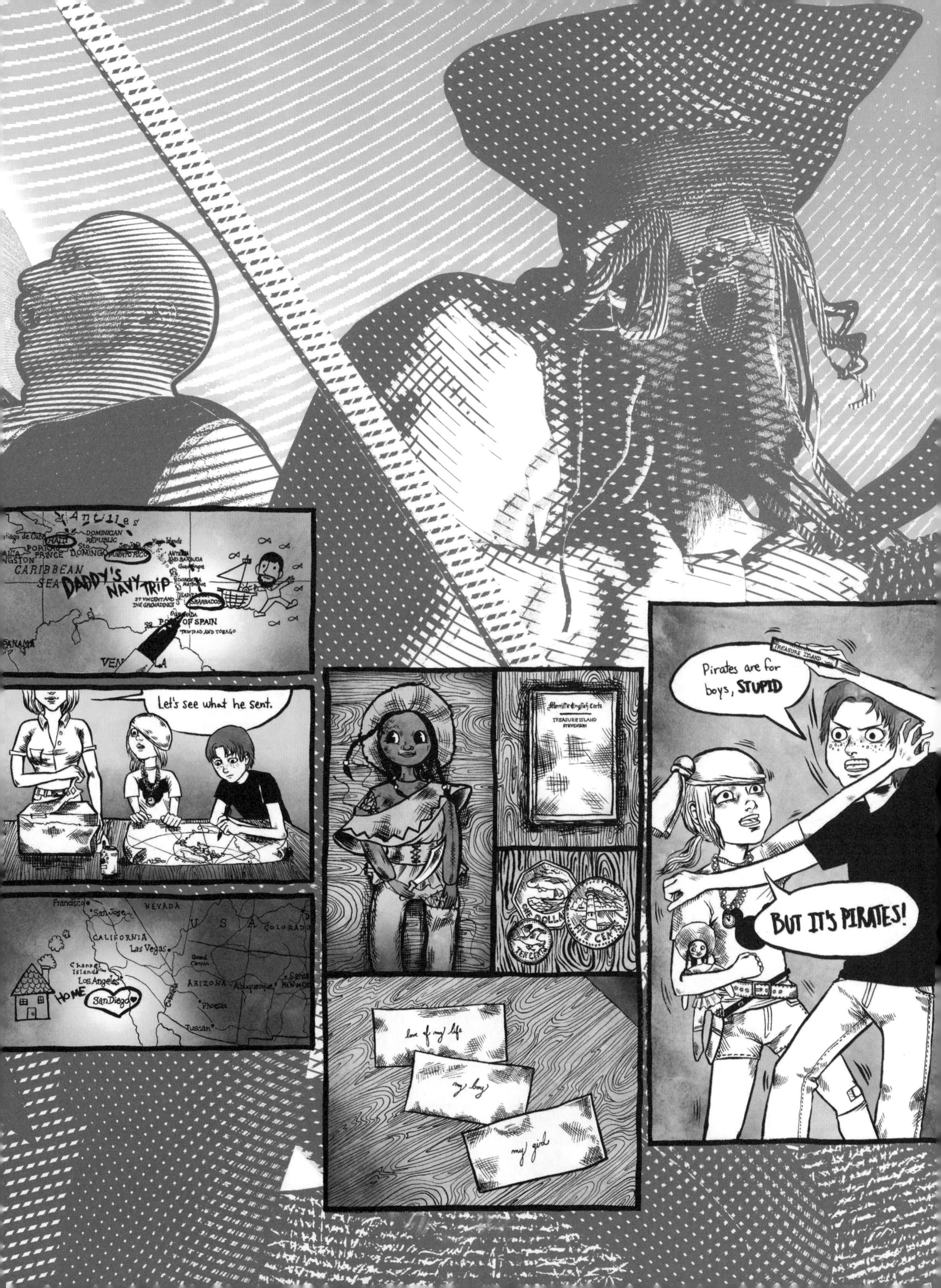
Antilles
HAITI
DOMINICAN REPUBLIC
PUERTO RICO
CARIBBEAN SEA
DADDY'S NAVY TRIP
ST VINCENT AND THE GRENADINES
BARBADOS
PORT OF SPAIN
TRINIDAD AND TOBAGO
PANAMA
Let's see what he sent.
NEVADA
CALIFORNIA
Las Vegas
Grand Canyon
Los Angeles
HOME
San Diego
ARIZONA
Tuscan
Merrill's English Texts
TREASURE ISLAND
STEVENSON
FIVE CENTS
TEN CENTS
love of my life
my boy
my girl
TREASURE ISLAND
Pirates are for boys, STUPID
BUT IT'S PIRATES!

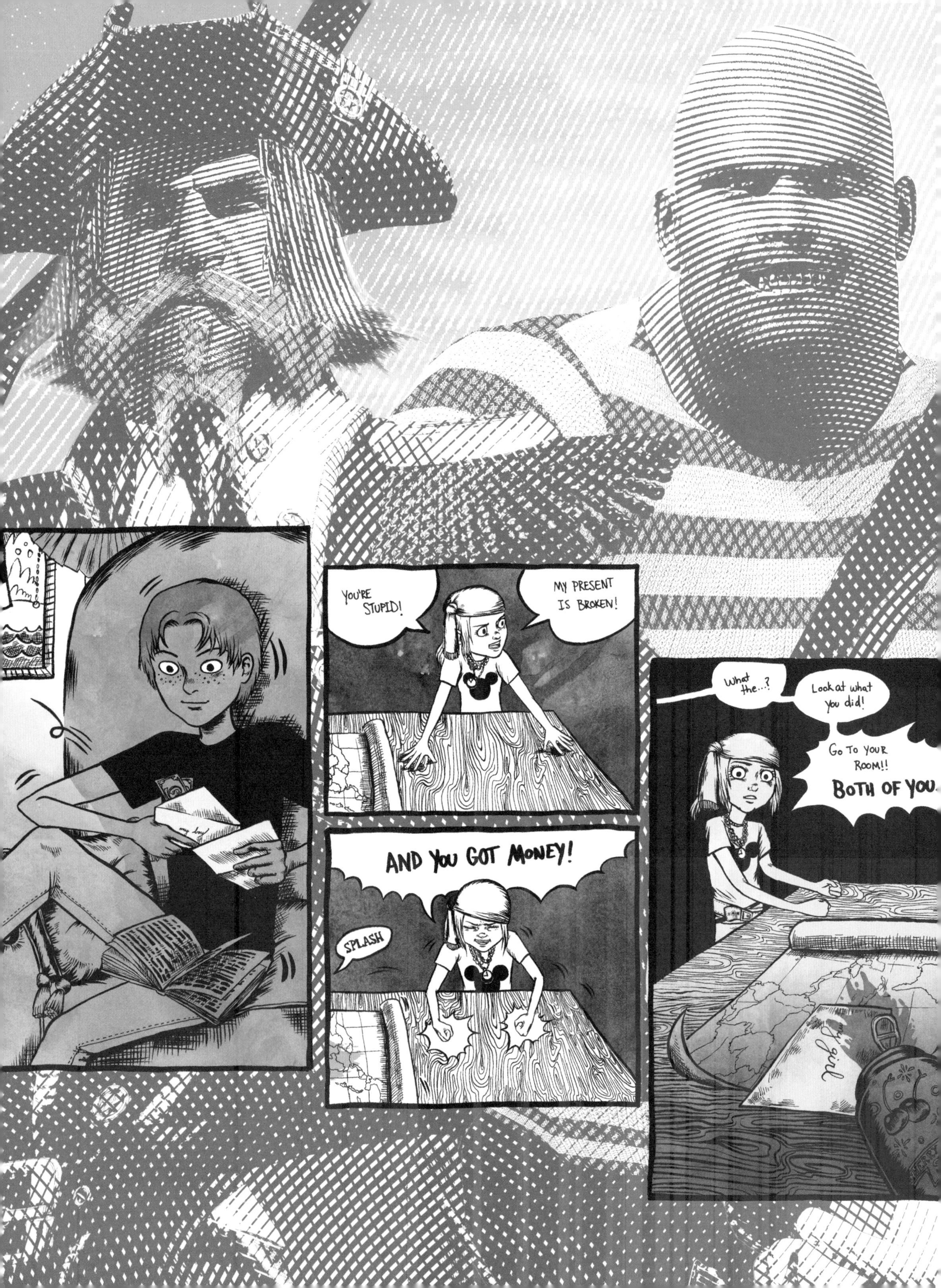
YOU'RE STUPID!
MY PRESENT IS BROKEN!
AND YOU GOT MONEY!
SPLASH
What the...?
Look at what you did!
Go TO YOUR ROOM!!
BOTH OF YOU.
my girl

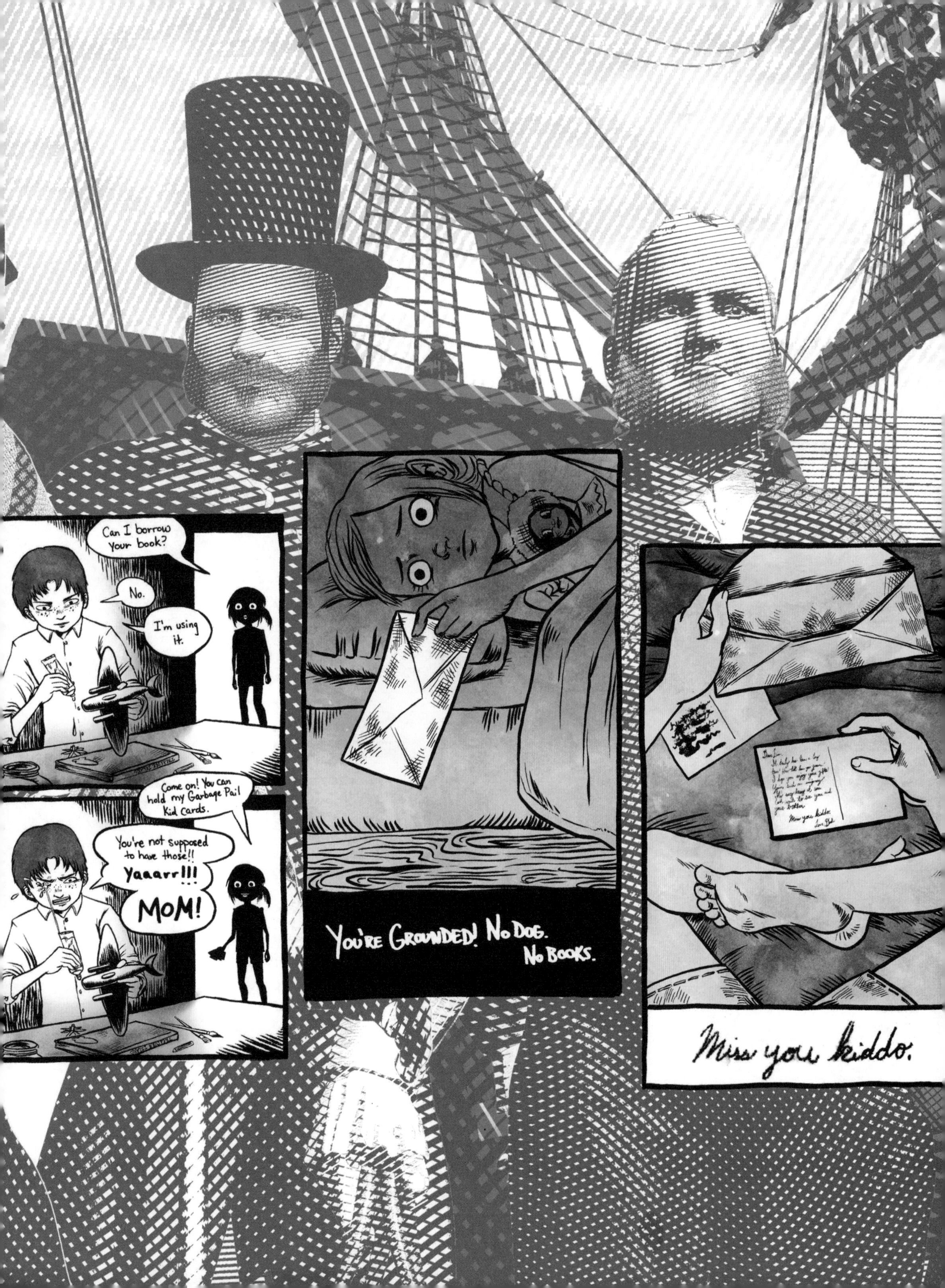
Can I borrow your book?
No.
I'm using it.
Come on! You can hold my Garbage Pail Kid cards.
You're not supposed to have those!!
Yaaarr!!!
MOM!
You're Grounded! No Dog. No Books.
Miss you kiddo.

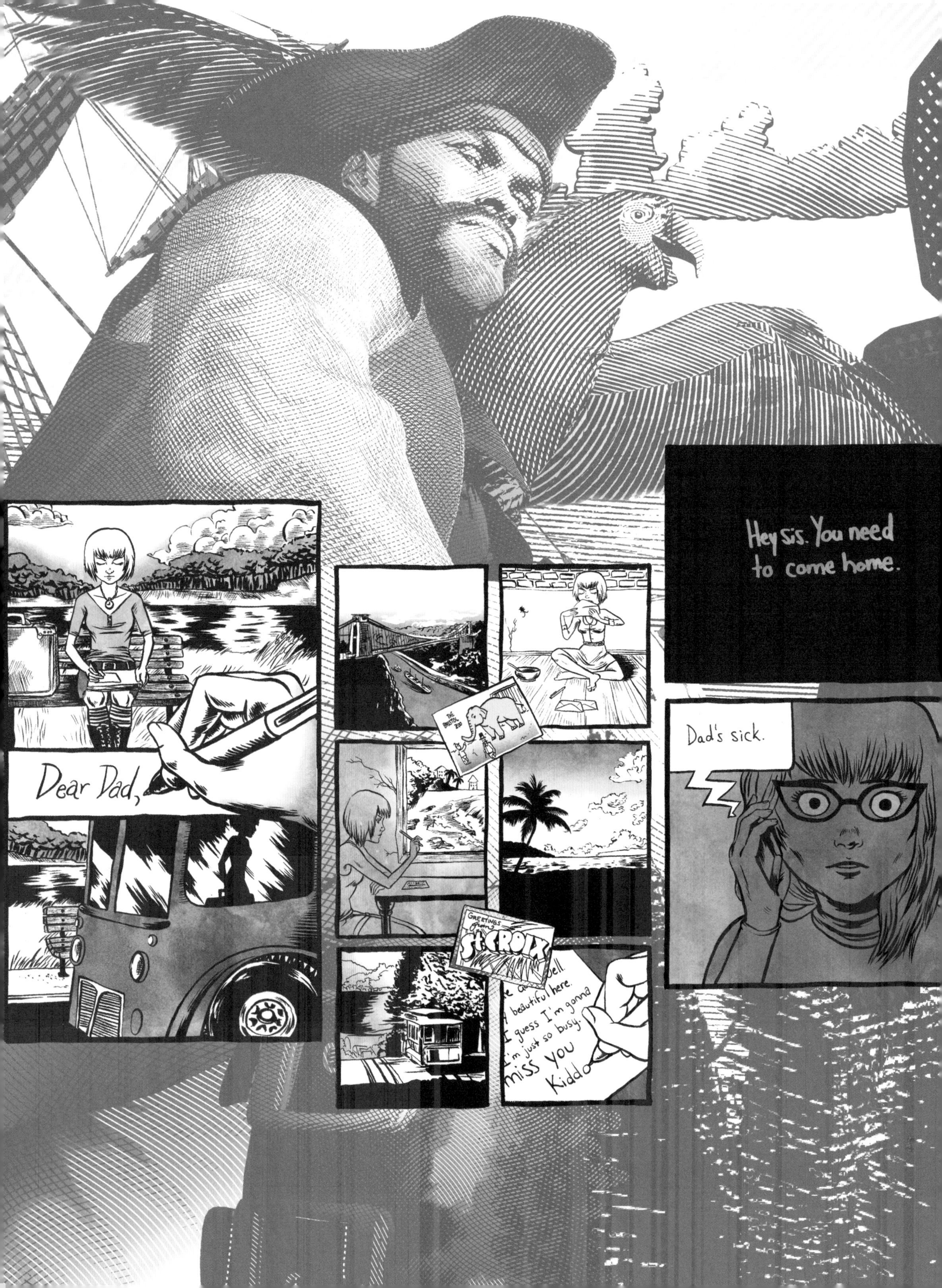
Dear Dad,
THE BRISTOL ZOO
GREETINGS from St. CROIX
beautiful here.
I guess I'm gonna
I'm just so busy.
miss you
Kiddo
Hey sis. You need to come home.
Dad's sick.

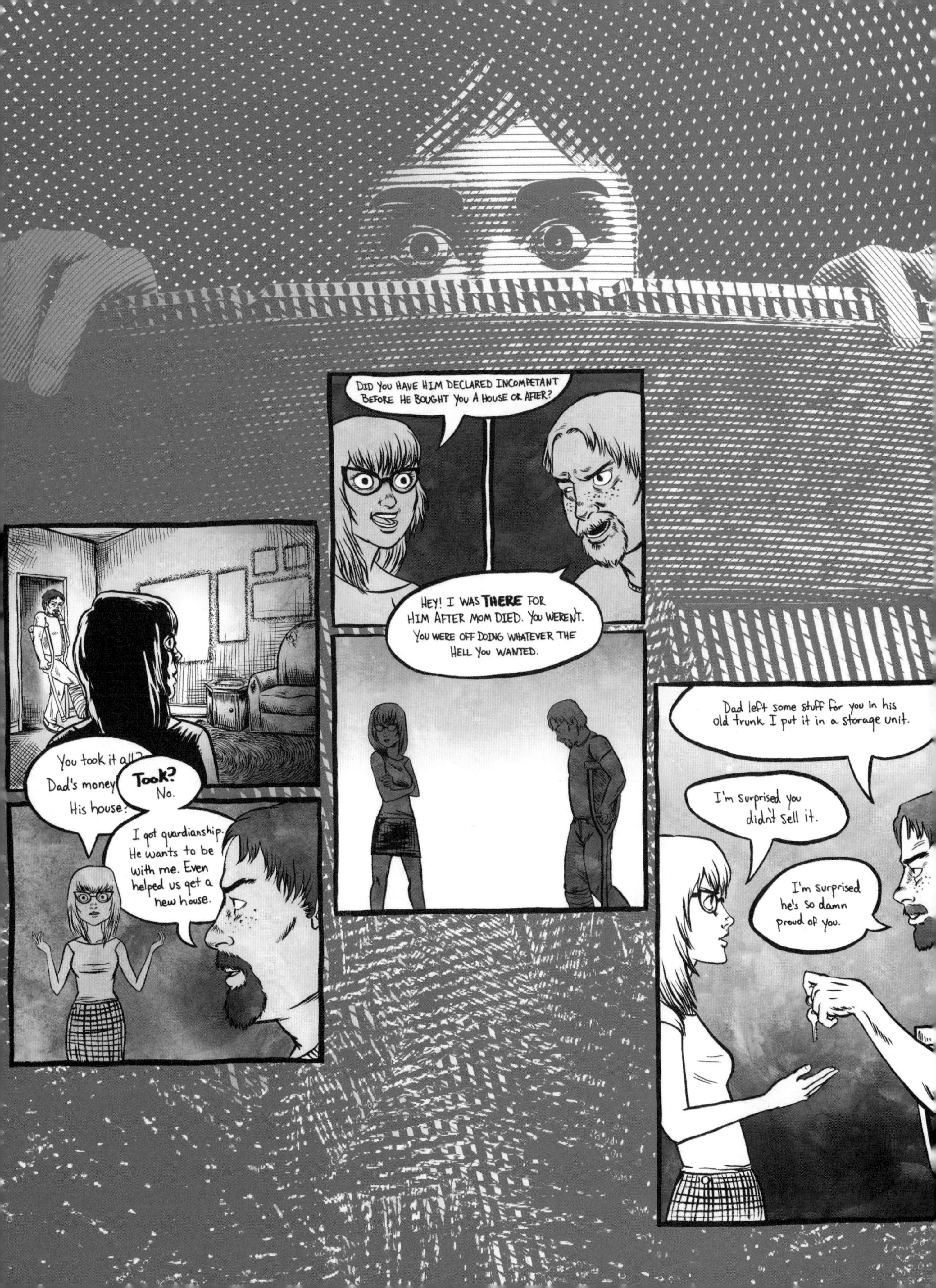

You took it all? Dad's money? His house?
Took? No.
I got guardianship. He wants to be with me. Even helped us get a new house.
DID YOU HAVE HIM DECLARED INCOMPETANT BEFORE HE BOUGHT YOU A HOUSE OR AFTER?
HEY! I WAS THERE FOR HIM AFTER MOM DIED. YOU WEREN'T. YOU WERE OFF DOING WHATEVER THE HELL YOU WANTED.
Dad left some stuff for you in his old trunk. I put it in a storage unit.
I'm surprised you didn't sell it.
I'm surprised he's so damn proud of you.

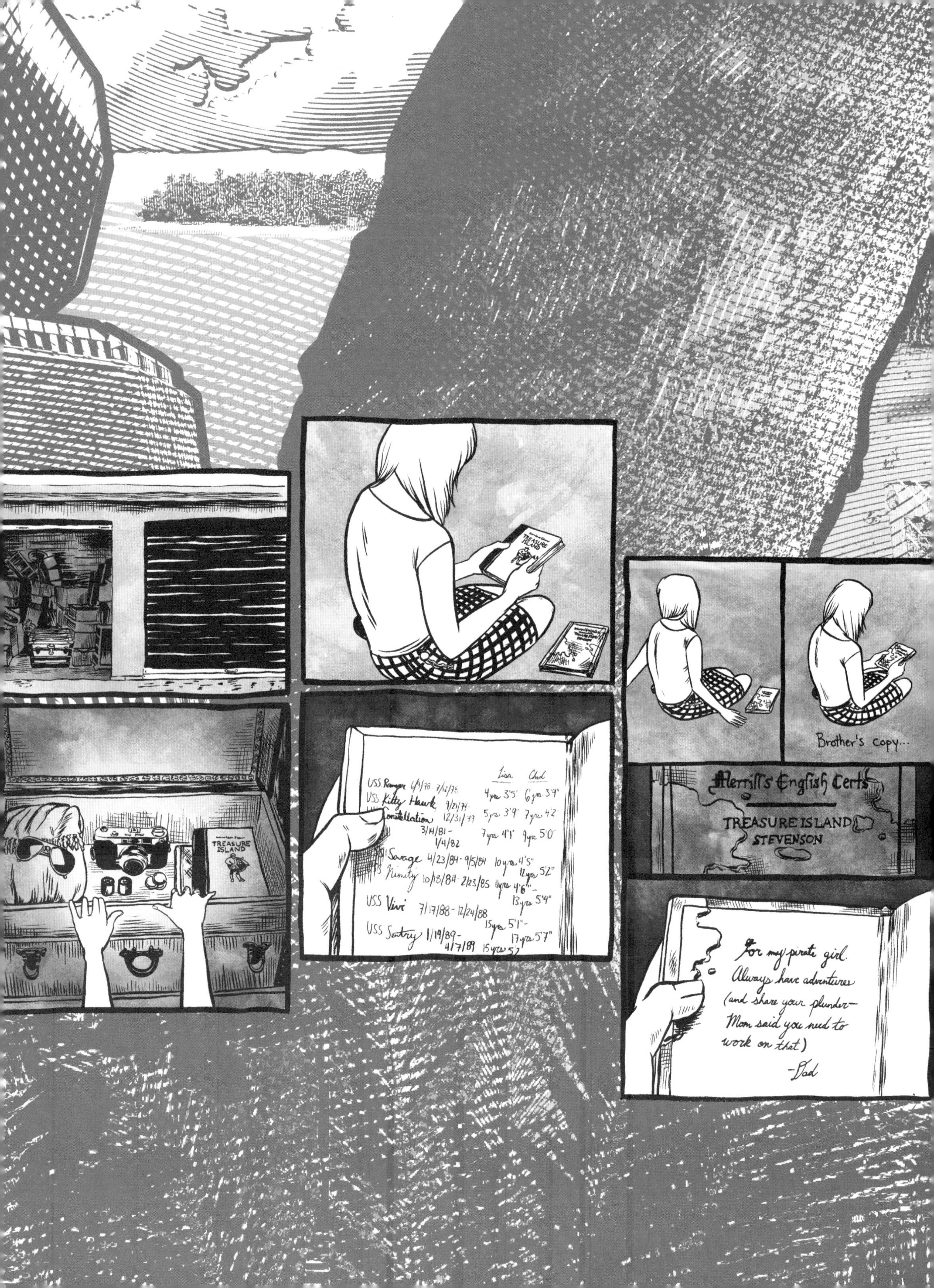
TREASURE ISLAND
TREASURE ISLAND
Lisa Chad
USS Ranger 6/9/76 - 7/12/78 4 yrs 3'5" 6 yrs 3'9"
USS Kitty Hawk 9/21/77 - 12/31/79 5 yrs 3'9" 7 yrs 4'2"
3/14/81 - 1/4/82 7 yrs 4'1" 9 yrs 5'0"
Savage 4/23/84 - 9/5/84 10 yrs 4'5" 12 yrs 5'2"
Nimity 10/18/84 - 2/23/85 11 yrs 4'6" - 13 yrs 5'4"
USS Vivi 7/17/88 - 12/24/88 15 yrs 5'1" - 17 yrs 5'7"
USS Sentry 1/19/89 - 4/7/89 15 yrs 5'2
Brother's copy...
Merrill's English Texts
TREASURE ISLAND
STEVENSON
For my pirate girl.
Always have adventures
(and share your plunder—
Mom said you need to
work on that)
-Dad

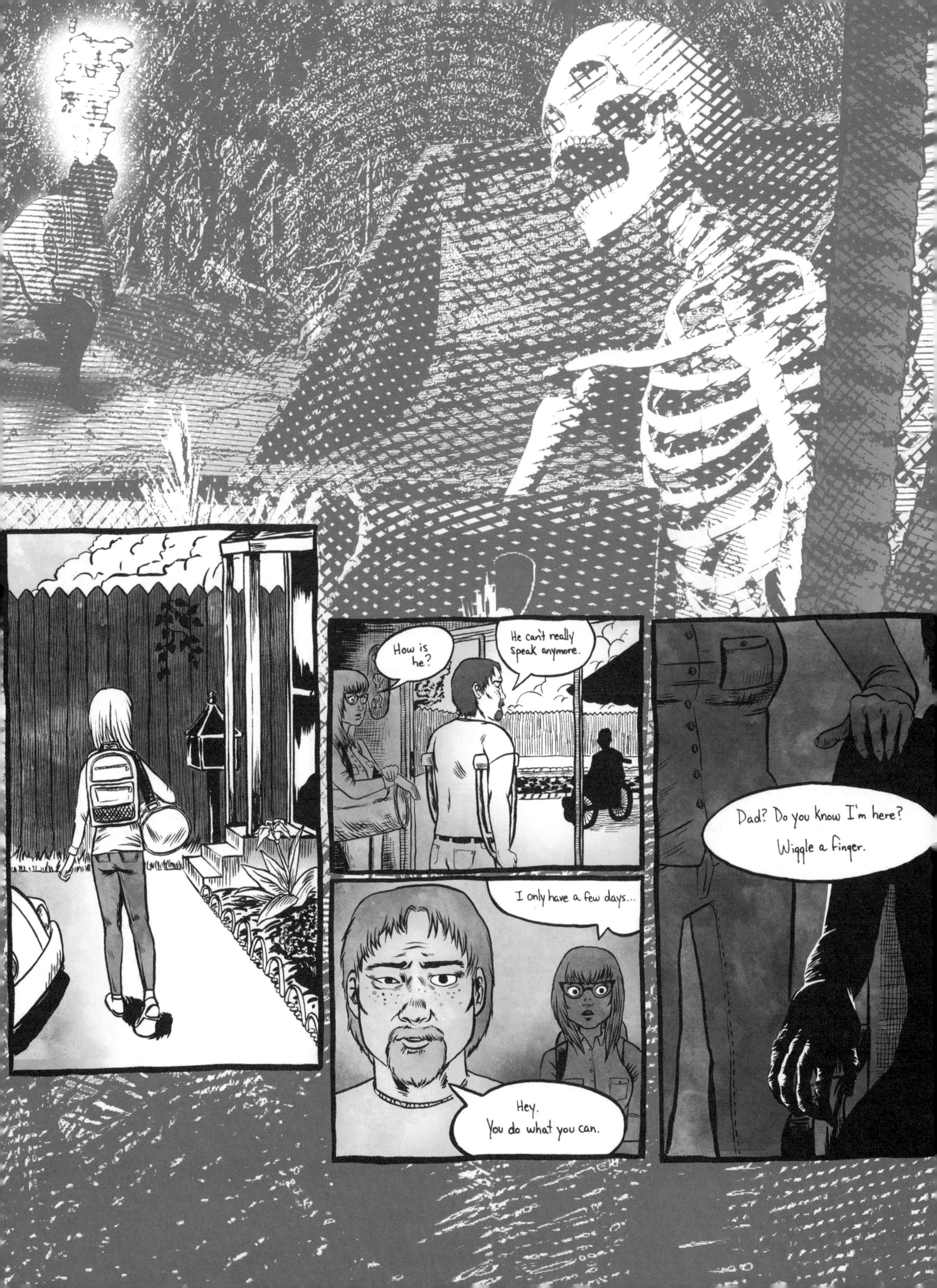
How is he?
He can't really speak anymore.
I only have a few days...
Hey. You do what you can.
Dad? Do you know I'm here? Wiggle a finger.

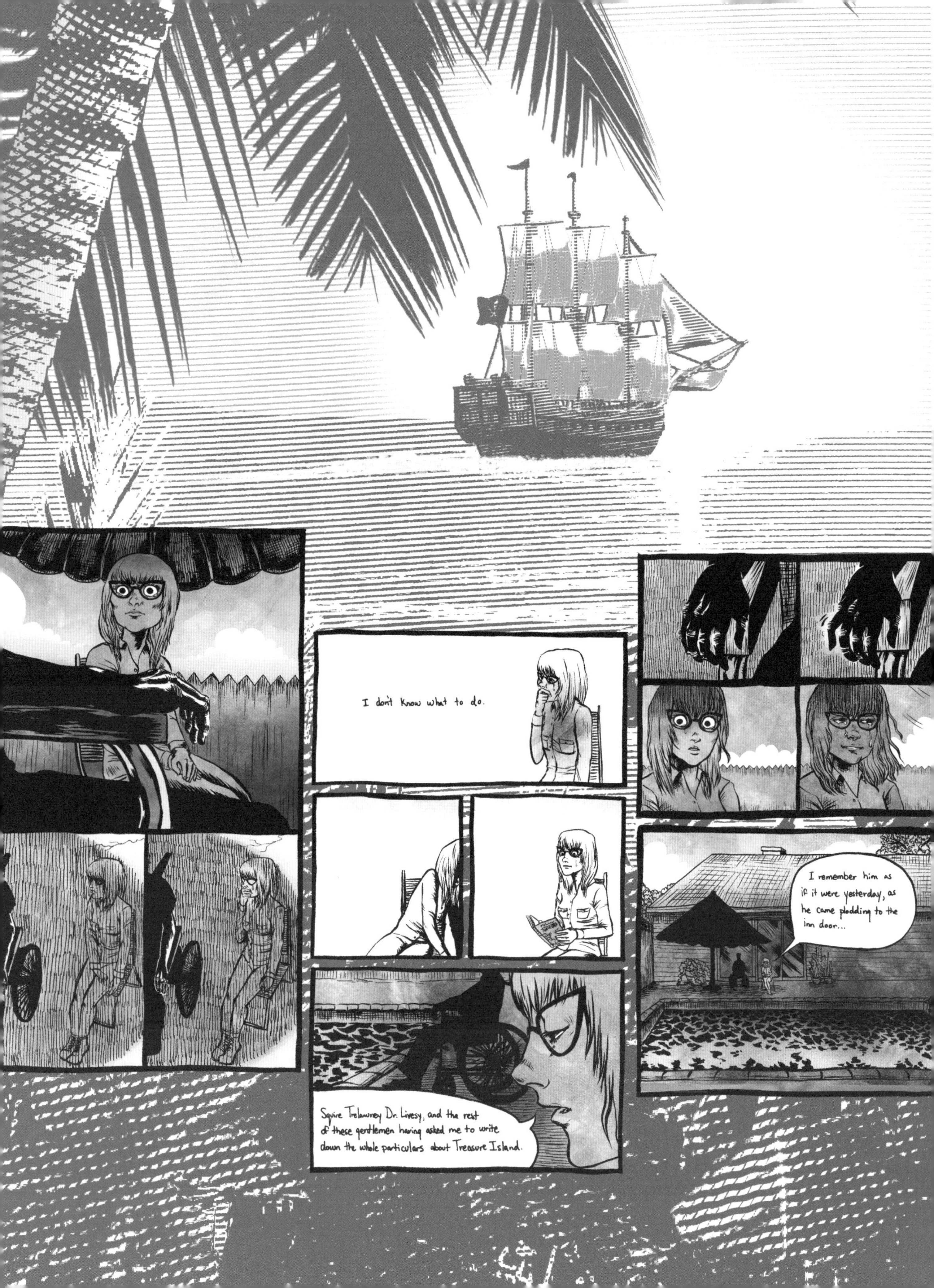
I don't know what to do.
I remember him as if it were yesterday, as he came plodding to the inn door...
Squire Trelawney, Dr. Livesy, and the rest of these gentlemen having asked me to write down the whole particulars about Treasure Island.

# "The Nightingale and the Rose"

## Oscar Wilde

ART/ADAPTATION BY **Tara Seibel**

**WRITTEN AT THE START OF OSCAR WILDE'S CREATIVE** flowering (which would yield *The Picture of Dorian Gray* and *Salome*, among other works), *The Happy Prince and Other Tales* and *A House of Pomegranates* have been causing confusion ever since they appeared in 1888 and 1891. Seemingly written for children—and indeed written while his two sons were tots—the stories are actually complex, often dark statements about the human condition. There seems to be no doubt that they can be fully appreciated only by adults, but are they meant at all for children? At times they're cynical and caustic, while at other times they seem to celebrate selflessness and humility. Or maybe they're both ways at once, creating ambiguity? Over 120 years later, opinions on these matters still differ widely.

"The Nightingale and the Rose" encapsulates this yin-and-yang approach. It serves up a bleak view of romantic love, but the self-sacrifice of the nightingale—though wasted—could be seen as noble and Christ-like. Or was it just stupid and naïve? You can decide as you view this adaptation by Tara Seibel, who often combines illustration, design, hand-lettering, unusual type, and flourishes and patterns to create a complex visual treat.

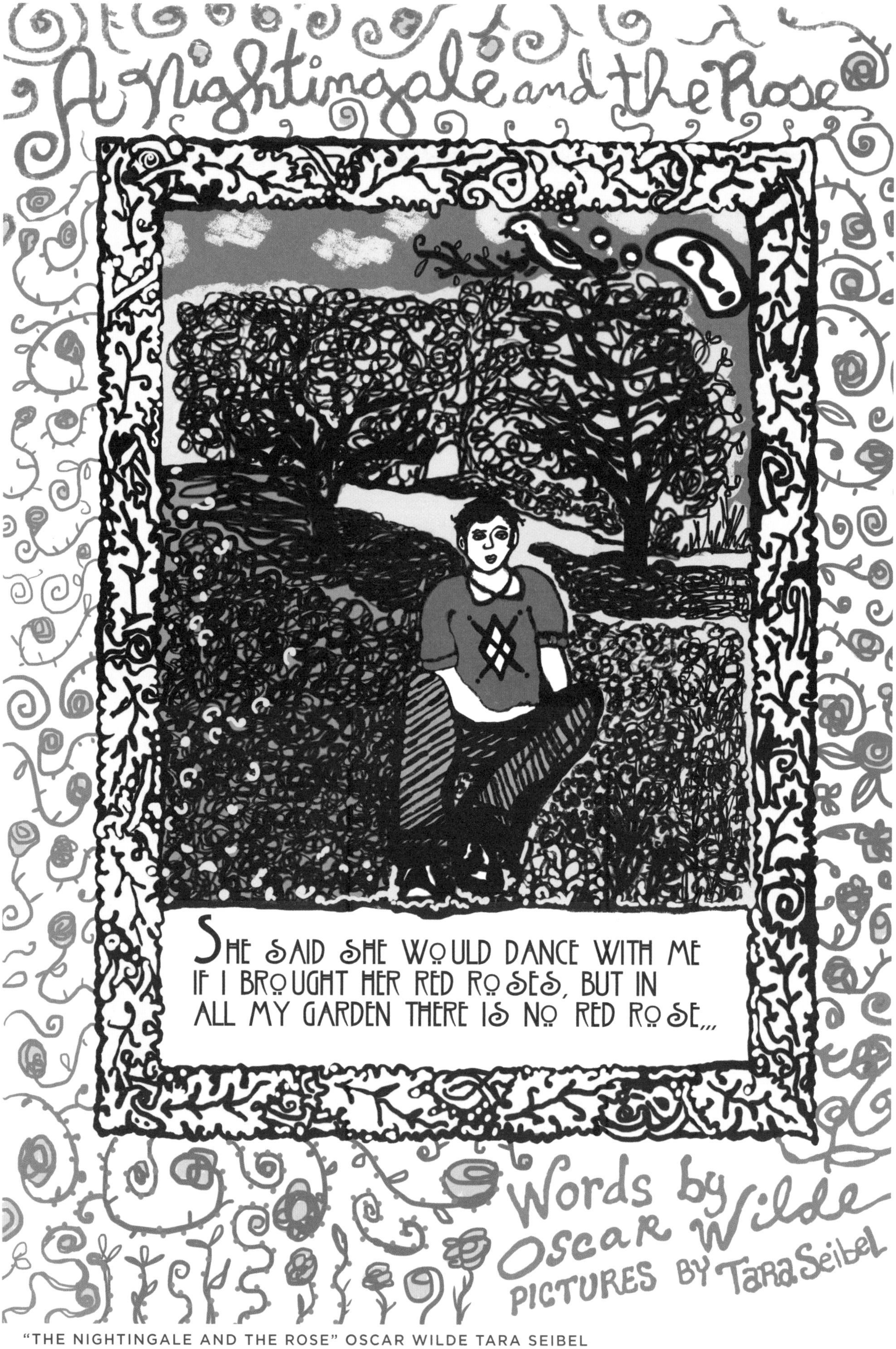
A Nightingale and the Rose
?
SHE SAID SHE WOULD DANCE WITH ME IF I BROUGHT HER RED ROSES, BUT IN ALL MY GARDEN THERE IS NO RED ROSE...
Words by Oscar Wilde
PICTURES BY Tara Seibel

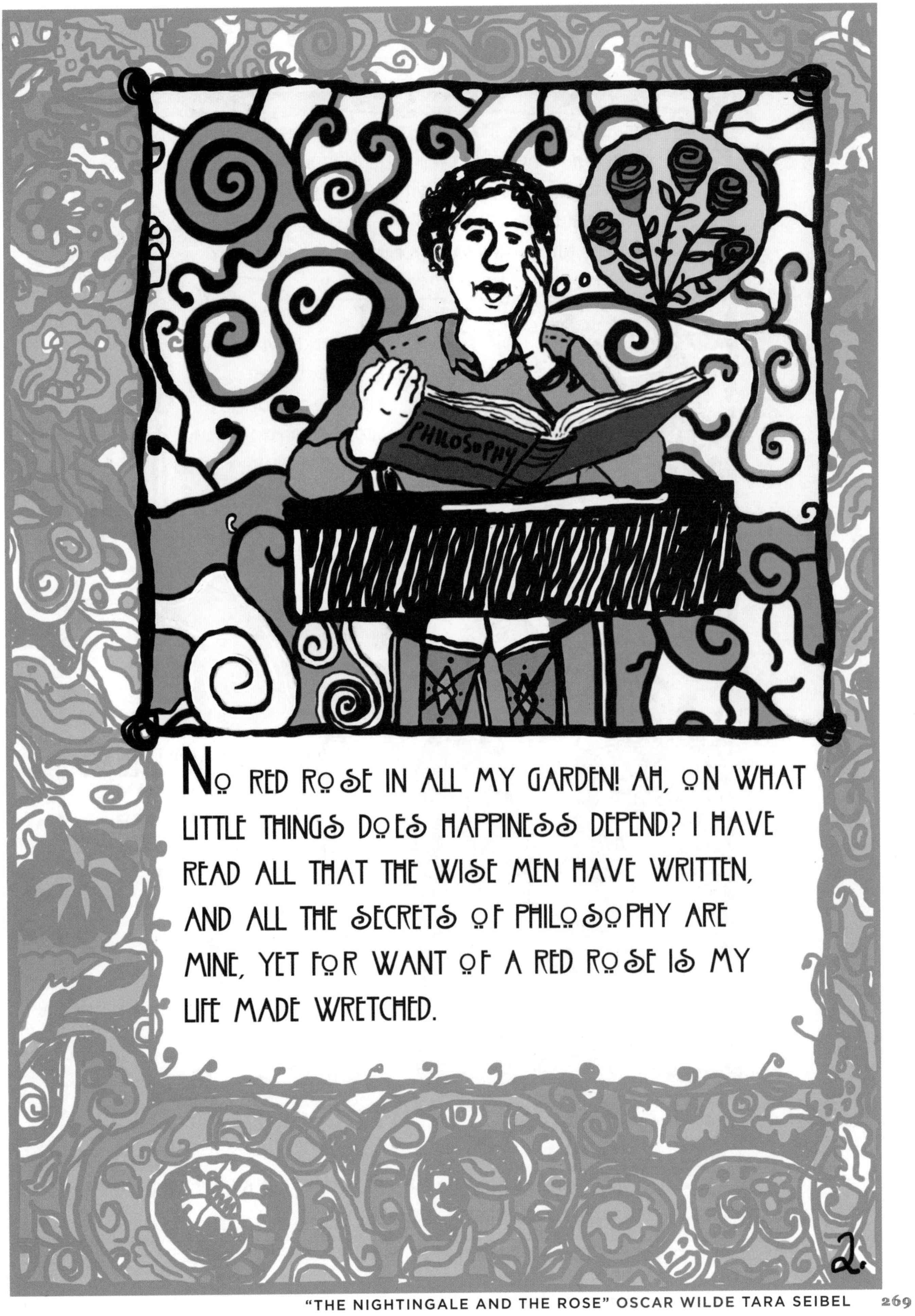
PHILOSOPHY
NO RED ROSE IN ALL MY GARDEN! AH, ON WHAT LITTLE THINGS DOES HAPPINESS DEPEND? I HAVE READ ALL THAT THE WISE MEN HAVE WRITTEN, AND ALL THE SECRETS OF PHILOSOPHY ARE MINE, YET FOR WANT OF A RED ROSE IS MY LIFE MADE WRETCHED.
2.

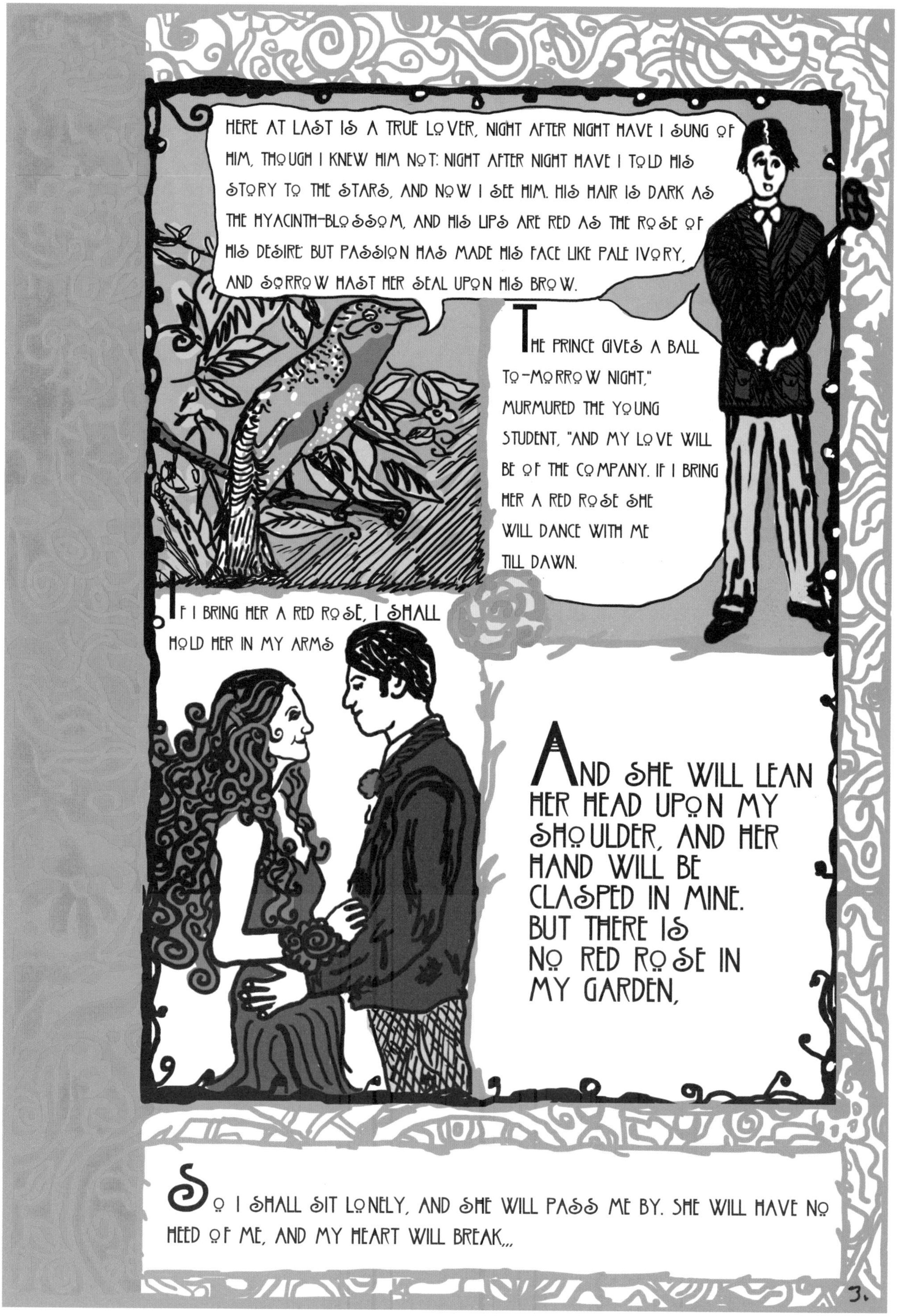
HERE AT LAST IS A TRUE LOVER, NIGHT AFTER NIGHT HAVE I SUNG OF HIM, THOUGH I KNEW HIM NOT: NIGHT AFTER NIGHT HAVE I TOLD HIS STORY TO THE STARS, AND NOW I SEE HIM. HIS HAIR IS DARK AS THE HYACINTH-BLOSSOM, AND HIS LIPS ARE RED AS THE ROSE OF HIS DESIRE: BUT PASSION HAS MADE HIS FACE LIKE PALE IVORY, AND SORROW HAST HER SEAL UPON HIS BROW.
THE PRINCE GIVES A BALL TO-MORROW NIGHT," MURMURED THE YOUNG STUDENT, "AND MY LOVE WILL BE OF THE COMPANY. IF I BRING HER A RED ROSE SHE WILL DANCE WITH ME TILL DAWN.
IF I BRING HER A RED ROSE, I SHALL HOLD HER IN MY ARMS
AND SHE WILL LEAN HER HEAD UPON MY SHOULDER, AND HER HAND WILL BE CLASPED IN MINE. BUT THERE IS NO RED ROSE IN MY GARDEN,
SO I SHALL SIT LONELY, AND SHE WILL PASS ME BY. SHE WILL HAVE NO HEED OF ME, AND MY HEART WILL BREAK...
3.

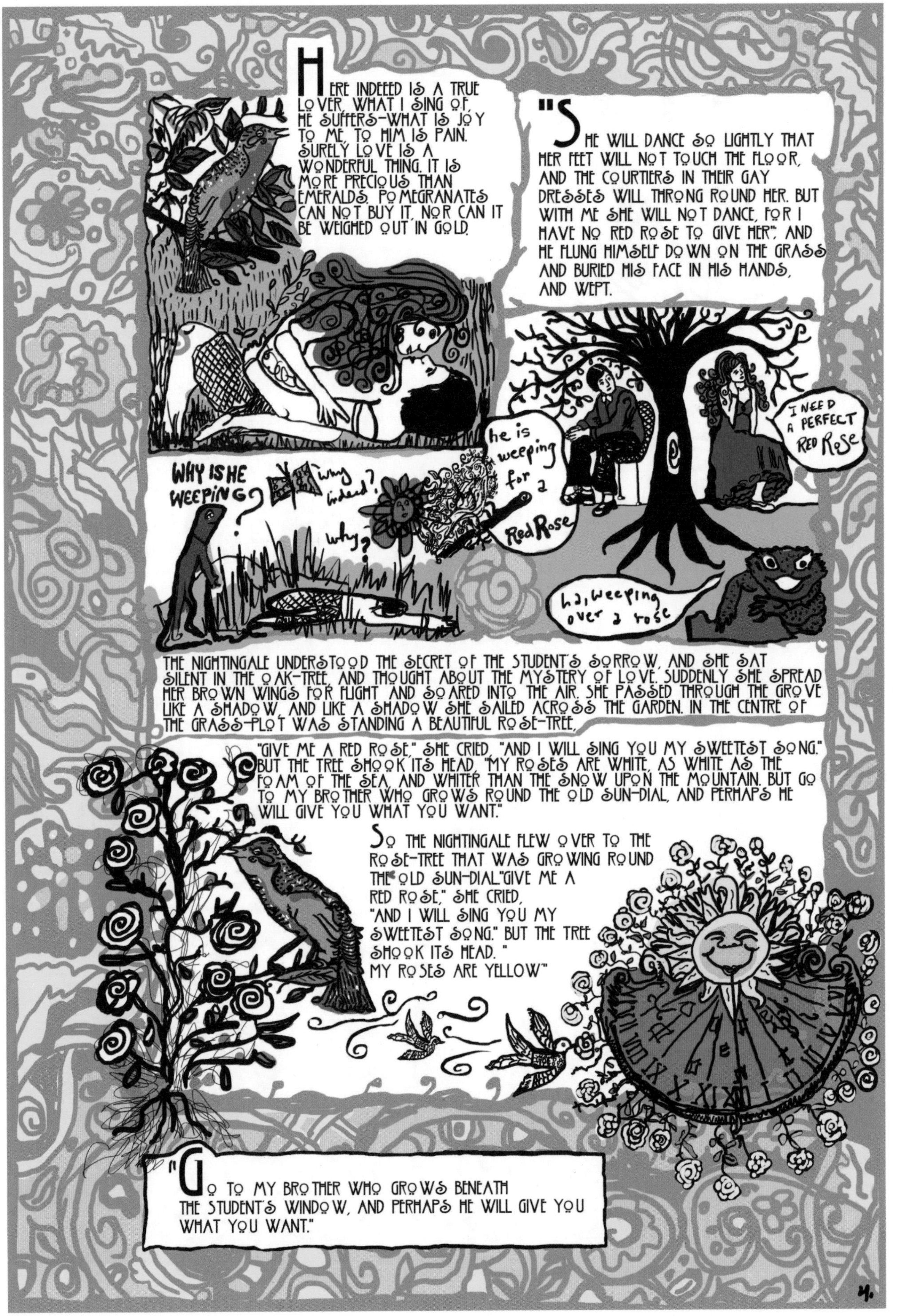
HERE INDEEED IS A TRUE LOVER. WHAT I SING OF, HE SUFFERS—WHAT IS JOY TO ME, TO HIM IS PAIN. SURELY LOVE IS A WONDERFUL THING. IT IS MORE PRECIOUS THAN EMERALDS. POMEGRANATES CAN NOT BUY IT, NOR CAN IT BE WEIGHED OUT IN GOLD.
"SHE WILL DANCE SO LIGHTLY THAT HER FEET WILL NOT TOUCH THE FLOOR, AND THE COURTIERS IN THEIR GAY DRESSES WILL THRONG ROUND HER. BUT WITH ME SHE WILL NOT DANCE, FOR I HAVE NO RED ROSE TO GIVE HER", AND HE FLUNG HIMSELF DOWN ON THE GRASS AND BURIED HIS FACE IN HIS HANDS, AND WEPT.
I NEED A PERFECT RED ROSE
WHY IS HE WEEPING?
why indeed?
why?
he is weeping for a Red Rose
ha, weeping over a rose
THE NIGHTINGALE UNDERSTOOD THE SECRET OF THE STUDENT'S SORROW, AND SHE SAT SILENT IN THE OAK-TREE, AND THOUGHT ABOUT THE MYSTERY OF LOVE. SUDDENLY SHE SPREAD HER BROWN WINGS FOR FLIGHT AND SOARED INTO THE AIR. SHE PASSED THROUGH THE GROVE LIKE A SHADOW, AND LIKE A SHADOW SHE SAILED ACROSS THE GARDEN. IN THE CENTRE OF THE GRASS-PLOT WAS STANDING A BEAUTIFUL ROSE-TREE,
"GIVE ME A RED ROSE," SHE CRIED, "AND I WILL SING YOU MY SWEETEST SONG." BUT THE TREE SHOOK ITS HEAD. "MY ROSES ARE WHITE, AS WHITE AS THE FOAM OF THE SEA, AND WHITER THAN THE SNOW UPON THE MOUNTAIN. BUT GO TO MY BROTHER WHO GROWS ROUND THE OLD SUN-DIAL, AND PERHAPS HE WILL GIVE YOU WHAT YOU WANT."
SO THE NIGHTINGALE FLEW OVER TO THE ROSE-TREE THAT WAS GROWING ROUND THE OLD SUN-DIAL. "GIVE ME A RED ROSE," SHE CRIED, "AND I WILL SING YOU MY SWEETEST SONG." BUT THE TREE SHOOK ITS HEAD. "MY ROSES ARE YELLOW"
"GO TO MY BROTHER WHO GROWS BENEATH THE STUDENT'S WINDOW, AND PERHAPS HE WILL GIVE YOU WHAT YOU WANT."

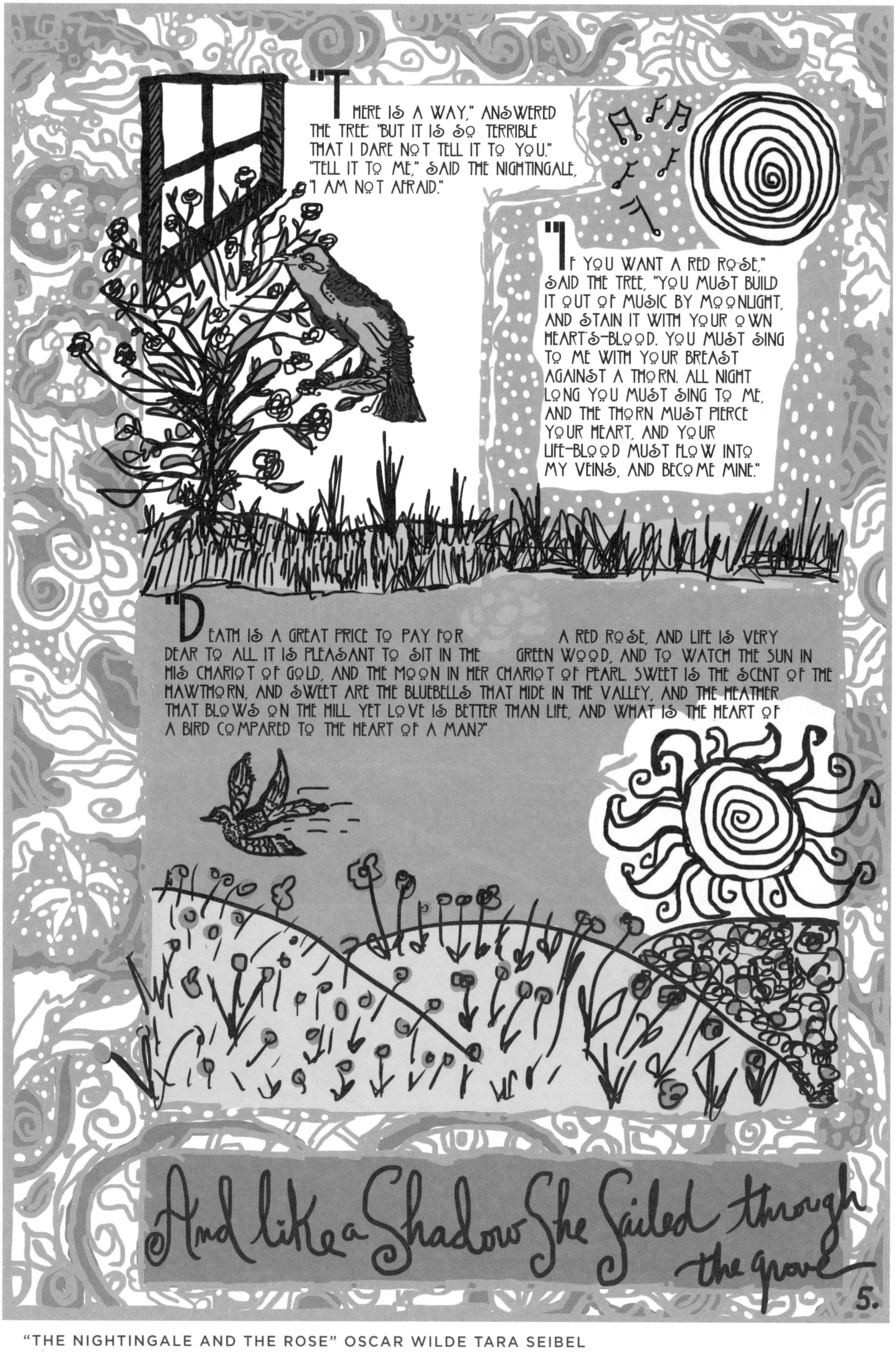
"There is a way," answered the tree: "but it is so terrible that I dare not tell it to you."
"Tell it to me," said the Nightingale, "I am not afraid."
"If you want a red rose," said the tree, "you must build it out of music by moonlight, and stain it with your own heart's-blood. You must sing to me with your breast against a thorn. All night long you must sing to me, and the thorn must pierce your heart, and your life-blood must flow into my veins, and become mine."
"Death is a great price to pay for a red rose, and life is very dear to all. It is pleasant to sit in the green wood, and to watch the Sun in his chariot of gold, and the Moon in her chariot of pearl. Sweet is the scent of the hawthorn, and sweet are the bluebells that hide in the valley, and the heather that blows on the hill. Yet love is better than life, and what is the heart of a bird compared to the heart of a man?"
And like a Shadow She Sailed through the grove
5.

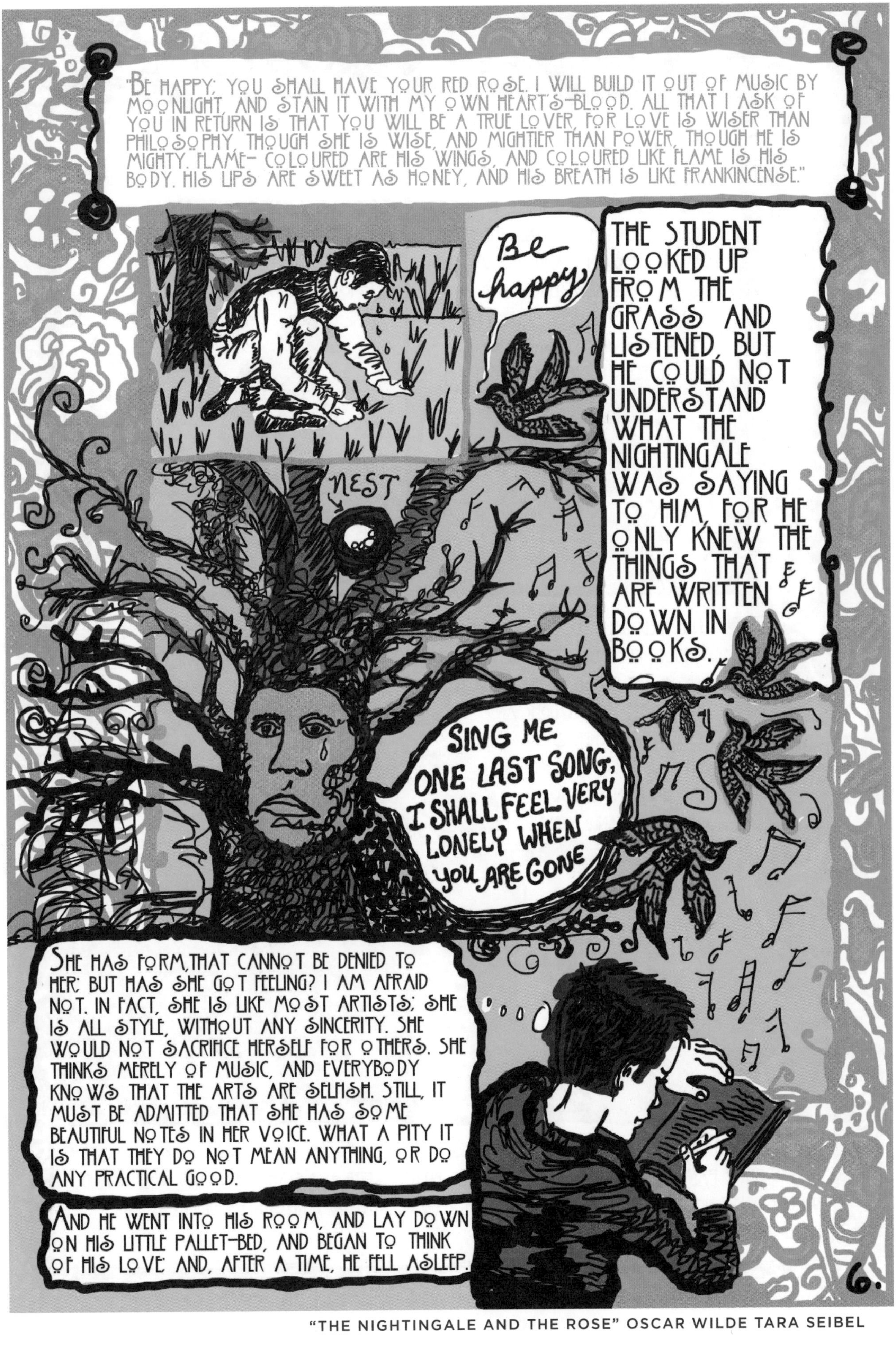
"Be happy; you shall have your red rose. I will build it out of music by moonlight, and stain it with my own heart's-blood. All that I ask of you in return is that you will be a true lover, for Love is wiser than Philosophy, though she is wise, and mightier than Power, though he is mighty. Flame- coloured are his wings, and coloured like flame is his body. His lips are sweet as honey, and his breath is like frankincense."
Be happy
The student looked up from the grass and listened, but he could not understand what the nightingale was saying to him, for he only knew the things that are written down in books.
NEST
SING ME ONE LAST SONG; I SHALL FEEL VERY LONELY WHEN YOU ARE GONE
She has form, that cannot be denied to her; but has she got feeling? I am afraid not. In fact, she is like most artists; she is all style, without any sincerity. She would not sacrifice herself for others. She thinks merely of music, and everybody knows that the arts are selfish. Still, it must be admitted that she has some beautiful notes in her voice. What a pity it is that they do not mean anything, or do any practical good.
And he went into his room, and lay down on his little pallet-bed, and began to think of his love and, after a time, he fell asleep.
6.

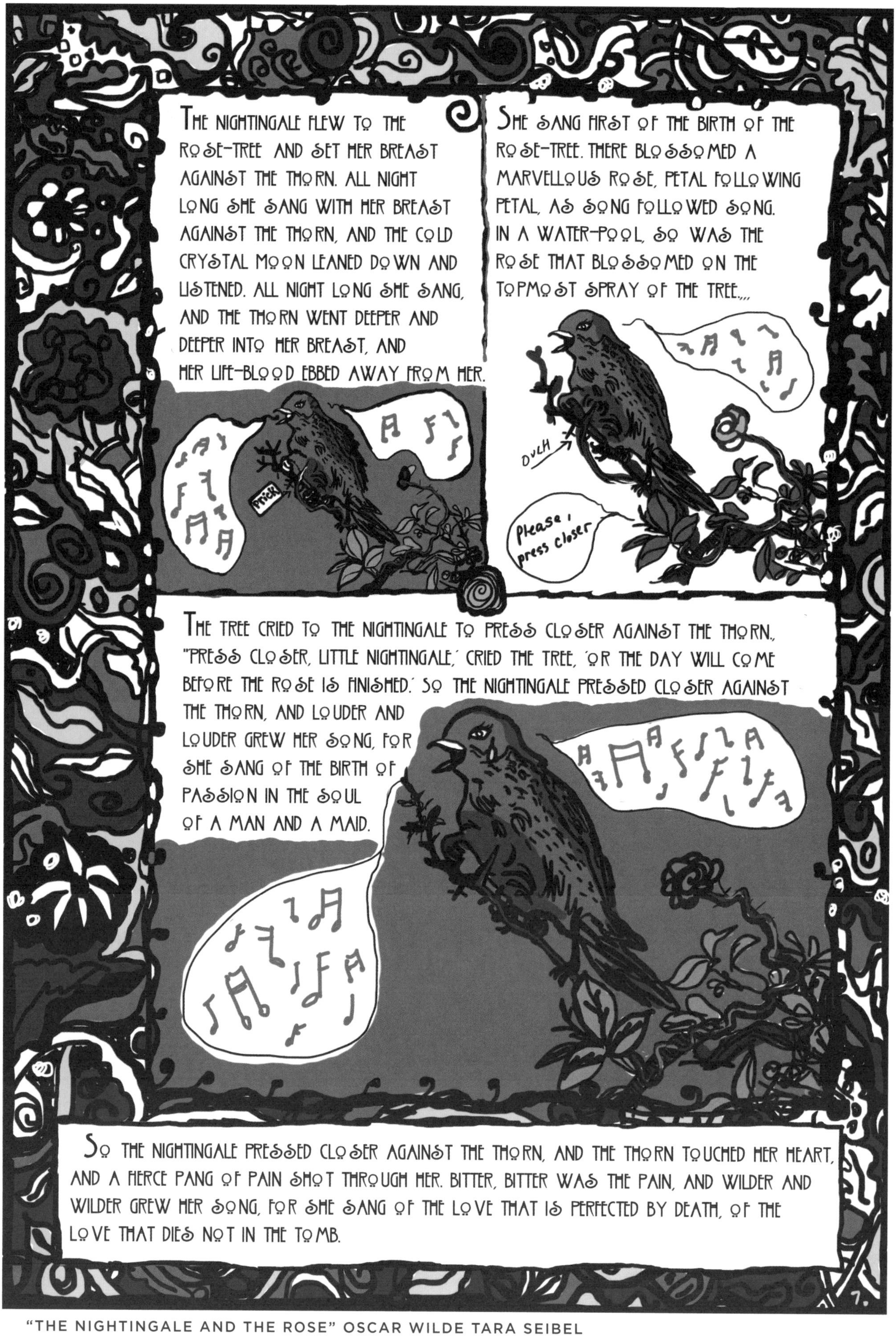
THE NIGHTINGALE FLEW TO THE ROSE-TREE AND SET HER BREAST AGAINST THE THORN. ALL NIGHT LONG SHE SANG WITH HER BREAST AGAINST THE THORN, AND THE COLD CRYSTAL MOON LEANED DOWN AND LISTENED. ALL NIGHT LONG SHE SANG, AND THE THORN WENT DEEPER AND DEEPER INTO HER BREAST, AND HER LIFE-BLOOD EBBED AWAY FROM HER.
PRICK
SHE SANG FIRST OF THE BIRTH OF THE ROSE-TREE. THERE BLOSSOMED A MARVELLOUS ROSE, PETAL FOLLOWING PETAL, AS SONG FOLLOWED SONG. IN A WATER-POOL, SO WAS THE ROSE THAT BLOSSOMED ON THE TOPMOST SPRAY OF THE TREE....
OUCH
Please, press closer
THE TREE CRIED TO THE NIGHTINGALE TO PRESS CLOSER AGAINST THE THORN. "PRESS CLOSER, LITTLE NIGHTINGALE,' CRIED THE TREE, 'OR THE DAY WILL COME BEFORE THE ROSE IS FINISHED.' SO THE NIGHTINGALE PRESSED CLOSER AGAINST THE THORN, AND LOUDER AND LOUDER GREW HER SONG, FOR SHE SANG OF THE BIRTH OF PASSION IN THE SOUL OF A MAN AND A MAID.
SO THE NIGHTINGALE PRESSED CLOSER AGAINST THE THORN, AND THE THORN TOUCHED HER HEART, AND A FIERCE PANG OF PAIN SHOT THROUGH HER. BITTER, BITTER WAS THE PAIN, AND WILDER AND WILDER GREW HER SONG, FOR SHE SANG OF THE LOVE THAT IS PERFECTED BY DEATH, OF THE LOVE THAT DIES NOT IN THE TOMB.

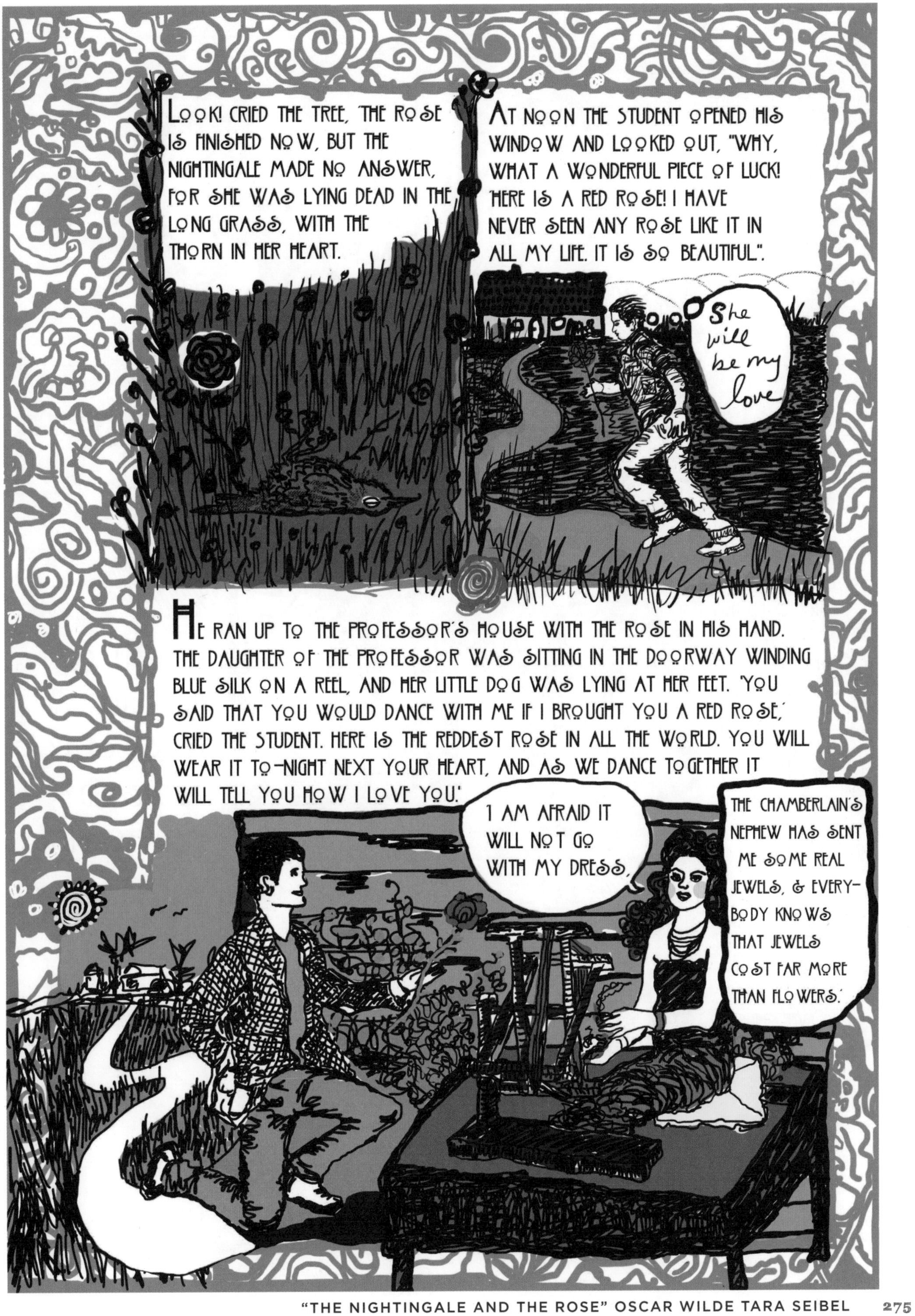
'Look!' cried the Tree, 'the Rose is finished now,' but the Nightingale made no answer, for she was lying dead in the long grass, with the thorn in her heart.
At noon the Student opened his window and looked out. "Why, what a wonderful piece of luck! 'Here is a red rose! I have never seen any rose like it in all my life. It is so beautiful".
She will be my love
He ran up to the Professor's house with the rose in his hand. The daughter of the Professor was sitting in the doorway winding blue silk on a reel, and her little dog was lying at her feet. 'You said that you would dance with me if I brought you a red rose,' cried the Student. Here is the reddest rose in all the world. You will wear it to-night next your heart, and as we dance together it will tell you how I love you.'
I am afraid it will not go with my dress,
The Chamberlain's nephew has sent me some real jewels, & everybody knows that jewels cost far more than flowers.'

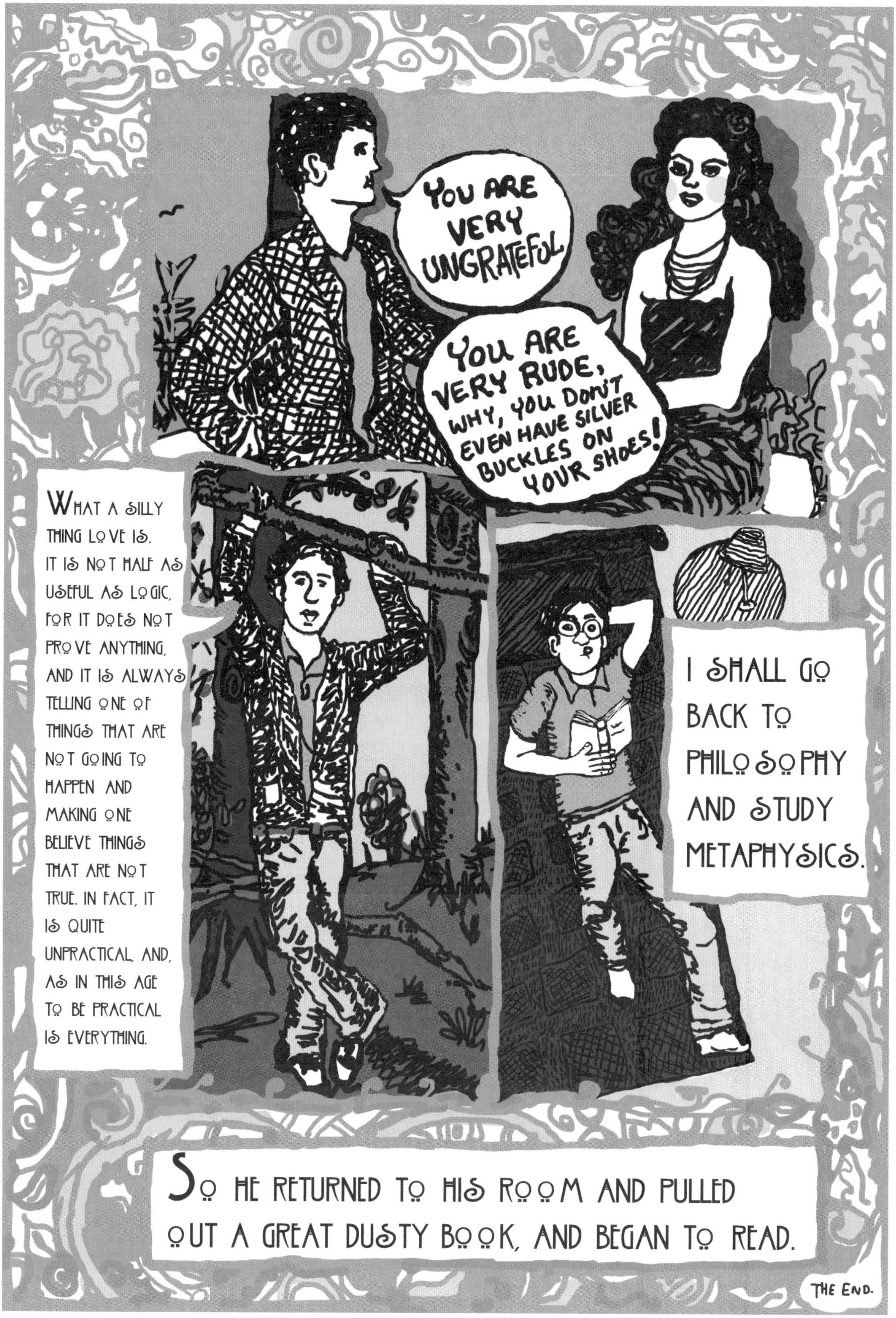

YOU ARE VERY UNGRATEFUL
YOU ARE VERY RUDE, WHY, YOU DON'T EVEN HAVE SILVER BUCKLES ON YOUR SHOES!
WHAT A SILLY THING LOVE IS. IT IS NOT HALF AS USEFUL AS LOGIC, FOR IT DOES NOT PROVE ANYTHING, AND IT IS ALWAYS TELLING ONE OF THINGS THAT ARE NOT GOING TO HAPPEN AND MAKING ONE BELIEVE THINGS THAT ARE NOT TRUE. IN FACT, IT IS QUITE UNPRACTICAL, AND, AS IN THIS AGE TO BE PRACTICAL IS EVERYTHING.
I SHALL GO BACK TO PHILOSOPHY AND STUDY METAPHYSICS.
SO HE RETURNED TO HIS ROOM AND PULLED OUT A GREAT DUSTY BOOK, AND BEGAN TO READ.
THE END.

# The Jungle Book

## Rudyard Kipling

ART/ADAPTATION BY **Caroline Picard**

**RUDYARD KIPLING WROTE PROLIFICALLY (HIS** collected writings take up twenty-eight volumes), achieving the rare feat of adding several works to the overall literary canon while penning some immortal works for children. Most famous writers managed to do one or the other.

In late 1893, Kipling started creating stories for kids involving Mowgli, a baby boy raised by wolves, a bear, and a panther after being stolen from his parents by a tiger in central India. The stories quickly expanded to focus on other animal denizens of the jungle. After appearing in magazines, these "children's beast-tales"—as Kipling called them—were gathered into *The Jungle Book*, which was instantly popular with critics and the public when it appeared in 1894.

Illustrator and publisher Caroline Picard is always experimenting with unusual and delightful ways to present narrative in comics form. When she chose to adapt four tales from *The Jungle Book*—including a Mowgli story and the well-known "Rikki-Tikki-Tavi"—I wondered what novel way she would come up with to present them. Now I see: each one starts on the first page and flows in a single seamless line across all seven pages.

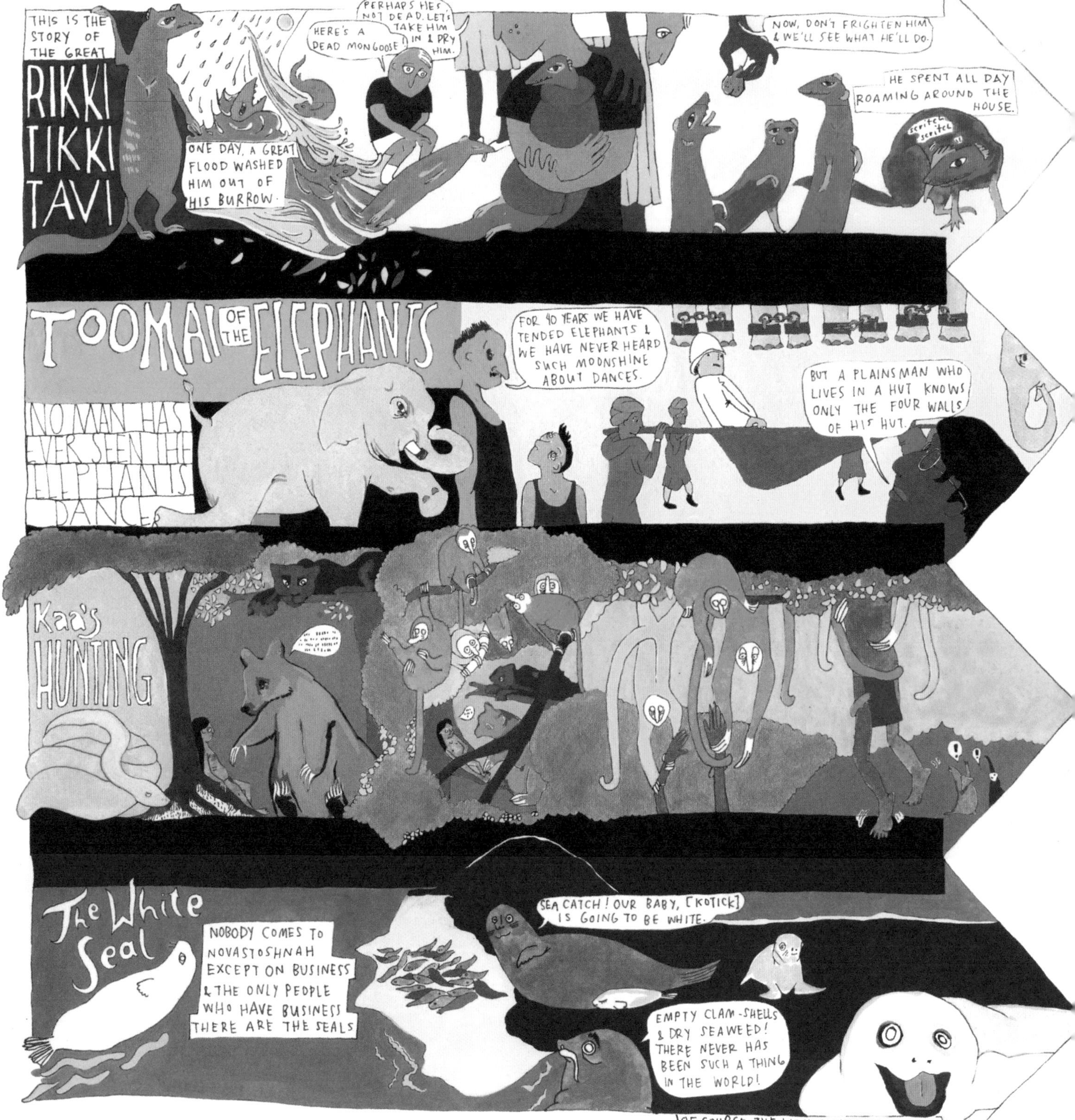
THIS IS THE STORY OF THE GREAT
RIKKI TIKKI TAVI
ONE DAY, A GREAT FLOOD WASHED HIM OUT OF HIS BURROW.
HERE'S A DEAD MONGOOSE!
PERHAPS HE'S NOT DEAD. LET'S TAKE HIM IN & DRY HIM.
NOW, DON'T FRIGHTEN HIM & WE'LL SEE WHAT HE'LL DO.
HE SPENT ALL DAY ROAMING AROUND THE HOUSE.
scritch scritch
TOOMAI OF THE ELEPHANTS
NO MAN HAS EVER SEEN THE ELEPHANTS DANCE
FOR 40 YEARS WE HAVE TENDED ELEPHANTS & WE HAVE NEVER HEARD SUCH MOONSHINE ABOUT DANCES.
BUT A PLAINSMAN WHO LIVES IN A HUT KNOWS ONLY THE FOUR WALLS OF HIS HUT.
Kaa's HUNTING
The White Seal
NOBODY COMES TO NOVASTOSHNAH EXCEPT ON BUSINESS & THE ONLY PEOPLE WHO HAVE BUSINESS THERE ARE THE SEALS
SEA CATCH! OUR BABY, [KOTICK] IS GOING TO BE WHITE.
EMPTY CLAM-SHELLS & DRY SEAWEED! THERE NEVER HAS BEEN SUCH A THING IN THE WORLD!
OF COURSE THE LITTLE FELLOW DID NOT UNDERSTAND WORDS FIRST. HE PADDLED & SCRAMBLED BY HIS MOTHER'S SIDE.

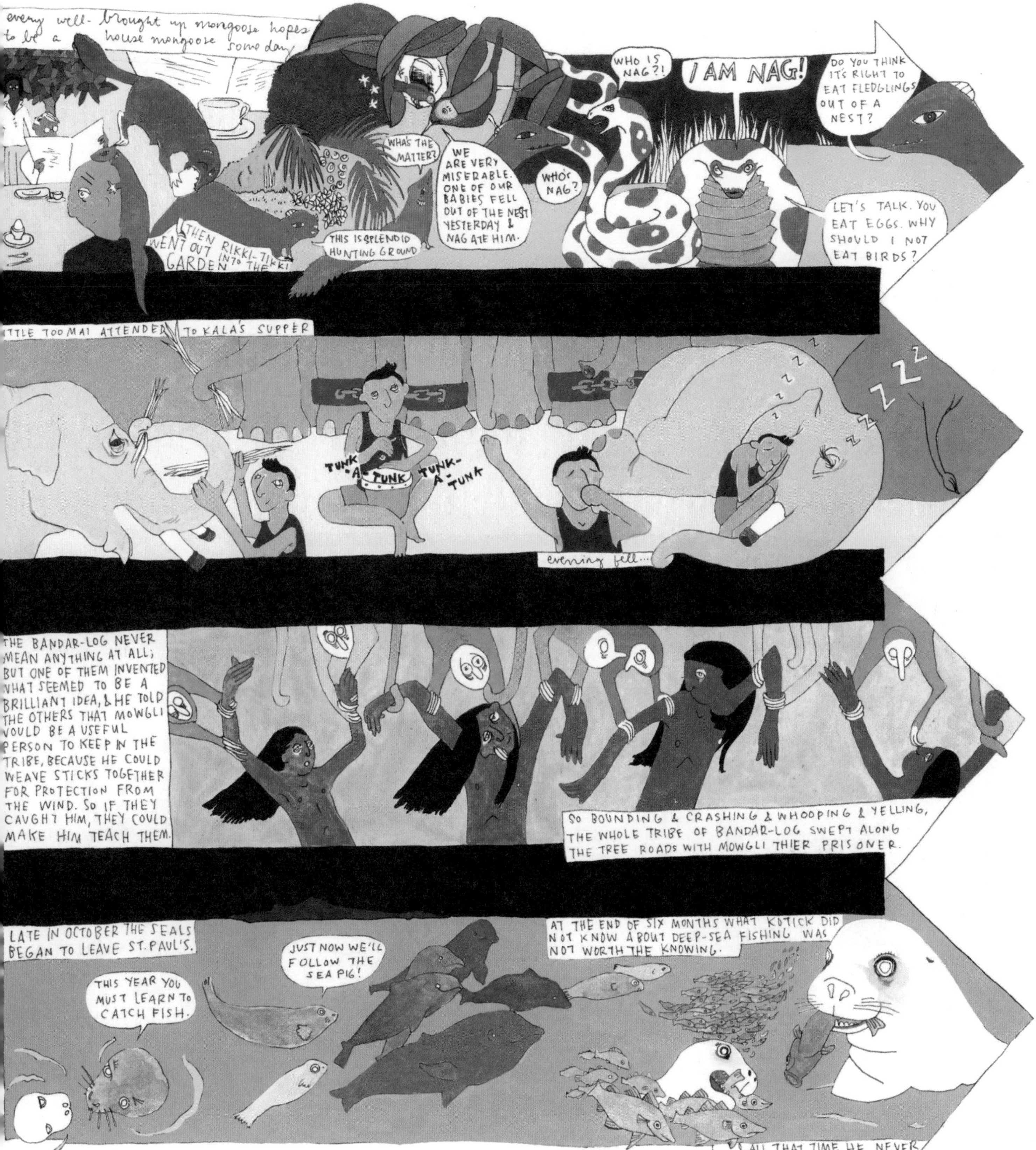
every well-brought up mongoose hopes to be a house mongoose some day
THEN RIKKI-TIKKI WENT OUT INTO THE GARDEN
WHAT'S THE MATTER?
THIS IS SPLENDID HUNTING GROUND
WE ARE VERY MISERABLE. ONE OF OUR BABIES FELL OUT OF THE NEST YESTERDAY & NAG ATE HIM.
WHO'S NAG?
WHO IS NAG?!
I AM NAG!
DO YOU THINK IT'S RIGHT TO EAT FLEDGLINGS OUT OF A NEST?
LET'S TALK. YOU EAT EGGS. WHY SHOULD I NOT EAT BIRDS?
ITTLE TOOMAI ATTENDED TO KALA'S SUPPER
TUNK-A-TUNK TUNK-A-TUNA
evening fell...
ZZZ
THE BANDAR-LOG NEVER MEAN ANYTHING AT ALL; BUT ONE OF THEM INVENTED WHAT SEEMED TO BE A BRILLIANT IDEA, & HE TOLD THE OTHERS THAT MOWGLI WOULD BE A USEFUL PERSON TO KEEP IN THE TRIBE, BECAUSE HE COULD WEAVE STICKS TOGETHER FOR PROTECTION FROM THE WIND. SO IF THEY CAUGHT HIM, THEY COULD MAKE HIM TEACH THEM.
SO BOUNDING & CRASHING & WHOOPING & YELLING, THE WHOLE TRIBE OF BANDAR-LOG SWEPT ALONG THE TREE ROADS WITH MOWGLI THIER PRISONER.
LATE IN OCTOBER THE SEALS BEGAN TO LEAVE ST. PAUL'S.
THIS YEAR YOU MUST LEARN TO CATCH FISH.
JUST NOW WE'LL FOLLOW THE SEA PIG!
AT THE END OF SIX MONTHS WHAT KOTICK DID NOT KNOW ABOUT DEEP-SEA FISHING WAS NOT WORTH THE KNOWING.
& ALL THAT TIME HE NEVER SET A FLIPPER ON DRY GROUND

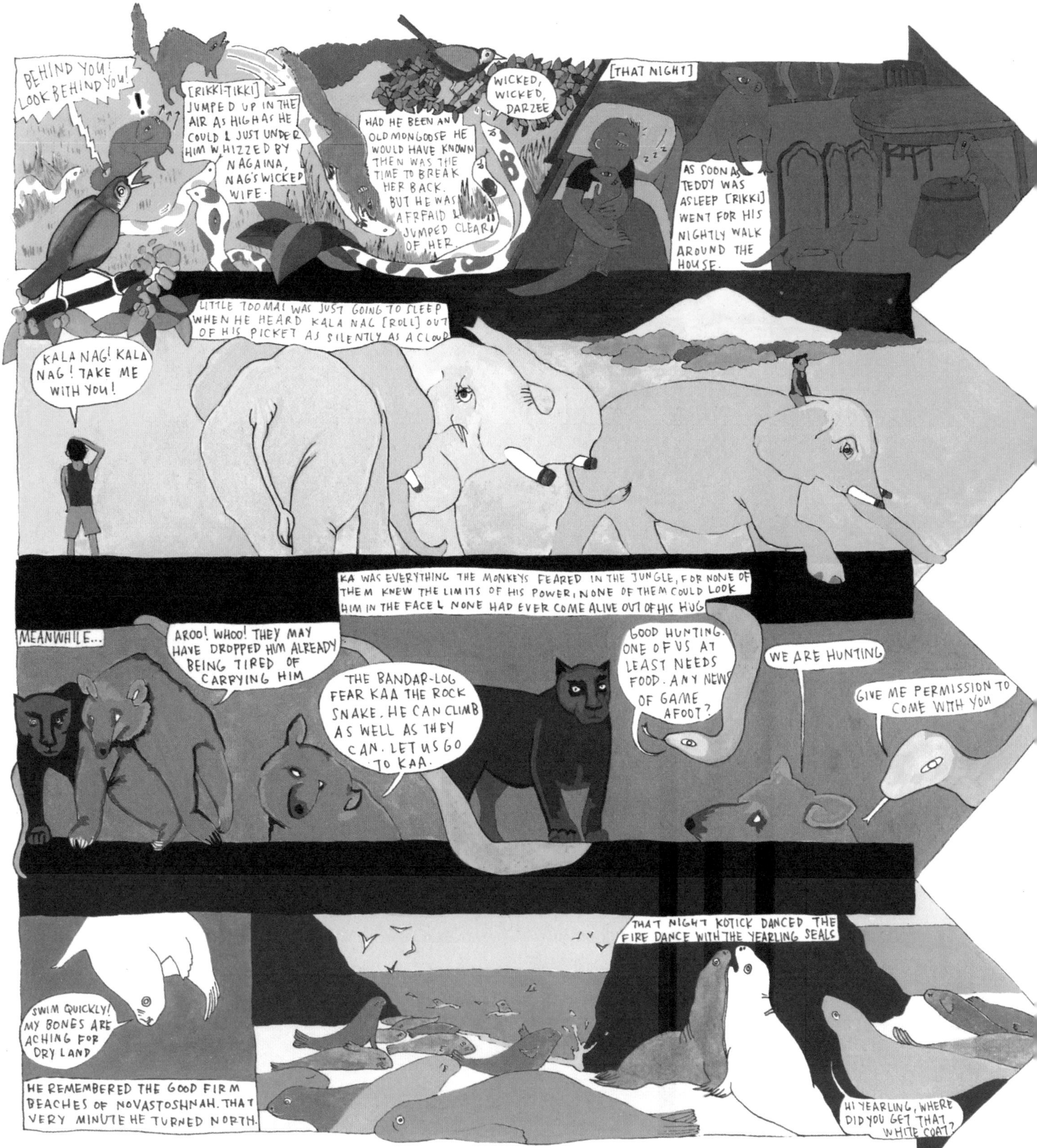

BEHIND YOU! LOOK BEHIND YOU!
[RIKKI-TIKKI] JUMPED UP IN THE AIR AS HIGH AS HE COULD & JUST UNDER HIM WHIZZED BY NAGAINA, NAG'S WICKED WIFE.
HAD HE BEEN AN OLD MONGOOSE HE WOULD HAVE KNOWN THEN WAS THE TIME TO BREAK HER BACK. BUT HE WAS AFRFAID & JUMPED CLEAR OF HER.
WICKED, WICKED, DARZEE
[THAT NIGHT]
AS SOON AS TEDDY WAS ASLEEP [RIKKI] WENT FOR HIS NIGHTLY WALK AROUND THE HOUSE.
LITTLE TOOMAI WAS JUST GOING TO SLEEP WHEN HE HEARD KALA NAG [ROLL] OUT OF HIS PICKET AS SILENTLY AS A CLOUD
KALA NAG! KALA NAG! TAKE ME WITH YOU!
KA WAS EVERYTHING THE MONKEYS FEARED IN THE JUNGLE, FOR NONE OF THEM KNEW THE LIMITS OF HIS POWER, NONE OF THEM COULD LOOK HIM IN THE FACE & NONE HAD EVER COME ALIVE OUT OF HIS HUG
MEANWHILE...
AROO! WHOO! THEY MAY HAVE DROPPED HIM ALREADY BEING TIRED OF CARRYING HIM
THE BANDAR-LOG FEAR KAA THE ROCK SNAKE. HE CAN CLIMB AS WELL AS THEY CAN. LET US GO TO KAA.
GOOD HUNTING. ONE OF US AT LEAST NEEDS FOOD. ANY NEWS OF GAME AFOOT?
WE ARE HUNTING
GIVE ME PERMISSION TO COME WITH YOU
SWIM QUICKLY! MY BONES ARE ACHING FOR DRY LAND
HE REMEMBERED THE GOOD FIRM BEACHES OF NOVASTOSHNAH. THAT VERY MINUTE HE TURNED NORTH.
THAT NIGHT KOTICK DANCED THE FIRE DANCE WITH THE YEARLING SEALS
HI YEARLING, WHERE DID YOU GET THAT WHITE COAT?

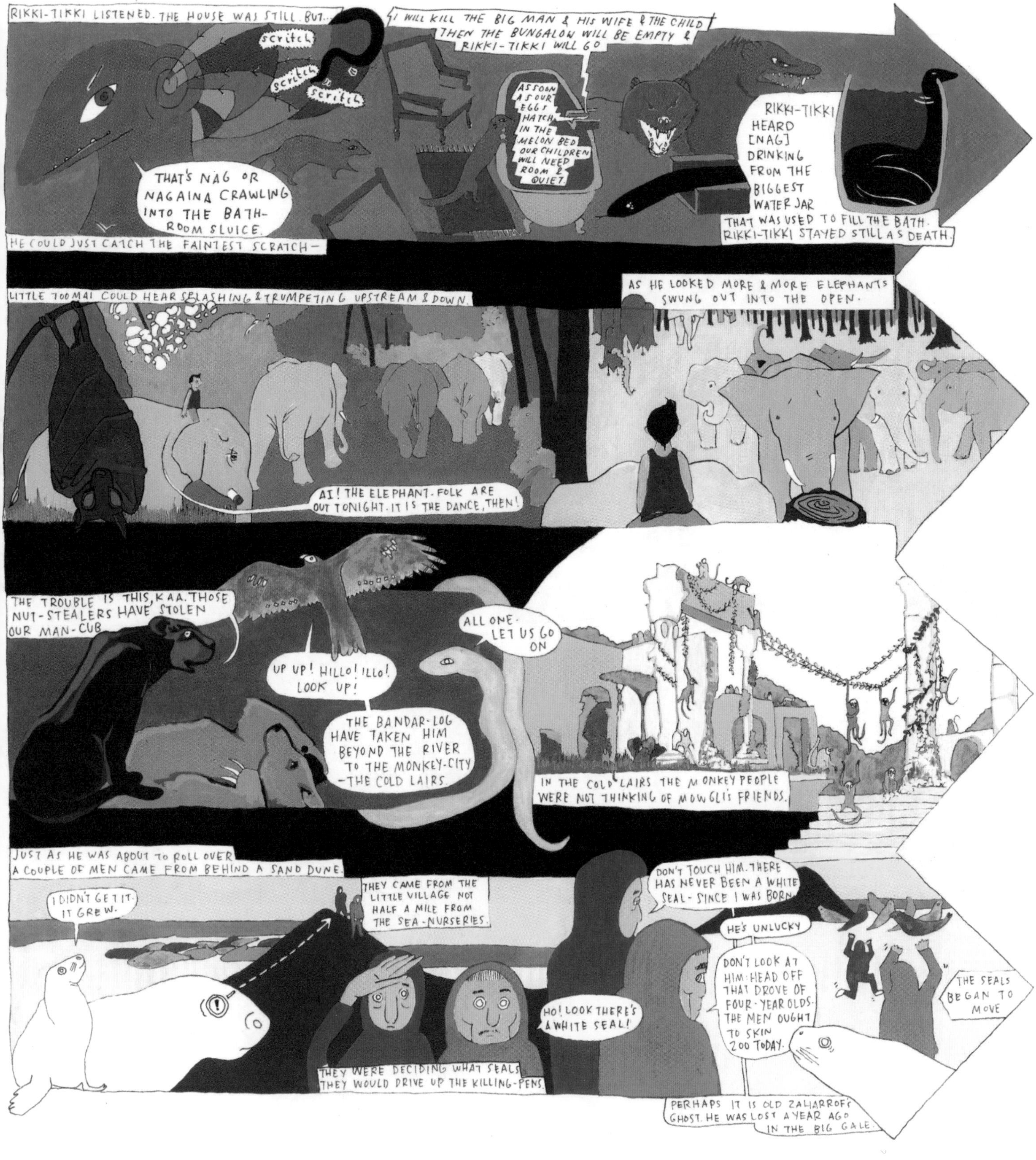
RIKKI-TIKKI LISTENED. THE HOUSE WAS STILL, BUT...
scritch
scritch
scritch
I WILL KILL THE BIG MAN & HIS WIFE & THE CHILD THEN THE BUNGALOW WILL BE EMPTY & RIKKI-TIKKI WILL GO
AS SOON AS OUR EGGS HATCH IN THE MELON BED OUR CHILDREN WILL NEED ROOM & QUIET
THAT'S NAG OR NAGAINA CRAWLING INTO THE BATH-ROOM SLUICE.
HE COULD JUST CATCH THE FAINTEST SCRATCH—
RIKKI-TIKKI HEARD [NAG] DRINKING FROM THE BIGGEST WATER JAR
THAT WAS USED TO FILL THE BATH. RIKKI-TIKKI STAYED STILL AS DEATH.
LITTLE TOOMAI COULD HEAR SPLASHING & TRUMPETING UPSTREAM & DOWN.
AI! THE ELEPHANT-FOLK ARE OUT TONIGHT. IT IS THE DANCE, THEN!
AS HE LOOKED MORE & MORE ELEPHANTS SWUNG OUT INTO THE OPEN.
THE TROUBLE IS THIS, KAA. THOSE NUT-STEALERS HAVE STOLEN OUR MAN-CUB
UP UP! HILLO! ILLO! LOOK UP!
ALL ONE. LET US GO ON
THE BANDAR-LOG HAVE TAKEN HIM BEYOND THE RIVER TO THE MONKEY-CITY —THE COLD LAIRS
IN THE COLD LAIRS THE MONKEY PEOPLE WERE NOT THINKING OF MOWGLI'S FRIENDS.
JUST AS HE WAS ABOUT TO ROLL OVER A COUPLE OF MEN CAME FROM BEHIND A SAND DUNE.
I DIDN'T GET IT. IT GREW.
THEY CAME FROM THE LITTLE VILLAGE NOT HALF A MILE FROM THE SEA-NURSERIES.
HO! LOOK THERE'S A WHITE SEAL!
THEY WERE DECIDING WHAT SEALS THEY WOULD DRIVE UP THE KILLING-PENS.
DON'T TOUCH HIM. THERE HAS NEVER BEEN A WHITE SEAL- SINCE I WAS BORN.
HE'S UNLUCKY
DON'T LOOK AT HIM: HEAD OFF THAT DROVE OF FOUR-YEAR OLDS. THE MEN OUGHT TO SKIN 200 TODAY.
THE SEALS BEGAN TO MOVE
PERHAPS IT IS OLD ZAHARROF'S GHOST. HE WAS LOST A YEAR AGO IN THE BIG GALE.

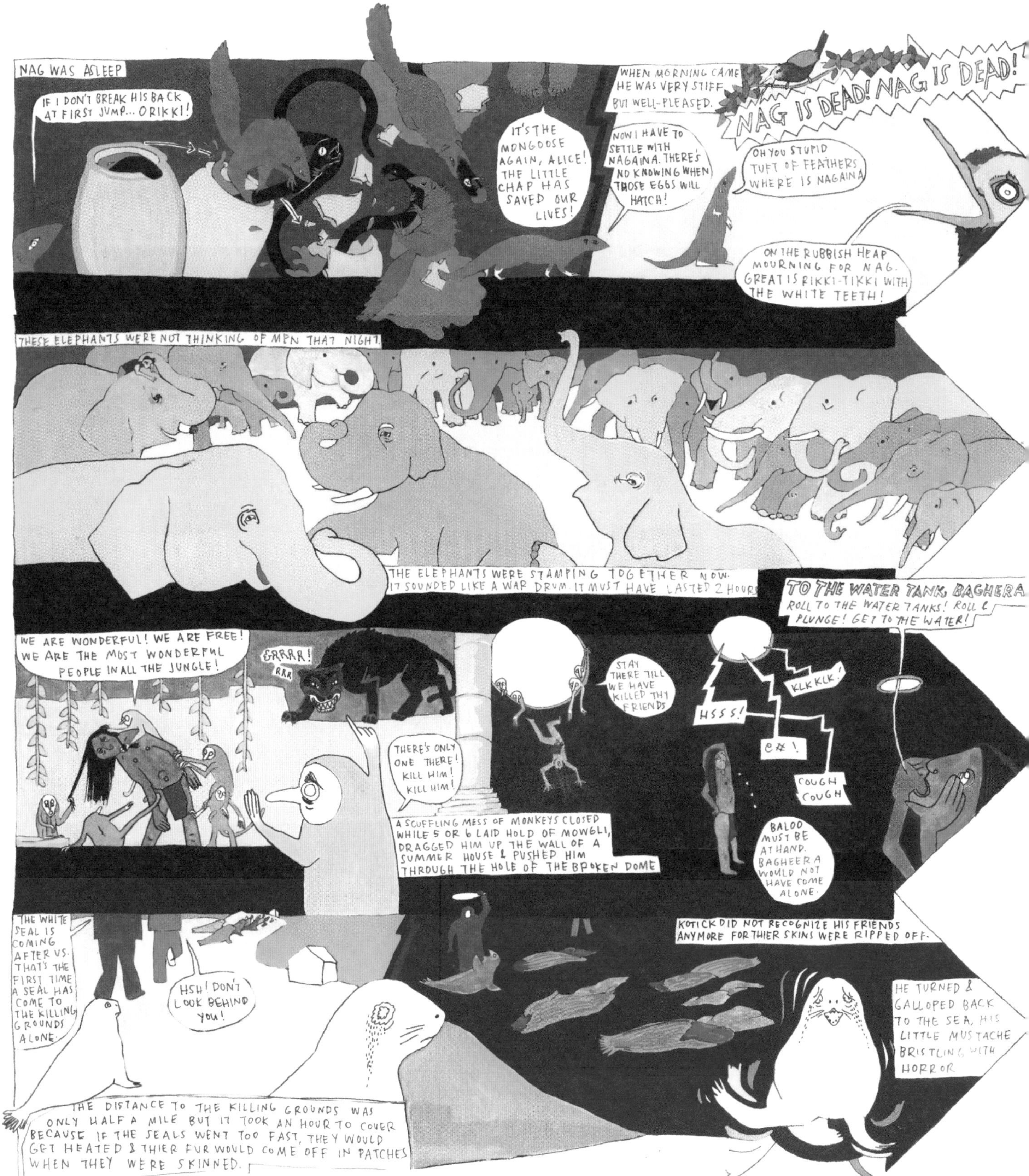
NAG WAS ASLEEP
IF I DON'T BREAK HIS BACK AT FIRST JUMP... ORIKKI!
IT'S THE MONGOOSE AGAIN, ALICE! THE LITTLE CHAP HAS SAVED OUR LIVES!
WHEN MORNING CAME HE WAS VERY STIFF BUT WELL-PLEASED.
NOW I HAVE TO SETTLE WITH NAGAINA. THERE'S NO KNOWING WHEN THOSE EGGS WILL HATCH!
NAG IS DEAD! NAG IS DEAD! NAG IS DEAD!
OH YOU STUPID TUFT OF FEATHERS WHERE IS NAGAINA
ON THE RUBBISH HEAP MOURNING FOR NAG. GREAT IS RIKKI-TIKKI WITH THE WHITE TEETH!
THESE ELEPHANTS WERE NOT THINKING OF MEN THAT NIGHT.
THE ELEPHANTS WERE STAMPING TOGETHER NOW. IT SOUNDED LIKE A WAR DRUM. IT MUST HAVE LASTED 2 HOURS
WE ARE WONDERFUL! WE ARE FREE! WE ARE THE MOST WONDERFUL PEOPLE IN ALL THE JUNGLE!
GRRRR! RRR
THERE'S ONLY ONE THERE! KILL HIM! KILL HIM!
A SCUFFLING MESS OF MONKEYS CLOSED WHILE 5 OR 6 LAID HOLD OF MOWGLI, DRAGGED HIM UP THE WALL OF A SUMMER HOUSE & PUSHED HIM THROUGH THE HOLE OF THE BROKEN DOME
STAY THERE TILL WE HAVE KILLED THY FRIENDS
TO THE WATER TANK, BAGHERA
ROLL TO THE WATER TANKS! ROLL & PLUNGE! GET TO THE WATER!
KLK KLK!
HSSS!
C#!
COUGH COUGH
BALOO MUST BE AT HAND. BAGHEERA WOULD NOT HAVE COME ALONE.
THE WHITE SEAL IS COMING AFTER US. THAT'S THE FIRST TIME A SEAL HAS COME TO THE KILLING GROUNDS ALONE.
HSH! DON'T LOOK BEHIND YOU!
THE DISTANCE TO THE KILLING GROUNDS WAS ONLY HALF A MILE BUT IT TOOK AN HOUR TO COVER BECAUSE IF THE SEALS WENT TOO FAST, THEY WOULD GET HEATED & THIER FUR WOULD COME OFF IN PATCHES WHEN THEY WERE SKINNED.
KOTICK DID NOT RECOGNIZE HIS FRIENDS ANYMORE FOR THIER SKINS WERE RIPPED OFF.
HE TURNED & GALLOPED BACK TO THE SEA, HIS LITTLE MUSTACHE BRISTLING WITH HORROR

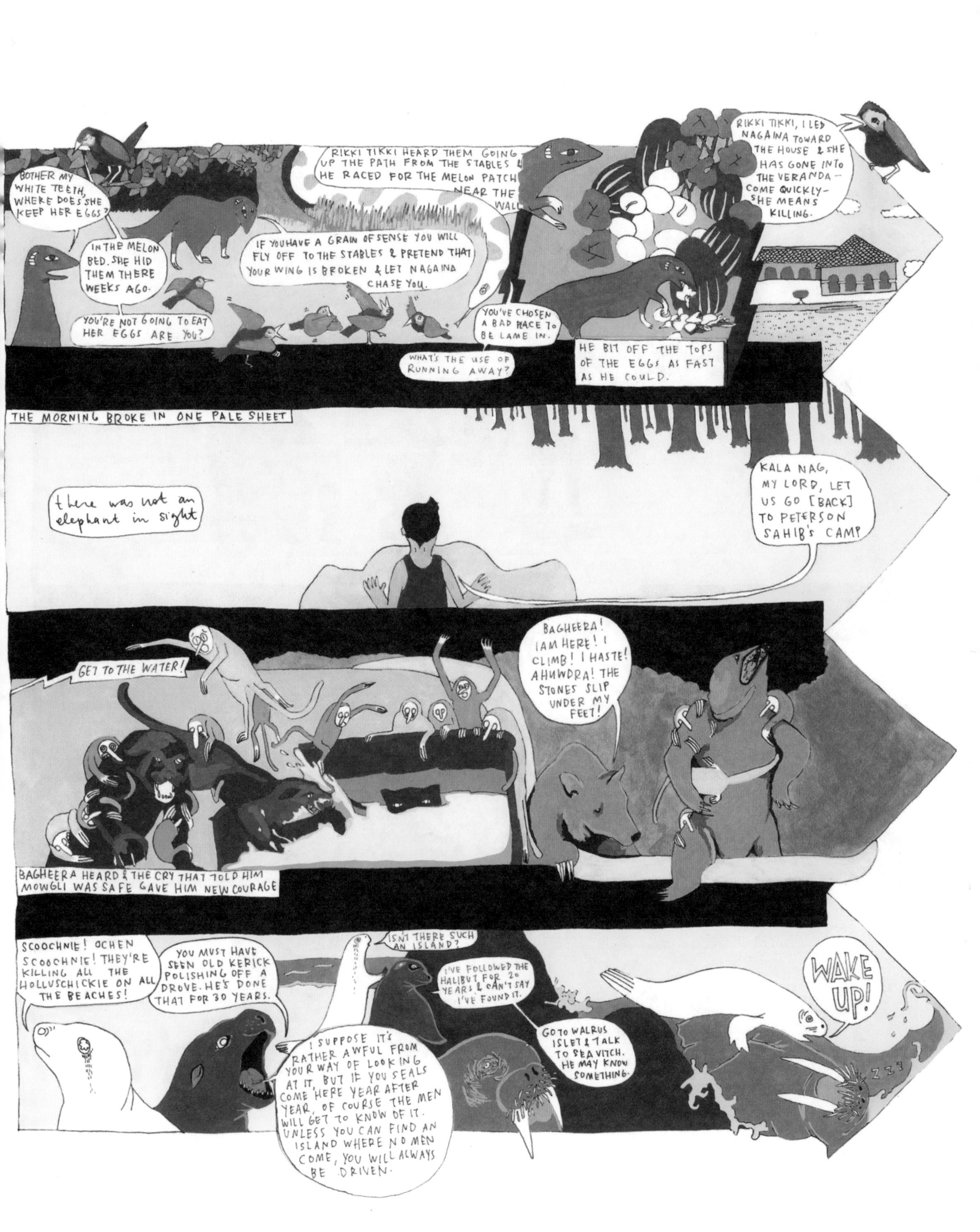
BOTHER MY WHITE TEETH, WHERE DOES SHE KEEP HER EGGS?
IN THE MELON BED. SHE HID THEM THERE WEEKS AGO.
YOU'RE NOT GOING TO EAT HER EGGS ARE YOU?
RIKKI TIKKI HEARD THEM GOING UP THE PATH FROM THE STABLES & HE RACED FOR THE MELON PATCH NEAR THE WALL
IF YOU HAVE A GRAIN OF SENSE YOU WILL FLY OFF TO THE STABLES & PRETEND THAT YOUR WING IS BROKEN & LET NAGAINA CHASE YOU.
YOU'VE CHOSEN A BAD PLACE TO BE LAME IN.
WHAT'S THE USE OF RUNNING AWAY?
HE BIT OFF THE TOPS OF THE EGGS AS FAST AS HE COULD.
RIKKI TIKKI, I LED NAGAINA TOWARD THE HOUSE & SHE HAS GONE INTO THE VERANDA — COME QUICKLY — SHE MEANS KILLING.
THE MORNING BROKE IN ONE PALE SHEET
there was not an elephant in sight
KALA NAG, MY LORD, LET US GO [BACK] TO PETERSON SAHIB'S CAMP
GET TO THE WATER!
BAGHEERA! I AM HERE! I CLIMB! I HASTE! AHUWORA! THE STONES SLIP UNDER MY FEET!
BAGHEERA HEARD & THE CRY THAT TOLD HIM MOWGLI WAS SAFE GAVE HIM NEW COURAGE
SCOOCHNIE! OCHEN SCOOCHNIE! THEY'RE KILLING ALL THE HOLLUSCHICKIE ON ALL THE BEACHES!
YOU MUST HAVE SEEN OLD KERICK POLISHING OFF A DROVE. HE'S DONE THAT FOR 30 YEARS.
ISN'T THERE SUCH AN ISLAND?
I'VE FOLLOWED THE HALIBUT FOR 20 YEARS & CAN'T SAY I'VE FOUND IT.
I SUPPOSE IT'S RATHER AWFUL FROM YOUR WAY OF LOOKING AT IT, BUT IF YOU SEALS COME HERE YEAR AFTER YEAR, OF COURSE THE MEN WILL GET TO KNOW OF IT. UNLESS YOU CAN FIND AN ISLAND WHERE NO MEN COME, YOU WILL ALWAYS BE DRIVEN.
GO TO WALRUS ISLET & TALK TO SEA VITCH. HE MAY KNOW SOMETHING.
WAKE UP!
ZZZ

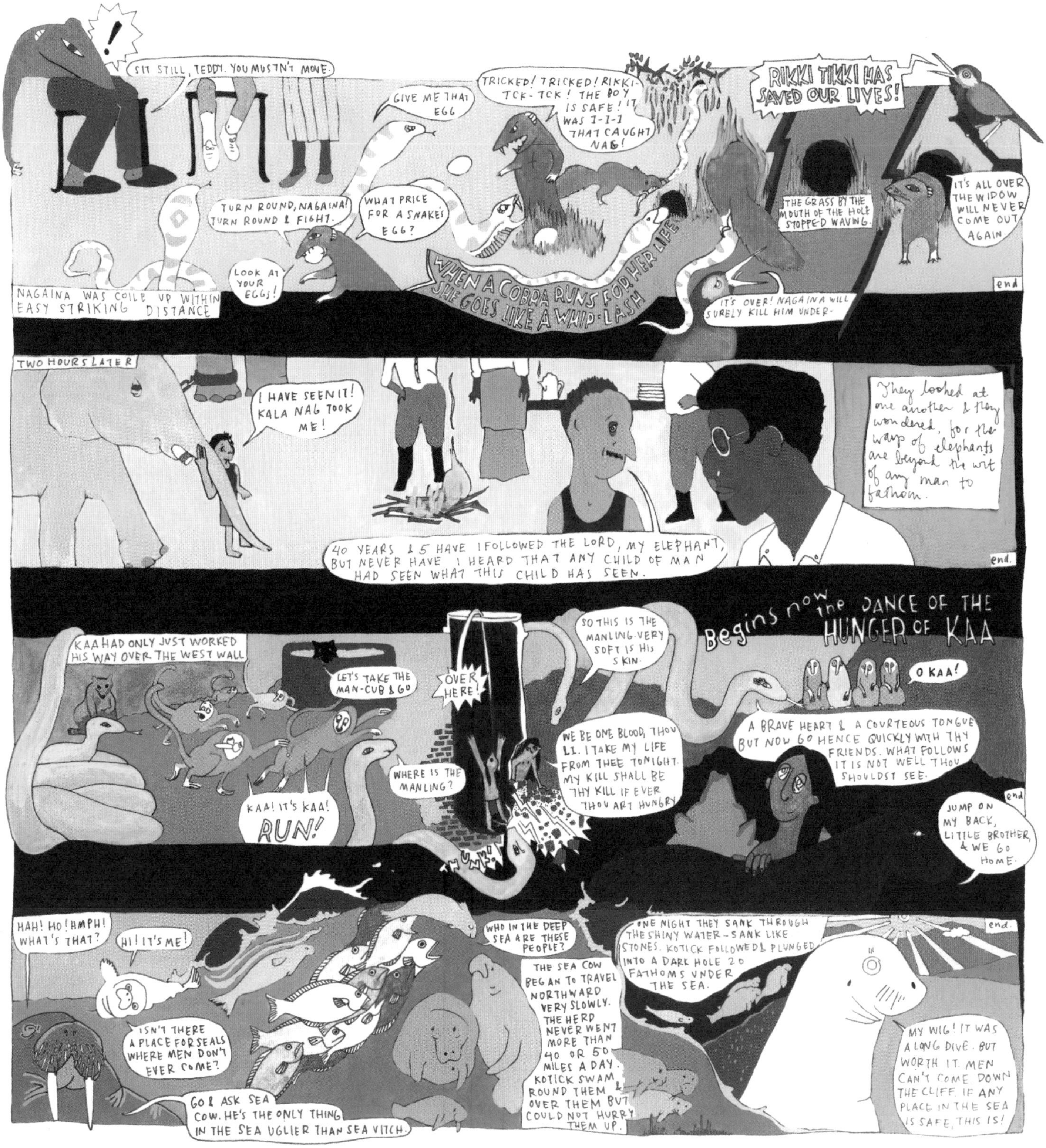
!
SIT STILL, TEDDY. YOU MUSTN'T MOVE.
GIVE ME THAT EGG
TRICKED! TRICKED! RIKKI-TCK-TCK! THE BOY IS SAFE! IT WAS I-I-I THAT CAUGHT NAG!
RIKKI TIKKI HAS SAVED OUR LIVES!
TURN ROUND, NAGAINA! TURN ROUND & FIGHT.
WHAT PRICE FOR A SNAKE'S EGG?
THE GRASS BY THE MOUTH OF THE HOLE STOPPED WAVING.
IT'S ALL OVER THE WIDOW WILL NEVER COME OUT AGAIN.
LOOK AT YOUR EGGS!
WHEN A COBRA RUNS FOR HER LIFE SHE GOES LIKE A WHIP-LASH
NAGAINA WAS COILE UP WITHIN EASY STRIKING DISTANCE
IT'S OVER! NAGAINA WILL SURELY KILL HIM UNDER-
end
TWO HOURS LATER
I HAVE SEEN IT! KALA NAG TOOK ME!
They looked at one another & they wondered, for the ways of elephants are beyond the wit of any man to fathom.
40 YEARS & 5 HAVE I FOLLOWED THE LORD, MY ELEPHANT, BUT NEVER HAVE I HEARD THAT ANY CHILD OF MAN HAD SEEN WHAT THIS CHILD HAS SEEN.
end.
KAA HAD ONLY JUST WORKED HIS WAY OVER THE WEST WALL
LET'S TAKE THE MAN-CUB & GO
OVER HERE!
SO THIS IS THE MANLING. VERY SOFT IS HIS SKIN.
Begins now the DANCE OF THE HUNGER OF KAA
O KAA!
WHERE IS THE MANLING?
WE BE ONE BLOOD, THOU &I. I TAKE MY LIFE FROM THEE TONIGHT. MY KILL SHALL BE THY KILL IF EVER THOU ART HUNGRY
A BRAVE HEART & A COURTEOUS TONGUE BUT NOW GO HENCE QUICKLY WITH THY FRIENDS. WHAT FOLLOWS IT IS NOT WELL THOU SHOULDST SEE.
KAA! IT'S KAA! RUN!
end
JUMP ON MY BACK, LITTLE BROTHER, & WE GO HOME.
HAH! HO! HMPH! WHAT'S THAT?
HI! IT'S ME!
WHO IN THE DEEP SEA ARE THESE PEOPLE?
ONE NIGHT THEY SANK THROUGH THE SHINY WATER-SANK LIKE STONES. KOTICK FOLLOWED & PLUNGED INTO A DARK HOLE 20 FATHOMS UNDER THE SEA.
end.
THE SEA COW BEGAN TO TRAVEL NORTHWARD VERY SLOWLY. THE HERD NEVER WENT MORE THAN 40 OR 50 MILES A DAY. KOTICK SWAM ROUND THEM & OVER THEM BUT COULD NOT HURRY THEM UP.
ISN'T THERE A PLACE FOR SEALS WHERE MEN DON'T EVER COME?
GO & ASK SEA COW. HE'S THE ONLY THING IN THE SEA UGLIER THAN SEA VITCH.
MY WIG! IT WAS A LONG DIVE. BUT WORTH IT. MEN CAN'T COME DOWN THE CLIFF IF ANY PLACE IN THE SEA IS SAFE, THIS IS!

# H. G. Wells

ART/ADAPTATION BY **Matthew Houston**

**H. G. WELLS WROTE OVER 120 BOOKS IN NUMER-OUS** genres over the course of fifty years, but we remember him mostly for several novels from the 1890s that helped to create and define science fiction. Under the guise of a groundbreaking story involving traveling through time into the far future, Wells speculates about the future of the human race, particularly social relations—class, work versus leisure, safety and violence, and other heavy issues.

The Time Machine has undergone the same cultural recat-aloging as 20,000 Leagues Under the Sea and Gulliver's Travels. These works are filled with trenchant sociopolitical commentary. They're complex, dark works of literature not intended for children. Yet, the surface action of each one can be immensely appealing to younger readers. Via adaptations for movies, TV, comics, and abridged texts, The Time Machine has been presented in a way that maximizes this appeal, and, in a case of self-fulfilling prophecy, it has become a children's classic (as have 20,000 Leagues and Gulliver).

Matthew Houston has several distinct styles of illustra-tion, any of which would've made a memorable visual treat of an adaptation. He chose to use his geometric style, with its flattened perspective and bright colors. The intri-cacy, simplicity, and repeating elements bring to mind diagrams and charts, perfect for a work of science fiction.

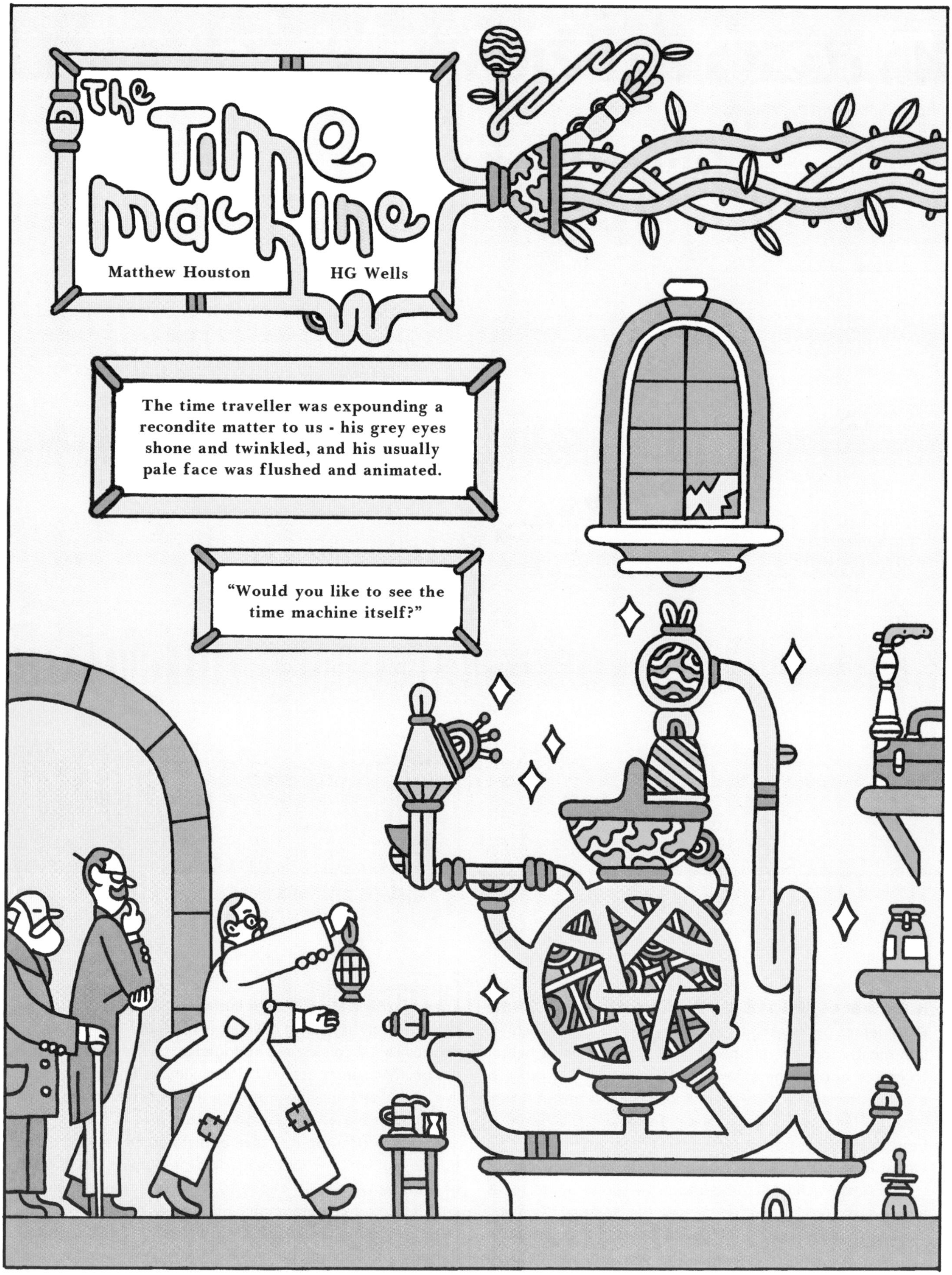
The Time Machine
Matthew Houston
HG Wells
The time traveller was expounding a recondite matter to us - his grey eyes shone and twinkled, and his usually pale face was flushed and animated.
"Would you like to see the time machine itself?"

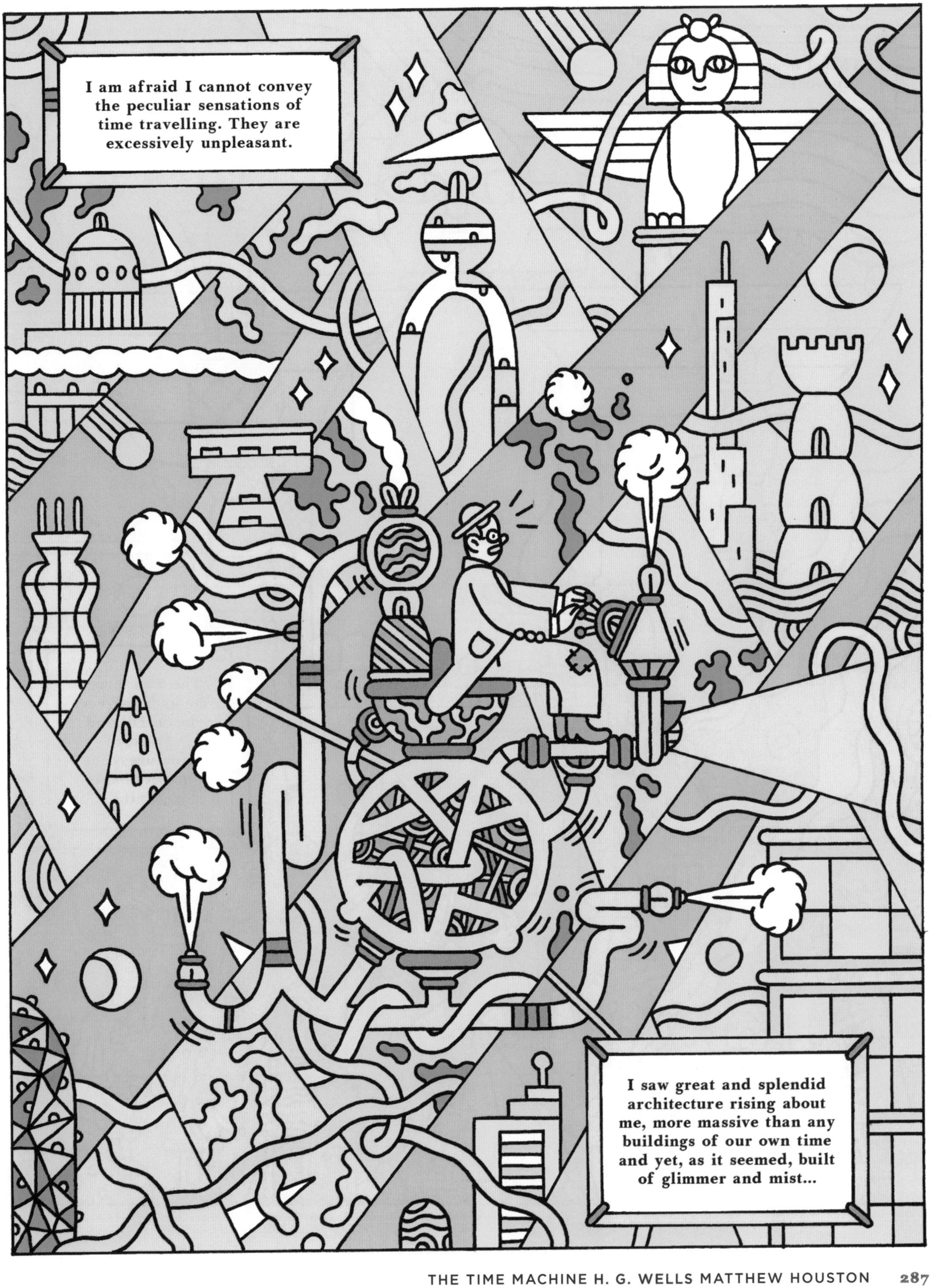
I am afraid I cannot convey the peculiar sensations of time travelling. They are excessively unpleasant.
I saw great and splendid architecture rising about me, more massive than any buildings of our own time and yet, as it seemed, built of glimmer and mist...

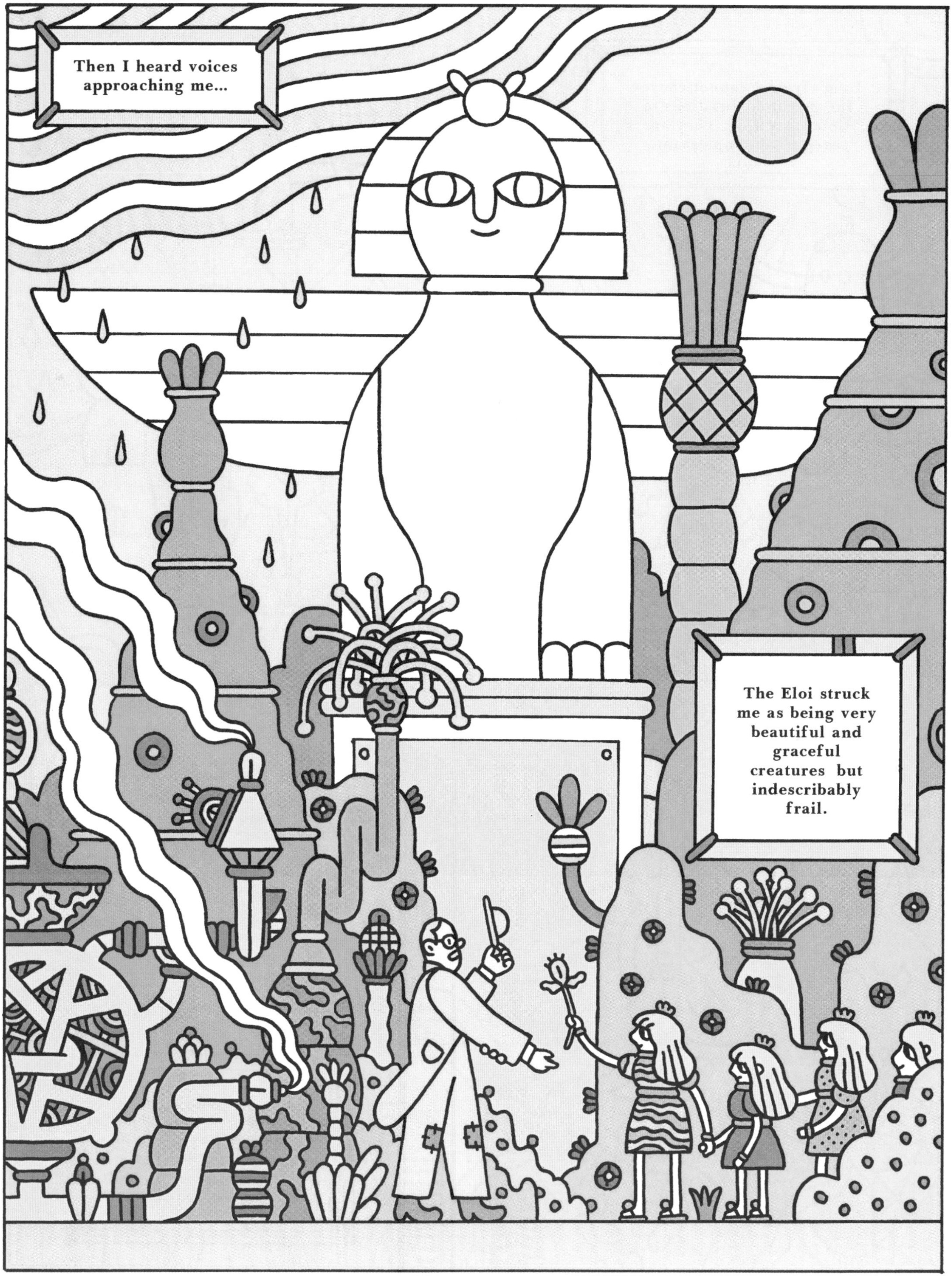
Then I heard voices approaching me...
The Eloi struck me as being very beautiful and graceful creatures but indescribably frail.

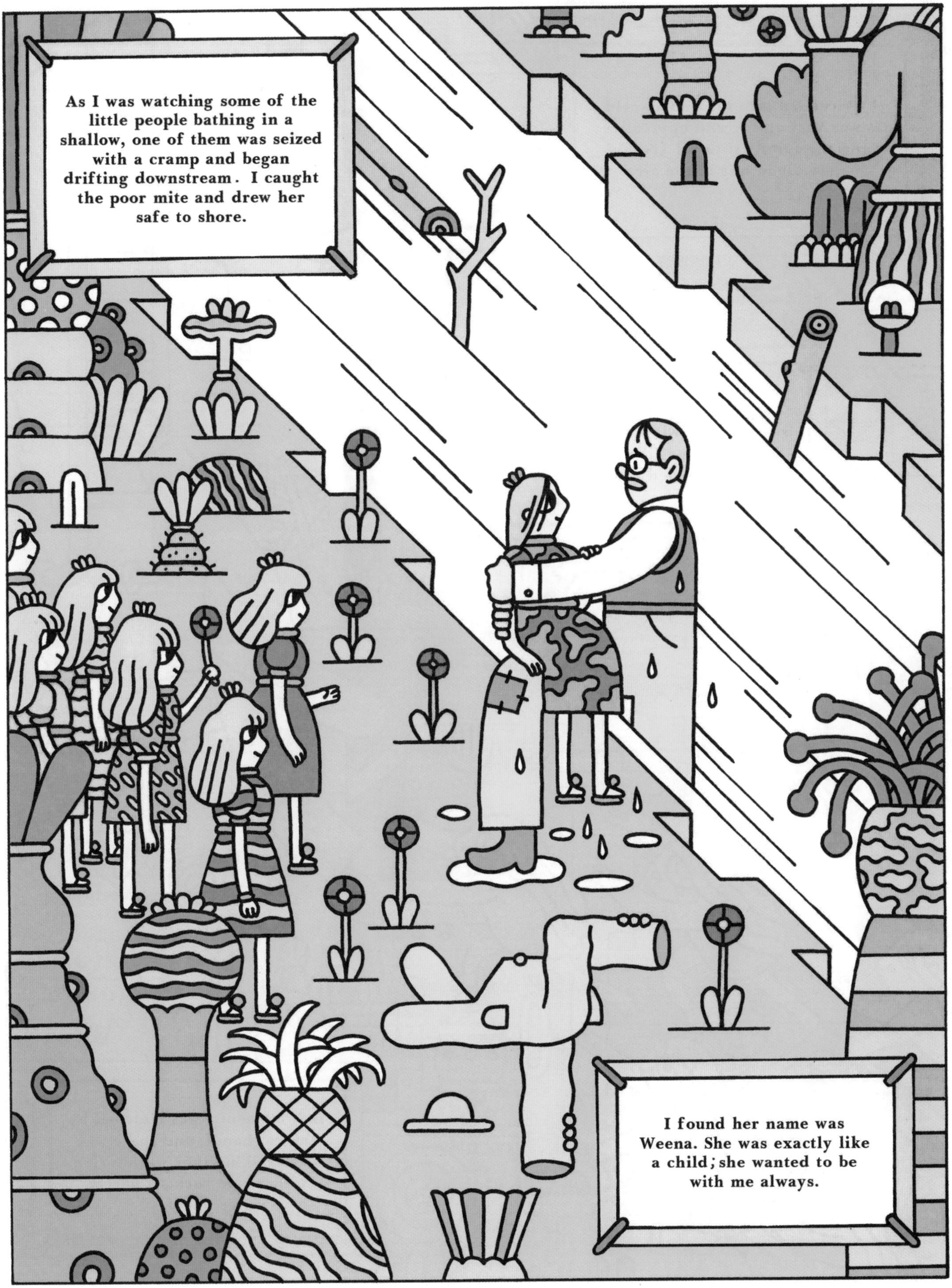
As I was watching some of the little people bathing in a shallow, one of them was seized with a cramp and began drifting downstream. I caught the poor mite and drew her safe to shore.
I found her name was Weena. She was exactly like a child; she wanted to be with me always.

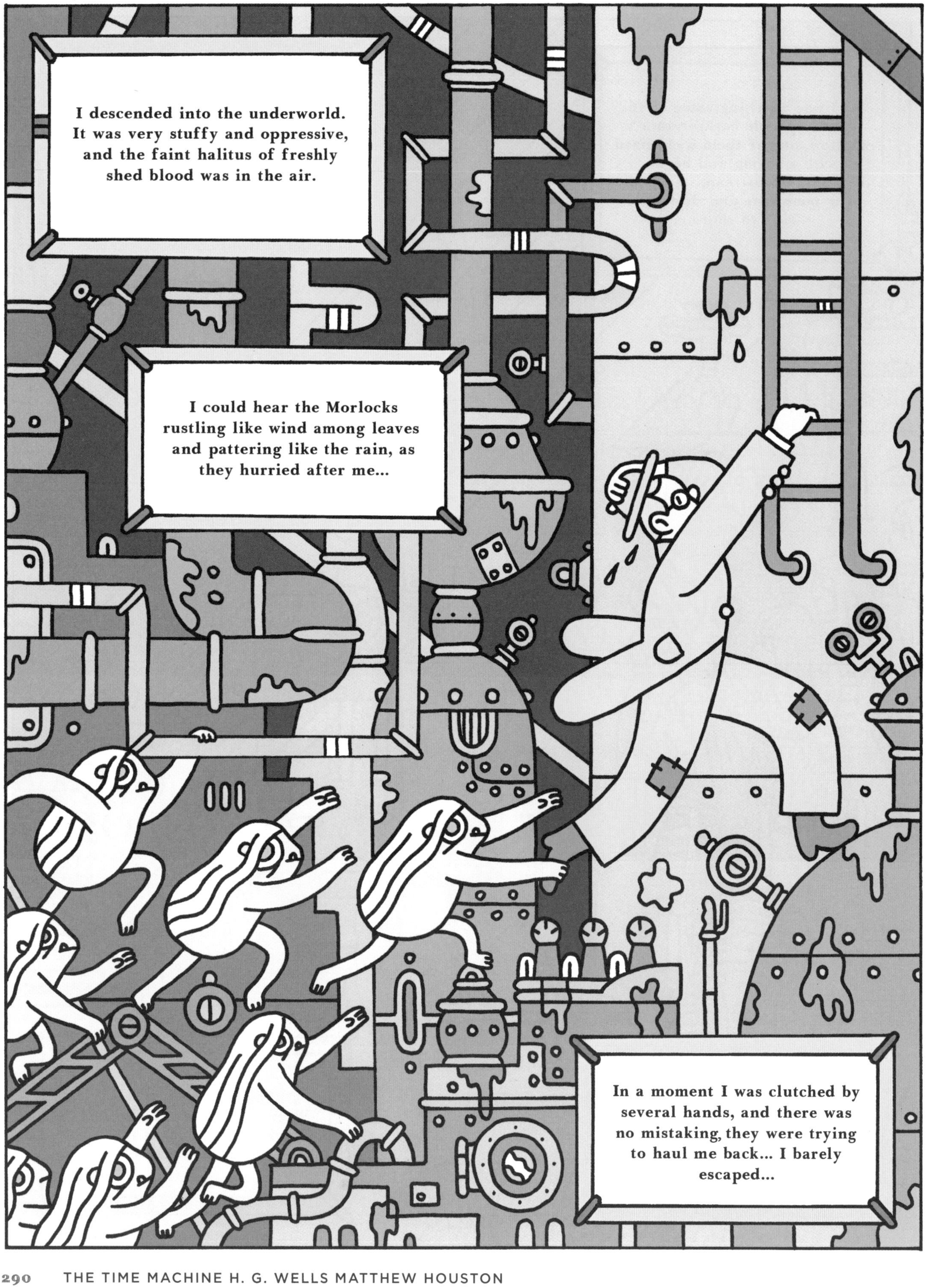
I descended into the underworld. It was very stuffy and oppressive, and the faint halitus of freshly shed blood was in the air.
I could hear the Morlocks rustling like wind among leaves and pattering like the rain, as they hurried after me...
In a moment I was clutched by several hands, and there was no mistaking, they were trying to haul me back... I barely escaped...

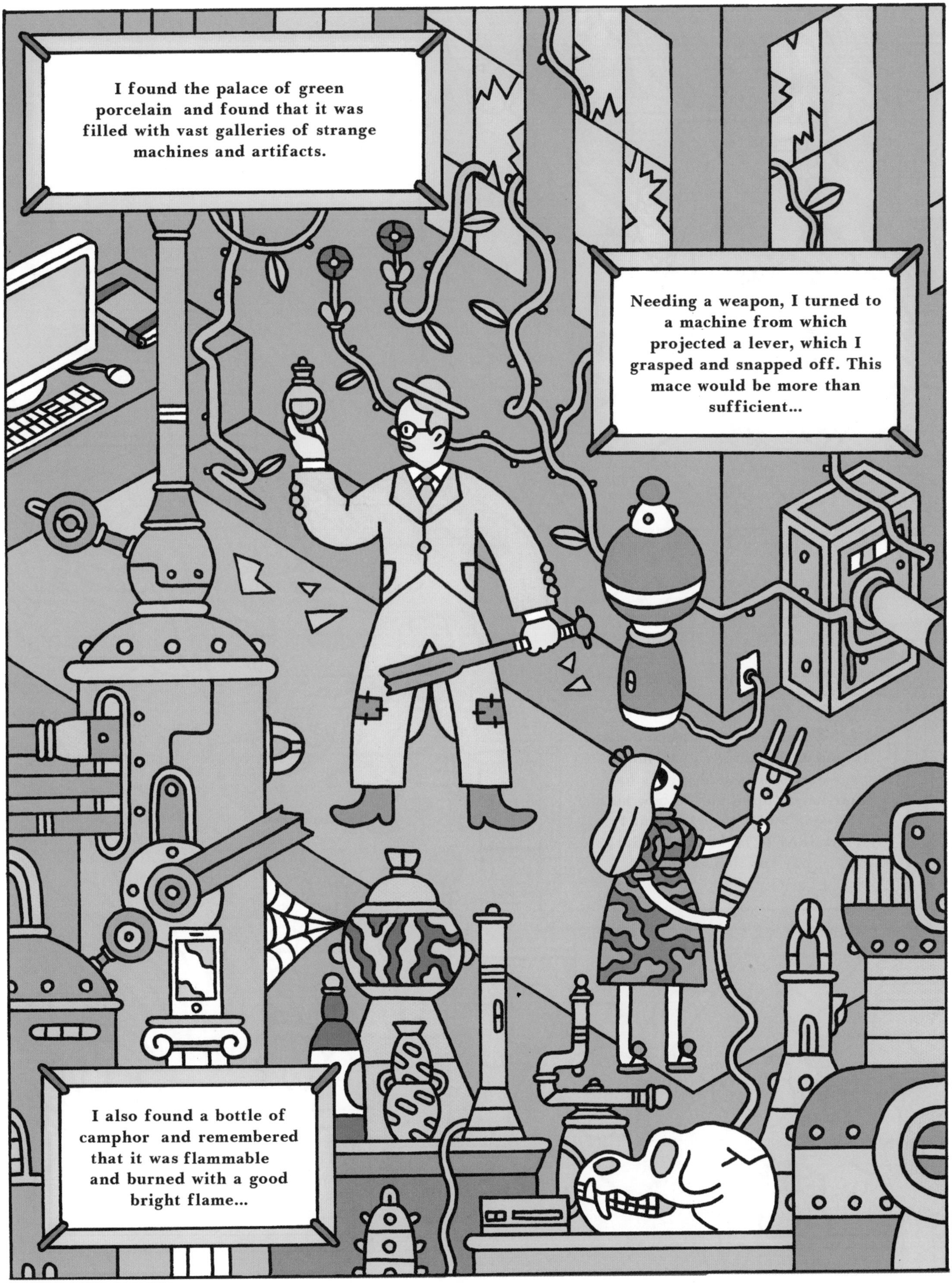
I found the palace of green porcelain and found that it was filled with vast galleries of strange machines and artifacts.
Needing a weapon, I turned to a machine from which projected a lever, which I grasped and snapped off. This mace would be more than sufficient...
I also found a bottle of camphor and remembered that it was flammable and burned with a good bright flame...

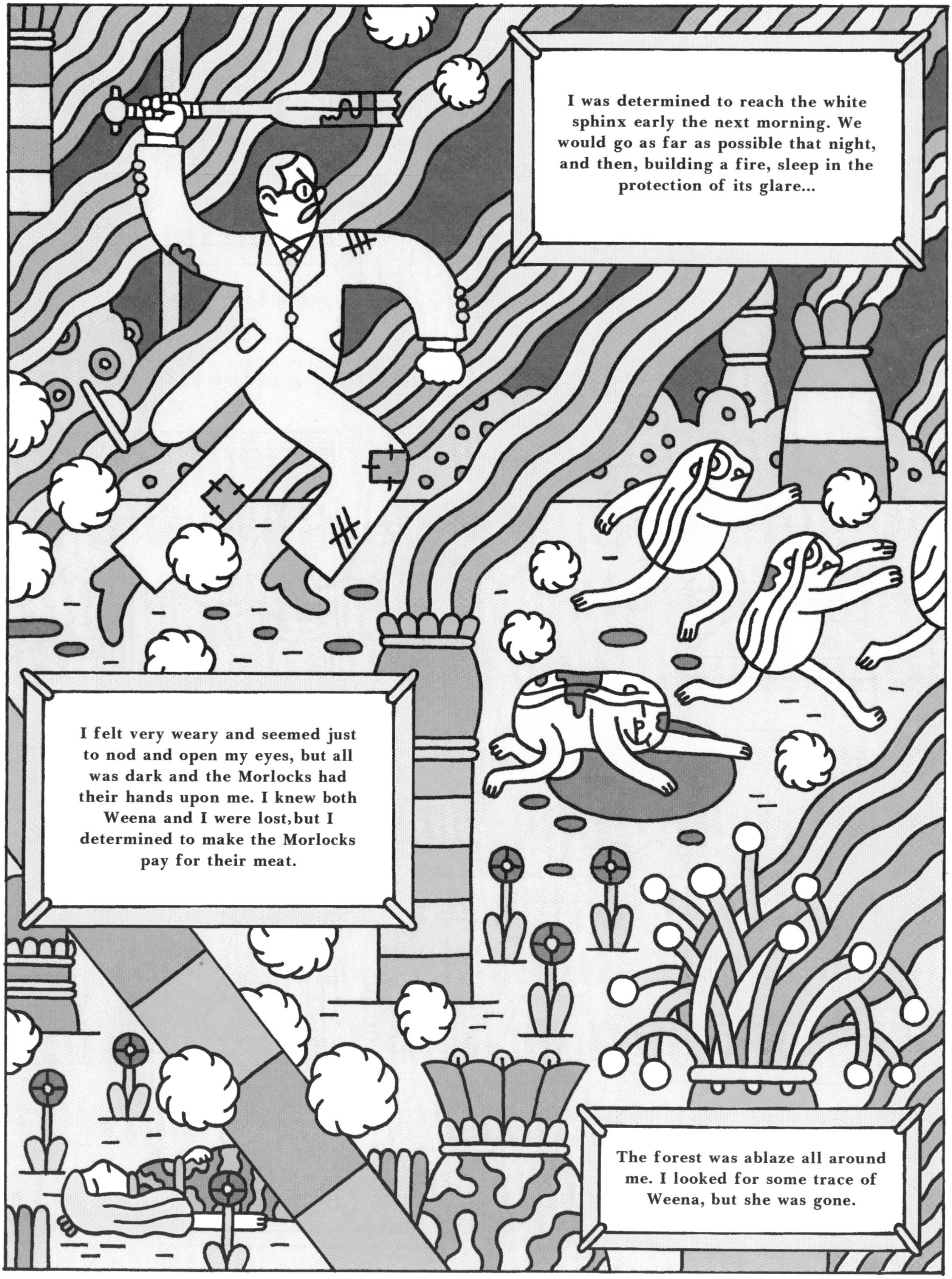
I was determined to reach the white sphinx early the next morning. We would go as far as possible that night, and then, building a fire, sleep in the protection of its glare...
I felt very weary and seemed just to nod and open my eyes, but all was dark and the Morlocks had their hands upon me. I knew both Weena and I were lost, but I determined to make the Morlocks pay for their meat.
The forest was ablaze all around me. I looked for some trace of Weena, but she was gone.

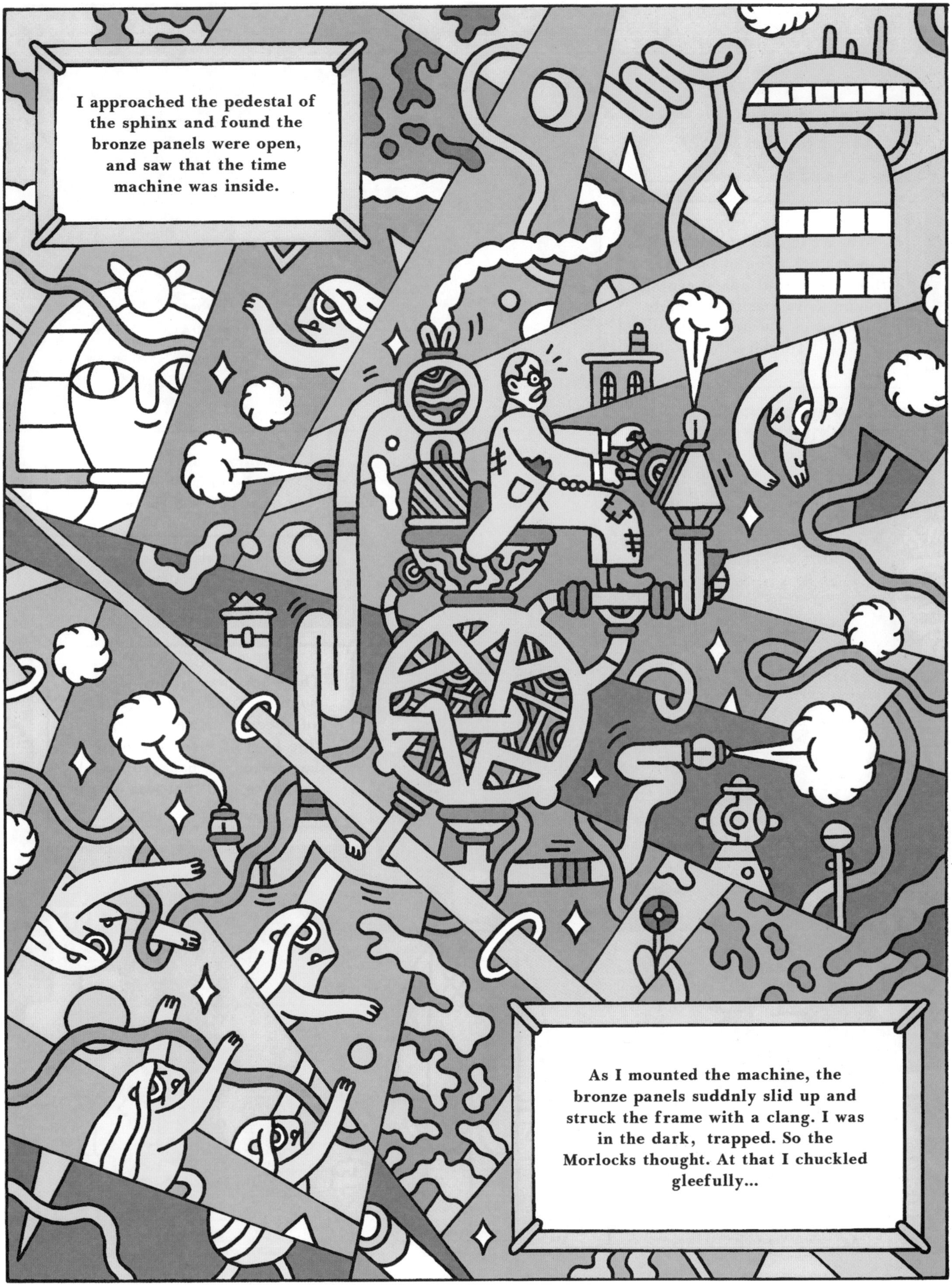
I approached the pedestal of the sphinx and found the bronze panels were open, and saw that the time machine was inside.
As I mounted the machine, the bronze panels suddnly slid up and struck the frame with a clang. I was in the dark, trapped. So the Morlocks thought. At that I chuckled gleefully...

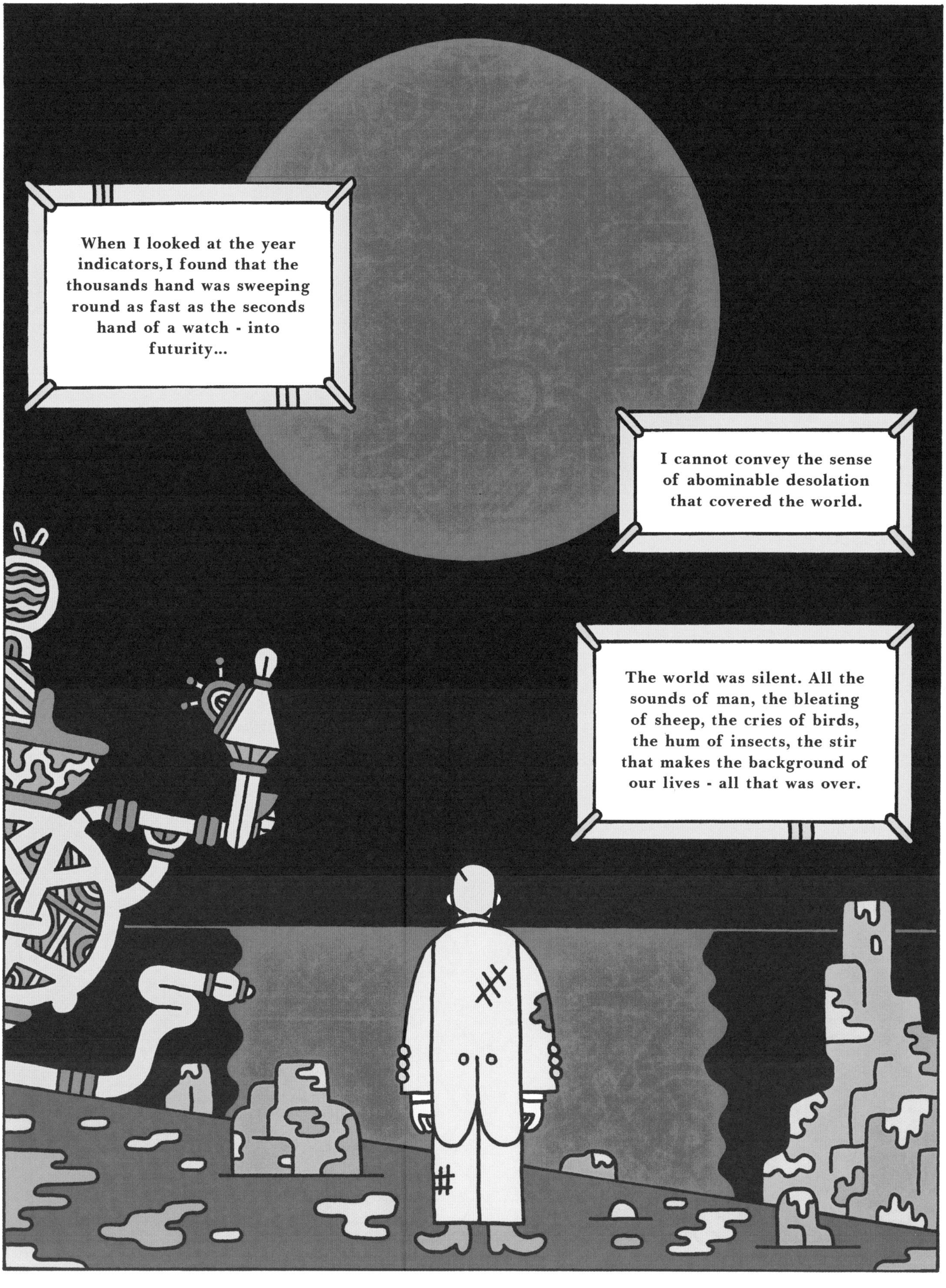
When I looked at the year indicators, I found that the thousands hand was sweeping round as fast as the seconds hand of a watch - into futurity...
I cannot convey the sense of abominable desolation that covered the world.
The world was silent. All the sounds of man, the bleating of sheep, the cries of birds, the hum of insects, the stir that makes the background of our lives - all that was over.

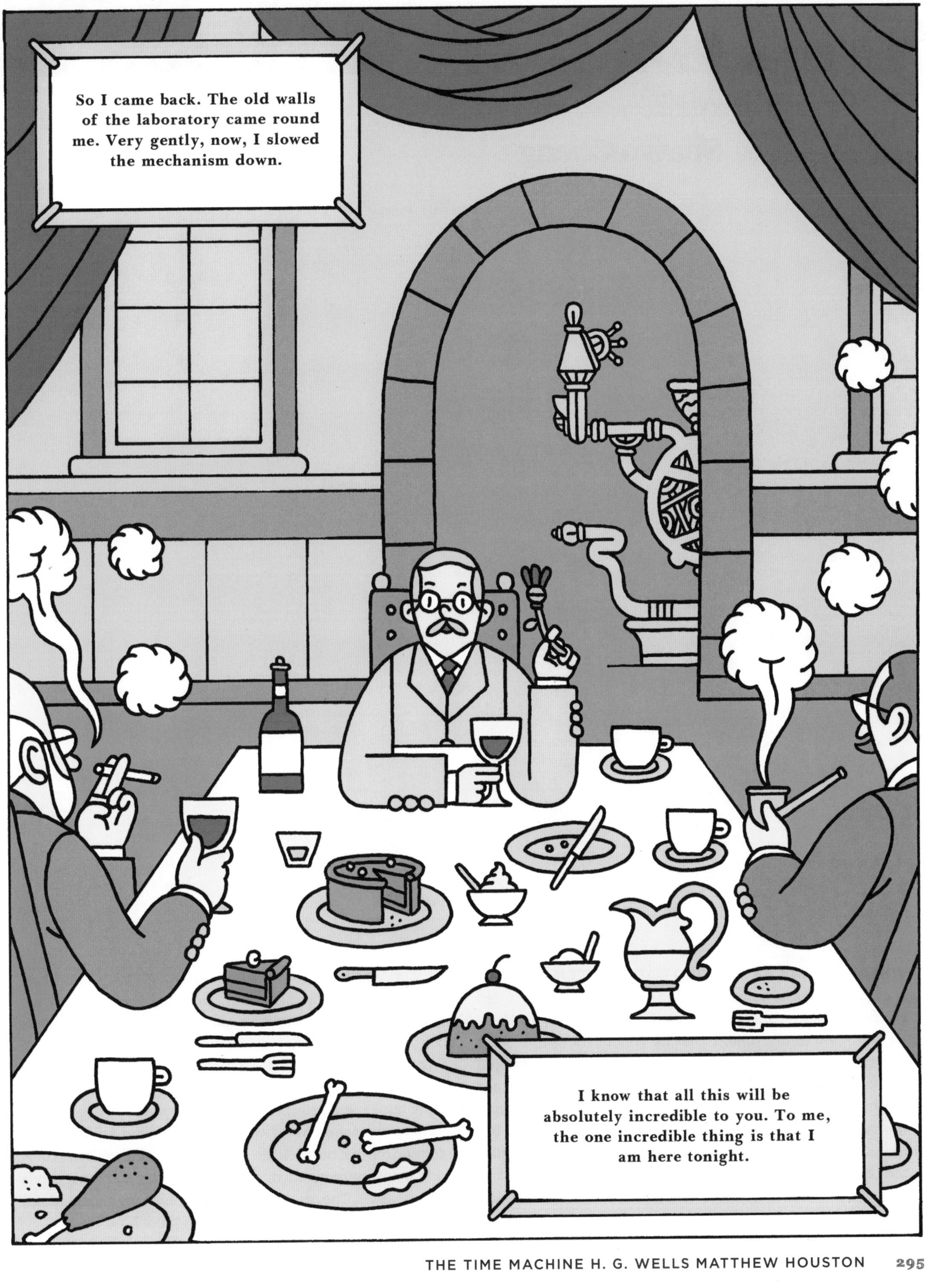
So I came back. The old walls of the laboratory came round me. Very gently, now, I slowed the mechanism down.
I know that all this will be absolutely incredible to you. To me, the one incredible thing is that I am here tonight.

# The Oz series

## L. Frank Baum

ART/ADAPTATION BY **Shawn Cheng**

**WHEN L. FRANK BAUM—WHO HAD WRITTEN A HIGHLY** successful book of nonsense poems—spontaneously started telling his kids about a land called Oz one day in 1899, he probably didn't realize that he was birthing the Great American Children's Novel. The gorgeous, lavishly illustrated book that resulted the next year, *The Wonderful Wizard of Oz,* was an instant smash success. A "musical extravaganza" based on the novel was a long-running hit in the first decade of the twentieth century, and the 1939 MGM film adaptation with Judy Garland—although overlooked at first—eventually became one of the most popular and important movies of all time.

Baum wrote thirteen further books in the series (two were published after his death). Imagine my delight when Shawn Cheng told me that he wanted to adapt *all* of Baum's Oz novels for this volume.

The quixotic nature of this scheme entranced me from the beginning. Shawn was to adapt each of the fourteen books in a single, huge page. (His original artwork measures twenty-four by thirty-six inches! Yes, two feet wide, a yard tall.) Then he informed me that he would be doing this epic adaptation in color, using a palette reminiscent of the old Sunday comics sections in newspapers. The results were beyond even my expectations: an instant comics masterpiece. Revel in them now. Go.

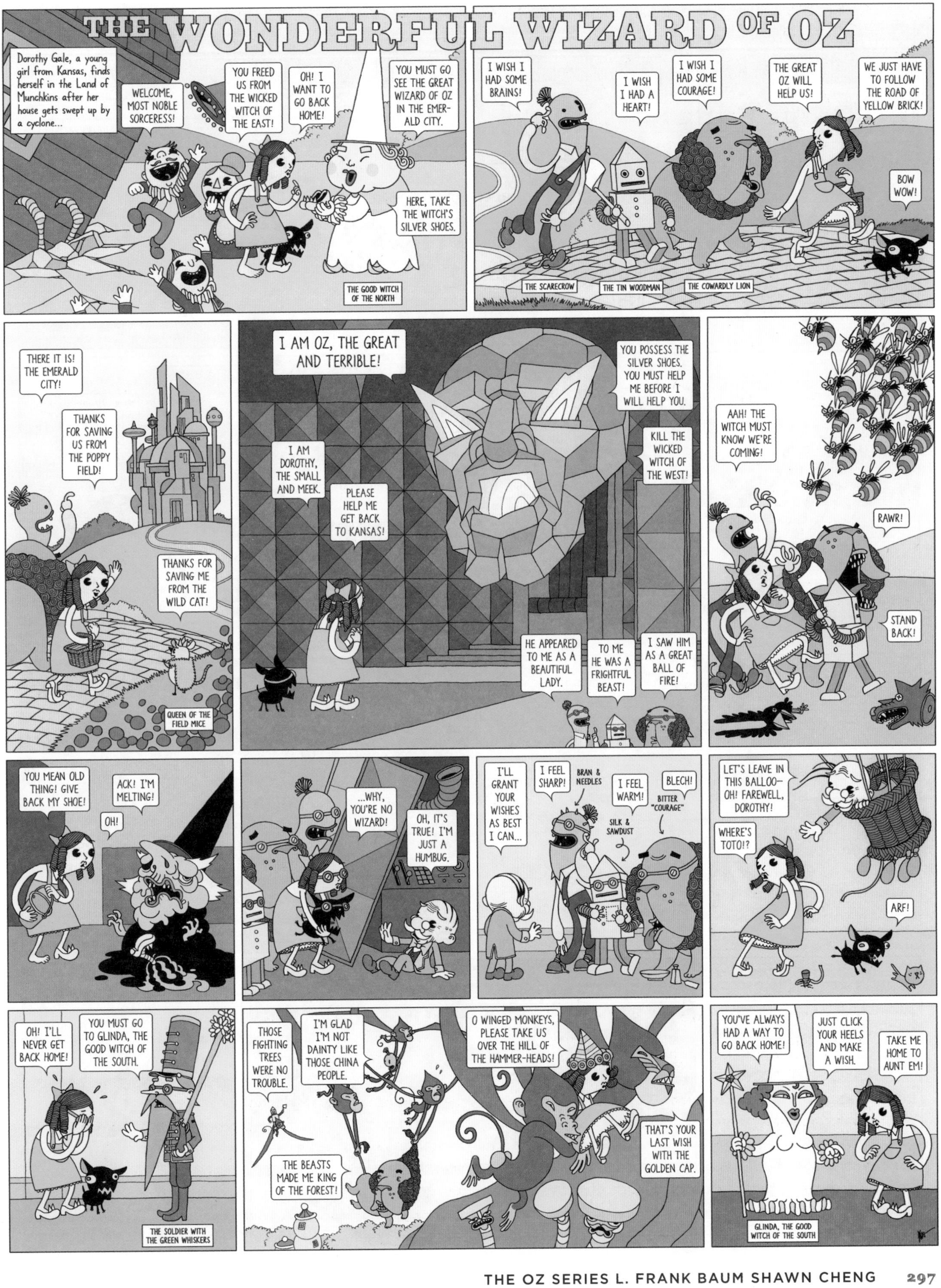
THE WONDERFUL WIZARD OF OZ
Dorothy Gale, a young girl from Kansas, finds herself in the Land of Munchkins after her house gets swept up by a cyclone...
WELCOME, MOST NOBLE SORCERESS!
YOU FREED US FROM THE WICKED WITCH OF THE EAST!
OH! I WANT TO GO BACK HOME!
YOU MUST GO SEE THE GREAT WIZARD OF OZ IN THE EMERALD CITY.
HERE, TAKE THE WITCH'S SILVER SHOES.
THE GOOD WITCH OF THE NORTH
I WISH I HAD SOME BRAINS!
I WISH I HAD A HEART!
I WISH I HAD SOME COURAGE!
THE GREAT OZ WILL HELP US!
WE JUST HAVE TO FOLLOW THE ROAD OF YELLOW BRICK!
BOW WOW!
THE SCARECROW
THE TIN WOODMAN
THE COWARDLY LION
THERE IT IS! THE EMERALD CITY!
THANKS FOR SAVING US FROM THE POPPY FIELD!
THANKS FOR SAVING ME FROM THE WILD CAT!
QUEEN OF THE FIELD MICE
I AM OZ, THE GREAT AND TERRIBLE!
YOU POSSESS THE SILVER SHOES. YOU MUST HELP ME BEFORE I WILL HELP YOU.
I AM DOROTHY, THE SMALL AND MEEK.
PLEASE HELP ME GET BACK TO KANSAS!
KILL THE WICKED WITCH OF THE WEST!
HE APPEARED TO ME AS A BEAUTIFUL LADY.
TO ME HE WAS A FRIGHTFUL BEAST!
I SAW HIM AS A GREAT BALL OF FIRE!
AAH! THE WITCH MUST KNOW WE'RE COMING!
RAWR!
STAND BACK!
YOU MEAN OLD THING! GIVE BACK MY SHOE!
ACK! I'M MELTING!
OH!
...WHY, YOU'RE NO WIZARD!
OH, IT'S TRUE! I'M JUST A HUMBUG.
I'LL GRANT YOUR WISHES AS BEST I CAN...
I FEEL SHARP!
BRAN & NEEDLES
I FEEL WARM!
SILK & SAWDUST
BLECH!
BITTER "COURAGE"
LET'S LEAVE IN THIS BALLOO— OH! FAREWELL, DOROTHY!
WHERE'S TOTO!?
ARF!
OH! I'LL NEVER GET BACK HOME!
YOU MUST GO TO GLINDA, THE GOOD WITCH OF THE SOUTH.
THE SOLDIER WITH THE GREEN WHISKERS
THOSE FIGHTING TREES WERE NO TROUBLE.
I'M GLAD I'M NOT DAINTY LIKE THOSE CHINA PEOPLE.
O WINGED MONKEYS, PLEASE TAKE US OVER THE HILL OF THE HAMMER-HEADS!
THE BEASTS MADE ME KING OF THE FOREST!
THAT'S YOUR LAST WISH WITH THE GOLDEN CAP.
YOU'VE ALWAYS HAD A WAY TO GO BACK HOME!
JUST CLICK YOUR HEELS AND MAKE A WISH.
TAKE ME HOME TO AUNT EM!
GLINDA, THE GOOD WITCH OF THE SOUTH

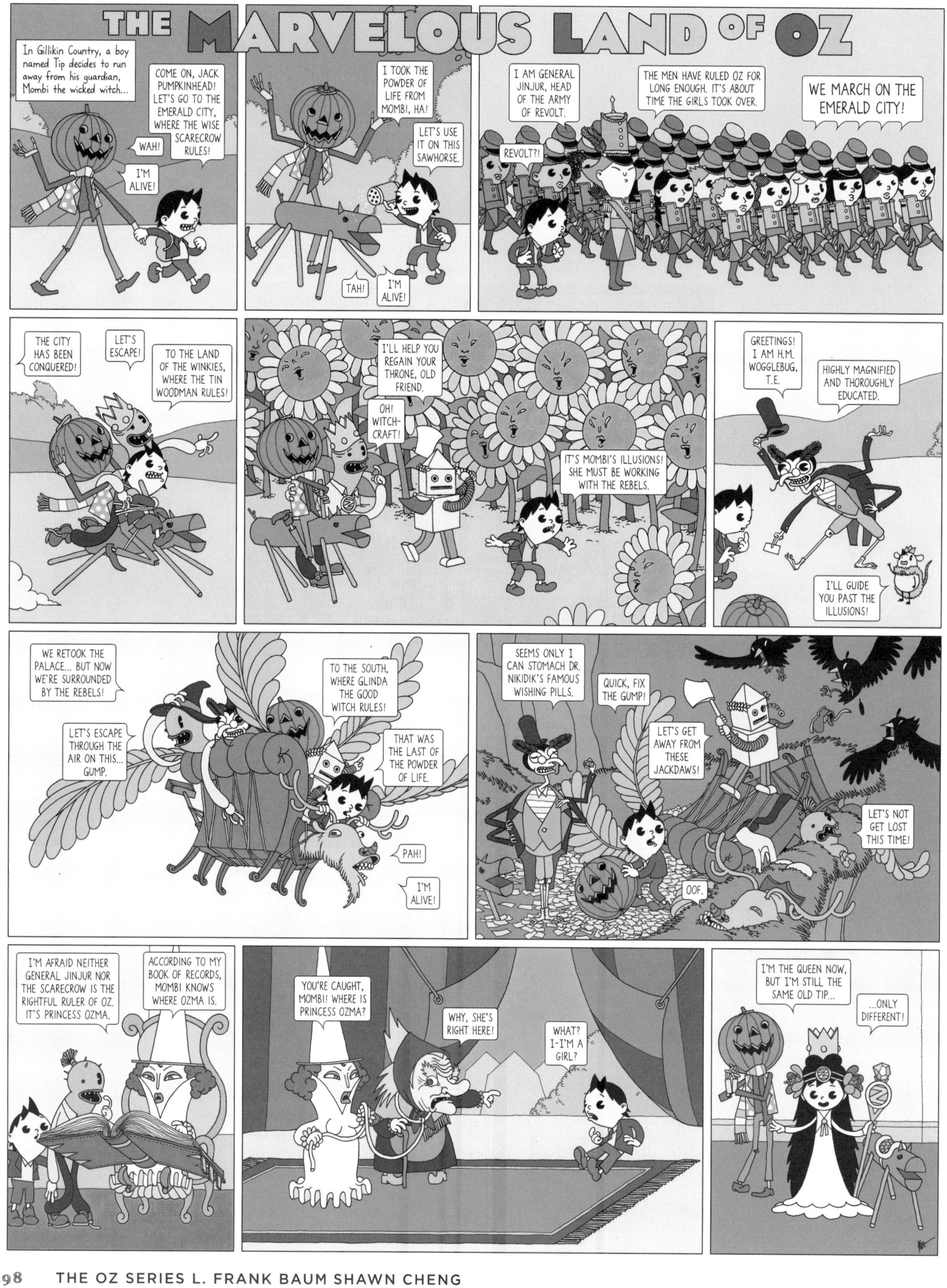

THE MARVELOUS LAND OF OZ
In Gillikin Country, a boy named Tip decides to run away from his guardian, Mombi the wicked witch...
COME ON, JACK PUMPKINHEAD! LET'S GO TO THE EMERALD CITY, WHERE THE WISE SCARECROW RULES!
WAH!
I'M ALIVE!
I TOOK THE POWDER OF LIFE FROM MOMBI, HA!
LET'S USE IT ON THIS SAWHORSE.
TAH!
I'M ALIVE!
I AM GENERAL JINJUR, HEAD OF THE ARMY OF REVOLT.
THE MEN HAVE RULED OZ FOR LONG ENOUGH. IT'S ABOUT TIME THE GIRLS TOOK OVER.
WE MARCH ON THE EMERALD CITY!
REVOLT?!
THE CITY HAS BEEN CONQUERED!
LET'S ESCAPE!
TO THE LAND OF THE WINKIES, WHERE THE TIN WOODMAN RULES!
I'LL HELP YOU REGAIN YOUR THRONE, OLD FRIEND.
OH! WITCH-CRAFT!
IT'S MOMBI'S ILLUSIONS! SHE MUST BE WORKING WITH THE REBELS.
GREETINGS! I AM H.M. WOGGLEBUG, T.E.
HIGHLY MAGNIFIED AND THOROUGHLY EDUCATED.
I'LL GUIDE YOU PAST THE ILLUSIONS!
WE RETOOK THE PALACE... BUT NOW WE'RE SURROUNDED BY THE REBELS!
TO THE SOUTH, WHERE GLINDA THE GOOD WITCH RULES!
LET'S ESCAPE THROUGH THE AIR ON THIS... GUMP.
THAT WAS THE LAST OF THE POWDER OF LIFE.
PAH!
I'M ALIVE!
SEEMS ONLY I CAN STOMACH DR. NIKIDIK'S FAMOUS WISHING PILLS.
QUICK, FIX THE GUMP!
LET'S GET AWAY FROM THESE JACKDAWS!
LET'S NOT GET LOST THIS TIME!
OOF.
I'M AFRAID NEITHER GENERAL JINJUR NOR THE SCARECROW IS THE RIGHTFUL RULER OF OZ. IT'S PRINCESS OZMA.
ACCORDING TO MY BOOK OF RECORDS, MOMBI KNOWS WHERE OZMA IS.
YOU'RE CAUGHT, MOMBI! WHERE IS PRINCESS OZMA?
WHY, SHE'S RIGHT HERE!
WHAT? I-I'M A GIRL?
I'M THE QUEEN NOW, BUT I'M STILL THE SAME OLD TIP...
...ONLY DIFFERENT!

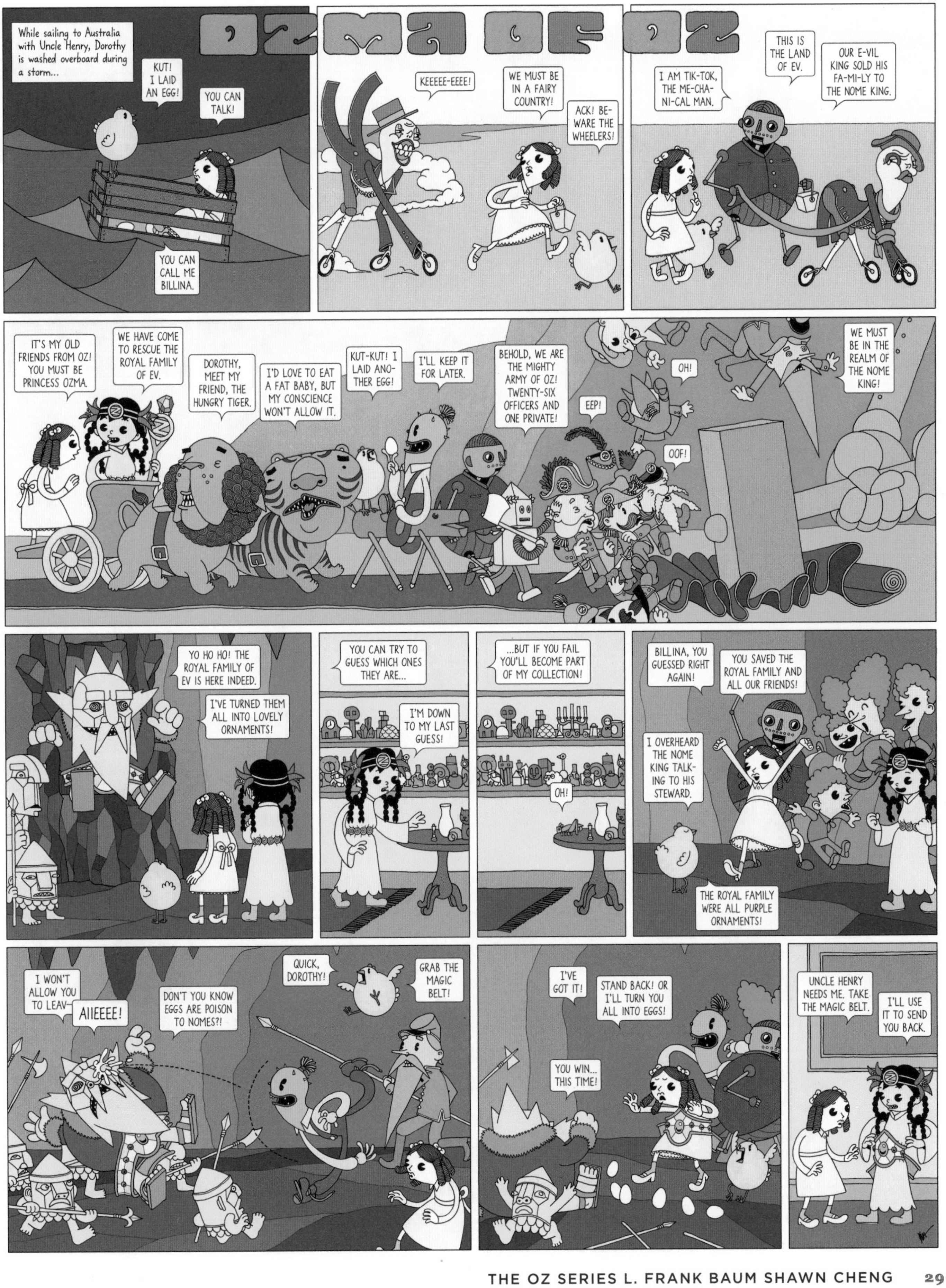
OZMA OF OZ
While sailing to Australia with Uncle Henry, Dorothy is washed overboard during a storm...
KUT! I LAID AN EGG!
YOU CAN TALK!
YOU CAN CALL ME BILLINA.
KEEEEE-EEEE!
WE MUST BE IN A FAIRY COUNTRY!
ACK! BE-WARE THE WHEELERS!
I AM TIK-TOK, THE ME-CHA-NI-CAL MAN.
THIS IS THE LAND OF EV.
OUR E-VIL KING SOLD HIS FA-MI-LY TO THE NOME KING.
IT'S MY OLD FRIENDS FROM OZ! YOU MUST BE PRINCESS OZMA.
WE HAVE COME TO RESCUE THE ROYAL FAMILY OF EV.
DOROTHY, MEET MY FRIEND, THE HUNGRY TIGER.
I'D LOVE TO EAT A FAT BABY, BUT MY CONSCIENCE WON'T ALLOW IT.
KUT-KUT! I LAID ANO-THER EGG!
I'LL KEEP IT FOR LATER.
BEHOLD, WE ARE THE MIGHTY ARMY OF OZ! TWENTY-SIX OFFICERS AND ONE PRIVATE!
EEP!
OH!
OOF!
WE MUST BE IN THE REALM OF THE NOME KING!
YO HO HO! THE ROYAL FAMILY OF EV IS HERE INDEED.
I'VE TURNED THEM ALL INTO LOVELY ORNAMENTS!
YOU CAN TRY TO GUESS WHICH ONES THEY ARE...
I'M DOWN TO MY LAST GUESS!
...BUT IF YOU FAIL YOU'LL BECOME PART OF MY COLLECTION!
OH!
BILLINA, YOU GUESSED RIGHT AGAIN!
YOU SAVED THE ROYAL FAMILY AND ALL OUR FRIENDS!
I OVERHEARD THE NOME KING TALK-ING TO HIS STEWARD.
THE ROYAL FAMILY WERE ALL PURPLE ORNAMENTS!
I WON'T ALLOW YOU TO LEAV–
AIIEEEE!
DON'T YOU KNOW EGGS ARE POISON TO NOMES?!
QUICK, DOROTHY!
GRAB THE MAGIC BELT!
I'VE GOT IT!
STAND BACK! OR I'LL TURN YOU ALL INTO EGGS!
YOU WIN... THIS TIME!
UNCLE HENRY NEEDS ME. TAKE THE MAGIC BELT.
I'LL USE IT TO SEND YOU BACK.

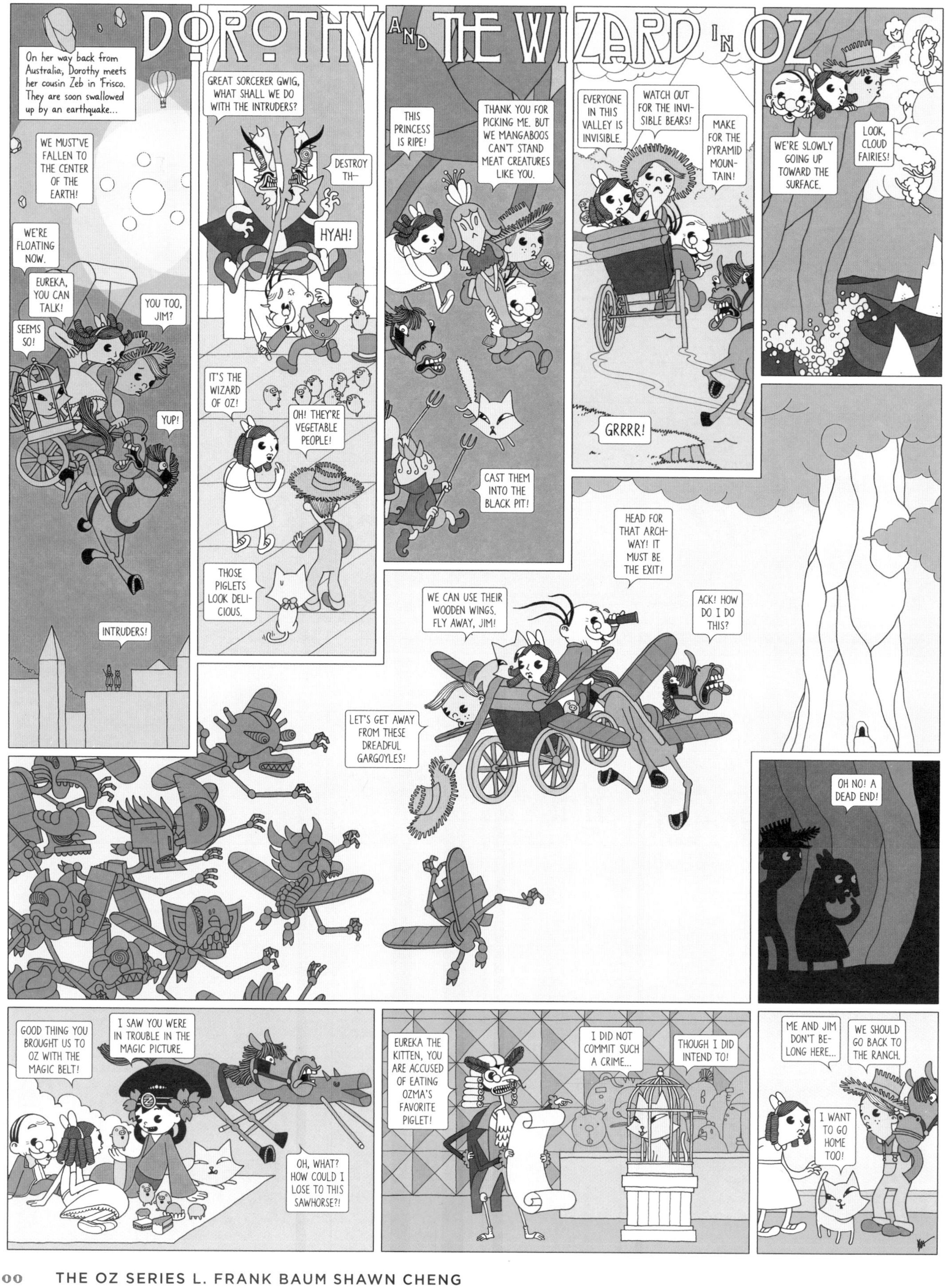
DOROTHY AND THE WIZARD IN OZ
On her way back from Australia, Dorothy meets her cousin Zeb in 'Frisco. They are soon swallowed up by an earthquake...
WE MUST'VE FALLEN TO THE CENTER OF THE EARTH!
WE'RE FLOATING NOW.
EUREKA, YOU CAN TALK!
SEEMS SO!
YOU TOO, JIM?
YUP!
INTRUDERS!
GREAT SORCERER GWIG, WHAT SHALL WE DO WITH THE INTRUDERS?
DESTROY TH-
HYAH!
IT'S THE WIZARD OF OZ!
OH! THEY'RE VEGETABLE PEOPLE!
THOSE PIGLETS LOOK DELICIOUS.
THIS PRINCESS IS RIPE!
THANK YOU FOR PICKING ME. BUT WE MANGABOOS CAN'T STAND MEAT CREATURES LIKE YOU.
CAST THEM INTO THE BLACK PIT!
EVERYONE IN THIS VALLEY IS INVISIBLE.
WATCH OUT FOR THE INVISIBLE BEARS!
MAKE FOR THE PYRAMID MOUNTAIN!
GRRRR!
WE'RE SLOWLY GOING UP TOWARD THE SURFACE.
LOOK, CLOUD FAIRIES!
HEAD FOR THAT ARCHWAY! IT MUST BE THE EXIT!
WE CAN USE THEIR WOODEN WINGS. FLY AWAY, JIM!
ACK! HOW DO I DO THIS?
LET'S GET AWAY FROM THESE DREADFUL GARGOYLES!
OH NO! A DEAD END!
GOOD THING YOU BROUGHT US TO OZ WITH THE MAGIC BELT!
I SAW YOU WERE IN TROUBLE IN THE MAGIC PICTURE.
OH, WHAT? HOW COULD I LOSE TO THIS SAWHORSE?!
EUREKA THE KITTEN, YOU ARE ACCUSED OF EATING OZMA'S FAVORITE PIGLET!
I DID NOT COMMIT SUCH A CRIME...
THOUGH I DID INTEND TO!
ME AND JIM DON'T BELONG HERE...
WE SHOULD GO BACK TO THE RANCH.
I WANT TO GO HOME TOO!

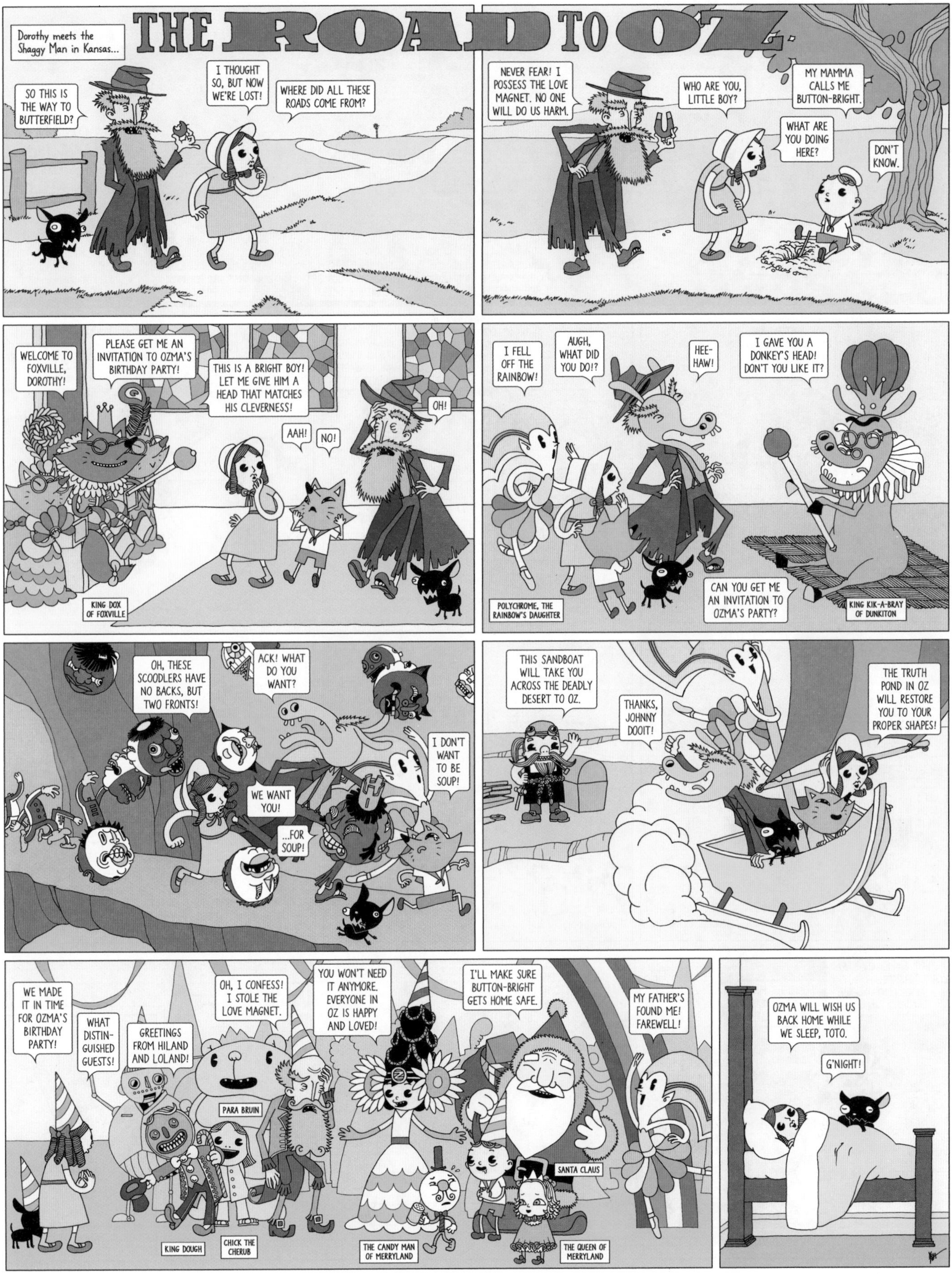
THE ROAD TO OZ.
Dorothy meets the Shaggy Man in Kansas...
SO THIS IS THE WAY TO BUTTERFIELD?
I THOUGHT SO, BUT NOW WE'RE LOST!
WHERE DID ALL THESE ROADS COME FROM?
NEVER FEAR! I POSSESS THE LOVE MAGNET. NO ONE WILL DO US HARM.
WHO ARE YOU, LITTLE BOY?
MY MAMMA CALLS ME BUTTON-BRIGHT.
WHAT ARE YOU DOING HERE?
DON'T KNOW.
WELCOME TO FOXVILLE, DOROTHY!
PLEASE GET ME AN INVITATION TO OZMA'S BIRTHDAY PARTY!
THIS IS A BRIGHT BOY! LET ME GIVE HIM A HEAD THAT MATCHES HIS CLEVERNESS!
OH!
AAH!
NO!
KING DOX OF FOXVILLE
I FELL OFF THE RAINBOW!
AUGH, WHAT DID YOU DO!?
HEE-HAW!
I GAVE YOU A DONKEY'S HEAD! DON'T YOU LIKE IT?
CAN YOU GET ME AN INVITATION TO OZMA'S PARTY?
POLYCHROME, THE RAINBOW'S DAUGHTER
KING KIK-A-BRAY OF DUNKITON
OH, THESE SCOODLERS HAVE NO BACKS, BUT TWO FRONTS!
ACK! WHAT DO YOU WANT?
I DON'T WANT TO BE SOUP!
WE WANT YOU!
...FOR SOUP!
THIS SANDBOAT WILL TAKE YOU ACROSS THE DEADLY DESERT TO OZ.
THANKS, JOHNNY DOOIT!
THE TRUTH POND IN OZ WILL RESTORE YOU TO YOUR PROPER SHAPES!
WE MADE IT IN TIME FOR OZMA'S BIRTHDAY PARTY!
WHAT DISTIN-GUISHED GUESTS!
GREETINGS FROM HILAND AND LOLAND!
OH, I CONFESS! I STOLE THE LOVE MAGNET.
YOU WON'T NEED IT ANYMORE. EVERYONE IN OZ IS HAPPY AND LOVED!
I'LL MAKE SURE BUTTON-BRIGHT GETS HOME SAFE.
MY FATHER'S FOUND ME! FAREWELL!
PARA BRUIN
SANTA CLAUS
KING DOUGH
CHICK THE CHERUB
THE CANDY MAN OF MERRYLAND
THE QUEEN OF MERRYLAND
OZMA WILL WISH US BACK HOME WHILE WE SLEEP, TOTO.
G'NIGHT!

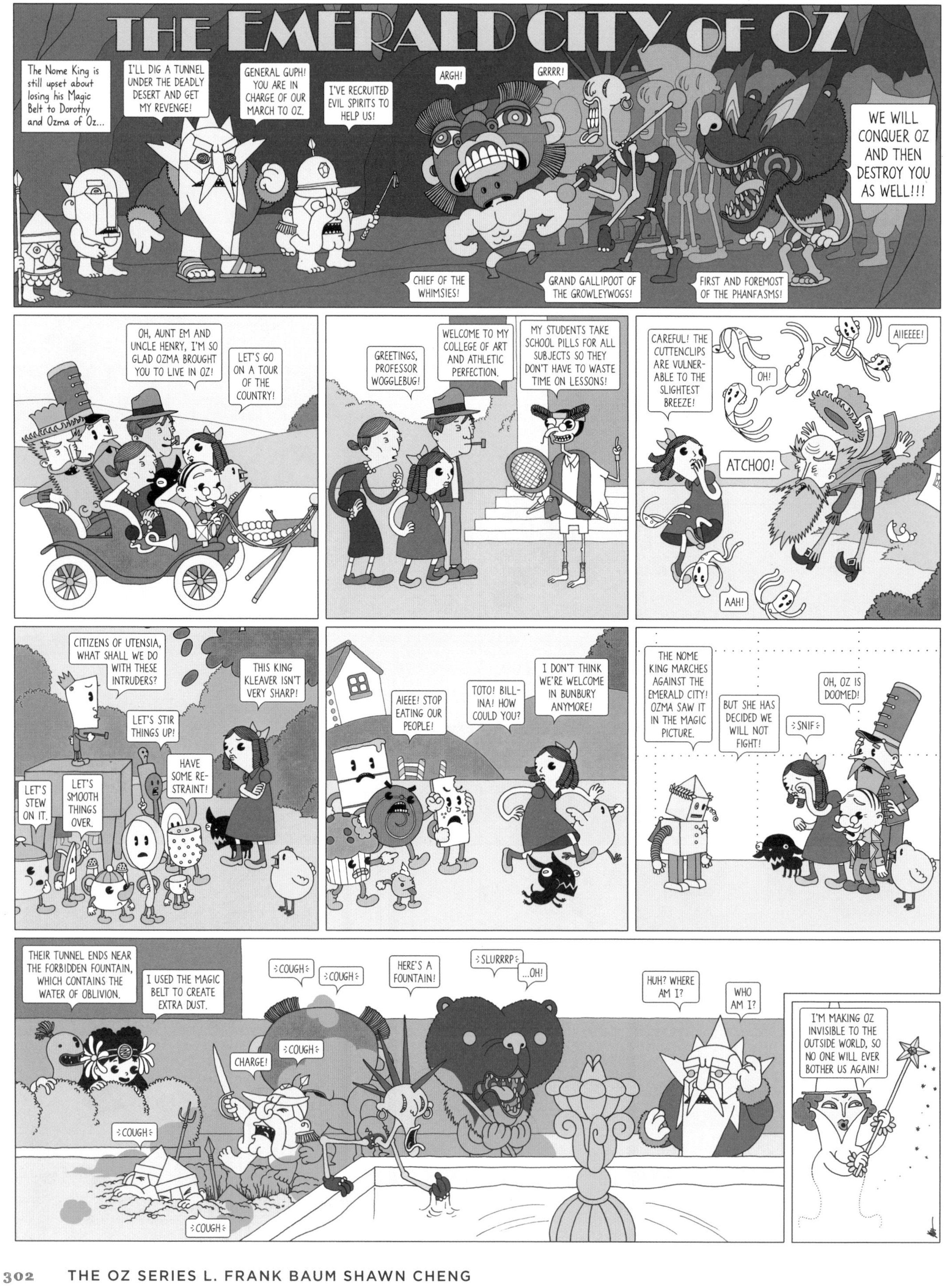
THE EMERALD CITY of OZ
The Nome King is still upset about losing his Magic Belt to Dorothy and Ozma of Oz...
I'LL DIG A TUNNEL UNDER THE DEADLY DESERT AND GET MY REVENGE!
GENERAL GUPH! YOU ARE IN CHARGE OF OUR MARCH TO OZ.
I'VE RECRUITED EVIL SPIRITS TO HELP US!
ARGH!
GRRRR!
WE WILL CONQUER OZ AND THEN DESTROY YOU AS WELL!!!
CHIEF OF THE WHIMSIES!
GRAND GALLIPOOT OF THE GROWLEYWOGS!
FIRST AND FOREMOST OF THE PHANFASMS!
OH, AUNT EM AND UNCLE HENRY, I'M SO GLAD OZMA BROUGHT YOU TO LIVE IN OZ!
LET'S GO ON A TOUR OF THE COUNTRY!
GREETINGS, PROFESSOR WOGGLEBUG!
WELCOME TO MY COLLEGE OF ART AND ATHLETIC PERFECTION.
MY STUDENTS TAKE SCHOOL PILLS FOR ALL SUBJECTS SO THEY DON'T HAVE TO WASTE TIME ON LESSONS!
CAREFUL! THE CUTTENCLIPS ARE VULNERABLE TO THE SLIGHTEST BREEZE!
OH!
AIIEEEE!
ATCHOO!
AAH!
CITIZENS OF UTENSIA, WHAT SHALL WE DO WITH THESE INTRUDERS?
THIS KING KLEAVER ISN'T VERY SHARP!
LET'S STIR THINGS UP!
HAVE SOME RESTRAINT!
LET'S STEW ON IT.
LET'S SMOOTH THINGS OVER.
AIEEE! STOP EATING OUR PEOPLE!
TOTO! BILLINA! HOW COULD YOU?
I DON'T THINK WE'RE WELCOME IN BUNBURY ANYMORE!
THE NOME KING MARCHES AGAINST THE EMERALD CITY! OZMA SAW IT IN THE MAGIC PICTURE.
BUT SHE HAS DECIDED WE WILL NOT FIGHT!
SNIF
OH, OZ IS DOOMED!
THEIR TUNNEL ENDS NEAR THE FORBIDDEN FOUNTAIN, WHICH CONTAINS THE WATER OF OBLIVION.
I USED THE MAGIC BELT TO CREATE EXTRA DUST.
COUGH
COUGH
HERE'S A FOUNTAIN!
SLURRRP
...OH!
HUH? WHERE AM I?
WHO AM I?
CHARGE!
COUGH
COUGH
COUGH
I'M MAKING OZ INVISIBLE TO THE OUTSIDE WORLD, SO NO ONE WILL EVER BOTHER US AGAIN!

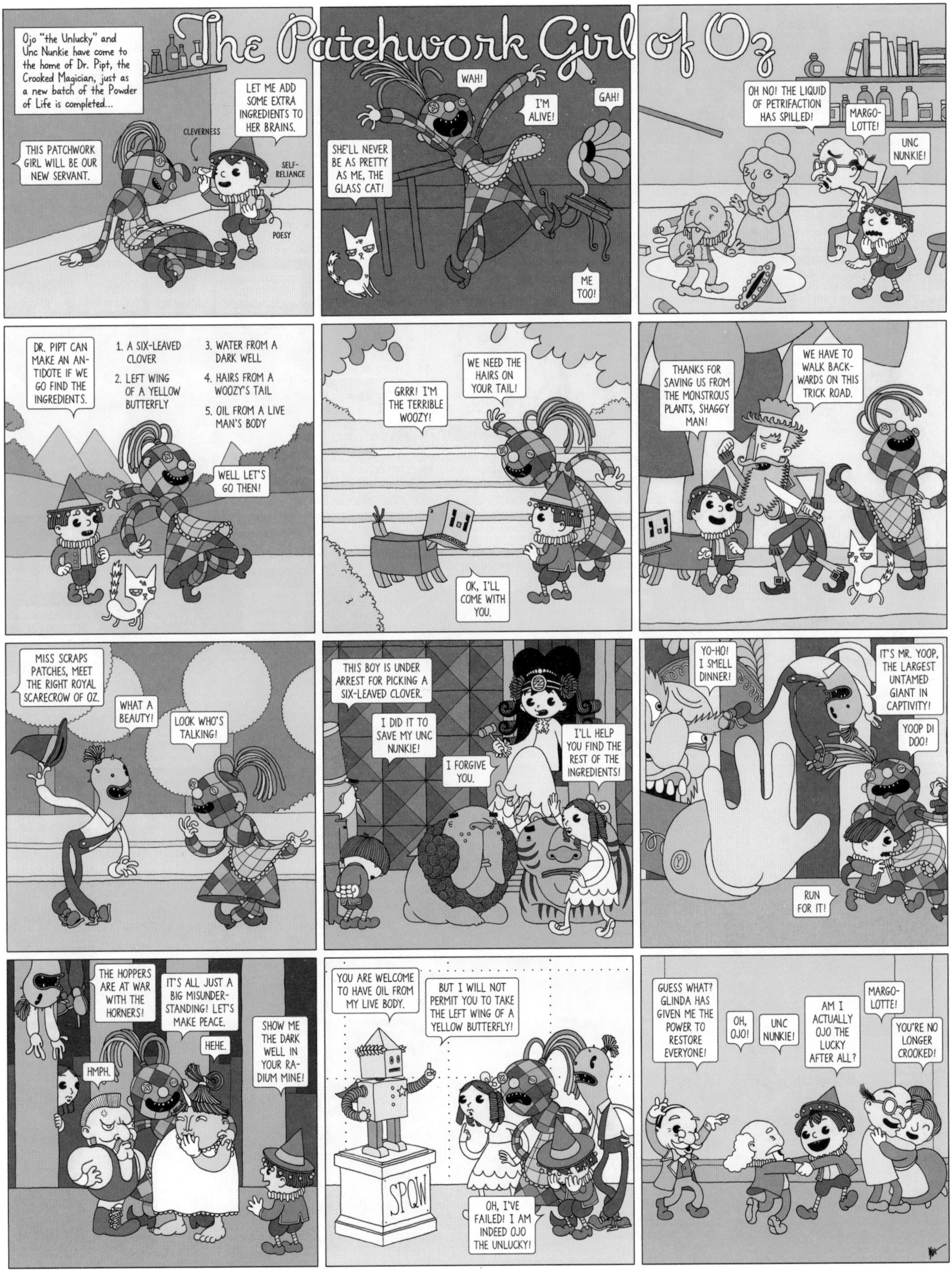
The Patchwork Girl of Oz
Ojo "the Unlucky" and Unc Nunkie have come to the home of Dr. Pipt, the Crooked Magician, just as a new batch of the Powder of Life is completed...
LET ME ADD SOME EXTRA INGREDIENTS TO HER BRAINS.
THIS PATCHWORK GIRL WILL BE OUR NEW SERVANT.
CLEVERNESS
SELF-RELIANCE
POESY
WAH!
I'M ALIVE!
GAH!
SHE'LL NEVER BE AS PRETTY AS ME, THE GLASS CAT!
ME TOO!
OH NO! THE LIQUID OF PETRIFACTION HAS SPILLED!
MARGOLOTTE!
UNC NUNKIE!
DR. PIPT CAN MAKE AN ANTIDOTE IF WE GO FIND THE INGREDIENTS.
1. A SIX-LEAVED CLOVER
2. LEFT WING OF A YELLOW BUTTERFLY
3. WATER FROM A DARK WELL
4. HAIRS FROM A WOOZY'S TAIL
5. OIL FROM A LIVE MAN'S BODY
WELL LET'S GO THEN!
GRRR! I'M THE TERRIBLE WOOZY!
WE NEED THE HAIRS ON YOUR TAIL!
OK, I'LL COME WITH YOU.
THANKS FOR SAVING US FROM THE MONSTROUS PLANTS, SHAGGY MAN!
WE HAVE TO WALK BACKWARDS ON THIS TRICK ROAD.
MISS SCRAPS PATCHES, MEET THE RIGHT ROYAL SCARECROW OF OZ.
WHAT A BEAUTY!
LOOK WHO'S TALKING!
THIS BOY IS UNDER ARREST FOR PICKING A SIX-LEAVED CLOVER.
I DID IT TO SAVE MY UNC NUNKIE!
I FORGIVE YOU.
I'LL HELP YOU FIND THE REST OF THE INGREDIENTS!
YO-HO! I SMELL DINNER!
IT'S MR. YOOP, THE LARGEST UNTAMED GIANT IN CAPTIVITY!
YOOP DI DOO!
RUN FOR IT!
THE HOPPERS ARE AT WAR WITH THE HORNERS!
IT'S ALL JUST A BIG MISUNDERSTANDING! LET'S MAKE PEACE.
HEHE.
HMPH.
SHOW ME THE DARK WELL IN YOUR RADIUM MINE!
YOU ARE WELCOME TO HAVE OIL FROM MY LIVE BODY.
BUT I WILL NOT PERMIT YOU TO TAKE THE LEFT WING OF A YELLOW BUTTERFLY!
SPQW
OH, I'VE FAILED! I AM INDEED OJO THE UNLUCKY!
GUESS WHAT? GLINDA HAS GIVEN ME THE POWER TO RESTORE EVERYONE!
OH, OJO!
UNC NUNKIE!
AM I ACTUALLY OJO THE LUCKY AFTER ALL?
MARGOLOTTE!
YOU'RE NO LONGER CROOKED!

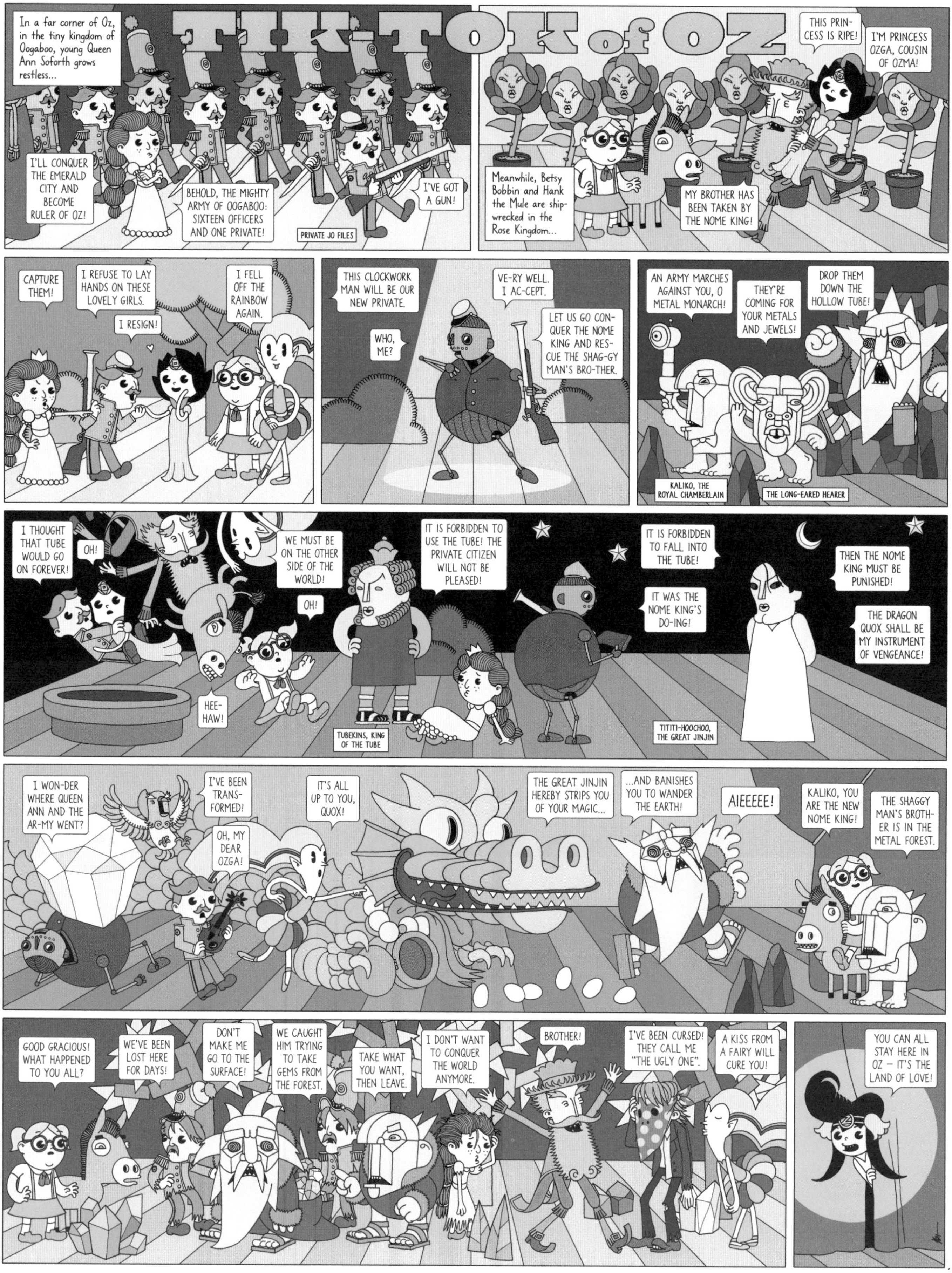
TIK-TOK of OZ
In a far corner of Oz, in the tiny kingdom of Oogaboo, young Queen Ann Soforth grows restless...
I'LL CONQUER THE EMERALD CITY AND BECOME RULER OF OZ!
BEHOLD, THE MIGHTY ARMY OF OOGABOO: SIXTEEN OFFICERS AND ONE PRIVATE!
I'VE GOT A GUN!
PRIVATE JO FILES
Meanwhile, Betsy Bobbin and Hank the Mule are shipwrecked in the Rose Kingdom...
THIS PRINCESS IS RIPE!
I'M PRINCESS OZGA, COUSIN OF OZMA!
MY BROTHER HAS BEEN TAKEN BY THE NOME KING!
CAPTURE THEM!
I REFUSE TO LAY HANDS ON THESE LOVELY GIRLS.
I RESIGN!
I FELL OFF THE RAINBOW AGAIN.
THIS CLOCKWORK MAN WILL BE OUR NEW PRIVATE.
WHO, ME?
VE-RY WELL. I AC-CEPT.
LET US GO CONQUER THE NOME KING AND RESCUE THE SHAG-GY MAN'S BRO-THER.
AN ARMY MARCHES AGAINST YOU, O METAL MONARCH!
THEY'RE COMING FOR YOUR METALS AND JEWELS!
DROP THEM DOWN THE HOLLOW TUBE!
KALIKO, THE ROYAL CHAMBERLAIN
THE LONG-EARED HEARER
I THOUGHT THAT TUBE WOULD GO ON FOREVER!
OH!
WE MUST BE ON THE OTHER SIDE OF THE WORLD!
OH!
HEE-HAW!
IT IS FORBIDDEN TO USE THE TUBE! THE PRIVATE CITIZEN WILL NOT BE PLEASED!
TUBEKINS, KING OF THE TUBE
IT IS FORBIDDEN TO FALL INTO THE TUBE!
IT WAS THE NOME KING'S DO-ING!
THEN THE NOME KING MUST BE PUNISHED!
THE DRAGON QUOX SHALL BE MY INSTRUMENT OF VENGEANCE!
TITITI-HOOCHOO, THE GREAT JINJIN
I WON-DER WHERE QUEEN ANN AND THE AR-MY WENT?
I'VE BEEN TRANS-FORMED!
OH, MY DEAR OZGA!
IT'S ALL UP TO YOU, QUOX!
THE GREAT JINJIN HEREBY STRIPS YOU OF YOUR MAGIC...
...AND BANISHES YOU TO WANDER THE EARTH!
AIEEEEE!
KALIKO, YOU ARE THE NEW NOME KING!
THE SHAGGY MAN'S BROTH-ER IS IN THE METAL FOREST.
GOOD GRACIOUS! WHAT HAPPENED TO YOU ALL?
WE'VE BEEN LOST HERE FOR DAYS!
DON'T MAKE ME GO TO THE SURFACE!
WE CAUGHT HIM TRYING TO TAKE GEMS FROM THE FOREST.
TAKE WHAT YOU WANT, THEN LEAVE.
I DON'T WANT TO CONQUER THE WORLD ANYMORE.
BROTHER!
I'VE BEEN CURSED! THEY CALL ME "THE UGLY ONE".
A KISS FROM A FAIRY WILL CURE YOU!
YOU CAN ALL STAY HERE IN OZ — IT'S THE LAND OF LOVE!

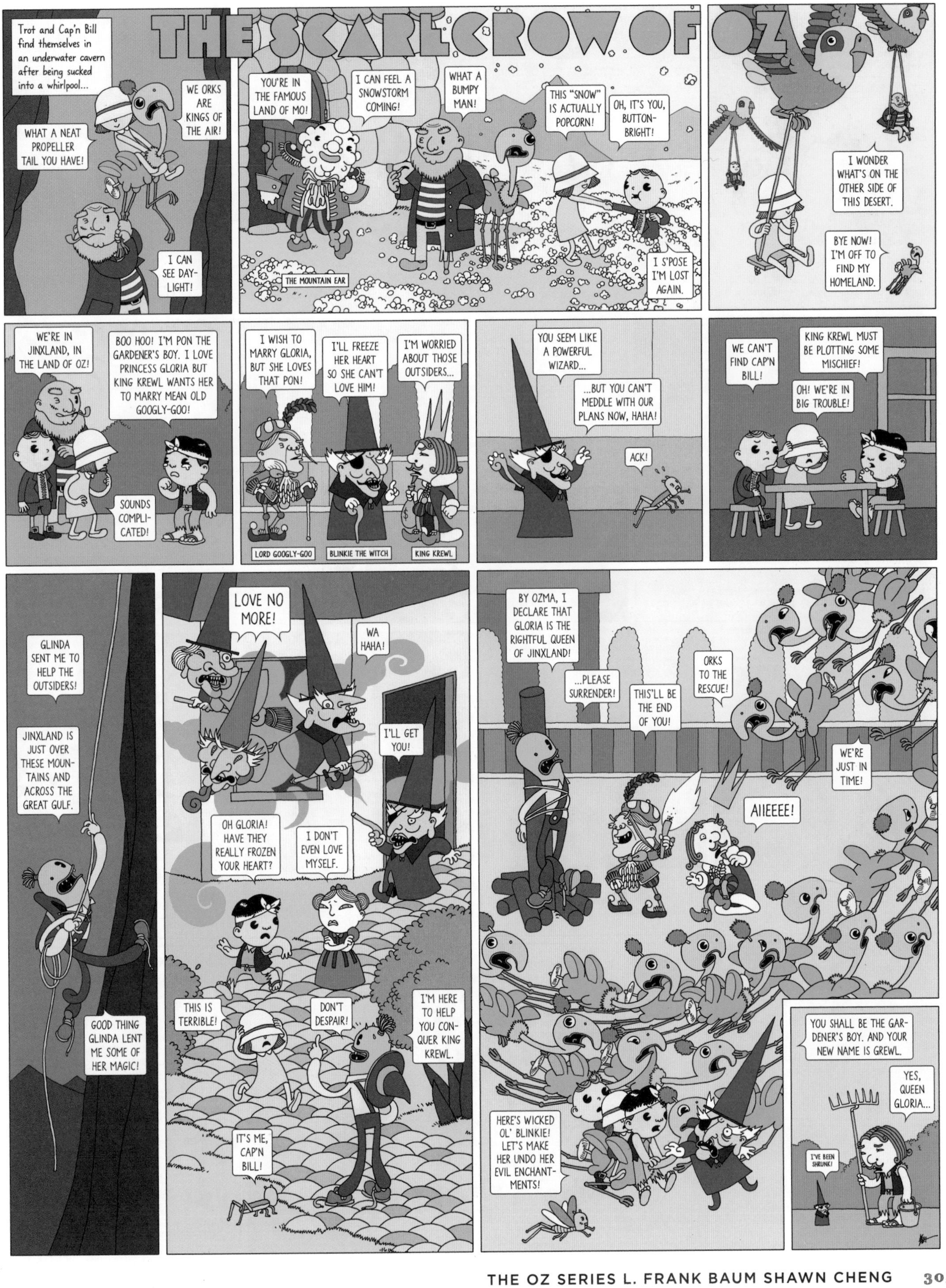
THE SCARECROW OF OZ
Trot and Cap'n Bill find themselves in an underwater cavern after being sucked into a whirlpool...
WE ORKS ARE KINGS OF THE AIR!
WHAT A NEAT PROPELLER TAIL YOU HAVE!
I CAN SEE DAY-LIGHT!
YOU'RE IN THE FAMOUS LAND OF MO!
I CAN FEEL A SNOWSTORM COMING!
WHAT A BUMPY MAN!
THIS "SNOW" IS ACTUALLY POPCORN!
OH, IT'S YOU, BUTTON-BRIGHT!
THE MOUNTAIN EAR
I S'POSE I'M LOST AGAIN.
I WONDER WHAT'S ON THE OTHER SIDE OF THIS DESERT.
BYE NOW! I'M OFF TO FIND MY HOMELAND.
WE'RE IN JINXLAND, IN THE LAND OF OZ!
BOO HOO! I'M PON THE GARDENER'S BOY. I LOVE PRINCESS GLORIA BUT KING KREWL WANTS HER TO MARRY MEAN OLD GOOGLY-GOO!
SOUNDS COMPLI-CATED!
I WISH TO MARRY GLORIA, BUT SHE LOVES THAT PON!
I'LL FREEZE HER HEART SO SHE CAN'T LOVE HIM!
I'M WORRIED ABOUT THOSE OUTSIDERS...
LORD GOOGLY-GOO
BLINKIE THE WITCH
KING KREWL
YOU SEEM LIKE A POWERFUL WIZARD...
...BUT YOU CAN'T MEDDLE WITH OUR PLANS NOW, HAHA!
ACK!
WE CAN'T FIND CAP'N BILL!
KING KREWL MUST BE PLOTTING SOME MISCHIEF!
OH! WE'RE IN BIG TROUBLE!
GLINDA SENT ME TO HELP THE OUTSIDERS!
JINXLAND IS JUST OVER THESE MOUN-TAINS AND ACROSS THE GREAT GULF.
GOOD THING GLINDA LENT ME SOME OF HER MAGIC!
LOVE NO MORE!
WA HAHA!
I'LL GET YOU!
OH GLORIA! HAVE THEY REALLY FROZEN YOUR HEART?
I DON'T EVEN LOVE MYSELF.
THIS IS TERRIBLE!
DON'T DESPAIR!
I'M HERE TO HELP YOU CON-QUER KING KREWL.
IT'S ME, CAP'N BILL!
BY OZMA, I DECLARE THAT GLORIA IS THE RIGHTFUL QUEEN OF JINXLAND!
...PLEASE SURRENDER!
THIS'LL BE THE END OF YOU!
ORKS TO THE RESCUE!
WE'RE JUST IN TIME!
AIIEEEE!
HERE'S WICKED OL' BLINKIE! LET'S MAKE HER UNDO HER EVIL ENCHANT-MENTS!
YOU SHALL BE THE GAR-DENER'S BOY. AND YOUR NEW NAME IS GREWL.
YES, QUEEN GLORIA...
I'VE BEEN SHRUNK!

# RINKITINK IN OZ

In the great Nonestic Ocean lies the peaceful and prosperous island kingdom of Pingaree...

"THE INVADERS FROM REGOS AND COREGOS WILL SURELY COME AGAIN," KING KITTICUT EXPLAINS TO HIS SON, PRINCE INGA. "OUR ONLY HOPE LIES WITH THESE THREE MAGIC PEARLS: BLUE GIVES YOU SUPER STRENGTH. PINK GIVES YOU INVINCIBILITY. AND WHITE GIVES YOU WISE ADVICE."

STRANGE SHIPS ARRIVE, BUT INSTEAD OF MARAUDERS THEY BRING JOLLY KING RINKITINK, WHO HAS RUN AWAY FROM HIS KINGDOM TO HAVE SOME FUN. HE IS ACCOMPANIED BY BILBIL THE TALKING GOAT.

SOON, INVADERS DO ATTACK! EVERYONE ON THE ISLAND IS TAKEN PRISONER EXCEPT INGA, RINKITINK, AND BILBIL. INGA RETRIEVES THE MAGIC PEARLS AND HIDES THEM IN HIS SHOES.

THE WHITE PEARL TELLS INGA: "A BOAT WILL WASH ASHORE. GO TO REGOS AND COREGOS AND FREE YOUR PEOPLE." SURE ENOUGH, THE NEXT MORNING A MAGIC BOAT APPEARS! THEY SET OFF ON WHAT SEEMS LIKE AN IMPOSSIBLE MISSION.

THEY ARRIVE ON REGOS. PROTECTED BY THE PINK PEARL AND STRENGTHENED BY THE BLUE PEARL, INGA EASILY DEFEATS KING GOS AND HIS WARRIORS AND TAKES OVER THE KING'S PALACE.

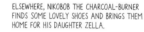

DISASTER! INGA DISCOVERS THAT HIS SHOES, ALONG WITH THE BLUE AND PINK PEARLS, HAVE BEEN ACCIDENTALLY THROWN AWAY.

ELSEWHERE, NIKOBOB THE CHARCOAL-BURNER FINDS SOME LOVELY SHOES AND BRINGS THEM HOME FOR HIS DAUGHTER ZELLA.

WITHOUT THE MAGIC PEARLS, INGA IS CAPTURED BY QUEEN COR OF COREGOS. HE AND RINKITINK BECOME HER SLAVES.

ZELLA COMES TO THE PALACE WITH SOME HONEY FOR THE QUEEN. LUCKILY, INGA NOTICES THAT SHE'S WEARING HIS SHOES!

HAVING RECOVERED THE PEARLS, INGA GOES INTO THE MINES AND FREES THE PEOPLE OF PINGAREE. ALAS, KING GOS AND QUEEN COR HAVE ALREADY FLED THE ISLAND, TAKING INGA'S PARENTS AS HOSTAGES.

FOLLOWING THE WHITE PEARL'S GUIDANCE, THEY SAIL TO THE REALM OF THE NOME KING. INGA SURVIVES THE TRICK CAVERNS AND CONFRONTS KING KALIKO, WHO REFUSES TO FREE INGA'S

HOLD IT RIGHT THERE! I'VE BEEN WATCHING EVERYTHING IN THE MAGIC PICTURE...

FREE INGA'S PARENTS OR I'LL USE THESE EGGS!

NOOOOOO!

AFTER RESCUING INGA'S PARENTS, THEY ALL VISIT THE MARVELOUS LAND OF OZ.

BILBIL IS ACTUALLY PRINCE BOBO OF BOBOLAND!

I WAS ENCHANTED!

LIFE IS FULL OF SURPRISES!

NEXT: A HAPPY RETURN TO PINGAREE!

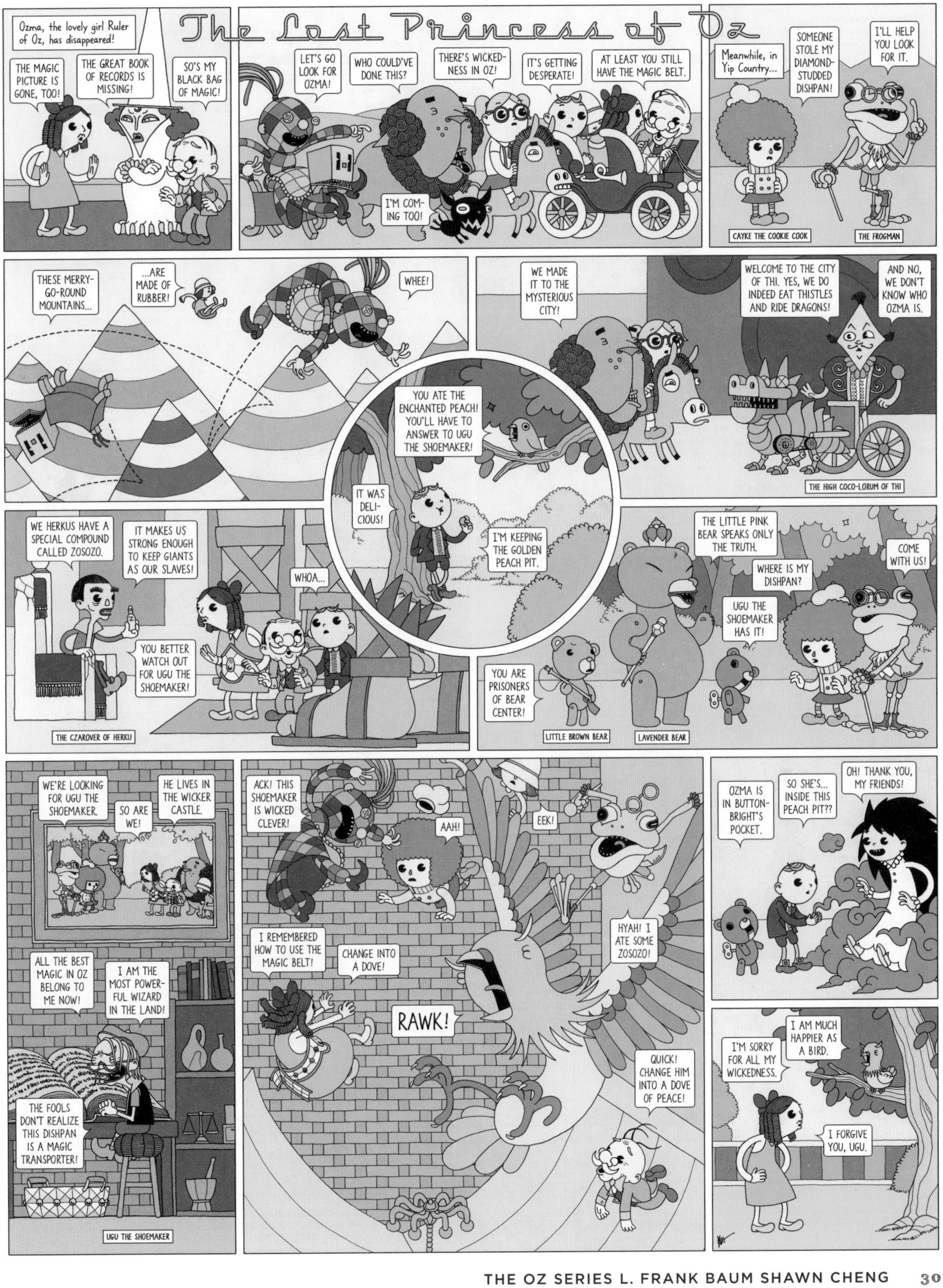
The Lost Princess of Oz
Ozma, the lovely girl Ruler of Oz, has disappeared!
THE MAGIC PICTURE IS GONE, TOO!
THE GREAT BOOK OF RECORDS IS MISSING!
SO'S MY BLACK BAG OF MAGIC!
LET'S GO LOOK FOR OZMA!
WHO COULD'VE DONE THIS?
THERE'S WICKED-NESS IN OZ!
IT'S GETTING DESPERATE!
AT LEAST YOU STILL HAVE THE MAGIC BELT.
I'M COM-ING TOO!
Meanwhile, in Yip Country...
SOMEONE STOLE MY DIAMOND-STUDDED DISHPAN!
I'LL HELP YOU LOOK FOR IT.
CAYKE THE COOKIE COOK
THE FROGMAN
THESE MERRY-GO-ROUND MOUNTAINS...
...ARE MADE OF RUBBER!
WHEE!
WE MADE IT TO THE MYSTERIOUS CITY!
WELCOME TO THE CITY OF THI. YES, WE DO INDEED EAT THISTLES AND RIDE DRAGONS!
AND NO, WE DON'T KNOW WHO OZMA IS.
THE HIGH COCO-LORUM OF THI
YOU ATE THE ENCHANTED PEACH! YOU'LL HAVE TO ANSWER TO UGU THE SHOEMAKER!
IT WAS DELI-CIOUS!
I'M KEEPING THE GOLDEN PEACH PIT.
WE HERKUS HAVE A SPECIAL COMPOUND CALLED ZOSOZO.
IT MAKES US STRONG ENOUGH TO KEEP GIANTS AS OUR SLAVES!
WHOA...
YOU BETTER WATCH OUT FOR UGU THE SHOEMAKER!
THE CZAROVER OF HERKU
THE LITTLE PINK BEAR SPEAKS ONLY THE TRUTH.
WHERE IS MY DISHPAN?
COME WITH US!
UGU THE SHOEMAKER HAS IT!
YOU ARE PRISONERS OF BEAR CENTER!
LITTLE BROWN BEAR
LAVENDER BEAR
WE'RE LOOKING FOR UGU THE SHOEMAKER.
SO ARE WE!
HE LIVES IN THE WICKER CASTLE.
ALL THE BEST MAGIC IN OZ BELONG TO ME NOW!
I AM THE MOST POWER-FUL WIZARD IN THE LAND!
THE FOOLS DON'T REALIZE THIS DISHPAN IS A MAGIC TRANSPORTER!
UGU THE SHOEMAKER
ACK! THIS SHOEMAKER IS WICKED CLEVER!
AAH!
EEK!
I REMEMBERED HOW TO USE THE MAGIC BELT!
CHANGE INTO A DOVE!
HYAH! I ATE SOME ZOSOZO!
RAWK!
QUICK! CHANGE HIM INTO A DOVE OF PEACE!
OZMA IS IN BUTTON-BRIGHT'S POCKET.
SO SHE'S... INSIDE THIS PEACH PIT??
OH! THANK YOU, MY FRIENDS!
I'M SORRY FOR ALL MY WICKEDNESS.
I AM MUCH HAPPIER AS A BIRD.
I FORGIVE YOU, UGU.

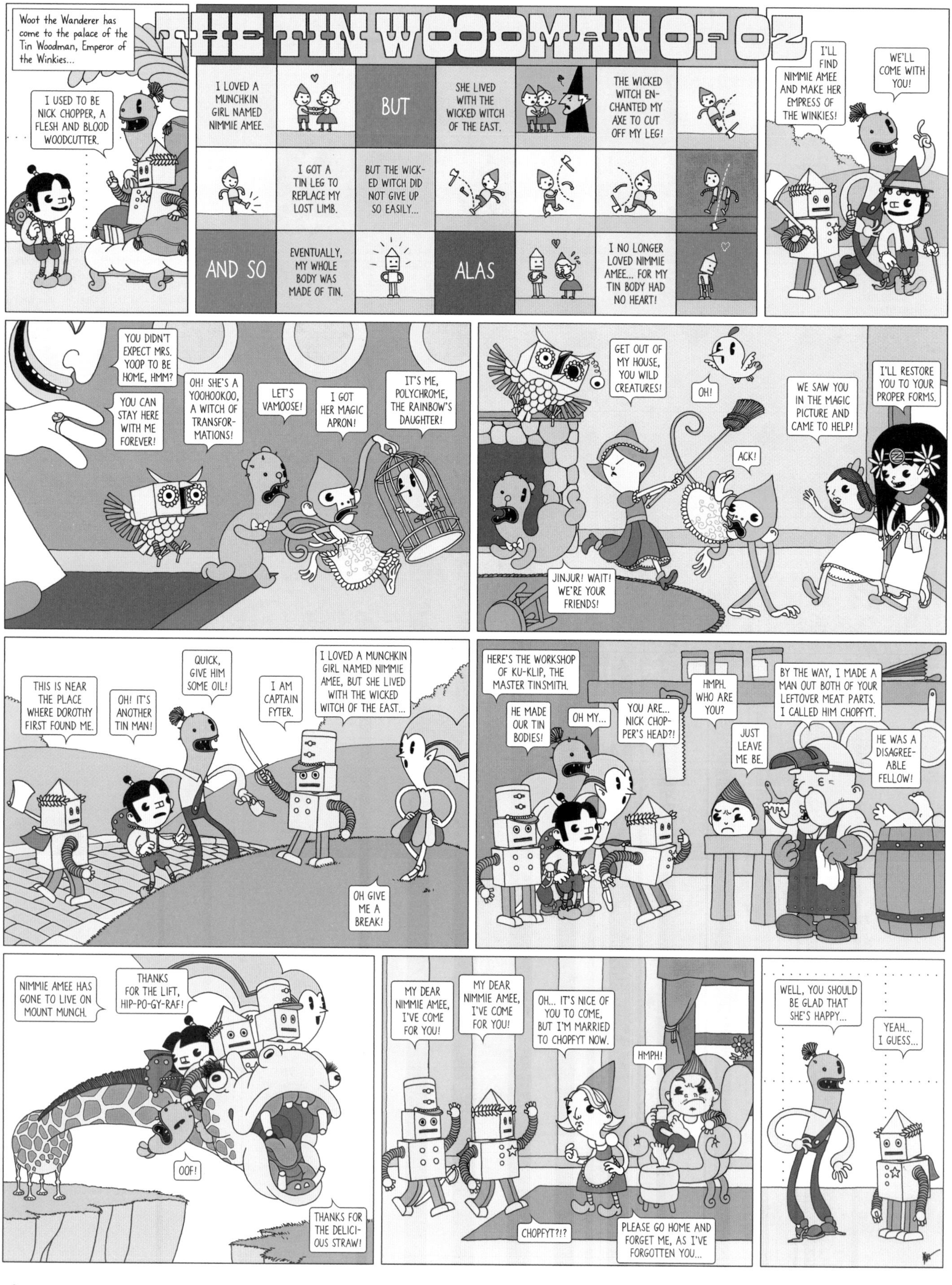
THE TIN WOODMAN OF OZ
Woot the Wanderer has come to the palace of the Tin Woodman, Emperor of the Winkies...
I USED TO BE NICK CHOPPER, A FLESH AND BLOOD WOODCUTTER.
I LOVED A MUNCHKIN GIRL NAMED NIMMIE AMEE.
BUT
SHE LIVED WITH THE WICKED WITCH OF THE EAST.
THE WICKED WITCH ENCHANTED MY AXE TO CUT OFF MY LEG!
I GOT A TIN LEG TO REPLACE MY LOST LIMB.
BUT THE WICKED WITCH DID NOT GIVE UP SO EASILY...
AND SO
EVENTUALLY, MY WHOLE BODY WAS MADE OF TIN.
ALAS
I NO LONGER LOVED NIMMIE AMEE... FOR MY TIN BODY HAD NO HEART!
I'LL FIND NIMMIE AMEE AND MAKE HER EMPRESS OF THE WINKIES!
WE'LL COME WITH YOU!
YOU DIDN'T EXPECT MRS. YOOP TO BE HOME, HMM?
YOU CAN STAY HERE WITH ME FOREVER!
OH! SHE'S A YOOHOOKOO, A WITCH OF TRANSFORMATIONS!
LET'S VAMOOSE!
I GOT HER MAGIC APRON!
IT'S ME, POLYCHROME, THE RAINBOW'S DAUGHTER!
GET OUT OF MY HOUSE, YOU WILD CREATURES!
OH!
WE SAW YOU IN THE MAGIC PICTURE AND CAME TO HELP!
I'LL RESTORE YOU TO YOUR PROPER FORMS.
ACK!
JINJUR! WAIT! WE'RE YOUR FRIENDS!
THIS IS NEAR THE PLACE WHERE DOROTHY FIRST FOUND ME.
OH! IT'S ANOTHER TIN MAN!
QUICK, GIVE HIM SOME OIL!
I AM CAPTAIN FYTER.
I LOVED A MUNCHKIN GIRL NAMED NIMMIE AMEE, BUT SHE LIVED WITH THE WICKED WITCH OF THE EAST...
OH GIVE ME A BREAK!
HERE'S THE WORKSHOP OF KU-KLIP, THE MASTER TINSMITH.
HE MADE OUR TIN BODIES!
OH MY...
YOU ARE... NICK CHOPPER'S HEAD?!
HMPH. WHO ARE YOU?
JUST LEAVE ME BE.
BY THE WAY, I MADE A MAN OUT BOTH OF YOUR LEFTOVER MEAT PARTS. I CALLED HIM CHOPFYT.
HE WAS A DISAGREEABLE FELLOW!
NIMMIE AMEE HAS GONE TO LIVE ON MOUNT MUNCH.
THANKS FOR THE LIFT, HIP-PO-GY-RAF!
OOF!
THANKS FOR THE DELICIOUS STRAW!
MY DEAR NIMMIE AMEE, I'VE COME FOR YOU!
MY DEAR NIMMIE AMEE, I'VE COME FOR YOU!
OH... IT'S NICE OF YOU TO COME, BUT I'M MARRIED TO CHOPFYT NOW.
HMPH!
CHOPFYT?!?
PLEASE GO HOME AND FORGET ME, AS I'VE FORGOTTEN YOU...
WELL, YOU SHOULD BE GLAD THAT SHE'S HAPPY...
YEAH... I GUESS...

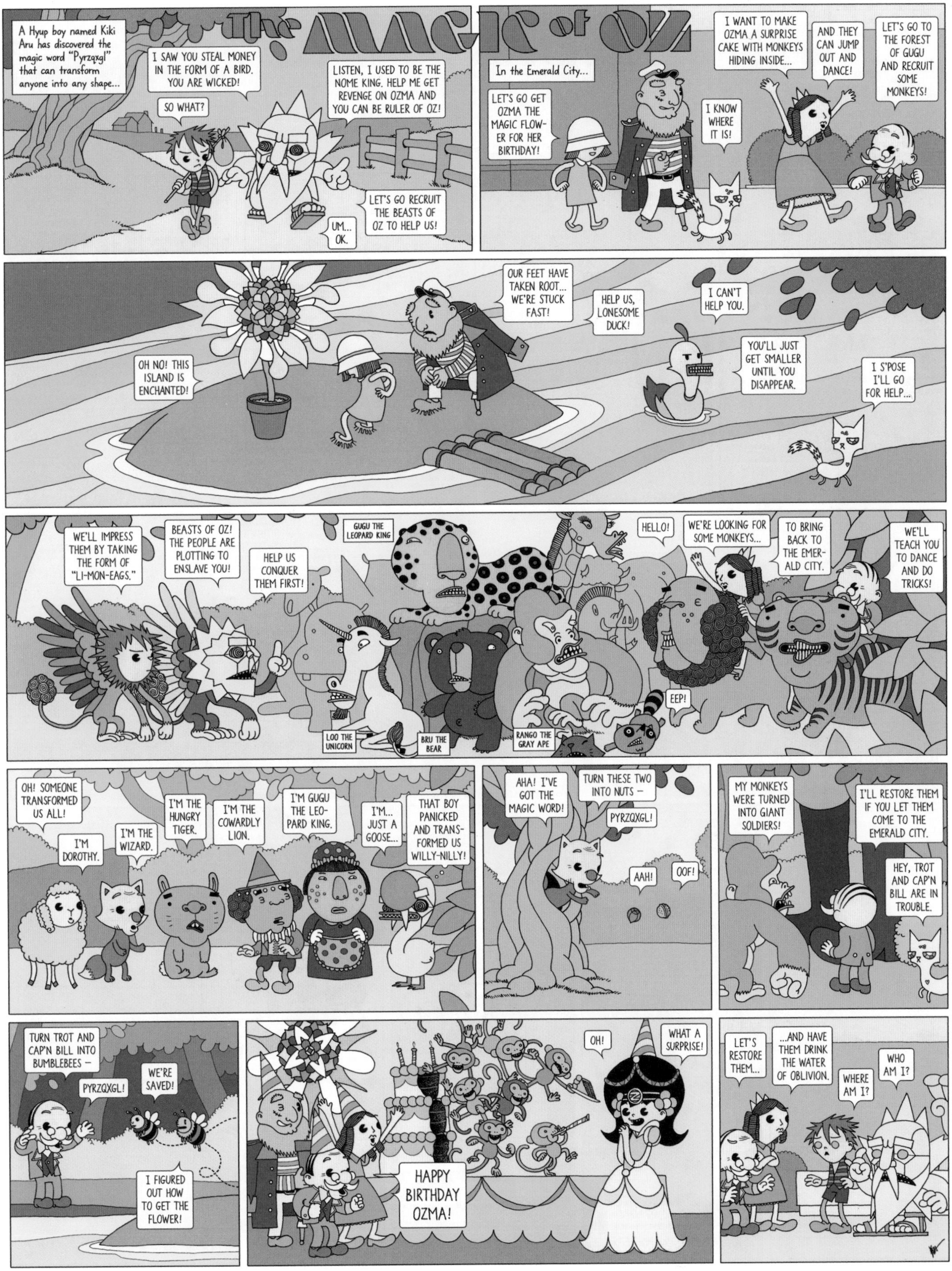
The MAGIC of OZ
A Hyup boy named Kiki Aru has discovered the magic word "Pyrzqxgl" that can transform anyone into any shape...
I SAW YOU STEAL MONEY IN THE FORM OF A BIRD. YOU ARE WICKED!
SO WHAT?
LISTEN, I USED TO BE THE NOME KING. HELP ME GET REVENGE ON OZMA AND YOU CAN BE RULER OF OZ!
LET'S GO RECRUIT THE BEASTS OF OZ TO HELP US!
UM... OK.
In the Emerald City...
LET'S GO GET OZMA THE MAGIC FLOWER FOR HER BIRTHDAY!
I KNOW WHERE IT IS!
I WANT TO MAKE OZMA A SURPRISE CAKE WITH MONKEYS HIDING INSIDE...
AND THEY CAN JUMP OUT AND DANCE!
LET'S GO TO THE FOREST OF GUGU AND RECRUIT SOME MONKEYS!
OH NO! THIS ISLAND IS ENCHANTED!
OUR FEET HAVE TAKEN ROOT... WE'RE STUCK FAST!
HELP US, LONESOME DUCK!
I CAN'T HELP YOU.
YOU'LL JUST GET SMALLER UNTIL YOU DISAPPEAR.
I S'POSE I'LL GO FOR HELP...
WE'LL IMPRESS THEM BY TAKING THE FORM OF "LI-MON-EAGS."
BEASTS OF OZ! THE PEOPLE ARE PLOTTING TO ENSLAVE YOU!
HELP US CONQUER THEM FIRST!
GUGU THE LEOPARD KING
HELLO!
WE'RE LOOKING FOR SOME MONKEYS...
TO BRING BACK TO THE EMERALD CITY.
WE'LL TEACH YOU TO DANCE AND DO TRICKS!
LOO THE UNICORN
BRU THE BEAR
RANGO THE GRAY APE
EEP!
OH! SOMEONE TRANSFORMED US ALL!
I'M DOROTHY.
I'M THE WIZARD.
I'M THE HUNGRY TIGER.
I'M THE COWARDLY LION.
I'M GUGU THE LEOPARD KING.
I'M... JUST A GOOSE...
THAT BOY PANICKED AND TRANSFORMED US WILLY-NILLY!
AHA! I'VE GOT THE MAGIC WORD!
TURN THESE TWO INTO NUTS —
PYRZQXGL!
AAH!
OOF!
MY MONKEYS WERE TURNED INTO GIANT SOLDIERS!
I'LL RESTORE THEM IF YOU LET THEM COME TO THE EMERALD CITY.
HEY, TROT AND CAP'N BILL ARE IN TROUBLE.
TURN TROT AND CAP'N BILL INTO BUMBLEBEES —
PYRZQXGL!
WE'RE SAVED!
I FIGURED OUT HOW TO GET THE FLOWER!
OH!
WHAT A SURPRISE!
HAPPY BIRTHDAY OZMA!
LET'S RESTORE THEM...
...AND HAVE THEM DRINK THE WATER OF OBLIVION.
WHERE AM I?
WHO AM I?

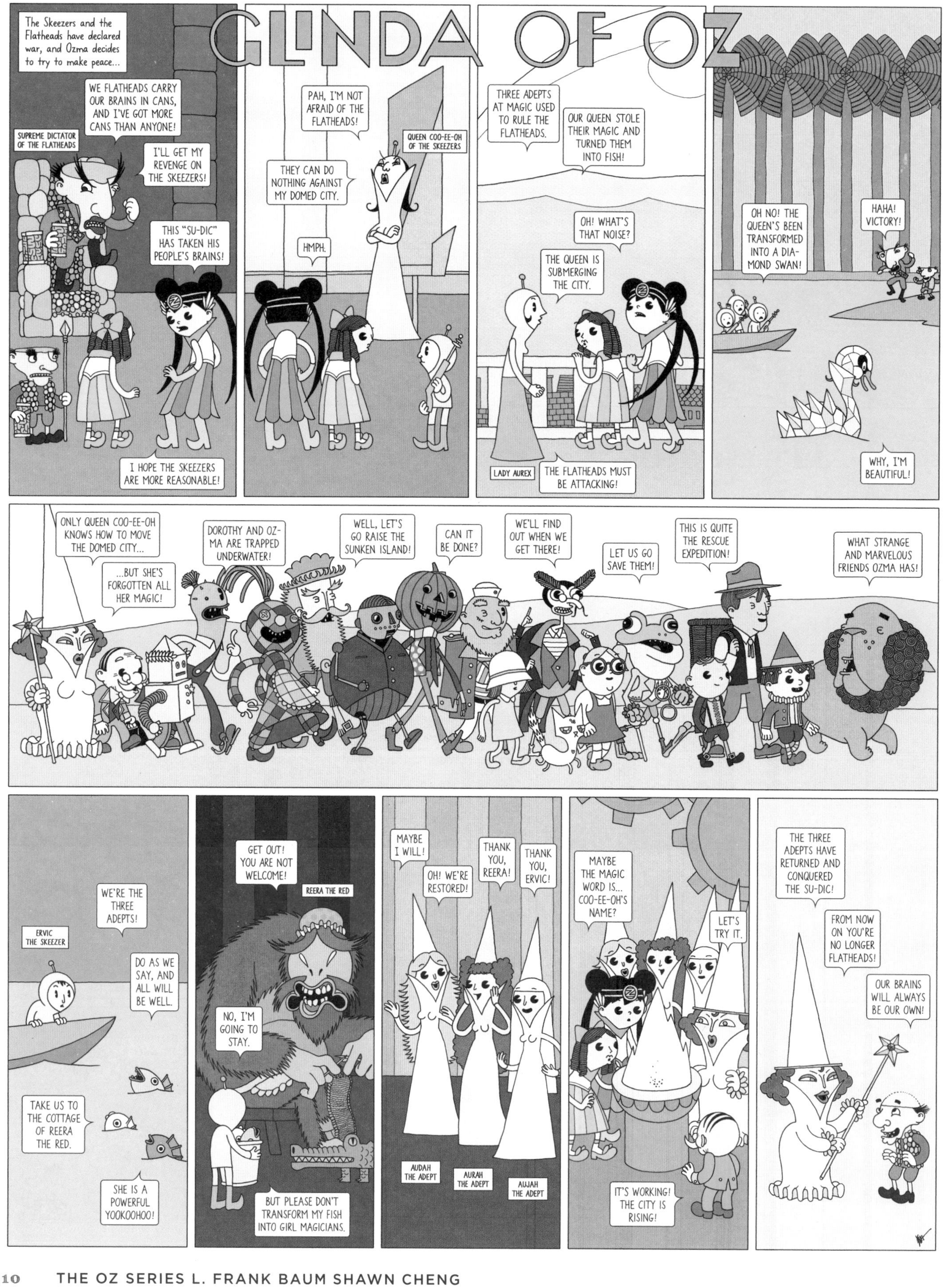
GLINDA OF OZ
The Skeezers and the Flatheads have declared war, and Ozma decides to try to make peace...
WE FLATHEADS CARRY OUR BRAINS IN CANS, AND I'VE GOT MORE CANS THAN ANYONE!
SUPREME DICTATOR OF THE FLATHEADS
I'LL GET MY REVENGE ON THE SKEEZERS!
THIS "SU-DIC" HAS TAKEN HIS PEOPLE'S BRAINS!
I HOPE THE SKEEZERS ARE MORE REASONABLE!
PAH, I'M NOT AFRAID OF THE FLATHEADS!
QUEEN COO-EE-OH OF THE SKEEZERS
THEY CAN DO NOTHING AGAINST MY DOMED CITY.
HMPH.
THREE ADEPTS AT MAGIC USED TO RULE THE FLATHEADS.
OUR QUEEN STOLE THEIR MAGIC AND TURNED THEM INTO FISH!
OH! WHAT'S THAT NOISE?
THE QUEEN IS SUBMERGING THE CITY.
LADY AUREX
THE FLATHEADS MUST BE ATTACKING!
OH NO! THE QUEEN'S BEEN TRANSFORMED INTO A DIAMOND SWAN!
HAHA! VICTORY!
WHY, I'M BEAUTIFUL!
ONLY QUEEN COO-EE-OH KNOWS HOW TO MOVE THE DOMED CITY...
...BUT SHE'S FORGOTTEN ALL HER MAGIC!
DOROTHY AND OZMA ARE TRAPPED UNDERWATER!
WELL, LET'S GO RAISE THE SUNKEN ISLAND!
CAN IT BE DONE?
WE'LL FIND OUT WHEN WE GET THERE!
LET US GO SAVE THEM!
THIS IS QUITE THE RESCUE EXPEDITION!
WHAT STRANGE AND MARVELOUS FRIENDS OZMA HAS!
ERVIC THE SKEEZER
WE'RE THE THREE ADEPTS!
DO AS WE SAY, AND ALL WILL BE WELL.
TAKE US TO THE COTTAGE OF REERA THE RED.
SHE IS A POWERFUL YOOKOOHOO!
GET OUT! YOU ARE NOT WELCOME!
REERA THE RED
NO, I'M GOING TO STAY.
BUT PLEASE DON'T TRANSFORM MY FISH INTO GIRL MAGICIANS.
MAYBE I WILL!
OH! WE'RE RESTORED!
THANK YOU, REERA!
THANK YOU, ERVIC!
AUDAH THE ADEPT
AURAH THE ADEPT
AUJAH THE ADEPT
MAYBE THE MAGIC WORD IS... COO-EE-OH'S NAME?
LET'S TRY IT.
IT'S WORKING! THE CITY IS RISING!
THE THREE ADEPTS HAVE RETURNED AND CONQUERED THE SU-DIC!
FROM NOW ON YOU'RE NO LONGER FLATHEADS!
OUR BRAINS WILL ALWAYS BE OUR OWN!

# J. M. Barrie

ART/ADAPTATION BY **Sally Madden**

**ADD J. M. BARRIE'S PETER PAN WORKS TO THE** list of classic children's literature that started when the author spontaneously created fantastical tales to entertain children of his acquaintance. The subject of a hugely successful 1904 play that was eventually turned into the novel *Peter and Wendy*, Peter is a parentless rapscallion-adventurer—a cross between Tom Sawyer and Huck Finn who can fly and will never be subject to the sadness and pain of growing up.

Beneath the adventures involving pirates, mermaids, fairies, and Native Americans (still the highly exotic "Other" in the early twentieth century), lots of weird, dark, and complex things are percolating. Sons without parents; parents who have literally lost their sons; Wendy being taken to be a mother to "the Lost Boys," who are only slightly younger than she; Peter's rumored role as an escort of dying souls, with Neverland as a way station to the afterlife; the idea that Peter himself might be a dead boy frozen in time; Peter's mutilation of Captain Hook; Peter's killing of Lost Boys who start to grow up; a jealous Tinkerbell trying to have Wendy killed. . . . Adding further complexity is the

fact that, starting with the original stage production, the role of Peter has always been played by an adult woman. Childhood, adulthood, parenthood, death, violence, homicidal jealousy, gender . . . Peter Pan sails into all kinds of hot waters.

Sally Madden brings her colorful, sprightly style to a rousing portion of the tale. **Spoiler Alert:** Wendy, Peter, and the Lost Boys are hanging out on Marooners' Rock ("so called because evil captains put sailors on it and leave them there to drown. They drown when the tide rises, for then it is submerged."). Peter hears pirates approaching in a dinghy; they're taking their hostage, the Native American princess Tiger Lily, to Marooners' Rock. Peter imitates Captain Hook flawlessly, telling the pirates to release their captive. Fooled, they do so, and Tiger Lily swims away. Then the real Hook shows up. A melee ensues, and Peter—fighting under Marquess of Queensberry rules—is badly injured. A crocodile chases the Captain away, and the Lost Boys assume that Peter and Wendy have flown to safety. But they're stranded on Marooners' Rock. The wounded Peter can't fly or swim. . . .

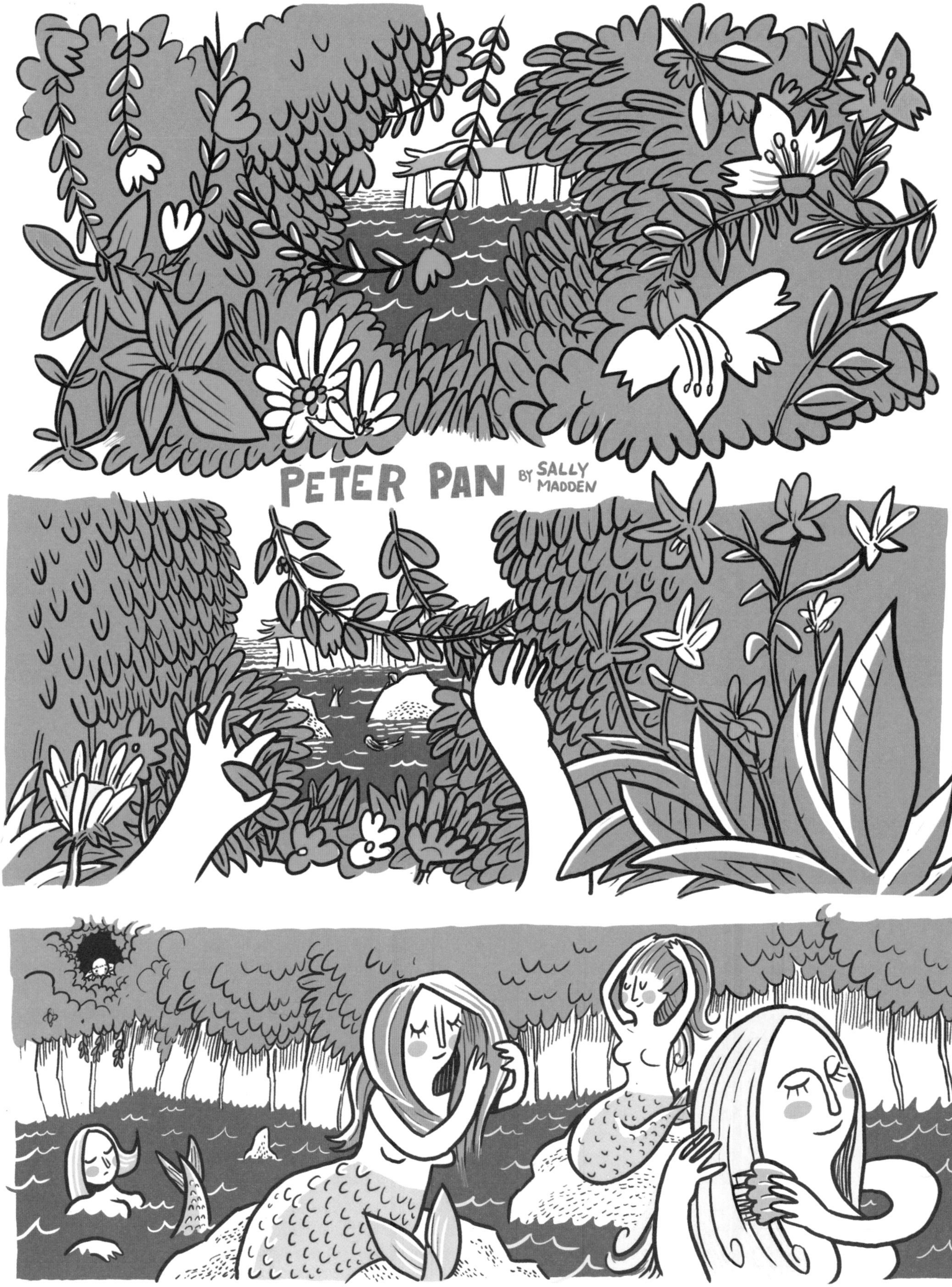
PETER PAN BY SALLY MADDEN

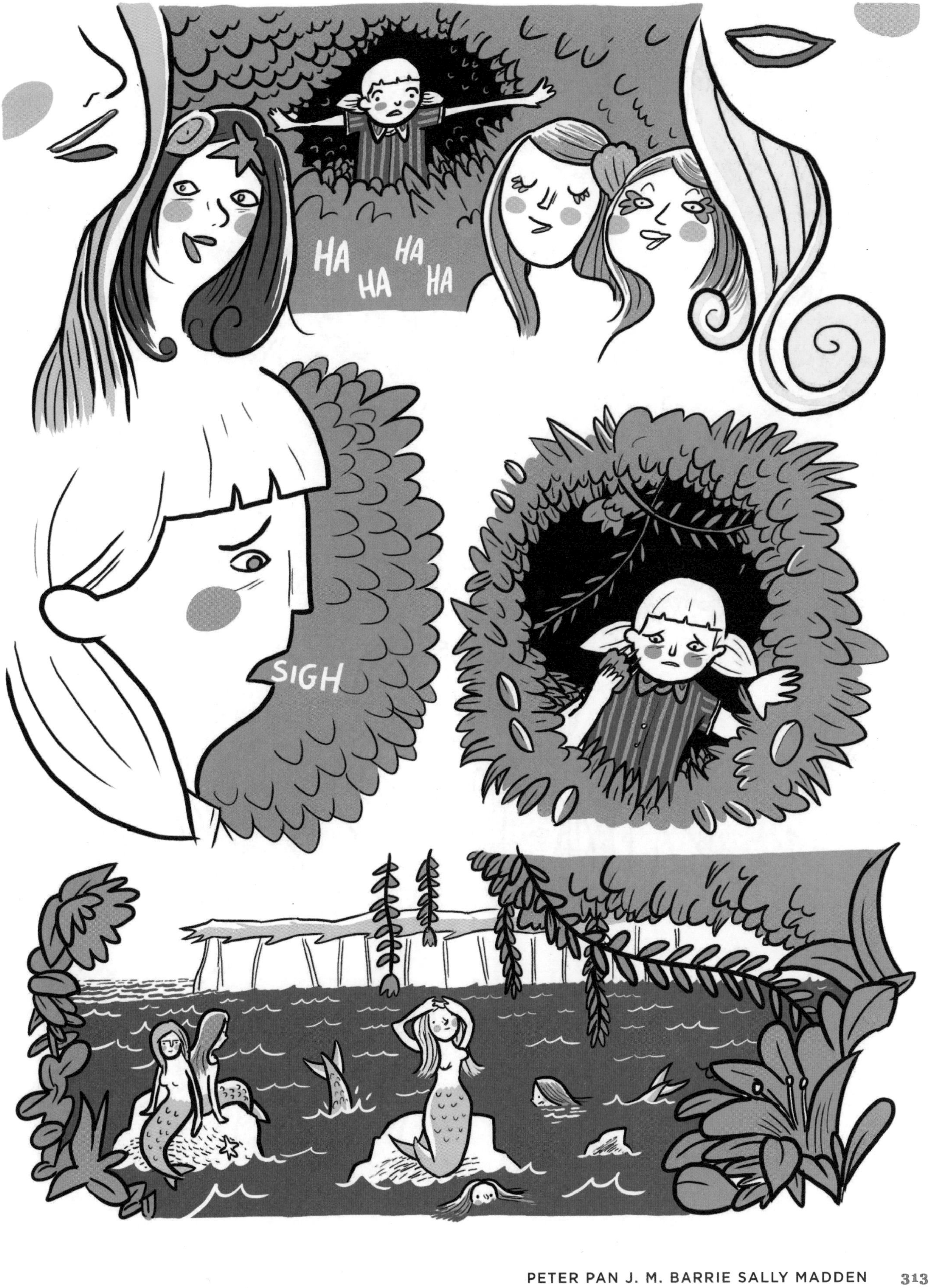
HA
HA
HA
HA
SIGH

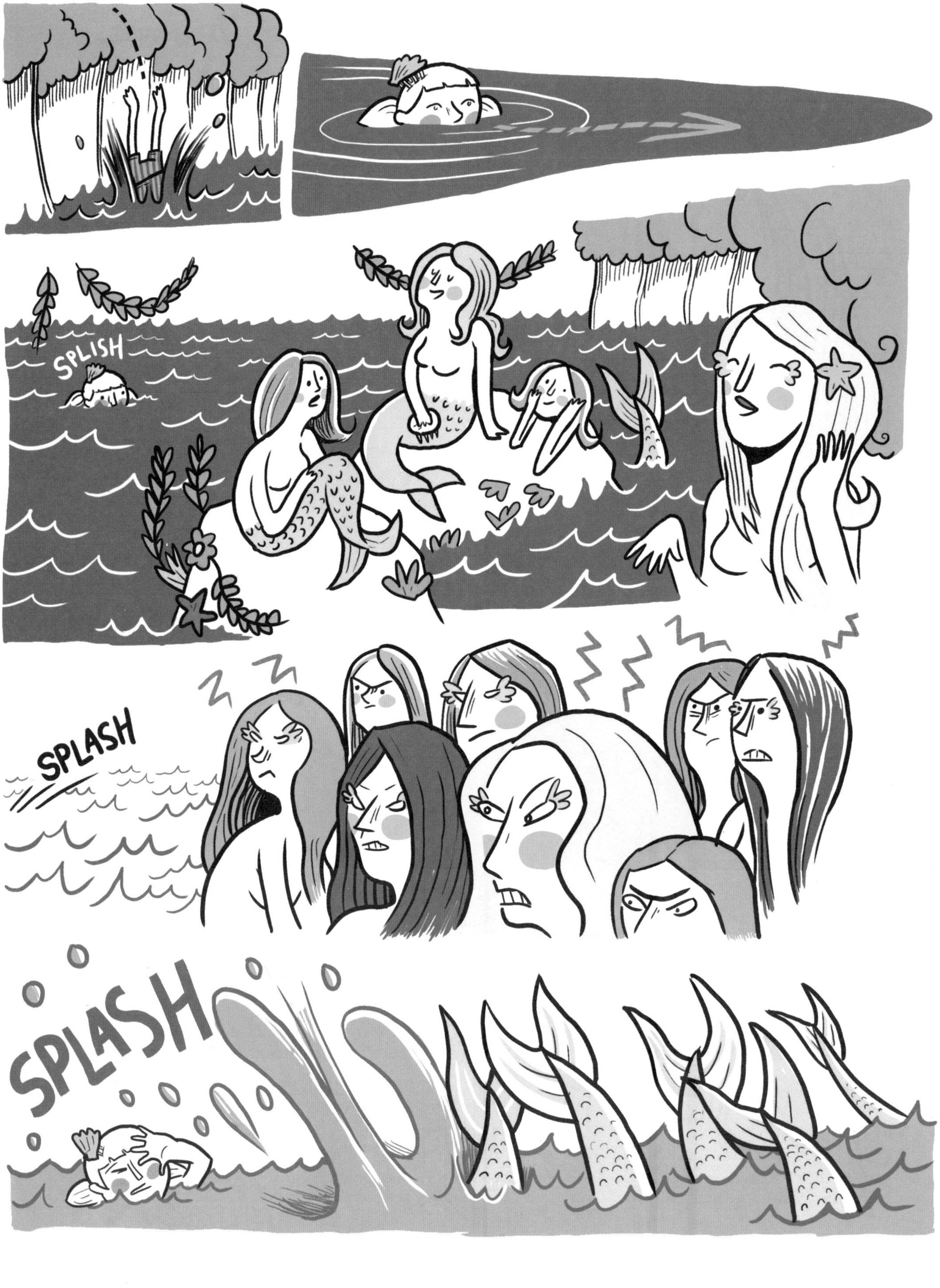
SPLISH
SPLASH
SPLASH

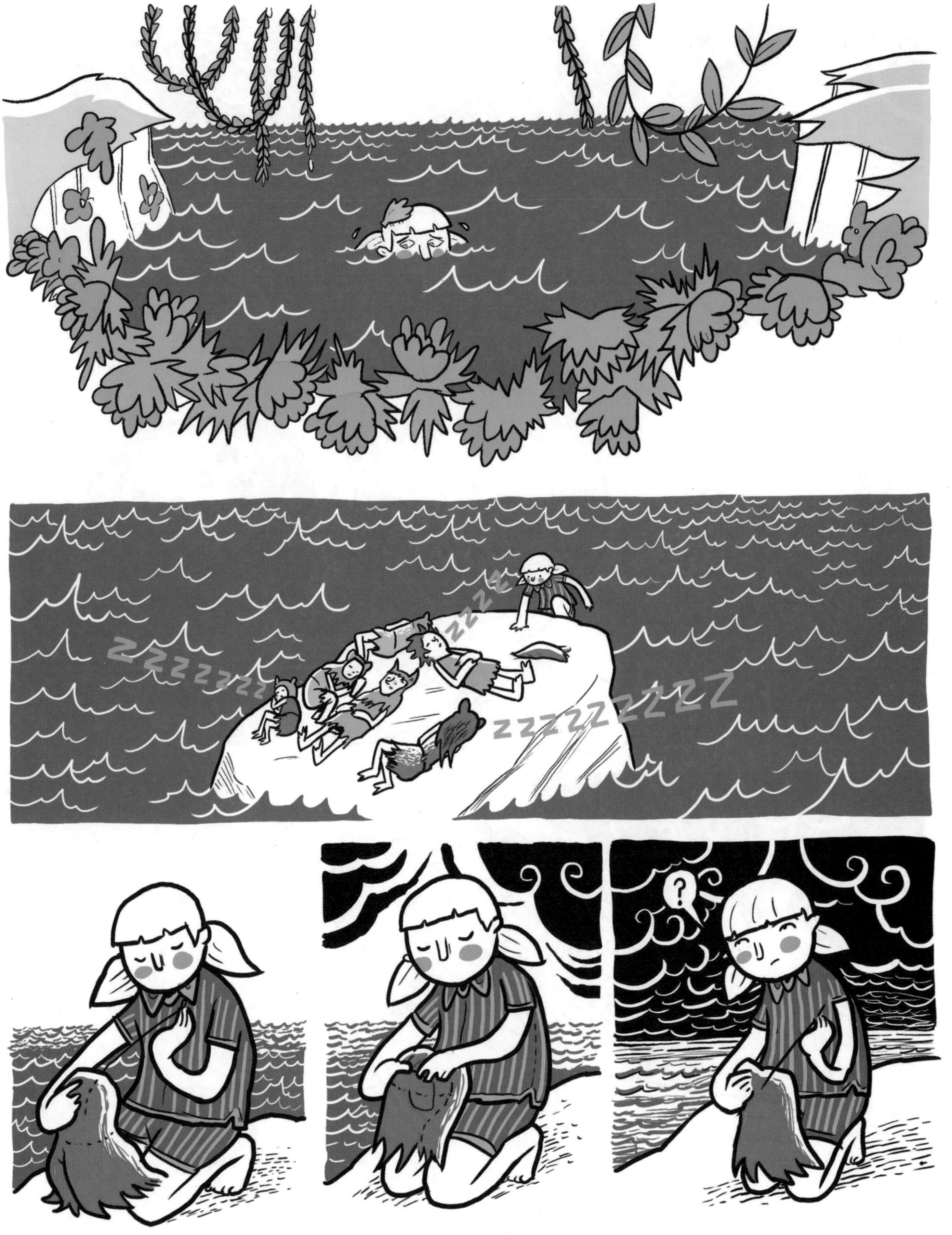
?

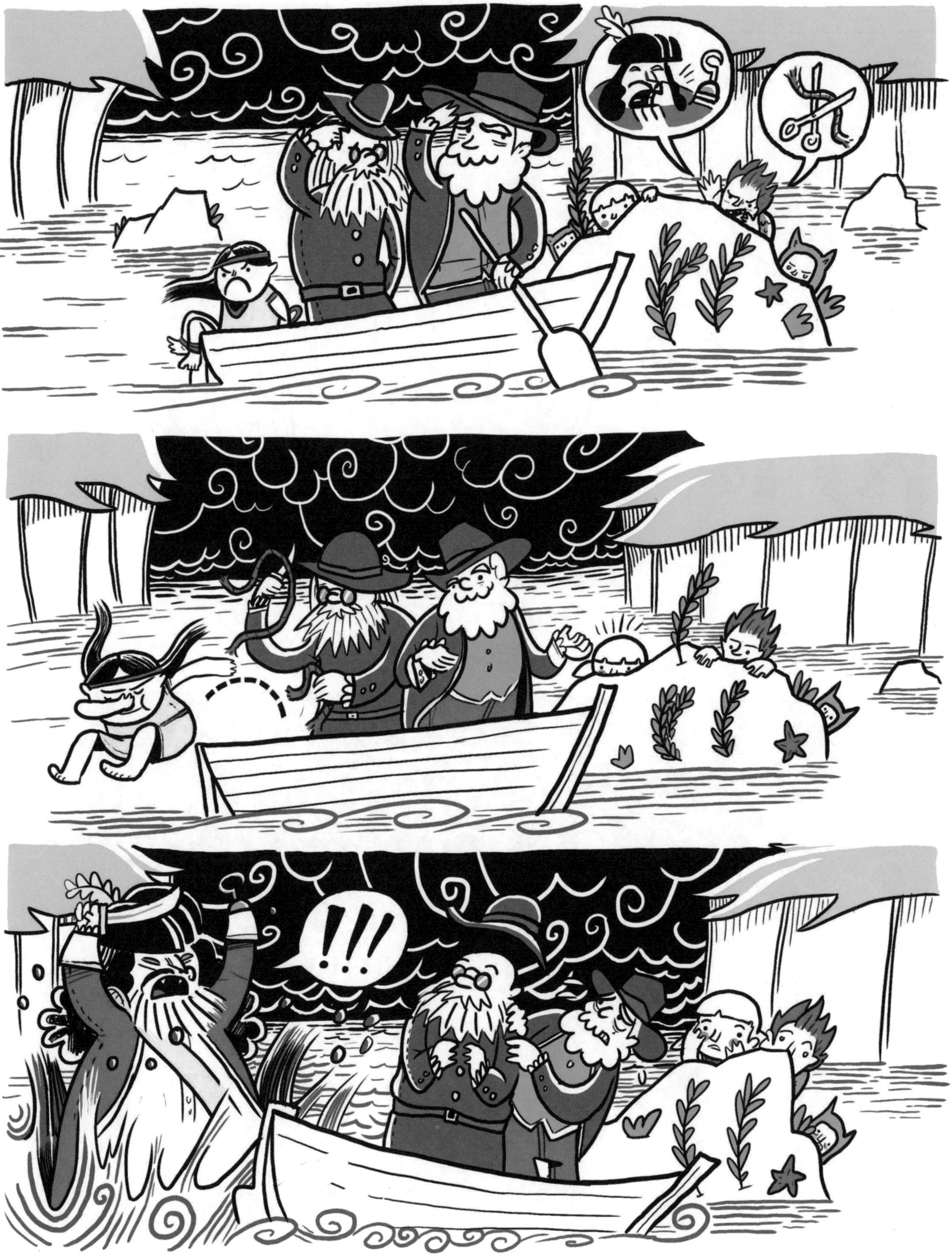
!!!

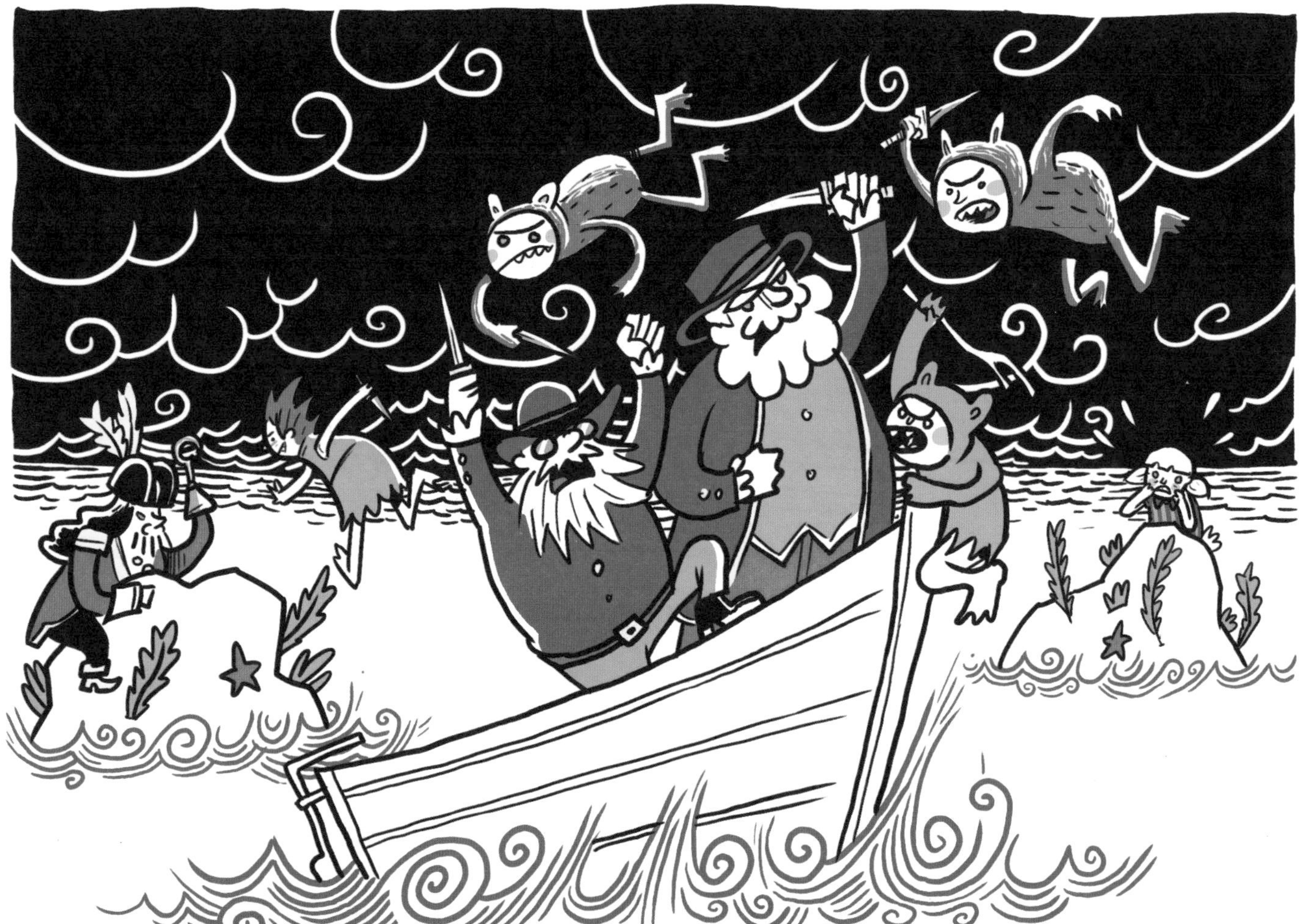

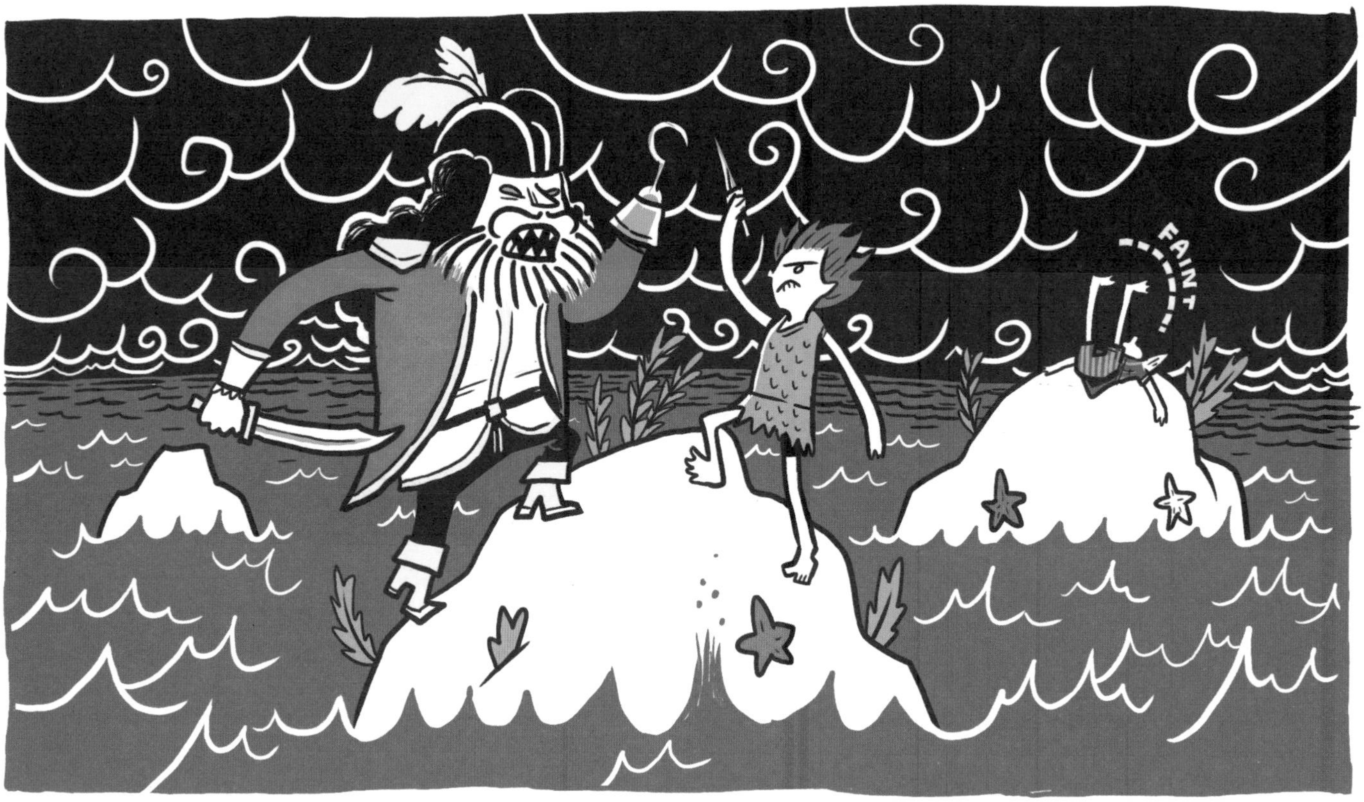
FAINT

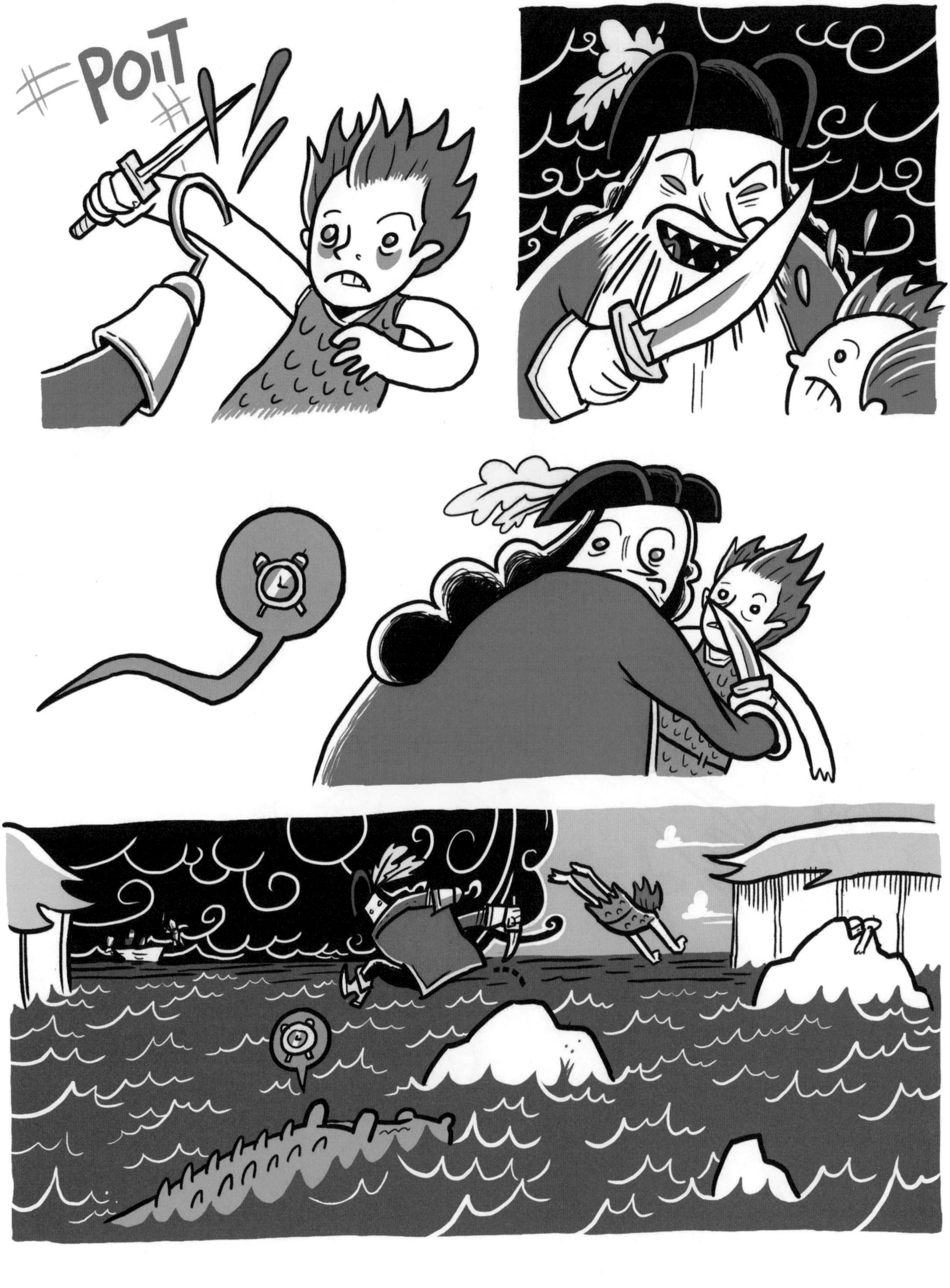
POIT

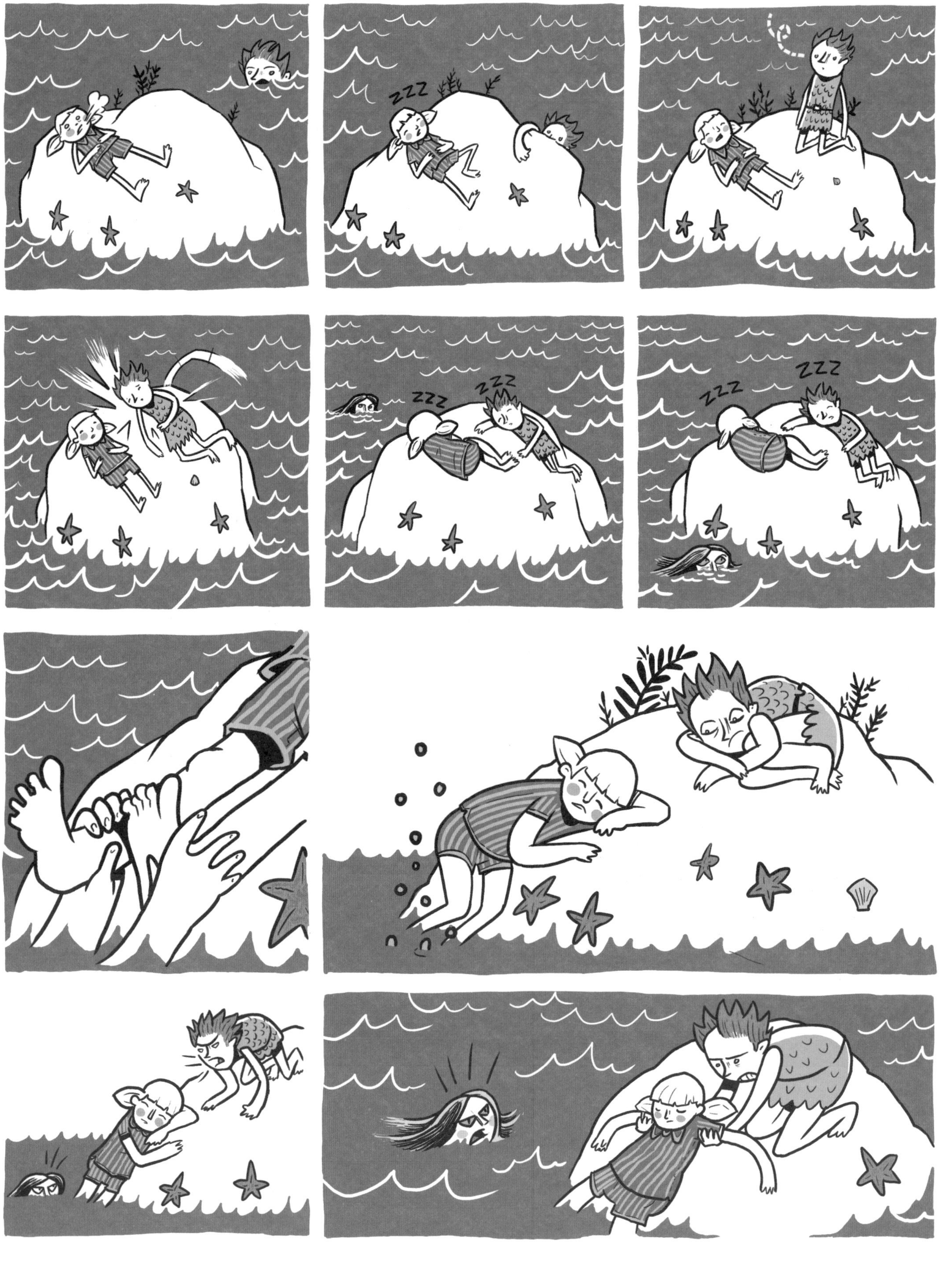
ZZZ
ZZZ
ZZZ
ZZZ
ZZZ

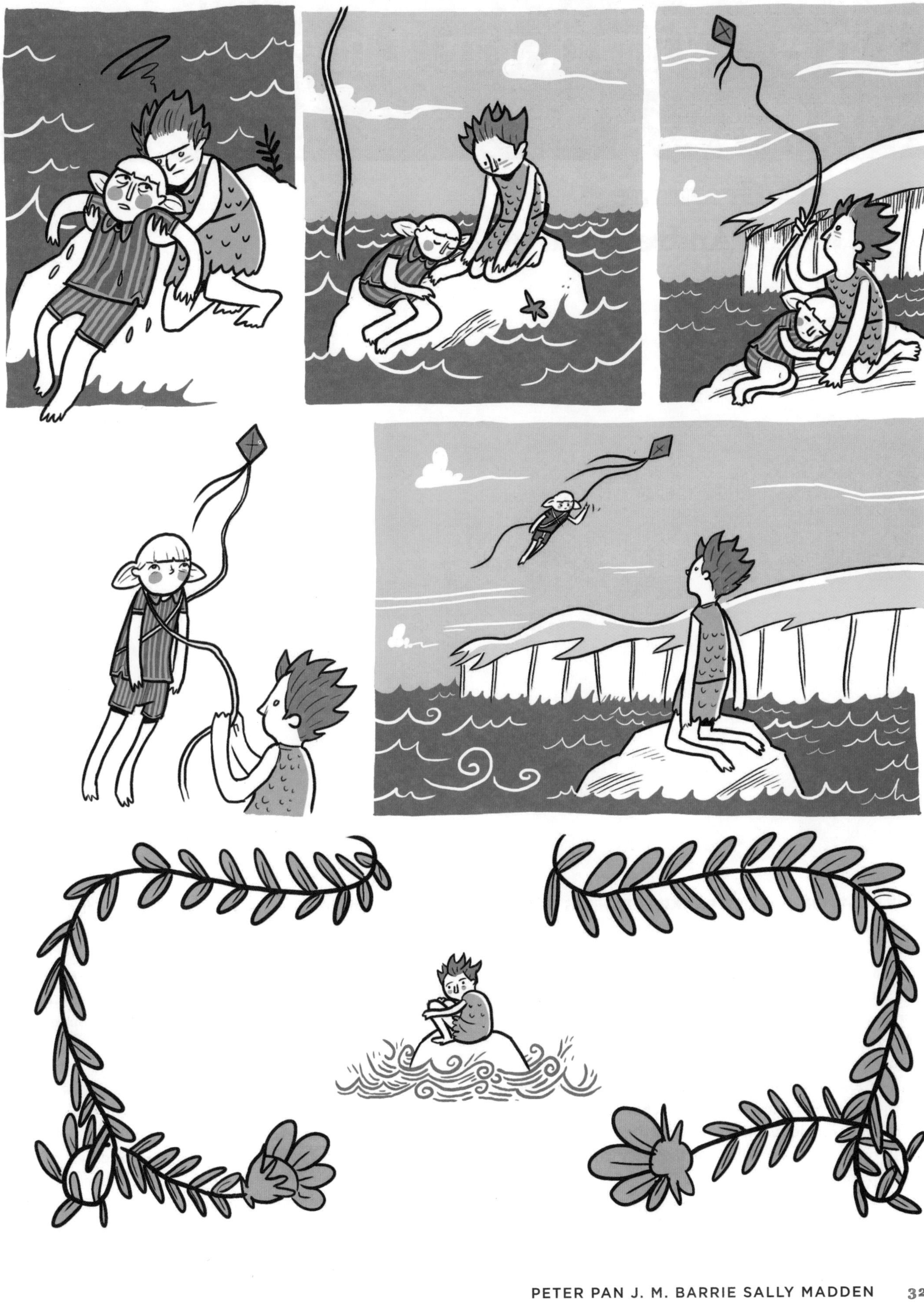

# The Wind in the Willows

## Kenneth Grahame

ART/ADAPTATION BY **Andrea Tsurumi**

**THE SCOTTISH-ENGLISH BANKER KENNETH GRAHAME** wrote two successful books of essays in the 1890s, but it wasn't until 1908, when he was forty-nine, that he produced his masterpiece, *The Wind in the Willows.* Like any number of classic works of kid lit, it gestated as bedtime stories for the author's own child (Alastair, who would commit suicide at age twenty). Set in an idyllic version of the British countryside, the beloved work principally involves four anthropomorphic animals—Ratty, Mole, Badger, and one of the most popular characters in children's literature, the unbridled, reckless, impulsive, boastful, rich badboy Toad.

Parul Sehgal, an editor at the *New York Times Book Review*, has written:

> It's the story of two little rodents, Mole and Rat, who carry on like bookish Edwardian bachelors, "messing about in boats"

and tramping in the snowy wood. But it's also the story of an intervention and a Bolshevik uprising, with a character based, it's believed, on Oscar Wilde. And these, mind you, are only the surface oddities. *The Wind in the Willows* is a book full of paradoxes—it's an ironical and deeply political nursery story, an ode to the hearth and the open road.

Illustrator and comics artist Andrea Tsurumi uses endlessly inventive layouts and Arcadian colors to adapt the climax of the book. Toad has managed to escape from prison, after being incarcerated for multiple destructive incidents involving his favorite new toy, a newfangled device called a motorcar. While away, his grand mansion, Toad Hall, has been taken over by weasels. Back in the day when characters in children's books could brandish guns, the four amigos hatch a plan to evict the squatters. . . .

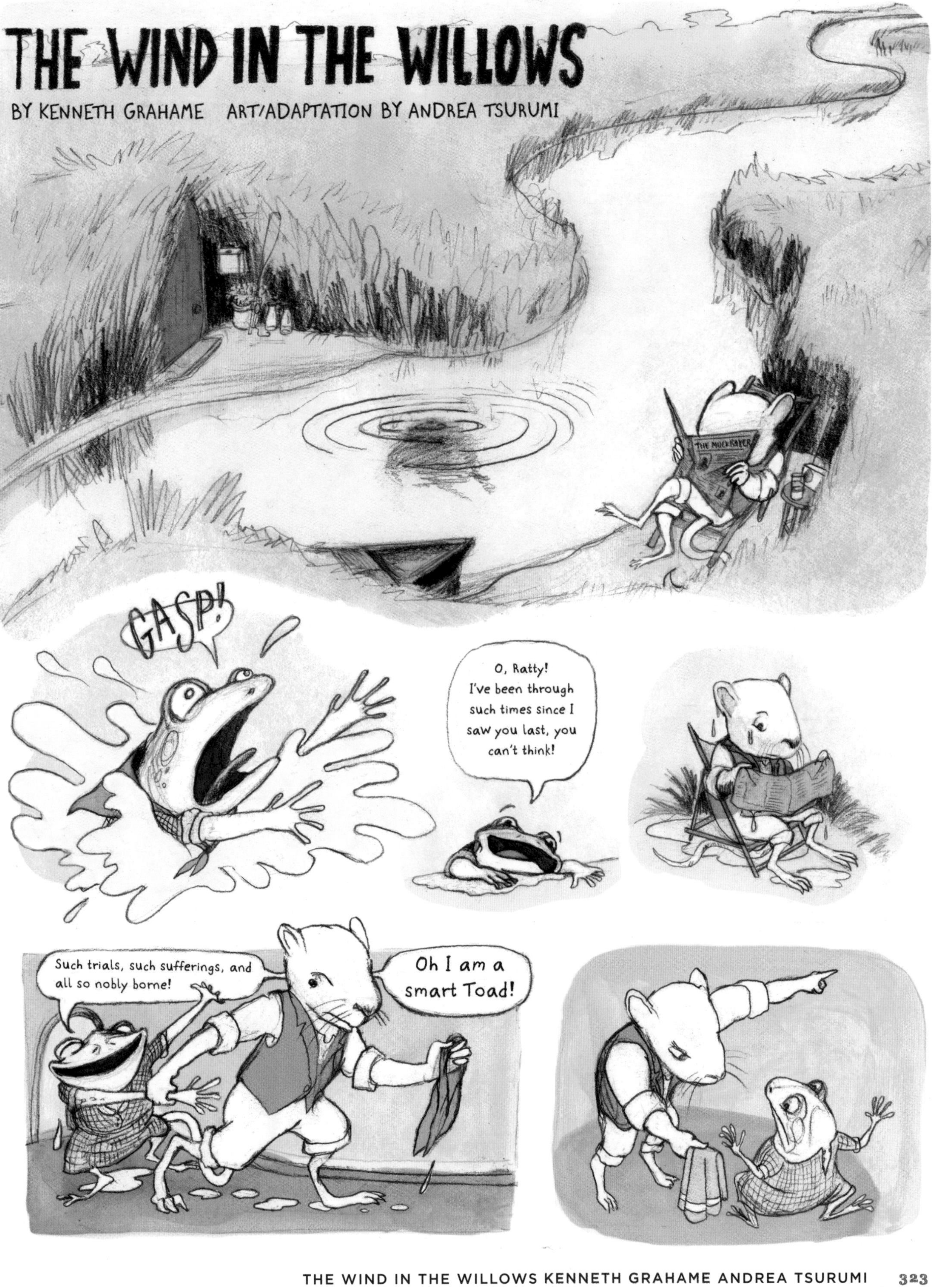
THE WIND IN THE WILLOWS
BY KENNETH GRAHAME ART/ADAPTATION BY ANDREA TSURUMI
GASP!
O, Ratty! I've been through such times since I saw you last, you can't think!
Such trials, such sufferings, and all so nobly borne!
Oh I am a smart Toad!

Such escapes, such disguises, and all so cleverly planned and carried out!

Been in prison—got out of it, of course!

Been thrown in a canal — swam ashore! Stole a horse—sold him for a large sum of money!

Humbugged everybody—made 'em all do exactly what I wanted! What do you think my last exploit was? Just hold on till I tell you —

SPLASH!

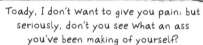
Toady, I don't want to give you pain; but seriously, don't you see what an ass you've been making of yourself?

You have been handcuffed, imprisoned, starved, chased, terrified out of your life, insulted, jeered at . . .

Where's the amusement in that? Where does the fun come in?

And all because you must needs go and steal a motor-car. When are you going to be sensible, and think of your friends?

...Quite right, Ratty!

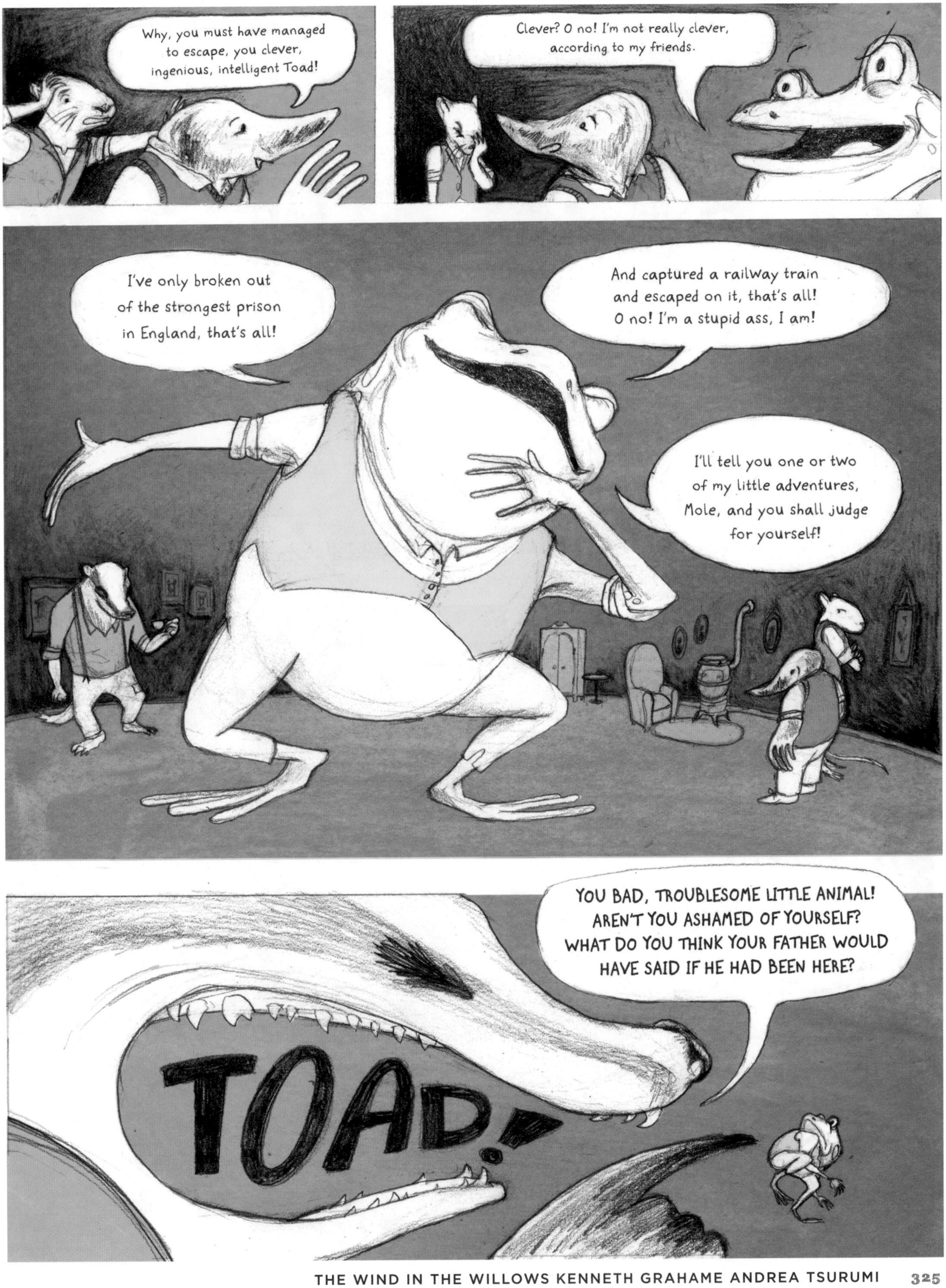
Why, you must have managed to escape, you clever, ingenious, intelligent Toad!
Clever? O no! I'm not really clever, according to my friends.
I've only broken out of the strongest prison in England, that's all!
And captured a railway train and escaped on it, that's all! O no! I'm a stupid ass, I am!
I'll tell you one or two of my little adventures, Mole, and you shall judge for yourself!
YOU BAD, TROUBLESOME LITTLE ANIMAL! AREN'T YOU ASHAMED OF YOURSELF? WHAT DO YOU THINK YOUR FATHER WOULD HAVE SAID IF HE HAD BEEN HERE?
TOAD!

There, there! We're going to let bygones be bygones.

Mole, please tell us what the position is.

PAT PAT

Bad.

Sentries posted everywhere, guns poked out at us, stones thrown at us, and when they see us, how they do laugh! That's what annoys me most!

There are more ways of getting back a place than taking it by storm. I haven't said my last word yet.

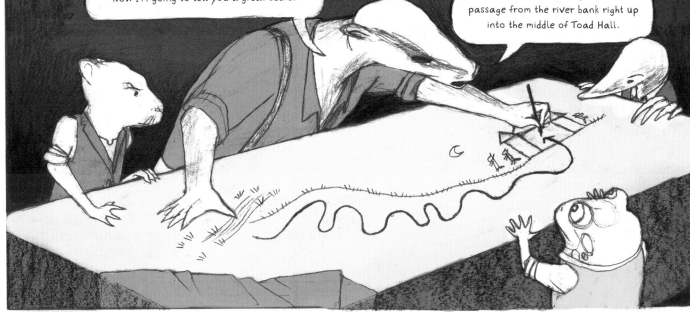

Now I'm going to tell you a great secret.

There is an underground passage from the river bank right up into the middle of Toad Hall.

O, nonsense! Badger, I know every inch of Toad Hall. Nothing of the sort, I do assure you!

My young friend, your father was a particular friend of mine and told me a great deal he wouldn't have dreamt of telling you.

?!

Well, perhaps I am a bit of a talker.

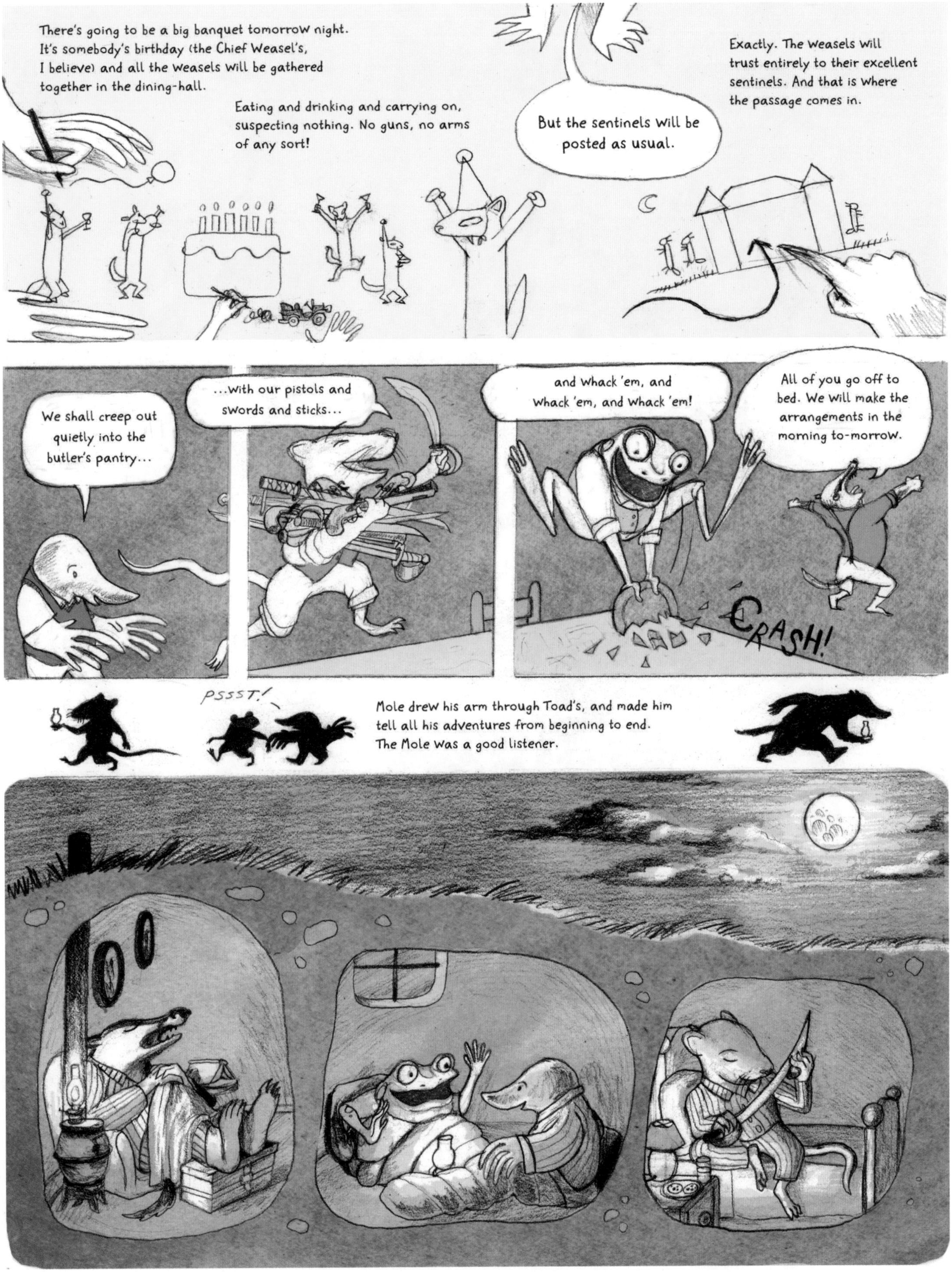
There's going to be a big banquet tomorrow night. It's somebody's birthday (the Chief Weasel's, I believe) and all the weasels will be gathered together in the dining-hall.
Eating and drinking and carrying on, suspecting nothing. No guns, no arms of any sort!
But the sentinels will be posted as usual.
Exactly. The weasels will trust entirely to their excellent sentinels. And that is where the passage comes in.
We shall creep out quietly into the butler's pantry...
...with our pistols and swords and sticks...
and whack 'em, and whack 'em, and whack 'em!
CRASH!
All of you go off to bed. We will make the arrangements in the morning to-morrow.
PSSST!
Mole drew his arm through Toad's, and made him tell all his adventures from beginning to end. The Mole was a good listener.

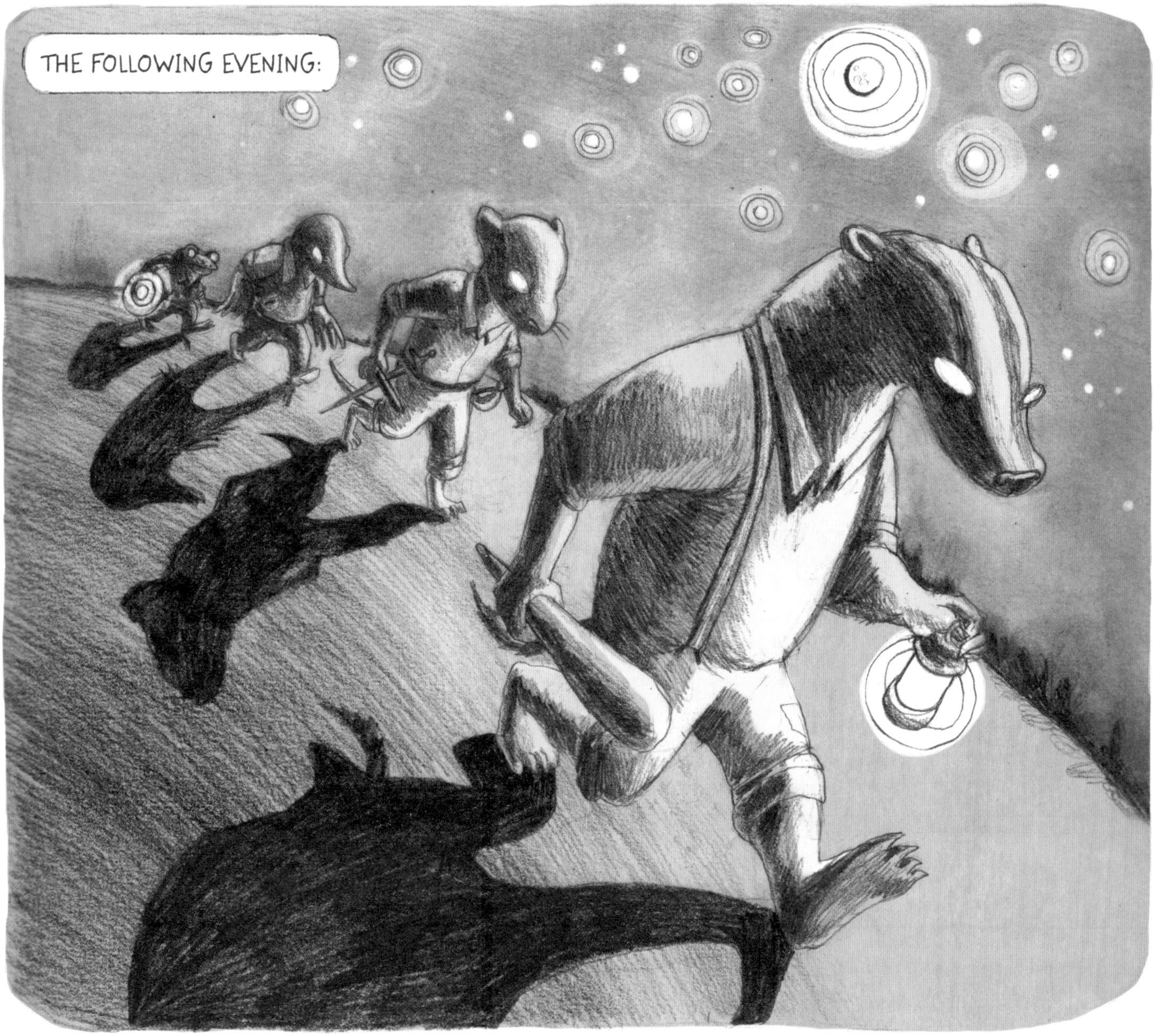
THE FOLLOWING EVENING:

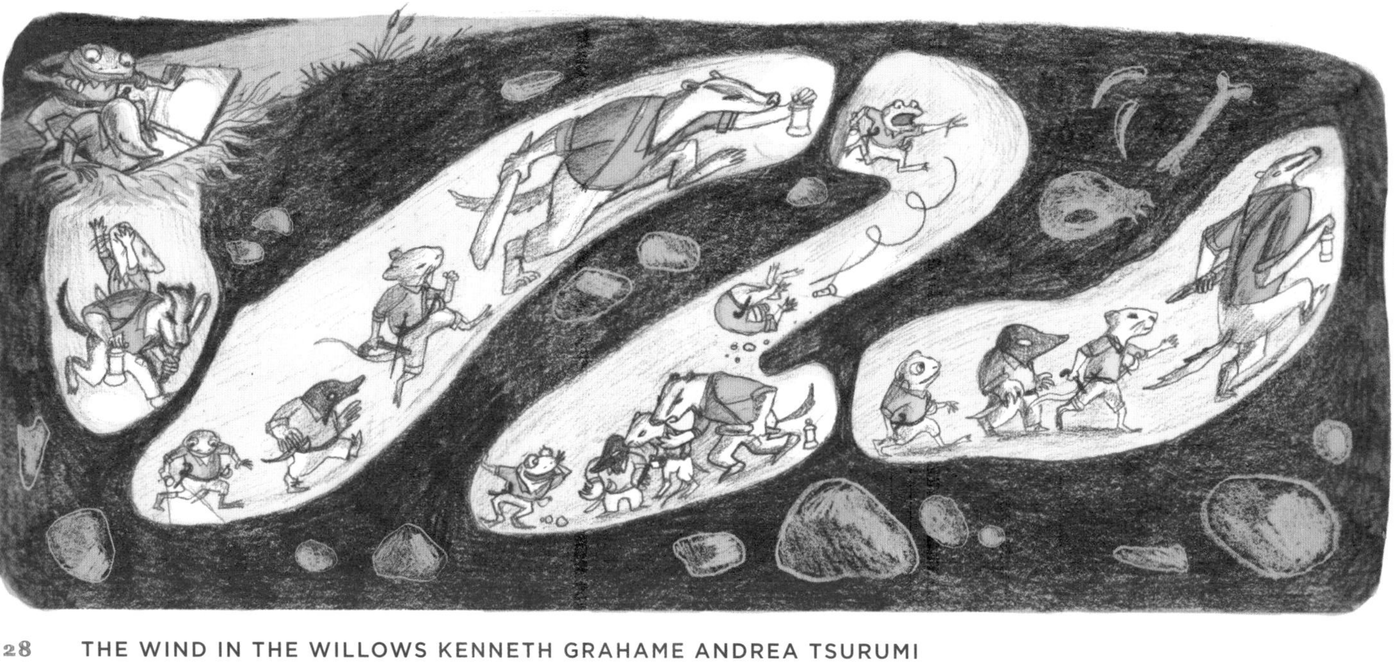

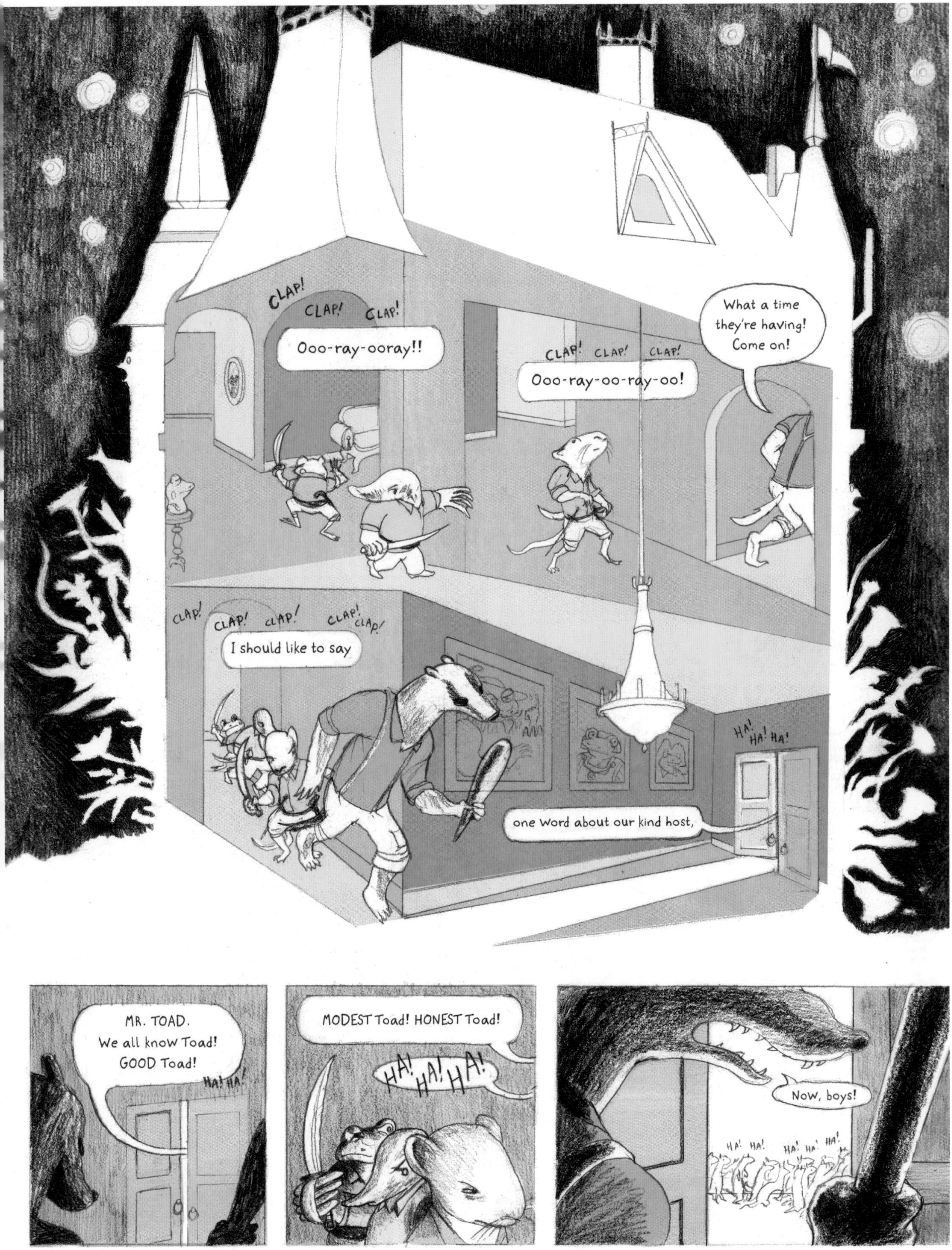
CLAP!
CLAP!
CLAP!
Ooo-ray-ooray!!
CLAP!
CLAP!
CLAP!
Ooo-ray-oo-ray-oo!
What a time they're having! Come on!
CLAP!
CLAP!
CLAP!
CLAP!
CLAP!
I should like to say
HA! HA! HA!
one word about our kind host,
MR. TOAD. We all know Toad! GOOD Toad!
HA! HA!
MODEST Toad! HONEST Toad!
HA! HA! HA!
Now, boys!
HA! HA! HA! HA! HA!

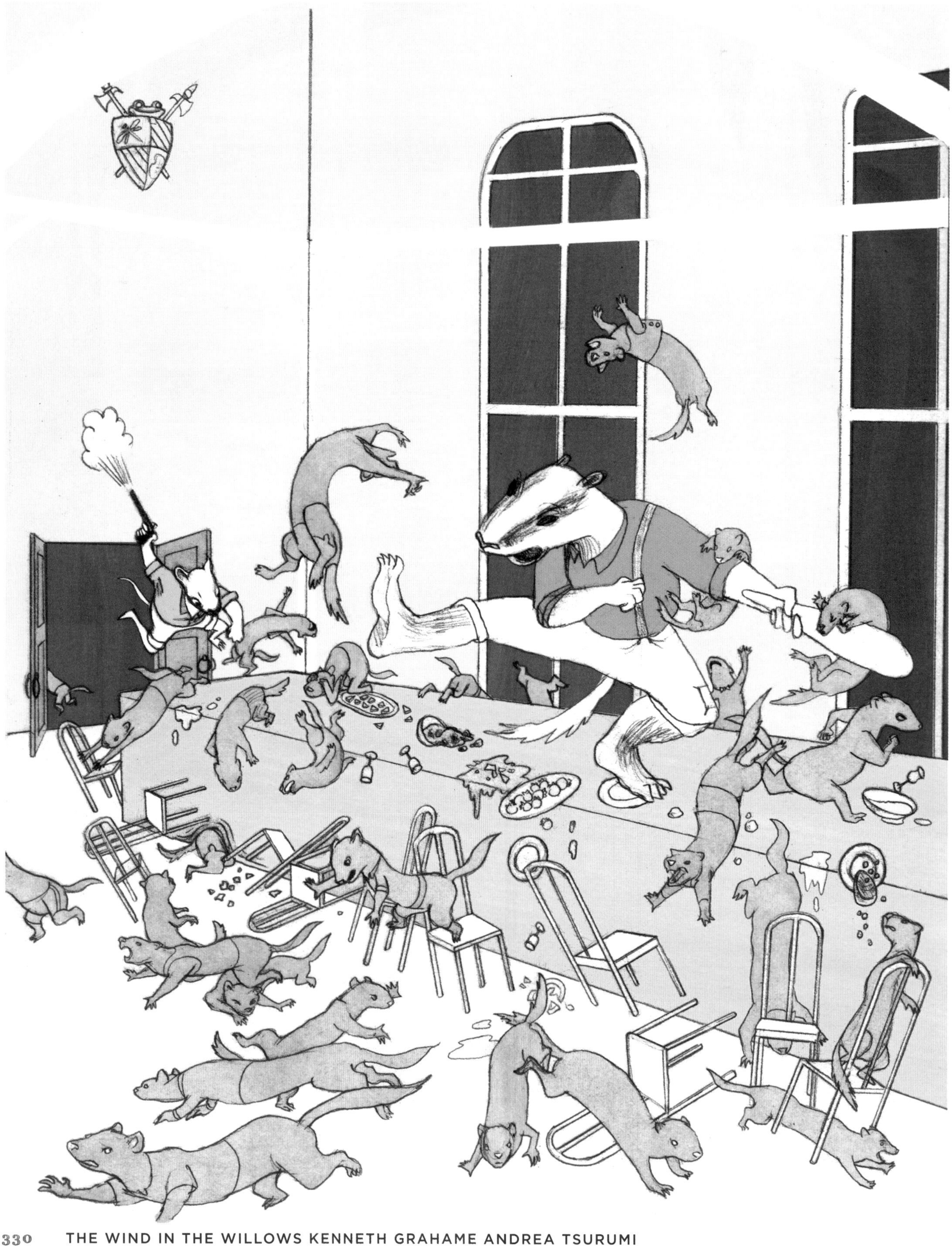

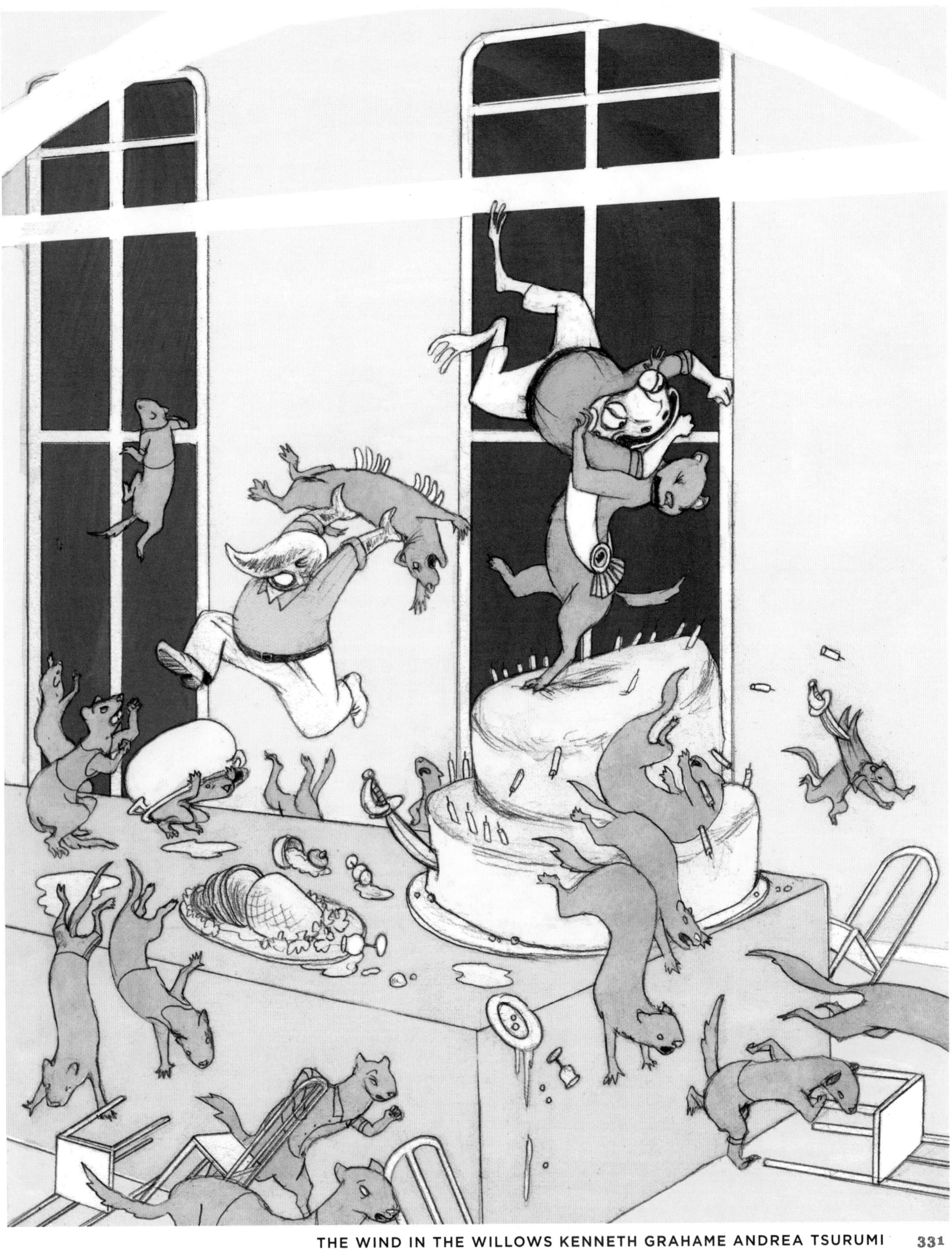

# The Secret Garden

## Frances Hodgson Burnett

ART/ADAPTATION BY **Juliacks**

**FURTHER BLURRING THE LINE BETWEEN CHILDREN'S** literature and great literature in general, *The Secret Garden* was originally published in serial form in 1910–11 in the *American Magazine*, which featured muckraking journalism and fiction from a who's who of great English-language writers from the first half of the twentieth century. The author, Frances Hodgson Burnett, is best-remembered for her so-called children's novels, which also include *Little Lord Fauntleroy*, but at the time was known as a writer of novels for adults.

*The Secret Garden*—which was quickly forgotten in its day but is now enshrined in the pantheon of the greatest children's novels of all time—follows the metamorphosis of ten-year-old Mary Lennox. She's a quintessential brat, a pill who dislikes everyone around her. When cholera kills her parents and all their servants in India, she's sent to live with her uncle, a widower, in a big, dark, dreary English manor. Slowly, she forms bonds with the maid, the gardener, a robin, her sickly cousin, and others. She finds a way into the secret part of the garden, which had been locked tight since her aunt's death. . . .

Juliacks is an avant-garde artist working in a number of disciplines. I was curious to witness the marriage between her cutting-edge sensibilities and this thoroughly Edwardian children's novel. The resulting mélange of ink, pencil, and paint has an edge to it while still capturing the gloomy, claustrophobic, then explosively bright feel of the book.

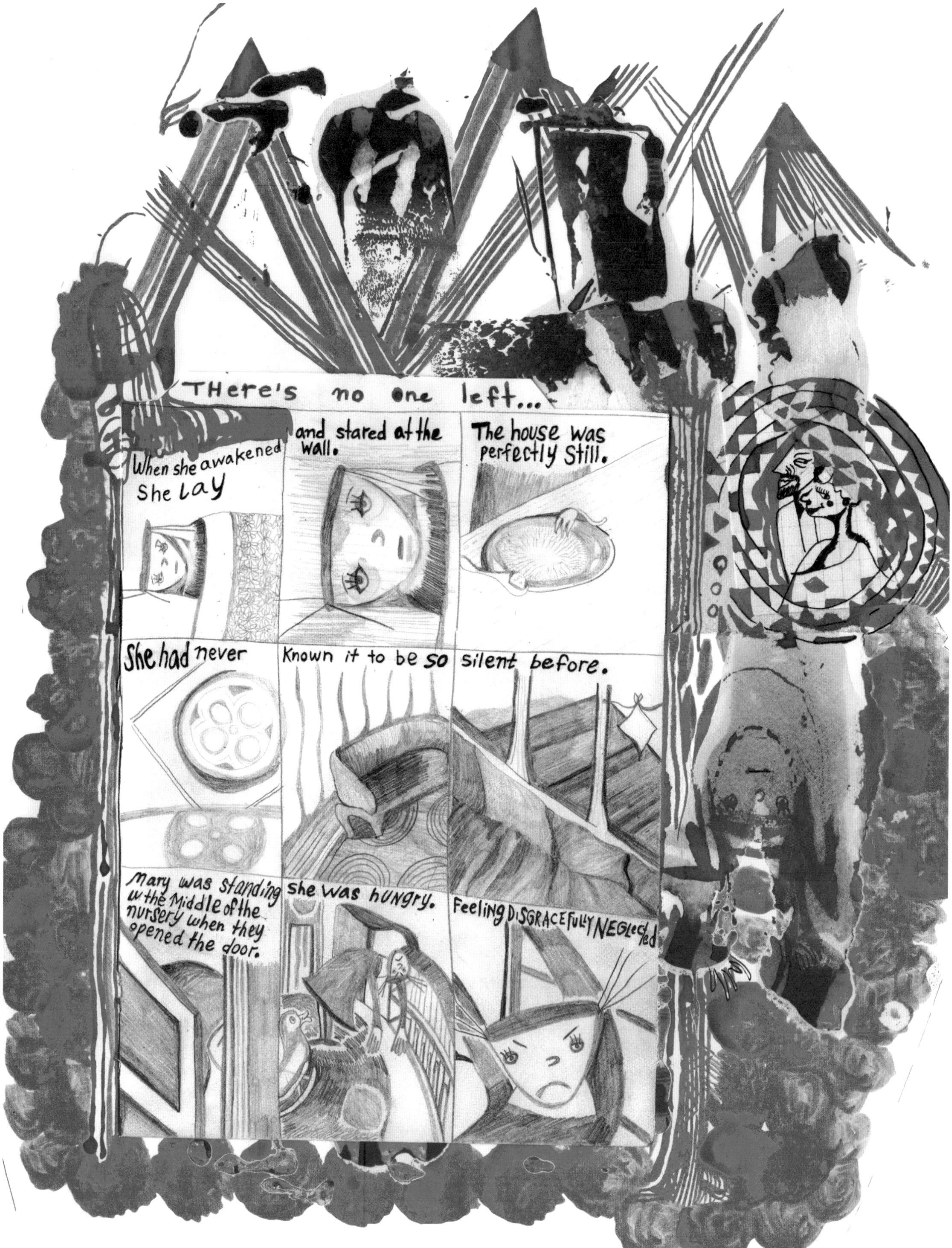
THere's no one left...
When she awakened She lay
and stared at the wall.
The house was perfectly still.
She had never
Known it to be so
silent before.
Mary was standing in the Middle of the nursery when they opened the door.
She was hungry.
Feeling DISGRACEFULLY NEGLected

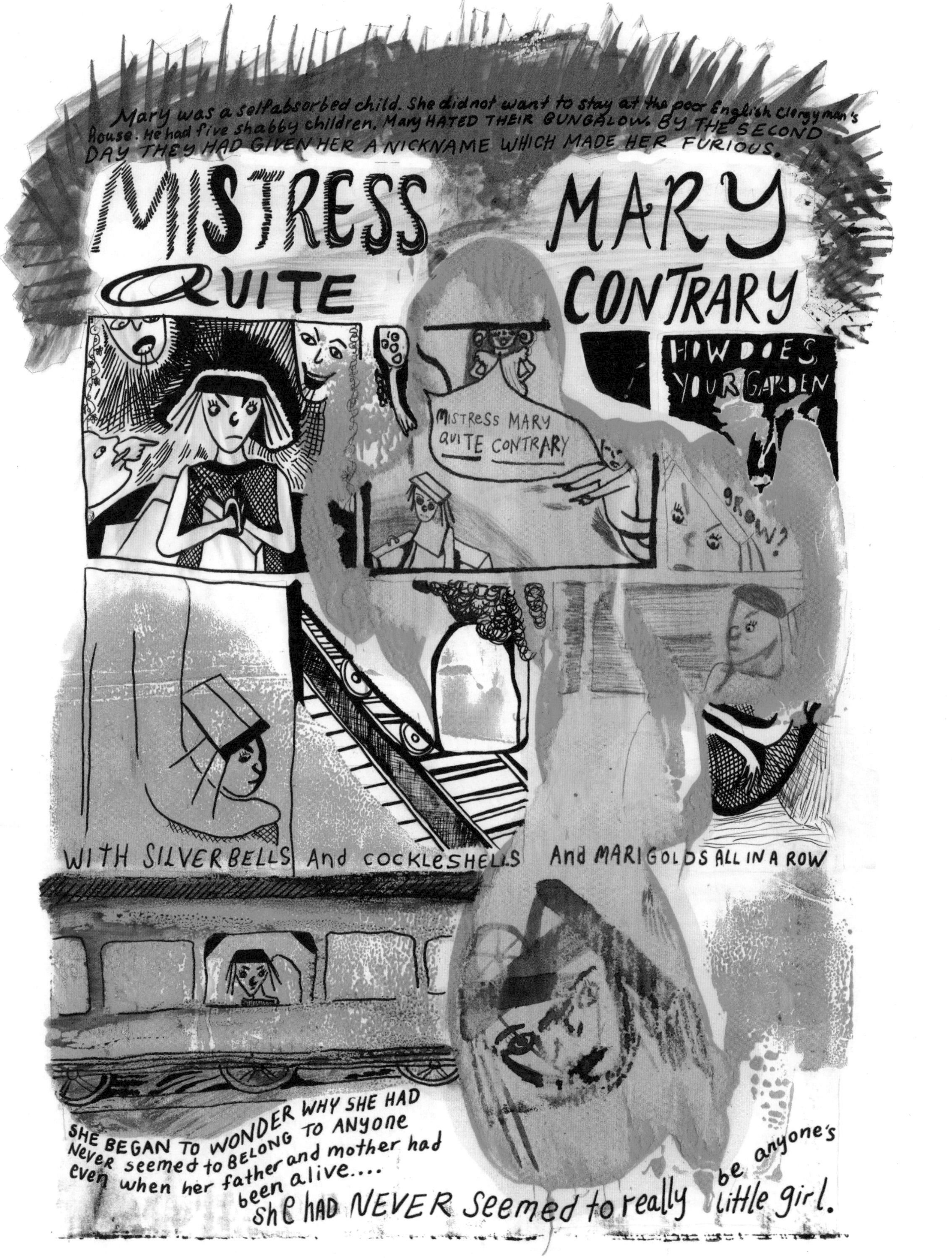

Mary was a selfabsorbed child. She did not want to stay at the poor English Clergyman's House. He had five shabby children. Mary HATED THEIR BUNGALOW. BY THE SECOND DAY THEY HAD GIVEN HER A NICKNAME WHICH MADE HER FURIOUS.
MISTRESS MARY QUITE CONTRARY
HOW DOES YOUR GARDEN
MISTRESS MARY QUITE CONTRARY
GROW?
WITH SILVERBELLS And COCKLESHELLS And MARIGOLDS ALL IN A ROW
SHE BEGAN TO WONDER WHY SHE HAD NEVER seemed to BELONG TO ANYONE even when her father and mother had been alive....
she HAD NEVER seemed to really be anyone's little girl.

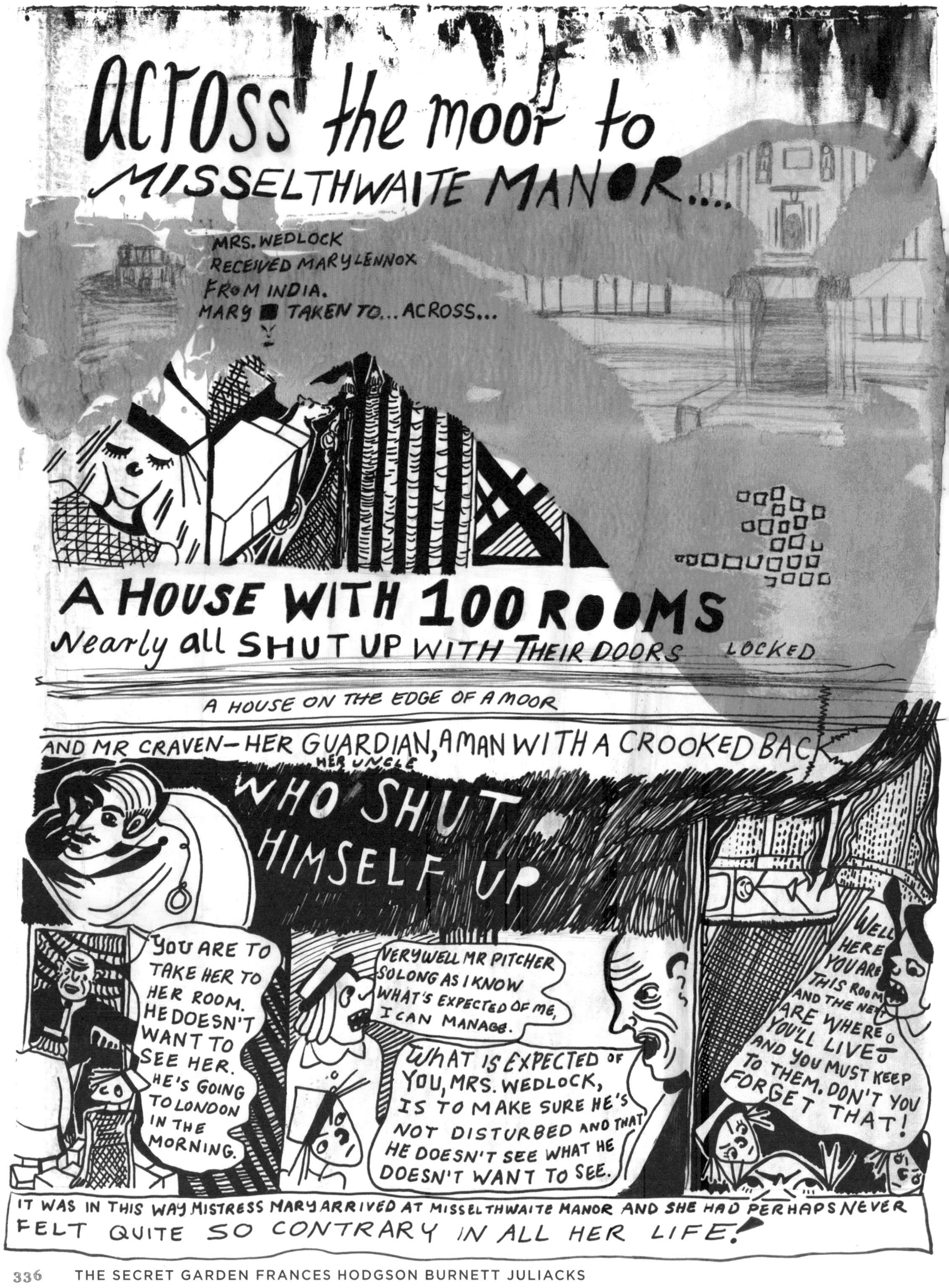
ACROSS the moor to
MISSELTHWAITE MANOR....
MRS. WEDLOCK
RECEIVED MARY LENNOX
FROM INDIA.
MARY [redacted] TAKEN TO... ACROSS...
A HOUSE WITH 100 ROOMS
Nearly all SHUT UP WITH THEIR DOORS LOCKED
A HOUSE ON THE EDGE OF A MOOR
AND MR CRAVEN— HER GUARDIAN, HER UNCLE A MAN WITH A CROOKED BACK
WHO SHUT HIMSELF UP
YOU ARE TO TAKE HER TO HER ROOM. HE DOESN'T WANT TO SEE HER. HE'S GOING TO LONDON IN THE MORNING.
VERY WELL MR PITCHER SO LONG AS I KNOW WHAT'S EXPECTED OF ME, I CAN MANAGE.
WHAT IS EXPECTED OF YOU, MRS. WEDLOCK, IS TO MAKE SURE HE'S NOT DISTURBED AND THAT HE DOESN'T SEE WHAT HE DOESN'T WANT TO SEE.
WELL HERE YOU ARE THIS ROOM AND THE NEXT ARE WHERE YOU'LL LIVE AND YOU MUST KEEP TO THEM. DON'T YOU FORGET THAT!
IT WAS IN THIS WAY MISTRESS MARY ARRIVED AT MISSELTHWAITE MANOR AND SHE HAD PERHAPS NEVER FELT QUITE SO CONTRARY IN ALL HER LIFE!

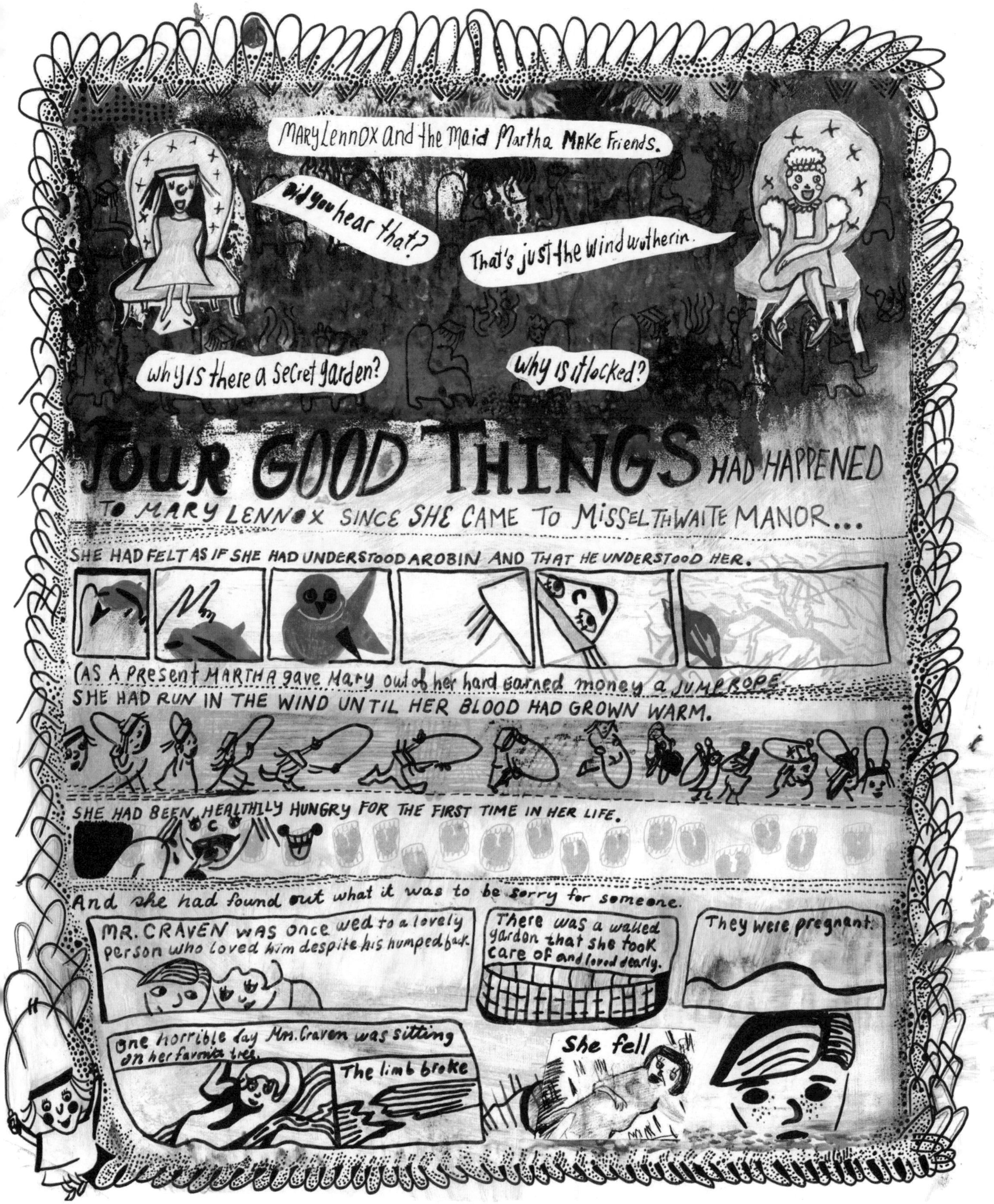
Mary Lennox and the Maid Martha Make Friends.
Did you hear that?
That's just the wind wutherin.
why is there a secret garden?
why is it locked?
FOUR GOOD THINGS HAD HAPPENED TO MARY LENNOX SINCE SHE CAME TO MISSELTHWAITE MANOR...
SHE HAD FELT AS IF SHE HAD UNDERSTOOD A ROBIN AND THAT HE UNDERSTOOD HER.
(AS A PRESENT MARTHA gave Mary out of her hard earned money a JUMP ROPE.
SHE HAD RUN IN THE WIND UNTIL HER BLOOD HAD GROWN WARM.
SHE HAD BEEN HEALTHILY HUNGRY FOR THE FIRST TIME IN HER LIFE.
And she had found out what it was to be sorry for someone.
MR. CRAVEN was once wed to a lovely person who loved him despite his humped back.
There was a walled garden that she took care of and loved dearly.
They were pregnant.
One horrible day Mrs. Craven was sitting on her favorite tree.
The limb broke
She fell

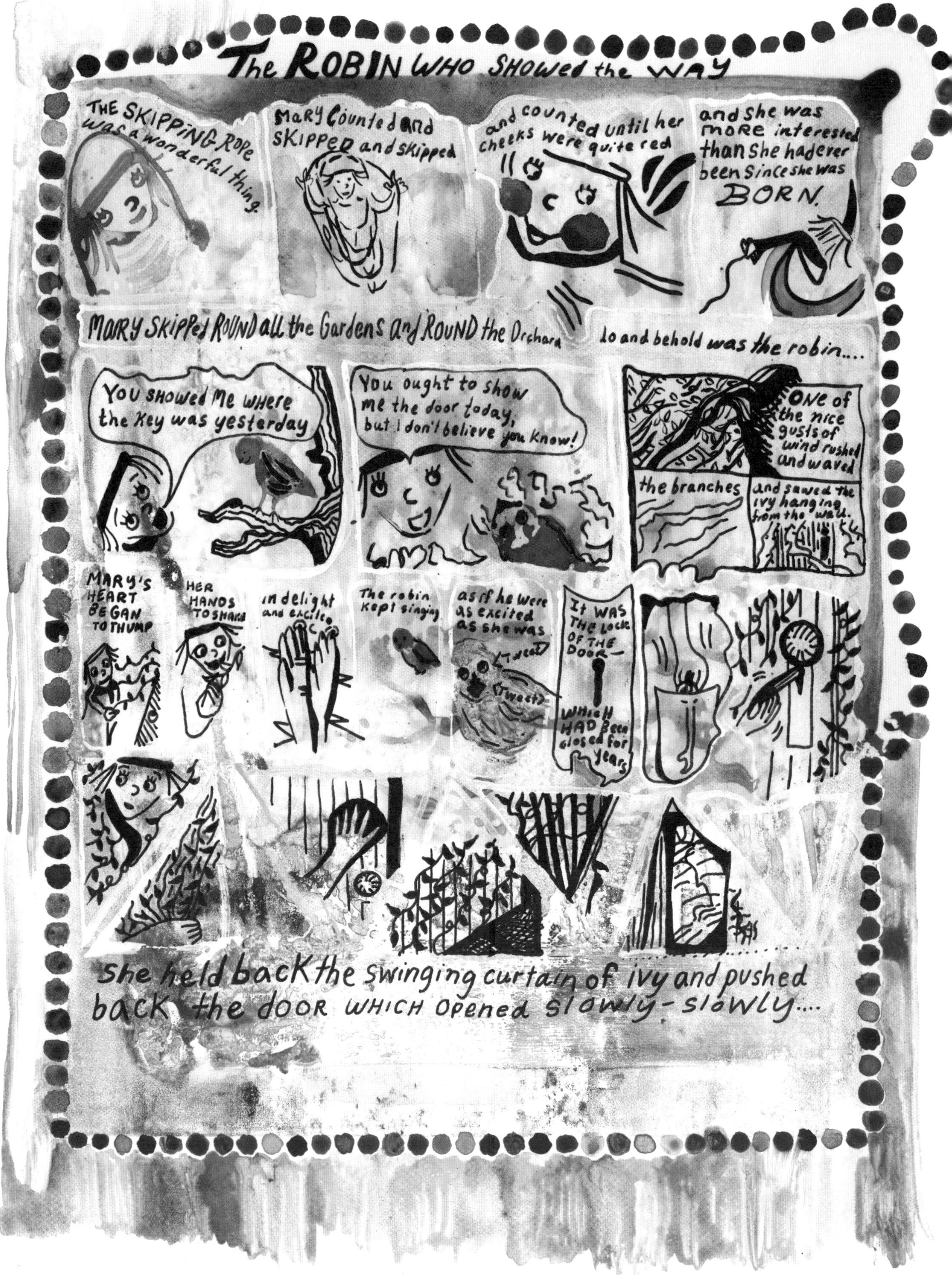
The ROBIN WHO SHOWED the WAY
THE SKIPPING ROPE was a wonderful thing.
Mary Counted and SKIPPED and skipped
and counted until her cheeks were quite red
and she was more interested than she had ever been since she was BORN.
MARY SKIPPED ROUND all the Gardens and ROUND the Orchard
lo and behold was the robin....
You showed me where the key was yesterday
You ought to show me the door today, but I don't believe you know!
ONE of the nice gusts of wind rushed and waved
the branches
and swayed the ivy hanging from the wall.
MARY'S HEART BEGAN TO THUMP
HER HANDS TO SHAKE
in delight and excite
The robin kept singing
as if he were as excited as she was
Tweet
Tweet
It WAS THE LOCK OF THE DOOR—
WHICH HAD Been closed for years
She held back the swinging curtain of ivy and pushed back the door WHICH Opened slowly - slowly....

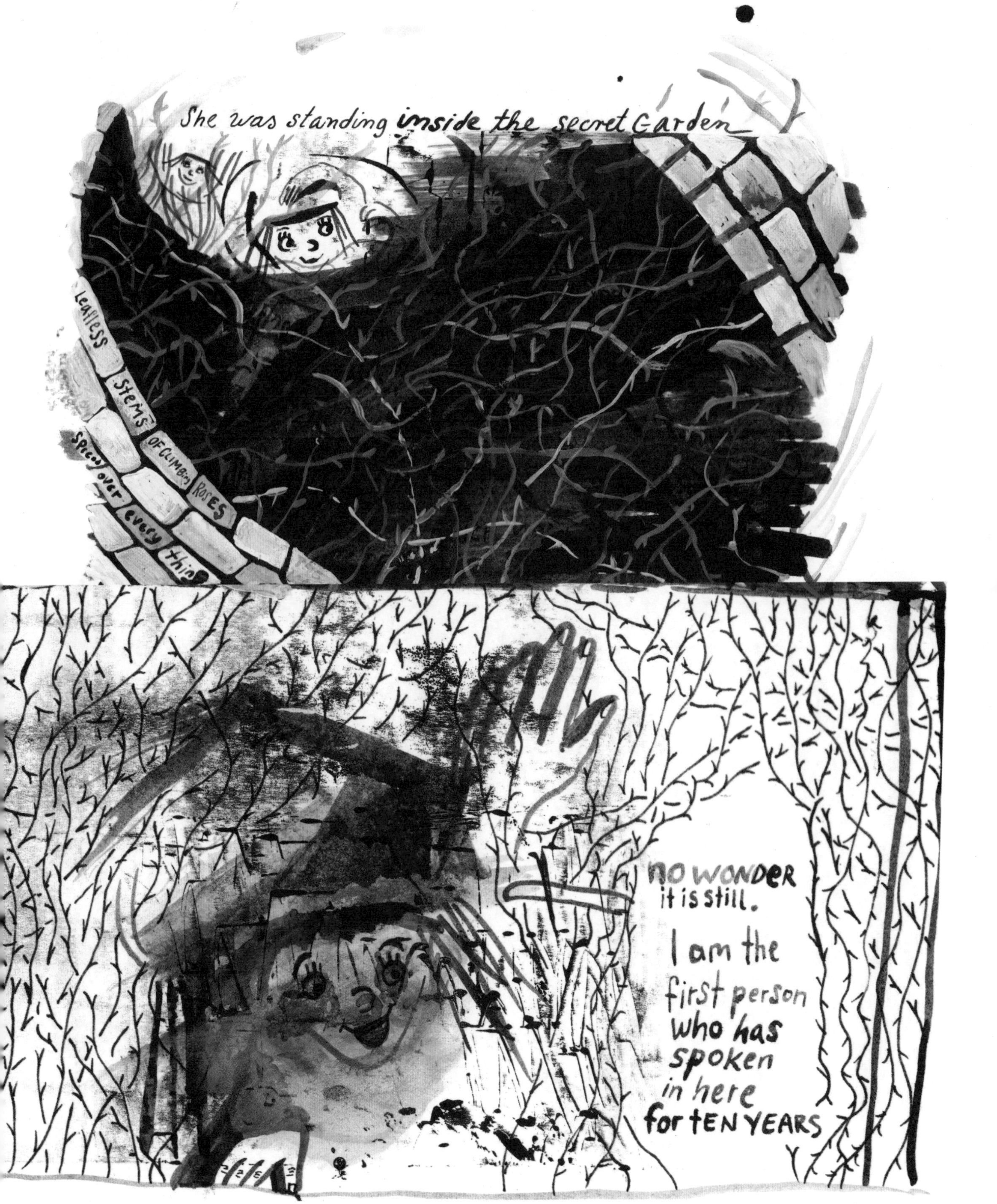
She was standing inside the secret Garden
Leafless
Stems
OF CLIMBing
ROSES
over
every
no WONDER
it is still.
I am the
first person
who has
spoken
in here
for TEN YEARS

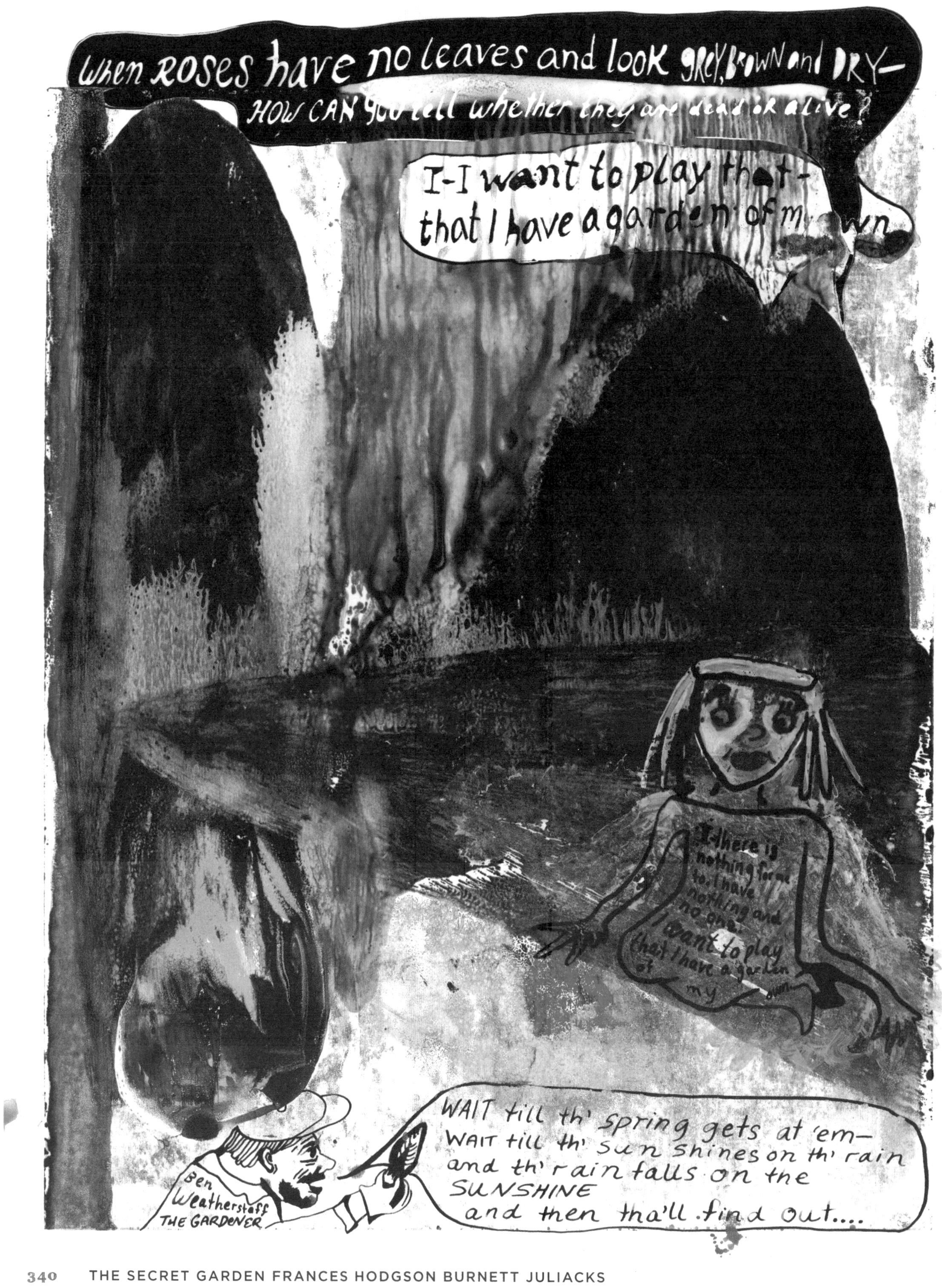
When ROSES have no leaves and look GREY, BROWN and DRY—
HOW CAN you tell whether they are dead or alive?
I-I want to play that-
that I have a garden of my own
I-there is
nothing for me
to. I have
nothing and
no one.
I want to play
that I have a garden
of
my own
WAIT till th' spring gets at 'em—
WAIT till th' sun shines on th' rain
and th' rain falls on the
SUNSHINE
and then tha'll find out....
Ben
Weatherstaff
THE GARDENER

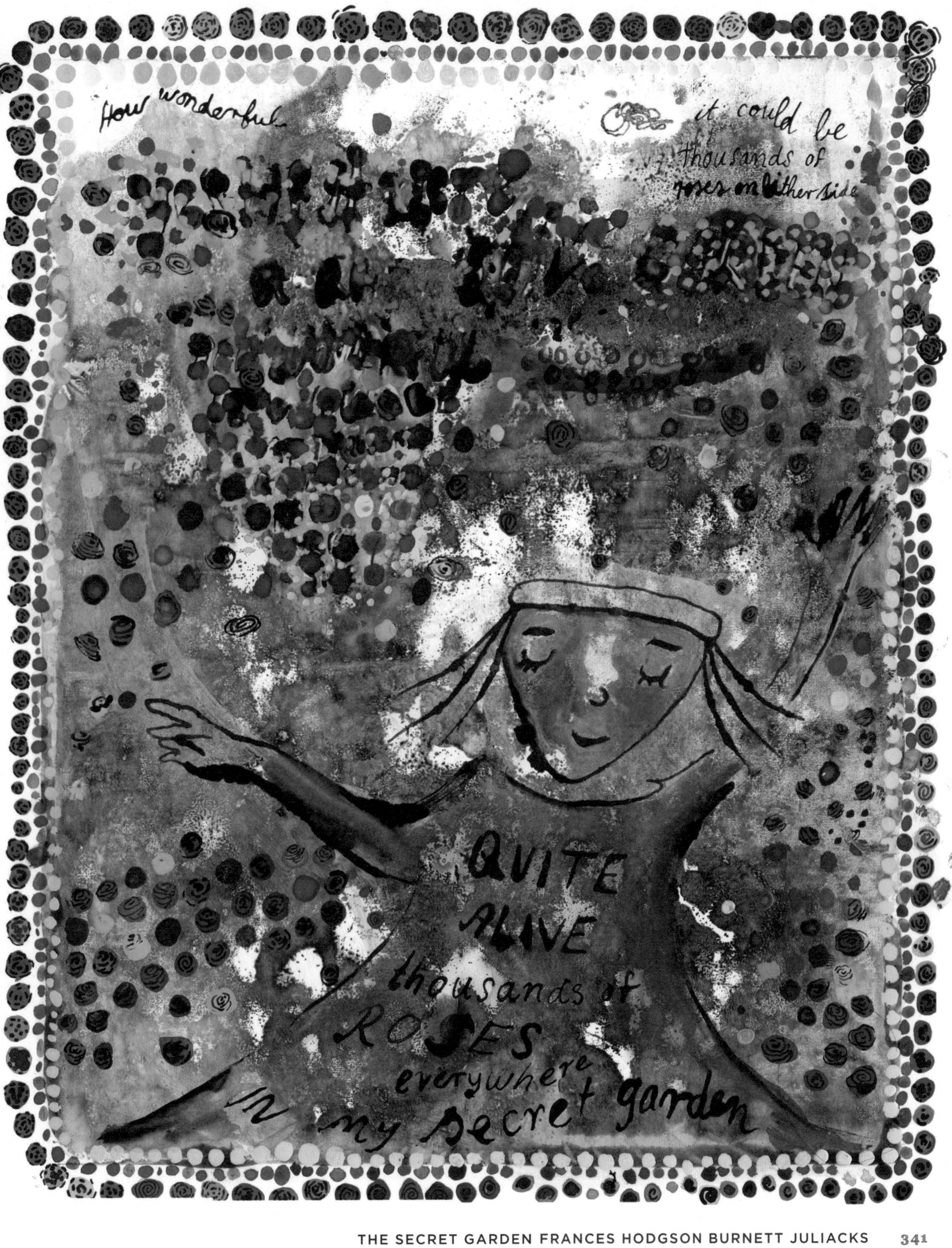
How wonderful
it could be thousands of roses on either side
QUITE ALIVE
thousands of
ROSES
everywhere
IN my secret garden

# The Velveteen Rabbit

## Margery Williams

ART/ADAPTATION BY **Kate Glasheen**

**BRITISH AUTHOR MARGERY WILLIAMS WASN'T** achieving any popularity with her novels for adults. After World War I ended, she and her Italian husband moved to the US. Then Williams wrote a novel for children, a story about a stuffed animal that is quickly forgotten by its owner but later, by chance, becomes the child's favorite toy. When the boy almost dies from scarlet fever, the bunny—because of the boy's love and the intervention of a fairy—becomes "Real," alive.

In the novel's most famous passage, the oldest, wisest animal in the nursery—the Skin Horse—tells the rabbit how stuffed animals sometimes come to life:

> "Real isn't how you are made," said the Skin Horse. "It's a thing that happens to you. When a child loves you for a long, long time, not just to play with, but REALLY loves you, then you become Real."

"Does it hurt?" asked the Rabbit.

"Sometimes," said the Skin Horse, for he was always truthful. "When you are Real you don't mind being hurt."

*The Velveteen Rabbit* was an immediate success upon publication in 1922, and, although its literary value isn't as high as many other classic children's novels, it remains unflaggingly popular, a beloved touchstone of countless childhoods.

Kate Glasheen—who drew the endlessly inventive *Hybrid Bastards!* graphic novel (written by Tom Pinchuk)—brings all kinds of goodness to this wordless adaptation of the entire book, including jaw-dropping use of panels, a buxom fairy you wouldn't normally imagine in a kids' book, and a quiet, touching final page.

# THE VELVETEEN RABBIT

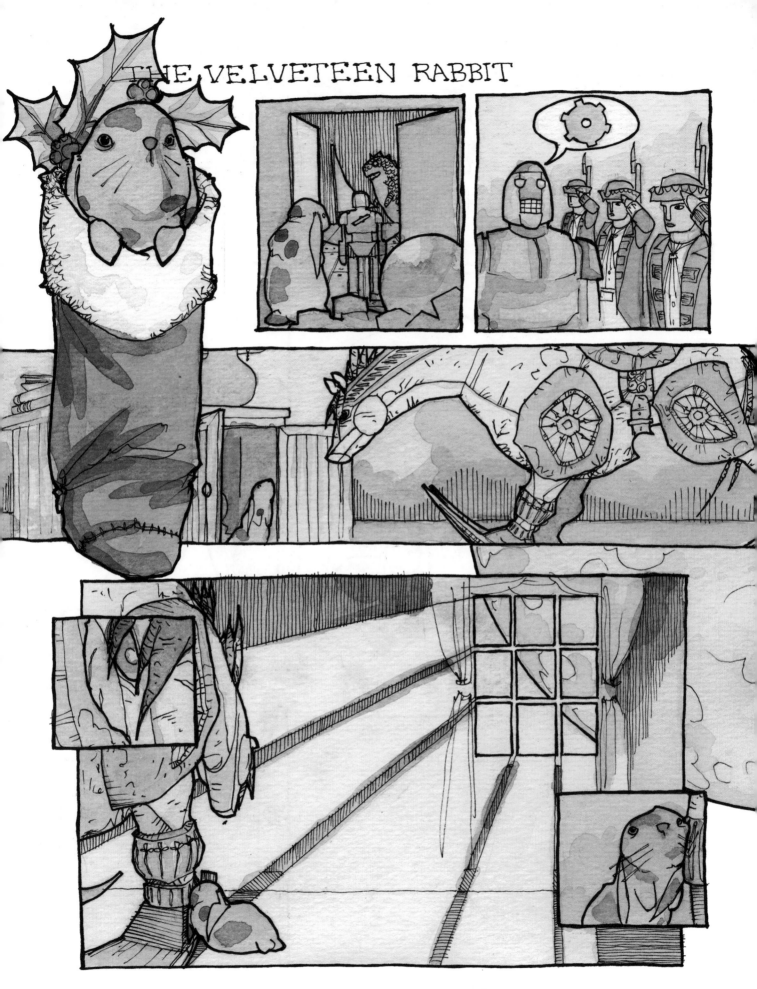

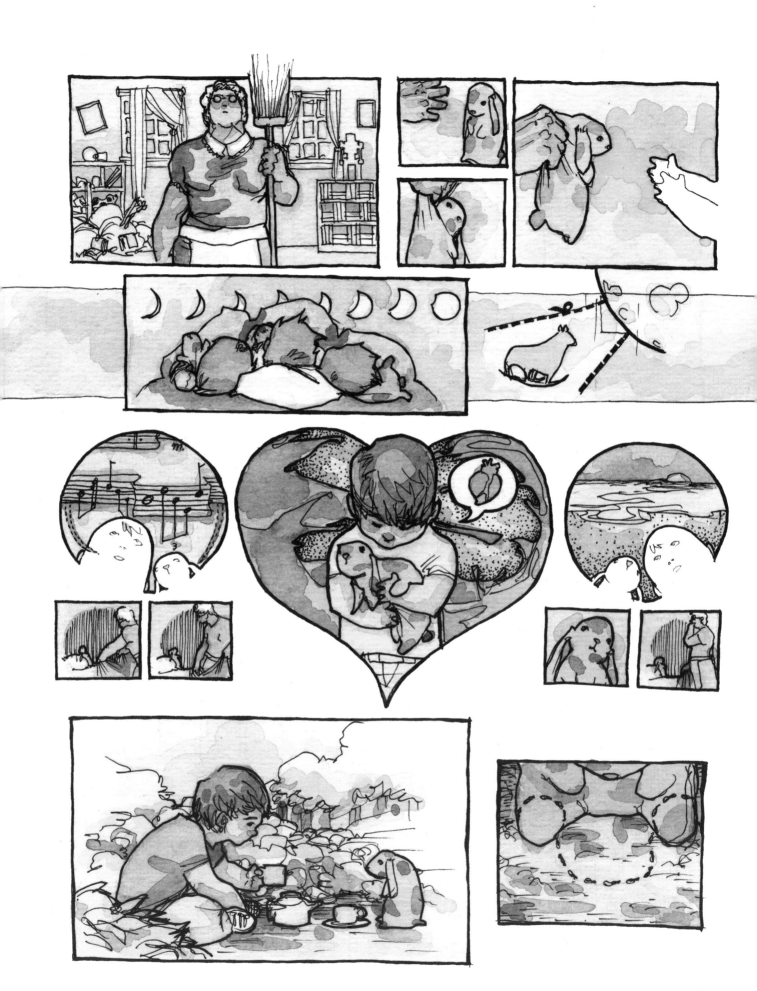

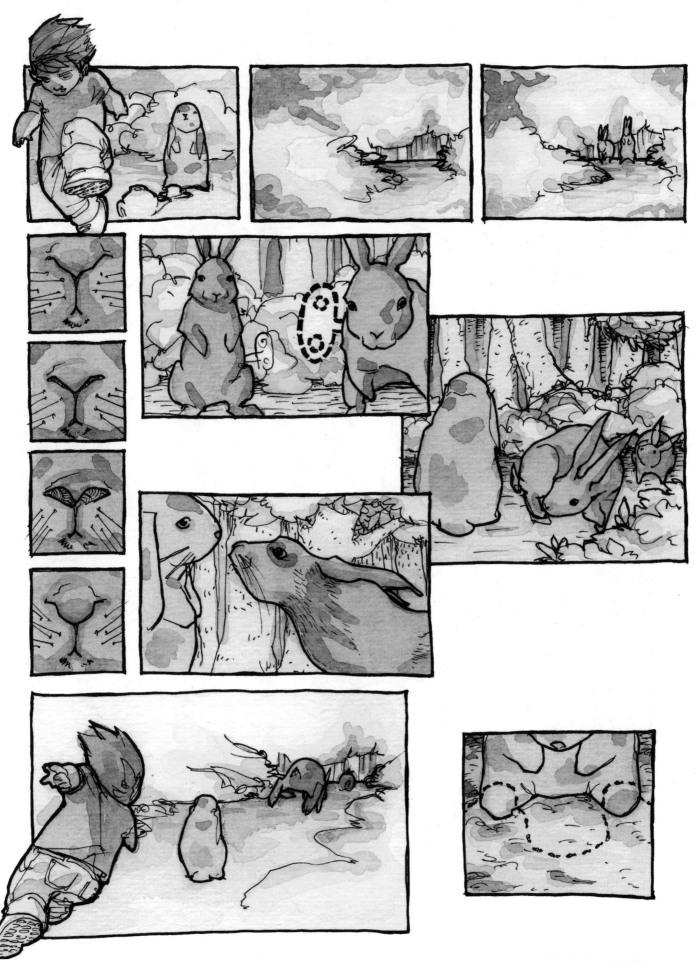

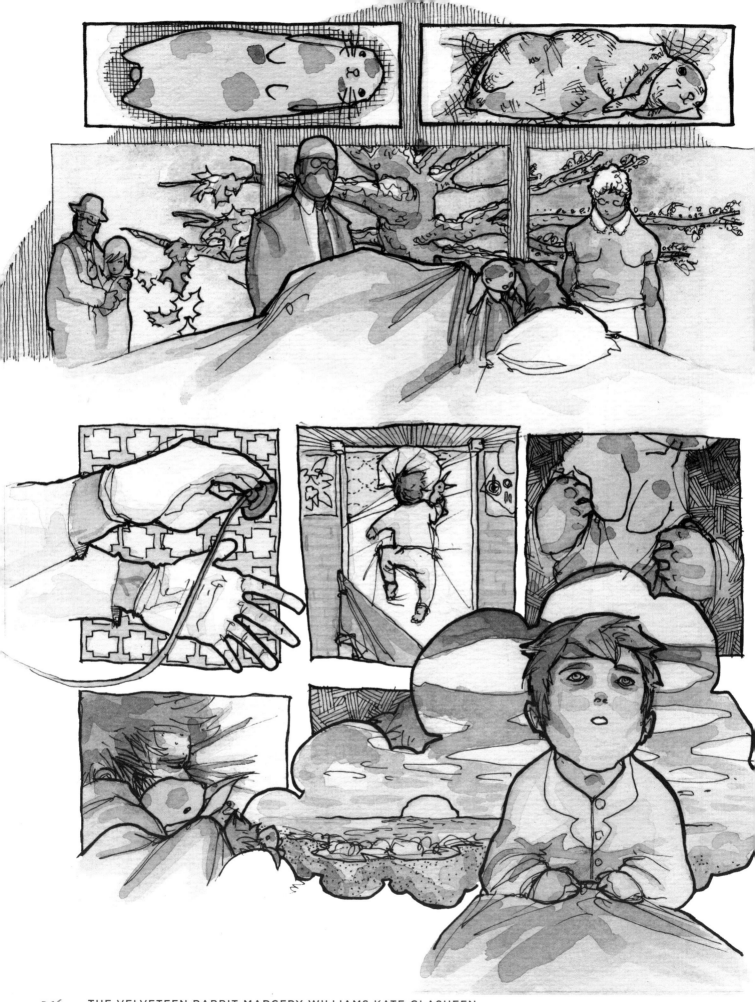

THE VELVETEEN RABBIT MARGERY WILLIAMS KATE GLASHEEN

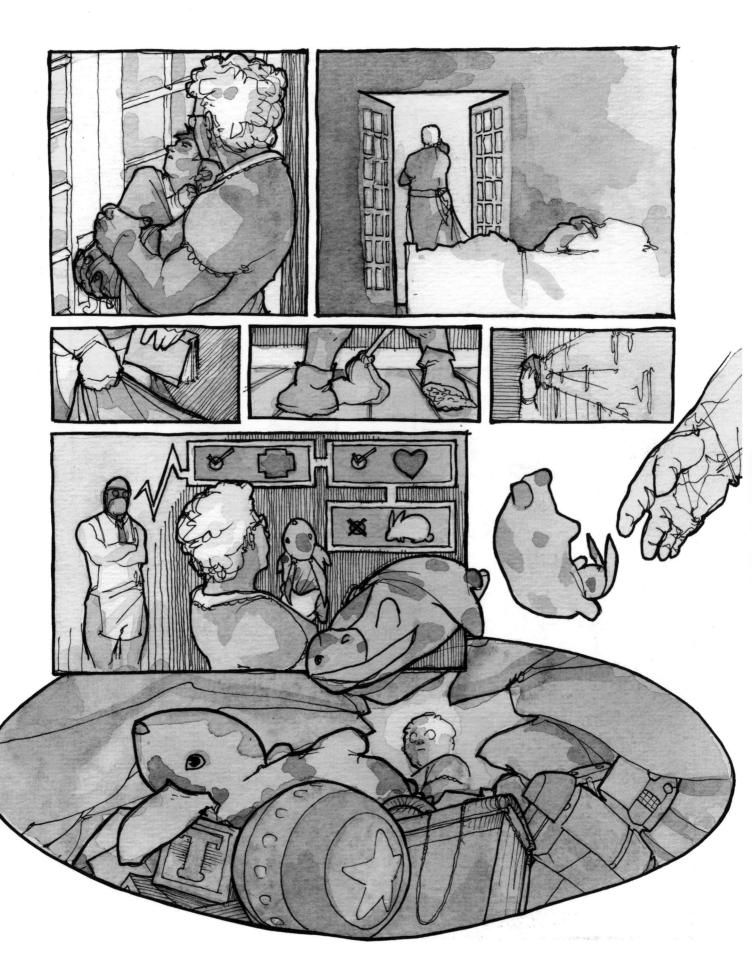

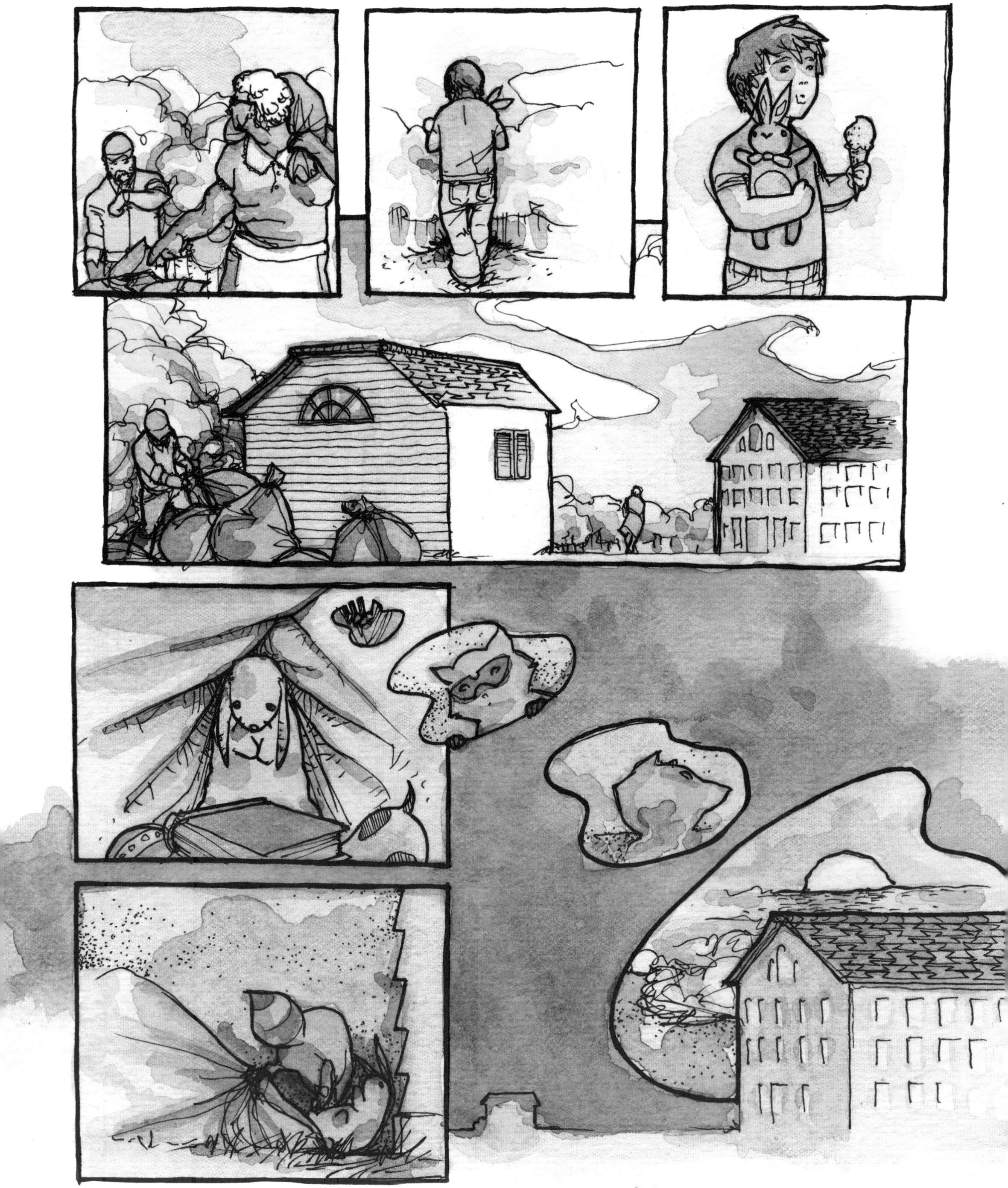

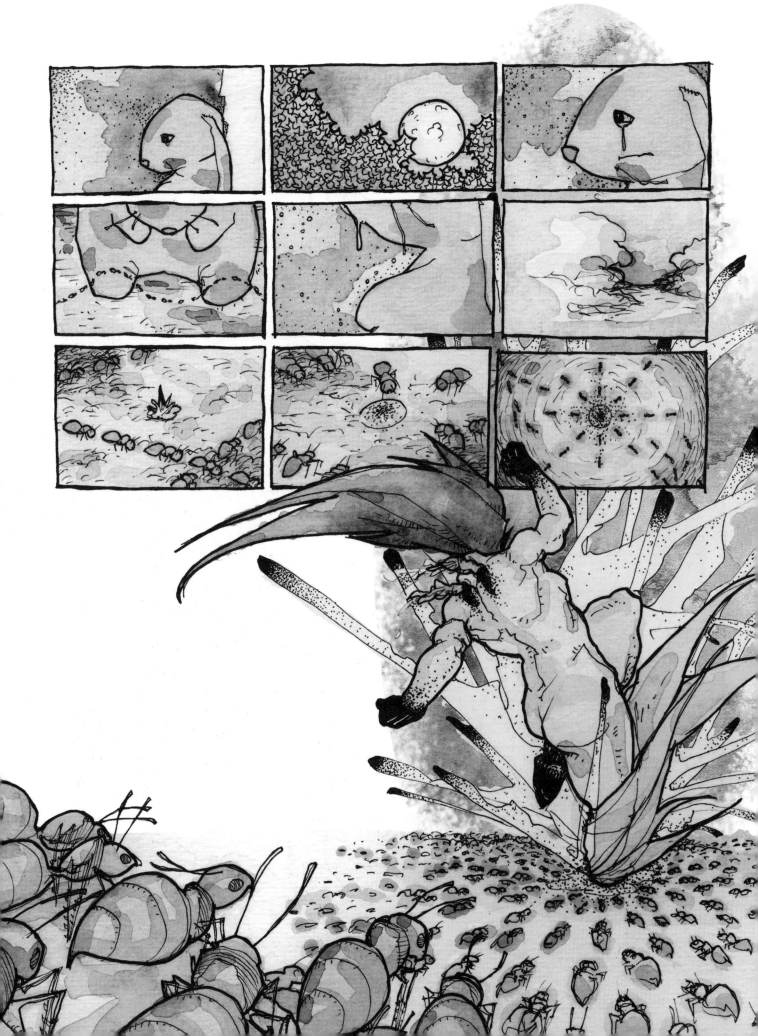

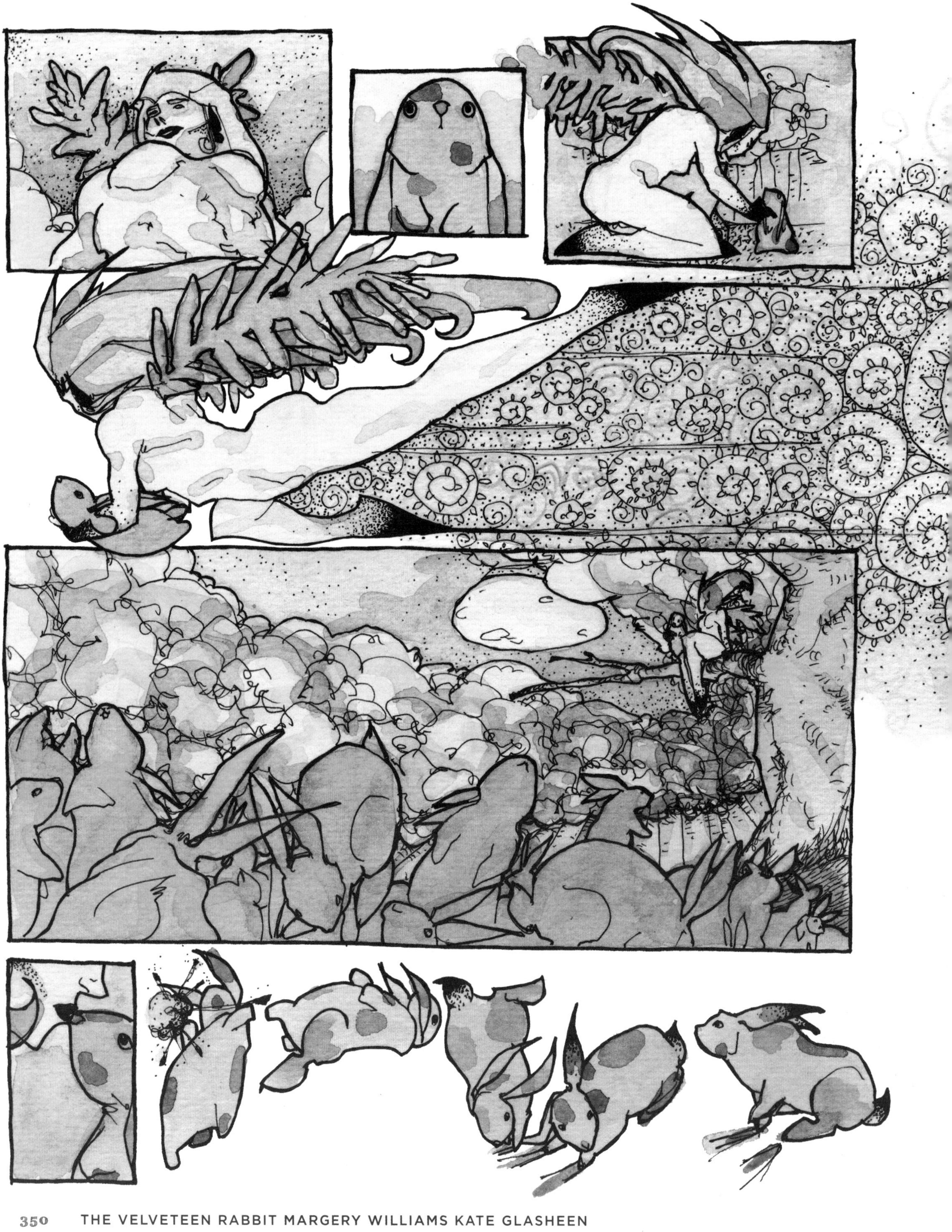

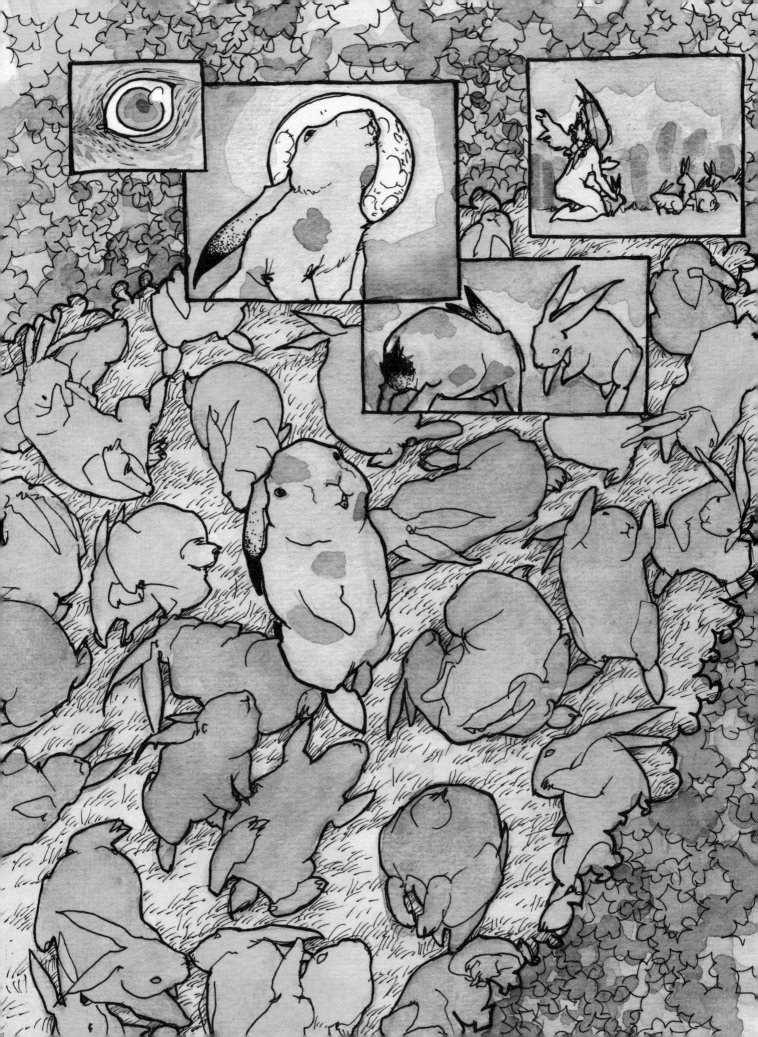

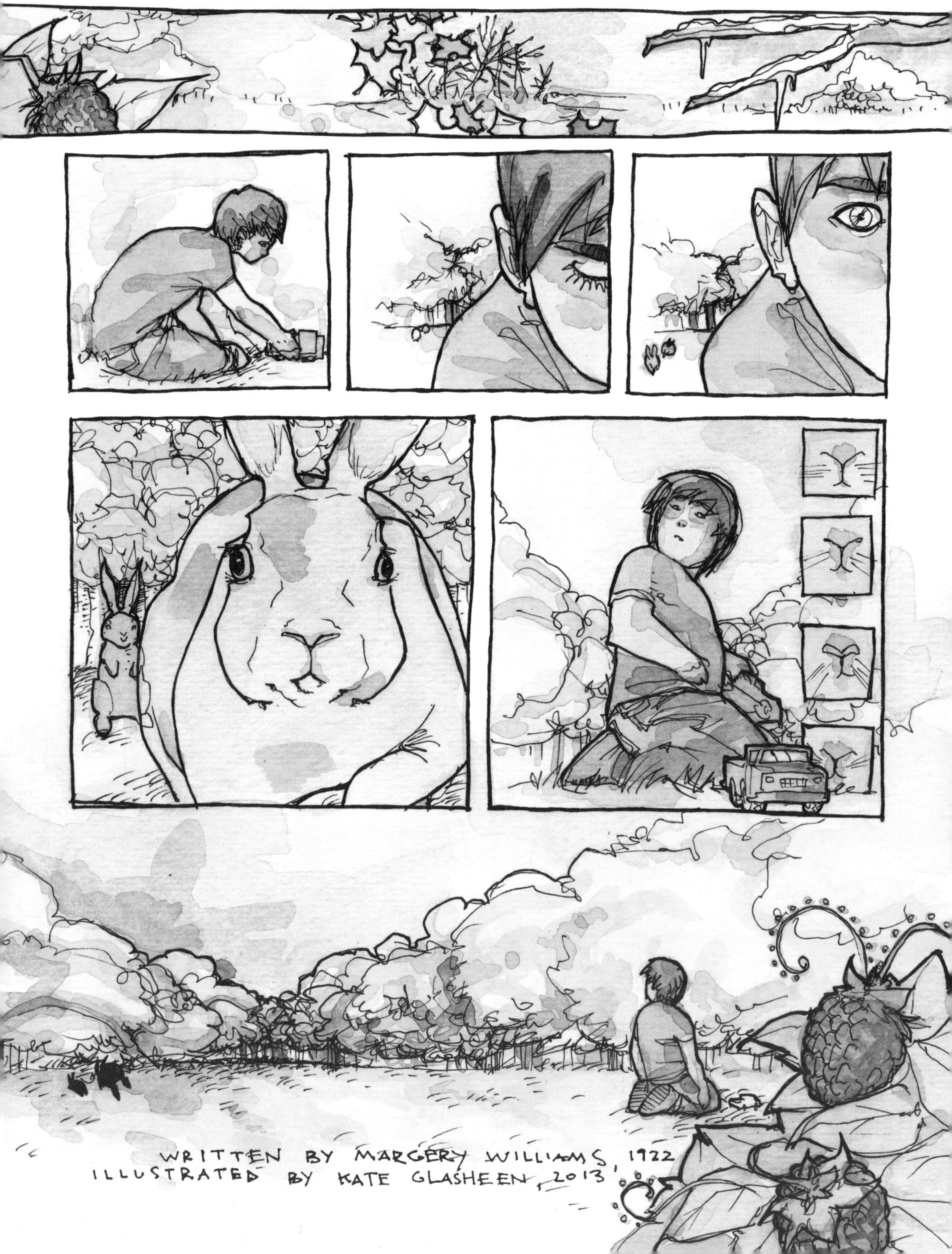
WRITTEN BY MARGERY WILLIAMS, 1922
ILLUSTRATED BY KATE GLASHEEN, 2013

# Rootabaga Stories

## Carl Sandburg

ART/ADAPTATION BY **C. Frakes**

**CARL SANDBURG HAD ALREADY WON THE FIRST OF** his two Pulitzer Prizes for poetry* when, in 1922, he put out the children's book *Rootabaga Stories*. Sandburg was an American and a Midwesterner to the bone—his collections include *Chicago Poems*, *Cornhuskers*, and *Smoke and Steel*—and he brought this identity to his fairy tales. He expressly wanted to get away from the European influence of the genre, the Grimm and Andersen stuff, and remake the fairy tale in a US mode. "I was tired of princes and princesses," he told an interviewer, "and I sought the American equivalent of elves and gnomes."

With his absurdist *Rootabaga Stories* (and the three follow-up volumes), he blended fairy tales and nonsense literature (as exemplified by Lewis Carroll and Edward Lear)

into yarns featuring the Pigs with Bibs On, the Village of Liver-and-Onions, corn fairies, and characters named Any Ice Today and Gimme the Ax. Regarding his foray into kid lit, Sandburg once said: "Children are the only people I never lie to."

C. Frakes brings her charming style and soothing palette to a couple of these tales, bravely offering to visualize Potato Face Blind Man, Picks Ups, Poker Face the Baboon, flummywisters, and other denizens of Rootabaga Country, none of whom are physically described by Sandburg. If you're expecting everything to make sense—grammatically or plot-wise—please don't.

*He also won a third Pulitzer for his biography of Abraham Lincoln.

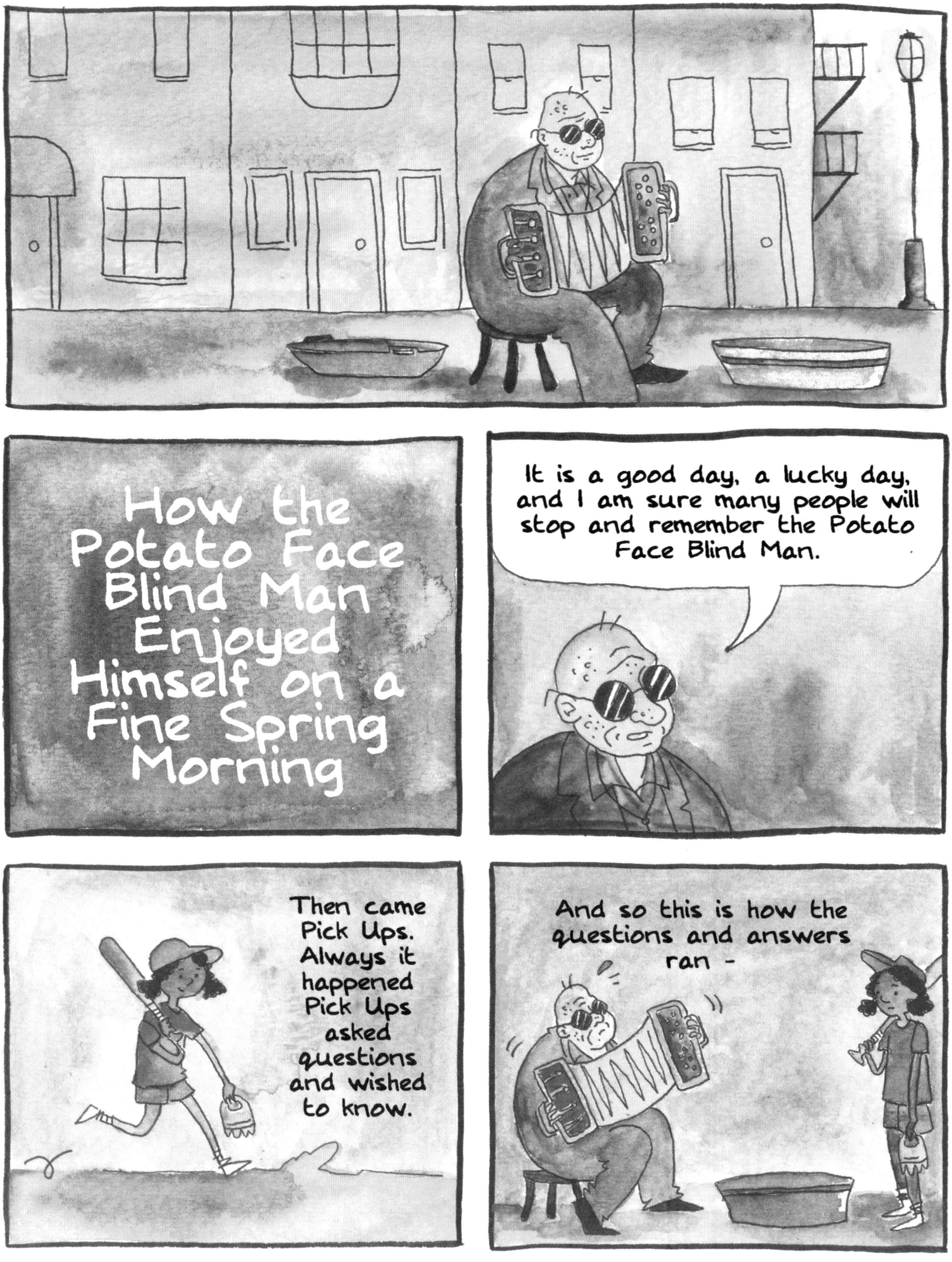
How the Potato Face Blind Man Enjoyed Himself on a Fine Spring Morning
It is a good day, a lucky day, and I am sure many people will stop and remember the Potato Face Blind Man.
Then came Pick Ups. Always it happened Pick Ups asked questions and wished to know.
And so this is how the questions and answers ran -

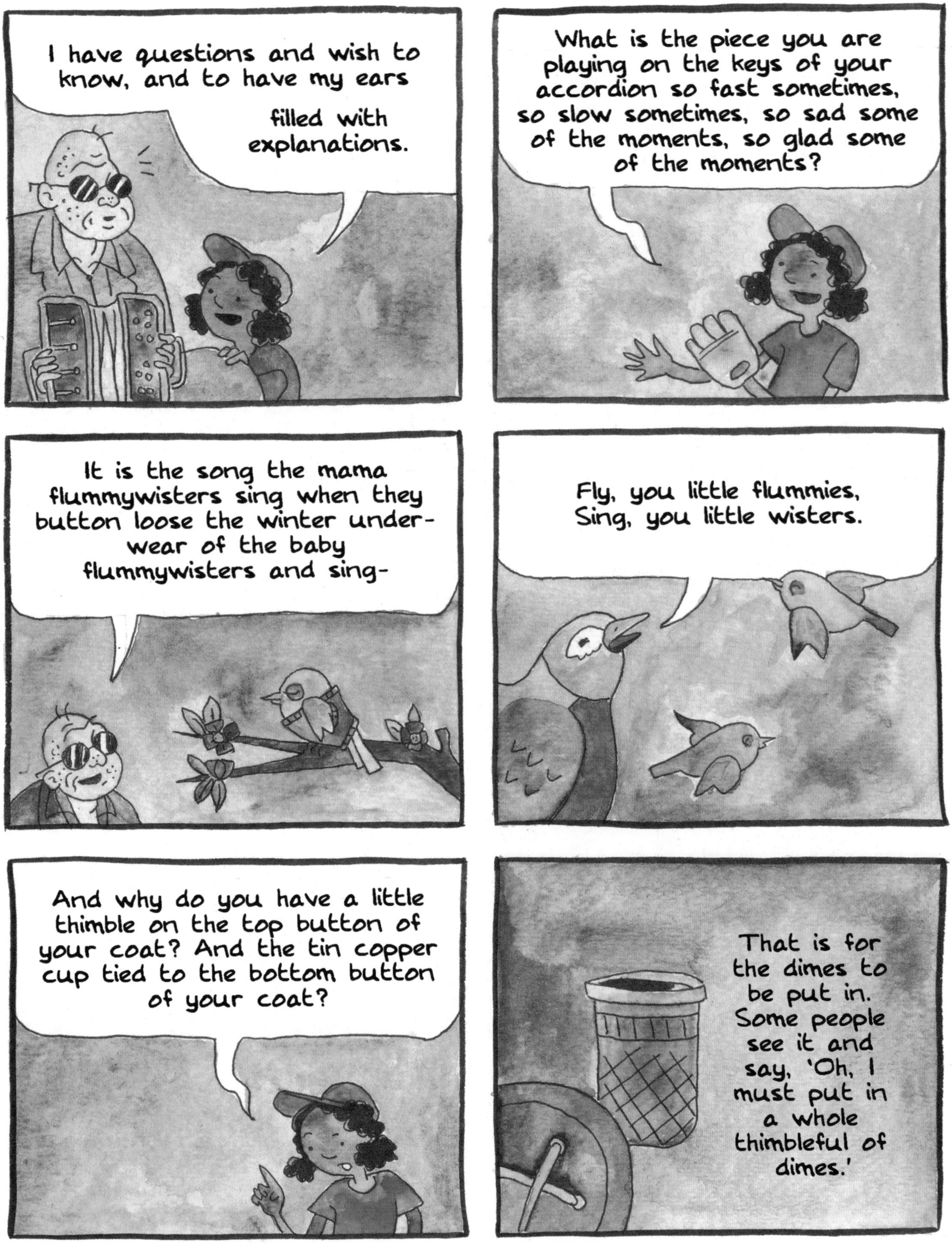
I have questions and wish to know, and to have my ears filled with explanations.
What is the piece you are playing on the keys of your accordion so fast sometimes, so slow sometimes, so sad some of the moments, so glad some of the moments?
It is the song the mama flummywisters sing when they button loose the winter under-wear of the baby flummywisters and sing-
Fly, you little flummies,
Sing, you little wisters.
And why do you have a little thimble on the top button of your coat? And the tin copper cup tied to the bottom button of your coat?
That is for the dimes to be put in. Some people see it and say, 'Oh, I must put in a whole thimbleful of dimes.'

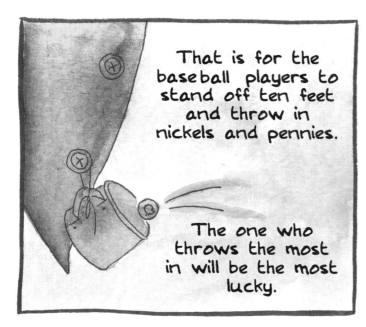

That is for the baseball players to stand off ten feet and throw in nickels and pennies.

The one who throws the most in will be the most lucky.

And the wooden mug? There is a hole in the bottom of it. The hole is as big as the bottom.

The nickel goes in and comes out again. It is for the very poor people who wish to give me a nickel and yet get the nickel back.

The aluminum dishpan and the galvanized iron washtub—what are they doing by the side of you on both sides on the sidewalk?

Sometime maybe it will happen everybody who goes into the postoffice and comes out will stop and pour out all their money—

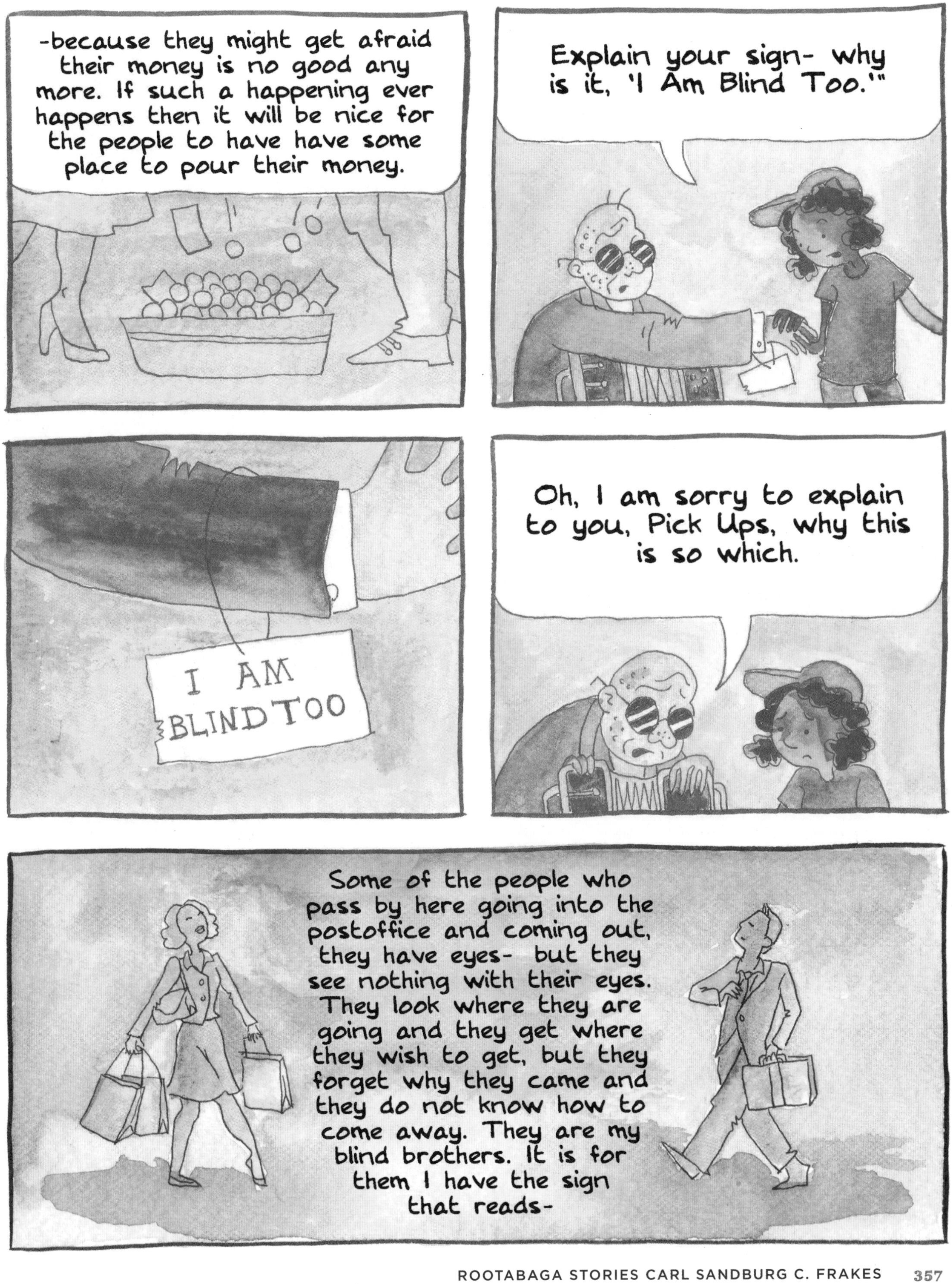
-because they might get afraid their money is no good any more. If such a happening ever happens then it will be nice for the people to have have some place to pour their money.
Explain your sign- why is it, 'I Am Blind Too.'"
I AM BLIND TOO
Oh, I am sorry to explain to you, Pick Ups, why this is so which.
Some of the people who pass by here going into the postoffice and coming out, they have eyes- but they see nothing with their eyes. They look where they are going and they get where they wish to get, but they forget why they came and they do not know how to come away. They are my blind brothers. It is for them I have the sign that reads-

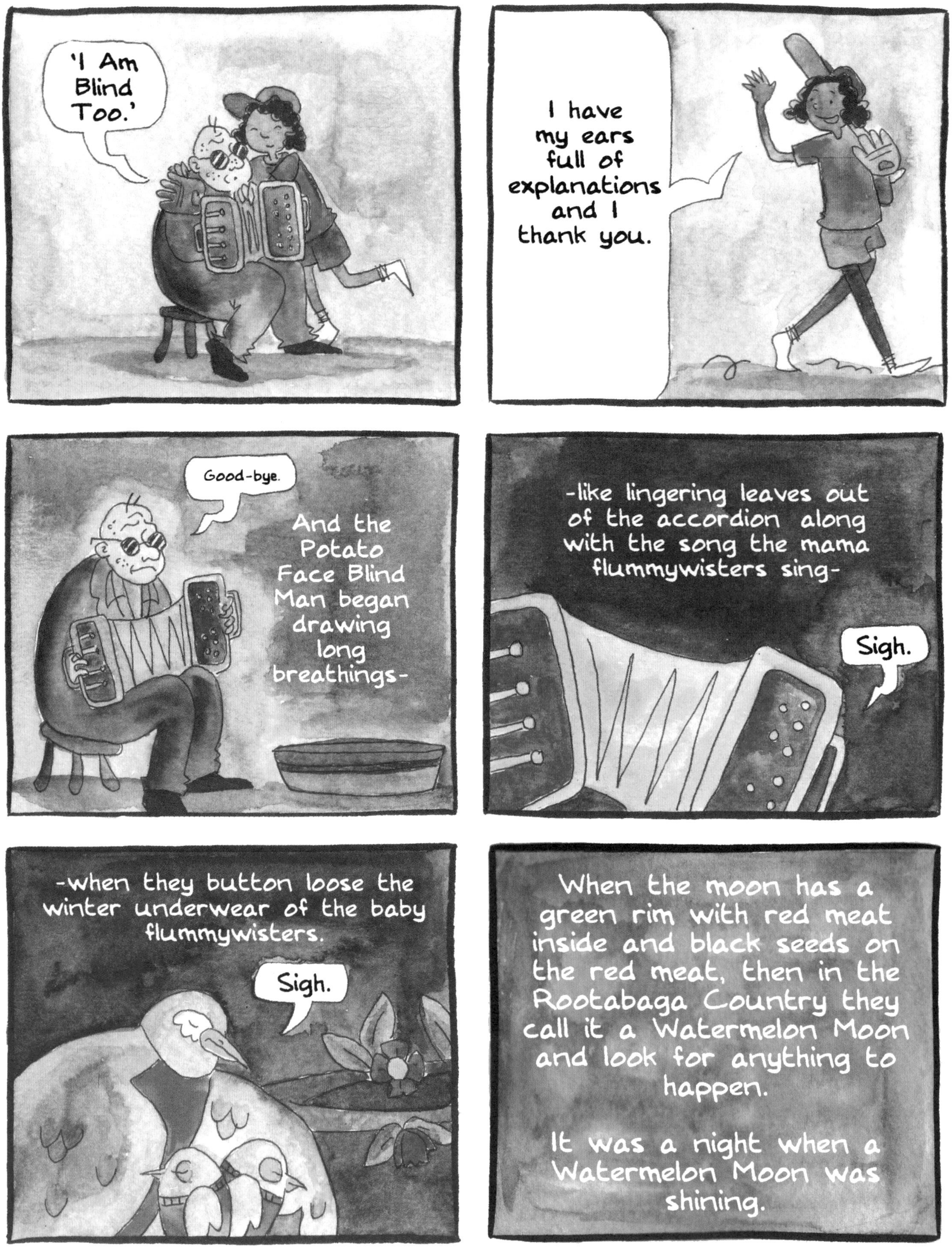
'I Am Blind Too.'
I have my ears full of explanations and I thank you.
Good-bye.
And the Potato Face Blind Man began drawing long breathings-
-like lingering leaves out of the accordion along with the song the mama flummywisters sing-
Sigh.
-when they button loose the winter underwear of the baby flummywisters.
Sigh.
When the moon has a green rim with red meat inside and black seeds on the red meat, then in the Rootabaga Country they call it a Watermelon Moon and look for anything to happen.
It was a night when a Watermelon Moon was shining.

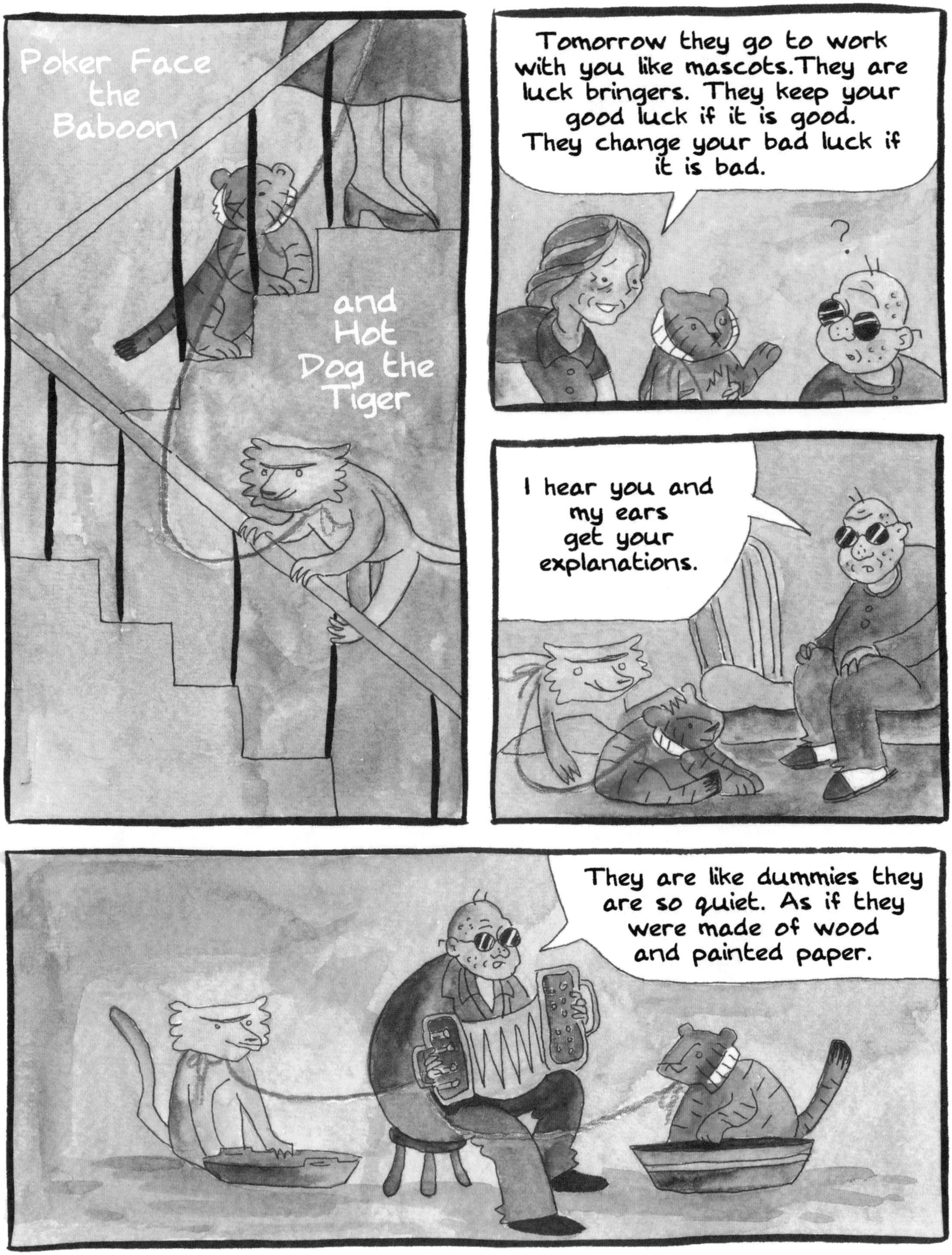
Poker Face the Baboon
and Hot Dog the Tiger
Tomorrow they go to work with you like mascots. They are luck bringers. They keep your good luck if it is good. They change your bad luck if it is bad.
?
I hear you and my ears get your explanations.
They are like dummies they are so quiet. As if they were made of wood and painted paper.

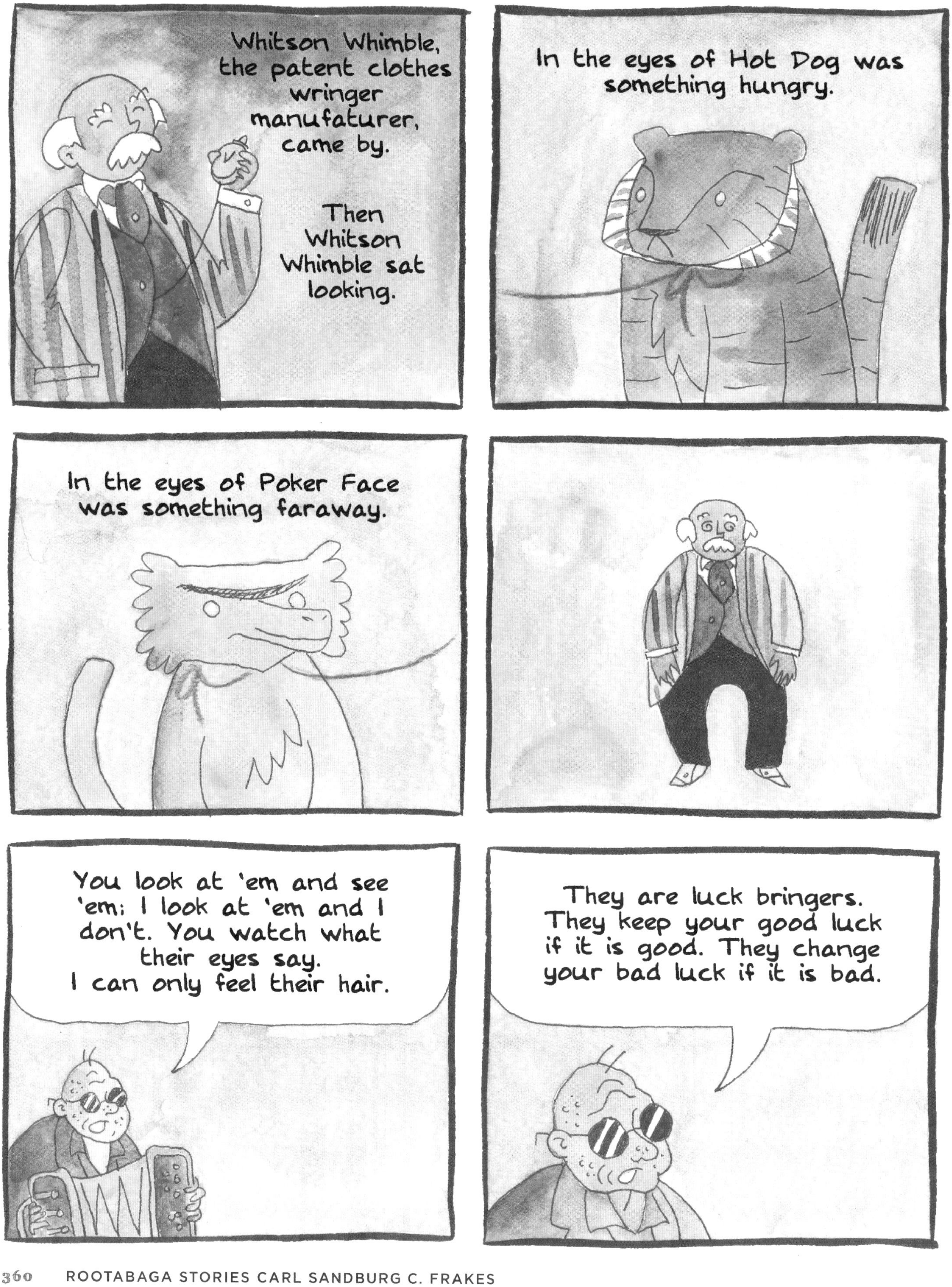
Whitson Whimble, the patent clothes wringer manufaturer, came by.
Then Whitson Whimble sat looking.
In the eyes of Hot Dog was something hungry.
In the eyes of Poker Face was something faraway.
You look at 'em and see 'em: I look at 'em and I don't. You watch what their eyes say. I can only feel their hair.
They are luck bringers. They keep your good luck if it is good. They change your bad luck if it is bad.

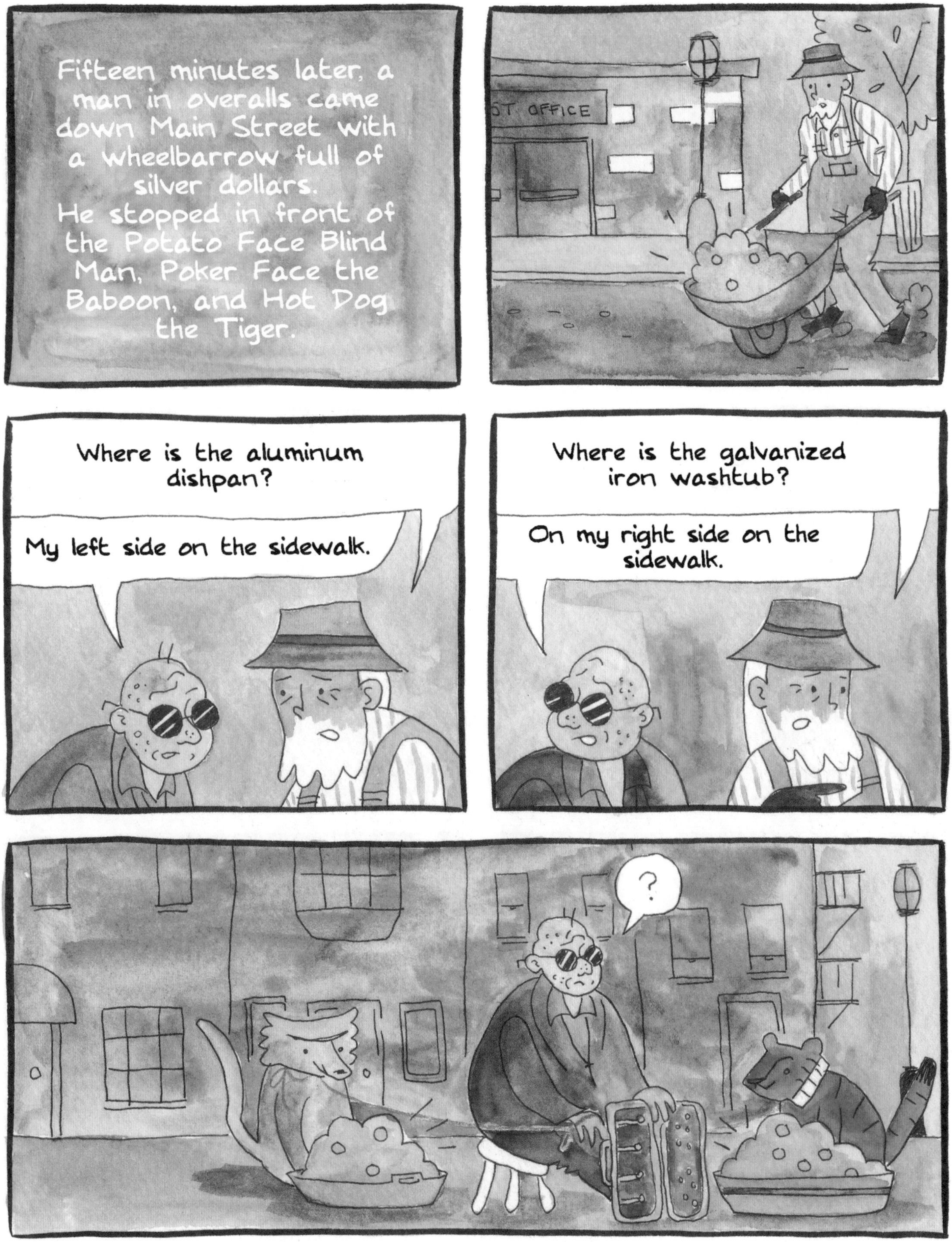
Fifteen minutes later, a man in overalls came down Main Street with a wheelbarrow full of silver dollars.
He stopped in front of the Potato Face Blind Man, Poker Face the Baboon, and Hot Dog the Tiger.
ST OFFICE
Where is the aluminum dishpan?
My left side on the sidewalk.
Where is the galvanized iron washtub?
On my right side on the sidewalk.
?

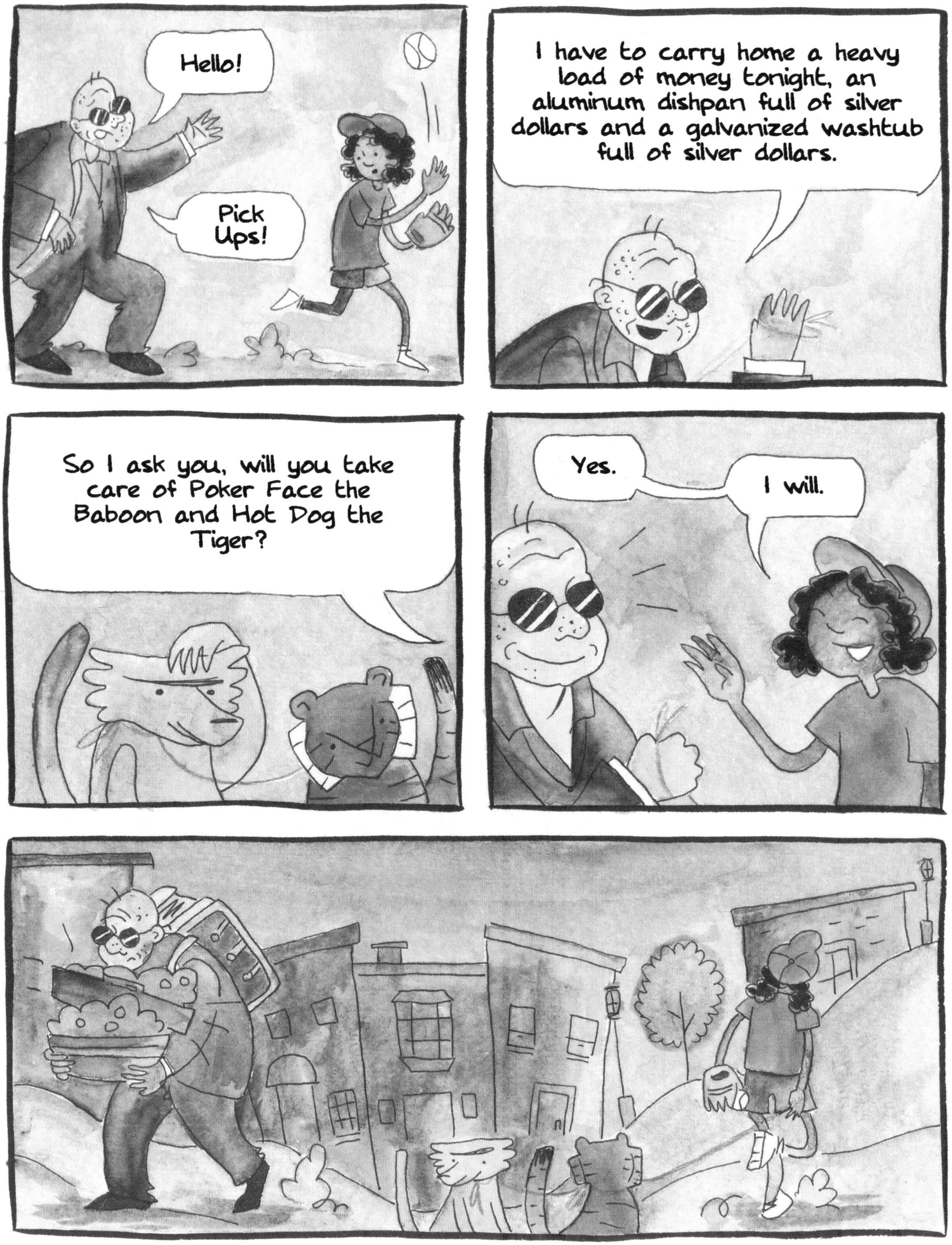
Hello!
Pick Ups!
I have to carry home a heavy load of money tonight, an aluminum dishpan full of silver dollars and a galvanized washtub full of silver dollars.
So I ask you, will you take care of Poker Face the Baboon and Hot Dog the Tiger?
Yes.
I will.

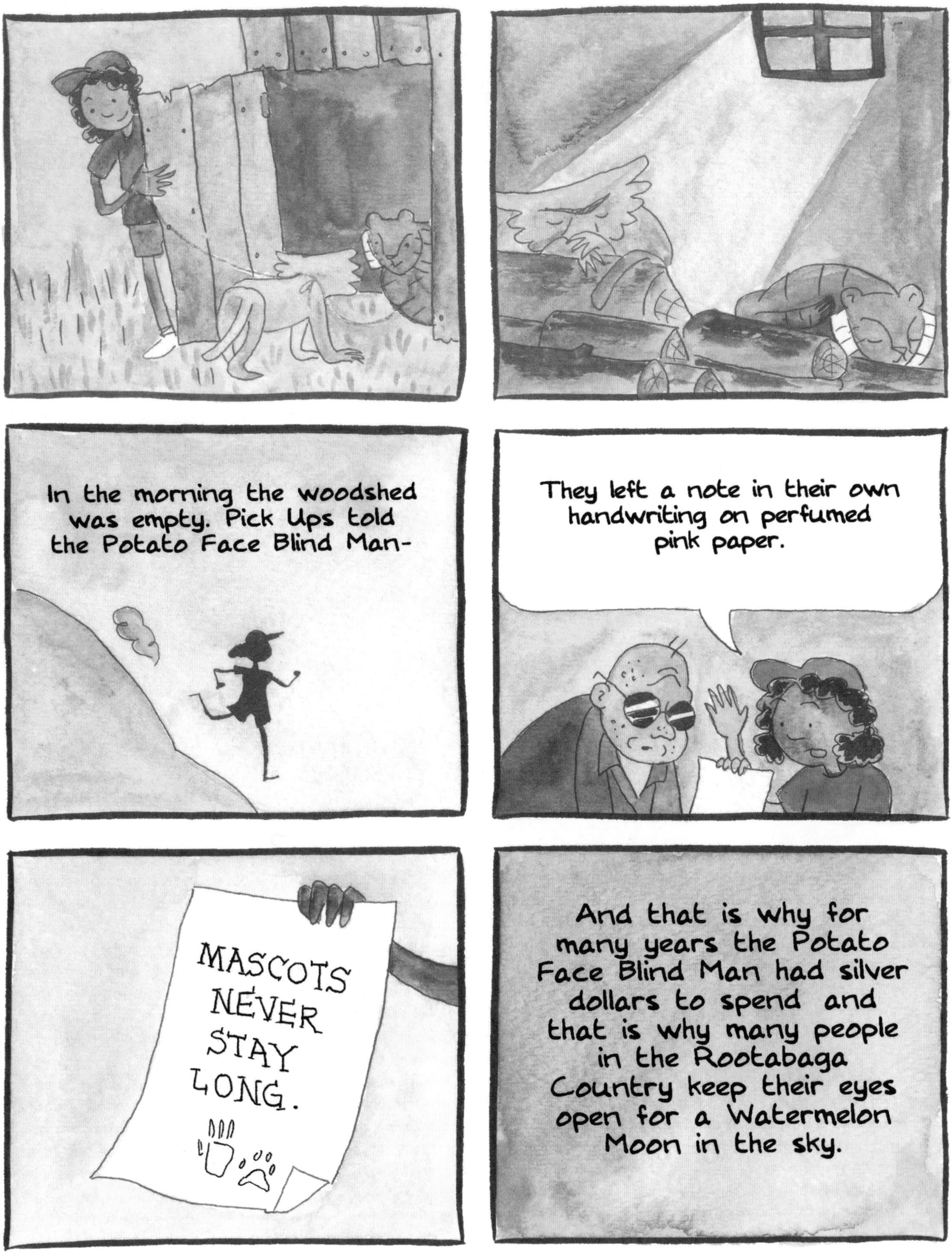

In the morning the woodshed was empty. Pick Ups told the Potato Face Blind Man-
They left a note in their own handwriting on perfumed pink paper.
MASCOTS NEVER STAY LONG.
And that is why for many years the Potato Face Blind Man had silver dollars to spend and that is why many people in the Rootabaga Country keep their eyes open for a Watermelon Moon in the sky.

# The Tower Treasure

## (A Hardy Boys Mystery)

### Franklin W. Dixon

ART/ADAPTATION BY **Matt Wiegle**

**EDWARD STRATEMEYER TRIED HIS HAND AT WRITING** pulp stories, dime novels, and series fiction for tweens and early teens in the late 1800s, but he realized that to really be successful, he had to be the one controlling this material. At the start of the twentieth century, he created a syndicate: he dreamed up characters that would form the basis of a series, wrote outlines for the books, then paid freelance writers a flat fee to churn out the volumes, which would be published under the name of a single, nonexistent author. He immediately hit pay dirt with the Rover Boys, followed soon after by the Bobbsey Twins and Tom Swift. His most monumental success was yet to come, though.

In the late 1920s, he had an idea for two teenage brothers in a small New England town. Sons of a former NYPD detective now in private practice, they would sleuth out all kinds of mysteries that popped up in their neck of the woods. Stratemeyer placed a classified ad for an experienced fiction writer; reporter and freelance writer Leslie McFarlane responded. Originally assigned to write for a different series, McFarlane would soon pen the first sixteen books (and three somewhat later ones) of the most successful juvenile fiction series in history—The Hardy Boys. The original series constitutes fifty-eight volumes, with another ninety-two in the next series, plus numerous shorter-lived series, all credited to the spurious Franklin W. Dixon. According to the *New York Times*, the series still sells over a million books a year, mostly heavily rewritten reprints of the original fifty-eight volumes.

Ignatz Award–winner Matt Wiegle brings visual inventiveness to everything he draws. For *The Graphic Canon of Children's Literature*, he wanted to work with the original Hardy Boys volume, *The Tower Treasure*, the one that started it all. One of Stratemeyer's instructions to McFarlane was to end every chapter as a cliffhanger. Matt runs with this, presenting the nail-biting conclusion of each chapter as a single panel—twenty-four chapters, twenty-four panels.

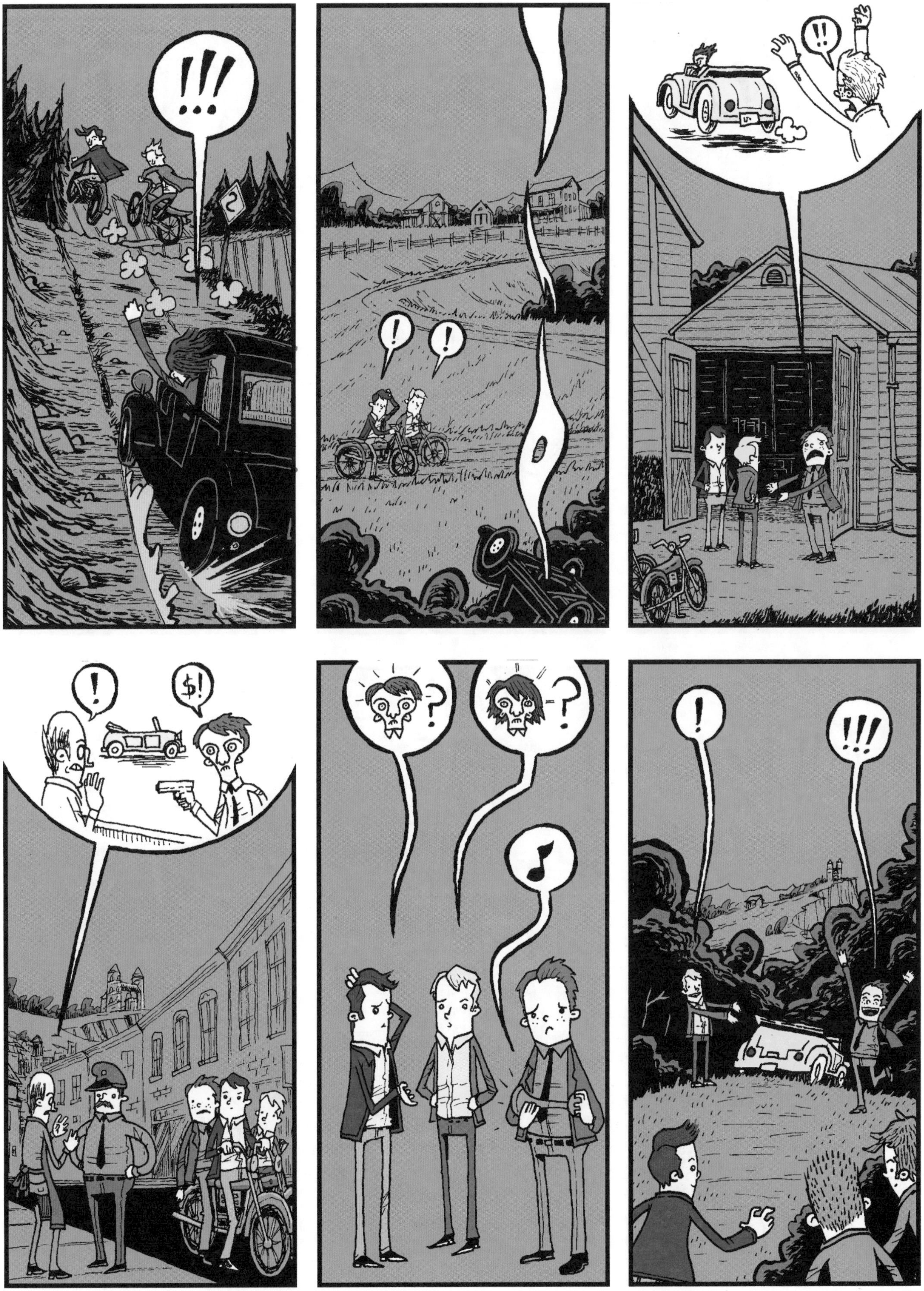
!!!...
!
!
!!
!
$!
!
!!!

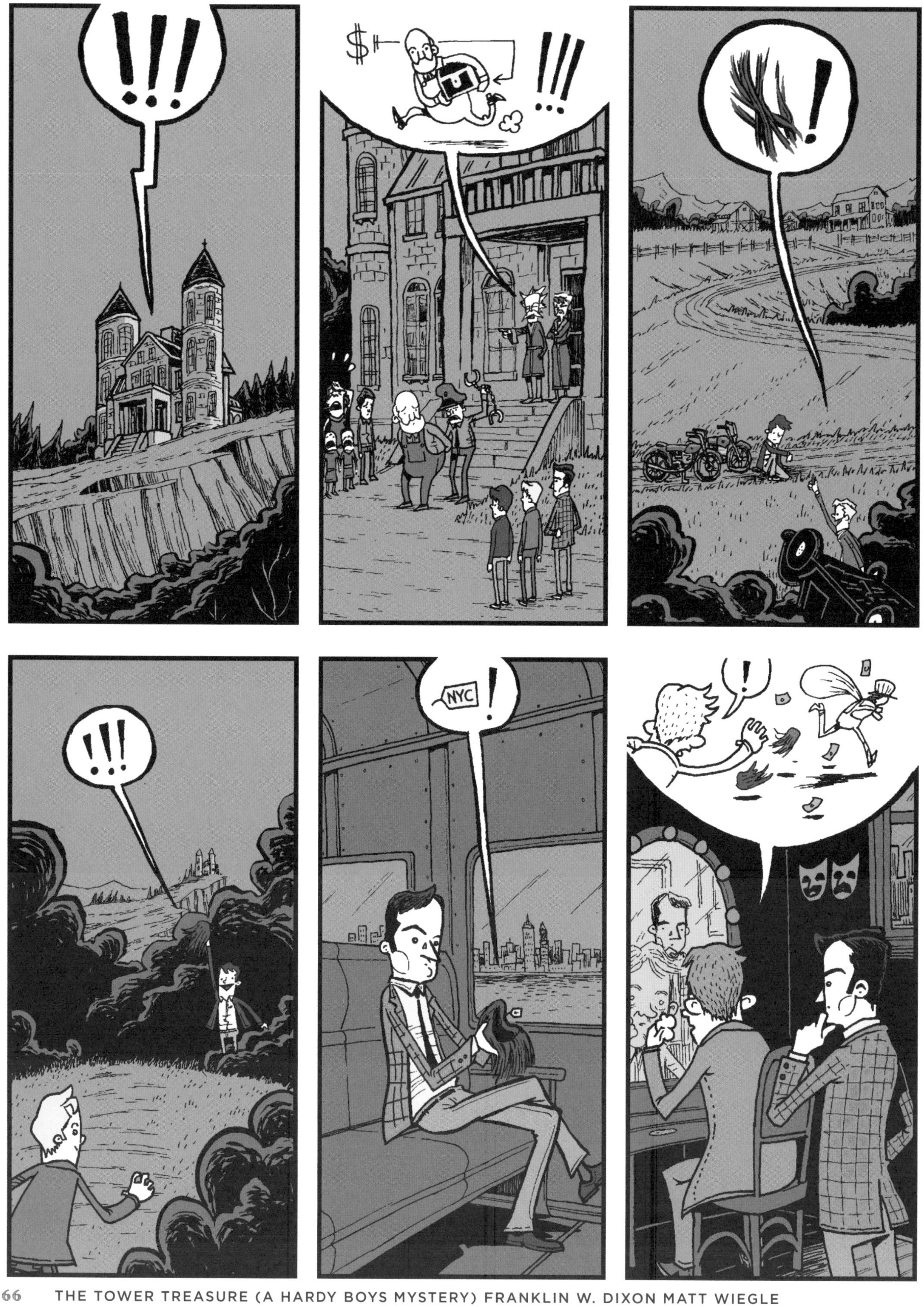
!!!
$
!!!
!
!!!
NYC
!
!

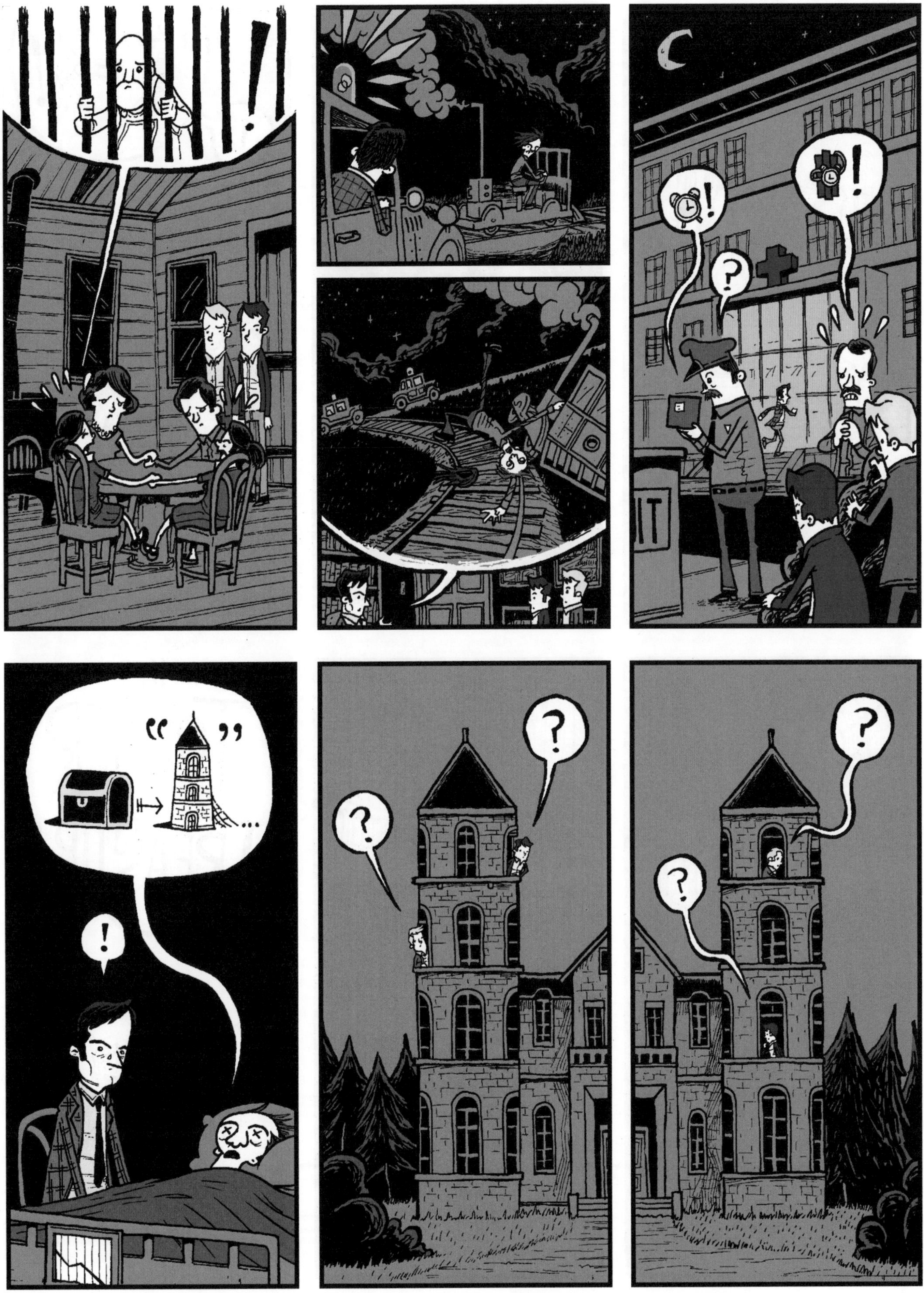
!
!
?
!
IT
...
!
?
?
?
?

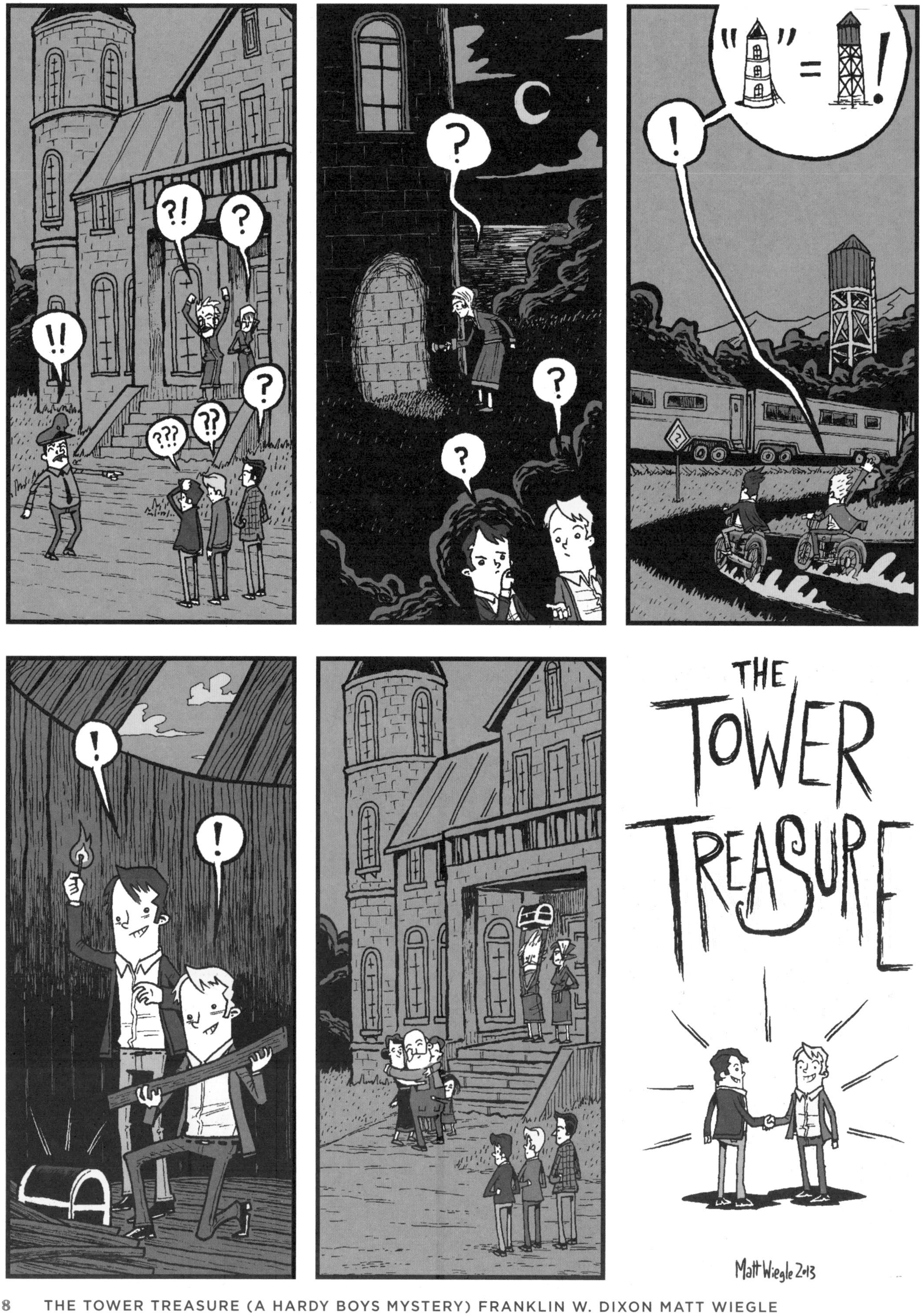
?!
?
!!
?
???
??
?
?
?
"" = !
!
THE TOWER TREASURE
!
!
Matt Wiegle 2013

# Sergei Prokofiev

ART/ADAPTATION BY **Katherine Hearst**

**A CHILD PRODIGY ON THE PIANO AND IN THE** realm of composition, the Ukranian Sergei Prokofiev went on to create more than 120 works, including operas, symphonies, and a number of pieces for children, including *Peter and the Wolf*. The 1936 musical composition accompanied by narration tells of a Russian boy who, aided by a bird, traps a vicious wolf; he and some hunters then take the captured beast to the zoo. In performances, each character is represented by a different instrument (including stringed instruments for Peter, French horns for the wolf, and flute for the bird).

The boy-vs.-wolf tale is perennially popular, constantly being performed and recorded umpteen times, with narrators including Sir John Gielgud, Sir Alec Guinness, Patrick Stewart, Sean Connery, Mia Farrow, Sting, David Bowie, and Captain Kangaroo.

London artist Katherine Hearst often works with fairy tales and folktales, transporting and updating them to contemporary Russia. She explains her stunning version of *Peter and the Wolf*:

> I thought it would be interesting to set Prokofiev's classic tale in the context of a modern-day wolf cull in Siberia. Peter is an Evenki reindeer herder, struggling to pursue the nomadic lifestyle of his ancestors. The Evenki are one of the indigenous peoples of the Russian North, among the last of Siberia's reindeer herding people. Their traditional way of life has been threatened by Cossacks, Tsarist taxation, collectivization under Stalin. It is now in danger of disappearing as oil pipelines are constructed across their territory. I wanted to explore the plight of this ethnic group through the lens of a children's tale. The menace of the wolf pales into insignificance when Peter is faced with the threat of modernity.

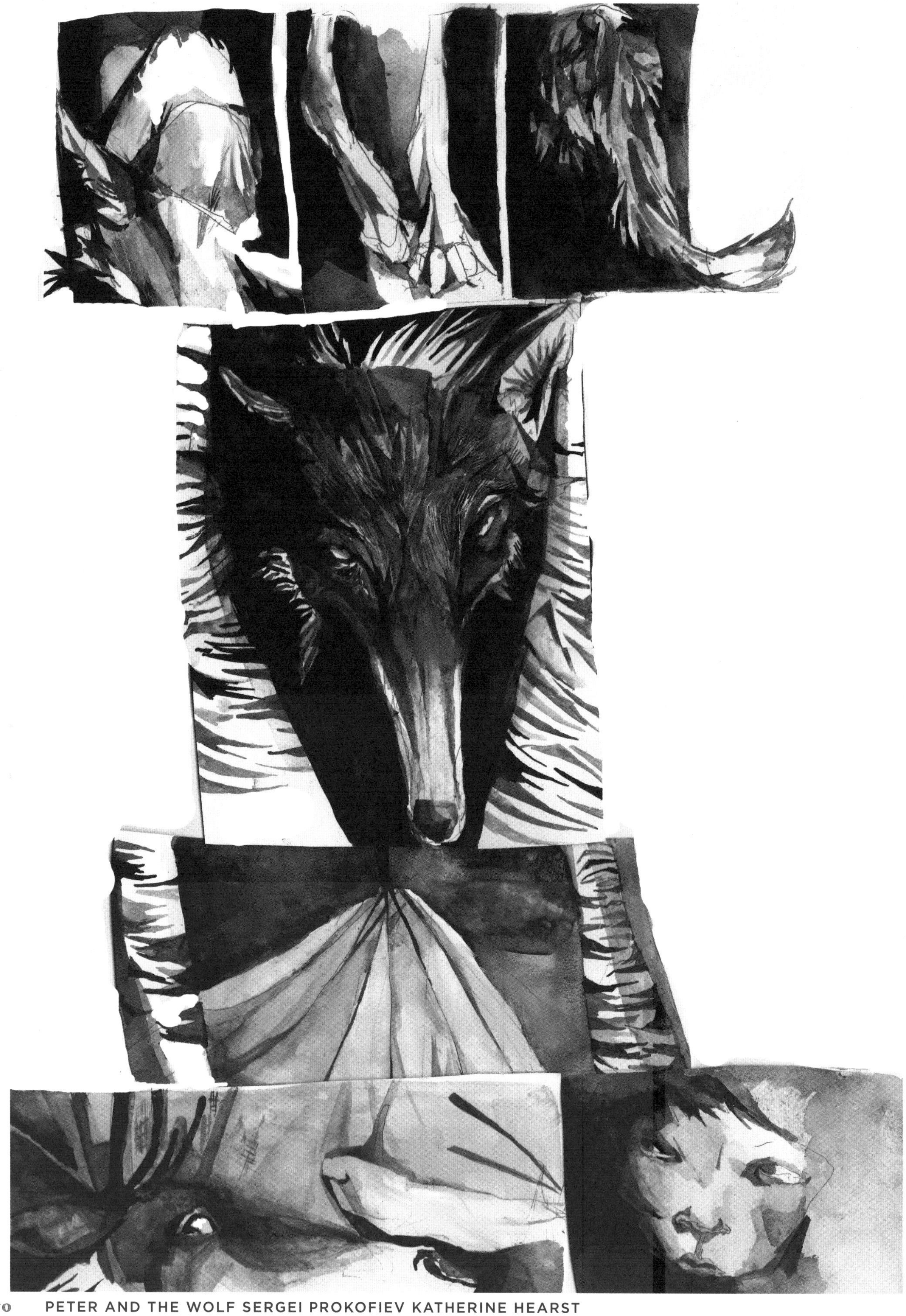

IT IS NOT FOR US TO FEAR THE WOLF, PETYA.

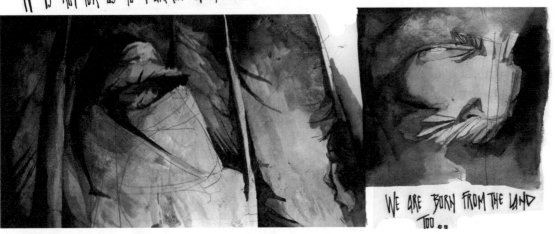

WE ARE BORN FROM THE LAND TOO..

...THERE WAS ...G BUT ICE

UNTIL THE SKY GOD 'HOVKI' CREATED REINDEER — THE GIVERS OF LIFE

AND IN THEIR TURN, THE REINDEER GAVE LIFE TO MAN

WHILE THE WOLF IS A HUNTER, MAN IS ALSO A TAMER..

HE ENTERED INTO A CONTRACT WITH THE DEER,

IN EXCHANGE FOR FOOD AND TRANSPORT.. MAN OFFERED PROTECTION

AND TO WOLF

IN THE ICY WILDERNESS MAN TAMED DEER

AND MAN HERDED

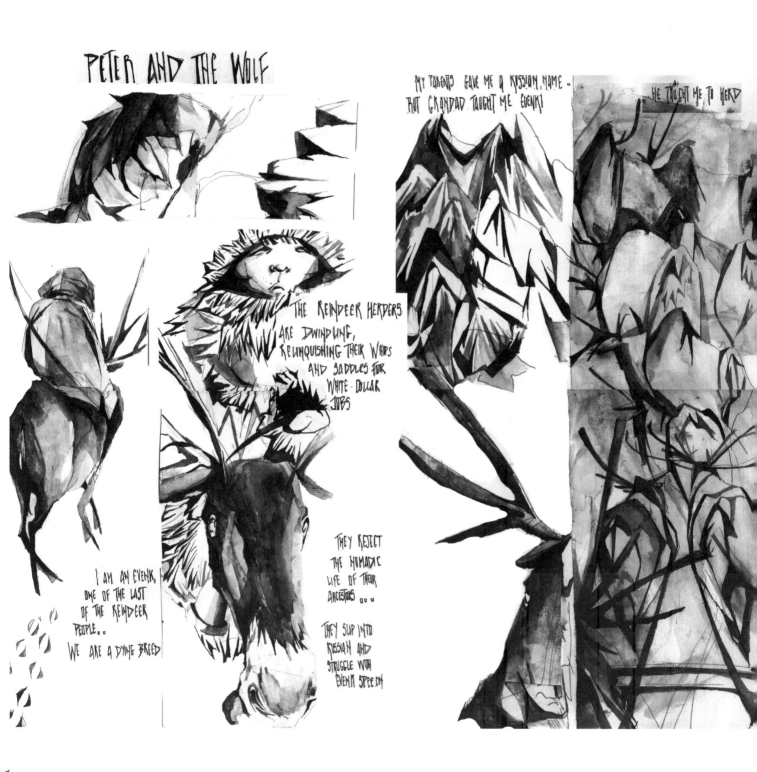

# PETER AND THE WOLF

MY PARENTS GAVE ME A RUSSIAN NAME - BUT GRANDAD TAUGHT ME EVENKI

HE TAUGHT ME TO HERD

THE REINDEER HERDERS ARE DWINDLING, RELINQUISHING THEIR WHIPS AND SADDLES FOR WHITE-COLLAR JOBS

I AM AN EVENK, ONE OF THE LAST OF THE REINDEER PEOPLE.. WE ARE A DYING BREED

THEY REJECT THE NOMADIC LIFE OF THEIR ANCESTORS ...

THEY SLIP INTO RUSSIAN AND STRUGGLE WITH EVENK SPEECH

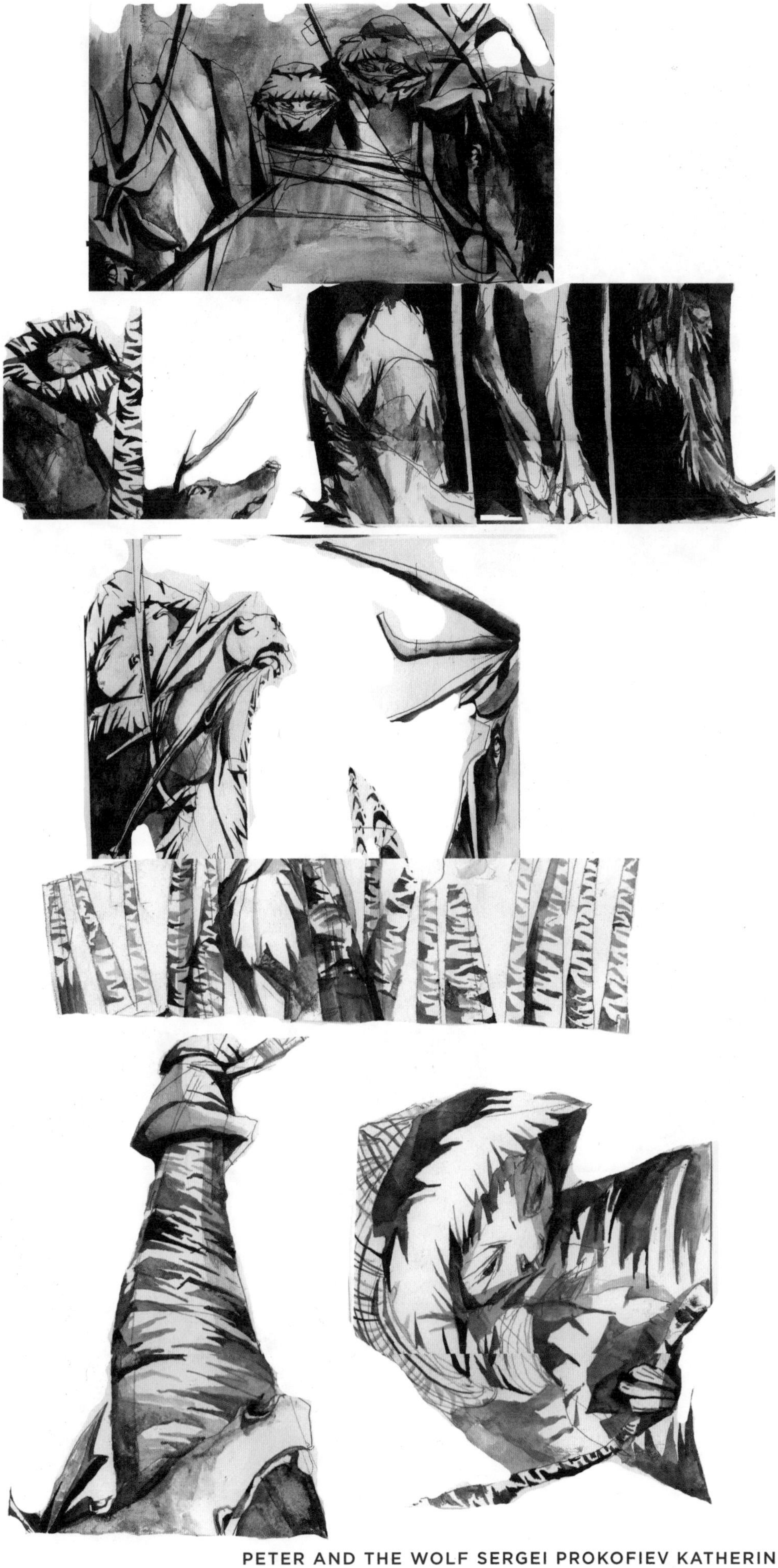

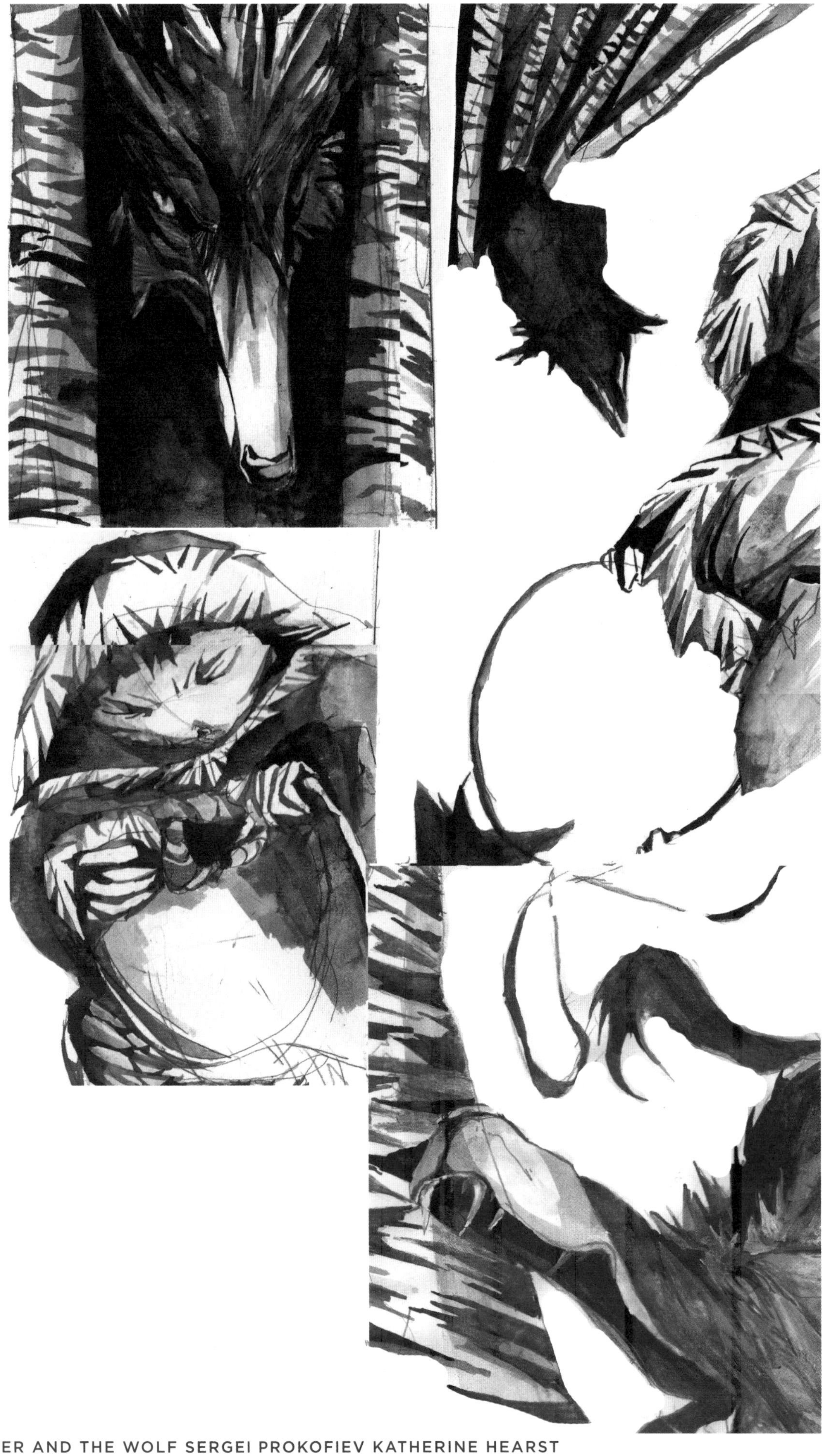

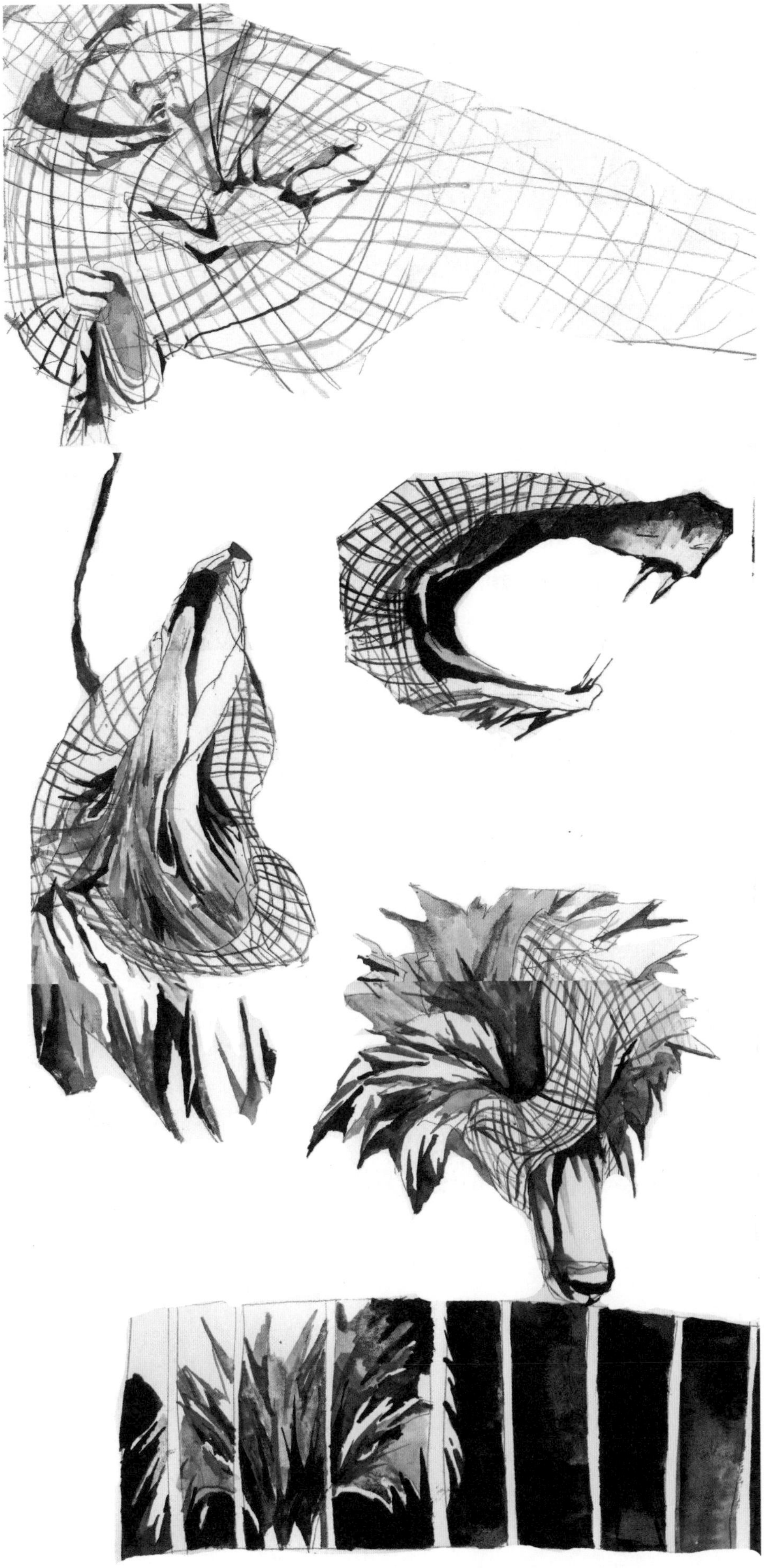

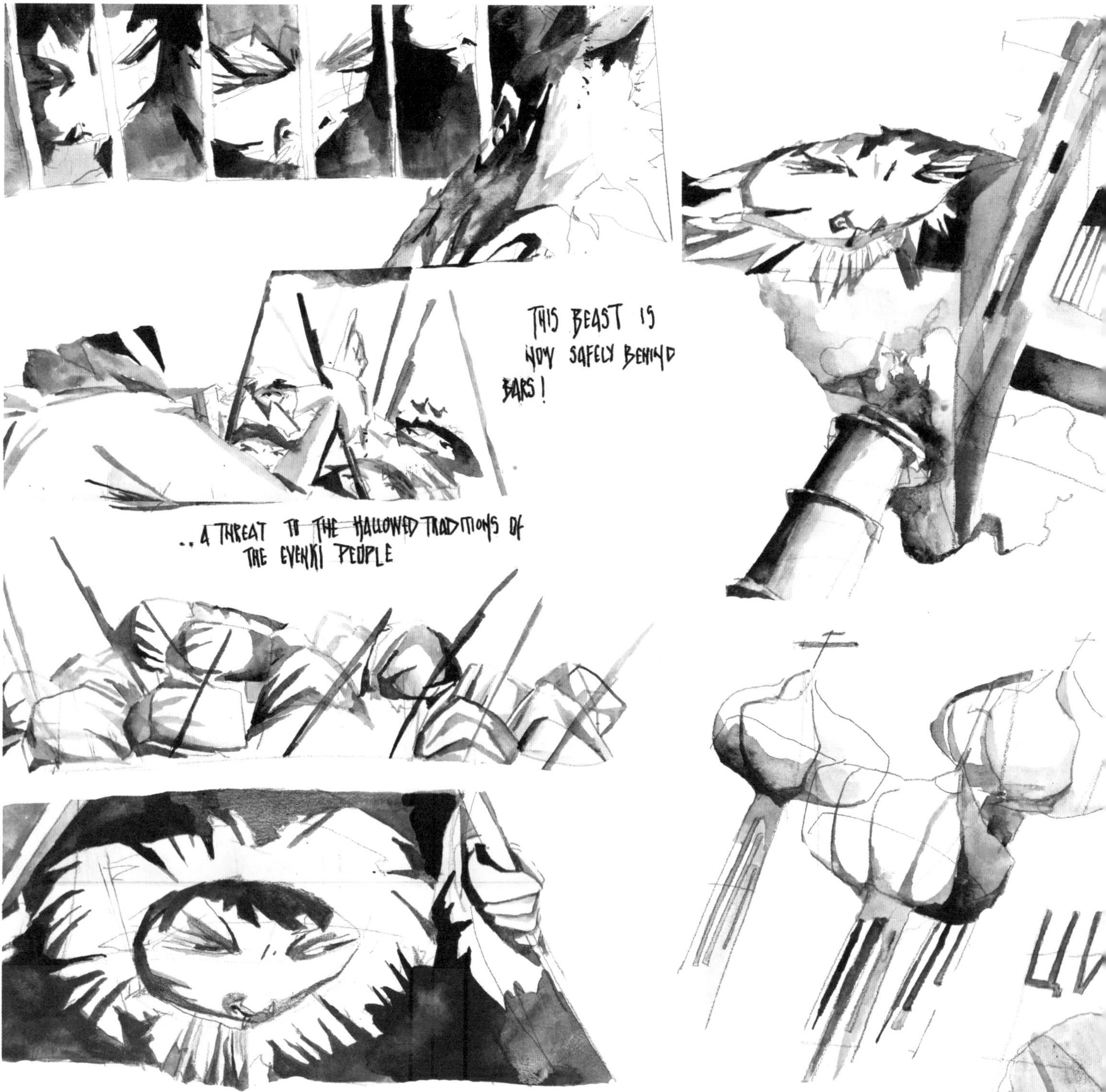
THIS BEAST IS NOW SAFELY BEHIND BARS!
..A THREAT TO THE HALLOWED TRADITIONS OF THE EVENKI PEOPLE

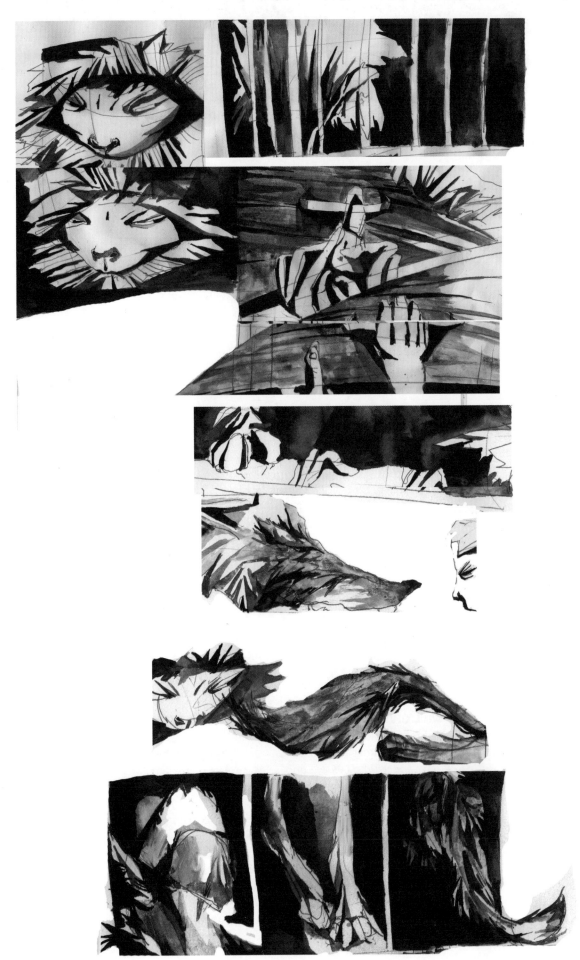

# Pippi Longstocking

## Astrid Lindgren

ART/ADAPTATION BY **Emelie Östergren**

**IN AN OCCURRENCE THAT WILL GIVE HOPE TO EVERY** struggling writer, the thirty-eight–year-old journalist and secretary Astrid Lindgren entered a contest put on by a publisher. Her manuscript—*Pippi Långstrump* (*Pippi Longstocking*)—won first prize in 1945 and went on to become one of the most translated, best-selling children's novels of all time. Lindgren continued to write books for children, turning into one of Sweden's most important writers. *The Historical Dictionary of Children's Literature* explains Pippi and her appeal:

> Pippi Longstocking, a self-assured, red-headed, nine-year-old orphan of supernatural strength, has a house and wealth of her own, is not subject to any adult supervision or rules, and lives and behaves exactly as she chooses. She refuses to be socialized and does not want to grow up.
>
> This anarchist protagonist, who fulfills every child's dream of freedom, was condemned by some contemporary commentators as a bad example for children; the novel is now acknowledged as one of the first to truly celebrate childhood autonomy.

Stockholm artist Emelie Östergren chose to illustrate her homeland's heroine. Emilie's work looks like children's book illustration at first glance, but the distortions and uneasiness on display take us to a strange parallel realm. This adaptation combines portions of two of the numerous Pippi books.

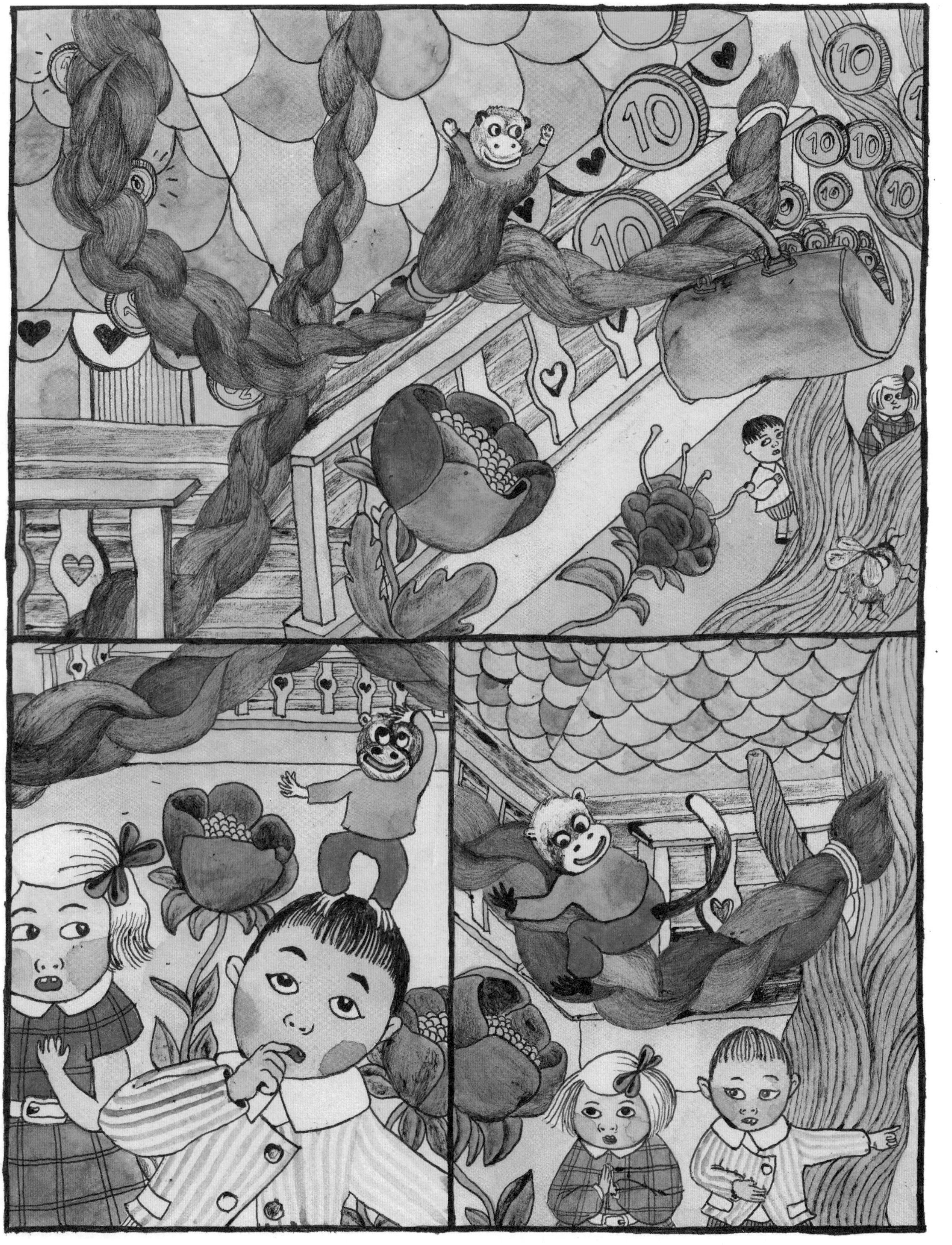
10

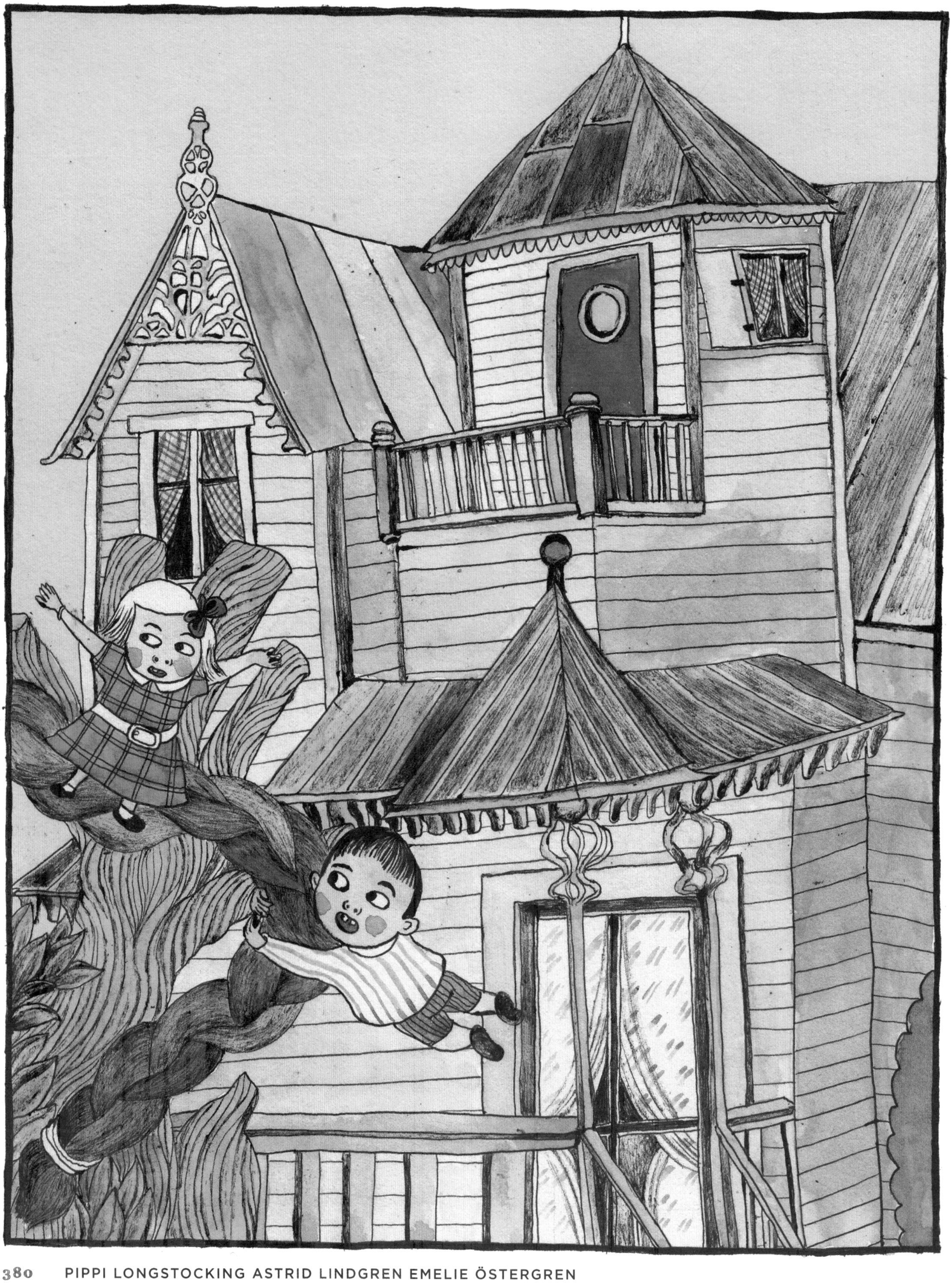

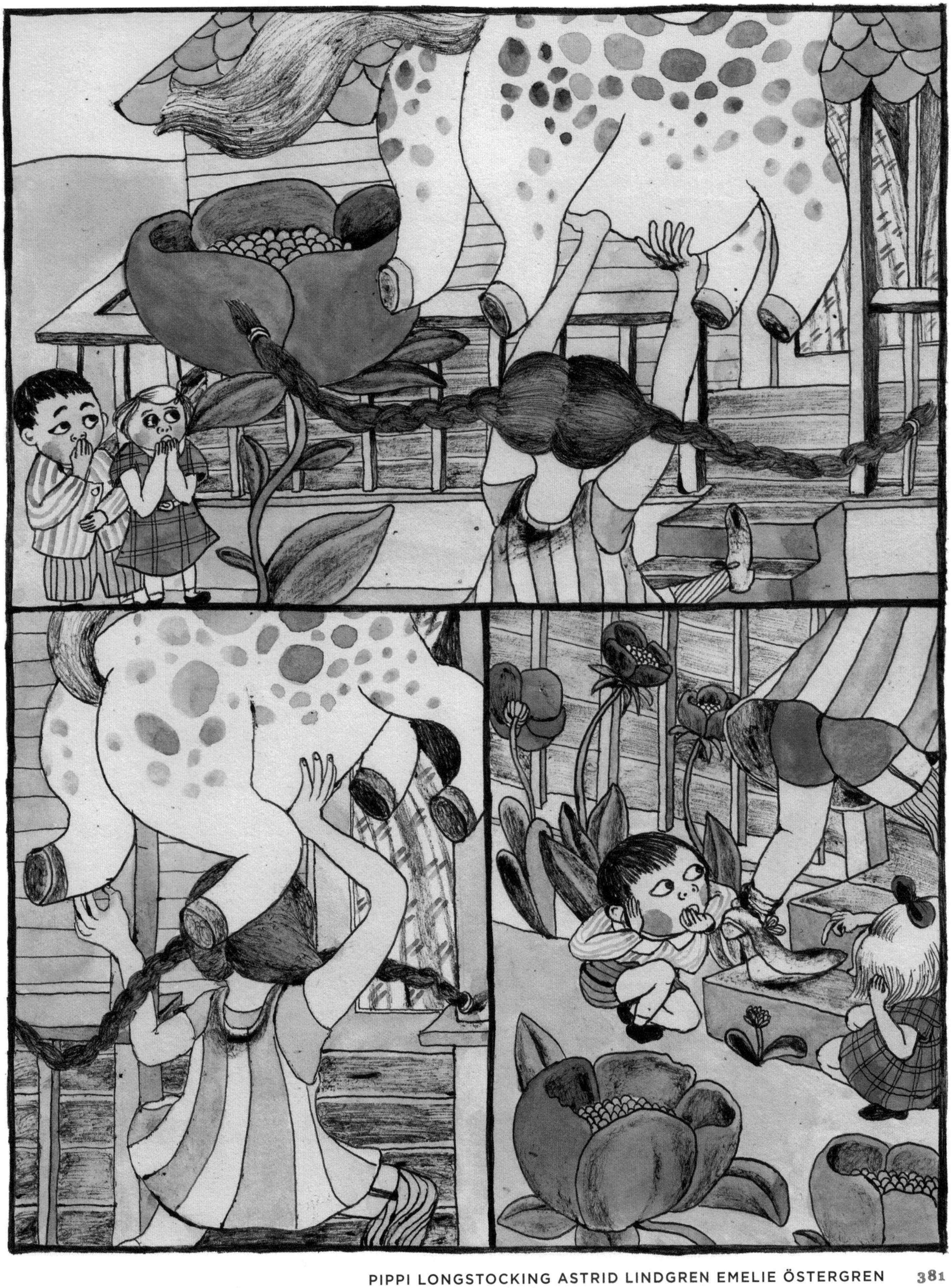

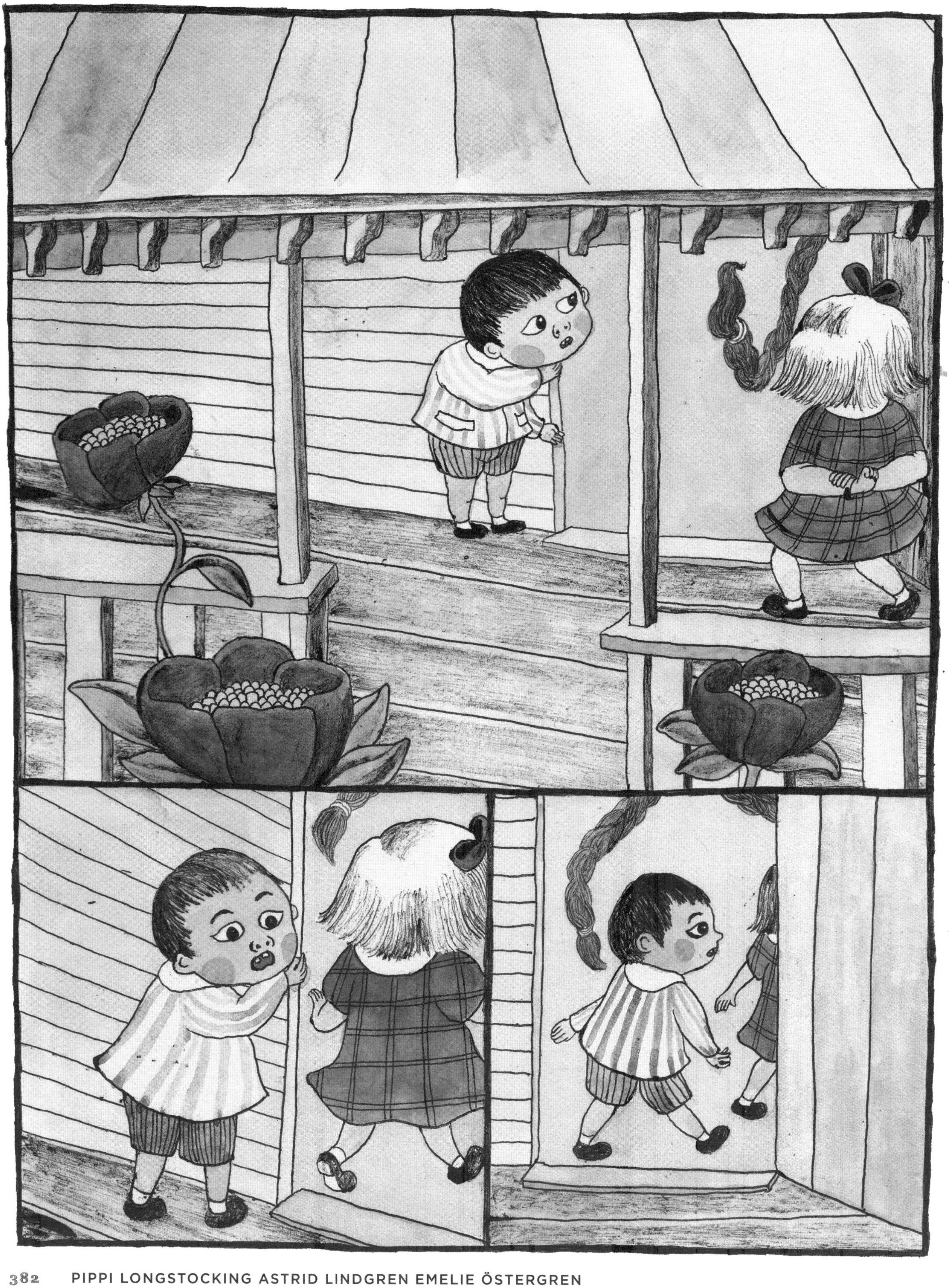

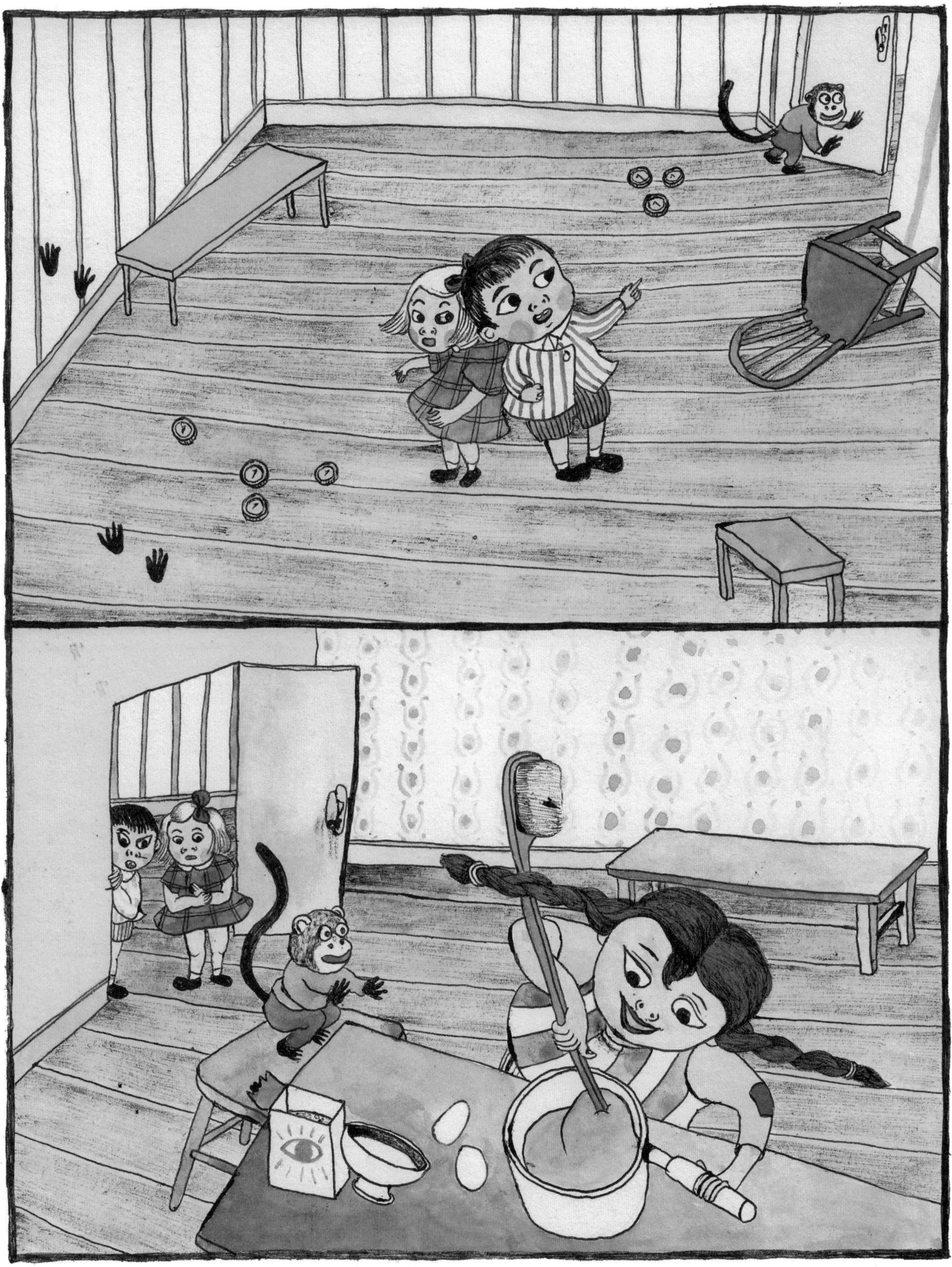

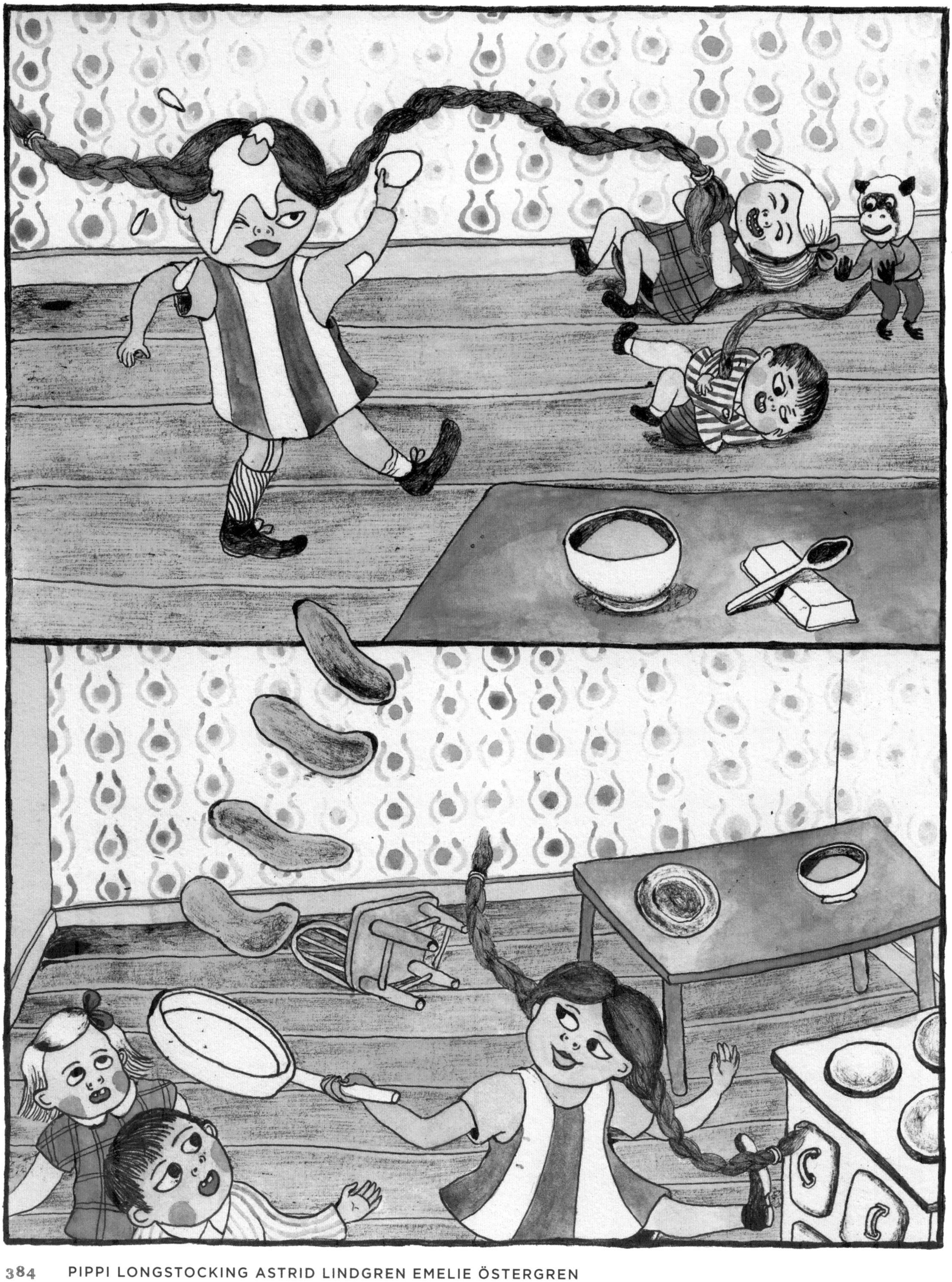

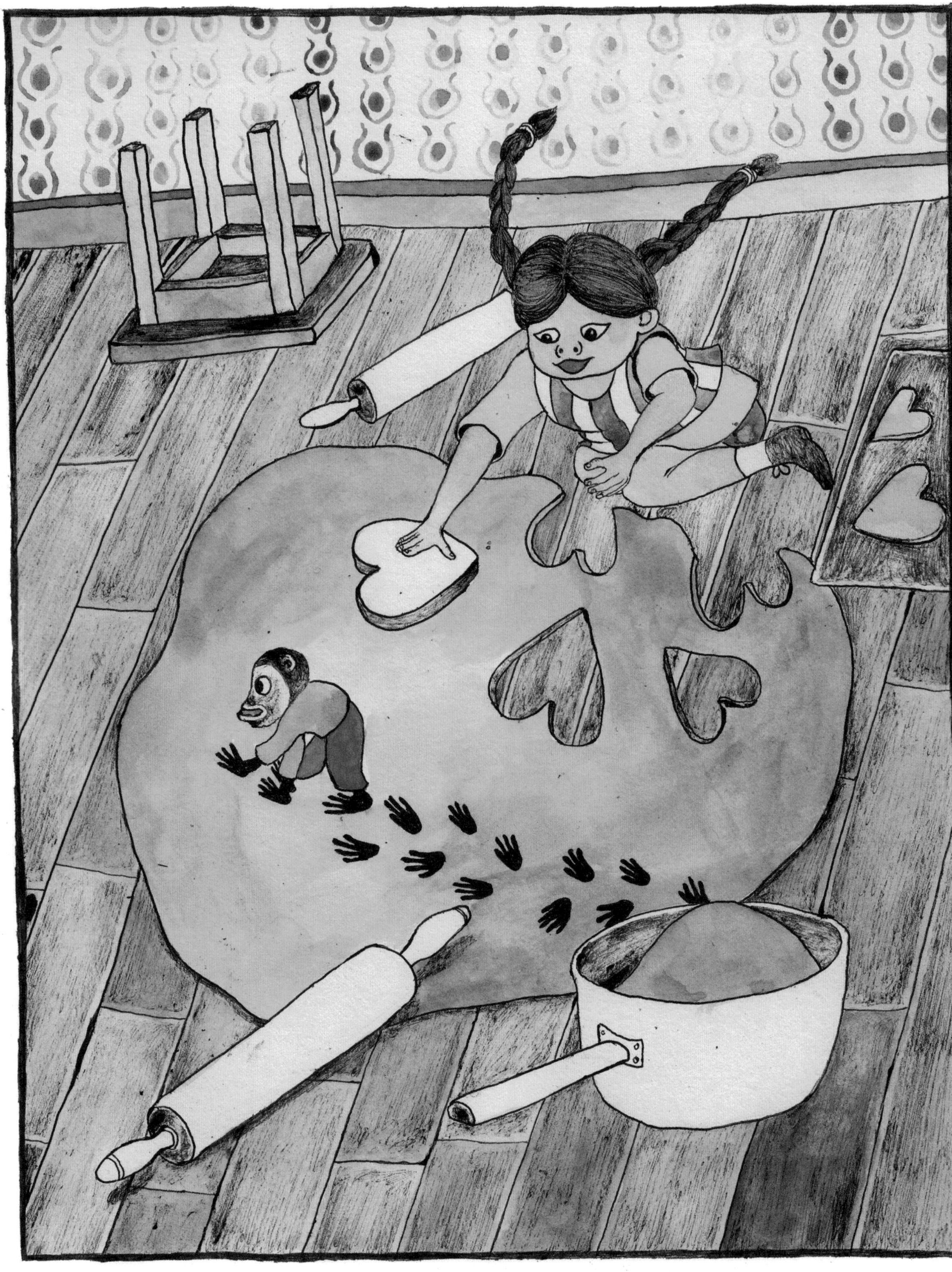

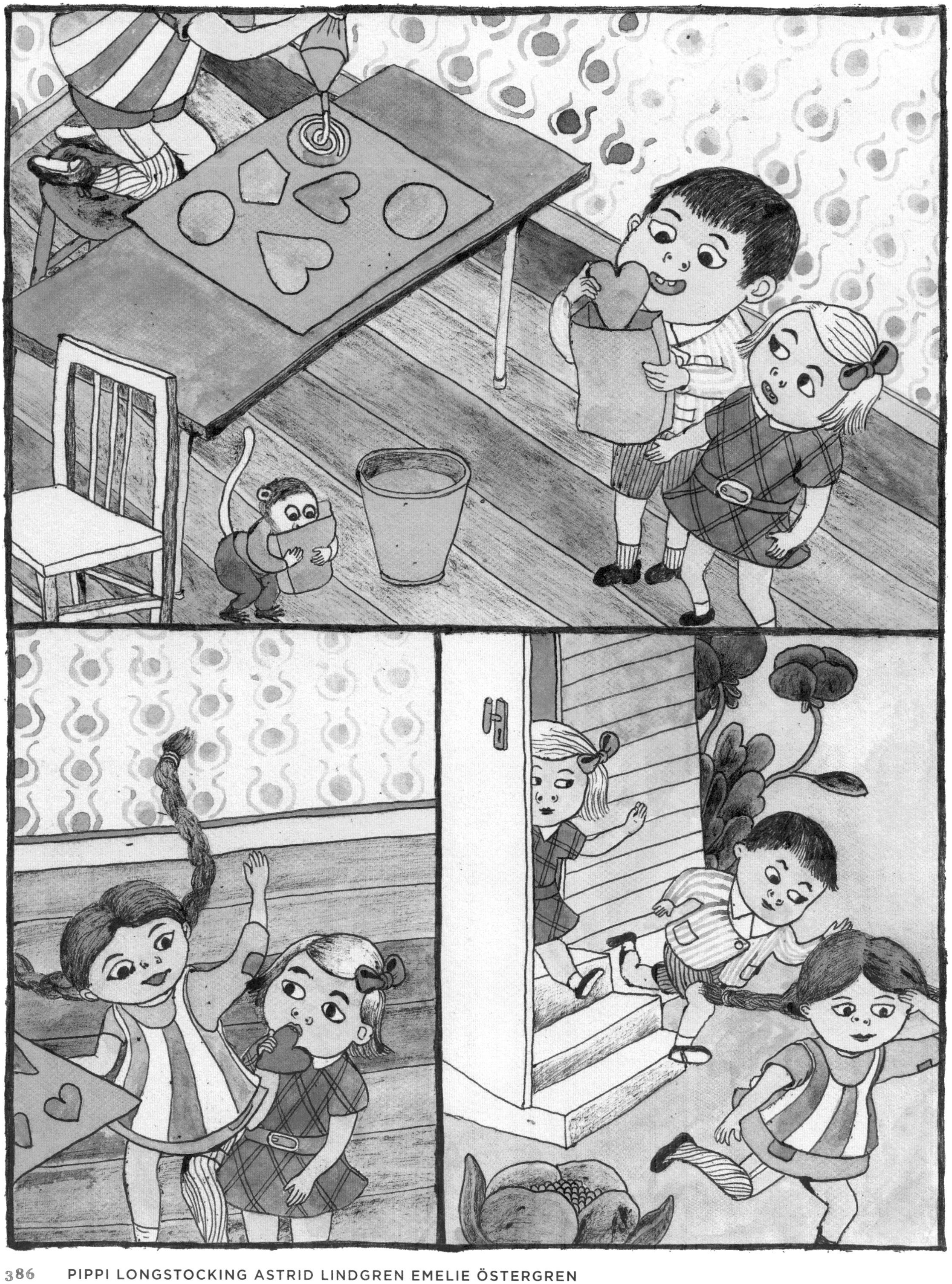

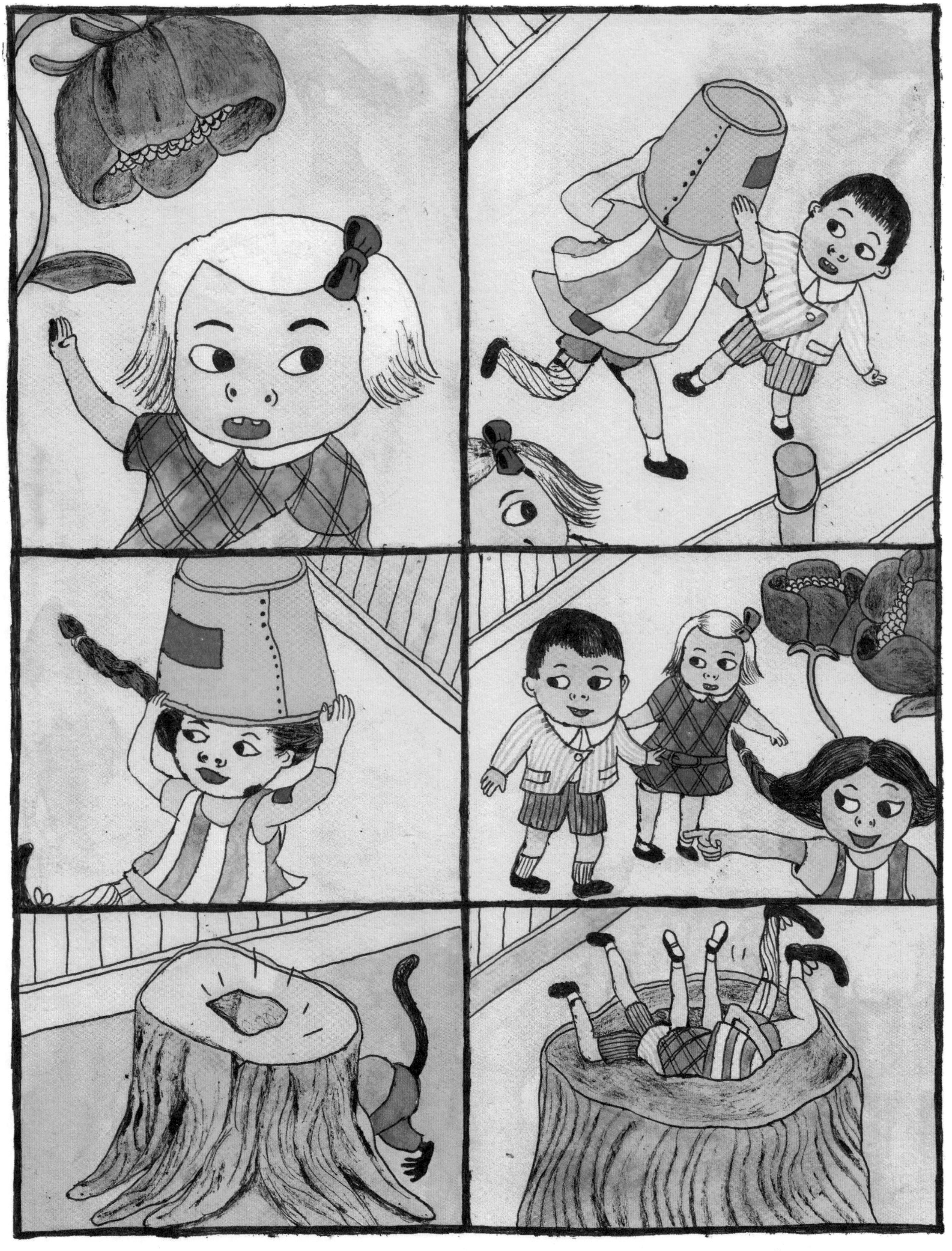

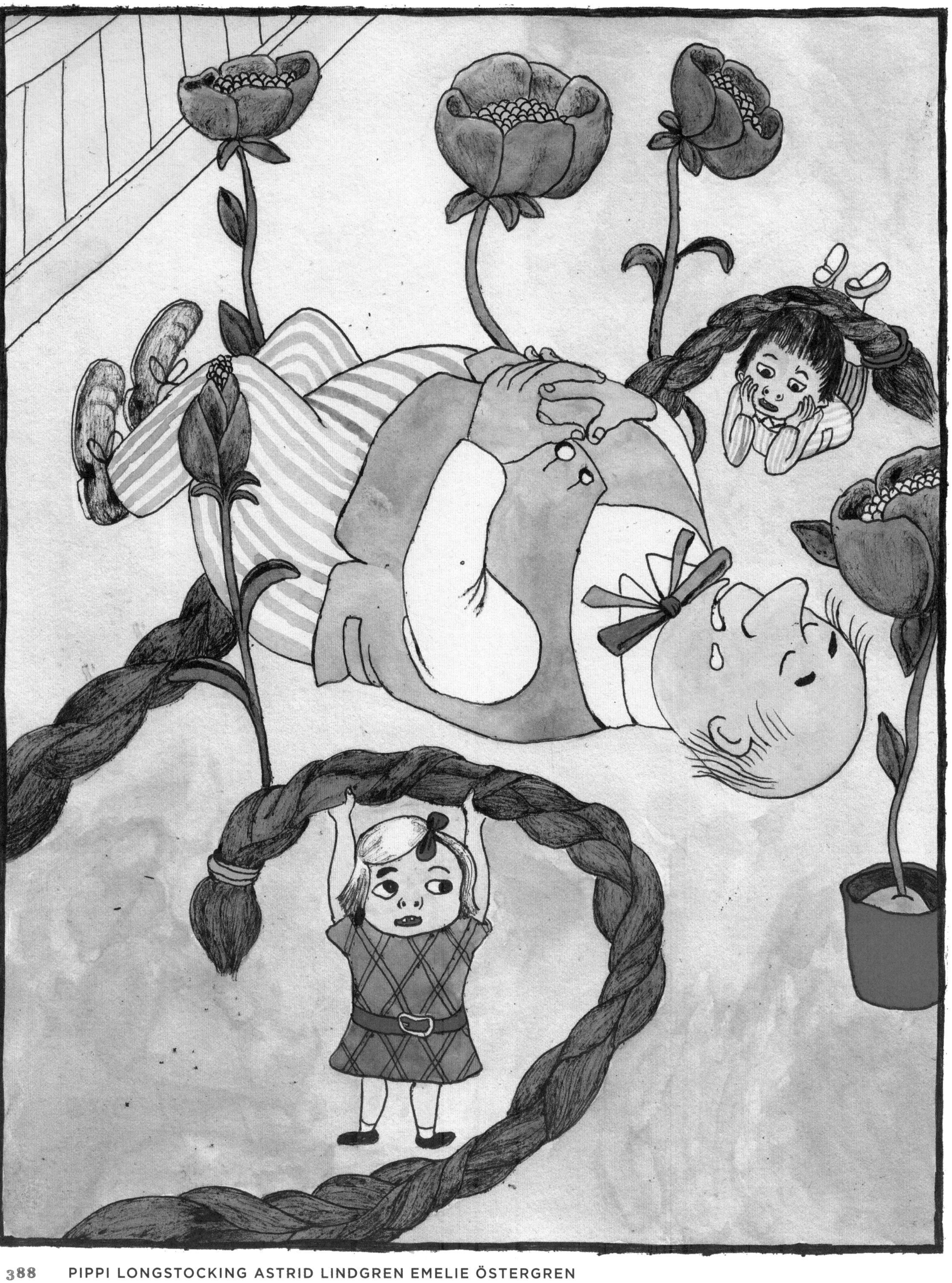

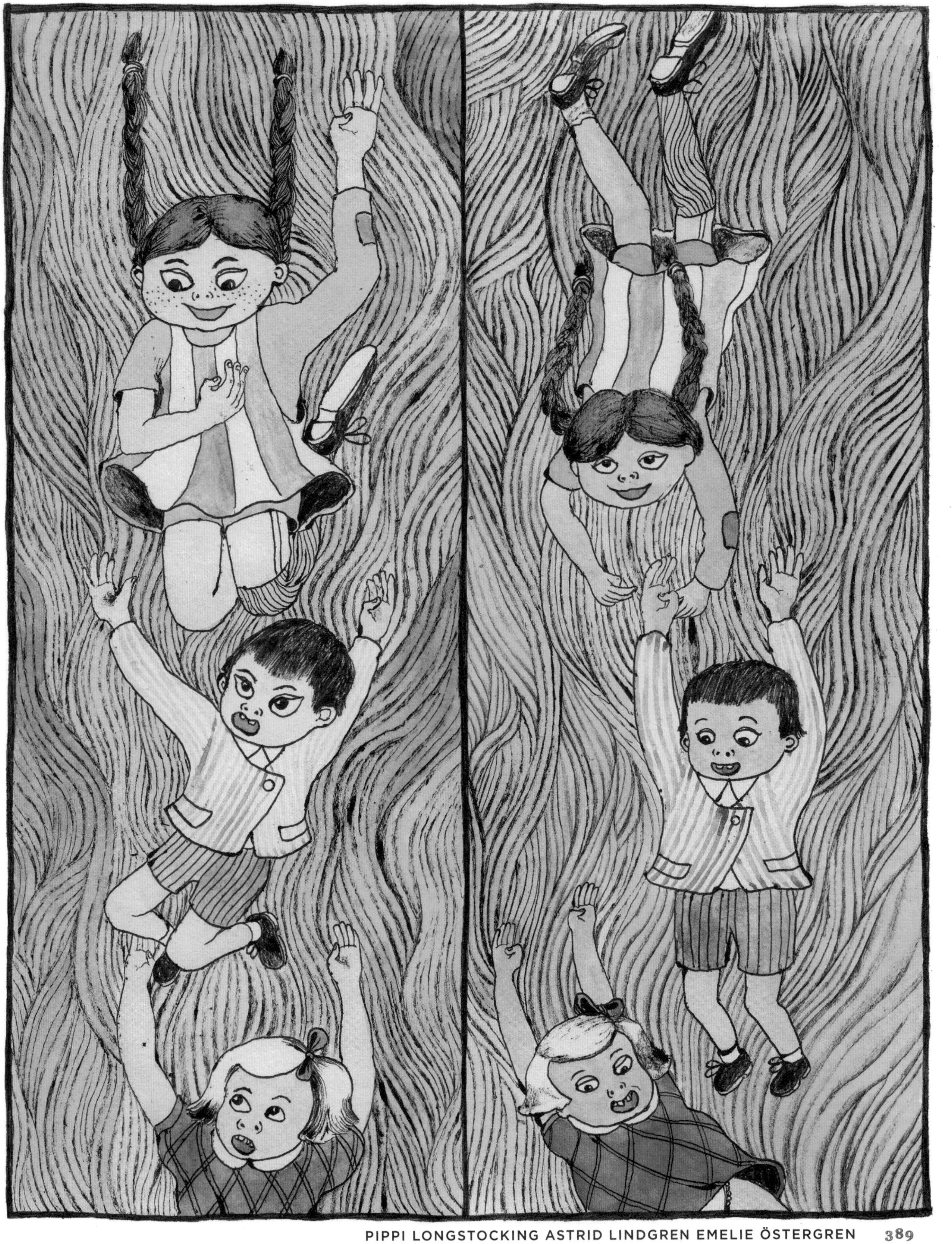

# The Diary of a Young Girl

**Anne Frank**

ADAPTATION BY **Sid Jacobson**

ART BY **Ernie Colón**

**AT THE BEGINNING OF 1933, ADOLF HITLER BECAME** the leader of Germany. Early the following year, the Frank family—father Otto, mother Edith, and young daughters Annelies (Anne) and Margot—moved to Amsterdam to escape the ever-increasing persecution of Jews. In May 1940, the Nazis invaded and occupied the Netherlands, and a little over two years later, Margot received orders to relocate to a labor camp. The family immediately went into hiding in a cramped, secluded annex attached to the headquarters of Otto's food-related business. They were eventually joined by several other Jewish friends: the van Pels family and Fritz Pfeffer. A handful of employees risked their lives to bring the hideaways food, reaching them via an opening hidden by a bookcase. The Franks stayed in this small, dreary space for a little over two years, literally never once going outside that entire time. In early August 1944, someone—we still don't know who—ratted them out to the Nazis, who stormed the annex and sent everyone to labor camps. Anne and Margot died of typhus, Edith of starvation. Otto survived, and one of the family's helpers gave him Anne's writings, created over the course of their entire hiding, from shortly after her thirteenth birthday to shortly after her fifteenth.

It turns out that Anne wanted to be a writer when she grew up, and she showed lots of promise in her diary entries, as well as the short stories, essays, fairy tales, and novel fragment she penned in the annex. Beyond her writerly talent, she was quite insightful about herself and her relationships. Her diary, as edited by her father and bowdlerized by publishers, became an instant worldwide best-seller and classic of twentieth-century literature. (The original, unexpurgated diary—with references to Anne's sexuality, family conflicts, and occasional despondency—has since been published.) It works on numerous levels, including as a literary diary, a coming-of-age story, and, of course, arguably the most important piece of writing to come out of the Holocaust.

Sid Jacobson and Ernie Colón specialize in graphic nonfiction and received official permission to create *Anne Frank: The Anne Frank House Authorized Graphic Biography*. The following excerpt covers events from August 1943 to the following April, as revealed by Frank's diary and her other writings.

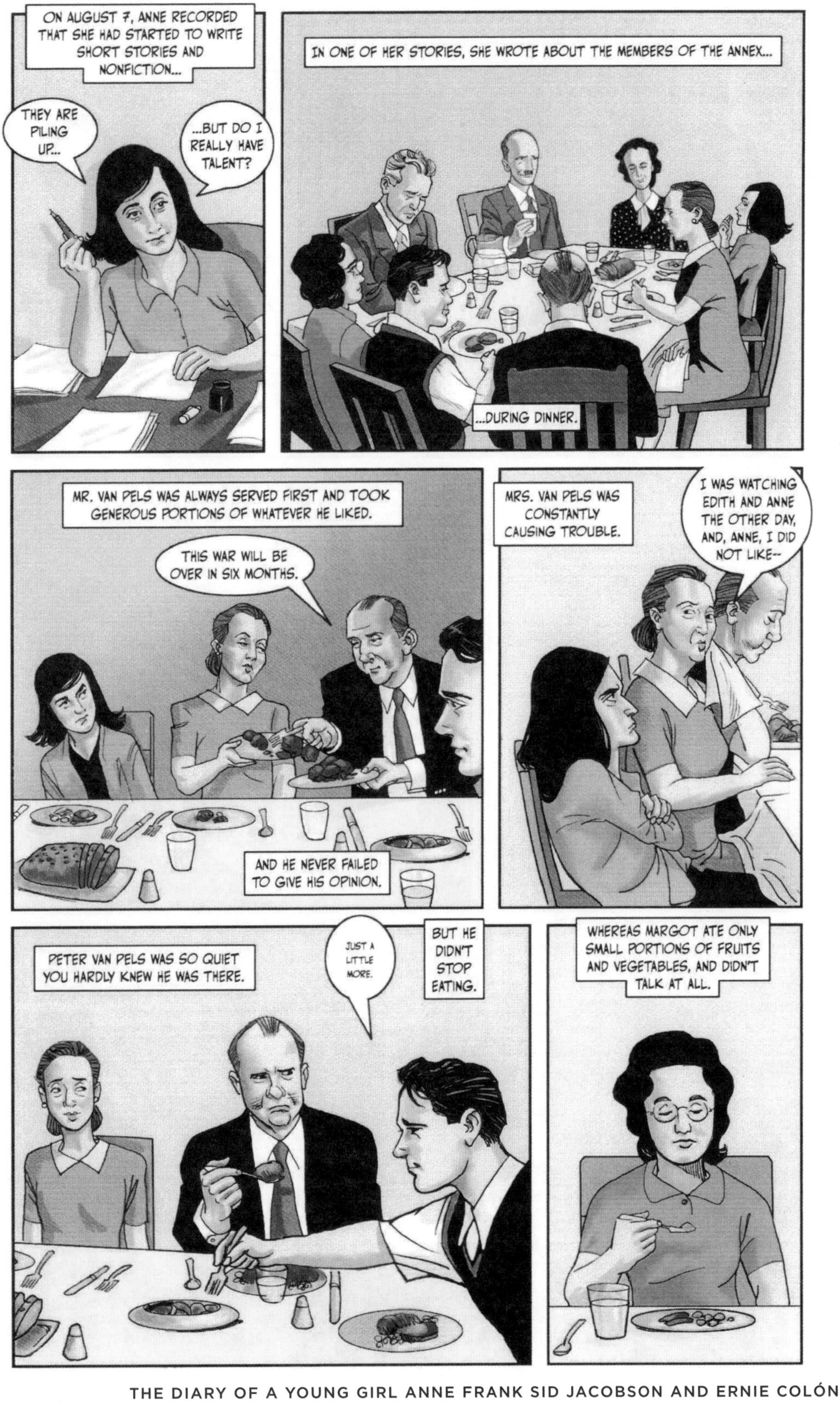

ON AUGUST 7, ANNE RECORDED THAT SHE HAD STARTED TO WRITE SHORT STORIES AND NONFICTION...
THEY ARE PILING UP...
...BUT DO I REALLY HAVE TALENT?
IN ONE OF HER STORIES, SHE WROTE ABOUT THE MEMBERS OF THE ANNEX...
...DURING DINNER.
MR. VAN PELS WAS ALWAYS SERVED FIRST AND TOOK GENEROUS PORTIONS OF WHATEVER HE LIKED.
THIS WAR WILL BE OVER IN SIX MONTHS.
AND HE NEVER FAILED TO GIVE HIS OPINION.
MRS. VAN PELS WAS CONSTANTLY CAUSING TROUBLE.
I WAS WATCHING EDITH AND ANNE THE OTHER DAY, AND, ANNE, I DID NOT LIKE--
PETER VAN PELS WAS SO QUIET YOU HARDLY KNEW HE WAS THERE.
JUST A LITTLE MORE.
BUT HE DIDN'T STOP EATING.
WHEREAS MARGOT ATE ONLY SMALL PORTIONS OF FRUITS AND VEGETABLES, AND DIDN'T TALK AT ALL.

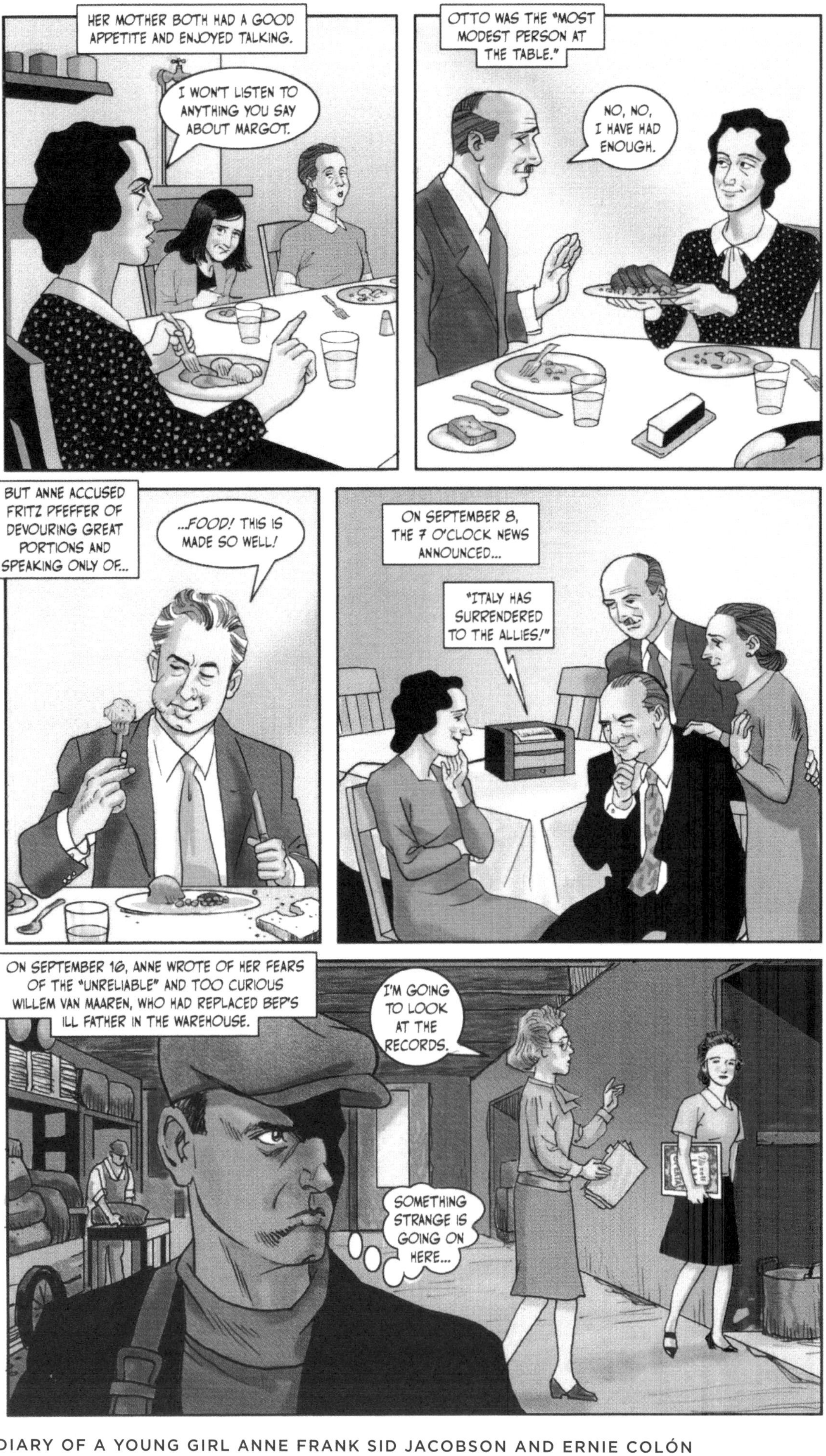
HER MOTHER BOTH HAD A GOOD APPETITE AND ENJOYED TALKING.
I WON'T LISTEN TO ANYTHING YOU SAY ABOUT MARGOT.
OTTO WAS THE "MOST MODEST PERSON AT THE TABLE."
NO, NO, I HAVE HAD ENOUGH.
BUT ANNE ACCUSED FRITZ PFEFFER OF DEVOURING GREAT PORTIONS AND SPEAKING ONLY OF...
...FOOD! THIS IS MADE SO WELL!
ON SEPTEMBER 8, THE 7 O'CLOCK NEWS ANNOUNCED...
"ITALY HAS SURRENDERED TO THE ALLIES!"
ON SEPTEMBER 16, ANNE WROTE OF HER FEARS OF THE "UNRELIABLE" AND TOO CURIOUS WILLEM VAN MAAREN, WHO HAD REPLACED BEP'S ILL FATHER IN THE WAREHOUSE.
I'M GOING TO LOOK AT THE RECORDS.
SOMETHING STRANGE IS GOING ON HERE...

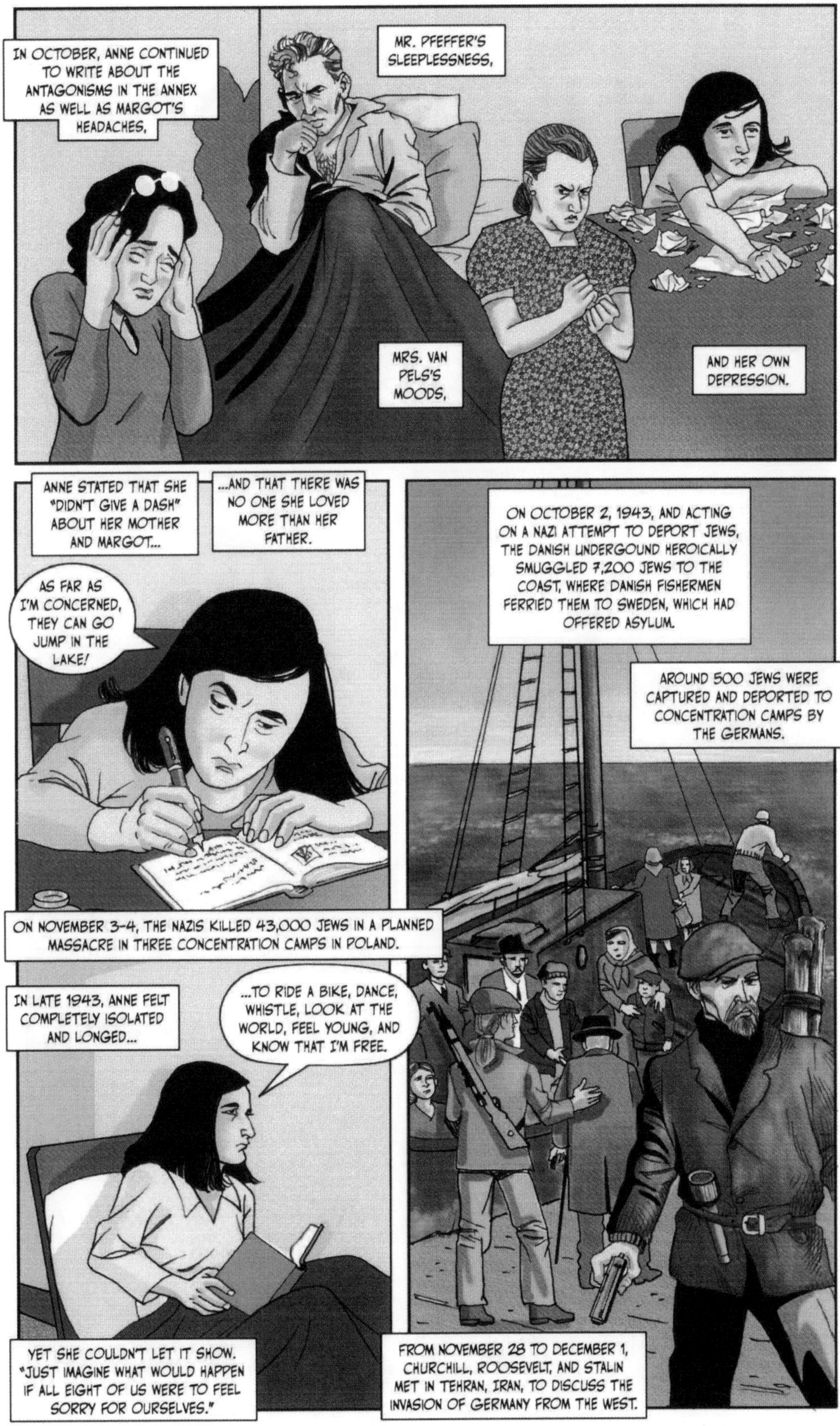
IN OCTOBER, ANNE CONTINUED TO WRITE ABOUT THE ANTAGONISMS IN THE ANNEX AS WELL AS MARGOT'S HEADACHES,
MR. PFEFFER'S SLEEPLESSNESS,
MRS. VAN PELS'S MOODS,
AND HER OWN DEPRESSION.
ANNE STATED THAT SHE "DIDN'T GIVE A DASH" ABOUT HER MOTHER AND MARGOT...
...AND THAT THERE WAS NO ONE SHE LOVED MORE THAN HER FATHER.
AS FAR AS I'M CONCERNED, THEY CAN GO JUMP IN THE LAKE!
ON OCTOBER 2, 1943, AND ACTING ON A NAZI ATTEMPT TO DEPORT JEWS, THE DANISH UNDERGOUND HEROICALLY SMUGGLED 7,200 JEWS TO THE COAST, WHERE DANISH FISHERMEN FERRIED THEM TO SWEDEN, WHICH HAD OFFERED ASYLUM.
AROUND 500 JEWS WERE CAPTURED AND DEPORTED TO CONCENTRATION CAMPS BY THE GERMANS.
ON NOVEMBER 3-4, THE NAZIS KILLED 43,000 JEWS IN A PLANNED MASSACRE IN THREE CONCENTRATION CAMPS IN POLAND.
IN LATE 1943, ANNE FELT COMPLETELY ISOLATED AND LONGED...
...TO RIDE A BIKE, DANCE, WHISTLE, LOOK AT THE WORLD, FEEL YOUNG, AND KNOW THAT I'M FREE.
YET SHE COULDN'T LET IT SHOW. "JUST IMAGINE WHAT WOULD HAPPEN IF ALL EIGHT OF US WERE TO FEEL SORRY FOR OURSELVES."
FROM NOVEMBER 28 TO DECEMBER 1, CHURCHILL, ROOSEVELT, AND STALIN MET IN TEHRAN, IRAN, TO DISCUSS THE INVASION OF GERMANY FROM THE WEST.

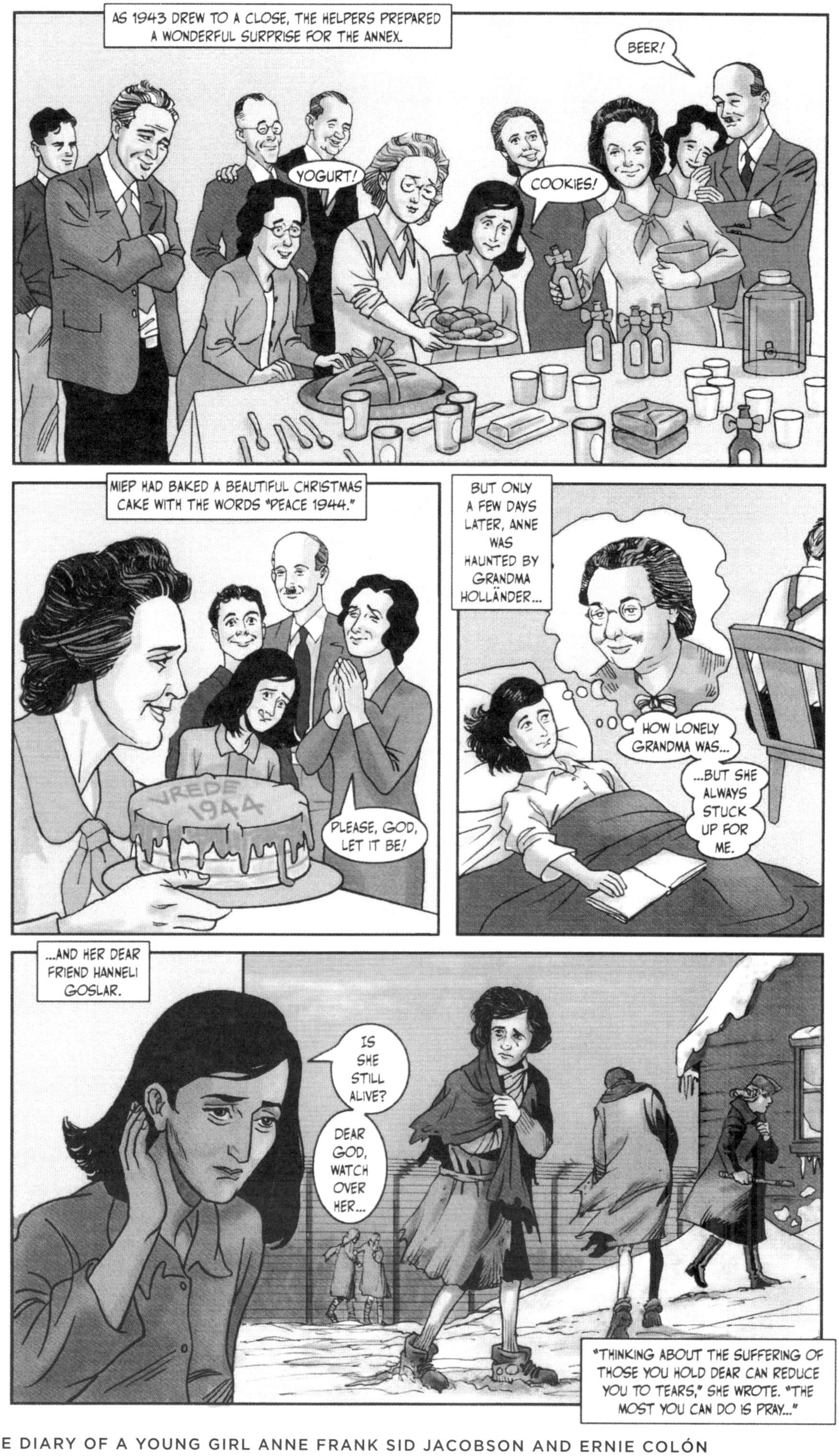
AS 1943 DREW TO A CLOSE, THE HELPERS PREPARED A WONDERFUL SURPRISE FOR THE ANNEX.
BEER!
YOGURT!
COOKIES!
MIEP HAD BAKED A BEAUTIFUL CHRISTMAS CAKE WITH THE WORDS "PEACE 1944."
VREDE 1944
PLEASE, GOD, LET IT BE!
BUT ONLY A FEW DAYS LATER, ANNE WAS HAUNTED BY GRANDMA HOLLÄNDER...
HOW LONELY GRANDMA WAS...
...BUT SHE ALWAYS STUCK UP FOR ME.
...AND HER DEAR FRIEND HANNELI GOSLAR.
IS SHE STILL ALIVE?
DEAR GOD, WATCH OVER HER...
"THINKING ABOUT THE SUFFERING OF THOSE YOU HOLD DEAR CAN REDUCE YOU TO TEARS," SHE WROTE. "THE MOST YOU CAN DO IS PRAY..."

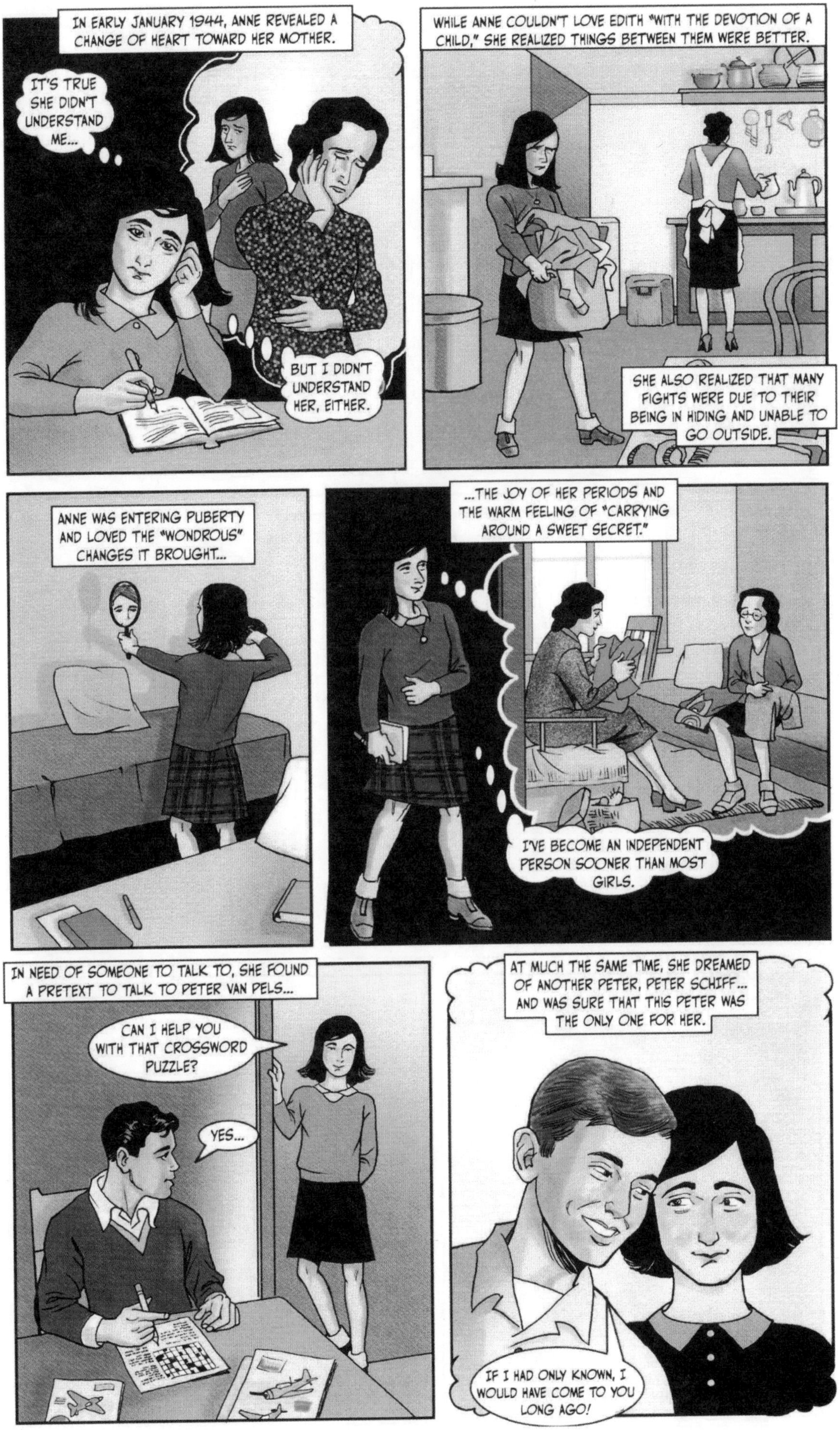
IN EARLY JANUARY 1944, ANNE REVEALED A CHANGE OF HEART TOWARD HER MOTHER.
IT'S TRUE SHE DIDN'T UNDERSTAND ME...
BUT I DIDN'T UNDERSTAND HER, EITHER.
WHILE ANNE COULDN'T LOVE EDITH "WITH THE DEVOTION OF A CHILD," SHE REALIZED THINGS BETWEEN THEM WERE BETTER.
SHE ALSO REALIZED THAT MANY FIGHTS WERE DUE TO THEIR BEING IN HIDING AND UNABLE TO GO OUTSIDE.
ANNE WAS ENTERING PUBERTY AND LOVED THE "WONDROUS" CHANGES IT BROUGHT...
...THE JOY OF HER PERIODS AND THE WARM FEELING OF "CARRYING AROUND A SWEET SECRET."
I'VE BECOME AN INDEPENDENT PERSON SOONER THAN MOST GIRLS.
IN NEED OF SOMEONE TO TALK TO, SHE FOUND A PRETEXT TO TALK TO PETER VAN PELS...
CAN I HELP YOU WITH THAT CROSSWORD PUZZLE?
YES...
AT MUCH THE SAME TIME, SHE DREAMED OF ANOTHER PETER, PETER SCHIFF... AND WAS SURE THAT THIS PETER WAS THE ONLY ONE FOR HER.
IF I HAD ONLY KNOWN, I WOULD HAVE COME TO YOU LONG AGO!

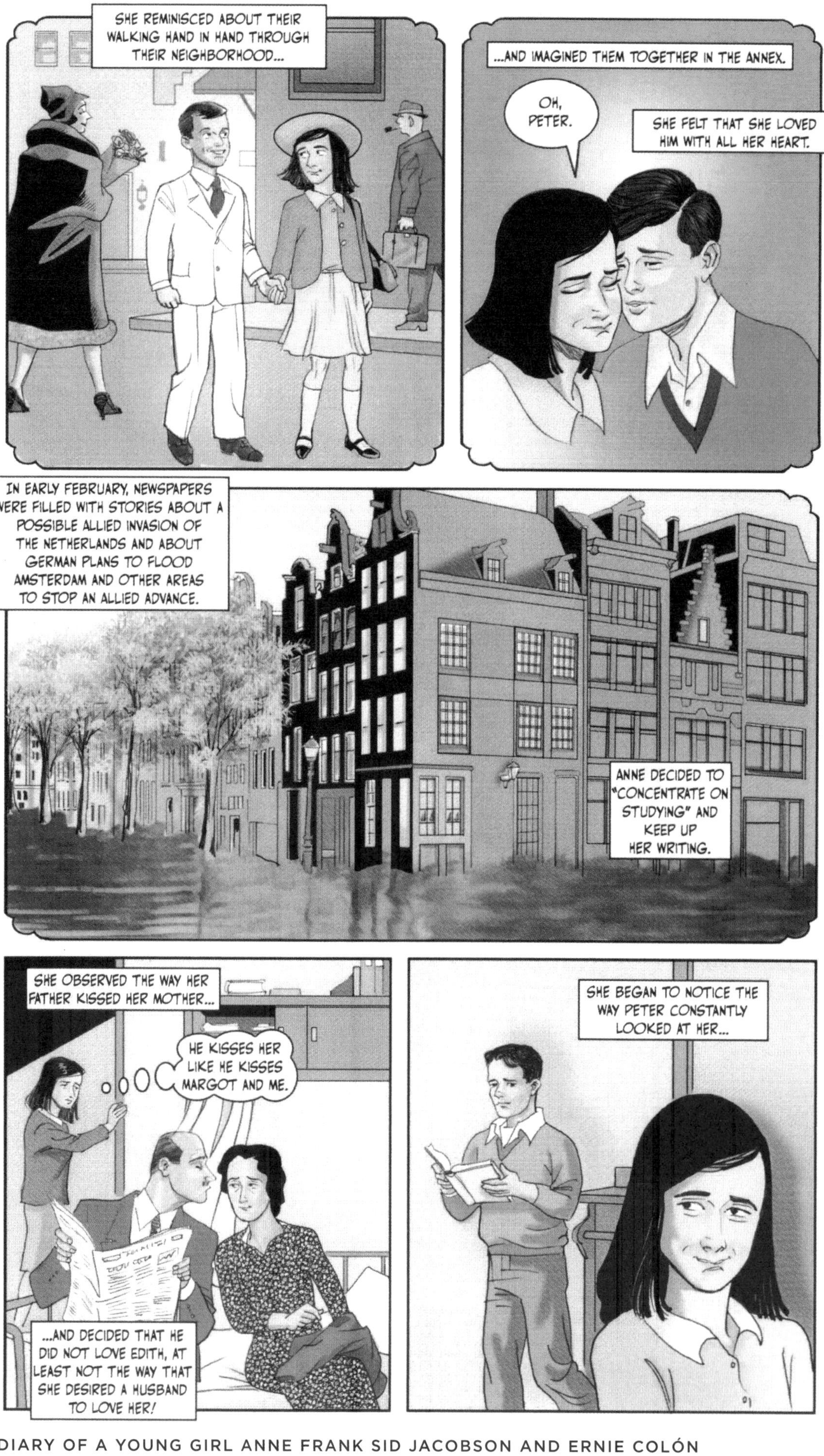
SHE REMINISCED ABOUT THEIR WALKING HAND IN HAND THROUGH THEIR NEIGHBORHOOD...
...AND IMAGINED THEM TOGETHER IN THE ANNEX.
OH, PETER.
SHE FELT THAT SHE LOVED HIM WITH ALL HER HEART.
IN EARLY FEBRUARY, NEWSPAPERS WERE FILLED WITH STORIES ABOUT A POSSIBLE ALLIED INVASION OF THE NETHERLANDS AND ABOUT GERMAN PLANS TO FLOOD AMSTERDAM AND OTHER AREAS TO STOP AN ALLIED ADVANCE.
ANNE DECIDED TO "CONCENTRATE ON STUDYING" AND KEEP UP HER WRITING.
SHE OBSERVED THE WAY HER FATHER KISSED HER MOTHER...
HE KISSES HER LIKE HE KISSES MARGOT AND ME.
...AND DECIDED THAT HE DID NOT LOVE EDITH, AT LEAST NOT THE WAY THAT SHE DESIRED A HUSBAND TO LOVE HER!
SHE BEGAN TO NOTICE THE WAY PETER CONSTANTLY LOOKED AT HER...

PETER, AFTER AN ARGUMENT WITH MR. PFEFFER, SOUGHT OUT ANNE IN THE ATTIC.

I DON'T USUALLY TALK MUCH BECAUSE I GET TONGUE-TIED.

YOU'RE NEVER AT A LOSS FOR WORDS. YOU SAY EXACTLY WHAT YOU WANT TO SAY.

YOU'RE WRONG. I TALK TOO MUCH AND THAT'S JUST AS BAD.

"I SENSED A STRONG FEELING OF FELLOWSHIP," ANNE WROTE LATER, SUCH AS SHE HAD ONLY EVER ENJOYED WITH GIRLFRIENDS.

IN THE FOLLOWING DAYS, ANNE VISITED PETER MORE AND MORE.

WHAT ARE YOU DOING?

I'M STUDYING FRENCH.

SHALL I HELP YOU?

ANY REASON BROUGHT HER UP TO THE ATTIC...THROUGH PETER'S ROOM.

I NEED SOME POTATOES FROM THE ATTIC.

I'LL GO!

"IT'S ALWAYS SO I CAN SEE HIM," ANNE WROTE ON FEBRUARY 18.

ON FEBRUARY 20, ANNE DESCRIBED A TYPICAL SUNDAY.

MR. PFEFFER WOULD RISE AT 8 O'CLOCK, SPEND AN HOUR CLEANING HIMSELF, THEN PRAY FOR FIFTEEN MINUTES WHILE MRS. VAN PELS USED THE BATHROOM.

BY 9:30 THE BLACKOUT SCREENS WERE REMOVED. THEN, WHEN OTHER PEOPLE MIGHT STROLL IN THE SUN, THEY BATHED AND CLEANED, KNOWING THEY WOULDN'T BE HEARD.

THE DIARY OF A YOUNG GIRL ANNE FRANK SID JACOBSON AND ERNIE COLÓN

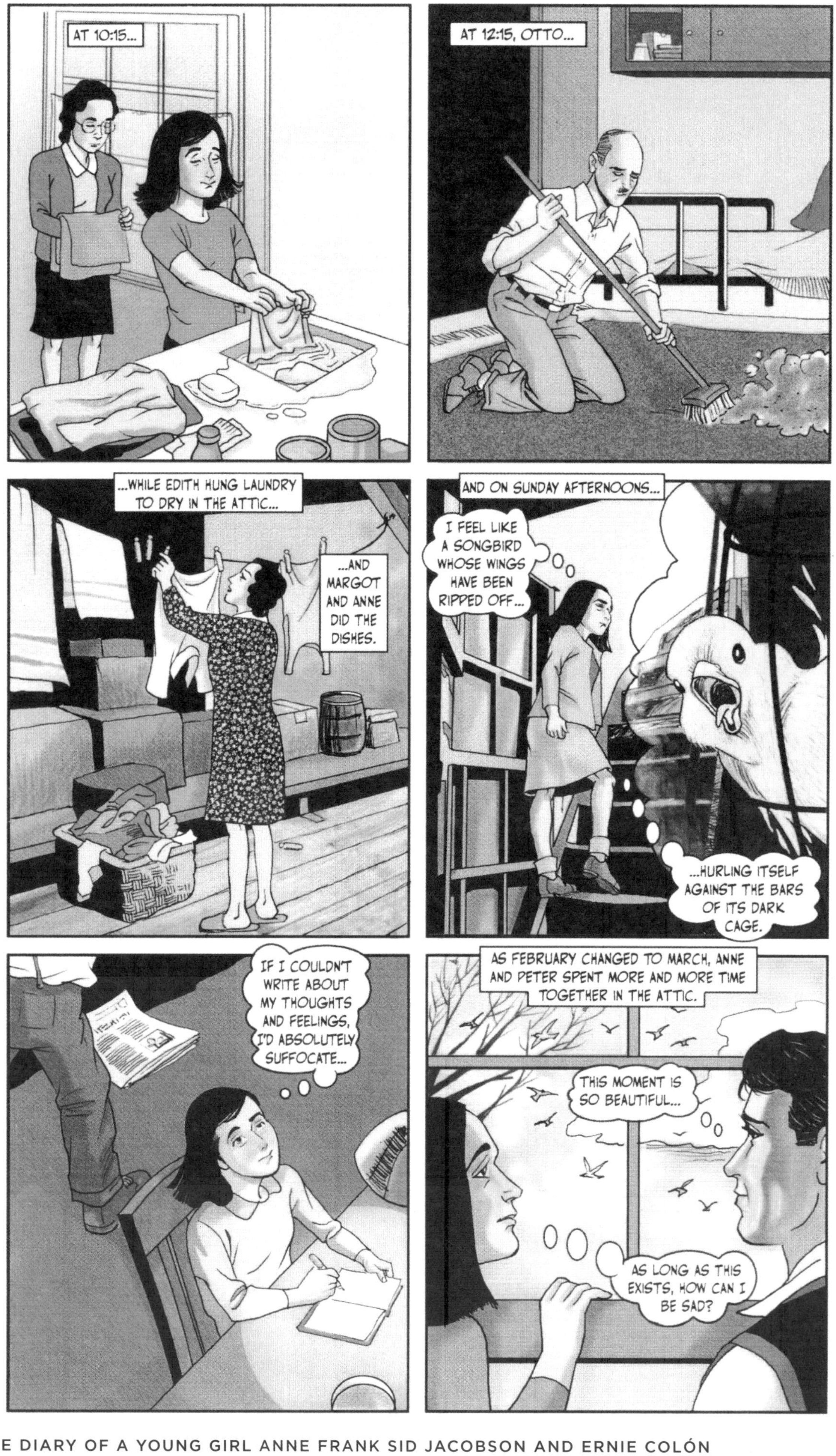
AT 10:15...
AT 12:15, OTTO...
...WHILE EDITH HUNG LAUNDRY TO DRY IN THE ATTIC...
...AND MARGOT AND ANNE DID THE DISHES.
AND ON SUNDAY AFTERNOONS...
I FEEL LIKE A SONGBIRD WHOSE WINGS HAVE BEEN RIPPED OFF...
...HURLING ITSELF AGAINST THE BARS OF ITS DARK CAGE.
IF I COULDN'T WRITE ABOUT MY THOUGHTS AND FEELINGS, I'D ABSOLUTELY SUFFOCATE...
AS FEBRUARY CHANGED TO MARCH, ANNE AND PETER SPENT MORE AND MORE TIME TOGETHER IN THE ATTIC.
THIS MOMENT IS SO BEAUTIFUL...
AS LONG AS THIS EXISTS, HOW CAN I BE SAD?

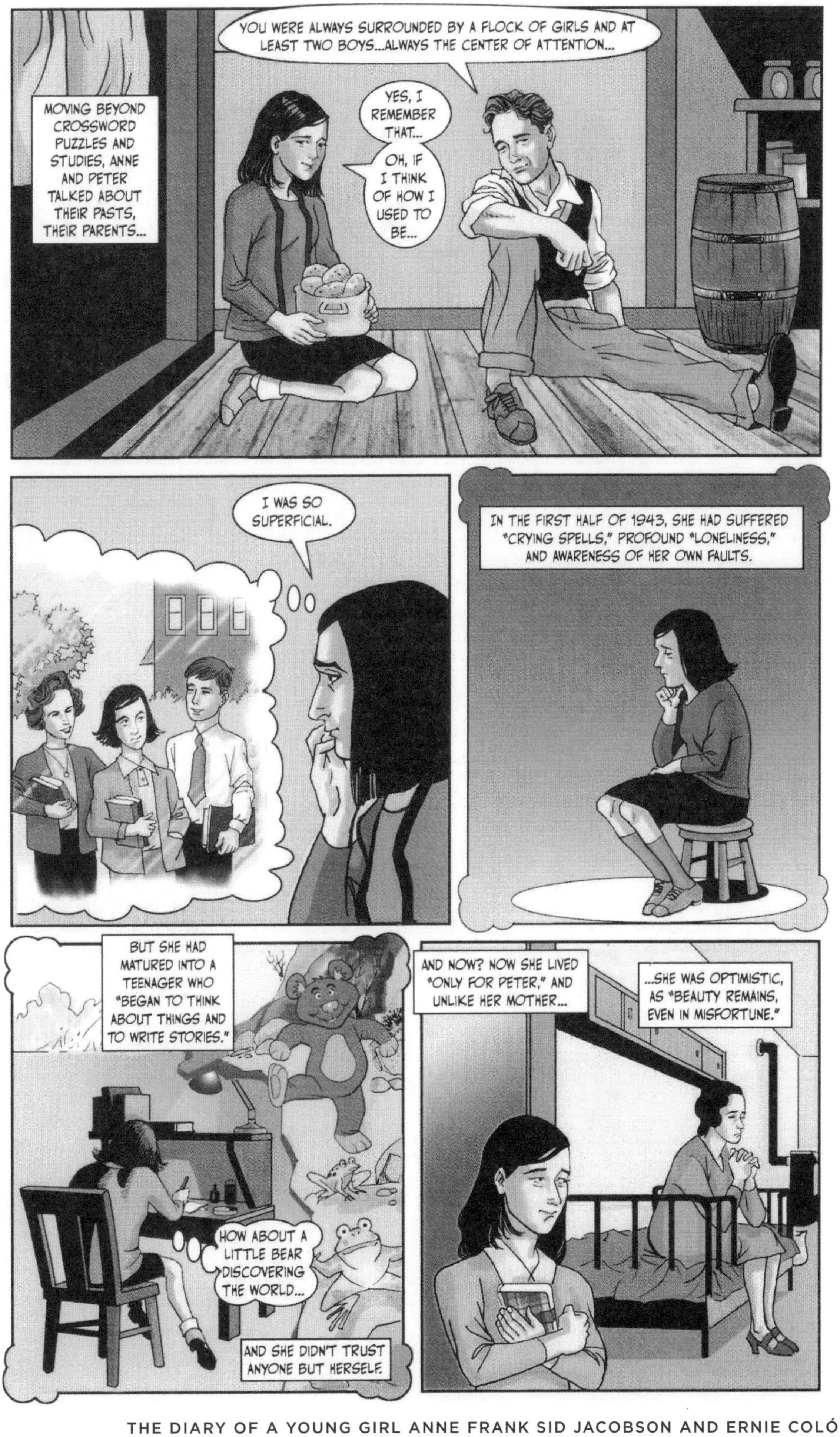
MOVING BEYOND CROSSWORD PUZZLES AND STUDIES, ANNE AND PETER TALKED ABOUT THEIR PASTS, THEIR PARENTS...
YOU WERE ALWAYS SURROUNDED BY A FLOCK OF GIRLS AND AT LEAST TWO BOYS...ALWAYS THE CENTER OF ATTENTION...
YES, I REMEMBER THAT...
OH, IF I THINK OF HOW I USED TO BE...
I WAS SO SUPERFICIAL.
IN THE FIRST HALF OF 1943, SHE HAD SUFFERED "CRYING SPELLS," PROFOUND "LONELINESS," AND AWARENESS OF HER OWN FAULTS.
BUT SHE HAD MATURED INTO A TEENAGER WHO "BEGAN TO THINK ABOUT THINGS AND TO WRITE STORIES."
HOW ABOUT A LITTLE BEAR DISCOVERING THE WORLD...
AND SHE DIDN'T TRUST ANYONE BUT HERSELF.
AND NOW? NOW SHE LIVED "ONLY FOR PETER," AND UNLIKE HER MOTHER...
...SHE WAS OPTIMISTIC, AS "BEAUTY REMAINS, EVEN IN MISFORTUNE."

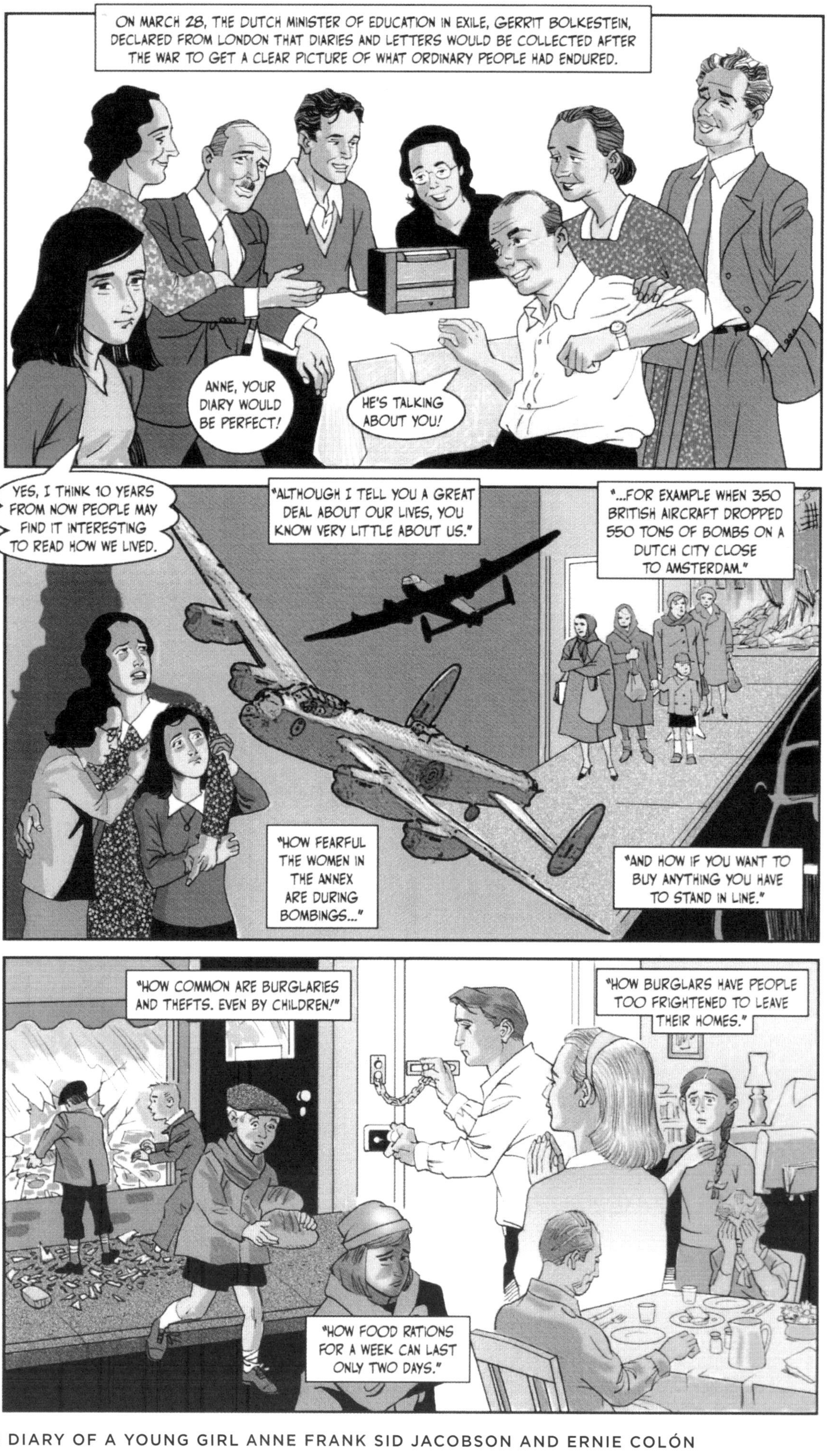
ON MARCH 28, THE DUTCH MINISTER OF EDUCATION IN EXILE, GERRIT BOLKESTEIN, DECLARED FROM LONDON THAT DIARIES AND LETTERS WOULD BE COLLECTED AFTER THE WAR TO GET A CLEAR PICTURE OF WHAT ORDINARY PEOPLE HAD ENDURED.
ANNE, YOUR DIARY WOULD BE PERFECT!
HE'S TALKING ABOUT YOU!
YES, I THINK 10 YEARS FROM NOW PEOPLE MAY FIND IT INTERESTING TO READ HOW WE LIVED.
"ALTHOUGH I TELL YOU A GREAT DEAL ABOUT OUR LIVES, YOU KNOW VERY LITTLE ABOUT US."
"...FOR EXAMPLE WHEN 350 BRITISH AIRCRAFT DROPPED 550 TONS OF BOMBS ON A DUTCH CITY CLOSE TO AMSTERDAM."
"HOW FEARFUL THE WOMEN IN THE ANNEX ARE DURING BOMBINGS..."
"AND HOW IF YOU WANT TO BUY ANYTHING YOU HAVE TO STAND IN LINE."
"HOW COMMON ARE BURGLARIES AND THEFTS. EVEN BY CHILDREN!"
"HOW BURGLARS HAVE PEOPLE TOO FRIGHTENED TO LEAVE THEIR HOMES."
"HOW FOOD RATIONS FOR A WEEK CAN LAST ONLY TWO DAYS."

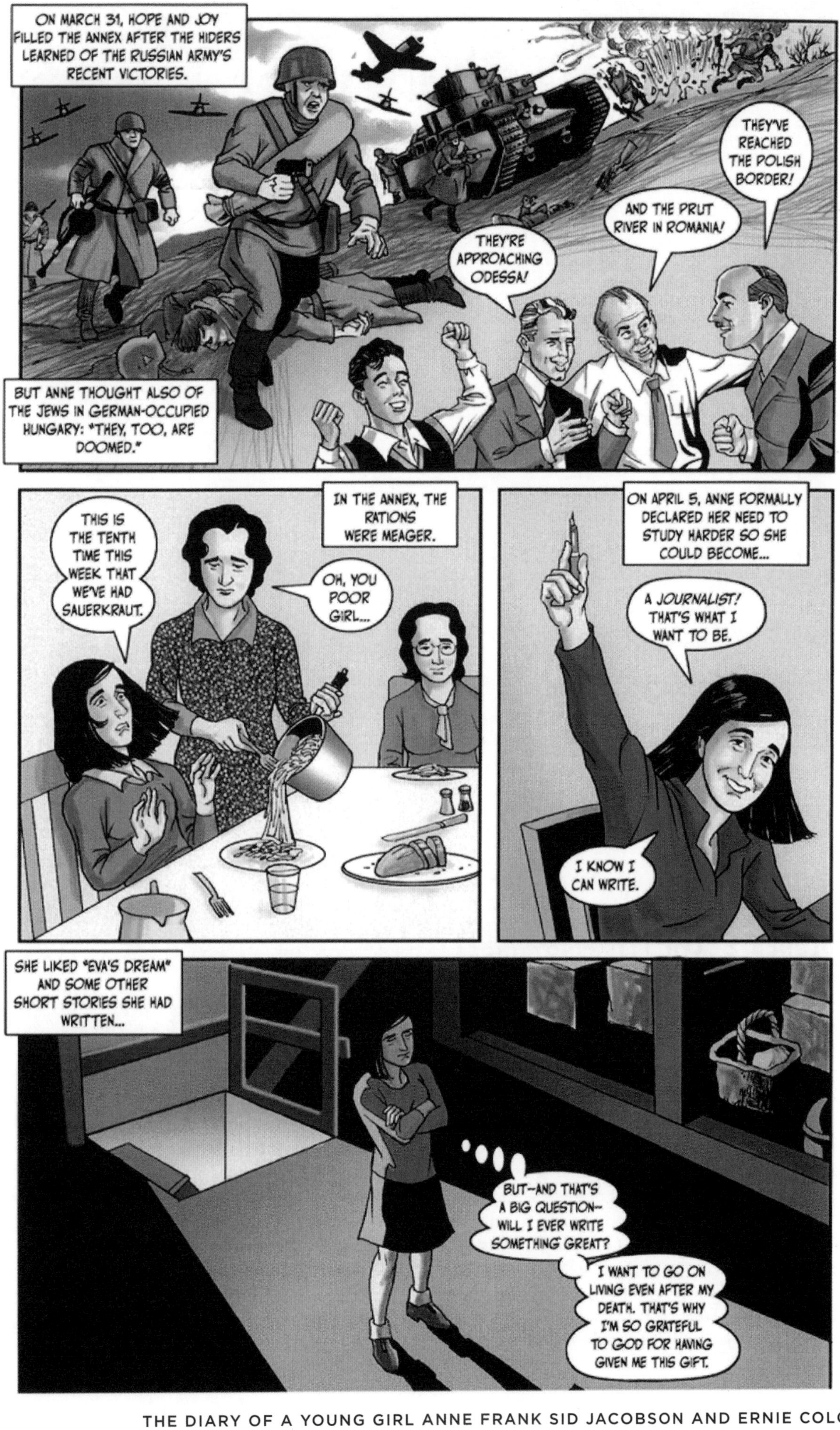
ON MARCH 31, HOPE AND JOY FILLED THE ANNEX AFTER THE HIDERS LEARNED OF THE RUSSIAN ARMY'S RECENT VICTORIES.
THEY'VE REACHED THE POLISH BORDER!
AND THE PRUT RIVER IN ROMANIA!
THEY'RE APPROACHING ODESSA!
BUT ANNE THOUGHT ALSO OF THE JEWS IN GERMAN-OCCUPIED HUNGARY: "THEY, TOO, ARE DOOMED."
IN THE ANNEX, THE RATIONS WERE MEAGER.
THIS IS THE TENTH TIME THIS WEEK THAT WE'VE HAD SAUERKRAUT.
OH, YOU POOR GIRL...
ON APRIL 5, ANNE FORMALLY DECLARED HER NEED TO STUDY HARDER SO SHE COULD BECOME...
A *JOURNALIST!* THAT'S WHAT I WANT TO BE.
I KNOW I CAN WRITE.
SHE LIKED "EVA'S DREAM" AND SOME OTHER SHORT STORIES SHE HAD WRITTEN...
BUT—AND THAT'S A BIG QUESTION— WILL I EVER WRITE SOMETHING GREAT?
I WANT TO GO ON LIVING EVEN AFTER MY DEATH. THAT'S WHY I'M SO GRATEFUL TO GOD FOR HAVING GIVEN ME THIS GIFT.

# Schoolyard rhymes

ART/ADAPTATION BY **John W. Pierard**

SEX, VIOLENCE, DEATH, PISS, SNOT, INCEST, insurrection. . . . You shouldn't let kids near this type of material. Oh, wait . . . kids are the ones *creating* this material.

The idea of folksongs seems like a quaint relic in the twenty-first century. Songs with no identifiable creator, not put into recorded form, simply passed along from one person to another, down through generations. But there is one group still singing folksongs to each other here in the post-postmodern age: children. From around the World War II era clear to today, children have been singing explicit, scatological, homicidal ditties to each other in schoolyards, summer camps, and anywhere else they congregate out of earshot of grown-ups. They deal humorously with the most taboo subjects in existence. Nothing is off-limits. The grosser and more disturbing, the better, the more likely the songs are to be passed from individual to individual through the decades. Indeed, I see several here that, with slight variations, my schoolmates and I were singing in elementary school.

John W. Pierard has previously illustrated children's books (*My Teacher Fried My Brains*, the P.S. 13 series). And classic literature (Jack London, Arthur Conan Doyle). And sex magazines (*Screw*, *Velvet Touch*). It's great to see all of these paths intersect in this piece, as he takes on the classic proto-literature of sex and grotesquerie that children tell each other. (John has framed these pieces as a talk by a moral do-gooder based on Fredric Wertham, who crusaded against comics in the 1950s, penning one of the great works of scare lit, *Seduction of the Innocent: The Influence of Comic Books on Today's Youth*.) The songs come from his childhood memories, those of friends, and the classic book on the topic, *Greasy Grimy Gopher Guts: The Subversive Folklore of Childhood* by Josepha Sherman and T. K. F. Weisskopf.

Greetings, Ladies, Gentlemen—concerned and pro-active parents, I have come to you to discuss a dangerous phenomenon festering in our community today which should be of gravest concern to all.

I present to you the results of my decades-long investigation into what I believe to be an insidious, subversive home-grown folk literature—a dysphemistic, barbaric amphigory of rude, unseemly and vulgar verse—spawned and nurtured, as it were, in the schoolyards, playgrounds and backyards of our nation.

I say to you that this creeping, noxious eruption of pre-pubescent discontent must be vigorously cleansed lest its corruptive influence spread like a wanton, pandemic subterranean fungus, contaminating the soil that is the collective soul and psyche of America's tender youth!

Hello, my name is Dr. Fredrich von Furtwangler, and my book, available in the lobby, is entitled:

"SEDUCTION OF THE INNOCENT, BY THE INNOCENT
A Brief Overview and Analysis of

RUDE SCHOOL-YARD RHYMES"

An unhealthy contemplation of wayward bodily fluids in awkward social situations.

WHENNN – YER DANCIN' WITH YER HUNNY, AND YER NOSE IS KINDA' RUNNY, PEOPLE THINK IT'S FUNNY – BUT IT'S NOT...!!!

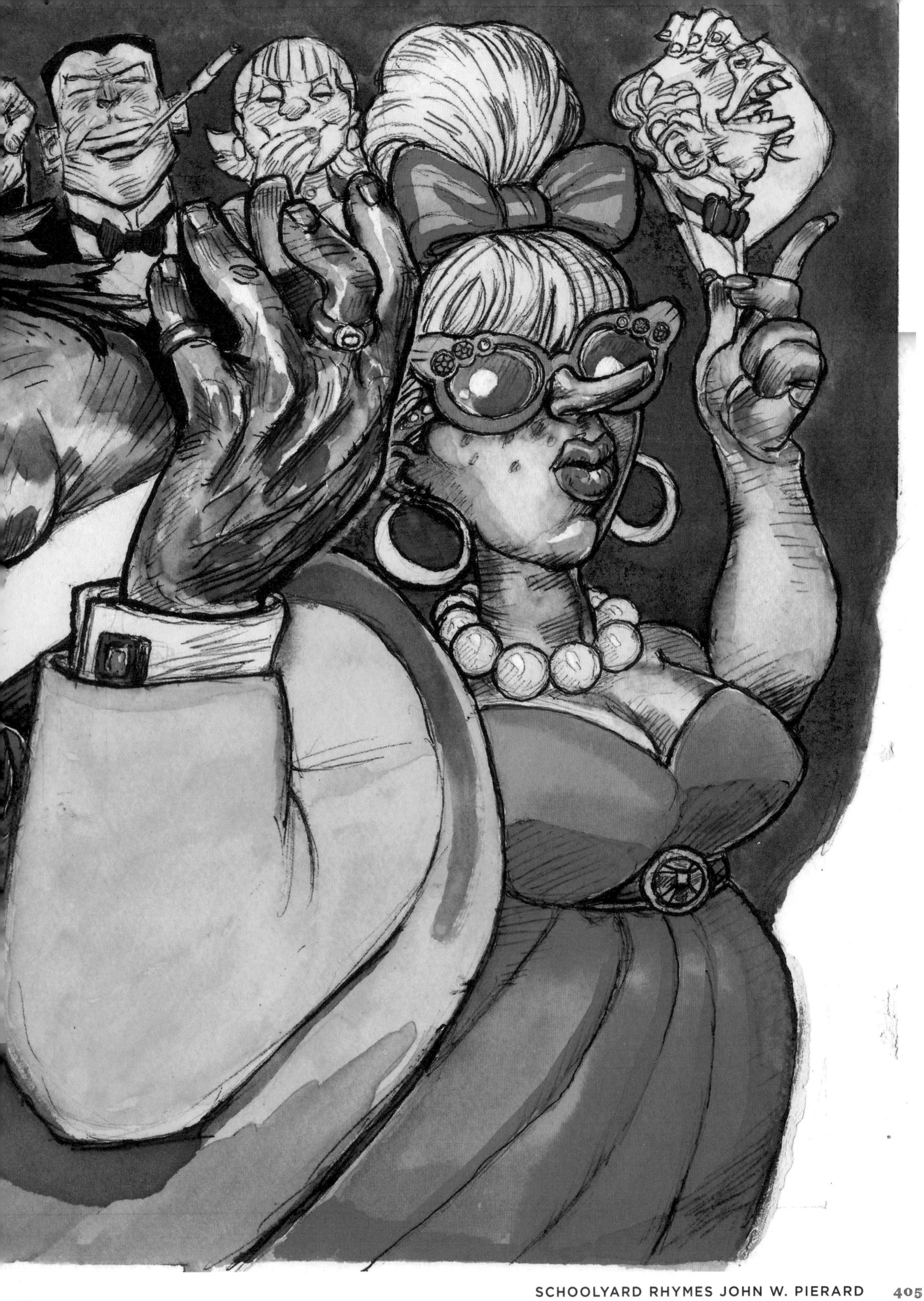

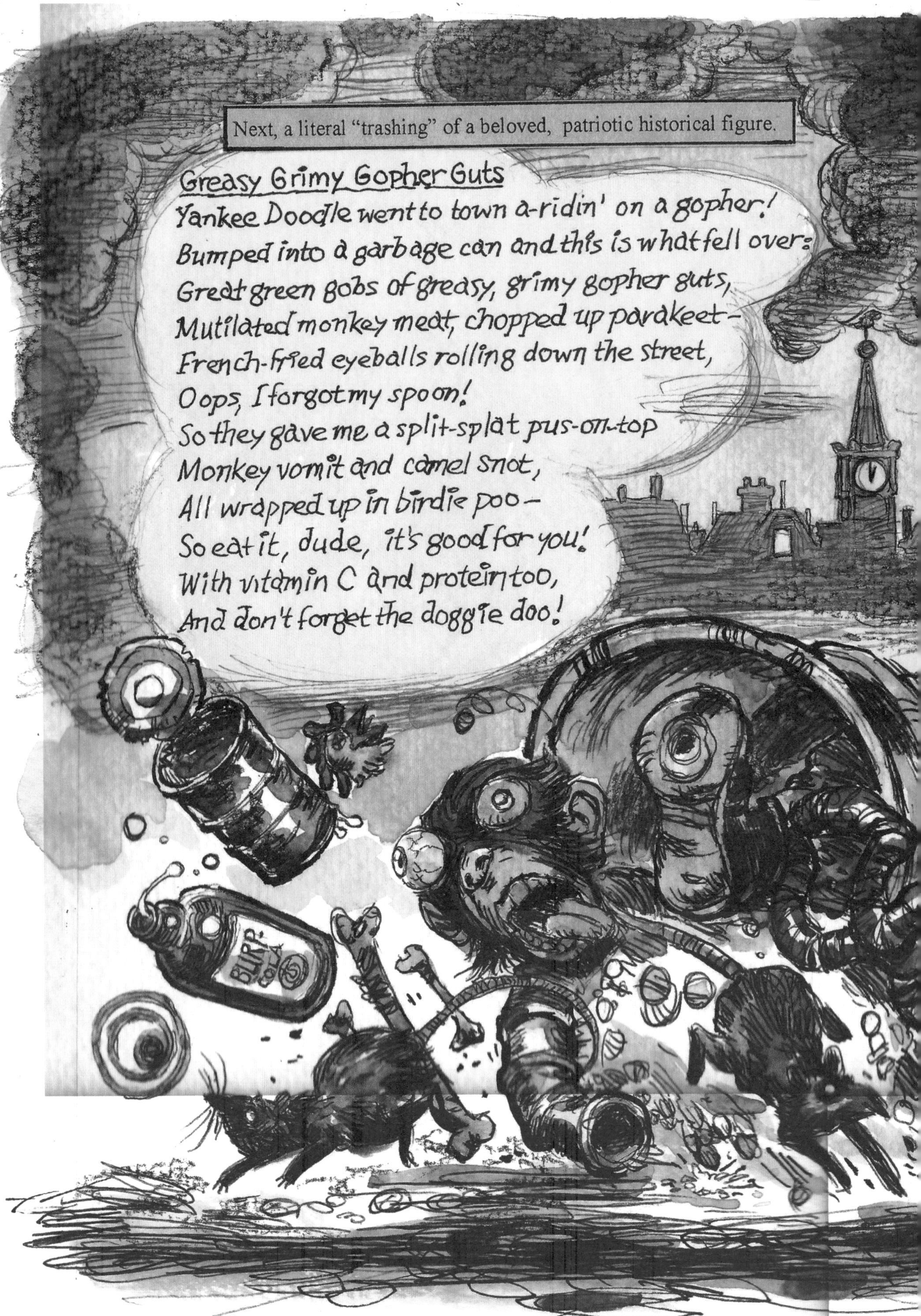
Greasy Grimy Gopher Guts
Yankee Doodle went to town a-ridin' on a gopher!
Bumped into a garbage can and this is what fell over:
Great green gobs of greasy, grimy gopher guts,
Mutilated monkey meat, chopped up parakeet-
French-fried eyeballs rolling down the street,
Oops, I forgot my spoon!
So they gave me a split-splat pus-on-top
Monkey vomit and camel snot,
All wrapped up in birdie poo-
So eat it, dude, it's good for you!
With vitamin C and protein too,
And don't forget the doggie doo!

Next, a literal "trashing" of a beloved, patriotic historical figure.

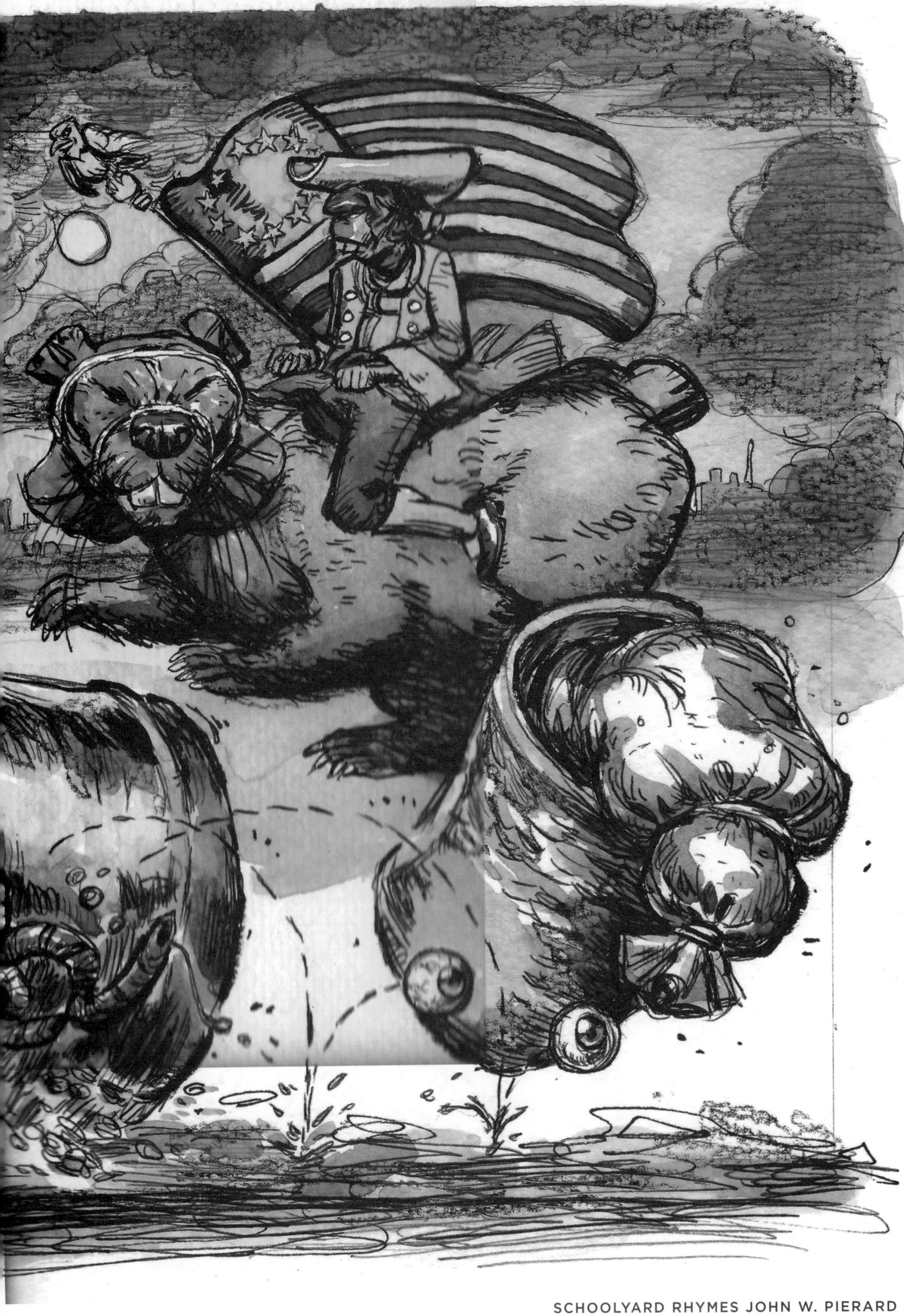

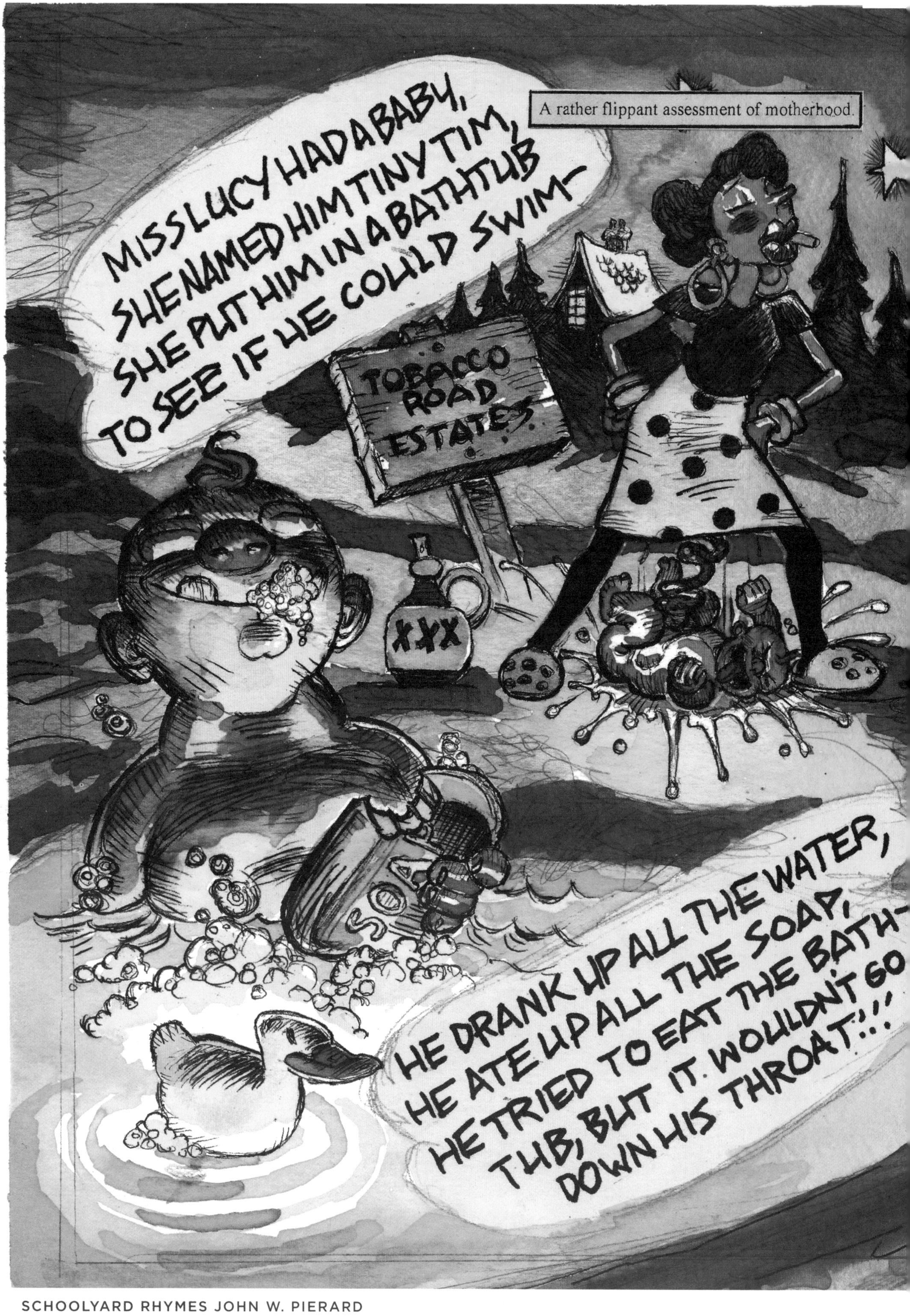
A rather flippant assessment of motherhood.
MISS LUCY HAD A BABY, SHE NAMED HIM TINY TIM, SHE PUT HIM IN A BATHTUB TO SEE IF HE COULD SWIM—
TOBACCO ROAD ESTATES
XXX
HE DRANK UP ALL THE WATER, HE ATE UP ALL THE SOAP, HE TRIED TO EAT THE BATH-TUB, BUT IT WOULDN'T GO DOWN HIS THROAT!..."

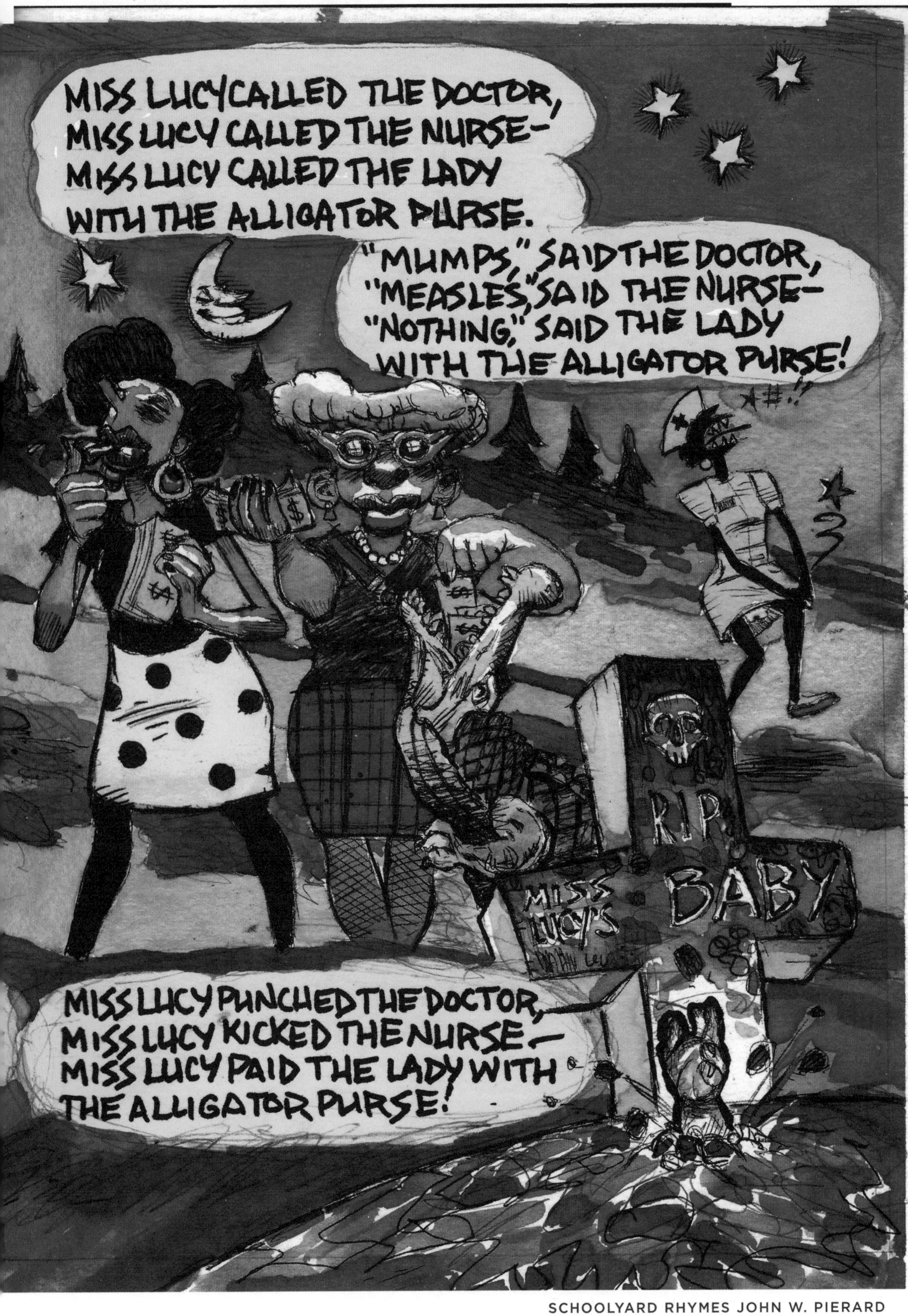
MISS LUCY CALLED THE DOCTOR,
MISS LUCY CALLED THE NURSE-
MISS LUCY CALLED THE LADY
WITH THE ALLIGATOR PURSE.
"MUMPS," SAID THE DOCTOR,
"MEASLES," SAID THE NURSE-
"NOTHING," SAID THE LADY
WITH THE ALLIGATOR PURSE!
RIP
MISS LUCY'S BABY
MISS LUCY PUNCHED THE DOCTOR,
MISS LUCY KICKED THE NURSE-
MISS LUCY PAID THE LADY WITH
THE ALLIGATOR PURSE!

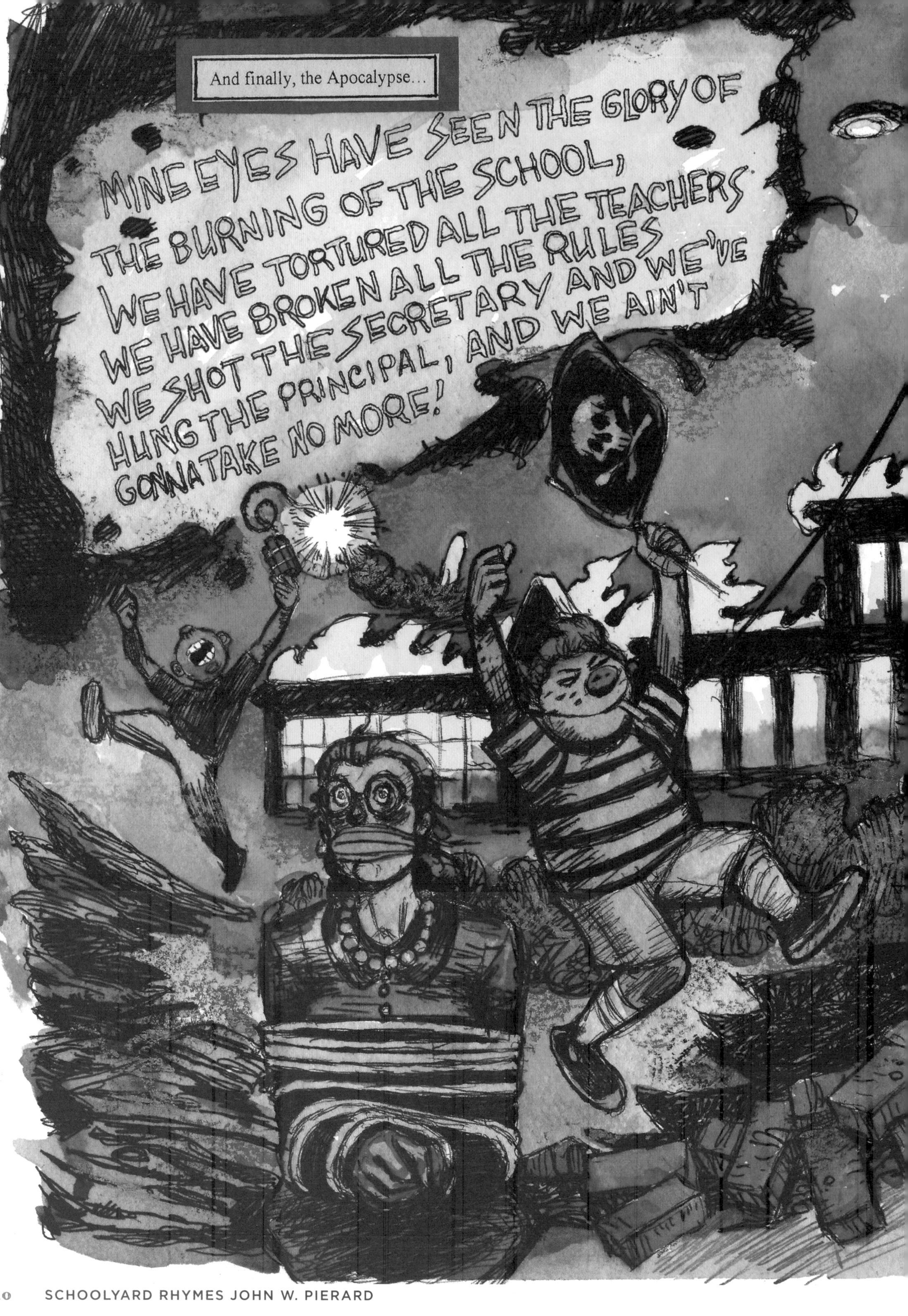
And finally, the Apocalypse...
MINE EYES HAVE SEEN THE GLORY OF
THE BURNING OF THE SCHOOL,
WE HAVE TORTURED ALL THE TEACHERS
WE HAVE BROKEN ALL THE RULES
WE SHOT THE SECRETARY AND WE'VE
HUNG THE PRINCIPAL, AND WE AIN'T
GONNA TAKE NO MORE!

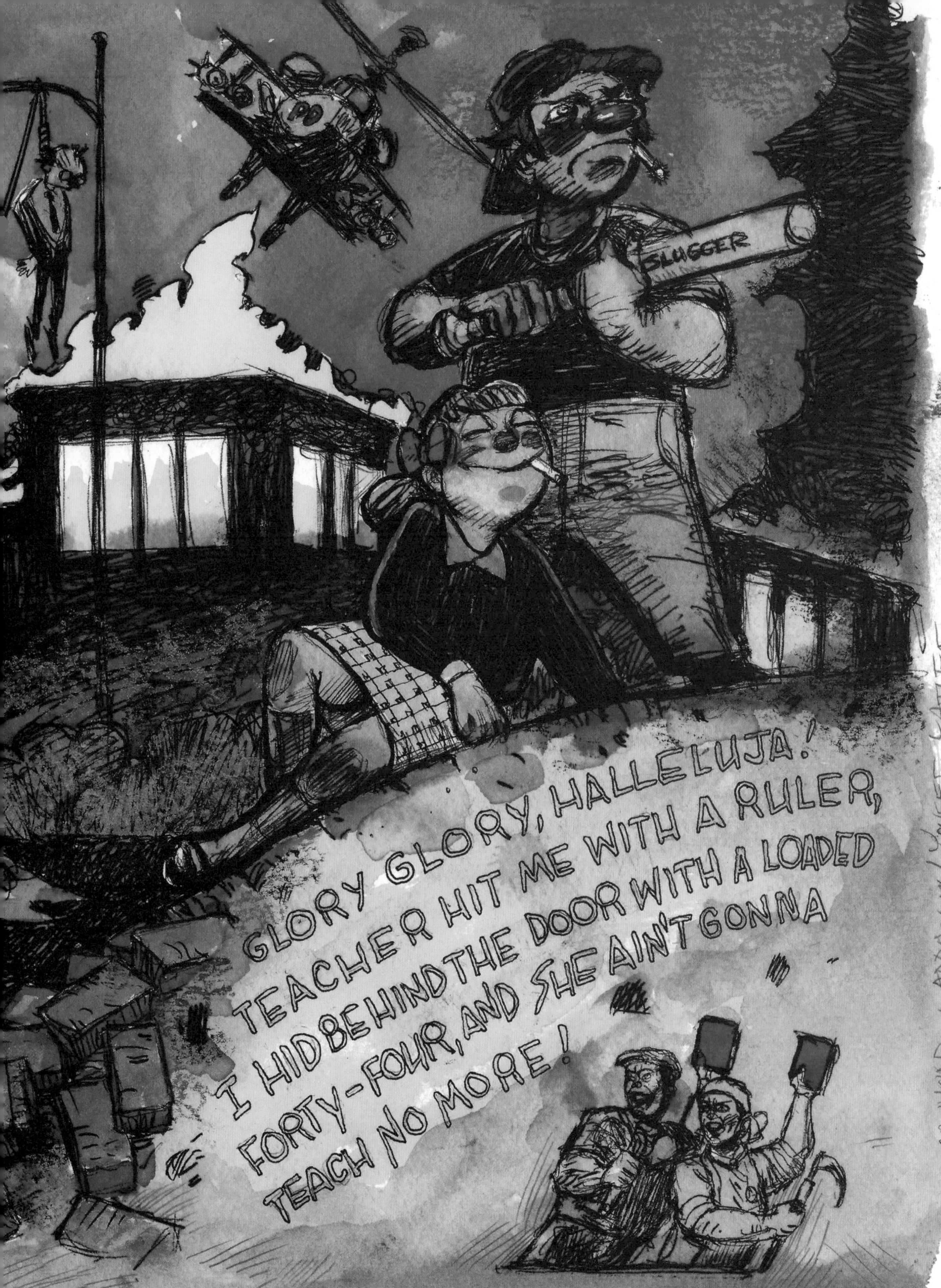
SLUGGER
GLORY GLORY, HALLELUJA!
TEACHER HIT ME WITH A RULER,
I HID BEHIND THE DOOR WITH A LOADED
FORTY-FOUR, AND SHE AIN'T GONNA
TEACH NO MORE!

# Watership Down

## Richard Adams

ART/ADAPTATION BY **Tori Christina McKenna**

**LIKE SO MANY GREAT CHILDREN'S NOVELS—INCLUDING** two of the greatest, *Alice's Adventures in Wonderland* and *The Wonderful Wizard of Oz—Watership Down* began its life when its author, Richard Adams, started spontaneously making up stories for kids, in this case his two daughters.

A British civil servant and former Royal Airman in World War II, Adams had been writing fiction only as a hobby when he decided to turn his rabbit tales into an epic adventure novel informed by *The Odyssey* and *The Aeneid*. *Watership Down* was rejected by numerous major British publishers and agents before being taken on by a one-person outfit, Rex Collings Ltd., in 1972. It was an instant commercial and critical success, winning major awards, going into numerous translations, and spawning a highly regarded animated movie. It continues to sell by the boatload.

Adams created an entire world for his rabbits—their own language, customs, history, folklore, etc.—yet he also grounded his book in the real world. As he explains in his introduction to *Watership Down*'s 2005 edition, all the places actually exist, many of the rabbits' personalities are based on people he's known, and he imposed the restraint that "although my rabbits could think and talk, I never made them do anything physical that real rabbits could not do."

Tori Christina McKenna has rendered the opening section of the novel wordlessly, with dynamic settings that are stylized, sometimes almost surreal, containing a cast of highly individual rabbits. The seer Fiver has a vision of the destruction of his warren. Like so many great prophets, he isn't taken seriously by most of his brethren, including those in power, but his brother Hazel believes him. They convince several other bunnies to join them as they seek a place to establish a new warren. **Spoiler Alert**: The original warren does indeed get destroyed during the construction of a new housing development, as Tori alludes to in the final panel.

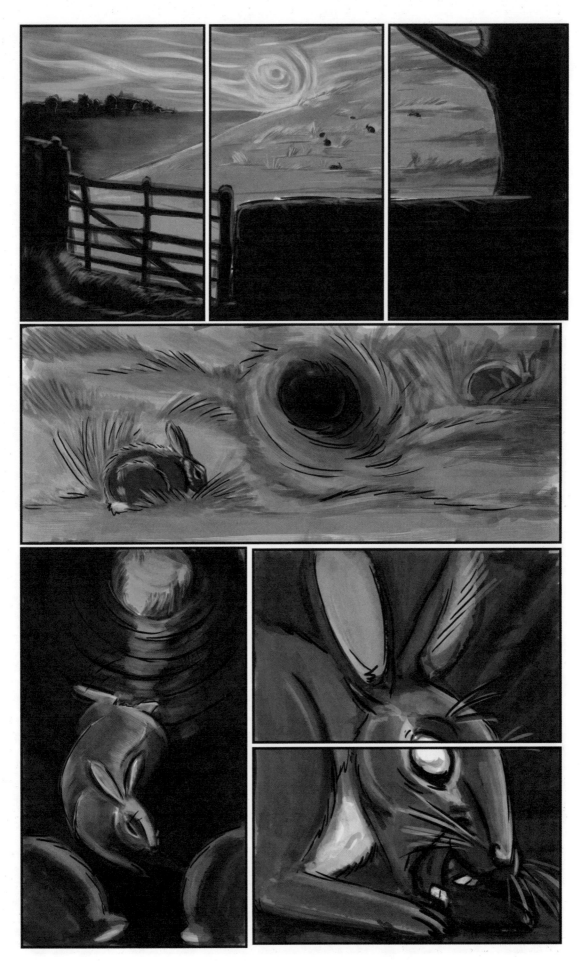

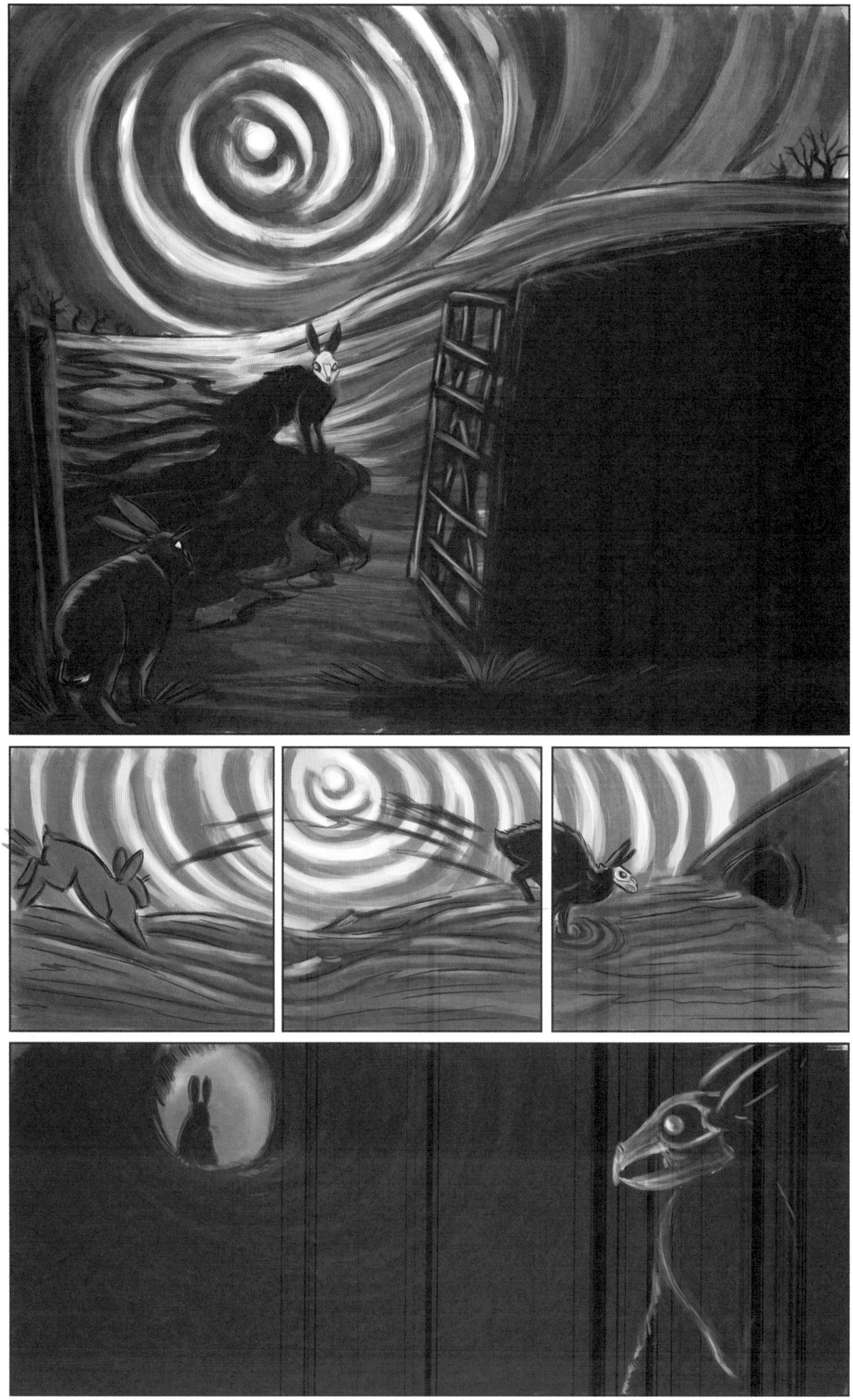

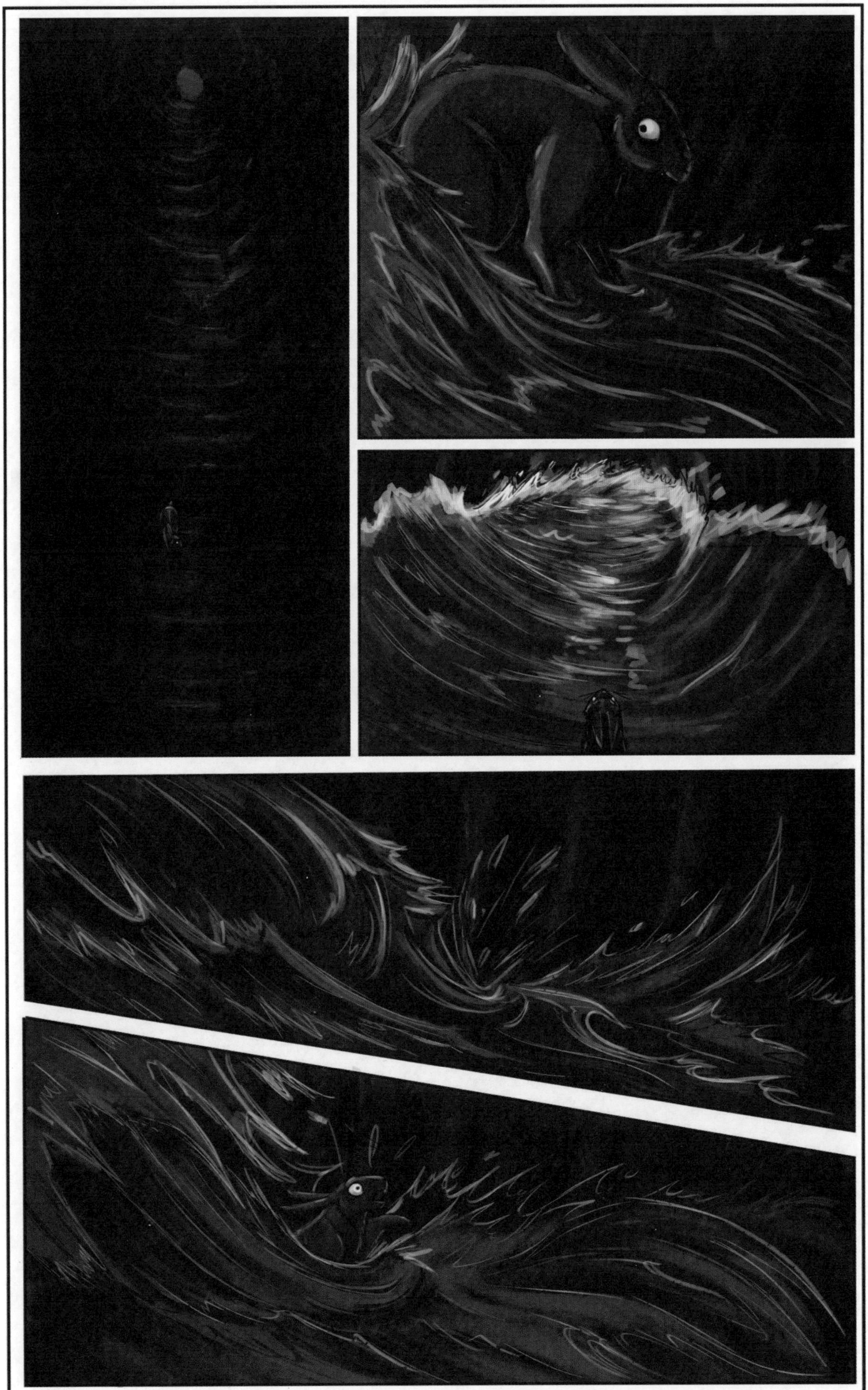

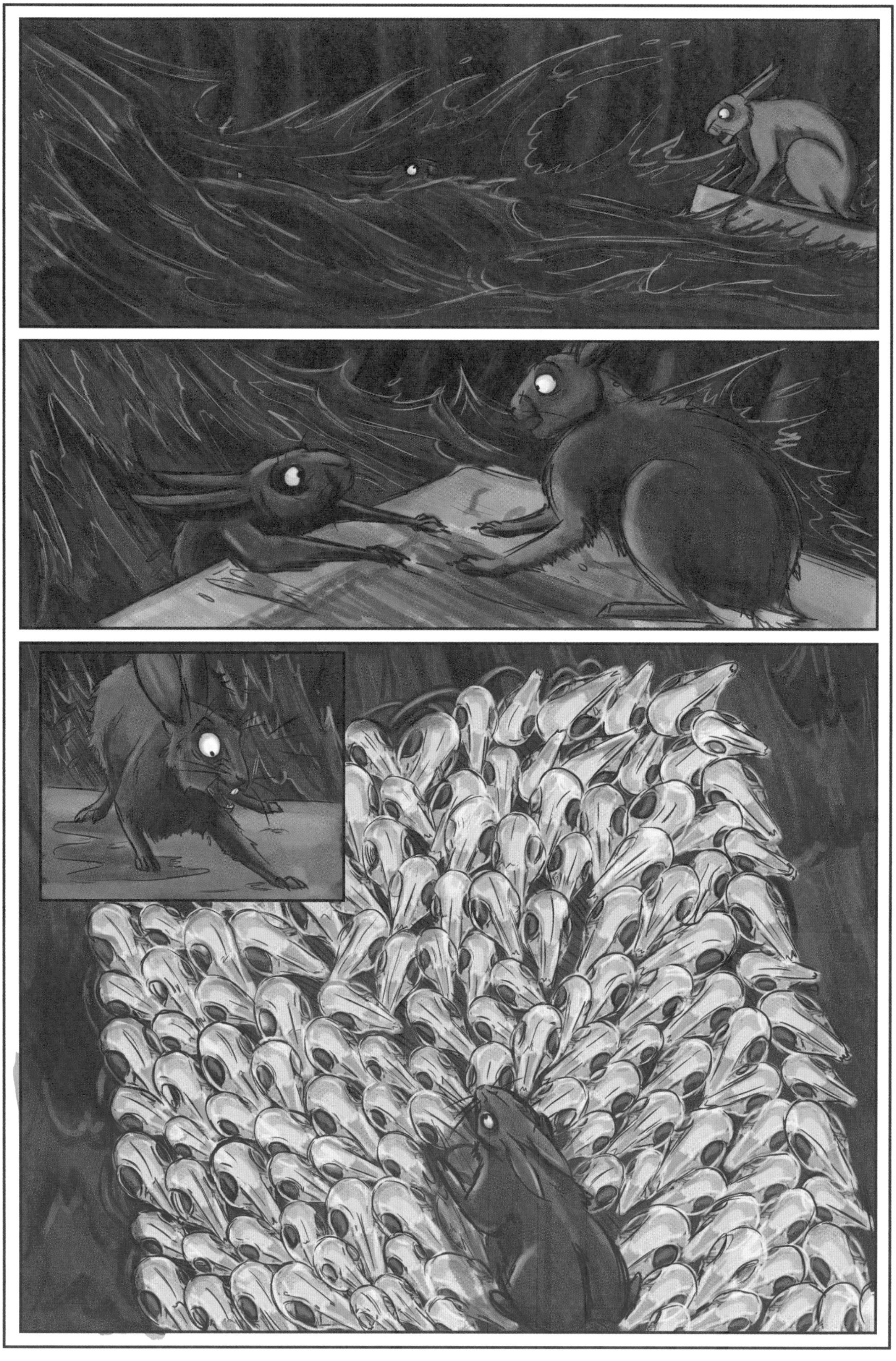

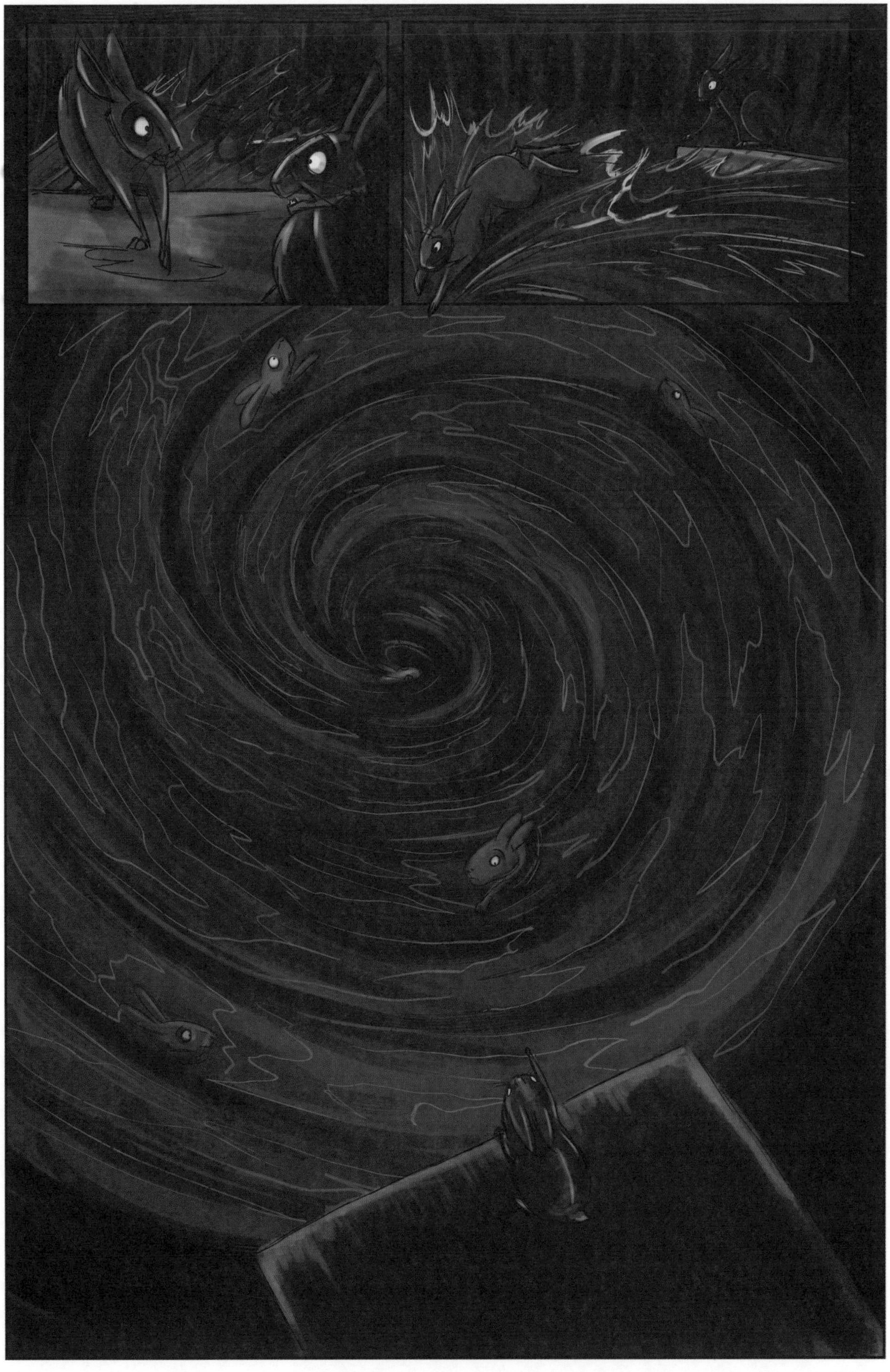

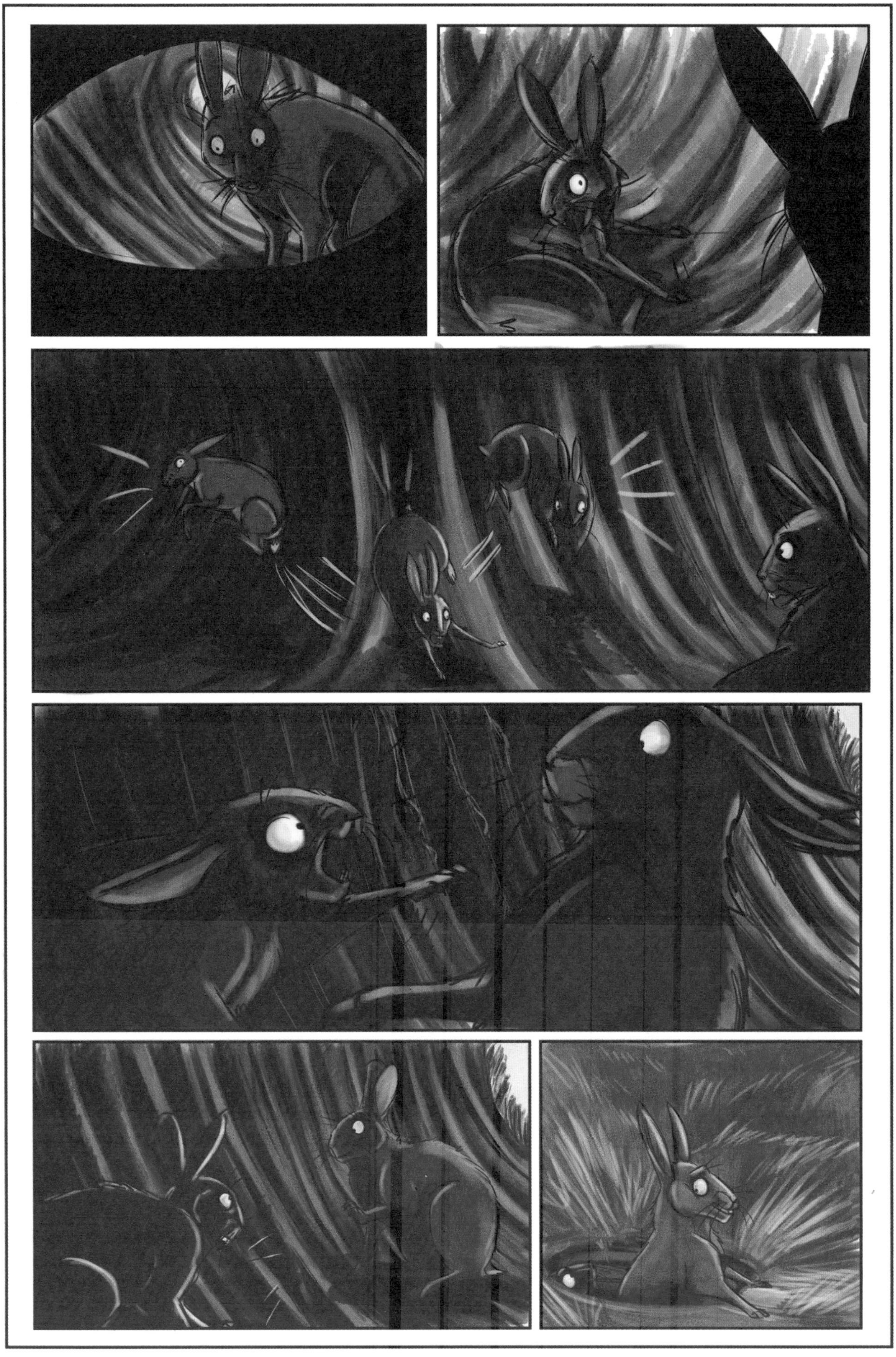

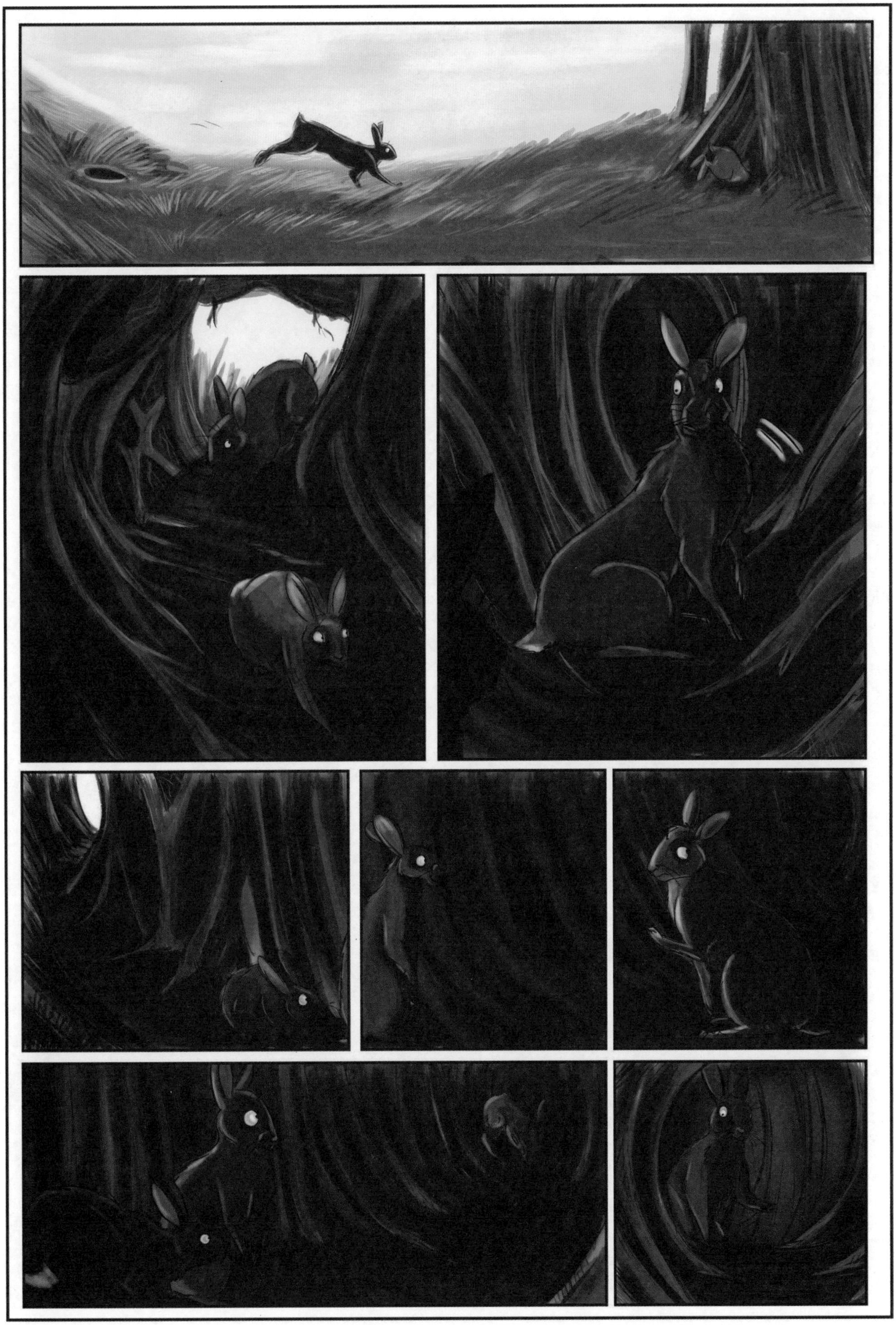

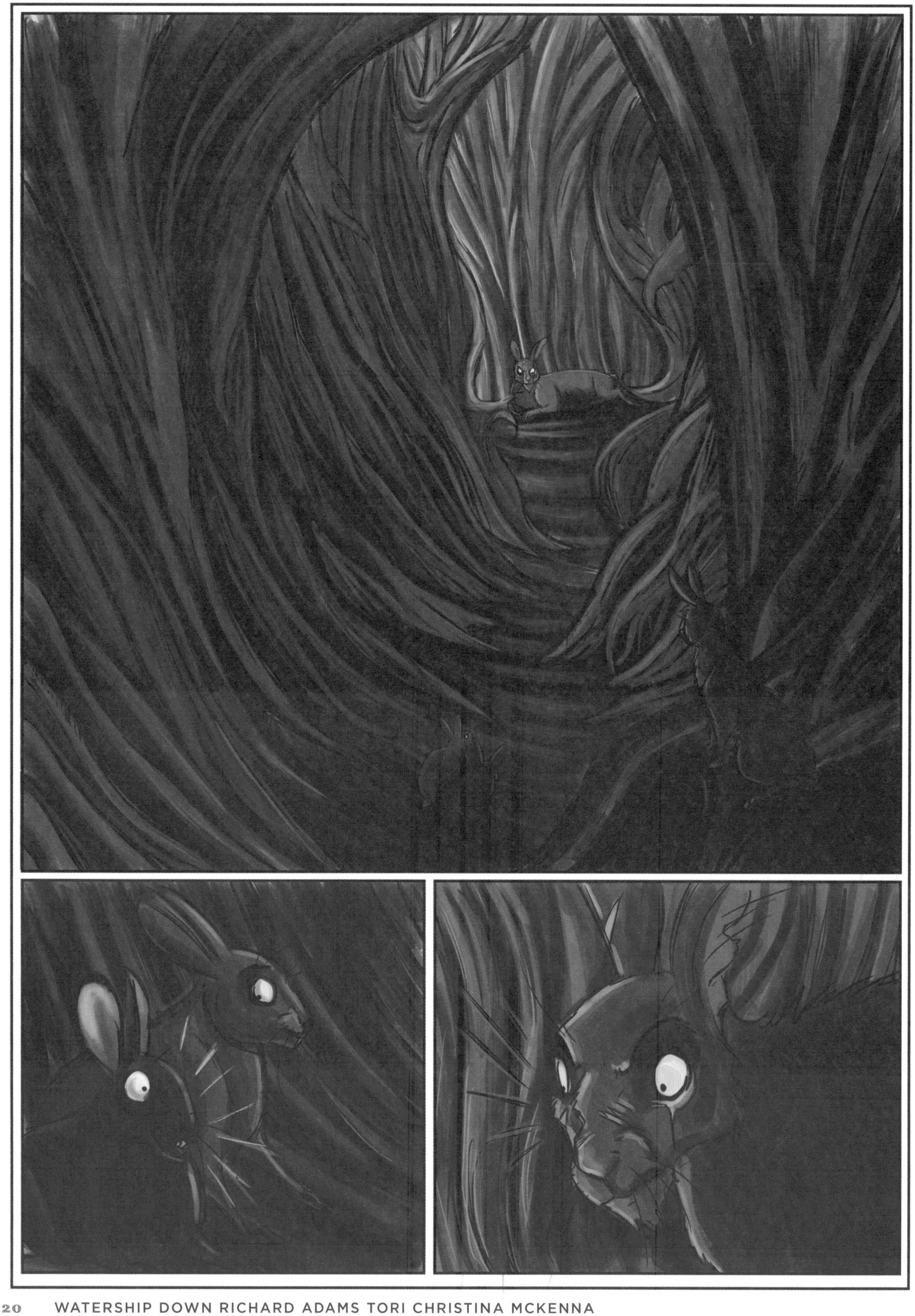

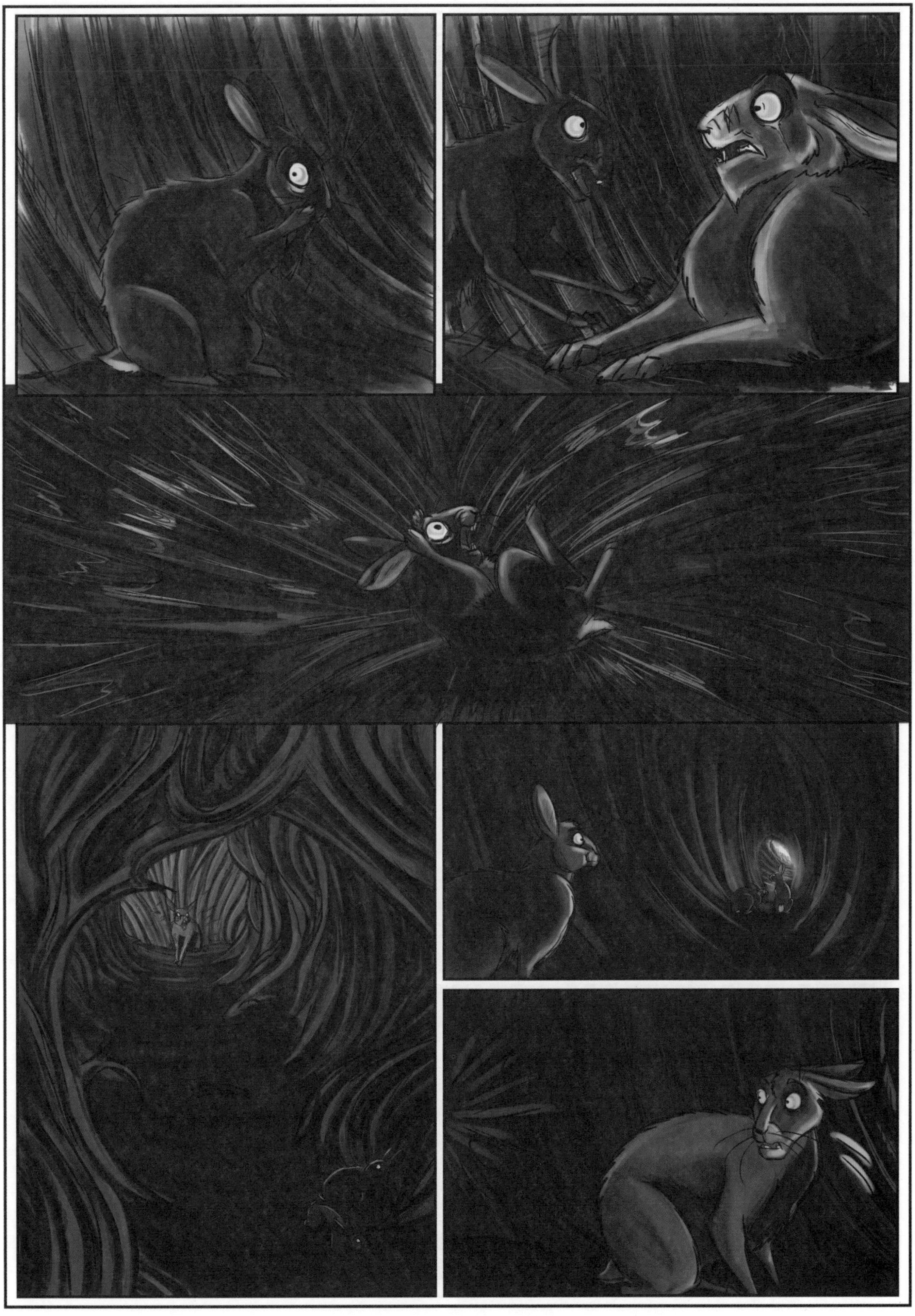

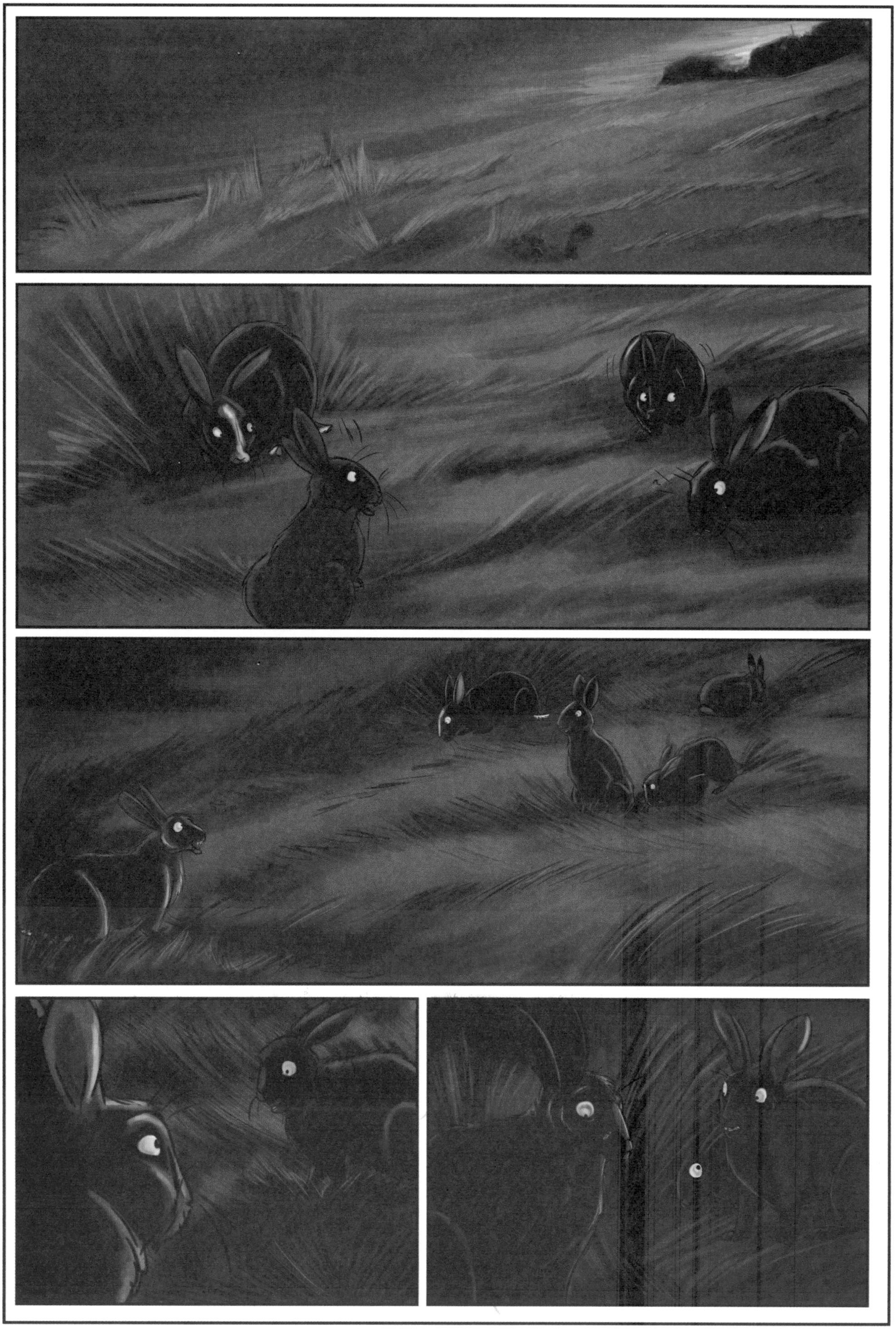

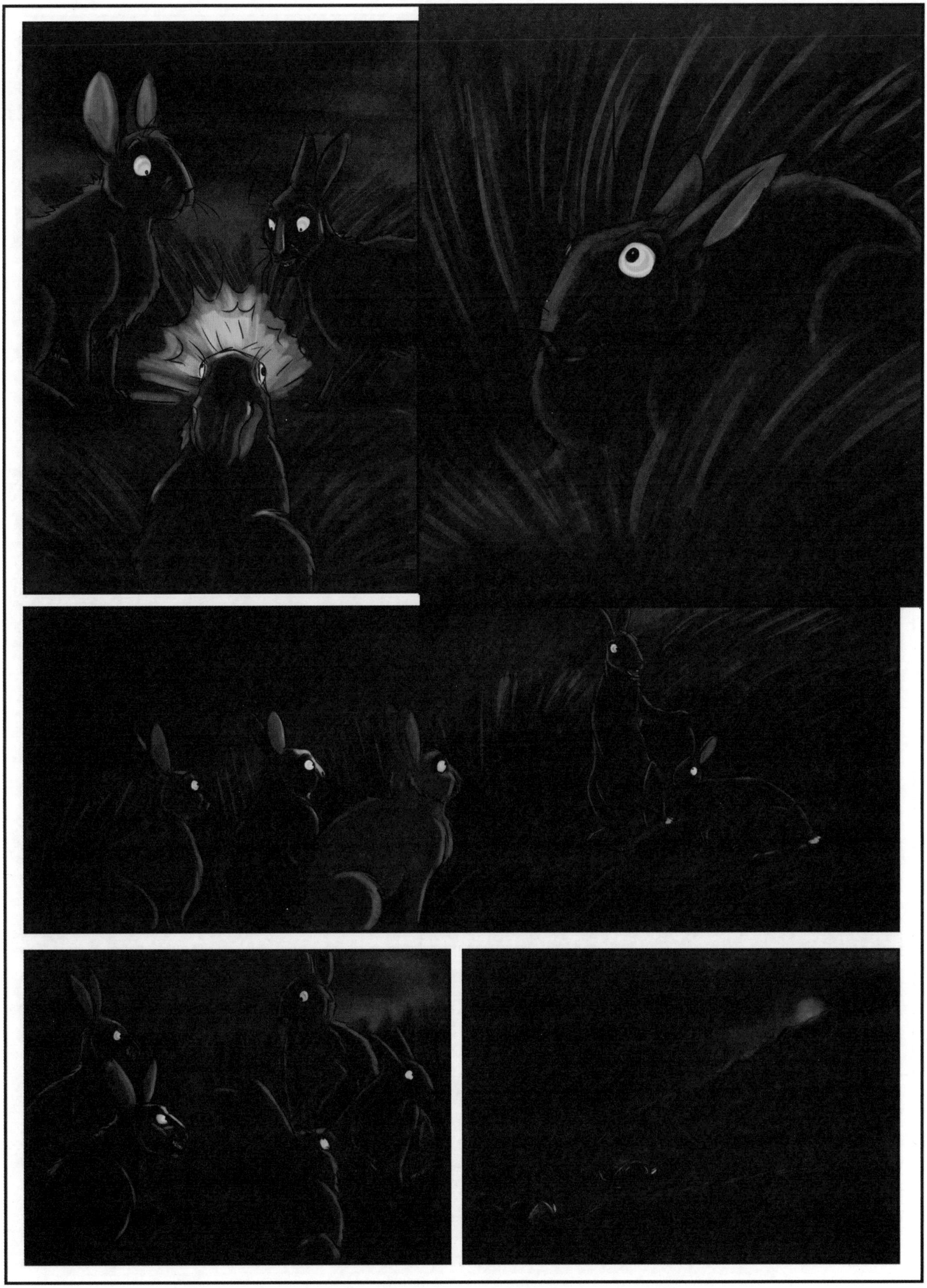

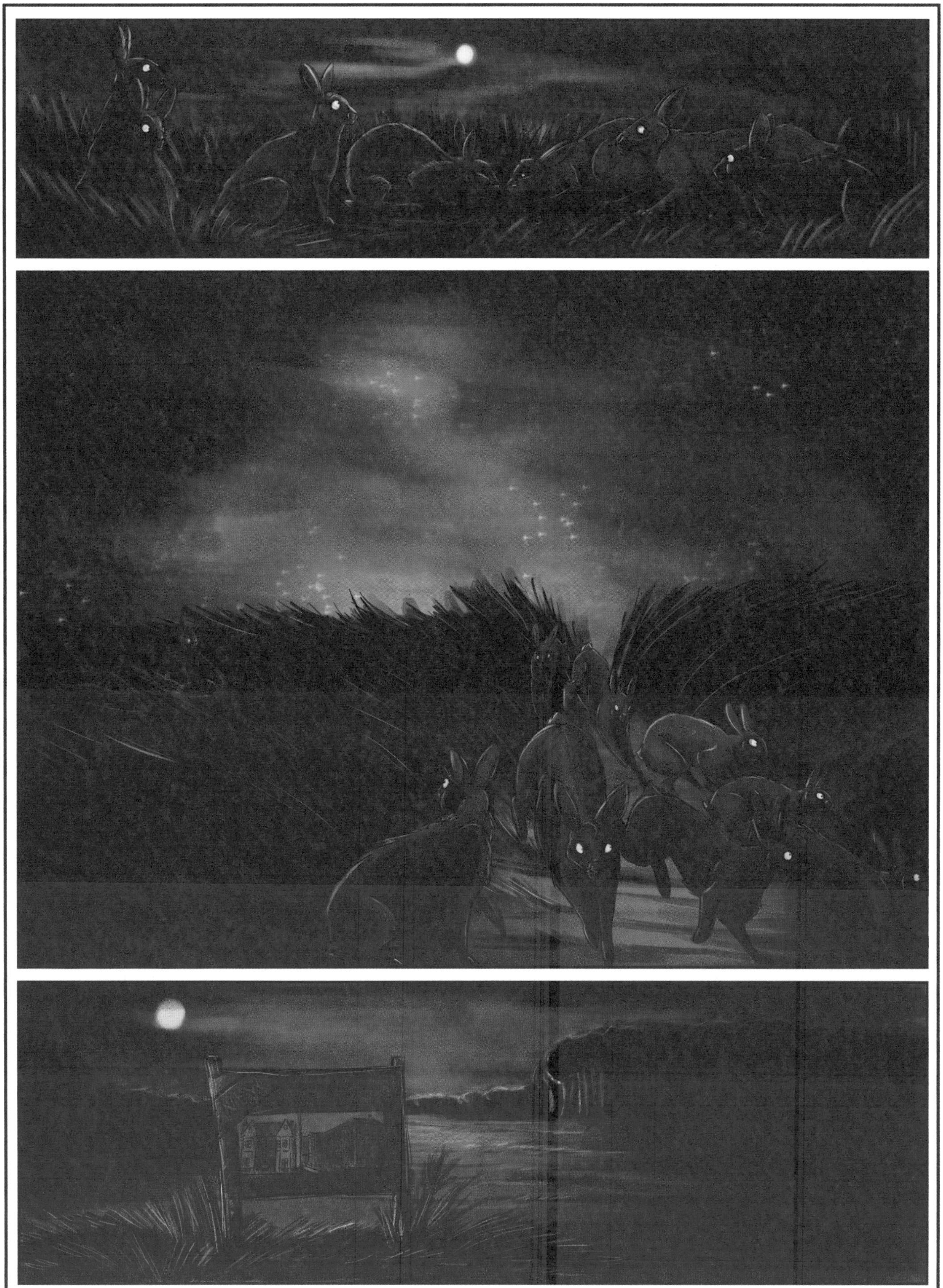

# The Harry Potter series

## J. K. Rowling

ART/ADAPTATION BY **Lucy Knisley**

**WHAT CAN BE SAID ABOUT THE HARRY POTTER** series? Joanne (J. K.) Rowling strode into familiar fantasy territory, with wizards, spells, and malevolent forces, but she put some less-common spins on it, making the protagonist and his comrades teenagers, and setting them in the current day, albeit an alternate version of Britain, one that hearkens to a semi-mythical bucolic time. Each of the seven books follows Harry & Co. through one year at Hogwarts School of Witchcraft and Wizardry, with the overall arc charting Harry's becoming a wizard of unprecedented ability, while battling the evil, megalomaniacal wizard Lord Voldemort, who wants to kill him.

The unbridled success of the Harry Potter series is astonishing. In 1995, when she finished the manuscript of the first Harry Potter book in Edinburgh, Rowling was a single mother of a small child, living on welfare benefits and dealing with depression and suicidal thoughts. A little less than a decade later, she was the first writer in history to become a billionaire, having authored one of the best-selling book series ever, which became the basis for the highest-grossing movie series ever.

Lucy Knisley's charming, often food-centric comics are in numerous anthologies, as well as her full-length graphic autobiographical works *French Milk* and *Relish: My Life in the Kitchen*. She read the first Harry Potter book when she was fourteen, growing up with the characters as the series progressed. Now an unapologetic adult Potterhead, she created a visually overwhelming, obsessive, playful series of posters—one for each book—that caused a storm of interest online.

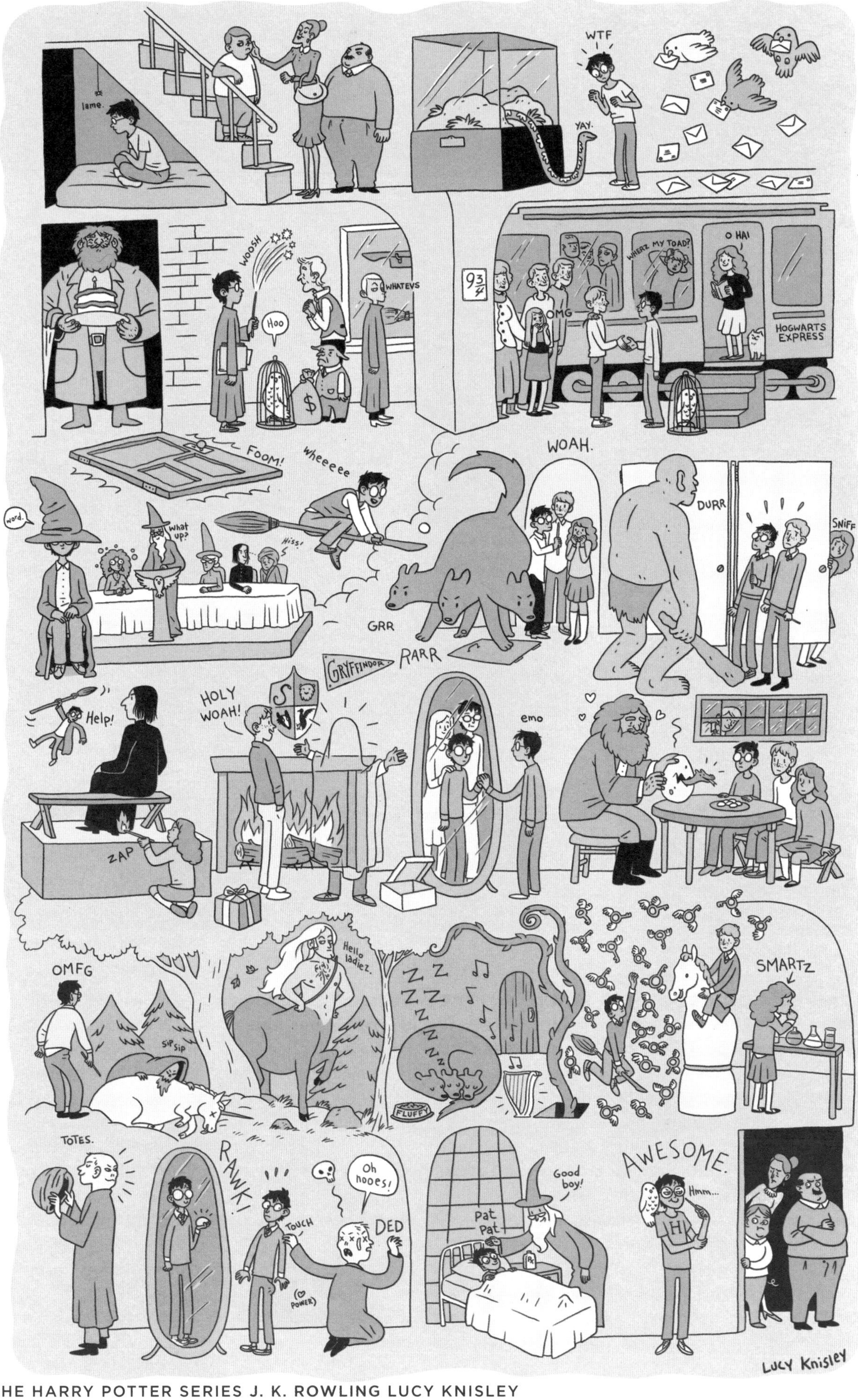
lame.
WTF
YAY.
WOOSH
Hoo
WHATEVS
9 3/4
OMG
WHERZ MY TOAD?
O HAI
HOGWARTS EXPRESS
FOOM!
wheeeee
WOAH.
word.
what up?
Hiss!
GRR
RARR
DURR
SNIFF
GRYFFINDOR
Help!
HOLY WOAH!
ZAP
emo
OMFG
Sip sip
Hello ladiez.
FLUFFY
SMARTz
TOTES.
RAWK!
TOUCH
Oh nooes!
DED
POWER
Pat Pat
Good boy!
AWESOME.
Hmm...
LUCY Knisley

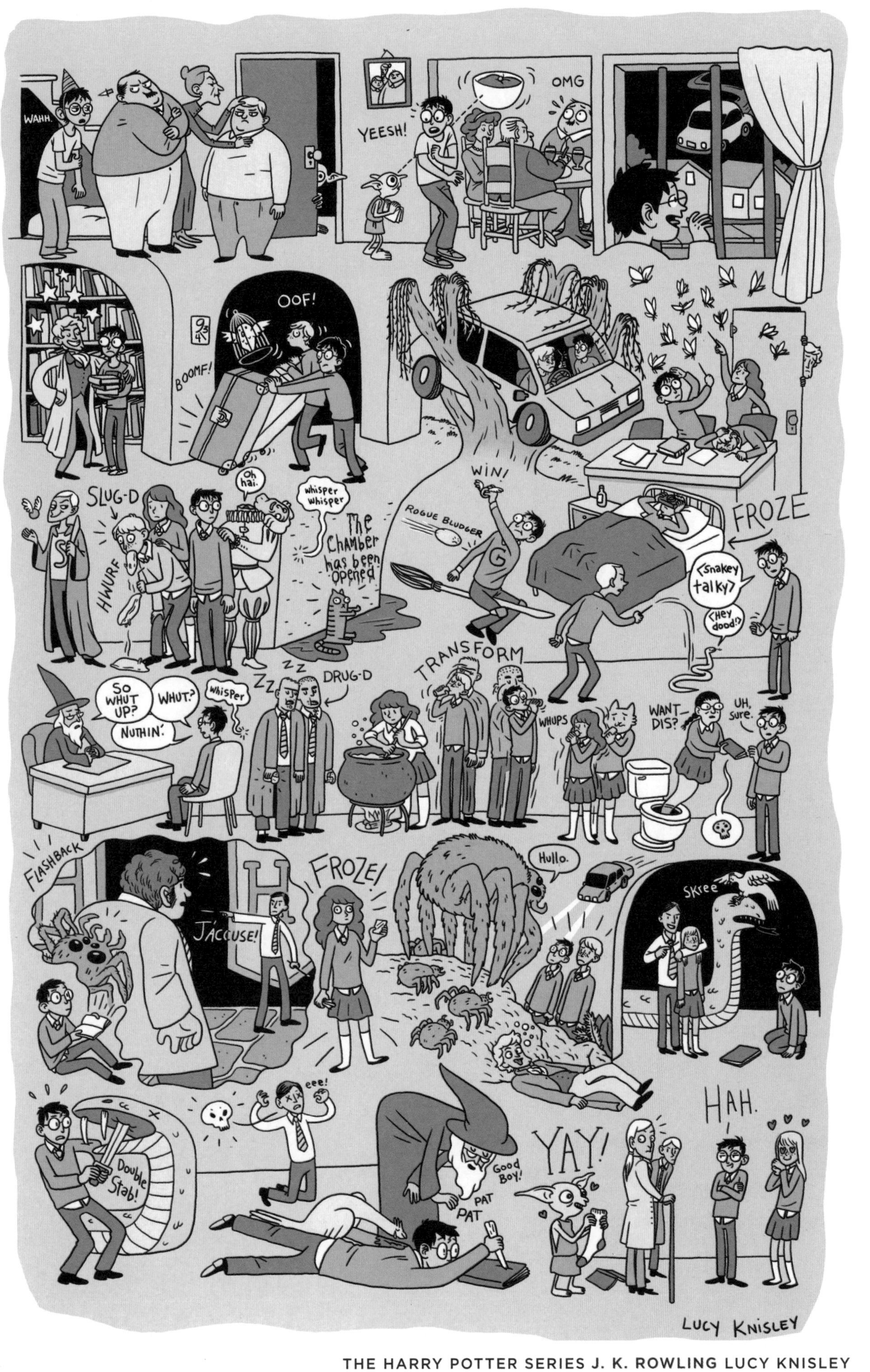
WAHH.
YEESH!
OMG
OOF!
BOOMF!
Oh hai.
whisper whisper
The Chamber has been opened
WIN!
ROGUE BLUDGER
SLUG-D
HWURF
FROZE
<snakey talky>
<hey dood!>
TRANSFORM
So WHUT UP?
WHUT.?
NUTHIN'.
whisper
DRUG-D
WHUPS
WANT DIS?
UH, sure.
FLASHBACK
J'ACCUSE!
FROZE!
Hullo.
Skree
eee!
Double Stab!
Good Boy!
PAT PAT
YAY!
HAH.
LUCY KNISLEY

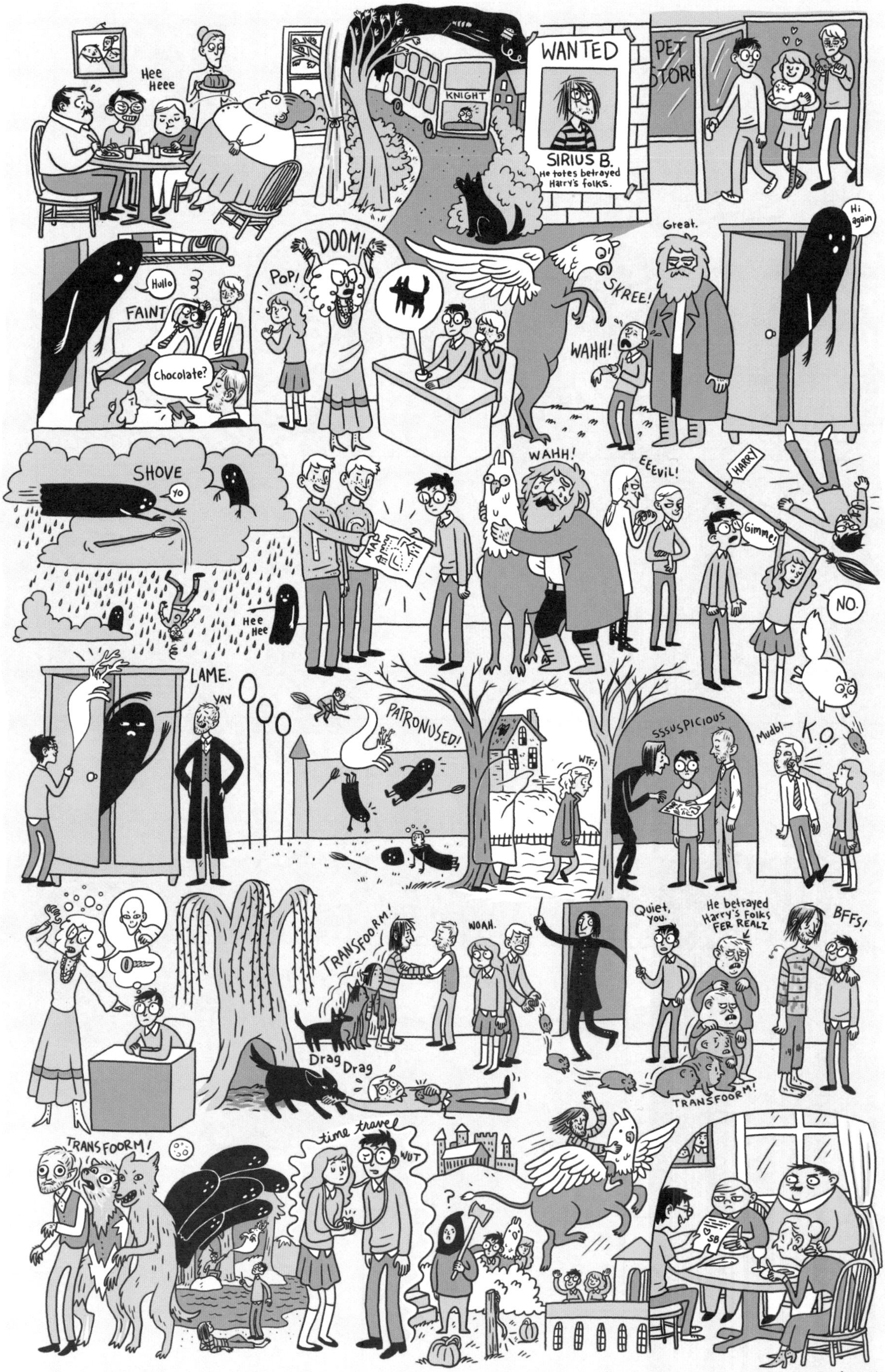
Hee Heee
KNIGHT
WANTED
SIRIUS B.
He totes betrayed Harry's folks.
PET STORE
Hullo
FAINT
Chocolate?
POP!
DOOM!
SKREE!
WAHH!
Great.
Hi again
SHOVE
YO
Hee Hee
MAP
WAHH!
EEEVIL!
HARRY
Gimme!
NO.
LAME.
YAY
PATRONUSED!
WTF!
SSSUSPICIOUS
Mudbl—
K.O.
TRANSFOORM!
WOAH.
Quiet, you.
He betrayed Harry's folks FER REALZ
BFFS!
Drag Drag
TRANSFOORM!
TRANSFOORM!
time travel
WUT
?
SB
LUCY KNISLEY

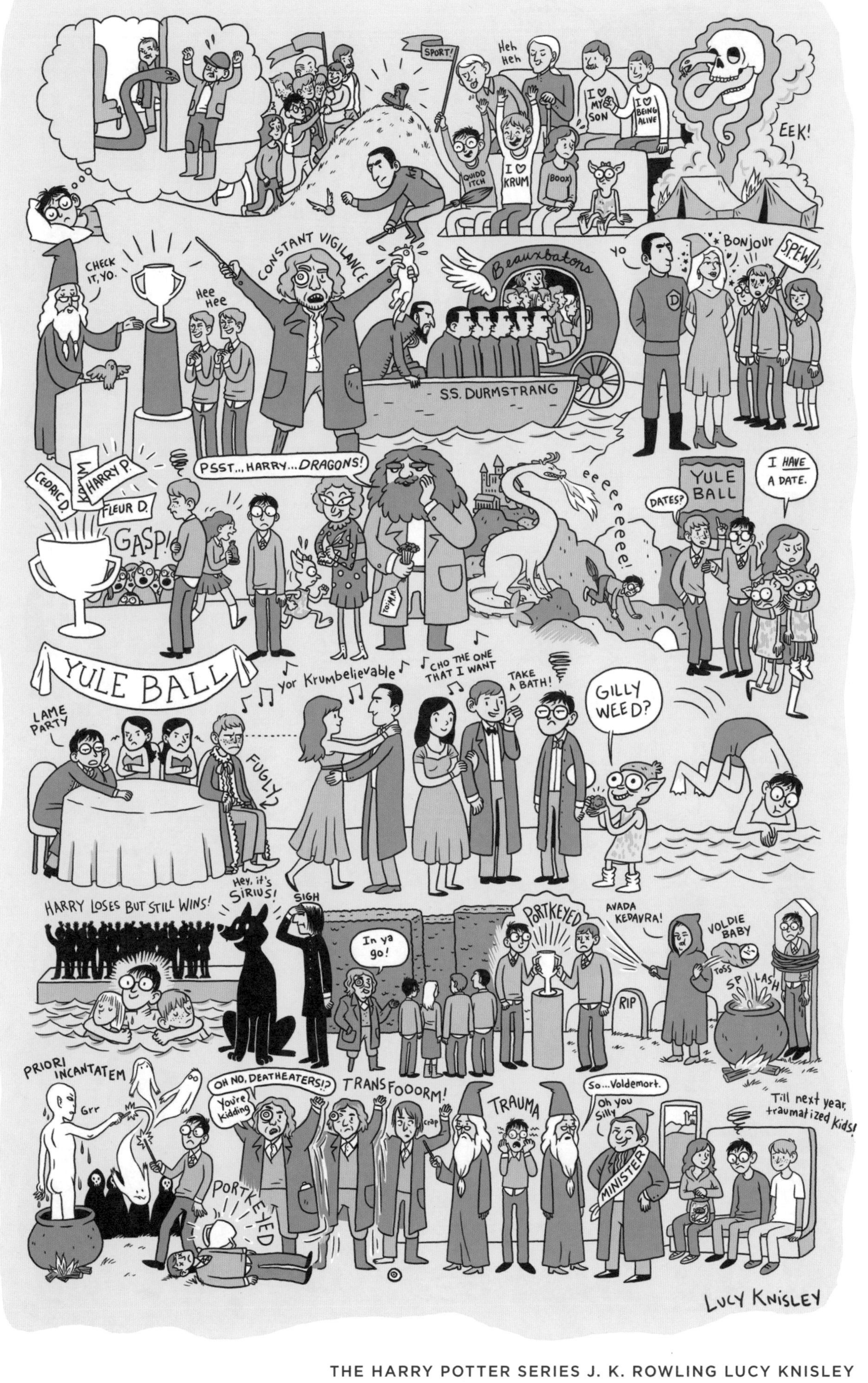
SPORT!
Heh Heh
I ♥ MY SON
I ♥ BEING ALIVE
EEK!
QUIDD ITCH
I ♥ KRUM
BOOX
CHECK IT, YO.
Hee Hee
CONSTANT VIGILANCE
Beauxbatons
SS. DURMSTRANG
YO
Bonjour
S.P.E.W.
D
CEDRIC D.
KRUM
HARRY P.
FLEUR D.
GASP!
PSST... HARRY... DRAGONS!
eeeeeeeeee!
YULE BALL
DATES?
I HAVE A DATE.
YULE BALL
yor Krumbelievable
CHO THE ONE THAT I WANT
TAKE A BATH!
LAME PARTY
FUGLY
GILLY WEED?
HARRY LOSES BUT STILL WINS!
Hey, it's SIRIUS!
SIGH
In ya go!
PORTKEYED
AVADA KEDAVRA!
VOLDIE BABY
TOSS
SPLASH
RIP
PRIORI INCANTATEM
Grr
OH NO, DEATHEATERS!?
You're kidding
TRANSFOOORM!
crap
TRAUMA
So... Voldemort.
Oh you Silly
MINISTER
Till next year, traumatized kids!
PORTKEYED
LUCY KNISLEY

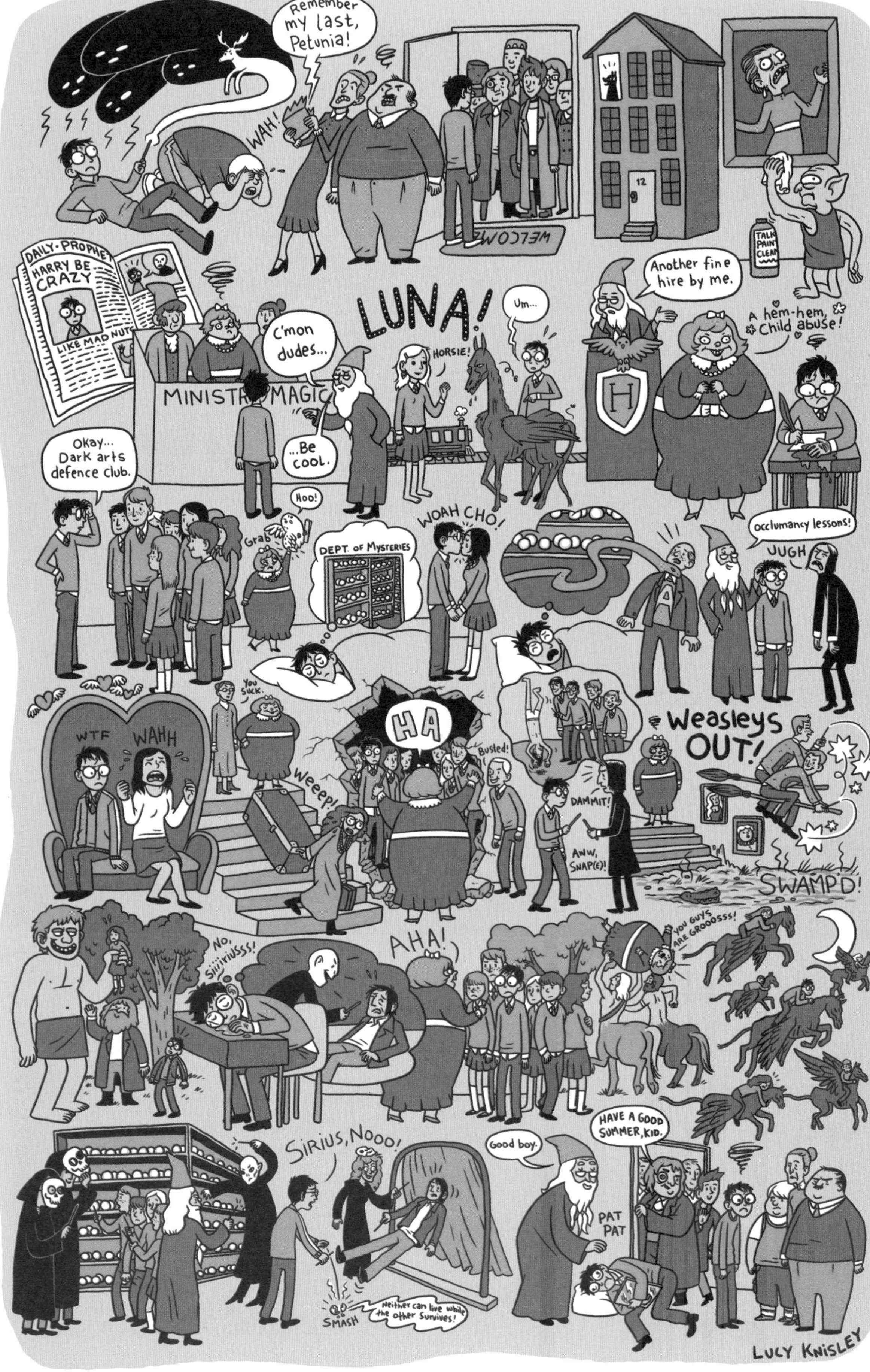

Remember my last, Petunia!
WAH!
WELCOME
12
TALK PAINT CLEAN
DAILY PROPHET
HARRY BE CRAZY
LIKE MAD NUT
MINISTRY MAGIC
C'mon dudes...
...Be cool.
LUNA!
HORSIE!
Um...
Another fine hire by me.
A hem-hem. Child abuse!
H
Okay... Dark arts defence club.
Hoo!
Grab
DEPT. of MYSTERIES
WOAH CHO!
occlumency lessons!
UUGH
A
You suck.
WTF
WAHH
HA
Weeep!
Busted!
DAMMIT!
AWW, SNAP(E)!
Weasleys OUT!
SWAMPD!
No, Siiiiriusss!
AHA!
YOU GUYS ARE GROOOSSS!
SIRIUS, NOOO!
SMASH
Neither can live while the other survives!
Good boy.
HAVE A GOOD SUMMER, KID.
PAT PAT
LUCY KNISLEY

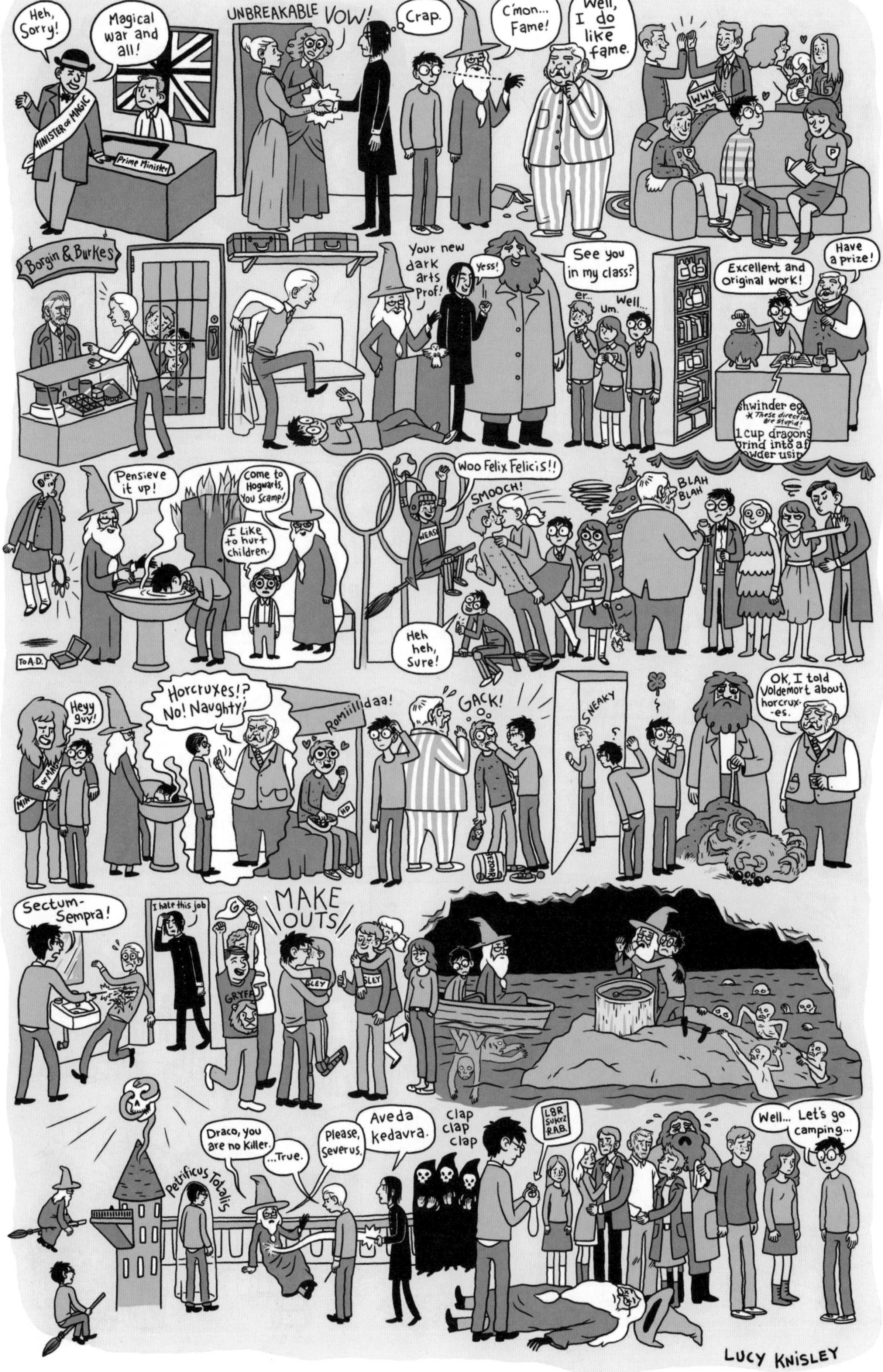

Heh, Sorry!
Magical war and all!
MINISTER OF MAGIC
Prime Minister
UNBREAKABLE VOW!
Crap.
C'mon... Fame!
Well, I do like fame.
WWW
Borgin & Burkes
Your new dark arts Prof!
Yess!
See you in my class?
er...
Um.
Well...
Excellent and original work!
Have a prize!
* These directions are stupid!
Pensieve it up!
Come to Hogwarts, You Scamp!
I like to hurt children.
To A.D.
Woo Felix Felicis!!
SMOOCH!
BLAH BLAH
Heh heh, Sure!
Heyy guy!
Horcruxes!? No! Naughty!
Romiiilldaa!
HP
GACK!
BEZOAR
SNEAKY
Ok, I told Voldemort about horcrux-es.
Sectum-Sempra!
I hate this job
MAKE OUTS
GRYFF
Petrificus Totalis
Draco, you are no Killer.
...True.
Please, Severus.
Aveda kedavra.
clap clap clap
LBR SUKRZ R.A.B.
Well...
Let's go camping...
LUCY KNISLEY

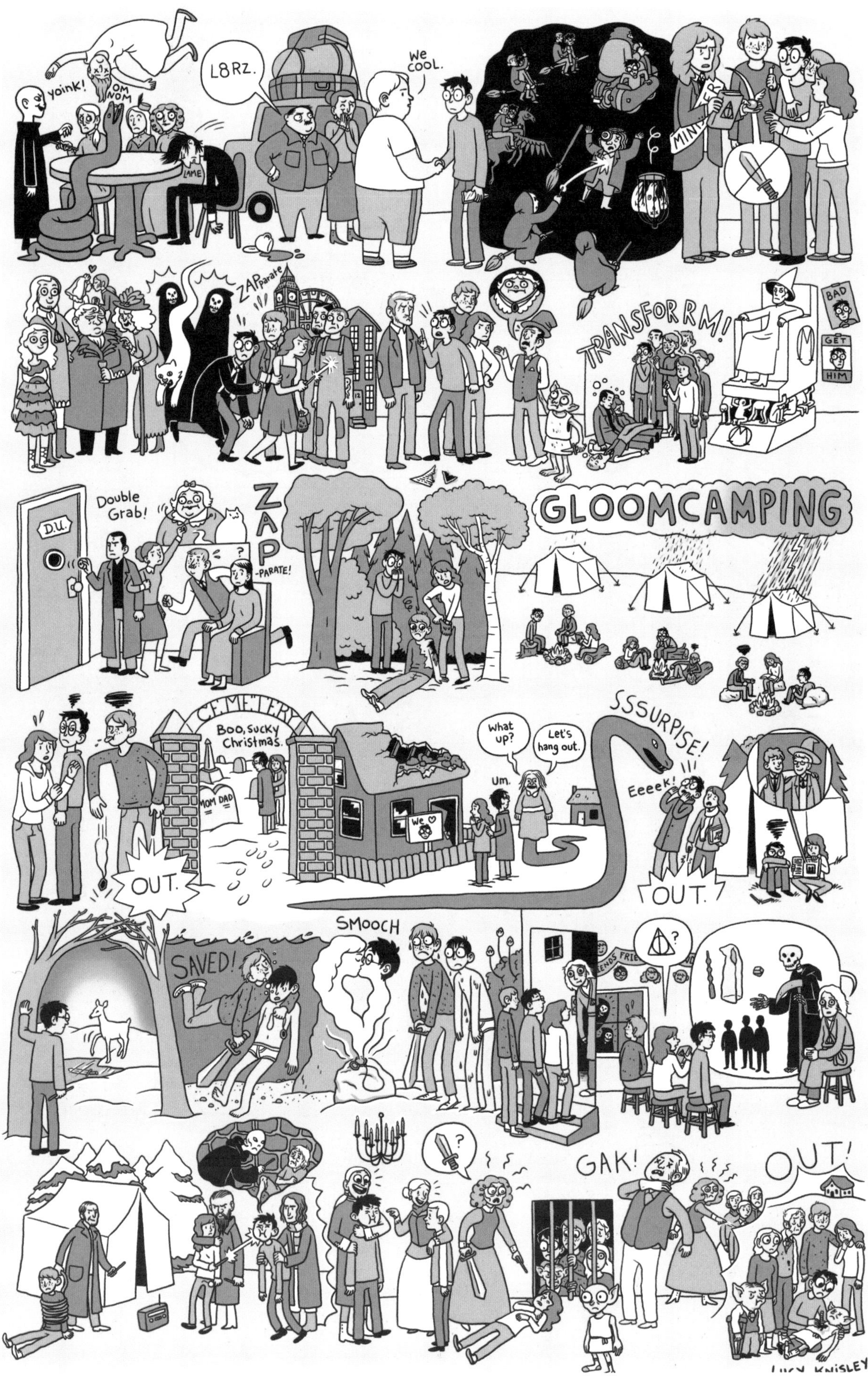
yoink!
OM NOM
LAME
L8Rz.
We COOL.
ZAPparate
TRANSFORRM!
BAD
GET HIM
D.U.
Double Grab!
ZAP -PARATE!
GLOOMCAMPING
CEMETERY
Boo, sucky Christmas.
MOM DAD
OUT.
What up?
Let's hang out.
Um.
SSSURPISE!
Eeeek!
OUT.
SAVED!
SMOOCH
GAK!
OUT!
LUCY KNISLEY

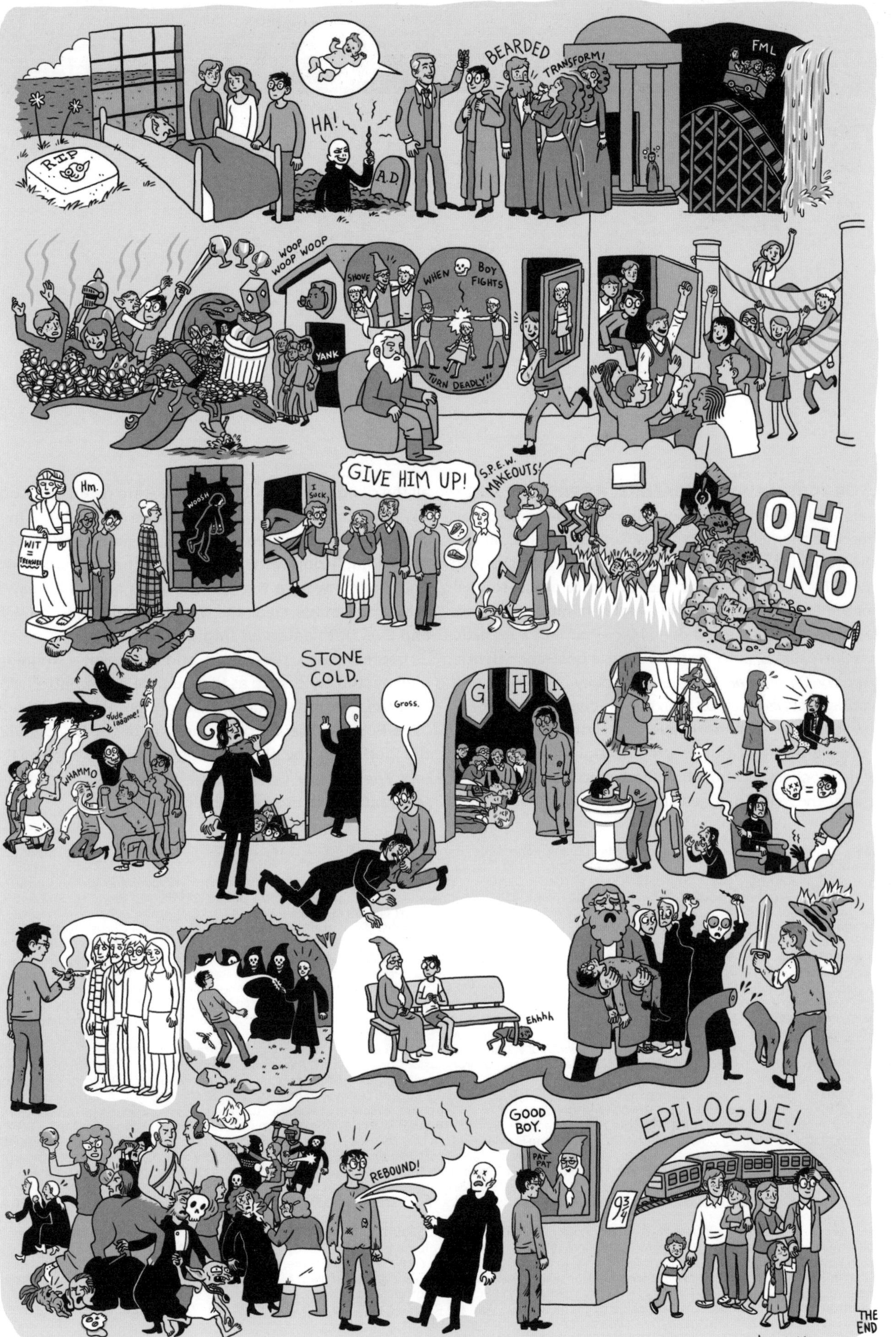
R.I.P.
HA!
A.D.
BEARDED
TRANSFORM!
FML
WOOP WOOP WOOP
SHOVE
WHEN BOY FIGHTS
TURN DEADLY!!
YANK
Hm.
WIT = TREASURE
WOOSH
I SUCK
GIVE HIM UP!
S.P.E.W. MAKEOUTS!
OH NO
STONE COLD.
Gross.
WHAMMO
G H
Ehhhh
REBOUND!
GOOD BOY.
PAT PAT
EPILOGUE!
9 3/4
THE END
LUCY KNISLEY

# Gallery
## Various artists

NOW, FOR YOUR VIEWING PLEASURE, WE PRESENT SIXTY stand-alone illustrations that radically reimagine some of the most famous characters and scenes from fairy tales, fables, and children's literature. As with the rest of *The Graphic Canon of Children's Literature*, the idea is for artists to give us something new regarding these highly familiar, endlessly illustrated works. Let's see a punk Mary Poppins, a realistic Babar, a Surrealist *Green Eggs and Ham*, a post-apocalyptic *Very Hungry Caterpillar*, the "Jabberwocky" in Africa, and *The Wonderful Wizard of Oz* in sixteenth-century China or in outer space. Show us a grotesquely distorted Wonderland, a hot Cruella de Vil, a truly horrifying Ugly Duckling, and Pinocchio receiving a wood-burning tattoo from Geppetto.

Some of these images pose intriguing what-ifs. What if all the gender roles in Snow White were reversed? And who says that the Seven Dwarves must be adorable? Why does Winnie-the-Pooh have to be bright yellow? What if Little Red Riding Hood were even badder than the wolf? What if Thumbelina were a warrior, à la Xena or Red Sonja? What if an artist made clear the parallels between Snow White and Eve, both eaters of tragic apples?

In other cases, these illustrations present a stunning and unexpected style, such as the multiple fabric patterns of *The Last Unicorn*, the snake-swallowing-its-tale motif of Aesop's "The Fox and the Grapes," the Day of the Dead styling of the Pied Piper, the photo-collage of the Cat and the Fiddle, and *The Hunger Games* done in the "chibi" manga style (characters as cute kids with big heads).

**Page 435:** "The Fox and the Grapes" (Aesop) - Ffion Evans. **Page 436:** "The Hare and the Tortoise" (Aesop) - David Whitlam. **Page 437:** Upper left: "The Pied Piper of Hamelin" (German legend) - Omri Koresh. Upper right: *Through the Looking-Glass* / "The Jabberwocky" (Lewis Carroll) - AngelusNoir. Lower right: *Through the Looking-Glass* / "The Jabberwocky" (Lewis Carroll) - Erin Taylor. Lower left: *Alice's Adventures in Wonderland* (Lewis Carroll) - *Alice and Mock Turtle* by Stéphane Bouillet (a.k.a. Remedact). **Page 438:** *The Adventures of Pinocchio* (Carlo Collodi) - *Pinocchio Begin* by SixSawSix. **Page 439:** *Through the Looking-Glass* / "Humpty Dumpty" (Lewis Carroll) - *Too Fragile* by Nicoletta Ceccoli. **Page 440:** "Cinderella" (Charles Perrault) - Alenka Sottler. **Page 441:** Top: "Snow White" (Brothers Grimm) - Rada Azolina. Bottom right: "Rapunzel" (Brothers Grimm) - Rachel Curtis. Bottom left: "Snow White" (Brothers Grimm) - Lia Perrone. **Page 442:** "The Emperor's New Clothes" (Hans Christian Andersen) - *Les Habits neufs de l'empereur* by Ian von Talee. **Page 443:** Upper left: "Snow White" (Brothers Grimm) - *Snow White: Gluttony* by Jonny Ruzzo. Upper right: "Snow White" (Brothers Grimm) - Steph Cherrywell. Bottom: *The Wonderful Wizard of Oz* (L. Frank Baum) - Billy Nunez. **Page 444:** Upper left: The Ramona series (Beverly Cleary) - *Beatrice "Beezus" Quimby and Henry Huggins* by Ricardo Cortés. Upper middle: "The Ugly Duckling" (Hans Christian Andersen) - Mimi Leung. Upper right: "Hansel and Gretel" (Brothers Grimm) - j-b0x. Bottom: *Alice's Adventures in Wonderland* (Lewis Carroll) - *Alice and the White Rabbit* by Stéphane Bouillet (a.k.a. Remedact). **Page 445:** "The Tinderbox" (Hans Christian Andersen) - Sharon Rudahl. **Page 446:** Upper left: "Three Blind Mice" (British nursery rhyme) - Aaron Fulcher. Upper right: "Snow White" (Brothers Grimm) - Bahar Karbuz. Bottom: *The Lion, the Witch and the Wardrobe* (C. S. Lewis) - *Edmund and the Witch* by Adam McLaughlin. **Page 447:** Top: *The Wonderful Wizard of Oz* (L. Frank Baum) - Joshua Heinsz. Bottom right: "Thumbelina" (Hans Christian Andersen) - Rebecca Dart. Bottom left: *The Story of Babar* (Jean de Brunhoff) - Chris Holbrow. **Page 448:** Top left: "Snow White" (Brothers Grimm) - *Someday My Princess Will Come* by Mira Ongchua. Top right: "The Little Mermaid" (Hans Christian Andersen) - Frances Alcaraz. Bottom right: "Rapunzel" (Brothers Grimm) - Victor Kolyszko. Bottom left: *The Hobbit* (J. R. R. Tolkien) - Zuzana Čupová. **Page 449:** *Winnie-the-Pooh* (A. A. Milne) - *Pooh and the Rabbit* by Joanna Pasek. **Page 450:** Top: "Beauty and the Beast" (French fairy tale) - Manuel Šumberac. Bottom: *Mary Poppins* (P. L. Travers) - *Chimney Sweep World* by Heather Dixon. **Page 451:** *Green Eggs & Ham* (Dr. Seuss) - Heather Watts. **Page 452:** Top: *Gulliver's Travels* (Jonathan Swift) - Pia Valaer. Bottom right: "Little Red Riding Hood" (Charles Perrault) - Eran Fowler. Bottom left: *The Hobbit* (J.R.R. Tolkien) - *Smaug* by Kateřina Čupová. **Page 453:** Top left: "Hey-Diddle-Diddle" (British nursery rhyme) - Kenneth Rougeau. Top right: "Beauty and the Beast" (French fairy tale) - Lia Perrone. Bottom right: *The Neverending Story* (Michael Ende) - *Moonchild* by Vilde D. Ulriksen. **Page 454:** Top: *The Hunger Games* (Suzanne Collins) - María Pérez Pacheco. Bottom right: *The Hunger Games* (Suzanne Collins) - *Peeta* by Maria Kartashova. Bottom left: *The Hunger Games* (Suzanne Collins) - *Katniss* by Maria Kartashova. **Page 455:** Top left: Harry Potter series (J. K. Rowling) - *The Three Broomsticks* by Tristyn Pease. Top right: *Coraline* (Neil Gaiman) - Abigail Larson. Bottom right: *Mary Poppins* (P. L. Travers) - Dumaker. Bottom left: *The Hundred and One Dalmatians* (Dodie Smith) - *Cruella de Vil* by Amaris Nicole Co Lim. **Page 456:** Top: Harry Potter series (J. K. Rowling) - *Harry Potter Years* by Valeria Bogado C. Bottom right: *The Last Unicorn* (Peter S. Beagle) - Katrina Young (KatArtIllustrations). Bottom left: *The Phantom Tollbooth* (Norton Juster) - *Symphony* by Sam Garvey. **Page 457:** *The Adventures of Pinocchio* (Carlo Collodi) - Eran Fowler. **Page 458:** *The Phantom Tollbooth* (Norton Juster) - *A Very Dirty Bird* by Elda The. **Page 459:** *The Very Hungry Caterpillar* (Eric Carle) - Alex Eckman-Lawn. **Page 460:** Top: *His Dark Materials* (Philip Pullman) - *Love for the Panserbjørn* by Katrina Young (KatArtIllustrations). Bottom right: *The Little Prince* (Antoine de Saint-Exupéry) - Dmitry (Lemon5ky) Dubrovin. Bottom middle: "Goldilocks and the Three Bears" (British fairy tale) - Kelly Bastow. Bottom left: *The Wonderful Wizard of Oz* (L. Frank Baum) - Andrew R. Chandler. **Page 461:** *Green Eggs and Ham* (Dr. Seuss) - *The Green Feast* by Jeff Christensen. **Page 462:** *The Wind in the Willows* (Kenneth Grahame) - Felideus.

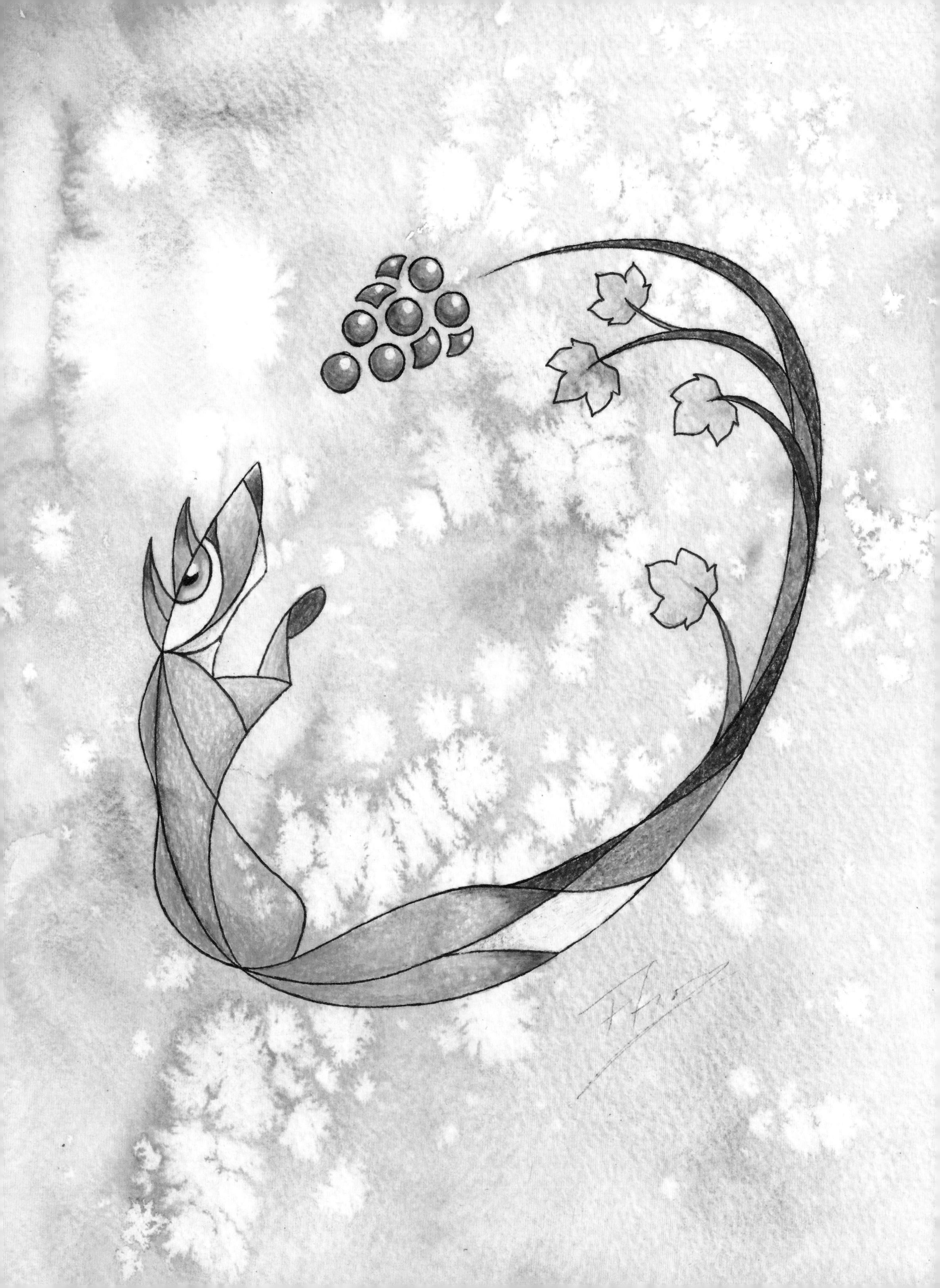

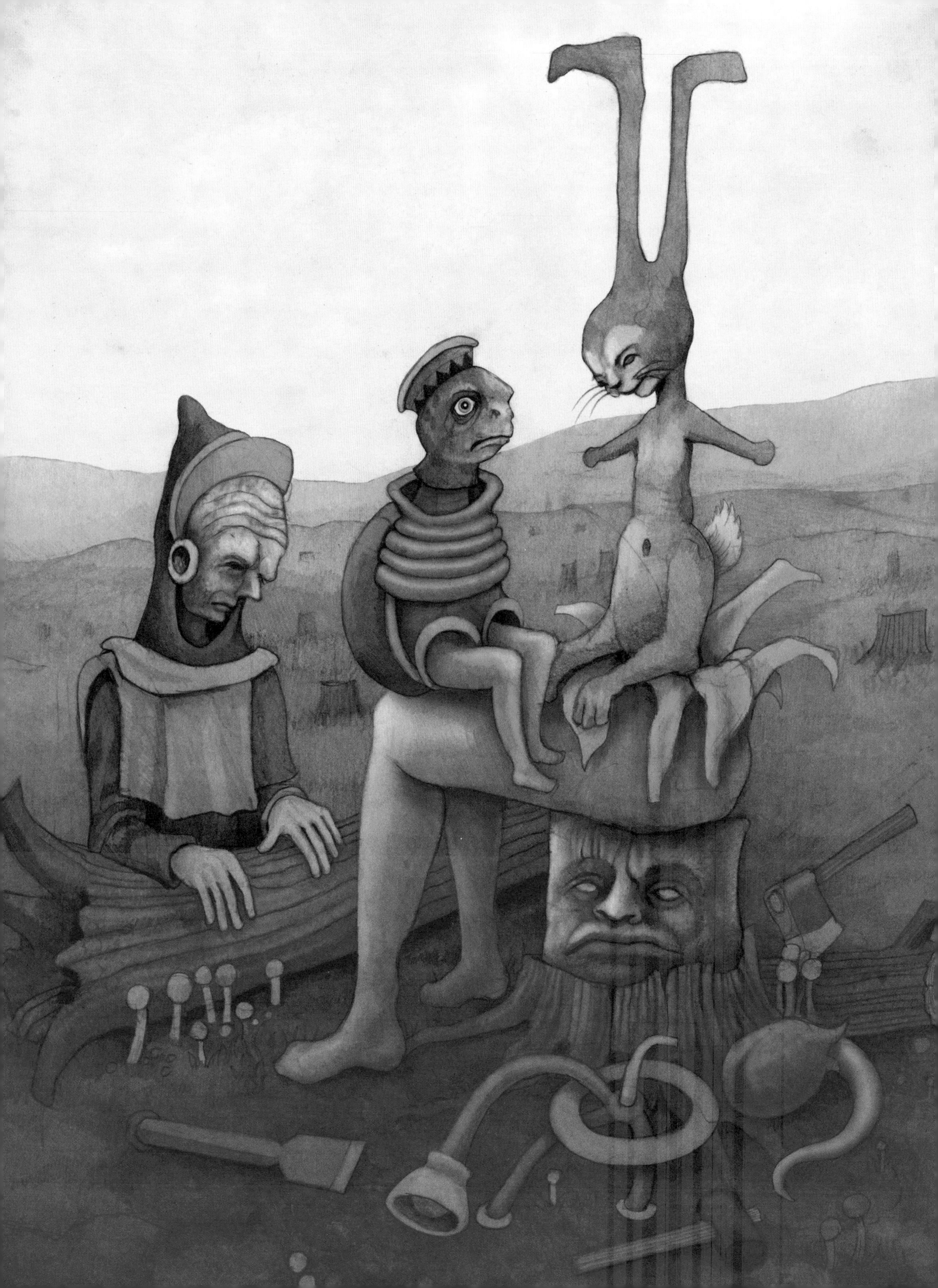

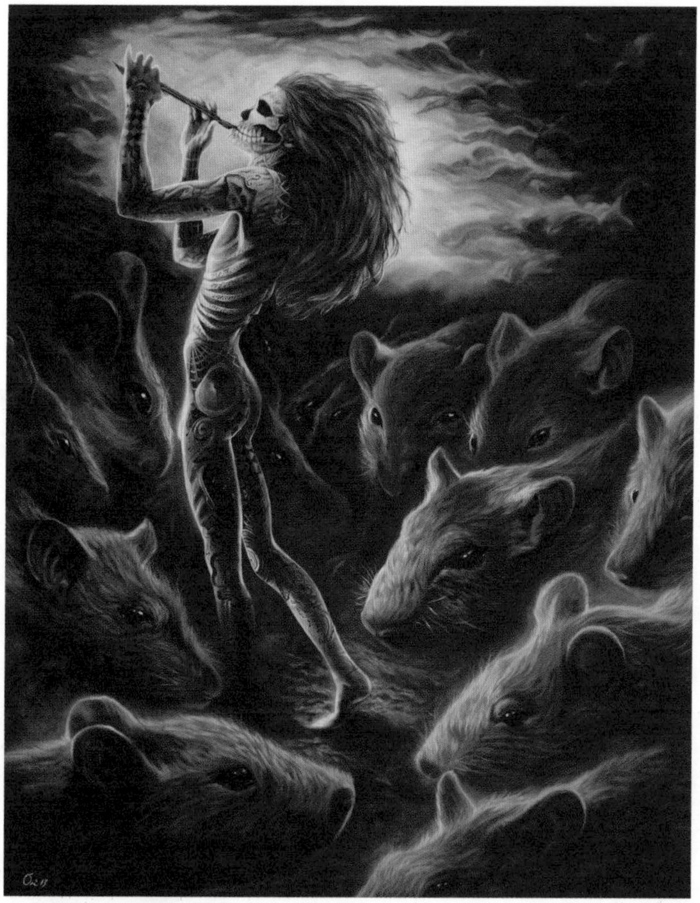

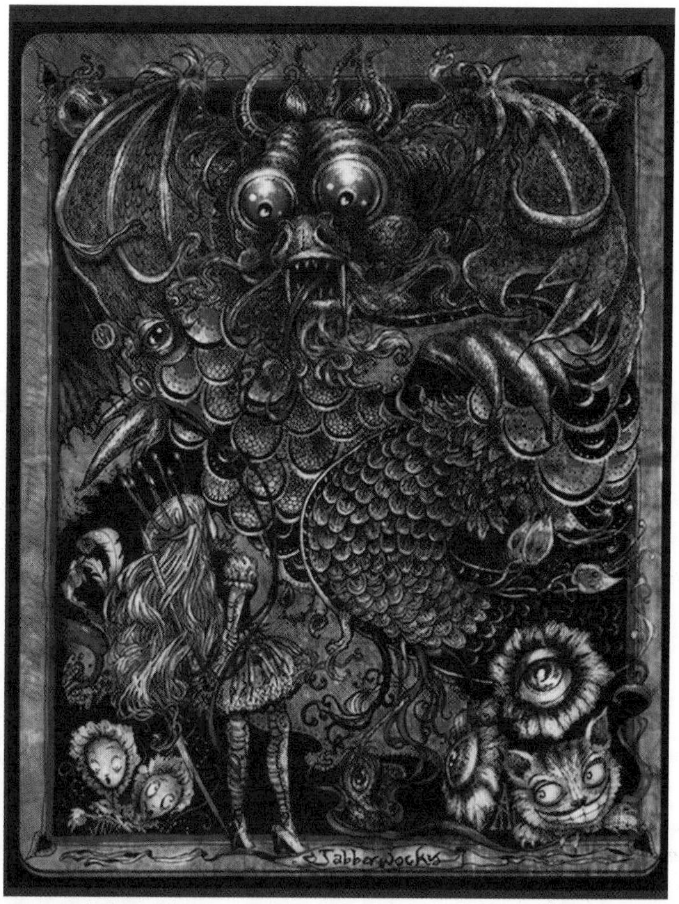
Jabberwocky

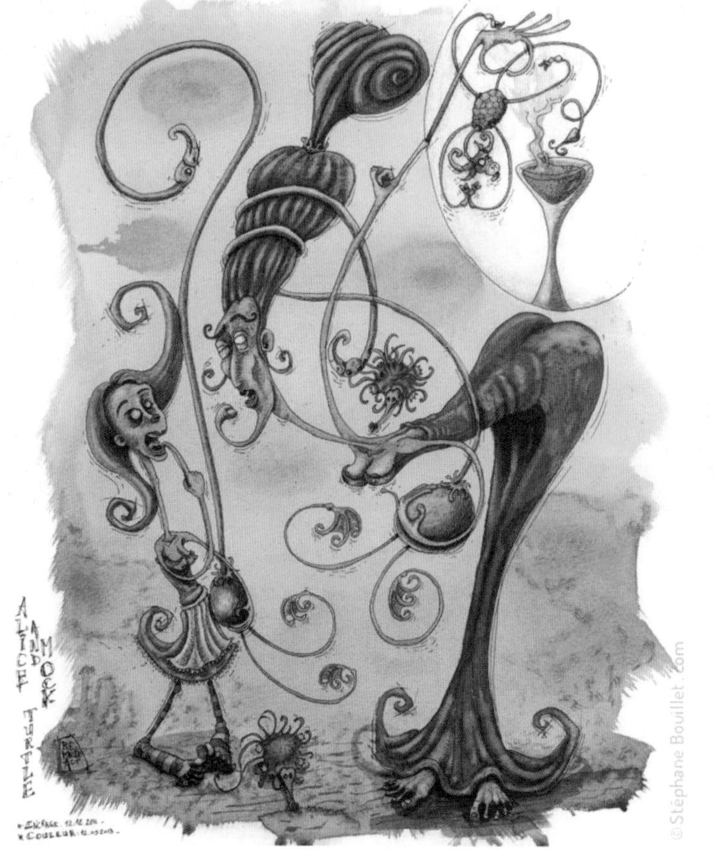
ALICE AND MOCK TURTLE
© Stéphane Bouillet.com

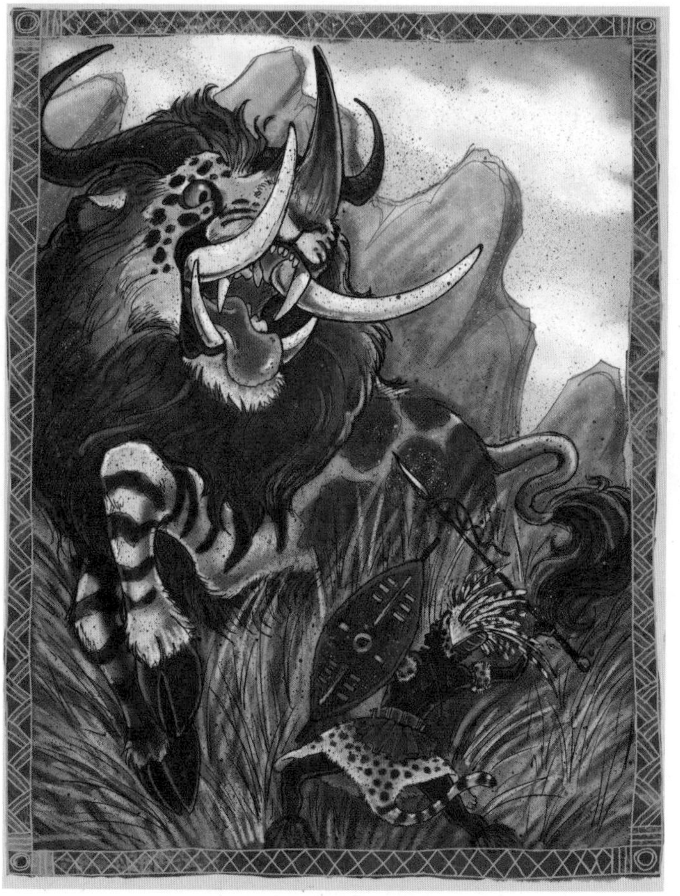

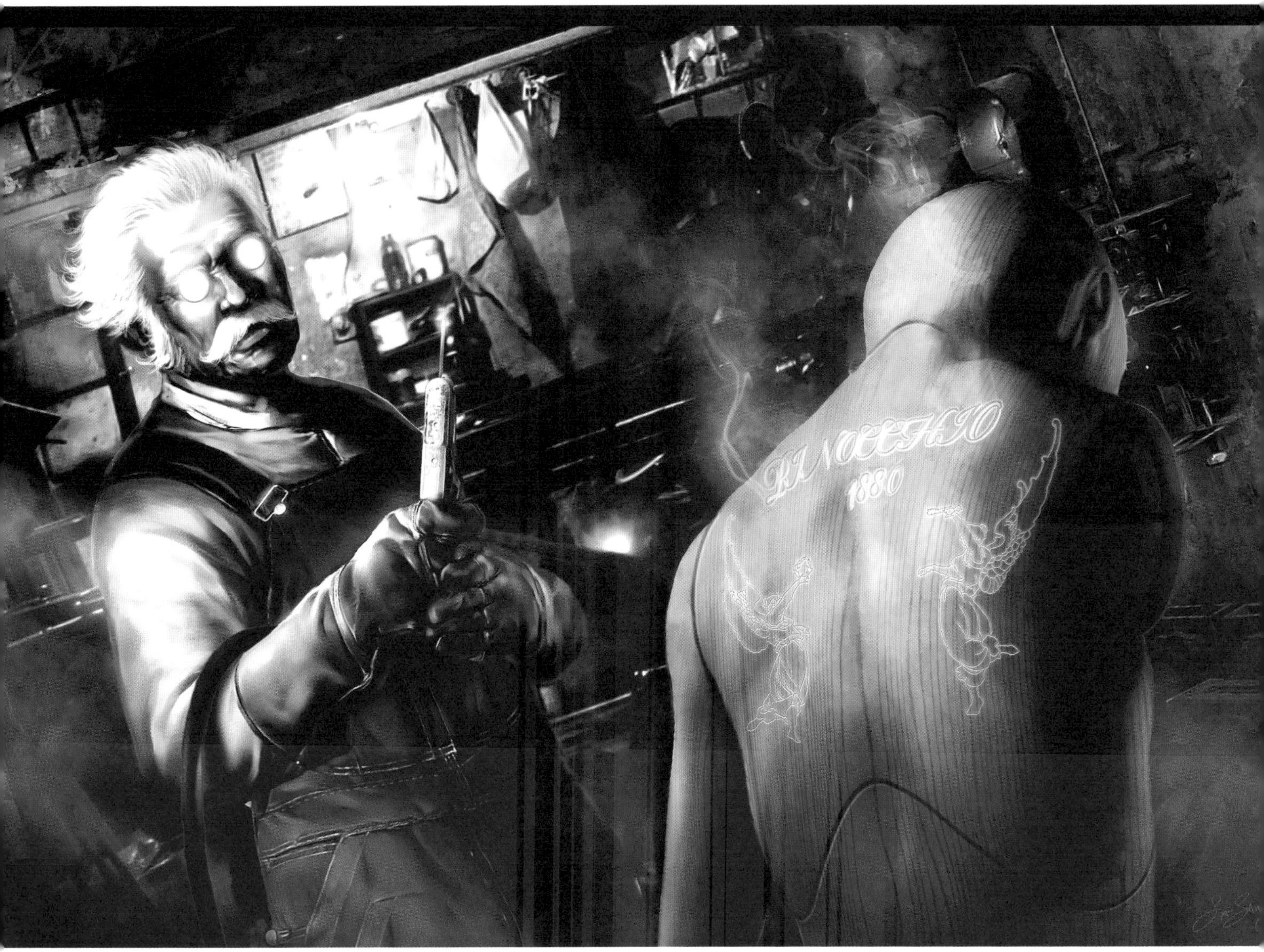
PINOCCHIO
1880

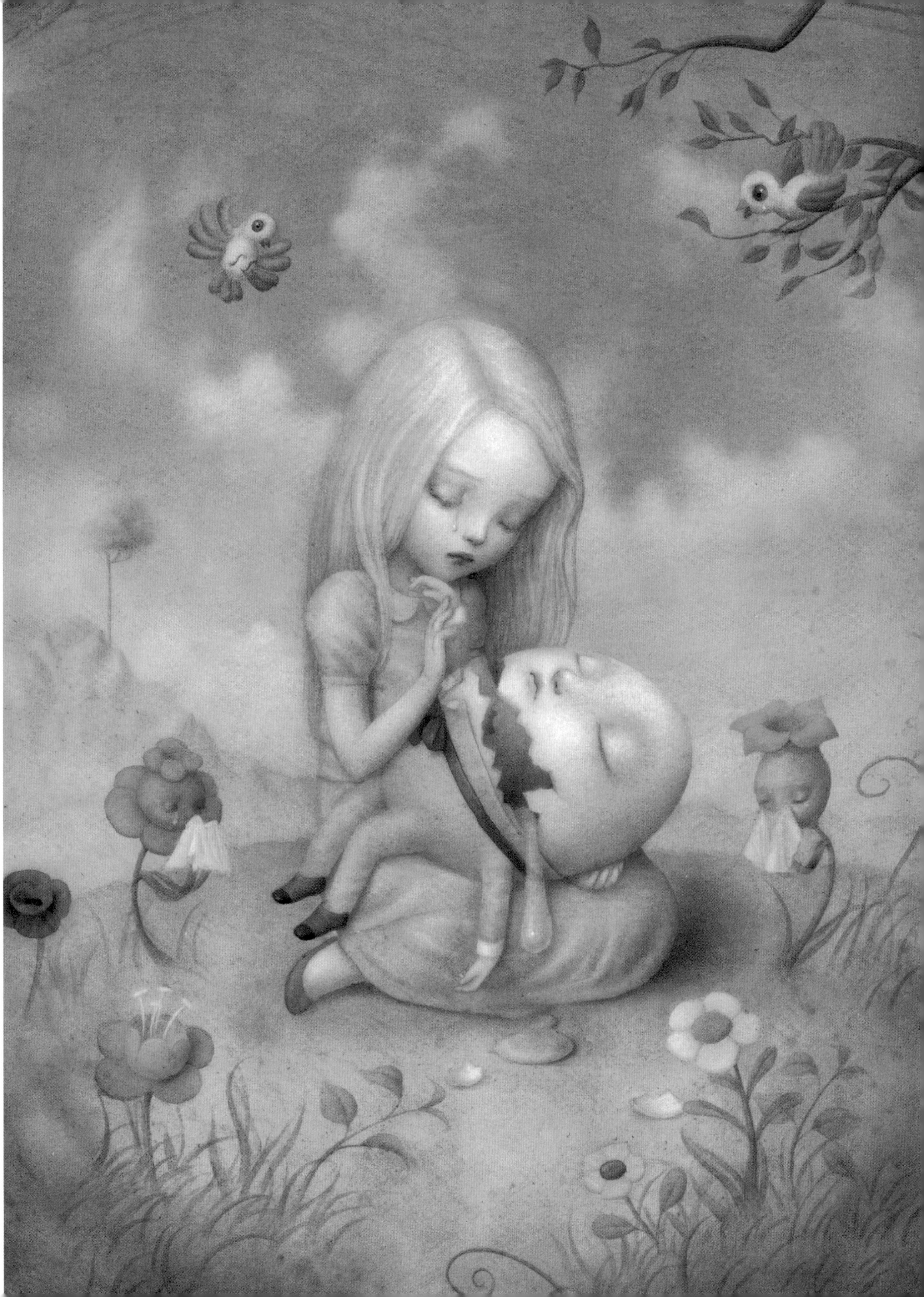

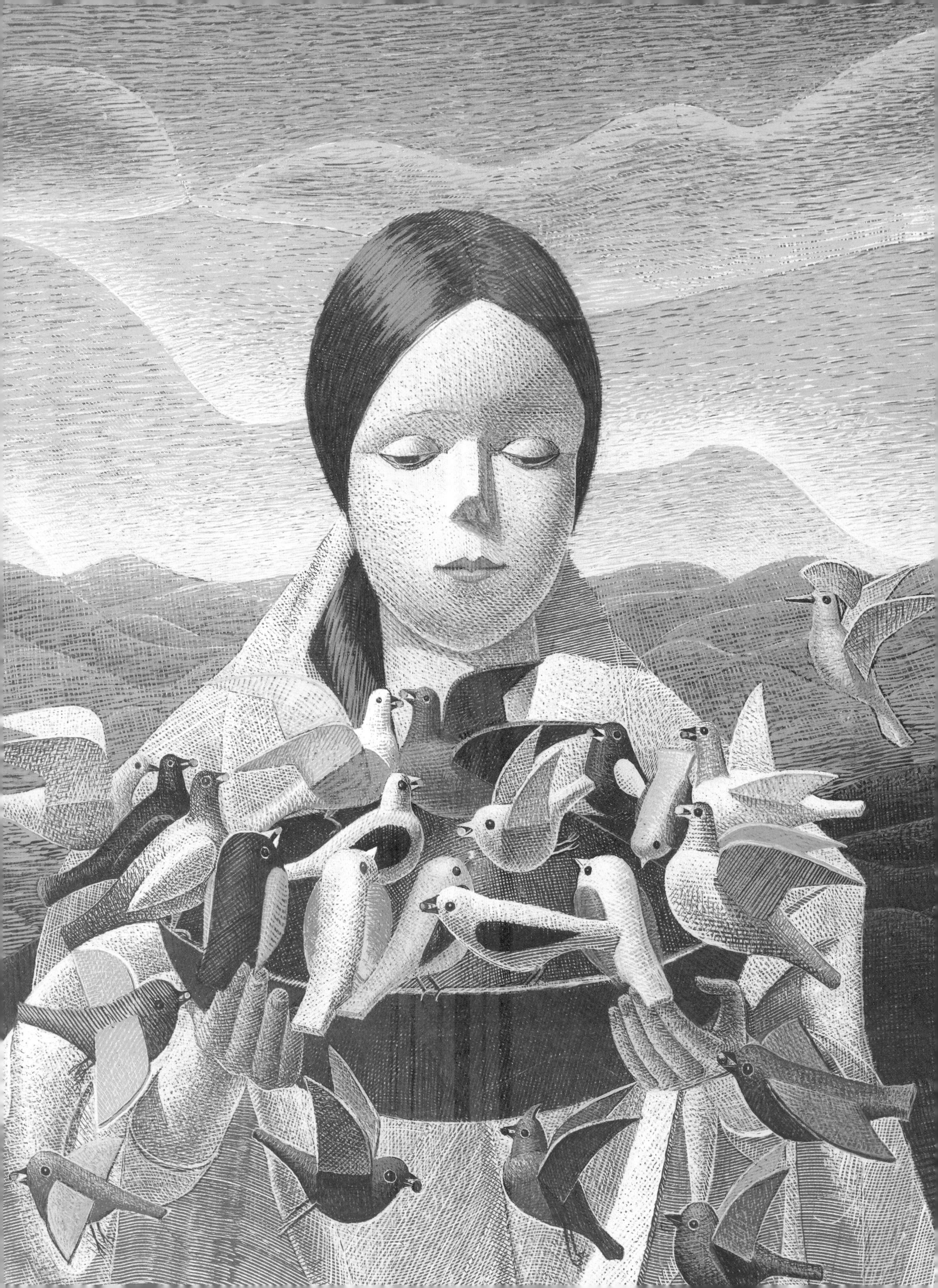

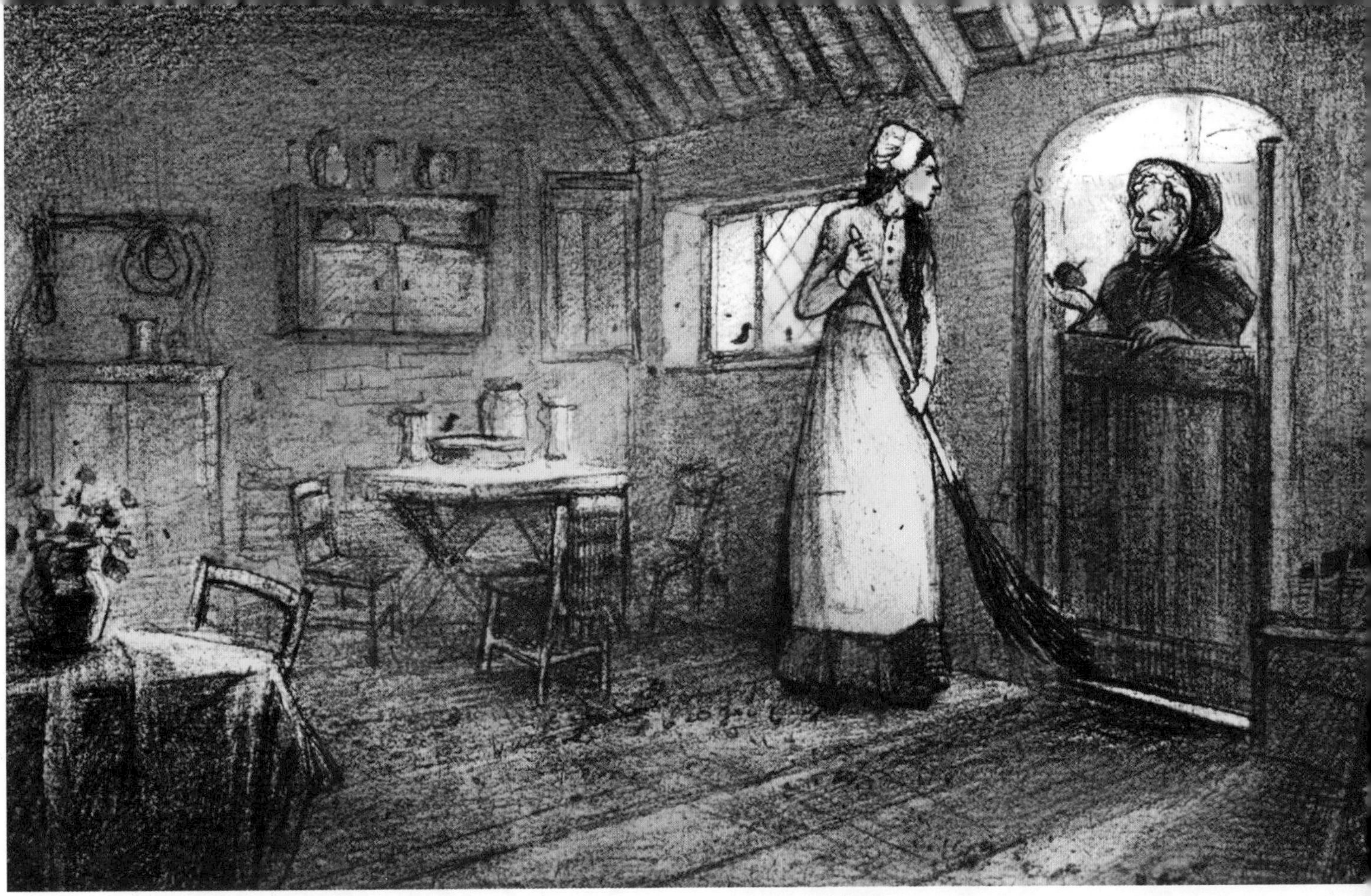

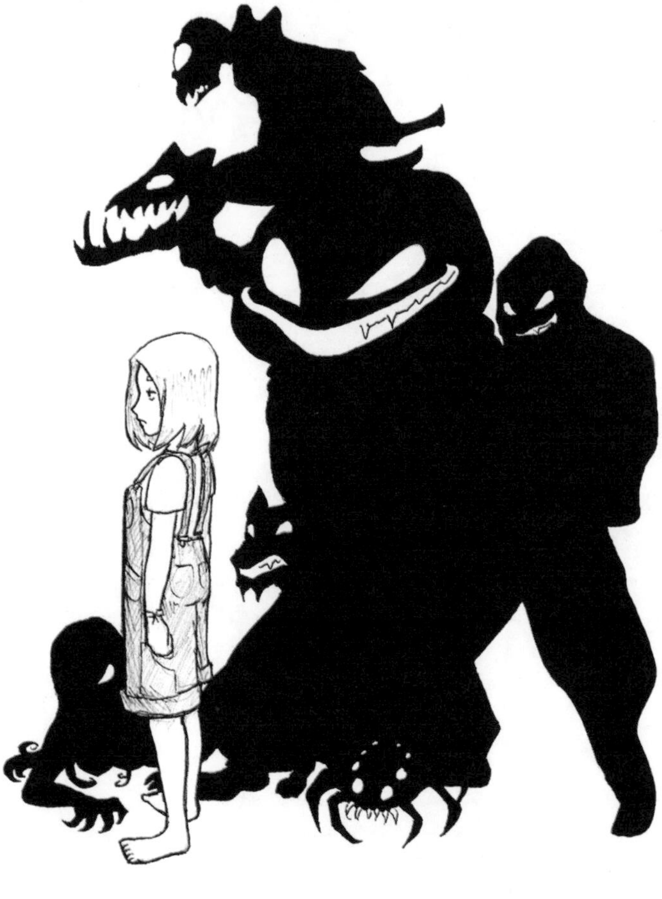

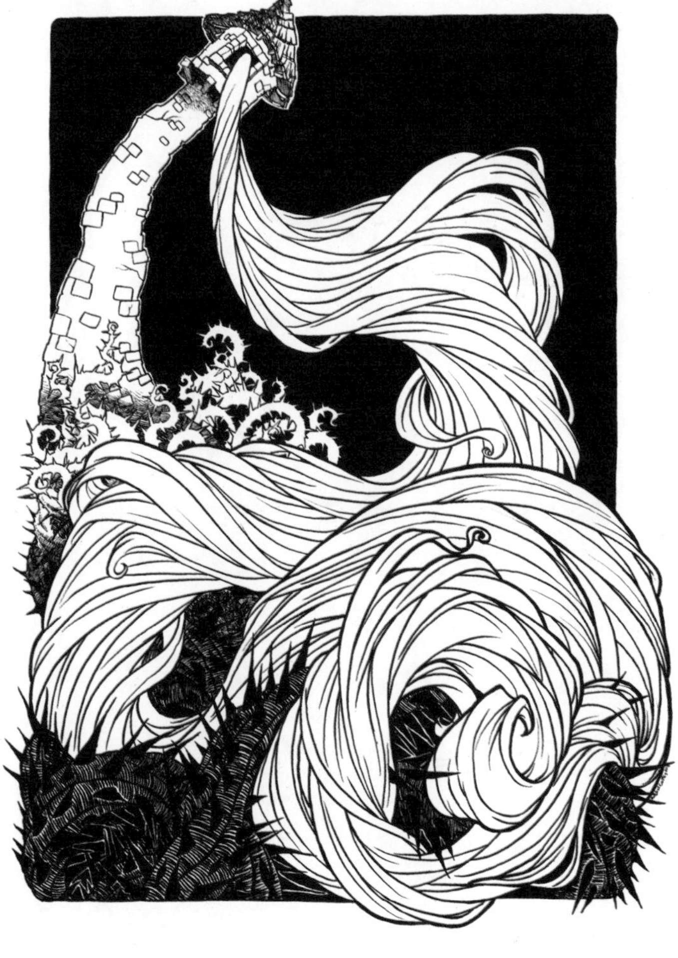

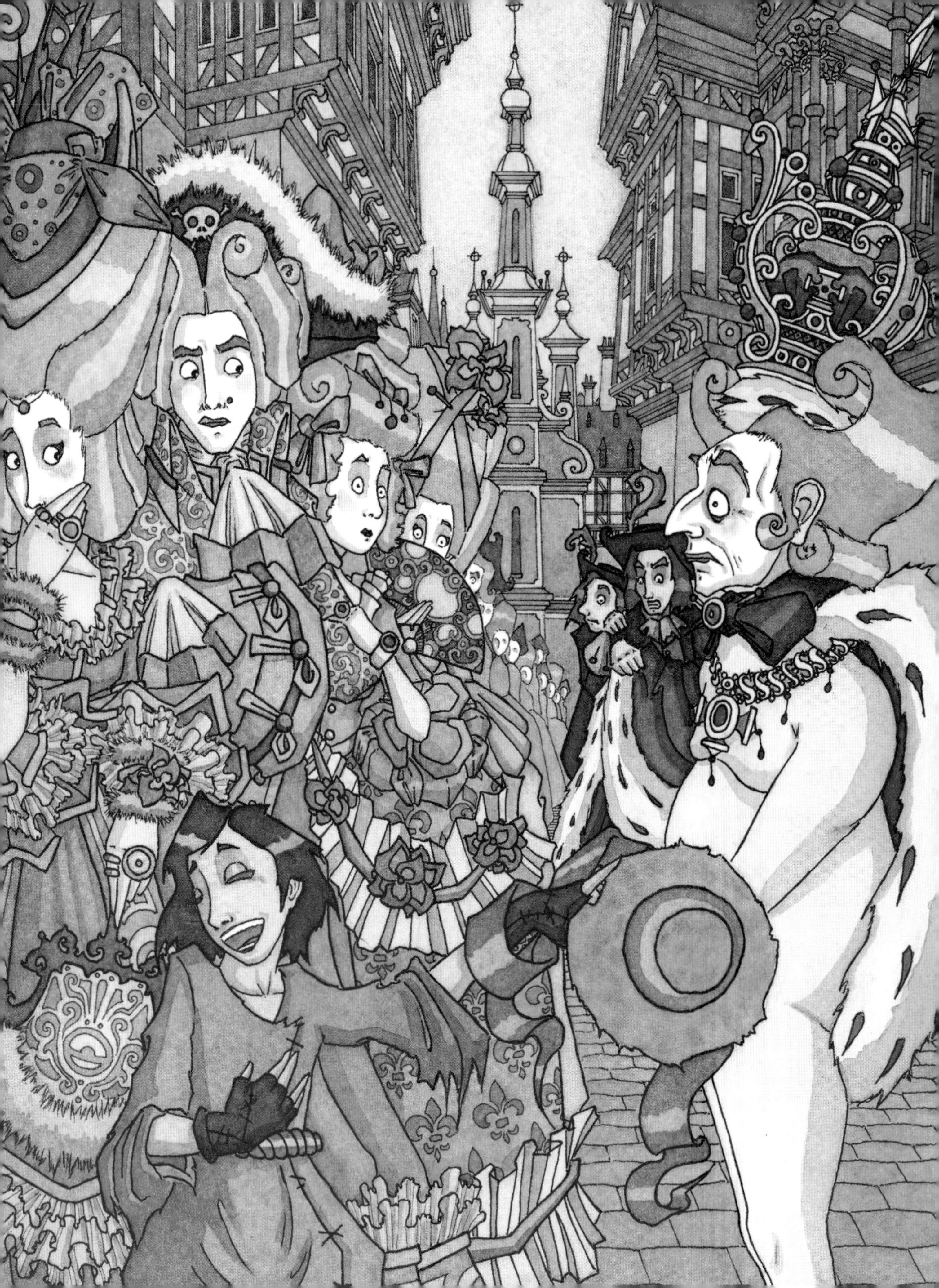

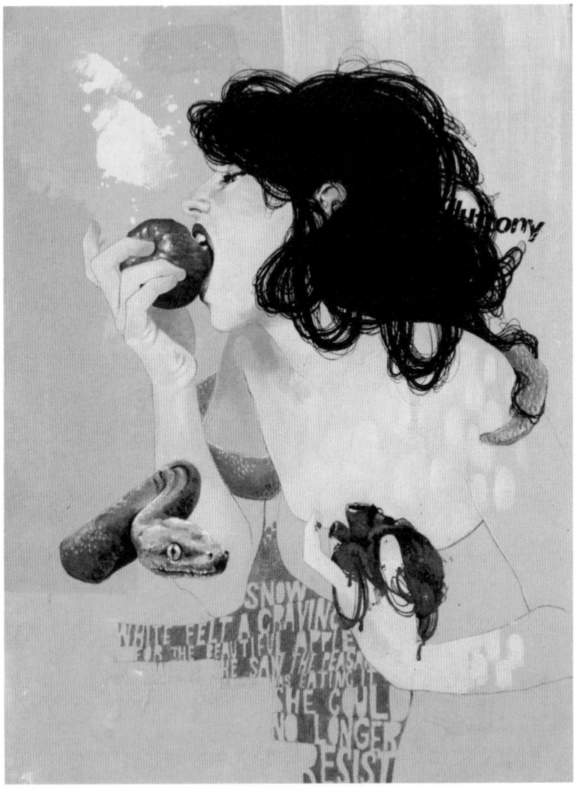
SNOW
WHITE FELT A
NO LONGER
RESIST

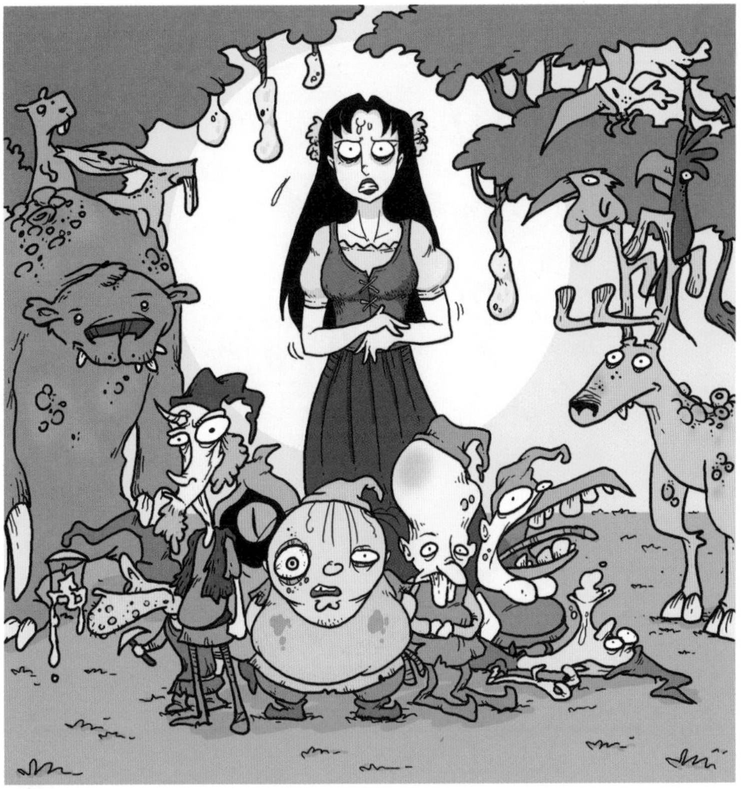

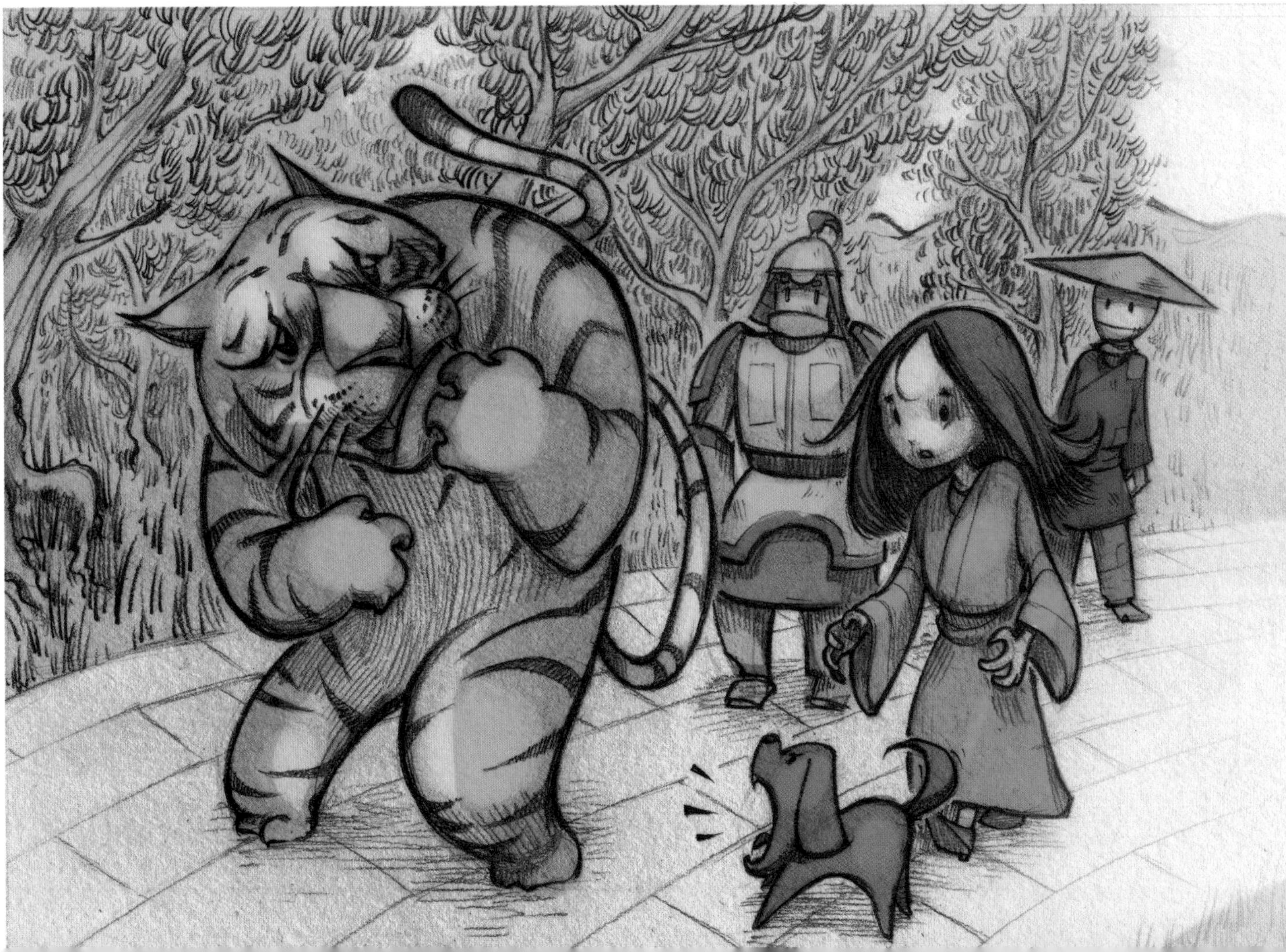

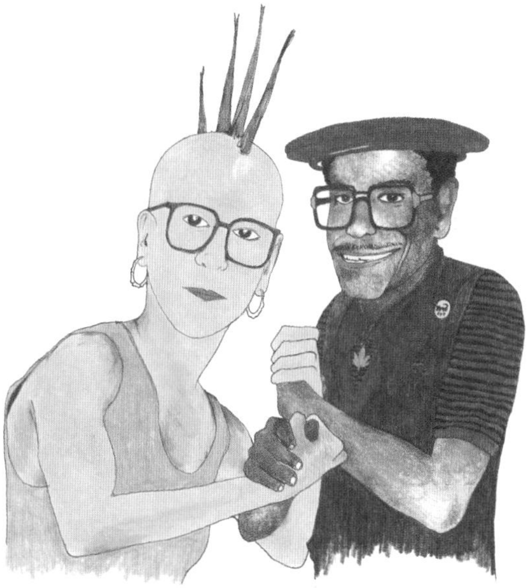

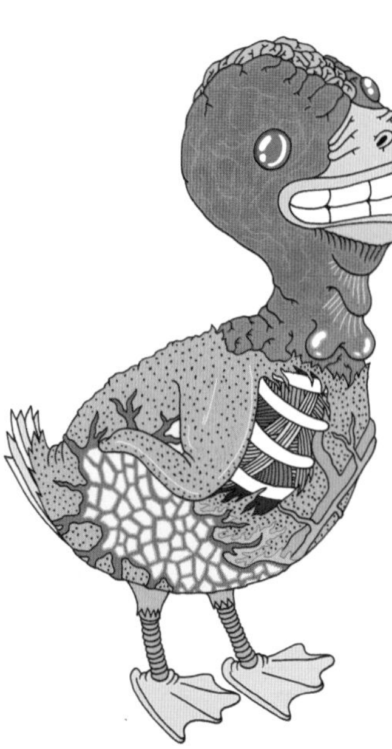

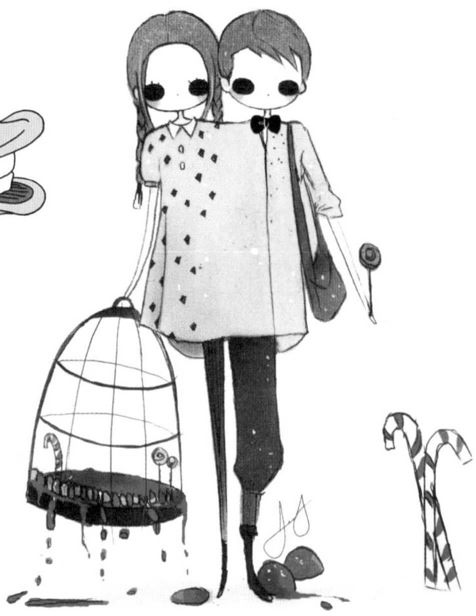

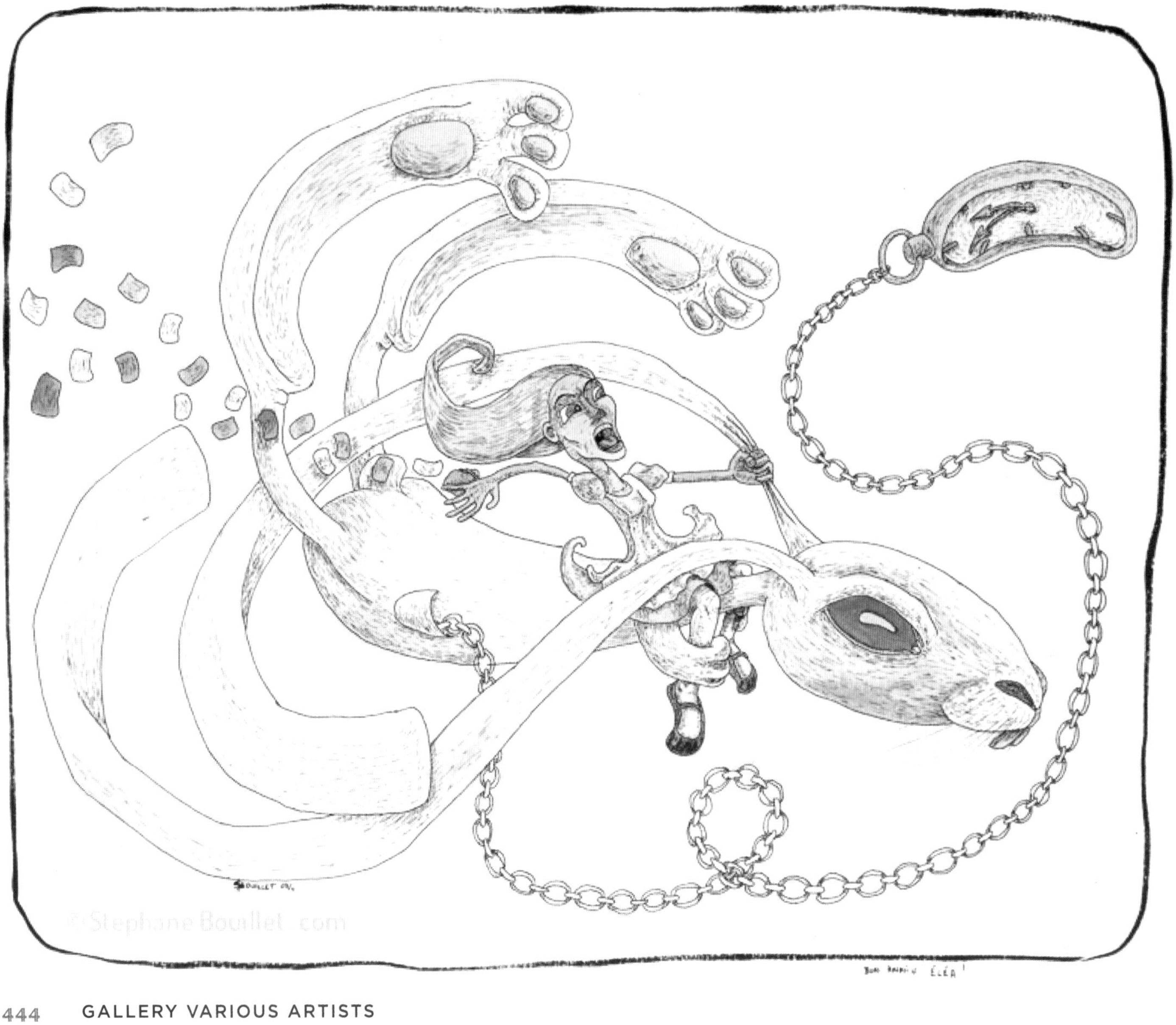
© StephaneBouillet.com

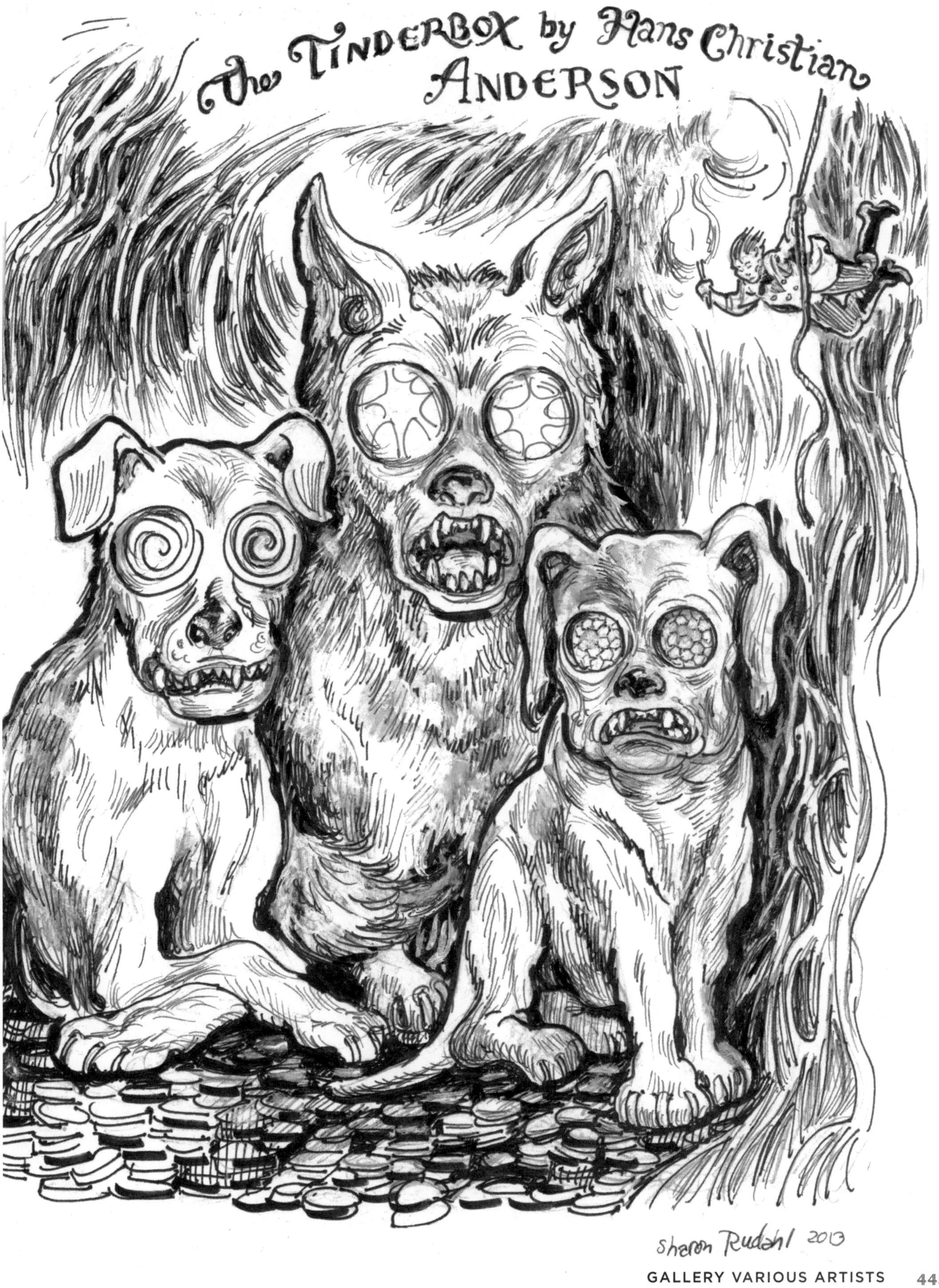
The TINDERBOX by Hans Christian ANDERSON
Sharon Rudahl 2013

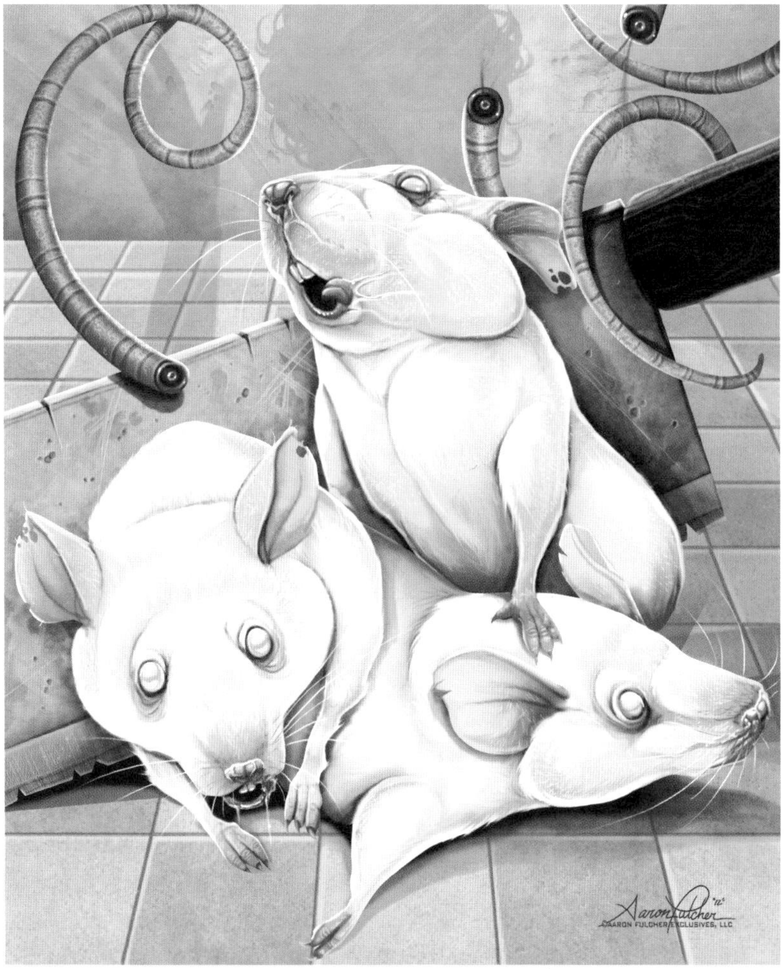
Aaron Fulcher
AARON FULCHER EXCLUSIVES, LLC

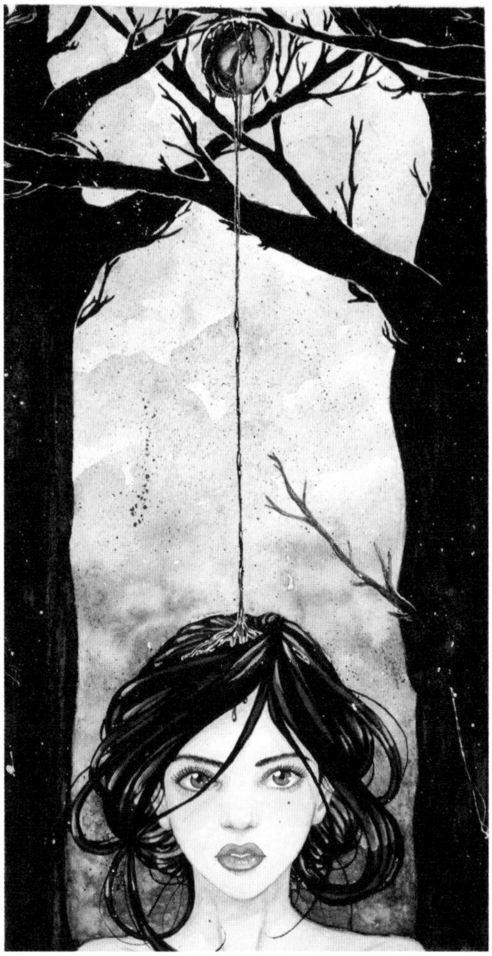

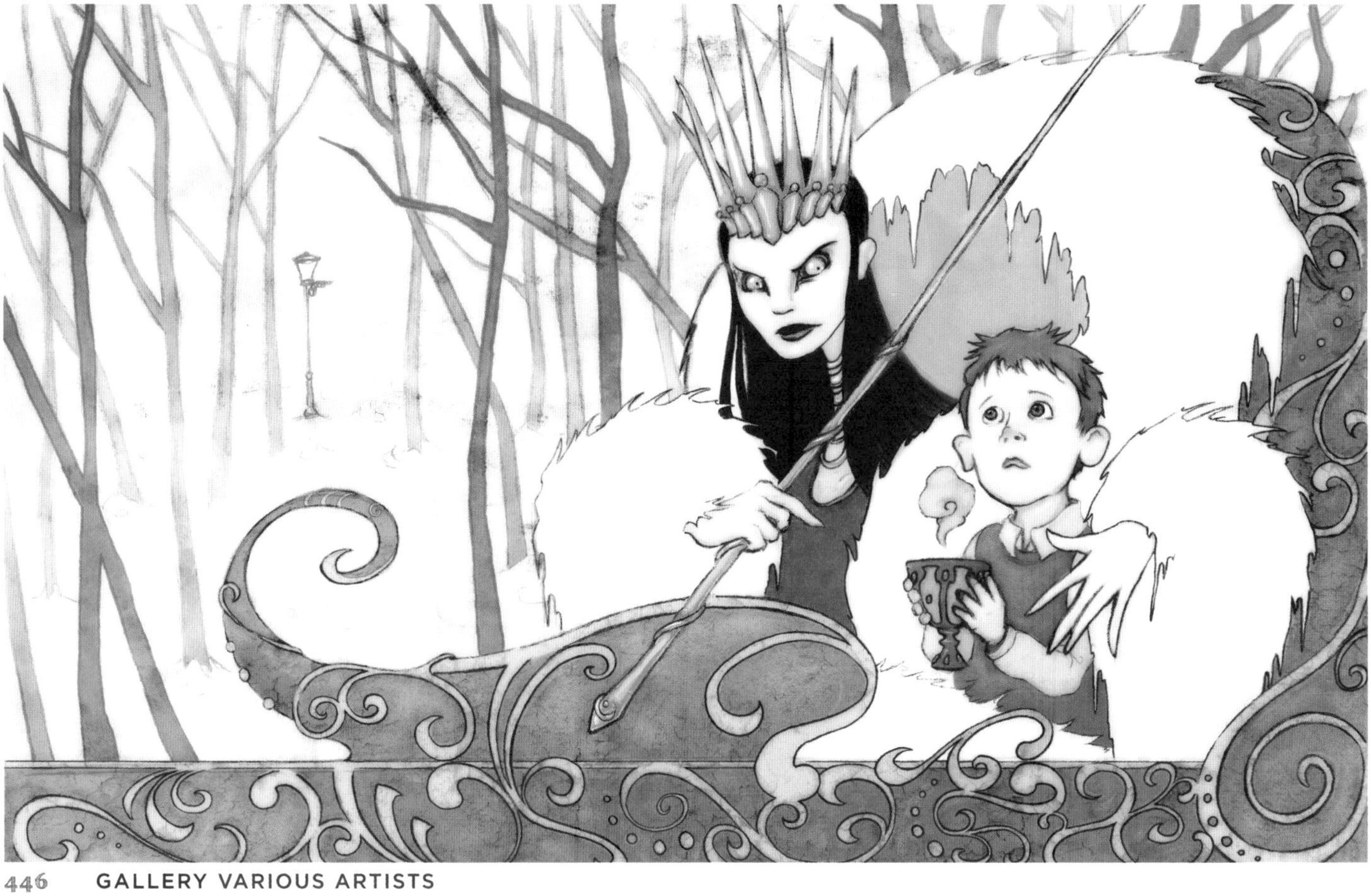

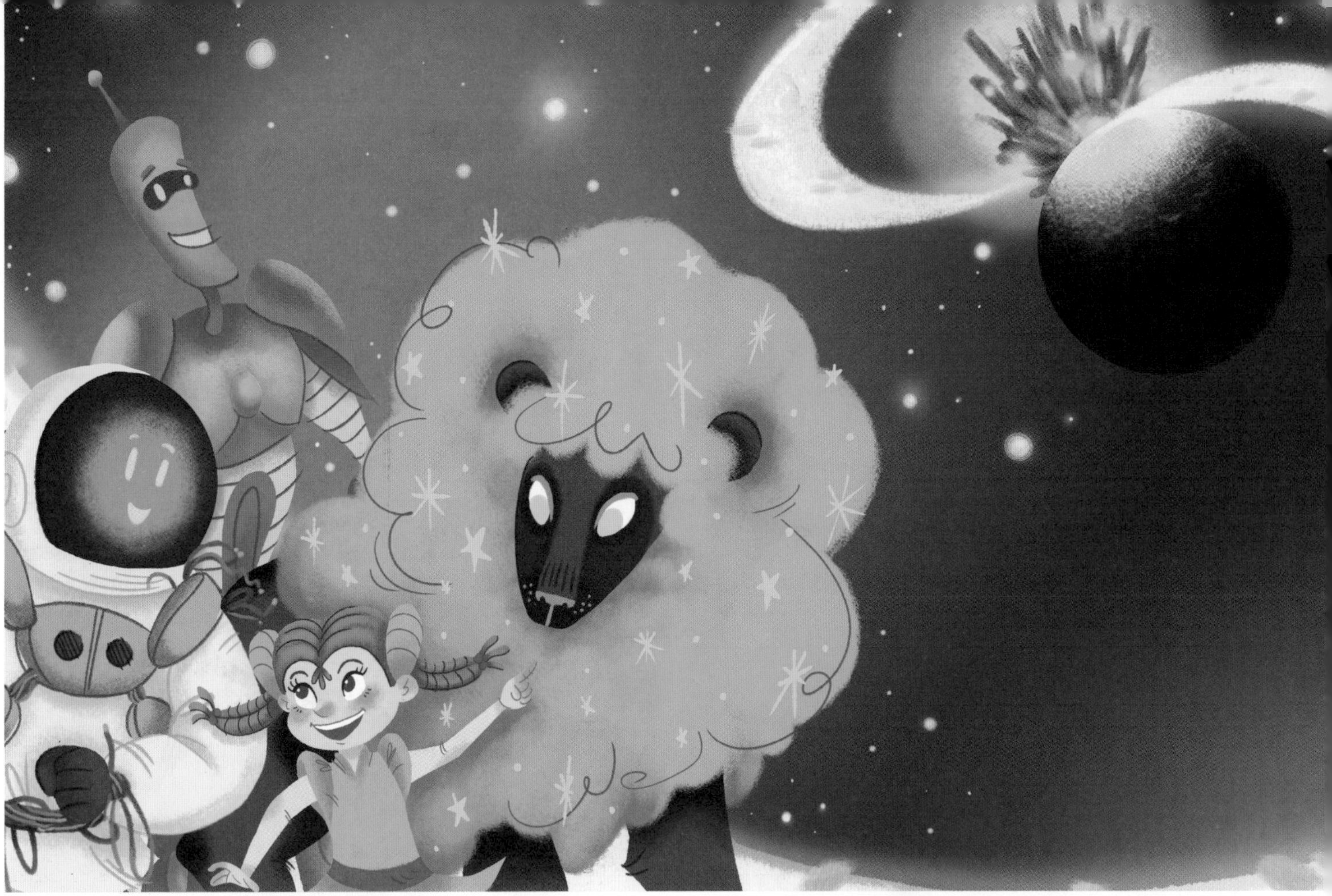

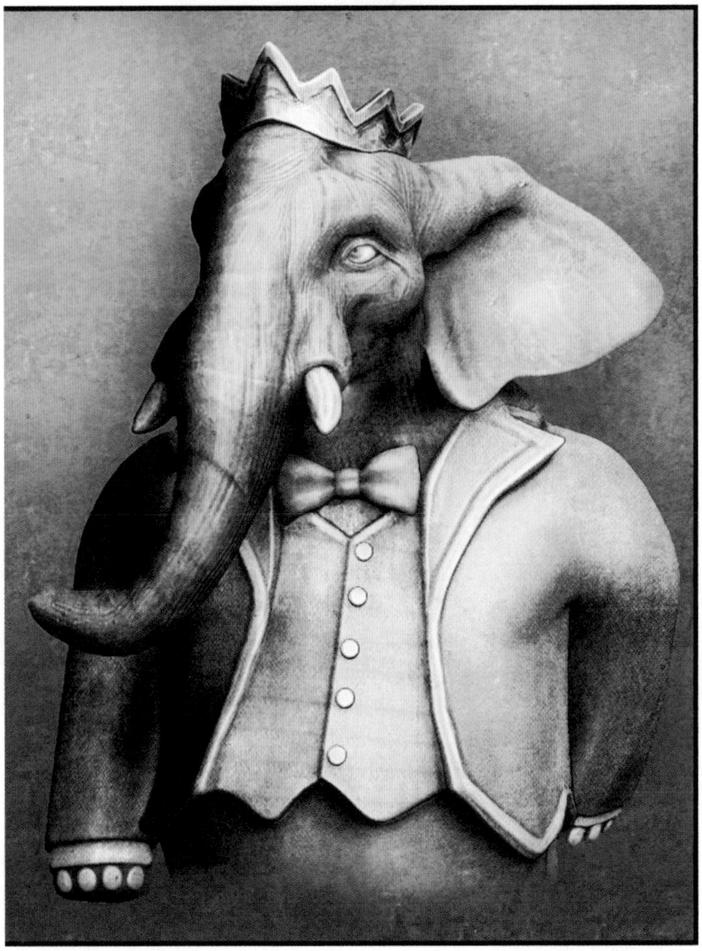

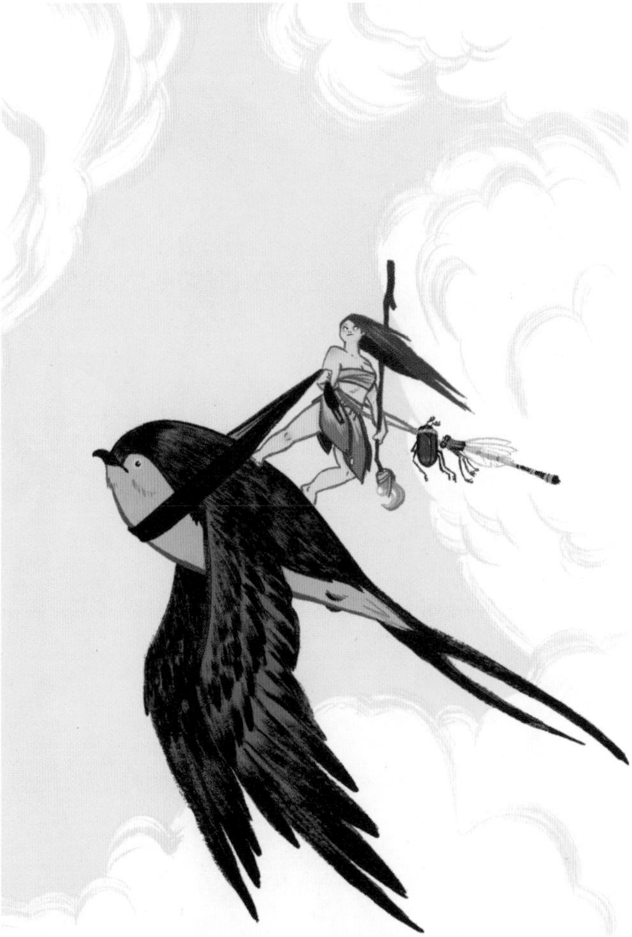

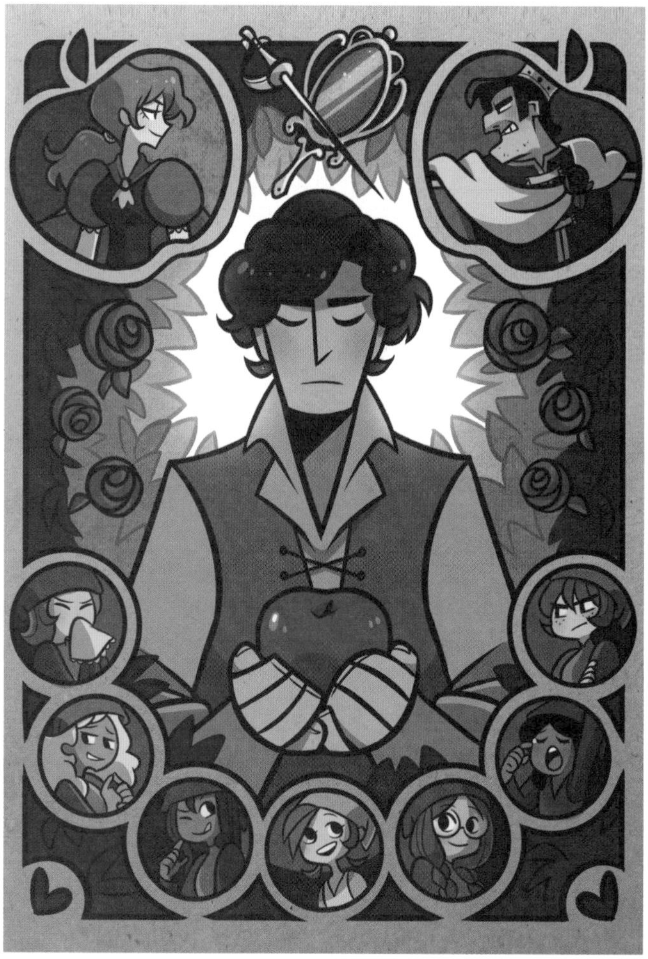

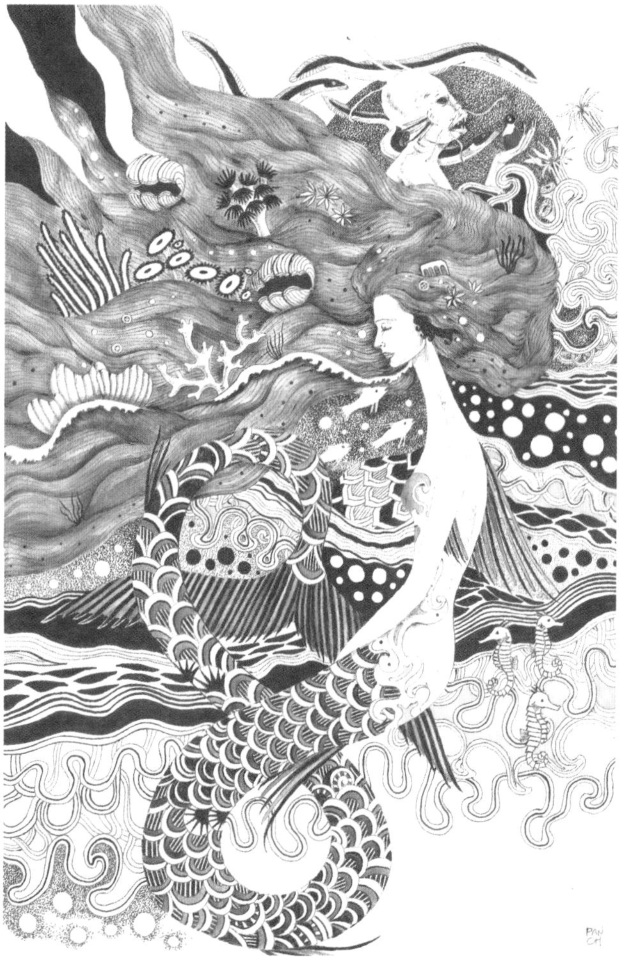

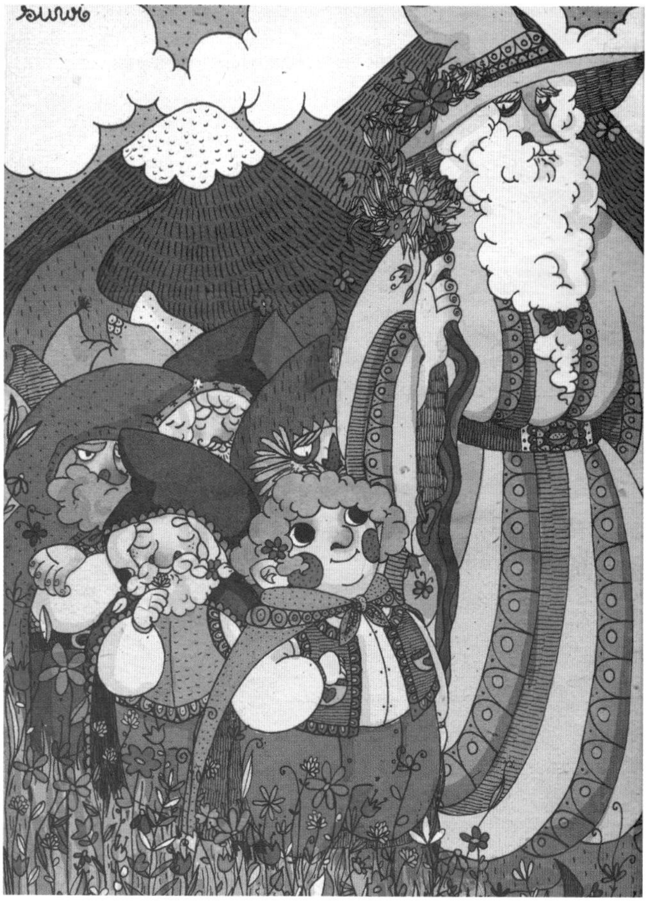

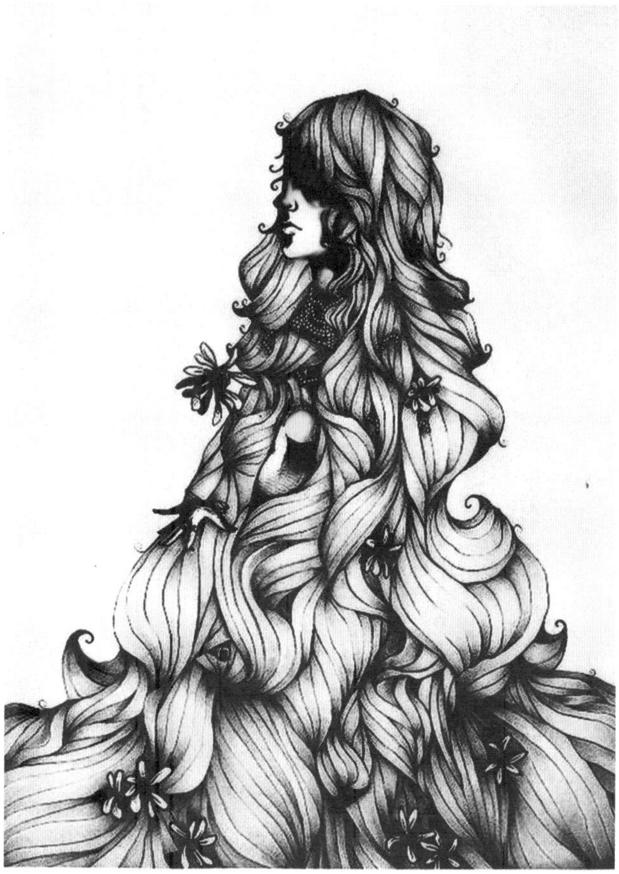

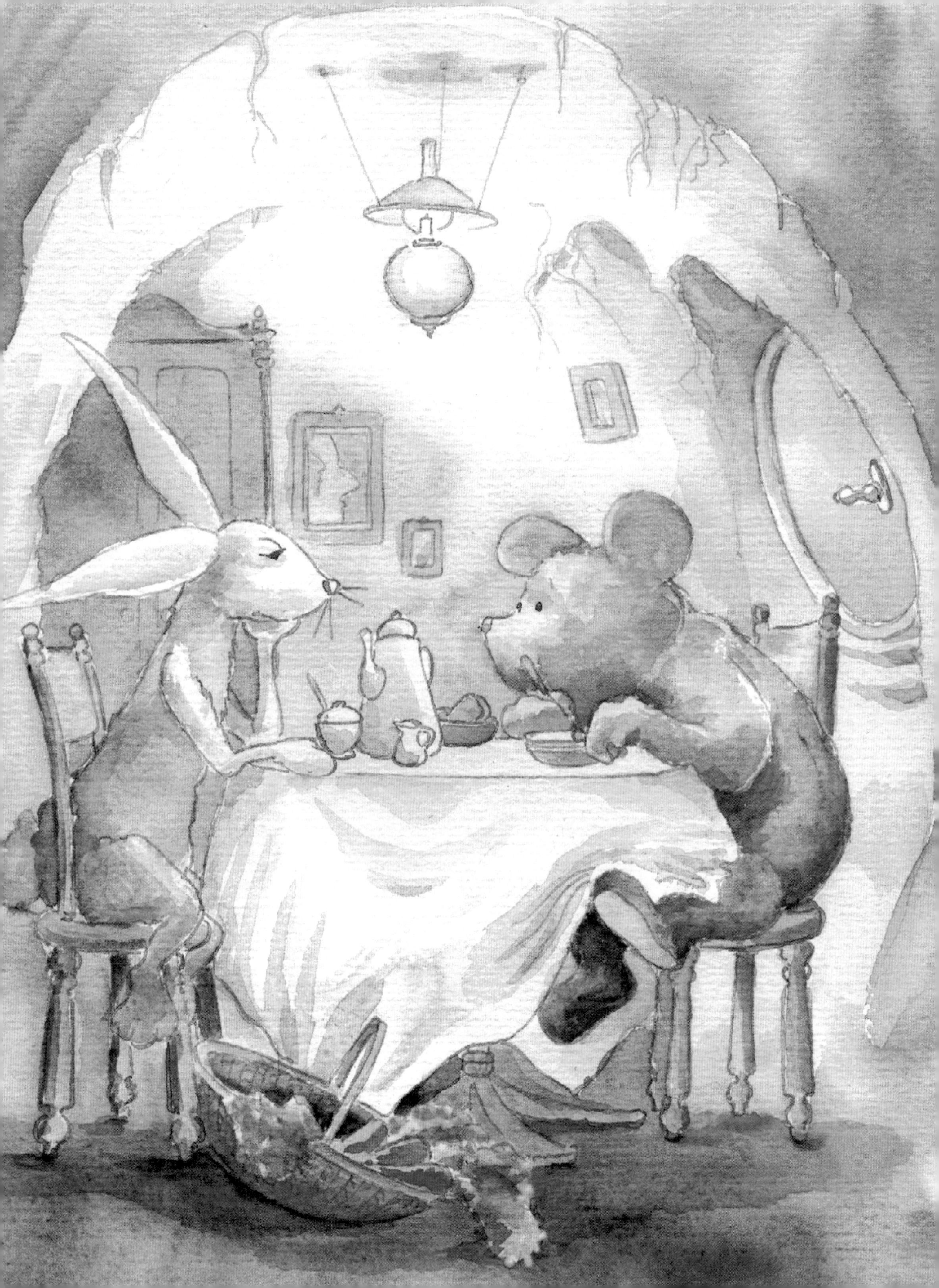

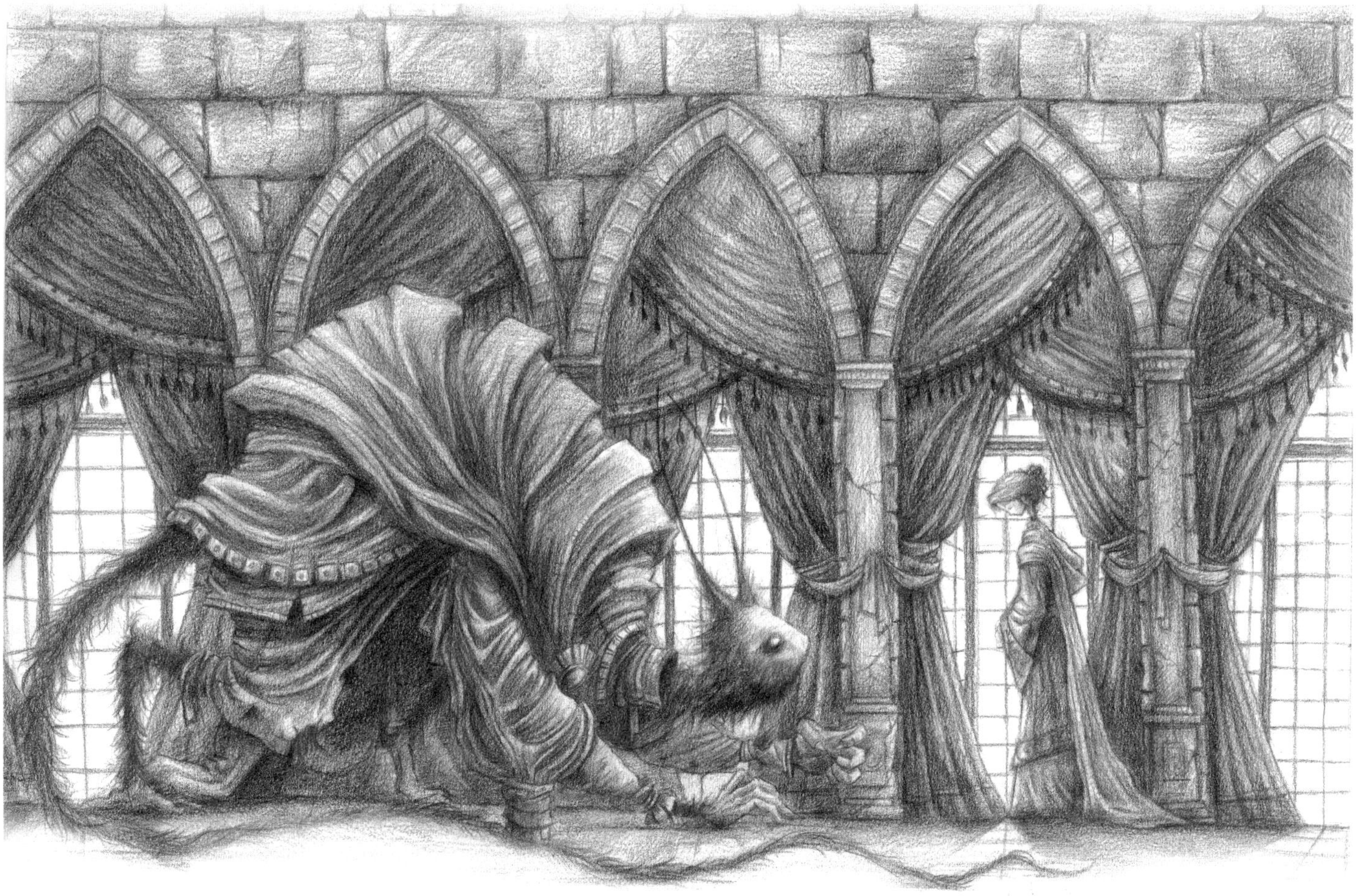

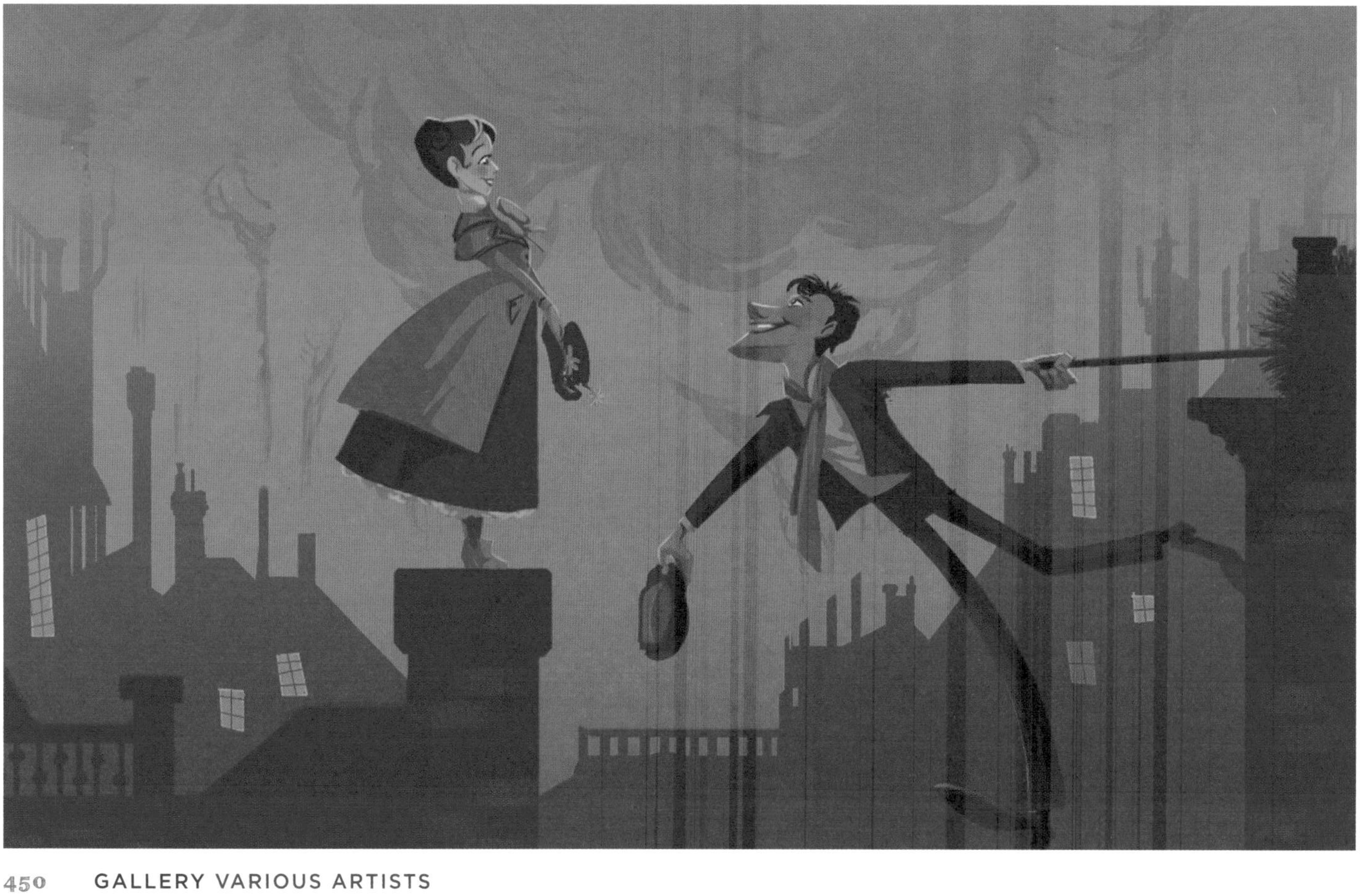

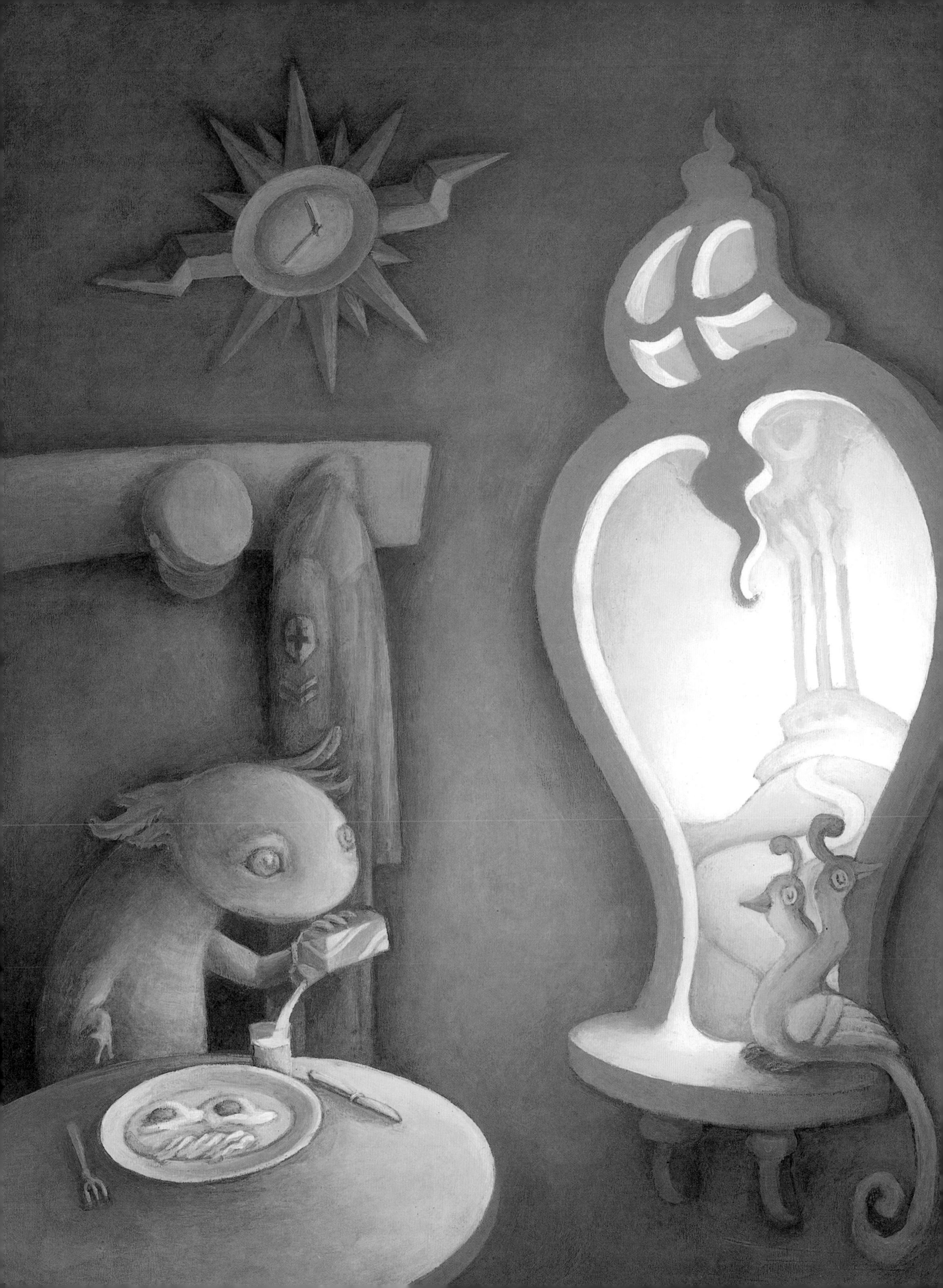

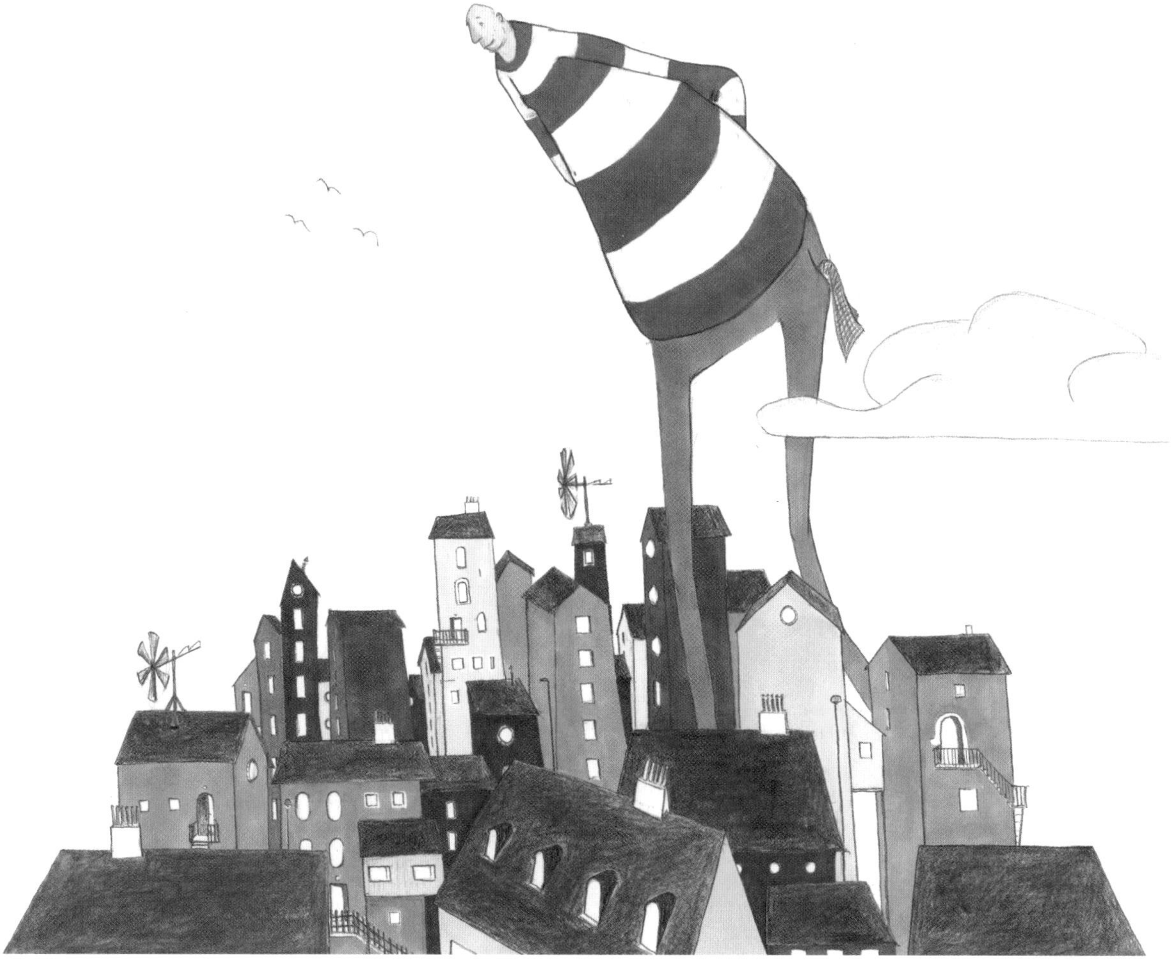

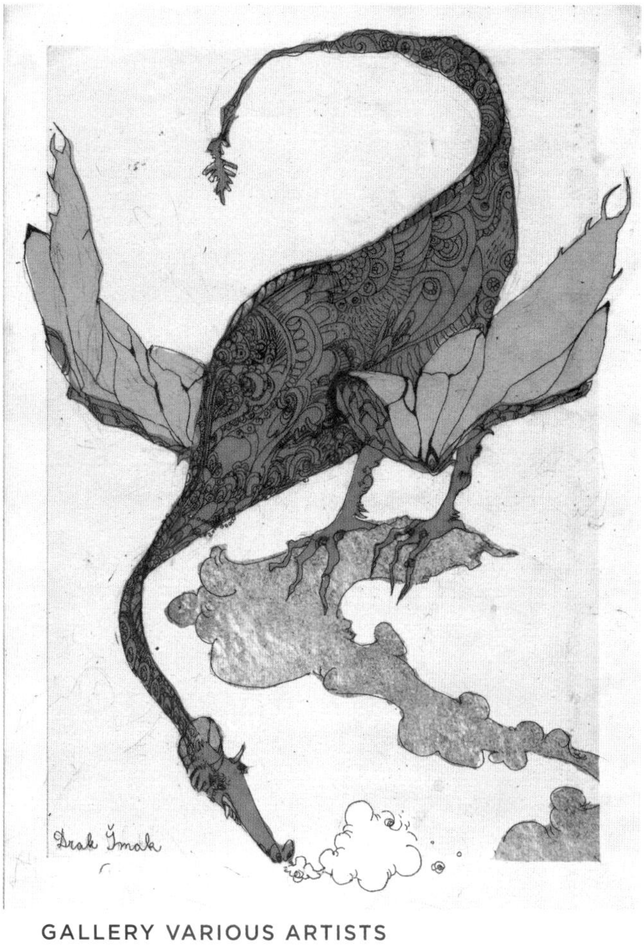
Drak Žmak

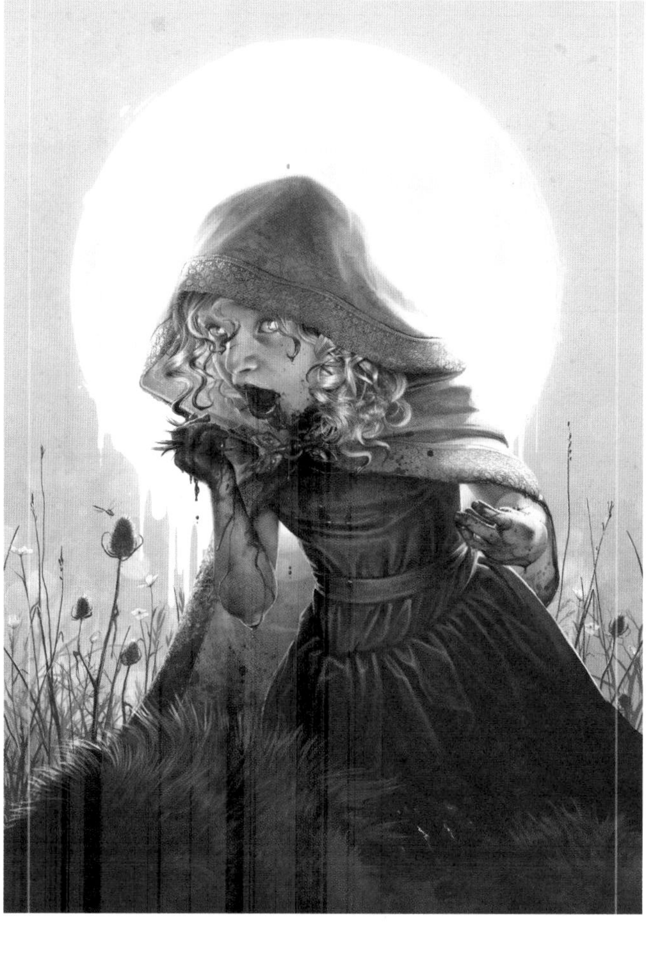

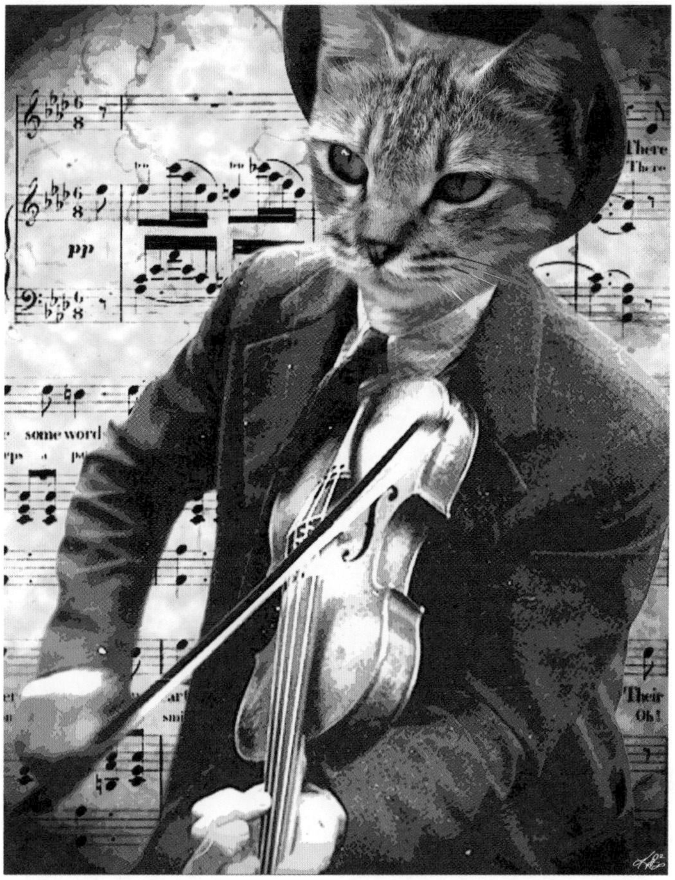
There
some word
Their
Oh!

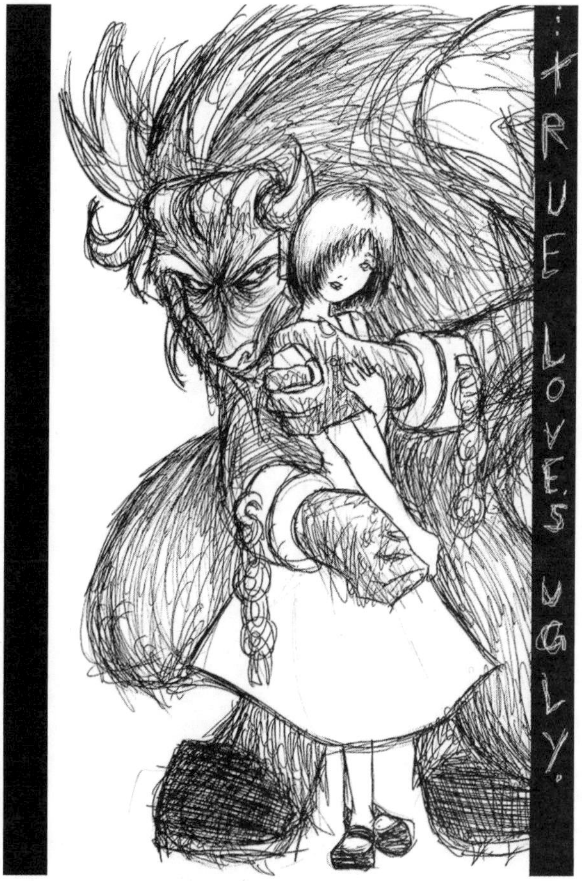
TRUE LOVE'S UGLY.

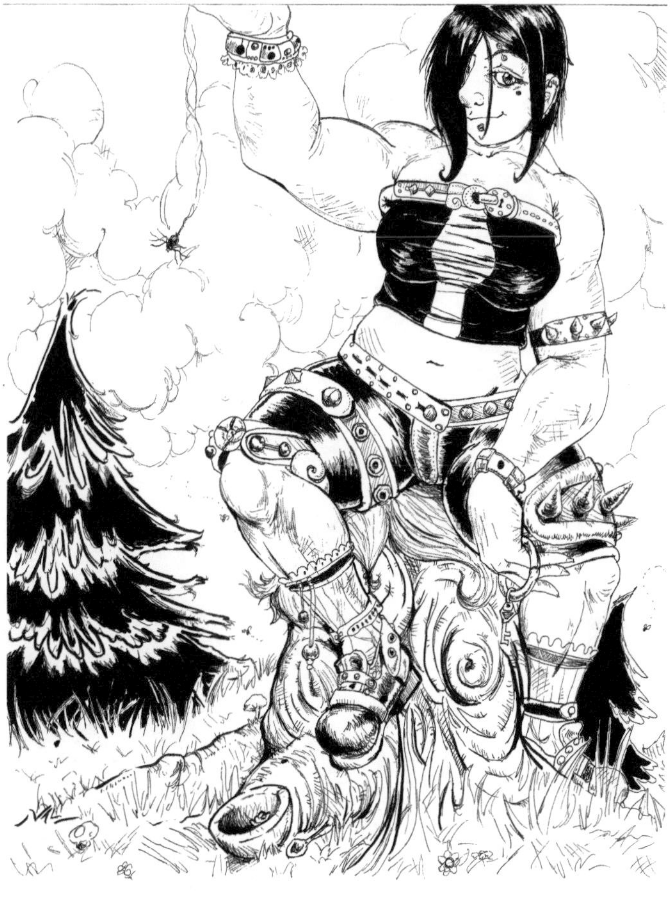

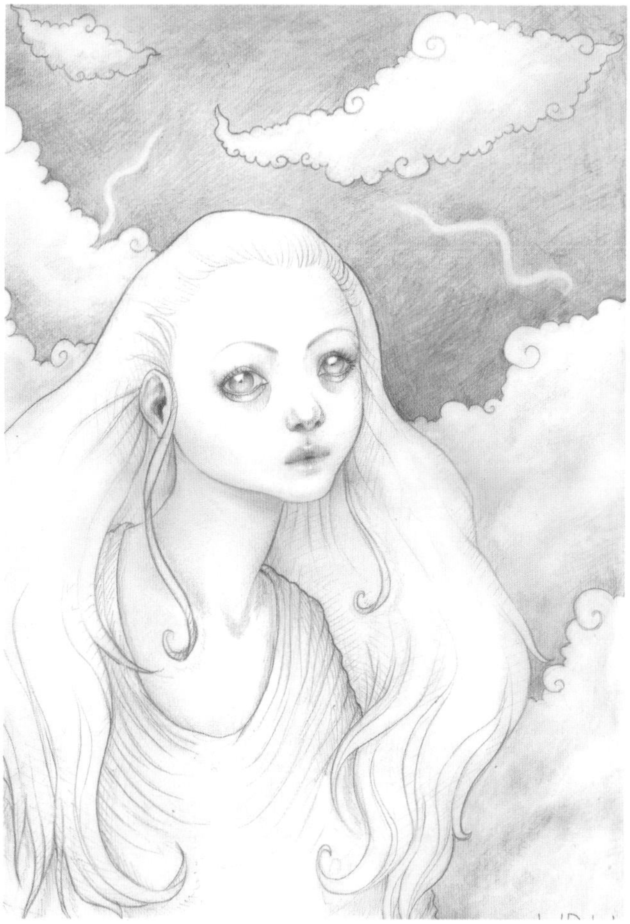

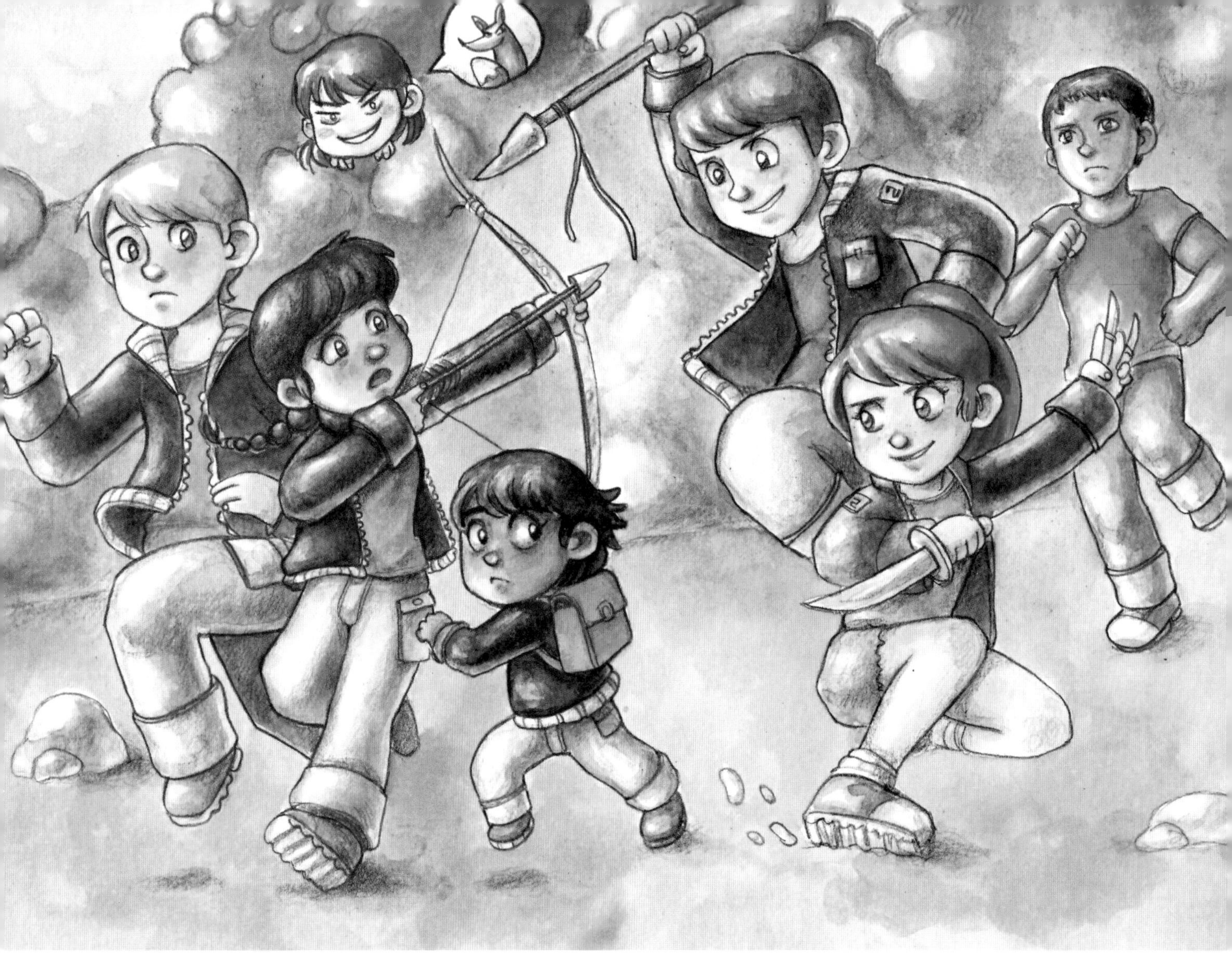

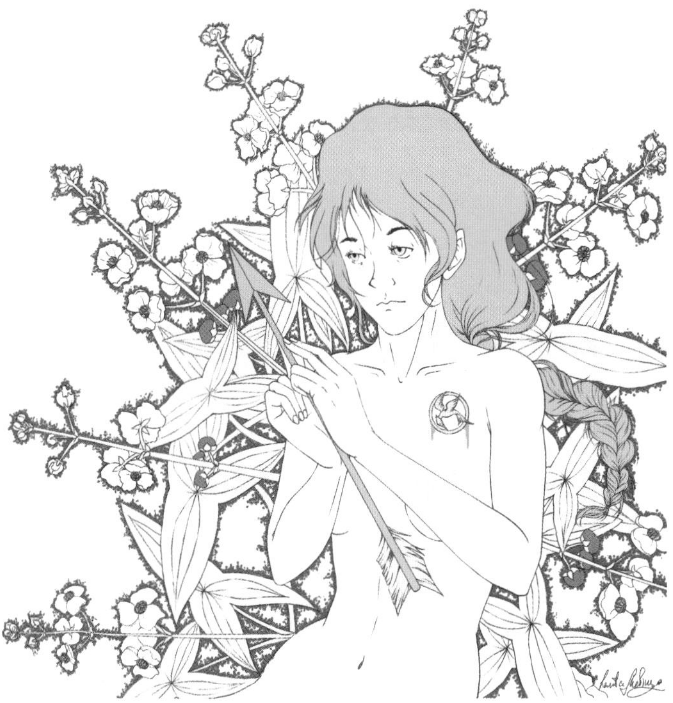

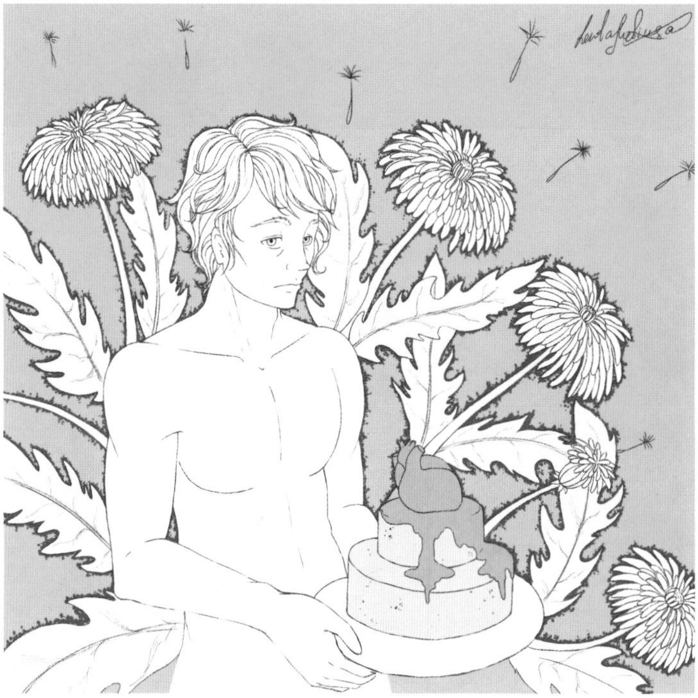

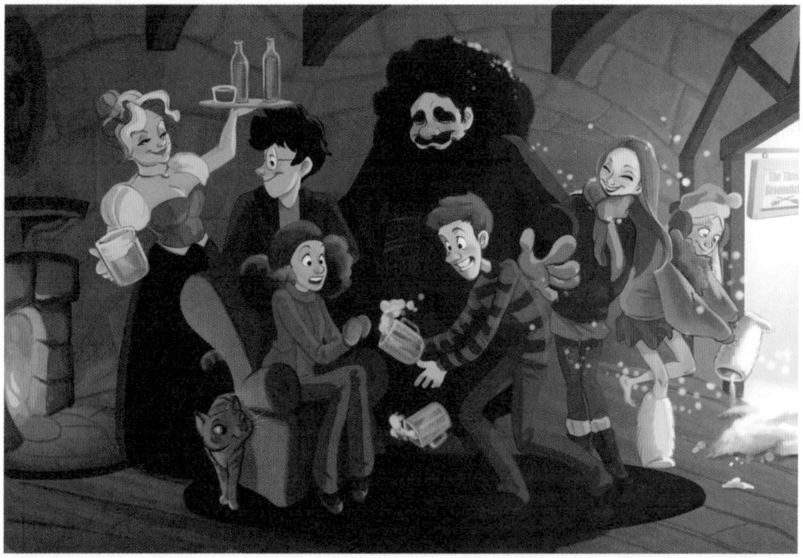

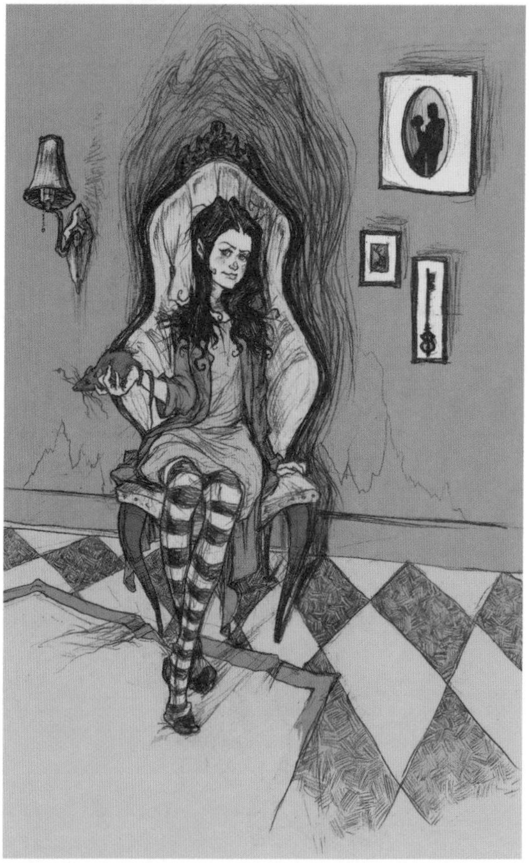

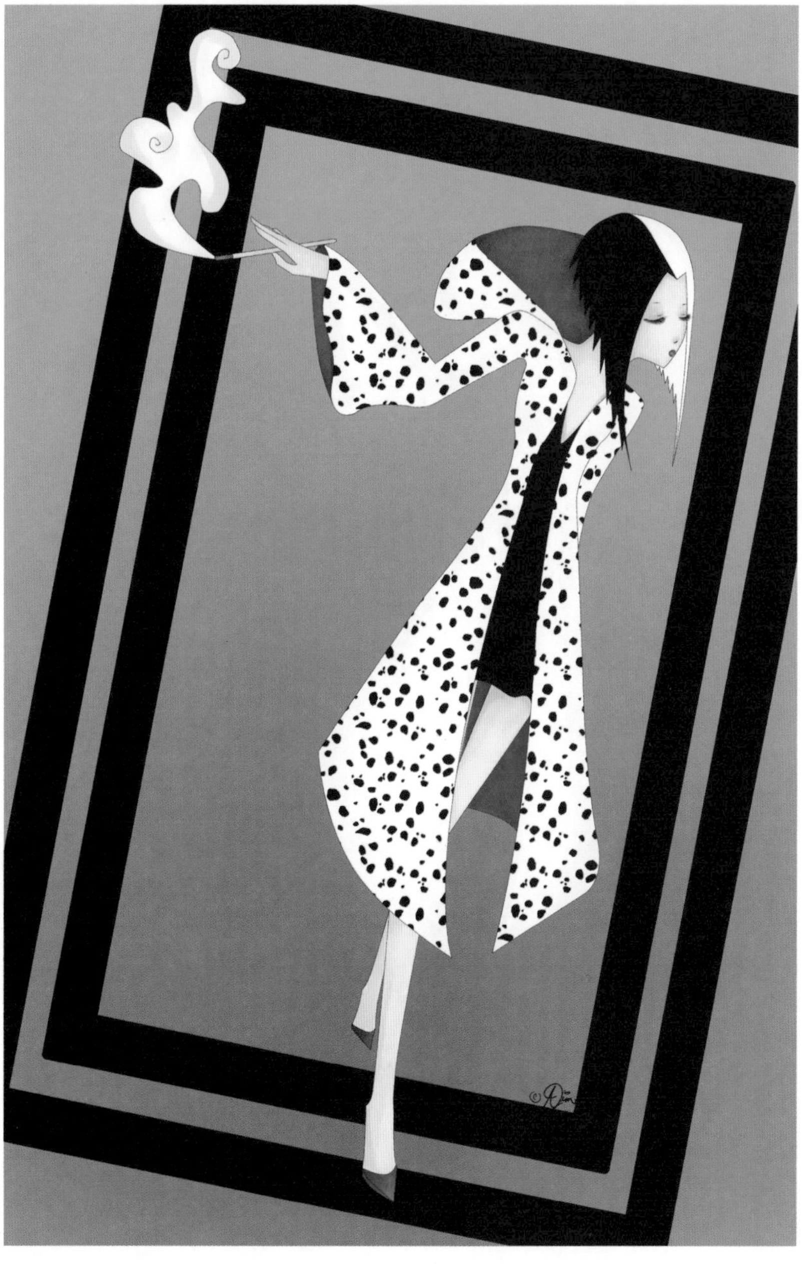

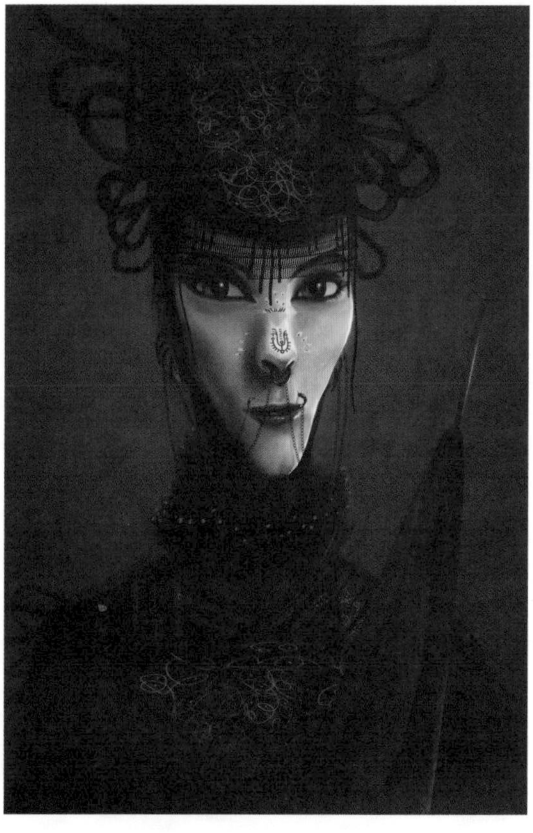

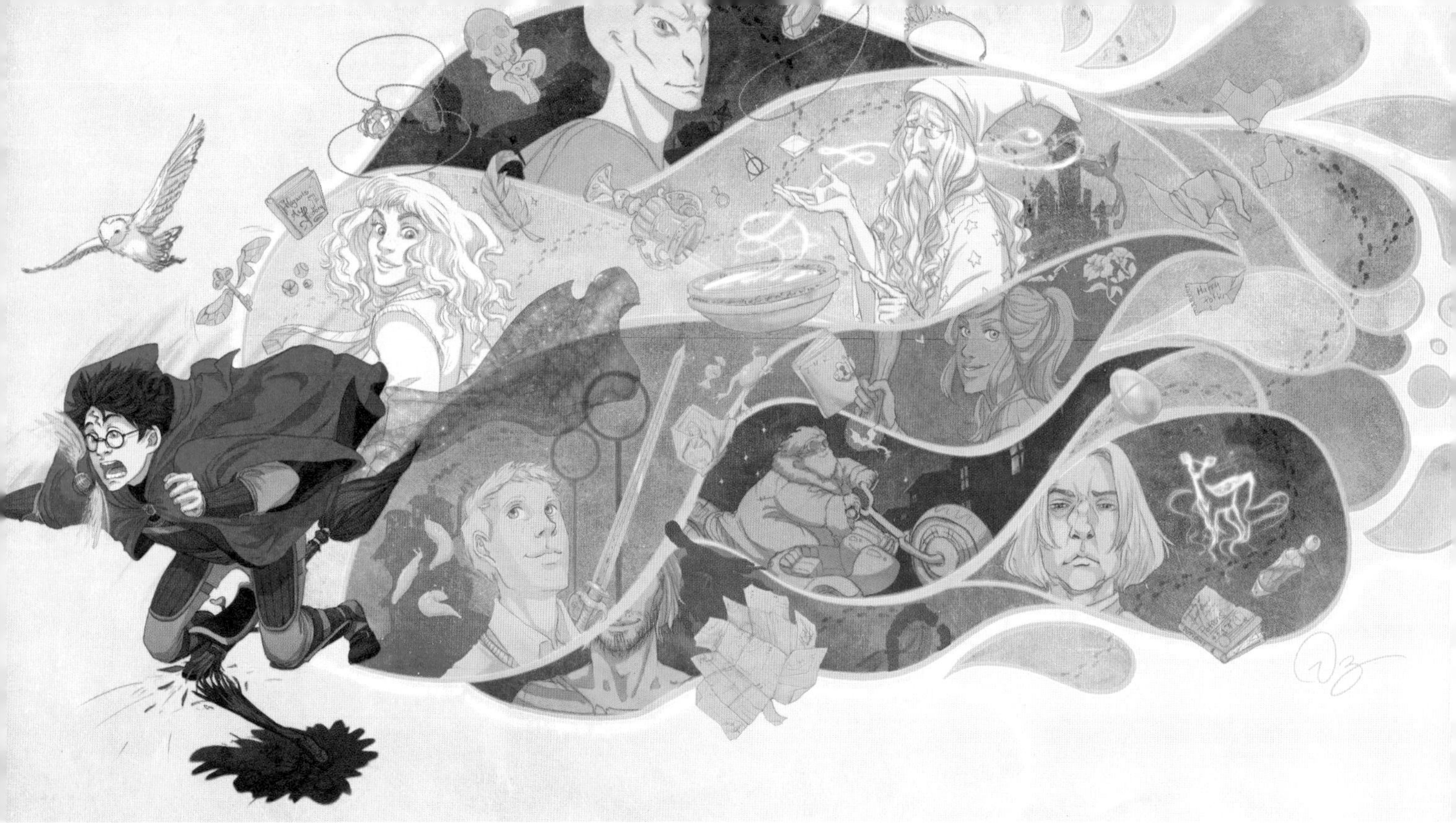

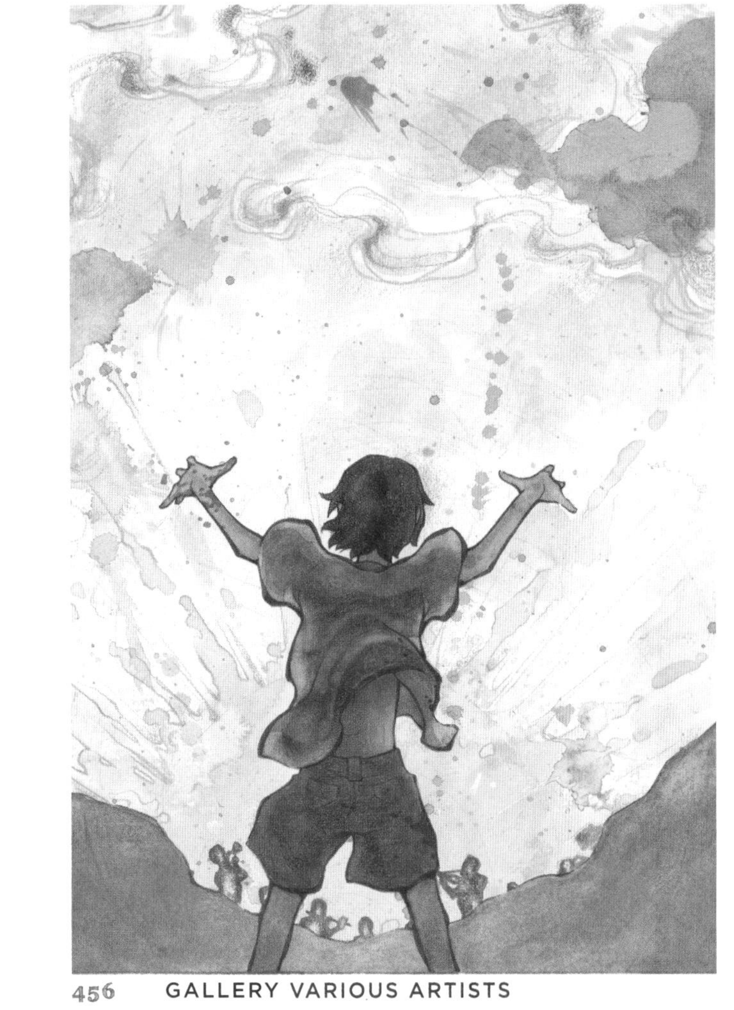

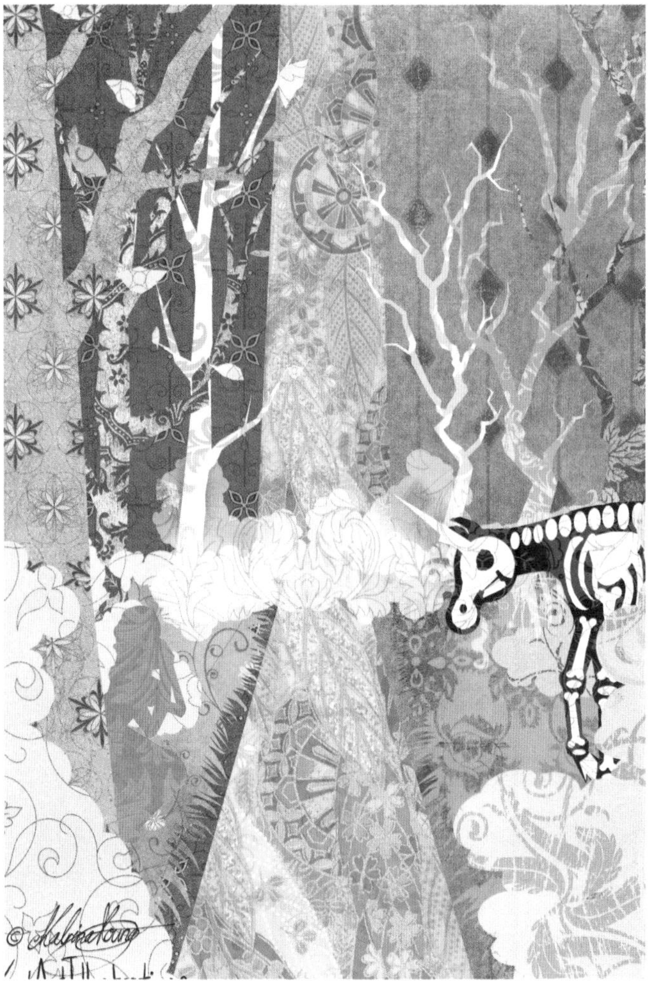

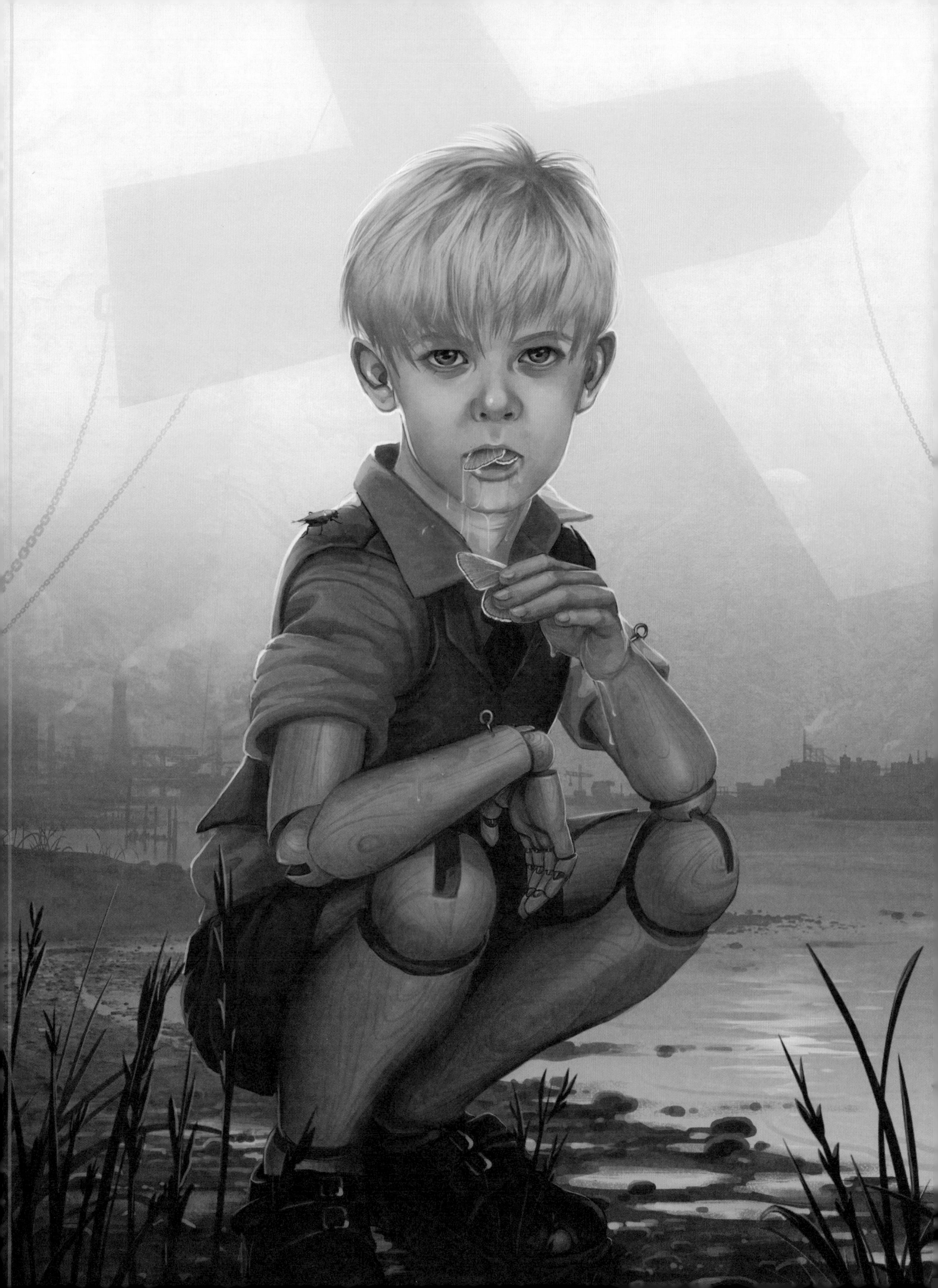

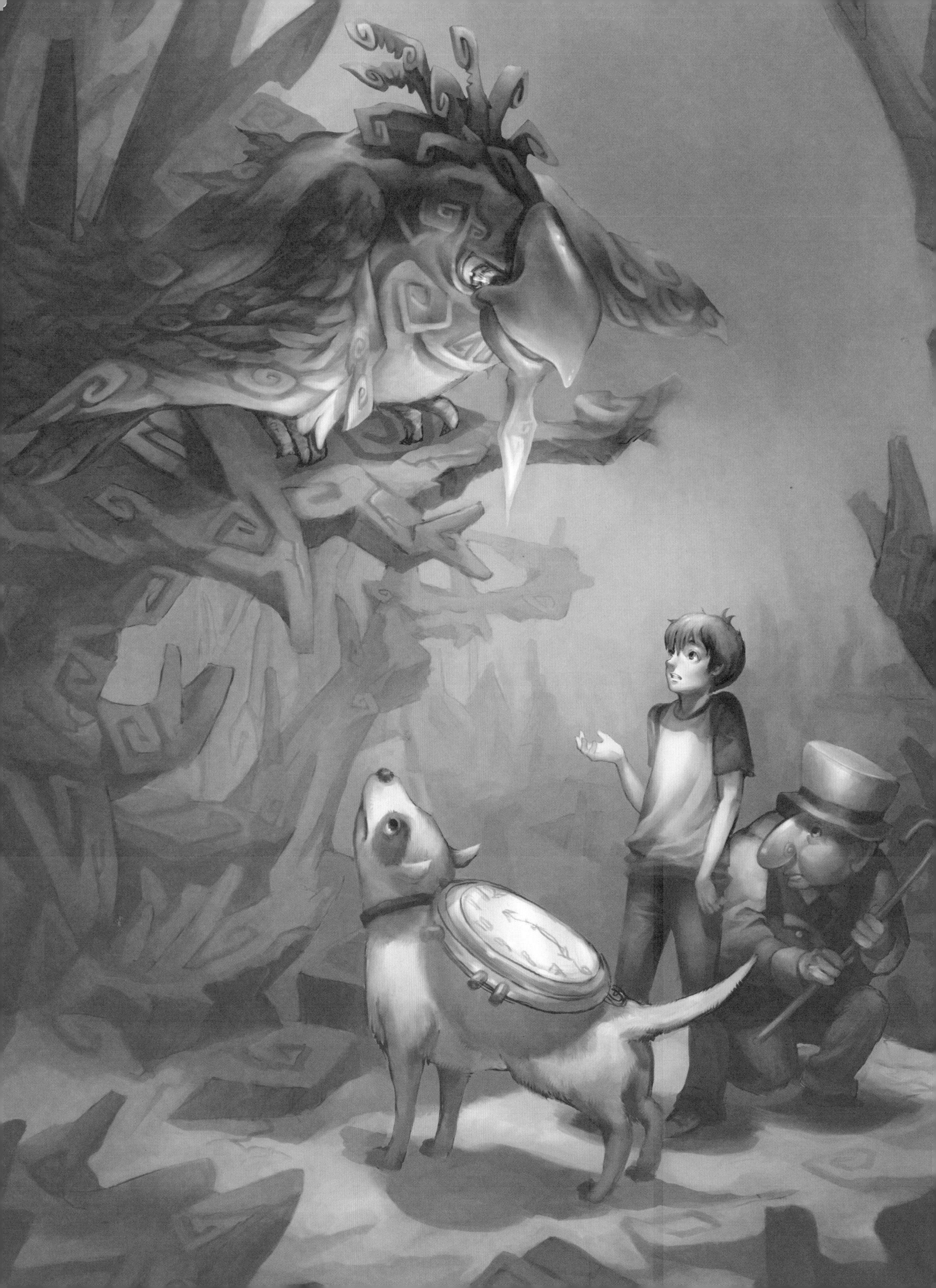

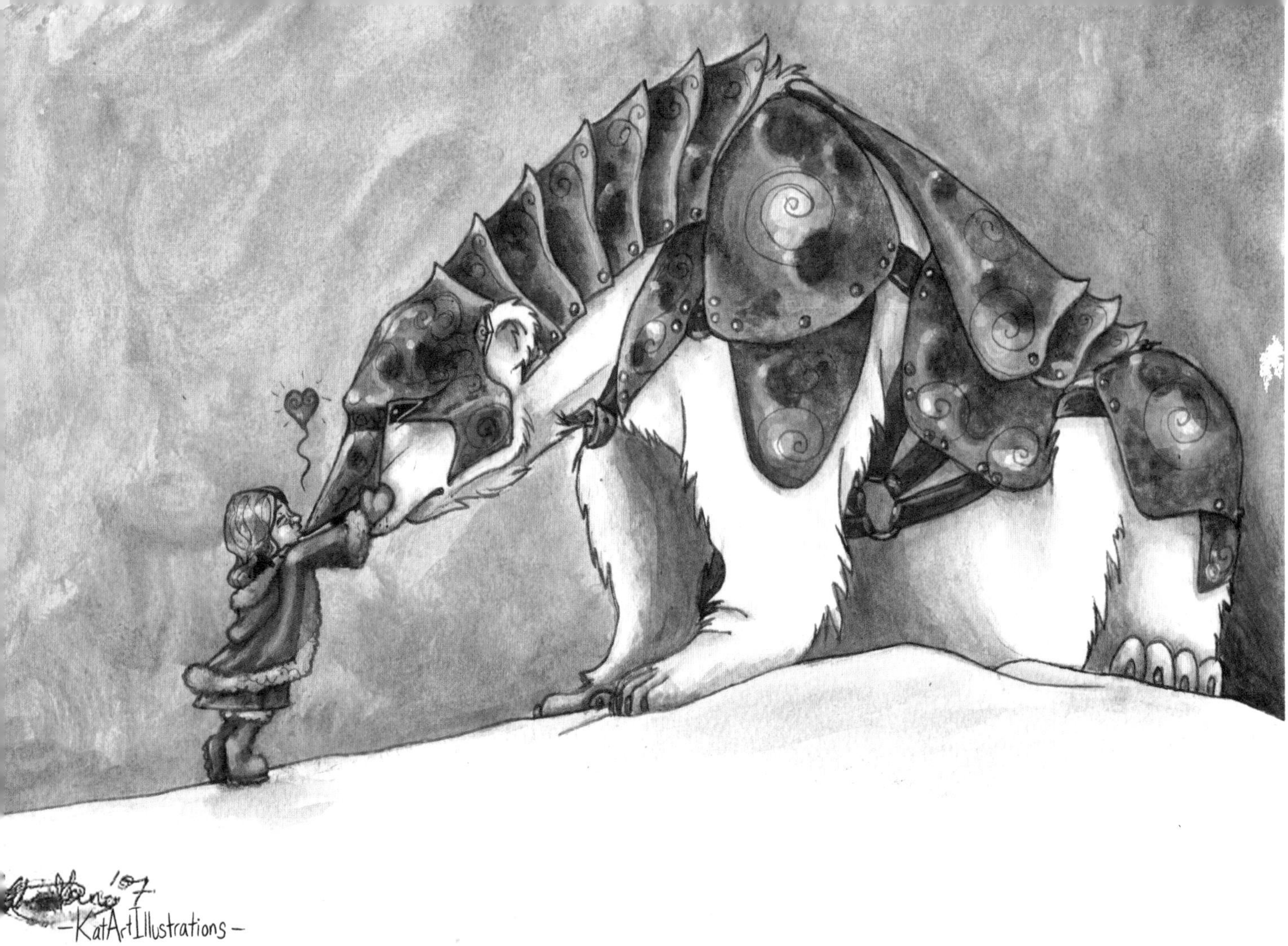
-KatArtIllustrations-

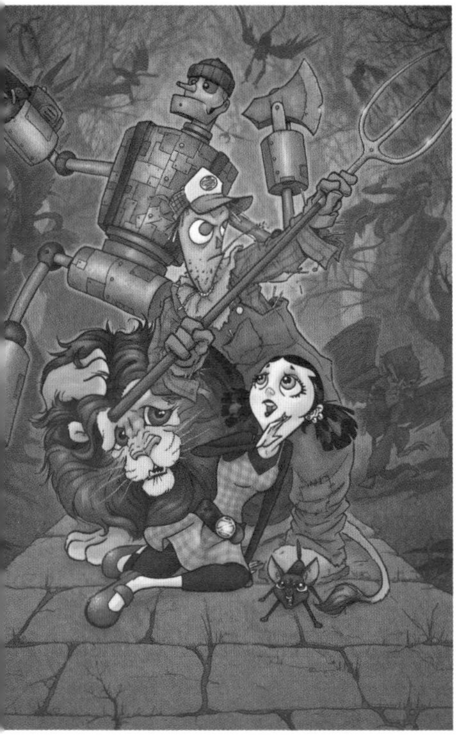

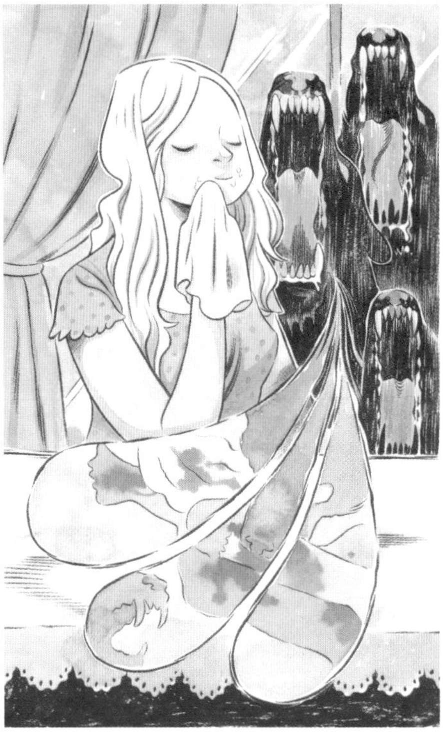

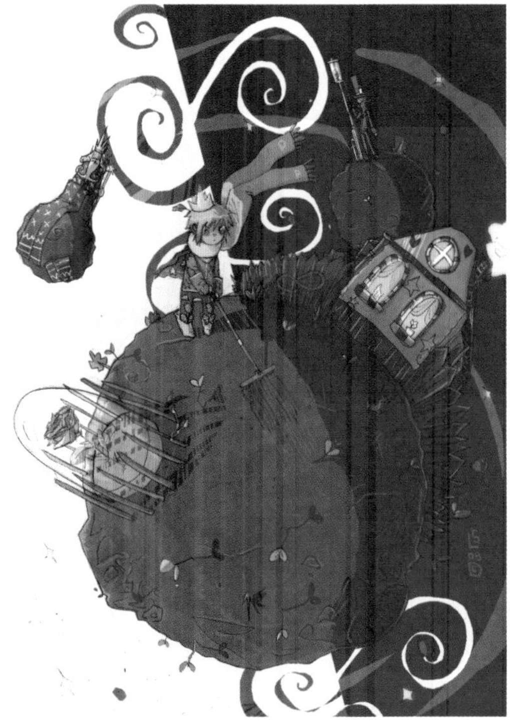

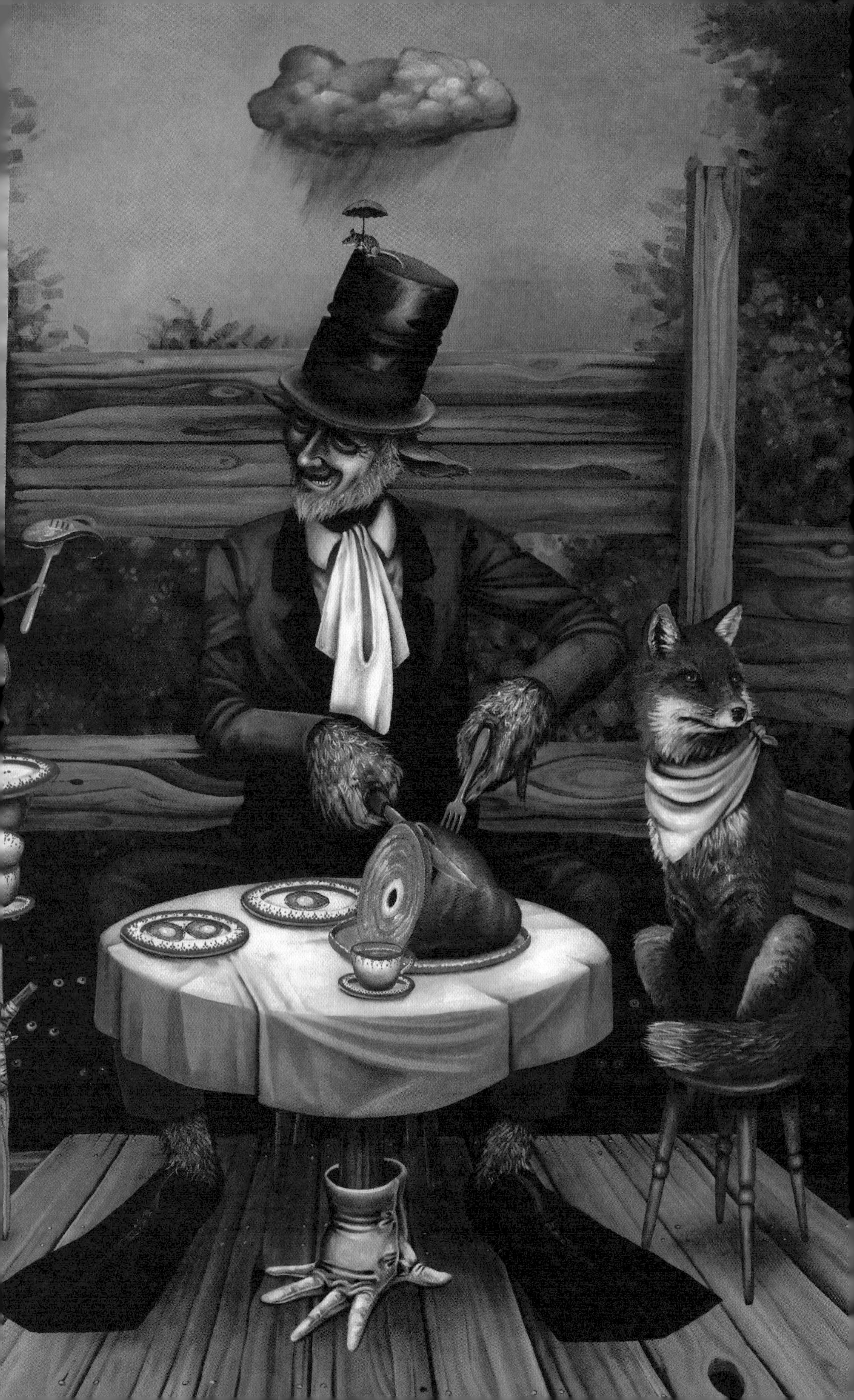

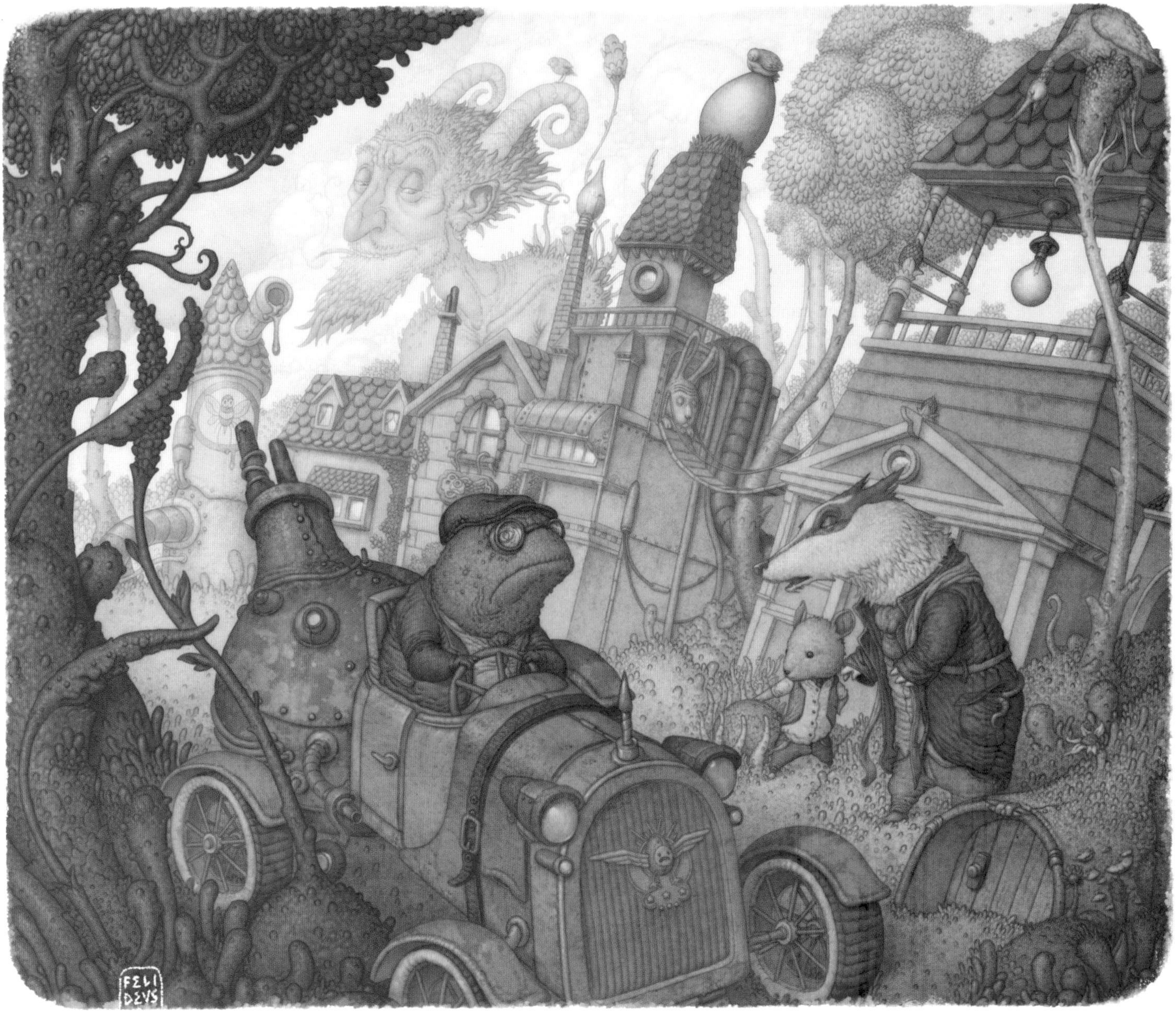
FELI
DEYS

# CONTRIBUTORS

**ANDRICE ARP** makes comics, paintings, illustrations, and small objects in Portland, Oregon. She was a coeditor of the Hi-Horse comic book series, which ran from 2001 to 2004, and the *Hi-Horse Omnibus*, which was published in 2004 by Alternative Comics. Since then, her comics and paintings have appeared semi-regularly in Fantagraphics' quarterly anthology *MOME*, among other places. Her paintings have been in group shows at Giant Robot and other galleries, and in solo shows at Secret Headquarters in Los Angeles and the San Francisco Cartoon Art Museum's Small Press Spotlight. You can see some of her newer work at interlineargloss.tumblr.com.

**RACHAEL BALL** is a cartoonist, illustrator, and art teacher. She produced regular cartoon strips for the iconic comic *Deadline* in the 1990s. Her illustrations and cartoons have also appeared in *The Times*, *Radio Times*, *Marketing Week*, MTV's *An Outbreak of Violets*, *Expresso*, Scholastic Books, and *The Strumpet*. She is currently working on two projects: *Shadows*, a fairy tale graphic novel, and *The Inflatable Woman*, a surreal take on her experiences with breast cancer, which you can follow at rachaelball.tumblr.com/theinflatablewoman.

**LESLEY BARNES** is an animator and illustrator from Glasgow. Her animations have shown in competition at film festivals all over the world and have won a number of awards. Lesley recently expanded into illustration, and her work has since been featured in publications such as *Grafik*, Puffin Books, *Time Out*, *Glamour*, and the *Sunday Times Style Magazine*, and at institutions such as the Victoria & Albert Museum in London. See more at lesleybarnes.co.uk.

**MOLLY BROOKS** is a highly sophisticated disaster machine fueled by green tea and jelly beans. Her illustrations have appeared in the *Village Voice*, *Time Out New York*, the *Nashville Scene*, the *Riverfront Times*, *The Toast*, *BUST* magazine, ESPN social, *Sports Illustrated* online, and others. She spends her spare time watching vintage buddy cop shows and making comics about knitting, hockey, and/or feelings. See more at mollybrooks.com.

**SHAWN CHENG** is an artist and cartoonist working in New York City. He is a member of the comics collective Partyka and a core contributor to the all-ages fantasy anthology *Cartozia Tales*. His comics have appeared in the *SPX Anthology* and *Best American Comics*, and his paintings and prints have been shown at Fredericks & Freiser Gallery in New York, and at the Giant Robot galleries in Los Angeles and San Francisco. Shawn was born in Taiwan and grew up on Long Island. He studied painting and printmaking at Yale University. Shawn currently lives in Astoria, Queens, with his wife and two daughters.

**ERNIE COLÓN** and Sid Jacobson first came together to create the *New York Times*-bestselling *The 9/11 Report: A Graphic Adaptation*. Since then, the pair have collaborated on *After 9/11: America's War on Terror* and *Che: A Graphic Biography*.

**JOHN DALLAIRE**'s first comics gig was as colorist and letterer on the Harvey-nominated *Black Cherry Bombshells* for DC Comics' Zuda imprint. Currently he is working as the colorist on Eric Shanower's *Age of Bronze*, and he draws/tones/letters the weekday comic strip *Zachary Nixon Johnson Adventures* at gocomics.com.

**DAME DARCY** has been known worldwide as a sequential artist for over twenty years. She is a cartoonist, illustrator, writer, fine artist, musician, animator, and filmmaker. Her self-publishing company (books, e-books, and e-cards), fine art (original illustration, paintings, art dolls), press kit, events, music, commissions, video, short film and animation, and all other multimedia can be seen and acquired at DameDarcy.com, where she can be contacted directly.

Using his father Kent Dixon's thoroughly researched rendition of *The Epic of Gilgamesh*, **KEVIN H. DIXON** has converted the world's oldest epic from cuneiform to comix. Kevin is also responsible for the autobiographical series *And Then There Was Rock*, true stories about playing in a crappy loser band. With collaborator Eric Knisley, he produced *Tales of the Sinister Harvey*, *Mickey Death and the Winds of Impotence*, and the Xeric Award–winning *Flavor Contra Comix and Stories*. His latest non-Gilgamesh project is *Mkele Mbembe*, which has nothing to do with the legendary modern-day dinosaur of Kenya. You can contact him at ultrakevin@hotmail.com.

**MAËLLE DOLIVEUX** is a French and Swiss illustrator who has lived all over the world, from New Jersey to New Zealand. She obtained a bachelor's degree in architecture from the University of Nottingham in 2008, and graduated from the Illustration as Visual Essay master of fine arts program at the School of Visual Arts in 2013. She is very honored to have received a silver medal from the Society of Illustrators for her work in this book. She has also been given recognition from the Art Director's Club, *American Illustration*, and *CMYK* magazine among others, and has worked for clients such as the *New York Times*, *Newsweek*, Motorola, Moleskine, and *Sesame Street*. In her perpetually diminishing free time, she enjoys performing improv, walking her dog, and messing around with animation. Her work is viewable online at maelledoliveux.com, and she is always happy to get an email at maelle@maelledoliveux.com.

**KATE EAGLE** studied illustration at the University of the Arts in Philadelphia, where she currently still lives. She's worked on a range of different projects from comics to store display. There's nothing she enjoys more in her life than seeing a happy dog. See more of her work at kateeagledraws.com.

**LISA FARY** is the founder and editor of PinkRaygun.com, where she's been writing about pop culture, politics, and fashion since 2007. She won the Abbey Hill Literary Short Fiction contest for her story "Dead Women Don't Throw Parties" and earned an honorable mention in the Garden State

Horror Writers 16th Annual Short Story Contest for "Bruja-ha." Fary cocreated and wrote the comic *Intergalactic Law* and currently writes the weekday comic strip *Zachary Nixon Johnson Adventures* for Go Comics.

**C. FRAKES** is a Xeric and Ignatz Award–winning cartoonist. She lives in Seattle and works in a library. See more at tragicrelief.com.

**CHANDRA FREE** is the writer and illustrator of the graphic novel series *The God Machine*. Born in Orlando, Florida, Chandra now resides in Brooklyn, New York, where she concocts her uniquely abstract and elongated art and comics. Intensely interested in the incorporation of psychology in her art, she focuses on the unconscious and human aspects of her characters. She is the art director at BLAM! Ventures; an illustrator on books like *Fraggle Rock*, *Conspiracy of the Planet of the Apes*, and *The Graphic Canon*; and the colorist for *Mice Templar* and *Sullengrey*.

**RICK GEARY** has been a freelance cartoonist and illustrator for around forty years. His illustrations and graphic stories have appeared in *National Lampoon*, *MAD*, the *New York Times*, *Heavy Metal*, *Disney Adventures*, and many other publications. He has written and illustrated five children's books. His graphic novels include the biographies *J. Edgar Hoover* and *Trotsky*, as well as nine volumes in the series *A Treasury of Victorian Murder* and four volumes in *A Treasury of 20th Century Murder*, the latest

of which is *The Lives of Sacco & Vanzetti*. In 2007, after thirty years in San Diego, Rick and his wife Deborah moved to Carrizozo, New Mexico. See his more of his work at rickgeary.com.

**KATE GLASHEEN** graduated from Pratt Institute in 2004, earning a bachelor of fine arts. Kate's artistic interests find communion in fine and sequential art under the notion that there's something hilarious about something that's not funny at all. Glasheen has been the artist for several critically acclaimed books, including *The Graphic Canon*, Volume 3, the full-length graphic novel *Hybrid Bastards!* (with writer Tom Pinchuk), and her own passion project, the Kickstarter-funded *Bandage: A Diary of Sorts*. Kate's commercial clients include Paramount Pictures, Lucasfilm Ltd., NBC, and AMC. Glasheen's gallery work has been exhibited throughout the country.

**SANYA GLISIC** is a Chicago-based artist and illustrator, working primarily in the fields of printmaking and drawing. She is originally from Bosnia. She has illustrated for Penguin Books, Seven Stories Press, Black Candy Records, Rotland Press, *Newcity*, and the *Chicago Reader*. Her work has been included in exhibitions at Whitdel Arts in Detroit and Rubin Museum of Art in New York. She teaches illustration and printmaking at Columbia College Chicago, as well as at Spudnik Press and Chicago Printmakers Collaborative. More of her work can be found at sanyaglisic.com.

**ISABEL GREENBERG** is a London-based comics artist and illustrator. She graduated in 2010 from the University of Brighton and has since produced work for a variety of clients and publications, including the *Guardian*, the National Trust, Nobrow Press, *Wrap Magazine*, Seven Stories Press, and the V & A. In 2011, she won the Observer/Jonathan Cape/Comica Graphic Short Story Prize. Shortly after, she began work on her first graphic novel, *The Encyclopedia of Early Earth*, which was published in autumn 2013 by Jonathan Cape, and was simultaneously released in the US, Canada, and Germany.

**ROBERTA GREGORY** has been creating her unique comics since the 1970s, with appearances in "undergrounds" like *Wimmen's Comix* and her own *Dynamite Damsels*. She was in almost all the issues of *Gay Comix* in the 1980s, and during the 1990s, she produced forty issues (and many collections) of her Fantagraphics solo title, *Naughty Bits*. Her Bitchy Bitch character has been translated into several languages and appeared in a weekly strip, live theater productions, and an animated cable television series. Roberta also created the *Winging It* graphic novel, *Sheila and the Unicorn*, and *Artistic Licentiousness*, and has appeared in many anthologies, including *The Graphic Canon*. She is currently working on a Bitchy graphic novel and the *Mother Mountain* series, and recently published her *Follow Your Art* book of travel comics and *True Cat Toons*, true cat comics. To keep up with her latest work, visit robertagregory.com and truecattoons.com.

**FRANK M. HANSEN** is a cartoonist, artist, and writer living in Los Angeles. He creates original cartoons for various print and digital publications around the globe in addition to creating designs for the clothing and animation industries. He is currently working to bring sound and motion to his cartoons in what he hopes is a fresh and new way, and posting satirical cartoons at AnimaticPress.com. To quench his desire to merge design and expression further, he creates ink and paint pieces, which have been shown at several galleries, including Gallery Nucleus, WMA Gallery, and the Red Gate Gallery in London. You can see more of his work at fmhansen.com.

**KATHERINE HEARST** is an illustrator and artist based in London, with a body of work ranging from illustrated stories to figurative painting. Since her childhood was spent in Moscow, Russian storytelling has exerted a powerful influence over her work. Her subjects are taken primarily from folklore or children's literature. She wants to bring these timeless stories into the context of modern-day Russia.

**MATTHEW HOUSTON** is an illustrator and character designer from Arizona who loves all things fancy, colorful, stylish, scary, heroic, villainous, curious, and cool.

**SID JACOBSON** and Ernie Colón first came together to create the *New York Times*–bestselling *The 9/11 Report: A Graphic Adaptation*. Since then, the pair have collaborated on *After 9/11: America's War on Terror* and *Che: A Graphic Biography*.

**SANDY JIMENEZ**, born in 1968, is an American comic book artist and filmmaker based in New York City. He has produced scores of varied and original illustrated stories since graduating from the Cooper Union in 1990, and he is best known for creating the independent comic book series *Marley Davidson* and the long-running and critically acclaimed "Shit House Poet" stories for *World War 3 Illustrated*.

**JULIACKS** makes worlds with comics, performance-installations, film, and theater. She is published in independent magazines and anthologies internationally, and in 2009, Sparkplug Comics published her collaborative comic book, *Rock That Never Sleeps*. While in Finland on a Fulbright grant for performance art, she made the comic art book and film *Invisible Forces*, which was taken on a mini-world tour. Her graphic novel *Swell* premiered as a play at Culture Project's Women Center Stage Festival in March 2012 in New York. Living in France, she's undertaking a new film, performance, and comics project: *Architecture of an Atom*, which has been published, screened, and performed at the Moderna Museum of Malmö, the Kiasma Museum of Art with the Helsinki Comics Festival, the Crack Comics Festival in Rome, and in other contexts in France, Canada, Denmark, and Portugal. The premiere of the comic book and feature film will be in January 2015 at the Moderna Museum in Sweden.

**KEREN KATZ** is the illustrating half of the Katz Sisters Duo. She is also the half that is not fictitious. She is a graduate of the Illustration as Visual Essay master of fine arts program at the School of Visual Arts, New York, and the Bezalel Academy of Art and Design, Jerusalem. She is always writing and drawing her next graphic novel—eight so far and counting. . . .

**ERIC KNISLEY** was born in 1961 in Asheville, North Carolina, began drawing comics shortly thereafter, and has continued without a break up to the present time. In addition to comics, he has designed scores of T-shirts, record covers, websites, and more, and has worked as an animator, photographer, voice-over guy, virtual-reality guru, videographer, musician, and sandwich artist. Most recently he helped to organize the Durham Indie Comics Expo (DICE) in Durham, North Carolina. Currently he works in a science museum and draws things.

**LUCY KNISLEY** is the author/artist for a number of graphic novels, including her most recent, the bestselling *Relish: My Life in the Kitchen*. She has published in a variety of magazines, papers, trades, and collections, and continues to churn out comics from her home in Chicago, where she also teaches comics workshops and camps to kids and adults.

**JOY KOLITSKY** is a freelance illustrator and storyboard artist. She also has a small greeting-card company called Sugar Beet Press, which features her artwork. She started making comics after college at the encouragement of comic-loving friends and has continued to enjoy doing so to this day. After many years in Los Angeles and New York, she now lives by the beach with her husband and son in Ocean City, New Jersey.

**PETER KUPER**'s illustrations and comics have appeared in magazines around the world, including *Time*, the *New York Times*, and *MAD*, where he has written and illustrated "Spy vs. Spy" in every issue since 1997. He is the cofounder of *World War 3 Illustrated*, a political comix magazine, and has remained on its editorial board since 1979. He has produced over two dozen books including *The System*, *Stop Forgetting to Remember*, and *Sticks and Stones*, which won the Society of Illustrators' gold medal. Peter has also adapted Upton Sinclair's *The Jungle* and many of Franz Kafka's works into comics, including *The Metamorphosis*, which is used in high school and college curriculums in the US and abroad. Peter lived in Oaxaca, Mexico, from July 2006 to 2008 during a major teachers' strike, and his work from that time can be seen in his book *Diario de Oaxaca*, published by PM Press, along with *Drawn to New York*, an illustrated chronicle of his three decades in New York City. He has been teaching comics courses at the School of Visual Arts for twenty-five years and is a visiting professor at Harvard University.

After failing as a medical illustrator, **SALLY MADDEN** turned to comic book illustration in 2005, the same year she cofounded the discontinued but still financially exhausting anthology *Always Comix*. A member of the Partyka Collective, she is working on a series of folktale adaptations with fellow member Matt Wiegle. She is supposedly illustrating a book of the Catholic saints with Marvel science-fiction writer Charlie H. Swift, who has been researching the book for over two decades with no end in sight. She has done cartooning work for Wide Awake Press and the online music magazine *If You Make It*. She lives in the city of her birth, Philadelphia, with her husband and no children.

**TORI CHRISTINA MCKENNA** first brought Euripides' *Medea* to life in place of a final paper for a Greek tragedy class at Beloit College. She graduated from there in 2006 with a bachelor's degree in both Classical Civilizations and Ecology, Evolution, & Behavioral Biology. After graduation she decided to pursue her love of art and furthered her education at both the Massachusetts College of Art and Design and the Center for Digital Imaging Arts at Boston University. She is well-versed in a wide variety of art forms in both digital and traditional art, from 3D modeling and animation, to costume and prop creation, to illustration and sequential art. She brings her love of biology and classics to all of her artistic endeavors. See more at coolbyproxyproductions.com.

**MIGUEL MOLINA**, a multifaceted Peruvian artist, was trained at the Escuela Nacional de Bellas Artes in Peru. His talent extends to various mediums of expression, such as ceramics, sculpture, mural and easel painting, as well as traditional Andean music. His body of work as an illustrator has been printed in numerous collections of books, stories, CD covers, posters, and more. He created the illustrations for the CD cover of *Serenata Inkaterra*, which was nominated for a Grammy in 2007 for cover design, and for the poster for the movie *The Power of Food*, which won Best Documentary in the Hollywood International Family Film Festival in 2011. Molina came to the United States in February 2008, signed on by Disney to perform in a musical revue of native dances in Orlando, Florida. He currently lives in Arizona, where Obsidian Gallery held an exhibition of his watercolor pieces in 2013.

There's some dude named **VICKI NERINO**. She grew up in northwestern Ontario among the cow pies, moose tracks, and bear logs, where she used to have farting contests with her father while her mother avoided them. Vicki makes weird comics about animals boinking and floppy boobies and awkward dates and stuff like that. She also draws and paints old people and naked stuff and that kind of thing. You probably shouldn't visit her website, vickinerino.com.

**BILLY NUNEZ** was born in the Dominican Republic and moved to the United States at the age of seven. His work as an illustrator and designer can be seen on his website, biz20.biz.

**MOLLY COLLEEN O'CONNELL** is an artist and curator based in Baltimore, Maryland. See her work at poetyunlimited.tumblr.com.

**EMELIE ÖSTERGREN**, born in 1982, was educated at Konstfack in Stockholm, where she received her bachelor's degree in 2007. Her comics and illustrations have been published in books, anthologies, comics, magazines, and fanzines both in Sweden and abroad. With a style that can be described as avant garde and experimental with elements of fantasy and surrealism, she has developed a mannerism that is quite unique. She is known for

her books *Evil Dress* and *Duke and His Army: A Dream Revisited*, published by Sanatorium Press. See more at emelieostergren.se.

**CAROLINE PICARD** is a Chicago-based artist, writer, and curator. Recent comics can be found in *Tender Journal*, *Projecttile*, *Diner Journal*, *Everyday Genius*, and *Bicycle Review*. Her new graphic novel, *The Chronicles of Fortune*, will be released in 2015 via Radiator Comics.

**JOHN W. PIERARD** works six months out of the year for the New York City Department of Parks and Recreation, where he 1) casts his steely gaze over the forest, looking for arsonists from a high tower, 2) picks up trash left by thoughtless proles, and 3) makes sure that tourists don't feed the owls. Owls are vicious and can turn on you in a New York second. DO NOT FEED THE OWLS. He lives in a two-room shotgun shack he built from plywood and some bits of old aluminum sheets he found out in the woods of Inwood Hill Park, where he works and lives with a bunch of mangy dogs. Doesn't talk much. Just spends the cold winter nights contemplating the meaning of existence and maintaining his smoky kerosene generator so that he can watch (and rewatch, endlessly) his stack of VHS copies of Tom Snyder's *The Tomorrow Show* and drawing pictures. In the off-season, he goes into town to recklessly spend his accumulated wages, drinking and whoring.

**TARA SEIBEL** is an alternative cartoonist, graphic designer, and illustrator from Cleveland, Ohio, who is best known for her collaborations with underground comix writer Harvey Pekar. Her work has been published in Chicago's *Newcity*, the *Austin Chronicle*, *Cleveland Scene*, *Juxtapoz Art & Culture Magazine*, the *New York Times*, and the *Los Angeles Times*, among other publications. After receiving a bachelor of fine arts degree from Edinboro University of Pennsylvania, Seibel illustrated restaurant menus and food packaging, then later worked as a line designer and illustrator for American Greetings before becoming a freelance editorial cartoonist. Seibel has taught illustration courses at Ursuline College in Cleveland. She lives with her husband Aaron, three children, and pets in Pepper Pike, Ohio.

**R. SIKORYAK** is the author of *Masterpiece Comics* (Drawn & Quarterly). He's drawn for the *New York Times*, the *Onion*, the *New Yorker*, *MAD*, and *SpongeBob Comics*, among many other publications, as well as the TV series *The Daily Show with Jon Stewart*, *Saturday Night Live*, and *Ugly Americans*. His comics have appeared in the anthologies *RAW*, *Drawn & Quarterly*, *The Graphic Canon*, and *An Anthology of Graphic Fiction, Cartoons, and True Stories*. He hosts the live cartoon slideshow series Carousel and has taught at the Center for Cartoon Studies and in the illustration department of Parsons The New School for Design. For more info, see rsikoryak.com and carouselslideshow.com.

**DASHA TOLSTIKOVA** is an illustrator, who just recently became an American. She now lives in Brooklyn. Her clients include the *New Yorker*, the *New York Times*, the *Wall Street Journal*, *Moscow News*, Rachel Antonoff, and Enchanted Lion Books.

The coeditor of African-American Classics, **LANCE TOOKS** began his career as a Marvel Comics assistant editor. He has worked as an animator on 100+ television commercials, films, and music videos; self-published the comics *Danger Funnies*, *Divided by Infinity*, and *Muthafucka*; and illustrated *The Black Panthers for Beginners*, written by Herb Boyd. His stories have appeared in Graphic Classics volumes of Edgar Allan Poe, Ambrose Bierce, Mark Twain, and Robert Louis Stevenson, and he collaborated with Harvey Pekar on *The Beats: A Graphic History* and *Studs Terkel's Working*. Tooks's first graphic novel, *Narcissa*, was named one of the year's best books by *Publishers Weekly*, and his four-volume *Lucifer's Garden of Verses* series for NBM Comics Lit won two Glyph Comic Awards. Lance moved from his native New York to Madrid, Spain, where he's hard at work on a new and very original graphic novel. See more at lancetooksjournal.blogspot.com.

**DAVID W. TRIPP**, born in 1971, lived in Maine the first half of his life, where he worked developing his artistic skills in the quiet, rustic environment that only Maine can give. In 2001, he moved to Philadelphia and attended the Pennsylvania Academy of the Fine Arts, where he received his undergraduate certificate and master of fine arts degree. His work can be seen in gallery exhibits and private collections around the world, as well as in numerous publications like *The Graphic Canon*, Volume 2, *Steampunk Originals*, Volume 1, and the ongoing Alice in Wonderland art project "What is the Use of a Book Without Pictures?," to name a just a few. You can see more of his art at davidwtripp.com.

**ANDREA TSURUMI** is a New York–based illustrator and cartoonist who likes history, absurdity, and monsters, in no particular order. She was included in the 2013 *Best American Comics* notables list, and her comic *Andrew Jackson Throws a Punch* won a MoCCA Award of Excellence. Her work has appeared in the *New York Times*, the *Boston Globe*, *Oh Comely*, and the *Brooklyn Rail*, among other places. After graduating with a master of fine arts degree in illustration from the School of Visual Arts, she now makes comics and picture books in Brooklyn. You can see her work at andreatsurumi.com.

**NOAH VAN SCIVER** was born in 1984 in New Jersey. He first came to readers' attention with his comic book series *Blammo*, which earned him an Ignatz Award nomination in 2010. His work has appeared in the alternative weekly newspaper *Westword*, *MAD* magazine, and multiple graphic anthologies. His first book, *The Hypo: The Melancholic Young Lincoln*, from Fantagraphics, is a graphic portrait of Abraham Lincoln's early years in Springfield, Illinois. Find more of his work at noahvansciver.tumblr.com.

**MATT WIEGLE** lives in Philadelphia and draws things. He received the 2010 Ignatz Award for Promising New Talent, and is a founding member of the Partyka comics collective. He is responsible for the minicomics *Is it Bacon?* and *Seven More Days of Not Getting Eaten*. He adapted the "House of Lac" section of *The Mahabharata* for Volume 1 of *The Graphic Canon* and portions of Kahlil Gibran's *The Madman* for Volume 3.

# ACKNOWLEDGMENTS

**ALL MY THANKS GO TO THE LOVELY, LOVING CYBELE.** And to my mom and my sister. My Chicago family. All my friends.

Endless gratitude is showered on Dan Simon, founder and president of Seven Stories Press, for taking on *The Graphic Canon* project and continuing it with this volume. Gigawatts of thanks to my main editor and project manager Veronica Liu, art director Stewart Cauley, managing editor Liz DeLong, marketing maven Ruth Weiner, operations director Jon Gilbert, global rights empress Silvia Stramenga, purse-strings puller Yves Gaston, production assistant Heather McAdams, and the rest of the good folk at Seven Stories Press. Praise to everyone at Random House Distribution, including Ann Kingman and Michael Kindness.

*Merci* to my other publishing peeps: Jan Johnson, Michael Kerber, Gary Baddeley, Kim Ehart, Matt Staggs, and everyone else at Red Wheel/Weiser and Disinformation.

Thanks to all the readers, reviewers, and bookstores who supported the previous volumes of *The Graphic Canon*, with special thanks to the Society of Illustrators.

Major thanks are due to everyone who makes this book and gets it into your hands: the paper-makers, the truck drivers, the printers, the distributors and wholesalers, the booksellers. . . . And of course the many trees who gave their all.

I'm grateful to all the writers who gave us these works of literature that have brightened, deepened, flavored, and occasionally traumatized so many of our childhoods, including mine. And I reserve a special place in my heart for all the artists and adapters, who enthusiastically produced amazing work. Without you guys, *The Graphic Canon of Children's Literature* couldn't exist.

# CREDITS AND PERMISSIONS

"The Miller, His Son, and the Donkey" and "The Eagle, the Cat, and the Sow" by Aesop were created especially for this volume. Copyright © 2013 by Roberta Gregory. Printed by permission of the artist.

"The Ape and the Fisherman" and "The Wasp and the Snake" by Aesop first appeared in *Aesop's Fables*, edited by Charles Santino, published by Fantagraphics. Published in color for the first time in this volume. Copyright © 1991 by Peter Kuper. Printed by permission of the artist.

"The Lion in Love," "The Fox and the Grapes," and "The City Mouse and the Country Mouse" by Aesop were created especially for this volume. Copyright © 2014 by Lance Tooks. Printed by permission of the artist.

"Little Red Riding Hood" (a European fairy tale) was created especially for this volume. Copyright © 2013 by David W. Tripp. Printed by permission of the artist.

"The Mastermaid" (a Norse fairy tale) was created especially for this volume. Copyright © 2014 by Andrice Arp. Printed by permission of the artist.

"The Firebird (a Russian fairy tale)" was originally self-published as a limited-edition concertina. Copyright 2014 Lesley Barnes.

"The Shepherdess and the Condor" (a Peruvian fairy tale) was created especially for this volume. Copyright © 2014 by Miguel Molina. Printed by permission of the artist.

"The Weardale Fairies" (a British fairy tale) was created especially for this volume. Copyright © 2014 by Rachael Ball. Printed by permission of the artist.

Four Fables by Jean de La Fontaine was created especially for this volume. Copyright © 2013 by Maëlle Doliveux. Printed by permission of the artist.

"Town Musicians of Bremen" by Brothers Grimm was created especially for this volume. Copyright © 2014 by Kevin H. Dixon. Printed by permission of the artist.

"A Tale of One Who Traveled to Learn What Shivering Meant" by Brothers Grimm was created especially for this volume. Copyright © 2014 by Chandra Free. Technical assists by BLAM! Ventures. Printed by permission of the artist.

"Star Dollars" and "The Water-Sprite" by Brothers Grimm were created especially for this volume. Copyright © 2013 by Noah Van Sciver. Printed by permission of the artist.

*The Nutcracker and the Mouse King* by E. T. A. Hoffmann was created especially for this volume. Copyright © 2014 by Sanya Glisic. Printed by permission of the artist.

"The Little Mermaid" by Hans Christian Andersen was created especially for this volume. Copyright © 2014 by Dame Darcy. Printed by permission of the artist.

"The Tinderbox" by Hans Christian Andersen was created especially for this volume. Copyright © 2014 by Isabel Greenberg. Printed by permission of the artist.

"Goldilocks and the Three Bears" (a British fairy tale) was created especially for this volume. Copyright © 2014 by Billy Nunez. Printed by permission of the artist.

"Advice to Little Girls" by Mark Twain was created especially for this volume. Copyright © 2014 by Frank M. Hansen. Printed by permission of the artist.

*Alice's Adventures in Wonderland* by Lewis Carroll were created especially for this volume. Copyright © 2014 by Vicki Nerino. Printed by permission of the artist.

*Fables for Children* by Leo Tolstoy was created especially for this volume. Copyright © 2014 by Keren Katz. Printed by permission of the artist.

*20,000 Leagues Under the Sea* by Jules Verne was created especially for this volume. Copyright © 2014 by Sandy Jimenez. Printed by permission of the artist.

"The Owl and the Pussycat" by Edward Lear was created especially for this volume. Copyright © 2013 by Rick Geary. Printed by permission of the artist.

"Calico Pie" and "The New Vestments" by Edward Lear were created especially for this volume. Copyright © 2014 by Joy Kolitsky. Printed by permission of the artist.

*The Adventures of Tom Sawyer* by Mark Twain was created especially for this volume. Copyright © 2013 by R. Sikoryak. Printed by permission of the artist.

*At the Back of the North Wind* by George MacDonald was created especially for this volume. Copyright © 2013 by Dasha Tolstikova. Printed by permission of the artist.

*Heidi* by Johanna Spyri was created especially for this volume. Copyright © 2014 by Molly Brooks. Printed by permission of the artist.

"The Tar Baby" (from *Tales of Uncle Remus*) by Joel Chandler Harris was created especially for this volume. Copyright © 2014 by Eric Knisley. Printed by permission of the artist.

*The Adventures of Pinocchio* by Carlo Collodi was created especially for this volume. Copyright © 2014 by Molly Colleen O'Connell. Printed by permission of the artist.

*Treasure Island* by Robert Louis Stevenson was created especially for this volume. Copyright © 2014 by Lisa Fary, Kate Eagle, and John Dallaire.

"The Nightingale and the Rose" by Oscar Wilde was created especially for this volume. Copyright © 2014 by Tara Seibel. Printed by permission of the artist.

*The Jungle Book* by Rudyard Kipling was created especially for this volume. Copyright © 2014 by Caroline Picard. Printed by permission of the artist.

*The Time Machine* by H. G. Wells was created especially for this volume. Copyright © 2014 by by Matthew Houston. Printed by permission of the artist.

The Oz series by L. Frank Baum was created especially for this volume. Copyright © 2014 by Shawn Cheng. Printed by permission of the artist.

*Peter Pan* by J. M. Barrie was created especially for this volume. Copyright © 2014 by Sally Madden. Printed by permission of the artist.

*The Wind in the Willows* by Kenneth Grahame was created especially for this volume. Copyright © 2014 by Andrea Tsurumi. Printed by permission of the artist.

*The Secret Garden* by Frances Hodgson Burnett was created especially for this volume. Copyright © 2014 by Juliacks. Printed by permission of the artist.

*The Velveteen Rabbit* by Margery Williams was created especially for this volume. Copyright © 2013 by Kate Glasheen. Printed by permission of the artist.

*Rootabaga Stories* by Carl Sandburg was created especially for this volume. Copyright © 2014 by C. Frakes. Printed by permission of the artist.

*The Tower Treasure* (A Hardy Boys Mystery) by Franklin W. Dixon was created especially for this volume. Copyright © 2013 by Matt Wiegle. Printed by permission of the artist.

*Peter and the Wolf* by Sergei Prokofiev was created especially for this volume. Copyright © 2014 by Katherine Hearst. Printed by permission of the artist.

*Pippi Longstocking* by Astrid Lindgren was created especially for this volume. Copyright © 2014 by Emelie Östergren. Printed by permission of the artist.

*The Diary of a Young Girl* by Anne Frank. Excerpts from "The Eight Hiders" and "The New Year" from *Anne Frank: The Anne Frank House Authorized Graphic Biography* by Sid Jacobson and Ernie Colón. Text copyright © 2010 by Sid Jacobson. Artwork copyright © 2010 by Ernie Colón. Reprinted permission of Hill and Wang, a division of Farrar, Straus and Giroux LLC.

Schoolyard rhymes was created especially for this volume. Copyright © 2014 by John W. Pierard. Printed by permission of the artist.

*Watership Down* by Richard Adams was created especially for this volume. Copyright © 2014 by Tori Christina McKenna. Printed by permission of the artist.

The Harry Potter series by J. K. Rowling was originally published online and as a highly limited series of posters. Copyright 2010 and 2011 by Lucy Knisley.

**Gallery**

All gallery artwork is copyrighted by the individual artists and reprinted by permission of the artists from their websites—see page 434 for complete credits—except in the cases below, which were created especially for this volume:

*Beatrice 'Beezus' Quimby and Henry Huggins*, based on the Ramona series by Beverly Cleary, was created especially for this volume. Copyright © 2013 by Ricardo Cortés. Printed by permission of the artist.

"The Ugly Duckling" by Hans Christian Andersen was created especially for this volume. Copyright © 2013 by Mimi Leung. Printed by permission of the artist.

"The Tinderbox" by Hans Christian Andersen was created especially for this volume. Copyright © 2013 by Sharon Rudahl. Printed by permission of the artist.

"Thumbelina" by Hans Christian Andersen was created especially for this volume. Copyright © 2013 by Rebecca Dart. Printed by permission of the artist.

*Gulliver's Travels* by Jonathan Swift was created especially for this volume. Copyright © 2013 by Pia Valaer. Printed by permission of the artist.

"Little Red Riding Hood" by Charles Perrault was created especially for this volume. Copyright © 2013 by Eran Fowler. Printed by permission of the artist.

*The Adventures of Pinocchio* by Carlo Collodi was created especially for this volume. Copyright © 2013 by Eran Fowler. Printed by permission of the artist.

*The Very Hungry Caterpillar* by Eric Carle was created especially for this volume. Copyright © 2013 by Alex Eckman-Lawn. Printed by permission

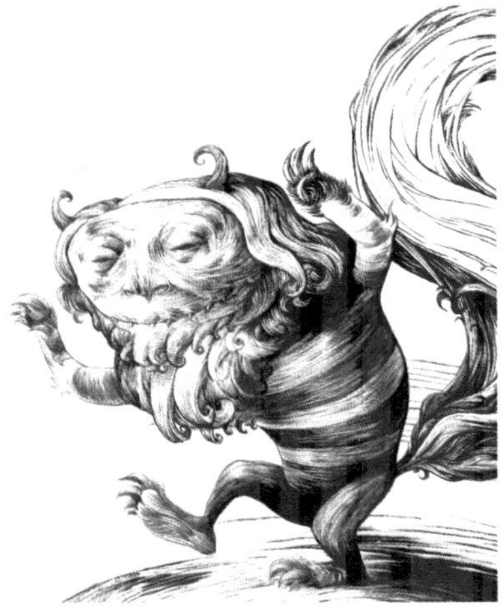

# INDEX

## TITLE



## AUTHOR/POET



## ARTIST/ADAPTER

Photo by Ross Smith

**RUSS KICK** is the editor of the three-volume, 1,600-page anthology *The Graphic Canon: The World's Great Literature as Comics and Visuals*. NPR said that it is "easily the most ambitious and successfully realized literary project in recent memory"; *School Library Journal* called it "startlingly brilliant" and "a masterpiece"; and *Booklist* declared it "a profound work of art." The third volume was a *New York Times* bestseller.

Russ has also edited the megaselling anthologies *You Are Being Lied To* and *Everything You Know Is Wrong*, and has written several nonfiction books, including the cult classic *100 Things You're Not Supposed to Know* (all from The Disinformation Company, now an imprint of Red Wheel / Weiser). His latest books for Disinfo are *Death Poems*, the first history-spanning anthology of poetry about death and dying, and *Flash Wisdom: A Curated Collection of Mind-Blowing, Perspective-Changing, and Eye-Opening Quotes*.

*The New York Times* has dubbed Russ "an information archaeologist"; *Details* magazine described him as "a Renaissance man"; and *Utne Reader* named him one of its "50 Visionaries Who Are Changing Your World." He resides in Tucson, Arizona.

**SEVEN STORIES PRESS** is an independent book publisher based in New York City. We publish works of the imagination by such writers as Nelson Algren, Russell Banks, Octavia E. Butler, Ani DiFranco, Assia Djebar, Ariel Dorfman, Coco Fusco, Barry Gifford, Hwang Sok-yong, Lee Stringer, and Kurt Vonnegut, to name a few, together with political titles by voices of conscience, including the Boston Women's Health Collective, Noam Chomsky, Angela Y. Davis, Human Rights Watch, Derrick Jensen, Ralph Nader, Loretta Napoleoni, Gary Null, Project Censored, Barbara Seaman, Alice Walker, Gary Webb, and Howard Zinn, among many others. Seven Stories Press believes publishers have a special responsibility to defend free speech and human rights, and to celebrate the gifts of the human imagination, wherever we can. For additional information, visit www.sevenstories.com.